MW00737865

The Saxon Chronicle

Jane Ellen Swan is also the author of:

The Saxon Chronicle, Volume I: The Capitalists
The Saxon Chronicle, Volume II: The Heirs

The Saxon Chronicle

Volume III
The Millers' Daughters

Jane Ellen Swan

VANTAGE PRESS
New York

FIRST EDITION

Copyright © 2004 by Jane Ellen Swan

Published by Vantage Press, Inc.
419 Park Ave. South, New York, NY 10016

Manufactured in the United States of America
ISBN: 0-533-14708-5

Library of Congress Catalog Card No.: 2003095136

0 9 8 7 6 5 4 3 2 1

TO

Karen,

Tim,

Jennifer

and Matthew

May they keep the story going.

"Let us now sing the praises of famous men, our ancestors in their generations. The Lord apportioned to them great glory . . . There were those who ruled, . . . those who gave counsel, . . . those who led the people, . . . those who composed musical tunes or wrote verses, rich men endowed with resources—all these were honored in their generations . . .

But of others there is no memory; they have become as though they had never been born, they and their children after them. But these also were godly men, whose righteous deeds have not been forgotten . . . Their offspring will continue forever, . . . Their bodies are buried in peace but their name lives on generation after generation."

—Ecclesliasticus 44:1–14

The Millers' Daughters

Book V
The French Time

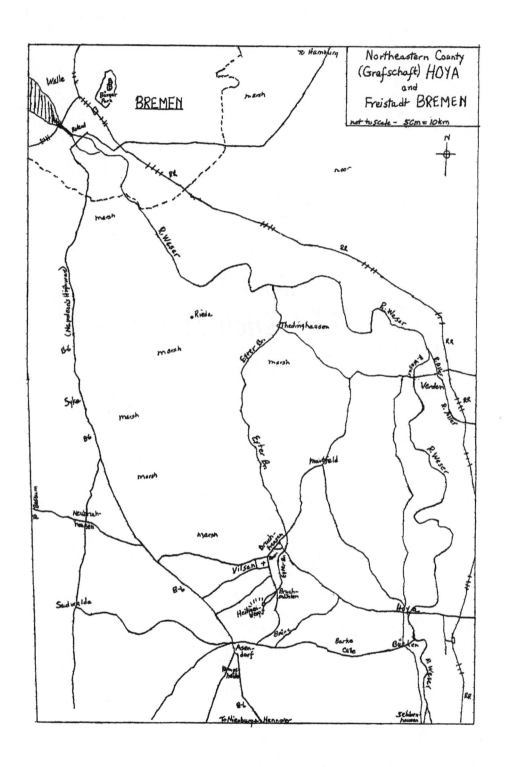

1

AD 1781

"Papa killed him," wailed Eleonore. "Papa killed my dear Fritzi."

"Hush, child, you must not say things like that," said Dorothea. "It was an accident."

"Nay, nay, I saw it. I saw it all," insisted Eleonore.

"You saw it? And how came you to be where you could see it?" queried Dorothea. "You know you are not supposed to go into the mill when they are working."

"I know. But I liked to watch them work. It was so—so interesting. And I was standing just inside the door very quietly. They never saw me."

"Oh, you wicked little girl! You could have been hurt as well. But you must not say that your Papa killed your brother. That is wicked, too."

"But he did. He did! Papa lost his temper and it was the same as though he pushed Fritzi."

"How so?"

"Fritzi was trying to fix something and Papa got angry and then he yelled and cursed so loud—you know Papa's temper—and it made Fritzi jump and his sleeve caught in that big shaft that makes the millstones go around. And then—and then . . . ," Eleonore started to sob and Dorothea put a comforting arm around her. "—and then it pulled his arm around it so he couldn't get free and the top stone was coming down. And—and—oh, Dorchen, it was horrible, horrible." Dorothea drew her close. "And all the while Papa was yelling like a crazy man instead of pushing the big handle to stop the stones. And it wasn't until Fritzi started screaming that Papa ran to turn off the machinery. Then I ran away but I could still hear Fritzi screaming. I still can," she cried.

Dorothea stopped in the middle of the street and embraced the weeping child. "Oh, you poor child to have witnessed that." She held her as closely to her bosom as she could with one arm. Her other hand was tightly holding on to Eleonore's younger brother Carsten, who immedi-

3

ately started wailing as well, although she doubted he knew what it was all about. Carsten was not too bright. He was not quite five years old; Eleonore was eight. They were on their way to their brother's funeral at the Vilsen church.

When Eleonore finally calmed down, Dorothea said, "Dry your tears now, Elli. We must hurry or we'll be late to church. We must pray for Fritzi's soul so that he will go to heaven."

"I know. And I shall pray for him. I love Fritzi. He's the only one I loved," she snuffled and then added, "I love you, too, Dorchen, but I hate Papa and I hate Heinzi."

"Child!" exclaimed Dorothea aghast. "But surely you love your Mama?"

"I suppose," replied Eleonore after a moment's hesitation, "but Mama's always so busy having babies, she never has time for any of us. You're the only one who takes care of us. That's why I love you."

Dorothea smiled ruefully. The child was right but too perspicacious for her age. "That's what I'm here for—to take care of you and help your mama." They arrived at the church. "Now dry your tears and no more crying until you are home in your bed tonight. Promise?"

"All right."

Dorothea hustled the children into the church and led them to the backmost pew. "Now kneel down and ask God's forgiveness before you pray for Fritzi," she urged.

"Papa says we don't have to kneel anymore," retorted Eleonore.

Dorothea rolled her eyes heavenward. "Then sit and bow your head, but pray."

Eleonore did so and Dorothea knelt. Her parents still kept to the old ways. She tried to pray for the fine young man whose life had been so suddenly snuffed out but her mind kept wandering to the intelligent, willful and confused child beside her. She needs my prayers even more, she thought.

Eleonore was the sixth child and second daughter of Miller Heinrich Anton Matthies and his wife Rebecke. Anton was considered the most competent, successful and, if rumor could be believed, wealthiest miller in all of County Hoya. He had held the lease on two important mills in the vicinity of Vilsen for over fifteen years. The larger of the two, Bruchmühlen, where the family lived, stood on the main road about a mile south of the village. The second, the so-called Klostermühle, lay about a half mile away on the same stream but back in the woods at a place called

4

Heiligenberg—Holy Mountain. It was very old, the original mill of an ancient monastery that had been there for centuries until it was destroyed right after the Reformation. Only the mill remained but many of the local farmers had an intense loyalty to the old Klostermühle, among them the Bruns family whose own patrimony in the area went back over a thousand years to old Saxon times. The Heiligenberg had been a sacred place for the ancients and many to this day held the place in awe. Moreover, the Klostermühle controlled the millpond and the dam thus making its importance far out of proportion to its economic value.

However, not many people in Vilsen and the surrounding countryside liked Miller Matthies. He was arrogant, loud-spoken, irrascible and too puffed up with his own importance. A stubborn contrarian, he never seemed to agree with anyone or anything and so, despite his affluence and status, he was never asked to serve on the Town Council or the Church Council. As a result he turned his back on his neighbors and the villagers except for strictly business transactions. This made it very difficult for Becke, who would dearly have loved to socialize, and for his children, who were shunned and snubbed in school. And Dorothea was well aware of his violent and sometimes frightening temper.

Dorothea was also a miller's daughter. Her father Wilhelm Koch, also an excellent miller, was as kind, gentle and forebearing as Anton was not. He was the miller at a fairly new mill in the tiny hamlet of Neubruchhausen, some six miles to the west of Vilsen. Her mother Elizabeth Margarethe was as bright, highly intelligent and vivacious as poor unhappy, downtrodden Becke Matthies was not. Lise loved music and saw to it that each of her children learned to sing and play the pianoforte that Wilhelm had bought for her many years ago. Dorothea came from a happy home.

Dorothea was sixteen. She had completed her schooling two years ago. When boys were then expected to enter an apprenticeship or attend one of the new Realschule (technical schools) or even go to the Gymnasium to prepare for university, girls, too, although it was still considered unnecessary to educate them beyond the age of fourteen, were expected to serve an 'apprenticeship' of sorts to train them to be efficient housekeepers, wives and mothers. Thus Dorothea had been living with the Matthies for well over a year.

The two families had been close for years. Becke liked to say that the closeness was because she and her dear beloved Lise had been friends ever since they were both married. But in truth, Lise did not even like Anton Matthies and only tolerated Becke because she felt sorry for her. The real friendship had been between Lise's father Cyriacus Lindemann and Anton's father Henni Matthies, both of whom had been dragoons and had served together in the many wars that had plagued Germany throughout most of the eighteenth century. Cyriacus had been a stalwart and well-beloved citizen of Bruchhausen, which in the intervening years had spread out so as to be almost a part of Vilsen. In fact, to hear Lise tell it, the family acquaintance had begun even a generation before that when her grandfather Johann Lindemann had been County Clerk and had welcomed the Princess Sophie Dorothea to the old castle at Bruchhausen and had there met the first Anton Matthies who was one of the Princess' lifeguards and escorts. Johann had taken the young dragoon under his wing and had given him some words of fatherly advice regarding Anton's unrequited and impossible love for the Princess.

The funeral service was beginning. Dorothea slid back into her seat, keeping a careful eye on both her small charges. She hoped Carsten would not fidget too much. Eleonore seemed to have calmed down. She was staring straight ahead at Fritzi's coffin resting on its bier before the chancel. In the front row on the right side sat Anton Matthies in black frockcoat and breeches, ramrod straight, as though he were the center of attention rather than his late son. With him was his second son Johann Heinrich—Heinzi—now almost sixteen, and his eldest daughter Adelheit, fifteen. Becke was not in attendance. Anton had forbidden her to come as she was close to her time with yet another child. The youngest daughter had been kept home as well.

On the left side were Dorothea's parents Wilhelm and Lise Koch, her brother Philipp, now fourteen, and her baby sister, another Adelheit, the same age as Eleonore. Dorothea hoped there would be a few minutes to speak with them after the funeral. She knew her mother would have some good, sensible advice for how to deal with Eleonore's bitterness. At the same moment she conceived the thought, Dorothea put it aside. The funeral was no place for that sort of discussion. Besides her parents would be in a hurry to return to Neubruchhausen having taken the day off from work to come here. No, better to wait until her half-day off on Sunday when she could tell Lise the whole story at leisure.

The service was mercifully short, the eulogy even shorter. Pastor made every effort to praise Heinrich Friedrich's virtues but what could one say of an eighteen-year-old who had barely begun his life? The church was less than half full and many of those that attended did so only because they felt obligated. Perhaps they owed Anton money. But many more stayed away. After the blessing, six sturdy young men, Fritzi's friends, hefted the coffin and carried it down the aisle while the organ wailed a mournful dirge. The Pastor, followed by Anton and his children, left next. Then the rest of the congregation filed slowly out of the church. Dorothea held the young ones back until the end of the procession.

"But I want to see Fritzi once more before they put him in the earth," objected Eleonore in a loud, frantic whisper.

"You will, my dear," Dorothea assured her. "They will wait for us."

Outside in the churchyard it was a blustery March day. Spring had been trying to come but without much success as yet. As the people gathered around the newly dug grave, it started spitting snow. Suddenly, as the young pallbearers were gently lowering the coffin into the grave, Eleonore pulled away from Dorothea and pushed herself to the front of the crowd. She would have fallen into the grave herself had not some woman restrained her.

"Fritzi, Fritzi," she cried, "I love you."

As the men started shovelling the dirt onto the coffin, Eleonore threw a tiny purple crocus on top of it. "Fritzi, it's for you. It's the only flower I could find," she sobbed and turned away into the kind woman's arms as though she could no longer bear to watch.

Dorothea had tried to catch up with her but Carsten had held her back. When she finally arrived at the grave's edge, she could see Anton's face black as thunderclouds. Only that the Pastor was saying the commital prayers kept him from venting his vehement temper. Oh, oh, thought Dorothea, we'll all hear about this before day's end. For herself she did not care, but she hoped he would not be too hard on Eleonore.

After the last shovelful of dirt was returned to the grave, the people drifted away in twos and threes. A few stopped to chat and several offered their condolences to Anton who acknowledged them briefly and with surprising courtesy. But most hurried off to homes and businesses as the weather was turning decidedly raw. Dorothea retrieved Eleonore.

"Thank you for catching her, Frau Meyer," said Dorothea apologetically, "else she would have fallen, I'm sure. Sorry to put you to so much trouble."

Frau Meyer was an impressive dowager, tall, very dignified, almost queenly in her black mourning clothes. Her late daughter had been married to one of the leading men on th Town Council, Johann Harm Hohnholz, who many thought would soon be elected Bürgermeister. Frau Meyer herself was one of the town's elite but she had no need to remind people of that fact. Her breeding shone through. And Frau Meyer was a very kind and gracious lady.

"Ach, no trouble at all," she replied. "The poor baby was over-wrought, and understandably so, to have lost her eldest brother in such a terrible fashion." She lowered her voice. "It can't be easy for her living with that pompous father of hers."

Dorothea nodded agreement as Eleonore said, "I am not a baby."

The two women smiled over her head. "Of course, you're not," replied Frau Meyer. "You're a fine young lass, growing up fast. I only said that because you reminded me of my own babies when I held you in my arms."

That seemed to mollify Eleonore. "I wish you were my grandmother. You're a nice lady."

Once again the two women exchanged meaningful glances. "Come now, children," urged Dorothea, "we must not keep Frau Meyer standing here in the cold. Say 'Auf Wiedersehen' and thank Frau Meyer."

Eleonore made her best curtsey and said, "Thank you, Frau Meyer, for catching me, else I'd have been buried along with Fritzi." Then she sobbed and said in a tiny voice, "Maybe I should have."

Frau Meyer gasped but quickly recovered her aplomb. "I don't think that would have happened."

Dorothea quickly shepherded her charges out of the churchyard. "Come, let us hurry. We've a long walk home and it is starting to snow harder. And you without your bonnet. Put your shawl up over your head so you don't catch cold. Why didn't you wear your bonnet, especially for church?"

Eleonore started to say, "Papa says . . . " and then thought better of it. "It was so nice when we started out this morning, I didn't think I needed it."

"Well, you do now. It's still March yet and one can't depend on the weather in March. And, by the way where did you come by that crocus?"

Eleonore did not know whether to hang her head or be defiant. "I picked it from Pastor's garden as we passed the parsonage. He has so many of them, I didn't think he would miss just one. They are so beautiful, Dorchen."

"I know, but that is still stealing. And you know very well that stealing is wicked."

"I don't want to be wicked, Dorchen, but it's Papa's fault. If he would let us have flowers in our own garden, I wouldn't be tempted to steal one.

8

Why won't Papa let us have flowers in our garden?"

"I expect because he does not think they are useful," she explained. Dorothea knew that Anton, although he claimed to be a staunch Lutheran, only paid the merest lip-service to religion and still had deeply ingrained beliefs from his Calvinistic-Huguenot forebears.

"But they *are* useful," insisted Eleonore. "If something beautiful makes people happy, it must be useful, mustn't it?"

"I expect you are right," agreed Dorothea, "but sadly not everyone thinks that way."

"I think Mama would like flowers but she doesn't even ask Papa anymore," said Eleonore thoughtfully. "Anyway, she's too busy making babies. How do the babies get in Mama's tummy, Dorchen? I know how they come out but I can't imagine how they get in there."

"You do?" asked Dorothea, shocked.

"Ja, I watched the last one come out. The midwife didn't know I was there because Mama was screaming so. And it came out dead anyway."

Child, child, thought Dorothea, you are just too precocious. "You shouldn't have been watching that," she said. "That is a very private thing."

"But I wanted to find out how they get in there. Is it something Mama ate?"

Dorothea almost smiled. She did not know what to say to that. "No," she replied very seriously, "I expect God puts them there."

"But if God puts them there, why do so many die before they're even a year old?"

"I don't know. It's God's will just as it was with Fritzi. Yet you never mourned them as you now do him." It was the wrong thing to say. Dorothea could have kicked herself the moment she uttered it.

"But they were nothings, not even people yet," Eleonore insisted. "But Fritzi—Fritzi," and she started to sob again, "was a grown man, a fine person. He was good and kind and cheerful and friendly and—and—the best one in our family. Why couldn't Heinzi have died instead of him? Heinzi is just like Papa—mean and stingy and cruel and not friendly at all."

"Elli! You must not say things like that. It was God's will."

"Don't call me wicked again, Dorchen," she begged. "I don't mean to be wicked. It's just—just that . . . "

"I'll not, little one," Dorothea assured her, "but you must learn to accept God's will. We all must." Dorothea could not bring herself to chide

9

the child again because so much of what she said was true.

When they arrived back at the mill, Eleonore's punishment was nowhere near as severe as they both had expected. Anton scolded her—and his scolding was loud and lengthy—not for stealing the flower but for embarrassing him. He did not dole out the usual harsh whipping but merely sent her to bed without supper.

After supper Anton called Dorothea into the cubbyhole that served as his office. He let the girl stand there for a while. He eyed her up and down—a fetching lass, light brown hair, a pert nose, small but well-shaped bosom, fast growing up into a tasty piece. She would soon be ripe enough to pleasure a man well. He would like to sample a little of that himself—and who would know? No. He quickly shook his head to dismiss those thoughts. She was not a demure miss to hide her shame. She would run right to her parents and Anton could not afford to lose their goodwill. Wilhelm and Lise were the only real friends he had.

He said sternly, "I am not pleased with your upbringing of my daughter."

"I am sorry, Master Matthies. The child is heartbroken over Fritzi's death and she was extremely overwrought. She got away from me ere I realized it, for I had Carsten to look after as well. I promise it will not happen again."

"It will not because I don't expect to lose another son in that foolish manner," he said callously. "But she is too willful. You must be more strict with her."

"I believe, Master Matthies," proffered Dorothea bravely, "that Eleonore would respond more readily to love and friendship than to punishment. Too strict a regimen only makes her more rebellious."

Anton grew livid. The presumptuousness of the chit. Oh, I'd really like to get between her legs and show her all a woman is good for. "Do you presume to tell me how to raise my children?" he asked.

"Nay, nay, Master Matthies, it was merely a suggestion."

"Then keep your suggestions to yourself and do as I say."

But Dorothea was not meek. And inwardly she seethed at the man's blindness and stupidity. "If you find my work so unsatisfactory, perhaps I should leave," she said. "I am sure my father can find me another place."

Anton was shocked. How dare she? But he did not want to lose her. Her work really was good and she came cheap because of the friendship with her parents. He made a valiant effort to keep his temper in check. "No, that won't be necessary," he said grudgingly. "My goodwife likes you

10

and needs you. Just don't put any ideas in my daughter's head. You may go now."

Dorothea nodded and left, glad that the confrontation had not been any worse.

After that Anton ignored Dorothea, Eleonore and all the rest of the family except for Heinzi, whom he now had to train to be his heir and sucessor—to be a competent miller. Competent was the best he expected. He secretly admitted to himself that Johann Heinrich had nowhere the brains—nor the personality and enthusiasm for the work—that Fritzi had. Well, so be it. He would make do with what he had. At least the lad was docile, obedient and willing. Anton was aware that Heinzi had a mean streak in him, that he often bullied the younger children. Mayhap now he will grow out of it, now that he was going to have some real work to occupy him.

When Becke was delivered of yet another stillborn babe, Anton turned away in disgust. What was wrong with the woman that she could not bear healthy children? What had he to show for all his efforts? Only six—no, five, now that Fritzi was gone—to live beyond infancy. And Carsten was not too bright. And how many had she lost? At least that same number. He had lost count. And each time Becke's post-partum depression had been worse than the time before—deeper and longer lasting. This time she did not even seem to recognize the people about her, did not seem to realize that she must be up and about to take care of her household. The burden of that all fell on Dorothea, while Becke lay there like a lump. Well, he would give her a little time. The midwife assured him she would get over it as she had before. But not too long. After all a man had his needs, too. Just as soon as she was well he would try again to plant another babe in her belly. Either that, or rape the Koch girl. No, best not think of that. Becke, the old cow, would have to do.

When Dorothea next visited her parents, she told her mother about Eleonore's bitterness and unreasoning hatred toward her father.

"I can well understand it—at least the bitterness," said Lise. "Don't you remember how I've told you about Anton's brother Jürgen? How I saw him murdered and was so frozen with fear that I couldn't do anything to prevent it?"

"Murdered?" queried Dorothea. "But I thought you said he was shot as a spy."

"A spy he was, but not killed by a firing squad. No, he was shot in the back trying to escape from a French soldier. And I witnessed the whole thing."

"What happened to the Frenchman, Mama?"

"I don't know. He ran away." Never *ever* would Lise tell anyone she had cut the man's throat and dumped his body into the river. Only her father had been privy to that secret and Papa had long ago gone to his rest. "And what was worse, I was in love with Jürgen, planned to marry him. I took to my bed, wouldn't eat or even talk to anyone. And I was much older than little Eleonore, older than you even. But gradually I took to riding again. That dear little mare helped a great deal in my healing. But it wasn't until my sister, your Tante Katinka, dragged me to Der Lustige Strumpf for dancing that I really came to life again. But the memory of that horrible day has never left me." She paused and sighed, looking back. "And I fear it will be the same with our Eleonore but you can do a great deal to help start the healing."

"That is what I wanted to ask you about," said Dorothea. "I don't know where to begin. Her father is not like your Papa."

"Definitely not. Don't expect any help there. He will only make her feel worse."

"Agreed. And I can't very well take her to Der Lustige Strumpf. I've never even been there myself."

Lise laughed. "Ach, some day some young man will say, 'Come, Dorchen, let us go dancing at Der Lustige Strumpf' and there you'll be."

"Not much chance of that as long as I work for Master Matthies."

Lise shrugged. "But seriously, you can get her out of a Saturday to meet and play with some of her friends. Does she have any friends her own age?"

"Not that I know of. She claims they snub her in school because they don't like her father."

"I think she is carrying this hatred of her father too far and using it as an excuse to make a martyr of herself."

Dorothea considered that for a moment. "I hadn't thought of it that way but I think you're right, Mama. She has no one her own age. She is very lonely even in that large family. She never goes anywhere except to church and that not every Sunday."

"How does she in school?"

"Well enough as far as I know. She's very intelligent but too knowledgeable about things she should not yet have any knowledge of."

"Then get her to read—happy stories and beautiful poetry. Take her

12

some of our books. I know they don't have a single book in that house."

"You're right. Mine are the only ones."

"And I have a new book of poems by that talented new poet from Weimar, Master von Goethe. Take it with you. You'll like it. But read it yourself first for some of them are sad and might upset her. Use your judgment."

"I shall and thank you, Mama."

The next Saturday, Market Day, Dorothea asked Becke's permission to take Eleonore into Vilsen for a little outing. So what if Becke, so sunken in her melancholy, would not remember granting it. She dared not ask Master Matthies, who would surely refuse. But she was certain they would not be missed for a few hours.

Eleonore was all excited at the prospect. "Can't you finish your chores after we come back?" she pleaded. "All the good things will be gone ere we get there."

"No, I can't. It would certainly call your father's attention to the fact that we've gone somewhere. He will be angry enough if he finds out, without my leaving chores undone. Besides, we are not going to buy anything. We don't have any money for that. We are just going to look and say 'hello' to people.

Eleonore looked a little disappointed at that. But still an outing was an outing and a rare experience for them both. She helped Dorothea as much as she could to hasten the time. She wore her second-best dress, her school dress, with, at Dorothea's insistence, a clean apron. And this time she willingly donned her bonnet because she wanted to look like a lady.

At last they set out. The weather was much better than it had been two weeks before. March was truly going out like a lamb and spring was bursting forth all over. Flowers were blooming and trees were in bud. The sun was beginning to feel a little warm on their backs as they walked down the road toVilsen.

They were not too late at all. The market stalls were still laden with crisp, fresh vegetables, pyramids of shiney white eggs, sqwawking chickens and row upon colorful row of beautiful flowers. They strolled around slowly taking it all in. Dorothea nodded and greeted many people she knew but Eleonore seemed to ignore them all. She was intrigued by the flowers.

"Have you seen any of your school friends here?" asked Dorothea.

"No."

"But I noticed there were some tried to greet you."

13

"I don't have any friends," said Eleonore.

"Whyever not? You have a pleasing demeanor when you aren't sulking about your father."

"They ignore me. So I ignore them," stated the child flatly.

"That is not right," said Dorothea. "To have friends, you must be friendly. Have you even tried?"

"Why bother? Papa would never let them come to the mill—even if they wanted to."

"Oh, Elli, Elli," remonstrated Dorothea. "Forget your papa for a moment and just be your cheerful self. I know you can. Let us enjoy our outing."

Eleonore was about to object when Frau Meyer walked up to them, her three grandchildren in tow. "Ah, children," she said, "I see you are out enjoying this lovely spring day. Much fairer than when last we met." Dorothea agreed. Frau Meyer turned to Eleonore. "The flowers are beautiful, are they not? Here, let me buy you one of these pansies to put on Fritzi's grave. You'd like that, wouldn't you?"

Eleonore was so flabbergasted, she did not know what to say. "Oh, oh," she sobbed, "ja, I'd like that very much."

"Then pick out which one you'd like and we'll all go with you."

"Why do we have to go with her to the graveyard?" complained Teddi, her eldest, who was lugging his grandmother's large, heavily laden market basket. He was not quite fourteen, but already chafing as he considered himself too manly for such chores.

"Because it's right on our way for one thing and secondly, I intend to invite them for kaffee and kuchen before they return home."

Seven-year-old Marie clapped her hands. "Oh, good," she said. "I like to have company." The youngest, Elisa, did not look quite so happy at the prospect.

"You will come, won't you?" Frau Meyer urged Dorothea.

Dorothea hesitated for a moment. It would make them miss their own afternoon coffee and Anton would be furious. But what did he ever have for the light meal but bread and butter? She was certain Frau Meyer would serve something delectable. It would be a treat for Eleonore. "Of course, we'll come," she replied. "It's kind of you to invite us, Frau Meyer."

In the churchyard they stood with bowed heads while Eleonore knelt down in the damp earth and planted the little pot of pansies on Fritzi's grave. "Dear God," she murmured, "please make sure that Fritzi gets to heaven." And after a moment, "And bless Frau Meyer because she's such a nice lady."

Frau Meyer smiled. "A fitting prayer," she said. "Come now, you must all be hungry."

They strolled through the churchyard and down the steep hill to the next street and soon arrived at Frau Meyer's spacious home. Eleonore was still sniffling, trying valiantly to hold back her tears. Frau Meyer put an arm around her. "I understand, child, how it is to lose someone you love. Less than two years ago I lost my own daughter—these children's mother—and my eldest granddaughter. But now they have a new mama who seems to be keeping their papa happy."

"And you are still not crying?" squeaked Eleonore.

"I wept terribly at first but time heals. Someday you will learn that death is a part of life. That is one reason why new babies keep coming."

"But most of Mama's babies die, too."

"Then they were not ready for life. Only the strong survive. You must be strong, child. Now dry your tears. I have some special treats for all of you."

After a delicious repast Frau Meyer sent the children out into the garden to play while she and Dorothea chatted. Suddenly a clock on the mantel struck four. Dorothea jumped up. "Oh, heavens, I had no idea it was so late. I fear Master Matthies will have our heads."

"Don't let him bully you, Dorchen. Stand up to him."

"I try to but I fear for Elli."

"Don't. Call his bluff. He is more bluster than anything."

Dorothea thought about this as they hastened home. Eleonore was obviously thinking about Frau Meyer's words, too. "I liked Marie," she said, "even though she is a year younger than I. She was never friendly in school but now we are going to be friends. I am going to be strong, Dorchen, strong. Thank you for taking me out this afternoon. And I'm not going to worry about Papa anymore. I'm not," she insisted determinedly.

In the event they suffered no punishment at all. Just a tongue-lashing, and that very mild for Anton Matthies. "Where have you been?" he started to storm. "I had to pour my coffee myself."

"Frau Meyer invited us for coffee," replied Dorothea quietly. "I did not know she was going to else I'd have told you."

"Frau Meyer, eh? Getting a bit above yourself, aren't you?'

"Not at all. Frau Meyer is a very gracious lady and she is very fond of Eleonore." There, let him think about that, she added to herself.

15

And Anton did think about that. Why, that uppity bitch. Best forget all about getting under her skirts. Her parents might forgive him if he had a little fun with her—just might, if he talked fast enough. But if she were cozy with Frau Meyer—God almighty, it could ruin all his carefully laid plans. That young son-in-law of hers, Harm Hohnholz, was already prominent on the Vilsen Town Council, soon to be Bürgermeister, 'tis said. He could not afford to antagonize any of them. He desperately needed the goodwill of every one of the powers that be.

When Dorothea next visited her home, she told Lise about the visit with Frau Meyer and casually remarked, "You know, Mama, Master Matthies did not punish us at all—only scolded me, and that very mildly. I couldn't believe it. Something has changed him."

Lise smiles. "That something—or rather someone is Frau Meyer," she said.

"How so? They didn't even speak."

"Dorchen, Frau Meyer is not only a very gracious lady but an important person in her own right as well as being connected with some very powerful people in Vilsen. And if that thick head of his wasn't so blown up with his own arrogance, Anton would remember that the Hohnholz, too, were very close friends with your grandpa Cyriacus and still are friends of ours. And right now Anton Matthies needs every bit of their goodwill and influence."

"But whyever for? He is very rich himself," said Dorothea.

"Indeed he is. Mayhap richer than they. But they have the political influence he needs at this time. You see, he has applied for the hereditary rights to both mills."

Dorothea looked puzzled. "No, I don't see. Hasn't he been miller there ever since I was born and was training Fritzi and now Heinzi to follow him?"

"Quite right, but he does not own the mills nor the water rights. The state owns them. We have the same situation here in Neubruchhausen."

"I know Papa doesn't own this mill, but Master Matthies—why I had the impression that he owned every bit of land for miles around."

Lise laughed. "He would like to give that impression and, in fact, he does own considerable property adjacent to the mills, but the mills themselves—oh, it's very complicated. Your father can explain it better than I. Ask him about it when he comes in for dinner."

"Ach, ja, it is a bit involved," agreed Wilhelm during dinner, "but not so once you understand the background. Both mills were built by the old monks who owned the entire Heiligenberg as well as many, many lucrative farms throughout the county. After the Reformation the Count of Hoya took over the property. By some legal arrangement the Dowager Countess Katharina received all the income therefrom but her children were not permitted to inherit. However, in her lifetime she did give away several prime acres on the top of the hill. That is how an ancestor of our friend Hinrich Bruns acquired his, for what reason is not clear. After her death Braunschweig-Lüneburg took over the county as well as the mills and all of the Heiligenberg except for those few bits of private property. There was also a third mill, the Wehlenmühle on the Maidamm, which your great-grandfather Johann Lindemann managed to buy from the Duke. Most probably because it had never been productive and is now falling into ruins since my parents died."

"I know about that," said Dorothea, "but why could Master Matthies not have done the same?"

"Because it was very important that the Duchy control the water rights, to say nothing of the lucrative revenues it receives from the mills themselves. Suppose, for example, a miller were to dam up or divert more water than he needed, all the mills as well as the farms downstream would suffer. If many millers were to do that, even the Weser could dry up."

Lise laughed. "Hardly that."

Wilhelm continued, "No, probably not. I exaggerate so that Dorchen will understand."

"I understand all that, Papa, although I did not realize it until now," replied Dorothea, "but why does the state still hold *all* of the Heiligenberg? And what is Master Matthies' present problem?"

"To answer your first question, because the source of the Eyter Brook which feeds all three mills is the so-called Sacred Spring at the foot of the ravine there. Surely you know of it. Even to this day foolish maids who still believe in the old heathen superstitions go to bathe there on certain of the old festival nights in the hope of being wed within the year."

"I know about that although I've never been there. Adi Matthies is full of those old beliefs but her papa would have her head if she ever went there."

Wilhelm laughed. "No doubt he would. As to Anton's current problem, other than the few millers who own their mills outright, there are two kinds of millers. Those that simply rent the mill from the state, such as he and I. When we retire or die, the position is put up for bid and the mill and all its rights goes to the highest bidder, provided he is otherwise qualified.

Then there are the hereditary millers who may bequeath the mill-lease and all its rights to his heirs in perpetuity. It is not very common but not unheard of either. Anton has applied to Hannover for this privilege."

"I see," said Dorothea thoughtfully. "But they must surely grant it. He is certainly experienced enough and well qualified financially. Why is he worrying?"

Wilhelm smiled. "Because there are a few stumbling blocks. None of them major. Nothing that can't easily be resolved, but politics being what they are, they were brought up and must be dealt with to everyone's satisfaction. First there is that little oil mill he built adjacent to the Klostermühle. It is nothing but a circular press driven by an old horse that walks around and around, but it stands part on state proverty and part on private. Also it provides Anton with a nice bit of extra income from the linseed oil for, as you know, the raising of flax and the weaving of linen is our major industry here in Vilsen. There are those who feel the state should have a share of that income.

"Then there is the fish pond which Anton restocks with thousands of carp every year at his own expense. He feels that he deserves some compensation for that. Thirdly and perhaps most important there is the new Forest Preservation Act of 1779 under which all the rest of the Heiligenberg was declared a state forest. There is even a proposal to build a forester's house on the site of the old abbot's dwelling. There are some who fear that the Matthies property, both private and state-owned will block access to the forest. All of which is not true at all but," Wilhelm shrugged, "that's politics."

"But all of these things seem so minor, so petty," remarked Dorothea. "It seems as though they could be easily resolved. They don't seem to be insurmountable problems."

"They're not," put in Lise. "What your father is trying to say is that there are many people who do not like Anton Matthies. Some are just jealous of his success but many have been offended or insulted by his abrasive personality. That is the real obstacle. Many do not wish him well and it's partly his own fault."

"I can well believe that," said Dorothea. "So that is why he suddenly does not want to offend me because he thinks I'm a friend of Frau Meyer." She smiled to herself. "That is very interesting."

"Now, lass, don't you breathe a word of this conversation to anyone," warned Wilhelm. "I mean not to anyone. It is for your information only so that you will be aware of the pressure your employer is under."

"Don't worry, Papa, I shan't. "But I was just thinking—why don't you apply for that same hereditary right for here?"

Wilhelm looked at her askance. "*You* would want to be a miller?" he asked, half joking.

"No, of course not," she relplied. "But there's Philipp."

Dorothea's brother Philipp, two years her junior, had been quietly eating his dinner during this conversation, presumably disinterested. But now he looked up, about to object.

But Wilhelm answered. "Philipp has already informed me that he has no desire to be a miller. In the fall he will be going to the gymnasium in Hannover and if he does well—and I have no doubt he will—he will then go on to the Georg-August University at Göttingen. So you see there is no point in worrying about hereditary rights."

"Good heavens, aren't we aiming high," exclaimed Dorothea. "And what would you like to be, Philipp, if not a miller?"

"I plan on studying law," replied Philipp very seriously. "You see, there is no legal basis whatsoever for any of those obstacles they are putting in Master Matthies' way. It's as Mama says, some folk simply don't like him. Yet he will succeed. A good lawyer could make mincemeat of those objections."

"Then I hope he has one," said his sister, "for if he doesn't get his way, I tremble to think what life will be like in that house."

"Snip, snap, schnur," chanted Dorothea. She was teaching Eleonore to spin—or trying to.

Adelheit was seated at the spinning wheel because Eleonore's feet could not yet reach the treadle. Eleonore, under Dorothea's guidance, was diligently feeding the linen fibres from the distaff to the bobbin. On the other side of the large room their mother Becke, who had finally recovered from her melancholy, sat at her loom, clacking away, oblivious to everything around her.

In almost every household in Vilsen—indeed in all of northern Germany—the spinning and weaving of linen was a skill every girl learned as soon as she was able. It was the most important cottage industry in the local economy. The blue-flowered flax flourished in the cool, damp climate. There was also a lucrative sideline in flaxseed and linseed oil, which is why Anton Matthies had built the funny little horse-driven oil mill next to the Klostermühle.

The two smallest children, Carsten and little Becke, were playing quietly in a corner. Dorothea had to keep an eye on them as well, lest they get in the way. "Snip, snap, schnur." She sang the spinning song again.

Suddenly Carsten stood up and shouted as loud as he could, "That's what the little man said in the story."

Eleonore jumped and the strands of linen slipped through her hands.

"Now look what she's done," screeched Adi. "The yarn is too thin here and all lumpy there."

"I'm sorry, Adi," pleaded Eleonore contritely. "Carsten startled me."

"And she's not twisting it right, either," continued Adi. "Dorchen, make her do it right."

Dorothea patiently tried once again to show Eleonore how to pull the fibre gently but quickly from the distaff and twist it properly before feeding it onto the bobbin. But the child was too nervous now and kept making mistakes. Meanwhile little Becke was tugging at Dorothea's skirt.

"Tell us the spinning story, Dorchen. Please," she begged.

Dorothea could see that Eleonore would not be learning any more spinning techniques today, so she acquiesced. "Come, Elli, enough for today. Let us tell the little ones the spinning story." She took her charge by the hand and they retired to the corner where the children were playing.

" . . . And the king said to the poor maiden, 'If you can spin this roomful of straw into gold by morning, I shall give you in marriage to my son' . . . and when the little man appeared and said to the weeping girl, 'I shall spin it for you if you promise to give me your first-born child — unless you can guess my name'. The poor lass, thinking she would never marry the king's son, readily agreed."

"His name was Rumpelstiltskin," shouted Carsten gleefully.

"Carsten!" remonstrated Eleonore. "That doesn't come until the third night, until she knew she was going to have the baby. Don't spoil the story."

Carsten hung his head for just a moment. Then he brightened. "But I knew his name before the girl guessed it. I'm the one that told her what it was," he announced proudly.

Dorothea blinked, Eleonore looked disgusted and baby Becke, bewildered. Dorothea was about to chastise him but then she thought, he's only five and none too bright. Let him have his fantasy. They all need that in this house.

Eleonore said, "Carsten, you are silly and you've spoiled the story. Besides I don't like that one anyway. My favorite is 'The Twelve Dancing

Princesses'. Dorchen, have you ever snuck out and gone dancing at night?"

Dorothea smiled and shook her head. "Nay, I can't say as I have. It sounds like fun, but princesses can get away with that sort of thing. Ordinary lasses such as you and I would be so looked down upon that no man would ever wed them."

Eleonore's face fell, "Really?" She lowered her voice to a whisper. "Adi keeps talking about going to the Sacred Spring some night to see who her future husband will be. In fact, I think she may already have gone once."

Dorothea was shocked. "How do you know?"

"Because one night I woke up and she was not in her place in our bed. It was the full of the moon and I could see clearly."

"Mayhap she just went out to the privy."

"Nay. It was a long, long time before she came back. And, Dorchen, when she came back she was fully dressed. She didn't know I saw her. I haven't told anyone until now."

"And you won't tell anyone again," warned Dorothea. "If your Papa ever found out, he would whip the hide off of her."

Nothing more was said about Adelheit's presumed nocturnal excursions, but it set Dorothea to thinking—not about the Sacred Spring. She considered that foolishness—but about her own life. Here I am a year older than she and I have never been dancing at Der Lustige Strumpf or anywhere else for that matter. I am old enough to be courting or at least have a beau but no one has ever looked at me. What chance did they have? I spend all my time as nursemaid to Master Matthies' children and housemaid to his slovenly, uninspiring wife. Why, I take better care of them than their own mother. I am going to speak to Papa about it when next I go home. How I should love to work for someone like Frau Meyer where intelligent conversation and elegant manners are the norm.

As it turned out Dorothea said nothing to her Papa when she went home. Wilhelm was sick—not gravely so, but in no mood to be bothered with her concerns. Lise was busy sewing clothes in preparation for Philipp's departure for the Gymnasium a few months hence. Dorothea decided to await a better opportunity.

June came and spread its warm embrace over the fecund land. Men shed their heavy woolen underwear in favor of loose fitting linen shirts; women gratefully exchanged their drab woolen gowns for brightly colored

21

linen or even expensive printed cotton ones. There was a feeling of freedom and gaity in the air. The festival of Pentecost—called Pfingsten—was upon them. It was the last great holy day of the church year, but most of the populace, especially the young people, looked forward to the fun and excitement of Pfingst Monday—Whitmonday. On this day the festivities took on the carnival air of a country fair, hearking back long before the church to ancient pagan times. The highlight of the day was the driving of the Pfingst-oxen. These normally placid and plodding beasts were decorated with flowers entwined about their horns and garlands of blooms around their necks, each one more elaborate and lovelier than the next. Young boys—farmers' sons and cowherds—drove them through the streets of Vilsen in a sort of race to a great open field that lay behind the houses below the church. No houses had ever been built there. Few, if any, of the participants or observers realized why. In ancient Saxon times the field had been sacred to the twin gods Freyr and Freya, the site of the spring fertility rites and also the bonfires of the Midsummer's Eve festival, now blessed by the church as the Eve of St. John the Baptist. Not many generations ago the winning ox had been driven directly into the huge bonfire to be roasted for the feasting later in the day, reflecting the ancient pagan sacrifices. It was thought to be a great honor but often it incurred economic hardship on the poor farmer who was the 'donor'. With the onset of the Age of Reason people began to frown on such cruel practices and, instead, prizes were awarded to the winner of the race. In recent years even the race was forgotten and the whole pageant became more of an exhibition with the prizes being awarded for the most beautifully decorated Pfingst-ox. Thus the decorations became more and more elaborate, many truly magnificent displays of floral artistry. And there were more participants than ever, since no one had to fear losing his precious and beloved ox to the fire.

Dorothea promised Eleonore that they would go into Vilsen to watch the parade. She hoped she would not have to take Carsten but in the end their mother insisted she take not only the little boy but also baby Becke as well. The two older children, Heinzi and Adi, were also eager to go, but Dorothea knew they would be absolutely no help with the little ones. She decided to let them go their own way only letting herself be responsible for shepherding them all home again at the end of the day. She was determined that Eleonore would have a good time. Becke pleaded fatigue as usual and Miller Matthies said he was too busy for such foolishness although everyone knew that not one farmer would be coming to the mill this holiday.

They left Bruchmühlen just as dawn was breaking, for the Pfingst-ox race—they still called it that—would start very early in the morning before the flowers wilted and, depending on how many oxen there were, would last until almost noon. When they arrived in Vilsen the streets were already crowded with onlookers. Dorothea tried to find a spot along the route where the little ones could see without being jostled. Then she spied Frau Meyer with her grandchildren. There seemed to be an open space around her. No one would dare to jostle that lady, thought Dorothea. Heinzi and Adi had already disappeared into the crowd, and good riddance, she thought uncharitably. Slowly she edged her charges toward where Frau Meyer was standing.

"Ah, good morning, Dorchen," said the lady. She put an arm lightly around Eleonore's shoulders. "I'm so glad you could bring this lovely lass this day. I know how she loves flowers."

Eleonore beamed.

Young Teddi seemed much more friendly than at their previous meeting. He placed himself squarely next to Eleonore obviously prepared to show off his vast knowledge of the qualities of the various animals and to whom they belonged. But Eleonore was more interested in the flowers than in the beasts who wore them. She continually surprised Dorothea with her knowledge of the various blooms although they had not one in their own garden. Secretly Dorothea hoped she would best the young man. Marie moved to Eleonore's other side and shyly took her hand.

"I'm glad you're here, Elli," she said. "I want you to teach me all about the flowers. You know so much."

Eleonore flushed with pride. She stood up just a little straighter. "They are easy to learn because they are all so different—different in size and shape and color and especially in the fragrances," she explained to Marie. "Ach, I think the smells of the spring flowers are the best of the whole year,"

Marie looked at her in awe. Teddi looked annoyed. "See, there is Farmer Bruns' ox, one of the finest bred in the whole county," he pointed out. "And the third one there belongs to Gerd Fallenkamp. That's my great-uncle on the other side." He glanced surreptitiously at Frau Meyer. "It, too, is a fine animal."

"Who? The ox or your uncle?" said Eleonore mischieviously. At Teddi's glare, she relented. "Ach, Teddi, don't be angry. I couldn't help but tease you. You are so serious. Oxen are oxen all year round but on Pfingst-montag it is the flowers that make them special. See there, the violets entwined with the lilies-of-the-valley. Wherever did anyone still find violets this late in the season? And look there, those peonies are not too practical for this sort of thing. Mind you, I love them. They smell the best of all the June flowers, but see how the petals are dropping already. They will be nigh onto bare ere the poor ox reaches the judges. A bit foolish, don't you think?"

Teddi looked at her. He could not believe this child was several years his junior. Too intelligent by far. Which somewhat annoyed his burgeoning maleness. And yet, yet, there was something about this spritely lass that intrigued him. Mayhap it was her jet-black hair and sparkling brown eyes, so unusual here where almost everyone was blond—or at the darkest, light brown like Dorothea's. He'd heard that Eleonore had some French blood. Mayhap that was it. She might grow up to be a sultry beauty. He wasn't quite sure what sultry meant but it had an enticing sound to it. Oh well, he shrugged, he wasn't about to wait all those years to find out. He started to survey the crowd for someone closer to his own age, while Eleonore prattled on about the flowers much to his sister's delight.

Little Eliza, meanwhile, had put aside much of her sulkiness in the company of the two youngest Matthies children. While she largely ignored Carsten, her own age, she seemed to delight in mothering little Baby Becke. All of which left Dorothea alone to stand beside Frau Meyer.

"How nice that they are all becoming such good friends," commented that august lady. "It is good for them. One cannot have too many friends. And what of you, Dorchen? Have you not a beau to walk out with yet?"

Dorothea laughed derisively. "Hah, what chance do I have of that, Frau Meyer? I spend all my time with the children and the housework. It is exceedingly rare that I can even come into Vilsen like this. And Master Matthies will not let anyone, even the children's friends, come to the mill. Very few people, let alone young men, even know I exist." She sighed bitterly.

"I think you are wrong," replied the older woman. "I have even now been observing a seemly young man across the way who has been watching you with great interest. Do you know him?"

Dorothea looked where she indicated. Her eyes locked with those of the handsomest man she had ever seen. And a mature man he was, no simpering youth. He was tall and strongly built. His light brown hair was almost the same shade as hers, his eyes seemed to be a startling mixture of green and brown, but she could not be sure from the distance if it were a trick of the light or not. When he caught her glance, his mouth spread into a broad, charming grin. She could see he still had all his teeth—and very good ones at that.

Dorothea quickly looked down. "No, I have never seen him before," she replied demurely.

"No doubt a visitor," commented Frau Meyer. "Folk often do come from afar for Vilsen's Pfingst-ox race. But it is strange that he seemed so interested in you." The wily lady raised her eyebrows to the man across the way and then glanced down at Dorothea. She turned her eyes back to the gaily bedecked oxen and hoped that he got her message. If he was as perceptive as he appeared to be, he would have.

When Dorothea next dared to look across the street, the man had disappeared. She felt a stab of disappointment and immediately chided herself. Good heavens, what could she be thinking of. The man was a total stranger. But he had been handsome.

A few minutes later Frau Meyer felt a light tap on her shoulder. Startled, she turned and looked up at the tall, green-eyed stranger.

"Good morning, Frau Meyer." He bowed deeply and courteously. "I hope I am not being too presumptuous but I believe you are chaperoning this comely lass who I am told is Miller Koch's daughter. I have long wanted to meet her and this seemed the ideal opportunity. I am called Christian Bergmann."

Presumptuous, indeed! Frau Meyer was shocked. But then she reflected, she herself had encouraged his flirtation. But she had not expected him to react quite so quickly—or so brazenly. Even that sedate lady lost a little of her aplomb. "How—how did you know my name?" she asked indignantly.

"Why, everyone in Vilsen knows Frau Meyer," he replied. He would never admit that he had discreetly inquired of her identity of local bystanders and had been delighted to learn that the chit accompanying her was indeed Miller Koch's daughter.

Frau Meyer accepted that although she did not quite believe him. She was beginning to regret encouraging him. He was too smooth by far and yet, somehow, she liked his daring. She nodded graciously. "And why are you so anxious to meet Miller Koch's daughter, Master Bergmann?" she asked. "She is certainly not so well known as I."

"I am no master yet, meine Frau," he demurred. "No but a humble journeyman miller, working at present with Miller Harries in Martfeld."

"Ah. Becke Matthies' father."

"The same. But in a few months I shall be moving to Neubruch-hausen to spend the last of my journeying years with Miller Koch."

Dorothea, who had avidly been taking this all in, gasped. "You? You will be working for Papa?" she exclaimed.

"Dorchen!" scolded Frau Meyer. "Mind your manners. You have not yet been introduced to the young man. You must not speak to him until you are."

"I'm sorry, Frau Meyer. It's just that I was so surprised."

"As was I," agreed the astute old lady. "Then, since there seems no help for it, I shall introduce you forthwith. Christian Bergmann, this is indeed Dorothea Koch, daughter of your future employer, Miller Koch. But mind you, don't get any notions. You will not see much of her. She does not live at home."

Christian took Dorothea's hand for the briefest moment and bowed low over it. "Charmed," he murmured. Then, "How so?"

"She is nursemaid and housemaid to Miller Matthies' children and a stern master he is," replied Frau Meyer.

Christian frowned momentarily and then brightened. "Then let us enjoy this lovely day while we may. May I buy you something delicious for the noon repast after the judging is finished, Fraülein Dorothea?"

"I—I—I—," she stammered. "But I must watch over the children," she objected half-heartedly.

"Go," said Frau Meyer. "I'll take care of the children for a little while." She pointedly emphasized 'a little while', but she smiled benignly. It would be good for the lass to have a little fun in her drab life.

Eleonore had not missed one bit of this exchange. She did not know whether to be glad for Dorothea or jealous of her. She turned from the flower-bedecked oxen, from Teddi, who no longer interested her, and her eyes followed her mentor departing through the crowd with that man. To her young mind he seemed awfully old. What can Dorchen be thinking? She quailed at the thought that she might be on the verge of losing her beloved companion.

"Come," she said to Teddi and Marie. "I want to see the judging."

"But there are still several more Pfingst-oxen to come," objected Teddi. "You can see them much better from here than when they're all crowded together in front of the judges." Typically male, he failed to see the motive behind Eleonore's sudden change of thinking. But Frau Meyer was quite aware of her intentions.

"No," she said firmly. "You will stay right here until the last ox has passed. Then we'll all go together to the field for the judging and some dinner. Let our Dorchen have a little privacy, lass. When you're older you'll understand. We'll meet them later on."

Eleonore's face fell at being caught out in her little ploy. "Very well," she murmured and turned back to watching the parade. But her heart was no longer in it. What was Dorchen doing with that man? Why did grown-ups always have to be so mysterious? What would she understand when she was older? She wished she would hurry and grow up soon.

Chris took Dorothea's hand and guided her through the press of onlookers toward the field where the judging would take place. She knew she should object to his forwardness but she did not withdraw her hand. She did not want to lose him in the crowd. Besides it felt nice to be led for a change instead of dragging several children behind her. They had little chance for conversaton until they reached the field and she was bursting with curiosity. When they arrived many of the flower-bedecked Pfingst-oxen were already lined up before the judges and more kept coming. Chris led her away from the multitude surrounding the oxen to the other side of the large field where tables and booths purveying all sorts of delica-cies were set up. A large ox was already turning on a spit over a pit of glow-ing coals—and had been since the previous night. This was not one of the Pfingst-oxen but one duly purchased by the village elders for the feasting. As various savory odors accosted her nostrils, Dorothea realized she was famished. Having left so early her breakfast had not been much.

"Let us find a table before the crowd breaks up," suggested Chris. "Are you hungry?"

"Starved," she admitted, "but the ox isn't ready yet."

"It will be soon. Meanwhile how about a nice bowl of soup and some fresh rolls and butter to start?" She nodded. He sat her down at a table. "Wait here. I'll be right back." In moments he returned with two steaming bowls of—what else?—oxtail soup and several crisp rolls slathered with butter. He placed them on the table and sat down next to her. "There. That should hold us for a while. They won't be carving the ox for another hour or more—until after the judging. I'd not want you to swoon from starvation ere we get to know each other."

Dorothea smiled and bit into a roll. "Not much chance of that," she said. "I've gone without before. But it does taste ever so much better out-of-doors, doesn't it? Especially when you're having fun."

"Are you having fun?" he asked.

"I think so," she replied hesitantly. "Tell me about yourself, Chris

Bergmann. How you will come to be working for Papa—everything. Aren't you a bit old to be yet a journeyman?"

He laughed. "I hope you don't think I am as ancient as all that, but yes, I am, a bit," he admitted. "The year I was born in Rodewald there was a terrible fire . . . "

"Where is Rodewald?" she interrupted.

"On the other side of the Weser between Nienburg and Celle."

"And when were you born?" she asked, very curious now.

"In 1750. I am thirty-one. Is that too old?" he replied.

A bit, she thought but she said, "No, not at all." He certainly looked—and acted—younger.

"Anyway—may I continue?"

"By all means. I'm curious," she admitted.

"Rodewald is a strange town—strangely shaped, that is. It is one of those called 'Strassendörfer'—all the houses are strung out on either side of one main street. There are no other streets except the high road from Nienburg to Celle which crosses it. Each family's garden or farm lies directly behind each house. Thus when this terrible fire came, it swept up both sides of the street consuming almost the entire village. It levelled the church and almost destroyed the mill at the far end where my father rented. My earliest memories are of helping to rebuild the village. It was a poor town. The farms were not rich, surrounded by moorland as they were. It took all of twenty years to restore it to some semblance of what it had been. I had almost decided that I wanted to be a carpenter instead of a miller. I had certainly gained enough experience. But several of my siblings had been lost in the fire. I was the only son left . . . "

Dorothea shuddered. "Oh, how tragic."

"Indeed. But I don't even remember them. I was no but a babe at my mother's breast. But the tragedy affected my mother deeply. She bore no more children after me. So my father decided that I must train to be a miller. I started my apprenticeship at eighteen, an age when most lads were already halfway through their journey years. Hence," he laughed, "you see here an old man still ajourneying."

Dorothea laughed with him. His grin was so infectious. "Then I admire you greatly," she said. "It must not be easy . . . "

He shrugged. "At my age? In a way, not. It can be difficult for the male conceit. Yet in other ways, it has been much easier. I was stronger than the younger lads and learned much more quckly. I am already qualified to be a Master Miller, but rules are rules and I must serve two more years as a journeyman. But I simply must get away from Master Harries and into a more congenial workplace."

"I can well understand that," she agreed. "I know him slightly. He can be quite—what shall I say—quite stifling."

"Exactly. Now tell me of yourself. May I look forward to breaking my fast each morning in your company once I join your father?"

"I'm afraid not. As Frau Meyer explained, I do not live at home and only visit but once a week on Sunday afternoon—if I am lucky. I am nursemaid and general helper to Miller Matthies' children. Mistress Rebecke is often ill."

"Ach. The stifled daughter of Master Harries."

"Indeed. And I am only beginning to realize that I, too, am being stifled. I should like to seek another position but I haven't yet had the courage to speak to Papa. Master Matthies is a hard master."

"Having been trained by Master Harries."

"Ja, and not only that but his own father neglected him having been away in the wars so much. He was raised by a Puritan mother. And of himself, he is of an extremely arrogant disposition. As I grow older, I get the feeling that he is not to be trusted." Chris looked at her askance and she quickly put a hand over her mouth. "Oh, I should not have said that. Please don't mention that to my parents. You are the first person I have ever confided in. Fear not, nothing has happened yet but I just feel that it will if I don't leave there soon."

"Have no fear, I shall respect your confidence," Chris assured her. "But it is good to have another adult to talk to, is it not? I hope I can be that person."

She nodded. Never had she felt so comfortable with anyone.

Just then a great cheer went up from the crowd around the judges' stand. "Oh, I wonder who has won the prize," she exclaimed. "Let us go and see."

"And lose our hard won place at the table?" he queried.

"You're right, of course," she replied. "You run. I'll hold our places and some for the children, too."

A few minutes later Frau Meyer came up with the children. "What happened to your young man?" she asked. "Has he left you already?"

"Nay, nay," replied Dorothea. "He has just gone to see who won the prize while I hold places at the table for all of us."

"It was one of the Bruns," Frau Meyer informed her. "I'm not sure which."

"It was Dieter," Eleonore said, clapping her hands. "I'm so glad. It really was the prettiest and the most—most—"

"Intricate," supplied Dorothea.

"Ja, ja, that's it," said Eleonore. "I shall have to ask him where he found violets so late in the spring."

"No doubt deep in the woods where it is still cool and shady," replied Dorothea.

"And how do you find your new friend?" inquired Frau Meyer.

"Quite well, Frau Meyer. Thank you for introducing us. He is very personable."

"Are you going to marry him, Dorchen?" chirped Eleonore.

Dorothea turned beet-red but was saved from answering that impertinence by Chris' return.

"The winner is Farmer Harm Bruns," he announced.

"Harm?" said Teddi, turning to Eleonore. "I thought you said Dieter. A lot you know, stupid."

"But I do know," retorted Eleonore sharply. "Harm Bruns is Dieter's father. He owns the ox but Dieter was leading him."

"Now children, stop bickering," scolded Frau Meyer. "Here, Teddi, take these pennies and fetch us some soup whilst we wait for them to carve that monstrous beast."

"I'm glad Harm Bruns won," said Dorothea to Chris. "They are good people and can certainly use the money."

"But how so?" asked Chris. "I thought all the farmers around here were quite prosperous."

"Prosperous, perhaps, compared to other places," replied Dorothea, "but with so many mouths to feed any little extra is bound to help."

"The Bruns have lived on that land for over a thousand years, back to old Saxon times," put in Frau Meyer.

"Ja, they are descended from our old hero Bruno, Wittekind's brother," added Dorothea.

"I reckon your Master Matthies might be a bit envious of that," commented Chris.

"My papa's family were Huguenots who come here over a hundred years ago with Duchess Eleonore d'Olbreuse. I am named after her," said Eleonore, proudly.

"My, my, I didn't realize I was in such illustrious company," said Chris. "And you?" he asked of Dorothea.

She blushed and Frau Meyer answered for her. "Dorothea has mayhap the best blood of us all. She is descended on her mother's side from two of the wealthiest merchants of Celle—the von Sehnden and the Stockman—back before the Reformation."

"Indeed?" said Chris. "Then I must admit that I am just a poor cousin to all of you. I know nothing of my forebears except my own parents."

Dorothea finally got her tongue. "But wealthy no more," she insisted. "All that was lost during the Thirty Years War—except for the stipendia."

"The what?"

"Each of these ancestors set up a foundation, one of which—the von Sehnden—would pay two years' tuition at a university once a generation for one of their descendants. My brother Philipp hopes to apply for it when he finishes at the gymnasium, but it's doubtful he'll get it. The other, the Stockman, pays a marriage portion to one descendant every year at Easter but I'm sure none of us will ever see that."

"How so?" asked Chris.

"Hundreds and hundreds of descendants. My grandfather was wed over thirty-five years before he got his and my mother is not even on the list yet."

"Interesting."

"Yes. Nice to dream about, but not to be counted on."

"I see."

Frau Meyer sought to change the suject. She was glad Dorothea had made it quite clear to this Bergmann chap that there was no money to be had there, although he did not strike her as a fortune-hunter. Still, one never could be sure. Best to be forthright from the start. She knew that Wilhelm Koch was more than comfortable, having gained an inheritance from somewhere. But that would not last long once Philipp was at University. "Teddi, they are starting to carve the ox. See if you can get us some nice slices." Teddi went eagerly. He was bored with the conversation. "Oh, how I wish I could find someone like you, Dorchen, to help us out. My son-in-law's new wife is breeding again and her first barely weaned. So the burden of these three falls more and more on me."

Chris looked at Dorothea encouragingly, as if to say, there's your chance. Speak up.

Dorothea caught the look. "Eleonore," she said, "why don't you go and help Teddi. He can't possibly carry all that by himself. Get me a slice from the rib, if you can, or off the rump. They're the best."

Eleonore needed no urging. She took Marie with her and hurried to catch up with Teddi.

31

"I did not wish to speak in front of her, Frau Meyer," continued Dorothea, "but I am thinking of leaving the Matthies. I've been meaning to ask Papa about it but I did not want to broach the subject until there was a possibility of another position. Are you serious about wanting me?"

Frau Meyer looked surprised. "I most certainly am but hesitated to ask. I thought you were well settled with the Matthies."

"Well settled, yes, but no longer happy. The atmosphere in that house is so—so—," she chose Chris' term, "so stifling."

"I rather thought that might be the case. But don't the children still have need of you?"

Dorothea shook her head. "The older two have no need of me. They are as arrogant as their father. Frau Matthies could easily take care of the little ones, if she would. Eleonore is the only one I really care about—the only one who shows some spunk, who has some real intelligence. And he tries to punish it out of her. I truly believe she would benefit more from an occasional visit with your grandchildren and other of her schoolmates than by my staying there merely to fend off his temper."

Frau Meyer looked thoughtful. Chris was intrigued by her concise analysis. He was mature enough to respect courage and intelligence in a woman. "Perhaps she could be boarded with some family here in the village," he suggested.

"Ach, don't even suggest it," exclaimed Dorothea. "He would never permit it."

"She's right," added Frau Meyer. "Mayhap in a few years when the child is older, but not now. However, we could invite her occasionally to study her lessons after school with Marie and some of the neighbor children."

"That's a good idea," said Dorothea, "but school is over now and a long summer lies before us. I don't think in all fairness I should leave ere then."

"Quite right," agreed Frau Meyer. "You must give them ample notice but you must prepare yourself. Would you want me to speak to your papa?"

"Nay, nay," said Dorothea. "Now that he is well again and I have an assured prospect, I can convince him, I'm sure. Mama may be more difficult. Her family has always been close to the Matthies. But she'll understand once I explain. My, my," she smiled, "I feel freer already."

"That's my girl," grinned Chris.

Just then Eleonore and Teddi returned bearing platters piled high with succulent ox steaks, potatoes and other vegetables. And no more was said on the subject.

After everyone had stuffed themselves, there were games of all sorts. Ring-around-a-rosie for the littlest ones; silly sack races for the boys and skip-rope for the girls of the next set; more serious races and contests of strength such as tug-o-war for the young men. Eleonore won a prize at skip-rope—a tiny figurine cleverly braided from the linen fluff left on the distaff. She was inordinately proud of it.

"Do you think Papa will let me keep it?" she wondered.

"Of course, he will. You won it fair," Dorothea assured her.

"He says things like that are pagan."

"Oh, don't be silly, child." But Dorothea wondered.

Frau Meyer pleaded fatigue. "All this excitement is fine for you young folk but an old lady needs her rest. Yet I hate to spoil the children's fun. Would you mind watching them for a while, Dorchen?"

"Not at all, Frau Meyer. I should be happy to."

"Just send Teddi home with the girls ere you leave."

All this time Chris had said very little. He seemed content just to absorb the ambience of happy village life. Now he took Dorothea's hand and asked, "And what contest will you join in, fair maiden? You must excel at something."

"Not much, I'm afraid, unless it be spinning and weaving and other household chores. And I'm sure every female, young and old, in Vilsen excels at that."

Just then a fiddler struck up a lively tune. It was one of the Bruns. It seemed as though every member of that ubiquitous clan played some instrument or other. Couples began to dance on the greensward.

"Now there is something I know you can do," said Chris. "Will you dance with me?"

"I'm afraid I am not very good at it," she demurred. "I've not had much chance to learn."

"Then I shall teach you. Come," he invited and led her out.

Dorothea was surprised at how easily she could follow his lead. Granted, some of the faster jigs caused her to stumble over her own feet but the music itself of the stately minuets and even the reels seemed to guide her toes of their own volition.

"That was fun," she gasped after one particularly spritely dance.

"It was," Chris agreed. "We must do this more often. Would you go dancing with me at Der Lustige Strumpf some Saturday evening?"

"I would but I could not," she replied sadly. "I only have Sunday afternoons free and that is my sole chance to go home."

"Then I shall happily wait until you are settled with Frau Meyer. I'm sure she will allow you more time off."

"Perhaps, but let us not count our chickens too soon. Now it grows late and I must gather up the children. Look, Baby Becke has missed her nap and there she is asleep on the grass. And we have a long walk home."

"Let me carry her for you," volunteered Chris.

"Nay, nay," she exclaimed almost in a panic. "Thank you, but no. I do not want Master Matthies to even know you exist as yet. I shall caution Eleonore to say nothing." She collected the little ones and sent Teddi homeward with the Hohnholz girls. "Now I must find the others. They are not to know either."

"Then, Mistress Dorchen, I shall bid you 'Auf Wiedersehen'," he said and placed a light kiss on her forehead. She nearly swooned with delight.

She found Heinzi and Adi at a shooting gallery and had to drag them away. They sulked as usual and the younger ones were tired and cranky. It would not be an easy journey home and yet Dorothea felt she was floating on air. She dared not look back but she could feel Chris' eyes follow her as she left the field.

Wilhelm, though puzzled by her motives, was not averse to Dorothea's leaving the Matthies for Frau Meyer's. "However, that would be up to your mother," he said. "She is the one who has always been friends with them. We shouldn't want to offend."

That was what Dorothea was afraid of. She approached her mother cautiously, quite prepared to extol Frau Meyer's virtues.

"Friends!" exclaimed Lise. "Hardly that. Yes, we have known each other all our lives. It was his father and mine who were the best of friends. At one time I was even considering marrying his younger brother Jürgen. They were as different as day and night. I have never liked Anton. In fact, I detest him. But don't you let a word of that be known. We only offered your services because I felt so sorry for poor Becke. But if he ever lays a hand on you, I want to know about it immediately. He hasn't, has he?" she asked vehemently.

Dorothea was shocked that her mother had gone right to the heart of the matter, a subject she had been afraid to mention. "No, he hasn't. But—but when he constantly talks about putting another babe in Mistress Becke's belly, I get nervous. It gives me a creepy feeling."

"He has said that in front of you?" Lise fumed.

"Often."

"I'll have his balls!"

"Mother!"

Lise laughed. "Sorry, Dorchen. But I grew up with stallions who had better manners than he. I have wondered how long this situation would last. I admire your fortitude. However, I don't want you flying out of the stewpot only to land in the fire. I am only slightly acquainted with Frau Meyer although she has a good reputation."

"She is a very gracious lady and intelligent. We have had some interesting conversations."

"But you would actually be working for her new daughter-in-law — or whatever the relationship is — would you not?"

"Her daughter married Master Hohnholz, but both her daughter and eldest granddaughter died about three or four years ago. Master Hohnholz remarried last year and there is already a new babe and another on the way. So most of the burden of caring for her own three grandchildren falls on Frau Meyer. In a way I'll be working for them both. And I suspect — although she didn't say — that it will be Frau Meyer who will be paying my wages."

"I see. Then I must call upon both Frau Meyer and Mistress Hohnholz. I would also see the house before I give my approval. But it seems as though you have already investigated that."

"You'll approve, Mama. I know you will."

Lise was charmed by the elegant Frau Meyer and found the new Mistress Hohnholz pleasant enough and the house well kept and spotless. To Dorothea the long summer ahead seemed endless. But soon it was time to harvest the blue-flowered flax, to soak the stalks in specially designed troughs, to beat the wet stems with wooden paddles in order to separate the fibres and to hang them on drying racks. They were so busy the time sped by. Ocassionally she received a note from Chris, inviting her to some special event such as dancing around the midsummer bonfire. But she could never go, was afraid to ask. She replied apologetically that hopefuly next year would be better.

One day toward the end of August Anton called Dorothea into his office. "So you will be leaving us soon," he said gruffly. "I call that mighty ungrateful after all we have done for you. We accepted you as a green, untried lass solely for the sake of your mother's friendship. And now that you are finally beginning to show your worth, you are going to desert us.

Have you no care for the children?"

"I am grateful for all I have learned here," insisted Dorothea timorously, "but it seems as though you are constantly complaining of my lack
of worth. I feel it is time for a change to somewhere where my humble talents will be better appreciated."

"Appreciated?" he stormed..

"And I *do* care for the children," she plunged on, heedless of his
anger. "More, I think, than you do, Master Matthies. But now that Mistress Becke is no longer constantly with child, I am sure she will be able to
devote more time to them."

"Insolent chit. You dare to question my manhood? The reason she
has not conceived again is because the last dead babe was born at the waning of the moon. It is all her fault and the midwife's."

"And no doubt, the moon's," retorted Dorothea, thoroughly disgusted now.

"Bitch!" he growled. "Methinks the real reason you are leaving is to
have more freedom to tumble in the hay with that churl you are seeing."

"I know no man, churl or otherwise," she denied hotly.

"Then wherefrom are those letters you keep receiving?"

"What do you know of my letters? What right . . . ?"

"I make it my business to know everything that goes on in this house.
And I think it's time you learned something else instead of panting after
some fool who has not the courage to show his face. I'll show you what a
good man can do for you."

Dorothea backed off, thoroughly frightened now. But he was
quicker. He grabbed her arm and drew her to him. His other hand
clutched her breast, squeezing until she cried out in pain. "Unhand me,
you beast," she screamed. She tried to twist away but he was too strong. He
flung her down on the floor, hiked up her skirts and straddled her, pinning
her helpless beneath him. She screamed again and again.

"I've wanted to do this for a long time," he leered as he unbuttoned
his breeches and his engorged penis sprang out. "Now I'll leave you with a
nice farewell present and you can tell your uppity mother it was a gift from
your lover, for I'll deny it."

Dorothea screamed again and tried to turn away from the ugly sight
but he held her firmly.

"Scream all you want, bitch, for no one dares to enter this room without my say-so."

Eleonore was looking for Dorothea. She could not imagine where she could have got to. Then she heard the scream emanating from Papa's office. Now who or what in the world could that be? It was definitely a woman's screams. Could Papa be punishing Adi for some infringement? But he rarely whipped Adi. Eleonore hurried to the main room. Adelheit was calmly spinning, studiously ignoring the noise, as was Mama at her loom. The only other woman in the house was Dorothea. Dorchen! Eleonore rushed back. She knew she was forbidden to enter Papa's office, but Dorchen was hurt. Her beloved Dorchen. She must rescue her. Heedless of her father's wrath, she burst through the door. There she saw the strangest sight. Dorchen was lying on the floor and this large stick-like thing was protruding from Papa's breeches. While she watched in horror, the thing shrivelled down to nothing and she could see it was is peepee-er. But she was more concerned with Dorothea.

She ran to her and knelt beside her. "Dorchen! Dorchen, are you hurt? I heard you scream."

Dorothea shook her head as though coming out of a daze. "No, Elli, I am all right, thanks to you. Here, help me up."

As Eleonore did so, she noticed Papa tuck the thing back in his breeches and stand up.

"Eleonore, get out of here," he shouted furiously. "You know you are forbidden to come in here."

"But, I heard Dorchen scream," she replied. "I wanted to help her."

"She did not scream. She merely swooned and I was trying to arouse her," he insisted.

"Liar," spat Dorothea, on her feet now but still visibly skaken. She smoothed down her skirts. "Come, Elli, neither of us have any business here."

"Eleonore! Come back here," he roared.

The two paused in the doorway, Eleonore looking hesitantly from Dorothea to her father and back again. There were tears of defiance in her eyes. "I'd best suffer the whipping now," she whispered, "or he'll only dole out worse later." Bravely she reentered the office, as Dorothea fled to her room.

But Anton did not dole out the expected whipping. He shook his daughter until her teeth rattled and she thought her head would fall off. He slapped her face several times, but nowhere near as viciously as he was wont, inflicting no serious damage. Then he took her by the arms so tightly she could feel them bruise, but she refused to cry out.

"I want you to forget everything you saw and think you heard here," he snarled.

"Yes, Papa."

"If you ever breathe a word of this to your mother or anyone else, I'll kill you with my own hands."

She had no doubt that he meant every word. "Yes, Papa."

"And I want you to stay away from that bitch Dorothea. She is a bad girl. She tormented me until I lost my reason. Do you understand?"

She did not quite understand nor did she believe any of it. Not her beloved Dorchen. But she knew better than to argue. "Yes, Papa," she said meekly. It was a promise she had no intention of keeping.

"Then get out of my sight. And mind you, keep your mouth shut."

Eleonore fled.

In her room Dorothea hurriedly packed as many of her clothes and other possessions as she could fit in her saddlebag. She regretted having to leave behind her books and other precious things but there was simply no room and she vowed she would never return. She just hoped she could escape before he came after her. Eleonore caught up with her in the stable as she was saddling her dear old mare.

"Dorchen. Dorchen, don't leave us," she cried.

"I must, little one, I must. I'll never return to this house again."

Eleonore clung to Dorothea. "Then take me with you." Weeping copiously, she let out all the tears she had held back during her punishment.

Dorothea held her closely for a moment. "I can't, dearest Elli. As much as I would like to, I dare not or it will go ill for both of us. Now calm your tears. He will get over it."

"I hate him. I hate him," Eleonore declared. "But he didn't whip me. I wonder why."

"But your face. Go and show that to your Mama and tell her I am sorry not to bid her farewell but I must hurry."

"But what can I tell her? He made me promise not to say anything about what I saw. But I don't really know what I saw. What did I see, Dorchen?"

"Nothing but a man trying to show his power over a woman he hates."

"Papa hates everyone, doesn't he?"

"It seems that way, but I really think he hates himself more. Now let me go." She quickly tightened the girth, threw her bag behind the saddle and mounted. "I shall try and arrange for you to visit me once I am settled at Frau Meyer's. Would you like that?"

"Oh, yes, Dorchen." A tearful Eleonore watched as her best friend hurried the mare down the road toward Vilsen.

Once Dorothea left Vilsen and headed west toward Neubruchhausen and was sure no one was following her, she slowed the horse down. When she was almost home, she suddenly heard hoofbeats behind her. Oh, no, she thought, he wouldn't dare molest me at my own home. Or would he? She was beginning to believe the man was crazy. She spurred her horse to a gallop and dismounted panting in the stableyard. No one seemed to be about but she would stand her ground. How dare he follow her?

Then when the rider drew near she saw it was not Anton Matthies at all but Chris Bergmann. She almost collapsed with relief.

"Dorchen," he called out cheerfully, "whatever are you doing here? I tried to catch up with you. Why did you run away from me?"

"It is my home after all," she replied more sharply than she intended.

"I know, but . . . " As he dismounted he could see she was very upset about something. He opened his arms and she collapsed against him.

"Oh, oh, oh," she moaned. "Something terrible almost happened. But—but—it didn't. I feel safe now."

He held her comfortingly. He longed to kiss her but was afraid of frightening her further.

"Tell me," he said.

"Nay, nay, I can't," she sobbed. "I must talk with my mother."

"Was it Master Matthies?"

She nodded and started to draw away from him. Just then Philipp emerged from the mill. What in the world was Dorchen doing home on a weekday? And more to the point, what was his sister doing in the arms of this stranger as though they were lovers?

"Dorchen, whatever . . . " he started to ask.

"Where is mother?" she inquired.

"She has gone visiting. She won't be back until near suppertime. And Papa doesn't even know you're here. The millstones are so noisy. I just came out for a breath of air or I'd not have known either. Dorchen, what is the matter?"

"Nothing," she said and headed toward the house. "Tell Mama . . . Oh, Philipp, this is Chris Bergmann, Papa's new journeyman."

Philipp looked from one to the other, perplexed. They certainly seemed well acquainted for strangers. He hoped it wasn't this man who had made his sister unhappy. Although that certainly did not seem to be the case the way he had been hugging her. "Nice to meet you," he said to Chris. "My father is in the mill. I'll take you to him. But, Dorchen . . . ?"

She shook her head. "Look after my horse, like a dear, Philipp and tell mother I'll be in my room. I must talk to her as soon as she comes home." And she fled into the house.

When Lise arrived home later, Wilhelm took her aside. "Dorchen is home," he announced. "I don't know what ails the lass. I didn't even see her but Philipp tells me she was very upset about something. I can't imagine what could upset her so much that she would leave Anton and Becke when she had no but a few more weeks to work for them."

Lise gave him a thunderous look. "Can't you? Well, I can guess," she said furiously. She threw off her bonnet and gloves and stormed up the stairs. She paused momentarily outside Dorothea's door to calm herself. The child needed comfort now, not anger. Time enough for that when she confronted Anton. And confront him she would. Oh, God, she prayed, I hope he hasn't raped her. She tapped lightly on the door. She expected her daughter to be lying on the bed weeping, but Dorothea was sitting by the window staring into space. Lise took her into her arms and said nothing.

"Oh Mama, Mama, it was terrible. I was never so frightened in my life. But I escaped him. I escaped."

"He didn't . . . ?"

"No, he didn't, but it was close. Eleonore rescued me."

"Eleonore? That poor little child to have witnessed that. Tell me."

"He grabbed me and started squeezing me here. Then—then he threw me on the floor and pulled up my skirts and petticoats. Oh, Mama, I was so ashamed. Then while he pinned me down he opened his breeches and his—his thing came out all by itself. It was so swollen and ugly." She shuddered at the memory.

"And then?"

"Eleonore burst in the door even though she was forbidden ever to enter there. Thank God, she heard my screams. It was a very brave thing for her to do."

"Ja, and thank God she did. But that poor child. What a scar it will leave on her soul." And on yours, too, Lise added to herself. Lord, I pray not.

"And then he had the audacity to lie and tell her it was I who enticed him beyond reason. Mama, I swear I didn't. I detest the man. If I ever were to do—to do that, it would be with someone I loved and who loved me. Not that beast."

40

"Of course, my dear. And someday you will find that someone. Don't let this one horrible experience turn you away from real love."

"And Mama," said Dorothea sadly. "I had to leave all my books and other precious things behind, I left in such a hurry."

"I'll fetch them for you tomorrow and you can be sure I'll give him a piece of my mind as well."

"Oh, Mama, don't. He swore Eleonore to secrecy. Said he would kill her if she ever told anyone, especially her mother."

"No doubt he would. But who were you to tell if not your very own mother? Don't worry. I have no fear of Anton Matthies. I rather think he fears me. I have ways of shutting him up ere he spreads his vile tale about you luring him on."

"You do? Oh, Mama." She smiled for the first time. "You are so brave. I feel so much better now that I know you are on my side."

"And whose side would I be on? Not his, for certain," Lise assured her, indignantly.

Dorothea smiled again. "Mayhap," she said mischievously, "you should take your butcher knife, if you mean to unman him."

Lise laughed and embraced her fondly. "That's my girl. Mayhap I should. He deserves it."

Wilhelm was as surprised to see his new journeyman as he was to see his daughter come home. "I didn't expect you until September," he said.

"Nor did I expect to come as yet," replied Chris, "but Master Harries has already obtained his new journeyman and there did not seem much point in staying with nothing much to do. But if I've inconvenienced you, Master Koch, I should be glad to put up at the inn in Vilsen until you are ready for me. I am not totally without funds."

"Nay, nay, I won't hear of it. It's no real inconvenience. It's only that I planned to give you Philipp's room and as you can see, he has not left yet for the gymnasium in Hannover. If you don't mind sleeping with him for a few weeks, there is no problem. I usually put the apprentices and the few journeymen I've had up over the stables. Some of them can be a bit rowdy. But since you are a mature man, I thought it would be nicer if you stayed in the house with the family."

"That's kind of you, Master Koch, but if Philipp is not agreeable, I should be happy to bed down over the stable for a few weeks. I've slept in worse places."

"No doubt you have. But Philipp will agree. In fact, I am sure he will enjoy your company—provided you can stand his interminable intellectual chatter."

"I'm sure I can. In fact, I look forward to it. It will be a welcome change from the silly inanities of most teenage boys. And if you're not prepared to pay me as yet, I should be happy to help out around the house and garden to earn my keep until you are ready for me to join in real work."

"Nay, as helpful as that might be at this time of year, that won't be necessary. Especially with my daughter home for a few weeks." Wilhelm decided he would get on well with his new assistant.

Very early next morning before anyone else was up, Lise left. She rode sedately not wishing her horse to be lathered or herself to be breathless when she reached Bruchmühlen. As she passed through Vilsen she nodded politely to acquaintances but did not stop. When she arrived at the mill, she walked straight into the house without knocking. Becke was still seated at the kitchen table drinking her morning coffee. Surprise and—what was it—disbelief, perhaps fear registered in rapid succession on her usually vapid face. She tried to recover.

"Why good morning, Lise," she said. "How nice to see you so early. Would you care for a cup of coffee?"

"No, thank you," replied Lise politely.

"I suppose you have come about your recalcitrant daughter."

"I have come to collect her things, yes. But I would speak to Anton first. My daughter is not recalcitrant. What fable did he tell you, Becke?" she inquired coldly.

"Why—why, nothing but that he was trying to discipline her for some minor thing Eleonore had done of which he did not approve and she lost her temper, spoke to him quite nastily and ran away."

"That is a lie," piped up Eleonore from across the table. "He—he— oh," she put her hand across her mouth. Lise could see the fear in the child's eyes, the bruises on her face and arms.

"No need to tell, Elli," she said. "I know." She paused significantly. "Where is he, Becke?"

"In the mill, I suppose. He starts early."

"Fetch him," ordered Lise. "I'll await him in his office."

"No, no, you can't go in there."

"What I have to discuss, Becke, cannot be said in front of the children." Or you, she felt like adding. "I'll wait in his office."

42

Becke could not understand all this fuss over a simple matter of discipline. But she had always been a little in awe of Lise—and that lady was obviously in a foul mood.

"Carsten," she said, "go fetch Papa quckly. Tell him Mistress Koch is here and would have words with him. That she is—is . . ."

"Very angry," Lise finished for her and swept out of the room.

Anton deliberately kept Lise waiting. Little did he realize that the calculated insult was only fueling her anger. He was prepared to bluff his way out. He was certain the chit would not have dared to tell her mother what had really happened. The man was totally foreign to such loving rapport as Dorothea had with her parents. He greeted Lise with feigned cheerfulness.

"Well, Lise, what brings you here so early of a morn? As you can see, I'm very busy but I can spare you a few minutes. I suppose Dorothea has told you some cock-and-bull story. It was really nothing . . ." She ignored his outstretched hand.

"My daughter told me the truth, Anton," she said frostily. "And you will spare me as much time as I want. It was rape, Anton—pure and simple, rape."

"She lies."

"My daughter is no liar. She is too innocent to make up tales of what she saw and suffered. And I have corroboration."

Anton fell into the trap. "I told Eleonore to say nothing. I'll kill her . . . " He forgot to control his mounting temper.

"Eleonore said nothing. She didn't have to. One look at her bruised face told me all. Your child , Anton, will suffer more from this than mine."

"I'll handle my children as I please."

Lise shrugged. "My main concern right now is that you do not spread your vicious lies about Dorothea. You know very well that she did not entice you, did not lure you at all. You will not mention the incident— ever—to anyone. Who would believe you?"

"Any man would," he replied. "Young Harm Hohnholz should be warned."

"You wouldn't dare!" she gasped.

"And how do you propose to stop me, Mistress Koch?"

"Very easily, Anton." Lise smiled and paused. He thought she was at a loss for words and smirked triumphantly, so that he was unprepared for her next remark. She asked slowly and deliberately, "How badly do you want the hereditary rights to this mill and Heiligenberg, Anton?"

His countenance drained to white, then turned red and purple with fury. "You wouldn't dare," he gasped.

"I would," she said calmly, "without a qualm. During the past several weeks I have become fast friends with Frau Meyer as well as her son-in-law Harm Hohnholz and his new wife. I am also well acquainted with all the members of the Council. You are already on shaky ground in this matter, as you well know. Many of the councilmen do not like you because of your arrogance. Several have been throwing stumbling blocks in your way. I believe that honor and personal integrity in a man are important factors in the granting of those hereditary rights. I know you have neither—never have. I doubt you know the meaning of the words. My daughter's reputation is worth far more than your rights to these mills. Think on it carefully, Anton. Whom do you really think they will believe?"

The man seemed to shrivel before her eyes, collapse like air let out of a bag. He gulped. "You drive a hard bargain, Lise."

"No bargain at all. Simply justice. You keep your mouth shut and Dorothea and I shall do likewise. But if you so much as hint at what happened here or imply in any way that my daughter is to blame, I shall blacken your reputation throughout the whole village. I shall shout the story all the way to Hannover. Do you understand, Anton?"

He nodded. "What do I tell Becke?"

"Simply tell her that it was a misunderstanding that has been cleared up and that you have apologized to me—although I doubt you know the meaning of that word."

"But—but—"

"No buts. On the surface we shall remain friends and she'll soon forget all about it. But your daughter is another problem. I would suggest that you treat her more kindly from now on. Perhaps a little kindness will help her heal. I hope it is not too late for she is the best of your motley lot. And if I ever hear of you abusing Eleonore because of this, I may still tell certain critical people the story. Dorothea and I shall do all we can to help her. I urge you to allow us."

"If you wish," he replied with surprising meekness. "I simply don't understand her. Never have. If I didn't know better, I'd think she wasn't mine."

"She is more like you than you realize, Anton. Probably a throwback to your dear father and grandfather. They were brave men without being arrogant, humble men without duplicity."

"If you say so." He shook his head, still not really understanding.

44

"And I do apologize, Lise. I am truly sorry for what happened. I don't know what came over me. May we still be friends?"

Lise knew how difficult it was for him to speak those words although she truly doubted his sincerity. But this time she shook his extended hand.

Chris walked into the Hohnholz house without ringing the bell and was greeted by the mouthwatering aroma of freshly baked bread and cakes. He was a frequent visitor here now and need not stand on ceremony. Since Dorothea had settled in well and seemed happy, he usually came once a month to see her, to take her dancing to Der Lustige Strumpf, or out walking or sometimes to just sit in the cozy parlor for good conversation. The Hohnholz permitted her to have not only all day Sunday off but once a month a Saturday evening. This was one of those Saturdays.

"My, Chris, you are early today," Dorothea greeted him. "We have just finished dinner. Have you eaten?"

"Enough."

"I was just about to take the chldren out. Leave your cloak on if you'd like to come with us."

"We are going for a sleigh ride," announced Marie.

"Not a sleigh ride, silly," piped up Eleonore from a corner where Chris had not noticed her. "We're going sledding down the hill. It's much more fun. And I'll bet Chris can give us an even better push than Dorchen can. Will you push us, Chris?"

"I'd be happy to," he replied. "And it's nice to see you again, Fraülein Eleonore."

"Oh, I can come here quite often now. I just ask Mama and Papa hasn't said 'no' yet."

Chris looked at Dorothea. Some radical change had come over Anton Matthies ever since that day last summer when Mistress Lise had charged off to see him with fire in her eyes. But Chris said nothing.

"It's the first snow we've had good enough to pack down," said Dorothea. "The children have been so looking forward to it. You don't mind?"

"Not at all. I haven't really played in the snow since I was a lad. Let's go."

In the flat land of north Germany the only real hill in Vilsen was the one on which the church stood. Behind the stately houses which faced the churchyard ran a very steep, roughly cobblestoned alley. The helter-skelter stones made it teacherous walking in summertime but with the snow packed down hard it was an ideal slope for sledding. Several neighborhood children were already screaming with delight as pigtails and scarves streamed out behind them. Some of the older boys took turns at the bottom watching for traffic as there was no way for the children, especially the littlest ones, to stop the speeding sleds if a horse or someone's wagon got in their way.

"Now, we'll have to take turns," said Dorothea. "We have only two sleds—unless you want to ride double."

"I'm not riding double with any girl," objected Teddi. "Besides they get scared the way I drive the sled. Watch."

With a push from Chris he zig-zagged down the hill shouting for everyone to get out of his way.

"I wish I could do that," sighed Eleonore wistfully.

"It's easy," said Chris. "I'll show you when your turn comes. You steer it with your body."

"Now Marie, you take Eliza in front of you," said Dorothea. "And hold her tight." With a gentle push from Dorothea the two girls sailed sedately down the hill. When Teddi returned, she said, "Now it's Eleonore's turn." Teddi yielded the sled reluctantly.

"Push me hard, Chris," ordered Eleonore. He did. She tried valiantly to imitate Teddi's maneuvers but only succeeded in almost upsetting herself as she reached the bottom of the slope. "I didn't do very well, did I?" she said as she trudged back up the hill with the sled.

"I'll go with you next time and show you how," volunteered Chris.

Girls, thought Teddi in disgust. But then he thought, it might be fun at that. I'll make her scream. To everyone's surprise he offered to take Eleonore the next time. "But you mustn't scream," he warned.

"I'll not," she promised.

He tried his wildest maneuvers while she hung on for dear life. And he had to admit—if only to himself—that it was kind of fun showing off to her while he held her in his arms, young as she was.

Returning to the hilltop, cheeks red with cold and exhilaration, she exclaimed, "That was exciting."

"She's game," admitted Teddi.

"Now it's Dorchen's turn," proclaimed Eleonore. "She hasn't been down once yet."

"Nay, that's all right. I enjoy just watching you have fun."

"Go down with Chris," urged Eleonore.

"Yes," chimed in Marie, "go down with Chris. It's ever so much better, Dorchen."

Soon everyone was clapping their mittened hands and singing, "Chris take Dorchen."

Chris took Dorothea's hand. "Come, my lady, it's your turn now." He led her to a sled and sat her down.

"Very well," she agreed, "but none of your fancy tactics. And who's to push us?"

"I shall." He sat down behind her, dug his feet into the snow and gave a mighty thrust. They went flying off. She felt so comfortable in his arms as though she belonged there. He whispered into her ear, "Happy?" She nodded. He kissed the back of her neck where the hood of her cloak had slipped away. She felt warmth surge through her despite the wintry air. All too soon they were at the bottom of the hill.

"Would you like to come back here this evening after the children are in bed?" he asked.

She hesitated a moment. But no. "I'd rather go dancing at Der Lustige Strumpf. Methinks it would be a mite warmer and we haven't been for a while."

He bowed over her hand. "Whatever you wish, my lady."

"And that reminds me," she said, "it grows dark so early this time of year and I promised to have Eleonore home before dark or she might not be allowed to come again. And I still have to see to the children's baths— and my own."

"No problem," said Chris. "Let them each have one more run down the hill and I"ll take Eleonore home on my horse while you bathe the children. Then we'll have supper and go dancing."

"Chris, you are so kind and Eleonore will be delighted, I'm sure."

"Poor mite, she deserves a little happiness," he replied.

That evening as they whirled around at Der Lustige Strumpf Chris realized suddenly that he, too, had found happiness. His life until now, while never really unhappy, had been rather bleak and drear. Unbidden the thought crossed his mind, this is the girl I am going to marry. Not yet, of course. She was still too young. Her parents would never approve. Chris got along well with Wilhelm Koch. The man was a hard worker, extraordinarily kind, if somewhat staid and unimaginative. He admired Lise greatly, the more liberal of the two. Truth was he was a little in awe of her—a true daughter of the Enlightenment. She was the one whose approval he must win. Well, he would bide his time and court Dorchen very slowly so as not to frighten her. He dared not even tell her that he thought he was falling in love with her. He could wait. She was worth waiting for.

When they sat down to rest, breathless from a fast jig, he said, "I have always wondered where the name of this place originated—Der Lustige Strumpf—the Merry Stocking. Do you know?"

Dorothea laughed. "According to my mother, who knows every bit of the history of the whole area, this is how the story goes. The house is very old as you can see—the oldest in Vilsen, I believe—about a hundred and fifty years or so. It was one of the few that survived the Thirty Years War or one of the first to be rebuilt after it—I'm not sure which. It has always been a tavern with this dance floor upstairs. In the old days the farmers who came into market of a Saturday would all come here to drink and dance after the market closed. They all wore wooden shoes—klompen—then. Many still do. Well, the wooden shoes made such a racket when they danced that the Pastor—you can see how hard by the church it is—the Pastor and several of the neighbors complained about the noise. So they made a rule that everyone had to take off their shoes before they mounted the stairs and dance in their stocking feet. Hence, Der Lustige Strumpf."

Chris laughed. "Only in Vilsen. But we did not have to remove our shoes."

"No, because they are leathern and don't make the clatter the wooden ones do. I believe anyone still wearing klompen must leave them belowstairs even now. 'Tis said that once the Princess Sophie Dorothea came here—long before Königsmarck—and refused to take off her shoes. Of course, they were soft leather slippers but everyone was so in awe of her that the fiddler couldn't even play his tune straight."

"And I suppose that was Vilsen's moment of glory."

"No, not really. Vilsen's history goes way back to ancient Saxon times. It has always been a market town. It stands—or stood—at the cross-roads of two of the old Volkswegs—the Amber Roads—from Roman times."

Chris held up his hands. "Enough. I didn't expect a history lesson when I asked."

Dorothea laughed. "My grandfather Cyriacus Lindemann was the real historian of the family. You would have liked him. Although my mother does pretty well at it, too."

"And I won't even ask where he got that strange name."

"No, don't because I don't know." They laughed together. He took her hand and led her back to the dance floor.

48

2

1783

Anton Matthies was happy—for once in his life. He was inordinately proud, but with only a touch of his usual arrogance. At last he was well satisfied with his life. And Anton proposed to give a party to celebrate. In rural villages such as Vilsen it was customary on occasions of great joy to call in one's friends and neighbors to a great fete to share that joy. But Anton had always been so anti-social he did not know how to go about it. He wasn't even sure if he had any friends. He decided to confer with the one person whom he trusted to advise him—if she would—Lise Koch.

On a bright April morning—warm for so early in the season—trees beginning to bud, spring flowers blooming, some hardy early birds even beginning to nest—Anton noticed the beauty around him for the first time in his life as he rode to Neubruchhausen. We should have some of those flowers around the house, he thought. Becke and Eleonore had always wanted them. Why hadn't he seen their usefulness before? He was in an expansive mood as he approached the Koch house. He had already told the family the good news; now, via Lise Koch, he would tell the world.

"Good morning, Anton," said Lise. "My goodness, something portentous must have happened to bring you so far and on a weekday. I hope it is good news and not bad."

"Good news, Lise, very good news," he announced cheerfully as he dismounted and drew from his pocket a large fancy document. "I am now the hereditary miller of both Bruchmühlen and Heiligenberg—at long last. And I wanted you and Wilhelm to be the first to know. See." He handed her the parchment.

She took it and read, 'In the name of King George the Third, etc., etc.' "I am so happy for you, Anton. Congratulations. You've certainly worked so long and hard for this."

"I know," he agreed. "And look, they approved on 28 February and didn't even write the thing until 28 March. A whole month I could have known without worrying."

"Now Anton, don't start complaining again. Be thankful it happened at all."

"You're right. I do complain too much, don't I?"

"A bad habit you have and one you should try to overcome," she agreed.

"And now I want to have a party to celebrate. You know, invite friends, neighbors, everyone. But I don't quite know how to go about it. Suppose no one comes. That would be awful. I need your advice."

She laughed. "They'll come, out of curiosity if nothing else, provided you behave yourself in the meantime. But first things first. Have you written to thank these three gentlemen in Hannover who signed the letter?"

"No. I didn't think . . . "

"Do so immediately. A brief note is all that is required but one to each of them."

He nodded. "The first two, all right. But that Kielmannsegge. He is the grandson of that—that . . . "

"I know," she interrupted. "Of George the First's fat mistress and no doubt his grandson as well, hence his high position. But no fault of his. And since when, Anton, are you, of all people, so full of moral rectitiude?"

He had the grace to hang his head. He didn't need to be reminded of that. "Very well, to all three. What else?"

"You must go to the next Town Council meeting and personally thank each of the members, even those who opposed you. Also to Bruchhausen to thank both the Amtsmann—the head of the County government—and the Amtsschreiber—the County Clerk." She smiled to herself. So many officials nowadays. Back when her grandfather Johann Lindemann had been County Clerk he had performed all the duties of both those offices all by himself. Well, that would certainly keep Anton on his toes.

"That's a lot of thanking," he remarked.

"But very necessary if you want their goodwill in the future. Also if you want them to come to your party."

"Shall I mention the party yet?"

"You could hint—to see what their reaction would be – but don't invite until you've set a firm date."

"But I want to have it as soon as possible."

"Wait just a minute." She looked at the document again. "This does not officially take effect until the first of May. Have it after that. The weather will be better then so people would have less excuse not to come. You might even have it picnic-style in that lovely little meadow next to the millpond. And have you no concern for your family? Give Becke and the girls a chance to plan and prepare. It is a big undertaking. And you might consider buying them some cloth for new gowns. I'm sure that has never occurred to you."

He shook his head. "God's balls, Lise, you drive a hard bargain as usual. I never thought it would be so complicated."

She laughed. "It's time you grew up, Anton—past time."

Previously a remark like that would have set his temper off. Now he simply nodded, thanked her and rode back to Bruchmühlen. She had given Anton a lot to think about.

In the event the party was held at the mill at Bruchmühlen, the family having decided that the meadow by the millpond was too far to carry all the food, drink, tables and other necessities. And what if it should rain? But so many people showed up that much of the party spilled out of the house into the garden where Anton had finally relented and allowed his womenfolk to plant flowers. Some of the guests merely dropped in for a few minutes out of curiosity and to offer congratulations, but many more stayed to eat and drink all they could. Anton Matthies could afford it and it was about time he did spend a little, was the consensus.

Lise was there with the whole Koch family. She was acting as co-hostess with Becke who was totally bewildered by the crowd and somewhat tongue-tied. Young Eleonore, however, was in her glory, acting with aplomb and a graciousness that belied her years. She offered the guests food and drink, thanked them for coming, told them how happy Papa was, even had intelligent conversations with some regarding such varied subjects as the state of this year's flax crop or the state of Hannoverian politics.

She listened avidly as Philipp, home for the summer, showed off his new knowledge of the latter to one of the town councilmen. "So you see, we are about to lose our American colonies," he was saying.

"We?" said the man.

"Our colonies?" queried another. "But they are England's colonies, not ours."

"But we and England are under one king," insisted Philipp, "therefore their loss could hurt us as much as England."

"I doubt it will affect us very much," said the first man.

"But the point is that they want a say in their own government—a constitution such as England has for herself and Hannover should have," proclaimed Philipp.

The first coucilman shook his head. "I don't know what they're teaching you youngsters nowadays. Are you at Göttingen already?"

"No, but I shall be in two more years. I intend to study law. That is their specialty."

"Ach," exclaimed the man, "then they'll surely fill your head with all that *Sturm und Drang* drivel. You'll be so bewildered you won't know what to think."

"But *Sturm und Drang* is literary, not the law," objected Philipp.

"Hah! That fellow Goethe combines public service with his literary work. Although I must admit I do like some of his poetry. But this new playwright Schiller I don't care for. He is sorry for the peasants and makes fun of the nobility."

"Ach," sighed the second man. "These poets should stay out of politics. Our government here in Hannover is good enough the way it is. It shouldn't be tinkered with. They leave us alone and that's all that matters. What need have we for a constitution?"

Anton was discoursing with another group. "The old Empire is dying and everyone knows it. Austria can't hold it together. Never has in a thousand years. We need a united Germany. Prussia is the one we should look to."

"I don't trust Prussia at all," disagreed Councilman Ravens. "Too militaristic. She'd like to gobble us all up—not unite us."

"Ja," sighed another man. "We no doubt admire Friedrich for building a state out of practically nothing but would you want to live under that sort of rigid discipline?"

"Many of the smaller states could well use that sort of discipline," said Anton. "I find no fault with it."

Ravens shook his head. "Maybe so, but we have no need of it here in Hannover. And what will happen when 'der alte Fritz' passes on? He's getting old, you know. That profilgate Friedrich Wilhelm will bring it crashing down in ten years. Prussia is Fritz. Without him it will be nothing because it has no basis in the estates—the people."

"I agree," said the other man. "Austria is our only hope, although admittedly a weak one. But the Emperor Josef's new Edict of Toleration shows promise. I read where over 70,000 people in Austria alone converted to Protestantism after it was passed."

"Something that should have happened two hundred years ago," declared Anton. "Austria is still in the dark ages. The Habsburgs have never cared about Germany. They look more and more to Hungary, Poland and the east to extend their personal empire."

"I say Hannover is fine by itself," stated Ravens. "We have no need of either Prussia or Austria. We have the best government in the whole Empire—the freest. Let them beat each other down and leave us alone."

And so it went. In the Germany of the Enlightenment where poets and philosophers, Bürgers, artisans and professors, even peasants and students dabbled in politics, the wave of nationalistic feeling was slowly emerging and growing stronger. Instead of religion dividing the land as in so many past centuries, the debate was of the merits or faults of the two great powers—Prussia and Austria.

But life went on.

The following year Christian Bergmann decided it was time to pursue his courtship of Dorothea Koch more ardently. She was nineteen now and ripe for marriage even if she did not realize it. He loved her dearly and he was quite sure she loved him in return although she had never said so.

During that summer the venerable Frau Meyer died and Dorothea decided it was time she went home. Lise agreed that she had probably learned all she was going to learn and she deserved to live her own life. Before she left they arranged for Eleonore Matthies to take her place in the Hohnholz household. Eleonore was thirteen now and mature for her age. Although the older children had no need of her, she had become fast friends with Marie and more importantly, Harm Hohnholz's second wife Catharine kept having babies. Anton Matthies drove a hard bargain as to her wages but since his own wife was no longer breeding, he willingly let her go. Eleonore rejoiced to be free of that dismal household and blossomed out in her new surroundings. With her dark good looks she was the most French-like of all Anton's children.

Lise was also aware that Dorothea was ripe for marriage. She was also very much aware that Chris Bergmann was in love with her daughter. But was he the right man for her? She wasn't sure. He had many good qualities. He was kind and considerate, stable and mature, and a very hard worker. Wilhelm said he was the best journeyman he'd ever had. She found no fault with the wide discrepancy in their ages. In fact, that might even prove to be an asset. There was only one problem. Although Chris had all the qualifications and had passed all the tests to be a Master Miller, he was not yet able to lay claim to that title because he did not have his own mill. Moreover, he did not seem to be seeking one. Was he lazy? She did not think so. Was he staying on because of Wilhelm? Because of Dorchen? She wasn't sure. Lise could not decide whether to start searching for another possible mate for her daughter or wait and see if things worked out. So she did nothing.

Chris and Dorothea were strolling hand in hand along the sparkling millstream. It was a very hot July day and they had just come home from Frau Meyer's funeral. Gladly they had divested themselves of the heavy black mourning garments and had donned cool linen gown and shirt. Chris could see Dorothea was still a little teary, so he said nothing until they were well out of sight of the mill. Then he turned her to him, enfolded her in his arms and kissed her deeply. At first she held herself stiffly but the gradually he could feel her melt against him and respond to his kiss.

"Don't keep weeping, my sweet," he said gently. "Frau Meyer led a full life and she was very old."

"I know," sobbed Dorothea, "but I shall miss her so."

"I am sure but methinks she would not have wanted you to mourn." They strolled on for a while in silence. Then he asked, "Tell me, what do you think is the most important thing you learned from Frau Meyer?"

Dorothea stopped and thought for a moment. "She taught me how to be a lady."

Chris had expected her to say that she had learned how to manage a household or even that she had become interested in local politics. Her answer puzzled him. "But—but," he objected, "how can that be? To be a lady one must be born to it. We are just simple peasants, not nobility."

"That no longer holds true," she replied. "And we are not peasants. We are Bürgers—or at least Papa is. But Frau Meyer said that many nobles are worse boors than the meanest peasant. Being a lady—or a gentleman—has nothing to do with blood but with manners and decorum, with courtesy and integrity, with being kind to everyone regardless of their social status."

Chris thought about that for a moment. "Methinks you have been reading too much of Master Schiller's poetry."

"I like Master Schiller's poetry. It is very beautiful even if a bit pagan."

"Have you read aught of Jean Jacques Rousseau? I believe he speaks of 'the noble peasant'."

"No, I haven't but I've heard a lot of his ideas from Philipp and even from Master Hohnholz."

"Then according to your definition, Frau Meyer, God rest her, and your mother and even you are ladies. Whereas someone like — er — Master Matthies is a boor."

She laughed. "I guess you could say that," she agreed.

"Then my lady, show me some of that kindness." He took her in his arms again and kissed her soundly. This time she did not hold back but responded ardently. "Ach, my Dorchen, if you only knew how I've hungered for you these many months – years."

She drew back a bit. "Hungered mayhap, but is it love or lust, Chris?"

"If what I'm feeling isn't love, I don't know what is. Yes, my sweet Dorchen, I've loved you for a long time. Do you love me enough to let me show you the difference between love and lust?"

"I — I think so," she replied hesitantly.

He led her to a grassy, hidden spot under a great linden tree, drew her down beside him and kissed her again, deeply. Thrills ran through her. Yes, she wanted this but she was still afraid. When he gently fondled her breast, she jumped and started to push him away. And yet — yet it excited her as nothing ever had before. She tried to dismiss memories of Master Matthies from her mind.

"I don't know, Chris," she murmured.

"Let me, sweeting," he insisted quietly. "You want it as much as I. You know you do."

Did she? Yes and no. But she lay back and made no objection when he carefully unbuttoned the bodice of her dress and withdrew one breast, kissing it as he gently fondled the other. Waves of heat washed over her. Her excitement mounted. Yes, she did want him, all of him. She put her arms around his head and held him tightly to her breasts as he nibbled on the taut nipples. Oh, God, she'd never experienced such sensations in her whole life. She no longer cared whether it was love or lust. She wanted more, more.

"Take me, Chris," she cried out.

"Not yet, sweeting. This is only the beginning."

"Only — ?" She gave herself up to pleasure. Before she was aware of it he had lifted her skirt, petticoats and shift and slid his hand up her smooth thigh. She almost jumped again when his fingers encountered something in her secret place that she had not known existed. Shock wave after shock wave jolted her. Oh, God, I never dreamed it could be like this. She arched her body toward his probing hand. She was on fire. How could he have brought her to this state? How would he put that fire out?

He unbuttoned his breeches and his manhood leapt out. She refused to look. She did not want memories of Master Matthies to spoil this ecstacy. She closed her eyes tightly and gave herself up to pure sensation. She willingly parted her legs and felt him push against her, very gently at first. Oh, don't be so gentle, Chris, she thought. Can't you see I'm on fire? But, of course he knew and so was he. He hoped he could hold back long enough to pleasure her. He thrust hard and she gasped at the sudden sharp pain. Then he was deep inside her and the momentary pain was forgotten as she welcomed him. Deeper and deeper he drove, until she caught the rhythm and rose to meet him. Then suddenly there were starbursts, comets, meteors, birdsong, heavenly choirs, rhapsody. She thought she heard someone scream, someone groan. Then all was quiet as they lay gasping in each other's arms.

After a while Chris murmured into her hair, "My sweet, sweet Dorchen," and kissed her gently.

"Oh, Chris," she sighed.

"Now, my sweet, will you marry me?"

"Oh, Chris, I don't know," she replied. "I love you dearly—especially after this—but I just don't want to get married yet. Can't we just stay like this for a while?"

Chris was surprised at that. Most girls, after what had just happened between them, would be forcing him into rapid wedlock. He forbore from reminding her what could result from their coming together. Mayhap his seed had already implanted a babe inside her. "If that's what you wish," he replied. But he was disappointed. Was she still holding it against him that he was not yet a master miller? He hoped not, but the doubt had crept in. So much for all her talk about ladies and noble peasants. He longed to tell her of his plans but they were too ephemeral as yet, too uncertain. Well, he would go along with her for now. As long as she wanted more of his lovemaking that would satisfy him for a while.

Within a few weeks Lise knew exactly what had happened to her daughter. Dorothea was no longer a young girl dreaming of love. She was a woman well satisfied. Now they would have to wed, and that right soon. There was no longer a question of seeking another mate for Dorchen. Lise hoped that she was not yet pregnant but that was bound to happen sooner rather than later. She thought it strange that neither Dorchen nor Chris had approached her about the inevitable marriage. She took her concerns to Wilhelm.

"I'm only surprised that it hasn't happened sooner," was his phlegmatic reply. "He has wanted to wed her for a long time. I believe it is Dorchen who is putting him off."

"Dorchen? But why? Doesn't she realize what can result from this?"

"I should think she does but I'm afraid she's been influenced by your uppity notions as to why he has not yet found his own mill."

"*My* uppity notions!" she exclaimed. "But then why hasn't he? You certainly can't be expected to support him and a wife and children forever."

"No, I don't intend to," replied Wilhelm calmly in the face of her fury. "I see I shall have to tell you of our plans although it is a bit premature yet."

"Whose plans? Not mine, certainly."

"Mine and Chris'. Anton Matthies has promised to give him the Klostermühle at Heiligenberg just as soon as he can safely rid himself of the drunken miller he has there. He has even agreed to build a new dwelling house at the mill."

"Is that so? Then why hasn't he? He should have sent that fellow packing long ago."

"The guild, you know. He must do something disastrous to warrant his dismissal—or else Anton must find him another place. I doubt it will be long now. His drinking is getting uncontrollable."

"I don't trust Anton Matthies."

"Well, I do—in this, at least," Wilhelm assured her.

"I shall go and talk to Anton."

"No, don't," he commanded. "It has all been arranged. To interfere now would only reveal to him what your daughter has been up to. You wouldn't want that, would you?"

It was like a dash of cold water. "No, I would not," she replied quietly.

"Then I would urge you to say nothing about this to Dorchen either. Let Chris tell her if he wishes. I think he meant to surprise her with the news when it became a fact. But obviously neither one could wait. I suggest you make plans for a wedding and let them work the rest of it out for themselves."

"Very well," said Lise, testily.

What Wilhelm did not tell his wife—and he was sorry he had upset her. It went against his grain to be stern and unkind—was that when he had been ill a few years ago the doctor had warned him that he had a very bad heart, that the next attack would surely carry him off. And it could happen at anytime. He had made Chris promise to stay with him until that time. He could not bear the thought of dropping dead in front of a new and untried journeyman. Chris he could trust to make all the necessary business arrangements and guide his family through what would be a most difficult time. Not that Lise was not capable of that. But somehow he did not want her to know—and worry.

Christian and Dorothea continued their idyll at every opportunity as long as the weather held. They could not make love in the house as she shared her room with her eleven-year-old sister Anna and Chris shared Philipp's room with her nine-year-old brother Johann. No further mention of marriage was made, although Chris was racking his brain as to where they could go once the weather turned cold and inclement.

Then one morning in October Dorothea awoke feeling terrible—nauseous and dragged out. This was not like her. She had never been sick a day in her life. She tried to think what she had eaten the day before. Something was making her very ill. She forced herself to get dressed and go down to breakfast. But a few minutes after she ate she had to make a mad dash to the privy and threw it all up. She went back to her bed and stayed there until midafternoon when she started to feel a bit better.

Lise tapped on her door. "Dorchen, may I come in?"

"If you wish."

"Feeling better now?"

"A bit. I can't imagine what I ate to cause this."

"Nothing at all. Don't you realize that it is the babe you are carrying?"

"Mother! How do you know? Do you really think so? Oh, Lord," she sobbed.

"I know so. How many courses have you missed?"

"Two, but I didn't think . . ."

"You? You who have seen Becke Matthies through how many birthings? And Catharine Hohnholz, too?"

"But Mistress Matthies was *always* sick and complaining—and Catherine never that I know of."

"Each woman reacts differently and even with the same woman no two carryings are the same. Let me see." Lise did a rapid calculation, "I should say sometime in April. You and Chris must be wed soon."

"But Mother, I don't want to be wed yet," Dorothea objected lamely.

"My dear girl, you have no choice now. I assume it is his."

"Of course," she replied indignantly. "I am not a whore."

"I was not implying that, dear Dorchen. But I understand he has wanted to wed you long ere this. Why won't you have him?"

"I have had him, as you have guessed. And I think I love him, but marriage! I had thought to wait . . . "

"Well, you can't wait any longer — unless you want to bear a bastard."

"Oh, no, but . . . "

"Does Chris know about this?"

"No. I haven't said anything to him yet because I wasn't sure."

"Then I suggest you tell him forthwith and start making plans for a wedding."

A few weeks later little Anna came dashing into the kitchen clad in nothing but her nightshift. "Mama, Mama!" she cried.

"Whatever is the matter, Anni?" asked Lise.

"Dorchen is gone and not come back yet," declared the child.

"What do you mean 'gone'?"

"She got up in the middle of the night and dressed herself and went away, I know not where. She didn't know I saw her but I woke up and did see her. I was afraid to say anything because she's been acting so strange lately. Anyway, I thought she would come back in a little while, but she did not."

"Dressed herself? Fully?" asked Lise, perturbed.

"Ja, Mama, even her cloak and boots," replied Anna.

"She has no doubt gone to the stable to talk to her horse. She does that sometimes."

"I know — but never for so long."

"Well, you get yourself back upstairs and dressed ere you catch your death in nothing but that thin nightshift. I'll go and find her." But Lise did not believe her own words. Dorchen *had* been acting strange ever since she had learned she was pregnant. Lise immediately went out to the stable. No Dorchen. And her horse was gone as well. Lise returned to the mill and sought out her husband and Chris. "Have either of you seen Dorchen this morning?" she asked.

"Why no," replied Wilhelm. "Is she not still abed? She has been quite the sleepyhead lately."

Chris shook his head.

"No," said Lise. "She went out in the middle of the night, fully clothed, according to Anni. And now I find her horse is gone as well. Where can she have got to?"

"Mayhap she went to the old wisewoman under the hill," put in young Johann.

"Why would you think that?" asked his mother.

"Well—well," he stammered, "I wasn't listening a-purpose, Mama, but just the other day I heard Papa and Chris saying as how Dorchen was going to have a baby. And the old wisewoman knows all about babies, doesn't she?"

"Oh, no," gasped Lise. "I hope she hasn't decided to take that route."

Johann looked puzzled and Wilhelm shocked, but Chris immediately flew into action. He threw off his apron, dashed to the stable, saddled his horse and in moments was riding out of the yard.

"I'll find her, never fear," he called out. "It's my child, too."

"Do ye crave to rid yourself of the child, then?" asked the old woman.

"Nay, nay," gasped Dorothea in horror. "I want the child. It's just that I—I don't feel ready to wed yet."

The old woman cackled in what Dorothea supposed was a laugh. "Hah! B'ain't that ye got no choice, girl, if'n he be willing. Is't that ye have no liking for the father? Was't rape?"

"Nay," replied Dorothea. "I went to him willingly enough, although I know now that I shouldn't have. And I *do* love him. It's just that I feel so sick, so rotten lately. My mind's all a-muddle. Not like a bride should feel. I don't know what to do."

"Ach, bein' that's the only problem, 'tis nowt but a passing thing. Every breeding woman suffers it the third, even fourth, month. After that you'll feel just fine again. If'n it troubles ye too fierce, there's a potion I can give ye that'll control the stomach heavin'."

"I don't know," said Dorothea hesitantly. "I don't have any money with me."

"Take it," insisted the hag. "If'n it helps, ye can pay me later. And the best thing of all is to bathe in the Sacred Spring at midnight at the full of the moon. A mite chilly for that now, I fear me. Too bad, for the waters of the Sacred Sprng will cure anything."

"I thought that was just for maidens to see what their future husbands would look like."

"That's only on two special nights—St. Andreas and St. Matthias—both in the bitter winter."

"But how can they see anyone's face if the spring is frozen?" asked Dorothea, intrigued now.

"Sacred Spring never freezes, but it cures all manner of ills all the year round. Croup and rheumatism, the flux and stomach upsets, everything."

"Hmm."

"Try it, if you will. Can't hurt and should help. But take the potion anyway. And listen, girl. Hindsight never served a body nowt. If ye truly want that babe, look forward to the joy it will give you, whether you wed the man or no."

Johann Justus Bruns was building a house. A very special house in a very special place, on the Heiligenberg—the Holy Mountain. Over two hundred years ago an ancestor of his had somehow acquired an extensive piece of land there. Family tradition claimed it had been a gift from the last countess of Hoya during the dissolution of the monastery after the Reformation for services rendered but no one knew what those services had been. Somehow the deed to the property had come down to his father Hinrich. Although most of the surrounding area had been declared a State Forest, the government had respected the few private holdings of which the Bruns' acreage was the largest. It consisted of a hay field, a grain field, a very rich orchard and a plot large enough for a good-sized house and garden. But no one had ever built anything on the latter part. There were four other cottages—very tiny, very ancient, said to have been the lay brothers' huts—along the lane that circled the top of the hill but few people lived in them. They were usually only used as temporary shelters during harvest time, when the family shared the rich bounty with their Bruns cousins, also descendants of the original owner, who still farmed the ancestral land near the Brüne spring which, according to legend, had been the wedding gift of the great Saxon hero, Bruno, Wittekind's brother, to his son Bruno.

But Johann Justus was not a farmer. He was journeyman cabinetmaker working for his father Hinrich in the village of Vilsen. Hinrich was the finest cabinetmaker for miles around and Johann Justus was proud to be working for him, learning from him and, in fact, was almost as good as he—but not quite, yet. And this was his first attempt at building a whole house all by himself. Oh, there was plenty of help that could be called on when needed—his brothers and cousins—and his father guided him every step of the way. But most of the work was his very own and he wanted it that way. He had already planned the words he would carve on the main beam—*Johann Justus Bruns fecit*—yes, he knew his Latin—and the date of whatever year he finished it. He was building it for his favorite sister

61

Sophie Amalia who was already being courted by a nice young man, although fortunately a betrothal did not seem imminent. The only condition Johann Justus imposed was that he could live there with her and her future husband. It was not that he disliked his step-mother. She was a very kind woman who tried to be a good mother to them, but it was not the same as their own. He wanted to get out of the house in Vilsen to make room for the new babies that kept coming along regularly.

But the work was going very slowly. He hoped Sophie Amalia would not decide to wed in a hurry. And now that the days were growing shorter he had less time to devote to the house, only a few hours at dawn before he had to start work in the woodworking shop. In the evenings there was already no longer enough light as there had been during the summer. It was nigh on Martinmas. Soon he would have to quit work entirely for the winter. He sighed as he began to pick up his tools.

Suddenly his horse whinnied. Now what has disturbed him, he wondered. Off in the distance he heard an answering neigh. Ah, someone out for an early morning ride, no doubt. Now where is that confounded dog, he wondered. I haven't seen him in the past hour or more. He whistled. No response. He called, "Klas, Kläsi, come on. 'Tis time to go home."

And now Johann Justus was truly puzzled. Klas, whose real name was Nikolaus after the beloved children's saint, was usually a very loyal and obedient dog. Even if he was off chasing rabbits he always came immediately upon hearing his master's whistle. He was a big dog, a mongrel, but with a lot of the great shepherd dog blood in him and therefore very intelligent. His one fault was that he tended to be overly friendly with strangers unless commanded otherwise. Ach, thought Johann Justus, I suppose I shall have to rescue that rider from his loving attention. Just then he heard frantic barking in the distance, from the same direction as he had heard the horse whinny.

Johann Justus recognized the bark. It was not the joyful greeting of a new friend. It was a bark signalling danger or some emergency. Klas was calling him — urgently. He headed his horse across to the other side of the hilltop. Now Papa would be angry because he would be late for work but he had to see what the problem was. Klas did not bark like that when he was merely chasing rabbits.

Ahead of him a rectangle of overgrown grassy mounds indicated where the monastery church had once stood. And to its left was the edge of the steep ravine at the bottom of which rose the Sacred Spring. There he saw the horse carefully tethered to a tree. No rider. The animal whinnied a frantic greeting to his own horse but Klas' barking echoed from deep down in the ravine itself. Oh, no, he thought, someone has fallen and can't get back up. He hoped he did not have to deal with broken legs or some other serious injury. He dismounted, carefully approached the edge and looked down. He could see Klas far below frantically running in circles and trying to claw his way back up. Beyond him he could see a scantily clad body lying deathly still. Good Lord, it appeared to be a woman, although he could not be sure. Pray God, she's not dead.

"Hold on," he called out. "There's another way out. I'm coming." He quickly remounted and dashed to the road leading down the hill. But partway down he turned his horse to the right onto a tiny track known to very few people. After a bit the horse could go no further. Johann Justus dismounted and carefully made his way down the opposite side of the ravine, slipping and sliding on the glossy pine needles. When he reached the bottom he saw her, half sitting, half lying on the other bank of the brook that led from the spring. Klas' barking changed to joyous welcome.

"Are you alive? Are you hurt?" he called out. "I'm here now."

She blinked her eyes open, pulled a cloak around her and nodded.

Here the brook was only about three feet wide but fast-running and treacherous nonetheless because both banks were spongy with sodden leaves and moss. No sun ever reached here. Rather than jump and risk falling himself, he plunged across water up to his thighs and reached her side. Klas was sitting next to her, tail thumping.

"Are you hurt?" he asked again.

"Nay," she murmured, "just wet and cold and exhausted. How does one get out of this accursed place?"

"From the other side. The way I came. And even that is not easy."

She nodded. "I should have used my head but I was afraid of getting lost. I tried and tried to climb back up the way I came but I kept slipping back until I was too exhausted to move." She shivered and he could see how tired she was.

"I'll get you out," he assured her. "I am Johann Justus Bruns. Who are you and how come you to be here in the first place?"

"Foolishness," she replied. "I am Dorothea Koch, daughter to Miller Wilhelm Koch of Neubruchhausen."

"A long way from home and that on a chilly November night."

"Foolishness," she said again. "The old wisewoman suggested I bathe in the spring."

"To see the face of your future husband?"

"Nay. I know who my future husband will be. Only to cure some of my ills."

"And you bathed with all of your clothes on?" he asked, startled.

She almost laughed. "Nay. I took off my cloak and boots. But then I changed my mind when I stuck a toe in and felt how cold the water was. Then—then before I could back away from the edge, I slipped and fell in—with all my clothes on. When I couldn't climb up the cliff, I took my gown off. It was weighing me down so heavily and making me colder than I am now. I wrung it out as best I could and sat down to pray that someone would come by daylight. Then your wonderful dog came and helped to keep me warm. How is he called?"

"Klas."

"Ach, ja, after the saint who rescues children. I am afraid I have acted like a child this night."

"Be that as it may, we have to get you out of here to some place warm where you can dry out ere you even think of going home. Can you walk?"

"I think so, but I could never cross the brook as you did. I don't want to get wet again."

"I'll carry you but after that you'll have to try and walk." He helped her to her feet and was slightly embarrassed as he could see right through the wet shift clinging to her body. "Wrap your cloak tightly around you and put your boots back on," he instructed. He turned away to retrieve her gown from the bush where she had hung it. It was still sodden. "You can't put this back on. Here, you hold it and I'll carry you." He picked her up easily and plunged into the icy stream. "Come, Klas." The dog followed willingly, shook himself violently on the other side and dashed merrily up the steep embankment ahead of them.

Dorothea was breathless with fatigue and still shivering when they reached the horse.

"We can't ride double on this track," said Johann Justus. "These slippery needles are difficult enough for him with just one on his back. So up you go and I'll lead him." He lifted her easily onto the saddle, but sidewise. "Sorry, I don't have a sidesaddle. I didn't come prepared for a lass," he quipped.

"I can ride astride," she said and promptly hiked up her shift and slung one leg over to the other side. At his obvious blush she carefully draped the sides of her cloak over her bare legs. He took the bridle and slowly led the horse back to the road.

"Now, where to? The Klostermühle is the closest," he said.

"No, no," she exclaimed. "Not to that drunken oaf. I'd as soon ride home wet as go near him."

"Then to the Matthies at Bruchmühlen."

"Please, not there either. I—uh—used to work for them and I'd not have them see me like this."

"Ah, now I know who you are. You also worked for the Hohnholz as well. I didn't recognize you—er . . . "

"In the condition I'm in. I can understand that. Just take me to my horse. I'll find my way."

"Nay, nay, never," he objected. "You'll catch your death, if you haven't already, riding so far in those wet clothes. I'd gladly take you to my step-mother in Vilsen, but, I trow, even that is too far. Nothing for it then but to come to my house."

"Your house?"

"Well—the house I am a-building. It's far from finished yet. Just the framing of the walls is up and no roof. But I've completed the fireplace although it has no chimney as yet. It won't afford us much shelter but we can build a fire to help warm and dry us a bit, especially that gown of yours ere you dare put it back on. Fact is my breeches are beginning to feel a little chilly, too."

'Twas then she realized that in her misery she had given no thought to the fact that this kind man waded twice through that icy brook for her sake. "I should like very much to see your house and sit before your fire, Johann Justus Bruns," she said.

He mounted and set her to ride pillion behind him. "Now hang on tight," he said. She put her arms around his waist and held on. They rode back up the hill and were just turning to retrieve her horse when they heard a clatter of hooves coming up the hill.

Chris arrived breathless and stopped so short his mount almost reared. His look of amazement quickly turned to a black glare of jealousy. "Dorothea!" he roared. "Whatever are you doing here in another man's arms? And out all the night and only half clad at that? I thought you were my true betrothed but now I know better. Now I understand why you hesitate to marry me. I should have suspected. Is the child his, too?"

Shocked at his unreasoning vehemence, Dorothea quickly unclasped her arms from Johann Justus' waist and sat up straight with as much dignity as she could muster. "Chris, Chris," she said, "it is not as it seems. This good man was kind enough to rescue me from near death and is even now taking me to where we can build a fire to warm me and dry my clothes. Think you that my gown became so drenched in the heat of betrayal? Control your unwarranted jealousy." With that she threw the sodden bundle at him. As he caught it something dropped out.

"And what is this?" he asked furiously. "A potion from the old witch to rid yourself of the babe? Whosever babe it is."

"Nay, nay, Chris," she denied. " 'Tis but some medicine to cure my stomach upsets. And it *is* your babe," she insisted vehemently. "How can you think otherwise? And I do *not* want to be rid of it."

Johann Justus did not know what to say or do. He did not want to get involved in a lovers' quarrel but something had to be done—and that right quickly. The man was plainly being unreasonable. And he could feel the lass shivering again.

"I assure you, sir," he announced formally, "I did the lass no harm. I no but rescued her from freezing to death by the Sacred Spring. In fact, my dog found her first. And we now but go to a place where we can build a fire to warm and dry her. Follow if you will and welcome, but I will hear no more of your disparaging remarks to this fine woman."

"The Sacred Spring? Freezing to death?" sputtered Chris.

" 'Tis true, Chris. He saved my life. He and Klas," said Dorothea.

"Klas?"

Whereupon Klas barked, "Rrrowf," not sure whether this angry newcomer was friend or foe.

"And I am still freezing," she added. "Come, Master Bruns, take me to your house. I have great need of that fire."

"To—his—house?" asked Chris, still wracked with jealousy.

Johann Justus ignored him and turned his horse to the circular lane. Christian followed. When they arrived, Johann Justus lifted Dorothea down and quickly set about breaking up kindling to lay a fire.

"This is a house?" asked Chris sarcastically.

"Still a-building," replied Johann Justus, his back to him, "but the fireplace is finished although it yet lacks a chimney." Soon he had a roaring blaze alight. Fortunately in the still morning air there was no wind and the smoke rose straight up despite the lack of chimney. "Now if you will hand me the lady's gown, sir, I shall spread it out to dry." That done, he stacked several boards in front of the fire. "That is the best I can offer for a bench, Fräulein Koch," he indicated.

Dorothea had been standing in front of the fire with her cloak slightly open gratefully absorbing its warmth. She wished she dared take the cloak off entirely in order to dry the back of her shift but she feared Chris' fur-

66

ther ire. She sat down on the boards, took off her boots and stretched out her toes to the flames. Chris glared but said nothing and sat down beside her. Klas sat on her other side and leaned toward her as if to share his own warmth. Johann Justus stood facing them, to one side, his back to the blaze in order to dry his own clothing.

"Now that you have a suitable escort, Fräulein Koch, I shall leave you as soon as my breeches are a bit drier. My father will be having fits that I am so late for work."

"Oh, Johann Justus, I thank you kindly for all your help," said Dorothea. "I am deeply grateful to you for saving my life. I shall never forget it. This fire feels wonderful. Fear not, we shall see that it is safely out ere we leave."

"See that you do," he replied coldly and then hesitatd. Should he speak out what was on his mind? Why not? The boor deserved it. He turned to Chris. "And I assure you, sir, that if aught had happened as you accused me of, my breeches would have been off and dry, not soaking wet as they are. You owe the lady an apology, if not me, for the crass words you spoke. And I urge you," he addressed Dorothea, "to think twice about taking on a jealous husband, child or no. Such a one is worse than no man at all. I bid you good day." He turned and went out, mounted his horse, called to Klas and disappeared down the lane.

"Well!" said Dorothea. "You certainly deserved that, Chris."

He turned red with embarrassment. "But—but, what was I to think seeing you half clad like that, clinging to another man, after being out the whole night?"

"No buts," she retorted. "You should have thought first of my wellbeing instead of your selfish, insane jealousy. Why could you not have waited to hear the truth of the matter before you spewed forth such invective? Why can't you believe the truth?"

"I—I guess I do now, but—"

"No buts, I said. And I *am* thinking twice about marrying you. A bad beginning such as this bodes ill for the future. Now, if you don't mind, I am going to remove my cloak, if you will permit it in another man's house. I wish to dry my back." She promptly did so and turned her back to the fire. After a bit she fluffed out her gown and turned it over. It was warm but still damp.

Chris stared at her lovely body through the thin shift. "Dorchen, I am sorry," he said. "I do love you, truly. I don't know what came over me, seeing you in another man's arms."

"I was hardly in his arms. He was in mine and that only so I should not fall off the horse. I was weak with exhaustion and cold. But what did you care?"

"I did care. I do care," he objected.

"Then you had a strange way of showing it. Just as soon as my gown is a bit drier I shall carefully douse this fire and head for home. You may acompany me or not as you choose. I find that my unintended dip in the Sacred Spring has indeed cured my morning sickness. I am famished."

However, Dorothea had caught a chill from her unexpected dip in the raw November weather. By the time they reached Neubruchhausen she was burning up with fever. Chris had to ride close to keep her from falling, but she refused to dismount until they reached home. Lise immediately put her to bed, dosed her with possets and laid a mustard plaster on her chest. For almost three weeks a wracking cough threatened to tear her apart. Every day from Martinmas to nigh on St. Nikolaus Eve Chris sat by her bed until Lise had to chase him out so that Dorothea could rest. "Don't you have work to do?" was all she would say to him.

As she slowly started to improve, Dorothea's first concern was for her unborn child. "Oh dear God, I hope I haven't hurt him," she prayed. She worried so that Lise finally called the midwife to check on her.

"Everything seems to be fine," said the woman. "In another month or so you should feel him kicking. Then we'll know better. But I don't think a little cold water hurt him. However, that cough of yours could. So stop worrying and get yourself better," was her advice.

Chris tried to talk to Lise. "I love her," he said. "I want to marry her. Have for ever so long. You know that. But now she won't have me."

Lise admitted that Dorchen had been foolish but she agreed with her daughter. "A jealous man is no good thing," she warned him. "You have got to prove that to her yourself. Nothing I can say would influence her." And she would say no more.

Chris went to Wilhelm. "Isn't there anything you can say to convince her that I truly want to wed her?"

Wilhelm shook his head. "Breeding women often act strangely. I think she'll wed you eventually but whatever problem there is, you have to solve that between you. Show her you're truly sorry for what you said. Women like apologies, not reasoning. That's why Lise and I get on so well. You know," he admitted, "I almost didn't wed my dear wife because I thought she had been defiled by some bandits. Turned out she was wiser than I and I soon got over it. Thank God. But don't you dare ever tell her I told you that."

Chris was totally surprised at that revelation and it set him to serious thinking. He vowed to try to forget the whole incident at Heiligenberg.

By the beginning of December Dorothea was coming down for meals but still rested most of the day. The fever had left her but she was still weak and tired, and the cough persisted though not as fierce as before. And, God be praised, the babe was beginning to kick. On the morning of the Eve of St. Nikolaus she had an unexpected visitor.

On the evening of 5 December it was customary for children to hang stockings from the mantelpiece with a letter to the good saint enclosed. The next morning they hoped to find the stockings filled with sweets, cookies, fruit and even tiny trinkets, if they had been good children, or the dreaded lump of coal if they had not. Sometimes they also left their shoes filled with straw for St. Nikolaus' white horse. Young Johann was getting a bit old for this but he went along with it for little Anni's sake. Besides it was nice to still receive the goodies. Dorothea wss determined to be up and about by then so as not to spoil the children's holiday.

Thus she was seated at the kitchen table having a late breakfast when Eleonore Matthies burst in the door. "Elli," she exclaimed. "What a delightful surprise. I haven't seen you in ever so long."

Eleonore hugged and kissed her. "Dearest Dorchen," she said, "I heard you were ill and I'd have come much sooner but as you may know Mistress Hohnholz has recently been delivered of another babe—a sweet, dear boy, but a mite frail, else I'd have come ere this. But how are you? I am happy to see you are out of bed."

"Ja, Elli, I am improving but, ach, it goes so slow. I can't seem to get my strength back. I'm almost ashamed to tell you about my adventure. It was so foolish of me."

"I've heard a little of the story."

"How so? And from whom?"

"Your friend Johann Justus Bruns."

"Ach! He's not spreading it all over the countryside, is he?"

"Nay, nay, only to me because he knows we are good friends. And he says you need a good friend right now."

"Ja, that I do, Elli. Chris is angry with me—unreasonably so. And now I'm not sure that I want to wed him at all."

"Oh, Dorchen, that's terrible. Why would he be angry? Just at some girlish foolishness. Why, half the maidens in the village have gone to the Sacred Spring at one time or another. My sister Adi has been there any number of times and still hasn't seen her lover."

Dorothea laughed at that. "Adi will catch some unwitting man one of these days whether she sees his face in the Sacred Spring or not. But seriously, Chris is jealous of Johann Justus because he thought we were having a lovers' tryst there when Johann Justus was only saving my life. He has stopped harping on it since I've been sick and has tried to make amends, but I don't trust him. I know it is still eating at his heart. I couldn't live with that, Elli."

"Indeed not. Oh, Dorchen, that is even more foolish than what you did. How can he believe something like that? Ach, men can be so stupid. Everyone knows you were a virgin ere you—er—ah—went to him."

Dorothea laughed again. "Everyone? Hardly that. But *he* knew and that is what hurts so."

"Well, he'll just have to get over that. The more fool he if he were to lose you."

"Easier said than done, I fear me," said Dorothea sadly.

"Then, before I forget, here is something to cheer you up. Johann Justus sent a little St. Nikolaus Day gift for the babe."

Dorothea looked surprised. "Indeed? But the babe is scarce born yet."

"He knows that but he thought to cheer you in your illness. And he could hardly send a gift to you, now, could he?" Eleonore drew a tiny trinket from her reticule. It was a baby rattle, so finely carved that, though of wood, it looked like tortoiseshell. In fact, on closer inspection Dorothea could see the tiny feet and tail of the tortoise and the rattle was in its mouth.

"Oh, that's exquisite," she exclaimed. "And no doubt he carved it himself." Eleonore nodded. "I shall cherish it and I'm sure my baby will love it. Thank him kindly for me, Elli. In fact, I shall write to him myself." She laid the rattle on the table and they spoke of other things.

Just then Chris entered the kitchen looking for a cup of coffee. When he sat down he spied the rattle. "And where did this lovely little thing come from? Did you bring it, Eleonore?"

Dorothea sought to hush her friend but too late. "Ja, I did," Eleonore blurted out. "It is a gift for the babe from Johann Justus Bruns."

"What?!" exploded Chris. "So your lover is sending you gifts now! I had hoped that you had forgotten him ere this. How long will his shadow hang over us?"

"Chris," said Dorothea, "Calm yourself. The gift is for the babe, not for me. And I can scarcely forget the kind man who saved my life."

Eleonore stood up. Her anger blazed. Her dark eyes flashed like Donar's thunderbolts. "You big, stupid oaf," she declared. "You men are all alike. You are no better than my father whom I detest. And I thought you were of a better ilk than that. He has beaten my mother down so that she is scarcely a real person anymore—a nothing. And not through jealousy of another man—Mama would never look at another man and she hardly goes anywhere—but through jealousy of his own children. Oh, yes, you men love putting the babes in there. Dorchen, remember how I used to ask you how they got in there? Well, I know now. But you hate it when the woman becomes gross and unwieldy and then a squalling brat appears. Even that kind of jealousy is slightly understandable in a selfish man like my father. But your kind is totally unreasonable—totally uncalled for. Dorchen is a good girl. I've known her all my life. Your kind of foolish jealousy will eat you up. It won't hurt her but it will break her heart. She loves you, you dumb fool, but you don't love her. I used to think you were the perfect man for her but no more. She would be better off without you—babe or no—unelss you grow up—and that right fast."

Dorothea watched Chris' face during this harangue. It went from anger to perplexity and then his mouth hung open at this tirade from so young a maid. Eleonore reached across the table and took a sip from Chris' coffee cup and sat down.

"There, I've said my piece," she said more quietly. "Sorry, Dorchen, if I've upset you but I simply couldn't hold back."

"You haven't upset me, dearest Elli. You've said it better than I could have. He won't believe me—or doesn't want to. I pray some of your words penetrated that thick skull."

Chris looked from one to the other. He did not know what to say or if he should say anything at all. "I—I guess I deserved some of that," he mumbled finally.

"All of it," said Eleonore.

"But to compare me with your father. That hurt. I am well aware of his violent temper. I am not like that."

"Do you deny that you lost your temper in a jealous rage no but moments ago over a tiny, innocent baby rattle sent by a friend who only wishes her well?"

"I guess—I fear I overreacted," he admitted.

Eleonore let the silence draw out. At last she stood up and went over to Dorothea and hugged and kissed her. "I must be leaving now, dearest

71

Dorchen. Mistress Hohnholz has only let me have this morning free to come and see you." She turned to Chris, wagging her finger. "And don't you pick on her the moment I leave either."

"I'll not. I promise," he said meekly.

"And oh, Dorchen," she said as she donned her cloak, "Mistress Hohnholz has said I may come to you to help with the birthing one week—even two weeks, if need be." And she departed.

Christian and Dorothea sat in complete silence for a while. Then he noticed the tears streaming down her cheeks. He went over to her, put his arm around her and wiped the tears with a napkin. Then he gently kissed her. "I love you, dearest Dorchen. I swear I do. I'll try to do better. I promise. I'll try to show you how much I love you."

She only nodded but her heart swelled with gratitude toward Elli. She would wait and see how much he meant it, but it was a start.

Christmas came and they passed the holiday quietly but with some joy and at least no rancor. Chris seemed to be bending over backwards to be kind to Dorothea. Since she could no longer ride, he would bundle her up and take her out for sleigh rides once there was enough snow. On winter evenings he would often read to her from her favorite new poets, Master Schiller and Master Goethe. Occasionally he would take over the household chores that she could no longer easily do. Although Lise was not always happy about that, she knew he meant well. No longer was marriage spoken of.

Soon after Christmas Lise took Dorothea aside. "When are you going to put the poor man out of his misery?" she asked.

"What do you mean, Mama?" asked Dorothea, although she knew full well what was meant.

"Marriage," stated Lise flatly. "Good Lord, girl, he is doing everything in his power to make amends. He is kinder to you, more thoughtful than any man I've ever known. Far more than the situation warrants. Methinks it is long past time you grew up and started to forgive."

"I know, Mama, and I do forgive him," she replied sheepishly. "It's just that—well—he hasn't asked me again and I doubt he ever will now."

"Ach, du lieber Gott!" exclaimed Lise, throwing her hands in the air, exasperated. "How many times must he ask you and be refused? If you think to emasculate him you will lose him entirely—to your regret. And hear me this too, you are about to become a mother. And an immature mother is the worst thing that can happen to a child. I have no desire to mother my grandchild while his mother still plays at childish games. Go and tell Chris you will wed him forthwith."

"Yes, Mama," said Dorothea meekly. "I shall." But she lost her courage and did not.

A week later Wilhelm decided to take things in hand. He usually left domestic issues to his wife and it had always worked out well. But this time Lise did not seem to be able to resolve the situation. Wilhelm loved Dorothea dearly, most of all his children, even his sons, but now he was deeply ashamed of his daughter. He regarded her as a trollop. Conceiving out of wedlock—well, that happened often enough and could be forgiven, especially when young people were hot in the loins. But to refuse to marry the man, when he so much desired it, that was incomprehensible. And such a good, kind, upstanding man as Chris. A man Wilhelm would have chosen for her even had this not happened. It was unconscionable.

"Dorothea," he said sternly one morning at breakfast.

Oh, my, thought Dorothea, he never calls me anything but Dorchen. This is serious. And what's more, he usually rushes right out to work in the mill and here he is sitting leisurely over a second cup of coffee. Her mild, gentle father. "Yes, Papa?"

"Dorothea, I am your father and you will obey me."

"Yes, Papa."

"I have had enough of this childish nonsense. I say, enough is enough. You will marry Christian Bergmann forthwith or you and your child will leave this house. I'll not have a bastard born under this roof."

"Papa! You can't mean that," she cried.

"I can and do. The choice is yours." It almost broke Wilhelm's heart to have said that and he hoped she would not put it to the test. He did not really think she would. Dorchen was a good girl, just a little crazy right now. "Furthermore," he continued, "there will be no fancy wedding in Vilsen with all your friends. Just a simple, quiet ceremony here at the church in Sudwalde. I have already spoken to the Pastor. He will start calling the banns this Sunday. I have told Christian my wishes and he agrees. Philipp will stand up for him. You may have one friend. I suppose you will want that Eleonore Matthies, child though she still is. It is all arranged. There will be no further discussion." He put down his coffee cup and left to go to the mill.

Dorothea sat stunned. She was white as a sheet. She wanted to cry and yet she could not. She sighed. Perhaps she was secretly glad that Papa had made the decision for her. She didn't know what was wrong with her.

Ever since she had become pregnant she couldn't make even a simple decision and she had always been a very decisive person. Her mind was always muddled and she had always known her own mind very clearly. She thought of poor, pitiful Becke Matthies. Oh, dear Lord, I hope I am not going to be like her.

Lise slipped quietly into the kitchen and sat down opposite her daughter. She could see the turmoil in Dorchen's face, in her eyes, in her heart. After a time she asked, "Well?"

"Mama, were you this stupid, this foolish, this muddled when you were carrying me?"

"No, I was overjoyed. But you were born a full year after your Papa and I were wed. I did a lot of foolish things before that. I was just as stubborn as you and so was your father in his own quiet way. But we learned to turn that strength to one another in love."

"I've always been strong-minded. You know that. What is wrong with me?"

"In part, guilt over conceiving out of wedlock. It happens often. Forget that and be thankful that he wants to marry you. And in part because of his foolish jealousy which I am sure he is over now and only awaits your forgiveness. You feel guilty because of that, too. And all that is dragging you down, muddling you. You are still a strong-minded and strong-willed woman, Dorchen. Only you have turned it in the wrong direction. Put that strength into forgiveness, into thankfulness, into joy in Chris' love and into joy for your coming babe."

Dorothea nodded. She knew her mother was right. She determined to be strong from now on.

Dorothea and Christian Bergmann were quietly wed in the Sudwalde church on the first Sunday of February. Johann Heinrich Reinhard Bergmann put in his appearance in mid-April 1785. He was a strong, lusty baby and seemed to have suffered no harm from his premature baptism in the Sacred Spring.

3

1789

Eleonore tripped gaily down the back stairs of the Hohnholz house. She was dressed in her new second best gown which she had designed and made herself—a charming, crisp, cool dimity embroidered with flowers that enhanced her ripening figure. And she was happy. She was happy because it was high summer and she loved all the lovely summer flowers and the warmth. She was happy because she had been given an unexpected day off in the middle of the week so that she could go and visit her dear friend Dorothea. And she was happy because Teddi would be coming home soon from the gymnasium. In the past year or so Teddi's attitude toward her had changed considerably. He no longer regarded her, condescendingly, as a mere annoying girl-child. Now he looked at her as a woman, nigh grown and very desirable. And she could sense the difference. No, she wouldn't mind at all if Teddi were to start courting her.

At the foot of the stairs someone suddenly grabbed her, lifted her off her feet and swung her around. "Happy sweet sixteen," he said and kissed her soundly.

"Teddi!" she screamed and nearly swooned with delight. "What are you doing here? I mean, I didn't know you were already home."

"I got in very late last night. You were already abed."

"Then welcome home and thank you for the greetings but my birthday was way back in January."

"I know but I wasn't here to help you celebrate."

"It wasn't much of a celebration. January is such a bleak month. I think that's why I love the summer so much."

"Ah, a warm girl born in a cold month."

She blushed becomingly. "How do you know I'm warm?" she asked flirtatiously.

"I can tell." He kissed her again. "There, now you can't say 'sweet sixteen and never been kissed'."

"Oh, my," she said. "You'd best not let your parents catch you doing that."

Just then Catharine entered the kitchen. The young people broke apart. She glared for a second and then quickly changed her expression to a smile. "Good mornng, Elli. I see you are all dressed up for your visit to Dorchen. The new gown is very becoming. Now hurry and break your fast and be on your way, ere the morning is half gone. Teddi, as soon as you have eaten your father wishes to see you. He and I have several things to discuss with you. I'll join you for a second cup of coffee."

Aha, thought Eleonore, that is why the unexpected day off. They want me out of the way so they can talk to Teddi before I do. And I trow, one of the subjects they discuss will be me. But Teddi seems to have anticipated that. She smiled to herself.

"So what news of Hannover?" she asked, as if she really cared.

"Nothing much from Hannover," he replied, "but have you heard what is happening in France?"

"No. Has Marie Antoinette a new gown or a new coiffure? Or perhaps a new diamond necklace?"

"Nay, nay. Far more exciting than that. The people have revolted. The news just reached Hannover the day before I left. No but a week ago they stormed the Bastille and the Tuillieries Palace and are even now marching on Versailles. They demand the King reinstate the Parlement and 'tis said he is quaking in his boots."

Eleonore was intrigued. She had read much lately of the new domocratic ideas that were sweeping across Europe, especially the writing of Master Rousseau. But at the look of shock on Catharine's face, she held her peace. She would find out more from Teddi another time.

"Ach, that's horrible," said Catharine. "What can they be thinking of? But then, the French are always a little strange." She glanced pointedly at Eleonore, who merely smiled. "Let's hope they keep their revoluton to themselves. They would never put up with that sort of behavior in Germany, especially here in Hannover."

Teddi thought it best to change the subject. "Then here is another tidbit of news that may appeal to your royalist sympathies. King George III is sending one of his younger sons, Ernst August, Duke of Cumberland, to start his studies at Göttingen next term."

"Oh, Philipp Koch is starting then, too," said Eleonore. "Maybe they'll be friends."

"I doubt that he would appeal overmuch to Philipp," said Teddi.

" 'Tis said he cares for nothing but the military and the hunt. He has done very poorly in his studies at the gymnasium or whatever they call it in England. He doesn't even speak German. His father insists he learn not only the language but how to *be* a German. I shouldn't think it will be easy for him, but I should still like to get to know him."

"But you *will* have that opportunity," said Catharine.

"No, dear Catharine," insisted Teddi. "We've gone over this before. I am not going to the University. I want to learn Papa's business as soon as possible."

"Theodor Ludwig, that is one of the things your father wishes to discuss with you, but I do not think it is meet or proper to speak of it in front of Eleonore. It is not something that concerns her."

Eleonore had not seen her dear friend Dorchen for many, many months—at least not for a good visit. And she was looking forward to it. They had met occasionally on market day and at church—enough to exchange news, but never for a good long gossip. And much had happened to Dorothea in the four years since she and Chris had wed. For one thing, they both seemed happy and very much in love. Eleonore hoped her little scolding had been instrumental in that, but whatever, she was grateful for it.

The year after Johann Heinrich's birth, Wilhelm Koch died suddenly. It was a shock to everyone except Chris. Wilhelm had not even told Lise about his heart condition. The family was told to immediately vacate the mill at Neubruchhausen, but eventually the government relented slightly. Chris put pressure on Miller Matthies to get rid of the miller at the Klostermühle and start building a new mill-house as he had promised. And Anton, unaware of the circumstances, chose none other than Johann Justus Bruns to build it.

Lise, too, had to make a decision. She would have been more than welcome to live with the young couple but she was an independent person and Wilhelm had left her a goodly inheritance. She chose to purchase a house in the tiny hamlet of Hoyahagen outside of Hoya where she had cousins her own age. The government, meanwhile, was lenient and let the Bergmann stay at Neubruchhausen for a nominal rent until they could move to Heiligenberg, especially since Dorothea was once again heavily pregnant.

This pregnancy seemed to bring her nothing but joy and happiness and Georg Wilhelm Bergmann was born in 1787. Meanwhile Dorothea wondered how to handle the situation with Johann Justus Bruns. She wanted to supervise as much of the building of the house as possible and to her surprise Chris made no objection to her riding over there frequently although he rarely accompanied her. Then one day when the house was more than three-quarters finished, he joined her. With great trepidation she introduced the two men as if they had never met before. Chris admired Johann Justus' fine work and soon was discussing technical details with him. Before long they became friends much to Dorothea's gratification. None of the three ever mentioned the incident at the Sacred Spring. A few weeks after Georg Wilhelm's birth the Bergmann moved into the mill-house at Heiligenberg.

Eleonore had seen the new house a few times since but it had been almost bare of furnishings. She knew that Dorothea had been lovingly furnishing it bit by bit as funds became available and now she was anxious to see the results. Eleonore took a well loved shortcut to the mill through the woods behind Vilsen. As she entered the cool forest a feeling of peace came over her. She knew every inch of these woods, having explored them since early chldhood. Her older brother Heinzi had often tried to frighten her with threats of demons and wolves, even with tales about Red Riding-hood and Hansel and Gretel. But since these stories always had happy endings, she refused to be intimidated by his dire warnings. As she grew older she could see nothing but beauty and peace in the lovely forest and she determined that if she ever had children of her own she would tell them wonderful tales of birds and trees, of benign fairies and elves. She followed the path over the hill to a tiny valley that sheltered the hamlet of Homfeld, then up another hill to a stairway cut into the hillside by people so ancient no one knew who they were. This set of steps led directly to the Klostermühle.

Dorothea met her at the door, arms extended. "Ach, Elli, it's so good to see you again," she said as they embraced. "Come, Johann Heinrich, and greet Tante Elli." The little boy, now four, made a courtly bow, took Eleonore's hand and kissed it.

"What a perfect little gentleman," exclaimed Eleonore.

Dorothea laughed. "Ja, for five minutes at a time. You may go and play now," she said to the child, "but mind you, come in well before dinnertime." The little boy ran out. Georg Wilhelm, barely walking and talking, did not seem interested in any of it. The two women sat down at the kitchen table over coffee.

"You have a lovely place here," commented Eleonore, "and you've done a magnificent job of furnishing and decorating it."

"Thank you, Elli. I thought your father would never get around to building it for us, but at last we're here and quite satisfied."

Eleonore nodded. "Ja, Papa was always one to be terribly impatient with everyone else except himself."

"And would you believe who made most of the furniture for us as well as building the house?"

"Johann Justus?"

"The very same. And now he and Chris are the best of friends."

"I'm so glad. They are both fine men. It was sad to see them at odds. And are you truly happy now, Dorchen?"

"Very, very much so. I can't believe I was so foolish but that is all in the past now. I am with child again and I am overjoyed. I hope it is a girl this time."

"I'm glad for you. When is it due?"

"Towards the end of the year—around Yule I reckon."

"Ah, that would be nice—a Chrismas baby. Of this one, I want to be a godmother."

"Indeed you shall, dearest Elli. Now, what of your news? Is anyone courting you yet?"

"Nay, nay, not at all. Although I suspect Teddi may be getting interested. He kissed me this morn." And she blushed.

Dorothea laughed. "That sounds just like Teddi. But be wary of him, Elli. He is such a self-centered, brash young man. I don't trust him. Don't let him cozen you. I'd hate to see you get into the fix that I did."

"Never fear, Dorchen, I'll not. I don't even know that I should want him should he be serious. He just likes to tease me. But I do think he has matured somewhat since he went to the gymnasium. And now he will be going on to the University. He doesn't want to but his parents are insisting on it. In fact, I just realized that that is why I was given this extra day off. They are even now talking to him, warning him against *me*."

When Chris came in for dinner, they changed the subject. "Have you heard what is happening in France?" asked Eleonore. "Teddi was just telling me this morning."

"Ja," said Dorothea. "Philipp has told us about it. I just hope they keep their troubles to themselves."

"Agreed," said Chris. "I'm all in favor of constitutional government myself, but those people are going about it in the wrong way. Such violence never solved anything. But I do fear that the fever—or fervor, whichever you want to call it—may spill over into Germany, especially into the universities. There are many radical thinking young men who would succumb to the trend. The problem here, however, is that no two Germans think alike as to what kind of government they really want. So I doubt anything serious will come of it. Mayhap not even in France."

1793 " . . . And now he has taken a regiment from Hannover into Holland," said Philipp. "In my opinion, we have no business there. It wll surely bring the wrath of the French mob down on our heads."

Just then Chris entered the kitchen. "Who has taken a regiment into Holland?" he asked.

"Philipp was telling me about Prince Ernst August," replied Dorothea. "He left Göttingen without even graduating, he was that eager to be in the military."

Chris shook his head. "Methinks he is more Prussian than the Prussians."

"Indeed," agreed Philipp. "His instructors in the classics and humanities were hand picked from amongst the finest professors at Göttingen but he had no interest, couldn't even pass some of the courses. He only enjoyed the martial exercises and the hunt. As soon as he left the university he was appointed captain of a cavalry regiment, the King's Light Dragoons, and now he is already colonel of the Second Cavalry Regiment out of Celle. At least he has learned to speak German, although not too well."

"He doesn't sound like a man we should want for a king," remarked Dorothea.

"I don't think we need fear that," said Philipp. "His eldest brother George is now Regent for poor old crazy George III and there are two others before Ernst August."

"And now you say he has taken his regiment to fight in Holland," said Chris. "How can that be when Hannover is not at war with France?"

"Because France has declared war on both England and the Netherlands," replied Philipp, "and where England leads, Hannover must follow. Besides, 'tis said she has sent us a huge subsidy to insure our cooperation."

"Then are we really at war again or no?" asked Dorothea. "Oh, Lord, I guess it has been peaceful for too long."

"That's hard to say," said Philipp. "The Emperor finally declared war on France back in March but Ernst August is actually fighting under Prussia's leadership."

"Who is actually more interested in carving up Poland," added Chris.

"I trust Prussia not at all."

"Nor does anyone else," agreed Dorothea, "except Master Matthies." Both men shrugged at that. "What is the purpose of this war anyway?"

"Ostensibly to save the monarchies of the world," said Chris, not without a touch of sarcasm.

"But now that the French have chopped off Louis' head, there is no longer a monarchy to save there," said Dorothea.

"Ah, but the Emperor and Friedrich Wilhelm of Prussia and Pitt in England are terrified that the French revolutionary ideas will spread across Europe," said Philipp. "Methinks they fear for their own heads."

"Well, I shouldn't worry about that," said Chris. "'Tis said the French army is nothing but an undisciplined rabble. Although Austria is weak, a good strong army such as Prussia's should be able to quell the disturbance rather quickly. That is, if Prussia and Austria can ever agree on anything."

"I hope you're right," said Dorothea doubtfully.

But Chris was to be proven wrong, however. In the spring of 1794 a French leader named Lazare Carnot arose who instituted the *levée en masse*. While desertions were frequent at first, this new army, instead of being governed by strict discipline as in the past, was held together by a patriotic *esprit de corps*. Moreover, they employed new military tactics. Instead of the entire army fighting a single battle, individual divisions engaged in what would later be called guerilla warfare and quick decisive victories were the norm over a wide area. In addition Carnot appointed several new, highly competent generals from the bourgeoisie. The combination was unbeatable. France conquered Belgium and the Netherlands. In Germany she occupied the Palatine and the entire left bank of the Rhein including Cologne, Bonn and Coblenz. And at the siege of Toulon a young captain-major of artillery, Napoleon Bonaparte, distinguished himself.

Meanwhile Prussia was having difficulties in the east. A revolt in her newly acquired territory in Poland led by Thaddeus Kosciuszko took up most of her remaining resources and exhausted her treasury. The alliance with Austria fell apart, primarily because Catherine of Russia negotiated the last partition of Poland with Austria without consulting Prussia. Prussia sued for peace with France at the Peace of Basel in July 1794. A secret provision of the treaty provided for the occupation of Hannover by Prussia in order to force the neutralization of Hannover with regard to France.

Eleonore Matthies could not have cared less what was happening with France had she even known. She did not care what was happening in Germany. Her own happy world had fallen apart. On a chill, dreary day towards the end of March she was seeking solace in her beloved Vilsen woods. She was warmly dressed in a heavy purple cloak. She even had a luxurious fur muff, a gift from Master Hohnholz this Christmas past. But none of it afforded her any joy. She wandered off the beaten path to a secret spot where she had often sought refuge as a child. The thicket that had once seemed such an excellent hiding place years ago had now grown up into trees and with the branches still bare provided no shelter at all. Spring had been trying to break through in Vilsen, but here in the deep woods snow still lay on the ground in places where the sun did not reach. When she came to the spot she barely recognized it. But, ah, her favorite rock was still there. How often she had sat on it and daydreamed when she was happy or nursed her hurt pride when she had been beaten by her father. She brushed the light covering of snow off the rock and sat down. What now? If Eleonore thought of France at all, it was to curse her hot French blood.

Eleonore's great-great-grandparents had been pure French, Huguenots come to Germany over a hundred years ago in the wake of Duchess Eleonore d'Olbreuse for whom she was named. Yet her great-grandfather, her grandfather and her own father had all married German girls so that the French blood was really quite dilute. And yet her father had always insisted that she and all her siblings be very proud of that bit of French blood. Truthfully she was the only one of the lot that even looked French with her sable, almost blue-black hair and dark eyes, with her sparkling, vivacious personality that Papa had tried to beat out of her. The others were all blond or brown-haired and, to be honest, rather dull people. She wished now she had curbed a little of that French blood and used some good German common sense. But she hadn't.

Why had she so deliberately and outrageously flirted with Teddi when she knew exactly what he wanted? When she knew there was no future in it? She had held him off for years, ever since she was sixteen, and now she was one-and-twenty. Mayhap that was it. Had she been afraid of being an old maid, bypassed by love, never having experienced that mysterious act which everyone else seemed to enjoy? Mistress Catharine would be bearing her third in a few months. No, she could not make that excuse. Suddenly, soon after her twenty-first birthday in January, she had felt such a longing, such a stirring of that damned hot French blood that she had decided to throw caution to the winds and experience that mysterious thing—to see what it was like.

Teddi had matured considerably since attending university but he was still somewhat arrogant and pompous as befitted—in his eyes—the scion of one of the wealthiest and most prominent families in Vilsen. His father had been elected Bürgermeister three years ago and looked to be reelected for many years to come. Eleonore knew that Teddi looked down on her as a mere servant although her own father Miller Matthies was almost as wealthy but not well liked. This dislike was often reflected in the Bürgers' attitude toward his children. Under the aegis of Teddi's grandmother, Frau Meyer, Eleonore had striven to rise above this stigma on the basis of her own personality and to some extent she had succeeded. She knew Mistress Catharine was fond of her and Master Hohnholz seemed to regard her well enough. And Teddi? She had always regarded Teddi as a teasing, often annoying, elder brother. How he had felt about her she was not sure.

And now they were lovers. Teddi was a fine lover. At least she thought so, although she had nothing with which to compare it. He had taken her maidenhead gently and considerately and thereafter brought her to ecstacy such as she could not have imagined possible. From then on she could not get enough of him and he seemed to feel the same. They made love every opportunity they could snatch until he had to return to Göttingen. But not one word of love passed between them. Did she love him? Eleonore did not think so. She was very fond of him or she would not have given herself to him. But Teddi was too selfish and self-centered to really love anyone but himself. Now she supposed she would have to marry him. Eleonore was pregnant.

And therein lay the next problem. Would he marry her? And more importantly, would his parents permit it? Teddi was due to graduate from the University this summer, so a livelihood was not a problem. But Eleonore was quite aware that Master and Mistress Hohnholz had tried to discourage any liaison between them as far back as when Teddi first kissed her at sixteen. Or could that have been because she was then so young and he had not completed his education? Could they perhaps have changed their minds by now? She was not aware of any other prospective bride being pushed forward by them. And she suspected that Catharine knew what was going on and had said nothing. Well, time would tell. And Teddi himself did not yet know about the forthcoming child.

Eleonore shivered. The cold from the rock was seeping through her heavy cloak. Her childhood hideaway no longer provided the consolation it used to. How insignificant those childish problems seemed now. The weather reminded her of the day her dear brother Fritzi was buried. She had been overcome with grief and hatred of her father. Kind old Frau Meyer had helped her get over that. She would have been the one to talk to Teddi—but she was gone now. And this was a problem that would not go away. In seven more months it would put in its appearance and long before that everyone would know that Eleonore Matthies was a wicked girl. She must prepare for the worst.

If the Hohnholz turned her out—as was their every right—she would go somewhere to bear the child and raise it herself. At least she would make sure that Teddi acknowledged it. But where to go? She could not go home. Papa would never even allow her in the door—or worse, would beat her to within an inch of her life and mayhap harm the babe. No, she would never chance that. What then? Her only true friend was Dorchen, who had warned her again and again not to get into this fix, to beware of Teddi. But Teddi had been no more than a very willing partner. It was her own hot French blood that had betrayed her. Damn!

Sitting here freezing will not make the babe go away. Eleonore was ever one for action. Brooding was not her wont. She stood up stiffly and brushed the snow off her cloak. I shall go and talk to Dorchen. She knew her friend could not solve the problem but at least she would lend a sympathetic ear—mayhap even have some ideas. She trudged through the woods toward the Klostermühle.

"Elli!" exclaimed Dorothea. "What brings you here on a Wednesday? An unexpected day off?"

"Nay, nay, I just took it."

"Without Catharine's permission?" Then suddenly Dorothea realized that this was not her usually ebullient friend. "Elli, whatever is the matter? Are you ill?"

"I'm not sick—sick at heart is more like," replied Eleonore. "Dorchen, I've something to tell you."

"Then tell. I'm listening." She put her arm around Eleonore. "Come, have a cup of coffee."

Eleonore shook her head. "You warned me, Dorchen. You warned me and I didn't listen."

Dorothea tried to think what it could be. She had warned the child of so many things over the years. Suddenly she gasped. "Elli, you're not . . ."

Eleonore nodded. "I am with child." And she burst into tears.

Dorothea led her to a chair and sat down beside her.

"Teddi's?"

Eleonore nodded again.

"Then he must wed you forthwith. Does he know?"

Eleonore shook her head. "Not yet," she sobbed. "He is still at Göttingen. And I doubt that he will—wed me, I mean."

"And whyever not?"

"He doesn't love me. He looks down on me. I was just a willing plaything—fool that I am."

"But surely Catharine and Master Hohnholz will insist on it," protested Dorothea.

"I think not."

"They haven't dismissed you, have they?"

"Nay, not yet. They don't know but surely they will find out soon. And then—then—"

"I doubt they will dismiss you," Dorothea tried to ressure her. "They are kind and honorable people, especially Catharine. And what makes you so sure that Teddi won't wed you?"

"He has never spoken of it, never said he loves me."

Dorothea almost smiled. "Men are like that. They are reluctant to express their feelings. Even my Chris asked me to marry him before he ever said he loved me. Yet he did."

"Teddi is not like your Chris. He thinks only of himself."

"Mayhap but he will outgrow it once he starts working for his father. And more so when the babe comes. My grandfather always said there is nothing like children to make a man grow up, especially if he has a good wife."

"But I am not good. I'm wicked. You've often said that yourself."

"Ach, dearest Elli, I never meant that as evil-wicked, only as mischievous or wrong-thinking, which you certainly are now. But you are a good girl. Don't ever let anyone say otherwise."

"It's that damned French blood in me. I couldn't help myself. I hate it."

"Now you *are* talking foolishness. You should be just as proud of your French blood as you are of your German. It's what makes you so vivacious and charming. Besides, if my arithmetic is correct, it's only one-eighth of your heritage. So stop blaming that. You were just curious. It happens all the time. So was I. It's nothing to be ashamed of. I know exactly what you were feeling and I don't have any French blood to blame."

Eleonore smiled through her tears. "Do you, Dorchen? Do you really understand?"

"Of course, I do, you silly goose. Now dry your tears and smile again. I want you to go back to Vilsen and act your usual cheerful self as if nothing were amiss."

"But what . . . ?"

"We'll cross the next bridge when we come to it. When does Teddi graduate from Göttingen?"

"In June, I think. And Catharine's next babe is due then, too."

"Then they'll surely need you that long. And if the Hohnholz really object to your marrying Teddi — which I don't think they will, mind you — then I shall go and talk to them myself."

"Oh, Dorchen, you are truly my best friend."

It was June, warm, wonderful June and Teddi was home at last. "Good morning, Teddi. Welcome home," Eleonore greeted him with all the cheerfulness she could muster. "It's good to have you back again."

"Oh, hello, Elli. It's good to be back."

"Teddi, there is something . . . "

"Not now, Elli. I have to discuss some things with Father before he returns to work."

"But Teddi, there is something I must tell you. Something very important."

"Eleonore, I said I am busy. I'll meet you in the stable loft later this afternoon."

"No, no stable."

"Well, then my room if you prefer. It will be safe. Papa will be at the Rathaus and Catharine is still abed with the newest offspring."

"No, Teddi. We must talk first."

He looked at her perplexed. Surely all she wanted was a roll in the hay. So did he, but that would have to wait. "Nothing can be as important as the dire news I have. Prince Ernst August has been severely wounded and fights for his life." He turned away from her and hurried to his father's study.

Eleonore was left standing there like a statue. She felt as if all the life had drained out of her. How can he be so cruel? No hug, no kiss, not even a kind word. Then the anger rose within her. Prince Ernst August be damned. Just wait until he hears my news. She wanted to rush upstairs to her bed and cry her heart out. But she had the after dinner cleaning up to do. She headed for the kitchen. Marie had already started clearing the table.

"Oh, Marie, you didn't have to do that," she said, fighting the tears. "I was coming."

"I know but Papa expects us all to help. Besides I thought to give you a few minutes alone to greet my brother," replied Marie with a twinkle in her eye.

"He wasn't interested."

"Not interested?" exclaimed Marie, astonished. "What do you mean?"

"He—he was so cold, as though I were a total stranger." And despite her best efforts the tears started to trickle down Eleonore's cheeks.

"Elli, whatever is wrong? You haven't been acting yourself lately and now this. I'll hang that brother of mine if he has hurt you. Tell me what is the trouble, Elli. I'm your friend."

"I can't, Marie, not yet. I must talk to Teddi first."

Marie examined her friend carefully. Yes, she had put on a little weight lately—she who was always so slim and tiny. Marie almost dropped the plate she was drying. "Elli! You're not—you're not—Elli, are you with child?" she blurted out. Eleonore stopped washing the dishes and hung her head, copious tears dripping into the sink. "How could you, Elli?"

"Very easily," murmured Eleonore.

"I knew what was going on between you two, of course, but I never thought . . . "

"It happens."

"And now he won't marry you. Is that it?"

"He doesn't even know yet," sobbed Eleonore.

"I'll hang him," declared Marie vehemently. "Let me talk to him."

"No!" Eleonore raised her head. "That is between us. I must be the first to tell him. I have to—to watch his eyes. Then I'll know. And don't you dare breathe a word to your father or stepmother either. Oh, Marie, I know you mean to be kind and helpful, but promise me that."

Marie nodded. "You're right, of course. I promise. But once it's all out, remember that I'll be on your side."

Eleonore smiled and wiped away her tears with the corner of her apron.

"I am terribly sorry to hear our young prince was so grievously wounded. Lost an eye, you say? But I fail to see what that has to do with us," said Harm Hohnholz.

"Ja," replied Teddi. "He suffered two sabre cuts to the head. One took his left eye. So now he has returned to England to recuperate—far sooner than he expected. He is very brave. There are all sorts of tales of his military prowess and courage."

"So?"

"Before he left Göttingen he was telling me about this new steam engine some fellow in Scotland invented. He was curious to see if mayhap there might be some military application, such as in siege engines. When I expressed interest, he invited me to accompany him back to England to investigate this phenomenon."

"Just you?"

"Well, several of us. He had thoughts of forming a sort of engineering corps in the army."

"What! You would join the army? I'll not hear of it."

"It's not exactly the army. We'd be building machines, not fighting at all."

Harm shook his head in exasperation. "There have been engineering corps attached to the army since time immemorial. The Romans had them to build roads in the wilderness and throw bridges across unbridgeable rivers. The old medieval knights had them to build siege towers and undermine castle walls. They were always in the forefront, in the most dangerous and vulnerable position, totally defenseless until the troops moved in. What did they teach you at Göttingen anyway?"

Teddi bypassed that question and tried a new tack. "I've also heard that someone in England has built a loom that uses this new steam power. I should like to learn more about it. Think what it would do for your business if you could build such a factory here in Vilsen. You could triple the output of linen."

"What?! And have every woman in Vilsen down on my head? We can only grow so much flax. It is a soil-depleting plant. If we wanted power looms, we have more than enough water power. Only that would mean dealing with Anton Matthies—which I mislike. But it would be much safer than this steam you speak of. I don't trust that at all—leaving people vulnerable to scalding and explosions. No, thank you. I can see you have a lot to learn, dear boy, that they did not teach you at Göttingen. And you will start tomorrow. First in the flax fields until you learn every bit of the processing. Then I would have you visit and observe some of our best spinners and weavers. Our friend Dorothea Bergmann is one such. You can learn a lot from her. Also several of the Bruns women both in town and out in the country. You might even try it yourself, if they'll let you, so that you can see for yourself how difficult it is to make fine linen. Some of these women amaze me. It looks so easy when they do it. Then, and only then, when you have learned all that, you may join me in the office and study the merchandising end of the business. After that, if you still have the itch to travel, you may visit our factors in Hannover and especially Bremen and Hamburg to learn from them. That should rid you of your high-blown notions and bring you down to earth."

Teddi was dismayed but said nothing. Up to now his life had been all fun and games. He had been a rich man's son with not a worry in the world. Now his father was insisting he work for a living—at probably very little pay—and at menial tasks at that. Teddi did not enjoy the prospect one bit. He had always thought he would start right at the top at his father's right hand. But Harm obviously had other ideas and he was very serious.

When Teddi made no comment, Harm continued. "Now if that is all clearly understood, there is another matter which has been brought to my attention. What are your feelings toward Eleonore Matthies?"

Teddi was shocked beyond belief. Could his father suspect their affair? He decided to play the innocent until he was sure. "Oh, she's a very nice lass, good with the children, a hard worker."

"You think no more of her than that?"

"Why should I? She's just a servant."

"You have no desire to wed her then?"

Shocked again, Teddi exclaimed, "Good heavens, no!"

"I only ask because Catharine suspects she may be with child. If that be the case, I suggest you reconsider. Although I'll not force you should you find the idea truly abhorrent."

Teddi gasped and turned red. "That—that must be what she was try-ing to tell me no but an hour ago. Are you sure?"

"No, we're not sure. You'll have to have the telling of it from her. But if it is so, I assume it is yours?"

"Uh—uh—it could be. But—but she led me on. If so, 'twas not my fault." Teddi was so flustered he could not think straight. How could this be? He was not ready for this. "Uh—and how did you know?"

Harm would have laughed had it not been such a serious matter. "Lad, lad," he said, "think ye that I have not fathered twelve children and know not what the result of swiving a lass can be—especially when both are young and hot-blooded and the lass is innocent?"

"But she did not act so innocent. I mean . . . "

"Was she virgin the first time?" asked Harm.

"She was," Teddi admitted, shamefacedly, "but—but I have been away these many months. It could be anyone's."

Harm shook his head. "I doubt it. You had more than ample opportunity during your winter holiday. If she is far enough along for Catharine to have noticed it, it must have happened then. Otherwise the chit leads a very circumspect life. We find no fault with her. Nor have we noticed any other male paying attention to her at all. Teddi, lad, you think you are a man because you have completed university and are hobnobbing with a prince. That is not the real world at all. Part of being a man is to accept one's responsibilities—especially towards women and children." Harm let that statement hang in the air. Teddi looked abashed but said nothing. "Now, go and seek out your Eleonore and find out the truth of the matter."

Teddi did not seek out Eleonore immediately. He needed time to absorb all this. He was forbidden to go to England; he would be doing peasant's work for Lord knows how long; he might possibly be about to become a father; and worst of all, his father had implied that he was not a man. Hell, if he could father a child, he was certainly a man. Immediately the fallacy of that hit him. Shit, even a fourteen-year-old lad could father a child. Suppose his father was right, that he was a trifle immature? God's balls, this being a rich man's son was not all the peaches-and-cream he had thought it to be.

Teddi headed toward his room. He had expected—half hoped—that Elli would be there waiting for him as she had so often in the past. By this time she would be lying on the bed, already partly undressed in anticipation of his lovemaking. He became aroused at the very thought of her warm body. He opened the door. The room was stark, empty. Even his bags had not been unpacked. His arousal quickly faded.

He found her in the back garden playing with the children. She seemed especially to favor his youngest step-brother, Harm Friedrich, now six, whom she always called Fritzi, although he knew all the other children adored her as well. She was pushing the little boy on a swing that hung from the huge linden tree. The lad screamed with delight as he flew higher and higher, while the girls clamored for their turn. Teddi remembered how he had loved that swing as a child. She will make a fine mother, he thought unwittingly. But not yet, he quickly thought in horror. He watched her for a few moments until she became aware of him.

"Ah, Teddi," she said "will you join us? The girls are awaiting their turn and I am a little tired."

"You wanted to speak to me?" he asked cooly.

"Indeed I do," she replied just as frigidly. "But not here. Let us go inside." She led the way into the Sunday parlor which was never used except on that day.

"Wouldn't my room—or yours—be more private?" he suggested, haltingly.

"No, this will do quite well. No one will bother us here and what I have to say will not take long." She sat down on a chair near the cold fireplace, not even on the divan where he could sit next to her. He took the seat opposite.

"Teddi, I am with child," she announced.

He had not expected her to be so blunt. "Uh—ah—er—are you sure?" he stammered.

"Of course, I'm sure. It is four months already."

"Four months! Er—Father rather suspected—or at least Catharine did."

"I'm sure she did. Women are more astute in these things but she has been kind enough to say nothing. But it will soon become very obvious to everyone. What are you going to do about it, Teddi?"

"I—er—I don't suppose there is any doubt that it is mine, is there?"

"Teddi! How can you think otherwise? How can you be so insulting?"

Teddi felt a momentary twinge of shame. This was not going at all well. "Then I suppose I shall have to acknowledge it. But marriage was not in my plans for a long while yet."

"Nor in mine. But nor was the child. Teddi, do you love me?"

Caught unawares, he mumbled, "I'm not sure." And quickly tried to amend that. "I'm very fond of you, Elli. You know that. We're very good in bed together. I suppose we could make a go of it, but . . . "

" . . . but you're not even sure what love is, are you?"

"I'm not really sure," he admitted. "Having lost my own mother so young—oh, Catharine is a fine woman, make no mistake—but I guess the only one I really loved was Grandma Meyer, although even she could be a bit austere at times."

"Ja, when she disciplined you."

"How so?"

"When you were so self-centered and thoughtless of others." Teddi looked amazed. He could hear the echo of his father's words. "Teddi, I'll not have a marriage without love—at least a little," Eleonore continued. "When you decide that marriage is in your plans, I may wed you. I'm willing to wait." She stood up and started to leave.

Teddi had not expected this at all. He had expected her to beg him, tearfully, to wed her at all costs. "What will you do—about the child, I mean?" he asked.

"Why, have it, of course. It is due the end of October, in case you are interested. You have several months to make your plans." And Eleonore fled the room.

Teddi felt relieved. It had not been as bad as he feared. And yet, why did he feel so terrible?

It was about a month later that Catharine called Eleonore to wait upon her. She still spent a great deal of time in bed. She was not recovering well from this last birth. And the little one, frail from the start, had turned sickly, would not nurse at all. Catharine despaired of his life. And now she had this odious task for which she had no heart.

Eleonore could no longer hide her swelling belly even though she had let out all her gowns long since. Everyone knew that she was a fallen woman and that Theodor Ludwig refused to marry her. Marie and most of the younger women sympathized with her. A few even envied her. Dorothea Bergmann had been a stalwart support. Everyone admired her courage. But some of the old hens were cackling, making remarks such as, "What can one expect from Anton Matthies' daughter?" forgetting that many of them had been in a like situation themselves only they had been lucky enough in that the man in question had eventually married them. Frau Meyer, had she lived, would have put a quick stop to the gossip, but no one seemed to remember that.

Eleonore held her head high through it all. But it was with some slight trepidation that she tapped on the door of the master's bedroom. Catharine rarely required her presence in midafternoon. It must be something wrong with the babe, she tried to convince herself.

"Come in, Elli," called Catharine.

Eleonore entered. "How fares the little one, Mistress?" she inquired.

"Not well, Elli, not well at all. He is sinkng so rapidly I fear for his life. Just look." The tiny mite was pale and so thin and gaunt he seemed to be shrinking away to nothing. Catharine held him to her breast but he would not suck. She sighed. "And now I must be the bearer of more ill tidings."

Eleonore looked attentive but said nothing.

"Master Hohnholz and I have discussed this endlessly," Catharine went on, "but he is adamant. There is no way I can put this gently, Elli, so I shall say it right out. He does not want you to bear your child in this house. He insists that you go home to have it."

Eleonore sat down heavily without asking permission. She had not expected this although she was not overly surprised. "You know I cannot do that, Mistress. My father has already disowned me—publicly. I would fear for my life and that of the babe should I go near him. I no longer have a home, Mistress."

"I am aware of that, Elli, and believe me, I argued against it vehemently. He is absolutely unyielding, unless, of course, Theodor were to marry you. Strangely, he has no objections to that. It is my stepson."

Eleonore nodded. "I know," she murmured. "But why? Why, Mistress?"

"He claims it will be unsettling for the younger children and set a bad example for the older girls."

"That's not true. Marie is already very sympathetic and understanding and I believe Elise is too, although it's sometimes hard to know what she is thinking. But they both already know about the child. What difference does it make where I actually have it? They are certainly not going to run right out and get themselves pregnant. If anything, my—my mistake should be a deterrent to them to—to succumb to a man's wiles as I did."

"I agree wholeheartedly. But men are peculiar. He is even afraid that it will damage the reputation of the whole household if we are to shelter a—a . . ."

". . . a fornicator? Is that what he said?" Catharine nodded. "When his own son is equally guilty?"

"I know, my dear. I fought against it. Lord knows, I fought against it but he would not listen to my pleas. I did at least convince him to let you stay until I am on my feet again and we see what will happen with this poor little one. A month or two at the most."

"I see," said Eleonore quietly.

"I shall try to find you a place for your lying-in, Elli, although I cannot promise anything until I am well again. But I'll do my best. Perhaps somewhere out in the country . . . "

"I understand, Mistress. I'll find a place even if it is a grotto out in the woods," Eleonore declared. "May I go now, Mistress?"

Catharine nodded as her own tears trickled down on the babe in her arms.

93

At the first opportunity Eleonore sought out her friend Dorothea. The trek over the hill and through the woods was not as easy as it had been with all the exra weight she was carrying. Her ankles began to swell and her back ached. She had to sit down to rest frequently. As she looked about her beloved woods she shivered slightly for although it was still summer the forest was deeply shaded and damp. So much for my bravado about bearing the child in the woods. She would have laughed at herself had she not been so worried and downcast. If I shiver now in August, what will I do at the end of October?

Dorothea welcomed her and listened to her whole sad tale. At the end, she said, "Elli, there is no question about where you will go. You will come here to bear your child."

"Oh, Dorchen, would you mind terribly?" sobbed Eleonore. "I hesitated to ask you since you already have five of your own. I don't want to be a burden."

"Nonsense. You won't be a burden at all. Besides I'm breeding again myself although my new one is not due until the spring. I am so happy bearing Chris' children and you must be happy, too, my dear, else you'll harm the babe. It matters not that that scoundrel won't wed you. I'd like to give him a piece of my mind. How can those people be so cruel?"

"Not all of them. Catharine is against it and Marie has been very kind but they can do nothing against the Master's wishes."

"Well, stop worrying and think only of the joy the babe will bring you. Be assured that you have a home here for as long as you will need it."

Eleonore felt as though a great weight had been lifted off her shoulders. And the walk through the woods was nowhere near as difficult as it had been a few hours ago. Dearest Dorchen.

Two weeks later Catharine's baby died. Eleonore was forbidden to attend the funeral, ostensibly on the grounds that she must stay home and care for the younger Hohnholz children but she knew in reality it was because the Master and Teddi were ashamed to be seen with her. She played quiet games with the children in the back parlor to distract them, although the younger ones did not understand what had happened. But little Fritzi did.

"Why did God take Mama's baby away, Elli?" he asked.

"I don't know," she replied. "Sometimes those things just happen." She no longer had a lap for him to sit upon but she held him close.

He put his ear to her belly. He liked to listen to the baby's heartbeat.

"But you have a new baby here to replace him, don't you?"

"It's not exactly the same," she replied. "No one could ever replace him."

Fritzi thought about that for a while. "But you once told me that you loved me in place of your brother Fritzi who died."

"In love, yes," she tried to explain, "but not in reality. He would be a grown man over thirty years old by now."

The disparity did not seem to bother Fritzi. "I love you, Elli," he declared. "If my brother Teddi won't marry you, I shall just as soon as I grow up."

Eleonore was shocked yet pleased that the small boy had had such deep thoughts. She hugged him to her. "Thank you, Fritzi."

Catharine recovered rapidly after the funeral and soon Eleonore received notice that she must leave. Marie made a tearful farewell and promised to come and see her. Eleonore packed as many of her belongings as she could carry and trudged through the woods to Heiligenberg. The walk normally took less than an hour. This time it took her the better part of a morning. She almost collapsed on the Bergmann doorstep.

"Elli," Dorothea scolded her, "why didn't you send word? I'd have sent Chris after you in the carriage." Dorothea had inherited her great-grandmother's fine English carriage from her mother. They seldom used it as they did not have enough horses, but Chris always kept it well oiled and sparkling clean. It was a vehicle of great beauty.

"I didn't think of it. They wanted me out of there so fast I left half my things behind."

"We'll send for them."

"No matter. I have no need of gowns that no longer fit. Besides I have a feeling they might have me back after—after things quiet down. Catharine certainly would want me."

"We'll worry about that if and when the time comes. If you even want to go."

"I'll have to earn money somehow to support my child."

"Well, don't worry about that now. Now you must rest. Come, I'll show you which room is to be yours. I've put the girls all together so that you can have a room all to yourself."

"Oh, Dorchen, I shouldn't want to put anyone out."

"Don't be foolish. Your namesake Eleonore is delighted and the little ones think it's quite a lark. They are happy that their Tante Elli is going to be living with us and soon her baby will be, too."

Marie never kept her promise to visit. Mayhap she could not. But to both Dorothea's and Eleonore's surprise Catharine came often. She brought baby clothes and warm, delicate wraps for the child. She brought delicacies from her own larder—ruby red jellies and golden honey, fine cakes and cookies. Although Dorothea claimed she did not need them, the chidren welcomed the treats. Once she offered the services of her own midwife. Dorothea was a little offended at that as she had a very fine one. But after some discussion they discovered that it was the same woman, Frau Schultze, the doctor's wife. They all laughed over that.

Then about mid-October Catharine surprised them once again by announcing, "Elli, I wish to be godmother to this child, if you'll have me."

Eleonore was astounded. "Why, Catharine, that is marvellous. Of course, I'll have you. And Marie, too, if Master Hohnholz will let her."

"He will. But what if it is a boy? He would need a godfather," asked Catharine.

Eleonore pondered that for a moment. "I have thought about that. Since there is no adult male in either family I've considered asking Johann Justus Bruns."

Catharine merely nodded. After she left Dorothea asked, "But what about your own brother Heinzi?"

"I'd not have him," Eleonore laughed derisively, "nor, I'm sure, would Papa allow him."

Two weeks later Johann Heinrich came running into the kitchen where Dorothea was preparing dinner. Eleonore had not put in an appearance all morning. "Mama, Mama, I heard Tante Elli crying. Not crying like she's sad but crying like she's been hurt."

"Oh, my!" Dorothea dropped everything and flew up the stairs. Eleonore was lying on the bed clutching her distended abdomen. She groaned as another spasm struck her. "Is it time?"

"I think so," she murmured. "Dorchen, don't leave me."

"Hold on. I'll be right back as soon as I've sent Chris for Frau Schultze. How far apart are the pains?"

"I don't know. A bit, I guess."

"Then there's time." I hope, she added to herself. Back in the kitchen she ordered Johann Heinrich, "Run and tell Papa to ride for Frau Schultze. Immediately!" The little boy hurried to the mill. With relief Dorothea heard the great millstones rumble to halt. She hated to do this to

Chris. It was harvest, his busiest season. But babies cared nothng for the calendar. She quickly set great pots of water to boil on the fire. All was silent. Then she heard hoofbeats as Chris rode out of the millyard and Johann Heinrich returned.

"Mama, what is happening? Is Tante Elli sick? Is she going to die?"

"Lord, I hope not. No nothing is wrong. It's just that her baby is coming."

"Oh." Johann Heinrich could not understand all the fuss over a mere baby.

"Now here is what I want you to do," said Dorothea. "Gather all the children here in the kitchen and keep them here. I do not want a one of you to go upstairs this afternoon no matter what you hear. Do you understand?" He nodded. "You are in charge here. Play with them. Keep them entertained."

"But I don't like to play with the little ones," he protested. "They don't know how to play my games. Besides they're girls."

"Well, today you must play their games. Remember, you are the eldest. I'm depending on you," said his mother.

Johann Heinrich nodded. He liked the idea of taking charge. Except— "But what about dinner?" he asked.

"That will have to wait until Papa returns. I must go up to Tante Elli now." She gathered up a pile of clean linen that she had already prepared for the purpose. "Remember now. No wild games and no noise." She went up the stairs.

Dorothea was bathing Eleonore's face with a cool cloth when Frau Schultze arrived. The midwife examined her patient carefully. "I was a little concerned because she is to tiny," she said, "but her hips seem quite flexible and she is dilating well. It may be an easier birth than I anticipated. But you can never tell with the first."

"Please, don't—oh—," Eleonore clutched her belly as another pain shot through her. "Please don't talk about me as though I'm not here," she said.

Dorothea smiled and Frau Schultze laughed. "Forgive me, my dear. It's just that so many of my patients are quite out of it by this time. Now, I'll tell you what you are doing wrong. When the pain comes, don't hold on to the babe as if you want to keep it there. Bear down with all your might to encourage it."

Eleonore nodded. How many birthings she had attended, even helped with—her own mother's, Catharine's—and yet she hadn't remembered this simple thing. How different it was when you were trying to do it yourself. When the next contraction came, she bore down but nothing seemed to happen.

"Good," said the midwife. "You're doing fine but it will be a while yet. Rest in between the pains. And Frau Bergmann, could I trouble you for a cup of coffee?"

"By all means," replied Dorothea, "and since it will be a while, I'd best feed my family."

They were just sitting down to dinner when in walked Catharine. "I just heard and came as quickly as I could. I hope you don't mind. I'd like to help if I can. After all it *is* my grandchild—or stepgrandchild. Has anything happened yet?"

"Nay," replied Dorothea, "not yet. Frau Schultze says it will be a while so there is nothing much to do yet but I am sure that Eleonore will be greatly cheered to know that you are here—and care. Go on up—or would you like some dinner first?"

"No, thank you. I've eaten," replied Catharine. "I'll just go up and try to cheer our girl. That is, if Frau Schultze will let me. She can be a bit of a tyrant when things start happening—as I'm sure you well know."

After Catharine ascended the stairs Chris said, "That was kind of her to come."

"Yes, it was," replied Dorothea, "even if she is no help at all. It will show her stepson where she stands in the matter."

"That gutless knave. I'd like to shake him till his brains rattle. If he has any."

Dorothea smiled. "As would I, but that's not the way to handle him. Frau Meyer taught me that. I've known him since he was a child. If this all works out well," she nodded upstairs, "I am going to talk to him myself."

Just then a piercing scream came from abovestairs.

"Mama, what was that?"

"Nothing. Finish your dinner. I must go." As Dorothea ran up the stairs another scream rent the air.

"Goodness gracious," said Frau Schultze, "it's coming quicker than I ever imagined. She's a strong little lass."

Dorothea rushed back down again to fetch a pail of warm water. Catharine stood there looking bewildered as though she had not borne several children of her own. By the time Dorothea returned, a tiny head was already emerging from between Eleonore's thighs. Frau Schultze was ready with a receiving cloth.

"One more good push, lass," she instructed, "and your work is done for today." Moments later she held the newborn up by the ankles and slapped it. A little mewl, a gasp and then a howl. "Ah, a good pair of lungs. And it's a dear little girl," she announced.

Together Frau Schultze and Dorothea washed the infant while Catharine bathed Eleonore's forehead. After the baby had been warmly wrapped and the afterbirth disposed of, they cleaned up Eleonore, dressed her in a fresh nightgown and tucked her in. Dorothea placed the little one in her arms.

"Rest now, child," said Frau Schultze. "You did remarkably well, especially for a first one. I predict you will easily bear many more."

"Not much chance of that without a husband," murmured Eleonore bitterly.

Catharine looked dismayed and the others ignored the remark.

"What will you call her?" asked the midwife.

Then Eleonore smiled, a radiant smile. "Catharine already knows." And that lady beamed.

In view of the circumstances the pastor decided that a private baptism would be in better taste and even he was surprised at the number of people that showed up. Eleonore had more friends than she realized. She was the best of the Matthies everyone said. Her years of working for the Hohnholz and especially Frau Meyer's sponsorship had made them see that she was different from the others. Her own sparkling personality had done the rest. Most still had no love for her father but they no longer held that against her. And some were even beginning to dislike the Hohnholz for the way Theodor Ludwig had treated her.

Chris had the rich carriage all ready for the party. Although they had no coach horses as such—only the horses that he and Dorothea rode—he hitched them to the coach and hoped they would run together the few miles into Vilsen to the church without mishap. Although Eleonore was barely out of bed, she insisted on going. The old taboo that women could not enter the church for forty days after childbirth had long been discarded. Besides she was proud of her daughter. She lovingly dressed her in the exquisite christening dress she herself had made.

When they arrived at the church Catharine with Marie and Elise were already waiting for them. Johann Justus carefully helped Eleonore and Dorothea down from the coach. A crowd of well-wishers welcomed them. Then Eleonore had another surprise. Her sister Adelheit emerged from the crowd to greet her. They hugged and kissed almost crushing the baby in Eleonore's arms.

"Adi!" exclaimed Eleonore. "How wonderful to see you. Are you visiting Mama and Papa?"

Adelheit was no longer the silly, giddy girl she had been. She had wed some years ago and now had three children of her own. She lived some distance away in Westen, a village on the far side of the Weser. "No, dearest Elli. I have come all the way from Westen just for you this day."

Eleonore was overwhelmed.

The christening party gathered around the font. Eleonore put the baby in Catharine's arms. The pastor intoned the brief baptismal service. After he finished the part about renouncing the devil and all his works and the sponsors had replied with a resounding 'I do,' he said to Eleonore, "Name this child."

"Catharine for Mistress Hohnholz, her step-grandmother, Margarethe for her great-grandmother Frau Meyer, Johanna for Johann Justus Bruns, her godfather, and Sophie because I like it."

The pastor smiled to himself inwardly. He hoped that the multitude of names would help make up for the child's illegitimacy. And so he baptized Catharine Margarethe Johanna Sophie in the name of the Father and of the Son and of the Holy Ghost. Later when he was making out the certificate for her, he asked Eleonore, "And who shall I say is the father?"

"There is no father," she replied bitterly.

Catharine spoke up. "The father is Theodor Ludwig Hohnholz. He has acknowledged the child even though he has not yet wed her mother."

The pastor did not blink an eyelid at this. It happened all too often but few men acknowledged their by-blows. "And what surname shall I use?"

"Matthies," said Eleonore quickly before Catharine could speak up.

Outside the church Mistress Hohnholz announced, "Everyone is invited to a huge christening feast at my house." In an aside to Eleonore she whispered, "Don't worry. The Master and Teddi have gone to Bremen for the day. I sent them." Then aloud she repeated, "Come all ye friends of our dear Eleonore. We can't have a christening without a christening party."

The group trooped cheerfully the short distance to the large Hohnholz house. Many had brought gifts for the baby but the most unusual and beautiful of all was from Johann Justus—an exquisite cradle made by the master woodcarver himself.

Several weeks later Eleonore had an unexpected visitor. It was the Eve of St. Nikolaus. Dorothea opened the door to him. "Master Matthies, this is a surprise. Is it Chris you wanted to see? He is in the mill. I hope nothing is amiss." For while Anton came frequently to the mill to check on things—after all he owned the hereditary rights—he had never come to the door of the millhouse.

"Nay, naught is amiss," he replied. "'Tis not Chris I am here to see but my granddaughter." At Dorothea's look of unfeigned amazement, he added, "I know, I know what you think of me, but 'tis never too late to make amends, now is't?"

Dorothea could see the effort it took for him to make that admission. "Come in," she invited, "but to see your granddaughter you must see your daughter as well. I'll not have her upset."

"Lass, you're as tough as your mother Lise," replied the old man. "I've said I've come to make amends, di'n't I?"

"Then well come you are. She is in the kitchen nursing the babe right now."

Eleonore, hearing the approaching footsteps and not knowing who it was, quickly covered her breast almost smothering the babe. "Papa!" she exclaimed and a deep look of consternation crossed her face.

"Elli, your papa has come to visit you and his granddaughter," said Dorothea. Noticing the look, she thought to herself, she is still afraid of him. If he hurts her, I'll throw him out forthwith.

"No need to cover yourself, lass," he said. "'Tis a beautiful sight, a mother nursing her child. How often I've watched your own mother nursing you and all the others."

"Thank you, Papa," said Eleonore, a bit nonplussed at this unexpected softening of her stern father. "And how fares Mama?"

"The same. Vaguer than ever, I fear. I'd have brought her along but the weather is so cold and she seldom wants to leave the house at all anymore. I fear I was too hard on her in our younger days." Eleonore was amazed at this admission. "Now, may I see my granddaughter? Hold her for a few minutes?"

"In a moment, Papa, as soon as she is sated. If I take her from the breast now, she will only cry."

Dorothea stepped into the gap. "Would you care for a cup of coffee, Master Matthies?"

"Ja, thank you. That would be nice." After he had taken a few sips of the steaming brew, he settled back in the chair and said, "I should never have denounced you. Adi made me see that. You know, after the christening she came to visit us and she scolded me, Elli. She actually scolded me. She reminded me of my own two brothers. How she knew about it, I'll never know. I thought it was a well-kept secret, although your mother knew about it, Dorchen. But I believed, and still do, that Lise was too honorable to say anything." Both women were extremely puzzled. What was he leading up to? "She knew I was so ashamed. But Adi pointed out that I had nothing to be ashamed about. I, after all, *was* legitimate."

Now the women were intrigued. "You mean Jürgen," asked Dorothea, "whom my mother almost wed?"

At the same time Eleonore said, "I know about Jürgen who died, but who else?"

Anton shook his head. It was obvious that the telling was very difficult for him. "Nay, nay, Jürgen, God rest him, was younger than I yet I was jealous of him—and for that I'm also ashamed. But, no, what I'm trying to say is that my parents had not one but two sons ere they were wed." He sighed with relief—remorse?—glad that it was out.

Eleonore exclaimed, "Papa! I never knew. Where are they now?"

"I never told any of you—or anyone else here in Vilsen. The eldest died when he was four years old. The second, Reiner, went back to Riede where my mother came from, where we also had cousins. I have not been in touch with him in years—again my foolish pride. I know not whether he is alive or dead, or where he might be. So you see, I had no cause to denounce you. It runs in the family."

"Papa, don't say that," said Eleonore, tear in her eyes. "It's that damned French blood."

"Nay, nay," he said, "never that. True, I admit, I tried to beat it out of you when I saw that you were the most French of all my children for fear this very thing would happen. But now I'm telling you to be proud of it. Those old Huguenots were very brave people." He paused a moment. "Nay, my parents never seemed to be ashamed of what happened. Mama seemed very happy that he married her at all. It was all the wars, you know. Papa was a dragoon and he was never home very much. Your grandfather, Dorchen, was often more of a father to me than he was. I never realized until after Cyriacus died how much he did for me." He paused again. "Nay, lasses, it was the changing times that made me such a prig, but I was unaware of it until Adi pointed it out. These new poets, whom I never much cared for, planted the idea in the Bürgers' minds—the vast middle class. They lost—looked down on—the easy-going morality of the peasants and they despised the licentiousness of the nobility. They became overly moral and pious, although they neglected the church itself. I strove to be like them. I was proud and ambitious and I was successful. I am a rich man now but at what cost."

Eleonore had never heard her father wax so philosophical. "I see," she murmured, although she was not at all sure that she did see. She was a little embarrassed at his confession.

"Well, enough of all that," Anton said more briskly. "I just wanted to ask your forgiveness and hope you will understand. I suspect your Theodor Ludwig is much as I was."

"He is not *my* Theodor Ludwig," snapped Eleonore.

"Not yet, mayhap, but I'll see that he is."

"No, Papa. I appreciate your intentions, but stay out of it, please."

"Very well," he agreed reluctantly. "Now may I hold my granddaughter for a moment?"

Eleonore placed the baby in his arms. Anton looked down into the little face. "Ah, another French one and pretty, too." He seemed very pleased.

"Papa, that dark hair is only baby hair. It will change. It's too soon to tell what she will look like."

"Nay, she's a French one, just like you. I can tell," he insisted. "And how is she called?"

"Catharine."

"Ah, Katinka, a nice name. It fits her. Dorchen, do you remember your Tante Katinka? Such a vivacious lass and that beautiful voice. Is she still alive?"

"Very much so," replied Dorothea. "She came to the christening. She is only a little over fifty and still sings in the choir."

"Is that so? I suppose I should go to church more often but there never seems to be time. Well, now little Katinka, see what I have brought for you." He handed the baby back to her mother and dove into a sack he had brought with him. "It is St. Nikolaus Eve and she must have her own stocking hung from the mantel."

"But, Papa," objected Eleonore, "she's too young to know what it is all about."

"No matter. She will learn." He drew out several tiny toys and trinkets and finally a large orange.

"Goodness, where did you ever get that?"

"An old pedlar, comes by once or twice a year, brings them all the

103

way from Italy. They keep well as long as they don't freeze. They're very good for the health."

"But, Papa, she can't possibly eat that yet. She has no teeth."

"For her, you cut it open and squeeze the juice out. Then let her suck it. Her teeth will come in good and strong. 'Tis said it's the best thing in the world to prevent the scurvy."

"Really?"

Christmas came and Dorothea and Chris tried to make it as happy an occasion for Eleonore as possible. Anton sent gifts but did not come again. Perhaps he felt he had said too much. He was such an enigmatic man it was hard to tell. Adi sent a doll by special messenger. It was almost as big as Katinka. Catharine also sent gifts from herself, Marie and Elise but pleaded the horrendous weather as an excuse for not coming. Philipp was their only guest. He spent much time regaling Chris with all the political news for which the women cared not a penny. The children, however, were joyous and made a great fuss over helping Katinka open her gifts and showing her theirs. And Eleonore noticed how her baby's eyes lit up at the sight of the brightly lit candles on the Christmas tree.

Then several weeks later during a January thaw when the fog lay so thick over the flat land that no one dared go far from home, they heard hoof beats in the lane. Chris was seated next to the cozy fire reading to the children. Now who in the world can that fool be, he wondered. The women were in the kitchen baking bread and heard nothing. The hoof beats ceased and moments later the bell jangled. Good heavens, it must be some sort of an emergency to bring a body out in this, thought Chris as he went to answer the summons. He opened the door.

"Teddi!" he exclaimed. "Whatever brings you out in this? Is something amiss at home? Catharine?"

"Nay, nay," replied Teddi irritably, "I am come to claim my bride."

"Your what?" shouted Chris in fury. And then he calmed down. "Perhaps you'd better come in and explain yourself."

Teddi stepped into the hall, deliberately took off his hat, scarf and cloak and shook the water from them. "Nothing to explain," he said. "My father convinced me that I should wed Eleonore and I am come to tell her the good news."

"If she'll even have you," muttered Chris, half to himself. "Come, warm yourself by the fire whilst I fetch her."

The children were suddenly very quiet as their father entered the parlor with this stranger. The baby was lying on her stomach on a wolfskin rug, gurgling and cooing. The older children gathered around her protectively. They did not know who this man was but somehow they felt threatened.

Eleonore, when she heard who her visitor was, first experienced anger, them some trepidation and finally curiosity. She entered the parlor head held high, with all the dignity she could muster. Carefully and deliberately she seated herself opposite Teddi and adjusted her skirts. Chris and Dorothea followed her. They were not about to leave her alone now. The silence was overpowering.

At last Eleonore said, "Well?"

Although Teddi had not expected her to fall into his arms, the chit was not making it easy for him. "Eleonore," he said tentatively, "I have come to make you a proposal."

"Indeed?"

"A proposal of marriage."

"Indeed? Methinks it is a bit late for that."

"It's never too late to—to make—er—amends."

"Indeed? And wherefor this sudden change of heart, Theodor Ludwig?"

"My father finally convinced me that it is the honorable thing to do."

"Indeed? And where was your honor when you seduced me?"

Teddi bit back the obvious retort. She was as guilty as he had been. She had welcomed his advances and she knew it. But Papa had warned him that she would throw this in his face. "I was young and immature then. I was thinking only of my own pleasure, not of any possible—er—results. I have matured a lot since then, Elli. Can I not convince you of that? Papa told me that a gentleman accepts his responsibilities. I am here to do that." It almost killed Teddi to eat humble pie but Papa had been very specific.

"I see," she said slowly. "So it is because of your papa that you make this proposal?"

"Well, yes—that is, sort of."

"And not because of any love you might have for me?"

Oh, shit. She would bring that up again. But he had come this far. Papa would be wroth if he returned with a negative answer. He hoped he sounded convincing. "But I do love you, Elli. I always have for years. You know that."

"Do I? 'Tis the first I've ever heard you say it." She knew his protesta-

105

tions rang falsely but it was nice to hear it just the same.

"I was just too young and shy to express my true feelings. But I swear I do love you, Elli. Now will you accept my proposal?"

"I'll think on it," she replied curtly. "Now, don't you want to meet your daughter?"

"What—er, oh, of course. Certainly. Which one . . . ? Oh, I assume it is the littlest one lying on that filthy wolfskin."

Eleonore grimaced with disgust. She went over and picked up Katinka and swung her high in the air. The baby gurgled happily. "The wolfskin is not filthy. It has been washed many a time. Chris shot it years ago and it has been the comfort of all Dorchen's babies and now mine." She carefully placed the little one in Teddi's arms. He held her awkwardly as if not sure what to do. "Cuddle her a little. She won't bite you."

Teddi was not sure how to go about cuddling so he said, "She is quite pretty, isn't she? Looks just like you."

"Perhaps. But there is also a lot of Hohnholz in her. See her chin. It is quite stubborn."

Teddi did not know quite what to make of that so he ignored it. "My step-mother tells me you named her after her. That was good of you."

"Ja, Catharine has been very kind and supportive. She is also named after your grandmother Frau Meyer. We call her Katinka."

Just then a large, fluffy gray and white cat came strolling along the hearthstone and jumped onto Eleonore's lap. Teddi clutched the baby to him and she started to cry.

"Why, Teddi, don't tell me you are afraid of cats," said Dorothea.

"No, of course not, although I don't care for them. Isn't it said that they will smother a babe?"

"Falderal. That's an old-fashioned myth," said Eleonore. "There's not a more gentle animal than this one. Here, let me show you." She pushed the cat to the floor, took Katinka from Teddi's arms and laid her on the wolfskin. The cat lay down amongst Dorothea's children. "You see, the cat won't even go near her because she doesn't like the wolfskin."

"Cats are very important to a mill," put in Chris, "else the rats will feast on the grain. We have half a dozen more out there and in the barn, but this is the only one we allow in the house. She is the children's pet."

"I see," said Teddi and for want of anything better to say he added, "So many cats and no dogs?"

"Oh yes," replied Dorothea, "two in the barn and one in the house." She called out, "Come, Wotan." A very large shepherd dog came loping in

106

from the kitchen. Did she imagine it or did Teddi cringe?

"Wotan?" he queried. "Do you believe in those old myths?"

"No, of course not but we think it is good for the children to learn of their Saxon heritage. Now let him sniff your hand so he will know you."

Teddi tentatively extended a hand. The dog sniffed it, seemed uninterested and went to sit with the children and the cat. Teddi visibly relaxed. At last he said, "It seems that I have now been introduced to the entire household. Let us return to the matter in hand. Elli, will you accept my proposal?"

"I said I would think on it," she replied.

"Well, think quickly. There is not much time. I have already told Pastor to call the banns."

"You what?" Eleonore had fire in her eyes. "Wasn't that being a mite presumptuous ere you had even asked me?"

"Well, Papa was sure," he stammered, "I mean I was so sure you would accept—I mean, honor me . . . "

"I fear you—and your papa—presumed too much," she replied indignantly. "I shall send you word of my decision in a few days. Now I think you had better leave." She stood up and extended her hand to Teddi. He took it and kissed it gently. Eleonore and Dorothea retreated to the kitchen while Chris escorted their guest to the door.

"Well!" said Dorothea when he had left. "That was interesting to say the least. What will you do, Elli?"

"I don't know. I just don't know. I am tempted just so Katinka will not be illegitimate but I don't trust him, Dorchen. His protestations of love were so false, I could see right through them. Think you not, Dorchen?"

"I agree, but he did say he had matured and I think he has—at least a little."

"Has he or is it his papa telling him to?" asked Eleonore doubtfully. "I still don't trust him and I know him far better than you do. I once told him long ago that I would never wed him without love."

"That may come. You could help him learn what love is. You have grown a lot, too, in the past year."

"I suppose."

"I think you should accept him," said Chris, returning. "It may be your only chance, Elli. I agree he is still a knave and a scoundrel—and, hah, afraid of cats and dogs. That kind of blow-hard often is. But if he should change his mind again, you will have nothing. Sometimes a marriage takes hard work—on both sides. And he did seem taken with the child."

"Was he? I couldn't be sure," said Eleonore.

"I think so," said Chris, "and don't forget, another child—born *in* wedlock—would make him proud and could go a long ways toward achieving that love you crave."

"Do you really think so?"

"I certainly do," said Dorothea. "Remember how foolish we were?" Chris walked over and put his arm arond his wife. Eleonore could see the lovelight shining from both pairs of eyes.

"Very well," she said, "I'll do it, if only for Katinka's sake. I guess I've got nothing to lose."

"And everything to gain," added Dorothea.

On 20 February 1795 Eleonore Amalie Matthies wed Theodor Ludwig Hohnholz in the Vilsen church. With some misgivings she left Katinka in the care of her mother Becke because Dorothea was to be her matron of honor and Dorothea's whole family was eager to attend, as were all the Hohnholz brood. Eleonore could not wear white and she had wanted to don a dark blue gown, but Dorothea insisted it was too sombre. In the end they decided on a deep rose that emphasized her dark hair. She was a beautiful bride as she walked down the aisle on her father's arm.

Before the organ started playing, Anton had whispered to her, "Well, we did it, Elli. I sure fixed the old man."

Eleonore wondered what in the world he was referring to but had no time to ask.

The bride and groom retired to the Hohnholz home for a lavish feast provided by Master Hohnholz. Catharine had already moved all of Eleonore's things from her old room into Teddi's. After the guests had left they went upstairs together. Eleonore wondered if his lovemaking would still be as gentle and exciting as she remembered it. For all her misgivings she looked forward to that. That, at least, had been good.

She sat on the bed and started to remove her gown but when she saw he was not undressing, she stopped.

"I'll bid you good night then," said Teddi and started to leave.

"Teddi," she exclaimed in consternation. "Where are you going? What is wrong? Come here. It is legal now." She tried to act flirtatiously.

"Well, you got your way," he said flatly, "or rather your father did. I hope you are satisfied."

"Whatever are you talking about? What had my father to do with this? It was *you* who came to *me*."

"Yes, but not before your father, the old curmudgeon, blackmailed my father into it."

"Blackmailed? Teddi, please explain. I have no idea what you're talking about."

"You don't? Perhaps you don't. You and your father were never on good terms so mayhap he didn't tell you. Well, I'll tell you of his nefarious scheme. He controls most of the farmers hereabouts. They have to bring their grain to his mill."

She nodded. "So?"

"So the farmers, including many of your Bruns friends, control their wives who usually sell all their linen output to my father. Anton Matthies threatened to take all their linen to another merchant in Hoya unless Papa agreed to our wedding. You must be quite proud of him."

Eleonore gasped. "I don't believe it."

"Well, it's true."

"And I always thought it was Catharine who finally influenced him—and you."

"That, in part, too. She and Marie."

"Marie?"

"Yes, Marie is being courted by a young man whose family was objecting to his marrying into a family already carrying the—er—stigma of bastardy."

Eleonore burst into tears. She did not know whom she hated more—her father, his father or Teddi himself. "So," she sobbed, "your father's business and Marie's courtship are more important than me."

Teddi could not stand to see her cry. She had always been so strong. And truthfully, he did still have some feeling for her. Perhaps she really did not know any of this—was just a pawn in their parents' machinations, as he felt he was. And she was wonderful in bed. He remembered that well. He sat down beside her and embraced her. Their kiss was long and deep and he quickly became aroused. Maybe just this once. He could not resist her.

Their lovemaking was as wonderful as they both remembered. He led her to greater heights than ever before. She forgot all the terrible things she had just heard in the ecstasy of it all. She welcomed him deep inside her. This was what she wanted—needed. At last she felt a whole woman again. And he wondered why he had ever stayed away from her so

109

long. Lord, she was good. Maybe this was love, after all. He wasn't sure.

After they were sated and lay gasping in each other's arms, he dreaded what he must next say to her. Mayhap he could softened it a little. "Dearest Elli, that was wonderful. I think I do love you."

"Oh, Teddi, and I you," she sighed. "It was just like old times, wasn't it?"

Maybe he should put it off until tomorrow. But no, it's best she know right now. "I hadn't planned on that happening," he said.

"But it did." She smiled bewitchingly. "And now we are right again."

"I did not want to get you with child while I was away."

"Away?" She sat up with a start. "What are you saying?"

"As part of the — the — er — arrangement, Papa has promised to let me go to England for a while."

"Arrangement? England?" she screamed. Eleonore felt totally betrayed.

He tried to speak calmly. "I've long wanted to go. I want to study those steam engines they have over there. Remember, I told you how the Prince invited me."

"But that was long ago and I thought, long forgotten. Teddi, how can you do this to me? And on our wedding night?" She burst into uncontrollable weeping, all pleasure from their ecstacy had fled.

He did not know what to do. He tried to console her. "I'm not going just yet. I have to wait until the weather improves for the channel crossing. And Elli, it won't be for long. Just a few months." He tried to embrace her but she turned away from him.

In silence she wept out her grief at his final betrayal.

4

 After Teddi left, Eleonore spent an increasing amount of time with Dorothea at the Klostermühle. At first she had left Katinka behind in Dorothea's care, not sure what sort of welcome the child would have at the Hohnholz household, and naturally she had wanted to see her as much as possible. But that had proven to be a foolish fear. Catharine doted on her godchild. But now Dorothea's time was drawing close and Eleonore felt she could be more help to her friend than at home. The Hohnholz had hired several servants after Eleonore's departure and now that she was a *Madame* Hohnholz there was absolutely nothing for her to do except sewing and embroidery which she detested, although she was very skilled at it.

Before Teddi had left they had made love several times more, albeit sporadically. At least in that they were well matched. But she soon learned that when she wanted it the most, he would deny her his favors, reasoning, probably correctly, that that was the time she was most fertile. Hence, no child was conceived from their eager coupling.

Eleonore often took little Fritzi with her on the excursions to Heiligenberg. He seemed to enjoy her company more than his own mother's and he loved playing with the Bergmann children. They were so much more fun than his own stuffy siblings and there were so many exciting things to do around the millpond and the barnyard. Johann Heinrich had even promised to teach him how to swim once summer came. He could hardly wait.

Sometimes Eleonore rode on of the Hohnholz's horses on these trips, with Katinka in a basket and Fritzi riding pillion behind her. But most of the time Eleonore preferred to hike the shortcut through the woods and so did Fritzi. Although the horse was very exciting, too. As spring began to break forth all over the land, she taught him all about the little flowers as they appeared and how to identify the various trees as they put forth their leaves. She pointed out the birds as they were courting and nesting and all the other little creatures of the woods as they emerged from their winter burrows. Sometimes they saw deer and occasionally heard a wolf howl. That frightened Fritzi a little but it was still very exciting.

Thus Fritzi was terribly disappointed when one day near the end of April, Eleonore told him he could not accompany her this time. "But why?" he asked.

"Because I shall be staying over several nights and you must be home in your own bed those nights."

"But you are taking Katinka," he remarked with a twinge of envy.

"Because Katinka is my baby. This time you must stay home with your own mama."

"But why?" he persisted.

"All right. I'll tell you but it must remain a secret. Promise?" He nodded. "Because Tante Dorchen is going to have her baby and no gentlemen or children must be around at that time."

"But Onkel Chris and all their children will be there," he argued.

"And he will keep them far away while it is happening."

"I see." Fritzi did not really see at all. He was not sure how this baby would come to Tante Dorchen. He had heard about storks bringing babies. Everyone said it was good luck for a stork to build its huge nest on one's rooftop. Mayhap that was it. Noisy children would scare the stork away. He was disappointed but he reluctantly agreed. Secrets were exciting, too.

On the last day of April 1795 Dorothea was delivered of a baby boy—her third boy, sixth child. She was happy to have given Chris another boy after such a string of girls. To her surprise Anton Matthies asked to be the child's godfather. It mattered not to Dorothea that the old miller rarely went to church, that he probably would not live until the lad was grown. She did know that he was extremely fond—and yes, proud—of Chris whom he was coming to regard more and more as a son. His own eldest son and heir Heinzi, although a competent enough miller, had nowhere near the brains nor the ambition as did her Chris. Heinzi had proven somewhat of a disappointment to Anton, who above all admired ambition. And so she was happy to accommodate Chris' mentor and employer. The babe was christened Heinrich Anton.

Eleonore was pleased as well. It seemed as though her father was mellowing in his later years.

The Peace of Basel was a desperate ploy on Prussia's part. Her treasury was nigh depleted; her troops were exhausted and decimated by desertions; the alliance with Austria had fallen apart after the third partition of Poland. And yet, aside from the obvious benefit of stopping France, at least temporarily, from invading north Germany, it was not without some benefit to that kingdom beyond the Elbe. For centuries, through marriages and inheritance, Prussia had held an assortment of small territories along the lower Rhein. The crucial position of Hannover separating these lands from the main part of Prussia had long been a thorn in Prussia's side. Her great desire had always been for a 'bridge' through Hannover to these territories. Although France now occupied those Prussian domains on the left bank of the Rhein, Prussia saw, or thought she saw, an opportunity to one day recover them by convincing France that she would keep Hannover, who naturally fought on the side of England, neutral in any future fighting. A secret provision of the treaty provided that Prussia would occupy Hannover in exchange for those territories in the Rheinland. A line of demarcation was drawn up on the right bank of the Rhein which left the southern states of Germany open to French depredations. King Friedrich Wilhelm thought it was a brilliant coup to ensure peace and keep the French out of all northern Germany. It proved to be otherwise. It earned Prussia the undyng hatred of all the southern states and especially of Hannover itself.

Thus it was on a late winter morning in 1796 that the Bürgers of Vilsen awoke to find a Prussian army camped on their doorstep—almost. Although the Prussians remained on the east bank of the Weser in the guise of an 'observation' army, their presence was strongly felt. The small red-coated garrison at Castle Hoya was helpless to object as the Prussians commanded the important bridgehead there, so they did nothing. Prince Ernst August had returned triumphant to Hannover with his regiment in late 1794 but had been recalled almost immediately to England leaving the country virtually leaderless and defenseless. England had more important things to think about than Hannover.

Ernst August had long forgotten that he had invited some of his fellow students at Göttingen to England. He was too busy being promoted and organizing the 'King's German Legion'. His greatest wish—to take them back to the continent to fight the hated French—was frustrated as he was ordered to take command of preparing defenses against the dreaded possibility of a French invasion of the island. He greeted the young men cordially and then promptly ignored them. If they weren't military he had no interest in them – or in steam engines or anything else of a civilian nature. Teddi soon became disillusioned with the Prince and with England. He did manage on his own to inspect one of the new steam-powered looms and watched it in operation. He was fascinated by the potential of this new source of power and was quite sure he could build one himself. The more he longed to go home, the more he realized that he truly missed his wife Eleonore. But once again he had to wait until the weather was favorable for the channel crossing.

Teddi had been gone almost a year when he finally arrived home in the spring of 1796. He had written to Eleonore few times during his absence and to his father even more rarely, so that she was totally unprepared for his arrival.

"Well," she said, "so the great engineer has finally decided to come home."

"I missed you, Elli."

She ignored that. "And did you learn all you wanted to about steam engines?"

"Yes, indeed—lots. I can't wait to tell Papa about it. But that can wait." He took her in his arms and kissed her. "Elli, I've missed you so. You can't imagine how much. I'm truly sorry I stayed away so long. I wanted to return sooner but I had to wait for the weather. But now I'm here, I want to make it all up to you." He kissed her again, deeply. "I love you, Elli. I never realized how much."

Overwhelmed, she let him lead her up the stairs. Katinka was playing on the floor of their room.

"Is that—" he said hesitantly, "is that our daughter? So big?"

"Babies do grow, you know. Katinka, come here, baby. This is your papa."

The little girl heaved herself awkwardly to her feet and went to Eleonore. "Papa?" she said. That was a new word.

"Walking already?" said Teddi.

"Of course and talking, too—endlessly." Katinka tried to hide herself in her mother's skirt. "However, she's a bit shy in front of strangers."

"But I—yes, I see. Point taken. I'll make it up to her, too. Now come here sweeting and let us make love. How I've hungered for you."

"Teddi! Not in front of the child." Eleonore swooped Katinka up into her arms. "I'll take her down to Catharine. Refresh yourself and I'll be back in a moment."

Teddi poured some water from the ewer into the washbowl on the dresser. He stripped off his coat, boots and shirt. He was going to take his breeches off as well but then thought better of it. Just the thought of

Eleonore's warm body aroused him. He washed his face and hands and lay back on the bed to await her.

"Your step-son has come home," said Eleonore to Catharine as she deposited Katinka on the kitchen floor.

"He has?" exclaimed Catharine, all aflutter. "I never heard him come in. Quickly, we must fix him something to eat."

"I think he has other things on his mind besides food," replied Eleonore with a twinkle in her eye as she went back upstairs.

They each disrobed slowly, prolonging the anticipation. Teddi drew her down into his arms and kissed her hungrily, all over—lips, neck, breasts. He nibbled on ther highly sensitive nipples until she was writhing with need for him. He kissed the little knob of womanhood between her thighs until she cried out in ecstacy. When he plunged into her she felt complete for the first time in over a year. He drove harder and harder, deeper and deeper and she welcomed him greedily. How could she have endured so long without him? Then all conscious thought left them both as they climaxed together in a whirlwind, a starburst of pleasure.

As they lay gasping entwined about one another, Teddi murmured, "Oh, Elli, dearest one, I've missed you so. I didn't realize how much until this moment."

She replied teasingly, "I suspect you were not without a woman all this time." But it was said without rancor nor a bit of jealousy. She knew he was telling the truth this time.

"I'll admit that I haven't," he said, "but those English women—ach, they are like cold fish compared to you. Elli, you are so good." Before long they made love again. Eleonore could not get enough of him.

And thus it was that she found herself pregnant again and this time she was very happy.

Teddi settled down to work for his father although he still had dreams of building a steam-powered loom. He fixed up a workshop in a part of the stable and whenever he wasn't working or making love to his wife, he could be found tinkering there.

Dorothea Elizabeth was born on St. Valentine's Day of 1797 and Eleonore's dearest friend Dorothea was godmother. "Surely this must be a love baby born on such an auspicious day," she said.

"Indeed she is," agreed Eleonore. "Teddi has changed a lot although he still chafes under his father's dominance. But he is ever so kind to me and just between us," she whispered, "I can't get enough of his lovemaking."

Dorothea smiled, happy for her friend at last.

Eleonore awoke in the middle of the night to the smell of smoke. She threw on her bedwrap and rushed downstairs, checking all the fireplaces, fearful that a careless servant had not banked them properly. Nothing was amiss. Even the kitchen was barely warm from the carefully covered embers in that huge fireplace. She could not even smell any smoke down here. She hurried back upstairs and threw open the bedroom window. The chill November wind rushed in bearing with it a much stronger smell of smoke. It was blowing down into the lower village from up on the hill. As she watched she thought she saw a glow against the sky. O God, she thought, with this wind it will send the whole row to its doom.

"Teddi, Teddi!" She shook her husband. "Wake up. There's a fire."

"Where away?" he mumbled, still half asleep.

"Up on yon hill," she replied, "and there's a sharp wind blowing right this way."

"Ja, I can feel it. Shut that window."

Just then the church bells started ringing the tocsin—wildly.

They both quickly donned warm old clothes and rushed out of the house. So did every able-bodied person in Vilsen, each one bearing a bucket. Vilsen was unusual in that it did not have an extremely poor section as did so many larger towns. It was primarily a middle-class artisan village. But up there on the hill above the church dwelt the less affluent folk in tiny cottages, all with thatched roofs. Fire was the most dreaded thing that could have happened.

As they ran up the hill Eleonore said. "Teddi, we should have wakened your father. I didn't want to disturb him. He's getting so old. But now I think we should have."

"Fear not. He'll have heard the tocsin. He'll be right behind us. And he's not that old—only fifty-five. Besides his honor as Bürgermeister wouldn't have it otherwise. He'll be up there directing things in no time."

"You're right, of course. A good part of his livelihood is up there." More than half the linen spinners and weavers, the fullers and dyers of Vilsen lived in the closely packed cottages that lined the Gartenweg, the lane that ran along the edge of the hill.

When they arrived at the scene, women had already formed bucket-brigades from several wells and even from the Eyter brook, some distance away. Men were throwing water on the fire and trying to beat out the flames with brooms and rakes. The first house was already an inferno and the thatch of its neighbor had ignited. Before Eleonore joined the bucket-brigade, she wanted to see if any of the occupants of the dwellings needed her help. After all, she was the Bürgermeister's daughter-in-law.

The mistress of the first house stood in the street with her children huddled about her, while her husband fought the flames with the other men. She seemed to be in shock but otherwise unharmed. The woman of the second house, however, was screaming hysterically, incoherently.

"My babies! My children!" she cried. "Help me! Help me! I'm a widow. I have no man. O help me." The men ignored her, too busy to help her.

"I'll help you, Tilde," offered Eleonore. "Where are your children? Still in the house? My God, woman, why did you leave them?"

"I—I just ran out to see what was happening," sobbed Tilde. "I didn't think my own house would catch. Now—now I'm afraid."

"Stop your screeching, Tilde, and show me where they are. Come now, hurry." Eleonore turned to one of the men with water. "Douse me," she ordered. "I'm going in there." He poured the water over her head and cloak. She ran into the burning cottage, the woman, somewhat calmer, following.

"Where are they?"

Tilde pointed up the ladder to the loft. "Up there." The smoke was already thick.

Eleonore climbed the ladder. She could hear the little ones scream-ing but up there the smoke was even denser and she could not see them. Stupid peasant, she thought. Then suddenly at one corner of the roof the thatch burned through. It gave her enough light to see by but she knew she had very little time. She located the youngest baby closest to the flames. Two others, one crawling, the eldest barely two, were sitting on the floor already half suffocated by the smoke and crying, "Mama, Mama."

She snatched up the baby, cradle and all, and went to the top of the ladder. "Tilde, catch him," she called. "I can't come down until I fetch the other two." She let the cradle slide down the ladder and hoped the woman had the presence of mind to break the baby's fall. Miraculously she did. "Take him outside and hurry back," ordered Eleonore. "I'll hand you the next one."

When she turned back the little boy flung his arms around her knees almost tripping her. "I want my Mama," he wailed. "Take me to my Mama."

"I shall in a moment but first I must save your little sister," she replied. "Can you climb down the ladder by yourself?"

The lad shook his head dolefully. "Mama won't let me."

"Ach," sighed Eleonore exasperated. "Then I'll carry you as soon as I rescue your sister." She swooped up the baby girl already half asphyxiated and took her to the head of the ladder. She held her by both hands and reached down as far as she could. "Catch her, Tilde." And let go. Tilde caught the second child.

Eleonore turned back to the little boy. "Do you know how to ride piggy-back?" she asked. The lad nodded. "Then climb on my back under my cloak and hold on tight." She knelt down and the little boy did so. She noticed that the main beam was already burning. She had only seconds. She took his knees under her arms and wrapped her steaming cloak tightly around them. She was just crawling to the head of the ladder when the remainder of the thatch burst into flames. The sudden explosion knocked her flat on her face. And the big beam was starting to sag.

Teddi was working furiously drawing bucket after bucket of water from a nearby well. He had no idea where Eleonore was. He simply assumed she was somewhere on the bucket line with the other women. He noticed his father had arrived and was directing operations. Two more cottages had caught fire as the wind picked up and blew sparks and flaming chunks of thatch down the line. Right now Harm was ordering a fifth house to be torn down in order to stop further spread of the flames. And the owners were stupidly arguing with him.

"Don't you touch my house," screeched the woman. "It ain't a-burnin' yet. We wetted down the roof. It'll be all right. Jakob's up there battin' out the sparks."

"I'm sorry, Mistress," said Harm as politely as he could, "it's got to go else the fire will take the whole street. That drop of water won't stop any-thing—especially with this wind. See, the thatch is steaming already."

The poor woman seemed to wilt. "Everything I own is in there," she sobbed.

"Then you should have dragged it out long since," said another man, "and not relied on a couple of drops of water."

Harm would never have said anything so cruel. He felt sorry for the woman but others had already lost everthing, some even having suffered serious burns trying to rescue precious household items. "I'm sorry, Mistress, but there's no help for it. Now stand back."

Several men attacked the house. With rakes they pulled down the thatch and dragged it far away from the flames; others chopped at the timbers with axes; while still others knocked the bricks apart with sledge hammers. It did not take them long to demolish the tiny cottage, leaving a wide space that the flames could not easily jump.

Harm stopped for a drink at the well where Teddi was still furiously bailing. "Hot work this," he said as he mopped his brow, "even though it is end of November. Wonder what started it. No doubt some fool didn't clean his chimney proper ere the fire season began. Where is Eleonore?"

"I don't know," replied Teddi, "probably down the line somewhere passing buckets."

"That's strange. She's usually at the forefront of something like this comforting the women and children."

Just then a man rushed up to them. "Masters Hohnholz," he gasped. "Tilde sent to tell you that your—your—that Mistress Eleonore ain't come out of her house yet where she was trying to save the children."

"What?!" they exclaimed in unison. Teddi handed the man the bucket. "Keep bailing," he said. "We're coming." He and his father raced toward Tilde's house. The thatch was already roaring but the walls still stood. Several men were inside calling to Eleonore.

The one on the ladder was Johann Justus Bruns. "Bruns, where is my wife?" asked Teddi officiously.

Johann Justus felt like ignoring him. "She's here, but I don't know . . . ," he called down. "Eleonore, are you awake? Can you hear me?"

Eleonore, only half conscious, was still groggy from the explosion and the smoke. "Help me down," she answered faintly. "I can't move my legs."

Johann Justus climbed up higher and looked down the length of her. A rafter, charred at both ends and smoldering although not actively burning, lay across her legs entrapping her. "I'll get you out," he assured her. He tried pulling on her shoulders.

She screamed and almost fainted. "Nay, take the child first."

"What child?"

"On my back—under my cloak."

He reached under her cloak and drew out the little boy, unconscious now whether from the smoke or fear, he knew not, but still alive and gasping for breath. He handed him down to one of the men. "Here, Dieter, take the lad out into the fresh air. Erich, I may need your help. I've got to go up and pull that rafter off her legs."

"Don't even try," warned Erich. "That big beam is nigh burned through. It's coming down on all our heads any second now. Just drag her out."

"Nay, nay." said Johann Justus, "it hurts her too much. I'll make it. Just pull her away when I lift the board." And he scrambled up into the inferno.

Erich took ahold of Eleonore's shoulders and, the moment Johann Justus raised the smoldering rafter, threw her over his own shoulder and clambered down the ladder. The next instant the big beam collapsed in a shower of sparks and flame almost catching Johann Justus. He dove for the ladder barely making it before the whole loft was aflame. His clothing was scorched and starting to burn but someone quickly wrapped him in a wet blanket and helped him outside. He lay down on the wet grass next to Eleonore.

Teddi was of two minds. He did not know whether to scold his wife for her foolishness or praise her for her bravery. It never occurred to him to worry about her injuries. Then he looked at his father. Harm had turned ashen gray. He clutched his chest and collapsed to the groound.

"Dr. Ewald! Dr. Ewald!" shouted Teddi. "Over here. Quickly." The good doctor had been working most of the night patching up cuts and abrasions, soothing burns, many serious, others not so.

"I'm coming," he replied. "What's amiss here?"

"My father," said Teddi. "I fear me his heart failed from all the excitement."

The doctor quickly knelt down by Harm and felt for a pulse. "He lives still but—I don't know." He dove into his bag and withdrew a tiny ampule. He forced Harm's mouth open and carefully placed three drops of the medicine on his tongue. "Tincture of foxglove," he explained. "It will either revive him in a few minutes—or—it may be too late. His heart is very weak."

"I've got to get him home," said a distraught Teddi.

"Nay, son, let him lie. If he wakes up by himself, it's time enough to help him home. Give the foxglove a chance to work. Now what else do we have here?"

Teddi had been so concerned over his father that he had forgotten all about Eleonore. "Uh, my wife, I guess, but I don't think she's hurt—just swooned."

Eleonore had been drifting in and out of consciousness as she lay on the cold ground. Every time she woke up the pain in her leg was excruciating and she could smell the stink of scorched wool and hair—her own. Her heavy wet cloak and gown seemed to have protected her from serious burns except where her hair had escaped from the hood, but her leg—what was wrong with her leg?

In one of her lucid moments Dr. Ewald asked, "Where is the pain, lass?"

"My legs," she moaned. "Especially the left one."

The doctor quickly hiked up her skirt and petticoats much to Teddi's chagrin. The very indecency of it that every male in Vilsen should see his wife's legs. But no one noticed at all. They were still too busy fighting the fires. Then the doctor said, "Oh my. For this we'll have to take her home to bed where I can treat it properly."

Teddi was even more annoyed. "She should never have come in the first place. And then trying foolish heroics just to rescue some slut's urchins. Eleonore, Eleonore, get up and go home. The doctor will treat you later."

"Teddi," shouted the doctor above the din, amazed at the man's callousness, "she's not going anywhere. She can't walk. Her left leg is fractured and both are seared. I'll give her some laudanum for the pain now and later when things have died down a bit so that men can be spared we'll make a litter out of her cloak and carry her home."

Teddi gasped. What next? Just when things seemed to be going so well. First his father, then his wife. Teddi could not stand to see illness or weakness in anyone. It turned his stomach. "Very well, then. I'll go back to fighting the fire." He turned away.

Dr. Ewald poured a spoonful of laudanum for Eleonore but before she would take it, she raised a hand and gasped, "Leave me and take care of Johann Justus. He risked his life to help me. His hands—his hands are his livelihood." Then she swallowed the opiate and soon drifted off into a troubled sleep.

All this time Johann Justus was sitting there half dazed but alert enough to have witnessed these exchanges. What a difference between those two, he thought. She so caring and selfless, he so arrogant and selfish. She deserves better that that for all their wealth.

The doctor turned to him. "Let me see those hands."

Johann Justus said quietly, "She's right, doctor. My hands are my livelihood and I fear—I fear—"

The doctor took one look and choked back a gasp. The palms were badly burned but the doctor had seen worse and he was very skilled. "I think I can save them, lad," he said. "What did you do—stick them straight into the flames?" He quickly applied his famous unguent.

"I lifted the rafter—aiyee, that hurts—off of her legs else I could not have freed her."

"That was a brave thing to do. The unguent will soon cool the pain and start the healing. I fear you will lose a month or two of work but not your livelihood. You must, however, be very careful while they are healing. Now I must have something to wrap them in. What can I use?" He looked about. "Ah, some strips of Eleonore's petticoat. I doubt she'll mind since you saved her life."

Johann Justus was almost too embarrassed to agree.

The doctor did not wait. Quickly he tore several strips from the hem of Eleonore's petticoat and wrapped Johann Justus' hands, one finger at a time, then the whole of each hand. "If I don't separate the fingers they could grow together as the skin heals and we certainly don't want that. You'll have to be extremely careful not to try to use them for a few weeks. Don't attempt to bend the fingers or put any pressure on them. I'll come and change the dressings every few days. And then we'll see."

Johann Justus looked at his hands. They were like two huge mittens. He laughed ruefully. "I doubt I could bend them if I wanted to. But they do feel better already. Take a look at my back, doctor. When that beam came down, some of the sparks caught me."

"Then let's get that shirt off." With the doctor's help Johann Justus complied. He shivered in the chill November air. The shirt was burned in several places and stuck to the skin but the burns were nowhere near as severe as those on his hands. The doctor applied the unguent. "You'll have to leave the shirt off for a while, so get yourself home ere you take a chill."

"But doctor, I can't leave Eleonore lying here," he objected weakly.

"We'll take care of her, lad, don't worry. You can't do anything for her with those hands. And if you take a chill, you could lose more than your livelihood."

Johann Justus could see the sense in that. Reluctantly he picked up his tattered shirt and headed for home. His own house also lay on Gartenweg but on the opposite side from the fire and fortunately a cross lane lay in between.

Just as a bleak dawn was breaking in the east a squad of Prussian soldiers marched up the hill. The ten men led by a sergeant halted at the corner of Gartenweg and lifted not a hand to help the exhausted villagers.

They merely stood there and laughed.

"Hey, lend a hand here," called Teddi, who was nearest to them. "We can use your help ere the whole village goes."

"Let it go. What do we care?" replied the surly sergeant. "We only came to be sure it wasn't the French attacking."

"They're not. But now you're here, help us. Every man is needed," said Teddi.

"Hah," laughed the sergeant, "we're here to protect you from the French, not to dirty our hands and uniforms in some filthy peasant's task."

Teddi could take no more. His temper exploded into fury. "Bastards!" he exclaimed. "I'll dirty your fancy uniforms for you." Whereupon he threw the bucket of water he was holding straight at the sergeant. The water hit the man directly in the chest, splashing up into his face and drizzling down onto his immaculate white hose.

"Arrest that man," sputtered the sergeant. Immediately two soldiers grabbed Teddi and pinned his arms behind him. The sergeant about-faced the men and marched them back down the hill dragging Teddi with them. When he yelled and struggled too much, a sharp clout on the side of the head silenced him.

So intent were the other men on fighting the fires that they scarcely noticed the altercation. But Johann Justus, limping his painful way home, did. He was about to intervene but then decided against it. What could he, a shirtless cripple, do against eleven well-armed men? There was no doubt Teddi had provoked them but the bastards *could* have helped instead of making fun of the struggling firefighters. And the punishment was certainly too severe, but that was the arrogant Prussian way. Johann Justus' blood boiled with hatred toward the Prussians. He would let Master Hohnholz handle it, *if* the old Bürgermeister survived. He turned toward his home and thanked God it still stood.

As a pale sun tried to rise through the overcast sky the fire ran its course and the exhausted men were finally gaining control. The equally fatigued women were still passing buckets of water until the last ember was extinguished. Seven homes had burned to the ground and two more were so badly damaged as to be uninhabitable. Men flung themselves down on the ground where they stood and women started dropping out of line to make them coffee and especially to comfort those who had lost everything. Almost the entire south side of Gartenweg had been devastated.

A wagon came trundling along from the opposite end of the lane.

The horses started to shy from the heat and the smoke. Heinzi Matthies drew them to a halt and his father Anton jumped down from the wagon. "Oh, my God," he exclaimed as he viewed the wreckage. "We heard the tocsin but never thought it would be this bad else we'd have come sooner," he said to the men nearest him. "I've brought a sack of flour and two sacks of grain. I feared some family would need them."

"Nine families," replied one of the men, amazed at the miller's generosity. Mayhap the old curmudgeon was having a softening of the heart in his old age.

"Then a good hot porridge will help them feel a little better," said Anton. "We've also brought a lot of grain sacks – good for blankets or cloaks. Now who needs them most?"

"Now you're here," said the man, hesitantly, "mayhap you'd best see to your daughter first."

"My daughter?"

"Ja. Mistress Hohnholz. I hear she's been grievously hurt trying to rescue some children."

"Eleonore! Where is she?"

The man pointed vaguely up the lane. "Ask Dr. Ewald. He's about somewhere."

"Heinzi," instructed Anton, "you take care of distributing the grain to those that need it. Be fair now. I must see to your sister."

Heinzi scowled as Anton ran off seeking the doctor or his daughter, whomever he came upon first. He actually almost ran over Harm Hohnholz. The old Bürgermeister was struggling to get up. He seemed to be dazed.

"Harm," said Anton, "what happened to you?" He tried to help the man up.

"I don't rightly know," replied Harm in a very shaky voice. "I had this terrible pain in my chest and that's all I remember. I seem to have been lying here a while. I'm all damp and cold."

Anton nodded. He knew exactly what had happened—a heart attack.

Just then Dr. Ewald came bustling up. "Leave him! Leave him!" he ordered. "He's had a severe heart attack and nearly died. It's only the foxglove that saved him, but he must rest."

"But surely not here. It's wet and cold," said Anton. "I'll help him home as soon as I find my daughter."

"I'm all right," insisted Harm, sitting up with an effort. "Are the fires out?"

124

"Just about," replied the doctor. "It has been a grievous disaster. Nine houses gone—this whole side of the street. But let others worry about it for now, else you'll fret yourself into another attack."

"But I must," objected Harm. "I am the Bürgermeister and these are my people. Any deaths?"

The doctor shook his head. "None that I know of—and only two serious injuries. Your daughter-in-law and Johann Justus Bruns, who rescued her."

"Elli!" exclaimed Anton. "Where is she? And how badly hurt is she?"

"Right over here, Master Matthies," said the doctor, leading the way. "I have given her laudanum for the pain. That is why she is sleeping. One leg is broken and both slightly burned. I have put unguent on the burns but we must get her home ere I can set the leg. We had to wait until the fires were out and men available to carry her, you understand," he added apologetically.

Anton nodded and knelt down beside his daughter. "I have a wagon," he said softly.

"Elli! Elli, it's your Papa."

"I doubt she hears you. 'Tis best if she doesn't awaken until I set the leg. The wagon will be a great help as I daren't let Master Hohnholz walk home either. And young Bruns—I fear for his hands. He lifted a red-hot beam off her legs in order to free her."

"Oh, God. The poor lad—his hands—his livelihood," exclaimed Anton.

"Indeed," agreed the doctor. "I sent him home. I had to peel the shirt off his back. He no doubt would appreciate a—a visit from you after we fix her up."

Anton nodded. "Then let me bring up the wagon forthwith. I'll have to drive it myself. I don't trust Heinzi to control the horses should they panic from the smoke and the heat." He hurried off. Moments later he returned, gently but firmly urging the skittish horses past smoldering embers.

Heinzi walked alongside. He couldn't care less about his sister. If the foolish woman got herself hurt, that was none of his concern. She was always getting into scrapes even as a child, whereas he had been his father's favorite son. He rather enjoyed being the benevolent benefactor, distributing the grain to the sorry victims of the fire. He had been rather annoyed when his father pulled him away from that task in order to help his sister.

125

"Let me turn the wagon around ere we load them," warned Anton. "The horses are nervous."

The doctor nodded and corralled two other men to help. "Try not to jar that leg any more than you can help," he instructed. When Eleonore was safely ensconced on the wagonbed, they tried to help Harm. It was actually more difficult because he tried to help himself and could not.

At last they were all set and Anton suggested, "Won't you ride up there with them, Dr. Ewald? You could help steady them as we go down the hill. It's pretty steep and they could slide." The doctor agreed, picked up his bag and climbed up on the wagon. "Now where, may I ask, is that foolish husband of hers — and Harm's son?" asked Anton, not without a touch of sarcasm. "He should be here helping with them both."

No one knew.

"The last I saw him he was drawing water from a well and passing buckets but that was hours ago," commented the doctor.

"Doesn't he even know she's hurt?" asked Anton.

"He knows all right, but he seemed more angry with her than concerned."

"That son-of-a-bitch. He should be horsewhipped," growled Anton.

"There was really nothing much he could have done."

Anton shrugged.

When they arrived at the Hohnholz house, they helped Harm into Catharine's waiting arms. The doctor explained what had happened. "Don't let him climb the stairs. Put him to bed down here. I'll leave you some more of the medicine but first I must see to Eleonore's leg."

The men carried her upstairs. She was still in the drug-induced stupor and only moaned a bit as the doctor manipulated her leg. He strapped it to two strong splints and warned Catharine, "She's not to attempt to walk on it for at least six weeks. I'll stop by to check on them both every day. I'll send Master Bruns over tomorrow to measure her for crutches. I have to go there anyway to see how his son fares."

"I'll go with you," said Anton. "I want to thank the lad."

"Would you want to stay the night here with Elli?" asked Catharine tentatively.

"Nay, I have to get the wagon and Heinzi back to the mill. I'm sure she'll be fine in your capable hands but thanks anyway. I'll return tomorrow on horseback — more freedom that way. And if that Teddi shows up, I intend to give him a piece of my mind."

At the Bruns house they found Frau Bruns fussing over her step-son.

Johann Justus did not seem to appreciate it. "Doctor," he asked, "do you really believe my hands will heal? Tell me true."

"I think so," replied the good man, "but I honestly can't tell you for sure for several days, mayhap a week. And I must emphasize again—don't put any pressure on them." The doctor knew his patient very well as he added, "Don't think it's unmanly to let your mother feed you and dress you for a while. You must. It's your livelihood, remember."

Anton watched Johann Justus' face fall. "Don't worry, lad, the good doctor assures me you will be just fine but it will take time. Is there anything I can do to help? I wanted to thank you for saving Eleonore's life."

If Johann Justus was surprised at Anton Matthies' visit, he was doubly surprised at his gratitude and offer of help. Anton was not known as a generous man and the families had never been close—the more so ever since the incident years ago at the Sacred Spring when Johann Justus had rescued Dorothea Koch—now Bergmann. He always seemed to be rescuing someone in some way connected to Anton Matthies.

"Thank you for the offer, Master Matthies," he replied, "but I can't think of anything at the moment—except perhaps your prayers. As for saving Eleonore, I was the closest one. Anyone would have done the same."

"Ja, that stupid ass husband of hers should have been the one. Where was he?"

"Didn't you know?" asked Johann Justus. "He was arrested by the Prussians."

"What?! Prussians? What in the world were they doing here?" exclaimed Anton.

"I don't rightly know. It was a small squad—about ten men and a nasty sergeant. They claim they thought it was a French invasion. Now I ask you—how could a French army get by their stronghold at Hoya without them knowing? They were just nosey is what. And then when Teddi asked them to help, they just stood there and laughed at our efforts to fight the fire. Teddi lost his temper—for which I can't blame him—and threw a pail of water at the sergeant. They immediately arrested him and marched off dragging him with them. Had I had my gun, I'd have shot them all. But what could I do?" Johann Justus held up his bandaged hands.

"The bastards! The fucking bastards!" declared Anton.

"Why, Master Matthies, I thought you liked the Prussians," commented the elder Bruns, Hinrich, sarcastically.

"You mistake my sentiments, Master Bruns. I do believe that Prussia is the only state that can bring about a united Germany. I seem to be the only one hereabouts that thinks that. Everyone still looks to Austria to accomplish that but she hasn't been able to do it in over a thousand years and in recent years the Habsburgs care even less about us. No, Prussia is the only one who could do it and even she is not strong enough yet. I had hopes under Fritz der Grosse but he is gone now and Prussia is weak again. And now she—and we—have France to worry about. I used to admire Prussian discipline, but this—this is not discipline. This is a—a gross abuse of power. They are not supposed to interfere with civilians—only observe what France is doing.

"I shall ride over there tomorrow. I know the commandant well. I sell them all their flour once a month. I'll get that stupid son-in-law of mine out of there. Meanwhile let him stew tonight. If he had been by Eleonore's side, this wouldn't have happened."

"Then it could have been someone else," remarked Johann Justus.

"I doubt anyone else would have been so foolish as to throw water at a Prussian sergeant."

Bruns father and son agreed. The Prussians were hated, even feared but not to be belittled.

"Anyway, lad," continued Anton, "I'm sure your hands will heal just fine. Ewald's a good doctor. And remember, if there's anything I can do, let me know. Just think of all the furniture orders you'll have from those people."

"Hrmph," said Hinrich. "They were the poorest among us. I doubt many of them can even afford to rebuild their houses."

Teddi sat on a filthy straw pallet, his head on his knees, in a cell in the oldest part of the ancient Hoya castle. It was damp, airless and very cold. He thanked God for only one thing—that they had not thrown him in the dungeon. He had heard horror stories about that. Apparently even the Prussians considered it uninhabitable. When they had arrived here yesterday morning, he had first tried his usual arrogant bluster. When that only seemed to irritate them more, he switched to humble, abject apologies. These, too, made no impression. The lousy bastard sergeant had magnified the incident out of all proportion. He even tried to imply to a young lieutenant that they had captured a French spy. This Teddi hotly denied.

"Can't you understand? We were exhausted from fighting the fire almost all night. And then your men came and laughed at our efforts. What would you have done?"

" 'Sir'."

"Sir." Teddi gritted his teeth. What a pompous ass, he thought.

"My men were only doing their duty and I can't believe they laughed at your—er—plight."

"You weren't there. I demand to speak to your commanding officer. My father is Bürgermeister of Vilsen and knows him quite well," he lied and wondered momentarily if Harm were still alive.

"Who cares?" replied the lieutenant sharply. "You'll demand nothing. The commandant is not here right now. He'll see you when he returns, if he decides it is worth his while."

Thereupon they had locked him in the cell. He had tried to stay awake in the hope that the commandant would return soon. But no one came and eventually sheer exhaustion drove him into a fitful sleep. He did not doze long, however. His mind was awhirl. How could he get out of here? How could he convince them he was not a French spy? Good Lord, the thought of what they would do to him if they really believed that was too terrifying to contemplate. The Prussians were not known for justice—or mercy. He wondered if the fires were out, what a blow to his father's business. Most of those women had been among his weavers and spinners. He supposed they would have to buy them new looms. It was doubtful that any of them could afford their own replacements. What a bother. But that decision would be up to his father. *If* his father was still alive. That brought another terrifying thought. If Papa died, he, Teddi, would be head of the household and owner of the business. Maybe then he could install those steam-powered looms. But where could he build a factory? He knew his father was not the only one to oppose modern machinery. The town fathers did not look kindly on such new-fangled devices either. Well, time enough to address that problem later. First he had to get out of here.

Lastly his thoughts turned to his wife. The doctor had said her leg was broken. That fool woman. What was she doing trying to be a heroine anyway? Those people weren't worth it. What were a few more starving children? They had too many anyway. But then he realized that he was well on the way to having a flock himself. He couldn't help himself. Eleonore was so enticing, so good in bed. He supposed he'd have to leave her alone for a while. How selfish of her, breaking a leg. Now he would have to go back to the whores he had used when she was in her last stages of pregnancy. He usually came here to Hoya for that purpose but no longer. If he ever got out of here, he would avoid the Prussian headquarters like the plague. He'd have to go farther afield. There were a few lusty wenches in Vilsen who he knew would accommodate him but he had to be careful there. Papa kept a watchful eye on such things in the village. He wondered how long it would be ere he could mount Elli. Damn the woman. He supposed he loved her in a way but he would never understand her. He fell into another restless sleep.

The next morning Anton Matthies rode up to the castle at Hoya. The old building was almost derelict. It had suffered many destructions, rebuildings and then neglect over the centuries. It could hardly be called a stronghold anymore but it was the only logical place for a headquarters since this particular regiment's prime duty was to safeguard the all-important bridge across the Weser.

"Good morning, Master Miller," the sentry addressed him cheerfully. "Here without your helper and your wagonload of flour? It must be important that you come alone."

"It is, rather," replied Anton. "Is Major Puckdorf about?"

"I believe he is reviewing the troops right now. It is rather a bad time to disturb him."

"I'll wait."

"Very well. Will you wait here or within? Or can someone else help you?"

"I'll wait in his quarters. It is a private matter." Whereupon Anton rode through the gate before the puzzled sentry could question him further. He settled himself in the major's room.

About an hour later the pompous little major came bustling in. By this time Anton was not only impatient, he was seething. He knew he had to keep his temper under control and that was not easy for him. The damn Prussians and their rules. They would never bend them much less break them. They were inflexible. He would have to be very diplomatic.

The major klicked his heels but did not bow. Anton did not rise.

"Ah, Master Matthies," said Puckdorf, "I was told you were here. Sorry to keep you waiting but duty, you know, comes first. Something I fear a civilian would not understand. No problem with our flour, is there?"

"No, no problem there. And I do understand," replied Anton. Then he plunged straight into the heart of the matter. "I also understand that you have no jurisdiction over civilians. You are holding a young man here, on what charge I know not, and not even a fair hearing." Anton was not sure of this last but he guessed it to be true.

"Oh, that," said Puckdorf. "I was going to talk to him later today when I had a free moment. But he did have a hearing before my lieutenant."

"A *fair* hearing? With your sergeant covering his own incompetence

130

by exaggerating the circumstances? I think not."

"He is accused of attacking an officer with intent to do bodily harm."

"Major, I too am a civilian but I know enough about the military to know that a sergeant is not an officer. Moreover, if there was intent, which I doubt, the man should be tried in a civil court. Your men were out of their jurisdiction."

"Our jurisdiction is all of Hannover."

"But as an *observation* army only. And that only to observe the French. Not to make war on innocent civilians fighting a disastrous fire. Moreover, the lad was provoked."

"Provoked? By my men? How can you say that? Were you there?"

"Witnesses. Several reliable witnesses. Picture this, Major, if you will. The men—and women—had been fighting a rapidly spreading, out-of-control fire through most of the night. They were exhausted, tired, burned, wet, many injured. On top of it all, this paritcular young man had just witnessed his father having a heart attack *and* his wife severely injured in an attempt to rescue several small children. Then at daybreak along come your men. When this man asked them to help, they not only refused—the exact words were they refused to dirty their uniforms—but they made fun of our people. They laughed at them. What would you have done, Major?"

"I'd have shot them."

Anton nodded. "Exactly. Now will you release this man to my custody and drop those spurious charges?"

Puckdorf grew red. "Forthwith, Master Matthies. And my apologies. The sergeant will be disciplined."

"Thank you, Major Puckdorf."

The moment Dorothea Bergmann heard the news of Eleonore's injury from Master Matthies—he had not mentioned Teddi's arrest—she gathered up her children and rushed to her dear friend's side. She found her sitting up in bed with young Fritzi waiting on her every whim. Eleonore was not in a good mood.

Dorothea leaned over and kissed her. "My dearest Elli," she said, "I was shocked when I heard how you were injured. It was a very brave thing to do. How do you feel today?"

"Terrible," replied Eleonore. "But I think it is more the after effects of that laudanum the doctor gave me. It was enough to knock out a horse but I suppose it was necessary. I feel like I'm having morning sickness and I'm not pregnant."

Dorothea laughed. "It will wear off. How about your leg?"

"Legs," corrected Eleonore. "The burns hurt more than the break. But the thing that bothers me most is my hair. It stinks where it was singed. I can't stand the smell of it. Dorchen, would you cut it for me?"

"Your beautiful hair? Oh, Elli."

"It'll grow back. It's all uneven and raggedy anyway and I don't dare do it myself until I can stand up. Oh, where is that Master Bruns? Doctor Ewald said he would send him over today to measure me for a crutch. I'll go crazy if I have to spend six weeks in bed when I'm not really ill."

"Now don't fret yourself, Elli. You need to rest so your leg will heal. Master Bruns will no doubt be along soon. I'll take care of your hair. Where would I find a big scissors?"

"In the kitchen probably. Fritzi, run down and ask cook for her kitchen shears," ordered Eleonore.

When Fritzi hurried to comply, Dorothea sought to change the subject. "I brought Heinrich Anton along to visit your Katinka. See how nicely they play."

Eleonore nodded. "They make a good pair. Dorchen, are you matchmaking already?"

Dorothea laughed. This was more like the old Eleonore.

Dorothea was in the midst of lopping off great chunks of Eleonore's raven tresses when Teddi came home. Dirty and dishevelled, tired and hungry, he had refused Anton's offer of a ride and had walked all the way from Hoya. It had embarrassed him that Master Matthies, of all people, had been the one to rescue him. He detested the man ever since Anton had forced him to marry Eleonore. Although grateful, his foolish pride had prevented him from accepting yet another favor. He first sought out his father. Catharine had met him in the hall.

"Papa? he asked. "Is he alive?"

"Ja, he lives," she replied dolefully, "but he is very weak and—and discouraged. It's almost as though he regrets that Dr. Ewald brought him back to life."

"How can he think that?" stormed Teddi. "He's too young to die."

"I know," she acknowledged wistfully. "Now don't you upset him. He must not be upset. He knows what happened to you. Master Matthies told us the whole story. So don't bring it up until he is stronger."

Teddi nodded and pushed past her into the parlor. "Papa, how are you?"

"Awful," groaned Harm, "and now I have to take this darn poison for the rest of my life."

"But it saved you. You'll soon feel better."

"Hrmph! And where have you been?"

"Uh—in Hoya, Papa."

"I heard. My son, when are you going to stop being foolish and grow up? How can you run the business when I'm gone?"

A damn sight better than you, thought Teddi. When is he going to stop treating me like a child? But he said, "Don't worry about the business, Papa. And don't you talk foolishness either. You're not going yet. Just rest and get yourself well again. And when the time comes, I'll manage. You've taught me a lot."

But Harm was not so sure. He did not trust his eldest son at all.

Nor did Teddi like the looks of his father. His color was deathly and he had never seen him so weak and downcast.

At length Harm said, "Hadn't you better see to your wife? She was grievously hurt. Leave me. I would rest now."

Grievously hurt, indeed. Foolish woman. He mounted the stairs and entered their bedchamber.

"Ah, the queen surrounded by her courtiers. Oh, hello, Dorchen. I didn't know you were here."

"Hello, Teddi," she replied. "I'm come to help where I can. We were wondering where you were. Elli needs you."

"And I need her."

"Then perhaps I should go downstairs for a bit while you—er . . ."

"Nay, nay, Dorchen," exclaimed Eleonore, "finish what you are doing."

"What *are* you doing?" asked Teddi abruptly. He could see the long hanks of cut hair lying on a white cloth around Eleonore's shoulders. The very thought of that lustrous black hair spread out on a pillow beneath him started to arouse him. "Stop that immediately," he shouted.

"No!" Eleonore shouted back. "Dorchen, finish what you are doing. It is all scorched and burned and it stinks. And from what I can see of you," she added to Teddi, "you stink, too. Go and take a bath."

Teddi shrugged and left.

Johann Justus accompanied his father Hinrich Bruns to the Hohnholz home. Not that he could do anything with his bandaged hands but he was anxious to see how Eleonore fared.

"Ah, the two lovliest ladies in all of Vilsen," he said as the entered the room.

Dorothea blushed at the remembrance of the time Johann Justus had rescued her from the Sacred Spring. "Hardly that," she demurred.

But Eleonore agreed, flirtatiously. "Of course we are, although I fear not so lovely now. How soon can you make the crutch for me, Master Bruns? I fear I'll go crazy if I must stay abed much longer."

"In a day or two," replied Hinrich. "I shall make you a pair. It will be easier for you. And also a leather strap to hold the bad leg up a bit so that there will be no chance of your putting weight on it, even inadvertently. Now lie down as flat as you can whilst I measure you." He carefully measured both sides from her armpit to her heel. "Very well," he said, "I'll have them for you as quickly as I can. You'll soon be up and about but you must follow my instructions carefully." Eleonore nodded. "And don't fret yourself, lass. Before long you'll be dancing at Der Lustige Strumpf again. Have you heard about this new dance from Vienna called a waltz? The most graceful thing I have ever seen." Hinrich still played his fiddle many a Saturday evening at Der Lustige Strumpf.

Both girls admitted that they had not heard about it although they knew that Vienna was rapidly becoming the music capital of the world.

"You must learn it," continued Hinrich. "I am teaching all my children and Johann Justus here can teach you and Teddi. He might not be able to use his hands as yet but his feet still work. By the way, was Master Matthies able to rescue Teddi from the clutches of the Prussians? A lot of foolishness that."

"Ja," replied Eleonore, "he did. Teddi came home a couple of hours ago. He's probably out tinkering in his workshop. Who knows?" She shrugged.

A few days later Eleonore was practicing using her new crutches when she had an unexpected visitor. Tilde, the woman whose children she had rescued, had disappeared. The ungrateful slut, Eleonore had thought at the time. But then, concerned with her own pain and disability, she had dismissed her from her mind. Now the woman, hesitant, apologetic, almost fearful, was on her doorstep.

"Mistress Hohnholz," she said, "I can never thank you enough for saving my little ones."

"I wondered where you had disappeared to," said Eleonore.

"I ran away. I took my babies and ran as far as I could get from the

134

fires. I was so afraid."

"I understand but where have you been?"

"We wandered around in the dark for a while, not knowing where to go. Then I remembered a cousin in Asendorf. The children are there now. I'm sorry I didn't come sooner to thank you but it is a long ways."

"It is—and you walked all that distance today?"

"Ja, Mistress. I had to thank you."

"I appreciate that," said Eleonore, "and what will you do now?"

"I want to come back to Vilsen, Mistress. These cousins can't keep us for very long. They are very poor—poorer than I was. At least I had my loom. Now I have nothing. I don't know what to do."

"I believe Master Hohnholz intends to replace all the looms and spinning wheels that were lost in the fire but that may take time. He has been very ill, too."

"Oh, no, Mistress, I didn't know."

"He had a heart attack from all the excitement but he is beginning to recover."

"I'm sorry to hear that. He is a good man, always fair to his workers. Not like—I mean . . . " Tilde blushed with embarrassment.

Eleonore knew exactly what she had been about to say. She ignored the implication. She was sure more than one of the weavers were wondering, with misgivings, what would happen when Harm passed on and Teddi took over the business. She changed the subject. "I don't know what, if anything, can be done about finding you a place to live."

"Ja, that is my biggest problem," agreed Tilde. "The others have men who can rebuild. I am a widow. It will be kind of Master to give me a new loom, but where would I put it?"

"I know. Let me see what can be done. I can promise you nothing but I'll try. I'll send word to you."

"Oh, thank you, Mistress, and thank you again for saving my babies. I am so sorry you were hurt. I shall pray for you."

As soon as Eleonore was able to negotiate the stairs with her crutches she went about her business as though nothing were amiss, albeit without her customary hustle and bustle. In fact, she took on more than her usual business of second in command of the household. Catharine was almost totally useless. She spent most of her time worrying and fluttering over Harm. Harm himself, while apparently recovering from the heart attack, could not seem to shake the deep lethargy that engulfed him. He simply assumed that Teddi was running the business. But Teddi was not.

135

Teddi kept himself locked away in his workshop in the barn tinkering endlessly with Lord knows what and permitted no one to enter there. Eleonore seldom saw him except at meals and then not always. He had even moved to another bedroom claiming the the very sight of her splinted left leg and even her shorn hair inhibited any amorous notions he might have.

If Eleonore was hurt by this, she said nothing. She had long since fallen out of love with Teddi the man but she still enjoyed his lovemaking—craved it, needed it. That and bearing the children that resulted were the only things that gave her some measure of contentment in the staid, uninspiring Hohnholz household. And now he was withholding even that. But Eleonore had also learned to keep her inmost thoughts to herself.

She soon realized that without any leadership the business was floundering. So she turned her energy to that. Certain that Harm had not done so, she wrote to their factors in Hannover, Bremen and elsewhere advising them of the disastrous fire and warning them that the shipments of linen cloth would for a time be severely curtailed. She tried to speak to Harm about living quarters for the burnt-out families.

"But I have promised I would replace all their wheels and looms," he responded vaguely.

"I know, Papa Hohnholz," Eleonore tried to explain, "but they have no homes to put them in."

"Well, then we'll just have to wait until they do."

"But meanwhile not only are those poor people losing income but your own business is suffering. Your competitors will quickly fill in the gap and soon you, too, will have nothing."

"Don't worry about that, lass. Teddi is taking care of it."

Mentally Eleonore threw up her hands in exasperation. The old man was obviously failing badly. She saw it would be up to her if anything was to be done at all.

Soon her hooded and heavily cloaked figure became a familiar sight hobbling about the town in the chill, dark days of December. Advent arrived and people were busy preparing for Christmas. Eleonore sought to make the most of the spirit of the season by pleading, begging, cajoling, even brow-beating those Bürgers who had rooms to spare into letting the extra space to those unfortunates who had lost their homes to the fire. She concentrated her first efforts on the wealthier Bürgers who had the largest homes starting with her own. Catharine was upset; Teddi was furious. But Eleonore held firm. "We must set an example," she declared. "How can we ask others to give up space if we do not? After all, they are *our* weavers and spinners," she reminded them. Tilde and her children were invited to move in with them.

She convinced the pastor to allow two families the use of the small house where the church held confirmation and Sunday School classes. It stood empty the whole rest of the week. Her greatest triumph was when the owner of Der Lustige Strumpf volunteered to open the lower floor of the building to one of the families. Everyone, even those reluctant to help her, admired her courage and tenacity. Some even compared her to the late Frau Meyer, which Eleonore considered the highest compliment.

Once the new looms and spinning wheels were in place the economy of Vilsen began to hum again, but it was far too late in the season to recover the losses they had suffered. To make matters worse Harm did not even seem to be aware of all Eleonore had done. The Bürgers and the church did what they could to alleviate the plight of the impoverished families with food and small Christmas trees. Hinrich Bruns put aside all his other work to create dozens of toys so that each child had at least one gift. Women sewed and knitted clothes often to the neglect of their own families. It was a sombre Christmas, indeed, in the ancient town.

Then on second Christmas Day Eleonore had good news. Doctor Ewald pronounced her leg healed and removed the cumbersome splint. Eleonore felt twenty pounds lighter and was overjoyed. Now Teddi will come back to my bed, she thought, but she was wrong.

"I'm too busy to change arrangements just yet. Let's leave things as they are for now," he said.

"But Teddi," she coaxed, "I can dance again. May we not celebrate the New Year at Der Lustige Strumpf? I'd like that."

"Not this year. I told you I'm too busy. Go yourself if you want to. I don't care."

Most of Eleonore's friends, especially Johann Justus, urged her to go. "You have been working so hard, you need some cheering up," they said. But she felt awkward going alone. She went instead to the church service which was attended only by the elderly and their very young grandchildren. All the rest were either at Der Lustige Strumpf or celebrating at gay parties at various homes. Even in church she felt out of place. She was in her lonely bed by ten minutes after midnight while the great bells were still ringing in the New Year of 1798.

Johann Justus, over thirty now, was still not wed. He often wondered if it were not because he was still secretly enamoured of two women, neither of whom he could possible have—two women so opposite from one another and yet the best of friends. Dorothea—closest to his own age, kind, thoughtful, hard-working, full of common sense and still very much in love with her husband. Eleonore—so much younger, bright, vivacious, sometimes a little foolish, exuding a sexual attraction she was not even aware of and obviously neglected by her husband. He thought perhaps the affinity existed because he had once saved each of their lives. 'Twas said that once a man did that he was bound to the other person for the rest of his life. Be that as it may—and that was best left to the philosophers—he realized that he must stop comparing every woman he met with these two. But it was hard not to.

Johann Justus' hands had healed well and he was now able to work again, although to a very limited extent. The new skin was still quite tender and sensitive but he was grateful for every day's progress. He had long since attained Master's status and could have left his father's atelier and set himself up in another town but he chose not to for several reasons. He loved Vilsen and preferred to stay there. His father was getting on in years and needed his help as his own two brothers had already left. His stepmother had given Hinrich another flock of children. Although not all of them had lived, there were still many mouths to feed. The two eldest of these had recently left for their journeying years but Hinrich had kept one behind. And Johann Justus was glad because sixteen-year-old Johann Heinrich was not only his favorite half-brother but seemed to be the brightest and most promising of the lot. Evidently his father had sensed that, too.

Good heavens, thought Johann Justus, he is growing up so fast he'll be wed before I. He vowed this new year to start looking for a wife and forget his *Minneliebe* for Dorchen and Elli. But that was easier said than done.

Eleonore was awakened with a start long before dawn by Catharine's screams. She threw on a bedwrap and ran to the elders' chamber.

"He's dead, Elli," Catharine cried hysterically. "My Harm is dead."

Eleonore held a sobbing Catharine in her arms for a few minutes until she calmed down a bit. Then she went over to the bed and took Harm's wrist to feel for a pulse. The hand was already ice-cold.

"We must send for the doctor quickly," cried Catharine.

"But it's already too late, Catharine dear. He is gone."

"But Dr. Ewald's medicine brought him back to life before. Maybe it can again. We must try. Send for the doctor, Elli," she insisted.

Eleonore knew it was hopeless but someone had to calm Catharine down. Reluctantly she woke Fritzi and sent him for the doctor. The doctor arrived just as it was growing light. He explained to the grieving widow that Harm had had another heart attack and had in fact been dead for several hours. "Mercifully he went quickly," he said and gave Catharine some laudanum.

And Teddi slept through it all.

Once again Eleonore took over the management of the business as well as the household. She importuned Teddi to no avail.

"There's no hurry now," he insisted. "It's the middle of winter. No one expects any shipments of linen until spring. The weavers have plenty to do to catch up on the time we lost. They know what to do. Besides I'll need a few of the better ones to make something special for me." When she looked puzzled, he added, "Don't worry, Elli, you seem to be handling things quite well. Just as soon as my project is finished I'll take over. It won't be long now. It's just too bad that the old man had to die right now."

Although for once he spoke kindly, Eleonore was still shocked at his attitude. "Teddi," she asked, "what is this mysterious project of yours? You're not building a steam-powered loom, are you?" She had visions of the whole barn being blown up.

"No, I'm not building a steam loom. You'll see. You'll see. Another month or so and it will be finished." And he would say no more.

Occasionally strange carters from far away would deliver several small but heavy wooden boxes containing she knew not what. She directed them to the barn. Teddi commissioned two of their best weavers to make a special fabric for him—no more that fifteen inches wide but ells and ells long, of the heaviest, coarsest thread, of the tightest weave they could possibly achieve. It grew ever more mysterious.

Finally in desperation Eleonore turned to her friend Dorothea—the one person in whom she felt she could confide.

"I don't mind being in charge of the household, Dorchen," she said. "It was what I was trained for and Catharine has become totally helpless in her grief. I don't even mind running the business. In fact I think I'm better at it than Teddi will be. But, Dorchen, he has not come to my bed since the fire. First there was the excuse of the splint on my leg, then his father's death, now this ridiculous project—whatever it is." She almost sobbed but then got ahold of herself. Dorothea watched in dismay as a tightly controlled seething fury took the place of her friend's sadness. Eleonore continued, "I need his lovemaking, Dorchen. I can't stand to be without it. He may not be the best husband in the world but I need him for that. What am I to do? Shall I take a lover?"

"No, not that," exclaimed Dorothea. "Give him a little more time. He said it would not be much longer. Mayhap then . . ." But Dorothea could see this was not the answer Eleonore sought.

"Another month," said Eleonore grimly. "It's already been three months. And what then? Will he find another excuse? I don't think he has even gone to his whores lately, so engrossed is he in this damnable project."

Dorothea shook her head. "I don't know what to tell you, dearest Elli. Perhaps if a man spoke to him . . . Shall I ask Chris?"

Eleonore pondered this a moment. "It can't hurt—if Chris is willing—but I doubt it would do much good. Yet—mayhap Chris can bluster his way into the locked workshop and at least learn what this foolish project is all about."

"It's worth a try. And I'm sure Chris would be willing," replied Dorothea as she put her arm around Eleonore. "And Elli, I understand how you feel. I, too, should be devastated if Chris were to turn away from me. But dearest lass, don't do anything foolish. Promise?"

Eleonore nodded, tearfully.

A few days later Chris came to the village. He did not stop at the Hohnholz house but went straight to the barn and pounded on the workshop door.

"Who is it?" called Teddi.

"Chris Bergmann."

Teddi opened the door the tiniest crack. "What do . . . ?" he started to say. It was the opportunity Chris was waiting for. The big, husky miller pushed right past the slightly-built Teddi and stopped in amazement. Before him stood the most beautiful, magnificent, finely engineered machine he had ever seen.

Teddi was furious. "Did my wife send you?" he yelled.

"No, she did not," lied Chris.

"Then why . . . ?"

"Because the whole town is wondering why you have become so reclusive, concerned about what ails you—you who were always so outgoing, so gregarious. Now I can see. Teddi, it is wonderful, ingenious."

Somewhat mollified, Teddi calmed down. "You really think so?"

"Indeed, I do and I know a lot about machinery. And you made this all by yourself?"

"Mostly. I had to order some of the special brass fittings from elsewhere. Old Schmidt would never have understood."

"I agree. A wise move."

"And I am waiting for the linen which should be ready any day now. The weavers don't even know what they are making."

Chris laughed. "Ah, yes, linen—the strongest material there is and it won't rot with use or age. Brilliant."

"Right. And then a little paint to brighten it up and it will be finished. I can't wait to display it." Teddi was becoming excited now in his enthusiasm. But then a shadow fell across his face. "Chris, you'll keep my secret, won't you? I want it to be a surprise for everyone."

"I'll keep your secret, Teddi," he assured him. "It will be worth waiting for. The whole town should be grateful."

"I hope so."

"But, Teddi, when I said your wife did not send me here, I spoke true, but my wife did. She is worried about Elli. The poor girl is terribly unhappy. You have neglected her shamefully since you started working on this and she simply does not understand why."

"I know. I know. But nor would she have understood this. She would soon have been out of patience with me. But I think you would understand, Chris. When a man is as deeply involved in a project such as this, he must live it, breathe it every waking moment. Nothing must distract him, not even lovemaking."

Chris nodded—and being a man he did understand.

Both Dorothea and Eleonore begged Chris, pleaded with him to tell them what Teddi's project was all about but he would not. They tried everything—Dorothea even accosted him during their pillow talk at night—but he refused to reveal Teddi's secret.

"I promised him on my honor and that's an end of it. You'll know soon enough." And she had to be satisfied with that.

To Eleonore he said, "Please be patient with him a little longer, Elli. I guarantee you'll be very proud of him."

"Hrmph," she replied.

A few weeks later Teddi announced that he was ready to display his invention to the world. He sent special messages to Chris and Dorothea inviting them to the great event—even one to Anton Matthies and his family. On the day he hitched their two strongest horses to the brightly painted red and gold contraption and had them draw it out of the barn. Teddi mounted to the driver's seat and slowly drove the strange vehicle through the village streets. Dogs barked at it; cats scurried away in fear; people came out of their houses and shops to stare at it. To all and sundry it looked like an ordinary, if somewhat garish, wagon but what was that odd-shaped thing mounted on the wagonbed? It looked like a greatly over-sized milk can and it was fastened securely to the wagon bed, not just set upon it. Instead of a lid two long T-shaped handles projected from either side of the top. There were two circular brass fittings—one at the top of one side and one at the bottom of the other. The whole was surrounded by lengths and lengths of the coarsest linen anyone had ever seen.

"I'd be ashamed to admit I wove that," remarked one woman.

Eleonore was so embarrassed she was tempted to run back into the house and hide, but eventually curiosity got the best of her and she followed the crowd of onlookers.

Teddi paused for a moment before the church.

"What is it? What is it?" everyone asked.

"You'll see. You'll see in a few minutes. Now I need four strong men to help."

Quickly several volunteered although they had no idea what they were volunteering for.

"Now follow me up the hill." Everyone followed.

There, to their amazement, chagrin, even fear, they saw a gigantic pile of wood on the site of two of the burnt-out houses. It was three times the size of any Midsummer's Eve bonfire. Teddi had already paid several village boys to stack the thing. He parked his wagon about a third of the way between the nearest well and the pile of wood. He and his helpers unravelled the two lengths of linen hose—for that's what it was. They fastened the brass fittings on their ends to the comparable ones on the huge can. He dropped the end of one down the well, instructing the man, "Be sure you keep it at least a foot beneath the waterline." Then to the boys, "Now, lads, light it." The boys rushed to thrust torches into the pile of wood.

A woman screamed.

Men cursed.

"Lord have mercy. He'll set the whole town afire again."

"He's crazy. Stop him. Stop him."

Teddi held up his hands. "Fear not, good people, your town is safe. We'll have it out in a few minutes. It must burn merrily ere I can demonstrate the efficiency of this wondrous machine."

No one believed him. Several men ran to get buckets but the man at the well fiercely guarded his hose and kept them away. Some women started to panic. Teddi calmly unravelled the second hose which had a long narrow brass fitting at its nether end. He set the two strongest men on platforms on either side of the can and instructed them to start pumping. At first nothing happened. The fire was burning ferociously. People backed away. Then suddenly the second hose kicked as a small trickle of water emerged. Teddi ran to help the man hold it and as the two men on the wagon pumped harder the stream grew stronger. They aimed the nozzle at the top of the inferno and a giant hiss of steam arose. They sprayed the water up, down and all around the pile of burning wood and within minutes the whole thing was reduced to a soggy black mound. The fire was effectively out.

People gaped in amazement and then someone raised a cheer. The pumpers stopped pumping and wiped their brows.

"Whew! That was hard work," commented one.

"But a lot easier than passing buckets—and quicker, too," rejoined his fellow.

The new Bürgermeister clapped Teddi on the back. "You are a genius, lad," he said. "Why, with that apparatus we could have saved all but the first house in the late fire, and even that might have only lost its thatch. Unbelievable!"

People were full of questions.

"Why does that brass thing at your end of the hose narrow down like that? Doesn't that restrict the flow of the water?"

"No. It's called a nozzle and it compresses the water so that the flow is stronger."

"That heavy, tightly woven linen was a clever idea. It will last forever. But how do you keep it from leaking?"

"Every inch of it is heavily waxed—inside and out."

"I wove one of them," boasted a woman, who had been ashamed to admit to it not a half hour before.

"And what if the well runs dry?" asked another man.

"I already have plans to have several more lengths of hose woven," replied Teddi, "so that eventually we can run it all the way to the Eyter brook. Then we'll never have that problem."

Chris came and embraced Teddi. "Congratulations," he said. "Although I understood the engineering principle of the thing, I must admit that I had my doubts as to how well it would work. But it performed beautifully. Now Elli will understand."

"I hope so," sighed Teddi.

Even old Anton Matthies came and shook his son-in-law's hand. "Well, that was very interesting. Seems you have more brains than I gave you credit for. But not enough to keep my daughter happy. See to her, lad, ere you lose her." Typically Anton could not express a compliment without adding criticism but Teddi knew he was right.

"What are you calling this thing?" asked the Bürgermeister.

"Why, a fire engine, of course," replied Teddi. "And I shall donate it to the town. We shall have to train a large number of men how to use it and divide them into teams of four or five to be on call for specific hours of the day and night. So that whenever the tocsin rings there will be no confusion as to who is responsible for operating it."

"A capital idea," agreed the Bürgermeister. "You have it all thought out, haven't you?"

"I've thought about it for a long time. You see I'd seen something similar in the bigger cities. And I just cursed myself that I hadn't built it before the fire. Had I, my wife and Johann Justus would not have been hurt, my father might not have died and nine families would still have their houses and livelihoods." Everyone was amazed at Teddi Hohnholz's humility, especially today when he had every right to be proud.

"And now, if you'll excuse me, I must see to my wife," he said and turned to Chris. "Where is she?"

"Last I saw her, she was with Dorchen way at the back of the crowd," replied Chris. "They've probably gone to your home. Say, why don't you go ahead and let me and these other fellows pack this thing up. We'll see it safely to your barn."

"Thanks, Chris, I'd appreciate that. But be sure they squeeze every drop of water out of those hoses but leave it in the tank. That way it won't take so long the next time."

"I understand," replied his friend. "Now go to Elli. Go."

That night Teddi crept into Eleonore's bed and held her in his arms. "Will you forgive me, dearest lass?"

"I was very proud of you today," she murmured into his shoulder.

They made such beautiful love that Eleonore was willing to forgive him anything. And before very long she was pregnant again.

144

5

1803

Heinrich Anton Bergmann and Catharine Hohnholz sat in companionable silence on the bank of the millpond. It was a beautiful June day and school was out for the summer. The sun was delightfully warm but not hot. The sky was cloudless. The trees, now in full leaf, lent a dappled shade. Heinrich liked being with Katinka even though she was a girl. She was sweet and intelligent and, above all, she knew when to keep quiet. She always seemed interested when he expounded on his vast—as he thought—knowledge of plants and animals, of field and forest. Yes, although he would never admit it, he enjoyed Katinka's company very much. They were both eight years old.

"See, the fish are jumping," he pointed out.

"I see," she replied. "That means they're happy, does it not?" she replied.

"I s'pose. Although I don't really know how fish can be happy."

"Why not?"

Heinrich shrugged. "You want to play Hansel and Gretel?"

"Ooo, I'd like to, but shouldn't we tell our Mamas first? They'll wonder where we've got to."

"Nay, we'll be back long before they miss us. They'll be talking about babies for hours."

"You're right. I wonder why they have so many babies."

"Mayhap because so many die."

"There's that. But you'd think two or three would be enough," said the ever practical Katinka.

"That's well enough for you to say. You're your Mama's eldest," replied Heinrich, "but I have two brothers and three sisters ahead of me. If Mama had stopped at two or three, I wouldn't be here."

"Oh. Then I should miss you very much."

They walked along in silence for a bit as each of them pondered this profound thought.

"I love these woods," sighed Katinka. "It's so—so quiet and yet you know there's life all around you. Oh! We forgot the bread crumbs."

"Ach, silly, you know even in the story the birds ate the crumbs."

"Well, pebbles then."

"Don't worry. We won't get lost. I know every inch of these woods," boasted Heinrich. "Did you know that we even have our own witch here?"

"Heinrich, are you trying to frighten me?"

"Nay, nay," he assured her. "She's a good witch, not a wicked witch. Would you like to visit her?"

"I—I don't know," Katinka said very hesitantly. "Why haven't we been to see her before when we've walked through the woods?"

"Because it's a bit further than I've ever taken you. But today, being it's nigh on midsummer, we'll have plenty of time. Come on," he urged. "I never knew you to be frightened."

"I'm not," she denied vehemently. "It's just that . . . What's the difference between a good witch and a wicked witch?"

"A wicked witch puts spells on people that make them sick or make them do bad things. A good witch helps people. Mama says I shouldn't even call her a witch. She's just an old wisewoman who helps women to have babies."

"She does? Does she put them in the mamas' tummies?"

"Nay, silly. A man does that."

"A man? But how—I mean, how do you know that?"

"My brother Georg told me. But he went off on his journeying ere he could tell more."

Hmm, thought Katinka. This sounds interesting. She was ever game for adventure, especially when Heinrich was along. "Very well," she said, "let us go and meet your good witch."

About a half hour later they come upon the tiniest cottage Katinka had ever seen. It was nothing more than a hut really. Just like the one in the fairy tale, she thought. It was surrounded by a well-tended herb garden but, other than that, it looked as though the enroaching forest would soon gobble it up. Two cats scurried away at their approach and a ferocious barking came from within.

Katinka clutched Heinrich's arm. "Is it a wolf?" she cried.

"Nay, nay," he laughed. "Nothing so fierce. You'll see."

Just then the door opened and a sleek little dachshund dashed out. He stopped barking when he saw Heinrich and his tail wagged merrily in greeting.

"See. Baldur knows me very well." He leaned down to pet the dog.

"Baldur?"

"Ja, she names all her pets after the old gods. The cats are Freyr and Freya. Her goat is Donar, of course."

"Of course. But is she not a Christian? Does she worship the old gods?" asked Katinka, horrified.

"I don't know. I suppose she's a Christian. I never asked. But she can tell the most wonderful stories about the olden times."

The old woman who stood in the doorway looked like a witch—that is, if anyone really knew what a witch looked like. Her face was so wrinkled and weather-worn it was hard to tell where her eyes and mouth began. She had no teeth. The hand clutching a highly polished, crooked staff was like a claw. She was very tiny yet stood surprisingly erect for one so ancient. She stared at the children with rheumy eyes.

"Who be it a-come to see the old wisewoman?" she cackled. Heinrich stepped forward so that she could see him better, although Katinka held back. Before he could answer, the crone cackled again with what they took to be a laugh. "Ach, if'n it b'ain't Heinrich Anton Bergmann. Well come, lad, and who be that with ye? Don't recollect seein' her before."

Katinka bravely stepped up beside Heinrich. "I am Catharine Margarethe Johanna Sophie Hohnholz," she announced proudly.

"Goodness gracious! A lot of names for a wee lass. And which one do you go by?"

"My family and friends call me Katinka."

"A goodly name. 'Twere a saint by name o' Catherine many hundreds o' years past down in a place called Italy. Then, too, an empress of Russia, died just a few years past. She weren't no saint though."

"Oh, I didn't know," replied Katinka, amazed at the woman's knowledge, for she was sure she must be illiterate.

"Indeed. Just so's they don't call you Sophie. Now there was a wicked woman."

"But I like 'Sophie'," protested Katinka.

"Who was a wicked woman?" asked Heinrich.

"Why, our duchess who missed bein' queen of England by one month. Knew all about her, I did."

"You knew her?" asked Heinrich in disbelief.

"Nay, nay, lad. I'm old but not that old. I was a-born the year after she

147

died. But I knew her sweet good-daughter Sophie Dorothea, her as used to bide a while here at Bruchhausen. But even that were afore my time. She was Princess of Ahlden time I got to know about it. So sad that. But come in, come in and set a bit. 'Tis coffee time and I've got some fine oat cookies you two will like."

As they followed the old woman into the cottage Heinrich whispered, "She's nigh on a hundred years old, methinks."

Katinka shook her head. Everyone knew the tragic story of Sophie Dorothea, estranged wife of King George I, who had been brutally exiled to Ahlden and her lover murdered on Sophie's orders. Katinka knew her history well and she was quicker at arithmetic than Heinrich. "Nay," she whispered back, "Sophie died in 1714. So if she was born the year after, that makes her eighty-eight."

"Still pretty old." Heinrich did not like it when she bested him like this.

They entered the tiny house. It consisted of only one room. On one side stood a table and two chairs, the wall lined with numerous cabinets and shelves, cluttered with assorted jars and crocks. On the other was a cupboard bed. In the very center was an old-fashioned round hearth with a smoke-hole through the roof above it. It was very dark. The fire gave the only light. A kettle hanging from an iron tripod bubbled with something that smelled strange—somewhat spicy but not at all appetizing. Katinka blinked her eyes and wrinkled her nose.

"Cookin' up a batch of one of my potions," the old woman explained. "Got to keep up a ready supply, never knowin' when a poor soul might have need of it. Here, have an oatcake—fresh baked this morn."

Katinka looked at Heinrich doubtfully. She had no desire to be bewitched by magic potions. But when she saw him munching greedily she tasted one and found it very, very good.

"So ye be Eleonore Matthies' eldest," pronounced the crone. Katinka nodded. She hoped the woman would not remind her that she had been born a bastard but the ancient one seemed to sense that and went on, "Used to come visit me many times when she was no but your age. Gave her comfort when her old man—your grandpa—was mean to her. Hear he's simmered down a lot in his old age. She minded me of a frightened doe a-runnin' through the woods. She loved the woods. She was like one of the forest creatures herself. Beautiful." She sighed.

Katinka smiled. She had not known this about her mother.

Suddenly while they were enjoying the delicious oatcakes they heard the raucous cawing of several crows—or was it their even larger cousins, the ravens? Seemed so, it was so loud. The old woman went to the door and stepped outside. "Got to see what they're goin' on about. Mayhap 'tis some dire news."

Heinrich and Katinka looked at each other. Mayhap the old witch *was* crazy although she had seemed perfectly coherent up to now. When she returned, her whole demeanor had changed. She seemed very upset, even irritable.

"You children best run along home now. Be goin' to rain afore long. Hurry now."

There still was not a cloud in the sky, although the sun was slanting towards the west and they knew they should be leaving. It was a long walk home.

But Heinrich had to question. "How do you know it's going to rain. Did the crows tell you?"

The ancient one cackled, "B'ain't no secret to that. My old bones tell me it's about to rain soon. And them weren't no crows. Them was Wotan's ravens and they brought fearful news indeed. Wasn't a-goin' to tell ye for fear of scarin' ye but 'tis best your elders know it. There's a terrible wicked enemy a-comin' from the west—Holland, methinks. Tell your Mas to gather in all the little ones and lock the doors. Tell your Pas to keep them ole muskets loaded and handy. It could be the French."

"The French? But . . . "

"No questions now. Run, run as fast as you can. Stick straight to the path and don't stop for nothin'—nothin' at all—till you're safe home in your beds." She shooed them away.

The two children were totally bewildered but they were truly frightened now. So they ran.

Dorothea and Eleonore were gossiping about babies just as their children had predicted.

"Dorchen," said Eleonore, "wouldn't you know—I'm carrying again."

"Well, I'm not—for a change—but I doubt it will be long ere I am again. And I'm not the least bit surprised at you. You love your Teddi as I love my Chris and we both love *it*. Some say that women are not supposed to enjoy lovemaking but we do. Is there something wrong with us?"

"No," replied Eleonore, "there's something wrong with them. They don't know what they're missing."

Dorothea laughed. "I know. I can't turn him away—don't want to. I just wish we didn't lose so many. It seems so futile going through all those months and months of carrying it, only to have the poor dear babe die in less than a year." She fought back a sob.

"I know. I've only lost one so far but you have lost—what is it now?—three. It doesn't seem fair."

"I just wish the change would hurry up and come to me so I could enjoy it without having to worry about getting pregnant."

"But Dorchen," exclaimed Eleonore horrified, "then you'd be *old*."

"Oh, I don't know. My mother always said those years after the change were some of the best in her life."

"Really?" said Eleonore doubtfully. "Ach, let's get off this dreary subject. Where do you suppose those two rapscallions have gotten off to? It's not like them to have missed these wonderful cakes you've served for coffee."

"I'm sure Heinrich Anton is lecturing her on all the wonders of the forest and Katinka seems to enjoy listening to him. I'd not worry if I were you. They'll not have gone far. No doubt with the days so long now they've lost track of the time."

Just then they heard hoofbeats pounding up the lane.

"Now who can that be?" wondered Dorothea. "I'd best go and see. Chris'll not have heard it with the mill running."

As she peered out the front door Fritzi jumped down from his lathered horse and ran toward her. "Tante Dorchen, Tante Dorchen," he cried out, "are Elli and the children still here?"

"Ja, they are," she replied. "But Fritzi, whatever is amiss at home? Is it Catharine?"

"Nay, nay, but the French are coming."

"What!" exclaimed Dorothea in disbelief.

By this time Eleonore was standing at Dorothea's side. "What foolishness is this?" she asked. "Who says the French are coming? And whyever for?"

"A fast courier just rode through Vilsen and warned everybody to gather in their womenfolk and children and livestock and lock their doors and arm themselves. He couldn't stop for long since he must ride all the way to Nienburg this night and warn every village along the way. Teddi can tell you more. He spoke to him and then sent me posthaste to fetch you and the children."

"Good heavens, I don't believe it," exclaimed Eleonore. "Whatever do the French want with us?"

"I don't know, but you'd better believe it," he urged. "The whole village is in an uproar. Hurry now."

"All right, all right. But you know I can't walk as fast you can ride, especially not now—and not with the little ones. I'll take the shortcut through the woods as I always do. We'll be safe enough there. Go ahead on home and tell Teddi we're on our way."

"Would you like me to take the baby up on the horse with me?" suggested Fritzi. "That way he won't slow you down."

"Ja, that would help. But Katinka . . . " gasped Eleonore. "Oh, Lord, where is Katinka? She and Heinrich Anton are off playing in the woods somewhere. I can't leave until she returns."

"Leave her," said Dorothea. "She can stay the night here. You know she'll be perfectly safe—no doubt safer than in Vilsen if what Fritzi says is true."

"It's true, all right," insisted the young man. "Now hurry, Elli. Make up your mind, else you'll all have to stay here."

"Oh, no, I couldn't impose on Dorchen to that extent. Besides I'd like to see what these Frenchmen look like." Fritzi rolled up his eyes and Dorothea shook her head. "Very well, I'll leave Katinka here. I'll come and fetch her on the morrow, Dorchen, provided things have quieted down."

"Don't worry, Elli, she'll be fine," Dorothea assured her. "This is like her second home. She'll no doubt enjoy the excitement. After all, she was born here."

Less than a half hour after Eleonore left ominous black clouds started rolling in, rapidly blotting out the sinkng sun.

"Ooo, look at that," pointed out Katinka. "It's going to rain any minute. Your old wisewoman was right."

"I see it," replied Heinrich Anton. "I wonder how she knew."

"Ach, that's nothing unusual," stated Katinka. "Lots of old people can tell when a storm is coming. They feel it in their bones. I've heard my Grandpa Matthies and my Grandma Catharine both say so."

Just then a bright flash of lightning and a loud clap of thunder startled them. Heinrich Anton took Katinka's hand. "Come on. We'd better run or we'll get drenched."

They were within sight of the mill when the heavens opened and the cloudburst hit them. And they still had to circle the millpond. By the time they reached the house both of them were soaked through to the skin.

Dorothea met them, scolding, "Children, children, where have you been? Couldn't you see it was about to rain? Come into the kitchen by the fire and get those wet clothes off ere you catch your deaths."

"Ja, we could see it," admitted Heinrich Anton sheepishly, "but—but we were kind of far away."

"Ja, Heinrich Anton's old witch told us it would rain," put in Katinka, "but the sky was all so blue so we thought we had time."

Heinrich Anton could have kicked her. "She's not my old witch," he retorted.

"The old witch," exclaimed Dorothea. "So that's where you were. And what other fables did she tell you?"

"That the French are coming," announced Katinka and suddenly looked around her. "Where is my mother?"

Dorothea did not know whether to be astounded or realistic. She hesitated a moment before she replied. "Ja, indeed, the French are coming. Fritzi rode up no but an hour ago and urged her to go home with the little ones. She couldn't wait since we didn't know how long you would be. You are to spend the night here with us."

"Oh, that will be fun," said Katinka.

"And tell me," asked Dorothea, "how did the wisewoman know the French were coming?"

"She said Wotan's ravens told her," replied Katinka succinctly.

When Heinrich Anton realized that his mother was not going to chide them for visiting the wisewoman, only for being wet, he bravely explained, "She said a terrible enemy was coming from the west. We heard all the cawing but it sounded just like a lot of noise to us. But she understood them. How can she do that, Mama?"

Dorothea shook her head. "I don't know but she is a very wise wisewoman."

In the event no one in Vilsen or Bruchhausen stayed behind locked doors. Eleonore was not the only one curious about the French army. Hundreds of men, women and all but the smallest children lined the streets of the two villages along which the troops must pass on their way to Hoya. French General Mortier had led them on a rapid march over difficult, muddy roads from Holland to Hannover. There were thousands upon thousands of them—infantry, cavalry, hussars and heavy artillery. Despite the downpour they seemed to be in good spirits, some of them singing a rousing marching song as they swung past the awestruck onlookers.

"They seem to be well disciplined," remarked Fritzi as he stood next to Eleonore.

"Perhaps," she said doubtfully. "They can't be otherwise marching at that pace. But what happens when they are turned loose on the town or countryside? Dorchen's mother Lise could tell you horror stories about the last time the French were here some thirty-five years ago. My own grandfather, too, although I never knew him."

"Still, they say this Napoleon keeps his troops under tight control."

Eleonore shrugged.

Just then a particularly handsome soldier looked straight at Eleonore and called out, "Ah, jolie Ma'm'selle, voulez-vous acoucher avec moi ce soir?"

Eleonore was shocked. She blushed and then turned white with fury. She put her nose up in the air and turned away. The soldiers laughed uproariously. And then she realized that her gesture was a mistake. Now they knew that she had understood the taunt. If she had only gritted her teeth and done nothing. But she had been too quick to react. No one else had understood the lewd remark.

"What did he say?" asked Fritzi.

"Nothing. Just something nasty I'll not repeat. Come, I'm going home. I've had enough of standing in the rain watching those boors simply walk in and take over our country. Where is the Hannoverian army anyway?"

"I was wondering the same thing," replied Fritzi. "In fact, why pick on Hannover at all?"

Eleonore shrugged. All she could think was, why me? Why single me out? Do I really look so French that they knew I'd understand?

The few German troops at the Hoya bridgehead surrendered without a struggle. What could they do against so many? They were disarmed and told to go home. At their look of puzzlement, General Mortier said, "The army of Hannover no longer exists. Now go." Thankful at not being taken prisoners, they went. Mortier left a small contingent of French troops at Hoya and turned his army south toward Nienburg.

Here he met with his first resistance. The German garrison defended the old fortress guarding Nienburg fiercely and valiantly but soon the sheer numbers of the French overwhelmed them and they were forced to an ignominious surrender. The survivors were taken prisoner simply for defending their homeland. Eleonore would have been gratified, had she known, that the French soldier who had insulted her was among the casualties.

The next day, on orders of Napoleon, the Hannover government sent delegates to a meeting at the village of Sulingen, some fifteen miles west of Nienburg. After seven hours of heated negotiations they were forced to sign the infamous, shameful Convention of Sulingen. The terms, in Napoleon's view, were lenient: the entire Hannoverian army was to be immediately disbanded; a war tax was imposed on all the people, noble and peasant alike; troops and horses were to be quartered on the citizenry, which was especially heinous to the peasants; and the entire land of Hannover was delivered up to France for ten years. Since both England and Prussia had long since left Hannover virtually defenseless, the delegates had no choice but to sign the disgraceful Convention. Not all agreed, however. A small remnant of the army, some 15,000 men, managed to escape to England and join the King's German Legion.

"But why pick on Hannover?" asked Dorothea. They were seated around her kitchen table. Her brother Philipp was visiting. Both she and Chris enjoyed his visits as he always had the latest news. In recent years he had been dividing his time between teaching at Göttingen and a successful law practice in Vilsen. When news of the French invasion reached him, he had hurried home.

"Because we're part of England," replied Philipp.

"But we're not *part* of England," argued his sister. "We simply have the same king is all."

"To Napoleon that is the same thing. And England is his bitterest enemy."

"I think what Dorchen is trying to say," put in Chris, "is that when Napoleon invaded the lands of southern Germany, granted he put in puppet governments in a few places, but he still let them remain sovereign states governing themselves. Why is Hannover to be forced under French rule as if it were a part of France?"

"Which it may soon be."

"What! Do you really believe that?"

"I fear it, yes," said Philipp sadly. "But to comment on the first part of our statement, don't be fooled by the phrase sovereign states. They are all tightly—and I mean tightly—controlled by Napoleon. Not a one of them has the same borders they had no but a few years ago. Napoleon has carved up the map of Germany as has never been done in its long history.

All of the ecclesiastical territories have fallen victim to his redistribution."

"And good riddance to them," commented Chris. "The Emperor's toadies."

"Agreed. But also every one of the smaller knightly domains has disappeared. Only six of the many Imperial Free Cities remain — Bremen, Hamburg, Lübeck in the north, Frankfurt in the middle and Nürnberg and Augsburg in the south. Even most of the larger states that are left had to relinquish pieces of their ancestral territory in exchange for others, depending on whom Napoleon felt he had to bribe or coerce. And, therefor, they are governing whole groups of disparate people who never lived together before, whose sense of Fatherland belongs elsewhere, thus weakening all those states. Hence the tight French control."

"I see," said Chris slowly. "So what you're saying is that all of Germany except Austria and Prussia is now under Napoleon's control."

"Exactly. And I predict they, too, will soon fall to him. His army is too strong and they both have been weakened by all these wars. And Germany is merely a stepping stone to further conquests. The man wants to conquer the whole world."

"But where else? He's already got Italy."

"Poland. Mayhap even Russia. And now with a new supply of troops from the German states, there'll be no stopping him."

"Heaven forbid," exclaimed Dorothea.

"And not surprisingly, all those so-called sovereign states in the south are actually welcoming the French — uh — interference, or whatever you want to call it, because they have long yearned to throw off the yoke of the Empire and at the same time it relieves them from the spectre of Prussian military might."

"But not Hannover," said Chris.

"No, not Hannover," explained Philipp. "Napoleon cannot afford to let Hannover be even a quasi-independent state and not only because of our connection to England, although that is a strong motivation for him given that the English fleet has frustrated his every effort to invade England. So he has turned to England's 'Achilles heel'. You may not like to hear that but even the English call us that especially after they left us defenseless by pulling most of our army over there to defend their damn island."

"That bastard Cumberland."

"I knew him at Göttingen and I agree. But no, the most important strategic reason why Napoleon must hold Hannover is our coastline. Do you realize that we have the only *real* coastline in Germany. Prussia's doesn't count. The Baltic is almost landlocked. Our great ports of Bremen and Hamburg are Germany's window to the world. And Napoleon cannot allow that."

"Ach, Gott," sighed Dorothea, "then we are truly a pawn of France."

"A slave, more like," said Chris.

"Indeed," agreed Philipp.

1804 For a while the tenor of life under the French occupation continued much as it had before. The French garrison at Castle Hoya was small, its primary duty to guard the strategic bridge across the Weser. Hence there was no need to quarter troops on reluctant peasants although a few pastures for their horses were appropriated. Their officers and even a number of non-commissioned officers moved into the former royal hunting lodge at Bruchhausen, newly rebuilt—again—in 1775. Individual soldiers occasionally came into Vilsen for personal needs but rarely mingled with the populace. With few exceptions they were always polite and courteous.

The war tax created the only real hardship but at first even that was not prohibitive as the nobles were no longer exempt and had to pay their fair share. However, Hannover, being primarily an agricultural country and having long ago freed her serfs, actually had very few landed nobility so that this was not the boon for the middle classes as it was in many other German states. The problem of the taxes was compounded by economic stress due to the lack of goods from England, particularly wool and small machinery, and the lack of a market for their own fine linen. Suddenly the rough, coarse wool of the beloved, but long neglected, Heidenschnucken became a valuable commodity. Food was still plentiful and everyone prayed that the country would be spared bad weather and poor harvests.

Once the people became convinced that this was not a rape and pillage conquest such as they had suffered from the last French occupation over forty years earlier, those who had a smattering of French began brushing up on the language, Eleonore and her father among them. Anton Matthies was able to reinstate his contract to deliver flour and grain to the barracks at Hoya and the castle at Bruchhausen. And Eleonore occasionally entertained some of the French officers with elaborate dinners at the Hohnholz home. Some of her neighbors were shocked and shunned her socially for consorting with the enemy. Others were envious and tried to emulate her but she had the advantage of the language and her French heritage.

156

"I don't care what they think," she declared to Dorothea one late spring day as they sat about the kitchen table at the Klostermühle. "We have to live with them. Why shouldn't we take advantage of it? Several of them are so intellectually stimulating. They've read Master Rousseau and Voltaire and even this new exciting female author Mme. de Staël, who I understand is a friend of Goethe and Schiller. I've needed that kind of conversation, Dorchen. I've been bored with Teddi for a long time but I didn't realize how very boring he could be until I met these gentlemen."

"Elli," exclaimed Dorothea, shocked, "that's your husband you're talking about."

"I know but you can't imagine how tedious he can be. His entire conversation revolves around the business—how bad thing are. You know it has never fully recovered since the fire and his father's death. But that is the fault of his own incompetence long before the French embargo." She paused and shook her head. "And at night—oh, Dorchen—even his lovemaking has become boring. And, of course, I'm breeding again."

"Oh, I didn't know. I haven't seen you, at least for a good visit, in so long."

"I know and I apologize but after losing the last babe I seemed to mourn longer than usual. I just moped about and with the weather so bad I hardly left the house all winter and I refused to let Teddi near me for so long. But once I started inviting the French gentlemen—oh, Dorchen, you have no idea how that has brightened my life—I figured I'd best let him back in my bed so he wouldn't become jealous."

"Indeed," agreed Dorothea, "that's the last thing you need is for Teddi to be jealous. He is so insecure, so unsure of himself anyway, although he still puts on his arrogant front. Not like my dear Chris, for which I thank God every day."

"You are so lucky, my dearest friend. When is your next one due?"

"August. And yours?"

"Not till December so I can be with you again." Eleonore was silent for a moment, obviously pondering something. "I fret so over how long I mourned this last one. Dorchen, you don't think I'm going to end up like my mother, do you?"

"Certainly not. You are too spritely and full of life. How fares your mother these days?"

"Not good. Some days she just sits in the corner at her loom and does nothing. The worst times are when she doesn't even know what day or even what time it is. Then again she'll bustle around as though she were twenty years old. Now that they are older Papa tries to be kinder to her but I fear me it is too late. Why didn't he do that when they were young? But no, he was so cruel to her, to all of us." Eleonore stifled a sob and fought for control. "No, Dorchen, I don't hate him like I used to but I can't say I love him. Pity is more what I feel. He put everything he had into being a successful miller and lost his family, one way or another, in the process. First Fritzi, who was the best, and then poor simple-minded little Carsten. Adi seldom comes all the way from Westen to see them although she does visit me once in a while. Even little Becke, now wed and living in Bensen, chooses to stay away. Only Heinzi is left and he is just like Papa was and is too stupid to realize it—cruel, selfish, arrogant without half Papa's brains. His wife is expecting another in December, too. Gerhardina. Did you ever hear such a foolish name? Her father must have wanted a boy. She creeps around like a timid little mouse afraid to open her mouth. I fear me if Heinzi doesn't mend his ways she will end up just like Mama. Only one thing is she firm about—Gerhardina. You must call her that. She will not tolerate any nicknames."

Dorothea laughed.

Heinrich Anton and Katinka were playing outside the mill. The spring had been cold and damp and it was the first Saturday afternoon that they could really enjoy the nice weather but their mothers had forbidden them to go wandering off in the woods as Eleonore would not be staying too long.

"That means we can't play Hansel and Gretel today," sighed Katinka.

"I know. I wish we could visit the old wisewoman though," replied Heinrich Anton. "We haven't seen her since last summer. I wonder if she is still alive."

"I expect she is or we would have heard. Do you think she still talks to the ravens? That was scary when they told her the French were coming."

"And they really came." He shook his head as if to expunge that idea. "I know. Let's play the princess who had to empty the lake with a sieve."

"Oh, that's a silly game because you never could do it even though the millpond is much smaller than a lake. Besides, if we ever fell in our Mamas would kill us."

"I s'pose."

"I have a better idea. Let's look in the brook for pretty pebbles and pretend they're jewels."

Heinrich Anton agreed very reluctantly after making a token objection. "But only ladies wear jewels."

Katinka had an answer for everything. "Some men do, too. My Papa has a ring with a pretty stone in it that he got from his papa."

Thus it was that the children were kneeling by the brook across from the mill when the stranger rode up. He was a young man, very thin but rather nice looking in a stern sort of way. His horse, however, was old and weary and had certainly seen better days.

Both children jumped up and Heinrich Anton, putting on his best company manners, asked, "May we help you, sir? Are you lost?"

"I don't think so," replied the stranger pleasantly. "Is this the Klostermühle of Heiligenberg? I am seeking Mistress Dorothea Bergmann."

"Ja, this is the Klostermühle and she is my Mama," said Heinrich Anton.

"Then I should like to meet her," said the man. "I understand she knows a lot of the old folk stories."

"If you mean fairy tales, that she does. Lots of them."

"My Mama knows lots of them, too," put in Katinka, "and she is here now so you can meet them both."

"Then you are not brother and sister?" asked the man.

"No, just best friends. But we are going to be married when we grow up."

"Katinka!" exclaimed Heinrich Anton, blushing to the roots of his blond hair.

Katinka ignored him. "You're not from around here, are you, sir? Where are you from?"

"I come from the University of Marburg in Hesse," replied the man smiling.

Neither child had heard of Marburg but they knew Hesse was another country. "Oh, that's a long ways away," said Katinka.

Heinrich Anton decided Katinka had dominated the conversation long enough. Besides, it was not polite to leave the nice man sitting here when he had come to visit his mother—*his* mother, not Katinka's. "Please wait here, sir, while I fetch my mother."

"Thank you, young man," said the stranger as he dismounted, "and may I water my horse in your brook whilst I wait?"

"Certainly. I'm sorry. I wasn't thinking. Katinka, see to it," ordered Heinrich Anton.

Katinka was about to stamp her foot and object. She did not want to be left out. But then she thought better of it. She took the weary horse's bridle and led him to the brook as Heinrich Anton rushed into the house. The man stood in the middle of the lane smiling.

"Mama, Mama," called Heinrich Anton, as he burst into the kitchen. "There's a man here wants to see you. Wants to hear you tell the old fairy tales."

Dorothea looked up perplexed. "What in the world are you talking about? Is he a crazy man?"

"No, Mama. He is a very nice man. Oh, do come, Mama. He's come all the way from Hesse just to see you."

"Indeed? Then I'd best go and see what this is all about. Are you sure he doesn't want to see Papa?"

"Nay, nay. He said *Mistress* Bergmann."

"And where is Katinka?" asked Eleonore.

"She's watering his horse."

Dorothea rolled up her eyes. "Then you'd best come along, too, Elli." She followed her son outside.

The young man swept off his hat and made a courtly bow. "Am I addressing Mistress Dorothea Bergmann?" he asked.

"I am she," replied Dorothea, "and this is my dear friend Mistress Hohnholz."

"Ah, then I have come to the right place. I am Wilhelm Grimm from the University of Marburg. My brother Jacob and I have a great interest in collecting the ancient folk tales of this part of Germany and I am told that you know a great number of them—a veritable treasure trove, I've heard."

Dorothea laughed. "A treasure trove I think not but I do know some. It's too bad my grandfather Cyriacus Lindemann is not still alive. He could have told you dozens."

"I'll listen to as many as you can tell me."

"My Mama knows a lot of them, too," put in Katinka leading the horse back from the brook.

"Catharine Sophie! Mind your manners," scolded Eleonore sharply.

"I'm sorry, Mama," apologized Katinka, not at all abashed, "but what shall I do with the horse? I want to hear the stories, too."

"Put him over in yon pasture," instructed Dorothea. She decided the young man was personable enough and not at all threatening. Chris would not mind if she invited him in for a little while. "Won't you come in and rest a bit, Master Grimm? We were just having our afternoon coffee and would like to hear more of your endeavor."

"Thank you, Mistress. Coffee would be most welcome," he replied as he followed Dorothea and Eleonore back into the house, the children trailing eagerly behind.

When they were all seated around the kitchen table, Dorothea said, "Now tell us a little about yourself and your—er—quest, Master Grimm. Why do you want to hear the old stories? Are you then professors at Marburg? History, mayhap?"

"Nay, nay. First of all, I am no master as yet. My brother and I are no but humble law students at Marburg."

"Ach, my brother Philipp is a lawyer and lectures betimes at Göttingen. But the study of law seems a far cry from collecting fairy tales."

Grimm smiled. "It would seem so, ja. But we were very fortunate to make the acquaintance of Meinherr Friedrich Carl von Savigny. You may have heard of his extensive library of medieval manuscripts. It is very famous." The women shook their heads. "Actually it was my brother Jacob who first impressed the professor with his brilliant scholarship. Jacob was invited to view his collection. I soon followed. Let me tell you, Mesdames, it was not long before we both—how shall I say it—became addicted to the ancient stories. Even though we both continue to pursue our law degrees, Jacob has become deeply intersted in studying the ancient German languages. He even plans on writing a dictionary some day. He is the scholar. I do most of the collecting because I get along well with the old women—begging your pardons, Mesdames, but it is the old women who usually remember the most tales, particularly those of the *Spinnstube*."

His enthusiasm was contagious. Dorothea nodded. "So now you would like to hear ours."

"Indeed, I would, Mistress, if you don't mind. My brother and I feel it is most urgent, especially now with the French occupation of our two countries, to preserve the old German culture and heritage before it becomes totally lost—suffocated under a blanket of—of Frenchifying."

"An admirable goal," commented Dorothea. "My husband would agree with you wholeheartedly."

Eleonore said nothing. She suddenly realized with a twinge of shame how her own social behavior was contributing to that 'Frenchifying'.

"We know Hansel and Gretel," chirped Heinrich Anton. "Katinka and I play it all the time."

"Ach," said Wilhelm Grimm, "that is a tale that is common all over Germany—all over Europe, for that matter. Sadly it was not unusual in the Middle Ages to send unwanted, excess children out into the forests in the hope they would never return."

161

Heinrich Anton was shocked. "Mama would never do that to us, would you, Mama?"

"Certainly not," exclaimed Dorothea. "Be assured that you are well loved."

Katinka said nothing but pondered this. She had never been sure if she had been wanted or not. But her natural mischievousness quickly put that thought aside. "Master Grimm mentioned the Spinnstube stories. Tell him ours. It was Mama's favorite."

Eleonore laughed. "It used to be until Carsten made me mess up all the thread when I was just learning to spin and Adi scolded me. After that I hated it. You tell it, Dorchen. I learned it from you."

"There are many, many Spinnstube stories," said Wilhelm. "I would hear yours."

And so Dorothea told him the tale of Rumpelstiltskin, the strange little man who helped the poor maiden spin a roomful of straw into gold so that she could marry the king's son.

"No, I have not yet heard that one," said Wilhelm. He quickly opened a box he had brought with him and extracted his journal, pen and inkpot. "Let me write it down." And promptly did so.

"My favorite was always 'The Twelve Dancing Princesses'," said Eleonore. "Are you familiar with that one? I always longed to go dancing like they did. Still do." She sighed wistfully.

"Can't say as I have. Tell me."

And so the afternoon sped by. All were thoroughly enjoying themselves.

Heinrich Anton spoke up. "Mama, tomorrow Master Grimm should go and see the old wisewoman. She knows even more stories than Mama does, Master Grimm. She even talks to Wotan's ravens."

"Does she indeed? Then I should like very much to meet her. Is she a real wisewoman and not a charlatan?"

"Very real and very ancient," replied Dorothea. "She knows more about healing than many doctors. But she may be reluctant to talk to you. She is very reclusive."

"I have spoken to many such," said Grimm. "Some fear the authorities, who often associate the old tales with witchcraft, will punish them but they usually open up to me once they understand that we, too, wish to preserve the old ways."

"She has a goat named Donar," offered Katinka.

Wilhelm laughed. "Then she is surely one of the old ones. I

162

should like to meet her."

"Then tomorrow the children can take you to her. But don't expect too much," warned Dorothea.

"Tomorrow," exclaimed Eleonore suddenly, looking at the clock. "I had no idea it was so late. It has been fun speaking with you, Master Grimm, but if I don't get home in time for supper my husband will be quite upset."

"I was wondering when someone was going to think of supper," said Chris from the doorway. "I've been standing here well over ten minutes and you people were so engrossed you never saw me. I felt as though I was back in the nursery again. May I meet our guest?"

Dorothea apologized, made the introductions and explained what the Grimm brothers were attempting to do.

"That sounds like a worthy endeavor," said Chris. "I am all in favor of anything that will preserve our heritage and our culture—our—our German-ness. 'Twas a sad day indeed when Napoleon simply walked in and took over—with no help from our British king, I might add. I abhor the fact that he wants us all to be part of France." He looked pointedly at Eleonore, who said nothing.

"Now, Chris, no talk of politics this evening," asserted Dorothea. "We have passed quite the most pleasant, cultural afternoon with Master Grimm and I would ask your permission to invite him to spend the night with us. He has been travelling all over Hesse and Hannover in his quest and would like to visit Mother Holle in the morning."

"Of course, he may stay," replied Chris. "I'd like to hear some of the old stories myself after supper. I don't suppose you have any about millers?"

"Oh yes, quite a few but usually the millers are the villains of the piece."

Chris laughed. "Then here you will find just the opposite. I am neither wealthy nor dishonest and I don't think I'm cruel, am I, Heinrich Anton?" He tousselled the boy's hair.

"No, you're the best papa in the world," said the boy, "not like old Master Matthies."

"Heinrich Anton!" exclaimed his mother, "you mustn't say such things. Master Matthies is your godfather and Katinka's grandfather."

Wilhelm Grimm could feel the tension building and thought, here is a living story, but said nothing.

Then Eleonore quickly diffused it by saying, "It's true, Master

Grimm, my father often was the typical miller of the stories although he has softened some in his old age. He was never dishonest to my knowledge, but cruel—yes. The lad speaks true. Well, I must take my leave. Master Grimm, it has been my pleasure. Katinka, would you like to stay the night here, if Tante Dorchen will have you, so that you can visit the wisewoman in the morning?" Eleonore knew her daughter well, knew that she often felt more at home in the Klostermühle than at the Hohnholz mansion.

"Oh, yes, Mama, I'd like that," replied the child.

The next morning Wilhelm Grimm was dismayed to learn they would have to walk for a half hour through the woods. Horses could not manage the narrow pathways. Always of frail health, ever since his years at the Lyzeum he had been prone to severe asthma attacks. He prayed the long walk would not bring one on but his curiosity about the old woman overcame his fear.

When they arrived at the tiny cottage, once again Baldur rushed out to greet the children, the old crone not far behind.

"Ach, Heinrich Anton and Katinka. Well come, childers. Ain't seen you in a snail's age. And who might this be with you?"

"This is Master Grimm come all the way from Hesse." explained Heinrich Anton. "He and his brother are collecting the old stories and want to hear some of yours."

The woman looked puzzled for a moment. Then she said, "Ach, I can tell lots of those but are you sure you're wantin' to hear them? Tales of Wotan, Frigga and Donar, of Baldur and Loki? Pastors don't like it one bit when I tell 'em but those old gods are still about in our woods and rivers and . . ."

"Er—that's not exactly what I had in mind," interrupted Wilhelm.

"Ach, then you mean the hero stories like Wittekind and Bruno and the thousand-year rose bush at Hildesheim," she said.

"Not really," he demurred. "Those are history. What my brother and I are seeking are the old folk tales for the children."

"Ach, you mean fairy tales. Don't know none of them." And she clammed up and would offer no more.

The children were perplexed. They knew she was lying. They had heard some of her fairy tales as well as the stories of the old gods and goddesses. Wilhelm tried diplomatically to coax her into talking but she refused. He realized too late that he had insulted her by not listening to her first offerings. Disappointed, he said, "Then I bid you farewell, Mistress—er—I'm sorry I don't know your name . . . "

"I don't have no name," she said. "Ach, there's them as call me Mother Holle but I can't shake no gold nor ashes from the sky." She cackled. "Can shake me featherbed right well though, which I'd best be about." She called to Baldur, reentered her house and shut the door.

Then Wilhelm, too, knew she had been lying.

On the way back Heinrich Anton said, "You should have let her tell you about the old gods and goddesses. She usually never mentions them in front of strangers."

Katinka, even more astute, added, "That's true. When you refused to hear about them, she thought you were a spy. The pastor and the doctor are quite jealous and would like to shut her up. But she does so much good for so many people, they don't dare."

And Wilhelm sadly admitted that he had handled this one all wrong.

As Wilhelm Grimm was riding down the lane from the Klostermühle, having refused an invitation to dinner, another rider came dashing up the lane.

"Dorchen! Chris!" called out Anton Matthies, "wait until you hear my news." He entered the house without knocking. The family was just sitting down to dinner.

"Ach, Master Matthies," said Dorchen, hoping she sounded welcoming, "would you care to join us? Or is it something urgent that you must discuss with Chris?"

"It is urgent but it will take a while in the telling, so I thank you for the invite. Becke's having one of her bad days so I doubt there's even any dinner on the stove." Anton sat down at the table. "Who was that fellow I passed on the road? Never saw him before." Anton seldom missed anything.

"He is Master Grimm from the University at Marburg," explained Dorothea. "He and his brother are collecting the old folklore in order to preserve our German culture for future generations."

"An interesting fellow and an admirable endeavor," added Chris. "One that is sorely needed in view of—of what has happened."

"Ach, German culture. What German culture?" asked Anton derogatorily. "Chris, you are way behind the times. We are governed by France now and soon there will be no such thing as German culture."

"That's what we're afraid of," murmured Dorothea.

"Ach, then listen to the latest news." The old man was more

165

excited—happily excited—than she had ever seen him. "Have you heard of the new *code civil* that the Emperor has promulgated?"

"Emperor!" exclaimed Dorothea. "I thought he was calling himself First Consul."

"He's even now had himself proclaimed Emperor. There was an elaborate coronation in Notre Dame Cathedral in Paris and 'tis said he took the crown from old Pope Pius and placed it on his own head. Don't you read the newspapers?"

"Chris reads them. I rarely have time," she replied. "In fact, I get tired of reading how wonderful he thinks he is."

"I read it and I was disgusted by his brazenness," said Chris. "And I'm not the only one. I read when the great composer in Vienna, Beethoven, who once admired him and had dedicated his third symphony to him, heard that, he changed the name of the piece to 'Eroica'."

Anton shrugged. "Call it arrogance if you will. I think it was a damned audacious thing to do. I admire the man's verve."

"But why are you so happy about that?" asked Dorothea.

"Not about that," replied Anton. "I don't really care what he calls himself. I'm excited about this new *code civil*. It's a new body of laws going back to the old Roman law codes. Not that I agree with everything in it, mind you, but there's an awful lot of good. It says that everyone is equal. No more nobility and no more peasants." Dorothea and Chris looked at each other. This coming from Anton Matthies was quite out of character. "The old ecclesiastical territories are totally gone, absorbed by the states nearest them. But best of all, the government will no longer own properties such as these mills. They will become private property owned—actually owned—by the folk who work them."

"Aha," said Chris. "So that is why you are so happy today."

"Indeed, I am. I don't yet know what is all involved in making the claim. I'm sure there will be a lot of papers to fill out. I may even have to go to Hannover. But I've leased these two mills for almost twenty years. I'm sure I'll have no trouble proving my claim. And then it will be mine—all mine. Isn't that wonderful? I wanted you to be the first to know. After all, you're like children to me."

"And what about the Klostermühle here?" asked Dorothea. "Can Chris make a claim as well?"

"Nay, nay," said Anton as if the thought had never occurred to him. "I hold the lease on both mills, therefore I shall own both mills. Don't worry. Nothing will change. You'll still pay me my rent as always.

Everything will go on as before."

Dorothea watched Chris' face fall. "I see," he said.

Anton did not even notice. "Just as soon as those deeds are in my hands, I'll have a big party. Remember the party we had all those years ago, Dorchen, when I fianlly was awarded the hereditary rights?" She merely nodded. "Well, this will be even more elaborate. I'm even thinking of having some boundary stones carved that will proclaim to all the world that this property belongs to Heinrich Anton Matthies—no other. Aren't you happy for me?"

"Indeed we are," replied Dorothea without much real enthusiasm.

"We surely wish you well, Master Matthies," added Chris. "Be sure to let us know how it goes."

After Anton left Dorothea asked Chris, "Do you really think it will go on as before? He is so puffed up with pride right now anything could happen. Boundary stones, indeed."

Chris laughed. "I think we can trust him—for a while at least. All of this will take some time. And, hard master though he is, he has always been fair. It's when he passes on and Heinzi inherits that I would fear. I trust Heinzi not at all."

"Nor do I," agreed Dorothea.

It seemed as though Anton Matthies and his daughter Eleonore were the only inhabitants of Vilsen who were content with the French occupation of Hannover, although Eleonore, truthfully, cared not a fig for the politics. She only enjoyed it because it brought a little excitement into her increasingly dull life with Teddi. Not so her father. Anton was enthusiastic about the new Code Civil and took every opportunity to brag about his bit of French blood. Many people had never liked him and now they detested him. Even those who had tolerated him now considered him a traitor. But the farmers roundabout still had to have their grain milled; the townfolk still had to buy flour. Anton had the local monopoly. So they shrugged off his arrogance, which they were used to anyway, and continued to do business with him. But they did not have to be friends.

In 1805 Anton finally received his deeds to both properties—Bruch-mühlen and the Klostermühle at Heiligenberg, including the mill pond and all the water rights. He immediately commissioned his boundary stones from a local stone carver. There were to be two—one depicting himself and Becke, the other depicting Heinzi and his wife Gerhardina. The man assured him that the likenesses would be quite true to life.

When Eleonore saw the work in progress, she shook her head. Her father was so proud of the stones she hesitated to criticize but she could not help herself. "Papa, why didn't you go to Hannover or somewhere and hire a real sculptor? These are so primitive looking they resemble gravestones."

Anton was not insulted at all. "I wanted a local man so I could keep an eye on him. He's making them exactly as I wanted them. And he does not charge Hannover prices. Besides they will be standing out by the roadside. If they were too fancy someone might steal them. They're not finished yet. Just wait. You'll like them."

Eleonore felt like saying, who would want them? But she could not resist commenting, "Cheap. Cheap. That's all you've ever been." Her words did not faze Anton at all.

On a raw, blustery November day threatening snow Katinka was taking her two younger siblings for a walk. Little Lise, eight, and Hans, five, were bundled head to toe against the cold, as was she, in heavy woollen clothes, mittens, scarfs and fur-lined bonnets. It was really no day for a pleasant walk but she simply had to get out of the drear house. Her step-grandmother Catharine lay very ill—Mama thought she was dying. And if that weren't enough Mama's newest baby was down with a severe croup. Papa, grumpy as usual when anyone was ill, had disappeared into his workshop.

Katinka held Hans tightly by the hand as Lise skipped alongside. They left Vilsen and turned onto the road to nearby Bruchhausen. They strolled under the once beautiful apple trees now shorn of their magnificence by the bitter wind. Katinka loved the apple trees in the spring when they put forth their delicate pink and white and so fragrant blossoms. She enjoyed their welcome shade in the summer and especially in the early fall when the rosy, luscious fruit hung heavy on the branches and everyone was allowed to pick all they wanted. Every road leading into Vilsen was lined with apple trees and they were famous throughout the countryside. Now only a few shrivelled brown die-hards hung from the bare branches.

"May we go to see the castle at Bruchhausen?" chirped Lise enthusiastically.

"We'll see," replied Katinka. "Only if Hansi doesn't get too tired and start crying. It's quite a ways, you know."

"I won't cry," insisted Hans, his chubby little legs plodding sturdily along. "I want to see the castle."

"Very well, if you promise," agreed Katinka. "But we can't go too near it. The French soldiers are there now."

"But we can see it from the road," said Lise. "Besides, Mama likes the French soldiers."

Katinka made no comment on that. They entered Langestrasse, the only real street in Bruchhausen. Bruchhausen was quite quite different in character from Vilsen. Vilsen was a much older, very charming, compact little village surrounding its lovely church. Bruchhausen was of the type known as a Strassendorf, all the houses strung out along one main street, the street in this case being the one that led to the so-called castle. Once the seat of the Counts of Hoya, later a royal hunting lodge for the Dukes of Braunschweig-Lüneburg, the buildings had been destroyed so many times in so many wars people had lost count. The present structure had been built in 1775 but still contained many stones from the earlier edifices, even from the ancient monastery at Heiligenberg. It was nothing more than a modest manor house but everyone still insisted on calling it 'the castle', more for nostalgia's sake than anything else.

As they drew near the castle Katinka heard the most unearthly noise approaching from the opposite direction. Soon the source of the noise became apparent as a large troop of the strangest, fiercest-looking riders thundered down the road towards the children. Katinka stopped in her tracks and tightly grasped the hands of the two little ones. The men were exceptionally tall, dark visaged, each sporting a thick, black, drooping mustache. Their horses, however, were shaggy and quite short-legged. The men wore baggy woollen trousers and heavy boots, colorful shirts beneath thick sheepskin waistcoats. In fact, some of them were bare-armed despite the cold weather. They were brandishing their guns in the air, all the while yelling their fierce battle cry at the top of their lungs. Katinka was momentarily petrified. Then Hans, thoroughly frightened, started to cry, which brought her to her senses. Quickly she turned around and started to shepherd the children back the way they had come.

Within seconds the first rider rode up to them, leaned down, caught her around the waist and swooped her up onto his horse. She screamed for all she was worth, although who would help her she knew not. Horrible thoughts raced through her head. But after riding but a few blocks he slowed the horse and gently set her down saying, "Fear not, little one, we are come to save your country from the French. But it is not safe here. There will be a small battle. So run, run home." Katinka could not under-

169

stand a word of what he was saying. It was a strange, gutteral language. But she understood well enough his gesture as he waved her away with both hands. A second rider deposited a screaming Lise next to her, while little Hans, forgetting his tears, was yelling, "Take me. Take me. I want a ride, too." A third horseman complied and soon set the laughing little boy down next to his sisters.

"Oo, that was fun," exclaimed Hans.

"Shut up," snapped Lise. "What are you laughing about? That was frightening. What did the man say to you, Katinka?"

"I don't rightly know," she replied. "It was a strange tongue I could not understand but he made it quite clear from his gestures that we should hurry away from here." She took the children by their hands and started to run down the street towards Vilsen. She glanced back once as it suddenly became very quiet behind them. The strange men had stopped yelling, no longer brandishing their guns in the air but holding them at a fighting angle. They rode swiftly up the avenue leading to the castle. Moments later they heard shots fired and shots returned and the yelling started again.

"I think these men just saved our lives, else we'd have been caught in the midst of a battle." She hurried the younger ones along as quickly as she could.

Before they got as far as Vilsen little Hans was lagging behind and stumbling. Katinka decided it was safe enough now, so she slowed her pace to a walk. She knew she could never carry Hans if the lad's little legs gave out. He had grown so much in the last few months. They arrived home breathless.

"Mama, Mama," Katinka called out. "We just met the strangest looking men I've ever seen . . . "

"There was a battle by the castle," interrupted Lise.

"And they gave us a ride on their horses," added Hans, delightedly.

"What?!" exclaimed Eleonore, coming down the stairs. "Hush now or you'll wake the baby. I finally got him to sleep."

"Mama," said Katinka lowering her voice, "they saved our lives."

"What!" said Eleonore again. "Then come into the kitchen where it's warm and keep your voices down so we don't disturb Grandma Catharine." When they had removed their heavy clothing and settled down to cups of hot chocolate, she said, "Now tell me all about it. Who were these strange men?"

"I know not," replied Katinka. "They spoke an outlandish language

I've never heard before. I mean, we speak German and you've taught us French and we've learned a little English and Latin in school, but it was not like any of those. But in all their fierceness, they were kind."

"They were like giants," said Lise, "but their horses were funny. They had short legs. It almost looked like the men were too big for the little horses. But Katinka's right. They were kind but we were still frightened."

"And they gave us a ride," added Hans again.

"Did they, indeed?" said Eleonore. "And how did that come about?"

Just then Teddi entered the kitchen. He had heard the last few exchanges. "So they've come then."

"Who has come?" asked his wife.

"Don't you read the paper, Elli?" he asked annoyed.

"You know I seldom have time for that," she snapped back. "Who are these strange men?"

"The Tsar has recently made an alliance with England and Prussia to drive Napoleon out of Germany. Soon we'll be rid of your beloved Frenchmen," he said sarcastically. Then he explained to the children, "Those men you met were Cossacks from far off Russia, the fiercest fighters in all of Christendom. In fact, I'm not even sure they are Christians. Their horses are called steppe ponies. Short-legged they may be, but 'tis said they are the fastest thing on four legs. And now Prussia will not be far behind."

"But I thought we didn't want Prussia either," said Eleonore.

"It will only be temproary until the French are defeated and driven back to France," he tried to assure her. "But come now. If there is to be fighting—and I'm sure it has already started—I want you and the children away from here. Quickly now. Pack a few warm clothes and get you off to Chris and Drochen at the Klostermühle. You should be safe there. Fritz can drive you in the carriage."

"What are you talking about?" demanded Eleonore. "I can't take the baby out in this weather. It would surely be the death of him. And what about Mama Catharine? She would never survive the trip either. No, I'm staying right here where I'm needed—here in my own home."

"Why are you always so stubborn, wife?" he growled.

"And why are you always so cowardly," she snapped back, "ready to run and hide in your workshop at the slightest provocation?"

He shrugged. "Do as you wish." He could never win an argument with Eleonore.

"I am sure there will be no fighting here in Vilsen," she said to

Teddi's retreating back. "The only French troops are at Hoya. If what the children heard is correct, the few French officers at Bruchhausen are already fled—or dead." Teddi had already left the room. Eleonore sighed to herself. That would be the end of her elegant soirées with the French officers. She was sure she would not care to invite any of the wild Cossacks—nor, heaven forfend, any of the Prussians, if they ever arrived.

The Prussians did finally arrive about three months later and occupied all of Hannover, while the Russians continued their sweep towards the Rhein driving the French before them. Meanwhile Napoleon was conquering all the territory south and east of Hannover, heading toward Vienna.

1806 was thus a momentous year: Prussia conquered long-coveted Hannover; Napoleon entered Vienna and forced the Emperor Josef to abdicate, thus effectively bringing the archaic Holy Roman Empire to an end; and Anton Matthies' boundary stones were finally completed and duly dated. He had them set up at Bruchmühlen on either side of the lane that led from there to the Klostermühle. He never did have his celebration. People were too uncertain as to what was going to happen next to be in a celebratory mood.

"You see, I told you Prussia would be the one to unite Germany," he said to Chris and Dorothea one day soon after.

"But Master Matthies," objected Dorothea, "I thought you liked the French."

"I said I liked their Code Civil. After all, it enables me to own all this," he spread his hands, "after I've worked like a dog for over twenty years to make it what it is. You must admit I deserved it. But I've always said Prussia is the one to unite Germany. Austria could not do it after a thousand years. She never cared about us."

"Nor does Prussia, I fear," argued Chris. "She is too militaristic for my taste. And too poor to hold it, methinks. Her serfs are still like slaves. I like not all Prussia stands for. And I fear me the French will be back. Napoleon cannot allow Prussia to stand if he means to conquer all of Europe and especially here in Hannover. He hates England too much."

Anton shrugged. "You may be right. But enough of this. Come walk down the lane with me and see my stones. I'm very proud of them."

Chris had better things to do than look at boundary stones but Dorothea urged him on in a subtle whisper, "Let him have his pleasure. He is getting so old. And don't laugh at them whatever you do."

Chris smiled. "You know me better than that. Very well, let's go."

At the junction of the main road Anton proudly displayed his boundary markers. The one on the right as they faced the road depicted him and Becke across the upper part with a tall crucifix rising between them. Anton was dressed in tricorn hat, breeches and an elegant frock coat, so long that it almost looked like one of the old medieval gowns. Becke wore a simple but stylish gown and a demure cap. It was a much, much thinner Becke than Dorothea had ever remembered seeing. The lower half consisted of a lengthy inscription declaring that this was the hereditary miller of Bruchmühlen and Heiligenberg together with their birth dates and so on. Around the top were all sorts of fancy curlicues and what appeared to be a coat-of-arms.

"What is that?" asked Dorothea. "I didn't know you had a coat-of-arms."

"Well, my family were nobility in France before they came to Celle," replied Anton, a bit flustered, "so I think I'm entitled to one. But since I don't know what it was, I chose this. The stone carver suggested it. It is a swan protecting her young. A nice touch, don't you think? It implies that now Heinzi's inheritance, and that of his descendants, is secure. Anyway," he added defiantly, "there are so many fake ones around nowadays, who's to know the difference?"

"I see," replied Dorothea. She crossed the lane to the other stone. In the same pattern as his father's, it depicted Heinzi wearing the slim trousers that were coming into vogue and the new style top hat. Gerhardina's gown had a much fuller skirt and lower neckline than Becke's. The inscription below declared that here was the favored son and heir to all this. The decorations around the top were similar and both stones bore the date of 1806. "Does Heinzi's have a coat-of-arms, too, or what is that?" she asked.

"Nay. That is just decoration." Anton replied. "I didn't want to overdo it."

They all laughed at that. And Chris and Dorothea diplomatically complimented Anton on the stones as if they had never seen anything more beautiful. The old man beamed.

As they walked back home, Chris said, "Well, that's that. It has decided me on something I've been considering for a long time."

"What do you mean 'that's that'? What have you been considering?" asked Dorothea, puzzled.

"Dorchen, my love, Anton does not have many years left to him and I trust Heinzi not at all."

"So you have said. Nor do I. But what are you considering? Chris, you're not thinking of leaving here, are you?"

"Nay, nay—at least not yet. But Dorchen, we must secure our own future—for our old age and for our own children."

Dorothea was thoughtful for a moment. "Ja, I can see the sense in that. What do you have in mind?"

"We need a home of our own."

"I agree and I can see you've already given it some thought."

"Quite a lot of thought. You know the widow Hirschfeldt's house?"

"Ja. Where Johann Heinrich works in the spice shop."

"The very same. The big house at the edge of the churchyard."

"Why, that is one of the biggest, most beautiful houses in Vilsen," she exclaimed. "Don't tell me you have that in mind."

Chris nodded. "The widow, as you know, died some years ago and her only daughter Sophie inherited. But now Sophie has married the Bürgermeister Tiensch and, naturally, is living with him. She has been renting the two upper floors aside from Johann Heinrich's rooms but now apparently she doesn't want the bother, so she is anxious to sell. I was lucky Johann Heinrich told me about it ere the word gets around town."

"But Chris, can we afford such a large house? What is she asking?"

"She is asking 400 Reichsthalers but I am sure I can get her to come down some, perhaps quite a bit."

"That's still a lot of money. Where would we get it?"

"My dearest Dorchen, you have that great coffer of yours stuffed with your inheritance from both your parents plus what we've added to it ourselves. How much have we used of it? For the boys' aprenticeships. That's all so far. Even if we set aside generous sums for the girls' dowries there will still be more than enough."

"But we are still having children, Chris. What of them?"

"I know and I thank you for them, sweeting. They'll not lack for anything, if, God willing, they live long enough to need it. I promise you that."

"That was to have been for our old age as well," she objected lamely.

"And what do you think this house will be? It's the first step towards a secure old age. You may even want to move in before we get that old. The kitchen has one of those new, modern iron cookstoves. No more cooking over the open hearth."

"Really? I should like to see that. But," and she laughed, "I'm afraid I should have to learn to cook all over again. Is it very complicated?"

174

"Much easier from what I'm told. Why don't you ask Elli? The Hohnholz have one."

"But Elli has a cook to do for her. I doubt she ever goes near it."

He laughed. "If you'll agree to spending the money, I really want to pursue this before the French come back and take it all away from us."

"Oh, Chris," she asked shocked, "do you really think that will happen?"

"That the French will come back? Yes, I do. That they'll steal our money, I pray not but it's entirely possible."

"Oh, no. Then let us hurry home and count it out right away. And first thing tomorrow, go and talk to Sophie Tiensch. But do haggle with her a bit. That's still a lot of money even though it is a beautiful house."

Chris smiled and stopped in the middle of the lane and kissed her warmly.

A few weeks later Dorothea was weeding her vegetable garden when Chris rode up the lane after a morning's visit to Vilsen. She ran out to meet him. "Well?" she asked.

He dismounted and took a paper out of his coat pocket, waving it triumphantly. "She accepted our offer," he said. He hugged her and danced her around in the middle of the lane.

"Wonderful," she replied. "Tell me. Did you haggle?"

"Did I ever haggle. And wait till you hear what all we're getting besides the house."

She blinked. "If there's that much to tell, we'd better sit down over a cup of coffee and not stand out here."

"An excellent idea. Just let me stable the horse and I'll be right in." A few minutes later as Dorothea was setting out the coffee cups, he strode into the kitchen, still waving the paper. "Tiensch wanted her to wait for other offers before she accepted ours. But she was anxious to sell. Moreover I convinced her that if the French came back, as I'm sure they will, no one will be in the mood to do any buying."

"Oh, Chris, wasn't that a bit underhanded?"

"No, not at all, because I firmly believe it. Don't you realize that after the battle of Austerlitz Napoleon is going after Prussia? Prussia will be stretched too thin. She won't care a fig for Hannover when her own heartland is being attacked. Once she is forced to withdraw her troops from here, it will leave the door wide open for the French to walk right back in."

"Oh. Well, never mind all that. Tell me about the house."

"I was able to get her down to 330 Reichsthalers which is a fantastic price when you hear what all we're getting." He paused a moment but she signalled him to go on. "The spice shop and business, of course, which I shall turn over to Johann Heinrich now that he's one-and-twenty. Then two pieces of cropland outside the village—and they're in a very good location—a large garden plot along Gartenweg and liberal wood-cutting rights in the Vilsen Woods."

"My goodness," she exclaimed, "all of that? Then you really did haggle. I was so afraid you wouldn't."

He laughed. "Do you think you are the only one who can strike a bargain?"

"Nay," she demurred. "It's just that men often don't—er—care to. When can we move in?"

"Whoa!" said Chris. "It will be a few months yet before everything is finalized. When is your brother coming back from Göttingen?"

"I think Philipp is back already but I haven't heard from him lately. I'll go and check on him this Saturday market day. Do you foresee any legal problems?"

"No, not at all but it's always good to have a lawyer look at all the papers just to be sure everything is in order. I'll come with you this week and show you through the house."

She clapped her hands. "I can't wait to see that stove."

In October 1806 Prince Ferdinand of Braunschweig, the brilliant hero of so many wars, was commander-in-chief of the Prussian army. But Ferdinand was not the same men he had been forty years earlier. He was seventy-one years old and in poor health. He could still conduct a battle as brilliantly as ever, had he been given a fair chance. But what Ferdinand could not contend with was the indecisive bickering among the other Prussian generals—the so-called High Command. When the King of Prussia himself stupidly interfered with the decision-making, Ferdinand knew all was lost before the battle was even joined. Nevertheless, when his army met half the French army under Marshall Davout at Auerstädt, he fought bravely but was mortally wounded. The battle ended in a complete rout.

On the same day, 14 October, Napoleon himself led the other half of his army against a Prussian army under Prince Hohenlohe at nearby Jena. This, too, ended in disaster. As the disorganized Prussians fled towards Weimar the pursuing French cavalry cut down thousands more. One cowardly general after another surrendered as Napoleon swept across Prussia.

Only at Lübeck did General Blücher put up a valiant resistance but his small force was soon overwhelmed. The famous Prussian army was no more. Thousands of the survivors deserted.

On 27 October Napoleon entered Berlin. The remaining cabinet ministers all swore an oath of fealty to him. He offered Prussia peace but Friedrich Wilhelm III stubbornly refused and opted to continue the war on the side of Russia. The court fled to Memel, the eastern-most Prussian outpost. In November Napoleon proclaimed the Continental System which stated that no English goods whatsoever were to be imported any-where into Europe and no Englishman was to set foot on the Continent.

In October the few remaining Prussian troops in Hannover were hastily withdrawn and in mid-November, just as Chris and Anton had pre-dicted, the French troops returned in force. This time there was no easy camaraderie with the conquerors. Napoleon was determined to punish Hannover for association with England and for her defection to Prussia. Thus began the Leidenszeit—the time of suffering, the time of sadness.

Troops were quartered on the peasants, officers on the Bürgers. Horses were stabled in their barns and even in their very houses. Every horse, even to the lowliest nag, was taken from them and sent to the bat-tlefronts. The famous flax fields were plowed under and planted with wheat for the soldiers and oats for the horses. Not that that mattered so much since, with trade to England at a standstill, there was no market for the linen. But the harvests were poor because flax is a soil-depleting crop and the fields should have been left fallow or planted with nourishing clover for a year or more. But the French insisted on planting grain imme-diately and then took every bit of the meagre harvests. Coffee, tea and other luxuries were distant memories. People struggled to live on what they could raise in their own tiny gardens and the conquerors even com-mandeered some of that. The war tax rose to astronomical heights. All over Germany Napoleon used the conquered states as a steady source of recruits for his army. And he 'played with the land'—that is, he broke up some states and patched them together with pieces of others. Groups of people of widely differing customs, religion and even dialects were forced to live together and were separated from the familiar. In the confusion, loyalties withered and often died.

6

In 1808 Napoleon gave the County of Bruchhausen —
i.e., the entire northeastern half of the former County
Hoya — to General Dupas as a gift. Theoretically this
meant that all the revenues of the county belonged to
him. In practice the reality was quite different, not only
due to the desperate state of the economy but also
because General Dupas was no businessman, not even a very brilliant general. Soon those who knew some French were making a pun of his name.
Since *du pas* meant *of nothing*, people were soon using it, behind his back,
to indicate a person with great pretensions who knew or did nothing.

Eleonore decided to take advantage of this. Although she was aware
of the fact that the French attitude toward the local people was quite different, harsher and more authoritarian, than it had been during the first
occupation, she had had such success with her previous soirées, she was
quite sure it would work to her advantage this time as well. Of course,
there was the problem of increasing food shortages but her cook was a
genius. And she still had her exquisite, alluring gowns which she hoped
would take the general's mind off the food. And fortunately, she was not at
the moment pregnant.

"You are crazy," said Teddi. "People will hate you even more than
before."

"Let them," she replied. "And you don't have to come if you don't
care to. Stay in your workshop. Fritzi can be my host."

Teddi sulked. And Fritzi, now twenty and very handsome, still adored
his beloved Elli. He rose to the occasion admirably and helped her plan.

"It should be a buffet instead of a sit-down dinner," he suggested.
"That way they won't notice the food so much."

"An excellent idea," she agreed.

"In fact, why don't we make it a ball and serve the supper late. We still
have enough wine, don't we, to get them a little drunk so they won't notice
the food at all."

"Oh, Fritzi, you are so clever. And certainly musicians are easier to come by than food these days. I shall speak to Johann Justus immediately."

"And you must invite Dorchen and Chris. The Bergmanns have a much larger garden than we and should be willing to help with the food. Mayhap you can talk Chris into shooting a deer or at least a few rabbits."

Eleonore laughed. "I wouldn't think of leaving them out. In fact, I'll ask Dorchen to help us plan and leave it up to her to suggest to Chris about the meat."

Fritzi nodded. "And be sure to invite most of the leading Bürgers and their wives. You can't be the only female with a lot of French officers."

She giggled. "As much as I should like that. But, no, you are right. It must look very decorous. Besides I can only dance with one at a time."

"What about your parents? Your father is always bragging about his French blood."

"No," she exclaimed. "Absolutely not. He is sure to say something offensive and mayhap even start a quarrel. And poor mother. She is so bewildered these days she would never fit in. I don't think she has ever danced in her life."

Dorothea was more than willing to contribute to the festive occasion, although in her heart she secretly agreed with Teddi that Eleonore was playing with fire. But Eleonore could be quite convincing.

"If we have to live with them we might as well make friends with them rather than enemies," she said. And again, "This town needs a little cheering up. Everyone is going about so glum."

And Dorothea had to agree with that. She promised as many fresh fruits and vegetables as she could spare including luscious tomatoes. Now that they had two large gardens the Bergmann were one of the few families to have enough produce and Dorothea often donated the excess to those in need. She could do no less for her best friend. Although the deed to the new house in Vilsen had been finalized in 1807 they had decided to continue living at Heiligenberg for the time being for several reasons, not the least of which was mistrust of the French. Johann Heinrich, who lived behind the spice shop, took care of the new house and they continued to rent the two upper floors.

In addition to the produce, Dorothea baked dozens of her famous gooseberry tarts and cooked bowls of a ruby-red, delectable pudding made from raspberries and currants. She inveigled her son into donating a few precious spices from his shop. She hesitated to ask Chris outright to provide some meat as game was growing scarcer and scarcer and much of

179

their own livestock had already been commandeered by the French. But Chris took the hint and a few days before the great event he presented Eleonore's cook with a string of a half dozen rabbits, some fresh fish from the millpond and one scrawny rooster.

"We were going to throw him in our own stewpot for Sunday dinner," he explained, "so we shall eat here instead. But mind you, cook him long and well. It might be wise to chop it up into a salad rather than serve the pieces. That way nobody will break their teeth on him."

The cook took one look at the old chicken and nodded. "You're right, Master Miller. I'll do that. Ain't it a shame what these damn French have brought us to? Time was, this house could have any kind of meat their hearts desired. No more. I don't hold with what the Mistress is doing but, mind you, don't tell her I said that. The poor lass needs some joy. Her life has been so sad. I'll make the finest buffet supper I can with whatever comes to hand." The old woman chuckled. "Why, I'll even make some pâté de foie gras with this old bird's liver and the rabbits'. That should please them Frenchies."

Chris laughed. "I'm sure it will."

Johann Justus graciously declined the invitation as his father, old Hinrich, had passed away not two months before and he was very busy with his cabinetmaking business—when he could get the proper wood, that is. Moreover he had recently taken a wife, a distant Harries cousin of Becke Matthies. But he promised to send two of his young step-brothers, whom his father had trained on the fiddle and fife, as well as another lad from the village, all of whom still played of a Saturday at Der Lustige Strumpf.

Eleonore sent out a carefully worded invitation to Bruchhausen Castle asking General Dupas and as many of his officers as he cared to bring to an intimate soirée to welcome him to Vilsen and Bruchhausen. The general promptly sent an aide with his note of acceptance. He had been bored to death in this rural backwater. Any opportunity for a little entertainment was welcome, although he did not expect much.

Once assured of her guest of honor's attendance Eleonore sent out even more carefully worded invitations to the leading Bürgers and their wives. The occasion was to honor the new Graf of Bruchhausen. A few refused out of pure pique, out of hatred for anything French or out of jealousy of Eleonore. But most accepted with alacrity, some simply curious but many deeming it wise to be on the right side of the powers-that-be. It promised to be an interesting evening.

The Hohnholz house, large as it was by Vilsen standards, had nothing that could remotely be called a ballroom. But it had two large adjoining parlors which were thrown open, carpets rolled up and furniture pushed out of the way against the walls. The food and punch would be served in the dining room. The withdrawing room was reserved for those who wished to rest from the festivities but Eleonore had also set up two small tables for cards. She knew from past experience that the French loved to play cards although they were not quite the avid gamblers that the English were.

On the evening in question the German guests, always prompt, began arriving in all their finery long before dark. Eleonore smiled to herself. Finery, indeed. How dowdy and old-fashioned most of them looked although she knew they were decked out in their very best for the occasion. Many of the women still wore the full skirts and the men the long frock coats of a by-gone era. Wigs were passé. That was their one concession to modernity—and a grateful one at that. The women wore their hair in curls around their heads or bunched into an elaborate snood; the men for the most part had theirs cut short, some even sporting bangs in imitation of Napoleon himself. Eleonore had always been very fashion conscious. So what if the French were hated for many reasons. Paris dictated fashion and she had tried to keep up as best she could, although good material was increasingly difficult to obtain.

But last Christmas she had made herself an exquisite gown in the very latest style. It was a dark red velvet trimmed with just the narrowest bit of white lace across the low, square neckline and at the edges of the large puffed sleeves. The waistline was cinched high directly under her bosom and hung from there straight to the floor. Another new mode for which she was grateful was no corsets. The restricting, cumbersome things were no longer necessary under this new style. She wore long gloves up over her elbows and the barest minimum of jewelry. Although she had plenty, this was one thing she was not about to flaunt before the conquerors.

The day had been hot and the evening was still sultry. Eleonore knew the velvet gown was too warm for this weather but the wine-red color brought out her best features—her fair complexion contrasted by her jet-black hair. So she determined to stay cool no matter how she suffered. People were milling about, women gossiping, men sampling the punch bowl, everyone wondering where the guest of honor was. Eleonore could smell their sweat under the heavy layers of perfume. She was beginning to get nervous herself and hoped she did not smell as bad as some of her guests. Where were they? She knew it was the custom in both France and England for important guests to be fashionably late. But how late? She ordered the musicians to begin playing for the dancing and hoped everyone would not be too bedraggled ere the general arrived. Fritzi asked her to dance but she tactfully refused. At least she would look cool and alluring for her guests.

At last! A maid signalled to her that a carriage had just drawn up in front of the house. Eleonore longed to peep out the window to see what he looked like but that would be gauche. Instead she went out into the hall and stood at the foot of the stairs as if she were only now descending. The maid answered the door.

"C'est la maison—the house of the Hohnholz?" asked a deep male voice.

Eleonore thrilled at the sound. She had never seen General Dupas before and her heart plummeted when in walked a short, very corpulent, past middle-aged man still wearing an old-fashioned powdered wig. So much for any thoughts of seduction. But she maintained her aplomb and stepped forward, graciously extending her hand.

"Welcome to our home, General Dupas," she said in French. "I am Eleonore Hohnholz. We are so happy you could join us this evening. We are honored."

The general bowed as low as his fat belly permitted and kissed the back of her gloved hand. "And we are honored to be here, Madame. Most gracious of you. We find so little social life here to—uh—to entertain us, we are most grateful for the opportunity." His voice was squeaky, almost effeminate. Definitely not the rich one she had heard at the door. "Permit me to introduce my aides." He indicated the two young officers behind him. "Le Capitain Jean-Marie Lescaux et le Capitain Jean-Paul Merot."

The men bowed and Eleonore's heart jumped up a few pegs. Mayhap seduction was still a possibility. Jean-Paul was the handsomest man she had ever seen.

All three men wore skin-tight buff breeches and the newest cutaway coats, higher in the front than a waistcoat with long tails at the rear. Obviously the shoulders were padded. The general may have had need of such padding but on the other two it looked a bit much. Their necks were swathed in such lengthy stocks it seemed as though they would choke. On the general the new style coat looked almost gross with his fat belly protruding beneath it. On the other two the new style was quite becoming.

Jean-Marie was of average height and looks, seemingly quite pleasant

182

until one looked into his eyes. They had a sly, weaselly look about them and immediately Eleonore did not trust him. Jean-Paul was considerably taller with clear skin, good teeth, merry eyes and dark curly hair that matched her own.

"Enchanté," he murmured over her hand. His was the deep, resonant voice. Eleonore's heart fluttered.

Quickly she took the general's arm and led him into the first parlor. "Come, mon general," she said in French, "our guests are eagerly waiting to honor you."

"Ah, you speak French," he said. "That is good. I am afraid my German is not very fluent yet."

"You will learn fast now that you are living here," she replied.

"Ah, oui," he sighed, "but it is always more comfortable to speak in one's mother tongue, n'est-ce-pas? You speak French very well, Madame. You even look French. Are you French, Madame?"

"I have a great deal of French blood," she exaggerated. "I am very proud of it. My great-grandfather was a Huguenot who fled from Louis XIV."

"Ah, so. Very sad that. But we no longer have that problem in France. Our Emperor has decreed full religious tolerance. Ever since our great Revolution we are all free and equal and brothers."

"Perhaps you would care to dance, mon General," said Eleonore, hoping he would not. "This new dance, the waltz, that has come from Vienna, is quite—er—spritely." She had been about to say seductive but that was definitely not the right word for the general. "Our musicians do it quite well."

"I am afraid I am not familiar with it," he replied. "A sedate minuet would be more to my taste. I leave these new dances to you young folk. My aides have my permission to dance if they wish."

Eleonore was glad to hear that. She instructed the Bruns brothers to play a minuet and danced one round with the general. Even after such a stately exercise he was sweating and breathless. She introduced him to several of the leading Bürgers and led him to the punch bowl. "Some refreshment, Your Excellency?"

"Ah, that would be welcome," he replied as he wiped his brow with a dainty lace handkerchief. "A warm evening, is it not?" Then he spied the card tables. "Now that is what I would enjoy—a sharp game of cards."

Eleonore was thankful she had primed some of the older men for this possibility. She gathered them up and sat the general down. "Now, no cheating under my roof," she teased flirtatiously as she fluttered her fan.

"Never fear, Madame," said Dupas. "I am the soul of honor and I trust these gentlemen are as well. We'll enjoy just a friendly game or two."

Grateful to be rid of him, Eleonore returned to the parlor where the dancing was in full swing. Fritzi was approaching her but Jean-Paul was already at her side.

"Ah, Madame Eleonore, now that you have done your duty to our general, the rest of the evening shall be ours. And I assure you I can waltz very well."

He took her arm as Fritzi came up and said, "Elli, you have not danced one dance with me yet this evening."

"Dearest Fritzi, I shall. I shall," she assured him, "but I must see to our guests first."

Fritzi turned away with a sad look on his face. She hoped he was not sulking. But no, he was not at all like his brother Teddi. Besides she could dance with Fritzi anytime. She was not about to let Jean-Paul go just yet.

"Your husband, Madame?" he asked.

"Nay, nay," she replied. "My brother-in-law. My husband is indisposed this evening. He regrets he was not able to be here."

"I am sorry to hear that but I rejoice in my good fortune. I shall be your escort for the entire evening. Shall we dance?"

He took her hand and led her out onto the floor. She thrilled as he fitted his arm snugly around her waist. He waltzed beautifully. She had never danced this close to anyone, let alone a stranger, before. She blessed whoever had invented the waltz.

Jean-Paul evidently had similar thoughts. "A tres seductive dance, n'est-ce-pas?" he murmured into her hair.

She smiled at his curious mixture of French and German. "It is indeed," she agreed. "And I do speak French if that is easier for you. It *is* the language of romance, n'est-ce-pas?"

"Ah, so you know that. But no, I wish to practice my German and you shall be my teacher." He drew her closer to him as they whirled around the floor. She thrilled with excitement as her breasts pressed against the hard surface of his chest. She could feel herself getting warm and it was not from the velvet gown but from the nearness of this magnificent male. At the end of the waltz he bent her backward in a deep dip and lightly kissed the tip of her nose.

"La, monsieur, you take liberties," she sighed and blushed.

"Pouf," he said, "that was no liberty—simply the proper ending for a beautiful dance. Besides, methinks you are not such the innocent as that."

Eleonore smiled but did not reply.

They danced several more dances together until Jean-Marie came up to them. "Hein, mon ami, are you going to monopolize our beautiful hostess all evening?" he asked. "Give the rest of us panting males a chance."

Eleonore took an instant dislike to him. Panting, indeed. But she knew he was right. "I really must attend to my other guests, Jean-Paul, but I shall give you another dance later, never fear. It has been my pleasure."

Reluctantly Jean-Paul turned her over to Jean-Marie. The captain held her even closer than Jean-Paul had but it was not the same. Instead of a thrill she felt a chill especially when his hand crept up her back and tried to reach around to touch her breast. She pulled away as much as she could without interrupting the rhythm of the dance. At the end he kissed her roughly full on the mouth and she could feel his tongue probing.

She gasped. "That, Captain Lescaux, is truly beyond the bounds of decorum."

"Hah!" he averred. "I had not thought you to be so prim and proper, Madame." And his sly eyes raked her lasciviously.

Eleonore escaped from his stare as quickly and courteously as she could. She made a pretense of seeing to the general's well-being. But that worthy was happily ensconced at a card table with a cup of punch at his elbow. He had no need of her attention. Jean-Paul was waiting for her near the punch bowl. Eleonore had been careful not to drink too much but now she felt the need of something to bolster her spirits. She accepted a cup from Jean-Paul.

"Did he offend you, cherie?" he asked.

"Who?"

"My comrade, Jean-Marie?"

"Oh, him. No, not really. It's just . . . No, not really," she replied.

"Ah, but he did. I can see it in your lovely eyes. He is like that—no breeding. But I must work with him so I seldom criticize. But I cannot have him offending our gracious hostess. It is very warm in here. Perhaps a stroll in the garden will make you feel better."

"I am afraid we don't have much of a garden," she demurred. Eleonore did not feel bad at all but the chance to be alone with him for even a few minutes was too tempting to forego.

"No matter. Come," he urged, "a breath of fresh air will do you good."

"They'll be serving the supper soon," she replied lamely.

"Ach, we have time for a short stroll and even one more dance ere they get to that." He took her by the elbow. "Which way?"

Since the front door of the house opened directly on to the street, she had to lead him through the back kitchen. The cook, maid and several girls hired for the occasion were busy arranging the supper. No one looked up as the couple passed by, but they noticed.

"Ah, that feels good," she sighed as she took a deep breath of fresh air. The night was still warm but nowhere near as stifling as in the house. "Now mind your step," she warned. "Much of this used to be my flower garden but since—since . . . er, now we have had to plant it all to vegetables."

"I understand," he murmured to cover her embarrassment. He knew what she had been about to say. "But a body must have food."

"But flowers are food for the soul. I have always liked to surround myself with them, since I was denied them as a child." Eleonore surprised herself confessing this to an almost total stranger. But she felt so at ease with him.

Jean-Paul put his arm around her. "And you shall have them again, cherie. Once the Emperor has united all of Europe and there is peace once more. We French love flowers, too. Surely you are familiar with our famous perfume industry."

Eleonore was not sure she agreed with all of this so she simply nodded. They reached the end of the garden and paused beneath the shadow of a great linden tree. Beyond near the stable the grooms were playing a game of jackstraws with the general's coachmen. But here under the tree they were secluded.

Jean-Paul took her in his arms and held her close. "A real kiss?" he asked. She did not have to reply. She looked up into his face and melted against him. He kissed her deeply and longingly. And again. She drew back breathless. It was as if she had never been kissed before. She fleetingly thought back to her early days—and nights—with Teddi. But that had long since palled. Now their lovemaking was boringly routine and rarely satisfying, only succeeding in getting her pregnant with children she no longer wanted.

Jean-Paul kissed her again. His hand slipped around to grasp her breast. She was on fire. This was real. This was lovemaking as it should be. She knew she wanted him as much as he wanted her. But she could not let it go too far—not yet. She slipped out of his embrace.

"We must go back," she said. "They will be serving supper and I, after all, am the hostess."

Jean-Paul was no fool. He would not rush her. He knew she was his for the asking. He could bide his time. "But I will see you again?" he asked. "I must see you again."

She nodded and started back. He took her arm and they strolled sedately back to the house. When they entered the kitchen, it was almost empty.

"Goodness!" she gasped. "They are serving already and I am not there."

But Dorothea had seen what was happening and had discreetly made herself temporary hostess. When Eleonore and Jean-Paul entered the dining-room, she was standing behind the buffet urging the guests to partake of the food. When she saw the couple enter, she winked at Eleonore and said, "Ah, our gracious hostess at the end of the line. She knows her manners, does she not? Letting her guests be the first to help themselves. Here, General Dupas, try one of these gooseberry tarts. I made them myself." And everyone's attention turned toward the general who was making a pig of himself. The front of his fat belly was already stained with bits of paté and grease from the rabbit.

Bless you, Dorchen, thought Eleonore.

When they reached the table Jean-Paul helped himself to a generous dollop of paté. "Your cook must be French," he said. "This is excellent. Try some." He took his fork and fed her a small bit.

It was good. "No," she replied. "She is all German but I taught her."

"Then that makes it all the better." He took a rabbit leg. "Lapin. One of my favorites." He held it out to her. "You take a bite. Then I shall and it will be like kissing you."

"Sshh," she whispered as she nibbled on the leg he held for her.

Just as this touching scene was being enacted, there was a commotion in the hall leading from the kitchen. All eyes turned in that direction as Teddi burst into the room. He wore old clothes. His hands were filthy from his workshop and he was drunk. Very drunk.

Eleonore was shocked. She had never seen Teddi drunk before. Teddi could not handle strong drink well and he knew it. Thus he had always been extremely abstemious regarding wine and beer. Whatever his other faults, drunkenness had never been one of them.

"You fucking, frog-livered French bastard!" he yelled. "Get away from my wife. She's a whore, I'll admit. But she's my whore, no one else's."

187

Eleonore gasped, horrified. She turned white and felt as though she were going to faint. She had never heard Teddi use such profanity either. "Get out of here," she screamed.

"I'd like some of your fancy punch," said Teddi, lurching toward the table. He reached for a crystal cup and missed. The precious cup went crashing to the floor.

Fritzi hurried up and tried to take Teddi's arm. "Come away, brother, you're embarrassing our guests."

"Embarrassing, huh? Well, she's embarrassing me, sucking up to these goddamned Frenchmen. Do you think I don't know what's going on? Her with her fuckin' French blood. And you . . . " He gave Fritzi a violent shove that almost threw the young man into Jean-Paul's arms. The captain steadied him. "And you," raved Teddi, "you're no better. You've been in love with her since you were six years old. You'd love to get under her petticoats, wouldn't you? If you haven't already."

The local Bürgers had not really cared how much Teddi cursed the Frenchmen but this—this shocked them beyond belief. Dorothea decided it was past time to take the situation in hand. She signalled to Chris.

The miller towered over Teddi and was twice as broad, probably the strongest man present. He firmly pinned Teddi's arms to his sides and gently turned him around, all the while saying, "Come, friend, let's go into the kitchen and have a cup of coffee. There you can tell me all your troubles. You've always felt comfortable talking to me, haven't you?" Teddi nodded and almost went limp as Chris quickly propelled him toward the kitchen.

The room was absolutely silent. Eleonore collapsed into a chair fluttering her fan. Jean-Paul was immediately at her side. He handed her his handkerchief with which she gratefully wiped her brow, at the same time telling herself, don't cry. Not now. Not until the guests have left. If she had been bored and disillusioned with Teddi before, now she hated him with all the vehemence both her German and French blood could arouse.

"Don't cry, cherie," whispered Jean-Paul comfortingly. "Don't be upset. It is not the first time we French have been cursed, nor, I fear, will it be the last."

She nodded. "Thank you, Jean-Paul. I need your strength now as never before."

"You shall have it, cherie. I see now why you are so unhappy. I shall make you happy again if you will let me."

She nodded and, gathering all her willpower, stood up. "I do apologize, my dear friends," she announced. "My husband is not himself tonight. And I especially beg your pardon, mon General. I hope it has not spoiled an otherwise gala evening."

"No offense taken, Madame," replied Dupas. "We Frenchmen are quite used to the—er—jealous husband." Eveyone chuckled at that and the room seemed to relax. "It has been a most enjoyable evening."

"Thank you, Your Excellency," said Eleonore. "Then mayhap there is time for one more dance ere you must leave." She instructed the Bruns brothers to strike up the music and she turned to Jean-Paul.

He held her close as they waltzed. "You are trembling, cherie," he said and drew her closer still. "Is he always like that?"

"Nay, nay," she replied. "I've never seen him drunk before. I can't imagine what happened. But he has been in a sulk all day. I don't want to talk about it. Make me happy again, Jean-Paul."

In reply he kissed her forehead. She hoped no one noticed but at this point she no longer cared.

"I shall, ma cherie," he said. "When can I see you again?"

"Soon, soon," she breathed. "But you see we must be very careful."

"I shall be the soul of discretion."

The dance ended and people were beginning to leave. She thanked them for coming and hoped they had enjoyed themselves. Even the old busybodies assured her they had. Oh, but they would have days of gossip over this. General Dupas thanked her for introducing him to the townspeople. It would make his job easier or so he hoped. Jean-Marie leered at her but Jean-Paul stepped in between and assured her, "You are tres galante, Madame. It has been my pleasure. À bientôt."

Dorothea and Christian were the last to leave.

"I got him to bed in that little room off the kitchen," said Chris. "He's passed out so I doubt you'll have any more trouble from him this night but he'll probably be sick and in a mighty foul mood in the morning."

Dorothea put her arms around Eleonore. "Don't worry, dearest Elli. We don't believe any of the terrible things he said and I doubt anyone else did either. Will you be all right tonight? Would you like me to stay with you?"

"Nay, nay. You've done enough and I thank you—especially you, Chris."

"If you need me in the morning, come quickly," said Dorothea, "or—or, if need be, send Fritzi and I'll come forthwith."

"Dearest Dorchen," said Eleonore, "you always seem to be helping me out of the messes I make of my life." After they left, Eleonore went up to her room carefully locking the door behind her. She stripped off the velvet gown, threw herself on her bed and wept.

A few days later a very young orderly came to the door with a note from Jean-Paul. The maid ushered him into the parlor where Eleonore sat staring into space. Since the night of the ball she had been unable to concentrate on anything—not her embroidery, not a book, not anything. Fortunately she had seen almost nothing of her husband in the interval. There had been no scenes, no recriminations, but no apologies either. He had kept to his workshop and still slept in the cook's little room off the kitchen. Cook, in turn, had been relegated to another maid's room in the attic. She was not very happy about this but Eleonore had assured her it was only temporary until the Master got over his—er—indisposition.

Eleonore took the note from the lad. A surge of excitement swept through her, also a frisson of fear. The very young soldier bowed and stepped back but did not leave. She looked at him questioningly.

"I am to await Madame's reply," he said.

Eleonore cautiously opened he note. 'Thursday at half after twelve take a walk out of the village towards Bruchhausen. I shall be there in a closed carriage. J-P,' she read. Thursday. Tomorrow. Could she do it? Easily. Teddi would never know she was gone. Would she do it? Of course she would. She wanted nothing more than to be with Jean-Paul again. Did she dare? If she was to be called a whore then she would be real one. And she had always risen to a dare.

She nodded to the boy. "You may tell Monsieur le Capitain that I agree to his request. Merci."

The boy said, "Merci, Madame. I shall give him your reply," and left.

Immediately Eleonore was in a flurry of activity. Her listless mood had completely evaporated. What should she wear? How should she dress her hair? What jewels, if any? Would he still be as exciting as the other night? Would he try to hustle her into bed the very first time? She had to be prepared for that. As much as she wanted him she hoped she could put that off for a little while. She dared not get pregnant. She would have to go to the old wisewoman for one of her potions. She wondered if she was still alive. She had not heard that she was not. She had tried the potion once years ago. She was not sure if it really worked or not. The stuff was so foul-tasting she had never tried it again and thus had borne Teddi seven children so far.

She had the maid carefully iron her coolest, prettiest summer gown. That evening she had a hot bath brought up to her room. She thoroughly washed her long hair and scrubbed herself. She wanted to smell like a spring flower for him. The warm bath relaxed her somewhat but she was so excited she could hardly sleep.

Next day at a quarter past noon Eleonore was just about to leave when Katinka said, "Mama, where are you going? It's almost dinnertime."

"I don't feel like eating today. I'm just going for a little walk. I should be back in time for coffee."

"May I come with you?"

"Not today, sweet girl. I really want to be totally alone. Mayhap tomorrow we can go and visit Tante Dorchen. You'd like that, wouldn't you?"

"Oh, yes, I should."

Katinka watched as her mother strolled sedately down the street, parasol open against the fierce sun for it was another very warm day. She had noticed Eleonore's strange mood the last few days, not at all like her normally vivacious mother. And now she was vivacious again. Katinka was now thirteen, almost a young woman. Although still very innocent, her budding female instincts told her that her mother was about to embark on a wonderful adventure. Although she would not have used the word sexual, had she even known it, to describe this adventure, Eleonore's excitement had been palpable—and contagious.

Katinka had heard about the terrible fiasco her father had created the night of the ball and this, no doubt, accounted for her mother's sad mood of the past few days. But this sudden change? What had snapped Mama out of the doldrums so quickly? Katinka's curiosity was piqued. She quietly slipped out of the house and followed Eleonore at a great distance.

Eleonore strolled sedately along the village street, nodding to acquaintances here and there but not stopping to talk. She felt like running and skipping like a young girl but that would never do. Soon she was out of the village and nearing the road to Bruchhausen. She hoped he would already be there. It was very hot and she would look like a fool standing in the middle of nowhere, waiting.

When she reached the crossroads she spied a small but exquisite closed coach parked under one of the apple trees. As she approached, the driver jumped down and opened the door for her. The next moment she was in Jean-Paul's arms.

191

Aha, said Katinka to herself. She'll not be back in time for afternoon coffee either. Although she had not seen who had been in the coach, she recognized an assignation when she saw one. She was happy for her mother on the one hand and worried on the other. She turned around and went home for dinner.

Jean-Paul kissed Eleonore deeply as the coach drove off. He could not get enough of her sweet lips. He hoped she would give him more very soon. "Ah, cherie," he sighed. "I was so afraid you would not come."

"You knew I would," she replied coyly. "Where are we going? Not to the castle, I hope."

"No, never," he declared, "and have every soldier in the French army know we are lovers? I'm not that much of a fool."

She laughed at that. He was so sweet. He kissed her again and his hand slipped over her breast. This time the cloth of her gown was sheer enough so that he could feel her nipple grow taut under his caress. She shivered with delight.

"We shall be lovers, shall we not?' he asked, not so much as a question but as a statement.

"Perhaps," she sighed.

"I have found the perfect spot," he said, "and there we shall have a picnic." He indicated a basket set on the seat opposite them. "There is enough there for both dinner and supper."

"But, Jean-Paul, I cannot stay that late," she protested. "I must be home in two or three hours."

"Then we shall enjoy a wonderful repast on the green and you may take the rest home with you. I know how increasingly difficult it is becoming for you to get good food. We have more than enough at the castle. Mayhap I can see that you get some meat from time to time."

"That is very thoughtful of you. It would be greatly appreciated." The coach left Bruchhausen and turned onto a smaller country road. "Now, where are we going?" she asked.

"Do you know Martfeld?"

"Fairly well." Oh, no, not Martfeld, she thought but then forced herself to relax against him hoping his 'perfect spot' was well hidden away from prying eyes.

Martfeld was a tiny hamlet a few miles to the north. It had not many inhabitants but it boasted two large mills—a watermill and a huge windmill right at the main crossroads. The coach pulled into the yard of the windmill.

"There is a lovely meadow behind the mill. Under shady trees beside the millstream is where we shall have our picnic." He stopped abruptly at the horrified look on her face.

"No!" she gasped. "No! Jean-Paul, my grandfather owns both of these mills. His house is right over there."

"Your grandfather?" he exclaimed. "But surely he is too old . . . "

"He is dead but my uncles run the mills and they know me very well. Jean-Paul, I shall not get out of this coach. We must go elsewhere or take me home, quickly."

"I am sorry, cherie. I did not know." He sighed. So much for the ardent lovemaking he had planned. He signalled to the coachman who deftly turned the coach around back the way they had come.

"Besides," she snapped, more sharply than she intended, "my husband may call me a whore but I am not some serving wench to be rolled in the hay—or the clover. I should think you would have the decency to treat a lady better than that."

"I do. I do," he demurred. "I do *not* think you are a whore. I honor you too much for that. I just thought it would be nice to sit in a lovely, shady place and—and . . . " He left the rest of the sentence hanging. He did not know what to say. "I am so sorry, cherie. I simply did not know. Am I forgiven?"

She nodded, somewhat calmer now that they had left Martfeld behind.

On an impulse he dove into the picnic basket and came up with a bottle of wine. "A little cup of wine will calm your nerves."

"Do not think to get me drunk, Jean-Paul," she warned.

"Never, never," he replied. "If ever I am to make love to you, as I so desperately want to, I should want you to be totally sober to enjoy every minute of it."

She smiled and accepted the wine. She sipped it slowly. It was a very dry French wine, not exactly to her taste. German wine was sweeter. But it helped her relax. She snuggled up against him once more.

After a time he asked, "How would a charming little coffeeshop suit you? I know of one in Hoya—very cozy and intimate."

Not too intimate, she hoped. "Yes, that would suit much better," she replied. "But coffee? They still have coffee?" She had not had a good cup of coffee in months.

"I believe so. Yes, I am quite sure they do. There are many French soldiers stationed at Castle Hoya and I am quite certain the army keeps this particular shop well supplied." He gave the coachman instructions to drive to Hoya.

When they returned to Vilsen late in the day the coach drove straight up to the Hohnholz doorstep.

"No, no," exclaimed Eleonore. "I can't be seen coming home like this."

"But, cherie, you cannot possible carry this heavy basket of food—and wine—all the way from the crossroads. I'll not get out of the coach. Tell your—er—family it is a hostess gift from General Dupas thanking you for the wonderful evening."

She laughed. "In that case, I shall accept it."

He kissed her hungrily. "And when may I see you again, dearest Eleonore? I promise I shall find a more suitable location for our rendezvous—suitable for a lady."

"Soon, dear Jean-Paul," she replied.

"Then Thursday next at the same time. This month Thursday is my afternoon off. I shall write should anything prevent." He kissed her again.

The coachman took the heavy basket and set it on the stoop. Eleonore stood watching until the coach was well away before opening the door.

The next afternoon Eleonore and Katinka strolled leisurely through the Vilsen woods on their way to the Klostermühle. Ever since she was a child, Eleonore had always loved this section of deep forest. Some children had been afraid of wolves and witches but to her it had been a haven. She felt that now, breathing in the clean scent of pine and fir, the sharp tang of oakleaf mold underfoot. The forest still worked magic on her.

When they arrived at the mill she greeted Dorothea briefly. "I am going to leave Katinka with you for a short while, if I may. I want to see the wisewoman."

Dorothea raised her eyebrows but said only, "You know she is always welcome."

Eleonore said, "Then Katinka, go and play with Heinrich Anton. I shall be back very soon."

"But Mama," Katinka objected, "Heinrich Anton is no longer a child nor am I. He has almost completed his apprenticeship and will be working. Can't I come with you? I'd love to visit old Mother Holle again."

"Mother Holle is it? No, not this time, Kati. I just have to fetch some medicine and I'll come right back."

"Medicine? But no one's sick."

"Well, it's just in case someone should get sick. I want to have it on hand."

Dorothea knew very well what 'medicine' her friend was seeking. She said, "Come, Katinka, help me bake some cookies for this afternoon's coffee. Then we'll eat them when your mother returns." She ushered the girl into the house and Eleonore continued on her way through the woods.

The old crone appeared at the door of her cottage as Eleonore approached. She went through the usual routine of letting the dog run out, bark and sniff the hand of her visitor. "Ah, Anton Matthies' girl," she cackled. "Kind o' thought ye might be a-comin' to see me soon."

Although Eleonore was well aware of the woman's second sight and the messages she claimed to get from ravens and other wildlife, she was always shocked at the old hag's perspicacity. "You did?"

"Course, I did. Heared tell yer flitty man ain't enough for you no more. Can't say's I blame ye. He weren't ne'er the man for you, young Nell. Playin' with those Frenchies, are ye? Well, more power to you, gal. B'ain't right to keep a good woman from her pleasure, now is't?"

Eleonore blushed to the tips of her ears—and she did not often blush. "You knew all that, old mother?" she stammered.

"Plain as the nose on yer face."

"And you approve?"

"Got the potion all prepared for you." The old woman led her into the dark cottage. "Best take two bottles. I'll not be around much longer."

"Oh, old mother, don't say that. We—everyone hereabouts depends on you."

"Lass, I be nigh on a hundred year old. Time to go. When the forest goes, I go. Wotan's ravens tole me."

"When the forest goes? What do you mean?"

"Don't know exactly," the crone replied. "Ye may like the Frenchie's diddling but they ain't got no love for the woods or the wild things. Forest be goin', mark my words."

Eleonore pondered this as she walked back through the woods but she could not imagine what the old woman was talking about. This forest had stood for hundreds of years and would stand for hundreds more. Germans were very proud—and careful—of their woods. Most people had only culling rights for firewood. Builders could construct an entire house from one or two large trees using the wood only for beams in the so-called

195

half-timbered style and for flooring. The gaps in the walls were filled with brick or even a sort of plaster liberally laced with straw. A few, such as Johann Justus Bruns, had special rights but from one or two oaks or maples a year he could craft dozens of pieces of fine furniture. The forest would never go.

When she reached the Klostermühle the family was just sitting down to afternoon coffee and kuchen—or what passed for coffee these days.

"Ah, you're just in time," said Dorothea. "Would you like some coffee or would you prefer chamomile tea?"

Eleonore hated the acorn mash that folk were forced to use for real coffee now. It was terribly bitter and seemed to stick to the roof of one's mouth. "I'd prefer the tea if you have enough," she replied.

"Ach, that we have a-plenty," said Dorothea. "Grows like weeds, that chamomile does and thank God for it. You can be sure I save and dry every last flower. Help yourself to some cookies. Katinka helped me bake them. I don't know how much longer we'll be able to enjoy those either. Sugar is getting scarce, too."

"So I heard but most of it comes from the French islands in the Indies, does it not? So why should it be scarce?" asked Eleonore.

"Because the British fleet is constantly harassing those islands," explained Chris. "Even captured some of them."

Eleonore shook her head. She could not understand why ordinary folk must suffer just because governments wanted to fight each other. She sought to change the subject. "Heinrich Anton, I hear you are almost done with your apprenticeship. Soon you'll be off a-journeying, no?"

"I'm going to be spending my journey years right here with Papa," the lad replied.

Eleonore looked askance at Chris. "Really?"

"Ja," said Chris. "I'm keeping him here right by my side for a number of reasons. I need him for one thing. Dieter and young Chris will just be starting their own apprenticeships and will be no help for the heavier work for several years. Another reason is for his own safety."

"Safety?" queried Eleonore. "You mean there might actually be fighting here?"

"Not necessarily that. But you are surely aware of this annual levy of recruits for Napoleon's army." She nodded. "If he is off journeying he could be snapped up in a minute. They start taking them at fourteen you know, and they demand a higher quota every year. Here at least I can offer him some protection. A miller's trade is vital to the army."

196

"I see," she said slowly. "I hadn't realized it was that bad."

"Because yours are still too young to worry about."

"Well, at least that will make Katinka happy." They all laughed and it broke the tension somewhat.

"And how fares your dear old papa?" Dorothea asked.

"Quite well as far as I know. I've not heard from him in two or three weeks."

"Then you didn't know that he suffered a near heart attack?" exclaimed Dorothea.

"What?!" shrieked Eleonore. "When? What happened? Is he all right now? Why didn't Heinzi send to me?"

Dorothea shrugged. "Heinzi being Heinzi is too thoughtless and careless to think of others," she replied. "And mayhap your papa didn't want to upset you. He refused to let them send for the doctor. So we're not sure if it was his heart although he showed all the signs of an attack. But he seems to be getting over it quite well now."

Eleonore felt a twinge of guilt. She had been so engrossed in planning her party for the French general that she had not given her parents a thought. She had even refused to invite them. And since then all her thoughts had revolved around Jean-Paul. "Thank God he is better," she murmured. "But why didn't *you* tell me?"

"We thought you knew."

"How did it happen?"

Chris took up the story from there. "You may have heard that Napoleon desperately needs battleships and frigates for his navy. The British nigh decimated what fleet he had at Trafalgar."

"What has that to do with Papa?" Eleonore asked sharply.

Chris held up his hand. "He has already looted the French forests beyond any hope of restoration. Now he is turning to the vast German forests—our forests. He needs oak for hulls and decks, pine for masts and spars."

"And?"

"Less than a week ago they started cutting your papa's prime stand adjacent to the state forest."

"Oh, no!"

"Anton went after them with his old musket. I tried to restrain him but you know his temper. There was no holding him back. In a way it was God's grace that he had the attack or he'd surely have been shot. He was yelling at them at the top of his voice and threatening them with the gun when he collapsed. I picked him up and tried to carry him off when he turned his temper on me. But it didn't amount to much as he was gasping for breath. I managed to help him home and to bed. By then he had calmed down enough to ask for some tea but he refused to let anyone ride for the doctor."

"But why didn't you anyway?"

"Elli, you know your papa. I didn't want to set his temper off again. No one crosses Anton Matthies."

"I know—only too well."

"When I left he was almost in tears. He kept crying, 'My forest. My beautiful forest that I fought so hard for'. For the first time since I've know him I felt pity for your father, Elli."

Eleonore was thoughtful for a moment. "So that is what the old wise-woman was referring to. She told me that the forest was going and when it was gone, she would go, too."

"She didn't need Wotan's ravens to tell her that," remarked Dorothea. "Walk a ways toward your old home and you can hear the axes and saws thumping and screeching all day long. It won't be but a month or so ere they reach here and then on up to where the old woman lives. She's right. The shock will probably kill her."

"Oh, no! That's horrible," said Eleonore. "How can they . . . ?"

"Very easily," said Chris with a touch of sarcasm. "Tell your General Dupas what we think of his depredations. Not that it would do any good." He rose and went back to the mill taking Heinrich Anton with him.

Eleonore had the grace to be embarrassed. She had not expected such vitriol from gentle Chris. As she rose to leave, Dorothea patted her arm. "Pay him no mind," she said. "We know it's not your fault but many people could be thinking the same thing. Be forewarned."

Eleonore nodded. Dear Dorchen was still her friend, no matter what she did. "Come, Katinka," she said, "we must pay Opa a visit on the way home."

"Do we have to?" objected Katinka. "It's much farther that way. And I hate young Heinzi. He is a nasty boy."

"The walk will do you good after eating sugar cookies all afternoon. And you must not say you hate anyone. You don't have to like your cousin but hate is a vile thing—a vile word." Eleonore well remembered her own hateful outburst against her father when her eldest brother was killed. Dorchen had helped her through that—and a dozen times since.

"But he tries to touch me in places where you said never to let *anyone* touch me," Katinka went on.

Eleonore was not in the least surprised. Like father, like son. "Well, we sha'n't let him, will we? You stick right close to me. We'll not be long. But I must see how Opa—and Oma—are faring."

When they arrived at Bruchmühlen Anton was sitting in the parlor sipping tea. Though the day was very warm he was wrapped in a heavy blanket. Eleonore was shocked at how he had aged. Becke was fluttering around almost cheerfully. It seemed her father's attack had given her mother something to do besides feel sorry for herself.

"So," grumbled Anton, "you've finally managed to tear yourself away from your French lovers long enough to see whether your old pa's dead or alive."

Eleonore tried to ignore that although actually it was a good sign. He was as irascible as ever. It would be a long time before he stopped fighting—even with death itself. "I'm sorry, Papa. I didn't know. Heinzi never sent word."

"Well, you can tell those French bastards to stay off my land."

"But, Papa, I thought you liked the French. You were always so proud of your French blood."

"No more, I ain't. I despise them chopping down all my beautiful trees."

"Now calm yourself, Papa. I'll mention it but I doubt it will do much good. The orders come from Paris—from Napoleon himself."

"Mention it!" he growled. "You're beginning to sound like that insipid, mewling husband of yours. Where is that fighting lass I raised? The only one of my children with enough backbone to best even me."

Eleonore smiled. "She's still here. But even I cannot take on the might of the whole French Empire. But if Napoleon is as arrogant as I've heard he will stumble and fall one of these days. The good Lord will see to it."

"Let us pray the good Lord doesn't take too long seeing to it or poor Hannover will be ground into the dust. This is only the beginning. I fear me the worst is yet to come."

Eleonore and Katinka left soon after that assured that Anton was well on the mend. But some of his words frightened Eleonore, as had the old wisewoman's. Was the worst really yet to come? She vowed to confront Jean-Paul the next time they met.

But the following week Jean-Paul was not interested in such sober things as politics. He was too pleased with his plans for ardent lovemaking—too eager to show her his latest choice for their rendezvous—quite sure that this time she would acquiesce.

"I have something very charming to show you, cherie," he said when they met. "You will adore it, certainement."

"Indeed?" she replied cautiously. "What or where is it?"

"You'll see. You'll see," he said. "I have rented a lovely little cottage. A private hideaway just for us."

"Not Martfeld again?" she queried skeptically.

"Non, non. You'll see."

The carriage turned onto the road to Hoya but long before they reached the village the driver turned the horses onto a narrow country lane. After a while they stopped before a tiny cottage.

Oh, Lord, thought Eleonore as Jean-Paul helped her down from the coach. It was not her idea of charming. While not exactly run-down, it was obviously very old and had seen better days. The proud crossed horses—the Sachsenross—at the gable peak was so weathered, it looked at though it would separate itself from the thatch at any moment. But she knew these old houses. It was sturdy, probably well over a hundred years old.

Jean-Paul produced a large key from his pocket and proceeded to open the door. At the same time he waved to the coachman who promptly drove off.

"Isn't he going to wait for us?" she asked, a bit apprehensive.

"Non, non, he will be back in three hours. That way, you see, no idle or curious passerby will know that anyone is here. I promised you privacy, cherie."

"That you did."

"Then entrez, entrez and see our petit love-nest."

Eleonore stepped inside and was pleasantly surprised. Though sparsely furnished the place was immaculate. The table and chairs before the hearth were highly polished and looked almost new. Across the room on a colorful braided rug were two comfortable chairs and a small wine cabinet. A central ladder that was almost, but not quite, a staircase led to the loft. Glancing up she could see a bed so huge it almost filled the entire loft. It was amply furnished with featherbeds, feather pillows and an exquisite lace coverlet.

"Very cozy," she commented. "And to whom does all this luxury belong?"

"I do not really know. The farmer who owns the house rents it to

General Dupas from whom I am renting it. The furniture belongs to the general. Several of my fellow officers have used it in the past but it is exclusively ours for two months. We'll not be disturbed."

"I see," she said slowly. And she did see. These French would have their liaisons no matter where. But she should not be shocked. She, after all, had agreed to be one of them.

Jean-Paul took her in his arms and kissed her soundly. "Come," he said, "let us have a little sip of wine ere we climb the stairs."

She sat down in one of the comfortable chairs and let him serve her. He deftly poured the wine and as he handed her the beautiful crystal his other hand grasped her breast and gently teased the nipple through the thin cloth of her gown. She jumped and shivered with delight, almost spilling the wine.

"Oh," she moaned and arched her back so that both breasts invited his touch. His hands willingly obliged. She was so hot aleady she did not need the wine but dutifully took a few sips when he backed off to drink his own. This was what she had been dreaming about for two weeks. She could not wait.

He set his glass atop the cabinet and knelt before slowly slipping his hands under her gown and caressing her thighs, teasing, teasing but not approaching her private place as yet. She longed to thrust herself toward those groping hands. But no. She would go along with his titillating game. It would be that much better later—if she could control herself.

He took her hand and bade her rise. He held her back against him gently massaging both breasts. She could feel his male hardness against her backside. "Shall we go up where it is more comfortable?" he invited.

"Oh, yes," she gasped.

She climbed the ladder with his hand on her thigh, sliding up and down with each step she took. She was so excited she nearly tripped but he held her firmly, urging her on. When she reached the top she looked around. It was as she thought. The huge, luxurious bed almost filled the loft. There was scarcely room to walk around. But then, no one was expected to walk around here. The bed was the only reason for being here—and it did look inviting.

Jean-Paul was behind her and immediately began undoing the laces of her gown. She blessed the new style—no corsets to get in the way or restrict her—or him. He grasped her breasts and then slid his hands down to her hips as the gown fell to the floor. She stood in her thin shift as he quickly shed his own clothes. She stared at his male magnificence. He was much larger than Teddi. Her loins trembled inside, wanting that beautiful piece of anatomy. He slipped her shift over her head and once again caressed her breasts, nibbling and sucking on the taut nipples until she was frantic with desire. He threw back the lace coverlet and led her to the bed. She sat down on the edge while he removed her shoes and stockings. One shoe, one stocking and a trail of kisses from her toes to her thigh. The other shoe, the other stocking and another trail of kisses. But this time he did not stop. He buried his face in the black triangle. She screamed with delight and fell back on the bed as his tongue found the center of her femaleness and brought her to ecstacy. And again. And again.

She could not get enough of him. Even in her younger days with Teddi she had never been loved like this. But suddenly she wanted more. She had to have all of him — and he knew it. She arched back against him, inviting. He rolled over her and gently teased with his rock-hard prick. Teased but did not enter. Instead he nibbled on her breasts again, sucking so hard she went wild with longing. She heard herself begging, begging him. At last he was inside, filling her exquisitely. But he pushed slowly and gently, bringing her to ecstacy several times more. She heard screaming and vaguely realized it was herself. She was crazy with wanting. When she thought she could stand no more, he suddenly plunged like a bucking horse, deep, deep. She met him eagerly. The stars burst, the heavens opened. She heard him groan aloud and she almost passed out from the sheer joy of it.

They lay gasping in each other's arms for a long while. At last he sat up, poured some more wine and handed her the goblet. She would much rather have had a cool sip of water but she was grateful just the same.

"So now you know what it is like to be loved by a Frenchman," he declared.

Conceited ass, she thought. But no. He was right. Conceited or not, she had never experienced such beautiful lovemaking. And she wanted more of it, as much as she could get.

"Shall we have a bite to eat?" he asked. "The basket awaits us down below."

"Not just yet," she murmured. "I just want to lie here a few moments and think about how lovely it was."

He laughed. "Lovemaking is not to be thought about, only enjoyed," he said. He leaned over and kissed her deeply. "My sweet Eleonore," he said and soon they were making love again. He had known right from the start that she could not get enough of him but now he realized, nor could he get enough of her. As he had said, no thoughts, just pleasure.

Much, much later, he rose on one elbow and said, "We really ought to eat some of that food. I'd not want you to faint. Unless you wish to carry it home with you again."

She smiled lazily. "Nay, this time I am hungry. In fact, ravenous. All that—er—exercise."

They laughed together. "Come, then, let me help you dress. Jacques will be here in less than an hour."

"I can dress myself. I think."

"But at least let me comb your hair," he pleaded. "I'd like that."

She agreed and once again felt sensuous tinglings as he part stroked and part combed her thick black hair.

The moment she arrived home Eleonore took a generous gulp of the old wisewoman's foul-tasting potion. She shuddered with distaste but she was still basking in the afterglow of their lovemaking. But the next day she suffered from belly cramps and debilitating diarrhea. For all her agony she decided it was worth it. It must be working, she thought, no seed could withstand that purge.

Several weeks later as they were heading home from the little cottage, Jean-Paul asked, "Can you come a little bit earlier next week? Like about nine of the clock?"

Somewhat surprised, Eleonore replied, "I suppose I could." She had never spent an entire day with him. "Why do you ask?"

"How would you like to go for a sail on the river?"

"A sail? In a boat?" she asked tremulously.

"Of course, in a boat."

"I've never been in a boat before," she admitted. "I—I can't swim."

He laughed. "No need to swim. I'll not let you fall overboard. It is very relaxing and peaceful out on the water. You will enjoy it."

"If you say so," she said doubtfully.

On the day in question they drove directly to the tiny boat haven on the Weser. It lay slightly downstream from the bridge just below the sheltering height of the ancient castle. Most of the boats were drawn up on the shore; a few were anchored out. Some belonged to fishermen but most of the river traders had not left the anchorage in many months because of the embargo. Except for increasingly rare local goods there was nothing to trade. But General Dupas had built a short jetty to which was tied his own boat. It was a small shallop, single-masted with a gaff-rigged sail and an extremely tiny cabin—if it could even be called a cabin.

Eleonore was surprised to see Jean-Marie already sitting in the cock-pit.

"Is he going with us?" she asked sharply.

"But, of course, cherie. I need him. I can't very well make love to you and sail the boat at the same time."

"But how . . . ?"

"Have no fear, my sweet. You see that little cabin? Small but very cozy. We just pull the hatch to and we are shut away from the world. After all, Jean-Marie *does* know what's going on."

"I'm sure he does," she replied. But she did not like it one bit. No, not at all. It was one thing, Jean-Marie knowing, but to witness . . . Neverthe-less she did not want to disappoint Jean-Paul. So she allowed him to help her aboard the small craft, while he handed the ever-present picnic basket to Jean-Marie. She staggered as the boat rocked and quickly sat down on the bench that ran along the gunwale. Jean-Paul helped Jean-Marie cast off and then sat down beside her and put an arm protectively around her shoulders.

At first she felt a little queasy but once she looked off into the distance the feeling went away and she began to relax and enjoy. The river was very calm with only a slight breeze to ruffle the water. And it was quiet. Oh, so quiet.

She noticed that they had not set the sail but that Jean-Marie had a long pole with which he was not only pushing the boat away from the shore but also steering it.

"If we are going sailing," she asked, "why do we not raise the sail?"

"We shall on the way back," explained Jean-Paul. "You see the wind here is always from the northwest—or sometimes from the northeast—but almost always northerly. If we were to set the sail, we should have to tack—that means zigzag—back and forth across the river. Very time-consuming and a lot of work. When going down river it is much easier to drift with the current and just use the pole to keep us off the shoals. On the return trip the wind will be behind us."

She snuggled into his shoulder and breathed deeply of the fresh air. His hand crept to her breast and she felt the usual thrill. But she gently removed it. Somehow it seemed profane in front of Jean-Marie.

"There is not much traffic on the river today," she remarked. "I can remember when we were little Papa sometimes would bring us to the bridge to watch the boats. It seemed as though there were hundreds of

204

them, coming and going. Where are they all now?"

"No doubt useless because of the embargo," he replied.

"But what are all those people who made their living on the river doing now?"

He shrugged a typically Gallic shrug. "Probably joining the Emperor's army."

"But surely not willingly," she protested.

"Some do," he insisted, "but I admit most are conscripted. But it is better than starving, non?"

The implications of the word conscripted chilled her. Already too many young men from Vilsen had been taken and, if rumor proved true, the levy would be even higher next year. As for starving—they would not be if it were not for Napoleon's bitter hatred of England and his damned embargo. Her family was not yet suffering, thanks in part to Jean-Paul's gifts, but she knew of many who were close to it. But she dared not voice these concerns. So she only said, "I suppose."

Suddenly she sat up straight. Another boat was approaching from downstream flying swiftly before the wind. There were three men aboard. When they spied the French boat they veered sharply across the river and hugged the farthest bank. She did not know two of the boat's occupants, but the third? Surely it could not be Fritzi but she was cetain it was. She was about to wave and call out but then thought better of it. The men obviously did not want to speak to the general's boat or even be seen. She had vaguely noticed that Fritzi had been disappearing every so often lately but had paid it no mind since she herself had been doing a lot of disappearing as well. What in the world was he up to?

"Ah, another boat," remarked Jean-Paul. "Do you know them?"

"No, not at all," she lied.

"Oh, the way you started up I thought you recognized them."

"No, I was just surprised to see another boat. The river has been so empty," she prevaricated, hoping he would not feel her rapidly beating heart. She settled back against him and pretended to doze.

They drifted past lush water meadows with a few cows grazing, whereas in years past there had been large herds. They passed once thick forests, now fields of ugly stumps. Tiny riverside hamlets looked nigh deserted. What had been a beautiful riverscape was a scene of desolation.

As the sun reached its zenith Jean-Marie turned the boat in to a small uninhabited island near the left bank of the river. Although long stripped of its large trees, there remained enough saplings and thick brush to provide welcome shade. Despite her black hair Eleonore's complexion was very fair and she could feel it burning under the noonday sun. She cursed herself for not bringing her parasol while admitting that it would have been quite awkward on a boat. She looked forward to collapsing onto soft grass in the leafy shadows. Not only was her skin on fire but her bottom was sore from rocking on the hard bench.

"Here we shall stop and have our dinner," announced Jean-Paul.

"Good," she said, although truly she was more thirsty than hungry. Then she watched with dismay as Jean-Marie threw the anchor onto the bank and the boat fell back some distance from shore. "But how . . . ?"

"Oh, we shall eat right here on board the boat," Jean-Paul replied to her unspoken question. "Then Jean-Marie will go ashore to hunt for a rabbit or two or a fat grouse for our supper. And we, cherie, will be in each other's arms all the rest of the afternoon. You'll like that, won't you?"

"Here? On these hard boards?" she said without much enthusiasm.

"Non, non," he assured her. "There are two bunks in la petite cabin. We shall be quite comfortable."

Eleonore looked at him askance. She had serious doubts about that.

After they had eaten, Jean-Marie took his gun, pulled the boat into the shore, hopped on to the river bank and let the boat drift out again.

"So you see, we are totally alone," said Jean-Paul. "Come." He took her hand and led her down a few steps into the minute cabin. There was an extremely narrow bunk on either side. She noticed gratefully that at least they were cushioned. But once he closed the hatch it was impossible to stand erect. She sat on one of the bunks. In moments it became stifling in the tiny enclosure.

"Oh, please, can't we have a little air?" she pleaded, fanning herself wih her handkerchief.

"But you wanted privacy, cherie," he insisted. "With all your clothes off it won't he so bad. I'll soon make you forget all about it." He started to undress her.

The narrow bunk was barely wide enough for a single person, let alone two. No way could he lie beside her. So the moment she stretched out on the cushions he was on top of her. He did nuzzle her breasts and stroke her thighs but in the cramped space his usual sensual foreplay was very awkward and she did not get the familiar thrill at all. He had barely aroused her when he entered her and it was quickly over. She had gained no satisfaction at all. In fact, she felt faint—and not from passion.

When she sat up, she was decidedly queasy. She quickly donned her shift, threw back the hatch cover and crawled out to the cockpit. She was promptly sick over the side of the boat, losing most of her dinner.

Jean-Paul looked abashed as he joined her. He dipped his handkerchief in the cool river and gently bathed her face which was a sickly white despite the sunburn. "I am sorry, cherie. It was a bit awkward, was it not?"

"A bit," she mumbled.

"And I had hoped it would be so nice here on the river. Perhaps later when it is a bit cooler and you are feeling better, we can try again. I want to please you, too."

"No, Jean-Paul. Take me home. I want to go home," she cried.

"But we have to wait for Jean-Marie."

"Surely the island isn't so big that you can't call him," she insisted.

"But, cherie, this may be our last time together."

"What!" She sat up straight. "What do you mean our last time together?"

"I am being transferred to the battlefront," he replied. "I'm not sure exactly when but I fear it will be very soon."

"No! Oh, Jean-Paul, no," she cried. Then more calmly, "I suppose I should have expected that, but I shall miss you terribly."

"C'est la guerre," he sighed.

After a while the fresh air revived her somewhat although the sun was still intense. Just the thought that this might be their last time together made her receptive to Jean-Paul's caresses and soon she forgot her queasiness for wanting him. But she refused to go back into that stifling cabin where she had felt trapped. She eyed the deepening shade on the bank of the islet.

"Jean-Paul, I simply have to get out of this sun," she declared. "Can't we, too, go ashore into that lovely shade?"

"But you wanted privacy, cherie," he replied.

"Not at the cost of being sick. Besides, you said Jean-Marie will not be back for some time. Please."

Jean-Paul was still naked beside her. When she fondled him in silent entreaty, he was quickly aroused and could deny her nothing. "Very well," he groaned. "If you will let go of me long enough for me to pull the boat in." He promptly did so and slipped into the shallow water still holding the line.

"But our clothes . . . " she said.

"Why put them on when we shall only take them off again? Besides they will get all wet. Take your shift off. As you can see, we have to wade a bit. Come now, cherie. Follow me."

Eleonore had never been naked outside of a house in her whole life—and in broad daylight at that. She hesitated a moment and then threw caution to the winds. She wanted him so badly, wanted him the way they usually made love. She pulled off her shift and carefully slipped into the river. Oh, how good that felt. She stood on the sandy bottom and let the cooling water caress her thighs and belly. She took some in her hands and splashed her burning face. It helped revive her. Jean-Paul took her hand and led her ashore to a mossy, leafy spot in the welcome shade. There they made exquisite love and it was as it had always been.

Afterward as they lay panting in one another's arms, Eleonore was torn between total bliss and deep sadness. She wished they could stay here just like this forever. But soon another vexation impinged on their idyll. As the sun slanted toward the west hordes of bugs swarmed in to attack them. Tiny midges whined in their ears and voracious mosquitoes bit them on every exposed part, which in their state of undress was all of them. Eleonore seemed especially vulnerable and soon red welts appeared all over her fair skin.

"Come quickly into the water," urged Jean-Paul, "that will scare them away and cool the stings."

Eleonore needed no urging. She hunkered down in the cool river until only her head stuck out. Jean-Paul hauled in the boat and boosted her aboard and nimbly followed. He handed her his shirt.

"Use this to dry yourself. I never thought to bring a towel," he said foolishly. "I didn't know we would be going swimming."

She smiled as she dried herself and quickly dressed. At least here they were free from the insects. Or so they thought. But the vicious mosquitoes had their scent now and followed them in droves. They even tried to bite through their clothes. They nearly went crazy swatting the creatures away. It was with great relief that they welcomed Jean-Marie back about a half-hour later.

As soon as they were out on the river with the sail set and scudding before the wind, their attackers disappeared. The sail back to Hoya would have been delightful had Eleonore not had to sit on her hands to keep from scratching the multiple mosquito bites.

The moment she arrived home Eleonore took a dose of the witch's brew and threw herself on her bed. She did not feel well at all but she was sure it was just a touch of sunstroke and would pass by morning.

The next day she suffered the usual after effects of the powerful potion—cramps and diarrhea. But after that she still felt terrible. She touched her forehead. It was burning. Still convinced it was only from the sun, she spent the whole day in bed. Cook sent her some nourishing broth. "Only liquids for a fever," she said, but Eleonore, although she forced herself to drink it, did not want even that. By the next day the fever seemed to have abated but she started trembling with the most violent chills. No matter how she wrapped herself in blankets and featherbeds she could not get warm. The family began to worry.

In a burst of unusual kindness Teddi sent their eldest son Hans to fetch the doctor. The fussy little man came promptly and pronounced, "It is a touch of the ague. I must bleed her."

Eleonore was half delirious but she heard that. "No!" she screamed. "I'll not be bled. Get away from me."

"But Madame Hohnholz," objected the physician, "I must draw out the evil humors that cause the sickness. It is the only way."

"It is not," she insisted. "Leave me alone. 'Tis no but a touch of too much sun."

The man shrugged and said, "Then there is nothing I can do for you, Madame. I bid you good day." And he left.

"And where did you get too much sun?" asked Teddi snidely. "I can't say as I've seen you working in the garden overmuch of late."

"I was out walking the other day and forgot my parasol. I stayed out longer than I planned," she mumbled. "Now let me rest. I'll be better by tomorrow." And she pulled the featherbed over her head.

Teddi thought dejectedly, whatever she had been doing out in the sun, it was not walking. He would like to kill the blasted Frenchman. But if he did, he would lose her, too. And he could not bear that no matter how often she betrayed him.

To everyone's surprise Eleonore was better the next day. Weak, but definitely herself again. After a hearty breakfast, she quickly wrote a tender lovenote to Jean-Paul apprising him of her illness, no doubt from the cold river water after the hot sun, else why would she have a fever one day and chills the next. She hoped he had not succumbed as well and longed to see him at least once more ere he had to leave her.

He sent back a bottle of wine with the messenger and a note assuring her that he was well and could not wait to meet her again. What he did not say was that her symptoms sounded suspiciously like *la malaire* and he had no intention of contracting it from her.

The next day the raging fever engulfed her again. Every muscle in her body ached. She took to her bed in agony. The following day the debilitating chills wracked her and she was forced to admit to herself that this was more than a touch of sun. She sent for Katinka.

"Do not come close to me, child, but run quickly to the old wise-woman. Tell her what is happening to me — first the fever, then the chills, then a brief respite and it starts all over again. She will know what to do. Now run."

Katinka ran.

Afraid to go all the way by herself to the wisewoman's through the wood where the French and many local men under guard were chopping down the trees, she went first to the Klostermühle. There she apprised Dorothea of her mother's illness. She collected Heinrich Anton and hurried on to the wisewoman's cottage. At the same time Dorothea quickly donned bonnet and shawl and set out for Vilsen to be at Eleonore's side.

The old woman met the two children in her usual way with the dog and goat greeting them first. "Now what's this fuss all about?" she asked them.

Katinka quickly delineated her mother's symptoms. "She said you would know what to do."

"Aye. Ja, ja." the old crone nodded knowingly. "That's the tertian fever for sure. And right deadly it is if it ain't cured quickly. Wait." She went back into the hut.

Katinka tried to be brave but she could not hold back the tears. "She said it is deadly. Oh, I don't want my Mama to die." Heinrich Anton took her hand as tenderly as an awkward fourteen-year-old could.

"Mayhap she won't. The old woman said it can be cured," he volunteeered.

"I hope so."

The wisewoman returned carrying a good-sized leather pouch.

"Mother Holle," wept Katinka, "is my Mama going to die?"

"Not if we can help it. Now mind me well. What's in this here bag is the only cure for the tertian fever. Most every time it cures it, if'n a body b'ain't too far gone with the shakes. At times it don't. Ye've got to know that. But ye say she's only had two attacks and them not a week gone."

"That's right," said Katinka, "and she seems well in between."

"That be the nature of the sickness. But don't let that fool you. Each attack will be worse until it carries her off, 'ceptin' she takes this medicine. This here stuff is called Peruvian bark, bein' it comes from a far-off land in America called Peru."

"I thought America was—well—just America," put in Heinrich Anton, always eager to learn. "I didn't know there was another country called Peru."

"Well, in the north it's all called America," the woman explained, "but this comes from the southern part—Spanish America. It comes to us by way of Spain. But now with that ass Napoleon a-fightin' in Spain, we can't get no more. There they call it Jesuit's bark but that name don't set too well hereabouts." She cackled at that. "Anyhow it's mighty powerful medicine fer what your ma's got. I'm a-givin' you all I have 'cause I'll not be around much longer. If'n it cures her, she won't be a-needin' all o' this—mayhap no but a quarter of what's here. But save the rest in case another body has need of it after I'm gone. Mind you keep it in a cool, dark place where no bugs or other vermin can get at it. Now, heed me well. You take a small piece of the bark and grind it up well, taking care to save the juice of it. Mash it into a pastille with its own juice. Should be about a half teaspoon's worth. Give it to her every morning and every eve for a week, ten days if need be—if the chills come back. Mind she drinks plenty of water with it. Keep her well wrapped up during the fever—even if she wants to throw the covers off—that way the chills won't be so bad next day. Strange as it may seem, the chills are more weakening to a body than the fever. Mind, feed her only liquids—good rich broth, cider and the like on the bad days. Make her eat hearty on the good days but don't let her do anything—nothing at all, even if she thinks she feels good. Rest, and only rest." She paused a moment. "Now did ye mind all I told you?"

The children nodded. The old woman made them repeat every word back to her. Katinka recited the instructions precisely.

"Now you, too, Heinrich Anton, just in case this lass gets devoured by a wolf ere she gets home." She cackled at her little joke. Heinrich Anton, too, repeated her orders. "Then off with ye. Frigga will watch over your ma, lass. She ain't about to leave you yet."

The children thanked her profusely and ran almost all the way home.

Dorothea was bathing Eleonore's forehead and trying to keep her covered when Katinka burst into the bed chamber. "Tante Dorchen, old Mother Holle said this would cure Mama." She handed Dorothea the leather bag. Dorothea opened the bag and sniffed. Each piece of cinchona bark was carefully wrapped in tightly woven linen.

"Ah, the Peruvian bark. Thank God," she said. "I was praying she still would have some. It is very precious now, you know. Johann Heinrich has not had any in the spice shop for years—ever since the French came."

"Then you know what it is?" asked Katinka, surprised.

"Ja, ja, I've used it before. The only cure for this malady. But tell me again what the old mother said just to be sure I remember the recipe."

Katinka duly recited the wisewoman's instructions. "She called it tertian fever."

"Ja. It's also known as swamp fever. I wonder where in the world she could have caught it. But never mind that now. Come with me to the kitchen and help me prepare it. It's as well you know how as I cannot be here all the time."

Under Dorothea's and Katinka's careful nursing Eleonore slowly improved. After ten days she pronounced herself well although weak, but Dorothea insisted she continue taking the medicine for a full two weeks. "You know, even when you're fully cured, the tertian fever comes back every seven years—mayhap for the rest of your life," she warned.

"Oh, no," exclaimed Eleonore. "I don't think I could go through that again. I've never been so sick in my life and I'm still so very weak."

"You've got to be prepared for it. Keep this bark in a safe place. It is more precious than gemstones. As for the weakness that will pass in a few weeks. You must eat well and rest, rest, rest."

"Eat well? That's a joke," said Eleonore. "This time of year all we have left in the garden are root vegetables—carrots, turnips and potatoes. We rarely see any meat, so we only have that on Sundays, if that."

"Speaking of meat—while you were delirious your lover sent a whole haunch of venison. Teddi was so furious he wanted to throw the whole thing to the dogs. I was able to prevent him and I made Chris come over and fetch it home. We're smoking it now. It's yours by right but I'll send it over in pieces. It will give you great strength."

"That damn fool," said Eleonore shaking her head. "Bless you, Dorchen. But you must share half of it. If it weren't for you, none of us would have any. I insist."

Dorothea nodded. "Thank you, Elli. And your friend also sent a note. I left it on the nightstand by your bed. Have you seen it?"

Eleonore nodded. "I am afraid to open it. I know what it will say. He is leaving for the battlefront. May be gone already. Tell me, Dorchen," she said hesitantly, "when I was delirious, did I babble overmuch?"

"Some, but don't worry. The few times Teddi was there we managed to keep you quiet. Do you want to tell me about it? Where were you that you managed to catch the tertian fever? It may help to get it off your mind."

212

Eleonore broke down and wept. Then the whole story of the river trip came out. "That man Jean-Marie, I don't trust him at all," she sobbed. "I am sure it was he who brought us the bad luck."

Dorothea wondered. "Perhaps," she said, "but I rather think it was the bad air on the island surrounded as it is by the river. It's too bad you went ashore."

"But I was burning up with the sun."

Dorothea shrugged. "Well, it's over and done with now and you are getting better. Try now to forget the whole thing and build up your strength."

A few days later Eleonore was sitting in the garden. Would she ever get her strength back? The shadows were lengthening and there was a nip of fall in the air. The late September sun was pallid and felt good on her fragile body. No chance of sunburn now. On top of everything else her monthly flow had begun for which she was grateful but there was no doubt that it weakened her further. She felt listless, unable to bring herself to do anything. Well, they all said rest, so rest she would. But it was beginning to annoy her—this inability to do anything. She longed for her former vigor.

Fritzi, coming in from the stable, found her there. "Dearest Elli, I've been looking for you. I have a present for you." He lowered his voice to a whisper. "But don't tell, Teddi." He dropped down beside her and handed her a small bag.

She looked at him askance. She took the bag and sniffed. "Coffee!" she exclaimed. "Is it real coffee? Wherever did you get it?"

"It is real coffee," he replied, "and only for you. There is only enough for mayhap a dozen cups in there. It is very precious as you know, so I don't want you sharing it with him—or anyone else for that matter."

"I know how precious it is. But surely he will smell it brewing. No one could miss the delicious smell of real coffee brewing."

"Ach," said Fritzi, "how often does he come in for afternoon coffee? Rarely, that I know of. Don't have it for breakfast then. Save it for your coffee and kuchen. If he should notice it, tell him the old hag sent it as medicine to perk you up. That would scare him off."

She laughed. "Fritzi, that's so kind of you and I thank you. But tell me, where did you manage to come by it?"

He put a finger to his lips and shook his head. " 'Tis better if you don't know," he said mysteriously.

Her thoughts flew back to the day on the river. "Fritzi," she asked, "what were you doing out on the river that day? You know I saw you but I said nothing. And who were those two men with you? I didn't recognize them."

"So you did see me. I was afraid that you had and I appreciate your not saying anything. The other two were friends of mine from Bücken. You wouldn't know them. They own the boat. We are partners in a small enterprise."

"Enterprise?" Her thoughts jumped rapidly ahead to rumors she had heard of rampant smuggling ever since the embargo on English goods. The French had established a solid west-to-east line of customs agents across northern Hannover and the line ran right through Bruchhausen and Hoya.

"Enterprise?" she asked again. "Fritzi," she whispered, "are you and your friends smuggling?" She looked down at the bag of coffee beans in her lap.

"Well, er—no—not exactly," he demurred. "It is just a small trading enterprise, but it's best you don't mention it to anyone."

Trading, indeed. She knew he was lying. "Oh, Fritzi, do be careful."

"Don't worry. I'm always careful. Enjoy your coffee." He got up and left her in the garden.

But Eleonore did worry.

The fact that her monthly courses had come and gone did not go unnoticed by Teddi. He suddenly was very attentive, almost kind. And Eleonore desperately missed Jean-Paul's beautiful loving. She determined to store away in her memory the recollection of that lovely idyll but she admitted that she was the type of person who could not do without a man's attentions for very long. So she resigned herself to allowing Teddi back into her bed. To her surprise he came more than willingly.

"I think it is time you had another child," he remarked casually.

"Oh, no. I don't think I am strong enough for that yet," she objected.

"It will strengthen you. You need something to keep you busy instead of moping about the house all day."

She seemed to have no willpower anymore. So she acquiesced. He tried to be kind and very gentle but it was not the same as she had experienced with Jean-Paul. But at least it satisfied her immediate longings. Since Teddi chose to spend the night in their bed for a change she could not immediately take the foul potion.

In the middle of the night when she was sure he slept Eleonore crept out of bed and looked for the bottle. It was not in its usual place. She felt around every piece of furniture, even on the floor but it was nowhere to be found. She supposed someone had moved it while she was ill. She dared not light a candle for fear of waking him. She climbed back into bed and hoped morning would not be too late.

At first light she was up again frantically rummaging through chests and drawers and the wardrobe.

"Are you looking for something, dear wife?" came a voice from the bed. She was so startled she turned white. "I threw it out whilst you were feverish. I had no objection to your dosing yourself with the witch's brew whilst you were screwing your French lover. I certainly wanted no Frenchman's get foisted on me. But now there's no need for it anymore, is there?"

Eleonore collapsed in a heap on the floor and wept.

Teddi got up and peed noisily into the chamberpot. He picked her up and carried her back to the bed. "I still have need of you," he said and took her quickly without any foreplay. This time she was not satisfied at all.

By November she knew she was pregnant again.

7

Fritzi peered through the dark as the little boat glided upstream. By November it was cold and they had to watch for ice forming along the edge of the river. Ever since they had been seen by Eleonore that time they had decided to make their monthly expedition at night. It could be a bit dangerous, but his companions from Bücken, Erich and Ernst, were river rats. They knew every stretch of the Weser by heart.

Suddenly he exclaimed, "What is my horse doing there? I left him in your barn." And a moment later in a whisper, "Turn the boat around, Erich! Don't go in. There's a French soldier there. No, wait. There's three of them. Ach, Gott!"

Ernst came to look. "Gott im Himmel! He's right. Swing back across the river, Erich, while I douse the sail. Hopefully they'll not have seen us yet."

"What do we do now?" asked Fritzi.

"There's another place downstream aways where we can put in. I don't think they'll know about it. If it's clear, we'll put you ashore and offload the stuff. Then we'll sail merrily home as if we were just out for a night of fishing. They can't arrest us if there's nothing on the boat. Now keep a sharp lookout."

"What about my horse?" Fritzi was very nervous now. He had known it was a dangerous game they were playing but everything had gone so well on previous trips he thought his fears were unfounded. But now they were very real. The French were merciless with lawbreakers—especially smugglers.

"We'll get him to you later. For now we're just minding him for our sick cousin."

"And my share of the—er—goods?"

"That, too," said Ernst. "For now, let's just hope we can get out of this with a whole skin."

Erich let the boat drift slowly downstream and then angled it once more back to the left bank. Fritzi continued to peer into the darkness although he had no idea what he was looking for. In a while Ernst joined him again on the bow.

"Lay out a bit, Erich," he instructed his brother. "We don't want to get stuck in those reeds. It should be soon." In a few moments he said, "Ah, there it is. Hold a bit. All right, in you go, Erich."

Erich turned the boat sharply and they entered a tiny creek that flowed through the swamp. Fritzi would never have seen it in a thousand years. He marvelled at their knowledge of the river. Both brothers were poling now as the creek meandered hither and yon. About fifty ells—he supposed Napoleon would call them meters now—up the creek the men gave a mighty shove and let the boat beach itself on the shore. Ahead of them, hidden in the tall reeds, Fritzi spied a tiny hut.

"Fisherman's shack," explained Ernst. "We've used it before."

"I'm afraid some of our goods will smell a little fishy after storing it here," added Erich, "but our customers are so desperate they won't mind."

"I see," said Fritzi. "How long will you have to leave it here?"

"Can't say. Until the area's clear of Frenchies and we can bring the wagon down," said Erich.

"Might be a while," added Ernst, "if they're suspicious of us and it sure looks like they are. Now, come on, let's offload this stuff and hide it away."

The three men worked in silence for about an hour carrying the contraband. The shack looked as though it would fall down any minute but Fritzi noticed it had a stout door with a heavy padlock. Erich had the key. They moved bolts of silk and fine English woolens, bags of coffee beans and tins of tea and spices, even some bottles of rum and Scotch whiskey. There was even a haunch of beef which they hung on a hook.

"Will that meat keep?" asked Fritzi.

Ernst shrugged. "It's cold enough now, it should keep for a while. We'll move that first. But if we can't, we'll just have to take the loss." He shrugged again. "It happens."

"Do you think we can get the stuff out afore Christmas?" asked Fritzi. "I was hoping to give my sister-in-law a length of that blue silk for Christmas."

"Depends on the Frenchies," said Ernst. "We'll know more when we see what they have to say."

"And don't you get any notions of coming here yourself," warned

Erich. "We made a bargain and we'll stand by it. You can trust us."

Fritzi was not so sure but he had no choice. When they finished unloading and storing, Ernst instructed him, "See you that path beyond the hut? Follow it carefully so's you don't fall in the swamp. It'll take you eventually to the road some miles north of Bücken. But mind you, stay off the roads. Cut across the fields. The Frenchies would surely question a lone man at this hour of the night wandering far from home. Go now. We'll send to you when it's safe."

Fritzi stumbled along the winding path for what seemed like forever. There was no moon to light his way, which was why they had chosen this night, although the stars were brilliant—and cold. But he did not dare to look up too often for fear he would miss the path. Occasionally he did and his foot sank into the mire along the edges. Once he almost lost his shoe. He had to kneel down and fish it out of the muck. But muddy or no, he was not about to go barefoot. Not in this weather. It was definitely getting colder and his wet knees and feet did not help. He had a warm cloak which he held tightly around him but cursed himself for a fool at leaving his hat and gloves in his saddlebags. They had seemed to be naught but encumbrances on the boat. Never did he think he would be traipsing for miles through swamps and fields at—what time was it? He was sure it was well past midnight. And walking, mind you. He who would never walk a mile if he could ride. He struggled on.

At long last the ground seemed somewhat firmer underfoot and in moments he burst through the tall grass onto a road. This had to be the Bücken to Hoya road. Just to be sure, he looked up to his right to find Polaris. Fritzi did not know much about the stars but the boatmen had taught him that much. Ja, there it was—right where it should be. Then he stood awestruck at what else he saw. Brilliant waves of red, green and white, powerfully undulating in the northern sky. The Northern Lights. Fritzi was not superstitious. He had scoffed at the old wives' tales that the Aurora portended some momentous event. Yet he felt gripped by the tremendous power of the display. A chill ran up his spine—and not from the cold. And he was more afraid than he had ever been.

That suddenly jolted him to his senses as he realized that he was standing, totally exposed, in the middle of the road. He wondered how far north of Bücken he was. Not too close to the French garrison at Hoya, he hoped. He reasoned that if he headed directly west he would eventually come to some road or path that he recognized as leading into Vilsen. He quickly crossed the road, climbed over a fence and entered the field oppo-

218

site. A pasture, evidently. But long deserted. Although the grass was now brown and sere from frost, it was too high to have been grazed in recent months. So, no animals or cowflops to worry about. Although grateful, he felt a momentary twinge of pity for the farmer. The French must have taken all his stock. He wondered who it was. No, he was too far from home to know anyone here. But soon, soon he would come to a friendly house and then home. He plodded on. Over fences, through grain stubble, more pasture but nothing familiar yet.

At last he came upon a narrow farm lane that he thought he recognized. If he were right, it should come out on the Vilsen road somewhere near Bruchmühlen. Then a horrifying thought struck him. He was a fugitive. He could not go home. That was the first place the French would look. Where then? If he was close to Bruchmühlen, then it would be logical to continue on to the Klostermühle. Chris and Dorothea would hide him for a few days. But then, he did not want to make any trouble for those good people. But mayhap they would have some ideas, some advice. He could not think of anything else to do. So he kept going.

When he finally reached the Vilsen road, he heaved a sigh of relief. Now, at least, he knew exactly where he was. He turned left, away from Vilsen. It was only a short distance to the lane that led to Heiligenberg. He wanted to run, for this was a main thoroughfare, but he was too exhausted. But who would be up and about at this hour of the morn? It had to be at least three or four of the clock. He slipped into the lane leading to the Klostermühle. Although the woods had been stripped of all large trees, the woodsmen had left enough underbrush to afford him some shelter. He was so weary that it never occurred to him that everyone at the mill would still be sound asleep. He went around to the stable. Securely locked. A dog started barking. Oh, no, he thought, Chris will shoot me ere he knows who it is. He hurried away from the stable, ready to identify himself if anyone emerged from the house. Finally the dog subsided. All was quiet and no one came. He spied a hayrick in the pasture across the millstream, probably winter fodder for the only cow they had left. He dug a little nest for himself, wrapped his cloak securely around him and was sound asleep in an instant.

It was Heinrich Anton who found Fritzi in the morning. He was hunting hen's eggs or he would never have gone over to the hayrick. He ran back to the house.

"Mama! Papa!" he cried. "Fritzi Hohnholz is sleeping in the pasture and I couldn't wake him."

"Fritzi? What in God's name is he doing here?" bellowed Chris. "Is he drunk?"

"I don't know. He didn't smell like it."

"Is he hurt?" asked Dorothea. "Is he dead?"

"Nay, nay. He's snoring but he's all muddy and covered with grass and burrs."

"Fine. That's just what I need. Burrs in the hay," growled Chris. "A great way to start the day, eh?"

"Now Chris, calm down," said Dorothea. "He may be hurt—or in trouble."

"Trouble, more like. Well, I suppose there's nothing for it but to see what's amiss, what foolish prank he's been into now." He stood up from the breakfast table and threw on his cloak. "Come with me, Heinrich Anton. I may need your help."

Together they went out to the pasture. Fritzi was still snoring blissfully. Chris looked carefully at his state of disarray. The man was filthy but there were no obvious signs of any injury—or of drunkenness. He was plainly exhausted. Chris hated to disturb him but they could not leave him here. He would soon freeze and then they would have a major problem. Chris gently shook him by the shoulders.

Fritzi jumped, startled, and screamed. Once he got his eyes open and saw who it was, he settled back in the hay and relaxed. "Oh, Chris, you scared me. I was waiting for you and I must have fallen asleep."

"You—were—waiting—for—me? And why were you waiting for me at this hour of the morning?"

"Well, I—er—I need some advice and—and—a place to hide."

"A place to hide?" exclaimed Chris, "and you chose me—us?"

"I couldn't think of any place else to go," said Fritzi forlornly. "I knew you would help me."

Chris was furious but he was too innately kind to refuse the poor knave. "I think you'd best come into the house first and get yourself cleaned up. Then over breakfast you can tell me what mischief you've gotten yourself into. And I'll want the truth—all of it."

"Thank you, Chris," Fritzi mumbled as he scrambled out of the hay and followed them into the house.

Dorothea was shocked to see the usually dapper Fritzi looking like a ragamuffin.

"Don't fuss over him," warned Chris. "Whatever he's got himself into is his own doing. After he's cleaned up, give him something to break his fast and then we'll listen to his latest escapade. I fear me this one may be serious."

Over breakfast Fritzi hemmed and hawed. "We—er, that is, I was just trying to help people."

Immediately that did not ring true. Chris had never known vain, self-centered Fritzi to help anyone, unless it be Elli, whom he adored. While far kinder and less thoughtless of others than his half-brother Teddi, nevertheless they were of an ilk.

"Help people, my ass," growled Chris. "Out with it. The truth now—all of it, or I'll not lift a hand to help you—if I even can."

Fritzi put his head in his hands. He had not expected this from gentle Chris. In moments he poured out the whole story. How he had put up the initial funds and the brothers from Bücken had supplied the boat; how once a month they had run far out into the North Sea to meet the British ship that lay there; how they had sold the contraband at exorbitant prices to eager buyers all over the county.

Although Chris was shocked, somehow he was not surprised. He had heard that rampant smuggling was quite commonplace and that most of the local people were quite willing to protect their suppliers, such was their hatred of the French or so great was their desire for the luxury items. Fritzi was not the only one. And the greatest danger was not being caught in the act but of jealous or envious neighbors. Obviously someone had tattled on Fritzi's partners.

"So the last place you can go is home," said Chris succinctly. "Don't think for a moment that they can't trace that horse of yours right quickly."

"I realize that," said Fritzi.

"And you can't stay here either. They'll surely know of the close relationship between our families."

Fritzi's face fell. "But where can I go? I daren't trust anybody else. I've got to let Elli know where I am. She'll worry. And what if my friends send to me that it is safe to come for my share? It's not that I don't trust them but—but . . ."

"I wouldn't trust them either," said Chris, "but that's not important now. We'll take care of Elli. The less she knows, the better. But what to do with you? Let me think a moment."

Chris was obviously turning several alternatives over in his mind. Fritzi waited. He was growing more and more nervous. If he could not stay here, he would really be a fugitive running from one hiding place to another. He tried to convince himself that maybe the soldiers had just

221

thought it a lost horse. But he knew immediately that that was a vain hope. Oh, why did I ever get tangled up in this? I really wanted to help people — and the money was fantastic, more that he had ever earned in the family business which was practically non-existent now between Teddi's neglect and Napoleon's embargo. Yes, it was the money, he had to admit. If the French were ever driven out, he intended to buy his brother out. He wanted to impress Elli. And, God have mercy, he wanted his brother's wife. Thou shalt not covet, whispered a tiny voice at the back of his mind. He put his head in his hands again to hide his tears while he awaited Chris' decision.

At last Chris spoke. "I can think of only one place where you would be relatively safe for a little while at least, until we see how the wind blows." Fritzi looked up expectantly. "The Forest House."

"The Forest House up on the Heiligenberg? But—but isn't that a royal preserve?"

"And what royalty do we have now except Napoleon himself who is off fighting in Italy somewhere?"

"That's right."

"Some of the French officers used to use it occasionally for hunting but now with most of the forest gone the hunting is no longer any good. No one has come there in over a year. You certainly don't expect mad George III or the Prince Regent would be allowed to come here. They never set foot in Hannover even long before anyone ever heard of Napoleon."

Even Fritzi had to smile at that. "So it stands empty?" he asked.

"Just about. There is one ancient watchman who is blind in one eye and can't see out of the other and is half deaf to boot. I don't think he even has a dog anymore, although I'm not sure of that. But he does faithfully make his rounds. You'll have to rise very early and make up the bed neatly just as you found it and scoot out into the woods while he makes his rounds. But then the rest of the time the place is yours. You'll soon learn his habits. He never deviates from his routine. They used to keep a well-stocked larder but I don't know what state it would be in now. We'll send food with you. The children play up there often so the old man knows them well. He would think nothing amiss were he to see Heinrich Anton. I'll keep the little ones away while you are there."

"Chris, how can I ever thank you?" said Fritzi. "It sounds perfect. How long dare I stay there?"

"As I say, let's see how the wind blows."

That evening when they knew the old watchman was settled by his fire in his cottage, three of them crept up to the Forest House. Heinrich Anton led. He knew the house better than his father.

"The door is never locked," he explained, "because royal places are sacrosanct. Who would ever dare rob one — or so the thinking goes." Once inside he lit a candle.

"Do we dare?" asked Fritzi.

"For now, ja. The old man can't see it from where he is. But I would not make a habit of it. I'll show you the back way out, too, just in case."

Fritzi was delighted with his refuge. He quickly learned the old watchman's routine and no dog was in evidence. He was up with the birds and retired with them. He dared not light a candle for Heinrich Anton had warned that sometimes lovers from the countryside came here of an evening, although that was unlikely in this weather. He tried a different bed every night and luxuriated in the deep featherbeds and pillows, in the pristine fine linen sheets and silken coverlets. He neatly made the bed every morning. He investigated the larder but was disappointed in that. Only a few hams and some shrivelled onions hung there. But Dorothea kept him well supplied with food. His only lack was the warmth of a fire and this he was afraid to attempt. The old caretaker might not be able to see or hear but he would surely smell smoke. But by and large he was quite satisfied with his royal hideaway.

On the third day Heinrich Anton brought him a note from Eleonore. They had not told her where he was, only that he was safe and that it would be dangerous for her to know more. She sent her love and promised him her prayers. At the end of the week he received another note. His horse had mysteriously reappeared in the stable during the night and in the saddlebags they had found, besides his hat and gloves, a bolt of the most beautiful peacock blue silk she had ever seen. Was it his? What should they do with it?

Fritzi gritted his teeth. He had meant it to be a surprise Christmas gift for her. Not only that but he had intended to give her only a gown-length of the precious cloth and sell the rest. He also now knew that his erstwhile partners were cheating him and had helped themselves to his share of the rest of the contraband goods. He fumed with helplessness. His first thought was to fetch his horse and ride straight to Bücken to confront them. No, that was stupid. He could not be seen in Vilsen. Mayhap Chris would lend him his horse. No, he never would. In his fury he knocked over a bedside lamp and the glass shattered all over the floor.

The next morning Eleonore sat in the parlor pondering the blue silk. Where had he come by it? For whom was it intended? Did he have a female friend of whom she knew nothing? These frequent all-night absences certainly hinted at a love affair although she definitely had seen no indication of it. Not from Fritzi. She felt a twinge of jealousy and quickly chided herself. What right had she, a married woman and pregnant, to be jealous of her own brother-in-law and he a young man over fifteen years her junior?

She heard the doorbell jangle. A moment later the frightened maid came in followed by a French officer.

"Madame," said the maid, "I told the captain you were indisposed, that you did not wish to see him but he insisted."

The man pushed the maid aside. "Madame *will* see me," he said. It was Jean-Marie.

Eleonore gasped. "What are you doing here?"

He leered. "I've come to make you a proposition. You may leave," he said to the maid. When the girl hesitated, he growled, "Get out," and shooed her out the door.

"And you can get out, too," snapped Eleonore. "I have nothing to say to you nor do I intend to listen to any proposition you might have."

"I think you will, Madame Putaine," he sneered.

"Don't you call me that," she screamed. "Get out of here."

He moved closer to her. She backed against a table. "We have proof that your brother-in-law Friedrich Hohnholz is part of a ring of smugglers in defiance of the Emperor's embargo edict. We have apprehended his partners and seek only him to complete the case for the crown."

"What?" she gasped and staggered against the table.

"However . . . ." His arm snaked around her waist as he bent her back over the table. His other hand grasped her breast. "However," he repeated, "if you were to be nice to me, the charges against him might be dropped."

"Unhand me, you filthy pig," she cried. The initial shock wore off and her brain started to function again. "You say, *might* be dropped. I wouldn't trust you for a copper penny. I hate you. Leave me be."

"You weren't so finicky with Jean-Paul, as I recall."

"Well, I am with you. Whatever was between Jean-Paul and me is in the past and not to be besmirched by the likes of you. Besides I am enceinte."

He backed away for a moment and she quickly slipped out of his embrace and fell into a chair.

224

"Is it his?" he asked.

"No," she snapped. "It is my dear husband's. We are quite reconciled."

"I see," he said deliberately. "Then it matters not to you that your husband's brother could hang."

"It matters not in the least," she lied. "You said you are still seeking him. Then seek. You will never find him." And she prayed she was right.

He grabbed her hand. "Where is he?" he hissed.

"I have no idea," she replied. "I pay no mind to his comings and goings."

He twisted her arm. "Where is he?"

"I told you I know not." She gritted her teeth against the pain. He twisted harder. She screamed and almost fainted.

Heinrich Anton always entered the Hohnholz house by the back door. He met Katinka in the kitchen. "Hello, love," he said cheerily. "I have a note for . . . "

"Sshh." She put a finger to her lips. "There is a French officer in the parlor with her."

"Do you think he is looking for Fritzi?" asked Heinrich Anton.

"I don't know. I hadn't thought of that," she replied. "Oh, I hope not."

"Let's go listen."

"But Heinrich Anton, that would be eavesdropping."

"I know. Come on." He took her by the hand and dragged her down the hall to the parlor door. Fortunately they did not overhear the beginning of the conversation but as they stood outside the door they heard him ask Fritzi's whereabouts and Eleonore's denial. Then they heard her scream.

Katinka cound not restrain herself. She burst into the room, Heinrich Anton close behind. "Mama, Mama!" she cried. "Did that—that man hurt you?"

Jean-Marie had quickly released her arm and pretended to be bowing over her hand. Eleonore, though white and shaken, recovered her aplomb and said, "Ah, children, come in. Come it. It is good to see you. Captain Lescaux was just taking his leave."

Jean-Marie straightened up. "And I suppose these two will lie just as much as you. Who are they?"

"My daughter and her friend," said Eleonore.

The captain stood in front of Katinka. "Do you know the whereabouts of your uncle Friedrich?" Katinka was dumb with fright. She shook her head, wide-eyed and tongue-tied. He turned to Heinrich Anton. "And you?"

Heinrich Anton bravely replied, "I don't even know who you are talking about."

Jean-Marie looked back at Eleonore. "Bitch," he hissed. "You'll pay. I'll see that you do." And he stalked out of the house.

Early in December Chris sent Heinrich Anton out into the woods to see if the woodsmen had left anything at all that might be used for a Christmas tree. "Even if it's small, by God, we'll have some Christmas cheer in this house despite Napoleon. I hope all his ships sink."

Heinrich Anton smiled. It was an ongoing theme with his father and his godfather and almost everyone else around Vilsen. "I'll find one, Papa, never fear. And if I can find two, I'll mark the other for Tante Elli. Don't you think?"

"Quite right. Teddi hasn't set foot in the woods in years. I doubt he even knows—or cares—what is going on. It was always Fritzi and the younger children who come for their tree."

Heinrich Anton set out. The forest close by the mill had long been stripped. The choppers and sawyers were working their way up towards the old wisewoman's cottage. Might even be there already. He wandered back and forth across the path seeking even the tiniest fir tree. So far nothing. He could hear the racket the woodsmen were making and then a dog barking. Oh my, he thought, they *are* there already. When he came upon the scene he noticed the two armed guards, one at either end of the strip of forest where the men were working. Not all the Vilsen men who had been forced to help the French were willing. Slave labor, they called it. Heinrich Anton stopped for a moment to watch. Yes, they were cutting right next to the old woman's cottage. Her little dachshund was barking frantically. Oh, please don't hurt him, Heinrich Anton thought. As he watched, the door of the hut opened and Donar, the goat, ran out. Whether she had ordered the animal or not, he could not tell, but the goat put its head down and charged directly at the nearest guard. The guard reacted quickly. As the boy watched in horror, he raised his gun and shot the animal through the heart. Immediately the old woman ran out and threw herself down on the goat, all the while screaming, "Murderer! Murderer! May Donar strike you dead. Donar's curse be on you and your foul Emperor and your children forever and ever." She collapsed against the dead goat.

Heinrich Anton froze in horror for a moment and then he ran to help her. She lay gasping, hugging and kissing the goat. He put his arm around her. "Come, Mother Holle, there is nothing you can do. Donar is dead. Let me help you back into the house."

"Donar will outlive the French Emperor and all his minions," she gasped. "His curse is on them now." She looked up then and recognized the lad. "Heinrich Anton, don't trouble yourself for this old woman." She seemed to be fighting for breath. "I am going now." He heard a strange rattling sound in her throat. She struggled for a few more words. "Tell your Ma—to take—all—all my—my things. She'll know—what . . ." A harsh gasp emerged from her mouth as spittle ran down her chin. She collapsed against the goat. Heinrich Anton knew without feeling her chest that she was gone. He knelt by her side and wept.

He did not know what to do. No way was he yet strong enough to carry her into the house. He hoped they would not harm her whilst he ran to fetch his father. A fury he had never known in his young life rose up in him. "You murdering bastard," he cried to the soldier. "Now you've killed her, too. A harmless old lady. And for what? The goat wasn't even a billie goat. It was a nannie goat she kept for milk. She would never have hurt you, you stupid fool." The guard turned away pretending not to hear. But he was a little nervous. A curse was a curse. Mayhap he should not have been so quick to shoot. But how was he to know a billie goat from a nannie goat when it was charging him? He was from the slums of Paris.

Heinrich Anton stood up. "I am going to fetch my father now," he yelled at the guard, "so that we can give her a proper burial. Don't you dare touch her—or the goat. Her curse is on you now. Anyone comes near them does so at peril of his life." The guard looked away. But all the Vilsen men heard. And while none dared lift his head from his tasks, they secretly admired the lad's courage.

By the time Heinrich Anton returned with his father and mother the woodsmen had moved further up the hill. The great trees lay stacked waiting for the wagons to come and haul them away. The guard was nowhere to be seen. To his great surprise—and relief—the old crone and the goat lay exactly as he had left them. He had fully expected the goat to be gone. It would have made a fine Christmas dinner for several families. The curse must have worked—at least on the French. The Vilsen folk would have had too much respect for the wisewoman to have disturbed her. The little dog Baldur was running around in circles, barking frantically, trying to nuzzle his mistress back to life. At least a half dozen of the great ravens

227

were perched on the rooftop, cawing loudly, and more kept coming.

"Wotan's ravens," remarked Heinrich Anton.

Chris nodded. "Ja, and they'll soon tear her to pieces. Help me to get her inside. Both of them. That goat will make several good dinners."

"Papa, how can you say that? She put a curse on it."

"Ach, that was just for the benefit of the gullible French. Meat is too scarce nowadays to leave it for the ravens or the wolves. Don't worry, son. I'm sure if she were able to say so it would have her blessing not her curse." Chris picked up the frail, withered old woman and carried her into the cottage. Heinrich Anton and Dorothea took the goat by the legs and hauled it inside as well. The little dog nearly went crazy as he followed them in.

Chris shut the door against any brazen ravens. It was suddenly very dark. He hunted around until he found flint and tinder and the stub of a candle which he lit. He sat down at the table. "Now what do we do with her?" he asked of no one in particular.

"We've got to bury her," said Heinrich Anton, sitting in the other chair.

Dorothea had brought two large baskets. She had been so pleased when she had heard of the wisewoman's last will. She had learned a great deal about herbs, simples and medicines from her own mother, Lise, although she knew she could never begin to approach the vast knowledge of centuries that the old woman must have had. She started packing the many jars and bottles, boxes and bags in her baskets. Most were clearly labelled although in strange cryptograms she would have to figure out later. Some were not and those she made careful note of where on the shelves they were. Harmless simples would be on the lowest shelf, poisons on the uppermost.

"I'd like to take her into Vilsen for a proper Christian burial for she was well loved," Chris was saying. "But was she a Christian?"

"I don't really think so," replied Heinrich Anton. "She was always talking abou the old gods."

"I believe she was a Christian," put in Dorothea, "but she wanted to be sure the people never forgot their ancient Saxon heritage. And she did have the sight. I know that."

"She certainly did," added Heinrich Anton. "Katinka and I have heard her talking to Wotan's ravens many a time. And the pastor didn't like her. He is always calling her a pagan and warning people to stay away from her. Not that anyone paid him any mind. But he might refuse to let her be buried in the churchyard."

"There's that," agreed Dorothea. "You're no doubt right."

"Then I think the best thing is to bury her right here," decided Chris. "The ground can't be too frozen yet in her little garden. Oh, but wait. Does she have any kin?"

"None that I know of," replied Dorothea. "I've never seen or heard her mention any and I've known her most of my life. She often bemoaned the fact that she had no daughter to pass her knowledge on to. That's why I'm doubly honored that she chose me."

"Then that's settled," said Chris. "Let's go home and have a bite to eat. After dinner we'll come back with shovels and lay her to rest."

"What about the dog?" asked Heinrich Anton.

"You might as well take him home, too, else he'll starve or the wolves will get him."

Word of the wisewoman's demise spread rapidly through the village and the countryside and almost every morning there was to be found a bouquet of fall flowers, a wreath of pine and holly or some other loving tribute on her grave.

Fritzi, meanwhile, unaware of all this, realized that he would soon have to leave his luxury accommodations. Although he had meticulously cleaned up all the glass and had disposed of the broken remainder of the lamp's chimney, he had watched with dismay as the watchman noticed the lamp. The old man mumbled to himself that it could not be squirrels or there would be a mess. A thief must have broken in.

Fritzi realized his mistake. He should have left the mess and let the squirrels take the blame. He spent the rest of the day hiding in the ravine near the Sacred Spring, the only section of the forest that had not been clear cut. There Heinrich Anton eventually found him, shivering and discouraged.

"I am going home," he announced. "Surely the hue and cry has died down by now."

"Nay, nay," said Heinrich Anton. "The French captain—the nasty one—has been badgering Tante Elli to reveal your whereabouts. 'Tis well that she does not know."

"Has he harmed her?" Fritzi exclaimed.

"Not that we could see, but he was threatening."

"Then that is all the more reason for me to go home. Teddi will never protect her. She needs me."

"Don't be a fool. That's the worst thing you could do. But there is another place for you to go." And Heinrich Anton told him how the old crone had died. "It's the perfect place for you. No one will dare to go there except Mama and I. You will be safer than here."

Reluctantly Fritzi agreed. That evening when the woodsmen had all gone home, he followed Heinrich Anton up to the tiny hut. He did not much relish staying in a witch's cottage. Further, he had been spoiled by more than two weeks in the opulent Forest House. He vowed it would not be for long. He was determined to be home by Christmas, and the French be damned. He wanted to see Elli's eyes light up when he told her the blue silk was hers. He wanted to hold her in his arms—even for a brief brotherly embrace. And Teddi be damned.

Fritzi felt more trapped than ever in the witch's cottage. The place stank. With the door shut, it was pitch dark, even in the daytime. He could not go outside by day as the woodsmen were still working nearby. He dared not light a candle even after dark because every night various folk, usually women, came to visit the grave. The straw bedding was damp and musty and he was sure it was full of fleas and lice. Only when Dorothea came and made a big show of lighting a fire did he have any warmth and hoped the embers would last the night.

On Christmas Eve he made up his mind. He was going home no matter what. Surely the French would not be vigilant this night. They had already searched the house and stable and ascertained that he was not there. If he could only get through the village without being seen, he would be safer home than anywhere else.

Although darkness fell about four o'clock this time of year, he dared not leave too early. People would still be abroad. He decided to wait until well after suppertime when most folk would be in their homes celebrating the holy eve. He slowly ate the cold supper Dorothea had left for him that morning. He was so nervous he could hardly swallow. He made sure the remains of the fire was safely out. No sense setting the shack on fire and set the whole woods a-burning. At last he shut the door behind him for the last time.

Fritzi did not know the forest well. He had never explored them as a child the way Elli had. He did not even know the shortcut to the mill, he had always ridden his horse on the roads. And he wanted to avoid the Klostermühle at all costs. The Bergmann would surely scold him and send him back. He set out along the first path he found. He did have the sense to remember what the boatmen had taught him. He looked up and found? Polaris. Vilsen lay directly north of Heiligenberg. That much he knew. So he reasoned if he travelled directly north he would eventually come to some part of the village. But the ancient, centuries-old paths did not go in a straight line. They meandered and twisted about according to the topography or followed even more ancient animal trails. He soon realized he was hopelessly lost.

When he came to a section of virgin forest he knew he had to be wrong. The French had been clear-cutting *up* from Vilsen. They would never have left a stand this large in between. And worse, when he looked up the trees were so dense he could not see his guiding North Star. He retraced his steps back to the last open space and to his shock he was right back at the witch's hut. He must have been going in circles. In frustration he sat down on a log and wept.

Soon he was shivering from the cold. He chided himself, what kind of a man are you, weeping like a woman? He simply would have to take the path by the mill and hope he could sneak past without rousing the dogs. When with relief he finally saw the mill ahead of him, he skirted it on the far side of the millpond. As he passed he could hear the family singing Christmas carols. A wave of nostalgia swept over him and he almost broke down again. He trudged on hoping he could find the short-cut to Vilsen. Dorchen, Elli, even the children knew it by heart, but he had been too proud to go that route, preferring to ride his horse. At last he came to a well-trodden path. That had to be it. He looked up. Yes, there was Polaris and the Big Dipper straight ahead leading him on.

The next problem confronting him would be how to sneak through the streets of the village without being seen. Well, he'd worry about that when he got there. Just let him get out of these woods. But the thought made him nervous and his belly started to cramp. Suddenly his bowels turned to water and he had to quickly squat down to relieve himself. He tried to clean himself as best he could with oak leaves. Oh Lord, now I'll stink. But then he reminded himself that he had not had a bath in over a month. I no doubt stink and am probably lousy as well. What will Elli think? Fool, he thought, just get yourself home first. He trudged on.

At long last he came to the large open field on the hill above the village where the town fathers were thinking of putting a new cemetery. And there in the distance was the top of the church tower. Joyfully he ran down the hill and then stopped abruptly when he came to Gartenweg, the first lane of the village. There was Johann Justus Bruns' house. He could hear them celebrating. He looked about. No one was in sight. Cautiously he crept down the nearest alley and arrived at the tiny square that led to the church. Should he cut through the churchyard? No, people would be arriving soon for the Christmas Eve service, although he had no idea of the time. He chose another alley on the far side of Bergmann's new house. It was steep and the cobblestones not properly laid. He was so tired he stumbled on the rough stones several times.

At the bottom he stopped and peeped cautiously arond the wall of the nearest house. Only four houses down the street was home but this was the main thoroughfare of Vilsen. Diagonally off to the left the inn was brightly lit. He could hear loud roistering and much drunken frivolity but no one was in the street. He looked the other way. All clear. He ran. He bypassed the front door and ducked into the alley leading to the stable just as he heard horses' hooves behind him. He plastered himself against the wall as a gig full of revellers swept past. He hoped thay had not seen him. He made his way to the back door and crept into the kitchen. Everyone was in the front parlor celebrating, exchanging gifts, singing carols. At least he was not too late.

Fritzi strode down the hall and stood for a moment observing them. At first no one noticed him. The children were scattered about the floor busily unwrapping their gifts. Marie and Lise and their husbands were there. Oh, oh, he had not counted on them being here. Teddi was complaining as usual.

"Couldn't you have found a better tree than this?" he asked. "It's so small and scrawny."

"Heinrich Anton brought it. It was the best he could find," replied Eleonore. "And we can be thankful for it. If you ever went up in the woods, you would know how bad it is."

Bickering as usual, thought Fritzi. Oh, my love, I'll cheer you up. At least I'm home now. He took a step into the room and called out, "Frohe Weihnachten."

Everyone looked up, startled. For a moment there was dead silence.

Then Eleonore cried, "Fritzi," and ran to embrace him.

He hugged and kissed her in a far from brotherly fashion. Then he suddenly stepped back. "Elli, I am filthy and lousy. You'll soil your lovely gown."

"No matter," she said. "It's so good to see you, but . . . "

"What are you doing here?" growled Teddi. "I'll not be arrested for harboring a criminal."

"I'm not a criminal," protested Fritzi.

"But it's not safe for you to be here," said Eleonore.

"Since the French have already searched the house, I am safer here than anywhere," argued Fritzi, "provided no one says anything." He looked pointedly at his step-sisters and their spouses, who looked away, embarrassed.

Teddi shrugged. "Well, you're here now," he said. "Let's not spoil the children's Christmas. I'll leave it up to my wife to handle the French officers. She seems to have a way with them." He turned away.

Fritzi stood forlorn and dispirited. Not the welcome he had expected. Even Elli, after that first fervent embrace, had been more worried than welcoming. He turned to go back into the kitchen. Then Eleonore, suddenly contrite, noticed his distress.

"Dearest Fritzi," she said. "I'm sorry. It was just the sudden shock of seeing you. Of course, you will be safe here. And I promise you no one will breathe a word. Have you eaten?"

"Ja, Dorchen left me some supper. What I should really like is a bath and some clean clothes."

Her face fell. "I have let the maid and the cook go to their own families for tonight since they will be so busy with Christmas dinner tomorrow. You'll have to heat the water and carry it up yourself."

"I'm sure I can handle that," he replied. "I'll clean up while you people are at church. Do I still have a room?"

"Of course you do, dearest brother. This is your home. And I *am* glad to see you regardless of the danger." She gave him a light peck on the cheek and turned back to the children.

Christmas dinner was a subdued affair. No goose or suckling pig graced the table. Only two chickens sacrificed from the precious few they had left. Vegetables were cabbage and turnips—no one's favorites—and pototoes. No fancy cake or creamy pudding for dessert for sugar was impossible to obtain. Applesauce sufficed. At least Vilsen boasted a plethora of apples.

Teddi was grumpy and almost totally ignored his brother. Eleonore was unusually quiet. She was so worried she could hardly eat. Only the children and the servants seemed to welcome Fritzi home. The children begged to hear stories of his escapades, which he promised to tell them someday, but not now. The two women fussed over him because he had always been kind to them. When evening arrived and nothing untoward had happened, they all began to relax a bit.

233

On second Christmas Day the axe fell. At daybreak a squad of French soldiers led by a grizzled sergeant arrived at the house. Two guarded the front door, two the back, and the remaining two went directly to the stable where they found Fritzi checking on his horse. In moments they had chains on him.

"How dare you?" screamed Eleonore. "By whose orders?" But she knew. She knew.

"By Capitain Lescaux' orders, Madame," replied the sergeant. "Whose else?"

Whose else, indeed. She almost swooned as they whisked Fritzi off to the dungeon cell at Hoya Castle where Teddi had spent some time so many years ago.

Eleonore tried to visit him taking food and his warm cloak. The guards accepted the food and cloak—Eleonore wonderd if Fritzi would ever see them—but they denied her access to the prison.

"You must obtain a pass from le Capitain Lescaux," they insisted.

Eleonore cringed at the thought. She knew what that would mean. No, even for Fritzi. She refused to demean herself to that level. At least not now. Only as a last resort to save him from hanging—and even then she did not trust Jean-Marie. The thought of his groping hands chilled her to the bone.

She turned to Dorothea's brother Philipp, the advocate. "Philipp, Fritzi needs an expert lawyer. I'll pay you anything. You must try and save him."

Philipp smiled ruefully. "For you Elli there will be no fee. Our families have been too close over the years. But I fear there's not much I'll be able to do for him. Under the new Code Civil many death penalties have been eliminated. However, under his Continental System, Napoleon has equated smuggling, especially from England, with treason. Mayhap since they did not actually catch him in the act, we can mount some sort of defense. I'll go and see him. But don't hold out too much hope. The *Code Napoleon* is a wonderful body of laws, but like any law it can be twisted to suit the occasion."

"Thank you, dear Philipp. I knew I could count on you."

He shook his head.

The next afternoon Philipp came to see Eleonore. He looked glum. "I talked to Fritzi for about a half hour this morning. They did not require a pass of me. Of course, he is entitled to a lawyer but they did not even ask. I thought that passing strange."

234

Eleonore then explained about Jean-Marie's importunities and threats.

"Ah, so that is what we have to deal with and not Fritzi's alleged crime at all. Their finding his horse down on the Bücken waterfront is purely circumstantial. It could have been stolen. And that damnable bolt of blue silk would have been more difficult to argue away, but I could have found 'experts' to swear it came from France or Italy. Why didn't you hide that away anyway?"

Eleonore hung her head tearfully. "It was his. I didn't know for whom he intended it. I thought mayhap he had a lover."

Women, thought Philipp. "He intended it for a Christmas gift for you, Elli."

"Oh," she gasped. "I didn't know."

"Never mind that now. The problem with Captain Lescaux puts a new light on things. I shall have to give some serious thought as to how we can outwit him. Meanwhile, don't despair, Elli. Fritzi is safe enough for a while. That old castle has more prisoners than troops to guard them, most of them smugglers apprehended long before Fritzi. Some have been languishing there for months. So I know it will be months ere he is brought to trial. Time is on our side because Lescaux could be transferred ere then."

"What makes you think that?" asked Eleonore.

"Rumor has it that Napoleon will be starting a new campaign in the spring now that he has conquered all of Italy and imprisoned the Pope."

"He has imprisoned the Pope? I didn't know that. Whatever for?"

"He claimed that the Pope has no right to rule temporal lands, with which I agree. But the Pope was also allowing British shipping into Rome and refused to stop it when Napoleon so ordered. So he conquered Rome itself and imprisoned the Pope, who is now threatening to excommunicate him."

Eleonore laughed for the first time. "Which he no doubt deserves and probably couldn't care less about."

"Agreed. So now he feels free to punish a recalcitrant Austria, who he feels is not behaving properly as a satellite state and must be made a part of the French Empire. And that will take a lot more troops than he presently has in the field."

"I see."

"So it is possible that this whole Hoya contingent may be sent to the front."

"Let us pray so," she said.

8

1809

Fritzi's neck was indeed saved from the hangman's noose by Napoleon's new plans but not in a way that anyone expected.

On the day after New Year's 1809 broadsides were posted all over the villages and throughout the countryside on trees and barn doors, town criers and riders throughout the county loudly proclaimed, announcements were made from pulpits and the steps of townhalls: the annual levy of troops from all over Germany was to take place in January instead of the usual April. And Napoleon demanded thousands of recruits instead of the hundreds conscripted heretofore. Every able-bodied man in the county from fourteen to forty-five years of age was liable to be taken. They were given lots and the lots would be drawn after the church service on the Sunday after the Epiphany. Any man who ran away or disappeared after his name was called would be summarily shot as a deserter.

The Sunday appointed was a raw day, blustery and threatening snow. But the entire populace of Vilsen, Bruchhausen and most of the surrounding district was gathered, elbow to elbow, in the churchyard. Mothers, wives, sisters, daughters clung to their menfolk as if they would never see them again. And many would not. General Dupas did the honors—if honors it could be called—while a decidedly nervous pastor held the basket with the slips of paper. An aide with quills, inkpot and a huge book sat at his side ready to inscribe the names as they were called out. The crowd was breathlessly silent.

"Johann Ludwig Matthies," announced Dupas.

"Heinzi's eldest," whispered Eleonore.

Gerhardina screamed and would have swooned had not old Anton held her up.

"Heinrich Christian Bruns."

"Johann Justus' stepbrother," said Eleonore to Dorothea.

236

"Fahlenkamp." "Diercks." "Meyer." "Erich Bruns — is that the same family?" Dupas asked the pastor.

"No, a second or third cousin," he replied.

After he called about a dozen names, the general turned the lottery over to Captain Lescaux. Not for him to be standing in this weather calling out hundreds of names. He entered his coach and drove off to Bruchhausen. The captain relished the assignment. He seemed to take great pleasure in the distress he was causing.

"Johann Heinrich Bergmann."

"Oh, no," gasped Dorothea and held Eleonore's arm for support while Chris put a comforting arm around her.

"Ravens." "Hegedorn." "Vasmer." "Mayer." "Schumacher."

"Theodor Ludwig Hohnholz."

Eleonore's intake of breath was so loud she was sure Lescaux would look right at her. She clutched at Dorothea but found she had to hold Teddi up who was on the verge of collapse from fright. Katinka on the other side took his arm.

"Come, Papa. I'll take you home if you'd like," she offered.

"Nay, nay, I'll wait," replied Teddi, trying to straighten up his shoulders as he imagined a soldier would stand. Oh, dear God, he thought, how am I ever going to do it? "Your mother will surely want to hear if they call out Fritzi."

"But they're not supposed to take more than one from the same household," put in Dorothea.

"Then at least your Georg Wilhelm is safe for this year," remarked Eleonore.

"Georg Wilhelm is in Liebenau," Dorothea stated. "He could be taken from there. I believe that 'household' is the operative word, not 'family'. Isn't that right, Chris?"

Chris nodded. "And so we're still worried about our Heinrich Anton because Johann Heinrich lives apart from us in the spice shop."

"But Heinrich Anton is only thirteen," asserted Katinka.

"He turns fourteen this very month," said Dorothea. "I'm not sure if they go by the exact birth date or merely the year."

And so they, and all the others, stood in the bitter January day until dark, listening as Lescaux called out name after name. Distant relatives, close friends, neighbors, mere acquaintances, unknowns.

At the final end of the roll, the captain announced, "All you who have been called are now part of the Imperial Army of France and subject to its discipline. You have three days to set your affairs in order. On Thursday at dawn you will report here in good order ready to march. Wear stout shoes and a warm coat if you have one. It is a long way to Bavaria where you will undergo your training."

"Bavaria!" came a concerted gasp from the crowd.

"Oui, Bavaria. There you will be joined by other recruits from every town, county and state in Germany. You will be a proud part of the greatest army ever to be assembled. And I am happy to announce that I will be in command of this Bruchhausen contingent. Vive la France! Vive l'Empereur!"

"Fuck the Emperor," shouted a voice from the crowd.

"Arrest that man," shouted Lescaux, turning red with fury.

But no one would admit to having spoken or heard the profanity. The crowd sullenly dispersed.

That evening Eleonore and Teddi sat alone in the parlor holding hands—something they had not done in years.

"I love you, Teddi," she murmured. "I may not have always shown it but I've always loved you. Still do."

"And I love you, Elli," he replied. "I know now it was my neglect of you with my endless tinkering that drove you away from me. And I was jealous before I had any reason to be. Will you forgive me?"

"I've always forgiven you, Teddi. And I'll pray for your safe return."

"Thank you, sweeting." He had not called her that in years.

She patted her still flat belly. "The midwife thinks it may be twins this time."

"And I'll not be here for the birthing."

When were you ever around for the birthings, she thought bitterly. But she said, "You may be. Let us hope the war will be over by then."

"I fear not. Napoleon will not rest until he has made all of Europe part of France."

"Then I shall write to you wherever you are. You must always let me know."

"I shall." He took her hand. "Come to bed, sweeting. Let me make love to you once more ere I have to leave."

After the men were gone, Dorothea came into Vilsen every day to work in the spice shop. She was determined to keep the business going for her eldest son. Although stocks were very low and exotic spices impossible to obtain, there were still sufficient supplies of the more common seasonings like pepper and cloves. Dutch ships still brought them from the East Indies when they could and since Holland was now a part of Napoleon's empire, she was able to obtain them sporadically.

She also brought into the shop most of the medicines the old wisewoman had left her and turned a corner of the shop into an apothecary. She was soon making many of her own simples and potions. People were grateful not to have to make the trip out to Heiligenberg and she did quite well.

Eleonore, too, was happy to have her dearest friend nearby as this pregnancy was not going well. With Lescuax gone, she was able to visit Fritzi occasionally. He seemed well enough physically—as well as the poor food and the dark, damp confinement permitted—but his spirits were understandably low. Her inability to cheer him depressed Eleonore as well. Then two weeks after Teddi had left, Katinka came down with a high fever and a severe croup. By the next day Eleonore realized it was far more than a croup. It was the dreaded and deadly whooping cough.

Eleonore watched in agony as her dearest daughter—her love child—struggled for breath against the strangling whoops of the disease. Katinka's lovely, newly maturing body fell away to nothing as the fever and coughing wracked it. Eleonore refused to let the doctor bleed her. Instead she ran to Dorothea for some of her cough syrup—a mixture of honey, cloves and whatever wine she could commandeer. Dorothea made gallons of it for the disease spread rapidly amongst the children of the village. She had endless arguments with the doctor who considered her not much better than the old witch. But when her syrup accomplished a few cures he reluctantly allowed her to have a small supply of laudanum of which she added a few drops to the syrup for the worst cases.

But not all were cured. Two weeks later Eleonore's other three children came down with the dreaded cough. Katinka survived but just barely. She was weak, thin as a rail and would always have bad lungs. Eleonore wore herself out nursing the other three and eventually lost one. Dorothea worried for her friend and gave her tonics to build up her strength. But it was the lack of nourishing food, especially meat, that devastated everyone. And the lack of sufficient firewood to keep warm added to their woes.

In February the weather worsened. It was not that cold but the damp wind from the North Sea brought sleet and freezing rain. And neither homes nor clothes nor people ever seemed to dry out. A drear, blustery March brought another dread epidemic—this time of measles. Katinka and Eleonore's second daughter Dorothea, now twelve, had already suffered that sickness but they were still too weak from the whooping cough to be much help to their mother. So once again Eleonore wore herself out nursing the younger children and sadly, lost another. And she did not even know where to write to Teddi to tell him.

Dorothea wisely forbade her own children to come into the village for any reason although Heinrich Anton pleaded to be able to visit Katinka. "Absolutely not," she refused. "You are much safer in the isolation of Heiligenberg than ever in the village. If she lives you can see her well enough in the spring after the sickness has run its course." She would not think about 'if not'.

At last in April spring made a hesitant appearance. And another of Napoleon's plans was put into effect. He had long been frustrated by the lack of good roads in northern Germany. The extensive river systems which had been the great highways of commerce since time immemorial were too slow and cumbersome to move armies rapidly.

A lumbering wagon dumped yet another load of stone in front of the sweating men as Fritzi swung the heavy sledgehammer down on a rock. He was so weak from the months of imprisonment he barely had the strength to lift the thing. But the armed guards were watching, just as they had overseen the woodsmen the previous year.

"What in hell are we smashing up these stones for anyway?" he grumbled to Gerd, the man next to him.

"Damned if I know," replied Gerd. "Just a new form of punishment for all I can see."

"But you weren't in jail. Why would they punish you?"

"I was forced into cutting down our beautiful forest on peril of my life," said Gerd. "It was almost as bad as prison."

"Never," said Fritzi. "I am so weak I almost get sick to my stomach every tme I hit that rock. At least you seem to have some strength left."

"Not much with the poor food we subsist on these days."

"You'll toughen up soon," put in Thomas, the man on Fritzi's other side whom he had met in prison. "And at least we're out in the fresh air, not in that stinking hellhole."

"You're right about that," agreed Fritzi. "And, glory be to God, we can go home at night. That's the only good part about this."

"If you have a home to go to," sighed Thomas.

"You don't?"

"My wife ran off with a French soldier. Took the babe with her," said

Thomas bitterly. "Lord knows where she is now, probably whoring for the whole army."

"My sister-in-law got mixed up with them, too," said Fritzi wistfully, "but at least she had the sense to stay home. But now my brother's gone, it's up to me to care for her and her children."

"Which I'm sure you'll do right willingly," said Thomas snidely.

Fritzi blushed at the implication and sought to change the subject. "But why *are* we standing here smashing these damned stones?" He leaned on the sledgehammer to rest his aching arms. Immediately the guard was on his back.

"Keep moving, man," the guard growled, "or it's back to the dungeon for you."

Fritzi picked up the sledgehammer and let it drop on the rock.

When the guard moved on, Thomas said, "That's it. Pace yourself. It don't matter to them how fast or how hard you hit the stones so long's you keep moving."

"But why?"

"Don't you know? This here's going to be a road—a real highway from Bremen to Nienburg and later on all the way to Hannover. Napoleon don't like our little country lanes."

"So that's it. Oh, God, my back aches."

"If he wants a straight road, well and good," commented Gerd, "but why not just cut a straight path through the farms and woods and let it go at that? Why haul all these rocks from God knows where?"

"Because that would be no better than the roads we got—muddy in summer and frozen ruts in winter," explained Thomas. "He wants a paved road with a good solid base that will be passable in all kinds of weather. A road that can support the heavy caissons and wagons."

"How do you know so much about it?" asked Fritzi.

" 'Cause I listen," said Thomas.

The men worked in silence for the next few hours, too exhausted for conversation.

Fritzi went home that evening and flung himself on the bed. Every muscle and bone in his body screamed with pain. His hands were raw and bloody from broken blisters.

"A nice warm bath is what you need," suggested Eleonore.

"But I just had a bath yesterday," he objected. Only the day before had Fritzi been released from the dungeon at Hoya and sent home.

Eleonore had insisted he have a bath before he even set foot upstairs. The prison filth was bad enough but she wanted no fleas or lice in the bed chambers if it could be helped.

"This would not so much be to clean you—although how you cannot be dirty after smashing rock all day—but the warm water will ease those aching muscles," she replied.

"But you yourself said there isn't enough firewood to heat much water," he argued.

"Hah! I anticipated that. I've had buckets of water sitting out in the sun all afternoon. It won't take but a moment over the fire to bring them up to a comfortable temperature."

Fritzi knew when he had lost an argument with his strong-willed sister-in-law. Reluctantly he agreed to soak in the warm water. But he made one last attempt. "But it won't help my aching teeth," he flung after her as she turned to leave.

"Your teeth?"

"Ja, they feel like they're all about to fall out."

"The scurvy!" she exclaimed. "That's from that rotten prison food. I'll have cook fix you some turnip greens and onions for supper."

"I hate turnip greens," he said petulantly.

"Stop acting like a child," she retorted, exasperated. "Do you want to lose all your teeth? Dorchen says it is the only thing to prevent the scurvy except when we can get oranges or lemons, which it's the wrong time of year for now."

"What does Dorchen know?"

"A lot." And she flounced out of the room to order the water heated.

Fritzi soaked in the warm tub for a long while. He had to admit Elli was right. He could feel the warm water drawing the pains out of his aching body. Why is it women always seem to know so much more about healing bodies than men? As he started to relax he daydreamed. How would Elli's body feel wrapped around his? Before he was aware of it, he sprouted an erection. Well! That had not happened since the first few days in the dungeon. Oh, Elli, he thought. As the water cooled so did the tumescence. And not beforehand, he thought. How embarrassing should she walk in and see that.

And in moments she did, carrying a large towel warm from the fire. "Here, dry yourself and then I'll massage your back with some of Dorchen's famous liniment."

"But—but—I'm not dressed," he stammered.

242

"Stop being such a ninny," she scolded, but gently. "You think I have not seen a naked man before?" She turned away politely as he climbed out of the tub and dried himself. "Now lie on the bed on your stomach," she ordered.

"Oh, oh, that feels cold," he said as Eleonore anointed his back with the liniment.

"In a few minutes you'll feel the heat of it," she said as she kneaded the tight muscles.

"Mmm, smells better than horse liniment." He moaned as he succumbed to her capable ministrations.

"It should," she replied. "It contains mustard, ginger, mint and some other things in linseed oil." She massaged his arms, neck and shoulders, his back and down to his buttocks.

He could feel the heat of the liniment draw the pain out of his aching body as her hands travelled up and down. Oh, those strong, beautiful hands. And suddenly he was aroused again. He could not help himself. Just the thought of her touch was enough. To actually feel it easing his pain was almost too much. Suddenly he rolled over and stood up. Before she was aware of it, he took her in his arms and kissed her fervently. He heard her tiny gasp at the sight of his erection but she did not resist him. She seemed to melt against him as he had always dreamed she would.

"Oh, Elli, Elli, I love you. I've loved you all my life," he murmured into her hair. "I need you. I want you."

She gently pushed him away. "I know, Fritzi, I know," she said softly. "But not now. I am six months pregnant."

It was like a dash of cold water. His ardor quickly cooled. He blushed with embarrassment. "I—I couldn't help myself. I'm sorry, Elli."

"Don't be," she whispered. "I understand." She picked up the liniment bottle and turned to leave. "Supper will be ready as soon as you're dressed," she said and left him.

He sat back down on the bed to pull on his drawers and hose. He felt like a fool. But then he could hear her saying she understood. And she had not resisted.

In late May Eleonore received the first letter from Teddi since the men had departed in January. She had read general war news in the newspapers. She had known he was still alive through correspondence from other Vilsen men to their families. Lacking an address she had asked Johann Justus to write the sad news of the deaths of two of their children to his brother in the hope that he would carry it to Teddi, although she had no idea if the men from Vilsen were still together as a unit or not. And now this very brief missive that made no mention of the children at all but was full of praise for Napoleon.

'Dear Wife,' he wrote, 'I have not written so far as the training was very strenuous. But now I am a man' (Oh, really, she thought.) 'and now can see what a glorious life is that of a soldier. I have now experienced my first real battle—four actually—and find it quite exhilarating.' (Teddi, you fool, still playing at games.) 'I have now seen the Emperor, actually fought under him. He is very short and a bit stout but what a genius! When Austria declared war on us' (us? she thought.) 'for the fourth time he dashed straight from Paris to Abensberg to personally take command. He is brilliant and although he drives us hard, the men love him.' (What propaganda they must have been fed during the training, she said to herself.) 'We had outstanding victories at Landshut, Eckmühl and Regensburg, where the Emperor was wounded in the Achilles heel. Everyone prayed for him and he was up and about the next day planning our assault on Vienna. What a brave man! There will be no stopping him now. I am well.
Yr loving husband, Theodor Hohnholz.'

Eleonore threw the letter on the floor and wept. Not one inquiry after her. Not one greeting to the children. The same selfish Teddi, only now worse than ever it seemed.

Fritzi found her there hours later staring into space in the lowering twilight. He sat down beside her and lightly put an arm around her shoulders. "What is it, Elli? Is the babe giving you trouble again?"

She shook her head and pointed to the letter which still lay where she had dropped it.

"May I?" he asked. She nodded. He picked up the missive and glanced at the signature. He could see it was from his brother. He deliberately took his time lighting a candle. Then he read it.

"The pompous fool," he exclaimed. "He sounds worse than Napoleon himself. Now he is a man. What falderal! He never was a man worthy of you, Elli—still isn't."

"I know," she admitted sadly, "but I was so young and so in love. He overwhelmed me with his sweet-talk. The same foolizshness as in that letter. I finally learned how false it all was. Now the only one he is fooling is himself."

244

Fritzi nodded. He himself was feeling more a man than he ever had. His muscles were now well developed; his hands hardened with calluses. But he knew that muscles and calluses no more than fighting battles made a man. The hateful labor on the road had also matured him emotionally and, along with most of the men, had instilled a deep hatred of Napoleon. But the new maturity also told him that this was not the time for more braggadocio.

"Teddi was always one to fool himself," he said. "Just let him suffer one battle wound and he will run crying home to you."

"Even I would not wish that on him," she said, "but I must admit it is more pleasant in this house without him. I don't constantly have to wonder what nasty remark he will make next. Is that very wrong of me?" Her plaintive tone touched his heart.

"No, it isn't. And you are absolutely right." He gently took her hand and patted it. "I shall always be here for you, dearest Elli—for you and the children."

She looked into his soft brown eyes and could see no sign of lust—only kindness. She placed her hand on his. "Thank you, Fritzi."

On the night of 3 July Teddi sat fully armed in the sultry weather. The sweat was pouring off him and he dared not even remove his hat to wipe his brow. These stupid shakos, tall, cylindrical and gaily plumed. What kind of a military hat was that? They wouldn't even stay straight on one's head if the chinstrap should slip—which it often did in this heat. Beside him sat Jobst Diercks and Erich Bruns, men he had scarcely known back home. But it was comforting to have men from Vilsen nearby. Teddi was scared. He had been frightened to death in each of the battles in April regardless of what he had written to Eleonore. And this promised to be fiercer than any of the others.

They were sitting waiting on the island of Löbau in the middle of the Danube very close to Vienna. Napoleon had been ferrying his entire army to the island from the right bank—still was, and probably would be all night. That damned river—how Teddi was beginning to hate it. They had crossed and recrossed it innumerable times, rebuilding bridges that the Austrians had destroyed only to have them swept away again in the torrential annual Danube floods.

A young corporal came by. "Get what sleep you can, mes amis," he suggested.

"Where are we supposed to sleep?" asked Teddi sullenly. "I don't see any tents."

The corporal smiled. "You are on dry land, are you not? Pity the thousands of poor wretches who are still crossing from the right bank and will be all night. Tomorrow we cross to the left bank and march out to meet the Archduke."

The men groaned. But Erich and Jobst flung themselves down on the ground and, using their heavy packs as pillows, were soon asleep. Teddi lay for a long time looking up at the inky sky. There were no stars. It was too humid and hazy. He was too nervous to sleep. His stomach twisted and his heart pounded at the thought of another march, another battle. But he must have dozed off because the next thing he knew it was cracking dawn and a sergeant was going up and down the ranks ordering them up.

"On your feet, lads, and march. Pick up breakfast as you pass the commissary and keep marching."

The weary men gathered up their weapons and moved out.

Once again they were ferried in great lighters across the remaining branch of the river. But this was a short trip. Less than four hundred feet separated them from the left bank. Then they marched at the double toward the northeast. The blistering July sun rose higher with each passing hour and beat down mercilessly on men and animals alike.

"Why are we going in this direction?" asked Teddi. "I thought we were about to take Vienna."

"It seems the Emperor Josef's brother, the Archduke Karl Ludwig, has led a huge army over this way thinking to lure us away from Vienna," replied Jobst.

"So why don't we just let him go and walk into Vienna if it is undefended?" said Teddi, puzzled.

"Because then he would be at our backs," explained Erich. "Any fool can see that. And that Napoleon would never allow."

"I see." Was Erich calling him a fool? Teddi's vanity bristled.

"Not only that," added Jobst, "but it is rumored that the Archduke's other brother, Archduke Johann, is hurrying up from Italy to help him save Vienna. So that's why we have to get there first."

"Ja," said Erich. "It's important that Napoleon subdue Austria once and for all to impress the Czar of Russia—to maintain his friendship."

"Friendship? I thought they didn't trust each other," said Teddi, more puzzled than ever.

"They don't but that's politics," replied Erich.

"Well, he won't have much of a victory if we all collapse from sunstroke," commented Teddi.

"Oh, Teddi, stop complaining," said Jobst. "He'll give us time to rest before the battle."

But Napoleon did not. All the long day of the fourth they pursued a fleeing Austrian army. At last the Archduke took his stand on a level area called the Marchfeld. He had approximately 150,000 men and 448 guns. Napoleon had almost the same number of men but many more guns. The Austrians were strung out along a several mile front with the tiny village of Wagram at its center. By early afternoon of the fifth most of the French army was in place. So anxious was Napoleon to attack the Austrians before help could arrive from Archduke Johann and his 30,000 additional men that he immediately threw his exhausted men against the Austrian line. They were handily repulsed.

Teddi practically crawled back to their tent at the hastily erected campsite.

"What's the matter?" asked Jobst. "Are you hurt? Can't you walk?"

"Nay, I'm not hurt, just exhausted," grumbled Teddi.

"A good night's sleep will take care of that," Erich assured him.

"Ja, let's sleep while we can," added Jobst. "Tomorrow will be the main battle. He made a mistake this evening but you can be sure tomorrow we shall prevail."

Teddi could not sleep. The intense artillery fire went on most of the night. His ears were ringing so he hardly heard the sergeant arousing the men before dawn. The Archduke was already attacking their southern flank in an attempt to cut the French off from the Danube. At the same time Napoleon's troops were thrusting against the Austrians' northern flank at the Russbach.

"What do we do now?" asked Teddi, timidly.

"Wait here for your orders," replied the sergeant. "The general will decide where you're needed most."

Teddi was grateful for the reprise but the waiting was as terrifying as the actual fighting. His hands shook on his gun with the deadly bayonet fixed and ready. The fighting was fierce, surging back and forth. The constant cannon fire ceaseless and deafening.

At last the order came. "In you go now, bayonets fixed," yelled the sergeant. "We are winning in the north. It's up to you to finish off their southern flank."

Teddi ran forward, his friends on either side of him. Before they even reached the enemy line, a cannonball cut a swath through their ranks and then another. Men were mown down like hay. Blood and guts, arms, legs and heads flew in every direction. Teddi gagged and was almost sick. He stumbled and would gladly have given up right there but the fixed bayonets of the closely packed men behind him would not permit that luxury. He lurched on.

Then came the order. "Hold! Kneel! Fire!" The front rank fired. "Fire!" The next rank fired over their heads. And the next. And the next. And they were fired upon just as rapidly. Teddi saw Erich go down. He wanted to collapse as well but he just kept firing blindly. A cavalry charge swept down on them. "Bayonets to the horses' bellies!" came the order. Teddi froze. At least shooting with a musket you did not see the man you killed. But waiting until lethal hooves were almost upon you was another matter entirely. Teddi kept firing instead, almost blindly. What did it matter? With men and horses so closely packed you were bound to hit something. He had lost track of Jobst. He suddenly felt alone and terribly vulnerable without his friends even though he was surrounded by thousands of men, friend and foe. He wondered if Erich were dead or alive. It occurred to him that if he were to lie down and pretend to be wounded he would not have to fight anymore.

But then the thundering cavalry were upon them. Instinctively he ducked from side to side to avoid the crashing hooves. He forgot to shoot. He did not use his bayonet. He wanted to run away but he could not move. Then the horses swept past and it was hand to hand fighting. Although he tried, he was still paralyzed with fear. Suddenly someone shoved him from behind and he was down on his knees. Before he could arise or even scramble out of the way the wounded man fell heavily on top of him knocking the breath out of him. The ridiculous shako flew off and he lay there helpless and unable to move. He did not know if the man were dead or alive but he could feel the warm blood trickling down on him from a grievous wound. Then he felt something even warmer seeping at his crotch and with a twinge of shame realized that he had wet himself. The man who had him pinned down was much heavier than Teddi but he knew that with great effort he could extricate himself—if he wanted to. But no, this was the perfect excuse he had been looking for. He remained where he was.

The incessant cannon fire never let up. It was said later that the artillery fire at Wagram was the heaviest in any war in history. Another ball cut a deadly swath nearby killing and maiming dozens of men. And two more bodies fell on top of Teddi. Now he was truly immobilized. Well, he had made his choice. He was safer here than if he had been up and then cut down by that ball. He tried to turn his head so that he could breathe more easily but it was difficult with the crushing weight on top of him. A particularly thunderous explosion reverberated nearby and all was quiet. Too quiet. Am I dead, he wondered. He blinked his eyes. No, he could still see the carnage going on around him but he was deaf—totally deafened by the concussion. It was quite peaceful now that he could no longer hear the noise of the battle, the screams of the dying. He decided to close his eyes and sleep until it was all over. But it was impossible. He could still see the horror, could feel the weight of the dead or dying men on top of him, could feel their life's blood oozing down on his back and neck.

Then he watched with dread as a wave of Austrians momentarily pushed the French line back and many of the soldiers were stabbing the wounded with their bayonets to finish them off. He wanted to scream out in panic, no, no, I'm not wounded, but a tiny glimmer of common sense kept him quiet. His dead friends were his salvation. The Austrians stabbed the topmost man, decided the rest were all dead and moved on. Soon the French drove the Austrians back once again.

Teddi did not remember when he passed out—or maybe he really had fallen asleep. As his hearing gradually returned he awoke with a start to what sounded like shouts of victory. It was late afternoon. He could tell because the westering sun was shining in his gritty eyes. He thought he heard someone yell, "MacDonald did it. MacDonald did it!" MacDonald? Then he vaguely remembered that there had been several regiments of Scots in the French army. Scots? Then with great effort he recalled hearing that the Scots, with their great hatred of England, had often fought on the side of the French for centuries, especially since the debacle at Culloden some seventy years before. Then he heard cries of "The Archduke Karl has called for a truce," followed by joyous cheering. Then "Johann got here too late." More cheers.

Now if only someone would come and rescue me, thought Teddi. This time he wanted to get up and join the cheering but he could not move. He could barely breathe under the crushing weight. Hours later the stretchermen finally came, desperately trying to sort out the living from the dead before dark. "Hilfe mir! Hilfe mir!" he cried out weakly and then decided he had better switch to French. "Aidez-moi," he gasped and could say no more. But in the stillness of the battle's aftermath they heard him.

"Sounds like a live one over here. We're coming, lad. Hold on."

"It sure ain't this one. Got no head or arms. Wonder who he was."

Teddi could feel them dragging the bodies off of him.

"Nor this one. Leg missing and his guts falling out."

If Teddi had known what was on top of him, he would have vomited—and thanked God that he hadn't.

"Now this one don't look too bad. Might have survived but for them corpses on top of him. Now was it him who called?"

"Nay, here, here," moaned Teddi.

"Ach, almost didn't see this little fellow 'neath that big lad. Here, roll him over. Merde, a ball right through his lungs—or heart."

With the weight removed, Teddi gulped a welcome breath of air. He tried to flex his arms and legs but could barely move.

"God, lad, you're covered with blood. Yours or his?"

"I—I don't think I'm hurt," he croaked hoarsely. "The ball knocked me over and I got buried under them. If you'd just help me up I think I'm all right."

The man shook his head. "Ball knocked you over, you'd look like them." He pointed to the decapitated and mangled bodies. Teddi looked and gagged. "Could be the concussion though. It happens." The man was willing to give Teddi the benefit of the doubt. He helped him up. Teddi's legs were so weak he almost fell down again. "Best get on that stretcher and let the surgeon take a look at you."

Terrifying dread of the battle surgeon engulfed Teddi along with guilt at his subterfuge. "Nay, nay, I can walk."

Just then a waterboy came up to them. He handed Teddi a dipperful. Teddi rinsed the dirt out of his mouth and spat. Then he drank deeply of the refreshing, reviving water.

"Well, make up your mind, lad," said the stretcherman impatiently. "We got others to look after."

"I'm all right," declared Teddi shakily. "I'll walk. But where is the camp?"

The men pointed him in the right direction and left him. He stumbled along. My God, the camp seemed to be miles and miles away. His legs and arms were shaking, his gut quivering. Once he sat down to rest but quickly got up again when someone offered to help him to the hospital tent. No way would he let that field surgeon near him. He staggered on.

Jobst was already lying on a cot when Teddi finally reached their tent.

"Ach, God be thanked, you're still alive," exclaimed his friend. "I feared for sure you were gone."

Teddi limped to his cot and sat down.

"Lord, man, you're covered with dirt and blood," said Jobst, "and pissed yourself, too." Teddi had the grace to blush. "Think nothing of it, lad. Happens to the best of us. Better that than shitting yourself—or did you do that, too?" Teddi shook his head. "Well, you'd best soak those clothes in cold water as soon as you can afore those blood stains set."

"What have we got laundresses for?"

"Hah, they won't be around till morning, if then."

"I don't care," groaned Teddi. He stripped off the offending clothing and dropped it on the ground. God, it stunk. He stretched out naked on the cot and closed his eyes. Then suddenly he remembered. "I saw Erich go down."

"Ach, ja, but he'll live. Nothing much. A ball through the thigh but a clean wound. He'll be up and around in a few days."

"That's good." But Teddi thought with repugnance, a clean wound. How can any wound be clean? It was a violation of one's body. He shivered involuntarily. He felt befouled just from other men's blood and his own piss.

Napoleon's army was encamped in a great meadow outside the walls of Vienna called the Prater. Teddi had quickly forgotten his cowardice caught up as he was in the general jubilation over the glorious victory. He had almost convinced himself that he, single-handedly, had played an important part in the battle. He was trying to write a long overdue letter to Eleonore.

'Dear Wife,' he wrote. 'As I write this I am enjoying the beautiful gardens of Schönbrunn Palace.' (What matter if he exaggerated a little?) 'The palace itself is much like our own Herrenhausen by Hannover but I think our gardens are far more elaborate. Last week we enjoyed a glorious victory at a place called Wagram, so that Austria will never bother Germany again. Many men from Vilsen were killed and wounded.' (He was tempted to say he had been slightly wounded just to gain her sympathy but then decided against it. Erich Bruns and several others would surely be sent home but at least they had not witnessed his cowardice.) 'But I am well,' he continued. 'The Emperor has moved into Schönbrunn and is setting the terms of a peace treaty before Josef. He has sent for his Polish mistress, the Countess Walewska, so it seems we shall be here a while. I shall write again when we move on. I believe Prussia will be next.

Yr husband, Theodor Hohnholz.'

251

Eleonore had heard the news about Wagram long before Teddi's letter arrived. All through April the congregation of the church had been asked to pray for victories for Napoleon and especially so when he had been injured at Regensburg. Many people, in disgust, had stopped going to church. Then in the latter part of July the Maire—the French commander of the village whose orders superseded even those of their own Bürgermeister and Council—had made the announcement about the great victory at Wagram and had demanded that a Te Deum of thanksgiving be sung in the church. Many more stayed away. They wanted no Popish Te Deums sung in a Lutheran church.

Eleonore also knew that Teddi was still alive. Johann Justus had brought her word of his survival when his cousin Erich Bruns had come home. She also learned that there would be no leaves for those who were not wounded. So she did not worry. She had more immediate concerns. The twins were due at any moment and the midwife *was* worried. She had not heard the second heartbeat for almost two weeks.

Dorothea and the midwife were in constant attendance when Teddi's letter arrived. Eleonore threw the missive aside unopened. "Just more of his lies," she said as another contraction gripped her. "I'm sure he will brag that he won the whole battle by himself. I'll read it later—after—after—oohh," she cried. "After this."

It was a difficult birth, especially for Eleonore who had borne so many so easily. For hours she strained, struggled and sweated in the humid July heat. She could hear the crowd in the churchyard cheering the Maire's announcement about Wagram. But the cheering sounded forced to her ears. She could even hear the Te Deum echoing from the church for the windows were wide open. It sounded like caterwauling to her—certainly insincere. She put her hands over her ears.

"Shall I close the window, Elli?" asked Dorothea. "I shall if it disturbs you."

"Nay, nay," she replied. "They'll be done in a minute and I need the air."

Oh, why was this taking so long? Is it punishment for my infidelity? Or because of the potion I took? Or is it because I don't really want this one? She tried to put such thoughts out of her mind. The contractions were almost continuous now and still nothing happened.

At last the midwife said, "Ah." A tiny head was appearing. She reached inside to help and extracted a tiny body—blue. She quickly handed the dead infant to Dorothea who wrapped it in linen and put it

252

aside. "Now bear hard," she instructed, "so we can save the other one."

Eleonore did so and with great effort brought forth the other twin. This one was alive but just barely. When the midwife held him up to clear his lungs, he just mewed like a tiny kitten instead of squalling as her other children had done. When Dorothea placed him in her arms, she burst into tears. Usually she felt relieved and a sense of joy after bearing a child but this time she felt only an overwhelming sadness.

She looked at the tiny boy in her arms. "What was the other one?" she asked weakly.

"A girl—already dead."

"Well, Teddi, your last gift to me."

Dorothea was not normally superstitious but she felt like making the sign against evil at Eleonore's statement. Was it a premonition?

About a week later Eleonore finally condescended to read Teddi's letter. Schönbrunn? Oh, I'm sure he's staying right in the Emperor's suite, she thought sarcastically. Herrenhausen? He knows I've never been to Herrenhausen and I'm quite sure he hasn't either. Of course, here it is—the great hero. And Walewska. What do I care how many mistresses Napoleon has? And Prussia next? Oh, he'll enjoy punishing them for arresting him those many years ago. Again, not a word of concern for her or the children. No mention of the two that had died.

She threw the letter into the fire and turned to her more immediate concern—trying to get this poor, frail, little mite to nurse. He would suck a few times and then the effort seemed to tire him so that he would fall asleep. I'm going to lose this one, too, she sighed despondently. She thanked God for dear Fritzi. He had been a pillar of strength and comfort through all her ordeals.

Napoleon lingered at Schönbrunn for three months while Josef II dithered over the terms of the peace treaty. The Habsburg kept hoping against hope that Prussia or Russia would come to his aid but no such aid was forthcoming. Napoleon knew that Prussia was weak, finished—no threat at all. To appease the Tsar he gave him portions of Poland that had been Austria's after the last partition. He set up the Grand Duchy of Warsaw from Prussia's share to the delight of Walewska. He placed all of Austria's Italian possessions under the aegis of France itself. Finally Josef realized he had no choice. The treaty was signed on 14 October 1809. Austria was forced to pay a huge indemnity in addition to losing a great part of her territory.

Napoleon was also overjoyed to learn that Marie was pregnant. No longer could he be blamed for Josephine's not giving him an heir. He sent Walewska home to her husband in Poland and departed Vienna the day after the treaty was signed. Immediately upon arrival back in Paris he announced to an hysterical Josephine that he was going to divorce her. He then started looking around for a new wife. Many people in Catholic France who had previously loved him now condemned him and predicted that his years of good fortune would soon be at an end.

He toyed with the idea of asking for the hand of the Russian crown princess although she was still a mite young. But it would be a way of avoiding war with Russia which now seemed inevitable if he wanted to advance east. However, he also knew that the Tsarina hated him bitterly and was sure to oppose any union with him. Rather than risk an outright rebuff he held his hand for the moment. Then Austria's crafty ambassador to France, Metternich, suggested why not a Habsburg princess? Josef's daughter Marie Louise was fully eighteen, mild, demure, obedient and properly trained. Napoleon considered it. It would guarantee war with Russia but it seemed as though that was going to happen anyway. On the other hand the Habsburgs were a fecund family and he could be almost certain of an heir, which he so desperately wanted.

On 11 March 1810 in Vienna Marie Louise was married by proxy to Napoleon. Like her ill-fated aunt Marie Antoinette before her she moved with eighty-three coaches and carriages to Compiègne where Napoleon met her on 27 March. On 1 April they were united in a civil ceremony and the next day in another elaborate religious rite at the Louvre. Almost all the cardinals refused to attend and Napoleon promptly exiled them to the provinces.

At the same time Napoleon made his feckless, immature and very profligate brother Jerome King of Westphalia. As far back as 1807 during his dismemberment and reorganization of the German states Napoleon had absorbed the northern third of Hannover, including Bremen, Hamburg and the entire coastline, directly into the French Empire. The remaining two-thirds of Hannover, all of Hesse and several minor territories became the 'Kingdom' of Westphalia. Now Jerome set up a luxurious, libertine court rivalling the worst of Louis XIV's at Kassel in Hesse. He enjoyed a constant round of balls and social extravagances including at least four mistresses, spending money meant for his brother's war chest. Napoleon, hoping that responsibility would mature him, sent Jerome letter after letter of sound advice.

To give him his due Jerome did promulgate the Code Napoleon giving Westphalia efficient administration, equality before the law and a jury system, uniform taxation and religious freedom. He encouraged free enterprise. Roads continued to be built and the waterways improved. Weights and measures were made uniform and tolls abolished. He decreed that every town be responsible for its poor (something that Cyriacus Lindemann, Dorothea's grandfather, had fought for unsuccessfully over fifty years before) and the town fathers still grumbled. He fostered Westphalia's already advanced culture by promoting public education and reorganizing the universities. He hired Jacob Grimm as his librarian.

But two heavy burdens counterbalanced all these blessings: taxation and conscription. And people were more inclined to see the bad than the good. And so did Napoleon. Taxes were increased hugely every year until they became prohibitive. Yet most of it went towards Jerome's lavish court instead of into Napoleon's treasury. The annual levies of troops were higher each year, yet Jerome could never seem to fulfill his quota, having spent the money beforehand. Napoleon became annoyed with his flighty brother, then aggravated and disgusted. By the end of 1810 he annexed all the remaining portion of Hannover into the French Empire, leaving Jerome a considerably reduced area to play with.

Meanwhile, immediately after the Treaty of Schönbrunn, Napoleon had sent all the Westphalian regiments east to the Oder River to keep an eye on Russia. This included Teddi and all the surviving men from Vilsen. There they were to spend the next two years. Teddi found that he had a new commanding officer, a young man from Asendorf named Carsten Campsheide.

Every year, aside from praying for Napoleon's victories, the churches had been ordered to celebrate Napoleon's birthday on 15 August. Anton Matthies had never attended one of these services. In fact, he seldom went to church at all. Now he pleaded old age and his wife's frail health. Becke, indeed, was failing rapidly—not physically but mentally. Anton never took her anywhere, fearful of being embarrassed by her maunderings or occasional hysterical outburst. Anton himself was still hale and hearty for all that he was seventy-eight years old.

When none of the Matthies family showed up at the church to celebrate the birth of Napoleon's son and heir in April, their absence was somehow brought to the attention of the Maire. In July that worthy per-

255

sonally rode out to Bruchmühlen to confront them.

"Ah, Monsieur Matthies, a good French name that," he said to Anton, "we are happy to see that you are enjoying good health."

"As good as can be expected for a man nigh on eighty," replied Anton.

"And with a name like that I am sure you are happy to be a part of France once again."

Anton was once very proud of his French blood. Now he was not too sure, especially after his daughter's escapades with those French officers. What in hell is this monkey leading up to, he wondered. "I am afraid the name goes way back to the seventeenth century. My ancestors were Huguenots fleeing the persecutions of Louis XIV. We consider ourselves thoroughly German now." There, he said it.

Heinzi and Gerhardina looked at him in surprise. They had never heard him say that before.

"Mais oui, of course," said the Maire. He had not expected that either. "Then you must be very proud of both your fine heritages."

Enough of this fencing. Get to the point, thought Anton beginning to be annoyed. "And to what do we owe the honor of a visit from the Maire himself?" he asked bluntly. "Surely not to discuss my ancestors."

"Non, non, certainly not. It has—er—come to my attention that you did not see fit to attend the Mass—er, I mean—the service celebrating the birth of our beloved Emperor's son and heir—the King of Rome."

"The king of what?" sputtered Anton.

"Of Rome, monsieur. Everyone was invited and expected to come."

"I don't recall receiving an engraved invitation," retorted Anton, his temper rising dangerously.

"Uh, well—it was announced all over the county. But never mind. That is past. Now I am officially inviting you and your family to the mass—er, that is—the celebration of the Emperor's birthday in August. Attendance is obligatory."

Anton was about to throttle the man. He gritted his teeth to calm down before answering. "I am an old man, as you can see, and my wife is in poor health. It is very difficult for us to get into Vilsen."

"But surely . . ."

Just then Becke burst into the room—all hundred and eighty pounds of her. "Oh, Anton," she burbled, "why didn't you tell me we had company? Who is this delightful man? Shall I put on some coffee?"

Anton would gladly have throttled her as well. He tried to be gentle.

256

"No, Becke. The Maire was just leaving. Go back to your loom like a good girl. We'll have coffee later."

Becke obediently left but the damage had been done. Obviously she was not as frail as her husband had claimed. The Maire did not like being taken for a fool.

"We shall expect you at the Emperor's birthday celebration. To do otherwise might be considered traitorous." And as a parting shot he added a not-so-veiled threat. "It would be a shame if we were to have to purchase our flour elsewhere. Au revoir, monsieur."

Anton's temper exploded. "How dare that son-of-a-bitch threaten me? Purchase his flour elsewhere, indeed. Where else? We're the only mill here except for Chris at Heiligenberg and all Chris' production belongs to me. I'd like to fill his flour with worms so he has the bellyache the rest of his misbegotten life. That damned prissy fop. I'll fix him. He'll not threaten me again."

"Papa, Papa, calm yourself," pleaded Heinzi.

Gerhardina burst into hysterical weeping. "Papa Anton," she cried, "we can't afford to lose that contract. It's our main livelihood. We have five children to feed and another soon to come."

"She's right, you know," agreed Heinzi. "We can't afford to offend him. Papa, you're as good as retired now. I'll make the decisions."

This brought forth another burst of temper. "And who taught you everything you know?" Anton shouted. "I still own both these mills and I'll still make the important decisions."

Gerhardina took a different tack. She tried to speak calmly. "But Papa," she argued, "this is not an important decision. What difference does it make if we go to some foolish celebration of Napoleon's birthday? It wouldn't hurt us and it will appease the Maire. That's all that matters."

"It matters to me," growled Anton. "I don't want to appease that mealy-mouthed bastard."

"But Papa," protested Heinzi, "we don't have to say the prayers or sing the hymns. All we have to do is show up. You mustn't upset yourself so."

"I'll be upset if I want to," grumbled Anton. "If you insist on telling me what I ought to do, I may just have to change my will."

Gerhardina gasped and Heinzi turned white. "You wouldn't," he said.

"Very easily," said Anton. "You were never the miller your brother Fritz would have been."

Heinzi had heard that all his life and was sick of it. "But Fritzi is long dead and I am here. I have work to do." He turned and left before he could lose his own temper, so very like his father's.

Gerhardina fled to the kitchen to start dinner. Although who would be in a mood to eat she knew not.

When she passed through the parlor, Becke asked, "What was all that shouting about? Is Papa angry again?"

"Nothing that concerns you, Mother Becke. Go back to your weaving."

Becke nodded. "That's good. I don't like shouting." And she sat there clacking away at her empty loom.

After a subdued dinner Anton saddled his horse and rode off to Heiligenberg to visit Chris and Dorothea. The Klostermühle was a sanctuary he sought more and more lately to get away from his contentious family. Although he finally admitted to himself that this time the aggravation was mostly of his own doing, he felt the need to talk the whole thing over with someone calm and sensible. Not his stupid, overbearing son or his greedy, bitchy wife.

Dorothea greeted him effusively. "Chris is in the mill," she said. "Shall I call him?" She could see that Anton was very upset.

"Nay, nay," he said, "not if he's busy. Mayhap just talking to you, Dorchen, will be enough. If you don't mind listening to an old man's concerns, that is."

But she called Chris anyway, after she had seated Anton at the kitchen table. "You know I don't mind at all," she assured him. When she thought of how she had hated this man years ago in her youth she was saddened because now she felt only pity for him. If ever there was a disappointed and unhappy man, it was Anton Matthies.

When Chris joined them, Anton spilled out the whole story of the Maire's visit and threats. And of the subsequent shouting match. "I lost my temper—again," he confessed. "But what was I to do? Take that French pipsqueak's threats? And I threatened to disinherit Heinzi."

Dorothea gasped. "You shouldn't have done that."

"No, you shouldn't," agreed Chris.

"I know," admitted Anton, "and I probably sh'an't but he infuriated me so. But I got to thinking on the way over here. I'd like to do something special for Heinrich Anton. After all, he *is* my godson."

"What do you mean 'something special'?" asked Chris.

"To protect him from Heinzi after I'm gone. I trust my son not at all.

258

How is the lad doing, by the way?"

"Very well," replied Chris proudly. "He's turning into a fine miller."

"Good. And who in hell is this King of Rome?" asked Anton in a complete non sequitur.

Dorothea laughed. "Don't you know? That is Napoleon's son by Marie Louise."

"No but three months old and already a king," commented Anton. "God help us then. We've only just gotten rid of one Habsburg and now we have another foisted on us."

"If you'd gone to the special service you'd have known," said Chris.

"You went to that?" asked Anton incredulously.

"We all did," replied Dorothea. "It was almost mandatory."

"So that's why that damned Maire came after me," mused Anton. "And the pastor permitted this?"

"He had no choice," explained Chris. "It was a direct order from the Emperor to every church in France, Germany, Italy—everywhere."

"Always thought he was a bit weak-kneed—the pastor, I mean."

"Take my advice, Anton," said Chris. "Close you eyes and ears if you must, but swallow your pride and go to this birthday thing even if it kills you. We can't afford to lose that flour contract. It will hurt us as well as your own family."

"I'll think on it," said Anton.

Dorothea tried to lighten the mood. "People are already jokingly calling 15 August St. Napoleon's day."

Anton smiled at last. "Well, he better start praying to himself then for I fear he's getting too big for his own breeches. He'll end up cutting his own throat. Mark my words."

Several days later, unbeknownst to anyone, Anton rode in to Vilsen to see Philipp Koch.

"How nice to see you again, Master Matthies," Dorothea's brother greeted the old man. "What can I do for you?"

"I want to add a codicil, or whatever you call it, to my will."

"Ah, so."

"I want to protect my godson's rights to the Klostermühle after I'm gone for I trust my son not at all."

Philipp looked askance and thought a moment. "You could declare him and his heirs hereditary lessees in perpetuity."

"That's what I had in mind. And Heinzi could not force him out?"

259

"Not at all—as long as the property is owned by one of your heirs. If they should decide to sell, the new owner could choose to honor it or not. There would be no guarantee in that case."

"But it will protect Heinrich Anton for his lifetime? That is really all I care about."

"Very definitely."

"Then do it ere I get any older," ordered Anton. "And don't you breathe a word to your sister."

On 15 August the entire Matthies family, even Becke and the youngest grandchild, piled into the old farm wagon they usually used to deliver flour and grain. For all his wealth Anton had never seen fit to purchase a carriage such as Dorothea had inherited from her mother. He saw it as a needless extravagance. Years ago had Becke or the children wanted to go to church or market, they walked into Vilsen. For longer distances he and Heinzi had ridden. The grandchildren still walked but Becke had not been any place in years. This time Anton decided they would all arrive together in style—as much style as the old wagon afforded them.

It was with great effort that Anton and Heinzi together got Becke into the wagon. "Oh, are we going for a drive?" she asked. "That will be nice."

"No, Mama Becke, we are going to church," replied Gerhardina.

"To church? On a weekday?" queried Becke, puzzled. She was pretty sure it was a weekday, although lately she often got mixed-up as to what day it was.

"Ja, Mama," explained Heinzi, "it's the Emperor's birthday."

"The Emperor? But I thought I heard that the Emperor abdicated last year. Or was it the year before?"

"That was Josef, the Holy Roman Emperor," said Heinzi. "This is the new Emperor Napoleon."

"Ach, the Frenchman who took away our Johann Heinrich. I don't want to see him."

"You won't see him, Mama Becke," Gerhardina assured her. "It's just a church service."

Anton gritted his teeth and laid the whip to the horses harder than he intended. The wagon jerked forward.

When they arrived at the church Anton led his family to the very front pew. He wanted to be sure that insufferable Maire and that lily-livered pastor took careful note of his presence. The pew was usually reserved for the Bürgermeister and Council and their families but no one was about to argue with Master Matthies, especially when they sensed that he was as tense as a volcano ready to erupt. Dorothea and Eleonore sat behind him. Anton smiled wanly at Dorothea, nodded cooly to his daughter and glared at everyone else. Chris laid what he hoped was a calming hand on his shoulder.

Then Becke spoke up in a loud voice, "Why is everything decorated in purple? Is is Lent?"

"Hush, woman," growled Anton.

"No, that is the imperial purple for the Emperor," whispered Dorothea.

"Oh, how nice," said Becke. "Then we must all curtsey when he comes in." She struggled to stand up. Eleonore pushed her down while Gerhardina held onto her arm.

"No, Mama," said Eleonore, "he won't be coming. We are just going to celebrate his birthday."

"Will you cackling hens shut up," snarled Anton and everyone turned to look. Becke wilted but at least it kept her quiet for a while.

The service began with a hymn of praise for Napoleon. Anton stood with the rest but refused to sing. Everyone close to him could see he was simmering. Then the pastor delivered a long and effusive sermon lauding all Napoleon had done for them. The simmering turned into agitation. The sermon was followed by a long and fervent prayer begging the Almighty to give Napoleon good health and a long life and continuing victories in all his undertakings. Anton's fist was thumping the rail in front of him at each petition of the litany. Everyone rose to sing the mandatory Te Deum. Anton exploded.

He turned purple and shouted, "I'll not sing any Popish song in *this* church. I'll not pray for the atheist who is killing our sons, who is taxing us to death, who is starving us. I'll not . . . " and he collapsed before anyone could stop him.

"Papa," screamed Eleonore.

Everyone rushed to the front of the church so that the doctor could hardly get through to him.

"Anton, you must not lose your temper in church," mumbled Becke, totally unaware.

The doctor felt for a pulse, put his ear to Anton's chest and shook his head. "He is gone," he said. "It was a massive heart attack. I can do nothing. No one could have. It was too quick."

Eleonore nodded, sat back down and wept. "It was his temper," she sobbed.

Later everyone said it was a bad omen. Napoleon would not have many more birthday celebrations in *this* church.

9

1812

Katinka, who wished to be known as Sophie, was now called Kati as befitted a grown woman of seventeen. She was walking rapidly through the Vilsen woods. It was still called that although it was mostly brush now. But here and there a sapling that had escaped Napoleon's woodsmen was growing to a respectable height that afforded some shade from the July sun. Kati did everything rapidly. She was an intense sort of person. She had developed into a lovely young woman although she was still thin and had never gotten rid of that nagging cough that had plagued her ever since the bout with the whooping cough. And this was what finally forced her to slow her pace.

She was on her way to visit her grandmother Becke on this fine summer Sunday afternoon. And she did not want to spoil it by coughing throughout the visit. Ever since her Grandpa Anton had died, Kati had made a point of visiting poor old Oma every few weeks. Becke's condition had worsened rapidly after Anton's death. Sometimes she did not even recognize Kati and those times could be very frustrating. At other times she was perfectly clear and lucid. Although her uncle Heinzi and aunt Gerhardina, neither of whom she liked, always put on a show of being kind to the old lady when Kati or Eleonore or Dorothea came visiting, Kati knew in her heart that they neglected Oma, mayhap even mistreated her abominably. Witness how much weight the poor dear had lost. She was now almost as thin as her granddaughter. So for this reason Kati kept up her routine of visits no matter how discouraging.

But Kati did not like to go to Bruchmühlen alone. She did not like her cousins either, had nothing in common with them. They were arrogant, mean and boorish like their father and had not inherited any of Anton's intelligence. She considered them stupid and beneath her. They in turn did not make her feel welcome. For this reason she usually asked Heinrich Anton to accompany her.

Heinrich Anton was more than willing for Sunday afternoon was the only time he was free to be with Kati. And Heinrich Anton was in love — that is, insofar as love could be distinguished from lust in a seventeen-year-old male. Ever since they were tiny children Kati had announced that one day they would marry. As a lad Heinrich Anton had not thought very much of the idea of marriage but now he rather liked the prospect of having Kati for his wife. In fact, he liked the idea very much although he knew they would have to wait until he finished his journey years and became a full-fledged master miller.

Heinrich Anton was waiting for her as she tripped gaily down the ancient steps from the woods to the clearing in front of the mill.

"My, don't we look pretty today," he said in greeting.

Kati twirled around in a little dance. "Why, thank you, Heinrich Anton." She tried to make light of his compliment but secretly she was pleased that he had noticed.

He took her by the hand and started to lead her down the lane.

"But shouldn't I at least say hello to your mother first?" she suggested.

"Nay, she's busy putting up cherries."

"But then we should help."

"Nay, nay," he objected. "My sisters are helping her. There'll not be room in the kitchen for anyone else. Besides it's my only chance to be with you."

Although Kati had been brought up to offer help where needed, she was grateful to get out of it. Stoning cherries was not an easy job. And he *had* expressed his preference to be with her. She smiled up at him and they headed down the lane.

As soon as they were out of sight of the mill he turned her toward him and kissed her soundly. It was a very inexperienced and chaste kiss but she had never been properly kissed before and it sent a delightful thrill through her.

She backed away slightly. "Ach, Heinrich Anton," she said, "you should not have done that."

"But we've kissed many a time when we were children."

"Ja, but we were but children then. Now you are a man and — and . . ."

"And you are a woman," he said.

She smiled and said, "Kiss me again, Heinrich Anton. I liked it."

He promptly did so — more lingeringly this time but still innocent. She leaned against him and he held her close. "Kati, you will be my wife, won't you? I want to marry you. I know that now."

She pulled away from him slightly. "We've always known that, Heinrich Anton, but it cannot be for a long time."

"I know," he sighed. "I must complete my journey years. But that will go by fast."

"There's more than that," she said wistfully. "I'll not be wed and bring children into a world controlled by France. They killed my grandfather, they degraded my mother, they took my father and thousands of other men, they destroyed our business, they've impoverished the country. Nay, Heinrich Anton, I love you dearly and you know I want to marry you some day, but until Hannover is free again I'll not wed you or anyone. Suppose Napoleon takes you. They say he is planning to declare war on Russia. I could be a widow before I'm eighteen. Have you thought of that?"

Heinrich Anton had thought of that but only in terms of his own life, never with the thought of leaving Kati a widow. He was also shocked at her vehemence. He had never stopped to think how devastated her family, who had always been so proud of their French blood, had been by the French occupation. He hung his head.

"I have thought of it," he admitted, "but never in the light of all you have said. I've only selfishly thought how lucky I've been so far to avoid the conscription. I'll wait, dearest Kati, as long as you want." He took her hand and they continued on to Bruchmühlen.

Becke was having one of her bad days and they did not stay long. She was back in some far-off time when Fritzi and Heinzi were babies and she was scolding her husband for something. Kati tried valiantly to make conversation but Becke did not even seem to know who she was. It was so pathetic. At last they took their leave.

"I've never heard her scold Opa in my whole life," commented Kati afterwards. "That must have been *really* long ago—even before Mama was born, I'll warrant."

About the same time over a thousand miles away Kati's father Teddi was saying to Jobst, "What do we do now?"

"Why, wait until someone tells us what to do, I expect," replied a bedraggled and disheartened Jobst.

"What a total waste of time trailing around this godforsaken country after our so-called king Jerome. He had no more idea of how to lead an army than that mongrel over there," said Teddi.

"Napoleon knows that now. He publicly chastised him and Jerome

265

resigned his command and is on his way back to Kassel."

"Good riddance. But as I say, what do we do now? It has been two weeks since we crossed the Nieman River into Russia and they only gave us food for five days. We've been roasting by day, freezing by night, drenched with rain and now here we are in Vilna expecting provisions and we have no commander."

Johann Heinrich Matthies joined them. "Teddi, why don't you stop complaining and do like everyone else?" He held up an icon in a jeweled frame.

"You can't eat that," rejoined Teddi.

"Nay, but you can trade it for food and the swill they call beer here."

"But Hans, that's looting," objected Jobst, "and we were forbidden to loot on pain of death."

"Ach, don't be so squeamish," said Johann. "Napoleon's not here yet and everyone's grabbing what they can before he gets here. You're foolish not to."

Jobst was about to reply when Carsten Campsheide walked up. Johann quickly slipped the icon into his coat pocket.

"The Emperor has just arrived and the commissary wagons will be here soon," said the young lieutenant. "After a few days rest to get the army reorganized, we'll be on our way to Vitebsk."

The men groaned. "Vitebsk? Where in the hell is that?" asked Johann. "I thought we were going to Moscow."

"I'm not sure," admitted Carsten, "but I understand it's on the way. In any event that is where the Scots-Russian general Barclay has retreated to. So we must follow. We've got to try to destroy his army before we get to Moscow."

"And who is to be our commander now that we have lost our 'king'?" asked Johann sarcastically.

"I don't know yet," replied Carsten, "but the Emperor has fifty generals with him. One of them will claim us, have no fear."

The men rolled up their eyes.

"And how far is it to this Vitebsk?" asked Teddi, dreading the answer.

"Oh, about a hundred miles or so," replied Carsten.

The distance from Vilna to Vitebsk was in actual fact 250 miles. On 16 July Napoleon led his reprovisioned army northeast in the hope of catching Barclay at Vitebsk. But the bird had flown the coop. The wily Scot had led his Russian army to Smolensk, a much larger and heavily fortified town. Napoleon arrived in Vitebsk near the end of July but there was further delay. Both reinforcements and supplies he had ordered to meet him there had gone astray. For two weeks he chafed at the bit but his men were grateful for the rest. Once again they had sweated under the merciless July sun, been drenched by downpours and shivered at night. Many had died en route and desertions were rampant. Several of his generals urged Napoleon to spend the winter there but he argued, rightfully, that it was poor country with little food and even less fodder to be had. Besides he had no intention of giving the Russians time to build up their armies. Smolensk would be better, if they could capture it. They left Vitebsk on 13 August once again on forced marches.

"Look at that!" exclaimed Jobst.

"Good heavens," said Teddi, "they're burning their own villages. These Russians are crazy."

"Not so crazy," said Johann. "Whatever food they can't carry with them, they are burning so there is nothing left for us to eat nor shelter either."

"Well, they won't burn Smolensk," Teddi assured him. "I've heard that town is sacred to their Blessed Virgin. We'll find shelter there."

"If we take it," added Jobst doubtfully.

They slogged on.

"What's wrong with those fellows?" asked Teddi the next day. He did not like to think that others were using his ploy of pretending to be wounded. The men were lying by the side of the road and appeared to be in great pain.

"Dysentery," explained Johann. "They'll be dead by nightfall. Nothing to eat but meat and most of that tainted."

"Ja," added Jobst, "and most of that from their own horses. Just last night I saw several of the poor beasts trying to eat the thatch of one of the farmhouses."

"Smolensk should be better," said Teddi, looking away from the dying men with distaste. "It's on a river and said to have good farmland around it."

"If they don't burn it first," said Jobst.

Meanwhile Barclay had been joined by another Russian army under General Bagration. They decided to make a stand at Smolensk to check Napoleon's advance to Moscow. Napoleon arrived there on 16 August with 160,000 exhausted men. He had already lost some 40,000 to death and desertion without yet having fought a battle. So anxious was he to join battle with the Russians at last that he immediately ordered his weary men into the fray. Fighting was bloody and vicious. He succeeded in capturing two suburbs and pounded the city with heavy artillery fire.

The next day they saw smoke rising from the town.

"The Emperor claims it is from our own artillery fire," Carsten told the men.

"But we know better, don't we?" said Johann slyly.

The Russians had fired their own town and both armies had slipped away under cover of darkness. Napoleon walked into a town devoid of food, supplies or shelter. The Russians had even carried away their famous and beloved Black Virgin with which to rally their troops. But Napoleon had no such icon and his troops were almost in revolt. The Austrians were fighting the Italians; the Prussians were quarreling with the other Germans; the Poles ignored all orders; and everyone hated the remaining French among them. Once again his generals urged Napoleon to winter here in Smolensk as it was already late in the season to get to Moscow and back before winter closed in. But the army was in such a state of disarray that Napoleon deemed it wiser to keep them moving since fear of furious and unexpected Cossack attacks was the only thing that held them together.

So after only five days in Smolensk the marching orders were passed. Shortly after midnight on 25 August they set forth on their way to Moscow.

"At least it's better than marching in the heat of the day," commented Jobst.

"But when do we sleep?" asked Teddi.

Jobst laughed humorlessly. "Whenever the general says we can." The Westphalian regiments, what was left of them, were now under the command of General Davout, a brilliant campaigner and one of Napoleon's favorites.

"Look at it this way," offered Johann practically, "you'd be shivering on the ground. At least the marching keeps us warm."

Murat and his cavalry led the vanguard constantly harassing the Russian rearguard. Their reckless bravery, almost comical were it not so serious, did much to lift the morale of the following troops.

"Will you look at that?" exclaimed Jobst. "He's riding straight into that band of Cossacks."

"And he'll ride right out again," declared Johann.

"The man is crazy," added Teddi. "He's a perfect target with all that gold on his uniform and those towering feathers on his hat. I can't believe he hasn't been killed yet."

"He leads a charmed life," said Johann, "or more like, he's just extremely clever."

"'Tis said even the Cossacks admire him for his bravery," commented Jobst.

At last on 5 September the French army topped a hill near the village of Borodino, still seventy-five miles from Moscow, and saw what gladdened Napoleon's heart and frightened most of his men. The Russians had finally dug in to fight. Around three hills they were hastily completing redoubts for their artillery and in the fields beyond at the confluence of the Moskva and Kalacha Rivers were thousands upon thousands of Russian troops.

Napoleon called a halt until the rest of the army could come up. All day of the sixth both armies prepared for the coming battle. Napoleon's own health was failing. He had painful urinary problems, dropsy in both legs and an irregular heartbeat. Nevertheless, he wore out three horses that day riding from one part of his army to another, checking their positions, cheering and encouraging the men. He consulted with his officers far into the night. There were heated arguments. Some of them feared his health was clouding his judgment for, instead of his usual flanking attacks that had won him so many victories in the past, he ordered a direct frontal assault, fearing that the flank attacks would allow the Russians to escape again. It was to prove a costly decision.

No one could sleep that night. At two o'clock in the morning Napoleon sent out a proclamation translated into every language his motley army spoke. "Soldiers. Behold the battle you have long desired. Now the victory depends on you." It went on to promise them a swift return to their various homelands.

"Do you believe it?" mumbled Teddi, half asleep.

"Which—the part about a victory or the part about a swift return?" asked Jobst.

"Either or neither."

"The victory is possible," said Johann. "Just possible but I doubt the swift return."

"Ja," sighed Jobst, "we'll end up spending the winter here and 'tis said the Russian winters are beyond belief, that it will be starting ere this month is out."

"And we'll never see our homeland again," said Teddi morosely. "I just know it."

"Ach, Teddi, stop being so negative," said Johann. "A victory tomor-

269

row will cheer us all up." Although he was not entirely sure he believed it himself.

At six in the morning of the 7 September the bugles sounded, the drums rolled. The call to arms! The battle was joined. It began with a heavy cannonade from hundreds of guns on both sides. Napoleon took up a position on the Shevardino hill where he could observe the whole battlefield. Bagration's great redoubt was less than a mile in front of him; the village of Borodino only a mile away. He sent two divisions against the redoubt and ordered Eugene to take Borodino on the right. But soon the smoke from the constant artillery barrages lay so thick that he could see nothing. Nothing at all.

Teddi prayed that he would not wet himself this time as he ran forward with Jobst and Johann on either side of him. Bayonets fixed, they shot at anything that moved opposite them. Suddenly they were slipping and sliding down the ravine in front of the redoubt. An earlier downpour had made the steep slope treacherous. Teddi tripped and sat down in the mud. At least he thought it was mud until he realized he was sitting atop a dead body. Revolted he struggled to his feet. Too soon yet to pretend to be wounded. The force of the men behind him threatened to trample him. No, that would never do. He kept on shooting. At least he knew he was momentarily safe from the big guns. The balls and shells were flying well over their heads. And suddenly he was face to face with a large contingent of Russians firing at the French just as fiercely as they were being fired upon.

Teddi's gut cramped and he was about to turn and run but his own companions prevented that. But gradually the whole French line was forced back by the Russian assault. Bodies were piling up all around them. It was difficult to know where to step. Soon it did not matter. Sliding back down the ravine he stumbled over one and fell down again. He was tempted to lie right there but someone hauled him up as they kept retreating. Then a new group of French soldiers joined them and they were able to push the Russians back. And so it went the entire morning. Back and forth, back and forth, neither side gaining, neither side losing. And the bodies piled up, six and eight deep in some places, littering the whole redoubt. The artillery fire was incessant and deafening. And this new invention called shells was especially frightening because one never knew where or when they would explode. The screams of the wounded were bloodcurdling. The stench of blood and death overwhelming. And over all hung such a thick pall of smoke, a man could not see more than a few feet around him.

Suddenly Teddi saw Jobst go down, half his face blown away. He tried to fight his way to him but could not. Once again they were pushing up the far side of the ravine and once again the Russians were repulsing them. Teddi's legs were shaking so he could hardly walk, much less climb. His fingers were numb on his musket. His shoulder ached from the constant kick of the gun. As they slithered back down into the ravine he stumbled over yet another corpse and fell down. This time he was not faking. He felt paralyzed although he was fairly certain he was not wounded. He hoped the Russians did not go about stabbing the wounded with bayonets as the Austrians had done. But they were too busy. He was kicked and stepped on as the fighting flowed over him and then he passed out.

Teddi had no idea how long he had been lying there in the mud and gore as he slowly regained consciousness. The heavy guns were still roaring continuously but the hand-to-hand fighting in his immediate vicinity seemed to have slackened some. Cautiously he tried to move his arms and legs. They seemed to function well enough, albeit stiffly. The pain in his back and chest, however, was excruciating. It hurt just to take a breath. Mayhap he was wounded after all. He blinked his eyes open. The thick smoke still lay over everything but what he saw made him want to vomit except that it hurt too much when he gagged. He was surrounded by bodies, piles of them, and here and there a few other wounded. He quickly closed his eyes again. As his head cleared he realized that he was soaking wet. No, he could not have pissed himself that much. It must have been another of those torrential showers. He had to get out of here but he did not know where to go. Which way was safety? His muddled brain refused to think. Much easier to rest here a while longer.

When Teddi awoke the second time his head was a bit clearer. His first thought was of Jobst. Teddi had never had many friends back in Vilsen. He had been too uppity, too introverted, looking down his nose at most people. Certainly the likes of Jobst Diercks had not entered the small circle of his acquaintances. But thrown together in the army these three years Jobst had become a good friend. Teddi had leaned on him for moral support. Oh,God, he could not lose him now. He needed him, had to find him. He tried to remember where he had seen him fall. He thought it had been on the downward slope of the ravine. But first he had to ascertain where he himself was. Cautiously he raised his head and looked about. He tried not to let the view of the dead revolt him. He was lying on the upward slope towards the redoubt but not too far from the bottom of the ravine.

Away to the right there was still fierce hand-to-hand fighting going on. To his left only sporadic and seemingly aimless shots of musketry. The big guns were demolishing the redoubt above him and dirt and debris kept raining down on him. Soon he would be buried! He had to move. He had to find Jobst.

Teddi managed to get his knees up under him but when he tried to stand the pain in his chest was too much. A wave of dizziness overcame him and he fell down, face in the mud. He wiped the dirt from his mouth with his sleeve. It was then he realized that he had lost his hat. Well, no matter. He hated the foolish thing anyway. Also his musket was gone and that was a more serious problem. Although he doubted he could even lift it much less fire the gun, its loss made him feel very naked and vulnerable. As he got to his knees again he found that one of his boots was half off. Evidently someone had tried to steal that too and had given up. He rolled over on his back and the stabbing pain in his chest almost made him give up, but he struggled and finally got the boot back on. He looked down at his chest. No blood, not even a tear in his uniform coat. What then was causing this pain? He dared not try to stand up again. He would have to crawl.

Teddi rolled over again onto his hands and knees. Slowly, painfully, half sliding, half wallowing on his belly he made his way to the bottom of the ravine. It was filled with about of foot of water. So it must have rained. But it was far from clear water. It ran red with blood and brown with what disgusting ooze he dared not think, but it surely was not mud. And suddenly he was so thirsty, so thirsty, but he would swallow his dry tongue before he would drink any of that abomination. Men had been dying of dysentery, typhus and other dread maladies from drinking supposedly pure water in this godawful land. Whatever was in that putrid water would surely kill him if a musketball did not. He forced the thirst from his mind. He tried chewing on his tongue to generate a little saliva. But he still had to cross that foul ditch.

If only he did not have to put his hands in it. But Teddi knew he was too weak to stand and if he ever fell face down in that—the thought was too horrible to contemplate. He looked up and down debating what to do. Then a thought came to him. Gruesome, but it might be his salvation. The ditch as everywhere else was filled with corpses. About ten feet to his right several were stacked so high they practically dammed the thing. There were his stepping stones! He crawled to the place. Putting aside his revulsion he forced himself to creep on to the back of the first unfortunate,

272

then the next. The bodies were slippery and foul-smelling but they were far cleaner than that putrid slime beneath them. When he at last attained the other side of the flood he lay down for moment gasping for breath. But each gasp caused him so much pain in his chest that he decided it was better to keep moving. He dragged himself back to the spot opposite his original path. Now he had to find Jobst—and that meant climbing this side of the damned ravine and this slope was steeper than the other side.

Desperately fighting his squeamishness Teddi pushed aside and rolled over corpse after corpse. After inspecting the third pile of bodies he was ready to give up. Was he in the wrong place? He did not think so. The path looked familiar. Resting a moment he glanced back over his shoulder. No, there was the spot on the redoubt they had been aiming for. At least he thought so. It was such a shambles now he could not be sure. But where was Jobst? He crawled a little higher. Suddenly without warning a hand reached out and clutched his wrist and a weak voice cried out something in a language he could not understand. Probably Polish or maybe Italian. Teddi screamed and almost fainted from the shock. But then he gathered his wits about him and realized it was no doubt a cry for help in whatever tongue and that the poor wretch was in far worse shape than he. He snatched his wrist away and mumbled in German, "No, no, I cannot help you. I am wounded, too." He dragged himself higher.

There! There! God have mercy. There was Jobst. At first it looked as though his friend were sleeping. Teddi put a hand on his shoulder and shook him gently. "Jobst, Jobst, dear friend. I am here," he cried. But his friend was already cold and rigor was setting in. Carefully he turned the body over—and retched. Jobst had only half a head. No eye, no cheek, no ear. Blood, pus and even brain matter were oozing into the mud. Teddi quickly turned the monstrosity that had been Jobst back into the dirt. With what remaining strength he had he threw himself on his friend's cold, wet back and wept.

Teddi had no idea how long he lay there draped over Jobst's dead body. He seemed to fade in and out of consciousness. At times he heard bits of conversation—shouts really—from the top of the ridge.

"Davout has been killed."

"Nay, nay, he is only wounded."

"Eugene has taken Borodino village."

"He did but the Russians took it back and blew up the bridge."

"Murat has been taken prisoner."

"Non, non, he escaped."

"Bagration has been mortally wounded."

"Is that true or just a rumor?"

"We're not sure."

And so it went. There was so much confusion, the smoke was so thick, the fierce fighting moved back and forth so rapidly that no one on either side, not even Napoleon, knew what was happening. The generals Davout, Ney and Murat knew no more than the commonest foot soldier. Subordinate officers were directing their small segment as they saw fit without orders from above. Cavalry dashed wildly into situations that made no sense. Some men continued fighting without any direction; others blatantly disobeyed orders and no one seemed to know or care. After ten hours of constant fighting the men were exhausted—hungry, filthy, wet and tired. And for what? Obviously neither side was winning. Morale was at its lowest ebb. Their spirit was gone. The losses on both sides were horrendous. About an hour before sunset a partial truce was called to gather up the wounded, although the big guns kept firing until dusk.

Through the fog in his brain Teddi heard the welcome cry of "Stretchers here. Stretchers here." Feebly he raised his head and lifted one arm. It seemed like forever before they got to him.

"Here, here," he called weakly.

"We're here, lad. Where are you hurt?"

"I don't think I'm hurt at all," he replied, "but I can't seem to walk and the pain in my chest . . ."

"Come on. We'll help you up."

"But my friend Jobst. He needs you more than I."

The man took one look at Jobst. "Your friend has no need of us. He is long gone. They'll take care of him tomorrow. Come now."

"I think I can walk," objected Teddi, "if you'll just point me to—to safety."

The men hauled him to his feet but his legs were so weak he would have collapsed again had they not held him up. "On the stretcher now, lad. We've hundreds of others to see to." Teddi cried out as they twisted his chest. "No doubt just hurt yourself when you fell. They'll see to you." They took him back behind the lines to the woods where three hospital tents had been set up.

Teddi dreaded the hospital tent more than the pain in his chest. Panic set in. No way would he let them chop off an arm or a leg. But the pain was in his chest. How would they handle that? Cut him open? His fear was so great he almost fainted again. They dumped him on the ground outside the tent. There was a line of at least a dozen men before him, some so severely wounded it was doubtful they would even live to see the surgeon. He could hear the sickening screams from within as arms and legs were lopped off or wounds stitched.

I don't belong here, he thought, terrified. Yet there was that sharp pain in his chest that prevented him from taking a deep breath. He tried to get up but it hurt too much. He sank back on the ground. "Oh, Oma, Oma," he cried. "Help me. Tell me what to do." He realized with a jolt what a fool he must sound like praying to his grandmother instead of to God. His grandmother, the devoted Frau Meyer, had been dead almost twenty years. Yet he could not help himself. "Oma, Oma," he sobbed.

"So there you are," said a weary but cheery voice. "I was wondering if you were alive or dead. We've lost so many." Johann Matthies was bending over him.

"Ach, Hans, I'm alive," croaked Teddi, "and not really wounded but this awful pain in my chest. I can hardly breathe."

"Sit up and let me see," said Johann, helping him to rise. "Unbutton your coat," he ordered. "Which side?"

"Here on the left," replied Teddi as he complied. "Do you think it's my heart?"

Johann smiled and shook his head. Teddi winced as Johann felt under his arm. "Nay, you'll live, I'm afraid. 'Tis naught but a couple of cracked ribs. Probably you fell against a rock—or more like, one of them kicked you in the ribs. See, there's a big bruise there. Ja, that's what it was. One of them kicked you when you were down. The bastards. Put your shoulders back like you were on parade. Does that help the breathing a little?"

"A little."

"It'll hurt like the devil for a few weeks but there's nothing they can do for you here. Let's get you out of here ere they do any real damage." Johann helped him up and half carried him back to their tent.

"How do you know so much about these things?" asked Teddi.

"Around the mill we're always having things like that happen—cracked ribs, sprained ankles, broken toes, pulled shoulders. Old Opa taught us how to fix all those little things. Never sent for the doctor 'cept for real bad sickness."

"Old Anton."

"Ja, God rest him. A hard master but a good man."

Teddi did not agree but forbore saying so. He looked around. The tent was empty. "Where is everybody?"

"Gone—and I thought you were, too. What of Jobst?"

"Dead. I saw it, Hans. Half his head blown away." Teddi shuddered. "I'll be having nightmares about it." And he started to sob again.

"Cry it out," Johann advised. "No shame in that. It'll help. And it looks like more of the same tomorrow. Napoleon won't give up this close to Moscow. I'd desert in a minute if there were any place to go."

"Would you really?"

"Ja, but a man wouldn't get a mile down the road ere a Cossack got him or he starved to death. No, the army is our only protection, like it or not."

General Kutuzov at first seriously considered renewing the battle the next day but when he was told of his great losses—fully half of his army was gone—he opted against subjecting his weary men to any more slaughter. He decided retreat was the better part of valor. Before the French were even aware of it, the Russian army was already several miles away on the road to Moscow.

Napoleon himself was as perplexed as any of his men. With the Russian retreat the French held the ground but it had not been a clear-cut victory. He had lost over 30,000 men, among them forty-three generals and innumerable other officers. Never before had he not experienced a decisive victory. It was a new and devastating situation for him. Yet his insatiable desire to reach Moscow, Russia's most holy city, drove him on.

Carsten Campsheide stuck his had inside the tent. He did not seem surprised to find only two men there. "Up and about," he commanded. "The Russians are retreating and we are bound for Moscow. Assemble in thirty minutes at the foot of the Shervardino hill."

"Oh, no," groaned Teddi.

Carsten looked at him. "Can you march or will you ride in a hospital wagon?"

The thought of riding packed together with bleeding, stinking wounded men was more distasteful to Teddi than trying to march with his sore ribs. "I—I think I can march," he said.

"But what battalion, what regiment, what division are we in?" asked Johann. "Are we still under Davout?"

"We are still under Davout," replied Carsten, "but of the two full Westphalian regiments we started out with there remains less than half a battalion."

"So many?" said Johann, shocked.

276

"So many," said Carsten sadly. "Davout is reorganizing his whole army, as are the other generals. I don't even know whom I am commanding. We'll find out at the muster."

On the twelfth through most of the 13 September the Russian army passed through Moscow finally stopping five miles beyond the city. It was a Sunday and the bells of all 340 of Moscow's churches pealed as though nothing were amiss. There was much looting, to the horror of the hapless citizens, and many desertions—and no one seemed to care. On the thirteenth Kutusov ordered the total evacuation of Moscow. Rich and poor alike loaded what they could into hundreds of wagons and left their beloved homes. On the afternoon of the fourteenth Napoleon arrived at the city gates.

He was dismayed to find the city deserted—totally empty except for a few prostitutes and vagabonds. Where was everyone? Vainly he awaited a welcoming committee from the city fathers—even if it was a grudging welcome. No one came. Vainly he looked for a letter from Tsar Alexander. None came. On the 15 September he moved into the Kremlin. Back in Vilna he had had thousands of counterfeit Russian rubles printed. With these he sought to purchase supplies for his starving men. No one would accept them, not even the whores. They had to be burned.

Then that night the fires started.

Awakened in the middle of the night, Napoleon ordered the army fire brigade to put them out, but new fires sprang up faster than they could control them. He ordered the arrest of the perpetrators. Four hundred were shot and each arsonist swore they had acted under orders of Count Rostopchin, the Governor of the City. On the 16 September Eugene and Murat, fearing that a powder magazine the army had stored in the Kremlin might catch, urged a reluctant Napoleon to leave the city. He took up residence in a palace in the suburbs. From there, with genuine sadness and dismay, he watched Moscow burn.

On the 18 September the fires finally died down and Napoleon returned to the Kremlin. He was appalled. Over two-thirds of Moscow lay in smoldering ruins. How crazy these Russians are to destroy such a beautiful city. The army reentered the town—a ragtag, undisciplined, totally disorganized army. Looting was endemic and widespread. And Napoleon let them. He felt the men deserved some compensation for entering an empty city.

"What in the world is that thing?" Teddi asked Johann. Young Matthies was carrying a large brass, urn-shaped thing with feet on the bottom, a spigot on the side and a fancy cover on top.

"It is called a samovar," replied Johann. "They brew tea in it. I'm taking it home as a gift for my mother."

"Your mother?" Teddi was thinking of old Becke. She would not know what to do with such a thing. Then he realized Johann was referring to Gerhardina, Heinzi's wife. Lord, my mind must be slipping, he thought. This was Elli's nephew. How old it made him feel. "Oh, ja, I'm sure she will enjoy it. But how do you plan on carrying it back?"

"In my knapsack, of course."

"But the thing is so huge, Hans. You won't have room for your clothes or food or anything else."

"I'll manage," replied Johann. "Why don't you help yourself to something, Teddi? You might as well. Everyone else is. With Napoleon's permission."

Teddi shook his head. He had no interest in art works or silver or anything that would make his pack heavier. Just the thought of carrying it made his ribs ache again.

Napoleon realized that the army's morale was at its lowest ebb. He organized small military exercises in the great square before the Kremlin but the men's hearts were not in it and the results were sloppy and disappointing. He tried to set up a miniature Comédie-Francaise with French emigrés who had been living in Moscow. He offered concerts and plays to his tired troops, but it all fell flat. Three times he wrote to Tsar Alexander in St. Petersburg offering peace terms but not one letter was answered.

Some of his generals urged him to winter in Moscow but the majority urged him to turn back soon as winter was closing in. What supplies they had found were rapidly being depleted. There would never possibly be enough to last the long winter. Moreover, his couriers had brought disturbing news of unrest in Paris. Another six months away could well mean his overthrow. That frightened Napoleon more than war, starvation or even the Russian winter. After a month he made the bitter decision to leave Moscow and head back to France.

On the 19 October the army moved out of Moscow, Eugene and Murat in the van, Napoleon in his carriage surrounded by the Imperial Guard in the middle, Davout and Ney bringing up the rear. Baggage carts with food and supplies for twenty days; many more wagons bearing the wounded; what artillery was left to them; 50,000 soldiers and 50,000 non-combatants, of whom only 25,000 were judged capable of fighting. They headed down the road to Smolensk where Napoleon had ordered new supplies to be delivered. As the last contingent left the gates of the city, the bells of Moscow—of every church still standing—began to peal—and peal and peal. The men heard them with both sadness and joy. Many wondered what Napoleon was thinking.

"I told you you wouldn't be able to fit that thing in your pack," said Teddi as they marched along in the crisp, cold air.

"You're right," admitted Johann, "but I've managed, haven't I?" He had the samovar dangling from his hip from a thong around his waist. With every step he took it bounced against his thigh.

"You'll soon tire of that. Why don't you just throw it on the cart with everyone else's loot?"

"And have our own men steal it from me? Not on your life," replied Johann.

On 24 October Eugene's vanguard met Kutuzov's army at a place called Maloyaroslavets. The French succeeded in driving the Russians back but in reality it was a defeat in that Napoleon had to take a longer route to Smolensk. He had hoped to avoid Borodino where the men had so many terrible memories. But it was not to be. A few days later it started to snow.

And it snowed and snowed, at times so blindingly they could scarcely see the men in front of them. When the sun did come out it turned everything to ice—glaring in the men's eyes, causing the horses to slip and slide. Kutuzov was following them but unseen, at a distance, along a parallel route. However, the troops were constantly harassed by fierce bands of Cossacks swooping down out of the hills. And any man who strayed out of line was quickly shot by jeering peasants. They huddled together for protection and soon, instead of orderly ranks, the army became a mob hastening towards Smolensk—and food.

Because of the longer route, the ice and the harassment, it took them far longer than twenty days to reach Smolensk. Soon they were eating their own horses which had simply dropped from exhaustion. On 13 November the vanguard entered Smolensk, there to be disappointed again. Napoleon had ordered 10,000 oxen, among other supplies, to be delivered there. Because of the long delay the local citizens and merchants had appropriated the oxen and clothing and resold them at exorbitant prices. The starving men went wild and looted the town unmercifully trying to regain food that was rightfully theirs. And there were no clothes or boots to replace their tattered uniforms.

"I can't go on," said Teddi. "I don't care if they take me prisoner. I'm staying here."

"Oh, yes you can," insisted Johann. Although back in Vilsen Johann had been taught to hate Teddi Hohnholz, he truly felt sorry for the older man and had grown to feel protective of him.

"But I'm so cold," replied Teddi. "Our German bodies were not made for this Russian climate. And it's only November."

Johann laughed. "Nor are the Percheron." He was referring to the giant dray horses from Normandy, said to be the most powerful in the world. "They are dropping like flies. But come. You need something hot to eat and then some warmer clothes."

"But they stole all our food and—and everything," sighed Teddi.

"And we have stolen at least some of it back. You'll see. Come over here." Johann led Teddi to where a group of men had built a large bonfire in the middle of the street. Over it not one but two spits were being turned. Each held a large ox leg complete with rump. In addition they had erected makeshift tripods from which hung kettles of simmering soup. The delicious smell made Teddi's mouth water so he almost felt nauseous from hunger.

"Here, sit by the fire and warm yourself," invited Johann. "Give me your bowl and I'll fetch you some soup. It even has a little cabbage in it, I think."

"Thank you, Hans," replied Teddi. "I don't know what I'd have done without you. I am so tired I don't think I could have found food by myself." He sipped the steaming broth. "Ah, that's so good."

Johann pitied Teddi. Teddi had been a businessman and a reclusive inventor but he had, even in the army, always had someone to set food in front of him. He had never had to fend for himself. Now it was a very different story. Johann vowed to watch out for him as best he could. When Teddi finished the soup, Johann brought him a slab of meat.

"Best cut it into small pieces," he warned. "It could be a mite tough."

Teddi did so and chewed and chewed. It tasted delicious but his teeth began to hurt. He remembered Elli, or was it Dorothea, saying he should eat turnip greens and he had refused. He wished he had some now. He swallowed some of the meat whole. At least it was filling. Warmed by the fire and the food, he felt somewhat better.

"Now let's go and find some warm clothes ere they're all gone," said Johann, "but first fill your canteen with some of that broth. With all this snow we can find water anywhere but this will give you strength on the road—just in case."

Johann led him to another part of town, a large square where scores of the baggage wagons were parked. Except for the one containing Napoleon's dwindling hoard of gold and his own personal trophies, none were guarded. Even the drivers were nowhere in sight. Men were helping themselves to whatever they found useful.

"Now, let's find ourselves a nice sheepskin coat—or would you prefer a cloak?" said Johann.

"But that's stealing," objected Teddi.

"Hah! And weren't they stolen in the first place? Do you see now why I didn't put my samovar on one of these wagons?" Johann dug through the load. "Now here's one should fit you quite well."

Teddi shrugged into the coat with the fleece on the inside. Immediately he felt a lot warmer. "It fits all right but it's so thick I can hardly move."

Johann laughed. "So what? It'll keep you warm. That's all that matters. Now let me see if I can find one for me." He continued digging and came up with a larger sheepskin coat. "Perfect. And here's a nice cloak as well. Be better at night than your blanket. Do you think you can carry it?"

"I'm tempted to."

"Strap it to the top of your pack. You'll be glad for it. If it gets too heavy, throw away some of your ammunition instead."

"But—but that's . . ."

Johann waved his hand. "Ach, I've seen men doing it all along the road. We're running, Teddi. Soon we won't need it at all."

Teddi had to agree, but not in the way that Johann meant.

"Now here's just what we need. Some rich Russian gentleman's hat. Try it on." Johann handed Teddi a strange round hat of black curly fur. "It's called astrakhan, I believe."

The hat came down over Teddi's eyes. "Too big," he mumbled from under it.

Johann laughed. "Well, aren't we the lucky ones. Some kind soul must have taken the whole stock of a hatter's emporium. There are dozens of them here. 'Tis a wonder he didn't steal the blocks as well. Here's one should fit you. And look, it's even got a flap you can turn down to cover your ears. I'll say this for the Russians, they know how to dress for their winters. Now let's see about mending our boots."

"Mending?" queried Teddi. "Since we're stealing already, why not boots, too?"

281

"I've already looked and there's none here," replied Johann. "The only one I found still had part of the man's leg in it. That was a little too gruesome even for me."

Teddi shuddered. "So what do you mean mending?"

Johann led him to another wagon. He pulled out a precious Oriental carpet. He unsheathed his knife and started cutting the carpet into strips.

"Hans, you can't do that!" exclaimed Teddi, horrified.

"Why not?' snapped Johann. "I got the idea from some cavlary officers I watched earlier. They were cutting up a similar one to tie around their horses' hooves to give them traction on the ice. It'll do more good tied around our boots than in whatever French parlor it was intended for. Help keep the damp out, too."

"Hans, you're so clever," said Teddi. "I'd never have thought of such a thing. And I must admit to a hole in one of my boots—damned uncomfortable—and the other's ready to go, too."

Napoleon had hoped to give his men a long rest in Smolensk but, aside from the lack of supplies, Kutusov was approaching with a new army of 80,000. And Naploeon only had about 25,000 in any condition to fight. The day after their arrival he marched out of Smolensk with one third of the army. Davout was to follow the next day and Ney on the sixteenth.

The road was hilly and covered with ice. The temperature plunged to below zero (Fahrenheit). The bitter wind whipped through their clothing as though they were naked. Two or three times a day Napoleon would climb down from his carriage and walk along with the men to encourage them. But they were spiritless. Exhausted men dropped in their tracks and quickly froze to death. The great Norman dray horses slipped backwards and fell so many times that hundreds of them simply refused to get up again. Descending the hills was just as treacherous. The cavalry dared not ride, men could not walk. Everyone, including the Emperor himself, slid down the hills on their backsides. Valuable artillery, spiked so it could not be used against them, was abandoned for lack of horses to haul it and lack of men to man it.

Eugene in the van fought off constant Cossack raids. Ney fought continued rearguard action against the following Russians. But very gradually they made progress, widening the gap between them and Kutuzov's army.

"Ach, ja, it's just like we were children again," chortled Johann, holding Teddi's hand as they slid down yet another icy hill.

Teddi grunted. He could see no pleasure at all in this. Although the sheepskin coat kept him a little warmer than he would have been, it was so stiff he could not comfortably put his arms down at his side. And it was heavy. He was tired, oh, so tired. If it had not been for Johann urging him on, he would have quit many a time. Dear Hans, what would he do without him? He plodded along setting one foot before the other like an automaton. My Lord, you could not even walk in a straight line without tripping over bodies. Oh, God, have mercy.

One night at a rest stop they were awakened by a horrid stench. It smelt like meat roasting but also like leather and wool burning. And the screams. Oh, Lord, the screams. They rushed to see what was happening. Two men were burning up.

"Poor fools," said someone. "They were so cold they lay too close to the campfire and in their sleep they rolled right into it. Time we got to them it was too late."

Their friends rolled the men into a snowbank but they were gone.

"Well, they won't be cold no more," commented another.

Teddi was nauseated for days every time he thought of it. He could not get the stench out of his nostrils.

On the 25 November they came to a town called Borisov on the Berezina River. There had once been a bridge but the Russians had blown it up. Napoleon, grateful for the engineers he always kept with him, ordered them to find a spot where they could build a pontoon bridge. The engineers found such a place about nine miles north of the town. Kutuzov was about forty miles behind them, so there was time. But then came word of two smaller Russian armies approaching from the north and the south. He sent Ney and another general to hold them off until the bridge could be constructed. The river was too swift-running to be frozen as yet but huge ice floes choked it, making the work extremely hazardous. Although several drowned, the valiant engineers struggled on until by one o'clock the next day one bridge was ready and the army started over it; by four o'clock another heavier bridge was completed for the artillery and heavy wagons. The cavalry—at least those who still had horses—swam them across. Napoleon made two new divisions out of 1,800 horseless cavalrymen, of whom only 1,100 still had weapons. He ordered most of the baggage wagons burned in order to free up the horses for the artillery. It took two days for the army to cross the river. One of the bridges broke, drowning hundreds.

With his inherent sense of honor still intact, Napoleon ordered all the eagles and regimental banners destroyed so they could never fall into the hands of the enemy. About this time the men noticed that he wore a small black bag hanging around his neck. Rumor had it that he had requested poison from his doctor should he be taken prisoner. To give him his due, he and all his generals waited until the entire army passed over the bridges before crossing themselves.

Carsten Campsheide said, "It's our turn now, men. Forward march and keep to the center if you can."

Johann took Teddi's arm and gingerly they stepped onto the floating bridge. It rocked beneath their weight. Teddi almost stumbled.

"Oh," he moaned, "it's like standing in a boat without anything to hold on to."

"You'll soon get your bearings," said Johann. "Don't look down at the river. Look straight ahead."

"I've never liked boats. I get seasick."

"Just keep moving. You'll make it."

They were slightly more than half way across when a giant ice floe smashed into the bridge separating the two sections. Dozens of men fell into the freezing water. Johann, who was on the outside, was thrown off balance by the weight of his samovar as the bridge canted alarmingly. He slipped and went over the side. Teddi tried to reach for him and nearly went over himself.

"Hans, Hans," he cried, "don't leave me."

Then he felt someone grab his coat from behind and pull him back. It was Carsten.

"There's no saving him, Teddi," he said. "Once they're in that frigid water, they're done for."

Teddi stared as the swift river carried his friend away but the foolish samovar floated for a long time. How ironic, he thought. In the ensuing panic, as men scrambled to get to the next safe section and the engineers hurried to fix the broken part, dozens more fell or were pushed over the side. Teddi almost joined them but Carsten had a firm grip on him.

"Come on, old man." he said, "just a few more steps to the next section and then we're almost across. It won't be long before we're back home."

Teddi followed obediently. He seemed to have no will of his own. Would he really get home? Did he even want to go home? Did he want to go back to Vilsen where no one seemed to like him—not even his wife? As much as he hated the army, here at least he had had friends. But now his last friend was gone. So what if he had been a hated Matthies? That did not matter here. Hans had been kind.

By the end of the second day the army was across the Berezina. Only 35,000 were left—half of them disabled or too exhausted to fight. The Russians had arrived and were shelling the remnant. At last Napoleon and his generals crossed. With some 8,000 non-combatants still left on the other side, Napoleon made the difficult decision to blow up the bridges and leave them to the doubtful mercies of the Russians. He hurried his forlorn troops westward to Vilna.

The temperature dropped to thirty below zero. The wind cut like knives. The snow blinded them. The only advantage of the bitter cold was that it enabled them to take a shorter route to Vilna by cutting across frozen marshes and small rivers. Without fear of the Cossacks, thousands more deserted, although few reached their destinations. Their bodies were found in the spring by the peasants.

Teddi limped along behind Carsten. He had lost one of the carpet coverings from his boot during the debacle at the bridge. It was the boot with the hole in it. During one of the infrequent rest stops he tried to shift the piece of carpeting from the good boot but his fingers were so stiff from the cold he could not tie it tightly enough and it kept flapping, making walking difficult. And he was tired. Oh, so tired.

Teddi plopped down in a snowbank beside the road. He could not take another step.

"Come on, Teddi," urged Carsten. "We'll be resting in a couple of hours."

"I've got to fix my boot. I can't walk with it like this. Go on ahead. I'll catch up to you."

"Well, all right," Carsten said, reluctant to leave him. "But don't sit there too long. Men have frozen to death simply thinking to take a few minutes rest."

"I know," replied Teddi. "I'll remember."

But Teddi had no intention of catching up—nor of fixing his boot either. As soon as Carsten was out of sight he unstrapped the sheepskin cloak from his pack—he had long since thrown away his musket and ammunition. He wrapped himself in the cloak and burrowed deeper into the snow. Ah, that was more comfortable. Just a short rest was all he needed. He felt so drowsy. His thoughts turned to Elli. He supposed he loved her in his way. But apparently his way was not the kind of love she had wanted. She had been good in bed though. And suddenly he was feeling warm—not the aroused type warmth that those thoughts usually provoked—but a cozy, comforting kind of warmth, inviting him to sleep. Teddi slept.

Before his body was totally frozen, someone stole the sheepskin cloak and astrakhan hat. Another took the heavy coat. The snow drifted over Teddi. Soon his tortured body could no longer be seen. At peace at last.

Napoleon left the army on 5 December, hurrying to Paris for fear of what was happening there in his long absence. He placed Murat in command. On 13 December his ragtag army, famished, undisciplined and mostly disabled, crossed the Nieman River. Fewer than 30,000 were left of the almost half million who had crossed here last summer. At Posen Murat decided to go back to Naples and left Eugene in command. As they passed through Prussia all the Prussian contingents defected and joined their own generals who had joined the Russians. When they reached the Elbe, almost all the remaining German troops also deserted leaving Eugene with a handful of loyal Frenchmen to make their way back to France as best as they could.

Near the beginning of March 1813 the maid said to Eleonore, "There is a Lieutenant Campsheide come to see you."

Campsheide. The name rang a vague bell. Some wealthy farmers over near Asendorf, if she recalled. What in the world did they want with her? "Show him in, please."

A very handsome blond officer entered the parlor. "Madame Hohnholz?" he queried.

"I am she," replied Eleonore.

Carsten bowed low over her hand and blushed. He could see she was quite pregnant. How could this be when Teddi had been gone almost three years? Mayhap there was another Frau Hohnholz. He cursed his fair complexion that made his blush so easily. "Are you the wife of Theodor Ludwig Hohnholz?"

"I am she," she answered testily. Good Lord, he might be handsome but his uniform looked as though he had slept in it for days. Mayhap he had. What now, she wondered.

"I am afraid I bring you sad tidings," he went on. "Your husband Teddi was lost during the Russian campaign."

Eleonore sat down quickly and put a hand to her mouth. "Lost? You mean killed?"

"Died—from the cold as far as we know."

"What do you mean, as far as you know?" she asked sharply.

There was no easy way to put this. "He fell into a snowbank and froze to death," he told her bluntly.

"You are sure?"

"Ja, his—er—body was seen by several men who followed after. We are sure."

Eleonore let the intitial shock of this news sink in. "Teddi would chose that way to die," she murmured. "He always was a coward."

"Au contraire, Madame," he refuted her. "Thousands died that way. It was not by their choice. Your husband fought bravely as long as he was able." She obviously knew Teddi well but Carsten had admired the older man. He would not let a charge of cowardice stand. "He held out far longer than many younger men. I was his immediate superior and I was proud of him."

"I see," she said quietly.

"And you should be proud of him, too," he added intentionally. Bitch, he thought, I believe she's glad to be rid of him. Poor old Teddi.

"Would you care for a cup of tea?" asked Eleonore. "I'm afraid I can't offer you coffee."

"Thank you, but no," he replied. "I have many more of these sad messages to deliver. As for the coffee—you may be getting it again sooner than you think."

"How so—with the embargo?"

"Prussia has already rebelled against Napoleon and has opened her ports to the English. The rest of Germany will soon follow her lead. My only regret is that most of the army of Hannover is not here but in England."

"But you still wear the uniform," she commented.

"This is my last duty as an officer of the Grande Armée. As soon as I have completed this unhappy chore, I shall gladly discard this uniform and don our own—or perhaps Prussia's."

"I see."

"Perhaps you can help me locate some of these unfortunate families." He read down the list and she was able to direct him to most of them. "Jobst Diercks."

"Oh, that is Dorchen's cousin."

"Heinrich Christian Bruns."

"Johann Justus' younger brother."

"Erich Bruns."

"Another branch of the family that lives out in the country. You'll have to inquire out towards Haendorf way."

"Johann Ludwig Matthies."

"Ach, no. That is my nephew. My brother, his father, is the miller at Bruchmühlen."

"I'm sorry then that you have lost two."

She shook her head. "My brother and I are not close but it is a shock just the same."

"Then I shall take my leave. You have been very helpful, Madame Hohnholz. And please extend my condolences to your children."

"I shall and thank you for bringing the news."

As he rode off Carsten wondered if she would now marry the father of the child she was so obviously carrying, whoever it might be.

Eleonore was sitting in the dark when Fritzi arrived home. Yes, he was still working on that confounded highway, although great sections of it were now complete. She had not even lit a candle. That was unlike her. She was usually so welcoming of him. What could be amiss?

"Elli," he said quietly so as not to startle her. "I'm home."

"Teddi's dead," she said flatly with no emotion at all.

"Dead?" he exclaimed. "How do you know?"

"A young Lieutenant Campsheide came this afternoon to bring me the news."

"Oh, God, have mercy. What battle was he killed in?"

"No battle at all. He froze to death on the Russian steppes."

"How—how dreadful. I've heard thousands died that way. It must have been awful."

"Yes," she said.

"Did they—er—bring him home? Will we have a funeral?"

"Fritzi, use your head," she snapped. "You just said they were dying by the thousands. Within minutes the snow had buried him. Fritzi, they were running. They didn't stop to pick up bodies."

"You're right, of course. But perhaps we should have a memorial service or something."

"I'm sure Pastor will see to it. There were dozens on the lieutenant's list—just from Vilsen alone."

"Oh."

Eleonore patted her belly. "Fritzi, you can marry me now."

He gasped. He had never given it a thought. It was the last thing on his mind. She had been so willing to have him come to her bed. And if she had gotten herself with child—well, they could always blame it on Teddi. But now . . . "Oh—er—I mean," he stammered, "I just don't know. I don't think we could right now. That is—it doesn't seem right with Teddi just dead."

"Fritzi, Teddi has been dead over three months and he was in Russia almost a year. I am six months with child. Everyone will know that it—that is, they—could not possibly be his." The midwife had already told her it would be another set of twins.

Fritzi wilted. "I know. I know. But it's too soon. I mean, it doesn't seem quite right yet. I mean . . . "

"Just what do you mean, Fritzi?" she snapped.

"I—I don't think I'm ready for marriage yet."

"And you never will be," she cried. "Yet you were ready enough to learn about lovemaking. You were ready enough for me to soothe your sore hands and aching back. You were more than willing to let me run the business—what is left of it—while you worked on that damned road."

"I had no choice in that," he protested lamely.

"But you had a choice in all the other things. And you have a choice now," she stated firmly, "but obviously you have already made it."

"I love you, Elli," he stammered. "It's just that . . . "

"You don't know what love is. You're just as self-centered as your brother. I should have known it, the more fool I. Get away from me, Fritzi. I hate you," she screamed.

Early the next morning Eleonore packed two saddlebags, mounted Kati pillion behind her on the only horse the French had not taken and left the Hohnholz house in Vilsen. She entrusted the care of her remaining son, little Georg, to her second daughter Dorothea and both of them to the old retainers.

"But why can't we all go with you, Mama?" asked Dorothea plaintively. She was sixteen.

"It is enough that I'll be begging Tante Dorchen to put up with me for three months. I can't impose further. She doesn't even know that we're coming," explained Eleonore. "You and Georg can come and visit us as often as you wish." Eleonore hugged her tearful daughter. "You be a good girl now and don't let your Onkel Fritzi near you."

"Never fear, Mama. I hate him as much as you do."

As they rode out of Vilsen on the raw, windy March day, Eleonore wondered if she would be as welcome at the Klostermühle as she always had. It seemed as though every time she got herself into trouble she turned to Dorothea Bergmann for help. But to whom else could she turn? Dorchen was her best friend—always had been. It then occurred to her to wonder about Johann Heinrich, Dorothea's eldest son. He had been recruited the same day Teddi had. Had he, too, frozen to death in far-off Russia? But he had not been on Lieutenant Campsheide's list, although he could have been in a different regiment. She hoped she was not heading for a house in mourning. What would she do then? Nothing until she knew for sure. She did not voice her concerns to Kati who was looking forward to spending three months or more in the company of Heinrich Anton.

They arrived at the Klostermühle to find instead a house of rejoicing. Johann Heinrich had arrived home just the evening before. He had lost two fingers to the Russian winter and many, many pounds. He had aged so his own mother Dorothea had not at first recognized this skeletal creature who had prsented himself at the door last night. But now they were celebrating his safe return.

"You have come just in time," Dorothea said to Eleonore, hugging her. "I was going to send word to you. And Kati, too. I'm so glad you're here. He was so exhausted last night, we just fed him a little and put him to bed, filthy clothes and all. I'm going to cook all his favorites for dinner. You'll stay, won't you? Right now he's soaking in a hot bath. I doubt not he'd stay there all day until Chris hauls him out." And Dorothea prattled on in her exuberance.

Eleonore hated to put a damper on her friend's happiness but she had to know. "Teddi's dead," she said as unemotionally as she had the evening before.

"Oh, Elli, I'm so sorry. I didn't know. And here I am chattering on like a magpie." She took Eleonore in her arms. "Forgive me?"

"Nothing to forgive," replied Eleonore. "And I don't want to spoil your happiness. And I *am* happy for you, Dorchen—and for Johann Heinrich. What a blessing that he is even alive. You should have seen the long list of the dead that young Campsheide fellow had—and that just from Vilsen. Jobst Diercks was on it and Heinzi's eldest."

"Don't tell me. I'm glad Tante Katinka passed on without knowing. And Heinzi's son—it's good that old Anton is gone, too. But what of you, Elli?"

Eleonore shrugged. "I would not admit this to anyone but you,

Dorchen, but I'm not sad at all. It's almost a relief that Teddi is gone."

Dorothea nodded. "I understand. You were never happy with him. But now you can marry Fritzi."

"That's just it," replied Eleonore gloomily. "He won't marry me."

"Ach, Gott," exclaimed Dorothea. "Just like his brother, isn't he? Damn him for a spoiled brat."

"Exactly. I simply had to get out of that house." Eleonore hung her head. "Dorchen, I've come once again to throw myself on your hospitality," she pleaded.

"And you shall have it," replied Dorothea. "Your first was born here and so shall these be. This has always been your second home."

"Oh, Dorchen, thank you. You are so good. But what of Johann Heinrich?"

"After a few weeks rest he will be going back to the spice shop. He can't wait. Although what he'll do for stock, I don't know. Don't worry, Elli, we'll manage. Now come and help me fix dinner."

Oh, the normalcy of it all in this wonderful house, thought Eleonore gratefully.

In the spring of 1813 Napoleon desperately reorganized his army. He put the new levy of that year into active service almost immediately and called up the levy of 1814 a year ahead of time. Although most of the new recruits came from a badly demoralized France, Westphalia and therefore Hannover was still technically a part of France but Jerome, in his usual lackadaisical way, did not enforce the conscription too stringently, especially in view of strong opposition from the populace. And Hannover's heart was still with her English sovereign even after ten years of French occupation.

Napoleon moved his army across Germany and met with Eugene who still commanded the veterans of the Russian campaign together with French forces pulled from fortifications all over Germany including those at Hoya. On 2 May they met a Russian-Prussian army at Lützen near Leipzig and defeated them although at terrible cost to the French. Napoleon was somewhat heartened when the King of Saxony, fearful of the growing power of Prussia, joined his army to the French. The Emperor moved his headquarters to Dresden. Meanwhile Austria hesitated to break her ties with Napoleon both for fear of Russia and for the sake of Marie Louise but at the same time the crafty Metternich was building up her own army. On the 18 May Napoleon, hoping for a more decisive victory, fought the Russians and Prussians again at Bautzen, defeated them but was too weak to follow up the victory.

At the beginning of June Metternich suggested an armistice with Austria as mediator. Napoleon suspected treachery but he had little choice, hoping to rebuild his battered army in the interim. Russia and Prussia hoped to use the truce to gain more allies.

On the very same day Eleonore brought forth another set of twins whom she deliberately named Herman Friedrich after Fritzi and Eleonore Amalie after herself. The boy died within a few hours and the girl died three days later. She herself was terribly weakened by the birth and exhausted as she had never been before.

Full of bitterness, she remarked to Dorothea, "So much for Fritzi." She stayed on at the Klostermühle, unable and unwilling to take up the pieces of her life.

10

 Heinrich Anton was teaching his youngest brother Christian the simplest basics of being a miller. Young Chris, now seven, was just beginning his apprenticeship and had a great deal to learn. But Heinrich Anton was not teaching very well today. His mind was on other things. His next two brothers Dietrich and Friedrich were nearing the end of their own apprenticeships and both had become reasonably adept although not quite skilled. Yet both were fully able to carry their weight around the mill with what little work there was to be had with the country near starvation due to the privations caused by ten years of French occupation and the exorbitant taxes demanded to support Napoleon's constant warfare. Heinrich Anton had to speak to his father before one of his brothers left for his journeying years.

He had been looking for an opportunity for weeks—ever since he had met Carsten Campsheide—but with all the excitement of Tante Elli having her babies and the subsequent funerals there had been no chance. But now Papa was just standing off to one side watching the four boys work. He looked as though his thoughts were miles away. Heinrich Anton told little Chris to work with Dieter for a while and approached his father.

"Papa, may I speak with you?" he asked. "I mean in private."

Chris, though startled out of his daydream, did not seem at all surprised. He looked at his son as though he had not seen him for a long time. "Ja," he replied, "and I've been wanting to speak with you. You've grown. Come, let's go outside in the fresh air where we can be alone. There's no privacy in here. Too noisy, too."

Chris led him around back of the mill and sat down in the shade on a rustic bench by the millpond.

"Papa, I'd like to go away for a couple of years. Oh, I fully intend to return and be the best miller hereabouts," he rushed on for fear Chris would interrupt him. "I'm well aware of my godfather Anton's legacy and I appreciate that. But you're not ready to retire yet and Dieter and Fritz are all the help you really need. There just is not enough work for all of us right now and I'd like to see a little of the world ere I settle down."

Chris listened thoughtfully until Heinrich Anton wound down. He had been aware for some time that his son was restless and felt superfluous. He also knew that Heinrich Anton had been attending meetings of the semi-secret 'Tugendbund' under the leadership of Hoya Secretary Mertens. The group of young men espoused unity for Germany under a constitution, a return to the old 'virtues' and, above all, freedom from Napoleon and the French domination. Chris also understood that his beloved son was just at that age when a young man felt the need to try his wings, to leave the nest. Hadn't he himself wandered around for years until he met his dearest Dorchen?

"And so where would you intend to go?" Chris asked.

Heinrich Anton was so surprised that his father had not objected, he hesitated a moment before answering. "Well, we—that is, I thought about going to England for a short while."

"England is it? And what would you do there?"

"You see, Papa, we have simply got to get the French out of Germany. Napoleon is faltering. All he needs is a good push and we'll be rid of him. But since Hannover doesn't have any army here—they are all over there in the King's German Legion—I—we—that is, some of us thought about going over there to join them."

This time Chris did object. "After I fought so hard to keep you out of the army, now you want to join up anyway?"

"But that was Napoleon's army," said Heinrich Anton. "This would be Hannover's own fighting for England. You know there will never be peace—or prosperity either—until Napoleon is done for."

"Agreed. But an army—no matter whose—means fighting and fighting can get you killed. I thought the Tugendbund was for peaceable solutions."

"So you know about that."

"Of course. I'm not blind."

"Those peaceable solutions are good enough for old men like Herr Sekretär Mertens but most of us young fellows are not content to wait."

Chris cringed. Secretary Mertens, though middle-aged, was younger than Chris himself. Old men, indeed. "And who put these ideas in your head? Who else is thinking of going?"

"Carsten Campsheide will lead us." And he named several other local young men.

294

"One veteran of the Russian campaign and a half dozen greenhorns," Chris commented. There was more to this than Heinrich Anton was admitting. Chris just knew it. "Now tell me the real reason you are so anxious to leave. Does Kati know of this?"

Heinrich Anton blushed and his father knew he had hit a raw nerve. "Not yet," admitted Heinrich Anton. He stumbled and stammered a bit. "You see, sir, she is part of the reason I want to go."

"Oh?" said Chris. "I thought you two were so eager to wed."

"I am but she said," and the words came tumbling out, "she said she will not wed until the French are gone out of Hannover. She will not bring any children into a starving and wartorn world. I cannot even touch her except for a little kiss here and there. She's driving me crazy without intending to. I love her dearly but, Papa, I'm a man now. I want her the way a man wants a woman. I have to get away from her and—and help drive the French out, so she will wed me. Until then . . ."

And at last Chris understood.

"I see," he said and was silent for a long time, thinking.

Chris was such a kind, even-tempered man that Heinrich Anton did not expect an angry outburst as some of his fiends had received from their fathers, but he did expect a lecture. Therefore, he was surprised at Chris' next question.

"Then you have not bedded her at all? I rather thought you might have."

Heinrich Anton shook his head. "Not at all. She won't even let me touch her—her—anywhere. She is not like her mother."

"I know she's not," replied Chris, "but it is not for us to judge Elli too hastily. She has not had a happy life. It might be good for Kati to get away for while, too." He paused for a moment. "I shall speak to your Onkel Philipp—on her behalf as well as yours."

"Onkel Philipp? On my behalf? I don't understand."

"Philipp once knew Prince Ernst August—whom I believe is now called the Duke of Cumberland—quite well at Göttingen. I understand he has been kept in England in charge of that country's defenses in case of an invasion by Napoleon. While he is not commanding the King's German Legion—I don't know who is now—he certainly has some influence. A letter of introduction would not be amiss."

"But I don't want to be shown any favoritism," objected Heinrich Anton.

"Don't be so innocent, my dear son. It *always* pays to know someone higher up and if you play it right, all your friends can be included, too."

"I see," replied Heinrich Anton, although he was not sure he did. "And what has all this to do with Kati? I'm certainly not taking her to England with me."

Chris laughed. "I should hope not. But bear in mind, she will be heartbroken when you leave and her mother at this time will be no help to her. That house is too gloomy by far. And she is such a bright, delightful child—er, I mean, young woman. It behooves her to get away for a while, too. Philipp has many connections at the court in Hannover as well as Göttingen. I'll see what he can do. Kati would fit in well there, I think."

It took Heinrich Anton a moment to digest all this. "Papa, I'm so glad I spoke to you and that you understand. I was thinking of running away but I couldn't do that. And you've told me so many things I would never have thought of."

"It takes a few years of learning the ways of the world. And I'm glad, too, that you came to me first. Your mother would have been heartbroken had you run off. She was not herself, just frantic with worry all the while Johann Heinrich was in Russia. So not a word to her yet—nor to Kati, either. I'll try to break it to her easily. Now when does your Lieutenant Campsheide and his little band of recruits plan on leaving?"

"Soon, I hope. Probably within a few weeks, I think."

"Good. The sooner the better. There is a truce in effect now. How long it will hold I know not. Right now Napoleon is too busy in Saxony to worry about British ships coming into Bremen and Hamburg. But he is also desperate for men. So the sooner you get yourself and your friends to England the better. I'll ride into Vilsen tomorrow and speak to Philipp. He is sure to have some worthy suggestions."

"Oh, Papa, how can I thank you? I knew you would understand."

"Just get yourself back here safe and sound. I'm not that young anymore."

The next day when Chris returned from Vilsen, he said to Heinrich Anton, "Your Onkel Philipp wishes to speak with you later this aftrnoon. He may also want to see your friend Campsheide. Can you contact him?"

"I can ride over there right now. But Onkel is not going to try to talk us out of it, is he?"

"Nay, nay. He thinks it is an admirable idea but he brought up the question of passports which neither you nor I nor, I'm sure, your friends have thought of. While England still considers herself the ruler of Hannover, technically we are still a part of France. Things could get a bit sticky if French officials stopped you. They might not honor the passports but having some sort of official document on you is better than none at all. At least it would prove you are not deserters, especially in Campsheide's case."

"I never thought it would be so complicated," sighed Heinrich Anton.

"Oh, I miss him so already, Tante Dorchen," sobbed Kati, "and he's only been gone a week. Mayhap I should have let him do—er—whatever it is men do to put babies in women."

Dorothea held her in her amrs. "Nay, nay, child. That would have been the more tragic. You were right to hold him off. He'll respect you the more for it someday."

"But I love him so. Do you think that's why he left—because he no longer loves me?"

"Nay, never that. He left because he loves you too much. Men, especially very young men, have certain needs and often feel they can't control them when they are near a desirable young maid. He did not want to hurt you. He felt that only by being away from you for a time could he control those needs. You'll thank him for it in the end."

"I shall?"

"Ja, dear Kati, he wants to defeat Napoleon just for your sake."

"For me?"

"Ja, ja, so that you can wed in a land at peace and free from France. Come now, dry your tears and let us work on those gowns you'll need for Hannover."

"But I don't want to go to Hannover. Mama needs me."

"No, she doesn't. She needs no one but herself. She is dragging you down into her own gloom and that is not right. A young maid like you needs to be happy and have fun. In Hannover you will be going to balls and soirées. You'll be dancing and having intelligent discussions and learning courtly manners and meeting other young people and wearing beautiful gowns. You'd like that, wouldn't you?"

"I guess so but I'm a little afraid."

"Fear not, Kätchen, I understand from Philipp that the Graf von Münster maintains an extremely decorous court in Hannover. Not like that wild, libertine Jerome in Kassel. God willing, if Napoleon is defeated, we'll soon be rid of that one."

297

"I hope it's not too stuffy in Hannover."

Dorothea laughed. "Don't worry, the young nobility would never permit that. Just a little spice is good, right? And this time of year you may get out to Herrenhausen as well. There they have a theatre and those beautiful gardens."

"Oh, I'd like that."

"Good. Then let's get busy on those gowns. We'll see that you're the most beautiful maid there."

At last Kati smiled.

In mid-July 1813 five young men from Vilsen trotted behind their leader Carsten Campsheide on the new highway to Bremen. Carsten was the only one with a horse which he led in order to walk with the men. At twenty-two Carsten was by far the eldest and the only veteran. Two like Heinrich Anton were eighteen and two as young as sixteen but all were eager to get to England and eventually fight Napoleon. Carsten had long since discarded his French uniform and was dressed exactly like the rest. The early morning was still cool and pleasant and even though it would get hot later, he knew it would never reach the debilitating heat of the Russian steppes. And for that he was grateful. He hoped they would reach Bremen before nightfall but he dared not push them too hard, especially this first day. These were not Napoleon's seasoned troops but raw young lads who would soon flag no matter how willing or eager.

"Riders coming," called out Gerd Meyer from the rear.

They dove into the ditch and scrambled into the woods beyond. They had decided beforehand to avoid all contact with mounted men until it could be ascertained that they were not a French patrol. Each of them had a weapon of sorts. Heinrich Anton had a beautiful, wickedly sharp knife sheathed in his boot. Chris told him it had been a gift to his grandfather from old Cyriacus Lindemann. Harm Bruns and Ludwig Schierhop also had knives but they were more the type for slaughtering pigs, deadly nonetheless. Erich Fischer had a brace of pistols from his father. Carsten doubted they could do much harm as they were duelling pistols but they could kill at close range. Gerd had only a stout stave knobbed at one end which he wielded like a club. Erich had offered to loan him one of the pistols but Gerd said no, he was quite capable of inflicting a lot of damage with his cudgel. Carsten, of course, had his sword as well as a pair of heavy military pistols, thanks to the French quartermasters. Although some of their fathers had offered muskets, Carsten had forbidden them as being too obvious. No need to call attention to their purpose. They would be well supplied with arms once they reached England. Besides he felt the fathers would have better use for the muskets in defending their homes, should the need arise.

"All clear," said Heinrich Anton. It had been small French troop but it apparently had not noticed the men as it thundered up the highway.

Carsten peered out cautiously. "Very well. Let's go," he said.

They paused at Syke for their noonday repast. It could hardly be called dinner. Each man carried enough food for five days just in case they had to wait that long in Bremen. Their food consisted mostly of boiled eggs, cheese, a few pieces of chicken, a lucky slice or two of ham, some fruit and lots and lots of bread which was already getting stale. One doting mother had foolishly included butter which had long since turned to soup. Carsten led them into a small copse near the cemetery.

"Here," he announced, "is the very spot where the great Duke Friedrich Wilhelm of Braunschweig and his 'black' army camped back in 1809 on their flight to England."

"I remember that," said Heinrich Anton. "They blew up the bridge at Hoya."

"I remember, too," said Ludwig. "They also stole some supply wagons, didn't they?"

"Yes, they did," replied Carsten. "A very daring escapade, right under the noses of the French."

"Why was he called the Black Duke?" asked Gerd.

"Because he and all his men were dressed entirely in black," replied Carsten, "so that they could travel unseen at night."

"Wasn't he killed in some battle?" asked Erich.

"Nay, nay," said Carsten. "That was his father, the old Duke, one of the heroes of the Seven Years War. He was killed at Auerstadt in 1806. A brilliant commander but his orders were countermanded by that foolish King of Prussia. So they lost the battle. One reason why I would not go to fight for Prussia, although a lot of our men have."

"Do you think we will meet this Black Duke when we get to England?" asked Heirnich Anton.

"It's possible," averred Carsten. "He should have a fairly high command since he brought them over two thousand men."

The little group passed into the territory of Bremen several hours later. Carsten had been afraid because of the lateness of the hour that they would be denied entrance into the town proper. But luck was with them.

Because of the long summer days the gates remained open well into early evening. A half hour later they were crossing the huge Weser bridge that led to the heart of the city.

"How big the Weser is here," exclaimed Gerd. "It's almost like the sea."

"Nay, the sea is several miles farther downstream," said Heinrich Anton from his superior knowledge. "And it is so big you can't even see land on either side."

"How do you know?" asked Erich. "Have you ever seen it?"

"Nay," admitted Heinrich Anton, "but my Tante Elli's husband—he who died in Russia—went to England once and told us all about it. Sometimes it makes you sick, but it won't if you have a strong stomach."

They all agreed that they would have strong stomachs.

"You'll see soon enough if we can find a ship," added Carsten.

Then they were overawed at the tall buildings, five- and six-storeyed with elaborate stepped gables. The ancient offices-cum-warehouses of the once powerful Hanse merchants lined the waterfront. None of them except Carsten had ever been more than a few miles outside of Vilsen and they marvelled that these handsome edifices could stand at all, much less for four or five hundred years. They also marvelled at the wealth they represented.

But the waterfront was remarkably quiet. Only a few riverboats and some fishing vessels heading out for their night's catch plied the river. Not a single large ship was in sight. The offices, too, were shuttered for the night but close up it was apparent that many had been closed for a long time. Napoleon's Continental System and the British embargo had hit Bremen hard because for untold centuries trade had been the former Free City's lifeblood.

The streets along the waterfront were also nearly deserted. Only a tavern here and there seemed alive. Apparently beached sailors and unemployed clerks still had some coin wherewith to drown their sorrows. Carsten decided to make his initial inquiries at one of these. Wharfrats always seemed to know more about what was going on than officialdom—provided they were at least halfway sober.

"Now you lads wait out here for me," he instructed. "I have to inquire as to where the harbor master's office might be."

"Why can't we go in with you?" asked Erich. "I am thirsty."

"Nay, it would never do to let them know our purpose in this neighborhood," cautioned Carsten. "Besides you'll be overcharged for no but

300

swill. Wait here like I tell you and don't go wandering off. I'll be right back." He did not want to tell them that they would be spotted immediately for country bumpkins, mayhap robbed or set upon, at the very least teased in order to start a brawl.

Erich grumbled but Heinrich Anton said, "We'll wait, Lieutenant. I'll hold your horse."

Carsten entered the tavern, hand quietly on the hilt of his sword. The place was so dark he at first could see nothing. Only a few candles stood on the back bar. The tobacco smoke was so thick it made his eyes water. The place stank of sour beer, rancid wine and human sweat. Carefully he made his way to the end of the bar where the barkeep was deep in conversation with a couple of patrons. He did not seem to be overly busy serving.

"Ho, mein Host," Carsten greeted him cheerfully. "We are just arrived in Bremen and I wonder if you could direct us to the Harbor Master's office. We had an appointment with him but I fear me we are a bit late. Had a little altercation on the road with a French patrol. None the worse for it though. Me hearties are well armed."

The host looked him up and down carefully before answering. There was obviously an air of authority about him. "We?" he asked.

"My men await me outside—all but two, veterans of the Russian campaign."

"Deserters then?"

"Nay, sir. Honorably discharged. We have most willingly shed the French uniform."

"I see," said the barkeep.

The two patrons seemed suddenly interested in the conversation at the mention of Russia. Carsten hoped not too interested.

" 'Tis strange that you should have an appointment with the harbor master," continued the host. "He only opens his office but once or twice a week and then only for a couple of hours. What, may I ask, is your business with him?"

Carsten lowered his voice conspiratorily. "We have heard that Bremen is opening the port to British ships in defiance of Napoleon's orders. We need to know when the next one is due in. We seek passage to England to join the King's German Legion."

"Ah, ha! Then I wish ye the best of luck but I fear me you'll have a long wait. 'Tis true the Town Council voted to open the port, under pressure from the merchants who run this town, but we've yet to see nary a ship nor has there been word of any a-coming, else these lads would be out there on the quay dancing and piping a welcome."

Carsten's face fell. "We had hoped . . . What do you suggest we might do?"

"Tell you what. You'd best go and talk to the Bürgermeister—not allowed to call him that no more, but we still do. Johann Schmid is his name. He's the only one as knows what's really going on. Can give you the best advice."

"And where can I find him?"

"Why, at the Rathaus, of course. Might even still be there. Works all hours of the night. A good man."

"Then I thank you for the suggestion. Er . . . ?"

"Take any one of these streets. They all lead to the Market Square. Rathaus is so big a blind man couldn't miss it. Better yet, Franz here lives over that way. He can show you."

"Be glad to," offered the younger of the two men. "I was about to be leavin' anyway. Ma'll be gettin' skittery."

Carsten was a little leery. He hoped it was not a trap. Then the older man clapped him on the shoulder. "I admire your courage, lad. I'd like nothin' better'n to join ye if'n I could." He clumped a wooden leg on the floor. "Lost it at Jena. That Napoleon's sure fearsome but he made a mistake goin' to Moscow. I guess I don't have to tell you that." Carsten nodded. "But his sun is settin'. It's up to you young lads to get rid of him once and for all."

"We'll try, sir," said Carsten.

Franz followed him out of the tavern. "What! Only six of ye?" he exclaimed. "Methought 'twas a whole army ye had." He burst out laughing.

"I never said how many," insisted Carsten.

"Nay, ye didn't. And smart thinking 'twas that," said Franz. "Old Nick Pegleg's a good man but some of them roughnecks might have started a little fracas."

"And three of them veterans of the campaign in Russia," Carsten said emphatically, hoping the boys would catch the ploy. He singled out the three eldest—Heinrich Anton, Ludwig and Erich. "They were all under my command. And the other two lost brothers there."

Harm, who rarely opened his mouth, surprised them all by catching the drift immediately. "Aye," he said, "and two cousins as well. All froze to death."

"Then I can see why you're all anxious to get to England," com-

302

mented Franz. "I'd happily join you, too, 'cept I'm a sailor not a soldier. Besides we got business to take care o'."

"Business?" said Heinrich Anton. "But I thought you had no business with the embargo."

"Hah." Franz winked broadly. "'Tis that we conduct our business by night and usually at the dark of the moon—if ye take my meaning."

Heinrich Anton immediately thought of Fritzi. "You mean smuggling?" he asked.

"Sshh—we don't use that word hereabouts," replied Franz. "For us, it's legitimate business. The biggest of the Hanse merchants are all involved. We be just their messengers, if you will. Pays well, too." He turned to Carsten. "Me and my friends could get you out to a British ship, an' you don't mind waiting a while. Ain't none out there right now, else I'd be workin'. And then too, were we to get you out there, ye might lay about three, four weeks whilst the ship awaits other men from other towns. No guarantee when you'd get to England. But we'd be willing to take ye, an' you're willing to take the risk."

Carsten thought about that for a moment. It was a tempting offer but so uncertain. "Then is it even worth our while to see Bürgermeister Schmid?" he asked.

"Ach, ja, it is," replied Franz. "He be the one as gets the word to us when there's a ship out there. Gets a message from the semaphore. He be the one can tell you best what's happening. And if it's too long to suit ye, ye can always go to Hamburg. Port's been open to English ships a long time. The Hamburgers don't give a f—— er, a damn for the Continental System."

"But doesn't that hurt your—er—business?" asked Carsten.

"Nay, not a bit. We don't pay no customs nor duties. 'Tis all clear profit."

"I see. But I'd really like to take my horse along. I assume that would be somewhat difficult on your boats. And then there's the time element. We'd really like to get to England as soon as possible. So mayhap we should try Hamburg. But I'll see Bürgermeister Schmid anyway, if you'll show us where the Rathaus is."

"Be glad to. Follow me. And I been thinking," continued Franz, "ye'll be needing a place to sleep this night. Ain't nothing around here 'cept fleabags."

"I'm sure we can find a suitable inn," said Carsten.

"Nay, nay, ye might be veterans of Napoleon's army but ye don't

303

know naught of big city ways. They'll charge ye double and you'd ne'er know the difference. Me Ma's got plenty of room for the lot o' ye, me brothers being all gone — two took by Napoleon, one dead already in Russia. The other two ran off and joined the British navy. Don't know if they're alive or dead but we suspect they're better off than the first two. And Ma won't charge you a penny 'cept for what ye might eat."

By this time they had reached the great Market Square, the heart of Bremen. All six of them stopped dead in their tracks in awe. Carsten had to admit the only big city he had ever seen was Moscow and that had been mostly in ashes by the time he got there. The Square was huge — so big the the whole village of Vilsen could have fitted into it with room to spare. And beautiful. Two sides were lined with elaborate step-gabled houses, far richer than those on the waterfront. At the far end stood a large and very ancient church, the Cathedral, with two towering, spear-shaped steeples in the old Romanesque style. And on their left, stretching the whole length of the Square, was the Rathaus, the most beautiful building any of them had ever seen. Eleven arches formed a portico in front of the ground floor. Tall stained glass windows with statues in between formed the upper floor and three gothic gables topped it all, the stonework as delicate as lace. Gargoyles and other fantastic creatures stood at the corners of the roof.

But what imprssed the young men the most was a gigantic statue of a medieval knight standing in front of the Rathaus and looking towards the Cathedral.

"What or who is that?" exclaimed Gerd as he and Erich ran over to it.

"That be our Roland," said Franz, "founder of our fair city."

"Ach, ja," said Harm, "my Pa told us all about him and the oxskin. He was a great one for history. Wanted us to know all the stories of old Saxony, he did."

"Now there be an educated man," acknowledged Franz. "Old Saxony, indeed. We here still think of it as that although another part of Germany bears the name now. They ain't got no right to it. This were Saxony long ere they even existed."

Heinrich Anton recalled with shame that Dorothea had also told him the story of Roland and the oxskin and the founding of Bremen but he hadn't remembered it until just this minute. He was also amazed that quiet Harm was far more intelligent than he had believed. "I remember that now but I never thought to see it. Gott, look. Gerd's head doesn't even come up to Roland's knee."

"I'll show you what else we have," said Franz, so obviously proud of his hometown. "Ye recollect the story of the Bremerstadtmusikanten? You know, the donkey, the dog, the cat and the rooster."

They all knew that one.

"Well, we got a statue of them, too, round side of the Rathaus. I'll show you later, but first let's see if Herr Schmid is still in his office. Come along, all of you. Ye must see the inside of the great hall. 'Tis so magnificent, it'll blow your eyes right out."

"But what of my horse?" asked Carsten.

"I'll take you and two others in first. Then when they come out, they can hold the horse whilst the other three see it. 'Tis something you don't want to miss. Come along then. And what be your name again?"

"Carsten Campsheide."

As they stepped through the entrance Franz greeted the guard familiarly. "Ho there, Alfi. Got some visitors who'd like to talk to the Bürgermeister. At least Carsten here does. Is he still about?"

"Ja, he is but best hurry," replied Alfi. "Last visitor just left so he's apt to be going home soon."

"Good. I'll take him up. The others here want to see the hall."

"Ah, I'm sure they do. Go ahead in, lads, and feast your eyes. 'Tain't nothing so grand in all of Germany."

And Heinrich Anton and Gerd did indeed feast their eyes. Although the sun had set, the twilight was still bright enough so that the tall stained glass windows glowed like jewels. Unlike in churches these depicted the powerful Hanse merchants who had made the city wealthy from the earliest days as well as the mighty guilds of all persuasions that had paid for this magnificent structure. Elaborately carved wooden seats like choir stalls lined the two ends and all over the walls were covered with exquisite wood carvings even lacier than the stonework outside. Huge chandeliers already lit with hundreds of candles hung from the massive ceiling beams. But what attracted their attention most of all were three large exact replicas of the old Hanse ships hanging from the beams in between the chandeliers. Each represented a different style from a different century and each was perfect down to the tiniest detail. Even the smallest model was a big as some river craft. With all sails set they gave the impression they were really sailing through the air. Therein was the wealth of Bremen.

"Is that the kind of ship we'll be sailing on?" asked Gerd.

"A bit bigger and more modern, I should think, but similar," replied Heinrich Anton.

They gazed around a bit longer drinking in the splendor. Then since Carsten had not yet returned, they passed out to give the others their turn before the light faded.

"Wait till you see it," said Gerd. "It's unbelievable."

Heinrich Anton agreed as he took the bridle of Carsten's horse in order to let the others see the hall before darkness fell. Soon they returned and Franz was with them.

"Where is Carsten?" asked Heinrich Anton.

"Still talking to Herr Schmid," replied Franz. "Come, I'll show you the Bremerstadtmusikanten whilst we're awaiting him. It's just around the corner."

"I'll wait here while you go," said Heinrich Anton. "It wouldn't do for Carsten to come out and find his horse gone. I'll see it when you return."

"That's really something," said Harm when they were all together again. "'Tis amazing how those old stonecarvers could make something so delicate yet so strong and all of a piece. There's the donkey on the bottom with the dog on his back and the cat on the dog's and the rooster atop them all—and looking so lifelike, too."

"Now let me get all your names straight in my head so's I can tell Ma. She likes to be able to call a body by his Christian name," said Franz, emphasizing the word Christian.

Hah, thought Heinrich Anton, no surnames then. But, of course, they wouldn't in their business. "I'm Heinrich Anton," he said.

"Ach, that's a long mouthful," commented Franz. "What does one call you when they're in a big hurry?"

Heinrich Anton laughed. "Then call me Anton. I've always preferred it anyway."

"I am Lude," said Ludwig.

"Erich." "Gerd." "Harm."

"Good enough. Can't get no shorter than that," said Franz.

At last Carsten reappeared. Anton thought he looked a little disappointed but he was smiling. "Well," he said, "it looks as though we have to continue on to Hamburg if we are to get to England in a reasonable time. It seems as though Bremen has decided to risk opening the port to British ships but the British haven't gotten the word yet. It will be up to Franz and his friends to get the message to the next ship that lays out there and that could be a while."

"I feared so. Didn't I tell ye?" said Franz.

"But the Bürgermeister also knows of at least a half dozen other

306

young men who would like to join us."

"That being the case, I can get you three or four more, an' ye want them," offered Franz.

"The more the merrier," said Anton enthusiastically. But then he caught himself. "But that's up to Carsten. He's our leader."

"I'd be glad to have them accompany us on one condition," said Carsten, "that I *am* the leader and that they will obey me in all things until we get to England. Also that these my friends from home will have precedence in case there is not enough room on the ship for all."

"Oh, there'll be room," said Franz. "Those ships bring in far more than they take out these days. But I'll tell them an' they don't like it, they don't have to go. There can be only one leader. Every sailor knows that. Come now, let's to home ere Ma goes to her bed."

Anton looked at Carsten questioningly. Carsten nodded and said aside, "The Bürgermeister vouches for him wholeheartedly and says his Ma is well-known for her willingness to help anyone who will oppose the French."

They arrived at a tiny house not far from the Square. Painted a gay pink and white, it was only one room in width but rose four storeys high.

"But shouldn't we get something to eat first?" asked Carsten. "It sure isn't fair to your ma to have six hungry men arriving without notice."

"Nay, nay, don't even think on it," Franz assured him. "She's always got a kettle of something good a-bubblin' on the stove. Never know who's apt to show up."

"But I thought your brothers were all gone," said Anton.

"True enough. But there's many another comin' by all hours of the day and night."

They then realized that Ma's house was a sort of refreshment depot for several of the smuggling crews. The front room was a sort of entrance parlor with a large kitchen in back. A spiral staircase between the two areas gave access to the upper floors. As they were to learn later, the first floor was Ma's domain—a larger parlor from which she could watch the street and a bedchamber behind. The second storey had two bedrooms of which they were offered only one but it had two large beds, each big enough for three. The sheets were clean and sweet-smelling, the straw mattresses were filled well enough to be firm but not lumpy and there were even real feather pillows. It was far better than any inn they could have afforded— and safe, which was even more important.

After a plain but hearty meal they willingly fell into bed for they were exhausted. None of them had ever walked that far in one day in their entire lives.

Carsten teased them. "You'd better get used to it. Napoleon marched his men twice that far in all kinds of weather with far heavier packs and weapons, bandoliers and powder horns to boot."

"We'll get used to it, Lieutenant," laughed Lude. "Just give us a couple of days."

The others laughed with him but some ached so they weren't at all sure.

They awoke before dawn the next morning to the delicious smell — could it possibly be? — of real coffee.

"Am I dreaming," asked Gerd, "or do I smell coffee?"

"Is it real?" asked Harm.

"Sure smells like it," said Erich. "Lord, I haven't sipped real coffee in years."

"Nor any of us," agreed Anton. "Seems it pays to be a smuggler."

"Hey, look ye outside," said Lude, peering out the window. "We got a welcoming party. Do you suppose all those are wanting to go with us?"

They crowded around to look.

"Not all, I would say," commented Anton. "There's some women and girls among them."

"I wouldn't mind having a few of them along," quipped Erich.

"Don't even think on it," said Carsten. "That's just begging for trouble."

After a light but delicious breakfast of hot biscuits, butter and real coffee, they went out to meet the new recruits. There were about fifteen who wanted to join the Vilseners. The rest were little brothers too young to go. The women were mothers, sisters or sweethearts here to bid their men farewell. Carsten looked them over. They were a mixed lot but all looked strong and healthy and reasonably intelligent.

Carsten repeated his conditions about being the leader and he added, "I was an officer in the French army on the Russian campaign. I know how to lead men and exact discipline. It any of you cannot agree to that, you had best drop out now." None did.

He also noticed that they seemed to be divided into two groups. "Now let me identify you," he said. "No names as yet. We'll learn those along the way. But tell me how you learned about us, what experience, if any, you've had and if you're willing to accept my leadership until we reach England."

Four young men stepped forward. Their spokesman was a homely fellow, short but heavily muscled. "I be Oskar," he said, "and we four be friends of Franz. We know how to fight real well but we didn't take too good to bein' sailors. Would much rather do our fighting on solid ground. And we'll gladly follow ye—er—sir."

Carsten smiled. "And the rest of you?"

A huge, burly redhead stepped up. "I guess I'm the leader of this bunch—or at least I got them together when Herr Schmid sent word as to your—er—intentions. Name's Wulfstan but call me Wulf. I was a corporal for Napoleon, honorably discharged, but there's a few here who took their leave afore we got to Russia—if you take my meaning. I won't say who right now but if that don't set well with you, we can leave them behind, but they're no cowards. They're just as anxious to fight *against* that atheist fiend as the rest of us. The others are longshoremen out of work, fierce brawlers if the need arises, but I can keep them in order. If you have need of a second-in-command, I'd be happy to serve under you—er—lieutenent, is it?"

"It is—or was," replied Carsten. "Thank you, Wulf. And I find no fault with any who deserted Napoleon. Thousands did. But if they're going to desert us, let them leave now for once we get to England there will be no place to go."

Several snickered and there was some muted laughter. One man called out, "We're with you, Lieutenant." "Fear not," said another, "we want to fight." "We weren't deserters," shouted a third from the back of the group, "just fed up with his wanting to be emperor of the whole world." "This ain't France. This be Hannover we want to fight for." "Right and our whole army's in England, so it's to England we would go."

That was enough to convince Carsten of their sincerity. "Thank you, men," he said. "Then we're leaving for Hamburg right now. Do you have enough food? Have any of you been to Hamburg?"

"I have," said Wulf, "many a time."

"Then you will be our guide for I have not. How long will it take us?"

"Four—five days. Depends," replied Wulf.

They headed east out of Bremen. The women and children accompanied them as far as the city gates where there was much hugging and kissing and fond farewells. Then they were out on the road which would eventually lead them to Hamburg. Those who had some military training marched along in good order while the others struggled valiantly to imitate them. Carsten noticed that several of them carried muskets, no doubt

French army issue. He decided to say nothing because, he reasoned, surely here in a walled city their families would have no need of them.

However, he gave his first order. "There will be no shooting, no fighting at all unless we are attacked. If we should come upon a French patrol, it's into the woods as quickly as possible and hide yourselves and especially conceal your weapons. We are not capable of fighting them and I want no heroics. All it will get you is being pressed back into the French army. And I'm sure none of you want that. Is that clear?"

"Very clear," replied Wulf. "We'll disappear so fast a mosquito wouldn't find us. But I should warn you, sir, as we get further east we'll be coming into the edge of the Lüneburger Heide and there won't be much in the way of woods to hide in. It's pretty open country. We'll have to have another plan."

"I see," said Carsten. "Are there villages? Farms with barns?"

"Few and far between and the villages are very small. There are some swamps and small streams that might do if we happen to be near one. Later on in the summer the heather would be high enough to hide us if we lay flat on our bellies, but right now, I don't know."

"Thanks for that information, Wulf. We'll have to worry about it when the time comes."

The first two days passed without incident. They kept up the pace Carsten set as well as untrained men could. At night since it was warm and clear, they slept under the stars for several had no money at all for inns, had there even been any. On the third day the stands of forest diminished rapidly and soon they were out on the open moor, scrub pine and oak affording little shelter. The road became sandy making walking difficult although it was paved here and there in the widely scattered villages.

Shortly after noon Wulf in the van cried out, "Riders coming! A lot of them!"

The little band dove into the nearest ditch, there being no other cover.

"Conceal your weapons and pretend you are dumb peasants," ordered Carsten.

It was indeed a contingent of French dragoons or cavalry numbering about fifty men. They were riding so hard and fast they never even noticed the men cowering in the ditch. They seemed to be fleeing something. No sooner had Carsten's men climbed out of the ditch, dusted themselves off and were about to continue on their way, when the call came again. "More riders coming!"

And now they saw what it was that the French were so desperately fleeing. It was a large troop of Russian Cossacks. At least a hundred fierce riders thundered down the road on their fleet steppe ponies after the Frenchmen. This time the men were not so fortunate. An alert rider spotted them and signalled to another who pealed off from the group and stopped. He levelled a huge pistol directly at Carsten's chest.

In extremely broken German he asked, "Are you German?" Carsten nodded. "Are you helping the French?"

"Nay, nay," denied Carsten, shaking. Everyone feared the ferocious Cossacks.

"Who are you and what is your business?" demanded the man.

Wulf stepped up. He had picked up a little Russian from guarding prisoners the previous year. "We are no but poor peasants on our way to Hamburg seeking work now that the port is open to the English who are helping you."

The man seemed relieved to hear his own language, mangled though it was. And he seemed satisfied with Wulf's explanation. "No one helps us. We Cossacks help ourselves," he declared. "We won't hurt you. We are saving your country from the French."

"Then is Napoleon defeated?" asked Wulf in disbelief.

"No, not yet. He and the Tsar have made a truce. Truce, bah! We Cossacks pay no mind to truces. We kill Frenchmen wherever we find them and chase the rest back to France."

"Good. Then good luck to you," said Wulf.

"Just stay out of our way," said the Cossack as he turned his horse around and rode hell-bent to catch up with his fellows.

"Whew," exclaimed Carsten. "That was touchy for a few minutes. I thought sure I was dead. Thank you, Wulf. I learned a little Russian while we were there but I couldn't follow all of it. What did he say?"

Wulf explained. "The truce is still in effect but these Cossacks are chasing after any French they can find."

"Then the Russians are not observing the truce?"

Wulf laughed. "The Russians are but Cossacks don't consider themselves Russians. They are fiercely independent. They recognize no leader but the man directly in charge of each group. We were very lucky. They usually kill and rob anyone they come across, even sometimes other Cossacks. If they had not been so intent on catching up to those Frenchmen, they'd have finished us. No doubt of it. But we weren't worth their time. We can thank those poor Frenchmen for that."

311

Carsten nodded. "Then I thank you again, Wulf. I've always heard that the Cossacks are more to be feared than any army in Europe but I never thought I'd have to confront them without an army behind me — and here of all places."

Wulf shrugged. "We were lucky."

Near the end of the fourth day they arrived footsore and weary at the banks of the Elbe. It was so wide here that they could barely see across. And there lay Hamburg, the greatest port on the North Sea, on the other side. And what a difference! The harbor was crowded with ships of all sizes and nationalities. The docksides were bustling. The great bridge that led them across the river was busy with traffic in both directions. Their spirits lifted immensely.

"Here surely we can find a ship bound for England," said Carsten.

"You can count on it," replied Wulf.

The bridge hop-scotched over several islands in the river and each of these was crammed with bustling warehouses. No depression here. The waterfront was equally crowded. They noted at least two English ships although neither seemed to be on the verge of leaving.

"Now where do you suppose the harbor master's office might be?" asked Carsten. "Do you know, Wulf?"

"Nay, I don't. Probably way downstream outside of the port," he surmised. "But why bother? There be two English ships docked right here and if I'm not mistaken another down there a ways. Just ask the captain or the officer of the watch. It's up to them anyway. Harbor master has nothing to do with passengers."

"Of course, you are right," replied Carsten, "but I don't speak any English."

"Oh, Lord, nor do I," said Wulf. "We'll have to find someone that does for I doubt they speak German."

Carsten turned to the group. "Do any of you speak English?" he asked.

Anton stepped forward. "I do but just a little. My mother taught us some when we were small but I've forgotten a lot. She had it from her grandfather who spent several years over there under George II."

"Well, give it a try anyway. It's better than nothing."

Anton threaded his way cautiously along the long wharf. Although work seemed to have ceased for the day, the place was jammed with bales, boxes and barrels. Great cranes stood ready to lift more goods from the cargo hatches of the great ship. Ropes, hawsers and cables snaked everywhere threatening to trip him. He approached the gangway. A sailor kept watch at the top.

Anton hailed him in very broken English. "Gut afternoon. Is the Herr Kapitän on board?"

"No, he's gone ashore. Won't be back till tomorrow morn. What is your business with him?"

"We are twenty men who need to get to England to join the army to fight against Napoleon. Do you take passengers?"

"At times. 'Tis up to the cap'n. Come back tomorrow."

"When will you be sailing?"

"Not for four—five days, I expect. We just got in this morn."

"Oh," said Anton crestfallen. "We had hoped to leave ere that."

"Try *Swallow*." The man pointed down the quay. "She should be ready to leave sooner. Cap'n MacLaughlin. He's a tough, old Scot but he won't o'ercharge you."

"Dankeschön," said Anton. "We'll try her. Otherwise we'll come back here tomorrow." He backed away almost tripping over a thick hawser. Anton had no idea what a tough, old Scot was but at least *Swallow* had some promise. He returned to Carsten and explained what he had learned.

They found *Swallow* some distance down the quay. The great cranes were still working, this time busy loading cargo. Anton had to duck the huge cargo nets a few times in order to get near the ship. He went through his speech again. This time the sailor called an officer over.

"Ferguson here. First mate," he said in passable German. "Captain's ashore. What can I do for you, lad?"

Anton was so relieved not to have to struggle with English that he rattled on in German until the mate held up his hand.

"Not so fast, lad," he said. "I understand your tongue but only if ye talk real slow and clear."

Anton apologized and repeated his request.

"Aye, we oft take passengers," said Ferguson. "Only one cabin taken so far this trip. Some Prussian nobleman and his family. How many did ye say you are?"

"Twenty, sir—and one horse."

"Och, I dinna know about that many. We only have one other cabin available."

"We'll sleep on the deck or in the hold—anywhere as long as you will take us. We aim to join the King's German Legion in England."

"Aye, so that's it, heh? Captain might be sympathetic to you then. I'll tell him about ye when he returns. Where can we find ye?"

"Uh—we just arrived in Hamburg and haven't looked for an inn yet."

"Best stay close by then. Try The Anchor Inn over there. Rough but handy—and cheap. We'll be sailing with the tide the morrow. Ebb turns about noon. I'll send word. What is your name?"

"Anton Bergmann but our leader is Lieutenant Carsten Campsheide."

"I'll remember."

Anton told Carsten the news. "Do you think they will take us?" asked the latter.

"I'm not sure," replied Anton. "He did say the captain might be sympathetic since we are going to join the German Legion. But, Carsten, it just occurred to me. This Ferguson didn't mention any charges but the other fellow did. Many of our men have no money at all and the rest of us not much. I guess we all thought they would take us for free like they did the Black Duke's army back in 1809."

"But those were British warships all ready and waiting for them. These are merchant vessels who have to show a profit. I fear you are right. We could have a problem." Carsten sighed. "And the next problem is how to pay for an inn—for the same reason."

"That might not be as much of a problem," put in Wulf. "I know these seamen's inns. Fleabags, most of them but not too fussy. They will say only three or four to a room but once the chamber is paid for, they don't care how many you cram into it as long as you don't wreck the place. Could we afford two rooms between us? That should do it."

"In a hovel like that I could probably pay for both rooms myself," replied Carsten, "but I'd rather the others contributed a little. We still don't know what the ship passage will come to or what we'll run into in England."

" 'Tis only fair," agreed Wulf. "The more as puts in the less for each one. Those as pays get to sleep in the beds, such as they are. The rest sleep on the floor."

"Agreed," said Carsten. "Let's go see if this Anchor Inn even has two rooms."

The Anchor Inn was more tavern than inn. The common room was crowded with boisterous off-duty seamen but it did have two rooms available. A sleazy barmaid took them up the stairs. The rooms were not as dirty as they expected although the beds were probably full of fleas.

"You can leave your packs here," she said. "You'll have the only keys."

Wulf nudged Carsten and subtly shook his head.

"We—er—still have need of them," said Carsten, "but thank you anyway."

She shrugged. "Supper be in about one hour," she said. "A groschen per head."

Wulf nudged Carsten again. "Nay," said Carsten, "we have other plans."

Downstairs Carsten paid the innkeep and received the two keys. "Do you have a stable and feed for the horse?"

"Livery two blocks down." The man pointed in the general direction.

Outside again Carsten collected a little from those who could pay.

"A groschen for supper, my foot," declared Wulf. "Probably give ye the belly gripes if'n it don't outright kill you. Over in the Market Square they got all kinds of good things to eat for just pennies—and a hell of a lot fresher, too. Wursts, puffer, and a new thing called hamburger."

"What is that?" asked Anton.

"Ach, they grind up the tougher parts of beef, fry it and slap it on a roll. Mmm—very tasty, too, and just great for us what don't still have all our teeth. Come on, you'll see."

The Market Square was even bigger than Bremen's but not so colorful. The Rathaus was even larger and beautifully ornate in the Gothic style but Wulf assured them it was not nearly so pretty inside. What interested them far more were the numerous stands purveying all kinds of food and drink. Mouth-watering smells assailed their noses and soon they were gorging themselves.

"Enjoy it while ye may, lads," said Wulf. "An' we get on that ship the morrow ye'll be busting your teeth on hardtack and dried beef a week or more."

While they were eating, Anton noticed Erich talking cozily with two of the former longshoremen. Not that there was anything wrong with that but they were two that Wulf had hinted had to be kept in order. Up to now they had done nothing to warrant suspicion but they seemed to be talking gullible Erich into something and Anton did not trust them.

On the way back to the inn Erich joined the men from Vilsen. "My friends are going to show me some of the sights of Hamburg after we get rid of our packs," he said. "Care to come along? It sounds exciting."

Gerd seemed tempted but was hesitant, waiting for the others' response.

"Me, I'm for bed, fleas or no," said Harm. "I'm exhausted."

Anton merely shook his head.

"Ach, don't be a baby," scoffed Erich. "You might not have another chance."

"I've never been here before," said Lude, "but I've heard plenty. The stews of Hamburg have a bad, bad reputation. I'm not interested."

That seemed to decide Gerd. "I think I'll sleep, too. I really am tired."

"Cowards!" said Erich. "Miss all the fun if you want to. I'll tell you about in in the morning." And he stepped back to the two longshoremen.

"Just be sure you're back to the inn by midnight," instructed Carsten, who had said nothing during this exchange although he was obviously concerned.

Wulf shook his head. "Have a care, lad," he warned. "This is the big city and you ain't used to it."

Erich ignored him.

When they had left most of the men and their gear at the inn, Carsten set off for the livery stable. Wulf and Anton accompanied him. When at first Carsten objected, Wulf explained, "Ye don't want to leave them saddlebags or even the saddle alone for five minutes in this neighborhood. Be gone in a wink. Ye'll be lucky if the horse is still there come morning. We'll help you carry them back to the inn."

"You're right, of course," admitted Carsten. "I didn't think. But the poor creature needs fodder and water. He's every bit as tired as we are."

"Then offer the groom a little bribe if the horse be safe and sound in the morning," suggested Wulf.

"Ja, I'll do that," agreed Carsten.

The men were all sound asleep, sprawled every which way on the beds and on the floor, when a pounding on the door awakened some of them. Carsten struggled out of bed, grabbed one of his pistols and cautiously opened the door an inch or two. It was a sailor from the *Swallow*.

"Carsten Campsheide?" he asked.

"Ja, I am he."

"Cap'n MacLaughlin be aboard now and is desirous of seeing you if you still be of a mind to sail with us in the morn. Right now."

"Wait a moment. Anton," he called, "come here and tell me what the man said."

Anton tumbled out of bed, rubbing the sleep from his eyes and translated.

"Right now?" asked Carsten. "What time is it?"

"About half after midnight, I should guess."

"Very well. Tell him just give me time to pull my boots on." The men had all slept in their clothes. "And Anton, call Wulf in the other room. 'Tis best he come along—and you, too. I'll need an interpreter."

In moments the three men were following the sailor through the dark streets. All was very quiet now. Even most of the taverns had closed for the night. So quiet that they could hear the river lapping against the pilings and the creaking and slapping of the rigging on the ships. The seaman led them up the gangplank and down a companionway to the captain's cabin. He was poring over charts when they entered.

"Carsten Campsheide and mates," announced the sailor.

MacLaughlin stood up. He was a huge man, taller than Wulf with hair even redder, if that were possible. A bushy red beard framed his face. "Welcome aboard, lads," he boomed. "I'm told you seek passage to England to take the King's shilling."

Anton attempted to translate that but the last phrase stymied him. In halting English he asked, "What means 'the King's shilling'? I don't understand that."

MacLaughlin laughed. "It means you want to join the King's German army. Is that so?"

"Oh, ja, ja. We want to fight for England and drive Napoleon out of Hannover."

"Good for you, lads. I admire your spirit. I tell you what I'll do for you. We dinna ha' a full cargo. B'ain't nae so much going out of here yet. I'll let you travel free bein' you're willing to work your passage. Mind, I'm only doing it for my son's sake. He's with de Barclay's Scots regiment fighting for the Russians."

Anton had trouble following the man's thick Scots accent but he heard the word 'free'—also the word 'work'. "Thank you very much, sir. But what sort of work? We are not sailors—or only two or three are."

"Nought you need to know about sailing but I'm sure you can swab the decks, clean out the bilges, mayhap aid the men on the sheets should there be a blow."

Anton did not understand the half of it but he tried to explain to Carsten and Wulf.

"I'm willing," said Wulf. "'Twon't be the first time I've swabbed decks."

"But what are sheets?" asked Anton. "Are we to make beds?"

Wulf laughed. "Sheets are the lines that control the sails. In a big

317

blow it takes a passel o' men to haul 'em around."

"Oh," said Anton. "I guess I don't know anything about ships."

"You'll learn fast."

"I'm more than willing to work," said Carsten. "Do you think the others will agree?"

"Depends on how bad they want to go to England," said Wulf. "If they don't want to work, they either pay or stay here. Methinks the cap'n is being very accommodating."

"What about the horse?" asked Carsten. Anton asked the captain.

"Och, the horse is less problem than the men," replied MacLaughlin. "So long's you take care of him and muck out his droppings. We'll tie him up good so's he don't break a leg. We've carried troops before."

"Then tell the captain we'll accept his offer," said Carsten. Anton translated again.

"Then be aboard no later than four bells of the forenoon watch. We sail at noon with the ebb."

"Four bells, I don't understand," said Anton.

MacLaughlin laughed. "That be ten of the clock in landsman's time. Bring your own food for a week. Might not be that long but with the sea you never know. I'll supply ye with water but if ye ain't paying I can't feed ye. Fair enough?"

Anton agreed and explained to Carsten.

On the way back to the inn Anton said, "Did you notice that Erich was not back by midnight?"

Carsten said, "I thought not but I was in such a hurry to see the captain I didn't pay it any mind. I'm sure he'll be there when we get back."

"Those other two weren't either," added Wulf. "They're probably good and drunk by now. I just hope the lad is not in any trouble—or worse yet, caught the French pox."

Anton was aghast. "Do you think that's where they went—to a whorehouse?"

"I'm sure of it," replied Wulf. "To most men that's all Hamburg is famous for."

"Then I shall discipline them severely," said Carsten.

Wulf laughed. "If ye can catch them. I'd not be surprised if those other two don't come back at all."

When they reached the inn, Wulf was proven right. None of the three had returned.

318

Carsten was all for searching for them immediately but Wulf restrained him. "Use your head, Lieutenant, if I may. There's nothing we can do till daylight. It'd be a fool's errand and far too dangerous right now. Besides we need a few more hours sleep. It'll be a hectic day the morrow what with loading all our gear on the ship—and the horse—and buying food for the journey and all. By daybreak all the whores and pimps and drunks will be sleeping and it'll be a lot safer. We'll find your friend and as for the other two, I say good riddance. I'm for a bit more sleep."

Carsten perforce had to agree with Wulf's more experienced judgment.

Dawn broke only three hours later. Anton rubbed his eyes. He wished he could lie abed a while longer but there was much to do today. He was exited about the trip to England but also worried. Erich had still not returned. He nudged Carsten awake and climbed out of bed.

"We've got to look for Erich," said Anton.

"I know," replied Carsten as he splashed water on his face, "but first I've got to tell the rest of the men the news. They don't even know we're leaving today. And I've got to give orders."

When Carsten had assembled all the men in one room and given them the news, they cheered. "However," he said, "we are missing three men. Two I don't care about but we must try and find our friend Erich if we can. Wulf and I will go. Anton, you may come, too, if you'd like."

"I'll come with you, too," volunteered Harm. "You may need some help."

"Very well. Gerd and Lude, you stay here and guard our things until we return."

"Oh, if only he'd taken his pistols," moaned Gerd. "He left them here for fear they would be stolen."

"No matter now," said Carsten. "The rest of you take your packs to the ship and stay there. It's the Swallow, Captain MacLaughlin, First mate Ferguson. He speaks a little German. Do whatever they tell you. I also would like a couple of volunteers to go to the market and buy food for all of us."

Oskar stepped forward. "I be your man for that. Used to cook aboard the old *Lorelei*. Remember her, Rolf?"

Rolf nodded. "A pretty good cook he was at that."

"I know what's best for shipboard, what'll keep and what won't. Tell me your favorites and I'll do my best to get them—just s'long's they ain't fancy pastries." Oskar laughed at his own joke.

319

"Very good," said Carsten. "Then those that can afford to give Oskar a few pennies and he'll be our victualler. And remember, all of you, we must all be on board the ship *before* ten of the clock. Not a moment later." He pulled a watch out of his pocket. "It is now a quarter to five."

"What about your horse?" asked Anton as they left the inn.

"Oh, Lord, I almost forgot about him for worrying about Erich," said Carsten.

"I'll take care of him for you on our way back," said Harm. "Livery sure ain't open yet. I'm a farmer, remember. I've got a way with animals."

"Thank you, Harm."

"Now come along," said Wulf, "and I'll show you the dregs of Hamburg—the Reeperbahn."

"The rope walk," said Anton. "That doesn't sound too bad. I understand all seaports have one. Unless he hung himself . . . "

"Let's hope that didn't happen. Nay, lad, they still twist and braid the ropes for the ships on the Reeperbahn—by day, that is. By night, they twist a lot of other things—if ye take my meaning."

Wulf led them at a fast trot through the Old Town, through the Neustadt which was still very old and out through the Miller's Gate to the Reeperbahn. It was a long, broad area, part workplace and part street. Ropes of all sorts lay stretched out where the wrights had left them the night before. There were lines thinner than a man's pinky and giant hawsers thicker than a man's thigh. But lining one side of the street were the infamous bawdyhouses, whorehouses and bordellos of Hamburg. Most of the houses and all the dance- and music-halls were closed now but some of the taverns were still open or were reopening, which was quite illegal but the watch studiously avoided this district unless they were called. And even then, they rarely came except for the most heinous of crimes such as murder or a major fire. Anton was glad there were four of them. He would not have entered one of these places on his life.

They carefully threaded their way through the ropes, stepping over numerous drunks, checking others that lay passed out in doorways or alleys. Wulf bravely inquired at some of the taverns but the keepers were closemouthed and claimed not to have seen the three men. Anton was beginning to get discouraged and Carsten nervously kept looking at his watch. But Wulf and Harm persisted.

"We'll find him an' he's alive," said Wulf. "We ain't half way down the street yet."

A little further on they saw a well. A crowd was gathered around it, more people than seemed usual for drawing their morning's water. As they drew near they could see a body lying in the midst of them and some of them were arguing heatedly.

"If'n he be dead, we got to call the watch, like it or not," said one onlooker, "but if'n he be alive, leave him be. He'll wake up soon enough."

"Throw some more water on him," said another and someone promptly did so.

"All that blood b'ain't no common drunk. He be beat and no doubt robbed."

"Probably trespassing on some pimp's territory, like as not."

"Whatever," cackled an old crone, "we don't want no watch down here. He be livin'. See, I saw him twitch with that last bucket of water. Leave him be, I say."

Harm ran ahead. "It's Erich," he called back. "Oh, Gott, it's Erich."

The others rushed up and the crowd parted willingly to let them through. Most of them quickly faded away. Wulf knelt by Erich's side and felt for a pulse. "He's alive but, Lord, is he bad hurt."

"See. I knowed he were alive," said the crone. "Could tell he don't belong down here. Must o' been a nice lookin' lad oncet. No more he ain't."

"Do you know who did this?" asked Wulf.

"Nay," she replied, "and no one here'd tell if they did. Don't waste yer time. Best take him home and fix him up." And she, too, sidled away.

In moments they were the only people on the street.

"Fetch some more of that water and let's get him cleaned up ere we try to move him," instructed Wulf. "He's bound to be mighty sore all over."

Erich's face was covered with blood and one eye was already turning purple. He seemed to have trouble breathing. Anton gently washed the blood and filth off his face while Harm felt for broken bones.

"Both arms and legs seem to be intact," pronounced Harm, "but I fear a couple of broken ribs."

"And a smashed nose," said Wulf. "I'm going to try to fix it a little so he can breathe better. Hold him in case the shock wakes him up." Gently he felt the torn cartilage, squeezed, pushed and kneaded it back into a semblance of a nose. Erich groaned and a great squirt of blood came out but then he seemed to breathe a bit more easily. They then could see that he had also lost some teeth as well.

"Hold his head up a bit so's he don't choke on those teeth if'n they still be in his mouth," said Wulf.

Erich sputtered, choked and then spit out a tooth with a lot more blood. He opened the good eye again. "Anton!" he croaked. "What are you doing here? Where am I? What happened?"

"Don't try to talk now, lad," said Wulf. "Can you rinse your mouth out? 'Twill make it feel a mite better."

Erich nodded. They got him to a sitting position and Harm brought more water.

"Rinse and spit first ere you drink any," warned Wulf. "Can't have you choking again."

When Erich had done so, Wulf asked, "Think ye can walk a bit an' we help ye?"

"I don't know."

"We'll carry ye if need be but 'twould heal ye better if ye could try and walk."

"I'll try."

"Gently now, lads. Let's lift him and watch those ribs. They're bound to hurt like hell."

They managed to get Erich to his feet but then he screamed and doubled over in pain. "My balls. O God, my balls are on fire."

"Ach, some bastard pimp tried to unman him, that's for sure. Easy lad, we'll hold you up."

Carsten was getting edgy. He looked at his watch again. "It's half after seven already," he said.

"What would ye have us do, Lieutenant," growled Wulf, "leave the lad here now's we found him?"

Carsten was immediately contrite. "Nay, nay, of course not. It's just that . . ."

"It ain't that late yet," replied Wulf. "Look, Lieutenant, whyn't you run on ahead and get your horse aboard. We'll meet you on the ship. And you might have those other lads take all our gear aboard, too. That way we can take Erich here direct to the ship. No sense jostling him more'n need be."

Carsten agreed and hurried off. Anton and Harm looked at each other.

"I bet he never saw any blood on the battlefield at all," commented Harm.

"Oh, he did. I know he did," replied Anton. "It's just his way. He thinks officers have to act like . . ."

"Like officers," finished Wulf.

With Wulf half carrying and the others supporting Erich they slowly made their way back to the Old Town and the waterfront. Carsten had sensibly taken his horse back to the inn and, after resaddling him and loading his own saddlebags, had put whatever of their gear Gerd and Lude could not carry on the animal's back. They arrived at the ship simultaneously.

"Didn't think he had that much sense," remarked Wulf snidely, "but he ain't showing much sense now."

The horse had balked at the gangplank and for all Carsten's urging refused to budge. Sailors on deck were laughing and Carsten turned red.

"Unload some of that stuff first and he'll be more amenable," called out Wulf. "Ship ain't going to leave without you. And while you're doing it, stand aside so's we can get this lad aboard right quick."

Carsten took one look at Erich. "Have you found out what happened to him?"

"Don't know yet and I doubt he'll remember much but he's bad hurt. We'll have to share out his work amongst us."

"And the other two?"

"No sign o' 'em, but to tell you true we didn't look too hard. So tell the cap'n we're only eighteen." He turned to Anton and Harm. "He's going to have trouble with that gangplank. I'll carry him." Whereupon big Wulf picked up Erich bodily and carried him on board.

Ferguson met them as they reached the deck. "What's this?" he asked, prepared to be angry. "We'll not have any drunks on board."

"He ain't drunk. Lad had a little run-in over on the Reeperbahn. Some's got to learn hard the first time."

Then Ferguson smiled. He understood only too well. "Then set him over there in the shade and out of the way."

"You got a doctor on board?" asked Wulf.

"Nay, I'm afraid not. Captain and I do what's needed."

"No matter. Harm here will take care o' him. He's good with animals."

At that even Erich tried to smile with his swollen mouth.

At last they managed to get the reluctant horse up the gangplank. Two sailors who had been waiting manhandled him down into the hold. "We'll show you where we'll put him and we'll tie him good. Then it's up to you to take care of him," said one to Carsten. "You got feed for him?"

"Oh, my God, I never thought of that," said an embarrassed Carsten, pulling out his watch.

"Go then. Run fast. You got plenty of time. Livery's closest although they'll overcharge you. They like oats best, though they're dearer. A little hay would do after he gets his sea legs."

Carsten ran off taking Lude and Gerd with him to help carry the fodder.

Just then a grinning Oskar and Rolf arrived alongside bearing sacks and sacks of edibles. Everyone crowded around to see what they had brought.

"Let them come aboard first," shouted Wulf above the din.

There were wursts of every length and variety, roasted chickens, a large sack of potatoes and even a dozen eggs.

"They'll be smashed the first wave we hit," remarked someone.

"I aim to smash them," said Oskar. "They be for our supper this very night."

"How you going to cook them?" asked another. "I sure ain't eating no raw eggs."

Oskar laughed. "You'll see. Just as soon as they show me where to store this stuff, I aim to cozy up to the cook. We'll be friends in no time." And everyone was sure he would.

"You only got two loaves of bread. That ain't enough for a whole week."

Oskar held up a bag of flour. "This be our bread."

"You aim to bake bread, too?"

"Sure enough. We'll be eating better than them Prussian nobles what's paying their way."

"Count on it," added Rolf. "I've et his cooking. Can't beat it. And look. We've even brung a sack o' fruit to keep yer teeth in."

"'Ceptin' poor Erich," said Anton. " He just lost a few."

Oskar looked at Erich. "Ach, lad, don't fret ye. I'll make ye some nice applesauce."

At last a very nervous Carsten returned with Gerd and Lude huffing and puffing under a huge bale of hay and a large bag of oats. Carsten took out his watch. "Are we in time?" he asked.

"Well, ship ain't sailed yet, if that's what ye mean," replied Wulf shaking his head. "Them sailors o'er there will show you where the horse be. He's all snug and secure. Harm checked on him just a bit ago."

Carsten went over to where Wulf indicated and one of the sailors led him down into the hold. He was dismayed to see how the horse was tied but realized how easily he could break a leg in rough seas had he any leeway. Gerd and Lude gratefully dumped the heavy fodder in a corner.

Then Carsten noticed that there were three other horses similarly secured nearby.

"Must belong to the Prussian nobles," said Carsten. "I hope they don't feed them any of ours."

"We'll see that they don't," promised Lude.

When they returned to the deck they found the men standing in a group ogling the other passengers. The Prussian nobleman and two women, presumably his wife and daughter, were promenading the deck. Although they ignored the men entirely, Ferguson did not miss the looks on the men's faces, nor did Carsten. It could be a potentially volatile situation.

"You men are not to mingle with the passengers," ordered the Mate.

"You hear that, men? Not even one untoward remark," said Carsten.

"But we can look, can't we, Lieutenant?" said someone.

"No more than that or you'll all have to remain below any time these people wish to stroll the deck," added Ferguson.

Just then the river pilot came aboard and the captain emerged to join him. But first he turned to the Prussian. "I would suggest you take the ladies to your cabin until we are at sea," said MacLaughlin. "There will be a lot of activity on deck here as we get under way and they could easily be hurt. You men may remain topside if you wish but *stay out of the way*." He roared the last words just as the ship's bell rang eight.

The men smiled at each other but no one said a word. Anton was glad because he had never been on a large ship before and the activity fascinated him. In fact, he had only been on a small Weser riverboat once in his life. Not that *Swallow* was very large. She was a barkentine, square-rigged on the foremast with fore-and-aft sails on the main and mizzen.

The gangway was withdrawn, mooring lines were cast and two small tugboats manned by sixteen oarsmen each slowly warped the ship into the river. The Elbe was a tidal river here and the flow of the river plus the ebb tide was so strong it hardly seemed as though any sails were needed. But MacLaughlin ordered a jib and the mizzen sail set to steady her. The pilot stood by the helmsman directing him, for rivers anywhere were tricky especially with the wind almost down their throats.

No one realized how far Hamburg actually was from the sea. When the tide turned six hours later they were still on the river but here the Elbe had widened out into a broad estuary and there was room to tack. It was almost fully dark when they dropped the pilot off.

By this time most of the men had gone to their hammocks or pallets on the lower deck but Anton was determined to wait until they were at sea. He had never seen the sea before. The crew set the foresails and main and another jib and the ship seemed to gallop forward. Suddenly there was a terrific lurch as the current of the river met the swells of the North Sea and Anton's stomach lurched as well. He was sure he was going to be sick. He rushed to the rail just in case.

"Take deep breaths and look off into the distance," advised a passing seaman. "Don't look down. Took ye by surprise, didn't it? Always happens."

Anton did as he was told and fought for control. The deep breaths seemed to help and as the ship lifted herself gently over the passing swells his stomach calmed down. But it had been a near thing and he was sweating from the effort. He looked up at the stars. They were brilliant.

"The stars are beautiful, are they not? So much brighter than on land," said someone at his elbow. It was the Prussian girl.

"I—er—yes, they are," he stammered.

"Have you ever been to sea before?" she asked.

"Nay, never. Have you?"

"Ja, many times. Papa goes to England often and sometimes he takes me and Mama. I am Charlotte."

"And I am Anton," he replied, "but I'm not supposed to be talking to you."

"Whyever not? People always make friends with perfect strangers aboard a ship."

"I don't know." Anton shrugged. "Captain's orders."

"Ach, wat ver Dummheiten," she said. "I won't hurt you."

Anton smiled. "Nay but he's afraid we might hurt you."

"Why that's ridiculous. We dine at the Captain's table every evening. I shall mention it to him."

"No, Charlotte, please don't. In fact, don't even mention that we have even spoken. I should not want to make trouble for my friends." Or myself, either, thought Anton.

"I'll not, if you insist but I still think it's silly," said Charlotte. "Are you going to Bristol or Glasgow?"

"We are going to England," replied Anton, a little puzzled.

"Bristol is in England. Glasgow is in Scotland," she explained.

"But—but I thought we were going to London," he said.

"I don't believe the ship is going to stop at London," she said. "Do your friends know that?"

She noted the look of horror on his face. "Oh, my," said Anton. "I'm sure they don't. How far is this Bristol from London?"

"Quite a ways," replied Charlotte. "It is on the far western side of England."

"Oh, my," he said again. "I shall have to tell them." Suddenly he yawned. "Oh, excuse me. I think it is time I sought my bed—or whatever serves for a bed."

She smiled—a very sweet, winning smile. "The sea air does make one sleepy. I usually take a walk around the deck every night before I go to bed. Will I see you tomorrow night?"

"Perhaps," he murmured. "I don't know if I dare."

"Ach," she said. "Don't be a coward. I won't eat you, Anton." She patted his arm.

"Good night, Charlotte," said Anton and fled. Before he went below he took another look at the stars. The North Star was directly ahead of them. Where in the world are they taking us, he wondered. He had thought England was to the west.

Swallow took a long tack along the coast of Denmark and then in the middle of the night while the passengers slept, she came about onto a westsouthwesterly course and, true to her name, flew towards England.

The next morning Anton said to Carsten, "Did you know the ship is not going to London at all but to some place called Bristol?"

"What? How do you know?" asked Carsten.

"Someone—that is, one of the crew told me. I think you should speak to the Captain."

"I certainly shall. But what if that is true and he refuses to take us to London?"

Anton shrugged. "Walk, I suppose."

Carsten and Anton had to wait quite a while before the Captain had time to see them.

"What ails ye, lads?" MacLaughlin said at last. "Ye be fretting like a caged tiger."

"We have just learned that your ship is not going to London as we thought," said Anton.

"Aye, that be so. We're bound for Bristol and then on to Glasgow, our home port. Did Ferguson nae tell ye?"

"No, he did not. We just assumed . . . How far is this Bristol from London?"

"About a hundred miles, give or take a little."

When Anton translated that, Carsten groaned. "That could pose a severe problem for my men. We only bought enough food for the voyage and several of them have no money at all. What shall we do?"

"Well, lad, I can't tell ye. Let me think on it a bit." After a moment MacLaughlin said, "I was under the impression that ye were off to join the King's German Legion."

"Yes, that's what we intend to do."

"Then the last I heard they were nowhere near London. They be guarding the south coast along the Channel in case ol' Boney has a mind to invade."

"Yes, we heard that, too," replied Carsten. Anton had not. "How far then . . . ?"

"Tell ye what," said MacLaughlin. "I canna promise nowt—nowt, ye understand—but depending on the time, the tide and the weather, mayhap we can drop ye off at Portsmouth. Be a lot closer to where ye want to go."

"That would be very kind of you, sir."

"But mind ye, there's a big naval base there."

"Oh, that would be fine. I'm sure they would be happy to direct us."

"Nay, nay, lads. I hate to do it to ye for it's like dropping lambs into a lion's den. Them press gangs, seeing a bunch o' bonny lads like yerselves, will grab ye in a twinkling and afore ye know what's happening, ye'll be under the lash of the British navy. I won't even let my own crew go ashore there, if any were so foolish as to want to."

"Oh my," said Anton and translated that for Carsten whose face fell.

"If we do go in—and mind I ain't promising," continued MacLaughlin, "we'll row ye in outside of the town and then hightail yerselves out o' there as fast as ye can. No stoppin' for beer nor bed nor whores, nor even to piss. Ask Ferguson to see if any of our men be from that area who could direct ye to the right road. Best I can offer."

Carsten and Anton thanked him profusely and went off to break the news to their friends.

Wulf took it with aplomb. "So if we have to run, we run. 'Twon't be the first time. In the smuggling business we did a lot of that. See if you can get a map from Ferguson. Be nice to know in which direction to run."

Later that day Anton inveigled Ferguson into showing them a map—or more properly, a navagation chart, but it showed enough of the south coast of England to orient them. A seaman was also found who hailed from Kent.

"Be a long hike even so from Portsmouth to Folkstone. Ye must head east through Sussex and most of Kent."

"Folkstone?" asked Anton.

"That's where their district headquarters be. But mayhap ye don't need to go so far. There be units of them scattered all along the coast. Any place east of Brighton ye may find them. Don't bother to stop at Brighton."

"Why not?"

"That's where Prinny's Chinee whorehouse be and the folk too la-de-dah for the likes of us."

Anton did not understand any of that but he only asked, "And who is Prinny?"

The man laughed. "That's what we call the Prince Regent. You know the old King's crazy, don't you?"

"Ja, we know that."

"And Prinny built himself this Chinee palace so he could take all his whores there. Ugliest thing you ever saw. The palace, I mean, not the whores."

"Do you know where we can find the Duke of Cumberland?"

"Oh, the one-eyed one. Mean bastard if there ever was. Last I heard he was at Folkstone but we been away for a while. You might run into Freddie of Brunswick a little closer. Now there's a gentleman."

"He means Friedrich of Braunschweig, the Black Duke," explained Anton to Carsten. "Oh, yes, we'd like very much to meet him. We admire him very much."

"Good luck then, lads, and keep your fingers crossed that Cap'n will stop at Portsmouth. He must either like ye a lot or want to be rid of ye. He seldom does favors like that."

Carsten and Anton pondered all that the man had told them and studied the chart more intently. Now at least some of the places had mental pictures attached to them.

The next day the cry from the masthead "Sail ho! Off the starboard quarter," brought everyone on deck to look.

"Masthead there, what colors?" boomed MacLaughlin.

"No colors but she looks French."

"Clear the decks for action," ordered the Captain and everyone but the crew were hustled below. The crew laid on every sail the ship could

329

carry. In those troubled times even merchant ships were heavily armed and the gun crews stood by their guns. *Swallow* was a small ship but she was fast. Soon the distance between the two ships slowly widened and in another hour she ran straight into the arms of the ubiquitous British warships of the blockade squadron. At her flag signal two frigates left the line to go after the Frenchman who beat a hasty retreat.

After a while the passengers were allowed back up on deck.

"That was a close thing," said Carsten.

"Does this happen often?" Anton asked a seaman.

"Often enough," he replied. "God bless the British Navy—as long as I don't have to serve in it. We were lucky this time. If we had been farther out or in a fog as is common in the North Sea, we might have had to stand and fight. A merchant ship will most always choose to run rather than fight, but if we have to, we do."

The fog held off and the weather was quite pleasant for the rest of the voyage. Soon they were in the English Channel where the swells turned to chop and was decidedly uncomfortable. They passed the mouth of the Thames and the chalk cliffs of Dover whose dazzling whiteness awed them. Then the sailor from Kent pointed out Folkestone.

"There be the German Legion headquarters where you'll want to go but 'tis most of another day's sail to Portsmouth," he told them.

Although they were too far out to see details, the men studied the coastline carefully to see what sort of country they would be traversing. There were many small fishing villages each with a likely harbor. Anton asked Ferguson why they could not be put in at one of these.

"Channel's too rough," the Mate explained. "We'll have to lie hove to whilst they take you in and that means we could be driven up on those rocks or blown so far out the boats could never find us. Closer in to Portsmouth we'll be in the shelter of the Isle of Wight and it'll be somewhat calmer. I expect Captain will let you know tonight."

"If we're going in by boat, what about my horse?" asked a worried Carsten.

"Oh, Christ! I forgot all about the damn animal," said Ferguson. "I assume he can swim."

"Ja, he can but he can't dive over the side."

Ferguson laughed. "No need for that. We have cargo hoists that can let him down as gently as can be, but then it will be up to you to hold him. He'll panic at first so I hope you've got a strong arm."

"I'll see that I do," Carsten assured him.

And so they awaited the Captain's decision. Tension ran high. Would the ship stop or would they have to go all the way to Bristol? Would they make it to shore? What would they find when they got there? Would the people welcome them or be hostile? Would they even be understood with none but Anton speaking a little English? And Carsten worried about his horse.

That evening, quite late, MacLaughlin sent for Carsten and Anton. "Looks as though we'll be able to drop ye off in the morning. I canna let ye know for sure until then. Channel's funny. Storms can kick up out of nowhere with no warning but I want ye to be ready so's we can do it fast. Have your men pack all their gear and saddle that horse but dinna put the saddlebags on him. There's two nice little coves this side of Portsmouth. We'll try to land ye at the easternmost one if we can. Cliffs are less steep. Smugglers coves they be."

"There are a few former smugglers among us," commented Anton.

"Dinna let that be known," warned MacLaughlin, "or the locals just might shoot ye on sight. They dinna take kindly to any might be rivals. Each band has its own territory and they guard it jealously. Howsomever, they can be mighty helpful to ye if they think ye are deceiving the King's revenuers. They know all the secret paths and hidden byways. I'll even give ye a letter telling of your intent. Most local folk can't read but most King's officers can read a little, should ye have the ill luck to run into any of them. Wouldn't do for ye to be locked up for smugglers ere ye meet your German friends."

Anton thanked him and they went below to prepare for their departure.

The next morning the men were roused out before dawn. They could barely see the coastline but the bulk of the Isle of Wight loomed ahead of them. *Swallow* lay hove to about two hundred yards off shore. Two ship's boats were already in the water with eight oarsmen and a coxswain apiece. Seamen were throwing their packs into the boats.

When some of the men objected, a sailor said gruffly, "Ye try climbin' down yon ladder with that on yer back and ye'll end up in the drink for sure. Ye can sort the stuff out when ye get ashore."

When the men looked over the side and saw the flimsy rope ladder they would have to descend, they shut their mouths. Most, especially the former smugglers, descended easily but a few were nervous and clumsy and had to be helped. Anton and Carsten were the last to leave. MacLaughlin gave them the letter he had promised and wished them luck. Just as they were about to go over the side Charlotte rushed up and handed Anton a slip of paper.

"That's my address in Bristol. Write to me, Anton. I've so enjoyed talking to you," she said. Anton blushed and took it because he did not know what else to do. "We'll see," he replied.

"I see you've made a conquest," remarked Carsten.

"Not that I was aware of," replied Anton.

They were half way down the ladder when Carsten looked up and saw his horse with a huge leather sling under his belly dangling in the air. "Oh, my God," he exclaimed and almost lost his footing. The first boat-load of men had already left and as soon as Carsten was seated, as instructed, in the sternsheets next to the coxswain, their boat pulled away as well.

"But the horse," shouted Carsten.

"Dinna fash ye," said the coxswain in broad Scots. "We'll catch him, but 'twouldn't do, now would it, to have those thrashin' hooves land on our heads."

And, of course, Carsten had to admit he was right. Slowly and gently the men on deck lowered the frantic horse into the cold water. After a moment the poor animal seemed to calm down and lay there, looking bewildered.

"Backwater now," ordered the coxswain. "Now grab a good hold on the gunwale so's he don't pull ye overboard and catch his bridle with the other hand and hold him close with his head up, else he'll panic again with that chop breaking over him."

After Anton quickly translated, Carsten did as he was told. The initial jolt nearly tore his arm out of its socket and Anton leaned over to help. As the boat moved forward the horse finally got the idea and started to swim and then it was somewhat easier. Half way across they met the first boat already returning to the ship.

As they neared shore the coxswain said, "See, I told you we've moved cavalry afore. Now gentle him when ye go ashore. Don't even ride him for a day or more until he gets his legs under him. Being tied all those days'll make him shaky as jelly." Carsten nodded. Once they were ashore, the coxswain pointed out, "There be a path yonder up that cliff. Have a care but it's passable. Smugglers use it all the time. When you get to the top head directly east. First town be Chichester. Nice town. Ye'll have nae problem there. Good luck to ye."

The men were busy sorting out their packs and other belongings but

Carsten's first concern was for his horse. Neither he nor the beast seemed to know what to do. Wulf decided he had better take charge.

"We'd best get off the beach right quick," he said. "In a few hours it will be covered with water. Look ye there." He pointed high over their heads to where the tide line showed clearly on the rocks. That woke Carsten up. "Track be over there," continued Wulf. "We scouted it out while we were awaiting you. Now lightest and nimblest go first. It's tricky but we can do it. Be hardest on the horse for it's a donkey track, not fit for a horse. We'll put him in the middle. Lieutenant, you lead him and I and the rest of us heavies will be right behind to catch him should he slip."

Slowly they made their way up the steep cliff. The path zigged and zagged. Several times they had to ease the horse around boulders that stood in the way. At last they reached the top safely and breathed a sigh of relief. Some of the men flopped down on the grass to rest. A few looked back down the cliff to where they had been. More than half the beach was already covered with water.

"Now where to?" asked Carsten. He was so shaken from the effort he was more than willing to let Wulf take command for the moment.

"We follow this track to wherever it leads. 'Tis a well-worn path so it must go somewhere," replied Wulf. "When we come to a real road we head east to Chichester."

They found that Chichester was only about five miles away. Since they had had no breakfast, the men were hungry. So they stopped to buy food. The inhabitants seemed to be friendly. One woman in a bakery, to their surprise, even spoke a little German.

"Ach," she said, "I've learned a few words. They come in here from time to time. Poor lads, so far from home and their land taken by that devil Boney. But most of them are stationed beyond Brighton."

"Do you know where we might find the Duke of Cumberland?" asked Anton.

"Oh, that one. Nay, I don't."

"Or Duke Friedrich of Braunschweig?"

"Ah, now there's a good man. Been in this very shop a few times himself. General Freddie, we call him. Last I heard his regiment was in the neighborhood of Eastbourne. Could have moved by now but they could tell you there."

"And how far is Eastbourne?"

"As far beyond Brighton as Brighton is from here," she replied. "A good two-three-day hike, depending on how fast you march. Some fifty miles, I'd say."

After filling their stomachs the men felt better. They headed east along the coastal road at a good pace, some of them even singing, a bit off-key but cheerfully. The south coast of England alternated between high chalky cliffs—heads, they called them—and rugged coves many of which had tiny fishing villages tucked into them. But atop the cliffs it was lush, green, rolling country which made for easy, even pleasant walking.

"How in the world did Napoleon ever expect to land an army on this coast?" asked Harm.

"Maybe he doesn't know," replied Anton.

"Ach, he knows all right. He's got spies everywhere," said Lude. "No doubt knows every inch of it."

"But he's got his hands so full now in Prussia and Saxony, I doubt he could even attempt it now," said Harm.

"Probably not," agreed Anton.

"In that case what are we doing here?" asked Erich whose wounds had healed during the voyage but who still spoke a little strangely due to the broken nose and missing teeth.

"Going to train to fight him properly," replied Lude.

"Right," said Anton. "And I have a feeling it won't be long before this whole German Legion goes back to Germany to drive him out of our homeland."

"You really think so?" asked Gerd.

Anton nodded. "At least we can hope so," he said.

They camped out at night because it was clear and warm but mostly because they had to save what little money was left amongst them for food. When they arrived at Brighton the next day a small argument arose. Most of them wanted to see the 'Chinee Whorehouse,' more properly called the Royal Pavilion.

"The Captain said to avoid Brighton," said Carsten.

"He said not to stop here," argued Wulf, "but he didn't say we couldn't stroll by and look at the thing."

Carsten sighed. "Very well. But look only and no stopping."

They strolled slowly around the perimeter of the Prince Regent's famous Oriental Palace and most of them agreed that it was certainly strange if not outright ugly.

"Much rather have seen his whores than the building," commented Wulf and the men concurred.

They camped out again that night and the next day they took a side road leading to Eastbourne. Upon inquiry they learned that Duke Friedrich's army was encamped only a few miles to the east of the town. Most of this time Carsten had been walking along with the men, leading the horse. Now he mounted up as he felt it was more fitting for an officer. The men brushed their clothes, straightened their hats and walked a little more erect. There was not much they could do, for after living in their clothes on the long walk from Vilsen to Bremen to Hamburg, five days on shipboard and two and a half days traipsing through Sussex, they looked like vagabonds and probably smelled worse. But their spirits were high as they marched into Friedrich's camp.

The sentries at the gate stopped them.

"I am Lieutenant Campsheide and these are my men. We have come even now all the way from Hannover to offer our services to the King's German Legion. Where will I find Duke Friedrich Wilhelm of Braunschweig?"

"Lieutenant, heh?" said the corporal. "Don't look like no lieutenant to me."

"Several of us are veterans of the Russian campaign on—on the other side."

"Deserters, heh?"

"Nay, nay. Honorably discharged but we feared not for long the way he is so desperate for men."

"How did you manage to get here?"

"A British merchant ship dropped us off near Chichester."

"Dropped you off? Just like that, in the middle of the Channel?" said the man sarcastically.

"Look," said Carsten impatiently, "is the Duke here? And if so, may I speak with him?"

Wulf looked as though he was ready to wring the man's neck. He took a step forward but said nothing.

The corporal took a step back. "No need to get upset. Just want to be sure you ain't French spies. Mighty strange you just dropping in out of nowhere."

"Ask the Black Duke how he got his men here," retorted Carsten.

"All right, all right. Hans," he said to one of his men, "go and tell the General's aide what we have here."

The man ran off and they waited. Very soon a dapper, young lieutenant returned with the sentry.

"Lieutenant Dornbusch," he said and shook Carsten's hand. That at least was promising.

"Welcome to the King's German Legion. I assume you have papers."

"Well, not exactly. We have come here under circumstances similar to the Black Duke's own flight from Germany except that there are only eighteen of us."

Anton spoke up. "But, sir, I *do* have a letter addressed to the Duke of Cumberland vouching for us and confirming our intent."

"Ah, so," said Dornbusch, much friendlier now. "The Duke of Cumberland is not here but I am sure the General will want to meet with you. Come this way."

Duke Friedrich Wilhelm of Braunschweig was everything one would want in a general officer—brave beyond the call, a superb tactician, a strict disciplinarian but so considerate of his men that harsh discipline was seldom needed and his men worshipped him. Descended from a long line of heroic generals—his father had died at Auerstadt, his great-uncle a hero of the Seven Years War—he was now well past middle age but carried himself like a much younger man and there was a twinkle in his eye that put everyone at ease. He welcomed Carsten, Anton and Wulf at his headquarters, a quaint little farmhouse on the downs of Sussex.

"So you want to join the German Legion," he said. "You know it was my 'black' army that was the start of it."

"Yes, sir, we know, sir," said Carsten, "and yes, sir, we want very much to join you."

"Ja, I remember when you blew up the bridge at Hoya," added Anton. "I was but a lad then."

The General smiled. "And have any of you had any training?" he asked.

"A few of us are veterans of the Russian campaign," replied Carsten, "on the French side, of course. No matter what you think of him, Napoleon's training was excellent."

"I agree. So we'll see how much you remember of it and the rest will have to start training immediately. I have mostly Bavarians and a few Braunschweigers here. The Hannoverian regiments are mostly under the command of General Carl von Alten. I'll send him a message and see what he wants to do with you. Meanwhile you can stay here."

"I have a letter addressed to the Duke of Cumberland," said Anton. "It is nothing much, merely introducing us and asking that you accept us. Mayhap I should give it to you."

"I am afraid that the Duke of Cumberland has left us—permanently."

"Really?"

"Ja, he has chafed under his brother's—the Prince Regent's—orders to oversee the defenses of England for so many years when he really wanted active fighting that he finally said 'enough' and simply left. I believe he has gone to offer his services to Prussia although I have not heard that he has arrived there. So I'll accept your letter on his behalf."

11

1813

Kati knew about the Duke of Cumberland's defection long before Anton did. Philipp had obtained a position for her in the household of Ernst Herbert Graf von Münster, the Prime Minister of Hannover in the absence of any viceroy from England. Kati was now happily ensconced in Hannover as a lady's maid to the Countess. She enjoyed the work and especially hearing all the court gossip and even an occasional state secret.

Thus she knew that the Prince Regent George did not like his brother Ernst August, Duke of Cumberland, at all. In fact, he hated him and did not trust him. Ernst August was as different from the rest of George III's sons as could be. While most of them ran to fat, he was very tall and thin, almost gaunt. He could have been considered handsome if one only looked at the right side of his face but when he turned the other side where he had lost an eye and been severely scarred by a saber cut in 1793, he was positively frightening. He was an extreme reactionary and from several earlier Georges had inherited a violent temper. It was even believed that he had murdered his own valet in a fit of jealousy but the case was never proven.

Thus when the Russians and Prussians were successful in driving most of the scattered French regiments out of Hannover and over the Rhein, it was deemed safe for a member of the royal family to return to Hannover as viceroy. Ernst August coveted the position and considered it his due but Münster none too subtly let Prince George know that he did not care to work with the independent and obstreperous Duke of Cumberland. So George sent their younger brother Adolph, Duke of Cambridge, instead. This suited Münster just fine as Adolph was easy-going, biddable and not too bright. Thus Ernst August had left England in a huff and going by a circuitous route through Sweden had presented himself at the Prussian army headquarters.

Count von Münster was himself a reactionary but only insofar as all

338

the nobility and royalty of Europe wanted a return to the *status quo ante* in the face of Napoleon's egalitarianism. He was a long-faced, rather dour man but highly intelligent and a superb diplomat. The Countess tried to make up for his stodginess by having a gay and light-hearted but also intellectual court. Although she was a bit in awe of the Count, Kati adored the Countess and was reasonably happy although there were times when she missed Vilsen—and especially Heinrich Anton.

She had had one letter from him late in August telling her a little about his trip and safe arrival in England. He also told her he was now called Anton which she did not much care for since it reminded her of her grandfather, who was also his godfather, but she supposed she would have to accept it. He ended by stating that they were now in training and he was very, very tired, promising to write a longer letter at another time. And nothing since. Her mother had forwarded the letter since Anton did not yet know that she was in Hannover. Kati had replied immediately to tell him of her new position but she had no way of knowing whether he had received her letter. Officially it was still forbidden to communicate with England but as Napoleon's Continental System gradually broke down, no one paid much attention to that. Yet the posts were very haphazard and uncertain. It was now late October and she worried that he might already be fighting somewhere and she not be aware of it.

Kati was dressing the Countess' hair in preparation for a ball in honor of the newly arrived Duke and Duchess of Cambridge. It was to be held at the ancient Leine Schloss but it was sponsored by the Graf and several other high-ranking nobles. All of Europe might hate Napoleon but Paris still dictated fashion. Skirts were getting slightly fuller again which Kati thought more becoming than the utterly plain straight lines of a few years ago but the high Empire waistline still prevailed. And some of the gowns were shockingly short ending slightly above the ankle and showing a woman's entire foot. Although the Countess always dressed in the height of fashion, she dared not go that far. Her husband was simply too conservative. If she had shown her ankles he probably would have sent her back to her chamber in disgrace. The Countess' hemline discreetly touched the floor.

Kati was winding a string of pearls into the elaborate coiffure and almost holding her breath as she had only recently learned how to do this, when the Graf burst into the chamber. Kati was so startled she dropped the pearls, pulling some of the elaborate headdress along with it.

"Now see what you have made her do," screamed the usually placid countess. "You gave me a fright as well. What is it?"

"I am sorry to disturb you at your toilette, Madame," said the Graf, "but I have the most wonderful news that I simply had to share with you ere we meet with the Duke and Duchess."

Kati had never seen the staid count so ebullient.

"Well?" said the Countess. "Out with it."

"Napoleon has suffered a horrendous defeat at Leipzig."

"And?"

"Austria has finally decided to get off the fence and join the Allies. Metternich's influence, no doubt. And what's more Bavaria has deserted Napoleon and joined her ancient archenemy Austria. Saxony even turned on the French right in the middle of the battle. It is even rumored that Napoleon's favorite Murat has defected and will fight against Eugene in Italy. The battle was so great and the victory so overwhelming that it is already being called the *Völkerschlacht*—the Battle of the Nations. 'Tis said that one German state after the other is withdrawing their troops from the French army and refusing to fight for him any longer. Napoleon is fleeing back to France with what few men he has left."

"That's nice, as long as he doesn't come this way."

"No, I believe he fled through Mainz and may be over the Rhein already. And hear this. Jerome has fled Kassel and is back in Paris."

"That should please the Duchess," replied the Countess. "Augusta is from Hesse-Kassel, you know. And now if you don't let Kati repair the damage to my hair that you have caused, you will complain that I am making you late for the ball."

The Graf looked down at the floor where Kati was still picking up pearls. "Never mind the pearls, Kati," he said. "Use Madame's diamonds instead. We have much to celebrate this night—and she looks better in them anyway. I am sorry to have disrupted your toilette, my dear, and I promise I won't complain. But I thought you would want to know." And the most powerful man in Hannover positively slunk out the door.

The Countess barely suppressed a giggle. "Ach, men, Kati. All I have heard for ten long years is war and battles. I'll believe it is the last one when Napoleon is dead and gone—not until. See what you can do to repair the damage. Tonight is a night for fun and dancing and gaity. Let us forget war for a few hours. I have heard they are going to let the townspeople dance in the castle courtyard. You might enjoy that."

"Thank you, my lady," replied Kati, who loved to dance. "I'd enjoy that very much."

"Just be sure you are back here in time to help me dismantle this," said the Countess, referring to the coiffure.

The Battle of the Nations, as the Countess predicted, was not the last but it was the turning point of Napoleon's career. From then on and well into the early months of 1814 the battles were fought on French soil. Blücher and his Prussians moved in from the north, after first aiding and abetting a revolution in Holland. Schwartzenberg, commanding an Austrian-Russian army with both Emperor Franz II and Tsar Alexander in tow, crossed Switzerland (with permission) and drove in from the south. The two generals promised each other to meet in Paris. Meanwhile Wellington had crossed over from Spain and was besieging the far south.

In January Napoleon released the Pope from his imprisonment at Fontainebleau and made arrangements to send him back to Rome. He gathered 60,000 new recruits to join the survivors of Leipzig and determined to keep fighting. He won several strategic victories and lost as many but the Allies were numerically stronger and kept pressing him back towards Paris. He sent Marie Louise and her son to Blois to set up a provisional government there. He left his brother Joseph in Paris as regent.

But France was on her knees. The economy was in shambles, the stock market had crashed, people were fed up with feeding all their sons into his war machine, the general attitude was one of weariness and apathy. The populace was finally tired of *la gloire*. Some French towns even welcomed the Allied armies as liberators.

Joseph urged Napoleon to surrender but he was determined to fight to the end. The Allies offered peace terms which the Senate urged him to accept. He replied with terms and conditions of his own which were unacceptable to the Allies. Fearing arrest if he entered Paris himself he retreated to Fontainebleau and left Generals Marmont and Mortier to defend the city. Soon Joseph, dreading the destruction of their beloved capital, transferred his authority to Marmont and left to join Marie Louise at Blois.

Finally after a day of bitter fighting, Marmont, too, decided not to sacrifice the beautiful town and capitulated to the Allies on 31 March 1814. On 1 April Tsar Alexander and King Friedrich Wilhelm of Prussia with the Generals Blücher and Schwartzenberg marched victoriously into Paris. Emperor Franz had chosen to remain behind at Dijon so as not to embarrass his daughter. On the same day the Senate enacted a new constitution guaranteeing all basic liberties and elected Talleyrand president.

On 2 April the Senate voted to depose Napoleon.

When word of this reached Fontainebleau his generals refused to obey Napoleon any longer. On 13 April he signed his first abdication and was escorted by four allied officers—Russian, Prussian, Austrian and English—to a British warship which took him to exile in Elba.

"You must have a new pretty gown," said the Countess.

"I?" said Kati. "But I am only your maid, my lady. What need would I have for a fancy gown?"

"Ah, but Vienna is such a liberal, gay city, 'tis said that even the common people are permitted to attend the musical galas, operas and concerts. While the men are deciding how to carve up Europe, there will be ample time for social life—even for you. You don't think the Emperor—or rather Metternich—would have invited all the wives had they not planned a good deal of social intercourse, do you? Of course, they have. The Viennese are famous for it. And the shopping. You will have to accompany me for shopping. Ach, I can't wait."

"Then you really think I should have an opportunity to wear a new gown?"

"By all means, you will. You may even meet someone to your liking."

Kati had not told the Countess about Heinrich Anton. "Have you been to Vienna before, my lady?" she asked.

"Nay. That is why I am looking forward to it. My husband, the Graf, was there once years ago when it was still capital of the Holy Roman Empire before—before Napoleon, that is. I am sure it has changed a great deal since then."

"I am looking forward to it, too, my lady." In fact Kati was so excited about the proposed trip she could hardly contain herself.

Graf von Münster was the delegate appointed to represent Hannover at the Congress of Vienna, that august body which was to decide the fate of Europe for many years to come. At first the four 'Great' powers wanted to be the only decision-makers at the Congress. Russia had the largest army; Prussia was still considered a nothing by the other three but she had the ablest generals; Austria, once considered the greatest but now feeble, had offered Vienna as the meeting site; and England had the money. Tsar Alexander himself represented Russia assisted by Count Razumovsky and Count Nesselrode. King Friedrich Wilhelm attended for Prussia but his active diplomats were von Hardenberg and von Humboldt. Austria, of course, had the highly talented Metternich and Lord Castlereagh spoke for England. The latter two were frightened of Russia, fearing that she would be the next conqueror to sweep across Europe and neither trusted Prussia, who was cozying up to Russia. Thus when Talleyrand insisted that France should be represented at the Congress they welcomed him knowing that a strong France would help maintain the balance of power against the eastern faction. Then all the other countries that had suffered from Napoleon's conquests—all the German states, Spain, Portugal, the Papal territories and, with the Tsar's permission, Poland—insisted on being represented as well. Within the Congress the larger German states—Austria, Prussia, Bavaria, Hannover and Württemberg—formed a Committee of Five to discuss a German constitution. Eventually, all told, about two hundred states and political entities were represented at the Congress.

Emperor Franz, while leaving the diplomacy to Metternich, provided ample entertainment for the delegates. At times it seemed as though there were more entertainments than diplomatic negotiations. Balls, concerts and elaborate galas resonated every evening at the imperial and other noble palaces. Beethoven performed a number of times for the delegates. Mistresses were provided for the top echelon and courtesans of every degree for the lesser nobility. Although Austria was nearly bankrupt, Vienna outdid herself to live up to her reputation as a gay, carefree, musical city.

Kati left the palace where the Hannover delegation was staying by the tradesmen's entrance. As she passed through the immense kitchen some of the servants looked at her oddly for she was wearing her new gown. It was a lovely pale yellow which set off her dark hair to perfection. She felt she looked just as fine as the Countess herself except without the jewelry. So she did not care what they thought. She had had few opportunities to wear it so far but this was one. She knew she had several hours of freedom for the Countess was sleeping. The ball the previous evening had ended at dawn.

She hurried through the kitchen courtyards and out a gate that led to an alley between this and the next palace and finally attained the street. She looked about for a moment to orient herself. She had had only a few opportunities to explore Vienna in the two weeks they had been there since most of the Countess' time, and hence her own, had been taken up by the lavish receptions for the delegates. She could still hear the Countess' words back in Hannover, 'You may even meet someone'. Well, she had met someone last night and now she was going to meet him again for afternoon coffee.

St. Stefan's was where they were to meet. Now that should not be too hard to find. The ancient cathedral lay at the heart of the city, its towering steeple a landmark visible for miles around. She could even see it from the upper floors of the palace where they were staying but here in the narrow, twisting streets of the old city her view was completely cut off. She did know that most of the palaces of the nobility fanned out in a semicircle from the Imperial Palace, the Hofburg, within the impregnable city walls. Walls no longer impregnable to modern armies as extensive damage from Napoleon's twice occupation of the city showed.

Kati plunged into one of the narrow streets that she hoped led in the right direction. The sharp November wind caught her as she turned the corner. She drew her shawl more tightly around her, wishing she had worn her cloak, but she had wanted to show off her dress. Her mind went over the meeting the night before. She had been watching the ball from a gallery at one of the princely palaces. She often accompanied the Countess to these affairs so as to be available to refurbish the gown or the hair of the lady after the innumerable visits to the powder rooms or even after a rest in one of the chambers provided for the purpose.

A voice at her elbow had said, "Don't you wish you were down there among them, dancing?"

"Oh, I do," she had replied, turning to face the speaker. He was a very handsome young man with dark hair and fair skin, a long straight nose and sultry lips.

"We can dance a few rounds up here," he had said. "No one will mind." Whereupon he had taken her about the waist without so much as a by-your-leave and had whirled her around and around in an exciting waltz until she was gasping for breath.

"La, sir, you are bold indeed," she exclaimed. "You are making me dizzy. I fear I shall fall off the balcony."

He laughed and she noticed his teeth were perfect. "Fear not, my lady, I'll not let that happen. I am holding you tight."

"Too tight for decorum's sake, I fear me," she replied as they slowed down and she backed away from him.

"But you enjoyed it, did you not? You are a natural dancer."

"Yes, I love to dance but not with total strangers."

"Then let me introduce myself. I am Ferenc. That translates into Franz."

"Then I shall call you Franz. It sounds better." Suddenly some instinct told her not to reveal her true name. "And I am called Sophie— no but a lady's maid."

"And I am personal valet to Count Razumovsky."

Kati did not know if he were lying or not. Count Ruzumovsky was the Russian ambassador to Austria and also well known as a patron of the famous composer Beethoven. "You are Russian then?" she asked.

"Nay. Hungarian. Since Hungary is now part of the Habsburg empire there are many of us here in the capital."

"I see." She thought that rather odd. A servant, perhaps, but one would think the Count would have one of his own in so personal a position. But then, what did she care? Then she noticed the Countess heading for the stairway. "Ach, but I must go. My lady will have need of me."

"I should like to see you again," Franz had said. "Have you ever been to one of our Viennese coffee houses?"

"Nay, but I hear the fare is quite delectable."

"Meet me tomorrow and I shall treat you to one. I'm sure you can escape for a few hours. They will be sleeping all day."

"I don't know," she said hesitantly.

"Yes, you can," he insisted. "Three o'clock at St. Stefan's. And if you can't come tomorrow, I shall wait for you every day until you do come. I am already enamored of you, dearest Sophie."

She did not believe a word of it but she was tempted. "Thank you, Franz. I can't promise but I'll try. Good night now." She quickly left ere the Countess should be looking for her.

Now Kati hurried down the street. She was very excited at the prospect of meeting Franz again although she told herself that she should not be. The small street opened onto a wide thoroughfare called Kärntnerstrasse and there at the end towered the 'Steffel', as the locals called their beloved cathedral. But here, instead of hurrying on, she paused and gaped with pleasure. She had heard that the Kärntnerstrasse was the finest shopping street in Vienna but she was unprepared for the elegance displayed in the many shop windows. Stylish gowns and elaborate millinery, delicate porcelain and gleaming silverware, priceless jewelry vied to attract the eye of passersby. And Kati was not immune to their seduction. How rich one would have to be to afford even the tiniest item displayed there. But how nice to be able to feast one's eyes on the luxury without the embarrassment of having to enter a shop when she knew she could not have afforded any of the merchandise.

After a few blocks of ogling she reached St. Stefan's. She looked up in awe at the Gothic splendor of the cathedral. The main entrance alone was unbelievable in its intricacy. She glanced around. There was no sign of Franz. Mayhap he was waiting for her inside. He had not specified. Kati had never been inside a Catholic church before. Ancient fears of being gobbled up by Jesuit proselytizers assailed her. She shook them off. If anyone accosted her, she would simply walk out. After all this was the enlightened nineteenth century. She set aside her fears and pushed open one of the huge doors. Inside it was very quiet. Fortunately there were no services going on at the moment. Once her eyes adjusted to the dimness she was amazed at the beauty surrounding her. The soaring height of the nave, the exquisite stone tracery especially of the pulpit and choir, the numerous lovely statues everywhere overwhelmed her. There were only a few people about, mostly sightseers, and still no sign of Franz. She decided to walk about a bit herself. Idolatrous it might be but it was certainly beautiful.

Kati was standing in front of a statue of the Virgin sheltering a number of people with her cloak, when a voice beside her said, "The Schutzmantelmadonna. Beautiful, isn't she?"

"Oh, hello, Franz. You startled me," replied Kati. "Beautiful? No. Charming perhaps, but we are taught it is heretical to worship her."

"Ach, we don't worship her—just honor her as protectrix of all people."

"I rather prefer the pulpit. The stonework is so delicate. I recognize some of the saints peeping out from it but who is that little man looking out of a window at the bottom?"

" 'Tis thought it might be the architect himself, Anton Pilgram. There is another self-portrait of him under the organ."

"He must have been a genius to design all this."

"Indeed he was. But enough of art and theology," Franz said. "Have you seen enough? I am sure you are ready for some good hot coffee and sweets."

"I guess," replied Kati as Franz took her arm and led her out of the church to a nearby coffee house.

"Kaffee mit Schlag?" asked the waiter.

"With whipped cream?" questioned Kati. "I've never had it that way before."

"Try it," urged Franz. "You'll love it. It is a Viennese specialty."

"Mmm," she murmured. "It is very rich. And these delicious cakes.

One could quickly get very fat here."

"You should," he commented. "You are too thin."

Kati ignored that and changed the subject. "If you are Count Razumovsky's valet you must know the composer Beethoven."

"I have met him but I do not know him well. Would you like to hear him play?"

"Oh, I'd love to. But how . . . ?"

"Very easily," replied Franz. "He practices almost every afternoon in the music room, sometimes in the grand salon of the palace. Do you know where the Razumovsky palace is?"

She nodded.

"Then come tomorrow afternoon—a little earlier, if you can."

"Oh, I could not be away two afternoons in a row," she said. "Perhaps next week. I'll send word when I can come."

"Fine, but address your note to Ferenc, not Franz, or they won't know whom it is for. Until then, sweet Sophie. I can't wait to see you again."

Kati went back to her lodgings with stars in her eyes. What a pleasant young man he was. This stay in Vienna should be most entertaining.

The following week Kati had another opportunity to escape from her duties. She quickly sent a note to Ferenc-Franz and hoped that Master Beethoven would be practicing that afternoon. This time she made sure she wore her cloak. Winter in this city surrounded by mountains closed in earlier than in her homeland. She hurried through the raw wind that threatened snow. Franz was waiting for her at the servants' entrance.

"I'm so glad you could come, sweet Sophie," said Franz as he kissed her on both cheeks in the French manner. If she thought that a bit forward, she made no comment. No doubt that is the way Hungarians were.

"Is Master Beethoven here today?" she asked.

"Indeed he is and working right now in the grand salon. Come," he said, "we'll go to the balcony where we can listen without being seen. But you must be very quiet. He does not like to be disturbed."

"I understand," she replied as she followed him up the stairs. If the other servants wondered who she was, no one gave any sign although a few knowing looks passed among them.

Franz led her to a gallery overlooking the vast hall and there beneath them was the master energetically playing some stirring music. Stirring but not exactly pleasant, thought Kati. Suddenly he stopped and made some notations on a score in front of him. When he played the piece again it sounded much better. How exciting, thought Kati, to not only hear him play but to actually watch him compose. She was so overawed by what she was hearing and seeing she almost forgot about Franz.

"Take off your cloak," whispered Franz. "It's much too warm in here for that."

She nodded and threw the garment over a nearby chair and returned to her enchantment. She knew not how long she stood there mesmerized but after a while she could sense Franz growing impatient.

At last he said, "Come, we must leave now. He will be quitting soon and it would never do for him or anyone else to see us lurking up here."

She hated to leave but realized he must know the master's routine far better than she. She allowed him to lead her out of the gallery and up two more flights of stairs. "Where are you taking me?" she asked. They were on the top floor in what must surely be the servants' quarters.

"I want to show you something," he replied. Part way down a narrow corridor he flung open a door. Within was a tiny, mean room with two cots—not even beds. "My room," he announced.

"But . . ." Panic started to rise within her. He took her arm and forcefully urged her into the room and kicked the door shut behind him. Suddenly he took her in his arms and was smothering her with kisses—lips, neck, throat, the tops of her breasts.

She pushed him away with all her strength. "No, no, stop that, Franz," she cried.

He looked surprised. "But surely you want me as much as I want you. I know you like me."

"But not that way," she said firmly. "What is it that you wanted to show me?" she asked as she edged towards the door.

He grabbed the obvious bulge in his breeches and shook it. "This," he said.

"No, no," she screamed. "Let me out of here. I am no whore."

"I know you're not," he replied smugly, "but all women want it. It's what they're made for."

"Not I," she retorted.

"Do you think I took you out to a coffee house or got you in here to hear Beethoven just for a kiss?" His voice had a mean edge to it now.

"My honor—and my virginity are worth more than one cup of coffee," she said haughtily. "Now let me out of here."

"Ah, so it's a virgin you claim to be. I doubt it but it makes it more interesting." He started to fumble with the buttons on her gown.

She slapped him hard across the face. Angered now he grabbed her and flung her on to the cot. It nearly knocked the breath out of her but she retained her presence of mind. He made the mistake of pausing to unbutton his breeches and that gave her the moment she needed. She rolled off the cot toward the opposite one. It was a flimsy thing so that she was able to pick it up easily. She threw it at him with all her strength and fled out the door. She ran down the corridor and almost stumbled down the first flight of stairs as there was no bannister. She tripped down the second flight, hurried past the gallery where only moments before she had been so enchanted. She tried buttoning her gown as she ran. She descended the sweeping main staircase. She was heading for the front door of the palace and be damned to anyone who questioned her. She was just passing the door to the grand salon when Beethoven himself emerged. She ran right into him. He caught her in his arms.

"Oh, ho, what have we here?" he said.

"Oh, your pardon, Master Beethoven, but I was in a hurry." She looked straight at him. He was not tall. He was undoubtedly the ugliest, most dishevelled, wildest-looking man she had ever seen but he seemed kind.

"In a hurry to get away from unwanted attentions?" he asked. He saw her glance over her shoulder. "Don't worry," he assured her. "He won't dare descend that staircase. He is not permitted in this part of the house. And what, for that matter, are you doing here?"

"He—he . . . " she stuttered.

"Speak up, child. My hearing is not what it was."

"He brought me here to hear you play, Master," she said as loudly as she could. "And I was enchanted. I wanted to hear more but he—he . . . "

"Had other ideas," he finished. "Would you like to hear more?"

"Oh, Master, very much so," she replied nervously, still glancing over her shoulder.

"Then I shall see that you get a ticket to my next concert. But I must know your name and where to send it."

She hesitated but the temptation was too great. She decided the truth was worth it. "I am Catharine Hohnholz but—but he thinks I'm Sophie. Please don't tell him. I'm lady's maid to the Gräfin von Münster of Hannover."

"Ah, yes, I know exactly where the Graf and Gräfin von Münster are staying. Dour old fool, isn't he? But the lady seems agreeable enough. Then, Catharine-Sophie, I shall see that there is a ticket to my next concert held in your name. Come, I'll escort you to the front door."

349

"Thank you very much, Master Beethoven," she said tremulously. "I shall look forward to it."

If the servants looked askance at his leading an obvious maid, and a stranger at that, out to the magnificent front door of the palace, they quickly looked the other way. The great composer was known to be somewhat eccentric and no one dared interfere.

When Kati hit the icy blast outside the palace, she realized that she had left her warm cloak behind. No way was she going to go back there. She ran instead—ran so blindly that she almost lost her way twice although it was not far to where they were staying. By the time she reached the mansion she was coughing and coughing and coughing. She sought her room and threw herself on her bed fully clothed and sobbed and sobbed between wracking coughs.

Hours later the Countess herself came seeking Kati. Her tears had dried and the coughing had diminished to an occasional hiccough. But she still lay inert, almost lifeless.

"What ails you, Kati dear?" asked the Countess. "Helga heard you coughing so violently she feared for you."

Kati sat up quickly and started coughing again. "Oh, my lady." she gasped. "I am sorry. I had no idea it was so late. I shall attend you forthwith."

"Nay, nay," said the lady. "It is obvious that you are ill. Ludmilla can attend me this evening. Her German is somewhat sketchy but she'll do. It is no special occasion tonight. We are dining in for a change, thank God. This constant social whirl does tire one. But I worry for you. How did you catch this chill?"

"Ach, my lady, 'tis a cough I have suffered all my life but it only comes on when I have done something foolish. I fear I inadvertently ran out without my cloak."

The Countess' eyes took in the girl's gown—her best, all rumpled now. She had obviously been crying as well as coughing. The Countess might be very staid and proper but she had not lived at court all these years not to know what went on. There was more to this than meets the eye. She would not have suspected it of Kati but the girl seemed so innocent she probably had not realized she was being seduced. "And where is your cloak now? We must wrap you in it."

"I—I left it behind," sobbed Kati.

"Behind? Behind where? I shall send a footman to fetch it. You need it in this weather."

"Nay, nay, my lady. I—I—," and suddenly she broke down. "Oh, my lady, forgive me. It had seemed like such a pleasant afternoon and it all turned out so terrible—so frightening."

The Countess nodded. She was right then. If a child resulted she would have to send Kati home immediately. She hated the thought of losing her. She had grown quite fond of the girl but the Count would never allow a pregnant servant in the household, let alone an unwed one. "And where did all this take place?" she demanded.

"At—at the Razumovsky palace." replied Kati.

"The Razu—" exclaimed the Countess. "However did you get in there?"

"I—I met this gentleman—that is, I thought he was a gentleman—who is the Count's personal valet. We had coffee a few times." She thought it better not to admit she had been so gullible after only one coffee tête-à-tête. "He offered to take me into the palace to hear the great Beethoven practice."

"And did he?"

"Oh, yes. And it was sublime, my lady, enthralling. But then—but then—he tried to rape me." Kati broke down into violent sobs again.

"And did he—did he have his way with you?" demanded the Countess.

"Nay. I managed to get away. In fact, Master Beethoven helped me escape. But I forgot my cloak." Kati hesitated tearfully. "I know you will want to dismiss me but I am still a virgin, my lady. I swear it," she declared.

The Countess then did something she had never done before. She took the girl in her arms and let her weep. "I believe you, Kati, but time will tell the truth of it, won't it?" she said. "But above all we must not let my husband, the Count, know of it. I shall send our most trusted footman after your cloak. And we shall speak no more of it—ever," she insisted. "Now get into your night dress and under those covers. I don't want you taking ill with that cough. I need you, Kati."

"Yes, my lady. Thank you for believing me, my lady," whispered Kati quietly.

"We were all young once," said the Countess and left.

The cook sent up hot, nourishing possets and Kati recovered quickly. The Countess had brought her own cook from Hannover, declaring the Viennese food was far too rich for her taste. Kati's cloak was retrieved the next day by a discreet footman who informed her the Count Razumovsky's

351

personal valet was an elderly, very dignified Russian and that *that knave* was only a footman and not even a first footman but of the lowest rank who frequently brought women into the palace and most probably would soon be shipped back to Hungary if he persisted in his deplorable conduct. The news did little for Kati's self-esteem. How could she have been so gullible?

She was afraid to go anywhere alone in her free time. The Countess noticed her despondency, which was so unlike the intelligent, vibrant girl Kati had been, and took pity on her. Having noted her love of music the Countess insisted she accompany her to various operas and concerts for which Vienna was so famous. Since it was almost unheard of for a mere servant to accompany her mistress to such functions, the Countess made the excuse that she required a companion since the Count did not particularly care for music and was too busy with the deliberations of the Congress. Kati was overjoyed at the privilege and soon came out of her self-imposed shell.

She had long since forgotten Beethoven's offer of a ticket to a concert. She heard he had played his martial *Die Schlacht bei Vittoria*, commemorating the last battle in Spain whereby Wellington had driven Napoleon out of Spain, for the delegates to the Congress. The music was terrible, not up to Beethoven's usual standards at all—one pundit had punned '*Die Schlacht* war schlecht (bad)' but it was received with great acclaim because it aroused a feeling of patriotism in the delegates regardless of what country they came from.

Thus Kati was delightfully surprised a few weeks before Christmas to receive a personal, handwritten invitation from the master himself. She ran to show it to the Countess.

"May I go to the concert, my lady?" she begged.

"Why, certainly you may," replied the Countess. "You will come with us. All the delegates have been invited. It is to be a great occasion. The Emperor has opened the doors of the Hofburg and the concert is to take place in the huge Redoutensaal. So the old rogue actually remembered you."

"Rogue?"

"Ach, ja. Master Beethoven is known to have quite an eye for the ladies," teased the Countess.

"But I am sure I shall be quite safe with you," replied Kati. And they laughed together.

On the evening of the concert Kati was so excited she could scarcely contain herself. Not only was she to see and hear the great composer in a real concert but she was about to enter into the sacred precincts of the Imperial palace—something she could never have conceived of in her wildest dreams.

The great salon was crowded with over six thousand people. Immense chandeliers of the famous Viennese crystal held thousands of candles so that the hall was as brightly lit as day. Kati stared goggle-eyed at the sumptuous gowns and jewels of the ladies, at the lavish uniforms of the men. Her best dress seemed positively drab by comparison. But she did not care. She was there.

Beethoven himself conducted the orchestra for two of his symphonies. Then he took to the pianoforte to play his Emperor Concerto. Kati had never been so moved in her whole life. The beautiful, piquant Adagio reminded her of the peace and quiet of Heiligenberg and Vilsen and she found tears of homesickness streaming down her face. But then the joy and fun of the finale brought to mind the dancing at Der Lustige Strumpf and she was smiling with rhapsody through her tears. After the composer played a few of his shorter pieces the concert ended with a standing ovation from the audience. Kati had never been so happy in her life.

"May I go and thank him, my lady?" she asked.

"Yes, go—if you can even get near him. I shall await you near the door."

"Nay, come with me, my lady. You certainly would like to meet him, too."

The Countess acquiesced while the Count frowned but said nothing. Kati took her by the hand and plowed through the crowd. Beethoven was surrounded by admirers and Kati feared they would never get near him but then she spied an opening and dragged the Countess through it.

"Master Beethoven, I want to thank you from the bottom of my heart," she shouted knowing he was almost deaf.

"Ah, the little waif at Razumovsky's," he said. "Did you enjoy the concert?"

"Oh, yes, Master. I especially liked the Adagio of the Concerto. It made me homesick."

He smiled. "Surely not for Hannover?"

"No, for a tiny village north of there called Vilsen."

"I shall have to remember that," said Beethoven.

Kati was about to introduce the Countess to him when they were pushed aside by other admirers. "I am sorry, my lady," she apologized.

"No matter," replied the Countess. "He remembered you. That is all that counts. It will be something to tell your grandchildren one day."

The main avowed purpose of the Congress of Vienna was a return to 'legitimacy', that is, a restoration of the reactionary absolute monarchies that had prevailed before Napoleon. England was the only constitutional monarchy although France had a semblance of one under Talleyrand which the restored Bourbon Louis XVIII was trying hard to abrogate. From no state was there any representation of the people, only the princes. And they agreed wholeheartedly that the *status quo ante* must be reinstated. However, in the wake of some of Napoleon's better reforms and the revolutionary ideas imported from France, a wave of popularism and liberalism swept over most of western Germany. But sadly the delegates in Vienna did not hear these voices—or chose to ignore them.

They were primarily concerned with dividing up Europe—once again—to preserve the balance of power. The three major western powers—Austria, England and France—feared Russia's determined push to the west. And no one trusted Prussia. Several of the German states realized that some sort of loose confederation would be to their advantage while still maintaining their sovereignty and independence. At first everything seemed to go well. Hannover was returned to England; Schleswig-Holstein to Denmark; France was allowed to keep Alsace. At England's urging Austria agreed to give up the Spanish Netherlands (Belgium) to the United Provinces (Holland) in exchange for large chunks of Italy in order to keep the mouths of the Rhein open for free trade.

But then the negotiations threatened to fall apart when Russia demanded all of Poland. The Tsar offered to give Poland a constitution but as a duchy subject to Russia. But Prussia wanted the parts of Poland that she had formerly held and in addition she coveted all of Saxony. The King of Saxony was still a prisoner in Berlin. Moreover, Austria felt that since her turning against Napoleon had decided the war she, too, should be compensated by gaining pieces of Poland and Saxony. The other powers did not agree at all.

The delicate negotiations went on and on. Delegates who had hoped to be home for Christmas had to make the best of it. Emperor Franz saw to it that the lavish entertainments continued over the holidays. The Tsar threatened to withdraw and 'twas said that only the wine, women and song of Vienna kept him there. On 3 January of the new year 1815 England, France and Austria signed a Triple Alliance for mutual aid and to maintain the balance of power. In the face of this Russia agreed to take only the Duchy of Warsaw, the greater part of Poland. Austria took Galicia. Prussia received a few small pieces of Poland and Swedish Pomerania and withdrew her demand for all of Saxony. She was allowed to claim only two-fifths of the kingdom and the King of Saxony was released and returned to rule the other three-fifths of the country. As a sop for not getting all of Saxony the powers gave Prussia a large piece of Westphalia along the left bank of the Rhein in order to tie together her former scattered counties.

Little did the delegates foresee the far-reaching effects of this decision. Prussia was a weak, poor, almost entirely agricultural country with few resources. The lower Rheinland was rich in iron and coal and had developed a fast-growing industrial complex. Friedrich Krupp had started an ironworks there in 1810 and had grown wealthy selling thousands of cannon and other armaments to Napoleon. The Congress, thinking to keep Prussia divided and therefore weak, had unwittingly given her the richest part of Germany.

Hannover was declared a kingdom although still under vassalage to England. With Castlereagh's help Graf von Münster acquired for her Osnabrück, East Frisia and a large part of northern Westphalia as well as Goslar and Hildesheim. Oldenburg should logically have become a part of the kingdom but the duke thereof vehemently refused. Still Hannover came out of the Congress a large, wealthy kingdom and she should have been happy. However, she was decidedly nervous with Prussia bounding her territory both to the east and to the west.

At various times during the Congress the question of what to do with Napoleon arose. No one expected him to settle quietly into a rural life and Elba was too uncomfortably close to Italy and France for peace of mind. Both Metternich and Castlereagh were in favor of moving him to a more distant and more secure location but the Tsar vehemently opposed this. So the matter was dropped.

By March most of the business of the Congress had been completed and the delegates were beginning to leave. At three o'clock in the morning Metternich was aroused from his bed. A breathless courier bearing an urgent message from the Austrian consul at Genoa was ushered into his bedchamber.

"Napoleon has escaped from Elba and has landed at Antibes on the first of March," he announced.

Metternich immediately recalled the delegates and they voted to declare Napoleon an outlaw whom anyone might kill with impunity. They also decided to defer the offical closing of the Congress until the former emperor was either dead or recaptured.

"What do we do now, my lady?" asked Kati.

"We go home as planned," replied the Countess. "Everything is packed." She indicated the mountain of trunks, boxes and baggage. "The coaches are waiting. The Graf, my husband, will have to follow when he can. I, for one, am sick of Vienna. I am tired of looking at mountains. I long for home."

Kati had long been homesick. And spring in northern Germany was indeed a wonderful season. "I, too, my lady. But what of Napoleon? Will there be more war?"

"Probably but it can't last long. Half of his own country is against him. I understand that General von Blücher is still in Belgium with a sizeable army. Wellington has returned to England so, weather permitting, he could have his army across the Channel in a few days. Come, Kati, our coach is waiting. You will ride with me since the Graf will be staying here a while longer."

Well wrapped in cloaks and blankets they settled into the coach for the long journey home. A heavily armed guard accompanied them. Five wagonloads of baggage and another coach jammed with servants followed.

At the mention of Wellington Kati thought about Heinrich Anton. Was he finally going to get his wish to fight Napoleon? She had only received two letters from him since his departure—one complaining of how tired he was with learning to be a soldier; the other complaining of the constant drilling, drilling and drilling, and going nowhere. Not one word about life in England. Heinrich Anton, bless him, was not a prolific writer.

They arrived in Hannover before the end of March. The sweet smell of spring was everywhere. Easter was approaching. After several days of unpacking and settling in the Countess said, "I think it is time you had a little holiday, Kati. A few weeks to visit your family and rest. Would you like that?"

"Oh, indeed, I should," replied Kati. "But how will you manage, my lady?"

"With the Graf still in Vienna, I shall be doing no entertaining nor much visiting. I, too, feel the need for a rest from the surfeit of social activities in Vienna. After a time it became a bit cloying, did it not? I long for the simple life for a while and you deserve some time to yourself."

"Thank you very much, my lady. I have not seen any of my family or friends for nigh on two years. It will give me great pleasure. When may I leave?"

"Next week would suit. That way you will be there well before Easter. If I have any urgent need of you, I shall send word. Otherwise, come back at the end of April."

"You are most generous, my lady."

Aside from her wages, a surprise gift from the Countess enabled Kati to take the postchaise from Hannover to Nienburg. She felt positively wealthy. After dinner at the posting inn at Nienburg she boarded another coach going to Bremen by way of Hoya. She wondered why the coach did not take the new highway. Did they refuse to acknowledge any work of Napoleon? But then she realized that the new road ran through absolutely nowhere—totally useless when the coach had to deliver mail to all the villages along the Weser. She wondered what she would find when she got there. In fact, where was home? She had had only one letter from Eleonore since she left. As far as she knew, her mother was still staying with the Bergmann at the Klostermühle. Tante Dorchen had written several times and sent occasional gifts but not much news. Well, she would soon see.

When the coach stopped at the Bücken post office, Kati asked the driver if he would drop her off at Bruchmühlen. She would go to the Klostermühle first.

"But, miss, you've paid all the way to Vilsen," said the coachman with surprising honesty.

"I know but I've decided I prefer Bruchmühlen, if you don't mind stopping. You may keep the difference."

"Ja, miss, certainly."

She gazed with longing at the familiar countryside. How good it was not to see snowcapped mountains. She agreed with the Countess. Once a Saxon—a north German, a flatlander—born and bred, one had no taste for mountains. Ah, there was the Bruns farm. Soon now, soon. She wondered again what she would find. She hoped her mother had received her note.

"Bruchmühlen," called out the coachman.

Kati leaned out the window. "Drive on a little further beyond the mill to that little lane yonder," she instructed.

He slowed the horses and stopped where she indicated. When he handed her down from the coach, she felt like a great lady. He climbed up top and brought down her portmanteau. "Will you be all right, miss?" he asked. "'Tis a mighty lonely place here."

"I'll be fine," she assured him. "It's home to me. I have cousins here at the mill and others at the Klostermühle where I am going. 'Tis but a short walk."

"Then I'll bid you farewell. Will you be returning to Hannover?"

"In about a month but I don't know exactly when."

"Our schedule is posted at the office in Vilsen but if you want me to stop here, you must let them know a few days before."

"I'll remember that and thank you."

The other passengers were becoming impatient at the unscheduled stop. One of them called out, "See your lover on the way back. We're late already."

Kati blushed and the coachman hurriedly resumed his seat and drove off. Kati picked up her portmanteau and headed down the little lane to Heiligenberg. She had no intention of visiting her cousins at Bruchmühlen just yet—if at all. She hoped she would not meet any of them right now.

"Katinka!" exclaimed Dorothea, embracing her. "You're here already! Your mama said you would be coming be she didn't know when. I'm surprised you didn't go straight to Vilsen."

"I wrote exactly when I was coming," replied Kati, "but I wasn't sure if she was still staying here or not. I gather she is not."

"Then she didn't tell you?"

"Tell me what?"

"Fritzi finally decided to marry her and she decided she could not live without a man. They were wed shortly before Christmas."

"Oh, no!"

"Katinka, your mama Elli is my best friend and I love her dearly but she has this obsession with lovemaking. Although they hated each other, she is exactly like your grandpa Anton Matthies, although she would never admit it. He was obsessed that way, too."

Kati nodded. "Lovemaking without love. Those twins that died were Fritzi's, weren't they?"

"Of course. They were sleeping together ever since she received the news of your papa's death."

Kati sobbed, "Tante Dorchen, may I stay here for my holiday? I can't bear the thought of staying in that house with him. I'll go to see Mama, of course, but I'd rather stay here, if I may."

Dorothea hugged her closely. "Certainly you may, liebchen. This has always been your second home, hasn't it? You don't need to ask."

"Oh, Tante Dorchen, thank you. It seems as though I've always had more love from you than from Mama."

"I'm afraid any love she might have had was driven out of her by her father. She can't help herself. She doesn't know what real love is. But I love you, dearest Katinka — and maybe soon you will really be my daughter."

Kati smiled ruefully. "Mayhap."

"Come then, let me fix you some supper. We've already eaten but you must be hungry."

"A little, but more tired than anything."

"Then after you've eaten, straight to bed. And sleep as long as you want in the morning. It's your holiday."

Kati was grateful that Dorothea had not yet mentioned Heinrich Anton other than the hint about being her daughter. She wondered if he had written as infrequently to his mother as he had to her. She wondered if he still loved her. She was unsure of her own feelings toward him. Well, not to worry about that now, she thought as she sank gratefully into the sweet-smelling featherbed under the eaves of the millhouse. An April shower pattering on the roof lulled her to sleep.

The next morning Kati awoke early as was her wont. Habit was hard to break. But she luxuriated in bed for a little while. No need to rush to the Countess' beck and call. A whole month of freedom! How she looked forward to it. When she arrived in the kitchen Chris and the younger children were just finishing breakfast.

"Welcome home, Katinka," he said. "You're looking well."

"Thank you, Onkel Chris. It's good to be here," she replied.

"I'm afraid we're still forced to drink this ersatz stuff we laughingly call coffee. Real coffee is still hard to come by. But have some anyway."

"They have plenty of the real thing in Vienna," said Kati. "They serve it with a huge dollop of whipped cream. It's unbelievably rich. Sorry, I don't mean to make you envious."

Chris laughed. "But you do. What we wouldn't give for a cup of that — even without the cream. They no doubt get it through Italy. Things are still very bad here. There's been much sickness, people dying for lack of proper food. But things are opening up a bit. The hope is that England can help us now—if she would. But it will take years for the farmers to get back on their feet and more years before the towns and villages can get any benefit from them. The soil is worn out from Napoleon's constant demand for food and fodder for his horses and troops. The farmers have no horses left to plow the fields. Would you believe two men are pulling the plows, where there are even any men left? There are no sheep, no pigs, no animals left to us—only a few scrawny chickens and here and there a skeleton of an old cow but no bull to service her—hence, no milk."

Kati was horrified. "I had no idea it was so bad, Onkel Chris. I have been living in the lap of luxury. I almost feel ashamed."

"No need for you to feel ashamed," put in Dorothea. "We are happy you were able to. It was all Napoleon's fault."

"Ja, and the princes and nobility can't—or won't—see it," added Chris. "Your Graf von Münster is one of the worst reactionaries. We can't go back to the old ways. People want a say in the government."

"Now Chris," interrupted Dorothea. "Let Katinka have some breakfast. You can talk politics later this evening. Don't you have some work to do?"

"Not much," he said as he stomped out the door, followed by his two younger sons.

As she ate her breakfast and swallowed the bitter acorn 'coffee', Kati asked, "Have you heard very much from Heinrich Anton, Tante Dorchen?"

"I wondered when you were going to ask. Truthfully, not much. Just an occasional letter every few months—and those very short."

"That's more than I've received. Only two in all the time he's been gone—and those all complaints."

Dorothea laughed. "I've gotten a lot of that, too. And then descriptions of a new kind of gun they have called a rifle. He claimed they can shoot three times as far and more accurately than a musket. What do I care about guns? Not a word about how he likes England or anything interesting."

"I know. Mine were the same. He might as well be in Timbuktu for all he tells about the country."

"He did mention that he now speaks English fairly fluently."

"That's nice. I hope he doesn't forget how to speak German."

"Not likely. He's in the King's German Legion under the command of officers from Hannover including the famous Duke of Braunschweig. He says very few of the men have learned any English at all."

"Do you think they will be coming back to Europe to fight now that Napoleon is back in France?"

"I'm sure of it. They say Wellington hastened from Vienna back to England the moment they got the word."

"I know. He left before we did."

"And that he will be bringing the whole English army as well as the German Legion to join the Dutch and the Prussians. Blücher is already somewhere in Belgium. Once they join 'tis said they plan on invading France immediately. That should put an end to the mad Napoleon."

"Let us hope so," sighed Kati.

"Are you going to see your mama today?" asked Dorothea.

"Perhaps this afternoon," Kati replied. "Right now I'd like to take a walk through the woods and enjoy the countryside for a couple of hours. Then when I'm refreshed mayhap I'll feel up to facing Mama."

Dorothea nodded. She understood.

Kati strolled up the hill behind the Klostermühle. The once shady path was brightly lit and full of weeds. The once stately virgin forest could no longer be called a wood. Here and there little saplings were beginning to grow but the scars left by the French clearcutting were still painfully obvious. All sacrificed to Napoleon's desperate need for ships most of which had subsequently been destroyed by Nelson and the British navy. The devastation would take years—nay, generations—to recover. But the birds were singing and Kati was happy to be home.

She climbed as far as the wisewoman's cottage. The tiny hut was long gone and even the old dame's grave was overgrown with weeds. Apparently no one left flowers there anymore. How sad. She shuddered at the recollection of that horrible day when the French had killed her. What a wealth of knowledge and history had been snuffed out that day. She suddenly thought of that gentleman named Grimm who had come to collect the old stories. She wondered if the brothers had ever had their book published. Dorothea would know.

Kati returned to the mill by another path through the grounds of the ancient monastery of Heiligenberg. The monastery had disappeared centuries ago but the orchards were still there just now coming into blossom. At least that remained but the fields lay fallow and the pasture was overgrown. Many of the peasant cottages still stood. She passed by the one that said on the main beam 'Johann Justus Bruns fecit 1795'. She wondered who lived there now. When she arrived back at the mill she was ravenous for dinner.

"Feel better?" asked Dorothea.

"Much. I think I feel up to visiting Mama this afternoon."

"Good."

"Do you think she's happy now, Tante Dorchen?"

Dorothea made a moué. "As happy as she can be, I should guess. Satisfied is more like it. At least she's mistress of her own home again. That counts for a lot with Elli."

Kati took the short cut through the wood to Vilsen. No one had any horses to ride but she preferred to walk anyway. It gave her time to collect her thoughts. She loved her mother dearly, had always been very close to her, but she often wondered if that love were returned. She cut through the churchyard. The lovely old church looked much the same although she had heard that Napoleon had stolen the magnificent bells and melted them down for cannon.

She approached the Hohnholz house. It had always been one of the wealthier homes in Vilsen but something looked different. Was there a slight aura of neglect about it? Or was her memory playing tricks on her since she had been away so long and lived in far more luxurious establishments in Hannover and Vienna? She was not sure. She hesitated a moment on the stoop and then walked in without knocking. After all, it was her home.

Her sister Dorothea came running from the back of the house. "Who is it? Ach, Katinka, Kati, you're home at last." She gave her a fond embrace. "Mama was wondering when you'd be coming." She looked about her. "But where are your things?"

"I'm staying at the Klostermühle. I prefer it there."

"Oh. Mama will be disappointed."

"I doubt it," replied Kati. "How is she?"

"Just fine. She'll be so happy to see you. Come along. She's in her office."

"Her office?"

"Ja. You'll remember that little room next to the kitchen where Onkel Fritzi used to sleep. That's her office. She runs the business now, you know."

"I see." Kati wondered what business was left as she followed her sister down the hall.

Dorothea flung open the door of the office and announced, "Mama, Mama, look who's here. It's Kati."

Eleonore looked up from her desk and smiled. "Ach, Kätchen, my dearest daughter, here at last. And all grown up into a lovely young woman, I see." She made no move to get up and embrace Kati.

Kati walked over to her, kissed her on the cheek and sat down. She was shocked. Her mother was fat. Fat! Eleonore, who had always been so svelte in between bearing children, who had always been so proud of her figure and her dress, was positively fat. It made her look much older than her forty-two years. Yet her thick, black hair had not one touch of gray in it.

"Thank you, Mama," said Kati. "It's good to be home for a while."

"Now tell me all about Vienna," said Eleonore. "I was positively jealous of you. What a wonderful opportunity. It must have been very exciting."

"It was. I even got to meet Master Beethoven and heard him play on several occasions."

"Oh, that musician. I've heard a little of him. But tell me about the balls and the soirées."

"Mama, I am only a maid. I only got to watch some of them from a balcony when I had to attend the Countess. But she was kind enough to take me to operas and concerts once in a while." But Kati knew what Eleonore wanted to hear. So she told about balls and galas and palaces, even if she had to make some of it up.

Eleonore was enthralled. "Did you get to see Schönbrunn?"

"Nay," replied Kati. "The imperial family was living at the Hofburg. Schönbrunn is their summer palace. We were there during the winter, remember? But I did once see the Empress riding to some affair in her ceremonial coach. It is the most eleborate thing I've ever seen — built for old Maria Theresia, I believe. It is totally gold-encrusted — real gold. Can you imagine such wealth?"

Eleonore shook her head. "Ach, I should love to see all that. Once I get the business back on its feet, I fully intend to take some trips. I owe it to myself. Vienna would be first and mayhap even Paris if things ever settle down over there."

Mama, Mama, thought Kati, dream on. A village peasant such as yourself would never be able to set foot in one of those palaces nor be invited to those balls. But there was no point in spoiling the dream. "So how is the business going?" she asked. "Do you actually have any business?"

"Oh, ja. It's starting to recover very well. And now that commerce is opening up with England again we'll soon be trading our linen for English wool."

"But do you have enough linen for international trade? I did not see one single flax field in bloom anywhere as I came from Hannover."

"That will come. Right now the farmers—those that can—are planting food crops because the people demand it. Which is somewhat foolish in my opinion. They should reserve at least some fields for flax. That has always been our cash crop. The linen would bring in the money they need to buy horses and other livestock."

"But I hear that many people are sick and starving. Shouldn't food come first? They can't eat linen."

Eleonore shrugged. "My dearest daughter, you simply don't understand business."

"I understand one thing," Kati replied. "England now has huge factories for wool and cotton, too. How can your little cottage industry compete with that?"

"Ach, factories," Eleonore said derisively. "Your father once had ideas of building a factory with steam-powered looms but his father and the Town Council would not permit it. Even I had to agree with that. It's quality, Kati, that counts. Quality, not quantity. Fine, hand-woven linen can compete with anything those smoke-belching factories can put out. You'll see. The Hohnholz were once one of the wealthiest families in Vilsen. We'll be rich again, I promise you."

Once again Kati thought, ja, Mama, dream on, but she knew better than to argue with her headstrong mother. She soon took her leave and was glad to return to the loving, common sense family at the Klostermühle.

That evening after supper Kati received the answer to one of her questions of the morning. Sophie, six, Dorothea's youngest, was seated on her mother's lap. Young Chris, eleven, sat on the floor at her knees. Dorothea was reading to them out of a large book.

"Why, those are the old stories we heard as children," exclaimed Kati, delighted. "And now they're in a book?"

"Ja," replied Dorothea. "The Brothers Grimm finally got their collection published. You remember the time the one brother Wilhelm came here asking about them, don't you?"

"Yes, I do. In fact I was just wondering about him this very morning."

"The first edition was published in 1812 but it was so scholarly it did not have a very wide appeal. Then Wilhelm, who was the better writer of the two and more sensitive, realized that their greater appeal would be to children. So he revised and shortened about fifty of them and changed the name to *Kinder- und Hausmärchen* (Children's and Houshold Tales). A third brother Ludwig drew the illustrations. Just look at this dragon, these elves. Aren't they fantastic? I understand it is now selling very well. I know these two love them."

"I know them all by heart," declared Young Chris, "and I can read them by myself." Then he added shyly. "But I like it better when Mama reads them. She makes them sound so—so—"

"Dramatic?" put in Kati.

"Ja, ja. Exciting," agreed Young Chris.

Little Sophie clapped her hands. "I love them, too. Sometimes I get a little scared of the wicked wolf or the dark woods but then everything turns out all right and they all live happily ever after."

Kati smiled. "Your brother Heinrich Anton and I used to play 'Hansel and Gretel' in these very woods when we were little like you."

Sophie's eyes grew wide. "And was there an old witch?"

"We used to call her a witch but really she was a very kind wise-woman. Her cottage disappeared long ago."

"Oh, tell us about her, Katinka," chirped Sophie.

Kati could have bitten her tongue off. No way would she tell these little ones that gruesome tale. "Not tonight," she said. "It's getting late."

"Ja, it's past bedtime," agreed Dorothea and hustled them off to bed.

Later Dorothea asked Kati, "Do you plan on visiting your grandma Becke while you're here?"

"I've thought about it but I hate going near the place. I trust Onkel Heinzi not at all."

"He's not as bad as he used to be," Dorothea assured her. "He's been sick a lot. Like so many others, lacking proper food."

"But they were so rich . . . "

"Ach, but Heinzi is not the manager old Anton was. Besides more and more of the farmers are bringing what grain they have to us instead of to Bruchmühlen. They know they'll get honest measure from Chris. And that makes the Matthies very, very jealous. Heinzi now has his second son Heinrich working with him and is starting to train the younger one Willi, but I'm afraid it is a case of the blind leading the blind. Heinzi was never a very good miller and he is teaching the boys all the wrong things."

"I'm not surprised," commented Kati. "I know his eldest son Hans died in Russia about the same time as Papa did. I remember him. He was always a kind of show-off. But I don't even remember the others. They have so many of them."

"This Heinrich is much the same. They all have a high opinion of themselves but no common sense and few brains. But never mind them. Old Becke is failing badly. I fear she is really losing her mind and they neglect her abominably. I don't mean they mistreat her. They simply ignore her. She would so enjoy a visit from you—if she is having one of her good days. But don't be upset if she doesn't recognize you at all. It's that bad sometimes."

"I see," said Kati, not looking forward to the prospect at all.

"I'll go with you if you wish," volunteered Dorothea. "I think I'm the only visitor she ever has."

Chris looked up from an old newspaper he was reading. "While you're planning visits," he said, "you should stop in and see Philipp sometime."

"I intend to," replied Kati. "I owe him a lot. Do you think he might have any news of Heinrich Anton?"

"No more than we have but he might have news of what the King's German Legion is doing." He waved the newspaper. "He lays hold of every out-of-town newspaper he can get. Even if they're a month or more old they have more news than our local sheet. Then he gives them to me. The ones I can read, that is." Chris laughed. "He even sometimes gets *The Times* from London. How, I don't ask. That is a little beyond me. But he tells me what it says. Often a totally different slant from what we hear."

"He is so brilliant," commented Kati.

"Ach, that he is," agreed Dorothea. She was so obviously proud of her brother. "It's too bad he never married. He is still teaching part-time at Göttingen. The Brothers Grimm are both professors there now and Philipp has grown quite close to them. He says they are dreamers but he agrees with their politics even if it is a little radical. Apparently they and several other professors are agitating for a constitution for Hannover."

Kati was not sure what the political significance of that was. So she simply nodded.

A few days later Kati and Dorothea strolled down the lane to Bruch-mühlen. Gerhardina let them in. "How nice to see you again Catharine," she said, although she obviously did not mean it. "What a lovely dress. Although isn't it a bit fancy for the country?"

"It's the only one I have," replied Kati.

"And how do you like Hannover?"

"Very well, thank you."

"I don't think I should care to live in the big city. Too crowded for my taste. Tell me, don't you find it a bit demeaning to be a maid?"

"Not at all. I find it can be quite educational."

Gerhardina's concept of education ended at age fourteen, once one had learned to read, write and cipher. Anything else was beyond her comprehension. "I suppose you've come to see your grandmother."

"Indeed, we have. Where is she?"

"In her usual place in the kitchen beside the fire even though it's so warm today."

"Not in the parlor with her loom?"

"Lord, no. We had to take that thing away from her. That constant clacking without any cloth in it was driving me crazy."

Kati looked at Dorothea, who shook her head as they followed Gerhardina into the kitchen. When she had left them, Dorothea said, "Don't mind her."

"I don't. She's always been like that. Nothing but criticism." Kati turned to her grandmother.

Becke Matthies had always been fat but now she was gross. Her hips overflowed the large chair she was sitting in. It looked as though she had not gotten up from it for weeks—if she were even able to stand. She had a shawl around her shoulders even though the kitchen was very warm—almost stifling. For all their wealth the Matthies did not yet have a modern iron stove so the kitchen fire had to be kept going day and night regardless of the weather. Becke had always suffered from bouts of depression and even at her best had been too timid and frightened of her husband Anton to dare to say much of anything. Kati noticed her rheumy eyes and the vague expression in them. This must be one of her bad days, she thought. She went over and kissed Becke on the cheek. She smelled bad. Thus Kati was quite surprised when her grandmother suddenly became quite voluble.

"Why, Eleonore Amalie," said Becke, "you naughty child. It's about time you came to see me. And who is this older woman? Ach, Dorchen, is that you?" She blinked her eyes as though trying to see better. "But your hair is turning gray. What a shame in such a young girl."

"But Becke," said Dorothea, "this is your granddaughter Katinka. Elli is her mother."

"I don't know any Katinka. You are lying again, Eleonore. I well remember the day you lied to save Dorchen from punishment. As if my dear Anton would ever hurt anyone. And you," she pointed at Dorothea, "you ran away. That was most ungrateful of you."

At Kati's look of puzzlement, Dorothea shook her head. "I had to, Becke, but that was long ago. We're friends now, aren't we? I'm the only one who comes to visit you."

"Ja, you are." The old woman started to cry. "My only friend. That one," she waved vaguely toward the front of the house, "she starves me. And she took away my loom. How can we make any money without my linen to sell? Oh, she's so cruel."

"You don't need that money now," said Dorothea gently. "The mill does quite well enough."

"Ach, the mill. That's all my Anton lived for. I got sick of hearing about it. But I tell you, not a one of them is half the miller he was."

"We'll let you rest now. Say goodbye to your granddaughter, Becke. We'll come again soon."

"Granddaughter?" Becke echoed.

Out in the lane Kati said, "How very sad. Is she always like that?"

"Nay," replied Dorothea. "Sometimes she's quite alert and aware but those times she doesn't say much. She was always afraid to speak up in front of your grandpa Anton. But at other times she doesn't know what day it is—or even day from night."

"I think she is losing her sight as well. Did you notice how cloudy her eyes are?"

"I've noticed. And that doubles the tragedy."

"Do you really think they are starving her? She doesn't look starved."

"Not at all. It's just her way of saying she feels neglected. But it can't be easy living with someone like that. I've never liked Gerhardina but I can feel sorry for her."

"What was Oma talking about when she said Mama was naughty and you ran away?" asked Kati.

Dorothea hesitated. She expected the question but did not want to answer it. "That is something you don't want to know about, dearest Katinka. It was long ago. Your mama was eight and I was sixteen. It was then that I left them and went to work for your papa's grandmother, Frau Meyer. Now there was a wonderful woman."

"And Mama?"

"Unfortunately she was left behind to bear the brunt of his—his temper."

"I understand," said Kati.

"Oh, look at the blossoms on those wild blackberries. We'll have some fine jelly this summer if the birds don't eat them first."

Dorothea was obviously changing the subject but Kati's curiosity was piqued. She was sure this had some bearing on why her mother was—as she was.

368

Kati tried to visit her mother at least two or three times a week. That way she could keep each visit short without giving offense. One time Eleonore begged her to stay for supper and she met Fritzi for the first time in years. He made a great effort to be polite and courteous.

To her unspoken question he explained, "I love your mother very much. Always have ever since I was a little child. She was more of a mother to me than my own and now she is the wife I've always wanted. The age difference matters not a bit when you're in love." Kati noticed he never tried to explain why he had refused to wed her back when he got her pregnant with the twins. Fritzi continued, "Besides this is her home. She has as much right to it as I. Not only that but I needed her help with the business. My half-brother, your papa, never let me have much to do with it. Elli actually ran it ever since our father died while Teddi was tinkering with his fire engine and Lord knows what else."

So that was the real reason. Kati murmured, "I understand." She knew he was twisting the truth a bit but if her mother was happy—and she seemed at least content—who was she to criticize? Let them have their dream of regaining the Hohnholz wealth. It would take years, if ever. Probably more than their lifetimes. Germany, France and all of Europe as well as England were in dire economic straits after twelve years of Napoleon's wars and disruption of normal commercial neworks. And now he was back again ready to cause more trouble. When would it ever end?

Kati paid a courtesy visit to Philipp Koch not only to thank him for placing her in the Count's household but in the hope that he might have some news of Heinrich Anton.

"Nay," said Philipp. "I had only one letter from him when he first arrived in England thanking me for my help and advising that Ernst August, the Duke of Cumberland, was no longer in England and therefore my letter was almost useless—but not quite. It did gain him entry to the famous Black Duke of Braunschweig and, last I heard, he was attached to the Duke's division. It seems they separated the original group from here and spread them out amongst various units. More I can't tell you."

"I see," said Kati. "Do you think they will be coming over to fight Napoleon?"

"Most definitely. I can give you a lot of general information. Wellington left Vienna right after the Congress learned of Napoleon's escape from Elba."

"I know that. He hurried back to England."

"Nay. He has made his headquarters in Brussels and has ordered his entire army, including the KGL, to join him there. Blücher and his Prussians are already there. Wellington intends to meet with him within the next week or two to plan an invasion of France sometime in July. Each of the major powers has pledged 150,000 men but Wellington is holding the others in reserve in various places around Europe: the Russians near Dresden, the Austrians on the upper Rhein and the Austro-Italians in northwestern Italy. You see, Napoleon is so foxy, no one knows for sure where he is apt to strike. But Wellington is commander-in-chief of the entire Allied army. Many of the smaller states are sending troops as well. The Dutch-Belgian army will be there under the Prince of Orange, whom no one trusts."

"Whom? The Prince or the army?"

"Neither. The Prince because he is a young, inexperienced, puffed-up know-it-all. And the Belgians because they love Napoleon and many are still loyal to him."

"Has Hannover sent any? I mean aside from the King's German Legion."

"Ja, she has. I believe they are already on their way. That is the one good thing Ernst August did in the few weeks he was here. He raised several divisions of Hussars—excellent fighters all."

"And where is Ernst August now? Why isn't he with them?"

"In Berlin and I hope he stays there."

"How so?"

"He is so reactionary he does not want Hannover to have a constitution which the people are demanding. We shall have a difficult enough time convincing your Graf von Münster of the right of it."

"He is a somewhat dour man but the Countess is so sweet."

"Good. I'm glad you're enjoying your work, Kati," said Philipp.

And so Kati returned to Hannover at the end of the month slightly confused as to the meaning of political terms such as reactionary and constitution, still not knowing what had happened to her mother and Tante Dorchen when they were eight and sixteen, and above all wondering where Heinrich Anton was and whether he would survive the next few months.

12

1815

Anton Bergmann sat in the shade cleaning his musket for the umpteenth time and for what? Nothing but the endless drilling and drilling. Word had been passed that there would be another inspection tomorrow—another of the innumerable inspections the Duke insisted on. Friedrich Wilhelm, Duke of Braunschweig—the Black Duke—was a fine soldier, a kindly man most considerate of his troops, but a strict disciplinarian. He always acted as though battle was imminent and expected his men to be prepared. No doubt he was as eager for real war as were his men and frustrated at the inactivity.

The little group from Vilsen and Bremen had been split up among several units of the King's German Legion. Only Anton, Wulf and Harm Bruns were still together with the Duke. The others had been scattered throughout the KGL. Carsten, only because he had a horse, had been placed with a unit of the KGL light cavalry. Anton wished he had one of the new guns called rifles that everyone was talking about. But they were reserved for a special corps of veterans from the Spanish campaign called Riflemen. To Anton that smacked of favoritism but then he supposed Wellington would naturally favor the veterans who had fought with him in Spain. Still the KGL numbered almost 4,500 men, a very large segment of Wellington's army.

Anton was homesick. Not that he disliked England. It was a pretty country especially here in Kent and especially now that spring had arrived. The local people were friendly enough and he had by now learned enough English to communicate with them. But the few times he and some of his friends had travelled up to London on short leaves he had been dismayed at the resentment, even hatred, some of the citizens felt towards Germans and especially toward the German kings who had ruled them for a hundred years.

For the past few weeks, ever since word had reached them of

Napoleon's escape from Elba, rumors had been flying thick and fast. Mayhap soon they would see some real action, fight a real battle for a change. Mayhap. But no one seemed to know anything for sure. Anton started putting his musket back together again.

He heard a great cheer arise over near their tents. Now what can that be, he wondered. A lieutenant and two corporals circulated among the men shouting something.

"Get yourselves ready, lads. We're going at last," announced a corporal. "We move out tomorrow."

"Tomorrow?" said one man.

"To where?" asked Anton.

"Ja, tomorrow. To Belgium, of course," replied the corporal. "We're finally getting our chance to finish Boney once and for all."

The men gathered around the lieutenant.

"This is it, men. We move out at daybreak tomorrow," he told them. "Get rid of your whores, your souvenirs and all your excess baggage. Take only your weapons and ammunition, canteens and blankets. The quartermasters will give you enough food for the crossing and the Duke's commissary wagons will meet us over there. An extra pair of stockings, if you have them, would not be amiss."

"Why stockings?" asked one man.

"Lad, we'll be marching over all kinds of terrain and in all kinds of weather—marching like you've never marched before. Let me tell you, nothing slows a man down more than a bare heel or toe rubbing against wet leather."

The veterans among them nodded. "He's right you know," said one as the lieutenant moved off.

"Ja," added another, "if you have them, another pair of underdrawers would come in handy, too. I've not seen a greenhorn yet who didn't shit himself or piss his drawers before a battle."

Anton did not much relish the idea of that but he believed the men. He decided to take all of his extra underclothing. Dorothea had insisted he take three pair of drawers and the same of stockings. He could still hear her saying, in case of accident, be sure your underwear is clean. He could never figure out, if he should be wounded in battle, how his smallclothes would remain clean, but there was no sense in leaving them behind. He had hardly ever worn the extras.

Early the next morning the men marched out. Spirits were high. Drums beat the cadence and many were singing old German songs and even some new English tunes they had learned during their long years in Britain. They were going to fight—really fight at last. They hoped the Prussians did not finish Boney off before they got there.

Anton had a slight disagreement with one of the quartermasters at the commissary that morning.

"How you gonna fit your victuals in that pack with all them drawers in there?" queried the man.

"I'll just push them down and make it fit," replied Anton stubbornly. "It's not heavy."

The man shrugged. "Hah! Just wait till you get to the other side and they load you with three times the bullets you got in there now. You'll know what heavy is. But have it your way. I ain't carrying it."

The army left England from several different ports on the southeast coast, mostly from Dover but also from every little town and village that could supply ships or boats. The local people willingly lent their vessels to their beloved Duke of Wellington. The cavalry, artillery and most officers travelled in the larger ships. The rest were sent in whatever was available, often as many as fifty men crowded into a fishing boat designed to hold only twenty. Fortunately the weather held and the Channel crossing was swift and uneventful.

At Ostend they mustered outside the town. They were issued more ammunition and more food until each pack weighed at least seventy pounds. Anton recalled the quartermaster's warning but he gritted his teeth, straightened his shoulders and bore it. Just as soon as a battalion was all present, they were immediately sent on their way to Brussels.

The men now realized they were indeed in a foreign country, and a somewhat hostile one at that. While the prostitutes and tavernkeepers welcomed the army, the citizens of Brussels openly showed their hatred of the English, Scots and Germans. The Belgians still considered themselves French and the majority were still loyal to Napoleon.

By the beginning of June the entire army had arrived and were bivouacked all around the environs of Brussels. At last Anton and the others got a glimpse of their commander-in-chief, Arthur Wellesley, newly made Duke of Wellington. He was a tall handsome man in his mid-forties. Long of face, clean-shaven, with piercing eyes, a hawk-like nose and a pointed, determined chin, he could act the noble dandy when he chose but he was more comfortable in the field among his men, where his top-sergeant voice could bellow out orders in language as crude as any trooper's. A brilliant tactician he demanded and got exemplary loyalty

373

from his soldiers. He understood his men and they loved him for it.

The other highly intelligent, eminently capable commander was the Prussian Field Marshal Gebhard Leberecht von Blücher. A heavy-set man, balding, gray-haired with soft brown eyes that missed nothing, a long nose above a luxurious mustache, he was seventy-three years old but as active as any younger man. He, too, was well loved hy his men who nick-named him old 'Vorwärts' since he refused to retreat if at all possible.

A third personage who considered himself a commander but who had no battle experience whatsoever was the very young Prince of Orange. A thin, callow, pimple-faced youth, he was in charge of the Dutch-Belgian contingent of the army. He let it be known that he knew more about fight-ing a war than anyone else and that he alone would be responsible for the glory they would soon achieve. No one liked him save a small group of sycophants who followed him everywhere and no one, even his own offi-cers, trusted his decisions, which were almost always wrong. Wellington detested him but he had to put up with him as he needed his troops.

Wellington and Blücher had met in May at Tirlemont near Brussels and discussed plans to invade France sometime in July when the Russians and Austrians could move up to join them. Blücher had moved his head-quarters to Namur in order to be closer to the British. Both commanders had fought Napoleon for years and knew his every trick and ploy. Although they despised him and vowed to rid Europe of him once and for all, as battle hardened soldiers they respected and admired his military prowess and did not fool themselves into thinking it would be easy.

Both the British and Prussians had numerous spies in France watch-ing Napoleon's every move. They knew that he had recruited an army of 150,000 men, mostly his old veterans. While many had refused the call, the majority were willing, overjoyed, to fight for him again. Leaving some twenty thousand to defend Paris, he had sent the remainder, the Armée du Nord, to the Belgian frontier. But there was no activity there. It appeared to be only a defensive maneuver. Napoleon himself was traipsing around Paris dressed in his coronation robes followed dutifully by four of his brothers. He was busy arguing with the Senate about a new constitution. All was quiet. Too quiet.

Blücher was not fooled. He installed Prussian garrisons at Mons and Charleroi, two logical crossing points on the River Sambre on two possible routes to Brussels. And all remained quiet. Suddenly on 13 June Napoleon dropped out of sight. And not one spy knew where he was or what was going on on the French side of the Sambre. It was too ominously quiet.

Many of the English nobles who had underwritten regiments, mostly cavalry, had brought along their wives or mistresses. Thus there was a constant gay social whirl in Brussels. Although few, if any, had any battle experience, their troops were well trained and made up the backbone of Wellington's light and heavy cavalry units. And they were all eager to fight for their Duke.

"You'd think they were going on a damned fox hunt. Tallyho!" grumbled Anton.

"I hope they know what to do when a thousand foxes run towards them instead of away," agreed Harm.

Wulf burst into their tent. "How would you lads like to go to a ball and dance with real women? Fine ladies, I mean, not tavern wenches."

Anton and Harm looked at each other. "A real ball? Whose?" asked Anton.

"And how did you manage to get invited?" asked Harm.

"The Duchess of Richmond's. I've been screwing one of her maids," replied Wulf with a grin.

"She is one of the richest of all the elite here," exclaimed Anton.

"And they are now inviting their maids' lovers?" said Harm skeptically.

"They are handing out tickets right and left to anyone and everyone. I trow there'll be as many common folk there as nobility. See, I've got four tickets." Wulf waved the cards at them. "Are you game?"

"Sure, we're game," said Anton. "Be nice to have some fun while we're sitting here waiting."

"Sure, why not?" said Harm. "Maybe if I meet a nice rich heiress to keep me, I won't have to go back to the farm when our enlistment is up."

Wulf laughed. "That's the spirit. Now whom can I give this fourth ticket to?"

"If we could find Lude or Gerd," suggested Harm.

"Ach, nay," said Wulf. "They're stationed way on the other side of the city. There wouldn't be time. How about one of the lads from our own tent here?"

"Then young Paul," offered Anton. "He is so shy a little social life might brighten him up. When is this ball then?"

"Tonight."

"Tonight?" ejaculated Anton and Harm together.

"Ja, tonight," said Wulf. "So brush up your uniforms, polish your boots and comb your hair."

That same afternoon Wellington was eating his dinner when he received word that a French force had crossed the Sambre and attacked the small Prussian garrison at Charleroi. There was no word of how large a force, who had prevailed and, most importantly, was Napoleon with them? The Duke held his army at Brussels believing that Napoleon would make his usual flank attack. Then he went to the ball.

But Blücher knew better.

The Prussians had set up a makeshift barricade at the end of the bridge over the Sambre. They mounted the few guns they had and raked the invading French unmercifully. But then a daring French officer drove his horse forward and cleared the barricade in one leap. He slashed the gun crews right and left enabling his troops to follow him. The Prussian major knew when to retreat in the face of overwhelming numbers. After losing a great number of men he gathered his little garrison and fled to the northeast. He sent an urgent message to Blücher.

Blücher had already guessed Napoleon's intentions but then a French general officer, Bourmont, defected to the Allies and confirmed Napoleon's plans. Some miles south of Brussels stood a few houses at a crossroads called Quatre-Bras. It was so tiny it could not even be called a hamlet but strategically the crossroads were of the utmost importance. It was here that the road from the east that Blücher would have to take met the road from the north that Wellington must use to meet the Prussians. Napoleon was determined to prevent that meeting and fight each army separately. That way he was assured of victory. If the two Allied armies were to join, even he was not so confident.

Anton had never seen such brilliance, such elegance. The truth of it was he had never been to a ball of any kind in his life. Kati had taught him to dance and, yes, they had gone dancing at Der Lustige Strumpf in Vilsen several times. But this was beyond anything he could have imagined. Jewels and gowns sparkled on radiant women. The men's uniforms glittered with gold epaulettes and all the medals they could cram on their chests and sashes. Harm gaped with open mouth and their new friend, young Paul, simply blushed and blushed. Only Wulf, who had been made a sergeant while they were in England, seemed at ease. He was dancing with every female who would accept him.

Anton had already gathered up his courage and danced with one girl, a pretty nobleman's daughter, and discovered to his surprise that they were just as raunchy as any tavern wench. This one had already implied, none

376

too subtly, that she would be more than willing to have him share her bed and he did not even know her name. He appreciated his dear Kati all the more. Around midnight he was about to approach another one when an urgent messenger rushed into the ballroom and sought out Wellington. The music stopped and all eyes turned in his direction.

The Duke opened the missive, quickly glanced at it and stuffed it in his pocket. Very quietly he passed the word, "All officers to their regiments." The Duke of Braunschweig spoke to his lieutenant who spoke to Wulf. Wulf signalled to Anton, Harm and Paul and led them out of the room.

Outside they were full of curiosity. "What has happened?" asked Anton.

"Something, but I don't know what," replied Wulf. "We are ordered back to our headquarters and must be prepared to march at dawn. More I don't know but I'm sure we'll soon find out."

Wellington, in order not to upset his hostess or her guests, continued to dance until three in the morning. Then he moved his headquarters to the little village of Waterloo, nine miles south of Brussels.

"Who is our nearest?" he asked his aide.

"Prince Bernhard of Saxe-Weimar, Your Grace."

"Send him to Quatre-Bras immediately. We must hold that crossroads."

"Saxe-Weimar just moved out," announced Wulf.

"At this hour of the night?" asked Harm.

"It's almost morning," replied Wulf succinctly.

"Where to?" asked Anton.

"A place called Quatre-Bras."

"Never heard of it."

"Neither has anyone else. It's no but a crossroads but apparently it's where we and the Prussians hope to meet. We can't let the French take it."

"Then it looks as though we'll be moving out soon, too," commented Anton.

"Count on it," replied Wulf.

Marshall Ney had already sent a few hundred scouts and skirmishers to investigate Quatre-Bras and when they returned reporting no sight of the enemy, he assumed he had plenty of time. Less than a mile south of the crossroads the main road from Charleroi to Brussels forded a small stream. When Ney returned late in the afternoon with fewer than three thousand infantry he ran up against four thousand men and eight guns of Prince Bernhard of Saxe-Weimar. The Germans stood in four solid lines across the road and west up to a dense wood. The moment the French were within range they opened a deadly musket fire. After several indecisive exchanges Ney realized he was outnumbered and ordered the French to retreat south to the village of Frasnes. He sent an urgent message to Napoleon for reinforcements. At the same time Bernhard sent an equally urgent message to Wellington stating that they were holding but that the French would attack in force by the next morning.

On Friday, 16 June, a series of misunderstandings atypical of both generals led to chaotic and near disastrous circumstances. Ney's message was delivered to Drouet d'Erlon whose reserve force Napoleon had ordered to stand ready to move either east or west as needed. Drouet immediately set out for Quatre-Bras but before he could reach there, Napoleon, unaware of Ney's plight and already desperately fighting the Prussians seven miles to the east at Ligny, ordered Drouet back to attack the Prussians' right flank.

Meanwhile Wellington was moving his army south to Quatre-Bras. When he saw no sign of the French and everything seemed to be under control, he rode off towards Ligny to see for himself what was happening, leaving the stupid, egotistical, intransigent Prince of Orange in charge.

Late in the day as the black-coated Braunschweigers under the command of their indomitable Black Duke approached the crossroads they could hear sporadic musketry and then the roar of cannon. Far to the east the more ominous sound of steady gunfire rumbled towards them.

"It has started," said Anton, a frisson of both fear and excitement running up his spine.

"Are we too late?" asked Harm.

"It's never too late," growled Wulf. "Just keep moving. We're almost there." Then a few moments later he exclaimed, "Lord, have mercy! They *do* need our help. On the double, march."

The men, already weary from the long march from Brussels, picked up their pace. The Duke and his cavalry spurred their horses on ahead. Then Anton and the others could see the cause of Wulf's dismay—the cause for haste.

Hundreds of Orange's Belgians were fleeing the scene—not retreating but running wild with terror and disloyalty. They still wore the French uniforms of their former emperor, the only change being that the N and eagle on their hats had been replaced by a W for King Willem of Holland.

The Prince of Orange waved his sword and tried to stop them but they swept right past paying him no mind. Apparently their own colonel, having seen his aide fall beside him from a musket shot and one of the Dutch guns at the ford destroyed, had ordered the retreat which immediately became a rout.

"Look at the cowards," exclaimed Harm. "What are they running from?" He could see no sign of the French.

"Cowards is too good a word," snarled Wulf. "Traitors is more like. I knew we could not trust those bastards to fight. They still love Napoleon."

"But where are the French?" asked Anton. As they arrived at Quatre-Bras the road to the ford was totally empty. On either side lay rich fields of grain. The rye was taller than a man's head. Off to the right was the dense wood that Saxe-Weimar's men were still valiantly defending.

"They're there all right," replied Wulf. "Watch the rye. When you see it bending, there's a whole battalion hidden behind it."

Then Anton could see and so did the Duke of Braunschweig. The doughty Duke ordered his men into a breech in the French lines between the road and the woods. The cavalry led the way, smashing down with their deadly sabres. The infantry followed. The advance French skirmishers fled like frightened rabbits before the onslaught. Just when the way seemed clear to the little stream, the cavalry ran straight into a French brigade hidden in the tall rye. They immediately opened fire and threw the German horsemen into confusion.

"Halt," ordered Wulf. "Form a square but hold your fire. Can't afford to cut down our own men."

The Duke ordered the cavalry to fall back but already wounded men were crying and horses screaming. Bloodied men were falling every which way and disemboweled horses lay kicking the air in agony. As the scattered remnants of the cavalry moved out of the way, an officer ordered, "Form a double line. Forward. Halt."

Wulf and the other sergeants took up the cry. "Present. Fire." And the deadly volley cut into the French square. Again and again they fired. The man beside Anton fell in a pool of blood.

"Paul!" cried out Anton, but the sergeants merely continued their litany, "Close ranks. Close up." And the carnage went on. The French ceased their pursuit of the German cavalry.

But then, just as the Black Duke and his aides, who had been the last to leave, were passing through their ranks an unlucky bullet struck the Duke directly in the back. As he fell from his horse, Harm broke ranks and rushed to catch him. As a captain was about to reprimand Harm, an unhorsed cavalry colonel ran to Harm's aid. Together they lowered their dying leader to the ground behind the lines.

"Auf Wiedersehen, my friends," gasped the Duke. "Fight to the end—for me—for Hannover." And he died in their arms.

"I'll see this man court-martialed for breaking ranks," grumbled the captain.

"No, you won't," ordered the colonel. "The lad did a brave thing. I'll see that he's rewarded, not punished. Now back to your position and hold as long as you can."

The captain sullenly obeyed and Harm could see that the colonel was openly weeping as they cradled their beloved Duke in their arms. Harm was so honored to have heard the Duke's last words that he vowed that he *would* fight to the end—for him and for Hannover. Together they lifted the Duke's inert body onto his horse which had stood loyally by as though he, too, were mourning.

"Now back to your ranks, soldier," ordered the colonel, "and if that captain gives you any trouble, let me know. What is your name?"

"Harm Bruns, sir."

"I'll remember. I am Colonel Auermann. Thank you for your help, lad." And he led the horse carrying the Duke's body back to Quatre-Bras.

Harm suddenly reappeared beside Anton and resumed firing at the French as though he had never been away.

"That was a foolish thing to do," commented Anton. "You'll be in trouble for sure."

"No, it wasn't and no, I won't," replied Harm. "I'll tell you later."

By this time the French brigade had recovered its order and was steadily advancing toward the decimated Germans. An officer ordered, "Fall back. But orderly now."

The sergeants echoed the order. "Fall back and fire. Fall back and fire."

The men obeyed and retreated as best they could, firing as they went. But they were suffering terribly. As they went Harm saw the nasty captain fall, half his face ripped away. As the man's brain oozed onto the ground, Harm felt only a pang of relief. No trouble from that one now, he thought.

Wulf had also noticed that they were now leaderless but for him. He had observed that many of the confused cavalry had fled to the woods, while others had galloped back to Quatre-Bras, some even joining the Prince of Orange. Without thinking twice he ordered his men into the woods. "Saxe-Weimar is still holding. There we'll be safe for the moment. To the woods, but keep firing as you go."

The men did so in a rapid but orderly fashion. Miraculously no more from their own contingent fell that day. As they gratefully entered the protection of the dense thicket, the men from Saxe-Weimar and Nassau welcomed them. "Brave lads," they said. "We tried to cover you as best we could but the range was too far. Now your Duke is dead, what will you do?"

Wulf shook his head. "Nothing but rest right now. Wellington will let us know soon enough."

The weary men threw themselves down on the soft, spongy earth taking care only to keep their powder dry as they might need it at any moment.

The last thing Anton noticed before entering the wood was towering, black thunderheads building up in the west.

"It will rain before morning," he said to Harm.

"Let it rain," replied Harm. " 'Twill wash away the stink."

When Wellington returned, he surveyed the carnage with disgust. "It looks as though we shall have to fight without the Prussians today," he commented. Then he saw the fleeing Belgians and the wide open road. "What is going on here?" he asked sharply of the Prince of Orange. "Have you issued an invitation to the French to walk up the road?"

"But we're holding, Your Grace," stammered the Prince.

"Never mind the formalities. I am merely the commander of this army. 'Sir' will do. Now explain yourself. Who? Where?"

"Ah — er —," the Prince turned to his aide.

"Saxe-Weimar is holding the woods over there, sir," pointed out the aide. "The Duke of Braunschweig has been killed."

"Oh, no," sighed Wellington. "And you let him go in there unsupported?"

"Well, er —," mumbled the Prince.

More British troops were arriving all the while and, at last, the British artillery. Wellington turned to General Picton who had brought a whole division, most of them veterans. The French had moved up their heavy guns and their infantry was now across the little stream. "Thomas," said Wellington to Picton, "lay three batallions across that road and drive them back. The French must not reach this crossroads."

Picton, a dour, blunt veteran, replied, "I'll not take orders from that bloody Dutch shit."

"I quite agree. I am giving the orders here," snapped Wellington. "Now move your men."

"At once, sir."

Picton placed three divisions as ordered, two of them gaily kilted Scots Highlanders, some of the toughest fighters in the entire army, accompanied by their pipers who never stopped playing while the battle raged. They launched a ferocious attack on the French, driving them back, only to be driven back themselves by the superior numbers of the French. Wellington threw in two more battalions. And so it went, back and forth, each side gaining ground and losing it moments later.

The men in the woods watched it all while keeping up their own deadly fusillade. They were relatively sheltered by the dense thicket in that the French could not see any discernable targets but every so often they raked the trees with volleys of their own and unlucky men fell. Saxe-Weimar sent an urgent message to Wellington, "We'll hold as long as we can but we're running out of ammunition." Wellington promptly sent them a whole wagonload of bullets and powder and an English regiment to reinforce them.

"Will you look at that," exclaimed Anton. "What is that damn fool up to now?"

"Looking to commit suicide is what," replied Harm.

The young Prince of Orange was leading his Dutch-Belgian cavalry directly toward the French guns.

"He thinks he can win the whole war by himself," commented Wulf and then laughed. "Watch what happens next. He doesn't see them yet but his men do. The bloody fool."

The front line of Belgian cavalry stopped dead in their tracks. Then the second line stopped. The Prince waved his sword in the air and shouted "Charge!" but not one horseman budged. Before them was a brigade of the famous French lancers, the most dreaded troops in the world. They held their eight-foot weapons tipped with razor-sharp stilettos vertical. Bright little pennants waved at their tips. A French bugle sounded, the lances were lowered and they advanced.

"Charge!" screamed the Prince but the Belgians turned their horses around and fled.

Suddenly realizing the danger the Prince, too, gallopped away passing his own men in his haste to escape. The faster-moving lancers skewered many, many of the fleeing Belgians and followed them right up to the British lines where the doughty Scots finally turned them back.

Wulf shook his head. "What a useless waste of good men," was his only comment.

"Ney is down," shouted someone.

"Nay, just unhorsed," said another. "See, they've already found him another."

"That's the second time today."

"You can see why Napoleon calls him 'the bravest of the brave'," commented Wulf.

"Too bad he's fighting on the wrong side," added Harm but no one thought it was funny at all.

Very gradually as Wellington poured more and more men into the field, Ney realized that he was outnumbered and, as darkness began to fall, he had the retreat sounded. Soon all was quiet except for the screams and moans of the thousands of wounded and dying. Now the regimental bandsmen who had played continuous encouragement during the entire fray went out into the field to bring in as many wounded as they could find before darkness set in. In the west the lightning flickered ominously from the towering black thunderheads.

"Ooh, my shoulder," moaned Anton rubbing the spot where the musket had kicked against it all day. He had hardly noticed it in the frantic heat of the battle, but now it was on fire. Would he ever be able to move it again?

"Look at my hands," said Harm as he showed his friend the powder burns.

"You'll live," said Wulf. "Better get used to it. There'll be a lot more tomorrow."

"It's going to rain tomorrow," said Anton.

"Good. Mayhap it'll give us a day of rest," replied Wulf. "Now make us a fire and let's have some supper."

"With what? Hardtack?" asked Harm. "Our kits are back with the baggage wagons."

"I'll find something," chuckled Wulf. "Just make a good fire. We'll need it ere morn."

Anton and Harm started gathering kindling and dry sticks for a fire. All around them Saxe-Weimar's men were building their own cookfires. Apparently most of them had some food with them. Anton wondered where Wulf was going to find any. He hoped he was not going to steal anyone's.

Wulf disappeared out onto the field. First he found three sharp bayonets. Then he lifted a full canteen of good French brandy from a dead lancer. Next with his knife he hacked a large chunk of meat from the rump of a dead horse. He returned to the wood triumphantly dripping a trail of blood behind him. "Voilá, our supper," he announced.

Anton and Harm stared at him aghast.

"You've never eaten horse flesh before?" said Wulf. "Just as tasty as beef if a mite tough. But we'll have it tenderized in no time. Now build up that fire."

The two young men watched as Wulf carefully stripped the hairy skin from the meat and cut it into three parts.

"We're going to eat *that*?" asked Harm.

"Nay, nay, you'll see," replied Wulf. He carved the slab of meat into three steaks, cut small cross-hatches on them and skewered each piece on a bayonet. He then wrapped a piece of the pelt around the end of each bayonet. "See," he said, "potholders. That steel will get mighty hot ere the meat is cooked." He handed a laden bayonet to each of them. "Now sear it in the fire to seal the blood in and then turn it very slowly for about a half hour."

They did as he instructed. The meat sizzled and the fire flared as the fat dripped but soon the tantalizing aroma did smell as good as beef and their mouths started to water. While they cooked the meat, Wulf uncorked the canteen and took a sip. "Mmm, good," he pronounced as he offered them the canteen. "Here, have a sip. 'Twill ease all your aches and pains. 'Tis brandy—powerful stuff. But mind you, only a sip at a time, else you'll fall asleep ere supper's ready."

Anton had never tasted brandy before. He choked and sputtered. But then he could feel its warmth spread through his body and ease his tired muscles. When the meat was cooked they gnawed on it. It was tasty enough although admittedly still tough. Anton thanked God he still had all his teeth. Harm was not so lucky. As young as he was, he had already lost several teeth and he had to chew and chew.

Towards dawn they were awakened by a torrential downpour. Lightning flashed and thunder rumbled louder than any cannon fire. Although the woods offered some protection the spongy ground soon became a quagmire. Their cloaks had been left behind with the baggage so the only protection for their precious powder was to shove it inside their coats but soon they were drenched through to the skin. Out in the field the trampled rye turned into a swamp and the dirt road became a river of mud. Then came the fierce wind and the men could scarcely see ten feet in front of them. The cavalry had to lean over their horses' necks and hang on for dear life to avoid being blown off their mounts.

Wellington received a message that the Prussians had been defeated at Ligny after six hours of hard fighting. Old Blücher had fallen from his horse and had to be carried off the field. Doom and gloom set in, not helped by the rain. Then a second message arrived from Blücher himself. He was unhurt, still in charge and had deliberately retreated in order to save his weary men. He promised to join Wellington the next day. Wellington sent back an encouraging reply ordering Blücher to head northwest and join him at a more defensible location called Mont-St-Jean three miles south of the tiny village of Waterloo. Meanwhile spies brought in the news that Napoleon had sent de Grouchy to pursue the retreating Prussians but de Grouchy, slow getting started, had lost his way and could not find the Prussians. The Emperor himself moved west to join Ney and in an unusual and unwarranted spate of anger accused Ney of cowardice and relieved his favorite of his command. Napoleon would show them how to win a war. More gloom and doom.

Wellington's orders to move out were sent to the men in the woods. They picked up their seventy-pound packs from the baggage wagons and slogged northward through the downpour. A few valiant French cavalry-men were still trying to attack the rearguard especially the artillery which was the last to leave but soon their horses' hooves were so encased with mud they could barely move and so had to leave off. The artillerymen whipped their horses flanks raw trying to get them to pull the heavy limbers through the mud. But finally they, too, were moving to the north.

After seven weary miles the men topped a low ridge and stopped for a moment to admire the view. To their right was a bright, white tavern called *La Belle Alliance*.

"What an ironic name under the circumstances," commented Anton.

"I wish we could stop there for a drink," said Harm.

"Not a chance," said Wulf. The doors and windows of the place were tightly shuttered.

"But look at that rich farmland," said Harm.

Before them spread a shallow, lush valley rich with fields of rye, oats, barley and hay. It was about three-quarters of a mile wide. On the opposite side another low ridge rose and beyond that, forest. The road ran straight across the valley and over the far ridge. They could see three prosperous-looking farmhouses. The one to their left, west, was large enough to be a chateau, a once fortified farm complex. It was called Hougoumont. Directly on the road ahead of them stood another smaller but sturdy walled farmhouse called La Haye Sainte and to the east a third, Papelotte. The heavy rain had subsided somewhat so that the men could see all this.

Anton peered through the drizzle. "Is this the place?" he asked.

"I think it might well be," replied Wulf. "See that ridge beyond. The men seem to be mustering there. But are they?" he asked himself, puzzled, for the men seemed to disappear before his very eyes. "Let's go see."

As they mounted the northern ridge Wulf could see why the men had seemed to disappear. The ground fell away sharply towards the forest of Soignes hiding the troops entirely from the view from the south ridge. Only the artillery was being placed on the edge of the ridge. Wellington had set up his command post under a huge elm tree beside the road and was issuing rapid-fire orders as the men mustered in. An aide called aside the remnants of the Duke of Braunschweig's men.

"You will report to General Karl von Alten," he ordered. "He is the new commander of the KGL."

"Ah, one of our own," said Anton.

"You know him?" asked Harm.

"No, but I've heard of him. He is from Hannover and said to be an exemplary leader."

"Good. That's what we need," said Wulf. "Just as long as we don't have to fight under that asshole of Orange." They all sighed with relief at that small blessing.

"Your position will be just to right of center," went on the aide, "right next to the Duke's own division."

They reported to von Alten and were told where to leave their packs and where to take up their stance. The idea was to crouch or lie down below the crest of the ridge so that the enemy could not see how many they were.

And so, drenched and weary, they waited in the steady rain for the French to appear.

As the dreary twilight on one of the longest days of the year began to close in there was still no sign of the French. Could they have given up? Not a chance, not with Napoleon in command. And where were the Prussians? No sign of them either. But then the food wagons, which had never made it to Quatre-Bras, began to appear and that somewhat cheered the soaking wet men. Although they could not find any dry kindling to build fires, the ravenous men, many of whom had not eaten since the previous night, gnawed with relish on cold salt beef and twice-baked bread. But their main concern was when their ration of rum would appear.

"What do we do now?" asked Anton.

"Sleep right where you are," replied Wulf. "The officers are spending the night, all cozy and dry, in the village of Waterloo, three miles to the north. But we stay right here and maintain our positions."

The men grumbled but there was little they could do. The infantry lay behind the concealed guns and behind them the cavalry horses were picketed in a long line. Their riders were busy cutting forage for their mounts and would sleep beside them.

"At least we don't have to feed two," mumbled Harm as he rolled over in the wet grass and tried to sleep.

The Duke had garrisoned the three outlying farmhouses.

"Lucky bastards," commented Anton. "At least they have some shelter."

"And they'll be the first to get hit," said Wulf. "I'd rather be back here, wet but safe."

Harm just groaned and rolled over again in the wet grass.

Few of the men slept that night. Most just sat huddled under their cloaks which did little good since their uniforms had already been soaked. They tried desperately to keep the waterproof sacks of powder dry under their coats.

Dawn broke early on Sunday, 18 June. It was still raining but it had slackened considerably and here and there were patches of blue sky. A thick morning mist settled over the valley but the men could clearly see the opposite ridge. Smoke from hundreds of cookfires rose into the air. Around La Belle Alliance a thick group of horsemen clustered around a small man astride a gray horse. The French had arrived during the night. And they were being led by the Conqueror of the World.

The British and Germans on the ridge waited—and waited. The tension grew palpable. When would it begin?

A chaplain led the Hannoverians in a psalm. Anton and Harm joined in lustily.

"That's right. It is Sunday, isn't it?" whispered Anton as they bowed their heads in prayer.

"Easy to forget out here," replied Harm.

Wulf seemed a little lost. He had not been a church-going man but if that cheered the others, then so be it.

Apparently the French artillery officers had convinced Napoleon to wait until the ground dried somewhat. But now the sun had broken through and the whole valley was bathed in bright light. On the far ridge the French were marching in parade ground order, regiment after regiment, battalion after battalion, showing off the Emperor's might. The strains of *La Marseillaise* echoed across the valley. A sudden shower temporarily obscured the view and the next thing the men on the north ridge saw was that the French were in battle order.

A single gun boomed. The gun was cold and possibly the powder was damp. The shot fell far short.

"Don't reply. Don't reply," shouted a gunnery officer as he moved from battery to battery. "Save your powder for the infantry and the horses. Don't try for their batteries," he kept repeating.

A second gun crashed. The ball landed in the middle of the valley.

"What time is it?" asked Wellington.

The gunnery officer opened his watch. "Nigh on half after eleven, sir."

A third shot reached to the bottom of the ridge sending up a shower of dirt.

It was Napoleon's signal.

The entire French battery opened fire. Hell had begun.

Two battalions and some cavalry of the KGL along with the Coldstream Guards had been sent to garrison Hougoumont and it was here that the French struck first. The chateau was a strong stone building surrounded by a wall. Behind it a kitchen garden provided another wall. Beyond was an orchard and then a small woods. The orchard had no wall but was enclosed by a thick, thorny hedge. The French infantry made their first attempt from the shelter of the copse and the orchard, chopping huge holes through the hedge in order to see their targets.

But the Germans and British were ready for them also having cut loopholes for their guns in the windows and walls of the farmhouse. A steady volley of musketry met the French and drove them back.

"I like these new long rifles," gasped Lude between shots. "Much longer range than the muskets."

"But much slower to reload," acknowledged Gerd as they kept on firing.

"I wonder where Anton and Harm are. They're missing all the fun," said Lude, exhilarated as he dropped another Frenchman.

"Last I heard they were with Braunschweig at Quatre-Bras," replied Gerd. "They might even be dead."

"Lord, I hope not. More importantly, where is Erich? Shouldn't he be here with us?"

Gerd shrugged between shots. "Knowing Erich, he's either hiding under a bed or showing off how brave he is. He's just like the Prince of Orange."

Lude laughed. "Even Erich isn't that stupid."

Gerd shrugged again. "Last I saw him early this morning he was crawling out from one of the artillery tents. No doubt screwing that bawd he picked up in London."

"Oh, Millie. She's here?"

"Sure enough. Passed herself off as a lady's maid to one of the officers' wives. Now all the women, high-brow and low-born alike are back there watching the show as if it were a circus."

"While we get our asses blown off," growled Lude. "Ach, du lieber Gott! Will you look at that!"

The British howitzers had unleashed their secret weapon—a spherical shell loaded with musketballs, invented by a Major-General Shrapnel. When the ball exploded over the heads of the attackers, it rained down hundreds of deadly musketballs and bits of metal on the unlucky recipients.

"God almighty! That's horrible," exclaimed Lude.

"But it will clear them out," said Gerd callously.

The French retreated to the relative safety of the woods and there was a temporary lull in the carnage. But it would not be for long. The men in the chateau could see the French dragging eight-pounder guns up to the edge of the nearest hayfield. The next assault was imminent.

At one-thirty Napoleon ordered Drouet d'Erlon—he who had been frustrated two days earlier—to launch a three-pronged attack: the easternmost against Papelotte where Saxe-Weimar's men were holding the farmhouse; the western column advanced on La Haye Sainte where Riflemen from the KGL were stationed; and the middle directly at the center of the British line on the ridge.

Wellington rode off to the center behind von Alten and Picton's divisions—the point of greatest danger—leaving the Prince of Orange at the command post, but not in charge. However, this meant nothing to the foolish Prince who wanted to show he knew more about winning a war than these stupid English or even stupider Germans.

The German riflemen were holding La Haye Sainte very well. From both sides of the farmhouse they kept up withering volleys of fire preventing the French advance. Soon thick clouds of smoke and dust obscured the entire farm.

"We must retake La Haye Sainte," screamed the Prince.

"But La Haye Sainte has not fallen," objected his aide. "We are still holding it."

The Prince ignored this. "Send in my battalion of Hannoverians," he ordered.

"But, sir, there is cavalry coming," cautioned the aide. "They will be caught on open ground."

"I see no cavalry," snapped the Prince. "Send them in."

Everyone but the Prince, blinded by his own ego, could see the Cuirassiers, the heaviest of the French cavalry, approaching. The German colonel, whose batallion of Hannoverians had been placed under the Prince's command, had no choice but to obey.

The Hannoverians marched bravely down the slope, bayonets fixed, colors flying. They scattered the French infantry before them. But just as they reached La Haye Sainte the Curassiers arrived and rode them down slaughtering hundreds. Blood spattered the riders' faces, their swords dripped with it. Some of the Germans' left wing managed to seek refuge with their fellows in the walled kitchen garden of the farm but the majority on the right side of the line stood not a chance. Bodies piled up as the cavalrymen slashed and cut and lethal hooves crushed them. A very few survivors managed to flee back up the ridge.

"Will you look at that," cried Anton. "That fool Orange again."

"Why doesn't somebody shoot him?" asked Harm, exasperated.

"In Russia that's what we would have done," said Wulf solemnly.

But now it was their turn.

The central column of French infantry was perilously close to the ridge.

"Stand," came the order. The French advanced hesitated for just a split moment. Where they had thought was nothing but a few guns was now lined four deep with men.

"Present." "Fire." Volley after volley decimated the French but their officers, realizing that they still vastly outnumbered the English, urged them on.

But the Germans and English held on and gradually advanced. "Fire in platoons," ordered von Alten and the rolling volleys started pushing the French back. The man next to Anton fell, guts pouring out of his belly. Anton thought for a moment it was Harm. But Harm was behind him.

"You still there?" shouted Anton above the din.

"I'm still here," replied Harm as they stepped over bodies. "Keep moving."

Suddenly a shout went up to their left. "Picton's hit." "Picton's dead." And so he was, a bullet though his head. Sergeants dragged the general back as they did all the other wounded. Von Alten temporarily took over command of his division. Wellington seemed to be everywhere.

Then a bugle sounded.

It was time for the cavalry to enter the fray. Almost twenty-five hundred men and horses had been waiting for this moment. The British heavy cavalry had the finest horses in the world but they were the worst led, in that each regiment had its own noble officer, the majority of whom had never ridden to anything more exciting than a foxhunt. Aside from the inexperienced officers, most of the men were die-hard individualists who did not know how to obey orders, seeking only their own glory. One duke even went so far as to pass a stirrup cup among his staff before they rode out.

At the next bugle call the heavy cavalry crashed down the slope and engaged the Cuirassiers, already tired from their attack on the luckless Germans at La Haye Sainte. Eager horses' teeth were bared as their riders slashed and stabbed and lunged with their swords, splitting heads, lopping off arms, stabbing bellies. This was easy—better than a foxhunt. They were drunk with bloodlust and some actually drunk from rum or gin. They attacked the French infantry decapitating hundreds, crushing the wounded with their horses' hooves. They cleared the field and as they approached the French guns on the other side some of the officers cried, "Halt! Back! Enough!" but the eager riders paid no mind.

Some fool called out, "On to Paris," and others took up the cry, "On to Paris," blinded by their desire for immortality.

Suddenly the foremost horses swerved to right and to left, uncontrolled. Before them were the French guns behind which stood rank upon rank of French infantry together with troops of Lancers and Hussars on fresh horses. The wild charge turned into a chaotic melée as the Lancers rode out to meet it. Panicked horses and men, suddenly sobered by fear, wheeled in every direction not knowing where to go except that they must get back to the safety of their own ridge. But their mounts were winded and the Lancers had no trouble catching up with them, slaughtering as they went. The easiest thing in the world was to stab a fleeing man in the back with a lance or hamstring the hind legs of a horse with a sword. The only obstacles were the hundreds of bodies of men and beasts strewn across the valley and to the Lancers these were no obstacles at all.

Moments before the cavalry charge, when they were successfully pushing the French infantry down from the ridge, Anton felt as though a giant fist had punched him in the left side. He staggered back and almost fell against Harm.

"You're hit," exclaimed Harm.

"Nay, I just tripped over something. I'm fine," protested Anton.

"Man, you're hit," insisted Harm.

But Anton kept firing his musket and plodding forward. Yet somehow it became increasingly difficult to move his legs. They seemed extra heavy. Just the mud, he convinced himself. But then he sensed something wet on the side of his coat. While reloading his musket he glanced down and saw a trickle of red staining the side of his white breeches. Just the dye running from these damn red coats, he told himself. He could not be hit. He felt no pain. Then just as suddenly he collapsed into Harm's arms.

Harm had been about to fire and thanked God he had not shot his dear friend. "Wulf, over here," he called out. "Anton's hit."

Wulf came hurrying over, took Anton under the shoulders and dragged him back, way back into the forest to a barn where the surgeons had set up their grizzly hospital. Harm wished he could go with them but his first duty was to kill more Frenchmen. And so he did.

Wellington rode back to the command post where the Prince of Orange was jumping with joy at the cavalry charge but the Duke had seen the debacle at La Haye Sainte.

"Why did you send those Hannoverians in there?" he asked, furious. "Good men, all of them—wasted."

"But—but they were under my command," replied the Prince petulantly. "We had to save La Haye Sainte."

"La Haye Sainte was not in any danger. Don't you dare give another order without my approval."

"But—but—," stammered the Prince who had been sure he could win the war all by himself.

"Get out of my sight," demanded Wellington.

The Prince slunk away.

Wellington had also observed with equal dismay the cavalry disaster. "Damn fools," he commented to no one in particular. "And where are the bloody Prussians? Blücher sent me a message during the night that von Bülow would be leaving Wavre at dawn with three other battalions soon after. We can't hold here much longer without them. Where the hell are they?"

But no one could answer him.

"What time is it?" he asked an aide.

"Three thirty, sir," replied the man.

And the Prussians still had not come.

Carsten Campsheide sat astride his horse well back from the edge of the ridge, waiting. He was a part of a battalion of German light horse that, together with several English and Scots battalions, the Duke had been holding in reserve. Carsten's patience was wearing thin. He itched to ride out with the heavy cavalry and slay a few Frenchmen for himself—just for Russia, he thought. But the Germans were disciplined and knew how to obey orders. And so he waited.

Now the bugle sounded and they were moving out—at last. The Duke's original intention had been for the light cavalry to help mop up after the heavies had done their work but now he sent them out to rescue the foolish riders instead. Although he had been an officer in the Russian campaign, Carsten had never actually fought with a cavalry unit but they had been well trained back in England. He remembered an old veteran saying, "Don't slash with your sword or you'll cut your horse's ears off. Stab and lunge instead." And again, "Don't be afraid of the Lancers. If you hold steady and your horse is smart, swerve at the last minute. Once you're past the blade, it's easy enough to cut the man's arm."

Carsten hoped he would be able to hold steady. Those lethal blades were indeed frightening. He carefully chose his target, a big Lancer coming right at him. He held his breath as the tip of the lance aimed for his chest. At the last possible moment he swerved. The horse responded magnificently. The long eight-foot shaft whistled past his shoulder. He chopped at the Lancer's arm. The man screamed and dropped the huge weapon.

Then he saw two Hussars who had dismounted and were searching a wounded officer's pockets for loot. This time he did slash splitting one's skull and decapitating the other with the back slash. He looked down at the wounded man and almost gagged. The upper half of the man's face was blown away and he was obviously blinded but his arms and legs kept twitching as if to fend off the looters. "I wish I could help you, friend, but there are more Frogs to be dispatched." The man moaned. Carsten doubted he had long to live. He turned his horse away seeking more Frenchmen.

At last the bugle sounded the retreat. Carsten skewered one more Frenchman and wheeled his horse around to join the others in herding the pitiful remnant of the bewildered heavy cavalry back to safety on the ridge, all the while guarding their backs from the few Lancers and Hussars left on the field.

Meanwhile at Hougoumont the French had reorganized, realizing that only a direct assault would take the place. Some of the bravest tried scaling the wall of the kitchen garden only to be shot or bayonetted back. Finally a great number at once succeeded in getting over and bayonetted the defenders in turn. They rushed towards the great wooden doors of the courtyard but the Germans and the Coldstreamers got there first and barricaded the doors.

"Wait here," said Gerd. "I'm going down to help and see if I can find Erich. Cover my back."

Lude shook his head and kept shooting every Frenchman he could, but it was getting dangerous up here, too. The French had moved up their guns and now the balls were crashing through the roof rafters taking men who had been firing through holes in the roof slates with them.

Gerd arrived at the kitchen garden just as the men were pushing back into the courtyard. But he had seen enough. His friend Erich lay gutted like a fish at the foot of the wall. He let himself fall back with the wave of men seeking the courtyard. He wanted to weep but was too proud to show it. What was one more man amongst the thousands killed that day? And yet—yet—Gerd made a pretense of holding his rifle at the ready but he was paralyzed with shock.

Then the French began chopping at the great door with the axes they had used earlier to cut down the thorn hedge. As soon as a crack was made in the old wood a musket was pushed through and fired blindly. Finally the axe connected with one end of the bar which flew up and the doors were opened. A stream of Frenchmen rushed in.

"Kill them. Kill them all and no quarter," ordered a colonel with a thick Scots accent. "And shut that goddamned door." A group of Coldstreamers rushed to the door and putting all their weight against it finally managed to get it shut and the bar back in place. The Frenchmen inside the courtyard were trapped.

It was really too close quarters for muskets let alone rifles. So most of the fighting was with swords and bayonets. Gerd saw the Scots colonel's fancy gold lace dripping with blood as he slashed and jabbed. The big Frenchman with the axe was swinging it lethally at anyone within range. He was fighting his way towards the Scots colonel and no one could get near him. That galvanized Gerd into action. He sidled back against the wall until he was behind the axe wielder. He waited for a moment until he had a clear shot. The Frenchman raised his axe and was about to lunge at the colonel when Gerd fired. The man raised his arms in the air and Gerd feared for a moment that he had missed but he could see the bloody stain spreading on the man's coat. Then the Frenchman tripped over a frantic pig that had escaped from the sty and fell on his face at the bloodied colonel's feet.

After the last Frenchman had been dispatched the colonel came over to him. "Thank ye, friend. Ye ha saved my life."

"That was for Erich," whispered Gerd.

The colonel looked puzzled for a moment. Then Gerd pointed to the kitchen garden. "My friend."

Then the colonel understood.

When Gerd rejoined Lude on the upper floor of the house, he finally broke down and wept.

Lude put an arm around him. "But you saved Hougoumont," he said.

Wellington was beginning to despair that his weary men could hold out much longer. He now had less then half the men and horses he had started the morning with and most had been fighting steadily all day long. Where were the damned Prussians?

Then the barrage started. Hundreds of French cannon fired ceaselessly at the ridge.

"Back, back a hundred yards," ordered Wellington. The order was passed up and down the lines. "A hundred yards back and keep to a crouch. Don't let them see you."

The men crawled on hands and knees towards the woods, grateful to be away from the deadly barrage. A shell hit an ammunition wagon which exploded in a display of fireworks and then burned with thick billowing smoke.

Then Wellington saw such a sight that even he, a veteran of ten years of fighting Napoleon, had never seen before. The French cavalry, lined up on the opposite ridge, sported uniforms of every color, stripe and style from everywhere in the entire former Empire. It was a magnificent and awe-inspiring display, just as Napoleon intended. And Wellington quailed with fear that his decimated, weary men should have to oppose that. It was time to set his trap.

"Form squares," he ordered.

A square was a unique British battle formation in which the men stood in squares four deep so that they could fire in any direction. The first two rows knelt with fixed bayonets; the second two fired over their heads. No horse would attempt to jump them and few riders were willing to try. And this time, instead of being in a row, the Duke ordered the squares placed alternately in checkerboard fashion, almost inviting the French cavalry to ride between them—to their deaths. Just in case any got through this gauntlet, the light cavalry was waiting behind the squares to finish them off.

At four o'clock the first wave hit—two battalions of Milhaud's—right in the center where von Alten's men were stationed. Harm pushed his knees into the mud as he stabbed at the bellies of horses while the men behind him shot the riders. The men in the front row of the square had to be careful that the heavy horses did not fall on them and crush them. But soon they were using the bodies of both men and beasts as barricades to fortify their square.

In the rear Carsten spotted a Frenchman who had somehow gotten through. The man seemed bewildered that he had made it so far. Then Carsten saw why. From the right side of the horse half the man's leg spurted blood. The foot and stirrup had been cut off. Carsten quickly ended the Frenchman's misery and commandeered the horse. There was a reward for recovered, sound horses.

Wellington's plan seemed to be working.

Then at five o'clock the second wave of French cavalry—two battalions of Kellerman's—hit a little further to the British right. How much longer could the men hold out? The number of French cavalry seemed infinite—inexhaustible. But then a cheer rose from the far left and quickly spread down the line. The advance guard of von Bülow's battalion had been sighted marching down the Wavre road. Wellington let them cheer but he knew it would still be a couple of hours before the Prussian infantry arrived in force. Could his beleaguered men hold out that long? Wellington was not a praying man but at that moment he addressed whatever deity could help them.

At six-thirty another wave of French infantry surrounded La Haye Sainte. It was the sticking point in Napoleon's advance toward Wellington's center. The German riflemen were still valorously holding out but they were running out of ammunition and there was no way to get any more to them. Wellington himself, since he seemed to be running out of officers, led a battalion in a successful delaying action.

Now far off to the left the men could hear guns crashing and heavy musket fire. The Prussians under Generals von Zieten and Dennewitz had attacked the French right flank at Plancenoit. Napoleon hurriedly diverted two battalions to capture the village but the Prussians were counterattacking.

And Wellington's British and Germans still held. At seven o'clock Napoleon in desperation sent in his famous Imperial Guard—his favorites, *les immortels*. Only the bravest of the brave were invited into the Guards and each man had to be at least six feet tall. They wore tall bearskin hats and carried their eagles proudly in their midst. Ney himself led them on his fifth horse of the day. They were fresh and eager—and the Imperial Guard had never been defeated anywhere—ever. But neither had they faced Wellington before.

Napoleon rode with them as far as La Haye Sainte. As the Guards passed him they shouted, "Vive l'Empereur" again and again. Surely now the French victory was assured.

The Guards were marching toward the ridge in columns but Wellington had his men spread out in lines. The English cannon fired and ten Frenchmen at a time fell. But still they marched on.

"Make every shot count," ordered Wulf. "Aim for their bellies." And then he fell, a bullet in his thigh. Tough as ever, he picked up a stick and limped back to the surgery barns.

Harm was shooting as fast as he could reload his musket. His shoulder felt torn from the gun's kick; his hands and face were black with powder burns. But he was no longer weary. He was running on sheer nerve now. He, a poor German peasant, was killing the famous immortals. It was a good feeling.

Von Bülow's divisions had now come up. His men, fresh, eager and still unblooded, attacked the French right flank with vicious savagery. The French panicked and ran, an undisciplined mob. Napoleon, seeing his beloved immortals crushed, ordered the retreat, wheeled his horse around and fled towards France. Only the Imperial Guard turned and marched in disciplined order. The rest of the French army was a shambles.

"Is it over?" gasped Harm, as the 'cease fire' command ran down the line.

"I think so," croaked the man next to him.

Harm sank back in the grass still, from habit, keeping his gun ready. "We did it," he said, looking up at the blue sky. "We fought to the end for Hannover—and for the Duke."

Wellington ordered all the able-bodied men to follow the French to take prisoners where possible. But there were not many. The valley was strewn with almost 50,000 dead and wounded—mostly dead. Wellington and Blücher met at La Belle Alliance and embraced and kissed each other.

"An appropriate name for the battle, La Belle Alliance, nicht?" suggested Blücher.

But Wellington insisted it be called Waterloo, only because he had slept in that village the night before. No one mentioned Mont-St-Jean where it had actually taken place.

"I have sent Gneisenau on to Paris in pursuit," said Blücher. "I am getting too old for that."

"And my men are too exhausted," countered Wellington.

"Gneisenau can handle it. He is excellent."

"Good," replied Wellington. "Then after my men have had two or three days rest we'll join you in Paris."

Once they had recrossed the valley back to the north ridge and put the prisoners under guard, Harm went looking for Anton and Wulf. Unbeknownst to him after Hougoumont, which was now a burning pile, had fallen, the surviving Germans and Scots had joined the ranks on the ridge. Thus Lude and Gerd were the first ones he met. They hugged each other in disbelief that they were still alive.

"Where is Anton?" askd Lude at the same time that Harm asked, "Where is Erich?"

"Erich is dead," replied Gerd flatly.

"Anton took a hit in his side some time ago," replied Harm. "I'm hoping he's still alive. I was just going to look for him now. Wulf, too, at the last minute, but I don't think that's so serious."

"Then let's go and find them," said Lude.

Anton was sitting on a tarpaulin under a tree, where the less serious casualties had been remanded. Several other wounded shared the tarpaulin with him, sprawled in various positions of discomfort and pain. But Anton refusd to lie down. He sat propped against the tree. The surgeon had said he would live to fight again and he was determined not to give in, although the pain in his side where the surgeon had probed hurt like hell.

The three men went first to the surgery barn where the growing pile of severed limbs—and bodies—almost made them gag. Blood was everywhere and the stench was appalling. But their friends were not there. Only the most serious cases lay on cots and pallets in the barn. They were directed to the woods.

"There he is," exclaimed Lude.

Harm ran to Anton. "Anton, Anton, my friend, are you all right?"

"No," sighed Anton and groaned at Harm's embrace. "But it seems I shall live—and carry this goddamned ball around with me the rest of my life."

"How so?" asked Harm.

"You were right. I was hit in the side but it didn't hurt at all—then," explained Anton. "Sawbones said 'cause it was in so deep. He tried to get it out but finally gave up. Said it was too close to my heart and lung and if he dislodged it the wrong way it could kill me. Cracked a rib but that will heal. The goddamned ball is wedged behind that rib and there it stays for the rest of my life."

"My God," said Harm and Gerd together.

"I've heard of that happening," added Lude. "Seems men can live for years with a ball in their chest."

"So they tell me," replied Anton without much enthusiasm.

Just then Wulf limped up. He was still leaning on a stick. His thigh was tightly bandaged. "So you're still among the living," he said to Anton.

"Barely," replied Anton.

Lude explained Anton's plight to Wulf.

"That's not so good," said Wulf. "But you'll make it. You've got the guts. Can't disappoint that pretty girl back in Vilsen, now can you?"

Everyone laughed at that, even Anton although it made his side hurt. "I hope not," he said.

"Just look as me," said Wulf pointing at his thigh. "A couple of inches higher and all the girls in Bremen would be in mourning. But I'll be marching to Paris in a few days. Count on it."

"So shall I," declared Anton. But his friends could not believe that possible.

Just then who should stroll up to them but Oskar. His uniform was clean and spotless although a bit sweat-stained.

"Where the hell have you been?" asked Wulf.

"Got myself a cushy job as cook to one of the English officers. Glad to see you're all still alive."

"You lucky bastard!" declared Wulf. "While we were fighting our balls off."

"Only danger I was in was from the ladies," smirked Oskar.

"Oh, shut up," said Wulf, but without rancor.

13

 Anton wrote his mother from Paris. Dorothea stared at the cover for a few minutes before breaking the seal. A few weeks ago she had a strange premonition. By this time word of the terrible battle of Waterloo had reached Vilsen and she had been praying ever since that he might be still alive. But it was his own hand, not that of some impersonal officer sending bad news. She tore open the seal. The letter was dated 14 July 1815.

'Greetings from Paris, dearest Mama,' he wrote. 'Paris is a beautiful city. Today is usually a great holiday here but this year King Louis XVIII, whom we brought back with us forbade any celebration. The people are sullen because Napoleon abdicated on 22 June, but everyone else is happy. The Prussians followed him right into the city but our Wellington bade us rest a few weeks as our men were very weary and it gave some of the less seriously wounded time to heal.' (No sense worrying her with details.) Was he among the wounded, she wondered. Why doesn't he say so? 'I had hoped for some leave time but it looks as though we shall stay here for a while. All the armies are here now—Russians, Austrians, Bavarians and others—and the word is that we shall occupy France for at least another year or two. We were also reminded that we had enlisted in the KGL for six years. So it will be some time before I can come home. But this is easy duty compared to before. So don't worry. Give my fondest regards to Kati. Tell her I think of her often and shall write to her next chance I get.

Yr loving son, Anton Bergmann.'

Ach, Gott, said Dorothea to herself. Why doesn't he tell how he is and what *he's* been doing? But then Heinrich Anton never wrote very detailed letters. She supposed she was lucky to have heard at all.

Dorothea showed Kati the letter when next she came to visit. "I suppose it will be three months ere he has another chance," commented Kati tartly. But she was pleased Heinrich Anton had at least mentioned her.

Kati was deep in thought about Anton as she strolled up the shaded lane towards the Klostermühle. She was enjoying an unexpected holiday at home since the Graf and Gräfin had decided to take the cure at one of the Bads in the mountains and the Countess had declared that there would be more than enough servants to wait on them hand and foot. The Graf had been grouchier and touchier than usual lately and Kati hoped that the holiday would restore him.

Kati had just made a duty call on her grandmother Becke Matthies and it had not been pleasant. The poor, pitiful old woman was vaguer than ever. She had not recognized her granddaughter at all. Kati was grateful her Onkel Heinzi and her nasty cousin Johann Heinrich had not been there. It was bad enough listening to Gerhardina's complaints. She had left as soon as she politely could. Now her good temper was being restored by the peace and beauty of the woods she loved.

Suddenly she heard footsteps crashing behind her as though someone were running. Now who could that be? She paused a moment and looked back. The cousin she had hoped to avoid slowed down as he caught sight of her.

"Ach, cousin Kati," he gasped, slightly out of breath, "I'm sorry I missed you at the mill. I wanted to walk back with you."

"You did?" Now that was a turnabout. "Cousin Heinrich," she said (they always called him Heinrich. Gerhardina did not approve of nicknames), "that is very kind of you but I assure you I know my way. In fact, I prefer to walk alone."

"But I've missed you. I wanted to see you." He put a hand on her arm.

She shook it off. "You did?" she asked again. "I can't imagine why."

"Well—you've been away so long and you've become a very beautiful woman."

"Indeed?" Now what in the world is this all about, she wondered.

"I know you miss Heinrich Anton and I thought—I thought—"

"You thought what?" she asked sharply. This was becoming tiresome.

"Well, cousin, I am a man now and I thought . . . "

"A man!" she gasped. This thirteen- or fourteen-year-old child, a man? She almost laughed in his face. But now she knew. "I think not, cousin Heinrich," she said as calmly as she could. "'Twill be many a year ere you can call yourself a man."

"I am. I am," he insisted. "Can't you see?" He rubbed his crotch which was too obviously swollen.

Kati turned away in disgust. "Go home and leave me be."

"But I want you, Kati." He grabbed her and tried to kiss her.

She easily pushed him away. "I said leave me alone," she spat.

He lunged at her again and squeezed her breast. "You know you want it," he leered. "Heinrich Anton has been away a long time. Give me what you've given him."

She fought and kicked. He was holding her too close for her to get her knee up to his crotch. But at last she extricated herself enough to give his face a resounding slap. It gave him enough pause so that she was free for the moment. "Don't you ever mention Anton's name in the same breath as your filthy thoughts," she cried as she ran up the lane.

She knew that she had infuriated him and that he would soon catch up to her. He was a big lad. Quickly Kati turned into the woods. She had once known a dozen secret paths through the forest but that was long ago. She prayed they were not too overgrown and that Heinrich was not familiar with them. She zigged and zagged through the trees. She could hear him crashing behind her. She picked up a stout branch to use as a weapon if need be. She had no qualms about hitting him over the head with it.

Suddenly all was quiet. Kati paused a moment in her flight and listened. Could he have given up? She hoped so but she doubted it. She knew her cousin too well. He would be too enraged by now to act with any sense. She stealthily took another turn onto a path that led to the last one going directly to the Klostermühle. Not far now. She could hear the mill-brook babbling off to her left. She took the last turn and ran right into Heinrich. He grabbed her so fast she did not have a chance.

"Now I've got you, you haughty bitch," he snarled. "I'll show you that I am a man." He held her so tightly she could not move. But she could scream. She screamed and screamed. He backed her up against a tree. She could feel his hardness poking into her belly. His hand snaked up under her skirts probing for her womanhood. "Shut up, slut. You want to wake the dead?"

"I intend to, pig. Onkel Chris! Somebody! Help me," she cried before he had to release her arm in order to clamp a hand over her mouth. This gave her a little purchase and she tried to twist away from his filthy fingers. But he threw her to the ground and fell on top of her. She could not move, could scarcely breathe. With one hand he hiked up her skirt again while the other tore at the buttons of his breeches. She screamed again at the sight of his swollen member. She tried to cross her legs but he planted a thick knee between them and gradually forced them apart. He grasped her breast brutally and tried to kiss her to still her screams. She bit him and drew blood but he did not even notice. She could feel his hard prick approaching her vital place. He did not seem to know quite where to put it. She would have laughed had she not been so terrified. But it would not be long before he found the opening. She clawed at his face and drew more blood. That only made him hesitate a moment because he could not catch her hands and still have one hand free to guide his prick into where he knew it was supposed to go. In fact, the bloody scratches only seemed to excite him more. She could feel his fingers and his prick pushing against her now. Any second he would destroy her maidenhead. Oh God, have mercy! Help me, she prayed. Suddenly he quivered violently and groaned. She could feel the hot slime of his seed spill all over her thighs and the ground. He fell on her gasping and she was pinned beneath him.

But she could still scream.

Suddenly someone took Heinrich by the scruff of his neck and hauled him to his knees. Chris was holding a musket to his chest. Heinrich turned white.

"You dastardly knave," shouted Chris. "What have you done to her?" He turned to Kati. "Are you hurt bad, lass? I'll kill him if you want me to. It would be within my rights." Heinrich quailed.

"No, no, Onkel," she whispered. "I am only a little hurt but I'm still a virgin," she declared. "I prayed to God and He heard me. This—this child let loose his—his disgusting filth ere he got to me."

Heinrich stammered, "But—but—how was I to know she was a virgin? I thought Heinrich Anton . . . "

Chris slapped him hard across the jaw. "Don't you defame my son with your filthy mouth. And don't you come near this lass again or I'll beat you to within an inch of your life, which is no more than scum like you deserve. Now get out of here before I kill you." He gave Heinrich a kick. "And see that you tell your Pa the truth for I shall sure see that he knows it."

Heinrich crawled on hands and knees until he was out of Chris' reach. Then he stood up and ran.

And thus was born a lifelong emnity.

Chris gently helped Kati up. "Come lass, your Tante Dorchen will clean you up and cosset you. 'Tis a woman's touch you need right now."

A few days later Kati said to Dorothea, "You see now why I can't stay here until Heinrich Anton comes home and we are safely wed. Besides I wouldn't be that much help to you. I'd only be in the way and another mouth to feed when times are so bad."

"That's not true," objected Dorothea, "but I can understand how you feel. The same thing almost happened to me once, long years ago—and from the same family."

Kati was shocked but not surprised at this revelation. When you were sixteen and Mama was eight, she wondered. But Dorothea would say no more.

"It's just that I am no longer content in Hannover," said Kati. "The Countess is still sweet but she is so edgy I never know what to expect from her. And it is all because the Graf is under such tension from this constitution thing. I don't even understand what it is."

"Philipp explained it to us," replied Dorothea. "A constitution is a legal document binding the king to share his power with a body of representatives elected by the people. Württemberg and some of the other southern states already have one based on the French *Charte*. Napoleon's ideas were not all bad, you know."

"I see," replied Kati. "That explains why the Graf is so vehemently against such a thing. He rules as if he were king, not wanting to share power with anyone, let alone representatives of the people. The Duke of Cambridge is nothing but a figurehead. The Graf von Münster's word is law."

"Indeed," agreed Dorothea, "but the times are changing. We have lived too long under the liberal French influence and people liked it—at least that part of it. He will have to give in eventually but it won't be easy for him. Philipp says that of all the states of Germany Hannover is the most reactionary. And all because of him. Even Prussia is leaning toward a constitution but it won't be easy there either because her kings have always had absolute power and have their huge military behind them. Nonetheless, Philipp tells us that there is a group of professors at Göttingen working on just such a document and soon it will be the law of the land."

"That's interesting," said Kati although she was not that interested at all. "But what do you suggest I should do? I'd like to seek another position but what is open to a woman besides dressing a lady's hair or laying out her clothes or being nursemaid to her brats?"

Dorothea shrugged. "I don't know. I just wish Heinrich Anton would

405

come home. That would settle everything. But meanwhile I'll speak to Philipp. He may have some ideas."

And so Kati returned to the Countess in Hannover but without much enthusiasm.

It was a dark, drear December day, threatening snow, as Kati entered the main entrance of the Leine Schloss. She no longer used the servants' entrance except when it suited her. She had been there so long the guards knew and respected her. Besides, as she expected, not a soul was in the great hall of the old castle. And it was very dark. The servants had not yet lit the wall sconces. It was the season of Advent and social activities had been curtailed. Thus she was more bored than ever. Instead of the three or four changes of dress the Countess required during the social season, Kati had only to dress her in the morning and help her to bed at night. She would have gone mad had it not been for her books. Kati loved to read. Dorothea had given her several of her own precious volumes and Kati had already read them innumerable times. So now she had taken to spending a part of her minuscule wages on books. She knew she should be saving her money towards her wedding and dowry but it seemed as though it would be many years yet before Anton came home and that dream took place. And so she was carrying two newly purchased books as she made her way across the darkened hall.

Just then a man came hurrying out of the Graf's office. He was evidently blinded by the dim light in the hall and she noticed he was wearing spectacles which no doubt contributed to his inability to see. He crashed right into her. Her books flew to the floor.

"Oh, Mistress—Fräulein, I beg your humble pardon," he apologized. "I did not see you. The light is rather poor in here, is it not? Here let me." He bent to pick up her books just as she was about to. He pushed his spectacles back onto his nose and looked at the books before he returned them to her. "I see you are a reader, and good taste, too. Master Goethe's sublime poetry and—oh, don't let the Graf discover you reading Master Schiller's works."

"Thank you, kind sir. No harm done," Kati replied. "And as to Master Schiller—I know the Graf has prohibited his plays but I don't believe he has forbidden the reading of them. I find them quite interesting and provocative. Makes one think."

"I quite agree. I only wish—er—certain people would pay attention to what he has to say." He pushed his spectacles another notch up his nose and peered at her. "A reader and intelligent, too," he commented. "An unusual attribute in a female."

"Not so unusual, sir," she bridled. "I find that many women are as intelligent as men, if not more so, if we should only be allowed to show it."

"My, my, that *is* a provocative statement. Yet I fear I must have to agree." He peered at her more closely. "Don't I know you from somewhere? Have we not met before?"

Ah, the usual ploy, she thought. And yet he did not seem *that* type. "I fear not," she replied. "I only work here in Hannover. I am from Vilsen, a little village you have probably never heard of."

"Vilsen," he said musingly. "I have never been there but some years ago I visited two lovely ladies at an ancient mill at nearby Heiligenberg."

"Master Grimm," she exclaimed.

"The very same," he admitted.

"I was but a child at my mother's knee and she and Tante Dorchen were telling you the old stories."

"I remember it well. Your mother was the dark-haired one who told me the tale of The Twelve Dancing Princesses. It was an unusual one that we hadn't heard before. I got the impression that she would like to have been one of them."

"And she still does, I fear me," said Kati sadly.

"And what do you here in Hannover?"

"I am no but a lady's maid to the Gräfin von Münster and to tell you the truth, I am bored to death."

"A person of your intelligence would be."

"I wish I could find another position—something more stimulating. But as you well know there is little such opportunity for a female, however intelligent."

Wilhelm Grimm thought for a moment. "Hmm," he murmured. "You are quite right in that. But still there is a chance I might be able to help you. Only a slight possibility, mind you, so don't get your hopes up. I must speak to my brother Jacob first. I assume you can write a fair hand?"

"Very fair, Master Grimm," she admitted.

"What is your name?"

"Catharine Sophie Hohnholz," she replied. "I am called Kati."

"Would you be willing to move to Göttingen?"

"Quite willing," she replied. "I should think it would be very interesting—and perhaps, stimulating as well."

"That it can be. That it can be," he said. "Well, Kati Hohnholz, I must hurry on now, but you will hear from us. It is too close to the Christmas season to—er—arrange anything now. But soon after the New Year I promise you will hear from us. Whether it be ja or nay, we'll not leave you wondering. Auf Wiedersehen."

Kati returned to her room in a cloud of excitement. She did not even have any taste for reading her new books. How wonderful it would be to work for the Brothers Grimm helping them collect their beautiful stories. And yet she knew she must temper her hopes and anticipation. It could all amount to nothing and she would still be here bored to death waiting on the Countess.

Nevertheless she threw herself with a gladdened heart into the preparations for the Christmas festivities. And when it came time to send her Christmas greetings home she thought it would not be amiss to ask Philipp Koch a little about Göttingen without actually telling him why she wanted to know.

'I can't imagine what sort of position you could find in Göttingen unless it be a governess to someone's children,' he wrote back, 'but in a university town there is no lack of those. Very few there have need of a lady's maid. Professors do not earn much money. And as for the students, beware that that they would want a woman for one purpose only.

'Yet I am assuming too much, dear Kati. You asked about the town not the possibility of employment. It is a lovely town dominated, of course, by the University. Therefore, the people, even the average Bürger, seem to be better educated than in most other towns. The students in general are far less rambunctious and obstreperous than at many other German universities, notably Heidelberg. The faculty specialize in history and politics but a growing number of new professors are adding disciplines in the various sciences and it is already far ahead of the other universities in scientific discoveries. The students, of course, have a Tugendbund, now called Burschenschaft, I believe, but they are far less the wild agitators as at Jena. Their goal is admirable—seeking the unification of Germany—but their methods are questionable, so you would be wise to distance yourself from their nonsense.

'All in all, I think you would enjoy a visit to Göttingen but be sure an older, honorable and steadfast woman accompanies you. It may also interest you to know that the Brothers Grimm, one of whom you met years ago, are now professors there. They are helping to frame a constitution for Hannover under the leadership of Professor Dahlmann. I count many of

408

my friends there. So if I can be of any further help, please don't hesitate to ask. Sincere greetings for the holiday season.

Yr friend, Philipp Koch'

Kati smiled at parts of the letter. Of course she remembered the Brothers Grimm. Had she not recently spoken to Master Wilhelm? But she had not mentioned that to Philipp. And if she heard good news from the professor it would not be for a visit to Göttingen but a move. And as for a steadfast chaperone, she had no intentions of any such person accompanying her. She felt sure that if the Grimms hired her they would see that she had suitable accommodations. Yet she hugged Philipp's letter to her and prayed that she was not dreaming impossible dreams.

By the end of January Kati was beginning to lose hope although she watched for the post every day. Then one day the Countess said, "There is a letter for you, Kati. It was mixed up with mine. I see it is from Göttingen not Vilsen so I thought it was for the Graf until I saw your name on it. Whom do you know in Göttingen?"

"Why—er—," Kati thought quickly, "just a childhood friend who writes occasionally."

"And does your mother know of this—this attachment?"

"It is hardly an attachment, my lady, and yes, she knows him quite well." She doubted Eleonore would even remember Master Grimm.

"I was merely concerned that you might be tempted to disavow your betrothed," said the Countess.

"I am not yet betrothed, my lady," objected Kati, "although I hope that will happen just as soon as Heinrich Anton returns from—from wherever he is. Until then I am free to choose my friends where I may." Afraid she might have been too outspoken, she quickly added, "Besides this is a very honorable clerk who is studying for the ministry. He has no designs on me."

"I thought Göttingen had done away with theology in its curriculum."

"Not in its curriclum, no. Just that the theologians no longer rule the University." She had heard this and hoped it was true.

"Well, a young lass such as you cannot be too careful. Remember what happened in Vienna last year."

And what happened this past summer on my very home ground, she thought. But the Countess did not know about that. "I have learned a lot since then, Madame," she said.

"Very well. You may have your letter," said the Countess imperiously.

Kati accepted the letter nonchalantly and put it in her pocket. She continued to attend to her duties but with such growing excitement she could hardly concentrate. At last when the Countess went to dinner was she able to rush to the privacy of her own room. Never mind her own dinner. She had to read that letter. She was shaking so she had to sit down as she tore open the seal.

'My dear Fräulein Hohnholz,

'I have spoken to my brother and he has agreed to offer you a position as clerk in our establishment at the University of Göttingen if you are still interested. The remuneration we can offer is not much but is comparable to that of other beginning clerks. I have taken the liberty of writing to our friend in Vilsen, Philipp Koch, who has attested to your excellence of character. Just as soon as you have received the requisite permission from your parents, we should like you to travel to Göttingen forthwith, but no later than the end of February when the new term begins. Be assured that we shall arrange suitable and decorous accommodations for you with a gentlewoman acquaintance of ours. Please advise the day and time of your arrival so that someone can meet your coach.

Yr. Obedient servant, Wilhelm Grimm'

Kati was overwhelmed with joy. She quickly scrawled a note of acceptance until she realized that they were hiring her for her handwriting. She carefully rewrote it in her best penmanship, assuring Master Grimm that her mother (of The Twelve Dancing Princesses) would surely grant permission, her father having died some years ago. She promised she would be in Göttingen before the end of February, time and date to be advised as soon as she herself knew. She painstakingly signed, sanded and sealed the missive and ran with it all the way to the Hannover post office rather than include it in the castle post where it could lie for days. She hoped to catch the returning mail coach to Göttingen.

When she returned she sat down to write a long letter to Tante Dorchen explaining everything. Kati knew if she wrote to her mother first Eleonore would have a burst of emotion at her leaving the castle (and the prestige therof) and going even farther away to live among strangers. It was not as though Eleonore missed her. Hannover might as well be the moon for all she heard from her mother. But Tante Dorchen would understand

and she could handle Eleonore.

The following week Dorothea's reply arrived saying how proud she was of her and wishing her all happiness and success in her new employment. She also assured Kati that her mother's permission was on its way to Göttingen by this same post. What she did not tell Kati was how long it took her to calm Eleonore's tirade and that she had stood right over her until she had written the letter and then had taken it to the post office herself. She also did not mention that she had asked Philipp's help in convincing Eleonore but that at first he had been extremely reluctant to do so. Philipp was a confirmed batchelor and knew very little about women. He could not imagine how a female, however intelligent, could possibly be capable of holding such a position. Dorothea had finally convinced her brother that Kati was quite capable of doing so and that she had every right to improve her situation.

But Kati did not know all this. She only knew that soon she would be going to Göttingen—to a new job, to a new world. She was not so innocent as to believe it would not be difficult to compete with male clerks but she was confident she could. Now she had only to tackle the Countess.

Kati chose a day when the Countess was in a rare good mood. It was Fastnacht—Carnival—the day before the gloom of Lent closed in. While not as uproarious an event as in the Catholic countries, it was still celebrated with foolery among the peasants and townfolk and with balls among the elite which ended the winter social season. The Countess was looking forward to the ball.

"My lady, I must tell you something," said Kati meekly.

"My dear girl, you look so serious," replied the Countess. "Can it not wait? Tomorrow would seem a better day for confessions."

"'Tis no confession, Madame, but simply notice that I shall be leaving your service in two weeks."

The Countess was thunderstruck—and immediately jealous. "What!" she exclaimed. "After all these years? That is most ungrateful of you." Then after a moment's thought she demanded, "What house is it? I shall better their offer."

"'Tis not another noble house, my lady. Have no fear I would leave you for that," Kati tried to explain. "I have accepted a position with the Brothers Grimm at the University of Göttingen."

The Countess was aghast. Just the word 'university' equated in her mind with 'den of iniquity'. "How can those two old batchelors have need of a lady's maid?" she begged to know.

411

Kati smiled at this. The Grimms were far younger than the Countess. "I shall not be a maid," she said, "but rather a clerk for their endeavor."

"What endeavor?" snapped the Countess. "That abominable constitution thing?"

"Nay, nay, my lady. They have also published a lovely volume of the ancient tales."

"I have heard of that. But how can a woman—? Ach, you young girls have been thoroughly corrupted by that hussy, Madame de Staël."

Kati shook her head. "Although I greatly admire her writings, I have not been corrupted by Madame de Staël or anyone else. It is by my own choice that I seek intellectually stimulating work."

"Intellect—," execrated the Countess, "but how can you? Women are not supposed to have—er—intellect."

"But unfortunately for men, my lady, some do, if we were only permitted to use it." Kati could not resist the jibe.

The Countess sighed with resignation. This was beyond her comprehension. "Whatever am I to do without you, Kati?" she grieved.

"I am sure you can easily find someone to take my place. Griselda would suit. She has long longed for it. And I had hoped, Madame, that you would be willing to give me a character reference but if you choose not to, I am leaving anyway."

The Countess put her head in her hands and sighed. "Go. Leave me. Send Griselda to help me tonight."

"Yes, my lady." Kati started to leave when the Countess called her back.

"No, wait, Kati. You had better be here to start training her. And—and, Kati, you shall have your character."

"Thank you, my lady." She curtseyed and left, thankful that that hurdle had been crossed.

Kati stepped down from the post chaise in Göttingen and wondered who would be meeting her. She knew she looked attractive in her new travelling outfit. At the last moment the Countess had been more than generous. The driver handed down her portmanteau and turned to help the other passengers. He, too, did not approve of women travelling alone. She pulled her cloak more tightly around her as the raw, cutting February wind blew down from the nearby Harz Mountains and looked around. She saw no one who looked as though they were seeking her. Well, she would wait. The little square was covered with snow and several paths had been shovelled across it. The coach had been somewhat late but not terribly so. The drivers and horses were quite familiar with this weather.

Then gratefully she spied Wilhelm Grimm himself hurrying towards her. He was coughing and coughing in the bitter air. He paused in front of her trying desperately to catch his breath.

"My dear Fräulein Hohnholz," he choked out with great effort. "I am so sorry to keep you waiting. I was here earlier but they said the chaise would be hours late with the snow. Fortunately, Marie heard the posthorn."

"I have not waited but a few minutes," she replied, wondering who Marie was. "And don't try to talk right now. I fear me this cold air will hurt your lungs." She herself felt on the verge of coughing along with him but she fought it back.

Wilhelm nodded and indicated she should follow him. After a few short blocks of trudging through the snow he stopped in front of a tall, stately house and rang the bell. A pretty, dark-haired woman in her mid-thirties opened the door and ushered them in.

"Ach, Wilhelm, that was quick," she said. "Now don't distress yourself." Wilhelm was coughing again. "And this must be our new clerk, Fräulein—ach, I forget."

"Hohnholz," supplied Kati. "But I am called Kati."

"And I, Marie."

Wilhelm finally caught his breath and made the formal introduction. "Catharine Hohnholz, be pleased to meet Marie Hassenpflug. Marie is our sister Lotte's best friend. You will be staying with her while you are here." He turned to Marie. "Is Jacob here? He will want to meet her as well."

"Mais oui, grumbling as ever. But that can wait," replied Marie as she put a welcoming arm around Kati. "Can't you see the poor child is blue from the cold? Come, my dear, a room is all prepared for you. After a little rest we shall have Kaffee and Kuchen and then you can meet that old curmudgeon and tell us all about yourself." Marie picked up Kati's portmanteau and whisked her up the stairs leaving Wilhelm standing there.

Kati immediately liked Marie and her easy-going yet taking-command personality. With her dark pert looks Kati had suspected she might be French and the woman's use of the phrase 'mais oui' convinced her. "You are French," she asked in that language.

"Ah, so," replied Marie, "an impoverished exile from the Revolution. And you? You speak it very well and you have the look, but I could not be sure."

413

Kati did not think the house looked very impoverished but she said, "Who could not learn it during these past years? But yes, I learned it long before that from my mother. We have a few drops of French blood in us and she is very proud of it but I fear it is quite dilute. It goes way back to the time of Eleonore d'Olbreuse."

"Ah, so, but it is enough, is it not, to still have the fire?' said Marie smiling. "I think we shall get along very well, ma Kati."

At coffee Kati finally met the redoubtable Jacob. The elder of the brothers by one year, he was very reserved and somewhat uncomfortable in social situations. He lived for and in his research and let Wilhelm make most ot the public contacts. Both men were handsome but Jacob could also be called distinguished whereas Wilhelm had a twinkle in his eye that made him look as though he were about to tell one of their wonderful stories.

The following morning Wilhelm called for her very early. In their bureau at the University she met the two male clerks with whom she would be working—Hermann and Gottlieb. Warned beforehand of her arrival, they greeted her courteously but very coldly. It was no more than Kati expected. She vowed to win them over in time. In his own domain surrounded by brilliant colleagues Jacob was more relaxed and forthcoming. Never once did he let her know of the violent arguments he had had with his brother about hiring her. He introduced her to several professors whose names she would have to sort out later.

"I noticed the sign on your door said Department of Philology," commented Kati. "I confess I don't know what that means."

"Philology is the study of languages—their origins, history and relationship to one another," explained Jacob.

"Ja," added Wilhelm, "Jacob has proven, for example, that the Romance and the Germanic languages are definitely related and that the changes from one to the other are governed by specific laws—just as in physics."

Kati looked blank but she said, "I see." Lord, what a different world I've entered.

"We have also begun work on a dictionary of the German language," said Wilhelm, "which will probably take us the rest of our lives to complete."

"That sounds interesting," she murmured.

"But right now the most important task on our agenda is the writing of a constitution for Hannover," pronounced Jacob. "That is what your work will consist of—making copies of each new draft. It may seem tedious to you after a while but it is extremely important that we get the wording just right so that the ministers will accept it."

Kati's face fell. "I see," she said. "I shall do my best." But that did not sound interesting at all. She had thought she would be working on their stories but no mention had been made of them at all. Well, she was here now. There was no going back. She would copy whatever they gave her.

She was shown to a tall slanted desk and was given an equally tall backless stool. She could hardly get her bottom up on it. Across the top of the desk from left to right were a candle, to be used only on the darkest days, a sand box and an inkwell. In a pocket at the side was supply of quills and the requisite knife for sharpening them. Just like the old medieval monks, she thought. Whatever happened to the printing press? But she dared not voice that question. It would have cost her her job. Later she realized that for the number of drafts required of this thing, the cost of printing so many revisions would have been prohibitive.

By the end of each of the first few days Kati was in agony, not only from writer's cramp but her back ached from the uncomfortable, backless stool.

"You'll get used to it," said Marie, massaging her shoulders. "That's what comes of wanting to do a man's job, I'm afraid."

Kati did not agree. "It's a job that women can do far better than men. It's just the furniture that is geared to men."

Marie shrugged. But Kati soon learned that she could trust Marie not to reveal her complaints to the Grimms. Marie also saw to it that she ate well. Although food was still scarce, especially in the towns, after two cold, wet summers and poor harvests from farms still desperately trying to recover from the French depredations. Meat and even fish was a rare treat. Yet Marie always managed to dress up bland turnips or beans with interesting French sauces that made them more than palatable.

Marie occasionally took her to some of the more reputable guest houses or Weinstube and there they listened to the students—the Burschenschaft—discussing the pros and cons of a united Germany. Some were in favor of Austria doing the job but they did not trust Metternich nor did they want a revival of the old Empire. Others looked to Prussia but most feared her militarism. The majority thought of union as a loose confederation of independent states but how this was to be accom-

415

plished among so many disparate entities seemed beyond their comprehension.

"Two women alone?" asked Kati when Marie had first suggested these excursions.

"Of course," Marie assured her. "The students are most liberal even if their elders are not. And believe me, they are more interested in your brains than your body."

What a refreshing change that was. And soon Kati lost her shyness and joined in the discussions. This led her to become more interested in the content of the documents she was copying. The constitution being promulgated by the professors of Göttingen provided for a bicameral parliament—something unheard of in the absolute monarchies of the last century. The upper chamber would consist of the landed nobility—the same oligarchy that had ruled Hannover ever since their kings went to England—but somewhat expanded to include some of the lesser nobility. The lower chamber was to be elected by the people of the towns—or at least some of them—the Bürgers, the wealthy merchants, bankers and industrialists. No mention was made of the vast number of people in agrarian Hannover—the peasants. This bothered Kati.

After that first day Kati saw very little of the Grimms, both busy with their students and their research and, occasionally, this blasted constitution. Then one day an opportunity presented itself to ask Wilhelm about her concern. She was still a little in awe of Jacob.

"Master Wilhelm," she asked, "why is it in this constitution that you propose is there no representation of the peasants provided? There is not even a mention of them. Yet they are the largest segment of our population."

"Ach!" Whilhelm threw up his hands. "Don't even speak of that around here." At Kati's puzzled look he continued. "We did not forget them. In the original draft they as well as the Bürgers were to be represented in the lower chamber. When your former employer, the Graf von Münster, saw that he stopped reading it then and there and threw the whole thing into the fire. I was so distraught I never saw you that day." Automatically he pushed his spectacles up on his nose. "It was like a ray of sunshine meeting you. I thought, if a simple maid is reading Goethe and Schiller, then there is still hope for Hannover. I simply had to rescue you from that. Although I'll admit now that Jacob did not approve."

"I thought not," said Kati.

"Oh, but he does now. He certainly does. He is very pleased with your work."

416

"Thank you, Master Wilhelm, and also for explaining about the peasants. I see now why every word of the constitution must be meticulously examined."

"Indeed," he agreed. "The peasants' day will come eventually but now it is more important to get the ministers to agree to *some* form of constitution. And unfortunately we must always remember who pays our salaries."

She smiled at that. "I do see what you are saying."

And so she copied yet another revision. For each new draft she had to make seven copies, one for each of the professors working on it. Then they would study it individually and in conference and she would be presented with still a further revision.

Besides her excursions with Marie the one bright spot in Kati's life was that she was now receiving numerous letters from Anton. Dorothea had written him of her new position and Kati wondered if he were just a little bit jealous or perhaps now had more leisure time in the army occupying France. Whatever the reason, she thought, good! Let him be a little jealous. It's about time he thought of me more often.

Kati worked for the Brothers Grimm for three years. Later she was helping with the dictionary and that she found much more interesting. At long last on 7 December 1819 the ministers in Hannover approved the final draft of the constitution and signed it into law. The Grimms and their colleagues were jubilant but Kati was not there to share their joy.

She had returned to Vilsen. Heinrich Anton was coming home at last. With luck he would be there by Christmas.

Book VI

'Heimat, liebe Heimat'
(Homeland, Beloved Homeland)

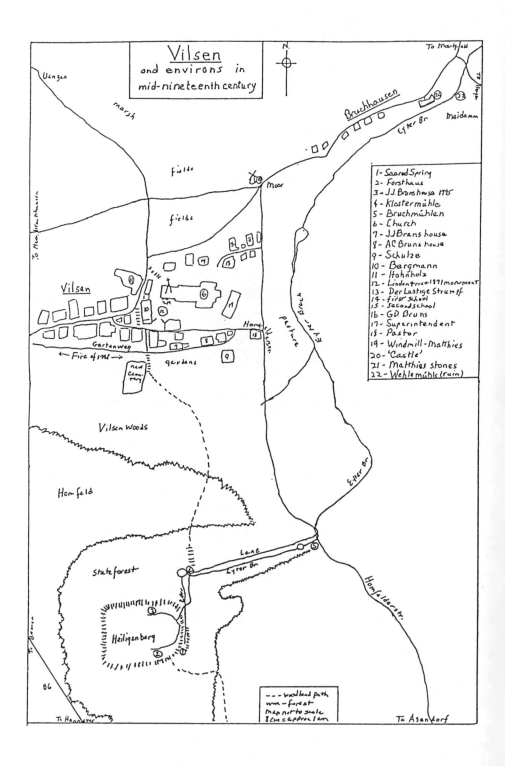

Vilsen
and environs in
mid-nineteenth century

N.

To Marklah

Uenzen

marsh

Bruchhausen

Eyter Br

Maidamm

fields

Moor

fields

To Nie derborehausen

Vilsen

1 — Sacred Spring
2 — Forsthaus
3 — J.J. Bruns house 1785
4 — Klostermühle
5 — Bruchmühlen
6 — Church
7 — JJ Bruns house
8 — AC Bruns house
9 — Schulze
10 — Bergmann
11 — Hohnholz
12 — Lindentree + 1871 monument
13 — Der Lustige Strumpf
14 — first school
15 — Second school
16 — GD Bruns
17 — Superintendent
18 — Pastor
19 — Windmill Matthies
20 — 'Castle'
21 — Matthies stones
22 — Wehlemühle (ruin)

Homfelderstr

pasture Bruch

Eyter Br

Gartenweg
← Fire of 1761 →
gardens

new Cemetery

Vilsen Woods

Homfeld

State forest

Eyter Br

Lane
Eyter Br

Homfelderstr

To Bremen

Heiligenberg

B6

To Hannover

--- woodland path
ᴡᴡ — forest
map not to scale
8 cm = approx 1 km

To Asendorf

14

1821

Eleonore was finally doing what she should have done years ago—paying attention to her eldest daughter, taking pride in her offspring. And now she was about to lose her. Eleonore's own marriage to Fritzi had gone much the same way as had her first to his half-brother. Although they still lived together and occasionally slept together, the marriage had disintegrated into a hollow, empty sham. The business had all but disappeared during the hardship of the French Time. And although she was working hard to revive it as the linen trade slowly picked up, they were poor as churchmice. Well, not quite. There was still enough for an elaborate wedding for her pride and joy—the only one of her many children that she actually loved and took pride in. Kati had wanted a simple, quiet wedding but Eleonore had insisted on trading on the former prestige of the Hohnholz name to make it the social event of the season. Kati had acquiesced knowing that once her mother had her mind set on something it was easier not to argue.

So now she stood on the kitchen table as erect as possible while Eleonore pinned up the hem of her wedding gown. The pins in the side seams and tucks stabbed her every time she turned the quarter turn that Eleonore indicated. She tried to hold her breath to maintain her posture when the pins scratched. In a few weeks she would be wed to Anton Bergmann and get on with her life—at last.

Kati let her mind drift back to the year and a half ago when Anton had come home. Although they had grown up together from babyhood they were like total strangers. The long years apart had taken their toll. Both had matured but in opposite directions. Anton was bitter, disillusioned, reserved and withdrawn. Kati was vivacious, sophisticated, intellectually alert and eager for life. It took them several months to get reacquainted.

Reluctantly at first, Anton told her about the battles at Waterloo,

421

carefully editing out the more gruesome aspects and never, *never* mentioning his wound or the bullet he still carried near his heart.

Kati in turn related the exciting gaity of Vienna and especially the glorious music of Master Beethoven and how she had met the great composer, deliberately omitting the unpleasant incident that had preceded it.

Anton told her about England—the lovely countryside, the terrible weather and the kind people, once you broke through their inate reticence and xenophobia—and about beautiful, elegant Paris and the many chateaux that literally littered the countryside. "It's too bad the French are so confused politically," he remarked.

And Kati told him about life at the court in Hannover, the Brothers Grimm and the lofty, ethereal atmosphere at Göttingen. She even explained, very knowledgeably, the new constitution.

But something was still amiss. She could sense it but she could not pinpoint it. What was wrong? Why has he holding back the final commitment to marriage. Finally, exasperated, she decided to tackle the question head-on.

"Anton," she said, "we have known each other since childhood, have always assumed that we should one day wed. Our families assumed the same. I have waited, holding myself inviolate, all these years for you and now it seems you no longer want me."

"Of course, I want you and I love you, dearest Kati," he objected, "but you refused to wed ere I went to join the Legion."

"What! And sit here all those years like a widow living a half-life? Naturally, I refused. We were too young then anyway and my excuse, if you recall, was to wait until Napoleon was vanquished. Well, he is off in St. Helena now and no threat to anyone. Everyone is free. Hannover is free. I have no more excuses. What is yours?" Unwittingly her voice became harsher as she spoke.

Anton looked as though he would burst into tears. "Kati, Kati, I did not wish to tell you but—but I am not sure—not sure that I can be a proper husband to you."

Kati was taken aback. "You mean—," she stammered, "you mean that something has happened to you so that you cannot perform as a man—so that your body cannot pleasure mine in the most precious, intimate act of marriage?"

"Kati," exclaimed Anton, "how do you know of such things?"

"Anton," she replied calmly, "I am not so innocent as to not know what goes on between a man and a woman. I grew up in the country, remember? I have witnessed horses and dogs mating. And, sadly, my mother's love affairs were notorious. What's more," her voice caught but she plunged on, "what's more I was almost raped on two occasions—one right here. But I am still an untried virgin—saving my love for you."

"What? Who?" he cried. "I'll kill him."

"Never mind that now," she asserted. "Your papa took care of it. It is long past. Let it be. But now you know my darkest secrets. What is yours? What are you not telling me?"

Anton's anger quickly cooled. He looked abashed. "Kati, forgive me. There is something I haven't told you. I haven't even told my parents. I *was* wounded."

"There?" she asked.

He smiled ruefully. "No, not there. The crown jewels are still safe and intact. Thank God for that. But I still carry a bullet in my side so close to my heart that I have been fearful of—of overexerting myself in that way. Although they tell me that men have lived for years with bullets in their bodies, I somehow fear that I shan't. I shouldn't want to burden you with that."

"Then we shall be most careful not to overexert you. Are not a few years of happiness better than none at all?"

He smiled again. "Kati, you beloved innocent, you probably don't realize that the act of making love puts a tremendous amount of strain on a man's body while the woman just lies there. Suppose the effort made the bullet slip into my heart?"

"Then you shall have to teach me how to make the effort while you just lie there. That is, if I don't get coughing my head off and spoil everything. We make a good pair, don't we?"

He laughed at that—really laughed for the first time since he had come home. "Ach, Kati, ever the optimist. I used to be optimistic, too, but . . ."

"And you shall be again," she insisted.

"Nay," he said, "those terrible battles took it all out of me."

"But you survived, didn't you? When thousands upon thousands died. That should be enough cause for optimism. Now stop your foolish worrying and let us plan our wedding."

And so they did.

"There, that's the last pin," said Eleonore. Now turn around very slowly and let me see how it hangs. I'm so glad that hoops are in style again

423

and the new crinolines make the skirt fall so softly and elegantly."

"But those pins at the waist are poking into me," complained Kati.

"We'll have them out in a minute." Eleonore looked approvingly. "After all, a woman is expected to suffer a little to be fashionable. Good! Now you may step down."

Kati jumped off the table in a billow of skirt and petticoats.

"I said step not jump," screeched Eleonore fearful that all her careful pinning would be undone. "When are you going to learn the manners of a lady? You should have stepped on the chair first and then on the floor."

"I don't think the manners of a lady customarily include standing on a kitchen table," retorted Kati.

But all the pins were in place and Eleonore sighed with relief.

The wedding took place on 29 June, a perfect bride's day, at the Vilsen church. Kati's gown was magnificent—layers and layers of white linen and lace and hoops so wide she could hardly pass down the aisle. Anton was resplendent in his KGL uniform although he was no longer a member of that corps. It was the only dress outfit he owned. (Dorothea had carefully patched the bullet hole.) He had by his side his brother Johann Heinrich of the struggling spice shop as groomsman. Kati had chosen her sister Dorothea as maid of honor but she had balked at having Fritzi give her away. Eleonore had been furious but Fritzi had not felt slighted at all. He had never really gotten along with his wife's eldest daughter. Kati would have preferred Onkel Chris but since he was the groom's father it would have looked rather odd. She finally settled on Philipp Koch who, although he was from the other family, was considered a neutral and uncontroversial personage who had long been legal advisor to both families. The Matthies attended in force and were surprisingly well behaved, although they had left poor blind, senile Becke behind.

At the dinner at the Hohnholz house Eleonore had obtained, among other treats, a huge baked ham. No one knew how she came by it nor dared ask. (Who is she sleeping with now, was the thought in many minds.) Gifts were simple because of the hard times but generous and well thought out. Linen predominated since that was the one thing of which Vilsen had an abundance. Even the Gräfin von Münster sent a lovely soup tureen of Meissen china. But the gift that Kati treasured most came from the Brothers Grimm—a beautifully bound and illustrated edition of their beloved fairy tales. 'For your first child' said the inscription. She recognized Jacob's hand but she was sure the idea had been Wilhelm's.

Before the festivities got out of hand Chris Bergmann stood up and rang for silence on one of Eleonore's crystal goblets. Everyone turned their attention to him expectantly. "I have an announcement," he said. "In order to complete the happiness of these two beloved children today, I have decided to transfer the tenancy of the Klostermühle to my son Heinrich Anton Bergmann," and he glared defiantly at Heinzi, "according to the agreement with your father Anton Matthies made these many years ago when he became godfather to the lad." Heinzi turned red but he was so surprised and flustered he could not think of anything to say. He could never object to a legal agreement before the whole company. He would think of something to circumvent it later.

Everyone then expected Chris to announce his retirement but he had another surprise in store. "There is a relatively new mill gone vacant in Sebbenhausen," he continued. "I have already paid the tenancy on it. So that these two fine children just starting out in life will not have two crotchety old folks underfoot, Dorchen and I shall be moving there in a few weeks."

There was a babble of astonishment, disbelief and some applause around the table.

Anton and Kati were the only ones not surprised. They had had long and sometimes vehement discussions about it during the past week.

"But Papa, you are seventy years old," Anton had objected.

"Seventy-one," corrected Chris.

"You should be thinking of retiring."

"I am still hale and hearty and I love my work. What am I to do—sit by the fire and knit stockings?"

"No, of course not, but—but what of the cost?" asked Anton.

"The deal is all cut. I have taken a mortgage on the house in Vilsen from Johann Heinrich and his father-in-law, Herr Schlöndorf." Johann had been married in 1818. "And I have turned the house over to Johann. We shall always be welcome there if we ever decide to retire. Moreover, the mill in Sebbenhausen has had poor tenants since its inception. I am certain that a competent miller can turn a profit within a year."

"But what of Anton?" put in Kati. "What will he do without you? How can he lift those heavy bags of flour with a bullet in his side?"

"He has been slinging them about very easily this past year," said Chris. "If the army surgeons pronounced him well enough to lug a seventy-pound pack plus a musket, lead bullets and powder, I am sure a hundred pound sack of flour seems light as a feather."

Kati could say nothing to that. Anton had filled out since he had been home even with the poor diet. She turned to Dorothea. "Oh, Tante Dorchen, I shall miss you so. What shall I do without you?"

"Now child—nay, you are no longer a child but a woman grown," replied Dorothea. "I have taught you all I know. It is time for you to use those skills. You now have a man to look after and, God willing, you will soon have children of your own."

So despite all their objections, Chris and Dorothea happily moved to Sebbenhausen and Anton and Kati took over the running of the Klostermühle at Heiligenberg.

The mill at Sebbenhausen turned out to be a disappointment for both Chris and Dorothea. Although it was less than twenty-five years old, years of neglect had necessitated many repairs. The dwelling house was damp, cold and barely habitable. Compared to it, the 600-year-old Klostermühle was an engineering marvel. One of the greatest problems was that there was no dam, the turning of the great mill wheel dependent entirely upon the flow of the stream which was not as uniformly reliable as Chris had believed. He cursed himself for having looked at it in the spring when the water was high. Now in the late fall the flow was down to a sluggish trickle. Morover with this arrangement the water flowed under the wheel turning it counterclockwise, if at all. Whereas with a dam the water flowed over the wheel to turn it clockwise and could be regulated. The inconsistent flow of the stream also permitted weeds to grow which often tangled in the wheel.

About a week before Christmas the mill wheel stopped entirely.

"I've got to get out there and clear that tangle," said Chris.

"No, Chris," objected Dorothea. "It's too bitter cold. You'll catch your death. We'll be going home to Vilsen for Christmas in a few days. Why not let it go until we return?"

"Because it will be far worse by then and the wheel may start to rust if it doesn't move."

"I should think the frost would kill those weeds."

"It would if they were out in a field but the moving water and the shelter of the wheel keep it above freezing. So they just keep on growing."

When Chris came in it was long after dark and he was soaked through, chilled to the bone.

"Here, come," cried Dorothea. "Get those wet clothes off and sit by the fire. I'll fix you a cup of coffee."

"I'd rather have wine," replied Chris, his teeth chattering.

Dorothea had brought with her a few bottles of her delicious elderberry wine but they drank it sparingly. She had not been able to make any in years due to the lack of sugar. She poured Chris the wine, rubbed him down with towels and wrapped him in blankets. She built up the fire but the chimney did not draw well and the fireplace emitted more smoke than heat.

"Mayhap you should go to bed. It would be warmer," she suggested.

"Nay. I'll be all right in time for supper. The wine is helping. What's for supper?"

"Egg dumplings."

"Again?"

"It's all we have. I could add some onions but I wanted to save them."

"Never mind. Save your onions. At least the dumplings will be hot."

By the next morning Chris was fine although Dorothea noticed he spent an inordinate time by the fire. There was no grain to mill this time of year anyway. The following day they left for Vilsen. They drove to Johann Heinrich's house in the village. There was far more room there for the Christmas festivities than at Heiligenberg. Anton and Kati joined them there.

Dorothea liked Johann Heinrich's wife Friederike. She was a sweet person, quieter and less forthcoming than Kati. But deep down she had an inner strength—much like her own, Dorothea noticed. She was a hard worker as well. She had already built the spice business back up to what it had been before, except for the fact that many products were still hard to come by. She and Johann Heinrich already had one son—a delightful toddler they had named Georg.

Christmas dinner was mostly vegetables but they did have a small goose that Friederike had bartered for some of her precious spices. It was filled with a savory, spicy stuffing.

The next day Chris begged to be excused. "I think I'll lie down for a while."

Dorothea was immediately concerned. Rarely did Chris nap in the afternoon. She felt his forehead. "I think you've got a slight touch of fever," she said. "I do hope it's not from that chill last week."

"Nay, nay," he objected. "Just too much food and excitement yesterday. We old folks are not used to that anymore."

Dorothea dosed him with her strongest posset and by the following

427

morning he pronounced himself well enough to return to Sebbenhausen. But the women were not so sure.

"Why not stay here through the New Year?" suggested Friederike. "The cold air will only make you ill again."

"Nay, nay, I am fine. I was not ill," insisted Chris. "I've got to get back to that blasted mill ere the wheel freezes up entirely."

Dorothea did not agree but she knew her stubborn husband. Cosseting him would only make him angry. She did take the precaution of borrowing an extra blanket to wrap around his shoulders. After they left the environs of Vilsen she knew something was very wrong when he started shivering and voluntarily moved over to let her drive the wagon the rest of the way.

By the time they reached Sebbenhausen the fever was raging again. She quickly hustled him into bed and built a new, roaring fire. She dosed him with ever stronger possets. For a few days the fever seemed to have broken by morning but was up again by evening. By New Year's he was delirious and less than a week later Chris was dead of the dread breast-water sickness—pneumonia.

Dorothea slowly and sadly drove the old wagon, laden with Chris' body and all their possessions, back to Vilsen. The roads were snowy, iced in places, and she hoped the old sway-backed horse would make it—the horse Chris had traded for ten bags of flour after the French had stolen all their finely bred animals. She let her mind wander back to the wonderful horses her grandfather, Cyriacus Lindemann, had bred, all descended from the royal Hannover stud, originally gifts from the Princess of Ahlden. Now there was a sad tale, she reflected. Anything to stave off her own grief.

She had always known that Chris would go first. He was so much older than she. She was so tired and exhausted, the full impact of her grief had not yet set in. She knew it would as soon as she moved into the house in Vilsen with Johann Heinrich and Friederike and slept in an empty bed. She tried to steer her thoughts to the long, happy, loving years they had spent together—how they first met at the Pfingst-ox race, how jealous he had been when Johann Justus Bruns rescued her from the Sacred Spring, how he first made love to her beside her father's millstream, how proud he had been of all their children, living and dead, what a fine miller he had been, one of the most respected men in the community, noted for his even temper and fairness. She let the old nag set his own pace. She was in no hurry.

Her second son Georg and his family came from Liebenau for the

428

funeral, as did her two youngest, still in their journeying years. She hardly knew any of them anymore. Her brother Philipp attended bringing some obscure Koch cousins. Of course, her best friend Eleonore was there with her children and Fritzi. And Heinzi Matthies with Gerhardina and their son showed up putting on faces of grief and offering false condolences. She did not believe a word of it. She would have to warn Heinrich Anton to be careful after this was all over. It did not pay to be careless or gullible where the Matthies were concerned.

And Dorothea was not far wrong. Beneath his professed grief Heinzi was gloating. The greatest obstacle was out of the way. He wanted to install his son Heinrich at the Klostermühle. But there was still that confounded legal document his father had made bequeathing the tenancy to Anton Bergmann and his heirs in perpetuity. And yet—yet now there was some hope of reaching his goal. Heinzi had somehow learned about the bullet in Anton's side, although Anton had never told him. And more importantly Kati did not seem to be breeding as yet. So Heinzi put on an appropriately long face and offered his condolences to the widow, whom he hated.

After a generous funeral repast provided by friends and neighbors, Kati, Friederike and Eleonore gently led Dorothea upstairs to her new room on the second floor of the large Bergmann house. It was a pretty room overlooking the churchyard, perhaps a poor choice at the moment, because she could see the raw grave from the window. But I shall enjoy it once the pain has healed, she told herself. Be strong, be strong. She had brought with her only her most cherished personal possessions and mementos. She had left everything else, including the Koch-Lindemann treasure chest, with Anton and Kati at the Klostermühle.

Dorothea had not yet broken down, holding her grief tightly within her broken heart. Some people thought it odd but those who knew her well—those whom she had nursed through illnesses that the doctors could not, those to whom she had extended kindness and compassion when others would not—these admired her all the more and respected her privacy. The three women who knew her best understood that. And yet they felt it would be better if she unburdened her grief. It would be a catharsis.

Eleonore, who never had trouble showing her grief quite dramatically, tried hugging her and holding her. But this annoyed Dorothea and she shrugged her off.

Friederike suggested reading from the Psalms. They had always comforted her.

"Lord, no thank you," replied Dorothea. "I heard enough of that outside there."

Kati, who probably understood her best, sat quietly holding her hand and patting it as she would a small child's. Dorothea appreciated that but she did not want any of them now. Only her dearest Chris whom she could not have.

"I know you all mean well, dear ones, and I appreciate your thoughtfulness," she said. "But I really want to be alone right now. Go, all of you. Leave me be. I promise you I shall be strong again tomorrow. But at this moment, I have no strength left."

The women left her reluctantly. Alone at last she threw herself on the bed and wept the torrents of tears that had been building up inside. "Chris, Chris, my love," she cried. "I can't ask you to come back but, wherever you are, send me your strength." Finally she slept, aware of his comfort and his love surrounding her.

Heinzi Matthies rode back from Hoya on a sweltering July day. He had on his best suit, the heavy wool adding to his discomfort. Heinzi was furious. He had been so sure a competent lawyer could break the agreement between his father and Chris Bergmann regarding Anton Bergmann's tenancy of the Klostermühle. He had not dared to consult Philipp Koch, who had drawn up the document, or anyone else in Vilsen who might carry tales of his intent back to Dorothea or Anton. So he had ridden all the way to Hoya in the oppressive heat of the dog days to consult a stranger who had charged a hefty fee only to tell him that the agreement was perfectly legal and valid and his only hope was if Anton Bergmann should die without producing a son. Heinzi was furious with frustration and especially at having had to pay a fee for what he already knew.

He took off his hat and mopped his brow with his handkerchief. He shrugged off his coat but that was worse. He could feel the July sun beating down on his neck and shoulders through the thin linen shirt. His mind raced crazily considering alternatives. He could not use physical force. That would be too obvious. He could burn them out but that was foolish, defeating his own purpose. He even considered murder. An accident at the mill, such as his brother had suffered many years ago? The thought was intriguing. But Heinzi doubted his own ability to be subtle enough to make it appear an accident. That was not his way. Heinzi's way was to charge in like a bull. And so his frustration grew.

430

"Well?" asked Gerhardina when he arrived home at Bruchmühlen.

"Well, nothing!" he stormed. "The damn, blasted lawyers are all alike. They all say the same thing. There's nothing to be done—legally. But I'll find a way. Just see if I don't. That mill belongs to us and I should have the right to choose the tenant—the miller."

Heinzi stormed around the house and the mill for the rest of the afternoon, talking to himself and anyone who would listen. Gerhardina kept the younger children out of his way. His temper was worse than his father's had been and truthfully she was afraid of him at these times. His son Heinrich bore the brunt of it. He had to keep working as it was the height of the season but he was so nervous that his father might harm the milling, the mill or even himself that he could hardly perform his duties. Heinrich was still struggling to learn. He was not yet a competent miller— probably never would be. Any mistake he made, however minor, was sure to bring on another fit of temper.

Heinrich was grateful, therefore, when his mother called them for supper and they were able to shut down the great millstones. As they entered the kitchen Heinzi was still fuming and cursing. Suddenly he turned purple, clutched his chest and collapsed on the floor in a fit of apoplexy. Gerhardina rushed to his side and moments later Heinrich rode for the doctor, supper forgotten.

But it was too late. Heinzi lay for two weeks, paralyzed and speechless, and then died.

"He brought it on himself," commented Kati when they heard the news. "His temper was as bad as Opa's without Opa's brains."

"And now we have to deal with Heinrich, which I greatly mislike," said Anton. "He has even less brains than his father and is as devious as a snake. At least with your grandfather, as miserable as he was, one knew where one stood. This one I totally mistrust."

"I agree. And then there's Gerhardina. She will guide him and he will do as she says. That woman hates me with a passion and for what reason I know not. I have never done, or even wished, her any harm."

"Jealousy, no doubt."

"Jealous? But of what?" asked Kati. "I can understand that Heinrich might be jealous of you for you have taken a lot of business away from Bruchmühlen. But it's certainly not your fault that he is so incompetent that the farmers, other than those who have fixed contracts with him, choose to bring their grain here. But Gerhardina jealous of *me?* I can't imagine why."

Anton shrugged. "Mayhap because you are happy and I doubt she has ever known happiness in her entire life. I don't pretend to understand women but that seems to me a female sort of motive."

Kati laughed. "But you understand me."

Anton put his arms around her and hugged her. "I try to but it's not always easy. When do you suppose we might try again to make that heir?" he teased.

She kissed him and smiled. "Tonight after supper. Now get back to work ere the farmers begin to think you are as neglectful as Heinrich."

As time went on Gerhardina had another bone to pick. She had never really cared for her mother-in-law Becke. Not that she actively disliked her. Becke was so mousy, so blank, so colorless, there was nothing much to like or dislike about her. While old Anton was alive, Gerhardina had dared not show her feelings. Besides back then Becke had still been able to care for her family in her ineffective, feckless way. Even while Heinzi still lived, although he had little respect for her, still he had loved his mother in his own peculiar way. So Gerhardina had cared for her as best she could even though she was disgusted by the older woman's senility and growing blindness.

But now, now Gerhardina decided it was time to rid herself of this increasingly difficult burden. Heinrich had been too young to remember his grandfather Anton at all and had never known Becke as a vibrant person, a force in the household. He respected her only in a general way as was a grandmother's due but to him she had been, and still was, merely a colorless fixture about the house—almost a nonentity. She had never shown him any love that he could remember. She was just there.

So Heinrich was sympathetic to his mother's concerns but had no idea what to do about it. Truthfully, he really did not care. That was women's business. "What can we do with her?" he asked, petulantly. "We can't throw her out in the street."

"No, of course not," replied Gerhardina. "I've heard that in some of the larger towns there are homes for people who are old and infirm. It's too bad we don't have such a thing here in Vilsen."

"Well, we don't. And she's hardly infirm."

"No, but she's senile. That's worse. You don't know the half of what I have to go through to care for her."

Heinrich ignored that. "Besides," he said, "doesn't one have to be—

uh, what's the word they use?—uh, indigent—poor. They would charge us."

"There's that. Maybe we could pretend."

"Ach, Mama, let it be," said Heinrich, tired of the discussion. "Oma's old. She can't have much longer to live."

"So you say. She'll outlive us all," said Gerhardina, bitterly.

"Why don't you talk to Tante Elli? After all she's her mother, too. She's rich and has a big house with servants. That would be the solution for you."

"Eleonore has never been very friendly towards us."

"Nor have you towards her. I have work to do." Heinrich stomped back to the mill.

But Gerhardina would not let it be. She tried to think of how she might approach Eleonore.

Johann Justus Bruns sat on the floor of his former home in the Gartenweg playing with his small nephew, godson and namesake. Both Johann Justus' mother and stepmother had preceded his father in death and when the elder Bruns died in 1808, Johann Justus had inherited the house and the well-established, lucrative cabinetmaking business. Since several of his stepbrothers were still young at the time, Johann Justus, being the eldest, had acted *in loco parentis* to them. When his favorite amongst them, Johann Hinrich, married and began having children of his own, Johann Justus decided it was time to move out. There were just too many children in that tiny cottage.

Johann Justus already owned a large house he had built himself many years ago up on the hill of Heiligenberg. His sister Sophie who had lived there for a while had died and the house had stood vacant. So Johann Justus, his wife and children had relocated there. It was a beautiful location on the property of the former monastery—land which an ancestor had received from a dowager countess of Hoya some two hundred years earlier. Johann Justus still walked the mile or so into Vilsen every day to work in the cabinet shop. He let his brother do most of the ordinary, unpretentious work, while he specialized in only the most intricate fancy work such as bedpost finials, balusters, mirror frames and the like—and especially, toys.

Today was the last day of May, young Johann Justus' fifth birthday, and his uncle had brought him the most beautiful, intricately carved little wagon complete with horse and driver that anyone had ever seen.

The little boy's eyes glowed with pleasure. "Danke, Oheim, it's very pretty."

"Push it around the floor and see what happens," replied his uncle.

Johann did so and as the wheels on the horse's feet and the wagon turned, the miniature driver's arm moved up and down cracking the tiny whip. The little boy clapped his hands. "It's just like he's alive," he exclaimed. "When I get big I'm going to make toys just like this."

"Of course, you are. The family has been fine cabinetmakers for many years."

"But I like the shiney ones better. I'm going to make the silver ones."

"Shiney? Silver?" asked Johann Justus, puzzled.

Hinrich laughed. "He means pewter," he explained. "Johann show your uncle what I brought you last time I went to Celle."

The child ran to a toy chest and brought out a tiny pewter horse. He carefully polished it on his sleeve before presenting it to his uncle. "See, Oheim, that's the kind I want to make. Only I like yours better because it has wheels on it. Will you teach me how to put wheels on it when I'm big?"

Johann Justus laughed at his nephew's enthusiasm. "Indeed I shall. But first you must go to school and learn to read and write and cipher. You'll be starting school in the fall, won't you?"

"Ja, but I can already write my name and I can tell time, too. Mama taught me."

"That's wonderful. And then after school you can learn to work with wood like your papa and I."

"Nay. I want to make things out of the shiney stuff—little things like knives and spoons and toys. I don't want to make big things like tables and chests."

Johann Justus shrugged. "Ach, lad, you'll change your mind ten times ere you're grown."

"That's what I keep telling Margarethe," put in Hinrich. "This one's so bright he'll find his way."

Johann Justus agreed. "And yet there's always some that break away from the old mold. Look at my son Georg David. He's set on becoming a musician. He has the talent for it, I admit. But how, I ask you, can a man make a living at being a musician?"

Hinrich shook his head. "Yet we must remember it was our father's uncle who first broke away from the farm to become a cabinetmaker. And some of us still play at Der Lustige Strumpf."

"Ja, there's that. And now some young men from our class even want to attend university."

"Not so many now as a few years ago with those heinous Karlsbad Decrees."

"That's true but Philipp Koch tells me it's not too bad at Göttingen yet. Göttingen always has been more conservative than many of the others."

"True, but what I can't understand is what right Metternich and his police have to come into Hannover and tell those professors what they can teach?"

"Don't forget our own Graf von Münster was a signatory to those decrees. He would like us to go back fifty years to an absolute monarchy."

"Well, he can't as long as we have our constitution."

"Which he'd dearly like to do away with."

"Ach, he'd have a revolution on his hands."

"No doubt. But I fear he would like to try."

Little Johann Justus did not understand a word of what his elders were speaking about but he listened avidly just the same.

The Karlsbad Decrees were a panic response of the old guard to the new liberal and revolutionary thinking brought to Germany by the French, and Metternich, Prime Minister of Austria, was the most reactionary of all. All over Germany student unions took on a more political character, not only promoting unity but unity with some form of representative democracy. In general these unions were harmless with no clear goal other than keeping the liberal spirit alive. Unfortunately one foolish act by a young, stupid student—the senseless assassination of the playwright Kotzebue—so frightened Prussian King Friedrich Wilhelm III that he met with Metternich to devise plans to stamp out what they called 'demagoguery'.

Metternich called a conference of ministers of the major powers of the German Confederation—Austria and the five kingdoms (Prussia, Bavaria, Saxony, Württemberg and Hannover) and the three archduchies (Baden, Oldenburg and Luxembourg)—in Karlsbad in Bohemia in order to draw up a list of decrees to suppress 'demagoguery', i.e., any statement, spoken or written, that appeared to criticize the absolute powers of the rulers. The universities, the newspapers and even the diets of the individual states were the targets of the purge. Commissioners were appointed by the states to each university to overhear the professors' lectures. Special police had powers to zealously enforce the decrees. The student unions were banned. The article governing 'freedom to the press' was actually a wide license for censorship. Other commissioners watched over the doings of the various parliaments. Even leading ministers' sermons were openly spied upon. This was especially true in the north as Catholic Metternich regarded Protestantism as a hotbed of liberalism. Although only two or three professors were actually arrested and removed from their posts, many others fled to France and England. And the fear was there. Those who remained retreated to their ivory towers and their research. Representatives in the diets could not get their ideas before the public because of the newspaper censorship. It seemed as though the tenuous nationalism and democracy of Germany were to die aborning.

But the constitutions still stood and, although temporarily balked in their intent, they would become a rallying point for a new rebirth ten and even twenty years in the future.

Carsten Campsheide was getting old. Carsten had been already in his late thirties, although he looked much younger, when he was conscripted by Napoleon to serve in the Russian campaign. He had been married with several children at the time but he went to war willingly enough for the honor and glory. When he returned from that disastrous campaign he was a changed man—not filled with bitterness as were so many but overwhelmed with hatred for the French emperor who had laid waste so much of Europe. But Carsten was a proud man who still longed for honor and glory. When the French had been driven out of Hannover, he had taken his little troop of recruits to England to join the King's German Legion. After all, wasn't the Duke of Braunschweig, the Black Duke whom he greatly admired, already an old man? And look at the Prussian General Blücher, a still virile man in his seventies.

Carsten had been proud of his exploits in the battle of Waterloo. Although he had received no special commendation, he knew he had done his part bravely and well and who was to know in the telling long afterward that he had not been a hero. Carsten had lost touch with his comrades during and after the battle, partly because he had been placed in the light cavalry and the rest of them in the infantry, but also because he had never been comfortable with the easy camaraderie the others had enjoyed. Until they came home he had not even known that Erich had been killed or Anton wounded. Good men all, Carsten had always intended to visit some of them but the years had slipped by and he had done nothing about it.

Carsten was a very proud man—proud of his farm, one of the largest and wealthiest in all of County Hoya, and proud of his ancestry. Family legend had it that in 1503 a knight named Jürgen Campsheide first settled on the land. Whether the story was true or not, Carsten chose to believe it. What he did know was that since the devastating Thirty Years War each generation had added to and enriched the land through purchases, marriages and other means. Although not technically noble, the family acted like it and many of the local people regarded them as such.

Although the Bruns farm was far older, going back a thousand or more years, the Bruns always seemed to be poor, often to the point of destitution. Although the branch in Vilsen, fine artisans, seemed to be doing as well as people in that class could. Carsten had always liked Harm, a brave, honest and forthright young man. He wondered what he was doing now, if Harm was caught in the inevitable cycle of poverty. He should really inquire. Perhaps he could help. But inertia had discouraged that intent.

Carsten's favorite of the group had been Anton Bergmann, a highly intelligent and congenial young man. Anton seemed to he doing fairly well at the Klostermühle despite his wound, although Carsten still looked down at the Bergmann as upstarts, the father after all had been a newcomer to the area. Although, in truth, the mother was granddaughter to Cyriacus Lindemann, one of the county's most beloved philanthropists in the last century, and through him claimed descent from some of the wealthiest merchant-mayors of Celle. Carsten did not know if that were true or not for they never bragged about it. But old Lindemann's type of philanthropy was not to his taste. Carsten often thought about the possibility of helping individuals less fortunate than he but never did anything about it. Carsten did, however, send all his grain to the Klostermühle to be milled although he had never been there himself. He often wondered why Anton did not buy the mill outright from the Matthies instead of leasing. Probably could not afford it or mayhap the Matthies would not sell. Now there was a family Carsten despised.

As for Gerd Meyer, he came from a well-to-do Bürger family that was already a power in local politics, both village and county, and was rapidly growing more so. Carsten did not like that. Well and good for Bürgers to be involved in the running of the village, but the county? Or mayhap even in this new state body of representatives? Moreover, the Meyers had sent a number of sons to the university to become lawyers, doctors and teachers.

Of course, someone had to perform those necessary tasks but they should come from the higher ranks of society, not from simple Bürgers. Carsten had no use for universities. To him they were merely hotbeds of liberals and radicals. He wondered if Gerd was one of them. Gerd had been a pleasant lad, friendly yet quiet and self-effacing, and with a shrewd intelligence that often surprised Carsten. He had been a hard person to get to know well.

Ach, thought Carsten, what need had a man for all that when he had the land? The land was wealth and power and security. The white petals of his favorite pear tree drifted down in benediction as he looked out over his vast farm. Carsten was very proud of his land. Carsten was a proud, proud man.

Carsten let his mind drift back a few years. In 1820 insane old King George III finally had died and his son, who as Prince Regent had been virtual ruler for many years, ascended the throne as George IV. The following year George IV made the first visit in sixty-six years of any Welf monarch to their former homeland Hannover. People cheered wildly along the King's route and since the Campsheide farm at Asendorf was bounded by that route, the new highway from Bremen to Hannover built by Napoleon, the whole family went to see their new ruler. And many were disappointed. George IV was fat, past middle-age and grossly unhandsome, with the long Stuart nose of his ancestor, the Electress Sophie, and the bull neck and double chins of the earlier Georges. His unsavory reputation as a profilgate womanizer was well known but people hoped that he might settle down now that he was finally king. Not so. The liberals hoped that he might do more towards expanding the new constitution—after all, England was a consitutional monarchy—to extend the franchise to the peasantry. The monarchists hoped he would do more to actually rule Hannover. Neither thing happened. In fact, nothing at all happened. It appeared that the King's visit was nothing more than a Royal Progress through the Welf homeland. But the people had their entertainment. If Carsten thought about it at all, it was to wish that Hannover had her own king and not these distant English Welfs.

But Carsten really did not care. What he cared about now was that his eldest son had finally produced an heir, a healthy boy who seemed to be thriving. He hoped, of course, that there would be several more sons. Children's lives were so precarious. But at least there was this one. Carsten felt that perhaps he could now relax a little. He had not intended to daydream. The reason he had come out here to sit under his favorite pear tree where he could think best, was to review his son's marriage settlement. He looked again at the paper in his lap. He was glad he had had the forethought to write in provisions for his and Marie's old age. Yes, it was ample. He and Marie could now enjoy a comfortable old age.

His daughter-in-law Anna came out to join him. She was carrying the new heir, baby Hinrich. "Ach, Papa," she said, "you are covered with pear petals. It looks like snow. Here let me brush them off."

"Nay, nay, let them be. I like them," replied Carsten. "But you should not be bringing that little one outside yet. He may catch a chill."

"Ach, nay, Papa," she insisted, "it is a beautiful spring day. And now that his eyes are focussing, I want him to see this fine farm you are so proud of. Some day it will all be his."

"Ja, some day," he mused, "but that will be long years yet."

Anna opened her bodice and began nursing the baby. Carsten was a little embarrassed at first—these young people had no modesty—but then he realized what a beautiful picture it made. He had missed so many years of his own children's growing up—years in Russia, years in England and then Waterloo—that he made up is mind then and there not to miss any of this grandson's. And his heart swelled with pride.

Harm Bruns struggled through the snow. It was up to his thighs and he waded rather than walked. Usually he could easily make the twenty-some mile distance from Bremen to home in one day. What was twenty miles to a veteran of Wellington's army? It was already almost dark. The darkness he expected. It was nigh on Christmas. But this much snow in this part of Germany was almost unheard of, especially so early in the season. It presaged a hard winter. And the summers the past few years had been terrible as well—cold and damp, crops rotting in the fields. People were still starving everywhere, even these many years after the French occupation.

And that was the main reason why Harm had been to Bremen. The land could no longer support them. Harm had not yet married but he had several brothers and sisters who had, leaving him to be the only one free to go elsewhere to find work that might help them. The Bruns were a large but close knit family—always had been. Early last summer he had gone to Bremen to seek employment, any kind. Fortuitously he had found Wulf still on the waterfront. Wulf had helped him get a job stevedoring, loading and unloading the great sailing vessels that traversed the globe from the old Hanse seaport. Unloading mostly, goods and products from far off Australia, South America and especially North America. Unloading because he was surpised to learn that a large portion of the outbound 'cargo' consisted of emigrants seeking new homes in these distant places. Now why in the world would these thousands of people want to leave their beloved homeland in favor of a foreign wilderness, which was all Harm knew of places like America.

Speaking with some of them he soon learned why. Many were still fleeing religious intolerance, especially from the Palatine, but the vast majority were from Prussia, fleeing both poverty and the Prussian military. Nothing wrong with the military, thought Harm but then he asked, "Why does Prussia need such a large army now when it's peacetime?"

They replied, "Because Prussia wants to conquer all of Germany."

"Oh, no, but not Hannover. Never Hannover," he declared.

"Especially Hannover," they told him. "Hannover has been a thorn in Prussia's side for years."

And on another occasion, "But I thought Prussia was going to have a constitution."

"Ach, what constitution? Friedrich Wilhelm is an absolute monarch and intends to stay that way. There is no hope for any of us peasants. Even the Junkers are not happy. We are going to a place where there really *is* a constitution—and freedom."

"And where is that?" asked Harm.

"To North America, of course."

"And what's more," added another group, "the King has arbitrarily combined the Lutheran and Reformed churches into one church, which is neither fish nor fowl. We can't put up with that. We are staunch Lutherans and we mean to go where we can worship as we please."

All this had given Harm much food for thought. He had mulled it about quite a bit earlier in the day on his lonely trek from Bremen. But now he was tired and cold and just the effort of plowing through the snow drove all deep thoughts from his mind. He had stopped a short while ago at his cousin's in Vilsen for a quick cup of hot coffee. They had urged him to stay the night but he had refused. After all, home was only a few miles further. He was glad he had kept this old army knapsack. Every trip home he had stuffed it with as many pounds of food he could squeeze in. This time he even had a few small Christmas gifts and tied to his belt was a goodly purse of coin, his wages for the past few months. Ja, he would see that the family had a good Christmas.

Harm was so bent over from the weight of his pack and the effort of trudging through the deep snow that he almost did not see the snow-covered mound beside the road in the dark. As he passed it, he thought he heard a moan. He stopped to listen. Then a tiny, hoarse voice emerged from it.

"Ach, there you are at last. I've been waiting so long," it said.

Harm made his way over to the lump. To his shock he discovered it was an old woman. She was sitting propped against one of the boundary stones Anton Matthies had so proudly erected years ago. Harm did not know the Matthies well. His brothers always took their grain to Anton Bergmann for milling, although he knew the Matthies profitted from it. But everyone knew who they were. This then must be the grandmother, old Anton's wife, whom no one had seen in years. He noticed she wore neither cloak nor hood and her feet were clad in the thinnest of house slippers. He gently brushed some of the snow off her head and shoulders.

"What are you doing out here, old mother?" Harm asked. He could not remember her name.

"I'm waiting for my son, Fritzi. But you're not Fritzi, are you?" she said plaintively.

Harm had no idea who Fritzi was but he said, "No, I'm not. But hadn't you best wait inside by the fire? You'll catch your death out here in the snow."

"But they don't want me there. They took Fritzi away, you know. But he'll come back. I know he will."

"I still think you should wait inside. Come, I'll help you," he insisted. He took her withered hand, already turning blue from the cold, and helped her up. She did not resist. He had to hold her up she was so stiff from the cold but she followed meekly. Just like an abused dog, he thought.

Bruchmühlen was only about a hundred yards down the road. That must be where she belonged. Harm had difficulty pushing through the snow to make a path for her. There was no sign of her outward path. He wondered how long she had been sitting there. He pounded on the door of the millhouse. After some time Heinrich answered, an annoyed look on his face.

"Who are you?" he demanded. "What—oh—"

"I am Harm Bruns, your neighbor down the road a ways. I believe this is your grandmother, is it not? I found her sitting beside the road covered with snow."

"Ach, so that's where she'd got to. We wondered," replied Heinrich, decidedly annoyed.

Gerhardina came bustling up. "Why, that crazy old woman," she screamed. "You should have left her there. She's nothing but—" Suddenly she stopped at the shocked look on Harm's face. "That is—I mean, she's not right in the head. We didn't know where she was. Come, Oma, let's sit you by the fire." She took the old woman's hand from Harm.

"She said she was waiting for Fritzi," said Harm.

"Ach, Gott," exclaimed Gerhardina. "Fritzi was my husband's elder brother. He died over forty years ago in a tragic accident. That was even before my time. You see what I mean."

Harm nodded. "Well, take good care of her. I'm glad I could help."

"Er—ja—uh, thank you," said Heinrich and shut the door in his face.

Harm had heard many unpleasant things about the Matthies but this beat all. How could people be so cruel to their very own? He was glad he was going home to a loving family.

"Why did you have to say those stupid things?" Heinrich shouted at his mother. "Now it will be all over the village."

"Ach, he's just a stupid Bruns," replied Gerhardina. "He won't say anything. Besides everyone knows she's senile. What harm did it do? Now do you see why we have to get rid of her?"

"I thought you were going to speak to Tante Eleonore."

"I shall but I just haven't had the right opportunity."

"You mean you haven't had the courage."

"Don't you accuse me of not having courage. It'll take a lot of courage taking care of her now. If she catches a chill it will be double the work than when she is well."

"Then take care of her now." Even Heinrich suddenly felt a twinge of sympathy for his grandmother, who was shivering by the fire. "Get those wet clothes off of her and give her some hot broth."

"While you sit there and dictate to me? At least you can help. Put that soup pot back on the fire whilst I rub her feet dry."

Gerd Meyer had not wanted to go to university. It had become a tradition in the family. His father and two uncles as well as his grandfather had all graduated from Göttingen with law degrees. But after six years in the army and especially after the horror of Waterloo, the whole idea seemed a bit childish to Gerd. He was clerking in his father's law office for want of something better to do until he could decide what to make of his life. But he seemed no closer to that decision than a year ago.

The Meyers were one of the wealthiest, most powerful and most respected families in Vilsen. But they were not ostentatiously wealthy nor avariciously powerful. They quietly did what they could to make Vilsen a desirable place to live and work—and to keep it that way. Although none of them actively sought political office, it was rumored that Gerd's father might soon be appointed district judge but the elder Meyer was too modest to speak of it. "If it happens, it happens," was all he would say.

Not like the boastful Hohnholz who had precipitously fallen from the political pinnacle under the dubious leadership of the last stepson and his profligate wife Eleonore, who had been born a Matthies. Back a generation or so a great-aunt—or was it great-great-aunt—had married into that family but the Meyers preferred to forget that connection.

Unexpectedly it was Philipp Koch, his father's competitor and friend—a friendly rivalry, they called it—who helped Gerd make his decision.

Gerd was desultorily dusting his father's law books with a feather duster, trying to make himself look busy, when a cheerful voice asked, "And how is our junior advocate this fine day?"

Gerd blushed and looked up to a grinning Philipp. "Oh, hello, Master Koch. I'm quite well, thank you."

"'Tis best you keep them dusted else you might sneeze when you open them. Have you even cracked a one of them?"

"Ach, Master Koch, you're teasing me," replied Gerd, "but truthfully, no, I haven't even read the titles. Papa is insisting I go to the university but I have no interest in studying for the law. No offense."

"None taken. The law is not for everyone. What is it that you like to do? There are many other professions, you know."

"I like helping people, but not in the legal sense."

"Have you considered becoming a doctor or a pastor?"

"No, neither. I saw too much of what doctors have to do at Waterloo. It turned my stomach. As for a pastor—I've never been much of a church-goer, much to my mother's chagrin. Wouldn't it be hypocritical if I were to start telling people what they should believe? No, I like telling people stories—like about Waterloo, about the places I've been and seen. What kind of a profession is a story teller?"

"Aha!" said Philipp. "Then you would make an excellent teacher."

"A teacher?"

"Ja, a schoolmaster. There is a great need. You're probably too young to remember but back just before the turn of the century and even after there was a great to-do about parents living south of the village not wanting to send their children to the new school in Homfeld because the schoolmaster was so incompetent. Both Chris Bergmann and old Miller Matthies were fined for failing to contribute to the Homfeld school. I was in Göttingen at the time, so I forget how it came out but I believe they both paid the fines and continued to send their children to school here in Vilsen."

"Yes, they did," replied Gerd. "I mean, I don't know about the fines but that is where I first met Anton—here in the Vilsen school."

"So you see there is a great need for well-educated teachers. And I'm sure you would enjoy studying under the Brothers Grimm."

"The Brothers Grimm?"

"Surely you know of their wonderful collection of fairy tales?"

"I've heard of them but I was at Waterloo when they first came out. But what have fairy tales to do with—with . . . ?"

"Both brothers took their degrees in the law," replied Philipp, "but they now are professors of language and language history and their closest colleagues teach history and geography—all things you like."

Gerd pondered this. And so he finally agreed to go to Göttingen—still reluctantly, until he met the Brothers Grimm. They changed his whole outlook on life.

Kati rolled out of bed slowly. What was wrong? She did not feel her usual buoyant self. She was about to shed her nightgown when—oh, my! She grabbed for the chamberpot and was promptly sick.

Anton held her and wiped her forehead. "What's wrong, dear sweet? Are you coming down with something?"

"Nay, nay," she replied when she could. " 'Tis nothing. I'll be fine in a little while. Go and have your breakfast. I just want to rest a few more minutes until this passes."

Anton left her but he was worried. There was so much sickness about. People all over were weak and starving—still suffering in the aftermath of the French Time. What would he ever do if he were to lose his dearest Kati? He could not bear the thought. He tried to eat but he almost choked on the food. A half drunk cup of coffee sat before him getting cold.

The next thing he knew Kati came bounding down the stairs, smiling broadly, eyes aglow. "Guess what," she said. "I am finally carrying. I hoped so but I wasn't sure until just now. Aren't you pleased?"

He hugged her and kissed her. "You're sure?" he asked.

"Of course, I'm sure. It's three months," she replied.

"I did wonder," he mused. "It semed a long time since you had a flux but I don't keep track of those things like you women do. I could have slept right through it. Oh, Kati sweet, that's wonderful. When do you think it will be?"

"End September, I think," said Kati.

Anton chuckled to himself. "Heinrich Matthies will be furious."

"Ach, curse Heinrich Matthies. We won't even tell him until I start to show. Besides it could be a girl."

"Then Heinrich will be overjoyed."

"Ach, never mind. Now that I know I am not barren we can have as many as both our mothers had."

"A few too many, that," said Anton, "but four or five would be nice. I'll enjoy working on it."

"Oh, you shameless wretch," she chided, "but I'll admit I'll enjoy it, too. I only hope my cough doesn't harm him. I have been afraid that was why I could not conceive."

"I don't see how it can. You were really worried about that?"

"Some. But I'll try to keep it under control now. Oh, I can't wait to tell your mama."

Two months later when Heinrich Matties learned the news, he was indeed furious. "Now there's no chance at all of breaking that agreement," he moaned.

"Oh, stop it," said Gerhardina. "She could lose it. It could be a girl. Anything can happen. Isn't it time you found a wife of your own and quit worrying about them?"

"I'll find one in time. I'm not ready for marriage yet. I'm too young."

"You weren't too young to try and rape that girl ten years ago—and I wonder how many others."

"How did you know about that?" he snarled.

"I knew. And you'd better start looking for one ere you get too old, never mind too young."

"I'll not bring a wife into this house as long as *she's* here. It wouldn't be fair to any woman. Have you spoken to Tante Eleonore yet?"

"Not yet but I intend to soon."

In the end it was Eleonore who came to them.

Eleonore had not been to visit her mother as often as she ought and she sometimes felt a little guilty about that. But not too guilty. Eleonore rarely felt guilty about anything. But it was frustrating when Becke did not recognize her, which was at least half the time. It was like talking to a stranger—or a ghost from the past. And then the past winter had been especially severe and the Hohnholz no longer had a coach or even a horse. While the business was slowly improving—spinners and weavers were working again, turning out as much as they could considering the dearth of flax—Fritzi was just not capable of getting the best prices from the factors and shippers in Bremen. Eleonore knew she could do better but he would not let her go claiming it was unseemly for a woman. Never mind that she oversaw the weavers, kept all the books, paid the taxes, wrote all the correspondence—in short, ran the business singlehandedly except for those crucial trips to Bremen. But Eleonore, too, was starting to feel her age. She was getting too old to bother arguing with Fritzi.

And she was getting too old to hike all the way to Bruchmühlen very often—she who used to love running like a deer through her beloved woods. She had heard the story of Becke's getting lost in the snowstorm from Johann Justus who had it from his cousin Harm Bruns. Eleonore would have enjoyed a leisurely walk to her childhood home on this fine summer's day had she not been boiling over with anger. Thus she was in fine fettle when she pounded on the door of the millhouse.

"Ach, Elli, how nice to see you," said Gerhardina, surprised into being polite for a change. "I suppose you're here to see your mother. It's been a long time."

"I simply wasn't able to get here with one thing and another," replied Eleonore. "But I have just now heard of how she was lost in the snow and nearly froze to death. I assume she has recovered else you'd have sent word. How is she?"

"As well as ever, physically, but even more muddled in the head. Oh, there was a touch of frostbite in her fingers and toes but I took care of that and I don't see any aftereffects."

"Didn't anyone miss her? Didn't anyone think to look for her? What's wrong with you people?" Eleonore could hardly control her anger. A touch of frostbite, indeed.

"Well, we don't pay much attention—." Gerhardina suddenly realized how that sounded. "That is, she is always just *there*," she amended. "We never thought she would take it upon herself to go outside, especially in a blizzard."

"Say what you mean, Gerhardina," snapped Eleonore. "You don't really pay any attention to her."

"More than you do," retorted Gerhardina. "I devote more than half my time caring for her. I can't cope anymore, Elli." Gerhardina started to sob, something Eleonore had rarely witnessed before. "I simply can't cope. We have to do something with her."

Eleonore could not decide whether the tears were false or genuine but she did sympathize. *She* would not want that burden. "What do you suggest?"

"Couldn't you take her, Elli? You have a large house and servants. Your daughter could help. I only have Heinrich who is busy all day and the younger children who need care as well."

"Only one already overburdened servant," replied Eleonore. "And you know Mama's sight is almost gone as well as her mind. She would surely break her neck on all the stairs we have. No, Gerhardina, this has been her home for over fifty years. Let her spend her last few years where she's comfortable."

"What about my comfort?"

Eleonore could see that further argument was useless. "I came to see her, after all. Where is she?"

"In her usual place by the fire even though it's stifling hot."

Eleonore swept past her sister-in-law and entered the kitchen. She was shocked when she saw Becke. Instead of the grossly overweight woman she had been, Becke was now skinny and shrivelled up as a withered apple. "Hello, Mama, it's Elli."

The rheumy eyes seemed to brighten a bit. "Ach, Elli, I'm so glad you're here." She extended her hand. "Come here, my dearest daughter. You're the only one I have left."

Thanking God that her mother at least recognized her, Eleonore took her hand and patted it. It was ice cold. She leaned over and kissed the wrinkled cheek. "How have you been, Mama? Are they treating you well?"

Becke ignored that and went on with her theme. "They took Fritzi away. They took Carsten away. They took Heinzi away. Adi and Young Becke—I don't know if they took them away or not but I never see them."

"Fritzi and Carsten and Heinzi are dead, Mama," said Eleonore gently. "God took them away. Adi and Becke are happily married but they live far away so they can't come to see you very often." And I live the closest and I'm just as bad, she thought.

"But you were always the smart one. You're too smart to let them take you away, aren't you?"

"I hope so."

"And now they want me to go away, too. I tried to go away a few weeks ago but some man made me come back. Is it still snowing out?"

"No, Mama, it's summertime now."

"I know I'm a foolish old woman now, Elli. I can't see too well to weave anymore. Weaving and making babies, that's all Anton ever wanted from me. But I loved him, my dear Anton. When he was alive I was strong but now I'm weak and useless. And they want to get rid of me."

Eleonore could not ever remember her mother being strong but she was disturbed that, senile or no, Becke was aware of the antagonism toward her in this house. She wondered what could be done.

"No one wants to get rid of you, Mama," she lied. "This is your home and you have as much right to it as they do."

Becke shook her head. "That old woman and that young man, they hate me."

"Do they mistreat you, Mama?"

Becke shook her head again. "Oh, I don't know. I just want to go home."

Eleonore could see the light in the old eyes fading. "You *are* home, Mama." But she knew her words did not register. Becke was retreating into her own private world.

As Eleonore turned to leave, Gerhardina accosted her. "Well, what are you going to do about it?"

"Nothing at the moment. I'll give it some thought. You know she's aware of how you feel about her."

"Ach, she's not aware of anything. Give it some thought. Hah! You'd better think. You're rich. Why don't you hire a nursemaid to take care of her? Then I wouldn't mind keeping her here."

"I am no longer rich, Gerhardina, as you well know. We can barely make ends meet." No way would she give one penny to Gerhardina or Heinrich. A nursemaid would never see any of it. "As I said, I shall think about what can be done."

A few days later, when her anger had cooled, Eleonore went to consult with her dearest friend Dorothea. Dorchen was always so sensible and she knew a lot about sick people. Hopefully she would have some ideas.

Dorothea had heard the story of Becke's misadventure in the snow from Johann Justus. So she was not surprised to hear of Eleonore's dilemma.

"I think they're deliberately mistreating her," said Eleonore. "She has lost so much weight."

"Nay," replied Dorothea, "old people in that condition often lose weight. I've seen it happen many a time. They do not want to eat and have no sense of time. And Gerhardina is not the type to coax her."

"True. I could almost sympathize with Gerhardina if only she weren't so—so mean."

"Ja, and remember Gerhardina has had the burden of her these many years. She's no doubt at the end of her tether—and she isn't the brightest person to begin with. Nor is her son."

"They want me to take her but I can't. Dorchen, I know she's my mother but I just couldn't stand living with her. Besides she'd be so disoriented at our house."

"I know. Truthfully you are not the right person to care for her. No offense, my dearest friend, but I know you too well. She is better off with Gerhardina. At least she's at home there."

Eleonore smiled. "At least you're honest. But, you know, Dorchen, Mama is aware that they don't want her. She was surprisingly lucid the other day. I fear me that she may wander off again." She hesitated a moment. "Dorchen, do you suppose that Kati might . . ."

"Elli," exclaimed Dorothea, "your daughter is very pregnant with her first due in a few months. And she is not strong herself. How could you possibly ask her to assume such a burden at this time?"

"I wasn't thinking of right this minute," replied Eleonore somewhat abashed. "But after the babe is born and she is well again . . . You know I think she's the only one who truly loves Mama and Mama seems to enjoy her company."

"Don't even think of it," said Dorothea. "I'll try and visit Becke more often but I've been so busy. There is so much sickness about. Meanwhile I'll enquire about, very subtly, of course. There may be someone who would welcome her and be willing to care for her. For a fee, mind you."

"Ja, that's another problem," sighed Eleonore. "Although I admit I'd rather pay a stranger than give one penny to my nephew and sister-in-law."

A few weeks later Dorothea walked slowly down the lane from the Klostermühle to Bruchmühlen with a very cumbersome Kati. Dorothea had increased the frequency of her visits to Becke to check on her but she had found nothing really wrong with the old woman except for her fears. But these were quite valid. She knew that Kati wanted to visit her grand-

449

mother at least once or twice more before her lying-in.

"Sorry to be so slow, Mama Dorchen," said Kati. "I feel so clumsy these days."

"Naturally. You're walking for two. But walking is good for you. 'Twill make the birth easier. How is your back?"

"Managing, but just about," replied Kati.

"Don't be surprised at anything your grandma says. She has a new set of fears, probably groundless."

"I know. She thinks they want to be rid of her, which is probably true."

"But they won't do anything about it. Not yet anyway."

"I hope not. But nothing surprises me there. I'm only glad when she recognizes me. Mostly she thinks I'm Mama. Calls me Elli."

"You and your mother do look a lot alike."

"But as different as day and night in every other way."

"God be thanked," said Dorothea.

The visit was unproductive and frustrating as usual. Becke kept pleading with 'Elli' to take her home. And Kati and Dorothea kept insisting just as firmly that she *was* at home.

"I can't help you now, Oma," Kati tried to explain, "but maybe after my baby is born, we might make some arrangement."

"Ach, babies," sighed Becke. "I know a lot about babies. I thought I was breeding again not long ago but Anton said it was only the full moon. The moon has a lot to do with babies, you know. When they're born on a waxing moon they will be happy and if they're born on a waning moon they'll know nothing but sadness. That's why I lost so many. It was the wrong time of the moon."

Kati and Dorothea looked at each other but Dorothea nodded. "It's an old folk legend," she said, "but I often believe there is some truth to it."

"Then let us hope this one is born on a waxing moon," said Kati, patting her belly. She turned back to Becke. "After he's born, I'll bring him to see you, Oma."

"Ja, that would be nice," replied Becke, dreamily.

On 22 September 1823 during a violent equinoctial storm that lashed tree branches and slashed torrential rain against the windows Hermann August Bergmann put in his appearance. It was so dark and dreary that Kati had no idea what the phase of the moon was. She was only grateful for a short, four-hour labor and that the baby was whole and seemed to be healthy. Dorothea and the midwife were grateful, too, for towards the end Kati had had a violent coughing spell, which may have helped propel the baby out but which left the mother exceedingly weak and exhausted. So much so that she had difficulty expelling the afterbirth. But after the midwife succeeded in manipulating that out, Dorothea was ready with a strengthening posset that promptly sent Kati to sleep.

The baby thrived but the mother took a long time to recover her strength. Winter closed in early and once again was far more severe than was usual for that part of Europe. People died by the hundreds from disease, starvation and the bitter cold. Thus it was late spring before Kati felt able to walk even the short distance to Bruchmühlen to have her grandmother meet the baby. Little Hermann was a joyous child, sitting up well by now and even trying to crawl. Kati carried him in a sling on her hip for he was a heavy babe and promised to be a mischievous imp. She had not gone far when to her surprise she found Becke sitting on a tree stump.

"Oma," she exclaimed, "what are you doing here?"

"Just resting a bit," replied Becke in a quavery voice.

"But you shouldn't be out here in the woods all by yourself so far from home."

"I was just going to see Kati. It is Kati, is it not?" She peered with her failing vision. "Or is it Elli?"

"No, it's Kati, Oma. And I was just about to bring my baby to see you."

"You're a naughty girl, just like your mother. I've missed you," sobbed Becke. Then something seemed to penetrate the fog. "Baby? You have a baby?"

"Ja, Oma, and that is why I could not come to visit, besides the winter being so long. See, here he is. His name is Hermann."

"Is it a boy or a girl?"

Kati shrugged mentally. "He's a healthy boy. Come, Oma, let me help you up and I'll walk home with you."

Becke seemed glued to the tree stump. She stubbornly refused to get up. "I have no home," she moaned. "That's why I was coming to see you."

Kati did not know what to say or do. Since they were far closer to the Klostermühle than to Bruchmühlen, she decided to get Anton to help. "You wait right here now, Oma. I am going to fetch Anton to help you. Don't go anywhere, you hear? I'll be right back."

Becke nodded and Kati hurried back to the Klostermühle. Anton was very busy but he quickly shut down the millstones and followed her.

"We can't leave her sitting there," said Kati.

"Of course not," Anton replied. "If she won't come along, I'll have to carry her. In that case we'd best bring her here. Then at the end of the day I'll hitch up the wagon and take her back."

"Good idea."

Becke was still sitting on the tree stump when they returned.

"Come, Oma Becke, I'll help you home," offered Anton gently.

Becke refused to budge. "I have no home," she repeated. "I was going to see Kati but no one will let me."

"Would you like to come to our house and visit for a short while?" asked Anton.

"I want to go to Kati's house."

"Our house is Kati's house. Come now, I'll take you."

He picked her up. She was light as a feather but suddenly she fought him like a wild cat. "Don't take me back there," she screamed.

"I shan't."

"Who are you?"

"I am Anton, Kati's husband."

"Oh, Anton." And suddenly she was meek as a kitten. She put her arms around him, cuddling like a lover. "Oh, Anton, I've missed you so."

Kati would have laughed at the look on Anton's face had the whole thing not been so tragic. "She thinks you're *her* Anton."

"I know," he replied. "Let's get her home while she's quiet and willing."

They settled Becke in a rocking chair by the fire and she seemed quite content to be there. Anton went back to work and Kati sat on a hard chair to nurse the baby. We'll need another rocking chair, she thought. She knew then that her grandmother was here to stay. Becke was sound asleep.

When Anton came in for dinner, Kati said, "We must send word to Gerhardina."

"I said I'd take her back at the end of the day," he replied.

"No, Anton. I think we are saddled with her, like it or no. Look at the poor dear. I believe she's happy for the first time in years."

"Are you sure that's what you want?"

"It's what she wants. I'm sure she'll be no bother."

"But Kati, I'll not have her taking any of your time—or strength—away from our son."

"She won't, I promise you. Hermann might even be some entertainment for her. She's so lonely. And she sleeps most of the time. She still

452

knows how to use the privy—not like some senile old people I've heard of. Although I'll have to take her since she can't see her way. She'll be no bother, I'm sure."

"But another mouth to feed."

"Ach, Anton, look at her. How much can she eat? I'll probably have to coax her to eat at all."

That evening after supper Kati insisted on accompanying Anton to Bruchmühlen to break the news to Gerhardina and fetch Becke's things. "She'll cetainly hoodwink you," said Kati. "I don't trust her to give us everything."

"I doubt she had much," he replied. "They'll have helped themselves to most of it by now. And you'll leave Hermann alone with her?"

"He's already asleep in his crib and she is snoring away in my rocking chair. She's not the old witch Gerhardina makes her out to be. They'll both be fine in the short while we are gone."

Kati was all full of fire, ready to scold Gerhardina for letting Becke wander off again. But when Anton quickly explained that they were willing to keep the old women in their home, Gerhardina was so effusive with cousinly bonhomie that Kati held her peace.

"We have come for her clothes and things," she said.

"Ach, that is so kind of you," said Gerhardina. "I'll fetch them in a moment."

"Would you care for a glass of wine?" offered Heinrich.

Kati was so surprised she nearly fell over. "No, no thank you. We have to get right back."

Gerhardina returned very quickly. "Here is her other dress—her Sunday dress which she hasn't worn in years. It's probably too big for her now. Two petticoats, her Sunday stockings and her other apron. That's the lot of it."

"Doesn't she have a cloak for winter?" asked Kati. "She always did."

"Not that I remember. Well, there is her old shawl. I didn't think you would want it."

"Of course, I want it. She'll need it come cold weather. The shawl, Gerhardina."

Gerhardina reluctantly produced the shawl. It was very large of fine wool. Gerhardina was obviously thinking of keeping it for herself.

"Doesn't she have another pair of shoes?" asked Anton. "Hers seemed quite worn."

Gerhardina looked at him as though he were crazy. "Who these days has two pair of shoes? Take 'em to the cobbler and get 'em fixed like everybody else does. She did have an old pair of house slippers. Maybe they're around some place."

Kati knew that to be true about the shoes so she did not argue. "We'll take the slippers. They will be more comfortable for her. And what about her jewelry? I know she had some."

Gerhardina looked flustered for a moment. " 'Twere only a few trinkets. I let my girls have the pick of them. Nothing valuable."

"I remember a pair of gold and pearl earrings she always wore when Opa Anton was alive. Also some garnet studs. Where are they, Gerhardina?"

"Uh—well—er, mayhap I can find them. I put them away when she no longer wore them."

"While you're looking, fetch her brush, comb and mirror. They were silver-backed as I recall."

Gerhardina looked fit to be tied but she disappeared into her own bedroom and shortly returned with the requested items. She also handed Kati an ancient leather bound book and a smaller one. "Her Bible and Catechism," she explained. "You might as well have them although what use they'll be to her I don't know seeing as how she can't see."

"I'll take them anyway," replied Kati. "It may comfort her just to hold them."

"What about her distaff and things like that?" asked Anton.

At this Gerhardina bridled. "Nay, nay. Those things belong to the mill, not to her personally."

"Never mind, Anton," said Kati. "We have enough. We have to get back. And Gerhardina, should you find any more of her *personal* belongings, send them along with one of the children."

"I'll do that," agreed Gerhardina, glad to have gotten off so easily.

In the lane back to Heiligenberg Anton said, "I'm glad now that you came along. I'd never have thought of jewelry or her brush and comb."

"I know," said Kati. "It takes a woman to think of those things. And I'm sure there is a lot more but we'll never see it. Old Opa Anton may have been mean but he loved Becke in his strange way. And when it suited him he was not ungenerous."

"I know. Look what he did for me, of which Heinrich is still jealous."

Becke settled into life at the Klostermühle more readily than anyone expected. She enjoyed baby Hermann and the child took to her immediately. He was too young to care whether she knew who he really was or thought he was one of her own. It did not matter to either of them. When he was not quite a year old she helped him to learn how to walk. And both cooed like infants at his accomplishments.

When winter closed in — and it was another harsh one. The kind the old folk and farmers called a 'wolf-winter', when wolves as well as people were starving and the beasts came daringly close to homes and even the village and often stole chickens, young livestock and even small children — everyone stayed close by the hearth afraid to venture beyond the barnyard or the privy. Although food was still scarce and the diet often monotonous, the Bergmann were better off than most. The millhouse was warm and cozy and the little family content.

Kati rejoiced to see the growing relationship between her grandmother and her son. Once Hermann began to talk, Becke would take him on her lap and tell him the old stories. Often she would lose her train of thought half-way through and Kati had to finish the tale. But Hermann was an exceedingly bright child and once he heard the whole story a few times, he seemed to sense when Oma Becke's mind started to wander. Then he would finish the story, telling it to her.

Perhaps because of the 'wolf-winter', when the wolves were howling in the woods dangerously near the mill, Hermann especially liked the tales where the wicked wolf was fooled by a girl with a red hood or by little pigs or goats. Thus he learned to have no fear of the animals. Kati was a mite concerned about this and made sure that either she with a stout stick or Anton with his musket or one of their dogs was with him whenever he ventured outside.

One unusually mild day late in January the little boy was playing in the yard with their largest dog standing guard. Kati was in the kitchen baking; Anton was in the barn tending to the cow and pigs. Suddenly they heard a shot. Hermann screamed and the dog yipped and howled in agony. Kati ran out of the house, Anton from the barn. There to their amazement they found Heinrich Matthies with a musket still smoking. And the gun was aimed directly at Hermann. The dog, although bleeding profusely from the thigh, was still trying to guard the child, growling and snarling at Heinrich with bared teeth and raised hackles.

"What do you think you're doing?" screamed Kati.

"I—I thought it was a wolf," stammered Heinrich as he backed off a few steps. But the gun was still pointed at the little boy, who was screaming with terror.

"Put that thing down and get off my property," yelled Anton. "You damned fool, you could have killed my son." He lunged toward Heinrich.

Heinrich smirked and lowered the gun. He backed out of Anton's reach. "I could have, couldn't I?"

"And you damn near killed my dog," shouted Anton. The dog now lay whimpering but was still alive. "Whoever saw a black wolf with brown floppy ears?" asked Anton.

" 'Twas hard to tell. Didn't have time to think."

"You never do. Now get off my property."

"It's *my* property," insisted Heinrich. "In case you forgot, I own the land, the mill and everything that's in it."

"Not everything that's in it," said Anton. "You may own the land and the mill but as long as I pay the lease-rent, this is private property and if I ever catch you near my son or anywhere near here with that gun in your hands, I'll kill you."

"Are you threatening me?"

"Not yet but I will if you ever come here with a gun again."

As soon as Heinrich had lowered the gun, Kati had swooped in and gathered up the baby. Hermann had stopped crying the moment he felt his mother's comforting arms around him. Now he watched the proceedings with great interest. Although he did not understand any of it, his inate child's instinct told him that this was someone not to be trusted.

"He bad man, Mama," he said, pointing at Heinrich.

"Hush, child," whispered Kati. "You mustn't say that but I am afraid he is." Aloud she said, "You heard what my husband said, Heinrich. Now begone with you."

Heinrich smirked again. "Frightened you, didn't I, bitch? Good. You're too haughty by far."

When Anton looked about to punch him in the nose, Heinrich turned his back on them and sauntered down the lane. Anton gritted his teeth and knelt down to see to the dog. He carefully felt the leg. The dog yipped once but lay still.

" 'Tis only a flesh wound. That's why it's bleeding so much. But the bone doesn't seem to be broken."

"Ach, that's good," replied Kati. "He's a fine dog—and just doing his duty."

"Ja," agreed Anton. "Take the babe into your Oma and come help me hold him. I'll have the bullet out in a trice."

Heinrich chuckled to himself all the way down the lane. He had hated Kati ever since the foiled rape many years ago. Serves the bitch right, he thought. Too bad I didn't really kill the brat. Heinrich hated the Bergmann for a number of other reasons. Anton was taking more and more business away from him through no fault of his own—or so he told himself. They were rich and he no longer was. Never mind that he had squandered a large part of his grandfather's wealth. They were happy and he was not. That probably more than anything made him hate them with a passion.

By the time he reached Bruchmühlen Heinrich had worked himself into a fine fettle. He slammed the gun down on the kitchen table instead of putting it in the rack.

"What's eating you?" asked Gerhardina.

"Oh, nothing. Had a little run-in with Anton Bergmann, 'tis all. He ordered me off the property. *My* property."

While Gerhardina always took her son's side, she also knew him very well. And as much as she disliked the Bergmann, she also knew Anton to be a very mild man.

"What did you do to provoke him?" she asked.

"Nothing. Nothing at all."

Gerhardina looked at him askance. She knew her son for a liar. It was something he could not help.

"Well," he admitted. "I was out hunting wolves and shot one of their dogs by accident."

She frowned. "By accident?"

He smirked. "Too bad I didn't hit the brat as well."

"What!" she exclaimed. Gerhardina could condone a lot of her son's foolishness—what she thought of as mischievous pranks—for she, too, was jealous of the Bergmann. "But that would be murder."

"Not if it was an accident."

"Heinrich! Don't you even think such a thing," she cried.

He shrugged.

"No," she said. "I'll not condone murder. There must be some other way to fix them without any blame attached to us. Let me think on it."

"The same way you thought about getting rid of Oma and never did anything about it until they solved the problem for you?" he said sarcastically.

"That was entirely different," she insisted. "I'll think of something. Meantime don't you do anything foolish."

457

He shrugged and went out to the mill.

Johann Justus Bruns rode down from his home on the Heiligenberg. Although he left the major part of the work to his younger brothers, he still made the trip to his shop in Vilsen every day regardless of the weather. But today was a fine spring day and he felt in no hurry. He let his old horse amble along at his own pace. Suddenly, as he passed through the State Forest that bounded the Matthies property, he pulled up the reins and stopped. He had caught something strange out of the corner of his eye. It was a man he was sure. But who would be skulking through the forest like that? Poachers were an occasional problem, to be sure, but rarely in broad daylight. Once in a while Gypsies would find their way back here but they usually were in groups and stuck to the main road. This man acted as though he were up to no good, not wishing to be seen. The woods were still fairly open, the trees not yet in full leaf. Johann Justus watched for a while as the man slipped clandestinely from tree to tree. He was too far away and moving too stealthily to be easily recognized but Johann Justus thought he looked suspiciously like young Heinrich Matthies. He seemed to be watching the Klostermühle. Now why in the world, wondered Johann Justus, would a man be sneaking through the woods next to his own property like a criminal, watching his own mill? Johann Justus shook his head and rode on. Heinrich Matthies, if it was Heinrich, was a strange person.

A few days later Johann Justus observed the same thing. This time he was sure it was Heinrich. He saw him sitting concealed at the edge of the forest, staring so intently at the mill that he never saw Johann Justus. How very odd. Johann Justus was in no hurry. So when he came up to the mill and saw Anton working in the yard, he stopped to pass the time of day.

"Ho, Anton," he called out as he rode into the barnyard. " 'Tis a fine spring day, is it not?"

"Grüss, Johann Justus," replied Anton. "It is that. It's good to see things getting green again. 'Twas a fierce winter. Glad to see it past."

Johann Justus nodded. "And how is your dear little wife and that fine new babe?"

"Very well, both," replied Anton. "And Hermann is not so new any- more. A year and a half and chattering like a magpie."

"And the old mother?"

"As good as can be expected. She enjoys the child although she's not always sure who he is."

"Did you have any trouble with the wolves this winter? There were many who did."

"Nay, we were lucky. They were all about. Could hear them howling many a night. But my dogs are very good. Kept them away."

"That's good. With a young babe like that you can never be too careful." Johann Justus had been wondering how to broach the subject of Heinrich Matthies' strange behavior without directly accusing him of something when Anton gave him the opening.

Anton and Kati had never told anyone but his mother Dorothea about the incident last winter, but Johann Justus was a good friend and could be trusted. "Had a little trouble with Heinrich Matthies, however."

"How so?"

"Claimed he was out hunting wolves. Marched right into the barnyard here and shot one of my dogs. Damn near shot the babe. I almost think he intended to."

"What!" exclaimed Johann Justus in disbelief. "Yet I can't be too surprised. He's a mean bastard—and a strange one. Then I'd better tell you what I've noticed these past days. I wasn't going to mention it but this puts a new light on it."

"And what is that?"

"Do you know he has been skulking about the woods lately acting very strangely? Sometimes he just sits and watches the mill and presumably what you're doing."

Anton blinked. "Now why would he be doing that?"

"I can't imagine but it strikes me as though he's up to no good. You'd better tell your goodwife to keep a sharp watch over that dear babe."

"I shall. And thanks for the warning."

Johann Justus rode on to Vilsen and Anton ran into the kitchen to tell Kati.

"Why, that—that dastardly knave," she said. "What trouble is he going to make for us now?"

"Lord knows but at least we're forewarned."

"Well?" said Gerhardina. "Where have you been this time when you should be working?"

"I was working," said Heinrich.

"Doing what?"

"I—er—was out scouting the woods for possible firewood."

"It's too early for firewood with the spring sap running. And you know it. Hegedorn left several sacks of winter wheat to be milled. He wondered where you were."

"Screw Hegedorn. I'll do them when I get around to it."

"And you'll soon lose him to Bergmann if you don't mend your ways."

"Then I'll threaten to charge him an extra five percent if he dares to move."

"That's stupidity. You'll lose him all the quicker. Listen, I've been thinking."

"You're always thinking."

"Ja, but this time it's a good idea. You know the Bergmann are wealthy—far beyond what he earns at the mill. And you always say that everything that's in the mill and millhouse belongs to you."

"As far as I know," he replied a little doubtfully. "Everything except their clothes and personal belongings, that is."

"I've always heard that Dorothea had a goodly inheritance from her father, old Miller Koch, as well as another from her grandfather Cyriacus Lindemann through her mother Lise. Do you suppose that treasure is still there at the millhouse?"

"How would I know?" snarled Heinrich. "But wait—it might be. Most times when I've gone to collect the rent they had it ready for me on the kitchen table but a few times when they didn't expect me, Kati would go upstairs to fetch it. Why? Do you mean to steal it?"

"Not steal it," objected Gerhardina, "simply claim it as part of your rights to the mill's furnishings."

"That would never work. They'll say it is part of their personal belongings. Don't forget, Anton's uncle is a lawyer and he's good friends with the Meyers in the village. And if you start claiming rights, they'll trace it right to us. I'm not that stupid."

"Then suppose we make it look like an outright theft," she suggested. "The Gypsies are already coming and by summer there'll be many about."

"Nay," said Heinrich. "I'd like to get my hands on some of that money just to spite them. And we could certainly use it. But it's a bad idea."

"Any worse than you trying to kill their child?"

"That was entirely different. Besides it was an accident. I thought the dog was a wolf. Nay, keep thinking, Mother. You'll come up with a better idea."

But Heinrich's greed was overwhelming. He could not get the

thought of that treasure out of his mind. The treasure just lying there, asking to be taken.

Anton had just finished dinner and was returning to the mill when a stranger rode into the yard. It was a hot July day and Anton was looking forward to the mill where at least it would be cool—dusty but cool. But he supposed he might as well be courteous. Mayhap it was someone lost or just seeking a refreshing cup of water. He went out into the yard.

"Ho, Anton. Do you remember me?" asked the rider.

Suddenly Anton recognized him. "If it isn't the lieutenant," he exclaimed. "Ach, how do I call you now?" He laughed.

"Carsten is good enough. Always was. I apologize for never coming to visit all these years. Don't know where the time has gone to. But now I'm getting old I decided it was time to renew old friendships ere it's too late."

"Lord, man, you're not that old," replied Anton.

"Older than you think," said Carsten. "After Moscow, I wanted so badly to defeat the Emperor—er, that is, Napoleon—that I lied about my age when we went to England. As you no doubt recall, they wanted troops so badly they didn't care."

"I do recall."

"Our family—or most of it—has always been blessed with looking younger than our age. As a lad I hated it but now I can see its value. That is, if the old body keeps up with it."

Anton laughed. "Ja, my mother's family is like that, too. And most of them live to a ripe old age. I doubt I'll make it though."

"How is your wound?" asked Carsten. "Still have that bullet in your hide?"

"Still carrying it around with me. But I've heard there are some doctors now with new procedures that can remove a touchy thing like that. There's one such in Lüneburg, I'm told. If I ever have enough money and can find the time, I might go there."

"Ach, I don't trust these doctors with new procedures. If it doesn't bother you, I'd say, leave it alone."

"On a day like this I don't even know it's there, but come rain or in the winter are days when I can hardly breathe or move. I've got a son to think of now."

"Good for you. I've got a grandson and another due in a few weeks," said Carsten. "That's one reason I'm out riding. Good time to stay out of the house. Grandfathers aren't too welcome when the women take over."

461

Anton laughed. "Now what of some of the other lads?" asked Carsten. "Do you see any of them?"

"Ja, from time to time. Gerd graduated from Göttingen and has just been appointed the new schoolmaster here in Vilsen. He starts in the fall. Of Lude I know nothing."

"What of that Bruns fellow who always seemed to be fighting next to you?"

"Harm. He's still working the farm part-time with his brothers but mostly he has been working in Bremen on the docks with Wulf. He's always talking about the people who are emigrating to America—thousands of them. I shouldn't be surprised if he wasn't thinking of going there himself."

"Ach, America. Who would want to go there? Not I," declared Carsten.

"Nor I. But you should hear the tales he tells of those who are going. Nightmare tales of poverty and persecution, especially in Prussia."

"Ach, in Prussia I can believe it. But Hannover seems to be recovering well from the French time. I know our farm is. All it takes is hard work and perseverance."

"Yours might be," replied Anton, "but there are many that are not. I see it here at the mill. And the linen industry—our mainstay here about Vilsen—is suffering from the competition from the huge factories in England. My mother-in-law speaks of it constantly. Our little cottage industries cannot long survive in the face of that."

"I hadn't realized that. We only make enough for our own use. Well, I must let you get back to your work. 'Twas good to see you again, Anton. I promise I'll not stay away so long again."

Anton nodded and Carsten rode off more thoughtful than he had been in a long time.

"It has to be on a Sunday," said Heinrich to Gerhardina.

"Nay, never on Sunday," she exclaimed. Gerhardina was not a very religious person but she still had the ancient dread of mortal sin. Committing a crime on a weekday might be acceptable but perpetrating it on Sunday more than doubled the offense in her opinion. "Why must it be on a Sunday?"

"Sunday morning to be exact," replied Heinrich, "because that's the only day they are both gone. I know. I've been watching them."

"So that's what you've been doing when you should have been

working—spying on them."

"Call it spying, if you will, but we have to know their habits, don't we?"

"I know. But Sunday? Isn't there another possible day?" she asked.

"Nay. She goes to market in Vilsen almost every Saturday but he rarely goes with her. He goes into town for whatever reason every so often but it's too irregular to be counted on. It's only on Sunday that they both go to church together and that not every Sunday."

"Then how would we know?"

"We have to watch and be ready."

"Oh, right. We can be walking along the road here as if we were taking a stroll and as soon as the wagon exits the lane we'll know it's safe."

"Nay, nay, Mother. For one thing they don't use the wagon. He spares that poor old nag he has as much as possible. They walk."

"Then that gives us more time."

"True but when the weather is good as it is now they usually take the shortcut through the woods. We have to be well hidden right up there by the mill watching carefully."

"And what of the child? Do they take him along or no?"

"Sometimes yes and sometimes no. It doesn't matter. He's not yet two. Who would take the word of a babe? We can always shut him in a wardrobe or something."

"Nay! You'll do no harm to the child," exclaimed Gerhardina.

Heinrich shrugged.

"And what of your old Oma Becke?" she asked.

"She's totally blind now from what I can tell. If we're very quiet and don't speak she won't even know we're there much less who it is."

Gerhardina shook her head. "I don't know. It's very risky."

"Not if you do what I say. I have it all planned. You want that money, don't you?"

"Naturally. That should have been ours—or most of it, anyway. We'll need the wagon, won't we? That coffer could be heavy."

"Don't be foolish, Mother. Where would we hide the wagon? Besides we're not taking the coffer. What if anyone saw it here? We'll take a flour sack with us, just remove the coin and leave whatever else there is. Then we'll bury it in the garden for a year or two until everything quiets down."

"A year or two? But—but . . ."

"Mother, use your head," said Heinrich exasperated. "If we suddenly start spending money, it will point right to us. You've done without it all this time. Another year or two won't matter."

"Ja. I suppose you're right," sighed Gerhardina, dreams of a new gown and bonnet flying out the window.

A few weeks later while Heinrich and Gerhardina sat hidden in the woods watching the Klostermühle, Anton and Kati were dressing for church.

"You know, I rather like these new-style trousers," said Anton. "At first I didn't but they're much more confortable than the old breeches. And one doesn't have to worry if one's stockings are falling down."

Kati laughed. "Ja," she agreed, "and I am glad the fuller skirts have come back. Much more graceful and feminine. And those sweet new bonnets—so much prettier than a saucy hat perched atop swept-up hair. A lot easier, too."

"Aren't we just the fashion plate?" Anton teased. "Are we taking Hermann with us today or no? I hoped to show Mama the new tooth."

"I think not," she replied. "He has been so fretful and cranky with cutting those teeth he would disturb the whole congregation. I've put him in his crib. He'll be all right with Oma Becke until we come home. And we could bring your mama back with us for Sunday dinner. She hasn't been for a while."

"Ja, she'd like that."

Arm in arm Anton and Kati ascended the ancient steps up to the shortcut through the woods. As soon as they were out of sight Heinrich whispered to Gerhardina, "Come on. Let's go."

"They didn't take the child," she objected.

"I told you that's no problem," said Heinrich. "Remember, no talking now. Be very quiet."

They crossed the lane and went boldly up to the front door. It was unlocked as they expected. Inside a door to the left led to the mill and a door to the right led into the house. Directly ahead a steep staircase between the two led to the first floor. The door to the parlor stood open and they could see Becke dozing in her rocking chair. Dozing but not asleep.

"Is that you back already? My, that was quick," she called out. "The little one hasn't cried a bit."

Heinrich put a finger to his lips and they crept up the stairs. The ancient steps creaked and groaned under their weight. Damn, thought Heinrich.

"Is that you Kati? Or is it Anton?" Becked called out again. "Who is it?" she demanded. But when no one answered she decided she must have been mistaken and made no move to get up.

"Hurry," whispered Gerhardina.

"Sshh," replied Heinrich.

They reached the top of the stairs and looked about. Heinrich was not sure which room was the main bedchamber. There were several. In one the little boy lay whimpering in his crib. Another appeared to be a girl's room, no doubt left from Anton's sisters. At the far end they finally reached the master's bedchamber. A large chest stood at the foot of the bed. Probably nothing but clothes. But could the coffer be hidden in the bottom?

Heinrich was about to dig into it when Gerhardina whispered, "There." She was pointing to a gaily painted box sitting on the top shelf of a book rack in the corner. It was quite large for a coffer and looked heavy. He was glad he had brought the flour sack. He struggled to lift it down. It *was* heavy. His eyes glinted at the thought of all that money.

"Careful. You'll knock the whole shelf over," warned Gerhardina.

"I told you to hush," growled Heinrich. He knew she wouldn't be able to keep still. The coffer was locked. "Oh, shit," he growled again. "Where is the key?"

"You don't think they were going to leave it for you, do you?" whispered Gerhardina. "You should have thought of that."

"No problem," he replied. "It's a small, simple lock." He took out his pocket knife. He easily splintered the ancient wood and pulled out the lock. "Gott, this thing must be a hundred or more years old," he remarked, forgetting his own prohibition on talking. "Ach, what's this? Nothing but papers."

"Let me see," she said. He handed her a thin paper browned with age. "Look at this," she exclaimed. "1695 it says and Cyriacus Lindemann. That was Dorothea's grandfather, I think. I wonder what all these names mean."

"Never mind. Put it aside." He pulled out another. "The deed to the house in Vilsen and a mortgage paper. I often wondered how they could afford that. Baptismal and confirmation certificates. Marriage certificate. Anton's Master Miller papers. Ah, the testament from my grandfather making him hereditary miller here. How I'd like to burn that but I suppose Master Koch has a copy. But where is the money?"

"Keep digging. It's got to be there," urged Gerhardina.

He flung aside letters and other papers. "Lord, they keep everything. Ah, at last!" Before his eyes at the very bottom of the coffer glinted silver coins—hundreds of them.

"Hurry. I'll hold the sack for you," said Gerhardina, decidedly nervous now.

Heinrich scooped the money into the sack as quickly as he could, but he could not help but admire some of the hoard. "Look, there's even some from the old Empire."

"Never mind. Keep going."

So engrossed were they in their looting that they nearly jumped out of their skins when a tiny voice said, "Bad man. Bad man." Little Hermann stood in the doorway pointing at them and crying, "Bad man. Bad man." He started to approach them but Heinrich knocked him aside with the back of his hand. The little fellow screamed as he fell back but he quickly scrambled to his feet and headed for the stairs.

"Don't hurt the child," cried Gerhardina.

"He's not hurt," retorted Heinrich. "See? Grab him."

But Gerhardina had her hands full holding the flour sack. Little Hermann almost tumbled down the stairs and ran to Oma Becke still crying, "Bad man!"

"Now the fat's in the fire," said Gerhardina. "Have you got it all? Hurry!"

"Most of it." Heinrich quickly tied up the top of the sack and threw it over his shoulder. "Let's go."

Becke was waiting for them at the bottom of the stairs, Hermann in her arms. "Who is that?" she asked. "What are you doing here? It's Heinzi, isn't it? I know it's Heinzi."

Heinrich pushed her aside so that she almost dropped the child as they fled out the door.

Out in the lane Gerhardina gasped breathlessly, "She knew. She knew who it was."

"Nay," said Heinrich, "she said 'Heinzi' and Papa's dead. Besides who would believe a senile old woman?"

But Gerhardina was not so sure. "I know we shouldn't have done this," she said as they hurried down the lane ready to duck into the woods should anyone come. "I should have thought of something else."

"Well, it's too late now," retorted Heinrich. The coins in the sack clinked pleasantly against his shoulder as they ran.

Becke recovered her balance and clutched the child to her. Not for the first time she cursed her blindness and her failing mind. Slowly she made her way back to her rocking chair and comforted little Hermann. I wonder what mischief they were up to, she thought. They think I didn't know who it was. But she knew. She knew.

Back at Bruchmühlen Heinrich slammed the sack on the kitchen table. The tinkle of the coins was music to his ears.

"Go and bury that thing quickly now," urged Gerhardina, holding her hand to her breast as she tried to catch her breath.

"Shouldn't I count it first?" suggested Heinrich. "I'd like to know how much we have."

"Get it out of here," she screeched. "You can count it in a year or two—after I'm gone."

"Mother!" he exclaimed. But he fetched a shovel and did as he was bid.

Some time later Anton and Kati returned home accompanied by Dorothea. They were in a good mood looking forward to a pleasant Sunday afternoon. Becke and Hermann were asleep in her rocking chair, the child cuddled protectively in her arms. Anton and Dorothea tiptoed into the parlor while Kati said, "Just let me run upstairs and change my clothes and I'll have dinner started in a few minutes."

"Isn't that a sweet picture?" whispered Dorothea. "Don't disturb them yet. The teeth will bother him less if he's sleeping."

Suddenly they heard Kati scream. "Anton! Tante Dorchen! Come quick!"

Anton jumped to his feet and ran for the stairs, Dorothea following. "What's amiss, Kati?" he asked.

"We've been robbed!" came the reply.

"Ach, du lieber Gott, no!" cried Dorothea when they saw the mess. It had been her coffer and most of it her money, left here at the Klostermühle for safekeeping. She fell to her knees with tears in her eyes and started sorting through the mess. "Who could have done this?"

Anton was holding a hysterical Kati in his arms. "We failed you, Tante Dorchen. We failed you. You left it with us for safekeeping and we failed you," she wailed.

"Stop that now," replied Dorothea from the floor. "It's not your fault. It could have happened anywhere. But who . . . ?"

"Mayhap Gypsies," suggested Kati, somewhat calmer now.

"I haven't heard that there were any about lately," said Dorothea.

467

Anton had let Kati go and was studying the room. "Nay, it wasn't Gypsies," he said. "Look." He pointed to a line of white on the floor. He knelt down to look at it more closely. "Flour," he announced. "Now who but a miller would have a large flour sack?"

Kati gasped. "Heinrich Matthies. But I can't believe even he would stoop to such a thing."

"I can. Very easily," said Dorothea.

"So can I," agreed Anton. "After he tried to kill my child, I'd believe anything of him. I feared he was planning something else after Johann Justus saw him watching us but I couldn't imagine what it could be."

"Oh, no. But why?" asked Kati.

"Who knows? Jealousy, I suppose," replied Anton. "In his twisted mind that would be reason enough."

"But how can we prove it was he?"

"I don't know. That could be difficult without witnesses," said Anton.

Dorothea had been sorting out the papers scattered about the floor. "Ach," she said holding up the ancient brown paper dated 1695, "God be thanked they didn't destroy this."

"What is that, Tante Dorchen?" asked Kati. "I've often wondered. It's a family history of some sort, isn't it?"

"Ja, my grandfather Cyriacus Lindemann's genealogy and therefore yours, Anton. This may be the means of recouping some of our loss. It has to do with the two family stipendia. I should have explained it to you at the time of your marriage but since we were well enough off, there didn't seem any need. I'll tell you all about it another day. Right now is not the time. Let's get this mess cleaned up. Did he take every penny? I was afraid to look."

Anton looked into the broken coffer. "Just about. There lie two half-groschen and a few pennies in the corner. He must have been interrupted."

Just then little Hermann appeared in the doorway. He ran to Kati. "Mama, Mama," he exclaimed as she embraced him, "bad man hit me, Mama."

"Ach, Gott," swore Anton. "There is your witness and who interrupted him. There's only one person Hermann calls 'bad man' and that is Heinrich Matthies." He went over to his son. "Did the bad man hurt you, baby?"

From the folds of Kati's skirt Hermann shook his head. "Hermann run away to Oma," he peeped.

"Good boy," said Kati soothingly.

"Becke," said Anton. "Do you think she saw—I mean, heard anything?"

"She may have—if she remembers. We can only ask," said Kati.

Dorothea shook her head. What witnesses! A babe not yet two and a blind, senile old woman. Who would believe either one? But she followed them downstairs to question Becke.

The old woman was lucid enough to be shocked when she heard what had happened. "It was Heinzi," she declared. "I know it was. I recognized his voice."

"But, Oma Becke," objected Anton, "Heinzi is long dead."

"No, *his* Heinzi," she insisted.

"She means Heinrich," said Kati explaining. "Even though he didn't like it she always called him Heinzi. *Her* Heinzi was the father and *his* Heinzi is the son."

"Ja," said Becke, "and that woman who was so mean to me. She was with him."

"You mean Gerhardina?"

"Ja, her. And he tried to knock me over when I had the babe in my arms."

"My God, that beast," said Anton incredulously.

"Bad man. Bad man," piped up Hermann.

"Ja, they're all bad," sighed Becke and sank back in her chair, exhausted from the telling.

"We'll have to go to the constable immediately," said Kati.

"On a Sunday?" said Dorothea. "They don't work on Sunday. I'll see Philipp first thing in the morning. He'll know what to do."

"It's a matter for the police," said Anton, "but I'd appreciate it if he went with me."

"Ja," agreed Dorothea, "and Herr Meyer should be willing to help, too. He's my good friend and he's a judge now. But you can't walk all the way to Hoya. Come to our house in the village first thing and we'll all go in my coach."

"But Mama, it isn't necessary for you to go," objected Anton.

"My dear child," said Dorothea deliberately, "you seem to forget—it was *my* money."

Anton blushed to his ears. "Forgive me Mama. I wasn't thinking."

"You were thinking it is unseemly for a woman," said Dorothea. "Let me tell you, dear son, I am more respected in this village than many a man."

Anton had never heard his mother speak so sternly but he knew her well. She was fighting back the tears. "Of course, Mama," he said meekly. "May I ask how much it was? We never touched it."

"I know," she replied. "That's why I trusted you with it. It was 3542 Thaler, five Silbergroschen, two half-groschen and some pennies." She fought back a sob. "Johann Justus made that coffer for me when your papa and I first were wed. And now look at it. Ruined." And then she broke down.

On Monday afternoon, Dorothea, Philipp, Anton, the chief constable and his assistant paid a visit to Heinrich Matthies. Heinrich tried to be polite and nonchalant although he was shaking in his boots. Gerhardina was nowhere to be seen.

"Well, this is quite a delegation," he said as he invited them in. "Something amiss in the neighborhood? Gypsies up to no good again?"

"There have been no Gypsies reported lately," said the chief constable. "Why? Have you seen any?"

"As a matter of fact, I did. Just yes—er, the other day two wagons went by on the road. Have no idea where they might be camped." Ah, this was going to be easy, thought Heinrich. Let the Gypsies take the blame. "Why do you ask?"

"There was a robbery at the Klostermühle yesterday," the chief constable informed him. "A considerable sum of money was taken."

Heinrich feigned surprise. "Ach, that's too bad. I didn't know you kept much money there. Not a good idea."

"It was my money," put in Dorothea. "I assumed it would be safe there."

"So that's why you're here. I wondered." Heinrich was dying to know what his take had been. Should I risk asking? He did. "Was it very much?"

"Quite much," she snapped. "My entire inheritance and dowry— 3542 Thaler."

Heinrich was astonished. He had not expected so great a sum. "I'm sorry to hear it," he mumbled.

"Master Matthies," said the constable, "witnesses have placed you at the scene during the time that Master and Mistress Bergmann were at church."

Philipp could have kicked him. Why give away all their knowledge?

"Witnesses!" exclaimed Heinrich. "There were no—that is, there couldn't have been since I never left the house all day. My mother is ill.

470

She's suffered a mild heart attack and I was by her side the entire day Sunday."

"And did you see anyone—stranger or otherwise in the lane yestermorn?"

"No one at all. I told you I was by my mother's side all day. Scarcely had a chance to even look out the window."

"Then, since you claim to be innocent, you won't mind if we search your house," said the constable.

"What? I have my rights," Heinrich flared. "Under our new constitution you can't . . . "

"I have a warrant here signed by Judge Meyer," the constable interrupted, waving a paper under Heinrich's nose.

"Oh, him." Heinrich glared at Anton. He glared at Dorothea and Philipp. But to the constable he smiled sweetly. "Then search away. You'll find nothing. I promise you."

While the two policeman searched the house from top to bottom, Dorothea took the opportunity to check on Gerhardina. She found her lying in her bed, moaning and clutching her breast. Dorothea could not tell if the 'heart attack' was real or faked.

"Why didn't you send for the doctor or even me?" she asked. "I have a powerful drug that would have checked it immediately."

"Ach," moaned Gerhardina, "who would have come on a Sunday night?"

"It happened last night?"

"Ja, right at suppertime. But it's some better today. I'm sure I'll be all right with a day or two's rest."

So it happened last night, thought Dorothea, hours after the theft. Real or feigned, it had no doubt been brought on by a case of nerves and guilt at what they had done. So much for Heinrich sitting by her bedside all day. "I'm sure you will. Rest is the best thing," said Dorothea and left her.

As they left the millhouse the assistant constable noticed a newly dug place in the garden. "Strange time of year to be digging up your garden," he remarked.

"Ach, a fox I shot last week," said Heinrich. "Stealing my chickens, he was. I buried him there. Must be pretty ripe by now."

Since the assistant constable did not relish exhuming a rotting fox corpse he said nothing to his chief who had not noticed. But Anton did.

Out in the lane they gathered for a moment. "He's lying," said Anton. "I know he is."

471

"How can you be sure?" asked the chief constable. "We searched the whole house and the mill and found nothing."

"The way he started to say 'there were no witnesses' and then amended his statement," said Anton.

"A slip of the tongue, nothing more."

"But," added Dorothea, "Gerhardina—Mistress Matthies—told me she only fell ill last evening around suppertime. She was not in bed all day nor was he by her side. I doubt it's even a heart attack. A bad case of nerves, is more like."

"Only a doctor could know that. Are you a doctor?"

Dorothea gritted her teeth at the constable's thickheadedness.

"Can't you dig up that so-called fox?" asked Anton.

"The warrant only covered the house and the mill," replied the constable officiously. "We can't search every inch of the property. It would take days and I don't have the manpower for that."

"I have a good mind to come back and dig it up myself," said Anton.

"That would be trespassing. Then you'd be in trouble yourself."

"That's correct, I'm afraid," put in Philipp. "And he'd have every right to shoot you."

"No. I'm afraid there's nothing we can do unless the treasure turns up. Or a reliable witness," said the constable.

"But there were two witnesses," objected Anton.

"Ach, a baby barely able to talk and a blind woman." He was kind enough not to add senile. "It was all their imagination, I'm sure. My guess is that it was some vagabond come upon it by accident. You are quite isolated back there, you know."

Anton shook his head. "Nay, it was no stranger. Of that I am sure."

"Master Bergmann," said the chief constable, "I sense there is no love lost between you and Master Matthies. I fear me your prejudice has clouded your judgment. As I say, if you can come up with any hard evidence, just let us know and we shall be happy to pursue the matter further. Until then, I bid you good day."

Anton fumed as the two policemen rode off.

Dorothea sighed, "So much for our vaunted justice system."

Philipp, the lawyer, who had experienced many such frustrations in his career, had to agree. But it was doubly hard when it involved his own loved ones.

Several weeks later on a Sunday afternoon Dorothea said to Anton and Kati, "I think it is time I explained to you about the family stipendia. It is probably too late for you but it could be of help to your son."

Anton and Kati sat down to listen.

"Many, many years ago," she began. It was just like a fairy tale except that it was true. "Back in the fourteen and fifteen hundreds two of my ancestors—your ancestors, Anton—were very wealthy merchants in Celle. One moved from Uelzen to Celle and did very well. The other actually was a very poor orphan who by hard work and perseverance became very wealthy. Both set up foundations to benefit their descendants. The first one—the von Sehnden—paid a stipendium to one descendant per generation in order that he might study at a universtiy for two years. The second—the Stockman—paid a stipendium *every* year to one descendant, either male or female, upon the occasion of their marriage. And after all these hundreds of years they are still paying it."

The young people's eyes flew open in wonderment.

"I didn't know our family came from Celle," said Anton.

"Way back, yes," said Dorothea.

"I never knew you had such illustrious ancestors—and so ancient, too," said Kati. "I thought the Matthies went pretty far back, always bragging about their French blood and Eleonore d'Olbreuse. Well, we won't talk about them now."

Dorothea smiled. "Nay, don't spoil a good story. Anyway, a person had to apply for this stipendium. It was not automatic. They had to be legitimately wed—for the Stockman—and most importantly, they had to prove direct descent from the founders. That was the purpose of this very old genealogy."

She carefully unfolded the ancient brown paper dated 1695 and handed it to them. "Careful. The paper is very fragile. Cyriacus Lindemann whose name is at the top was my grandfather as you know. He could only have been a small child at that time. So it's my belief, although I'm not sure, that *his* grandmother Anna von Sehnden had it written for him ere she died. He was the last one in our line to have received it. My mother never even applied for it since my papa Wilhelm Koch had inherited a goodly sum—which is now gone." Her voice choked up for a minute. She cleared her throat and continued. "For the same reason I never registered you, Anton, or any of my children. It's not too late to do so although don't expect to collect on it. Your brother Johann Heinrich is also interested now that he has a son. I've been very remiss in not putting your names on the list and for that I apologize. But I didn't think we had any need of it.

473

How wrong that has turned out to be. It could be very helpful now."

"Why do you say 'don't expect to collect on it'?" asked Kati.

Dorothea laughed. "Hinrik Stockman had a dozen or more children and each of those . . . You figure out the arithmetic. There are hundreds and hundreds of descendants by now. My grandfather Cyriacus received his payment when he was over thirty-five years wed. They make lists of what they call *exspectans* projected twenty or more years ahead. So the sooner you get your name and that of your son on it the better chance you have."

"Why a person could be dead ere they collected," said Anton, "so why bother?"

"Many do die and then they move the next person up on the list. And you have to be registered first. But believe me, it's worth it."

"How much is the payment?" asked Kati.

"I'm not sure what it amonts to now what with all the currency changes in the last several years. The original payment was twenty Lübeckerthaler. It was equal to more than the average family's annual income at that time. I don't know how Lübeckerthalers translate into Reichsthaler but Reichsthalers are almost the equivalent of Hannover Silbergroschen. It's still a goodly sum."

Anton whistled. "I'll say it is. If the average artisan earns about six pennies a day . . . That's far more than a year's wages for most."

"Indeed it is. So you see why this little paper is so valuable," said Dorothea. "I shall take care of getting copies of all the baptismal and marriage records you need. I shall no doubt drive our old pastor crazy with all that copying but I'll see that the church is well paid for his effort. Then we'll send it all to Celle. To Uelzen, too. Might as well try for both."

Kati marvelled at how Dorothea could be so cheerful in the face of their terrible loss. It seemed as though Dorothea was always coming to the rescue. Might as well give her some more news.

"We'll soon have another to register besides Hermann," announced Kati. "I am with child again."

Anton rushed to embrace her. "Why didn't you tell me?" he said.

"I was going to but this seemed to be the right occasion," she said.

Dorothea smiled at their happiness. The Lord taketh away but He also giveth, she thought.

15

1831

The economy of Hannover was very slowly improving. There had been a few good harvests and the recent winters had not been so severe. Food that had not been seen in twenty-five years was gradually appearing on tables. The famous Hannover stud had recovered and was breeding well, enabling those who could afford it transportation and plow-horses at more reasonable prices. The flax fields dotted the landscape with their heavenly blue flowers and the linen trade, despite the competition from England, had found a new customer, surprisingly, their old enemy France. Although the French economy still lagged the rest of Europe after the depredations of the Napoleonic era, those who could afford it, a growing number, preferred the fine handwoven linen of Hannover to the factory made cloth of England. Everything pointed to better times.

But then a dark cloud fell over Europe and spread rapidly. No one knew where it came from. Was it from the air they breathed or did it rise like a miasma from the ground beneath them? Some said it was even because some dead creatures had been found in the Sacred Spring which flowed into the millpond and thence into the Eyter Brook, the source of most of Vilsen's water. But that did not seem likely since it struck indiscriminately, although those few with deep wells seemed to suffer less. The most probable source of blame fell on the Gypsies, the perennial scapegoats in any kind of disaster. Surely they brought it with them from somewhere else because they were known to be filthy, lazy and untrustworthy. But wherever it came from the disease struck young and old, rich and poor, men and women. After three days of agony, most died quickly. Very few survived. The name of the beast was cholera.

Anton and Kati now had four children. After Hermann, they were all girls—Hanne born 1825, Friedrike born 1827 and Dorothea, less than a year old. They hoped that their relative isolation at the Klostermühle would protect them from the epidemic. Kati would not let the children stray too far from home and she herself avoided going into Vilsen. But the farmers still came with their grain to be milled and Anton himself occasionally went into the village for supplies. Then one of the Bruns brothers announced that an old uncle had contracted the disease and even now lay dying. Kati made Anton scrub his hands thoroughly after handling their grain. She even washed all his clothes although it was not laundry day.

Not long thereafter Kati was nursing Kleine Dorchen but the baby would not suck. She was whimpering and fretful and seemed to be developing a fever. At last Kati gave up and laid her in her cradle. She put cool cloths on her forehead and tried to get her to swallow one of Dorothea's possets but the baby only threw it up. Kati was frantic. Was is just a colic or was it the dread sickness that was sweeping the country? Should she send for Dorothea or not? She hated to bother her. She was so busy tending the desperately ill. But her own grandchild? At last the baby fell into a fitful sleep although she still felt feverish. Kati decided to wait until morning. Simple fevers usually broke by morning. Mayhap Kleine Dorchen was just cutting a tooth.

By the next morning Kati knew it was not a tooth. The poor baby's body was burning up with a raging fever and the watery flux had begun. Her little cradle was soaked with it. Kati sent Anton for his mother. She worked diligently to clean up the mess but the violent diarrhea kept flowing out of the tiny body. She wrapped her in cool cloths but the fever only rose higher. She tried to force liquids down the baby's throat. They said that was the best. But the infant regurgitated it immediately. Every place Kati touched the child seemed to give her pain and at first she cried to the point of exhaustion. But then she sank into a whimpering torpor. Kati knew even before Dorothea arrived that she was going to lose her youngest.

Dorothea came almost immediately, riding pillion behind Anton. She stood by the little cradle shaking her head. She tried everything but this time even her most efficacious possets were to no avail.

"I'm afraid," she said, "I'm afraid it's too late. We are going to lose her." She took Kati in her arms.

"I should have called you last night," wept Kati.

"It wouldn't have mattered," said Dorothea. "Once it takes hold there is nothing anyone can do except pray. It is the worst with the very youngest and the very old but also the quickest. Thank God at least that she won't suffer long."

"Mama, Mama," said a little voice, "what's wrong with Baby

Dorchen? Is she sick? Can we help?" Hanne and Friedrike were standing in the doorway.

"Keep the children away from her," warned Dorothea.

"Go away. Stay away," screeched an overwrought Kati. "Ja, she's sick. Get out of here fast and don't come back."

Hanne took Friede by the hand and the two little girls fled.

Hanne took it in stride. Nothing seemed to bother her overly much. But Friedrike was more sensitive. And she had never seen her sweet mother in a fit of temper before. She started to cry. Hermann was waiting for them in the kitchen. From the lofty height of his eight years he tried to take command and comfort his little sisters. He put his arm around Friede and let her cry for a moment.

"Friede, Friede," he said consolingly. "She's not angry with you. Probably not angry with anyone. She's just upset that Kleine Dorchen is so sick."

"But she said 'Don't come back'," sobbed Friede. "Where can we go, Harm?"

"Ach, she didn't mean go away from our home," he replied. "She just meant stay away from Dorchen so you won't catch it. You don't want to catch it, do you?" Friede shook her head. "People are dying all over the country."

"How do you know that?" asked Hanne.

"Papa said so," declared Hermann.

"Is Dorchen going to die?" asked Hanne.

"I don't know. She could," stated Hermann profoundly.

Friedrike started crying again. "Am I going to die?" she asked bewildered.

"Nay, you won't die," Hermann assured her. "Not if you obey Mama and stay away from Dorchen."

"Now you've frightened her, you big know-it-all," scolded Hanne. "I'm hungry. What are we going to do for dinner?"

"I don't know. Here comes Papa," said Hermann.

But Anton ignored them and went directly up the stairs. "How is she?" he asked the women.

Dorothea shook her head.

"She's dying," sobbed Kati. "My baby is dying. Dear God, how could this happen?"

Anton had no answer. He had never seen his strong Kati so completely broken.

477

Little Dorchen died the next day. Dorothea tried her best to comfort Kati. Anton was at a loss to know what to do.

"I suppose I'd better notify Pastor," he said.

"Ja, you must," said Dorothea, "but there's no hurry. He is overwhelmed right now."

"But the funeral?" asked Anton.

Dorothea shook her head. "They won't let you bury her in the chruchyard anyway."

"Whyever not?" asked Kati.

"They're not allowing any of the cholera victims to be buried there. There are so many of them. They have opened a mass grave out on the moor. Pastor has blessed the ground but they just dump them in. No stones, no markers, no flowers."

"How horrible," said Kati.

"Ja, you would do better to bury her right here. Then you'll always have her with you. I'll see to it that Pastor comes if I have to bring him myself."

Kati looked at her husband through her tears. "Anton?"

"I think Mama's right. I'll go out and dig a grave immediately," he said, glad of something physical to do.

"Go and tell Pastor first," said Dorothea. "The ground must be consecrated. I'll see to the laying-out. And Kati dear, remember you have three other children who are lost and bewildered and wondering what has happened. They need you now more than this one."

The cholera epidemic claimed dozens in the village, thousands in the country, many thousands throughout Europe. Johann Justus Bruns succumbed as did his half-brother Johann Hinrick and some of their children. Johann Justus bequeathed the house on Gartenweg to his nephew and godson Johann Justus.

"I shall miss him terribly," sighed Dorothea. "He was a good friend."

"The very best," agreed a tearful Eleonore. "I should have married him instead of either of my husbands." Her Fritzi had been one of the victims yet she seemed to mourn him not at all.

Dorothea smiled ruefully. "I could have but I loved my Chris more."

Dorothea herself was bereft not only of her granddaughter but also of her eldest son. Johann Heinrich, Anton's brother, came down with the dread illness a few months later and died an agonizing death. He left to Dorothea's able care his widow Friederike and three small children.

Gerhardina Matthies succumbed as did two of her younger children. Heinrich, who had finally wed a girl named Adelheit from Uenzen in 1828, survived but lost his first two babies.

"Serves him right," remarked Anton. "It's their just punishment, well deserved."

"Don't say that," cautioned Kati. "It will bring bad luck."

Out in the country the farming branch of the Bruns family lost several including Anton's friend Harm.

"Ach, what a pity," said Anton, "to have survived those terrible battles and then to go like this. He was a good man. I shall miss him."

"It was God's will," said a resigned Kati.

"Ach, it's no wonder," said others, "they were so poor. But such good people. It's a shame."

Even old Carsten Campsheide fell to the dread disease.

"You see," said Anton, "even great wealth is no protection."

"Mayhap," said Kati, "but I'd rather have some of our wealth back. Much good it did the Matthies—or whoever stole it."

Kati had changed a lot in the last few years. The bitterness at the cruel blow of fate in the theft of Dorothea's inheritance never really left her. Old Becke had died peacefully in her sleep back in 1827 and the relief of being free of that increasingly onerous burden should have cheered her. But it did not. One of Becke's last coherent statements had been, "I know it was Heinzi," which left Kati with an additional feeling of guilt which she knew in her heart was unwarranted. But it was there just the same. Other than Hermann none of her children remembered Becke, which was just as well since the old woman had become so mean-spirited and abhorrent towards the end.

Kati should have rejoiced in her children but the overwhelming happiness at her first one was just not there for the others. She loved them as much as she was was capable, but it seemed as though the bright light of her spirit had been extinguished at the death of her youngest. The children, of course, were not aware of this. They had never known her to be otherwise. To them she seemed sweet, kind, ostensibly loving if somewhat stern—but distant. It was no wonder little Friedrike was so sensitive, longing for warmth that was not there. Hanne reminded Kati of her mother Eleonore. Events, both great and small, washed over her like water off a duck's back. Yet she was a secretive child. One never knew what she was thinking. Kati hoped she would not turn out like Eleonore. That was the road to unhappiness. Hermann was becoming too mature for his eight years. Although unwarranted, he seemed to feel he had to take responsibility for his younger sisters, as though he sensed that his mother was not quite able to give them the love they needed. He was a bright child doing very well in school. He seemed to enjoy learning but he never spoke of it with either the delight or dislike that most young children showed.

Kati was only vaguely aware of all this. Her children were healthy, well-behaved, highly intelligent and loving. What more could a mother want—or do? So she was content to let things drift. Her perennial cough had gotten much worse since the baby's death. And she felt so tired all the time. So very tired.

Anton, always busy at the mill, was totally unaware of his children's emotional needs. He loved them dearly and was very proud of them. He sometimes played with them on the long summer evenings or during the winter but he sensed nothing amiss. He assumed that their mother was supplying all their needs—food, clothing, even story-telling. It simply never occurred to him that they, so young yet, would have any needs other than physical.

He was, however, very aware of the change in Kati and did not know what to do about it. Whenever he asked, she would say she was just fine, just a little tired at the moment. He would liked to have had more children but Kati failed to conceive. Even their lovemaking had lost its bright luster. She never refused his overtures but the spark seemed to be gone. He was concerned enough to mention it to his mother Dorothea.

"Perhaps she's coming early into the change," suggested Dorothea. "It happens to some women, you know."

"Do you think that might be it?" he asked, slightly embarrassed at having to speak of 'female things'. But his mother was a healer. She would know.

"It could be," she replied. "I don't see anything wrong with her except that wracking cough which, admittedly, has gotten worse. Even my strongest potions only seem to ease it temporarily. But she's had that most of her life so I shouldn't worry. In any case give her lots of loving care. A woman needs that at that time in her life."

"I always do, Mama. Oh, Lord, I don't want to lose her."

"You won't."

But even wise Dorothea was not always right.

Several months later on one of the bleakest days of winter Kati suffered an especially violent coughing spell. She looked in horror at the bright red staining her handkerchief. She quickly hid the offending cloth from sight and told no one, not even Anton.

Eleonore was wondering what to do with her life. After the cholera had taken Fritzi and her youngest child, she had tried—really tried—to run the business by herself. But it was impossible. Even his contribution, small as it had been, had been enough to keep things going. And they even had started to prosper again. But no way could she make all those trips to their factors in Bremen and Hannover and beyond and still oversee the weavers here in Vilsen much less take care of the bookkeeping and correspondence.

Eleonore was sixty years old and tired. At first she thought to hire some younger people but there was no one she felt she could really trust. So she made the heartbreaking decision to sell the business. She was still the able businesswoman and skillfully maneuvered the bidders into stiff competition. One Herr Tiensch, a former mayor of Hoya and a Vilsen merchant, offered the best price and she shrewdly lured him into renting an apartment in a house the Hohnholz had owned for many years as well.

This together with investing some of the money assured her a small but steady income. Then a very satisfied Eleonore splurged with the balance. She bought a beautiful matched pair of gray horses and refurbished the family coach which had not seen a horse since the middle of the French time. And she gorged herself on food—long longed-for delicacies which were slowly becoming available for those who could afford them. She even considered taking in boarders. The big Hohnholz house seemed empty now with only her, her second daughter Dorothea, who had become an avowed spinster, and the old cook-housekeeper rattling around in it. There were always young journeymen in various trades in need of accommodations. Eleonore longed for youthful company again.

Then one day Eleonore looked in her mirror and was aghast. She was getting fat just as her mother Becke had. She quickly dismissed the idea of taking in boarders—young men who would laugh at her instead of wanting to sleep with her. She also stopped eating all the rich food and confined herself to a breakfast of coffee and a roll, a sparse dinner and almost no supper. The weight fell off rapidly but then she was tired. Eleonore attributed it to boredom.

Oh, yes, she was bored. She missed the business. She had never enjoyed the Kaffee-klatches of the women, none of whom trusted her. She had regarded men as mere playthings to be lured into bed, nothing more. Thus she had no real friends.

481

Suddenly it occurred to her that she had three lovely grandchildren whom she rarely saw. There was the youth she so desperately needed. And Kati, the daughter she had always claimed as her favorite. How she had neglected her. So Eleonore took the old coach and the beautiful horses and began making frequent, impromptu visits to the Klostermühle.

"Mama, you look so well," said Kati. "You've lost a lot of weight."

"Thank you, my dear," said Eleonore. "I simply had to. I was getting to look just like my own dear mother and I certainly didn't want that."

"But she became quite thin towards the end. It was because she wasn't eating right. Are you eating well?"

"As much as I want. Although I do feel a bit tired at times. But I'm sure that will pass."

"And your cheeks are so pink. Is that real or rouge?"

"It is real. I don't use rouge anymore. I thought at first I was a bit feverish but now I'm used to it. Do you think the children would like to go for a ride in the coach? I noticed young Hermann admiring my new grays. Aren't they beautiful?" asked Eleonore.

"Indeed, they are," agreed Kati, "and I'm sure the children would enjoy it. Just be sure to have them back in time for supper."

"I shall. I promise."

These coach rides quickly turned into almost weekly excursions during the summer of 1832. Although Eleonore faithfully returned the children before supper, they seldom had appetite for the evening meal because she invariably stopped during the coffee hour at a coffee house or a pastry shop and let them eat their fill of the richest treats they could choose. Kati became concerned.

"Mama," she said, "please don't let them stuff themselves at coffeetime. They are not eating their supper."

"Ach, it won't hurt them to miss a meal once in a while," replied Eleonore. "They enjoy it so, picking out all those delicious cakes and pastries. I wish I had had that opportunity when I was their age."

And because Kati knew of her mother's very unhappy childhood, she indulged her. Also because she felt the children deserved a little excitement now and then and she herself was getting more and more tired so that she barely had time for them.

In the fall the problem partially resolved itself. Hermann had to return to school and Hanne was just starting, leaving little Friedrike home alone with Kati. So the coach rides were limited to Sunday afternoons. Then Anton objected.

"It's the only time I have to spend with my children," he said. "And she is monopolizing them. Even my own mother doesn't see them very much anymore. And she needs a break from caring for my brother's three. *They* don't get to ride all over the countryside in a coach."

So Kati had to limit the excursions with Eleonore to once a month. The children did not seem to mind too much. Although Hermann enjoyed hearing his Oma Elli's tales, much elaborated upon, of the French Time, the two little girls seemed to prefer their Oma Dorchen's company.

"I like when she tells us the old fairy tales," said Hanne.

"And she loves us more," chimed in Friedrike.

"She does? How do you know that?" asked Kati.

"Because she hugs us and cuddles us," said Friedrike. "She's warm."

"I see." Kati considered that for a while. Admittedly Eleonore was not a warm person. She was too self-centered. Kati felt sorry for her although she would never let her mother know that.

One day in December after the St. Nikolaus holiday Eleonore arrived early at the Klostermühle and announced that she was going to take the children to see all the prettily decorated shop windows. By this time she had decided she was too tired to drive the coach herself. Besides the weather was too cold to be sitting outside on the driver's seat. Thus she had the groom, whom she had hired when she purchased the horses, drive them so that she could sit inside the coach with the children.

"But Hermann and Hanne see the shops everyday when they go to school," objected Kati. "Only Friede has not seen them. The others will be bored."

"I'm aware of that," replied Eleonore. "I am going to take them to Hoya where there are many, many more shops. Even the streets are decorated."

"But the shops are not open on Sunday."

"Ach, we're not going to buy anything—just look."

Kati sighed. "Very well but Hoya is a long ways and it gets dark so early this time of year."

"I'll have them back before dark. You worry too much, Kati."

So off they went all bundled up against the cold for it was a raw day threatening snow. They stopped briefly in Vilsen to let Friede see the pretty shop widows. It was so blustery that even after the short few-block walk Eleonore was shivering uncontrollably.

"Hurry, children. Let us get back into the coach out of this wind," she urged through chattering teeth.

Back in the coach she sat in the middle with Hanne on one side and Friedrike on the other. Hermann sat on the seat opposite.

"Oma, you're shivering," said Hanne.

"I'll be all right in a few minutes with two warm little girls beside me." But she was gasping for breath.

The coach drove off. Barely were they halfway through Bruchhausen when Eleonore suffered a violent coughing spell, so much so that she did not have time to pull her handkerchief from her reticule before a bright shower of blood splattered all over her gown and Hanne's clean white apron. The frightened little girl tried to mop it up with her own handkerchief which she then put back in her pocket.

"Oma, are you sick?" she cried. But Eleonore lay back and could not answer.

Hermann had the presence of mind to rap on the coach roof. The vehicle stopped, the groom climbed down and opened the door. "Yes, Madame?" He quickly backed off when he saw the blood.

"Oma is sick," said Hermann. "I think we should take her home."

The groom looked hesitantly at Eleonore, who simply nodded. She still had no breath to speak. He turned the coach around and drove to the Hohnholz house. He opened the door but was afraid to touch his mistress to help her. Eleonore stumbled down the steps by herself. By this time she had recovered somewhat.

"Will the children be coming in with you, Madame?" asked the groom.

"No, no, take them back to Heiligenberg," she whispered. "And say nothing of this to anyone. I'll be all right after a little rest. 'Tis only this cold wind brought it on." And to the children she said, "I am so sorry, dear ones. We'll go again in a few days." She haltingly made her way into the house and the groom drove the children back to the Klostermühle.

Hanne was crying. "Mama will be angry with me. It is my Sunday-best apron."

"No, she won't, silly," said Hermann. "It wasn't your fault. Oma Elli is sick."

"But she said not to tell anyone," wept Hanne.

"She didn't mean Mama. Mama will wash it for you and it'll be as good as new. Now blow your nose and dry your tears. We're almost home."

"Is Oma going to die?" piped up Friedrike, who had been terrified at all the blood.

"No, of course not," replied Hermann. "It was just the cold wind."

Hanne blew her nose into her blood-stained handkerchief and tried to wipe more of the blood off her apron. She was still determined not to let Kati see the damage. She would wash the offending garment herself. But it was not to be.

Kati was in the barnyard feeding the chickens when the coach arrived. So surprised to see them home so early, she ran to the coach to meet them. "Whatever is amiss?" she cried. "You're home so soon. Where is Oma?"

"Oma got sick from the cold wind and we had to take her home," explained Hermann.

Then Kati saw Hanne's apron. "Hanni, whatever happened? Is that your blood?"

Hanne burst into tears and shook her head. "Oma—Oma coughed and coughed and—and it came out all bloody. I'm sorry, Mama. I'll wash it myself."

"Don't be silly, Hanni," said Kati. "It's not your fault. Let's get you into the house quickly and get that foul thing off." Kati was so concerned with Hanne that she did not even notice that little Friedrike was sobbing woefully. It was up to Hermann to comfort his sister.

A few days later Kati made the effort to go into Vilsen to see her mother. Eleonore was still in bed although seemingly much recovered from her attack.

"Have you seen the doctor, Mama?" asked Kati.

Eleonore shook her head. "What's the use? I know what it is. Stay away from me."

"Nay, Mama, I shan't. You see, I have it, too."

"What?!" Eleonore almost flew out of the bed. The two women embraced and wept on each other's shoulder. "How long have you known?" asked Eleonore at last.

"I don't know. Almost a year, I should guess," replied Kati. "I haven't told anyone up to now, not even Anton. And you?"

"About six months, I think. It's hard to tell. Oh, if it were only summertime," moaned Eleonore, "we could go to the mountains and rest. The doctors say there is no cure but I have heard that the clear mountain air cures a lot of people."

"That's as may be," said Kati sadly, "but it's the depth of winter now. We could not even get to the mountains for the snow. Besides I have heard that the cure, if any, can take months—even years. I can't leave the children that long."

"Then you'd better tell Anton. He deserves to know."

"I suppose you're right," admitted Kati, "but after the New Year. I don't want to spoil their Christmas."

Another of the horrendous aftermaths of the French Time was rapidly spreading across the country. It was more insidious than the cholera. People were infected months—even years—before they were aware of having contracted the disease. It struck indiscriminately, young and old alike. It seemed to have been brought from somewhere by the war veterans—those who had fought across Europe from Russia to Waterloo. It appeared first among the wounded—those already weakened by their injuries. Subsequent starvation and severe winters without adequate firewood did the rest. It was highly contagious and spread quickly through the general population. The doctors called it tuberculosis; the people called it consumption, for, just as a fire could consume the heart out of a log without showing a flame until the entire log collapsed, so it was with the afflicted. Outwardly they seemed healthy until close to the end.

The year 1833 was a tragic one for the little family at the Klostermühle. Little Hanne was the first to succumb in June. Kati was already too weak to care for her. Steadfast Dorothea was there for them both, always careful to scrub herself diligently and change her clothes lest she carry the germ back to the already half-orphaned children at the spice shop. They buried Hanne beneath the apple trees at Heiligenberg next to her baby sister Dorchen.

Eleonore went in July. Kati was too far gone to attend her mother's funeral. Anton and Hermann were there as was Dorothea and a few of the Bruns. Not one Matthies saw fit to come to their aunt's funeral, although Eleonore's sister Adelheit came all the way from Westen.

By the beginning of August Kati was delirious with fever and struggling from the incessant bloody cough. All Dorothea could do was give her potions to ease the stress of the coughing. She devoted most of her time to consoling the two remaining children. On the 11 August after a particularly bad spell Kati left them. Few friends were left to come to the funeral but to everyone's surprise, Adelheit, Heinrich Matthies' wife, showed up. She had grown to like Kati even though her husband had discouraged much social contact. Adelheit did not know the background of the enmity between the two families and was surprised when Heinrich seemed to gloat over Kati's death. She felt she should do something to heal the breach.

Dorothea promptly whisked Hermann and Friedrike off to the Bergmann house in Vilsen, there to live with their cousins, Johann Heinrich's children. She felt it was no time to leave the bereft children to fend for themselves with a grieving father who was already neglecting them as well as his business. She religiously took them back to the Klostermühle every Saturday afternoon and Sunday to try and cheer Anton up. But it seemed to be a losing battle.

Anton's work was slipping. Not in quality. He was still the finest and most honest miller thereabouts. But often the farmers had to wait days and days for their flour. At first people attributed it to his great grief and were tolerant. What Anton mentioned to no one was that the bullet in his side was becoming more and more painful making it almost impossible to lift the heavy sacks of grain and flour. Whether this was due to the severe emotional blows of the past few years or would have happened anyway, he did not know. But very gradually he began losing his customers to Heinrich Matthies.

Hearing the rumors, Gerd Meyer, his last living wartime companion, came to visit him. Outside of the family Gerd was one of the few who knew about his wound.

"Anton, you've got to try and pull yourself together," said Gerd. "I know you've got a lot to grieve over but your children need you."

"I know, Gerd, and I appreciate your concern," replied Anton, "but I feel they are better off with my mother and sister-in-law than with me. I don't know how much longer I'll be around."

"How so? Is it the bullet acting up?"

Anton nodded. "Sometimes the pain is so bad I can't work at all. I fear me the damn thing is going to move to my heart any day."

"I have heard there is a doctor in Lüneburg who is able to remove them from such a—a delicate position."

"I've heard that, too, but that will cost money which I no longer have."

Gerd thought a moment. "Let me speak to my father. He knows every judge in Lüneburg. Surely one of them must know this doctor."

"I'd appreciate that, but not yet. I want to start Hermann on his apprenticeship even though he's a bit young yet."

"Hermann does not want to be a miller," said Gerd.

"He doesn't?" said Anton, surprised. "He's never told me that."

487

"Sometimes children tell their teachers things they are afraid to admit to their fathers. He would like to be a doctor and I believe your mother is encouraging that after all the sickness they have seen."

"A doctor!" exclaimed Anton. "But that will take a lot of money, too. He'd first have to go to the gymnasium and then university."

"If he's determined enough, funds will be found. But he's young yet. Give him time. He may change his mind."

1837 In England King George IV had died in 1830 and was succeeded by his brother William IV. The third son of George III, Edward, Duke of Kent, had died some years prior leaving a young daughter Victoria. The fourth son was the redoubtable, extremely reactionary Ernst August who felt that he should be the next king. However, when William died in 1837, English parliamentary law was very clear on the subject and Victoria was awarded the throne. Ernst August was livid and rumor had it that he even plotted to do away with his niece. As a sop (and no doubt to get him out of England) he was handed the Kingdom of Hannover because the old Salic law prohibited a female from reigning in Hannover.

In general the people of Hannover welcomed the dissolution of the 123-year bond with England hoping it would give the country a chance to develop on its own. However, very few relished the idea of having Ernst August as their king. His unsavory reputation as an alleged murderer and womanizer preceded him. His violent temper was well known. His close personal and military ties to Prussia were mistrusted. And above all, all but a few archconservatives feared his reactionary politics. People had grown to love his younger brother Alfred, Duke of Cambridge, the easy-going and do-nothing viceroy, and were sorry to see him leave. Even the extremely conservative Graf von Münster preferred the malleable Alfred to Ernst August who was stubborn and refused to listen to anyone's advice.

Ernst August arrived in Hannover on 28 June. He was accorded a royal if somewhat insincere welcome by the mayor Rumann. The very same evening he met with the opposition leader of the conservative nobility, Georg von Schele. Within days he prorogued Parliament and on 5 July ordered the repeal of the constitution, claiming it was not compatible with his views. Von Schele was made Minister of State.

Immediately seven professors at Göttingen, citing their oath—and presumably the King's—to uphold the constitution, strenuously objected. Among them were historian and public law specialist Friedrich Dahlmann, who had written much of the constitution, and the brothers

Jacob and Wilhelm Grimm. Quickly known as 'the Göttingen Seven', these brave men risked their professional lives to speak out against what they considered the reprehensible and illegal acts of Ernst August. The King retaliated by dismissing all seven from their posts and ordered Dahlmann, Jacob Grimm and Gervinus into exile. The rest left Hannover soon thereafter.

While the majority of the populace at first passively accepted the actions of the king, the dismissal of the Göttingen Seven aroused a firestorm of protest which quickly spilled over the borders of Hannover to all the constitutional states of the Confederation. Only the two largest and most reactionary, Prussia and Austria, backed the king but that was enough to enable him to refute and forbid any motions the Parliament tried to make.

"This is absolutely outrageous," said Dorothea to the elder Herr Meyer.

"Agreed," said the old judge, "but one must be careful to whom one expresses one's opinion — especially someone in my position."

"I understand. Do you think there will be more dismissals at Göttingen? Philipp tells me there are several other professors trying to plead the case of 'the Seven' before the King's ministers."

"I don't know. It's hard to say. The latest rumor is that the King intends to shut down the University entirely."

Dorothea gasped. "How can he do that? It's the finest university in Germany."

"Very easily, I'm afraid. The government pays the faculty's salaries. But it may not come to pass. Most of the other universities — Heidelberg, Jena, Tübingen, to name a few — have objected strongly to Ernst August's action. Most except those in Prussia, that is. In addition many of the governments of the constitutional states — Baden, Bavaria, Saxony, Hesse, among others — have condemned the King. Although that doesn't seem to bother him a bit."

"Then there is hope that he may relent?"

Meyer shook his head. "I doubt it. He is very stubborn and will never admit when he's wrong. To make matters worse, the Queen, Friederike, has now arrived and they have gone to Karlsbad, ostensibly to take the cure, but everyone knows he has gone there to meet with Metternich. If that old tyrant convinces him to enforce the Karlsbad Decrees, which are largely ignored here in Hannover thanks to England's influence, then we shall have policemen on every corner and a conversation such as this could not be held in public."

"Ach, how horrible. Do you really think it will come to that?"

Meyer thought for a moment. "Nay, not quite that bad," he said thoughtfully. "There is a strong opposition movement under the leadership of the young Bürgermeister Stüve of Osnabrück. It will be difficult for a while since Ernst August has taken away the freedom of the press but they are speaking out all over the country. Poor Rumann was suspended, as you may know, and the Appeals Court in Celle *had* to find him guilty but the fine was so light as to be negligible and he is still speaking out."

Dorothea sighed. "I wish there were some way to help those professors—brilliant men deprived of their livelihoods and honor just for refusing to break their oath."

"Their livelihoods, yes, but not their honor. Other universities are clamoring for them. It is Hannover's loss not theirs. And there *is* a way to help. I have heard that funds are being donated by people all over to help pay their salaries until they find other positions."

"Philipp mentioned something about that. Do you think we could start such a collection here in Vilsen? I should especially like to help the Grimm brothers, particularly Wilhelm who is in poor health and has a wife and children. He came to the Klostermühle years ago collecting their wonderful stories. A fine young man. And our dear Kati worked for them both before she and Anton were wed."

"I know and we certainly can start such a fund. I should be happy to contribute although I, understandably, cannot be an obvious part of it."

"But I could," declared Dorothea. "I have no office or tenure to be deprived of. I am simply a private citizen trying to right a terrible wrong. And I know almost everyone in Vilsen and the country roundabout. They'll give. I'll make them."

Meyer smiled. "That is the spirit that makes Hannover great. But be careful, Dorchen, and remember someone has to get the money to them. Are you capable of that?"

"Philipp would go. He has known them longer than I and he is no longer actively practicing law due to ill health. And Hesse is not so far."

"Wilhelm we know has returned to Hesse but rumor has it that Jacob has gone to London."

"Then for Wilhelm it shall be."

So Dorothea began her campaign to help Wilhelm Grimm, begging, cajoling, intimidating, even threatening. Most contributed willingly as they were able, a few reluctantly. She used the political argument on the younger ones; to the elders, she reminded them how much their children and grandchildren loved the brothers' fairy tales. Gerd Meyer enlisted the schoolchildren to help. Although not one child had a single penny of their own, many were able to influence their parents. For the littlest ones he used the story of Mother Holle who rewarded the good sister with a shower of gold and the wicked sisters with a shower of ashes. For the older ones he carefully explained the meaning of the Goose that laid the Golden Egg.

Dorothea drove out through the surrounding countryside. Many of the farmers were still poor and some did not really understand but when she explained that they had suddenly lost their new and hard-won vote so painstakingly included in the revised constitution of 1833, they were almost ready to take up arms and willingly gave what they could. Her Anton, she knew, gave far more than he could afford. The only outright refusal she had was from Heinrich Matthies.

"Why should I support that bunch of radicals?" he grumbled. "It's time we had a strong arm here just like in Prussia."

"You seem to be the only one that favors Prussia," she retorted. "If she ever takes over the rest of Germany as she'd like and everyone else prays will not come about, I fear you will live to regret it. I bid you good day."

Heinrich shrugged and Dorothea picked up her skirts and flounced out of the millhouse.

Adelheit followed her out onto the garden. Dorothea felt sorry for Adelheit, a small, timid creature who always seemed to have bruises on her arms and probably elsewhere.

When they reached the gate Adelheit whispered, "Sometimes I don't understand him, but I feel sorry for those poor professors just standing up for their rights. Here take this." She dug into her apron pocket and came up with a half-groschen and a few pennies. "I always keep a little back from the household money. He's so miserly."

"Thank you, Adi," replied Dorothea. "I'll pray for you." She entered her coach and drove away wondering how so wealthy a man could be so stingy for she knew well that he had not yet spent a penny of the treasure he had stolen from her. She had been watching.

Philipp agreed to take the money to Wilhelm Grimm at Marburg in Hesse. Her brother was getting so frail that Dorothea insisted he take her coach rather than ride. Although the people of Vilsen had been more than generous the sum did not amount to much as the village was small and the country people were still struggling to recover from the French time. But

491

it might be enough to buy a few weeks' bread and milk for his children or pay a part of his rent. Wilhelm sent back with Philipp a gracious note thanking her profusely and advising that he and his brother had not yet decided which offer to accept but were seriously considering the Royal Academy of Sciences in Prussia. Good heavens, she thought, Prussia of all places.

Johann Justus Bruns tramped through the streets of Celle along with a hundred or more other young men and even a few women. They waved flags; they sang patriotic songs; and they chanted 'Freiheit—Freedom, Freedom'. Johann Justus had just completed his apprenticeship with Master Pewtermaker Meinecke and was now considering where to spend his journey years. The first few with the master, of course, if he would have him but then he would like to go to other masters in other cities to broaden his knowledge. Each town specialized in designs and decorations unique to itself and Johann Justus wanted to learn as many styles as he could.

Meanwhile the young men of Celle—students, apprentices, journeymen, artisans of all trades—were protesting in favor of the 'Göttingen Seven' and their lost constitution. By implication they were protesting against the king although no one dared say so openly. That would be treason resulting in immediate arrest and loss of all they had worked so hard for. But the feeling was there, an undercurrent of their fervor.

"A penny for your thoughts, Johann," said the young man marching beside him. Alfred Krupp was a second-year journeyman for the same Master Meinecke. Johann Justus knew him but not well. The journeymen rarely mixed with the apprentices except at meals. "You're supposed to be singing, not daydreaming."

Johann Justus laughed. "I was just wondering where I should spend my journey years," he said and started singing lustily again.

"Why, the first two or three right here with Master Meinecke of course," replied Alfred between snatches of song.

"Of course. But there is so much out there to be learned and I would learn as much as I can."

"You're right but be patient. They don't call these the Mutjahre—the years of courage—for nothing," replied Alfred. "Oh, look! Good heavens, what is going on up front there?"

The young men had started their march at the Stechbahn, the ancient tilting ground beside the Stadtkirche. From there they wound their way through the Market Square, past the Rathaus of old Lüdeke von Sehnden and were now turning into Ritterstrasse, now being called Kanzleistrasse, with the intention of ending up before the castle gates to voice their support of the 'Göttingen Seven'. But as the front ranks neared the end of Ritterstrasse, some sort of altercation seemed to be taking place. Suddenly the word was passed back through the ranks. "Police. Police. Run. Run."

Alfred grabbed Johann's arm and pulled him into the Kalandgasse, a tiny, quiet street that led past the famed Latin School and back to the church. "Come on, let's get out of here. I have a friend around the corner who will hide us."

"But why?" objected Johann Justus. "We have done nothing wrong. We were just going to march peaceably past the Castle, which is almost empty anyway, and return to the church for a prayer service."

"I know," replied Alfred, "but evidently the police don't agree that our intentions are peaceful. Listen to that."

They could hear shouts and screams behind them as the police batons collided with unsuspecting heads and mounted troopers blocked their way. Alfred hurried Johann along and ducked around a corner behind the church. Far beyond on the other side of the church they could see the tail end of the parade—dozens of young men milling about uncertain as to what to do. Alfred pushed open a door in one of the ancient houses and hurried up some stairs.

"I hope my friend is at home," gasped Alfred out of breath. "If not, we'll hide under the stairs until things quiet down." But his friend was home and quickly let them into his tiny apartment.

"What is going on out there?" he asked. "I heard a lot of noise."

"Pauli, this is my friend Johann," introduced Alfred. "The police evidently didn't like us supporting the 'Göttingen Seven'. There'll be some sore heads and broken bones and lost livelihoods out there. We thought it prudent to get away while we could."

"Wise," said Pauli reflectively. "Of course, you have been here all afternoon discussing intellectual matters, such as my indexing of the old church books."

Alfred smiled. "Of course."

Johann Justus was perplexed. "I don't understand," he said. "We have the right of peaceable assembly under the constitution."

"A constitution which no longer exists," commented Pauli.

Johann Justus stood up. "I'm going back," he declared. "There are friends of mine who may be hurt. I have to help them."

"Don't be foolish," said Alfred. "You may be hurt or arrested yourself."

"I don't care. They are my friends standing up for our rights and they need help. Hide here like a coward if you wish but I am going back." Johann Justus stormed out the door.

The remark about being a coward hurt Alfred to the quick. He looked at Pauli and said, "I'd better go with him." Pauli shook his head as his friend followed in Johann's wake.

Alfred caught up with Johann Justus in the Kalandgasse. "I'm not a coward, you know. Just thought it the better part of common sense."

Johann Justus did not reply. He was only of medium height but broad-shouldered and husky. Although usually of a mild and loving disposition, he was a fighter when circumstances warranted. Alfred was much taller and thinner but wiry. Although he could and would fight when necessary, he much preferred negotiation.

When they reached Kanzleistrasse things were still in a turmoil. Several young men were lying on the ground, others milling about in confusion, shouting deprecations at the police. The police did not seem to be arresting anyone as yet but they were still laying about with their batons and those on horseback still blocked the way to the empty castle.

Johann Justus spotted a youth he knew lying in the middle of the street and ran to him. "Gottfried," he cried and reached the man just as a horse was about to trample him. Johann Justus swatted the horse on the rump and ducked the officer's baton. He gathered up the lad and carried him to the sidewalk. "Godke, are you all right?"

Gottfreid shook his head. "Ooo, my head," he moaned. "What happened?"

"You'll have a sore head for a few days but I don't think anything else is broken. Try your arms and legs."

Gottfried gingerly moved his limbs and nodded. "I—I think so," he murmured. He looked about to faint again so Johann Justus propped him up against a wall.

"Sit here until you regain your senses," instructed Johann. "I have to help others. I'll be back."

Alfred, not willing to be called a coward again, waded into the throng and dragged another young man, whom he did not know, to safety.

"He's not one of ours but no matter," said Johann Justus. "I think his name is Peter." He dove back into the melée again and helped another.

This one was conscious but limping badly. He leaned gratefully on Johann Justus, favoring a badly sprained or maybe broken ankle. "Here, Willi, sit down with these two and see if you can revive them. We'll help you out of here as quickly as we can."

Then Alfred led another to the sidewalk. He was bleeding profusely from a smashed nose and broken teeth.

"Ach, Karl," said Johann, "can you see?" The man shook his head. Johann Justus took his own handkerchief and wiped some of the blood, tears and mud from Karl's eyes and the man nodded gratefully but he could not speak. His mouth was too badly smashed.

Johann Justus and Alfred managed to rescue six in all. Things were beginning to quiet down. Many of those uninjured had fled and the police were turning their attention to those seated or lying around the perimeter.

"We've got to get them out of here," said Johann Justus. "But where?"

"Not to the hospital, although some of them need that care," said Alfred. "That is the first place the police will go to arrest them. Let us take them to Pauli's and get them cleaned up. Then we'll decide. He won't mind. He could use a little excitement."

Pauli almost screamed when he saw the wounded men but then he rose to the occasion and set water to boil, fetched clean cloths and soap and water, gave them water to drink and brandy in some cases to dull the pain. He fussed over them like a little mother. Johann Justus had to laugh but was grateful for his help.

The men sat around the floor as Pauli did not have enough chairs. Gottfried held cold cloths to his head which was rapidly growing a large lump. Johann Justus bound up Willi's ankle which seemed to be just badly sprained. Pauli took special pains to clean up Karl's bloody face.

"Here, let me see that nose," said Johann Justus. "My mother taught me how to do it. My brothers were always having fights. But it has to be done right away else it will set wrong. Now hold on, lad. It will hurt like the devil for a minute but you'll be able to breathe more easily if I can just get it right." Karl screamed and held tightly to Pauli's hand as Johann Justus maneuvered the nasal cartilage. And then he nodded gratefully and pointed to the water pitcher. They gave him water . He rinsed his mouth and spat out blood, phlegm and a broken tooth. Then he began to talk.

"Ach," he mumbled with great difficulty, "I think I bit off the end of my tongue."

"Let me see," said Johann Justus. Karl opened his mouth as best he could. "Nay," Johann assured him, "you bit it but it's still all there, just

495

bloody and, I'm sure, damned sore."

"Thank you, Johann. I'll not forget this."

They were most worried about Peter, who was still only half conscious.

"Does anyone know what guild he belongs to?" asked Alfred.

"Hush, you're not supposed to use that word anymore," joked Johann Justus.

"Trade, then," said Alfred.

"I'm not sure but I think he may be a smithy's apprentice," replied Johann Justus.

"I think you're right," put in Gottfried. "I've seen him around Master Schmidt's forge."

"Then I shall take special pains to see that he gets well," said Alfred.

"How so?"

"My father has an iron foundry in Essen," said Alfred Krupp. "Didn't you know?"

"No," replied Johann Justus. "And yet you're learning to become a pewtermaker."

"I'm interested in all kinds of metalwork but I prefer making the smaller, more delicate things," said Alfred. "Papa made cannons for Napoleon until 1813 and then supplied the Prussian and Russian armies to help drive him out of Germany. I am not too proud of that but that was before I was born. If I ever inherit the business I intend to do things differently," he declared.

And that thought pleased the men. From that time on Johann Justus Bruns and Alfred Krupp became lifelong friends.

1839   Dorothea was happy—as happy as she could be with so many dear ones missing. But she was surounded by her five loving grandchildren and that was enough to make an old woman very happy. Dorothea had long since—after Kati's death—moved her beloved pianoforte, which she had inherited from her mother, from the Klostermühle to the big Bergmann house in Vilsen. She had tried to imbue each of the children, with varying success, with her love of music.

It was New Year's Eve and the children were gathered around the pianoforte singing Christmas carols. It had been a nice Christmas although it could have been so much better—ach, she chided herself, I must not let thoughts of Heinrich Matthies' treachery spoil our festivities. Even though we are poor, 'tis better that we are happy. And they were not *that* poor. Diminutive Friederike, Johann Heinrich's widow was doing quite well with the spice shop. Anton seemed finally to have recovered from his grief and was regaining many of his former customers at the Klostermühle, although Dorothea still worried about him. There were times when he simply sat morosely staring into space. His mother knew something was troubling him but she could not imagine what. She hoped that in time he would tell her. Anton and Friederike sat opposite each other by the fire while the children sang. Wouldn't it be nice if those two wed, she thought, but Dorothea doubted that that would ever come to pass. Friederike had become too independent managing the spice shop and Anton had lost his former sunny disposition.

The children had no such sad thoughts as they sang 'Stille Nacht, Heilige Nacht', the beautiful new hymn that was sweeping the country. No matter that it had been written by an Austrian Catholic priest and his organist. Protestant north as well as Catholic south had embraced it wholeheartedly. They sound like angels singing, thought Dorothea. Then they burst into 'O du Fröhliche, O du Selige', the happiest of Christmas carols. And then their favorite of all, a song each had learned in earliest childhood, 'Ihr Kinderlein, Kommet'. It brought tears to Dorothea's eyes, thinking back over all the Christmases since they were babies. But they were no longer babes, not even little children anymore. How time flies, she thought.

Georg, Friederike's eldest, was already a young man of nineteen and had just begun his first year at Göttingen University where he intended to study theology. Everyone regarded him as the most talented of the lot. And he had been very, very lucky in securing the grant from the von Sehnden stipendium which would pay for his studies for at least two years. He was also a talented musician.

"Here, Georg, you play for a while, while I direct the choir," offered Dorothea.

"Nay, Oma, you play so well. I prefer to direct the choir. I am starting to study conducting at the University and the practice will do me good."

"Then why don't you prepare to be an organist instead of a pastor?" she asked.

"Because I believe the two things go together," replied Georg.

"Then, if I'm to continue playing, I'll need another cup of coffee."

"Tiete, fetch Oma a fresh cup of coffee," instructed Friederike. "The pot's on the back of the stove."

Henriette, whom they called Tiete, hurried into the kitchen. She called back over her shoulder, "Don't start another song without me." Everyone liked Henriette, now fourteen. She had an outstanding personality and was also highly intelligent. She had just finished her schooling and was now helping Gerd Meyer with the younger children at the school. Many people were outraged at this, saying a female had no business teaching school. Henriette claimed she was only helping to maintain discipline and to clean up after the children but everyone knew she was also helping to teach the very youngest. How sad that girls cannot attend university, thought Dorothea. She would be a natural for it. But Henriette also had stars in her eyes these days. She had just met a friend of her brother's, a fellow student at Göttingen named Ludwig Schulze, who was planning a career in medicine. Henriette's plans included getting to know him much better.

Dorothea, called Doris, Friederike's youngest at ten was already showing signs of becoming an astute businesswoman like her mother. She loved helping out in the spice shop and especially enjoyed toting up their profits at the end of the day.

Hermann, Anton's son, now fifteen, was still not sure what he wanted to do with his life. Since finishing school last year he had been working with his father at the mill but he still had dreams of becoming a doctor. He knew he would have to make up his mind very soon because if he did not go to the gymnasium he could never attend university. But where would the money come from? He knew Oma would try to help but, oh, if only those thieving Matthies had not stolen Oma's money. He also decided to talk with Georg's friend Ludwig while they were home for the Christmas holiday.

His sister Friedrike, now eleven, was the most serious of them all. Just as intelligent as the rest, she nevertheless was so quiet it often did not show. Dorothea feared she was still grieving the loss of her mother, or, to put it more accurately, simply missing the fact that she had no mother. While both Dorothea and Friederike tried hard to fill that role, it was often difficult to know what the child was thinking. She often could be found with her nose buried in a book rather than be playing with the other children. She seemed to prefer her own company.

Tiete returned with the coffee and Dorothea gratefully took several sips. "Now just a few more songs and then we shall have our cookies and wine to see the New Year in. Then quickly to bed for tomorrow I have a surprise for you."

"Who?" "What?" "When?" "Where?" they chorused.

"Georg David is having a New Year's party tomorrow at his new house to introduce us to his new bride and we are all invited."

The boys cheered, the girls squealed with delight and young Friedrike clapped her hands.

Georg David Bruns, a middle son of the late elder Johann Justus, had also broken with family tradition and and become a musician—a very talented one. As each of Dorothea's grandchildren had become old enough she had sent them to Georg David for music lessons. Once again Georg was the most talented. He learned to play and sing to an almost professional level. Tiete was not far behind and she seemed to enjoy the music the most of all of them. Hermann and Doris were adequate but did not have the same enthusiasm for it as the other two. Friedrike was the enigma. She was learning quite well and decidedly preferred singing to playing but it was hard to tell whether she really enjoyed it or not. Oh, well, thought Dorothea, they cannot all be alike. Thank God they are all so different.

They arrived at Georg David's house shortly after dinner. The house was already crowded with numerous Bruns relatives as well as most of Georg David's pupils and their parents and many other friends and neighbors. They were introduced to his bride Christine, born Büchte from Neustadt-am-Riebenberg, a charming, if somewhat shy, blond, blue-eyed little lady. She made them feel welcome as though she had lived among them in Vilsen all her life.

Georg David had arranged a recital of some of his most talented students, Georg Bergmann among them.

"You never told me," chided Dorothea.

Georg laughed. "Nay, Oma, it was to be a secret surprise, even from you."

During the performance Christine provided plenty of cookies, cakes and wine for the audience and the proud parents. Everyone enjoyed the recital immensely especially, of course, the parents. At the end Georg David made an announcement.

"I now have a special treat for you. Let me introduce my cousin Johann Justus Bruns, whom some of you may not know as he has been away many years in Celle. He is a talented violinist and why he wants to be a pewtermaker instead of a musician I'll never know." Johann Justus blushed and bowed while the audience laughed and clapped. Friedrike sat up straight and suddenly seemed interested.

"He is going to play some of the old Lieder for you beginning with

Franz Schubert's beautiful *Serenade*. Also some of the new songs by the upcoming composer Robert Schumann. Then," he paused a moment, "then he and I shall play some music for dancing and singing." Everyone applauded at that.

During the playing of the *Serenade* Friedrike seemed to come alive. Dorothea watched her carefully. Is it the music or the young man that intrigues her, she wondered. It's almost as though she is in love. But no, it couldn't be that. She's too young and he a young man of nineteen. It must be the music. Perhaps I should have had her take violin lessons, but who could afford the fiddle?

In the fact, it was both. Friedrike felt herself transported to realms of beauty she had never known existed. And it was Johann Justus who was creating that beauty. She looked at him more carefully. He was a nice looking man—not handsome by any means—rather plain, in fact, but with a *joie de vivre* that brightened his face as he played. Something told her that he was also a kind and considerate man. Anyone who made such beautiful music had to be. Freidrike, of course, did not understand all these feelings but she decided then and there that she wanted to know Johann Justus better.

At the end of his performance Johann Justus said, "Now I am going to teach you all the newest waltz that has become very popular all over Germany and then we'll dance to it. It is called 'Du, du liegst mir im Herzen'. He promptly played and sang the lilting melody and soon everyone was singing lustily. Then he and Georg David played while everyone waltzed around the small parlor. Or almost everyone.

Johann Justus noticed little Friedrike sitting by herself watching the dancers longingly. None of the boys her own age cared for dancing—or even girls—as yet. He could see her feet tapping. He put aside his fiddle, while Georg David kept playing, and walked over to her.

"Good afternoon, Jungfer, are you not one of the Bergmann?"

Friedrike was so flustered at his attention she could scarcely answer. "I—I," she stammered. "Ja, my name is Friedrike."

"And I think you would like to dance. Would you dance with me?"

"I—I don't dance very well," she murmured. Dorothea had taught them all to dance but obviously Friedrike had not had much practice. Then she mentally straightened her spine and her innate determination came to her rescue. She tried to act like Tiete would have. She held out her hand graciously and said, "I should like that very much."

Johann Justus took her hand and whirled her out onto the floor. At first she felt as though she had two left feet but then the lilting three-quarter rhythm of the waltz took over and she felt as though she were floating on air.

On their way home through the snowy evening Doris teased her. "Friede has a boyfriend," she singsonged.

"I have not," Friedrike snapped back. "He was just being kind because he knew I wanted to dance and most of the boys are so—so stupid. I'll never see him again." But secretly she hoped she would.

After the New Year Anton sought out Dorothea. "Mama, there is something I wish to discuss with you."

Ach, here it comes, she thought. Now I'll find out what is bothering him. "You know I always have a ready ear, dearest Anton," she said.

"You know about the musketball in my side," he began hesitantly.

"Certainly, I know. Is it bothering you?"

"For years I was hardly aware of it except in bad weather but in the last few years—ever since Kati's death," he choked back a sob for a moment and went on, "it has been—how shall I describe it?—not painful exactly but like a heavy weight making it more and more difficult to breathe. Do you think it could be growing?"

Dorothea turned white but she strove to remain calm. "Musketballs don't grow," she said slowly, "but there could be scar tissue around it that is. Or, God forbid, it could have moved closer to your lung with all the heavy lifting you do."

Anton thought about that for a moment. "You may be right. It is what I feared."

"There is also the possibility of lead poisoning, although I hate to even think of that."

"I don't think so," he said slowly. "I don't feel sick otherwise—just that terrible pressure. But this is what I wanted your advice on. I have heard that there is a doctor in Lüneburg, a surgeon who is an expert in this sort of thing. 'Tis said he uses a new kind of drug discovered by some doctor in Scotland—it's called chloroform—that will put a man so soundly asleep that he will never feel the knife or the probing or anything. It enables the doctor to dig much deeper without the patient thrashing about and therefore makes the surgery much safer. I want to go and consult with this doctor. What do you think?"

"I have heard a little about this Scottish doctor's new drug but I know nothing about how effective—or dangerous—it might be. It is so new and experimental that I can't give you any sound advice. Remember, however, that with any drug of that kind an overdose could put you to sleep permanently."

"I know but if the damn bullet moves to my lung or heart I'll die soon anyway."

"Ach, Anton, don't say that," she exclaimed. "And it seems as though you've already made up your mind to go to this doctor in Lüneburg. Who recommended him?"

"Gerd Meyer, whose father knows a judge in Lüneburg who had an appendix operation with this same doctor."

"And he lived?"

"Lives yet and feels very well."

"That's certainly a good recommendation. Then go if you must," Dorothea said hesitantly. "I shall pray for you with all my heart. But shouldn't you wait until the weather is better? It's a long ways to Lüneburg and you could get stranded in a blizzard on the moor or worse."

"Possibly but I'm told the doctor prefers to operate in the cold weather. That way the blood doesn't flow as freely."

"But you could also catch pneumonia."

Anton shrugged. "I'll take that chance. There is just one thing that concerns me."

"And that is?"

"Can we afford it?"

Dorothea had not thought of that. "Probably not," she replied, "but if it will save your life, I'll find the means—somehow. Go now and make your plans. We'll worry about that when you are well again."

"There is one other thing I intend to do while I'm in Lüneburg," said Anton.

"Yes?"

"Judge Meyer said his friend the judge there might be able to help us recover the money Heinrich Matthies stole from us."

"Hah!" snorted Dorothea derisively. "We'll as soon see the cow jump over the moon as see that. I have more faith in your doctor than in any far-off lawyer, especially after all this time. Don't get any false hopes. If Philipp and Judge Meyer himself could do nothing back then, no lawyer in Lüneburg will be able to either. Put that out of your mind and concentrate on your operation."

Two days later Anton was ready. He hugged Hermann and Friedrike fondly as he explained to them what he was about to undergo. They deserved to know — just in case. But best not to think of that. He promised to return in about a month if all went well. He rode out into the bleak January day. The weather was cold but not unbearably so and fortunately it did not snow. He could have made better time but he became exhausted so quickly that he took a leisurely pace. Two and a half days later he arrived at Lüneburg. Dr. Zornweiss was waiting for him.

The doctor listened to Anton's heart. "Sounds strong enough to me. The ball hasn't reached there yet. You'll do. Come back here at first light tomorrow."

"But," said Anton dismayed, "I don't have any place to stay."

"Then sleep on that cot over there," said Zornweiss. "It's where you'll be sleeping for several days after the operation anyway."

The room was very cold and not even a blanket had been offered. Nor had Anton had any supper. He had not expected this. Truthfully he did not know what he had expected. He went outside and fetched the last of his stale bread and a few crumbs of cheese from his saddlebag but his mouth was so dry he could hardly swallow it. Nowhere could he find any water with which to wash it down. He stretched out on the cot fully clothed and wrapped his cloak around him but between shivering and nerves he could not sleep. He wondered what the morning would bring. He prayed as he had never prayed before. He must eventually have dozed off from sheer exhaustion because he woke up towards dawn, screaming, from that old nightmare about Waterloo that he had not dreamt in years. He made no more effort to sleep even though he still felt exhausted. He lay there trembling the rest of the night.

At last just as dawn was breaking a young man entered the room bearing one of the new-type oil lamps from which he lit four more lamps — two at the head and two at the foot of a higher long table. The room was soon blindingly bright.

"I am Erich, Dr. Zornweiss' assistant."

"Good morning, Erich," said Anton, "and what will you be doing to assist?"

"Handing him his instruments mostly and mopping up the blood but it is I who shall be administering the chloroform. Don't worry. I am a medical student at Edinburgh and have been taught by Dr. Simpson who discovered this wonderful drug. It is so simple really. You just breathe a little bit instead of having to drink enough rum to make you pass out. Which can also make you sick to your stomach and undo all the surgeon's work."

"I see," said Anton.

"Now take off all your clothes and lie down on this table."

"But it's cold in here," objected Anton halfheartedly.

"You don't expect the doctor to operate through your clothes, do you?"

"No, of course not but couldn't I just leave my drawers on? He won't be operating down there—I hope."

Erich shook his head. "Suit yourself but I must warn you. This drug relaxes the body so much that all the humors flow out. Everyone shits and pisses all over the place. You wouldn't want to sleep in shitten drawers for the rest of the week, now would you?"

"No, I guess not." Anton removed all his clothing and climbed up on the table. Erich had placed a sheet under him but the table was as hard and cold as stone. Anton shivered.

Erich proceeded to strap down Anton's legs.

"Why do you do that?" he asked.

"Because even though a man is asleep and can feel nothing the body seems to sense the pain and will thrash about sometimes causing the surgeon's knife to slip. You wouldn't want that, would you?"

"No, I wouldn't."

"Now put your arms up over your head so they're out of the doctor's way." Erich tied Anton's wrists securely. Anton felt as though he were being crucified.

The doctor came in then. He was all cheerfulness and encouragement. He must have slept well, thought Anton. "Now let's listen to that heart again." He put his ear to Anton's chest. "Sounds fine," he pronounced. "A little fluttery but still strong."

"From the cold," murmured Anton.

"And no doubt a little fear," said Zornweiss, "but no need to be afraid. We'll have that old bullet out before you know it and you'll feel much better. Now my assistant will hold a cloth over your nose. Just close your eyes and breathe deeply. You'll be asleep in a trice and never feel a thing."

Erich poured something from a bottle onto a cloth and held the cloth to Anton's nose. It had a sicky-sweet smell. Anton breathed as he was told. He felt his head go swimmy and then nothing more.

The doctor quickly cut open Anton's left side and laid back the flaps of skin. Erich was busy mopping up blood. "Ah, there it is behind this rib. Hand me the tongs." Erich did so. "I'm going to have to move this rib a little to get at it. Let's pray it doesn't crack."

As Zornweiss moved the rib Anton screamed.

504

"He still feels it," exclaimed Zornweiss. "Quick, give him some more chloroform."

"But Dr. Simpson warned about an overdose," objected Erich.

"The hell with Dr. Simpson," shouted Zornweiss. "Can't you see the man is in pain? Do as I say."

Erich reluctantly soaked the cloth again with chloroform and held it to Anton's nose. Both men watched as his tortured body visibly relaxed.

Zornweiss moved the rib again, took his tongs and snatched at the musketball. "There, I've got it." He pulled the offending bullet out with a jerk and let the rib fall back into place. This time there was no reaction from Anton but a great spurt of blood followed the extracted ball. "Now mop that blood up so I can see if it's clean and we'll sew him up."

Erich sponged and the doctor peered into the chest cavity. "Looks good and—Oh, my God! His heart has stopped!"

The two men stared as Anton's lifeblood slowed to a trickle. "That should not have happened," said the doctor, perplexed.

"It was the overdose," insisted Erich. "Dr. Simpson told us that too much can slow the heart down so much that it fails."

"I don't want to hear Dr. Simpson's name again," screamed Zornweiss. "And don't you breathe a word of what happened outside of this room. The cause of death is simply heart failure due to loss of blood."

Erich, shocked, merely nodded. He made up his mind to go back to Scotland as soon as possible.

Dorothea was dozing on the settee in the parlor. Oh, my, she thought, this old age nonsense is catching up with me. I never needed these afternoon naps before. Suddenly there was a pounding on the front door—the front door of the house, not the spice shop. The children were still at school and Friederike was busy in the shop. Now who can that be? Reluctantly Dorothea got to her feet and went downstairs. The pounding continued.

"All right, all right, I'm coming." She opened the door.

A poorly dressed man stood without holding a paper and a little bag in his hand. Dorothea gasped. She looked beyond him and saw his cart standing in the chruchyard with Anton's horse tied behind it on a leading rein.

"Mistress Bergmann?" asked the carter.

"I am she."

The carter touched his cap. "Sorry to bring ye bad tidings, Mistress, but I brung yer son's body home from Lüneburg."

Dorothea, who had never swooned in her life, collapsed on the floor.

The carter did not know what to do. He started yelling, "Anybody else t'home?"

Finally the ruckus penetrated through to the spice shop and Friederike came running. "What's amiss here?" she cried.

"I comed just now all the way from Lüneburg bearing this corpse and the mistress done swooned. I reckon 'twas a mighty shock for her but I got to have my money."

Friederike was so concerned with Dorothea that the man's words did not immediately sink in. "Oma Dorchen, shall I fetch some smelling salts? What happened?"

Dorothea was beginning to wake up. "Nay," she whispered. "Help me up. Anton's dead."

"What?!" This time the awful news registered. "Oh, no, I don't believe it."

"I knew it the moment I saw his horse," sighed Dorothea.

"Mistress, if'n ye don't mind telling me where to put this here coffin," said the carter, "I'd like to be on my way. Doctor said as how you'd pay me."

"Bring it in here," directed Friederike.

"B'ain't no man around as can help me?" asked the carter.

"Nay, we have no man here. He—was—our—man," said Dorothea through her tears. "We'll help you."

The two women together with the carter struggled to get the heavy pine box into the house. Dorothea quickly pried the lid up. She had to be sure. She almost swooned again at the white bloodless face of her dearest son, clothes bloodstained where the doctor had hurriedly stitched up the skin. She shut the lid.

"Friederike, pay the man and get rid of him. We have to be alone and think what to tell the children."

"How much are you asking?" asked Freiderike.

"Half a groschen," replied the carter.

"Half a groschen!" exclaimed Friederike. "Why that's . . . "

"I been three days on the road from Lüneburg and going back empty. That's more'n fair," insisted the carter. "Doctor said as how . . . "

"Never mind," said Dorothea. "Just pay him."

"Thank ye, Mistress, and here's this." The carter handed her the paper and the little bag.

"What's this?"

"Can't say as I can read it but I figure 'tis the reckonin' from the doctor. An' this here's the bullet. He wanted ye to know he truly dug it out even though the man's heart gave out."

Dorothea gasped. She felt like throwing the filthy thing at the man. She dropped it on the floor as though it were a live thing ready to kill again. "I'll not pay that butcher a penny," she said.

The man shrugged and left. Dorothea and Friederike fell into each other's arms and wept.

Later they were sitting at the kitchen table awaiting the children. "We'll lay him out tonight after the children have gone to bed," said Dorothea.

"We have to tell Pastor," said Friederike. "He'll have to have the funeral right away. It's been three or four days already."

"I know. I'll go and see him later—after we've told the children. Although I imagine our dear Anton was pretty well frozen on the trip here." Dorothea started sobbing again and tried to get ahold of herself. "But there is one thing we must do ere word of his death reaches Heinrich Matthies."

Friederike looked puzzled.

"Ja," explained Dorothea. "That knave will steal everything that isn't nailed down. He's already stolen far too much from us. First thing tomorrow we must move every stick of furniture and their other possessions out of the Klostermühle. Do you think some of our neighbors here will help? We'll need two or three strong men."

"I'm sure they will. Anton was well respected. The Bruns brothers I know we can count on."

Just then Hermann burst through the door followed by his sister Friedrike and his cousin Doris.

"Harm, what are you doing home already?" asked Dorothea, surprised. Hermann had long since given up his dream of going to the gymnasium and becoming a doctor due to lack of funds. He had apprenticed himself to Johann Justus Bruns' elder brother, the cabinetmaker. Anton Christoph Bruns had been named after Hermann's father and grandfather and that had seemed especially propitious to young Hermann. He also enjoyed the work.

"Is Papa home?" asked Hermann. "I saw his horse nibbling grass out in the churchyard as I passed."

"Ach, Gott," said Dorothea, "I forgot all about the horse. Come here, children. I have something to tell you." She put an arm around each of Anton's children and held them close. "Dearest ones," she said solemnly, "your Papa has died."

Doris ran to her own mother and for once had no teasing remarks to make.

Much later, after the funeral, Hermann came to the girls' room. He took his little sister Friedrike in his arms and held her. Henriette took Doris aside. She knew what was coming. Friede had held up well during the obsequies and all that followed. She had barely cried at all. Henriette knew she was holding her grief tightly inside. Apparently Hermann understood that as well.

"Let it out, Kleinchen," he urged. "Don't hold it in. You'll feel better for it. We must be brave."

"Brave? How can I be brave?" Friedrike sobbed. "First God takes our Mama away. Now our Papa. We are all alone. Oh, Harm, what's to become of us?" Her voice rose in pitch to near hysteria.

"We are not alone. We still have Oma."

"But Oma is old. She won't be with us much longer. She will die, too. Oh, Harm, what are we to do then?"

Hermann held her tight. "You have me. I'm a man now. I'll take care of you, dearest Friede. You always can count on me to be there for you."

"Oh Harm, you will, won't you?" And then she started to weep in earnest. Hermann held her in his arms and let her cry it out. It was the catharsis she needed.

When her tears were finally spent Friedrike murmured, "Thank you, dearest brother. I'll try to be brave. Nay, I *shall* be brave."

"That's our girl," said Hermann.

"We all have to be brave," added Henriette, "and we'll help each other to be brave. We'll always be there for you, too, Friede." She surreptitiously gave her sister Doris a nudge to keep her quiet. "And Georg will, too."

Whereupon Friedrike began to weep again but it was short-lived this time. She knew she could count on her brother and cousins. These five children were a close-knit group. They had grown up together, had suffered hardship and sorrow together and in the end they would all be stronger for it.

A little more than a month after Anton's funeral Heinrich Matthies said to his wife Adelheit, "Just as soon as the weather breaks we'll start construction."

"Oh, I'm so happy for you," said Adelheit.

"You should be. I've waited long enough."

"How so? I thought you did not have the money ere now."

"I've always had the money. I saved it up years ago but I had to wait until the Bergmann was out of the way."

"What do you mean? I don't understand. What had the Bergmann to do with building a new mill?" she asked, puzzled.

Heinrich realized he had said too much. "Uh—er—he might have objected. Never mind that now." He quickly got off that track. "It will be the finest, most modern windmill in all of County Hoya. And, Adi, you shall have a brand new house right next to it. I'll even buy you one of those new iron cookstoves for the kitchen so you won't have to cook over the fire anymore."

"That will be nice," said Adelheit although she was not at all sure. "I shall have to learn to use it."

"You will. There's nothing much to learn."

"Heinrich, can't we stay right here in Bruchmühlen?" she asked timidly. "I like it here. Why go to the expense of building a new dwelling house? The mill will cost enough as it is."

"I *want* everyone to know how successful Heinrich Matthies is. We shall have a new house. This old place is too damp and drafty."

Adelheit made one more attempt. "But it's so nice out here in the country. I don't know as I shall be comfortable with close neighbors." Adelheit was very shy and timid.

"You won't have any close neighbors. The new windmill will not actually be in either village but rather at the crossroads between Vilsen and Bruchhausen." Heinrich was growing angry. "Mayhap in a new house you won't lose so many babies."

"Oh, Heinrich, how can you say that?" But she feared it might be true. Out of six births so far they had only two living children, Anna Dorothea, almost nine, and Friedrich, less than a year old. Adelheit started to cry.

"Stop it. You know how I hate that snivelling." He lost his temper— the infamous Matthies temper. He took her arm and squeezed it painfully. Oh, not another bruise, she thought. "The next babe I plant in your belly will be born at the new windmill. And that's all there is to it." He twisted her arm and threw her from him. She almost fell and fled toward the kitchen.

"I wish him well of it," said Dorothea when she heard the news.

"But you must admit it is going to be a beautiful mill," replied Hermann, "and in a superb location, too."

"Ja, built with stolen money—our money," she said bitterly. "And located where he can rub our noses in his ill-gotten gains every day."

Hermann shrugged. "But, Oma, it was never proven that they took the money."

"You were a witness," she insisted.

"Ach, Oma, I was so little I don't remember it at all. All I recall was running to Oma Becke because I was frightened of something, I knew not what. Although I must admit that for years as a child I was afraid of Master Matthies. Now I realize that he is nothing but an arrogant, pompous fool."

"His crime will come back to him," said Dorothea. "I may not live to see it but you will. Just wait and see. The Lord will punish him someday. Count on it."

16

1841

Dorothea was well satisfied with the progress her grand-children were making. She had prayed that the good Lord would let her live long enough to see them to adulthood or at least until they were able to fend for themselves. She had other grandchildren, of course, in Liebenau and elsewhere from her other sons and daughters. But they were all far away and she rarely saw them. These five orphans or fatherless she accepted as her special responsibility. They needed her far more than the others.

Georg had completed his studies at Göttingen and was now an assistant pastor at a church in Hannover. No worry there. She was very proud of him. He was also directing the church choir and Dorothea was happy that he was able to exercise his considerable musical talent.

Henriette was now actively teaching alongside Gerd Meyer who paid her a small pittance out of his own fees. But it was enough because, although a few die-hard parents had threatened to withdraw their children from the school, many pleased parents supplemented her meagre income with gifts of all sorts, even money. But no worry there either because Henriette was being actively courted by young Ludwig Schulze and Dorothea was sure they would wed in a few years as soon as he received his medical degree.

Doris would be no problem either. As young as she was, she was capable of running the spice shop almost as well as her mother Friederike. She showed a good head for business and could already drive a hard bargain. If she was not yet as knowledgeable about mixing the simples and potions of the apothecary side, Dorothea felt that would eventually come. Dorothea was trying to teach her all the knowledge her own mother and the old wisewoman had passed down to her. Doris was bright and quick if a trifle impatient—which could lead to serious mistakes. But Dorothea did not worry overly much about that. After all Doris still had two more years of school.

She was somewhat concerned about Hermann. Now eighteen, he was just completing his apprenticeship with cabinetmaker Anton Bruns and doing very well. He would soon begin his journey years which meant he would no doubt have to leave Vilsen for several years. Hermann took great pleasure in making beautiful things. He also was more interested than any of the others in learning about Dorothea's simples and potions. She knew he was still disappointed at not having been able to go to university to study medicine. But that could not be helped. He also seemed to have set himself up *in loco parentis* to his sister Friedrike. They were closer and clung together more than the other three. Both Anton's children were also more sensitive than the others. Was that because they had lost both parents while the others still had a mother? Or was it something inherent in their natures from both Anton and Kati? Dorothea did not know but she hoped they would both survive the separation. And what worried her more than anything is that Hermann occasionally expressed a desire to emigrate to America. That shocked her and she prayed it was just a passing fancy.

Dorothea was most concerned about Friedrike. In less than a year she would graduate from school and be confirmed in the church—the rites of passage to adulthood. And then where to place her? Not in any ordinary Bürger's home. The child was too intelligent and sensitive for that. She already could weave the most beautiful linen Dorothea had ever seen. She was an accomplished needlewoman, almost an artist, with embroidery, smocking and lace. No doubt from her touch of French blood. And one would almost think she was noble born, such was her demeanor. Dorothea thought back to her ancestor Anna von Sehnden. Mayhap that inheritance was strong in Friedrike as well.

If only, Dorothea thought, we still had some contact in Hannover. But her brother Philipp was long dead and the Grimm brothers were off in Berlin. Then she wondered if the old countess for whom Kati had worked were still alive. She knew the Graf von Münster had died some years ago, some said of a broken heart, less than two years after he had been summarily dismissed by King Ernst August. Münster was not Hannover but it would be a noble house where Friedrike could learn fine manners and possibly be happy for a few years until it was time for her to wed. And if Dorothea meanwhile passed on to her forefathers, at least the child would have some security.

Dorothea took up pen and paper and started to compose a letter to the Gräfin von Münster.

To her surprise and delight about a month later she received a reply.

512

It was written in a spidery, shaky script but in the Countess' own hand. She wrote that she did indeed remember Dorothea's gooddaughter fondly and had been saddened at her untimely death at so young an age. She did not realize that Kati had had a daughter of her own, now almost grown. Sadly her own household had diminished so in size since she was alone that she had no need of someone of Kati's talents. However, she still had many friends in Hannover and, she wrote, 'it may interest you to know that young Georg, Duke of Cumberland, the King's son, is now betrothed and should be wed next year. The young couple will not live at the Leine Schloss but in a new Fürstenhof in Neustädte Markt, a suburb of Hannover. The house is already being prepared for them. I have succeeded in securing a position as lady-in-waiting to the new crown princess for my own granddaughter and see no reason why a post for yours could not be accomplished as well. I shall write to Hannover and advise you forthwith.'

Dorothea wondered what Friedrike's reaction to the news would be, even debated telling her granddaughter until the appointment was confirmed. In the end she dropped broad hints and was delighted that the girl seemed to find the prospect of serving the new crown princess exciting.

"Just like Mama," she exclaimed. "Do you think they might take me to Vienna as well?"

Dorothea smiled. "Not likely, my dear. That was a special occasion for the Peace Congress. But there is the possibility of perhaps going to England. 'Tis said Queen Victoria is very family-minded. But don't get your hopes up yet. There is no guarantee that you will be the Duchess' personal maid as your mama was to the Countess. You could be nothing more than a second parlor maid or even a scullery maid."

Friedrike made a face. "Nay, Oma. I shall be a fine lady's maid. They'll like me as soon as they get to know me. You'll see."

Dorothea smiled. She did not doubt the child's confidence in herself.

Several weeks later another letter arrived, not from the countess this time but from the head housekeeper of the new Fürstenhof, one Frau Gnevkow. She wrote that she would be happy to accept such a highly recommended young maid into the royal household but no way could she promise an appointment as a lady's maid. That would be entirely up to Her Grace, the new Duchess, once she arrived.

Although Dorothea's fears were confirmed, Friedrike seemed to mind not at all. "The new Duchess will like me. I just know she will," she asserted confidently and immediately started sewing new gowns, shifts, petticoats and other things she might need in a royal palace.

"New underwear, I agree with," said Dorothea, "but why that fancy gown? It's very pretty, I admit, but you'll have no need of it. They'll no doubt put you in a uniform."

"But I'm bound to have some time off—a half day at least," insisted Friedrike. "That is what this is for. I can't be seen in Hannover in these countrified gowns." And she continued sewing.

Then just as Friedrike was preparing to leave in a few weeks, a hurried note came from a hurried undersecretary. The wedding had been postponed. Queen Friederike was gravely ill, possibly dying. There was no need for Fräulein Bergmann's services at this time. They would advise when such services were required.

Dorothea was more disappointed than her grandchild.

"Don't worry, Oma," said Friedrike. "Princess Marie is bound to marry Prince Georg some day and then I'll have a place. Meanwhile I'll help you with your simples and weave my linen."

Dorothea wished she had her confidence. She was feeling her age more than ever lately. Although still in reasonably good health, her hands, back and legs had become so crippled with arthritis that even the simplest tasks were an effort. She prayed even more fervently that she would live long enough to see this child settled.

Friederike of Mecklenburg-Strelitz had buried two husbands before she wed Ernst August. He had had innumerable mistresses and affairs. She was a determined, head-strong woman and everyone predicted that they would buck heads so severely that they would soon be at each other's throats and the marriage would not last. But everyone was wrong. They fell in love and formed a perfect team of exquisite schemers. While Ernst August plotted to do away with his niece Victoria, Friederike plotted to marry their son Georg to the heiress to the English throne, despite the vehement objections of Victoria's tyrannical mother. But neither event was to take place. Victoria ascended the English throne and Ernst August was sent to rule in Hannover. A tragic accident was to prevent any chance of a royal marriage.

When Friederike died on 27 June 1841, Ernst August was so devastated that his political opponents perceived the first cracks in his armor of arrogance and stubbornness and had hopes that he would weaken enough to allow them to reinstate the constitution. He gave strict orders that the queen's room be left exactly as it had been in her lifetime. Not a thing was to be touched. He would visit the room several times each day and could often be heard talking to her. His grief was so intense, many feared for his sanity. Friederike had been the only one who could soothe his violent temper. The following year he had a chapel built in her memory at Rehburg near the ancient Kloster Loccum. The Friederiken-Kapelle was dedicated on 23 August 1842. This seemed to have served as the necessary catharsis for the king and only then would he allow plans for his son's wedding to go forward.

Georg of Cumberland was the only son of Ernst August and Friederike, a daughter born two years later having died a few months after birth. He was born in 1819, the same year as his first cousin Victoria. The two had played together as children and the future queen had even looked fondly on him as they reached their teens. But a tragic accident when he was fourteen—a childish prank at a party in Kew Gardens—had left Georg totally blind. Nonetheless he was still very handsome and as different from his parents as could be possible. Georg was sweet-tempered, mild-mannered and far more interested in pursuing and sponsoring the arts, especially music, than he was in politics. However, he was deeply imbued with a sense of his God-given grace to rule and in many ways was just as reactionary as his father. Ernst August had tried to bring him up in as normal a manner for a young prince as his blindness permitted. He was taught to ride and trained in sword-play and military tactics although obviously the use of any firearms was beyond him. Georg had been betrothed to the Princess Marie of Sachsen-Altenburg but the wedding had been postponed due to his mother's death. At last Ernst August had agreed to set a date for the royal nuptials in February 1843.

Friedrike Bergmann received the news shortly before Christmas. She was to report to the new palace in Hannover before the end of January 'for training'. The whole household was in a flurry of excitement.

Johann Justus Bruns had been working with pewtermakers in many different towns during his journey years but, if at all possible, he tried to be home in Vilsen for Christmas. Each time he came home he made a point of visiting the Bergmann household. He had been fascinated by the young girl who had wanted so badly to dance that New Year's long ago. This year to his surprise and gratification he found a near-grown young woman all excited about embarking on the adventure of a lifetime in Hannover. Johann Justus looked at Friedrike with new eyes—as a man to a woman, instead of a mentor to a child.

Johann Justus picked her up and swirled her around and kissed her lightly on the tip of her nose.

"Johann Justus," she screamed with delight, "put me down. How dare you?" She blushed but she was smiling.

"Very easily," he replied. "If your grandma wasn't looking, I'd kiss you again."

Dorothea laughed. "I can close my eyes but remember, Johann Justus, she is still a young, innocent maid and you a man grown. Don't rush her."

"I'll not, Frau Bergmann. Fear not," he assured her. "But I wager she'll lose that innocence quite rapidly at the court in Hannover. The King is said to be the worst kind of womanizer."

"I think not," replied Dorothea. "Friede is a good girl, properly brought up. Besides she will not be at the Leine Schloss anywhere near the King. She will be serving the Duchess of Cumberland at the new Fürstenhof. The crown princess-to-be is said to be very strict on decorum."

"Then I shall not worry about her but I shall miss these Christmas visits."

"She is sure to have some free time occasionally but probably not at Christmas. So then you may kiss her again—but only a quick one, mind you, just for Christmas."

Johann Justus took Friedrike in his arms and kissed her quickly but soundly full on the lips.

Friedrike was a little bewildered by this whole conversation. She knew of the King's reputation as a womanizer but she was not exactly sure what that entailed. What she did know was that when this kind, jolly man had kissed her she had felt a thrill right down to her toes.

Just then her cousin Doris entered the parlor, clapping her hands. "See, what did I tell you?" she said. "Friede has been in love with Johann Justus for years."

This time both young people blushed. "Ach, Doris, stop your teasing," snapped Friedrike. "You know that's not true. We're just good friends is all." But she wondered.

Dorothea thought it best to change the subject. "And how goes your journeying, Johann Justus?"

"Quite well, thank you," he replied. "Hard work and long hours with meagre pay. But I have learned so much. I think I shall be ready to make my masterpieces in another year and I shall go back to Celle for that." Celle was the undisputed capital of the pewtermaking craft.

"Indeed? An ambitious undertaking," commented Dorothea.

"I feel I am just about ready. I have been practicing making the pieces I must do for the Master's examination and they have been well received."

"And what sort of pieces will you be making? Or is that a secret?"

"The type of pieces is no secret. Those have been the guild requirements for centuries and are well known. But the style and design, ja, that is my secret. There are three pieces that must be made—a coffeepot or some sort of beaker with an attached cap, a large water pitcher and," Johann Justus laughed at this, "in years past the third used to be a key fully one ell long and four to five inches wide. Since we no longer have doors that require such a key, the guild will now allow us to make a set of tableware—knife, fork, spoon and some sort of serving spoon such as a soup ladle."

"I see. Very interesting," said Dorothea. "And once you attain Master's status, you will be free to marry, is that not so?"

Johann Justus wondered what she was leading up to but he answered forthrightly. "That is so, although since the guilds were temporarily outlawed during the French Time the rules have not been strictly enforced. I haven't really given it much thought but, I ask you, what man could afford to support a wife on a journeyman's pittance?"

"Ach, ja, I know about that," sighed Dorothea. "My dear Chris and I ran into that same problem. And where do you intend to settle once you have become a master?"

"Why, right here in Vilsen, of course. There has long been a need here for a maker of fine tableware. Methinks we are overburdened with cabinetmakers."

Dorothea laughed. "Ach, ja, the ubiquitous Bruns. Yes, it will be nice to buy plates and bowls, ewers *and* coffepots right here instead of paying extra to have them carted from Celle. Then you should have no trouble with the Bürger oath."

"I don't expect any. My family have been well-respected Bürgers of this town for over a thousand years."

"Indeed they have."

Friedrike had said nothing during this entire conversation but had listened avidly with growing pride in her dear friend Johann Justus. She wondered why Oma had been asking so many questions about Johann Justus' prospects. And suddenly the thought occurred to her, could she be falling in love?

After he took his leave Johann Justus wondered the same thing. Was the old lady's inquisition a prelude to matchmaking or was it just friendly curiosity about an old friend's great nephew? He did not know. What he did know was that Friedrike would be ripe for marriage by the time he became a master pewtermaker. It was worth thinking about—and worth waiting for.

The whole family turned out to see Friedrike off at the Vilsen post office. It was a sunny but bitterly cold January day. The mail coach was late.

"Oh, I hope it doesn't snow. Then I shall be even later," said Friedrike through chattering teeth. She wrapped her new cloak tighter around her and pulled her bonnet down over her ears.

"It's too bad we don't have a railroad here yet like they do in Berlin," said Hermann.

"Ja, they already have one from Dresden and Leipzig as far as Magdeburg," added Henrietta. "That's not that far away. It may come here someday."

"I've heard the merchants in Hamburg and Bremen want to build a line from there to Hannover but old Ernst August won't permit it."

"Whyever not? Friede could be there in three or four hours instead of taking almost two days."

"He claims he is protecting the livelihoods of the boatmen on the Weser and the Elbe but the truth of it is the old fool is against anything modern and progressive," replied Hermann bitterly.

"Hush, Harm," warned Dorothea, "right or wrong, it's the King you're talking about."

Hermann shrugged.

"Ach," said Friedrike, "I don't think I should want to go on one of those things anyway. I'd be frightened to death. Have you ever seen a real one, Harm?"

Hermann admitted that he had not.

"Well, I saw a picture of one in the newspaper and it is truly frightening. The smoke and ash is so thick one can hardly breathe. Your clothes get filthy and you're lucky if they don't catch fire from a flying cinder."

"Ach, that's your imagination," objected Hermann. "It can't be that bad."

"Nay, it's true. They interviewed some of the passengers. I read the whole article."

"Ach, you read too much," derided her brother but secretly he wished he had read the account himself. He was fascinated by the Iron Monsters, as many were now calling the massive engines.

"Nonetheless," said Friedrike. "I'd rather trust the horses. At least you can see where you're going." Just then from down the street came the blast of the posthorn. "Ah, here it comes at last." And a quiver of both fear and excitement ran through her. She had never been away from home before.

The coach made its overnight stop at the staging inn at Nienburg. The cost of the accomodations was included in the price of the ticket but the meals were not. Dorothea had given Friedrike some money but not sure how long it would last, she ate very frugally. The next morning at dawn another young girl joined the passengers. A somewhat pretty, buxom blonde, she plopped herself down next to Friedrike.

"Good morning. I'm Inge," she said. "What is your name?"

Friedrike was a little shocked at her forwardness. She had been taught never to speak to strangers. But then she had noticed most of the other passengers, obviously strangers to one another, had chatted quite freely yesterday. "I am called Friedrike," she replied shyly.

"Are you going all the way to Hannover?" asked Inge.

"Yes, I am. Are you?"

"Indeed, I am. All the way to the new Fürstenhof where I am to be a nursery maid."

Friedrike's mouth hung open in surprise. "You are? I—I am going there, too. But how can you be a nursery maid when the Prince and Princess are not even wed yet?"

Inge laughed. "Well, just a plain maid for now. But I shall be a nursery maid ere long. I've had a lot of experience."

"How can you be so sure?"

"Ach, lass, you've got to look to the future—always. In these noble houses one has to push oneself forward else you'll be trampled upon. How old are you?"

Friedrike thought that a bit of impertinence but she replied, "I am fifteen."

"And I am seventeen—well, almost seventeen. I see I shall have to take you under my wing."

Friedrike did not want to be taken under anyone's wing, least of all brazen Inge's. "That's very kind of you," she said, "but I don't think it will be necessary. I'll manage."

They sat in silence for a while. Then Inge asked, "Have you ever

519

been to Hannover before?"

"Nay, I haven't. Have you?"

"Many times. So you see you'll even need someone to guide you around the town."

"I don't expect I'll be doing much exploring at first. They'll keep us too busy. Besides I feel as though I know the town very well. My great-uncle used to travel there on business often and he told me a great deal about it ere he died. And my mother was a lady's maid at the court before she married."

"Ah, so. And whom did she serve?" Inge wondered if this girl might have important connections to be cultivated.

"No one who is there now," said Friedrike.

"And did your mother obtain this position for you through her—er—connections?"

"Nay. My mother died when I was no but a small child."

"Oh, I'm sorry." And that shut Inge up for a while.

As they approached Hannover a man in the corner seat spoke up. "Forgive me if I seem bold, ladies, but I could not but help overhear your conversation. My coach will be meeting me at the staging inn and I shall pass right by the Fürstenhof on my way home. I should be happy to drop you there if you would like to accompany me."

Friedrike had wondered how she would get to the palace with her heavy box and portmanteau. She had been told it was a considerable distance. The gentleman seemed to be harmless enough, a benign, grandfatherly type. She looked to Inge for a decision.

"Nay, nay," replied Inge. "Thank you for your kind offer, sir, but we are being met."

Sometime later when they alighted at the post office right in the heart of Hannover near the ancient Marktkirche Friedrike asked Inge, "How do you know we shall be met? I see no one here. We should have accepted the man's offer. He seemed harmless."

"Those are the worst kind," declared Inge. "Ach, girl, I see you have a lot to learn. To answer your question I was told they are sending a coach or some sort of vehicle to meet the mail coach every day because so many new servants are arriving daily. They have a whole new palace to staff. That's why it was so easy to get the job. We just wait here. Someone will be along."

"I see." But some of Friedrike's enthusiasm faltered. Is that what she was to be—just one of hundreds of faceless retainers? It seemed a far cry from what her mother had experienced in the countess' household where the inside staff consisted of only twenty or so. Well, she was here now and she would make the best of it. She hugged her cloak tighter around her against the bitter wind.

At last trundling down the road came a strange-looking vehicle. It appeared to be a landau but why would the roof be folded down in this weather? As it drew closer Friedrike saw that it had no roof at all. The coach had definitely seen better days. It drew to a stop in front of them and a very handsome young groom jumped down and addressed them.

"Holthus?" Inge nodded. "Bergmann?"

"I am she," replied Friedrike.

"I knew it had to be you two, standing there like frozen waifs. I'll soon have you where it's warm."

"In that?" queried Friedrike.

"What did you expect—the coronation coach?" But then he relented a little and explained. "You see, they are painting and refurbishing all the coaches for the wedding so we have to use this old thing for the nonce. Are these your boxes?"

"Ja," they said.

"Good. Then climb in and we'll be on our way."

Inge climbed into the landau and Friedrike followed carrying her own portmanteau. The groom easily threw Inge's box on the seat opposite. Friedrike's was smaller but much heavier.

"Lordy, what have you got in here? Gold?"

Friedrike smiled. "Nay. If 'twere gold would I be sitting here? 'Tis no but a few books besides my clothes."

"Books! Can you read?"

"Of course I can read. Can't you?"

"Not very much," he replied. "No need for it in my work. Now here's a nice blanket to tuck around your knees. Don't think I didn't have a thought for your comfort. He threw them an old horse blanket. Friedrike hoped it was not full of fleas. But it did cut the bite of the wind. Lord, we'll smell like a stable ere we arrive, she thought.

Friedrike noticed that as the groom tucked the blanket around Inge's knees his hand rested on her thigh momentarily. She expected Inge to cry out or at least object. She did neither. She was actually smiling at the man. Friedrike automatically disliked the groom. Aside from his surliness, she now marked him as a lecher, handsome though he might be. Oh, what sort of a world am I entering, she wondered.

As they drove off through the growing darkness the first wave of homesickness hit her. The words of the *Lorelei*, that beautiful poem by the upcoming poet Heinrich Heine kept running through her head. 'Ich weiss nicht was soll es bedeuten, dass ich so traurig bin . . .'*

On the 18 February 1843 it was snowing hard. Not a propitious day for a wedding. Many expressed the fear that it was a bad omen, predicting much sadness. But nonetheless crowds gathered outside the old Leine Schloss where Prince Georg and Princess Marie were married in the royal chapel and all along the route to the Fürstenhof hoping to catch a glimpse of the newlyweds who were now to be known as the Duke and Duchess of Cumberland. People cheered mightily as the royal coach passed by but their hoped for glimpse was not to be. The coach was tightly shut against the weather. Yet thousands were to tell their children and grandchildren that they did indeed see the Prince or the Princess waving at them through the windows. Perhaps they really did.

All the inside servants were lined up in a semicircle outside the front door of the palace to greet their new master and mistress. Frau Gnevkow and the butler stood in the middle like generals inspecting their troops. Although Friedrike was tall for her age, she was wedged so far back in the ranks she could barely see over the heads of those in front of her. But at least their bodies as well as the roof of the porte-cochère sheltered her somewhat from the inclement weather. She pitied the gardeners, grooms and other outside help who had to stand out in the drive. At last the royal coach appeared and a cheer went up. At glares from the butler and the housekeeper the cheers quickly subsided into decorous applause.

The Prince's valet helped his blind master out of the coach and Georg in turn helped his bride down. She was followed by her personal maid who carefully adjusted the train of her exquisite gown. The bridal couple stood for a moment facing the drive and waved to those waiting there. Then they quickly turned towards the door of the palace. Prince Georg shook the butler's hand and embraced Frau Gnevkow. He appeared to be introducing the housekeeper to his bride.

Friedrike stood on tiptoes and tried desperately to see the Duchess but her view was blocked by other heads and shoulders. All she caught a glimpse of was part of the skirt of the beautiful gown. Tired of craning her neck she settled back down. Oh well, she sighed to herself, at least I saw the beautiful, dappled-gray horses. Hannover was famous for its magnifi-

---

*('I know not what it should mean that I am so sad . . .')

cent horses bred at the stud farm near Celle. Her great-grandfather had once bred them from that same stud but Napoleon had stolen them all.

The royal couple passed into the house and the servants were dismissed. Frau Gnevkow and the butler barked out orders. "To your stations now and no slouching. The wedding feast is in two hours."

Late that evening Friedrike wearily climbed three flights of narrow, steep stairs to the room under the eaves that she shared with Inge. She had been up since before dawn polishing furniture and silver, helping to arrange flowers, ironing endless yards of damask tablecloths. She had never been so tired in her life. Thank goodness, the Duke had finally wanted to bed his bride for no servants, however lowly, had been permitted to leave until after the royal bedding ceremony took place. After that the lesser retainers had been allowed to seek their beds or go out to the stables where the servants were having their own party. The feasting both there and within the palace would no doubt go on until dawn. Friedrike had no enthusiasm for either. And she still had not seen what the Duchess looked like.

When she reached their tiny room, Inge was not yet there. Friedrike was so exhausted she was tempted to throw herself on her cot with all her clothes on. But, no, that would never do. If Frau Gnevkow spied one wrinkle on the drab black uniform, she would be severely reprimanded. She carefully shed the garment and hung it up. She donned her nightshift, blew out their one meagre candle and fell into bed. Hours later she thought she heard Inge arrive but she had no desire for idle chatter. She pulled the cover over her head and went back to sleep. Dawn would arrive only too soon.

When the girls had first arrived at the Fürstenhof, Frau Gnevkow had said, "Since there are still many more to arrive, there is still ample choice of rooms. I can put you in a room for four on the third floor or one in the attic for just the two of you."

"May we see them?" asked Inge.

Friedrike had never dreamed she would be sharing a room with Inge. She almost opted for the room for four until she saw how cold it was. "Uh—is there no fireplace here?" she asked timidly.

Frau Gnevkow looked at her as though she were crazy. "In servants' quarters, never. But if that is going to bother you, you'd be better off upstairs. There are two rooms left that back against the chimneys. You may have one of them."

And so they had settled in in the tiny attic room. What little warmth seeped out of the great chimney was very welcome.

Johann Justus returned to Celle to work on his masterpieces. He had already completed two of them and was working on the third. And on this he had to be extremely careful. Hundreds of years ago when it first became known to men that lead was poisonous, most governments, especially those of the pewtermaking centers, had enacted strict laws governing the proportion of lead to tin in pewter. Tin alone was too soft and brittle to be practical so the lead was vital to give it strength and weight but those utensils connected in any way with food could have no more than one part lead to ten of tin. Other things such as candlesticks, hot water bottles and the like were permitted a higher portion of lead.

First the pewterer had to design a form or mold which could be made of brass, iron or even stone into which was poured the molten mixture of tin and lead. Clay or plaster laced with calve's hair formed the interior mold. When the hardened pewter was removed from the mold it was placed on a special lathe to burnish all the rough spots off. This could be extremely difficult and time-consuming. Elaborate artistic relief or embossed decorations were usually carved into the mold before casting or the piece could later be engraved or etched with designs or someone's initials. Hinged caps were cast separately and then soldered on. Finally the piece was highly polished so that it almost resembled silver.

Johann Justus was making the mold for his set of tableware. In this case the high relief was cast right with the piece. Therefore the mold had to be painstakingly designed. He was concentrating so hard on the elaborate details that he never heard someone approach his corner of the master's workshop.

"Ah, the master at work," said a voice quietly so as to not startle him.

Johann Justus turned around. "Ach, Alfred Krupp, my old friend," he exclaimed. "I never expected to see you back here in Celle." The two men embraced warmly.

"I had to come here on business," explained Alfred, "and I heard you were about to take your master's examination."

"Ach, not that soon. I have just started on the third piece—or pieces actually. It will be quite a while yet, I fear me."

"Then I shall wait."

"Weeks?"

"No, I guess not that long. Could I not have a glimpse of the first two pieces?"

"Nay, nay, my friend. Not even for you. You know they must remain a secret until the masters have passed on them."

"I know. Then will you send word when the examination is to be? I shall most gladly return."

"I can surely do that but it seems a long way to travel just for that," said Johann Justus.

"Not at all. I want to see those masterpieces. Even when we were working here together you had a touch of artistic genius. I am sure it is more highly developed now."

"I don't know. I just design whatever comes into my head," replied Johann Justus modestly.

Alfred laughed. "Then I must admit I had another motive for coming to see you. You know that I am now the owner of the foundry in Essen."

"So I have heard."

"And the business is doing quite well. I now have a hundred and forty men working for me. I have come to ask you—again—to come and work for me—or rather, work with me," he quickly amended. "I could even make you a partner eventually. Have you given it any thought since we last spoke?"

"I have, dear Alfred, and the answer is still 'no'. I do not like working with iron and I have no taste for making cannon. I prefer making smaller more useful things—or perhaps I should say, more peaceful things."

Krupp laughed. "Admittedly your skills in design would not be necessary for cannon. But we also make stoves and suchlike. Have you ever seen the fancy embellishments on some of the new stoves?" Johann Justus nodded. "And I'm even thinking of going into those new locomotives. There your artistry could go wild—as long as they also run. Although I fear I should have a great deal of competition there."

"Stick with what you know best—your cannon," advised Johann Justus. "But as much as I appreciate the offer, Alfred, the answer is still 'no'. Aside from the reasons I mentioned, I do not want to live and work in Prussia. Hannover, specifically Vilsen, is my home and there I shall work. There is a great need for a skilled pewterer there. I have already been promised the use of a vacant barn just behind my house for a workshop."

"But these days Hannover under Ernst August is even more repressive than Prussia. Besides we in the Rheinland are not overly bothered by Berlin. We do pretty much as we please."

"You, maybe, but not the common people. And as far as Hannover is concerned I hope we can soon change that and reinstate our constitution.

Stüve is working hard in the opposition party."

"So you're still as active in politics as ever."

"Not so active anymore." He pointed to his workbench. "But still very interested. Hannover is largely an agrarian country. The vast majority of people are farmers and peasants, yet for less than four years did they have the franchise. They barely had a chance to use it ere it was taken away from them. I and many others hope to restore that privilege. I don't know how or when but it will happen."

"Don't count on young Georg. He has been too well trained by his father, your king."

"We're not. Besides he's too busy with his new bride right now. I wonder how it must be not being able to see one's wife."

"He has hands, has he not? And I'm sure his prick still works," remarked Alfred lasciviously. They both laughed at that. "Then I shall wish you the best of luck with your master's examination. I shall try to be here but if not, write me. You have my address in Essen. I want to keep in touch."

"Thank you, Alfred. I should like that."

Friedrike was polishing silver, a job she particularly detested. The thick paste made from baking soda and wood ash cleaned well enough but it would stick in the grooves of the heavily embossed handles of knives, forks and spoons and it was almost impossible to get it out. And out it had to come or Frau Gnevkow would be wroth. Friedrike put the cloth over her fingernail and tried to dig it out but it was tedious and time-consuming work and the housekeeper was sure to complain that she was too slow. Gradually she became aware of another maid watching her, a maid she had not seen before. At least she thought it was a maid although the young woman wore no uniform, just a drab gray housedress and a plain old mobcap over her hair.

"Here, let me show you an easier way to do that," said the woman. Friedrike thought, now what? Is she going to report me? The woman went over to the huge sideboard and selected three or four toothpicks. "Place your polishing cloth over the tip of one of these and you can pick it out much more quickly, polishing the groove at the same time."

"Thank you. That does make it easier. I don't recall seeing you before. What is your name?"

"I am Marie. And you?"

"I am called Friedrike."

"Ah, a worthy name. And what do you do besides polish silver, Friedrike?"

"I polish furniture and sweep the carpets. Sometimes they let me help arrange the flowers. I like that best."

"No, I meant what do you do in your spare time? Not go out to the stables, I hope."

"Nay, I have no taste for that. I read and—don't breathe a word of this—sometimes I sneak into the music room and play the pianoforte."

"What! A maid who can read and also play. Your talents are being wasted here."

"I know but I am young yet. I can bide my time. I hope someday to be a lady's maid."

Marie looked at her strangely, as though appraising her. "And what sort of things do you read?"

"Ach, Goethe, Schiller, the new poet Heine. I even brought my copy of the Brothers Grimm's Children's Tales with me. I know I'm too old for them but sometimes they console me when I'm feeling a little sad."

"Oh, my. That is a name we don't mention around here."

"I know. But somehow I felt I could trust you, Marie. You won't betray me, will you?"

"Nay, child, never. I loved those stories as a child and even my husband grew up with them until my father-in-law sent those worthy professors into exile and forbid the mere mention of their names."

"Your husband? Your—your father-in-law?" Friedrike fell into a deep curtsey. "Oh, Your Grace, forgive me," she whispered. "I did not realize who you were."

"Up off your knees, child," said the Duchess. "There is nothing to forgive. Of course, you did not know me. I look more the scullery maid than you in that crisp white apron but that is the only way I can get to know my people. And, Friedrike, someday if Frau Gnevkow can spare you for a half-hour or so, I should like you to play for me."

"Oh, Your Grace, that is very kind of you," she stammered, "but I'm afraid I'm not very good. My cousin Georg, who is assistant pastor at St. Peter's, is the real musician of the family."

"I have heard of his excellent choir. A talented family, indeed. Then you cannot be far behind. I should still like to hear you play. And don't worry, Friedrike, I shall keep your secrets."

Friedrike was permitted to go home to Vilsen for a week or two once a year, usually in the summertime when the royal couple went off to the baths or the mountains or even to England. It was the best time of year to enjoy the beautiful countryside around her hometown, although she did miss celebrating Christmas at home. But terribly busy though it was, Christmas at the Fürstenhof was a gay, sparkling, festive time and on second Christmas Day all the servants were awarded lavish gifts for all their hard work.

On her visit to Vilsen last summer she did notice that her dear Oma Dorchen seemed to have shrunken and to be failing a little. After all she was almost eighty. But Dorothea had always been a pillar of strength, not only to her own family but to the whole community. It seemed to Friedrike that her grandmother would go on forever. Thus she was surprised and dismayed to receive an urgent letter from Henriette stating that their Oma was failing rapidly—not sick really, just sort of fading away. Her cousin urged Friedrike to come home quickly, if at all possible, as Dorothea was especially asking for her.

At the first opportunity Friedrike went to Frau Gnevkow and showed her Henriette's letter.

The housekeeper was skeptical. "It's just an excuse to go home for Christmas. I know you young girls. Homesick after the first year. No, I simply can't spare you."

"But meine Frau, it is not an excuse. And I'm not homesick," insisted Friedrike, although in truth she was. "See my cousin's letter. Read it for yourself. I am not lying. My dearest grandmother is dying."

Frau Gnevkow shook her head. "For a mother or a father I might consider it but simply for a grandmother, no. Can you not imagine what would happen to my staff if I were to allow that? Every young maid has four grandparents. They would be absent more than they are here."

"But this is different," objected Friedrike. "Both my parents died when I was very young. Oma is the only mother I have ever known. She is my only grandparent left. And she is dying."

"I am sorry to hear that but the answer is still no. Now go about your duties like a good girl and try to put it out of your mind."

But Friedrike could not put it out of her mind. Dearest Oma, what shall I do? She was tempted to run away but she knew even Oma would not approve of that. She decided to seek her cousin Georg's advice. She had visited with Georg a few times since she had been in Hannover but not as often as either would have liked. He was always very busy with his pastoral duties and his choir and she had very little time off. But this time she would make the time. Thank goodness today she had worked for breakfast and dinner and was not required for supper. The moment she was free she forgot her own supper. She threw on her cloak and bonnet and ran to find Georg.

St. Peter's church was a long ways away, all the way across town and she ran almost the entire distance. It was already dark and she prayed that Georg would be there. Also that she would not get lost. She was breathless by the time she reached the parsonage and pounded on the door.

The maid answered and peered at her warily in the darkness.

"Is Pastor Bergmann in?" Friedrike gasped. "I am his cousin Friedrike Bergmann and it is most urgent that I speak to him."

The maid looked at her more closely. "Ach, ja, I remember you now. Come in. Come in." She ushered Friedrike into the parlor. "And whatever is a young lass like you doing out in the dark?"

Friedrike ignored that. "Is he here?" she asked. "I must speak to him forthwith. Please."

"Ja, ja, he's here. He's just having his supper. Now sit you down and catch your breath. I'll tell him you're here."

Georg came out immediately and embraced his little cousin. "I can guess why you're here. It's about Oma Dorchen, isn't it?"

She nodded. "I had a letter from Tiete."

"I had the same," he said, "and, of course, we must go and I pray we won't be too late. Even though it's our busiest season here in the church, Pastor Bödeker has been very kind and understanding. How soon can you be ready?"

"I can't go." Friedrike started to sob. "That mean, wicked old housekeeper will not let me."

"She won't let you?" exclaimed Georg. "I can't believe that."

"It's true." And Friedrike wept openly.

Georg held her close until her crying subsided. "We'll find a way," he assured her. "Come now. Dry your tears. I'll warrant you've skipped your supper to come here. That will never do. Come into the dining room. Frau Pastorin Bödeker always has more than enough."

"I don't feel like eating."

"You must. We'll figure out something."

While Friedrike picked at the food set before her by the kindly pastor's wife, Georg told them what had happened.

"Why, that is unconscionable," exclaimed Pastor Bödeker. "What can the woman be thinking of?"

"Only her own rules," replied Georg. "I have heard she will not bend an inch from them."

"Ach, then I shall go to the King," said the senior pastor. "I am not his personal pastor for nothing."

"No, not the King," gasped Friedrike in horror.

"Whyever not?" asked Georg. "This calls for stern measures."

"Because I am afraid of him."

"Afraid of him? How so?"

"He has only come to the palace a few times but every time he looks over all the women and girls as if—as if . . . oh, I cannot say it," she sobbed.

"You mean in a lewd manner," suggested Bödeker gently.

Friedrike nodded and tried to get ahold of her emotions. "His reputation as a womanizer is well known. I fear me any favor from him would have to be repaid in his bed. I could never do that—even for Oma."

"I'm afraid she's right," agreed Georg.

Pastor Bödeker nodded ruefully. "Then we shall find another way. Let me think on it. Now finish your supper, child, and Georg will walk you home ere you are missed."

The next morning Friedrike was on her hands and knees carefully sweeping the grand staircase with a dustpan and brush. Frau Gnevkow called to her from the foot of the stairs. Her face looked like thunder. Now what have I done, wondered the girl.

"Her Grace, the Duchess, wishes you to attend her forthwith," said the housekeeper.

Friedrike started to tremble with fear. And yet—Marie had been kind the one time she spoke to her. She stood up and shook out her skirts and apron. "Yes, Ma'am. Where shall I find her?"

"In her morning room. But first put away that dustpan and brush or someone will surely trip over them. You can finish up here later."

Friedrike quickly put away the tools and with much trepidation re-ascended the stairs to the Duchess' apartments. She was greeted by the same woman who had shown her the trick of polishing silver but she certainly did not look the same. Marie was dressed in a soft blue morning gown and had jewels all over her hands and around her neck.

The Duchess smiled as she said, "Come in, Friedrike."

Friedrike curtseyed deeply and said, "You sent for me, Your Grace?"

"I did. Come, sit here by me." She indicated a stool just to the right of her feet.

Friedrike sat on the stool, still a little apprehensive. But the Duchess seemed to radiate warmth and that served to calm her somewhat.

"I have just had a visit from a Pastor Bergmann—your cousin, I believe. Pastor Bödeker sent him to me." Friedrike looked up in surprise. The Duchess went on, "He told me at great length about your close-knit family and your wonderful grandmother. I am so sorry to hear she is failing but that must come to all of us in time. He told me how she kept the family together when your parents died and of all the good works she has done in Vilsen over a long lifetime. Also that she is an accomplished, highly respected healer. I sincerely wish I could have known her."

Friedrike nodded, trying to fight back the tears.

"Your cousin is a most persuasive young man. 'Tis no wonder he is such a fine pastor. I have made arrangements for both of you to travel on the stagecoach first thing tomorrow morning. It is much faster than the mail coach. Your passage has been paid for both ways. Your cousin insisted on paying his own way. I shall expect you back immediately after the funeral."

"Your Grace," Friedrike choked out. "Your Grace, how can I ever thank you? But—but what of Frau Gnevkow?"

"I have already spoken to her."

"Ach, that is why she looked so stormy when she said Your Grace wished to see me."

Marie smiled. "She always looks like that. Even I was a mite terrified of her when I first came here. But one learns to deal sternly with such as she. They expect it. Now back to your work ere the madame looks even stormier. And pack your things tonight. I shall send you and your cousin in the gig to the staging inn as the coach leaves very early."

"Oh, thank you. Thank you, Your Grace."

"Please send my fondest regards to your grandmother if she still lives. And if not, convey my deepest condolences to your family. And Friedrike, when you return you must play and sing for me. Your talented cousin has told me how very talented you are also."

"I shall, Your Grace, with all my heart."

The stagecoach was indeed much faster than the plodding mail coach which must perforce stop at every little village that had a post office. It covered the ground in one day that took the post coach two. The only prolonged stop was at Nienburg for the noonday meal. In fact, they learned later that it would not have made the stop at Vilsen but for the

Duchess' influence—and probable bribery. They arrived just as it was growing dark on the day before Christmas Eve and the coach continued on to Bremen.

The Bergmann house looked just the same as always, welcoming them home. And yet, when they entered they were struck by an eerie, sombre silence. No one seemed to be about.

"Oh, Georg," said Friedrike clutching his hand, "are we too late? Is she gone already?"

"I don't know," he replied. "We shall soon see. Is anyone at home?" he called out loudly.

There was no answer.

Friedrike peered into the parlor. "Oh, Georg, look," she exclaimed. "There is no Christmas tree."

He shook his head. That was an ill omen. "Maybe they're in the kitchen and didn't hear us."

They started down the hall just as Doris burst in from the spice shop. "Ach, welcome, welcome home," she said as she embraced them both. "I heard you come in but I had to close up the shop first."

"Oma?" asked Georg.

"She's still hanging on but barely," replied Doris. "Come, take your wraps off and go up to see her. She'll be so happy you're here. Especially you, Friede. She keeps asking for you. Mama and Tiete are with her."

To their surprise Georg and Friedrike entered a room of joy instead of mourning. It was gaily bedecked with evergreen boughs and in the corner was a festively decorated little Christmas tree surrounded by gifts. Dorothea was sitting up in bed and held out her arms to hug and kiss them. They were shocked by her appearance. She seemed to have shrunken away to nothing. Her frail body looked lost among the pillows and the pallor of her skin almost matched the white of the sheets. But she was smiling.

"Ach, dear ones, I am so glad you could come all the way from Hannover. I told Tiete not to summon you but she insisted. Now I'm glad she did. It's so good to have my whole family around me again so I can say goodbye to you all." She fell back against the pillows, exhausted from the effort of speaking. "Ach, you see how weak this old woman has become. I told Friederike and Tiete to help me up when we heard you come in but I can't sustain it for very long." Her voice was barely a whisper but she seemed to be laughing at her own frailty.

"We are so glad to be here, too," said Friedrike. "I almost couldn't come but thanks to Georg I'm here. But where is Hermann?"

"He will be here just as soon as he is finished with his work," replied Tiete. "Never fear. He has been here with Oma every free moment he has."

"Ja, and we are going to have our Christmas up here," added her mother. "We don't want Oma to miss a moment of it."

"Ah, so. We wondered why there was no tree in the parlor," said Georg. "That's an excellent idea."

"And with you here, Georg, you can lead us in the Christmas carols since we can hardly move the pianoforte up here," said Friederike.

"As for that, we have another surprise for you," said Henriette. "Johann Justus Bruns is home for the holidays and he will be here tomorrow eve to play his fiddle for our carols."

Friedrike clapped her hands. "That's wonderful."

"You know he'd be here anyway once he heard you were home," teased Doris. "He's always been sweet on you."

Friedrike blushed but she was happy for the news.

Just then Hermann rushed in. He went straight to Dorothea and kissed her before he even greeted his sister and his cousin. "Ach, Friede, I'm so glad you're here. And Georg, too. It would have been terrible if Oma . . . " Doris gave him a kick. "Oh — er — I mean, what's for supper? I'm hungry."

"Ach, young men," put in his aunt. "All they can think of is food."

They all laughed — even Dorothea.

"I know," she murmured. "I raised six of them. Feed them, Friederike."

"Ja, ja, come now, children," agreed Friederike. "Let Oma rest a bit. Too much excitement and she won't want to eat."

The next day was Christmas Eve. After all the cooking and baking was done, they all dressed in their best clothes although they had no plans for going to church this year. Pastor Georg would conduct a short prayer service later. They all trooped up to Dorothea's bedchamber. They were determined to make it a merry Christmas for her even though each one was on the verge of tears. It was hard to believe that their dear Oma was about to leave them, she who had been such a stalwart pillar of strength for each of them throughout their lives. So they put on happy faces for her sake.

Just then Johann Justus arrived. The first thing he did was pick up

Friedrike, swing her around and kiss her soundly.

"Johann, put me down," screamed Friedrike with delight.

"Why should I? I like kissing you," he replied with a chuckle. "Besides it's Christmas. Merry Christmas everyone." Only then did he pay his respects to Dorothea.

The old lady was smiling at his antics. "She'll make you a good wife someday," she said, "if that's what you have in mind."

"I'll admit that has crossed my mind, Oma Dorchen, but there's time," he said. "I have to get settled first and get my business going. And she's young yet. We can wait."

Friedrike blushed. "Don't talk about me as if I weren't here," she said indignantly. "Don't I have anything to say about it?"

"Not until I ask you," teased Johann Justus.

"You could do worse," said Dorothea. "The Bruns are a fine family. Why, I remember fifty—nay, almost sixty years ago this young man's uncle of the same name rescued me from the Sacred Spring . . . "

"Ja, Oma," interrupted Henriette, "you've told us that story many a time. Don't tire yourself now."

Dorothea sank back against the pillows. "You're right, my little nurse. I must save my strength for giving my gifts."

"Gifts? Oma, when did you . . . ?" began Henriette.

"How could you possibly . . . ?" asked Friedrike.

"Oma, we don't need any gifts," objected Hermann.

"I'm sure she's thought of something to surprise us," said Doris.

"I'm certain she has," added Georg.

"It wouldn't be Christmas without gifts, now would it?" whispered their grandmother with great effort. "Nay, I did not steal out of bed to make things or go shopping. These are special. You'll see. Ach, now I'm going to be scolded. Here comes our almost-physician."

Ludwig Schulze entered the room. The first thing he did was go over to the bed and feel Dorothea's pulse. "It's too fast," he pronounced. "You've been exciting yourself, Mistress Bergmann."

Dorothea waved him away. "Ach, it's Christmas. My last. Let me excite myself if I want to. Go and kiss your almost-betrothed. Johann Justus was not so hesitant."

Ludwig blushed. He took Henriette's hand and gave her a tiny peck on the cheek.

How staid he is, thought Friedrike, smiling inwardly. She much preferred Johann Justus' exuberance.

Now Johann Justus took up his fiddle and they sang several choruses of carols. All the old favorites and some new ones as well. Then it was time for the gifts. Friedrike was embarrassed.

"I didn't bring any presents," she said apologetically, "because I didn't know until the night before that I should even be able to come."

"Never mind, child," said her aunt Friederike. "You brought yourself. That's all that matters."

"Ja, that's the best gift of all," chimed in Johann Justus.

"Now, before anything else let me bestow my gifts," said Dorothea, sounding for the first time more like her old self, "just in case I should fall asleep ere I have a chance. Georg, Lude, help me to sit up again."

"Just one gift ere you start, Oma," insisted Doris, "so you won't catch a chill while you sit up."

"Very well, just one then."

Doris brought a large package from under the tree. She helped Dorothea unwrap it. It was a beautifully crocheted shawl of the sheerest wool in a heavenly pale blue. "Ach, little one, this is exquisite. And you did it all yourself?"

"Ja, Oma. It took me a long time. I prayed I would have it done ere— er—in time for Christmas."

"Then your work has certainly improved since I was last below stairs."

"You taught me, Oma."

"It's a shame that I'll not be here long enough to enjoy it very often."

"Ach, Oma, yes, you will. But that is why I chose my own favorite color so that . . ."

Dorothea laughed. "The ever practical Doris. Thank you, my dear. It is lovely. Now, Georg, if you would be so good as to fetch my coffer over there and set it beside me here on the bed."

Georg did so. It was the same coffer that had been broken into years ago. The lock had never been repaired. Dorothea slowly opened the lid. They all wondered what was coming next.

The first item she tried to extract from the box was so heavy she could hardly lift it. "Here Georg, help me. It is to be your gift. The family Bible."

Georg was overwhelmed. "Oh, thank you, Oma. I shall treasure it."

"You are the eldest," she said, "and you must keep all the family records as I have. It was started by my grandfather Cyriacus Lindemann. He gave one to each of his daughters. That was my mother Lise's copy."

"I shall be honored to do so, Oma."

Then she carefully withdrew from the coffer the ancient, fragile bit of paper dated 1695 that each of them had been shown but were never allowed to touch. "Tiete, you are to be the trustee of this genealogy that my grandfather had from his grandmother Anna von Sehnden. Make sure that the very moment any one of you marry you will enroll them in both the von Sehnden and the Stockman stipendia. Georg has already studied under the von Sehnden for your generation but the children any of you might have would be eligible. As for the Stockman you are all eligible the moment you wed but you must apply. So Tiete, see that they do so quickly as I fear they are very far behind. Here are the addresses in Celle and Uelzen where you must write."

"Oh, Oma, I shall take good care of it," said Henriette, "and you can trust me to do exactly as you say."

Dorothea lay back against the pillows for a moment.

"It's too much excitement for her. She must lie down again," pronounced Ludwig.

"Oh, hush, Lude," objected Dorothea. "I'm just resting a minute. And I'm having fun. Don't deprive an old lady of her last pleasure." She took a sheaf of papers out of the coffer.

"Hermann," she said. "This isn't worth very much but I feel you should have it. It is your papa Anton's Master Miller papers *and* the testament from old Anton Matthies making you hereditary lessee of the Klostermühle. I know you don't want to be a miller but that legal document just might someday be the means of bringing Heinrich Matthies to justice for what he did to us."

"Thank you, Oma," said Hermann, "but don't upset yourself over that. It is long past."

"Ach, I know but it will come back to him someday. Building that windmill with illicit gains. The good Lord will see that justice is done. Some day. I predict it. And now, my dearest little Friede," she dove into the coffer again and extracted a small notebook. It looked quite new compared to the treasures she had already dispensed. "For you, something special that I did make myself. Last summer when I knew I would be leaving you soon, I wrote down all the recipes for the simples, potions and medicines I had from the old wise-woman, from my dear mother and some I made up myself. I leave all that knowledge to you."

"Thank you, Oma. It is a great honor," replied Friedrike, "but I don't have the time. I'll not even be here in Vilsen."

"You will. You will. In two or three years you will be back here and take up where I left off—curing the sick and comforting those you cannot cure. You will be very good at it. Meanwhile study the book until you learn them all by heart and know what illnesses they are useful for."

Ludwig Schulze made a face. He did not intend for Dorothea to see it but, frail as she was, her mind was still sharp and she missed nothing. "Ach, Lude, I know what you're thinking," she chided, "but I'll wager in my lifetime I've cured more unfortunate folk than all the doctors we've ever had here in Vilsen. Ja, some so weakened by the bleedings and purges that the doctors gave them up for dead. The old ways are still the best. I trow, the old wisewoman knew more than any ten doctors—even if she did occasionally speak to Wotan's ravens."

"Well, it's true, I must admit," replied Ludwig, somewhat flustered, "that bleeding and purging are falling out of favor and that the theory of the four humors causing disease is no longer so widely believed. I have even seen through the microscope some of the 'wee animales' that van Leeuvenhoek spoke of but whether they are for good or ill or why they exist sometimes and not at others we do not know. It is a great mystery."

"Not so to those of us versed in the old ways," insisted Dorothea. "It would behoove you to learn some of it yourself. Anyway, Friede here shall be Vilsen's next wisewoman."

"Oh, Oma, that is too great a responsibility," demurred Friedrike. "I don't know that I am capable of it."

"Of course, you are. And now to Doris, I leave all the simples and medicines already in my apothecary corner of her shop. That should fetch you a tidy sum. And once Friede starts making them, you are to receive half the profits."

"Thank you, Oma," said Doris. "I wondered about that."

Dorothea laughed. "You would. And lastly to my dearest gooddaughter who has done so much to make my last days comfortable . . . "

"Oh, no," objected Friederike. "You are the one who has done so much, Mama Dorchen, and have given everything you have to the children. There can't be anything more."

"Ah, but there is," said Dorothea. "When my dearest mother passed on a few years ago, I learned that the Matthies had not stolen all of the Koch inheritance. There is a small sum still at interest in Wernigerode. Since Philipp and my little brother and sister are all dead, it has passed to me. It isn't much but it will help. And I have left instructions that after your death it is to be divided equally among these five children."

"Oh, Mama Dorchen!" exclaimed Friederike.

537

Dorothea held up her hand. "And," she added, "whatever money is left here in my coffer after you pay for my funeral is yours to keep as well. It even includes the two half-groschen and few pennies the Matthies left behind. I kept them for good luck," she said laughing.

After all that the gifts under the tree seemed superfluous.

At the end of the evening Johann Justus took Friedrike's hand. "Will you walk out to the gate with me?"

She nodded and donned her cloak. They walked hand in hand a short distance through the churchyard. He stopped under the great linden tree. It was very still and cold but the stars shone brilliantly through the bare branches. He kissed her lightly and held her close.

"I had no intention of speaking of marriage yet," he whispered into her hair. "I want to get my business well established which may take three or four years. But since your grandmother brought it up, I'm simply asking, will you wait?"

She backed off and held him at arm's length. "I don't know. I honestly don't feel ready for that yet. I'm still young."

"I know."

"Besides, I, too, have to wait three or four years. I'm supposedly committed to the Duke and Duchess until I am one-and-twenty. Would *you* wait?"

He took her in his arms again. "I'll wait," he murmured. "And you know what? I am going to start calling you Fritzi. There are just too many Friedrikes in that house. It's confusing."

She laughed. "But my aunt spells hers with an extra 'e'."

In response he kissed her deeply, longingly and she felt her whole body thrill.

"I'll wait," she said at last.

They could hear the Christmas Eve service just ending in the church as the doors were opened and the joyful music poured out.

"Merry Christmas, dearest Fritzi."

"Merry Christmas, Johann Justus."

On 29 December 1844 Dorothea passed peacefully into her last sleep. No doubt her illustrious ancestors welcomed her into their heavenly ranks.

Back in Hannover after the New Year Friedrike noticed some

changes, some subtle, others more obvious. Inge was bubbling with excitement. "Did you have a nice Christmas?" she asked. "You missed a good time. It was simply dazzling here."

"My grandmother died four days after Chirstmas," replied Friedrike.

"Oh, I forgot. That's why you went home, isn't it? I'm so sorry. It can't have been very pleasant."

"But it was. She made Christmas Eve one of the loveliest I can ever remember. And look what she gave me."

She pulled the little notebook out of her portmanteau. Normally Friedrike did not share her inmost thoughts with Inge. They were two such different people. But she just had to share her joy in the treasure she had received from Dorothea with someone.

"What is that?" asked Inge, obviously not impressed.

"It's all the recipes for her simples and potions and medicines."

"Whatever would you want that for?"

"So I can have an income after I leave here."

Inge blinked. "You don't want to get married?"

"Someday perhaps but not for quite a while."

"Does it have a potion in there to prevent conception?"

This time Friedrike blinked. "Probably. I'd have to study it carefully first. Why do you ask?" Although Friedrike already knew the answer to that question. Inge was still running out to the stables to her groom every chance she got.

"Because the King has taken a fancy to me."

"The King!" exclaimed Friedrike.

"Ja, the King himself. He noticed me at Christmastime and during the New Year's ball he took me to one of the fancy bedchambers. I could hardly refuse, could I? Despite his age he is still a very virile man. And if you don't look at the terribly wounded side of his face he is really quite handsome. Isn't that exciting?"

Friedrike should have been shocked but she was not. "Inge, Inge, do be careful," she warned. "He is known to be very cruel."

"A little rough, maybe, but he was not cruel to me. Aren't you excited for me?"

"No, I'm not. Inge, you are playing with fire."

"Ach, don't be so stodgy. 'Tis the only way to advancement in this place. And I don't mean to be a second maid all my life. You'll see."

Friedrike could only shake her head at her friend's foolishness.

Two months later there was another bit of news that set the whole palace to rejoicing. The Duchess Marie was with child at last. If all went well, it would be born in late September. The following month Inge was transferred to the future nursery. She was set to stitching infant clothes which she was not very good at. But it did not matter. Everyone knew how Inge had achieved her promotion.

One day the Duchess sought out Friedrike. "I am sorry, my dear," she said. "I requested you, you know, and the Duke agreed but the King overrode our decision. I don't know why."

"I am afraid we all know why," replied Friedrike bitterly. "But thank you anyway, Your Grace, for thinking of me."

"Is it so obvious then?" asked the Duchess horrified.

"She brags about it to me, Your Grace."

"Oh, he would not like that one bit."

"I'm sure he would not."

"Don't worry, Friedrike, your turn will come. I'll think of something."

"Thank you, Your Grace. I should only want a promotion on my own merits—not that way."

"Good girl," said Marie.

Late in the spring Inge returned to their tiny attic room and started slamming things into her travelling box. Friedrike could see she had been crying but now she seemed more angry than sad.

"Whatever is wrong, Inge?" she asked.

"Damn him. Damn that wretched old woman. Damn them all," she cried. "I am to leave forthwith."

Friedrike was astonished. "But why, Inge?"

Inge pulled the skirt of her gown tight and stuck out her belly. "That's why. Haven't you noticed? Did you think I was just getting fat? My God, you are the innocent. That is a babe in there," she said bitterly.

Friedrike was not surprised. "Is it—is it the King's?"

"Nay, no such luck," moaned Inge. "If it were, I'd be sitting pretty. But no, he hasn't been near me since that one time at New Year's. Now that he has taken the Countess von Grote for a mistress, he has lost interest. I doubt she'll let him near any other woman. Nay, it is the by-blow of that fool Roland. And the old witch Gnevkow has finally noticed and has summarily turned me out."

"Oh, Inge, I'm so sorry. But can't—er—Roland—(it was the first time she had ever heard the groom's name) marry you? Or won't he?"

"I didn't ask. Nor would I want him even if he did. He was a good lay but too stupid to spend the rest of my life with. I had hoped to conceal it until the Duchess had hers—this one is due only a few weeks later—and then apply to be wet nurse for the new princeling. But Gnevkow wouldn't hear of it. Nay, I shall go back to Nienburg and try to find a rich old man who would be sympathetic to my plight."

Friedrike shook her head. Oh, Inge, she thought, it is you who are the innocent one.

The next morning Inge departed.

A few days later the Du chess of Cumberland summoned Friedrike to her apartments.

"Sit down by me here," she invited. "I suppose you can guess why you are here."

"Dare I hope, Your Grace?" asked Friedrike.

"Yes, you may dare," said Marie. "This time *I* have overruled the King. You shall be my nursery maid. Nay, not just a maid but in charge of the nursery. There will be a wet nurse, of course, and a laundry maid, perhaps some others under you. The midwife, naturally, will rule all—even me—but if all goes well she will only be here for a few weeks before and after the birth."

"Oh, Your Grace, I am deeply honored. Thank you so much. But I fear I do not have much experience with babies. I was the youngest in our family."

"Then we shall learn together," said Marie. "The midwife will tell you all you need to know and from then on it is simply common sense and loving care."

"I shall do my best, Your Grace. And Frau Gnevkow?"

"She will have nothing to do with the nursery except to send in a girl to clean. You will be responsible only to the midwife and to me."

"That is a very pleasant prospect, Your Grace."

Marie smiled. "Then you may move your things into your new room today. Come, I'll show you."

The room off the nursery, though small, was three times the size of the attic cubbyhole Friedrike had shared with Inge. And, what's more, it had a private sitting room attached with its own cheery fireplace.

"Oh, Your Grace," she exclaimed, "this is sheer luxury compared to that—that . . ."

"I know. I hope you will be happy here. And raise a happy child for me."

"Indeed, I shall, Your Grace."

One of the first things Friedrike did after settling in was to rip out most of Inge's atrociously incompetent stitching. She spent most of her time resewing dozens of tiny baby clothes and decorating the nursery for the eagerly awaited princeling. Marie was so sure it would be a boy that no thought was given to the possibility of a princess.

That summer Friedrike was not allowed to go home to Vilsen but it did not matter. She was happy in her work and with Dorothea gone, it would not have been the same, perhaps even sad. And the Duchess needed her. By this time Marie was heavy and cumbersome — restless, bored with waiting. The oppressive summer heat also made the carrying more uncomfortable. Although her personal maid did all she could to make it easier for her lady, Marie often called on Friedrike to keep her company and sometimes to entertain her.

One day they were in the opulent music room of the palace, just the two of them. The Duchess was lolling languidly on a silken chaise-longue while Friedrike played soothing melodies and joyful tunes on the pianoforte. The baby had been more restless than usual and its kicking had made Marie edgy. Friedrike could sense her gradually relaxing to the calming music. She was wlling to play all day if the lady so desired. Besides she was enjoying it, too.

Suddenly they were interrupted by Marie's personal maid bursting into the room. "My lady, Your Grace, I am sorry to bother you but the King has just arrived," she exclaimed.

Friedrike stopped playing and Marie looked decidedly annoyed. "He has no doubt come to confer with the Duke," she said. "It is no concern of mine."

"But he was asking specifically for Your Grace," said the woman.

"Then let him come to me," said the Duchess haughtily. The woman looked shocked but left.

Moments later Ernst August entered the room. "What are you doing down here?" he demanded to know. In the presence of the monarch only two postures were acceptable. One either stood or bowed low. No one sat without the royal permission. Friedrike immediately jumped up from the bench and sank into a deep curtsey. The Duchess did not move.

"I am enjoying some lovely music," she replied succinctly.

"You should be up in your chamber for your lying-in not down here parading your—your condition for all the world to see." He glared at Friedrike who was still trembling in her curtsey.

"My condition is due to *your* heir and I am sure all the world is aware of it. Moreover, Sire, I find your attitude towards women's affairs as archaic as your politics."

Ernst August looked as though he would burst a blood vessel. He started to fume but then thought better of it. "Modern women," he grumbled under his breath.

Meanwhile Marie noticed Friedrike's discomfort. "Rike dear, you may arise and sit you back down ere you fall down."

"And who is this?" growled the King.

"My new nursery maid," replied the Duchess.

"What! A peasant who can play the pianoforte!" he exclaimed. "I suppose she can read, too. I'll not have it. They are the ones who are stirring up all this unrest."

"She is a far better maid than the one you chose, Sire, and a very talented person as well."

Friedrike could take no more of this. If she lost her job, so be it. She had to speak up. "Begging Your Majesty's pardon," she said, "but I am no peasant. My family have been Bürgers in Vilsen for centuries. I *can* read and write and play music, too, which I believe my lady enjoys."

This time Ernst August fumed. "Why, that impertinent hussy. Dismiss her immediately."

Marie replied as calmly as she could although she was seething inside. "Nay, Sire, I'll not dismiss her. She is a fine companion as well as a maid. And if you don't stop upsetting me, you could well harm the babe. Now, with your permission, I'd like to continue our music."

The threat of possible harm to the babe stopped Ernst August in his tracks. That would never do. He turned and marched out of the room without saying another word.

On 21 September 1845 the long awaited prince was born. Her labor had been relatively easy and after her maids and the midwife's assistants cleaned her up, the Duchess Marie sank back against the luxurious pillows and sighed with relief at a job well done. Now mayhap the old boar will be happy. For that is how she thought of her father-in-law, the King— a boar, the strongest, meanest, most unpredictable animal known. The midwife placed the babe in her arms and she described to her blind husband how beautiful and healthy the boy seemed to be. But Georg, in awe and wonder that this could really be his, insisted on feeling every part of the tiny mite's body.

"He is perfect in every way," Marie assured him.

And Georg, finally satisfied that his son had all the necessary equipment, leaned over and kissed his wife. "I am very proud of you, my dear," he said. "We shall name him Ernst August."

"Of course," agreed Marie. She had expected no less.

But little Ernst August did object to all the fondling and started squalling.

"Put him to the breast, Your Grace," urged the midwife.

"Nay, nay," objected the Duke. "How can you even suggest that? Only peasants nurse their own children. We have hired a wet nurse."

Marie would have liked to nurse her baby for a while but she dared not go against her husband's wishes. Such a thing was just not done in royal circles. "Give him to Friedrike," she instructed the midwife. "The wet nurse is awaiting him in the nursery."

Friedrike wrapped the baby in a delicate receiving blanket and bore him off to the nursery. No swaddling clothes for this one, she thought, as she handed him over to the wet nurse. The midwife had told her that such wrappings were a thing of the past, in fact, could inhibit the child's growth. And since no one else had mentioned the swaddling Friedrike was determined to care for this princeling herself in every way except the actual feeding. She felt very protective of the tiny mite and already loved him dearly.

As soon as word of the birth reached the King, Ernst August hurried from the Leine Schloss to the Fürstenhof and went directly to the nursery. The baby had just finished suckling his first meal and Friedrike was cuddling him a little before laying him in the magnificent royal cradle, when the King burst in. It was impossible to curtsey properly with the babe in her arms so Friedrike merely executed a half bow.

"Never mind all that," said Ernst August. "Let me see him. Is he whole?"

"He is beautiful, Your Majesty," she replied turning the little one's face toward him.

"I would see all of him," demanded the King.

"Perhaps Your Majesty would like to hold him whilst I remove the blanket," she suggested.

"Ja, give him here." The King held out his arms. As Friedrike placed the baby in his arms, she felt his hand brush against her breast. Was it deliberate or simply accidental? She could not be sure but she backed away a little as she unwrapped the blanket. "I would see all of him," insisted Ernst August.

"But, Sire, he must not catch a chill," she replied.

"Ach, with that roaring fire you have in here, how can he catch a chill? The room is stifling."

"To us it may seem warm but he has just emerged from the warm womb where he has been sleeping these many months. To him it will seem chilly." She was aghast at her own bravado in speaking thus to the King but she did not care. What did this fool know about babies?

"Do you deny your king the right to view his own grandson?"

"Nay, nay, never, Your Majesty. But please be quick for the child's sake." She removed the tiny shirt while the King carefully counted the correct number of fingers and toes. She hesitated over the diaper.

"Take if off. That is the most important part of a man, is it not?" He leered at her. "How can I know that it is not a girl unless I see for myself."

As Friedrike bent to untie the diaper, she felt once again the tips of his fingers touching her breast. This time she knew it was deliberate and she could not back off. She quickly removed the diaper and stood aside.

"Ah, so," said the King.

"He will be tall like Your Majesty, I trow," she said. "See how long he is already."

Just then the tiny penis stood up straight and squirted all over the King's fancy uniform.

Friedrike nearly choked trying to suppress a giggle. "Ah, Sire, I am so sorry," she apologized. "He has just been fed and that is the way of babies." And it serves you right, she thought mischievously.

"Here, take him. I have seen enough," sputtered Ernst August as he thrust the child back into her arms. A maid rushed up and dabbed ineffectually at his coat with a cloth. He hurried from the room. After he left Friedrike and all the maids burst into gales of laughter.

Ernst August stopped briefly to visit his daughter-in-law, the Duchess Marie. "Thank you, my dear," he said. "Now the inheritance is secure. I am afraid I cannot linger. Your son has already annointed me." He fled from the palace.

Later when Friedrike told Marie the whole story, they fell into each other's arms and laughed to the point of tears. "Serves him right," said the Duchess.

Although the King's mistress kept him on a tight rein, rumor had it that he still laid any number of willing, and some not so willing, servant girls at both the Leine Schloss and the Fürstenhof as well as having frequent liaisons with noblemen's wives. Friedrike always kept her distance from him whenever he visited the nursery. But soon it became apparent that he had lost interest in the child and was more interested in her. She hesitated to mention her fears to the duchess as she knew Marie would have no power in this situation. Yet his attentions made her nervous.

One day he took her by the hand and led her into her own private sitting room. Friedrike tried to hold back but his grip was strong.

"Sire," she exclaimed, "I do not believe it is seemly for you to be alone with me in my private quarters."

"Anything your King does is seemly. Do you wish the others to overhear all our conversation?"

"I can't imagine what Your Majesty could have to say that is not fit for their ears."

Ernst August ignored that. "A young maid like you who plays the pianoforte and can read and write could go far with my help." He tried to put his arm around her but she pulled away.

"Sire, you may consider me a mean peasant but I am from a Bürger family and although persons of royalty may not think so, we have our honor. I am quite content with my position here and have no desire to go farther. Moreover, I do not intend to stay here all my life. As soon as my agreed upon time of service is completed, I shall return to my home. Meanwhile I am quite certain that Her Grace is well satisfied with my work."

Suddenly without warning the King swept her into his arms and kissed her full upon the lips. "Ah, a tasty little bitch you are. I like a wench with spirit."

Friedrike was aghast. She pushed him away. Without thinking of the possible consequences she declared, "I will not sleep with you, Sire. Not for any promotion nor any promises of royal largess. You are acting beyond the bounds of propriety. And if you see fit to have me dismissed, I beg you to tell Her Grace the *real* reason for it. Now get out of my rooms and the nursery ere you disturb your grandson as much as you have upset me."

Ernst August stood for a moment looking perplexed. Rare was the woman, peasant or noble, who had refused him. And she such a fiery bitch—the kind he enjoyed. Well, he would bide his time.

Friedrike was not dismissed. And she never told Marie of the incident. The king avoided the nursery when at all possible after that. Only after the child learned to walk and talk did he visit occasionally and then quickly took the little boy out for a ride on his horse.

Life went on peacefully for a time. In the summer of 1846 Friedrike was able to go home to Vilsen for a short leave but it was not the same without her Oma Dorchen. Henriette was still not wed and she was beginning to fear her Ludwig would never ask her. Friedrike had hoped to see Johann Justus but he was off somewhere. Christmas was the best time for that and she knew she would never again be allowed to leave Hannover at that time. Although she heard that Johann Justus had achieved his master's status, he still had not settled down and she was afraid he never would. He had not written to her at all since her grandmother's funeral a year and a half ago. Best forget about him, she told herself, although she really did not want to.

The following year, 1847, she could not leave at all as the Duchess had borne another child—a fragile, little girl this time, whom they named Friederike.

"Not after you, my dear," joked Marie, "although I'd have liked to say so. But after my husband's late mother, Queen Friederike."

" 'Tis a good name, Your Grace, no matter whom she is named after. I am proud to bear it."

But later when she heard the duchess calling the tiny girl Fritzi, it brought tears to her eyes. At home she was usually called Friede. Marie called her Rike. But only Johann Justus had called her by the endearing diminutive Fritzi. She often wondered where he was and what he was doing and if she would ever see him again.

17

1848

Dwelling in the rarified atmosphere of the royal palace Friedrike heard little of what was going on in the rest of the world—partly because of her isolation in the nursery but also because Ernst August censored every bit of news that came to the Fürstenhof. Thus she had no idea, because she had been home so seldom, that there had been three years of bad, even disastrous, harvests. Famine was rampant in the land and disease quickly followed.

A growing undercurrent of restlessness and resentment swept the country and permeated all levels of society. The farmers bemoaned their lost franchise—and blamed Ernst August; merchants, hoping for renewed trade after the separation from England, decried the lack of railroads and factories—and blamed Ernst August; statesmen and politicians chafed under the censorship of the press—and knew the King was to blame. With three years of poor harvests the entire economy regressed to a state worse than at the end of the French time. The smoldering embers of dissatisfaction and anger needed only a breath of wind to turn it into a raging bonfire.

On 24 February the bourgeoisie of Paris rose and swept Louis Philippe from the throne.

A firestorm of revolution spread across every German state, indeed across most of Europe. The princes shook with fear. Before the end of February uprisings occurred in Baden and other southern states and their rulers were forced to obey their quasi-dormant constitutions and invite liberal ministers into their cabinets. The revolution spread to Vienna and became bloody and violent. The Habsburg empire nearly fell apart as Hungary demanded its own parliament; Bohemia, Croatia, Lombardy and Venezia all rose against the crown. The archconservative Metternich was forced to resign and fled first to Prussia and eventually to England.

A few days later on 16 March news of Vienna reached Berlin. A dithering, timid King Friedrich Wilhelm gathered his troops around him but hesitated to act. At last on 18 March he issued a proclamation that parliament and the constitution would be reinstated and other rights of the people restored. But he had hesitated too long. Instead of the joyous crowd he had expected at the palace gates the people were sullen and distrustful. The mob pushed forward demanding concrete promises instead of vagueness. The troops fired on the crowd and two people were killed. This set off bloody street fighting that engulfed all of Berlin for several days. Prince Wilhelm, the King's even more reactionary brother, was quickly sent out of the city on a vaguely conceived diplomatic mission to England. Wilhelm stopped en route at Hannover and was warmly welcomed by Ernst August. This was a grave mistake.

Friedrike had heard the horrifying news from Berlin and Vienna as had everyone else but they were far away and she was more concerned with her own immediate problems. The King's unwanted overtures had become more frequent and persistent. Just this afternoon he had, in a fit of temper at her constant refusals, dragged her into her own bedchamber and flung her on the bed. He had stood over her menacingly, threatening all sorts of punishment if she would not comply with his desires.

"Never, never," cried Friedrike.

"Hush! Do you want the whole palace to hear you?"

"Yes, I do," she replied.

But Ernst August stopped short of outright rape. Not from any consideraton for his victim, she was sure, but more likely from fear of ridicule. He was, after all, almost eighty years old. He turned away and stalked out of the room.

Friedrike lay shaking on the bed for a long time. Her arm was still sore where he had twisted it. No doubt it would show huge bruises ere long. She finally made up her mind that this time she had to tell the Duchess Marie, perhaps even tender her resignation. She needed an ally. The burden was becoming too heavy to carry alone. But first she would seek out her cousin Georg's advice.

That evening after supper she donned her heavy cloak and set out. It was a very mild evening, almost too warm and springlike for March. The heavy cloak soon became too warm. She threw back the hood and let the cloak hang open, but she still did not take it off. She needed the garment more for a disguise than for warmth. She wandered aimlessly through the streets of Hannover, as much to calm down as to get her thoughts organized before telling Georg her plight. She soon realized she was nearing the ancient Leine Schloss where the King was busy entertaining his cousin-by-marriage, Prince Wilhelm of Prussia. It was entirely opposite to the direction in which she had intended to go. She turned to the left down a small street leading back to the center of town. And then she heard it.

At first it was like the roar of ocean surf—which she had never seen or heard in her life but which she had read about. And she had seen waterfalls. This was like the roar of the mightiest floodwater. She stood still for a moment wondering what it was and where it was coming from. Then in the far distance she spied the twinkling of numerous torches and bit by bit she could distinguish individual voices rising above the uproar. She froze in her tracks as she realized what all the noise portended. A crowd of shouting people was marching towards her—thousands upon thousands of them. As yet the mob was not unruly. They strode along in good order but the press of humanity filled the street wall to wall. She did not know whether to flee or hide or keep moving for that was the direction in which she wanted to go. Surely they would let her pass. They still seemed peaceable enough.

Just then a uniformed horseman rode out of a nearby alley and saw her hestitating.

"You'd best seek shelter, lass," he called out. "That mob will run you down. I'm off to warn the Schloss." And he galloped on.

Then she was truly frightened. She realized then that the revolution had come to Hannover.

Friedrike looked frantically for a place where she could hide but the house walls were solid, flush against the street. The alley from which the horseman had emerged was too far ahead. The insurgents had almost reached it. She flattened herself against the nearest building and hoped they would pass her by unmolested. As the first ranks approached she noticed two men proudly bearing a large banner—the black, red and gold flag that the student groups some years ago had determined would be the new emblem of a united Germany—if it could ever be united.

The first groups that passed her seemed orderly enough, marching along in almost military fashion, shouting benign slogans like 'Freedom', 'Give us our constitution back', 'Reinstate Parliament', 'Let Stüve be heard', and so on. Friedrike thought she even recognized a few familiar faces—but men from Vilsen here in Hannover, so far away? In the growing darkness she could not be sure. It was probably just a trick of the light.

Friedrike clung to her wall. So far no one had bothered her, in most cases had not even seen her. But then the later ranks of the mob became more obstreperous. They were not marching at all but pushing ahead trying to get to the forefront. There were even several women among them. And the slogans became cruder, even obscene, and much louder.

"Send the Prussian pig back to Berlin," yelled one.

"Ja, and why not send Ernst August back to England as well," shouted another.

"Ach, he's too well protected between his whores' legs," came the reply.

"I'd like to get him between my legs," screamed a disheveled woman. "I'd bite his shrivelled old balls off—'ceptin I ain't got no teeth." The crowd guffawed loudly at this. "I'd still have 'em," she continued, "had we not been starving these past years."

Friedrike pulled her hood over her head and closed her eyes to try and shut out the sound and the sight of them but the noise was too great. And she could smell them—unwashed bodies, onions and garlic—and the alcoholic fumes told her that many were very drunk. Suddenly she felt someone grab her arm.

"Come along, girlie. What you doin' cringing there? Don't you want to see the King?"

Friedrike screamed. "No, I don't," she cried. "Unhand me, you beast."

The man was black-haired, red-faced, unshaven and missing several teeth. "Now that ain't no way to talk to someone who's just fighting to get his rights back but mayhap you don't understand that. You look mighty uppity to me. You one of the King's whores?" He was so repulsive she tried to ignore him.

"I am not," she snapped. "Just leave me alone."

But the man would not let go. Against her will he dragged her along with the crowd. "Come on now," he urged. "We need every body in Hannover to stand up to the King. Why, a pretty face like yours might just be the thing to soften up his cold, black heart."

Friedrike calmed a little when she saw that he was not about to rape or otherwise harm her. She tried another tactic. "I agree with all you are trying to do," she tried to explain, "but I do not want to see the King. I hate him, too." And that, she admitted, was the truth. "Just let me go about my business."

"Now that's a right-thinkin' lass," said her captor, "but right now your business is here with every other right-thinkin' Bürger in Hannover."

551

She doubted that he was a Bürger but nowadays, who knew? They were swept along by the mob and she realized she was so enclosed by the press of bodies that she could not have extricated herself had she wanted to. Also by now she was becoming curious as to the outcome of this insurrection. But then she began to worry. Surely Ernst August would call out his troops. She knew that he had only the highly trained, crack Palace Guard with him at the Leine Schloss and they alone could not possibly overcome this mob—unless some hothead started shooting, as had happened in Berlin. But the rest of the troops were just outside the city gates. They could be there in less than half an hour. And then things could turn bloody. She noticed that not one of the men in the crowd appeared to be armed. It would be a massacre. But would even Ernst August stoop that low? Yes, he would, she realized, thinking of her own predicament.

The man's grip on her arm relaxed as he became aware that she could not escape. She tried to sidle away from him but then a new surge of humanity swept her forward. The excitement of the people grew palpable as they neared the ancient Schloss. When they reached the great square before the castle, the crowd fanned out into ever larger semicircles. Now she might have a chance but looking back she realized she was trapped. Hundreds and hundreds of people kept pouring into the square from every side street and alley. There was no way out.

Friedrike watched intently as the men in front surrounding the flag-bearers lined up before the portico of the Schloss and shouted, "Your Majesty, come out. Your subjects would have words with you." Their tone was respectful enough but there was something else. Was it hatred, disgust or even despair? Probably all three. And Ernst August did not appear.

The crowd behind the leaders took up the cry. "Sire, hear us. We only want justice." "Give us our constitution back." "Freedom—freedom from tyranny." The demands grew wilder, louder and coarser as the outcry spread back through the mob. And still no one appeared.

Friedrike realized that the temper of the crowd was building towards a volatility that needed only a spark to touch off a full scale riot. Oh, why doesn't that arrogant fool come out and talk to them, she thought. Just then the Palace Guard appeared and lined itself up across the portico. Oh, please God, don't let them shoot, she prayed. But the guardsmen stood at ease, rifle butts on the ground before them. Yet they remained very alert to every nuance. Then one of the leaders who presumably could see more than the rest held up his hand for silence. And just in time, for the presence of the Guard had had an incendiary effect. The mob's shouts diminished to an ominous rumbling.

Friedrike tried to push ahead to see what was about to take place. But everyone else had the same idea and the sudden surge knocked her off her feet. Inadvertently she screamed as she fell. Several of the forward ranks turned around to see what was amiss. Two kindly men helped her up ere she was trampled by those behind.

"Are ye hurt, lass?" one asked in homey Low German.

"Nay, nay," she replied in the same familiar language. "I'm all right, thank you. Just a little shaken." She made a pretense of brushing dirt off her skirt to hide her embarrassment. But then her curiosity got the best of her. "Where are you from," she asked, "that you speak Platt?" For that was what the old Low German was beginning to be called.

"I hail from Bücken," the man replied. "And you?"

"Not so far. From Vilsen," she said.

"Ach, I believe there are several men from Vilsen here. Mayhap you know them."

"Oh, where?" she queried anxiously.

The man shrugged and waved vaguely. "Somewhere about. Who knows in this mob?"

Then another surge of humanity separated them. She strained to look about for familiar faces but could not see over the heads of those immediately in front of her. After a few moments she sensed rather than saw someone pushing *backward* against the flood tide of the crowd. The fool, she thought. But then, maybe I should follow him and get myself out of this mess. Suddenly she felt an arm snake around her waist.

She gasped and was about to scream when the man whispered into her ear, "Hush, Fritzi. It is I, Johann Justus."

She nearly swooned at the familiar voice. "Ach, Johann, you startled me," she said as she fell against him. "I am so glad to see you. But whatever are you doing here?"

"I might ask the same of you," he replied.

"I was going to visit my cousin Georg when I got caught up in—in this mob and—and I could not get away. Just what is it all about?" she asked.

"It is about freedom," replied Johann Justus. "We only want the bas—er—tyrant to restore to us those rights and freedoms he took away from us over ten years ago. People are rising up against tyranny all over Europe. It is time these despots saw the light."

"And you came all the way from Vilsen?"

553

"Several of us did. These are not just people from the city of Hannover. Almost every town and village in the entire kingdom of Hannover has sent a delegation here."

"But how do you propose to convince him if no one has been able to so far?"

"We hope to strike fear in his heart by sheer numbers. Let him see how the majority of people really feel. There has even been some talk of assassination."

Friedrike gasped. "Not you?"

"Nay, not I. That is not the way to go. But if he does not redress the wrongs soon I fear me this crowd could take matters into their own hands."

"Oh, I hope not but I fear there will be trouble very soon. He is sure to have called in the troops. They could be here any minute and then — then . . ."

"Ja, let me try to get you safely out of here. Then I shall come back."

"Nay, nay," she objected. "I want to stay with you. Then I shall feel safe enough. Besides, now I am curious as to what will happen. He is very stubborn, you know."

"Very well but promise me, the minute any commotion erupts, you will let me hustle you out of here forthwith."

She nodded as they turned their attention once more to the men in the front ranks who were calling for silence. The crowd waited with baited breath. Would the King finally show himself? But Ernst August did not appear. Instead a short but handsome man of middle age walked out on the portico of the castle. Everyone knew who he was although few knew much about him. He had been the vehement and intelligent opposition leader through all the almost eleven years of Ernst August's reign but because of the severe censorship of the press his speeches and ideas of reform had only been passed by word of mouth. It seemed as though that was about to change. He was Johann Stüve, Bürgermeister of Osnabrück. He held up his hand and even the rumblings and murmurings stopped. The people waited in absolute silence to hear him speak.

"My dear friends and people of Hannover," he began, "I know why you are here and I agree with every one of your goals." Cheers from the crowd. "Prime Minister Bennigsen and I have spoken at great length with His Majesty this afternoon and I believe he is finally beginning to see the light." More cheers. "It will not be easy and it will take time." Stüve did not mention how difficult it had been to make the stubborn, arrogant ruler agree but everyone there knew. They admired his courage. He could easily have been arrested and tried for treason. "The Prime Minister and I convinced him that absolutism is a thing of the past. The people will only be content with a democratic form of government. We pointed out to him how successful it has been in England, as he well knows but would never admit until now. We persuaded him to see that that is why England has made so much progress while Hannover, indeed all of Germany, falls behind." The crowd was grumbling again. They did not want to hear about England. Stüve held up his hand for silence. "It will take time and a lot of hard work and we must *all* work together but I promise you—" he paused significantly. He had everyone's attention. "I promise you I and my liberal party shall do all in our power to reinstate our constitution." Wild cheers. But what does that mean, wondered many. He went on to explain. "The vote will be restored to every man, peasant, Bürger and noble equally. The new parliament will be truly representative of all the people of Hannover. The judiciary will be separated from crown administration and we shall fight for trial by jury. The vast Welf fortune shall once again be merged back into the state treasury. And above all, we promise that censorship will end immediately. Freedom of the press, speech and peaceful assembly will once again prevail in the land." The crowd went wild with cheers and applause. When the tumult abated somewhat, Stüve continued. "Tomorrow at noon here in this place His Majesty will make a proclamation confirming all I have promised. But," he held up his hand, "I must emphasize, these things will take time. Until we have a new constitution and a duly elected parliament none of these promises can be fulfilled. So I bid you, dear fellow citizens, go now peacefully to your homes and await the King's proclamation tomorrow. I must warn you that before the King agreed to make this proclamation he had already called in the troops and *they do not yet know* what has been agreed upon. We do not want the bloodshed that happened in Vienna and Berlin to take place here in Hannover. Malcontents, malingerers and troublemakers will be swiftly punished. So go quickly to your homes and return here, peaceably, tomorrow to hear your King." This time there were no cheers and only scattered applause. Stüve bowed and went into the castle.

"Does he mean it?" queried Friedrike.

"Most assuredly he means it," insisted Johann Justus.

"But can he bring it about?" she asked doubtfully.

"He will certainly do everything in his power to make it so," he replied.

The crowd was slowly dispersing. Not as quickly as Stüve had urged but drifting in twos and threes into the side streets of the city. However, many still stood about in groups avidly discussing Stüve's chances of success. Many doubted that Ernst August would so easily give up the despotism he had so vehemently imposed upon Hannover these ten years or more.

"May I walk you back to the Fürstenhof?" asked Johann Justus.

"I'd like that," said Friedrike. "But where are you staying?"

"At a farm outside of town. That's where my horse is. But I've a mind to find a place somewhere in the city. I want to hear what Ernst August has to say tomorrow."

"I'd like to hear him, too, but I don't know if I should be able to come. I'll surely be chastised for staying out so late tonight."

He took her hand and they started strolling out of the castle square. "I hope you . . . Ach, Gott, here come the troops. Hurry, Fritzi." He dragged her along as quickly as she could run.

But it was too late.

The troopers, paying no mind to the fact that most of the people were peacefully leaving, rode into the square swinging batons and the flat of their swords. Heads were smashed, teeth knocked out, arms slashed, women were knocked to the ground. Johann Justus with Friedrike in tow weaved a zigzag path trying to avoid the horses' hooves and the lethal weapons. They had almost succeeded in leaving the square when a trooper turned his mount sideways and deliberately blocked their path.

"Where do you think you're going, rabble-rouser?" demanded the trooper.

"Peaceably to our home," replied Johann Justus politely. He pushed Friedrike away from him. "Run, Fritzi, run."

"And where might your home be?" asked the man. "Don't sound like a Hannoveraner to me."

Johann thought quickly. "Neustädter Markt," he said.

"Liar," spat the man. "Only rich people live there. Not the likes of you. You aiming to stir up more trouble there?"

"I am neither troublemaker nor rabble-rouser," insisted Johann. "Now let me pass."

"Why? So you can run after your whore?"

Johann Justus seethed but he refused to reply to that.

Friedrike had not gotten far. Another trooper caught her up and held her. She was about to scream when she heard that last remark. She squirmed out of his arms and ran back to Johann Justus. Her temper flared. "I am no whore," she shrieked. "He is my husband. And I shall see that Her Grace, the Duchess of Cumberland, hears all about this. What is your name, soldier?"

The trooper hesitated. "Ja, and I am the King of England," he said sarcastically but she sensed that he drew back a little.

"We both serve at the Fürstenhof," she continued. "I am nurse to Prince Ernst August, the King's heir. The King knows me very well. I shall report this incident to him as well." Too well, she thought, and hoped they would not put her words to the test. She haughtily put her nose in the air and took Johann's arm. "Come, love, let us hurry ere the Duchess misses us. Let us leave these pigs to their filthy work."

"Pig, is it?" yelled the trooper, infuriated again. He raised his sword and took a swipe at Johann Justus. Johann ducked but not quite far enough. The point of the sword caught him under his right eye. It was not a deep cut but it bled profusely.

"Now see what you've done, you pig," screamed Friedrike. "The King shall surely hear of this."

Just then a sergeant came over. "What is going on here?" he asked. "Did they refuse to leave?"

"We were trying to leave but they refused to let us," replied Friedrike as she held her handkerchief to Johann's face.

"They were running," mumbled the trooper.

"Running is not yet a crime that I know of," said the sergeant.

By this time several other soldiers were surrounding them. One spoke up. "The lass claims she knows the King personally. Says she works for the Duchess of Cumberland."

"Then all the more reason to let them go," said the sergeant. "She just could be telling the truth and then it could go hard with us. Hans, you always were too quick with that sword."

"Thank you, sir," said Friedrike. "I shall see that your kindness is also included in my report." She quickly led Johann Justus out of the square.

Several blocks away in a dark, quiet street they slowed their pace. "I need to catch my breath," she said and promptly sat down on someone's doorstep. Johann squeezed next to her. He could feel her trembling.

"You're shaking," he said.

"I know. It's just reaction from fear and, yes, anger. 'Twill pass in a moment now that we are safe. But, oh, Johann, your eye. 'Tis all my fault that I lost my temper. Let me see it."

"How can you see in the dark? Anyway he missed the eye—not by

557

much, I'll admit. 'Tis no but a nasty cut on my cheek." He took the bloody handkerchief away. "See, the bleeding has almost stopped. And it's not your fault. Don't ever think that. The bastard would have done it anyway."

"But it needs care," she insisted. "You cannot walk way out to some farm like that. You must stay at the Fürstenhof this night. I have an unguent that will help it heal and prevent infection."

Johann Justus had to admit that he felt a little weak from loss of blood. It was a tempting offer. "I?" he said. "At the palace? They'd never permit it. And it could make trouble for you."

"Nay, nay, it won't. There are plenty of places I can hide you in the stable loft. No one will ever know."

Some time later footsore and weary they arrived at the princely palace. Friedrike led Johann Justus directly to the vast stable. No one seemed to be about. The horses stirred quietly in their sleep. Just as they were about to mount to the loft a voice came from one of the empty stalls.

"So the haughty little mouse has found herself a lover. Seems she's not as timid as she made out to be."

She looked toward the stall. The groom she detested was lying atop a very young maid whose skirt was pushed up to her chin.

"Shut up, Roland," said Friedrike. "This is not my lover but a friend from my hometown who was injured tonight. He will stay here a few hours until he heals. And Roland, you will say nothing of this, else I'll tell Her Grace who got Inge with child."

"Ha, ha," he laughed. "That 'twere long past. She weren't the first nor, I hope, the last that I've planted a babe in." The girl under him squirmed and tried to get up and he turned his attention back to her. "Now, sweeting, don't let my boasting fret you. I'll be careful. Wouldn't want to knock a nice piece like you up too soon."

Friedrike and Johann Justus crept up to the loft.

She bedded him down in the sweet hay in a far corner. "Now you rest right here," she ordered, "and keep that kerchief against the wound so no dirt will infect it. I'll go and fetch my unguent and a few other things. I'll be back as quickly as I can."

"I don't want to make any trouble for you," he said.

"You won't. I'm no doubt already in trouble for being so late. A little more won't matter." As she left the stable she could hear Roland pounding away on the girl.

Friedrike hurried to the nursery. The young maid she had left in charge was totally distraught.

"Where have you been?" she cried. "The little princess has been fretting something terrible for hours. She won't settle down."

"I had thought to visit my cousin for a bit but I got caught up in that crowd going to the Leine Schloss and I couldn't get away. It was a little frightening but I'm all right now."

"Ach, did you hear Master Stüve?"

"Ja, I did. He spoke very well but how much is just a pipe dream remains to be seen. Now let me see to my little princess." Friedrike picked the child up and cuddled her. She quieted down immediately. "I think she is cutting a tooth. They're always more fretful at that time."

"I tried picking her up any number of times," said the maid, "but the minute I put her down she started crying again. I was afraid to do it too often. Her Grace doesn't want them spoiled."

"Ach, a little spoiling never hurt any babe, especially a girl. Now fetch me a clean sugar tit—a large one so she can bite on it but not swallow it. Her fussing didn't wake our little prince?"

"Nay. He sleeps like a log."

"Then I suggest you seek your bed, too. I'll rock her until she falls asleep."

Friedrike chafed at the delay but she had to be sure everyone—maids as well as the children—were sound asleep before she returned to Johann Justus. She rubbed some oil of cloves on the baby's gums and that seemed to help. She let her bite hard on the sugar tit and rocked her in her arms until the little princess dozed off. Gently she laid her in her cradle and watched for a while until she was sure she was slumbering deeply.

Friedrike quickly assembled the unguent and other things she would need in a small basket and crept cautiously out of the nursery. It was very late and the palace seemed quiet enough. In the kitchen she paused to light a lantern from the many hanging in the dairy room that the milkmaids used for the early milking. She entered the stable even more cautiously but no one seemed to be about. Even the empty stall was no longer occupied. She prayed Roland had gone to his bed.

"Ach, Fritzi," sighed Johann Justus sleepily. "I must have dozed off. I was beginning to think you were not able to come back and that I should get out of here."

"Not until I've seen to your wound and you've rested a bit more. I'm sorry it took so long but the baby was fretful and I had to wait until she was asleep. Now let me see your face." She held the lantern up high.

"Be careful of that lantern with all this hay," he warned.

"I shall. That's why I brought a covered lantern and I shall put it out the minute I've fixed you up." She carefully cleaned the wound and the blood on his face with a wet cloth. "Ach, it is deeper than you thought. It should have some stitches but I didn't bring my needle. It will leave a scar."

"Ach, then they'll think I've been to Heidelberg," he joked, referring to the duelling scars those students were so proud of. "No mind. It will heal soon enough with your loving care."

She carefully applied the unguent and tried to pull the torn flesh together as best she could with a clean bandage.

"So. That's the best I can do. Promise me you'll seek out a doctor tomorrow."

"Ach, it feels better already. You are a fine nurse. Now may I kiss you?"

She quickly put the lantern out and he took her in his arms. He kissed her deeply and longingly. She felt the tingle right down to her toes. Before she was aware of it his tongue was probing her lips apart. She opened her mouth slightly and let him enter, not knowing what to expect. Oh, Lord, she had never been kissed like that before. He drew her closer until his strong, firm body was molded to hers. She could feel his hardness rubbing against her thighs. Despite all the layers of their clothing it felt exciting. What would it feel like flesh to flesh, she wondered and just as quickly put that thought from her mind. Nay, I'll not let him—at least not yet. But then his hand slipped over her breast, caressing and teasing right through the cloth of her gown. She gasped at the thrill that surged through her. The heat of it centered right in her loins and she almost spread her thighs for him. But suddenly the realization of what was about to happen dawned on her—and she was afraid.

She pulled away and cried, "Nay, Johann, nay, nay. Not now, not yet."

"But I love you, dearest Fritzi. I want you so much."

"I'll not be treated like a light-o-love," she said indignantly.

"I never thought you were," he replied. "I've asked you to marry me long ago. Now you have to marry me."

She sat up abruptly. "And why do I *have* to marry you?"

"Well, for one thing you told those soldiers in the square that you were my wife."

"Hah! Total strangers. They didn't even know who we were."

"But now you spend most of the night alone with me here in the hay."

"No one at all need know. Oh — except that fool Roland."

"Whom I trust not at all."

"Nor do I. He will be sure to tell the palace guard. Johann, you must be gone from here before daybreak. And you are too weak to walk all the way to your friend's farm. Let me think. Ja, take one of the horses — the old mare way down at the end. They neglect her so they'll never miss her for a few hours."

"And be hung for a horse thief as well? How would I get her back?"

"Just slap her on the rump and she'll find her way. I guarantee it. Now get a little more sleep ere you leave. I must hurry back to my charges ere the baby awakes again. She's teething."

He took her hand. "I didn't mean to frighten you, dearest Fritzi. I do truly love you and you haven't answered my question yet. Will you marry me?"

"I'll think on it. And I, too, apologize for disappointing you but virgin I am and virgin I shall remain until we are wed. Besides, I may be home sooner than you think."

"Oh? How so?"

"The King has made some very unwelcome overtures and grows more persistent all the while. It is what I was going to discuss with my cousin Georg earlier tonight — er, last night. I intend to ask the duchess to release me very soon. I can't tolerate it anymore."

"Ach, my poor dear Fritzi. Then come, flee with me tonight."

"Nay, nay. I must do it the right way. I cherish her good will. And Johann, I do love you, dearly." She gave him a quick kiss on his cheek — the unwounded one — and slipped away in the darkness.

The next morning when crafty Roland raised the hue and cry the guards seached the loft thoroughly but Johann Justus had carefully stirred up the hay so that there was no trace of his having been there. He found he still had Friedrike's bloody handkerchief which he stuffed in his pocket. It was some while later that they discovered the old mare was missing. But while they were considering forming a search party, someone noticed her standing, bewildered and half asleep, in the stable yard.

"There's your mare. 'Twas your own carelessness, I fear, that let her wander out," said the guard.

And Roland was made to look like a fool.

That day neither Friedrike nor Johann Justus was able to go to the castle square to hear King Ernst August's proclamation. She because she

561

was too sleepy and afraid to leave her charges again; he because he was well on his way back to Vilsen. Not many others showed up either—a few hundred instead of the thousands of the day before. Many were leery of the troops' brutality. Many more did not believe the king would truly agree to Stüve's promises. So it was with great surprise that the few that were there heard Ernst August publicly—though no doubt reluctantly—confirm that he would reinstate parliament, that the people would soon have a new constitution and above all that the abhorred censorship would be lifted immediately. But the biggest surprise of all came when he announced—surely under pressure from von Bennigsen—that Johann Stüve would be appointed to the cabinet as Minister of the Interior. Ernst August was an arrogant, bigoted despot but he was no fool. As much as it must have galled him to have to relinquish over ten years of his self-centered autocracy, he realized he must face the inevitable or Hannover would be plunged into a bloody civil war. Besides he was getting old.

The welcome news of Stüve's appointment quickly spread throughout the city and out into the countryside. Johann Justus in Vilsen actually heard it before Friedrike, sequestered in the Fürstenhof. Most people rejoiced at hearing it but many others were dubious. Political freedom was a fine thing but would it put food on the table? The causes of the revolutions went far deeper than mere hatred of royal despotism. Three years of failed harvests had left many people on the verge of starvation. The artisans of many trades feared the big factories of the industrialization. Germany's rivers had been the major means of transportation for eons but now the railroads were supplanting them. And everyone feared Prussia.

Although there were still pockets of unrest everywhere, Hannover remained fairly quiet in the hope that Stüve could carry out his reforms and that Ernst August's wings had been clipped. But elsewhere the revolts, often bloody and prolonged, continued on through the summer of 1848. In the south a huge peasant uprising took place in almost the same area that had seen the great Peasant Revolt of three hundred years earlier. In Dresden in Saxony things got so out of hand that the king called in Prussian troops to help quell the revolt. In Baden the grand duke's own army sided with the people and almost accomplished their goals until he, too, called in the Prussian army. Even so they held out at Rastatt until mid-July. The brutality of the Prussian troops was decried everywhere. Stüve warned, 'A German Empire with Prussia at the head will be consumed by Prussia'. In Saxony a fiery young composer and head of the Dresden opera, Richard Wagner, fled into exile in Switzerland. In Baden a young journalist named Carl Schurz, after a daring escape, went to America where he continued to expound his ideas of moralistic reform. And thus began one of the greatest emigrations in history. In the next few years hundreds of thousands of people from all walks of life, from all parts of Germany, sought freedom and a better life in America. They were known as the '48ers.

Friedrike was aware of very little of all this. Her immediate concerns were far more personal. She feared the king more than ever. He would certainly be in a vile mood for having been stripped of so much of his power and he was sure to take it out on innocent underlings. And now she had another reason for wanting to leave the Duchess' service—Johann Justus Bruns. Day and night her thoughts kept reverting to those thrilling few hours in the hayloft. Should she have given in to him? One moment her body said yes; the next her sterner self rejected the idea. She would hold herself inviolate until marriage. He would appreciate her the more—*if* he was serious about marriage. But she was sure of one thing: He was the man for her. She *would* wed him.

Friedrike looked for an opportune moment to approach the Duchess. The young prince hardly needed her at all anymore. He was growing so fast. The little princess was sitting up by now and beginning to crawl. Already she was showing signs of her royal breeding. With the exquisitely delicate little dress that Friedrike had made for her spread about her, she would sit on the great bearskin rug before the fire and gracefully point. Her brother, little Ernst August, would run and fetch whatever favorite toy she wanted. She would then laugh and gurgle with delight but when he attempted to take back his own toys from her, she would screech like a hellion. Friedrike delighted in watching them but more and more the thought crossed her mind—I should much rather enjoy watching my own children.

"Oh, no, you can't leave me," cried Marie. "Whatever will I do without you? I need you. The children need you."

"Helga is every bit as capable as I," replied Friedrike, "and she loves the children dearly. And even the new maid Anke is learning very fast. In a very short time she will be just as good."

"But why? Why?" asked the Duchess. "Are you not happy here, Rike?"

"Your Grace, you know that I have been very happy here. But my agreed upon time of service is almost up. I shall be one-and-twenty in

August and I should like to go home. Besides," she hesitated a moment and decided to take the plunge, "I am afraid."

"Afraid?" exclaimed Marie. "Of whom? Of what?"

"Of His Majesty, Your Grace."

"The King?"

"Ja, Your Grace. His importunities have become unbearable. Lately he has tried to use force. I am afraid I cannot fight him off much longer."

Marie gasped. "I am shocked but nay," she admitted, "I am not surprised. The old lecher. So Madame Grote is not keeping him content. Only my late mother-in-law could do that. I shall speak to him immediately."

"I don't know as that would be wise, Your Grace," offered Friedrike.

"Nonetheless, I shall," insisted Marie. "I'll not have him molesting my maids. He thinks me meek and mild. He has never seen my temper." Friedrike smiled. "But," Marie went on, "could his advances be because he has heard the same rumor as I—that you have taken a lover?"

Friedrike was so shocked she could hardly reply. "That snake, Roland," she sputtered. "Nay, Your Grace, the king's advances started way back when Master Augi was born. And I have *not* taken a lover," she said indignantly. "I am still virgin and intend to remain that way until I am wed. However, I will admit that the night of—of Master Stüve's speech a very dear friend from Vilsen was severely wounded by the king's troops for no reason whatsoever. I let him rest in the stable here until I could dress his wound. He then left and I have not seen him since."

"I see," said the Duchess thoughtfully. "And is this the man you hope to wed?"

"Perhaps," replied Friedrike noncommitally. "I shall decide after I have been home in Vilsen for a few months."

"Then you can surely stay until your birthday."

"I had hoped to leave before summer."

The duchess thought a moment. "Then let us compromise. You may leave on the first of June. Will that be satisfactory?"

"Most assuredly, Your Grace. And I thank you."

"I shall miss you sorely, Rike, but you deserve a life of your own."

"Indeed, Your Grace. I should rather be nursing children of my own."

"Understandable."

On 18 May a pan-German diet, the Constituent German National

Assembly, was called at Frankfurt. Almost 800 duly elected delegates met with much initial enthusiasm at old St. Paul's Church in that city, although rarely did more that 500 convene at any one time. It was remarkable in that for the first time in German history a representative body from all the German states, large and small, met together to formulate a constitution for all of Germany which would supersede or override the constitutions of the individual states, where they existed. Professor J.C. Dahlmann, he of Göttingen Seven fame and author of Hannover's first constitution, was appointed head of a team of seventeen professors and lawyers to frame the new national constitution.

Dahlmann's team worked hard all summer using as much as they could of the United States Constitution as a model. But there were certain aspects of the American constitution that did not fit the German situation. The executive was to be an 'emperor' chosen by and from the ruling princes. They had not yet decided whether to make this office hereditary or for a limited term. The bicameral legislature was to consist of a State House and a People's House. The State House could not follow the United States Senate model because some states were simply too small and others too large to allow for equal representation. Instead half the members were to be appointed by the various princes and half elected by the states' parliaments. The People's House was to be elected by popular vote of every 'independent' male over age twenty-five. This brought a storm of protest from the delegates because the word 'independent' excluded factory workers, farm workers, in short, anyone who worked for someone else. This was quickly amended to include universal male suffrage.

Despite its avowed purpose of formulating a German constitution the Frankfurt Assembly soon deteriorated into heated discussions over German unity. The delegates separated into three basic parties: *Grossdeutsch*, who wanted Austria to head this new government, *Kleindeutsch*, who preferred Prussia, and those who wanted no executive at all, only a supreme parliament.

When the professors presented the first several articles of the proposed constitution to the assembly another furor broke out. One of the articles clearly stated that the constitution covered only the German states. All non-German states were excluded. This was clearly a slap in the face for the Habsburgs whose vast empire now included Hungarians, Croats, Italians and many others. Although the German states of Austria voted in favor of it, the Habsburgs and their prime minister Schwartzenburg were highly insulted and their delegates walked out of the assembly.

The assembly then offered the Imperial crown to King Friedrich Wilhelm IV of Prussia. This would have been Prussia's opportunity to unite Germany peacefully. But Friedrich Wilhelm, dithering as usual, refused the crown. His grounds: the article on univeral suffrage.

"I'll not have that common rabble telling me how to govern," he exclaimed. The princes heaved a collective sigh of relief and laughed at the dwindling efforts of the Frankfurt assembly. The more conservative among them went back to being as reactionary as before. Ernst August of Hannover remarked, "Those fools think they can make unity on a piece of paper. They can have unity if they want it but only by blood and the sword."

Friedrike knew little of all this and probably would not have cared if she did. It was the end of May and in a few days she would be going home. Home to Vilsen. She had written Henriette when to expect her but she had given no thought to what she would do once she got there. Perhaps she could help out at the school where she believed her cousin still taught or take care of children or sew beautiful clothes or even help Doris in the spice shop, the latter thought crossing her mind as she carefully packed Oma Dorchen's recipe book.

She had a hard time trying to shut the lid of ther travelling box. She had acquired two new gowns since she had come to Hannover—one she had sewn herself and the other an elegant hand-me-down from the Duchess. She doubted she would ever have the opportunity to wear it in Vilsen but she was determined not to leave it behind. The voluminous skirts of the two gowns near filled the box to capacity but the problem with trying to shut the lid was the hoops. Paris fashion had decreed that hoops be ever wider each year. Friedrike struggled with the foolish things, bending, twisting, flattening them until finally she was able to slam the lid shut. She dared not open it again until she was home for fear they would jump out at her like a jack-in-the-box. Anything left would have to be squeezed into her portmanteau.

She hoped the duchess would offer her transportation to the post office but so far nothing had been said. She knew if she offered Roland a little money he would take her with or without permission but no way did she wish to be beholden to that snake. This time Marie had not offered to pay for the stagecoach nor did Friedrike expect it. Therefore she planned on taking the much slower but much cheaper post chaise. It would take her two days instead of one but no matter. She had briefly toyed with the idea of taking the brand-new steam train. The line from Hannover to Bremen had opened just last year. It would have been exciting but when she learned that the line ran over on the east side of the Weser and that the nearest stop was at Eystrup which was about five miles from Hoya, itself about six more miles from Vilsen, she decided against it. Besides it was very costly.

On the Monday before Friedrike was to leave, Marie called her in to her sitting room.

"Well, my dear Rike, I am sure you are all packed and ready to go. I shall miss you so," she said.

"And I you, Your Grace. I shall be leaving on Thursday. It is the first of June."

"Thursday? Ach, child, don't you realize that Thursday is a holiday? There will be no post that day."

"Ach, in my excitement I had forgotten. Ascension Day isn't it? Then I must leave on Wednesday. But, no, then I'll be stranded halfway there. I guess I must leave on Friday then."

Marie smiled. "I have never known you to be so unaware of things," she teased, "but I can understand your excitement. Here," she handed Friedrike a small purse, "these are your wages until the first of June. I know it is not customary to pay until the end of the year but you have been such an excellent and faithful servant I did not think it fair to make you wait."

"Oh, thank you very much, Your Grace. I had not expected it. Thank you so much indeed."

"Now keep this and any other monies you may have saved under your skirt in a special pocket sewn into your petticoat. They tell me there is still much unrest in the land and highwaymen are robbing both the mail and stage coaches frequently."

"Oh, goodness. I did not know. Thank you for the advice, Your Grace. And may I also ask a small favor?"

"By all means."

"Could someone—someone other than Roland—drive me to the post office? I fear my box has grown terribly heavy over the years I have been here."

Marie smiled. "I have already spoken to old Jacob, the head groom. He will see that someone other than Roland takes you. Go and see him to fix the time."

The Duchess of Cumberland then stood up and, to Friedrike's surprise, warmly embraced her. "Do write to me from time to time," she said. "I want to hear everything you are doing. I hope we can always be friends."

If Friedrike was flabbergasted by the familiarity, she did not let it faze her. "I shall always be your friend, Your Grace," she replied. She had long known, that aside from rank, she and the duchess had much in common.

"And once you leave here," continued the Duchess, "between us, I shall be just plain Marie."

Friedrike laughed. "It shall be our secret."

The next day she went to see old Jacob.

"Of course, lass," he said. "I'll drive you myself. Wouldn't want that fool Roland playing any of his tricks. Madame said to take good care of you. You're her favorite, you know."

Friedrike was up before dawn on Friday. The post chaise left very early. Jacob sent two stable lads to carry her heavy box to the gig. A thick mist lay over the city and the river.

" 'Twill burn off in a couple of hours," Jacob assured her. "Never fear. Them posthorses could find their way blindfolded." He set her down at the post office but insisted on waiting until the coach came and she and her belongings were safely on board.

The first day's journey to Nienburg was tedious but uneventful. Oh, I'll be home in time for Pfingsten (Pentecost), she thought. I wonder if they still run the Pfingst-ox race. Of course, they do. It was a centuries old tradition and so colorful. She had not seen it in years. Oma Dorchen used to tell her that was when she and Opa Chris had met. She had never known her grandfather. He had died long before she was born. She let her mind drift to all the wonderful things she would enjoy in Vilsen—walks through the woods, the beautiful old church—and, she had to admit she would certainly enjoy seeing Johann Justus Bruns again.

Johann Justus was holding a meeting—or more properly, simply a gathering—in an isolated, desolate spot between Vilsen and Bruchhausen called Moor. The ground was too swampy for farming and the woods were thin. Most folk, even the authorities, avoided the place and therefor it was ideal for their purpose. Johann hesitated to call his friends 'rebels'. They were not revolutionists like those in Berlin or Vienna or even like the near-rioters in Hannover. They were simply men who desperately needed work but who did not understand or who were too stubborn to see that they must change with the times. Many of the old trades and occupations were rapidly succumbing to the industrial revolution. And a number of the

568

losers, unfortunately, were turning to highway robbery. This is what Johann Justus hoped to stop.

"What good is freedom of the press when a man ain't got a penny to buy the newspaper?" asked one man.

"Ja, a constitution and havin' the vote is just fine but it don't put bread on the table," said another.

"But robbing and hurting innocent people is not the answer," argued Johann.

"Them as has should be willing to share," shouted a big ruffian named Adolf.

"But those who ride in the post chaise or the stage coach are just ordinary folk like you and me. Could even be your mothers or sisters," replied Johann.

"Not on the stage coach they ain't. Them be the rich ones."

"Nay," said Johann. "The rich ones are the owners of the big factories and the investors in the railroads. And you could never get near them. Besides they do share their wealth by creating new jobs. If only some of you stiff-necked rogues would unbend a little and be willing to learn new work, you could have bread on your table."

"Never," declared one farmhand. "We should do what those cutlers over in Solingen did—burn down the iron foundry."

"Ja," agreed a Weser riverman, "and wreck those infernal steamboats like they're doing on the Rhein and the Danube."

"But there b'ain't nay steamboats on the Weser yet," commented someone.

"There will be sooner or later, mark my words. Besides it ain't steamboats what's hurtin' our trade. 'Tis the damn, friggin' railroad."

"You could easily get a job on the railroad, if you wanted to," suggested Johann. "Shovelling coal or loading cargo or even collecting tickets. I hear they're crying for help."

"What? And suffocate in that stinkin' hellhole," yelled the boatman. "I'd rather starve in the fresh air of the river."

"Then starve," said someone in the back.

The boatman clenched his fists and turned.

"Now, now," Johann sought to defuse the rising tempers. "We didn't come here to fight among ourselves but to discuss our problems and above all to seek viable alternatives to the highway robberies. The king has threatened to send in troops and then we'll all suffer—the innocent as well as the guilty."

"Let him. We'll fight."

"Nay, nay, that's not the way," urged Johann.

"Then what is the way? My woman's been a hard-working linen weaver all her life, like so many hereabouts. And the custom's fallen off so much we've barely enough to eat."

"But the textile mills are begging for help," replied Johann.

"What! And have her sit in the dark for sixteen hours? And who's to take care of the little ones?"

Johann Justus was at a loss for an answer. The meeting was going nowhere. The men were growing restless. Tempers would soon flare. Although most of the men had walked the short distance to Moor, he noticed that three had ridden their horses.

Now the ruffian Adolf growled, "I've heard enough of this drivel." He signalled to two of his cronies. "Come on, pals. It's time to share the wealth." They mounted their horses.

"No. Wait, Adolf, Veit, Izaak," cried Johann. "Come back." But the men laughed and rode off.

"What's he talking about—'share the wealth'?" asked someone.

"The post chaise is due soon," shouted Johann. "They aim to rob it. We've got to stop them. Hurry, Hermann, Peter and anyone else who has a horse."

"But our horses are home. We can't catch them on foot," objected Peter.

"Then we run and fetch our horses," urged Johann. "We still might be able to catch up with them. Better we stop them than the king's troops or we'll all suffer."

"Ja, we've got to try," agreed Hermann Bergmann as they rushed back to Vilsen. "My little sister's supposed to be on that coach."

"She is?" And Johann Justus' heart pounded with fear and anxiety for his love. He had not known.

The post chaise had left Nienburg right after first light. Friedrike had not slept well last night at the posting inn where she had had to share a bed with two other women. She had thought there were fleas but now she did not feel any of the vermin attacking her, so perhaps she was mistaken. She had dozed through most of the morning as the coach made stops at all the little villages along the Weser. But now she was wide awake as they left Bücken. Vilsen would be the next stop and then the coach would take its dinner rest at Bruchhausen where they would change horses before continuing on to Bremen. Vilsen! Home in less than an hour. She could hardly wait. She straightened in her seat and adjusted her bonnet. Ah, there were the apple trees—those wonderful trees that lined every road leading into Vilsen. A sure sign they were nearly there.

Friedrike felt rather than heard the slight change of pace of the horses' hooves. She was seated on the verge side and facing backwards so she could not see what was happening on the road. Why were they slowing down? This was an empty stretch of the road. Suddenly the coach lurched and swayed. Then amid screams and shouts, curses and the frantic neighing of the horses the coach slowly tipped over.

"I saw them," screeched the woman diagonally opposite. "They rode right into the horses." The man next to her tried to keep her from falling.

"Highway robbers," he said. "And my pistols are buried in our baggage. I told you I should have kept them on me." But his wife never heard him. She had swooned.

Friedrike and the other person on her side would have been crushed but for a fortuitous quirk. As the coach twisted with the poor horses struggling in the traces, the door next to her flew open. Although it was partially crushed it kept the coach from lying flat on its side. Friedrike thought frantically of the considerable sum of money sewn into her petticoat. She would not let them have that if she could help it. She saw that there was just enough room by the open door to crawl out. She motioned to the woman opposite.

"We can get out that way. Come on."

"But the whole coach could tip the rest of the way and we'd be crushed," said the woman, hysterically.

"Ja, and all the baggage could slide off the top, too, although I think it's pretty tightly lashed. We can't wait. I'm going."

"I don't know," sobbed the other.

Friedrike did not wait. On her hands and knees she crawled out of the restricted opening, careful not to jar the door that was holding the coach up. The ground was soft and damp. She knew she would be covered with grass stains and mud but that mattered not. She had heard that some of these highwaymen actually killed people if they could not find any money or jewels. She had no intention of dying just yet. When she was clear of the coach she quickly glanced about. The four passengers who had been riding atop the baggage lay scattered on the ground. One was unconscious, another screamed with a broken arm. The other two just seemed to have had the wind knocked out of them. But she did not wait to see. She dared not stand up or the robbers would surely spot her. She kept on crawling until she reached the trees of an orchard. She cautiously stood, gathered up her skirts and ran as fast as she could deep amongst the flowering trees. It did not afford much shelter but she hoped the thieves would be so busy with their mayhem that they would not look in her direction. She hid behind a tree, gasping for breath, and propped her chin in a fork. She was shaking all over as she watched the scene on the road unfold.

The highwaymen had cut the traces and freed the struggling horses. So they have a bit of kindness in them after all. Probably farmers. But nay, they will round them up later and steal them, too. Horses with broken legs would be no good to them. The coachmen always went armed but as the poor man had been struggling with the horses and the tilting coach, his musket had slipped to the ground. One of the thieves now held it on him as another tied the man up with the reins. This done, they joined the third who was systematically relieving the passengers, now pulled out of the coach and lined up on the road, of their jewels and purses, their watches and everything in their pockets. One even took a woman's fur muff, although what she had needed that for in this warm weather, Friedrike could not imagine.

Then the robbers started on the baggage and the mail bags. They cut the lashings and threw the boxes to the ground, pried open the locks and pawed through them. Most of the contents they threw aside mixing everyone's clothes and belongings into a jumble on the road. Once in a while they cheered when they came upon someone's life savings or family jewels. Friedrike cringed when she saw them pull her box down. Oh, please, don't let them take Oma's book, she prayed. Nay, they would be more interested in the duchess' fine gown.

Suddenly she heard hoofbeats in the distance pounding down the road. The thieves heard them, too.

"We'd best make tracks," said one fearfully.

"Nay, let 'em come," said their leader. "We're armed, ain't we? We'll fight 'em off. See, there's only two more boxes to check."

Then a strange thing happened. It was hilarious and Friedrike would have laughed hysterically had she not been frozen with fright. As one robber forced the lock on her box, the lid flew open of its own accord and the twisted hoops sprang out like a jack-in-the-box hitting the man right in the eyes.

"My God, it's a demon," screamed the man clutching his bloody

572

nose.

"It's a trap," declared the second. "I'm out of here."

The two mounted their horses and with their loot fled down the road. Their leader, not daring to stay without his aides, quickly mounted and followed them. Moments later three horsemen rode up, all of whom Friedrike gratefully recognized. They were her brother Hermann, Johann Justus and their friend Peter.

"Ach, Gott, we're too late," exclaimed Johann Justus. "Just look at this mess."

"Let's go after them. They can't be far," suggested Peter.

"Nay, they've too good a start and they're armed. We're not. But at least now we know who they are. We'll report it to the police."

"That's right," agreed Hermann. "Let the police take care of them. We've got to help these people."

The frightened passengers and coachman had not known whether these new men were more robbers or not. At Hermann's words they relaxed somewhat and all began chattering at once.

Johann Justus tried to take charge. First they untied the sputtering coachman who was more concerned with his horses than with the passengers.

"Your horses are fine." Peter assured him. "They're about a half mile up the road contentedly grazing. We'll round them up for you just as soon as we've righted the coach and helped anyone who is injured."

"But the bastards cut the reins," objected the coachman. "Couldn't hook 'em up anyway."

"We'll worry about that later," said Johann as he methodically checked the passengers for injuries. All those who had been riding inside the coach seemed to be unharmed although badly shaken up.

The swooning woman cried, "They took my muff. My dear grandmother's muff."

"Never mind that," exclaimed her husband. "They took all our money, too, and my pistols. I just knew I should have kept them on me." His wife seemed about to swoon again.

Hermann was more concerned with looking for his sister. She should have been on this coach but where was she? Mayhap she missed it or, God forbid, the highwaymen had kidnapped her. Then, "Ach, Gott, that's her box. I recognize it. Friede, Friede, where are you?" he called.

No one seemed to recognize the name but then, how would they? They were all strangers to one another. At last the timid woman, noticing his distress, spoke up.

"Is she a young lass of about eighteen with brown hair?" she asked.

"She's twenty but that could be her," replied Hermann. "What happened to her?"

"She crawled out of the other side of the coach and ran away," said the women. "She wanted me to go with her but I was afraid. I wish I had else I'd not have been robbed. And the coach didn't fall any farther after all. She was brave and I was afraid."

"Where did she go? Did you see her?"

"Nay, but she can't be far."

Johann Justus was examining the four men on the far side of the coach. They, as well as the postal helper who always rode standing on the back of the coach, had been thrown to the ground. Two seemed to be unhurt and were sitting up trying to get their wits about them. The coachman's assistant had a cruelly twisted leg, possibly broken.

"Them sons-o-bitches rode right into the horses," he told Johann. "'Twas a daring thing to do. They could have been killed themselves. Looks as though they had a lot of practice."

"I dare say they had," agreed Johann sadly. "Can you get up? Let me help you."

The man groaned. "Can't say as I can. Damn leg hurts something fierce."

"Then stay right there. We'll fetch a doctor as soon as we can."

"This one's got a badly broken arm," said Peter, "and the other one is still unconscious but breathing. I don't know as we should move him."

"Then let him lie there until the doctor comes. Meanwhile we have to try to set the coach upright until help comes."

Hermann came running around from the other side. "Johann, Peter," he cried, "Friede was on the coach but she escaped. Where can she have got to?"

"How?" asked Peter.

"Who said?" asked Johann.

"One of the women said she crawled out of the door on this side and ran away," replied Hermann.

The three men peered under the coach.

"That's a mighty small opening to have squeezed through. Do you think she could have?" asked Peter.

"By God, it was a smart thing to do—if she did," said Hermann.

"She could have," said Johann. "She's a very determined woman."

Just then all their questions were answered. A muddy, dishevelled, barely recognizable young woman came running out of the orchard. "Hermann, Hermann," cried Friedrike. "It's me. I'm safe."

Hermann ran towards her and caught her in his arms. "Ach, Friede. Thank God you're safe," he said as he held her close. "I was so worried about you."

"I'm so glad it was you who came. I feel safe now," she replied. She looked down at her gown. "I may look like a pig but they didn't get my money. But, oh, my box. I hope they didn't steal Oma Dorchen's book."

"Let's go take a look," said Hermann.

Peter cleared his throat. "Er—ah—there's someone else here who's glad you're safe."

Johann Justus blushed. "Ach, Fritzi, I was so worried about you."

She looked at him. "One would never know it for all you've written to me," she remarked.

"I—er—well, we'll talk about that later now that you're home," he replied with obvious discomfort.

"Ach, Johann, I'm sorry," she apologized. "That was a mean thing for me to say. But I did wonder."

"Let's go check your box," suggested Hermann diplomatically. They walked back around the coach.

Friedrike looked at her box. Except for the broken latch nothing seemed to have been disturbed. And then she started giggling. Lying in the middle of the road were the two troublesome hoops.

"What is so funny?" asked Johann.

She was laughing so hard she could not speak. She pointed to the two hoops. "That is what saved us."

The men looked at her as though she were crazy.

"I thought it was the sound of our hoofbeats that scared them off," said Johann.

"In part, ja." she said, "but when they broke open the lock, those foolish hoops jumped out and hit one of them in the eyes. He had a bloody nose. He thought it was a demon. It was just so funny." She turned apologetically to the other passengers. "I don't mean to laugh when all of you have suffered such grievous losses—but it was funny."

As they relaxed most of the other people could now see the humor in what had happened.

The timid woman spoke up.

"And that saved my box, too, from being rifled," she said. "See, it is the last one still on the coach. I'd like to give you a small token of esteem for your bravery if one of these kind gentlemen would fetch it down."

Peter promptly did so. The woman opened the box and dug down to the bottom. She came up with a tiny satin bag containing a pair of diamond earrings which she placed in Friedrike's hand.

"Oh, nay, nay, meine Frau," exclaimed Friedrike. "I cannot take them. They are too valuable. Besides it was not my bravery that scared them off. It was the hoops."

The woman laughed. "But you packed them so cleverly. Take them. I'd have lost everything had it not been for those hoops. I still have the necklace to match. It was a gift from the Empress."

"The Empress?"

"Ja. I am from Hannover originally but I have come all the way from Vienna, where I was a lady-in-waiting at the Imperial Court, and am going on to Bremen. A long trip but I face an even longer journey. The necklace is to pay my passage to America where my husband is awaiting me. Without your hoops I should never have been able to go at all. So take the earbobs as a token of my appreciation. I notice you have no jewelry of your own."

" 'Tis true, I don't. But—but . . . "

"Besides you have the look of a lass who is coming home to be wed. Is this the lucky man?"

This time Friedrike blushed. "I do? Nay, this is my brother." She glanced pointedly at Johann Justus, who blushed in turn.

"Ah, the shy one," said the woman.

"He's not really shy at all," replied Friedrike, "just tongue-tied."

The woman smiled. "Then consider it an advance wedding present."

"Then, thank you so much," stammered Friedrike. "And—and I don't even know your name."

"Rosa Schneider," replied the woman. "And yours?"

"Friedrike Bergmann."

"And you live here in Vilsen?"

"Ja, Frau Schneider. And where in America are you going?"

"To a place far in the middle of America called Illinois. He already has a rich farm there. I think we shall be very happy. And if it weren't for you, I should not be going at all."

Friedrike had never heard of a place called Illinois but she noticed Hermann's ears prick up at the mention of a rich farm. "Then I wish you the best of luck and happiness in your new home," she said.

"And I, you, young Friedrike. Once I am settled perhaps I shall write to you."

Johann Justus cleared his throat. "Come now. We've got to ride for help." It was the first he had spoken at all during this remarkable exchange. Fritzi never ceased to amaze him. He turned to the male passengers. "We shall be fetching the doctor and some other help in a moment but first we must try to set the coach upright, if you men are willing to help. It could be a long wait and we can't have the ladies standing out here in the noonday sun after what they've been through. Once the coach is upright they can sit inside it."

The four uninjured men and the coachman helped the three men from Vilsen. With all their strength they pushed and shoved and heaved and finally got the coach back into an upright position but just as they did so an axle which had evidently been cracked in the accident gave way and the right rear wheel of the coach fell off. They groaned with frustration.

"Well, we sure ain't going no place now," said the coachman in disgust.

"We've got to prop it up with something so at least it sits level," said Johann. "If we only had some rocks . . . "

"You know rocks are scarce as hen's teeth around here," said the coachman.

"If we just slip the wheel back on and then prop that with a piece of wood, it should hold until we get back," suggested Peter.

They scouted the orchard for a suitable piece of wood. By this time the farmer who owned the orchard had come out to see what was amiss. When he saw their plight, he said, "Don't you go chopping none of my trees down. I got a board in the barn that'll do just fine. Wait whilst I fetch it. Got to have it back though."

"Hurry," begged the man with the swooning wife. "My back is killing me."

"You can let go, mein Herr," said Johann. "Three of us can hold it. Meanwhile Peter, ride as fast as you can to Bruchhausen and tell them to send another coach."

"Ain't no spare coach in Bruchhausen," said the coachman. "Got to send all the way to Bremen for that. But they got a wheelwright—if they can find him."

"A wheelwright then and new set of reins. I'm off," said Peter.

"And tell them to send me a new musket," the man shouted after him. "The devils stole mine."

577

"Now, ladies," said Johann, "if you would set yourselves to sorting out these clothes and things and repacking your boxes, you can sit in the coach as soon as yon farmer returns with a board. But mind you, don't wiggle around too much or the whole thing may overset again. We'll be back with the doctor and other help as quickly as we can."

"I'm coming with you," announced Friedrike. "I can ride pillion behind Hermann."

"What about your box?" asked Johann.

"Send it on the doctor's wagon," she said.

"And what of these?" asked Hermann as he picked up the hoops.

"Oh, hang them around your neck," retorted his sister.

Hermann blushed at having to adorn himself with such intimate items of female apparel but he dutifully hung them around his neck. Everyone laughed at the sight. Then Friedrike hiked up her skirts and mounted astride behind him. This time Johann blushed at the sight of her shapely legs.

"Tiete, Tiete, I'm home," called out Friedrike.

Her cousin came running from the kitchen. "Ach, Friede," she exclaimed. "Where have you been? It's so late. I took the whole afternoon off from school so I'd be here for you. And then you never came. I was so worried, I was about to go to the post office for any news of the coach." Finally she noticed Friedrike's muddy gown. "You're all dirty. What happened? Was it an accident."

"We were set upon by highway robbers but I'm all right. I managed to escape. That's why I'm such a mess."

"Oh, no!" said Henriette as she hugged Friedrike tightly. "You poor dear."

Friedrike told her cousin the whole story and even staid Henriette had to laugh at the tale of the flying hoops.

"And where are they now?"

"Ach, Hermann must still have them."

Just then her brother walked into the kitchen. He threw the offending hoops on the table. "Here, take these afore the damn things strangle me."

"Hermann, your language!"

"Hello, Tiete. Sorry. But I must admit they did have their merit. Served a better purpose than holding women's skirts up." They all laughed at that. "Well, the people at Bruchhausen are looking for the wheelwright. Seems he only works for the post as needed, although I imagine that's quite often. Meanwhile they've sent to Bremen for another coach but that can't possibly be here until tomorrow. They gave Peter a new set of reins, for all the good that will do, and another musket for the driver. But they said they hope he still has balls and powder as they had none to spare."

"Why, that's ridiculous," commented Friedrike. "I thought Thurn and Taxis was such a wealthy company."

"They are," replied Hermann, "but Bruchhausen is only a small way station, meant only for a change of horses. They don't have much else in the way of supplies."

"Ach, those poor women," exclaimed Henriette. "They can't stay out there in the middle of nowhere all night. How many did you say there were?"

"Three besides me," replied Friedrike. "Two with husbands and that Rosa Schneider I told you about."

"Then, Hermann, tell them to come back here with the doctor's wagon," instructed Henriette. "They're more than welcome to stay here if they wish. We have the room. It's such a big house."

"Good idea," replied Hermann. "I'm sure they'll appreciate it. But let me have a cup of coffee first. I'll catch up to them. The doctor's wagon doesn't move very fast."

"Tell them to bring my box, too," added Friedrike.

"Ja, and send to Bruchhausen for their dinner," said Henriette. "I'm sure they're starving and after all, they did pay for it."

"Ja, ja, Herr Kommandant," said Herman as he gulped down his coffee and quickly hurried after Johann Justus and the doctor.

The women seemed grateful for the hospitality and a chance to freshen up, although the swoony woman kept complaining.

"We were going to Bremen for my niece's wedding and now we'll miss the whole thing," she moaned.

"When is the wedding?" asked Rosa.

"Sunday afternoon."

"If the new coach gets here before dark we may yet be there by midnight."

"If—if. . . Well, it was kind of you to send for our dinner but what about our poor men?"

"Their dinner has been sent out to them," Hermann assured her. "Someone has to stay to guard the baggage."

"Can't the police do that?"

"The police are looking for the culprits. We don't have as many here

579

as in Hannover," he explained.

But no one paid her much mind. Hermann and Friedrike were far more interested in asking Frau Schneider about America.

"I haven't seen much of you since you've been back," said Johann Justus to Friedrike some weeks later.

"You didn't seem interested," she replied. "You never once wrote me after the March riot."

"I thought you'd understand. I've been busy."

"What, stirring up more revolts?"

"Nay, trying to prevent them. But also I've been so busy setting up my shop and getting my business started. I thought you'd be interested."

"I am interested but I still don't understand. Besides I, too, have been busy trying to find some way I can earn my keep. I can't live on my savings for very long and I certainly can't expect Tiete or Doris to support me. It's quite a change coming back from the big city to a little country village, home though it may be."

"But Fritzi, you won't have to work if you are going to marry me. You did say you would marry me, did you not?"

"I said I would think about it."

"Ach, Fritzi, love." He took her in his arms and kissed her soundly. They were standing in the yard between his house and his new shop.

She melted against him. The old thrill was still there but she was not about to let him know that—not yet. "Oh, Johann," she sighed. Then more briskly, "Come, I thought you were going to show me the new pewterer's shop you've made out of Gätje's barn."

Puzzled as usual by her reaction, Johann took her by the hand and led her into the barn. He was very proud of his new shop.

"My, it's hot in here," she commented.

"Of course. I have to keep the fire going all day but it's not as bad as a blacksmith's shop. You see, instead of an open forge I use that brick stove. Tin and lead don't require as much heat to melt and forge as iron does."

"And what is this? It looks like a sculptor's studio."

"Those are the molds I must make for each piece—one inside and one out. Or rather, those are the master molds. The actual ones I use have to be broken each time to extract the hardened pewter. And this is the lathe to burnish the finished pieces and . . . "

Friedrike was still looking at the molds. "Some of these are quite beautiful," she interrupted. "You really are quite an artist, Johann Justus."

Johann beamed. "I'm glad you think so," he said. "And I play the fiddle as well. Remember?"

"I do remember. And do you still play at Der Lustige Strumpf?"

"Der Lustige Strumpf is no more. A family by the name of Schumacher bought it and turned it into a private residence."

"Oh, I'm sorry to hear that. Where do young people go to dance now? Or do they?"

"They do. My cousin Georg David opens his house to us almost every Saturday night. Sometimes there are so many they spill out into the street. The pastor doesn't look kindly on it but so far no one has tried to stop it. It is such fun."

"It sounds like it."

"Ja. In fact, I was about to ask you. Would you come dancing with me this Saturday?"

"I'd love to."

"No more shy wallflower?" he teased. She shook her head.

Hinrich Campsheide was a very proud man, just as his grandfather Carsten Campsheide had been a very proud man. At the age of sixteen, back in 1838 when his father died, Hinrich had inherited the vast and wealthy Campsheide farm just outside of Asendorf. Of course, his mother Adelheit had been a very able administratrix but after he reached his majority Hinrich felt that he had built up the farm and the family's wealth considerably, just as his grandfather Carsten had done. Hinrich had fonder memories of his grandfather than of his own father, whom he regarded as rather weak. Although he had only been eight when the old man died, he clearly remembered his stories of the Russian campaign with Napoleon and the battle of Waterloo. Hinrich was very proud of his grandfather's brave deeds and vowed to emulate him insofar as possible. Trouble was, there was no war going on right now.

Hinrich had a sister Marie and two brothers, Christian and Johann Hermann, all of whom he considered weaklings like their father. In fact, the youngest, Johann Hermann, still only sixteen, was somewhat of a dreamer, which exasperated Hinrich no end. But as long as they did their work around the farm he could not complain. None of them had married as yet although it looked as though Marie might do so soon. Well, that would be one less mouth to feed although his mother claimed she needed her daughter's help with the housework. He hoped his brothers would put off marrying for a long while so that he would not have to hire help on the

581

farm. Hinrich himself was somewhat interested in a girl from Ördning-hausen, daughter of an old neighbor of his mother, whom Adelheit was urging on him. But the family was very poor—in his opinion—and he was in no hurry to take on that burden.

But now something had happened of which his Opa Carsten would be inordinately proud. Due to the revolts of March and the civil unrest that still permeated much of Hannover, the king Ernst August had ordered local militia to be recruited and trained by the army. And Hinrich Campsheide had been appointed captain of the troop for the northern part of County Hoya. Hinrich was totally on the side of the king and his stern measures. He had no use for demagogues such as Johann Stüve who wanted a constitution and the vote for every man. What use was a vote? Military might—and, of course, wealth—were the only power with which to rule a country—or a family. Hinrich knew that there was still a bunch of rebels fomenting trouble in and around Vilsen and he vowed just as soon as his troop was fully trained and adequately equipped he would root them out to the last man. Problem is, he did not know who they were. The folk over there were very close-mouthed and protective. But he would find out.

It was a steamy day at the beginning of August and Friedrike was iron-ing her cousin's gowns. She had not yet been able to find any employment suitable for a young unmarried woman, although she had started making Oma Dorchen's potions and medicines for Doris and this had helped con-siderably in increasing the spice shop's revenues. With that and the wash-ing, ironing and other household chores she felt she was at least earning her keep. But why, oh why did they have to have so many damn—sorry, Tiete—darn ruffles? She wiped the sweat off her brow so it would not drip and stain the gown just as the doorbell jangled. Now who can that be? She set the iron back on the stove and wiped her face and hands again. She went to the door. A man, rather handsome, in a strange-looking uniform she had never seen before, stood on the doorstep.

"Good day, Frau . . . "

"Fräulein," she corrected.

"Uh—ja—Fräulein. I am Kapitän Campsheide of His Majesty's Own Hoya Militia."

"I never heard of them."

He ignored her remark. "We have orders from the King to search every household in Vilsen for the demagogues and revolutionists who have been stirring up so much trouble hereabouts."

"Revolutionists?" she exclaimed. "I can assure you we are harboring none such in this house," she asserted indignantly. But inside she was shaking for she knew that even now Johann Justus was having another meeting at Moor, partly to quiet the would-be insurgents but mostly to elect a delegation to go visit Minister Stüve in Hannover to find out what was taking so long with the new constitution and to hurry things along, if possible.

"Nonetheless we must search your house," he insisted. "I promise you we shall seek them out and arrest every one for treason."

"Treason?"

"Ja, Fräulein. And anyone who objects to the search will likewise be arrested for obstructing justice. If you are innocent, you have nothing to fear."

"I find your presumptions extremely offensive." She tried to sound haughty but inside she was quaking.

Just then Henriette came home. "What is going on here?" she asked.

"This is my cousin who is head of the household," said Friedrike. "You will have to explain your errand to her. I have no right to grant you entry into this house. I have ironing to do." She fled into the kitchen.

Passing strange, thought Hinrich, a household run by two maiden ladies. But perforce he was obliged to explain his duty all over again to Henriette. As soon as she heard what it was all about, Henriette tried to delay as much as possible. She knew where Friedrike was going. Hermann might be at that meeting, too, and a lot of other good men.

"I do agree with you," Henriette said slowly, tongue in cheek, "that demagoguery must be stamped out. But I fear I find your methods a bit high-handed, sir. And why pick on my house?"

"We are starting here in the center of town and will fan out from there. Yours happened to be the first house on the Kirchenplatz. We are not singling you out. Every house in Vilsen and Bruchhausen will be searched." Why did he feel as though he were apologizing to this woman? "I assure you, if you are innocent you have nothing to fear but if we become suspicious of any household, troops will be quartered on them until all the culprits are caught."

"Quartered! Culprits? Why, that is the most heinous thing I have ever heard. Disrupting innocent people's lives. And I assure you, Kapitän, we are three innocent maiden ladies and my cousin."

"Three?"

"Ja, my sister who owns the spice shop."

583

"And your cousin is a man?"

"Of course. Does being a man make him guilty?"

"Certainly not. Where does he work?"

"Wherever his work takes him. He is a furniture maker and must deliver to people's houses."

"But he must have a shop."

"He is very talented. You should see some of the beautiful pieces he makes. Perhaps your wife would like to give him an order for a chest or a clothes closet."

"I don't have a wife."

"Your mother, then."

"My mother has all the furniture she needs." Damn this woman. Will she never shut up? "Now Madame—er—Fräulein, if you would just permit us to inspect your house. 'Twill take but a few minutes and we shall continue on our way."

They were still standing on the doorstep. Henriette wondered if she had given Friedrike enough time. She also hoped enough of the neighbors had overheard the conversation. Word would spread through the village like wildfire and not a 'demagogue' would be found twixt here and Bremen.

"Well, if you insist," she said hesitantly. "But be quick about it. I assure you we have nothing to hide." She made a pretext of fumbling with the door latch and slowly let them in.

When one of the militiamen noticed the iron sitting on the stove, he said, "I thought your cousin had ironing to do. Where is she?"

"How would I know?" snapped Henriette. "You kept me standing out there so long. Mayhap she had to go to the privy. She is a very nervous person. You no doubt frightened her to death."

"I am sorry. I didn't mean to be so inquisitive," apologized Hinrich Campsheide.

Friedrike fled down the back street. She knew it would have been quicker to take the horse but she did not want to attract any attention to herself. Besides in the time it would have taken to saddle the animal she could be halfway to Moor if she ran fast. It was not far. And fast she did run, with her skirts hiked up almost to her knees.

As she raced down the street, all sorts of wild thoughts ran through her head. In a few days was her birthday—her twenty-first—and Johann Justus had talked Tiete into having a birthday party for her. Friedrike had not had a birthday party since long before Oma Dorchen died. And now these—these militia with the funny-looking uniforms were about to spoil it all. She must not let Johann be arrested. And, what was more, she had finally decided that if Johann asked her again to marry, she *would* wed him. She would be one-and-twenty in a few days. So what, if Tiete was the elder and should have wed her Doctor Schulze long ago. It did not look as if that were ever going to happen. She loved Johann and would not wait any longer. Therefore she must not let Johann be arrested. Lately she had become more interested in his politics as he had carefully explained to her the need for a constitution and an end to Ernst August's tyranny. A proper constitution would prevent this very thing—unreasonable search and seizure—from happening. Nay, she would not let them seize her Johann—or Hermann or anyone else.

She had a stitch in her side and was gasping for breath as she reached the swampy field in Moor where the men were meeting. After the post coach robbery, they had gotten rid of all the ruffians and troublemakers. This was a peaceful gathering of thoughtful men who only wanted freedom and justice.

"Go, go away. Go home. They are coming to arrest you," she cried out.

Johann caught her before she fell. "Fritzi, what are you doing here? What are you saying?"

She tried to catch her breath as she explained. "The King has sent troops to quell what they call a rebellion. They aim to arrest every one of you for treason. They are going to search every house and shop in Vilsen. They are even now at our house. Tiete is trying to delay them as long as possible so that I could come and warn you. So go, quickly."

Johann Justus immediately took charge. "She's right. Scatter quickly, men—in all directions. Don't go directly to your homes unless you would normally be there at this time of day. Come back into Vilsen from every road but from here. Peter, go and warn the folk in Bruchhausen. Hermann and I shall take care of Vilsen. At least we've elected our delegates to Stüve. We'll meet clandestinely after this blows over. Meanwhile, we barely know each other. Now, go."

The men scattered in every direction.

"Come, Fritzi," said Johann. "Mount up. I'll take you home."

"But we mustn't be seen together."

"Never fear, love. I'll drop you off before we reach the Kirchenplatz. Tell them you've been to the privy. I have to build my fires up again. I let them die down since it was so hot today and I wasn't going to be there."

Friedrike limped into the kitchen, pale and gasping, just as the soldiers completed their search of the Bergmann house.

"Where have you been?' asked Campsheide brusquely.

"Haven't you boors any consideration for a woman's modesty?" she croaked. "Or for her privacy? If you must know I have been sitting in the privy. Oooh, I think I'm going to be sick." She leaned over the sink and gagged.

The captain blushed. "I do apologize. It's just that—er, I mean—" He turned to Henriette. "Mayhap you should send for the doctor."

Henriette was furious. "It is you who have made her sick. She is a very frail, delicate person. I assure you, she will be quite well as soon as you leave. You see, you have found no 'demagogues' in this house. Now get out and leave us alone."

When Henriette had locked the door after them, Friedrike collapsed at the kitchen table with a cup of coffee.

"Wouldn't some chamomile tea be better for you?" asked her cousin.

Friedrike laughed. "Nay, nay. I'm not sick. Just out of breath."

"Then you're a very good actress. You even had me fooled. And he was actually apologizing!"

"It seems all of Vilsen must be good actors as long as those animals are prying into every corner of our lives."

"Did you get to your Johann in time?"

"I did. And they scattered to the four winds. And he's not *my* Johann—not yet."

Henriette smiled. "I guarantee he will be ere the year's out. Why do you keep refusing him, Friede?"

"I don't know. He's a lot older than I, for one thing. And he always seemed more interested in his politics than in me. But since I've been back home I understand a lot more of his thinking—especially after today. And speaking of marriage, when are you and your Doctor Ludwig going to wed? You don't seem in any hurry either."

"Oh, it won't be for a while yet. He's still studying, you know. And then he has to set up a practice. I think he is going to try to buy out Doctor Eichhorn but the old man seems reluctant to retire."

Later Doris came in for afternoon coffee. She was very annoyed. "The nerve of them," she complained. "They even went through my still room. I don't know what they expected to find there."

"Probably a corpse or two or some bats' wings," joked Friedrike.

"I don't know how you can be so flippant," said Doris. "And what about your birthday party? Now they've spoiled the whole thing."

"No, they haven't," said Henriette. "It will go on as planned. The most important thing for us—and for everyone in Vilsen—is to act as normal as possible."

Just before suppertime Hermann came in. He was covered with sawdust.

"What in the world happened to you?" screeched Henriette. "You look like a scarecrow. Don't get that all over the floor."

Hermann laughed. "It's part of my disguise."

"Disguise?"

"Well, I knew Johann Justus would warn his brother Anton Christoph of what was happening, so I went out to Süstedt to the sawyer I buy most of my wood from. I couldn't very well bring back wood without the wagon so I just brought back samples. But I stood behind his saw to make sure I was well anointed. They were just leaving our shop when I got back. I made sure they took careful note of my decoration."

They all laughed at Hermann's cleverness. Friedrike wondered how many other fanciful tales were being fabricated by the men of Vilsen that day.

Henriette was not so pleased. "Well, we've seen it. Now get out in the yard and brush that off ere you get it all over my clean floor and into our supper."

Hermann saluted. "Ja, ja, Herr Kommandant."

The next morning Captain Campsheide was back at the door accompanied by two very young soldiers.

"Good morning, Frau—er—Fräulein Bergmann. These two men will be quartered in your house until further notice. One to observe the household, the other the spice shop. Both will sleep and take their meals here."

"Well, I never . . . " sputtered Henriette. "You found nothing to interest you yesterday. I thought you said troops would only be quartered on those who aroused your suspicions. What do you suspect us of? Why us?"

"Nothing provable at the moment but you must admit that your—er, the other young woman acted very strangely yesterday."

"She was sick. You made her sick."

"I trust she is fully recovered. And your cousin Hermann Bergmann's story was not entirely plausible. His employer Master Bruns told us one story and when Bergmann arrived, he told us quite another."

"That's possible. Hermann uses their shop but works quite independently. They do not always know where he is working."

"No doubt true but unfortunately we do not believe him."

"How despicable of you," snapped Henriette. "And I suppose I have to feed these two mongrels."

"Watch your language, Madame," said Campsheide. "King's orders and the law of the land. Quartered troops must be supplied bed and board by the households to which they are assigned. If necessary, the family must give up their beds to the men."

"Never! We are not wealthy, Herr Kapitän."

"That is your problem. And I assure you, Madame, you are not being singled out. We have found evidence, or at least suspicion, of demagoguery in more than half the households of Vilsen. The troops will remain here until the rebellion is stamped out and the perpetrators are brought to justice. I bid you good day, Madame."

In actual fact troops were quartered on at least three-quarters of the homes and businesses of both Vilsen and Bruchhausen. Anton Bruns had to put up with one in his cabinetmaker's shop. Gerd Meyer had to be very careful what he said as he taught the children. Strangely enough, no soldiers were forced on Johann Justus Bruns, probably because his cottage was so small and there was no woman to cook for them.

Gerd Meyer's brother Dieter Meyer, who had followed their father as local judge, wrote three outraged letters post-haste to Minister Stüve in Hannover. Three, in case one or two should be intercepted. Stüve presented the case to Prime Minister von Bennigsen, who went to the King. The citizens of Vilsen felt as though they were walking on eggshells. Good friends passed each other on the street with barely a nod. Johann Justus devised a series of secret passwords to convey news and messages. Life in the village tried to go on as normally as possible but the open friendliness had gone. And still Kapitän Campsheide and his cohorts were not able to arrest one single person. The townfolk had unobtrusively closed ranks against them.

Meanwhile plans for Friedrike's birthday party went ahead. It was to be at afternoon coffeetime. They could not afford to provide a big meal for a large number of people but Friedrike and Henriette baked cakes galore—the delicate butterkuchen, a yeast cake with cinnamon, sugar and

butter topping that was everyone's favorite, and several fruit-covered con-
coctions, since it was summer and fruit was plentiful. The latter were
always served with generous dollops of *Schlag*—whipped cream. As they
worked they pointedly ignored the young teenage soldier sitting in the
corner of the kitchen, sweat pouring off him from the reflected heat of the
huge oven. Johann Justus had warned every guest not to speak a word of
politics, not even by hint or innuendo. Not that the warning was necessary. No one would have. Those who were fortunate not to have been saddled with troops felt sorry for the Bergmann girls—such nice people,
grandchildren of dear old Dorchen who had helped so many.

"I have asked Adi Matthies," said Friedrike.

Henriette raised her eyebrows. "Just Adi?"

"Well, no. I included him and all the children. But it's not likely he
will come."

"Nor is it likely he will allow her to come."

"I'm not so sure. Things seemed to have thawed a lot between the
families. After all, she did ask Doris to be godmother to this last baby. Adi
apparently still knows nothing about the—er—" she glanced at the soldier
in the corner. "—about the past."

"It's just as well," sighed Henriette. "She has enough troubles of her
own. Constant babies and only four still living."

"Ja, and this last doesn't look too strong. It's all his fault that so many
die, the way he brutalizes her. And I've heard he gets meaner every year."

"I hope she doesn't come with a blackened eye or covered with
bruises. Everyone feels so sorry for her but it embarrasses them. They
don't know what to say."

Georg David was playing Dorchen's pianoforte and Johann Justus
was playing his fiddle. People were singing and dancing and gorging
themselves on delicious kuchen. The party was in full swing when Adi
Matthies arrived with only one child, young Friedrich who was a precocious ten. She did not have a black eye or any obvious new bruises but
Friedrike noticed she was missing a few more teeth than when they had
last met.

"I'm so glad you could come, Adi," said Friedrike welcoming her.
"Come in and join the fun. But where is Anna Dorothea?"

"She had to stay home and take care of the little ones for me, else I
couldn't have come."

"That's too bad. She's just of the age to enjoy a party like this.

589

Couldn't Heinrich have watched them just this once?"

Adi laughed ruefully. "Him? Take care of children? He wants nothing to do with them except to make them." she said bitterly.

Friedrike ignored that. "Do come and have some cake and coffee. I'll wager Friedrich would like a piece of birthday cake. Wouldn't you, lad?" The boy nodded shyly. "And you'll have to take some pieces home for Anna Dorothea and little Caroline."

Friedrich greedily stuffed cake into his mouth. "Mmm," he mumbled between swallows. "Why don't you make good cake like this, Mama?"

"I simply don't have the time." replied Adi. "Now hush and don't make a pig of yourself." Just then she noticed the soldier sitting in the corner munching on a tiny bit of cake. Henriette had pointedly not offered him any but someone else had had pity on him. He was younger than many of their own children. "You poor dears, burdened with that," said Adi. "I guess we are very lucky not to have troops quartered on us. Heinrich is so loyal to the King."

"Papa likes Prussia, too," chirped Friedrich. "Papa says the Prussians would hang all those dema—demo—those bad men."

"Hush, Friedrich," said his mother.

But Friedrich would not be hushed. He wanted to show everyone how smart he was. "I know where they meet, too, not far from our windmill. But no one asked me."

Friedrike could have killed him. She did not know if the soldier had heard the child or not, but enough was enough. She took him by the arm and guided him across the room, as she whispered, "Friedrich, we don't discuss politics at birthday parties. It's not nice. Come, let's ask Master Bruns to play your favorite song. Wouldn't you like to dance?"

"No. I don't know how," replied the boy, sullen at being deprived of his audience.

"Or perhaps you'd like to sing with the other children. Master Georg David can teach you."

"No. Don't want to."

"Then have another piece of cake. Have you tried this cherry one?"

To that the lad agreed.

Friedrike glanced pleadingly at Johann Justus but he merely shook his head. He and Georg David struck up another lively tune and people began to dance again. But a definite pall had fallen over the festivities.

Whether Adi Matthies was embarrassed over her son's *faux pas* or whether she was just too dumb to realize he had even made a gaff, no one was sure. But very shortly she announced that she would have to leave as it was almost time to nurse the new baby. The guests heaved a collective sigh of relief when she and Friedrich left. Johann Justus could have kicked himself for not extending his warning to the Matthies with whom he was none too friendly but it never occured to him that Friedrike would ask them to her party. He should have known better because she, like her Oma Dorchen, had always tried to befriend the poor woman. But he did not worry overmuch. No more meetings had been held at Moor. He only hoped Friedrich had not recognized anyone but then—who would believe a child anyway?

After everyone had eaten their fill and the enthusiasm for dancing was beginning to flag, Johann asked his cousin to play a flourishing fanfare. He rapped for attention.

"I have an announcement to make," he said. Everyone was silent. Friedrike wondered, what in the world now? "Now that my dear Fräulein Friedrike is one-and-twenty and a woman able to think for herself—I hope—" He paused for the inevitable laughter and Friedrike turned red. "I want you all to know that I am going to make her my wife—and that within the next few weeks!" Everyone applauded for both young people were well liked.

Friedrike was appalled. She did not know what to say. Finally she stammered, "But—but you haven't even asked me."

"I've asked you so many times I've lost count and all you ever say is that you'd think about it. But dear friends, she has never said me 'nay'. So I think it is time she stopped thinking and says me 'ja'." More applause. He took her by the hand and drew her to him. Friedrike was thrilled but also a little apprehensive. She did love him. As strong-willed as she had always prided herself on being, mayhap that was what she needed—someone stronger to make up her mind for her. She melted against him.

"See how willing she is. Now say me 'ja', dearest Fritzi," he urged.

She would not let herself think anymore. In a clear voice she said, "Ja, I shall wed you, dearest Johann."

Everyone cheered and Georg David struck up the chords of 'Du, du, liegst mir im Herzen'. Johann took her in his arms and waltzed her around the room.

After the guests had left Friedrike knew she simply had to talk to Johann—but not under the eyes of their watchdog. She walked outside with him and they strolled arm in arm around the churchyard in compan-

591

ionable silence through the balmy evening. It was all so sudden—this idea of marriage. She strove to get her thoughts together. Johann sensed that and waited for her to open the conversation.

Suddenly she blurted out, "In just a few weeks? Johann, you must be out of your mind. I need more time than that to get ready. Any woman would."

He laughed. "That was just to shock you into saying 'ja'. You may have more time but not too much. I have already spoken to Pastor about announcing the banns."

"You have? Well, that was certainly precipitous of you. You could have consulted me first."

"Fritzi sweet, you have wanted to wed me ever since we spent the night together in the palace barn—mayhap even before that—but you would never admit it to yourself. I had to force your hand." He took her in his arms and kissed her hard. "I do love you so."

"And I you, Johann, but—but I need time to make a gown among other things, and I'm not sure that we can afford the material." She knew she was grasping at straws.

"What about that beautiful gown the duchess gave you? You've told me about it but I've never seen you wear it."

"I haven't since I've been back in Vilsen. I suppose it might do."

"Then that's settled. Besides we won't be wed until after the new constitution is in effect."

"The constitution?" she exclaimed, puzzled. "Whatever does that have to do with us?"

"A lot. It means freedom—freedom from the tyranny such as been happening right here these past weeks. I do not want to start a new life and certainly not bring children into a world that is not free."

"I see," she said quietly. "And when is that suppose to happen?"

"Very soon, I hope. Parliament is meeting at the beginning of September and it shouldn't take them but a few days to ratify it. All the arguments and discussions have been going on for months and they now have all the wrinkles ironed out. So, dearest Fritzi, we can be wed anytime in late September."

She shook her head. "That is no doubt the strangest reason I ever heard for setting a wedding date. But, dear Johann, I suppose I shall have to get used to it. Politics is your lifeblood and I would not have you any other way."

The following week Captain Campsheide made an arrest. His men had been watching the field in Moor very carefully ever since they learned about it from the soldier at the Bergmann house. There had been no sign of any meetings. In fact, folk rarely ventured near the place. But now they had captured two culprits—a very young teenage boy and an even younger girl. Campsheide hauled them before Justice Meyer on charges of treason.

Dieter Meyer was furious when he saw who the alleged miscreants were. The lad was his own great-nephew and the lass the daughter of one of the leading merchants in Vilsen. But Dieter maintained his judicial dignity as he seethed inside. He vowed to make a fool of this pompous jackass, Campsheide.

"What were you doing in Moor?" he asked the lad.

The boy was so embarrassed and nervous he could hardly speak. "Er—I—er—that is, we were just visiting."

"And why did you go all the way to Moor to visit when you see Hanne every day at school?"

"Ah—er—well—we wanted to be sort of private."

"I see. And did you kiss her?"

The boy turned beet-red. "I—I . . ."

Hanne was too young even to be embarrassed. She had no concept of the seriousness of the charges against them. Probably did not even understand the word 'treason'. She thought it was all a lark. "Ja," she admitted, "he kissed me—two times. It was nice."

Dieter tried not to smile. "And did he do anything else? Did he touch you anywhere?"

This time she knew enough to blush. "He tried," she said, "but I wouldn't let him. Mama said never, never . . . But then the soldiers came and brought us here. They weren't very nice. Why were they so mean? We were just—er—ah—having a little fun."

"Hanne, you are too young for that kind of fun. A lady does not do such things. Now, I want you to go straight home and tell your Mama everything, else I shall tell your Papa. And, Hanne, don't ever go near that field in Moor again until you are at least eighteen. Do you understand?"

The girl nodded and fled.

"Now, Dieter," the judge addressed his namesake, "how often have you gone to that field in Moor—either with Hanne or anyone else?"

"This was the first time, sir." The lad was so relieved that Hanne had told most of the story that he could now speak coherently, although he wondered what his punishment would be. "The other boys said it was a good place to go if you wanted to—er—that is, be alone with a girl."

"Dieter, do you know what the word treason means?"

"I—I think so, sir."

"Did you see or meet anyone else in that field, other than these soldiers?"

"No, sir. We were quite alone."

"Did you talk of any politics with Hanne?"

"No, sir. I don't know anything about politics. We didn't talk much at all. I just wanted to—er—that is—I mean . . ." And he blushed again.

"I think we all know what you wanted to do with Hanne. No need to describe it. Now, go straight home. I shall speak to your father later. Case dismissed."

The lad speedily left.

"Gentlemen," said Judge Meyer with all the dignity he could muster, "I find no cause for treason here. I am sure that no matter what town or village you come from there is a trysting place—a lovers' lane. That is what that field in Moor is. Nothing more. However, I shall send a report of the case to Hannover to prove you are doing your duty. I bid you good day."

Hinrich Campsheide was furious. He did not like being made a fool of.

A few days later an order came from the King via Prime Minister Bennigsen to withdraw all the troops from Vilsen and Bruchhausen. And gradually life went back to normal.

On 5 September 1848 Parliament ratified Hannover's new constitution and on the 29th of the same month Johann Justus Bruns and Friedrike Sophie Bergmann were wed. Her cousin Pastor Georg came all the way from Hannover to assist the pastor of the ancient Vilsen church in the ceremony. Her brother Hermann gave her away. Henriette, who acted as her maid-of-honor, and Doris put on the most elaborate wedding feast Vilsen had seen in a long time. Friedrike was resplendent in the duchess' lovely gown and Rosa Schneider's diamond earrings. The church was packed with well-wishers. Johann Justus did not play his fiddle at the party. He danced only with his bride. But Georg David and the other Bruns brothers and cousins more than made up for it. Georg David even wrote a special song celebrating the virtues and charms of the newlyweds.

After the lavish supper Johann Justus and Friedrike walked the short distance from the Bergmann house to his tiny cottage on Gartenweg followed by a merry crowd of revellers. Johann politely but firmly shut the door in their faces. Friedrike looked around. She had not been in the house for many years—not since Johann's mother had moved in with his brother Anton Christoph down the street, leaving Johann Justus alone. The place was spotlessly clean but so spare—so—so masculine. Immediately she started thinking of ways to soften it—to feminize it. In her mind she was already hanging pretty curtains and putting a linen cloth on the table.

, But Johann had other things on his mind. He took her hand and led her into the bedroom where fluffy, opulent featherbeds awaited them. He kissed her tenderly. He felt her body quiver against his. Was it a thrill of anticipation or a frisson of fear? He could not be sure.

"Are you frightened, my love? Don't be," he said.

"A little," she admitted as memories of the King's crude advances flooded her mind.

"I won't hurt you, sweet. I promise I'll be very gentle. I want to give you pleasure."

"I know, Johann. It's just that . . . "

"No more thinking. Let us just enjoy one another—very slowly. Here now, take off those pretty lace gloves. I never could understand how ladies can eat with gloves on."

She smiled. "But these are especially for that. See. They are only half-gloves. No fingertips." She stripped the gloves off and carefully laid them atop the chiffonier.

"Let me help you take off that beautiful gown. I shouldn't want to crush it."

She was a little hesitant at that but he was already unbuttoning the many tiny buttons. Just the feel of him undressing her was exciting.

"Where can I hang it?" she asked timidly.

"Oh, my," he said. "I see where my brother Anton will have to build us a new clothes closet. I never realized a woman needed so much more room for her clothes than a man. Let's just lay it carefully over this chair for now." He handled the gown as if it were the most precious thing on earth. When he turned back he saw that she had untied her petticoats of her own volition and was gingerly stepping out of the garments. That pleased him greatly but then he had to choke back a laugh.

"Those hoops. Are they . . . ?"

This time she laughed gaily. "The very same," she said. "And just as springy as ever." She dropped them to the floor and daintily stepped out of the wooden hoops.

"Now where in the world do we put them?"

"Leave them lay," she replied. "I'm sure your floor is cleaner than that road was." She hesitated a moment. "I'm afraid you'll have to help me unlace my corset. We usually do each other, but . . . " He did so eagerly.

He stared at her standing before him clad only in her shift. He could hardly drag his eyes away from her rising breasts, the nipples quite visible through the sheer material. "Let me take off your shoes and stockings," he said.

"But your only chair is covered with my gown. Where can I sit?"

"On the edge of the bed, of course."

"Oh," she said nervously. "But when are you—er—going to—er—undress?"

"Just as soon as I see you in all your splendor." But then he relented a little. Mayhap he was not being fair. He removed his coat and carefully hung it it the chifferobe. He quickly pulled off his shirt and threw it on the floor.

She gasped. She had never seen a naked man—or even a half-naked one—before. She stared at his broad chest, the hard muscles, the line of hair leading down below his trousers. She shivered without realizing it.

"There, is that better?" She nodded nervously. He took her by the hand. "Now, come, sit on the edge of the bed whilst I take off your shoes and stockings." Meekly she obeyed him.

Quickly he took off her shoes and then caressed her feet. He ran his hands up to the garters on her thighs. She nearly died with—was it fear, embarrassment or excitement? She could not be sure. Gently he rolled each stocking down.

"What exquisite clockwork," he commented. "Not many women wear lisle stockings."

"It was just special for today," she replied. Then an unwelcome thought crossed her mind. "How do you know what kind of stockings most women wear?"

He laughed. "Nay, my love, I have not been undressing other women. But sometimes a playful, cooperative little gust of wind will lift a lady's skirts above her ankles and it is in a man's nature to stare." He caressed her bare feet and started kissing his way up her legs. She promptly forgot her doubts as she succumbed to the exquisite sensation.

Suddenly he stood up and flung back the top featherbed. He picked her up and in one fluid motion had her shift up over her head and off and laid her down on the bed. For a moment he simply gazed at her naked body, drinking in her beauty. In less than two seconds he shed his shoes, stockings, trousers and long underwear. Friedrike gasped and stared. So that was the instrument men used to—to—she hesitated to think the word deflower. It did not sound right. She had known about it, of course. Even felt it as the lascivious king had pressed it against her. But she had never seen it fully aroused before. It really was rather ugly and yet it fascinated her. And also frightened her just a little.

Johann lay down beside her and began kissing her and caressing her. Gradually her fear was replaced by the thrills that swept through her. When he kissed and nibbled on her breasts the rapture centered on her loins and she had to keep herself from crying out how much she wanted him. When his fingers touched her secret woman's place her hips automatically rose up to meet him. At last he rolled over between her thighs and slowly guided himself into her. Suddenly he thrust hard. She felt a slight stab of pain and then he was inside of her—deeply. Pain and fear forgotten, she knew only ecstacy.

Afterward as they lay gasping in each other's arms, she thought, how come it is that women are not supposed to enjoy this? Am I peculiar or are they? When they made love a second time, she, now having an idea of what to expect, was able to respond to him more fully and it was as near perfect as anything could have been.

Johann held her in his arms for a while, kissed her good-night and fell asleep. Friedrike cuddled up against his strong body but sleep was a long time in coming. Those other women must be crazy not to enjoy this, she thought. But then mayhap they didn't have a man like her dear Johann. She remembered dear Oma Dorchen telling her a little about it before she went to Hannover. Oma always said she had loved Opa Chris making love to her. So mayhap I'm not so peculiar. She thought of staid Henriette. When is her Lude ever going to wed her? She wondered if he could arouse Tiete to passion such as this. She doubted it. And poor Doris, who doesn't even have a beau as yet. She finally fell asleep and dreamed wonderful dreams.

The next morning she awoke early as was her wont despite the lack of sleep. She felt more joyous and happy than she had ever felt in her life. She was eager to fix their first breakfast together to show Johann what a good wife she would be. She wondered if he had any food in the house. Just as she was about to get up he encircled her waist with his arm and pulled her to him.

"Where do you think you're going?" he asked, grinning.

597

"I—I thought to get your breakfast," she murmured.

"Later. Right now we have more important things to do."

"Oh. But aren't you going to work today?"

"Not today, love. Today is our wedding day."

"But that was yesterday. Oh—I see."

"Today the door is barred against all comers. We can stay abed all day making love if you'd like. Tomorrow we shall rise early and go to church like a proper married couple to show all the village how happy we are."

And Friedrike agreed that Johann knew best. She loved him all the more as she turned into his arms.

And not long after the New Year of 1849 Friedrike knew she was pregnant.

18

1849

Friedrike was not particularly overjoyed at finding herself with child so soon. She had hoped for at least a year of having Johann all to herself. But with their frequent and rapturous lovemaking what else could she have expected? She tried to think back to the days when, caring for the little prince and princess, she had longed for babies of her own. It had seemed so simple then. With the finest doctors and all the money in the world, the Duchess' pregnancies had seemed like a breeze. She had been too young to remember her own mother's last time. No one had warned her that she was to be sick in the mornings, that she would be cranky or have wide mood swings. It was not like her at all. So much for living in a household of three maiden ladies. She wished she had someone older to talk to. At times like these she missed Oma Dorchen and even her own mother terribly. Having been away at Hannover for so many years she did not yet have any close friends in Vilsen except Adi Matthies—and she was the last person she wanted to ask.

Friedrike thought of Gerd Meyer's wife Mathilde. Now there was a fine lady, like all the Meyers. She was probably in her mid-fifties, too old to be bearing any longer but young enough not to be a grandmother—as yet. But she was such a fine lady Friedrike hesitated to ask her about such mundane things as morning sickness and mood swings. Yet she had a vague remembrance of both Oma Dorchen and Oma Eleonore speaking of an older Frau Meyer, a very gracious lady who had helped them both so much when they were young. Friedrike was not sure of the relationship but she knew it was the same family. She made up her mind to consult with Mathilde—as soon as she felt a little better.

Meanwhile, Henriette, oblivious of her cousin's discomfort, kept urging her to enroll her marriage with the Stockman Foundation in Celle as soon as possible. One blustery March day Friedrike was seated at her kitchen table attempting to do just that. She had a clean piece of paper, a newly sharpened quill and the inkpot sitting before her but instead of writing she was staring out the window at the raw day thinking back to how warm March had been just a year ago when she and Johann had met in Hannover during the riot. Little did she think then that in one year she would be sitting in her very own home expecting their first child.

She tried to shake her lackadaisical mood. Come now, she chided herself, 'tis only a brief letter that is required. She picked up the quill, dipped it in the ink and wrote the salutation. Then she remembered that she must enclose a letter from pastor attesting to the marriage. That put a further damper on her spirits. She certainly did not want to go out into that cold wind today.

Suddenly the door burst open and on a gust of wind in flew her brother Hermann.

Friedrike was startled out of her reverie. "Hermann! Shut that door. All the leaves are blowing in. Whatever is wrong?" But immdeiately she knew it was nothing terrible because he was grinning. Hermann always approached everything with infectious enthusiasm. Right now she envied him that trait. "Aren't you working today?"

"Oh, ja," he replied. "I just delivered a beautiful chest of four drawers to Herr Putzer and he paid me handsomely, his Frau was that pleased. So I can take the rest of the afternoon off to visit my favorite sister."

"Hermann! I am your only sister." But she smiled. His ebullience was hard to resist.

He sat down at the table opposite her. "Have you heard the latest news?"

"What news? Has the King died that you are so happy?"

He laughed. "Nay, not yet. Although that won't be long a-coming, methinks. Some say he is doddering. He's over eighty, you know."

"How well I know," she replied.

"Nay. This is news from America. They have discovered gold in California!"

"Gold? And where might California be? I never heard of it."

"It's on the far, far side of America, right on the Pacific Ocean. It's part of the territory they recently acquired from Mexico."

"After another foolish war. I don't understand the Americans. The place is so big, why did they want more territory?"

"So that it will all be free from one ocean to the other."

"Free? When half of them own slaves and the other half want to free them? They can't even decide amongst themselves what they want."

"Agreed. But it's not much different here where Prussia still holds her serfs to the land while Hannover freed hers ages ago."

"Another reason for not wanting Prussia to head a united Germany."

He shrugged. "And Austria would have us all be Catholics. But I didn't come here to rehash old politics. Let me tell you about the gold."

"What about it?"

"They say thousands and thousands of people are hurrying to California to seek more gold. In fact, it is being called 'the Gold Rush'. They are going in droves by covered wagon or by clipper ship."

"What is a clipper ship? And how can they sail across solid land?"

"It is the fastest, most beautiful ship ever built. I've seen pictures of them. And they don't sail across the land, silly, but all the way around the southern tip of South America—a much longer distance but they are so fast they actually get to California quicker than the wagon trains. And it's much safer, too. No fear of animals dropping dead or people being killed by Indians or dying of thirst in the deserts. I hear that many men from Germany are going, too."

"Hermann!" she exclaimed. "You're not thinking of going to America, are you?"

He chuckled at her look of horror. "Nay, not at the moment. But I would like to go someday, at least to see it even if I didn't decide to settle there."

It was the most he had ever admitted concerning his thoughts about America and it worried her. "Dearest brother, you have a good trade here. You are not starving. I can understand a family emigrating if they'd lost all their land or were in trouble with the law like some of the '48ers or even to escape the brutality of Prussia. But why anyone else would want to go to that wild, crazy place is beyond me. What you need is a good wife to settle you down. Are you still courting that Dora?"

"I never was courting her. But that's over now. Her father didn't seem to like me." Hermann shrugged. "Tell me, have you ever heard from that Rosa Schneider?"

"Ja, I have. One letter just before Christmas. They have a fine farm in a place called Elgin not far from Chicago but she hates the house. It's nothing but a log cabin with sod for a roof. Sod, can you imagine? She also says it is very lonely but they are starting to build the railroad so more people are coming there—mostly from Germany."

"See. What did I tell you?"

"Hermann! Please don't get any foolish ideas about America," she begged. "You said you would always be here for me."

"I know I did but you have Johann now."

"I know. And I thank God every day for him. He is such a good, kind man. Ach," she said, "I am sorry to be so moody but I might as well tell you—I am to have a child."

"Wonderful," he exclaimed. "And I shall be the godfather."

"Ach, you men." But she smiled. His enthusiasm served to brighten her spirit immensely. "You know, there is one thing I should like to have from America."

"And that is?"

"A gentleman over there has invented a sewing machine."

"A sewing machine? Where did you ever hear of that?"

"Tiete gets a ladies' book from Paris every year and it told all about it. It is quite wonderful. You just step on a treadle like on a spinning wheel and a belt makes the needle go up and down. Think of the time and sore fingers it would save."

"Remarkable."

"So you see—I am not totally illiterate. I should rather have something practical like that than all your gold from California. Although it would no doubt take some of that gold to buy one."

After Hermann left she put aside the letter she had started. That could wait another day. It was almost time to get Johann's supper. Hermann always cheered her up and she began to count her blessings. Johann Justus was the finest, most considerate husband any woman could want. And so talented, too. His business was going well. Now that the economy was improving somewhat, every bride in Vilsen and for miles around had to have as complete a set of his beautiful flatware and tableware as she could afford and older women were requesting pieces for anniversaries and birthdays to add to or replace theirs.

And when Johann played his fiddle just for her, all thoughts of sadness left her and she would sing and dance around by herself to his great delight. She vowed then and there to keep doing so until she became too cumbersome. She wanted this to be a happy child.

Johann came in to supper with more news. His was always of the political kind.

"Friedrich Wilhelm has called a conference in May in Potsdam. He has invited the princes of all the major German states to discuss a German

Union. Not unification under Prussia or even a confederation like the old one but something like an alliance."

"That sounds like a step in the right direction." replied Friedrike.

"On the surface it would seem so but we liberals are firmly against it because he is also proposing that the governance of this union be a new constitution drawn up by his favorite minister von Radowitz which cancels out most of the best provisions of the Frankfurt constitution. It would make Prussia hereditary head of this so-called empire with a council of six princes to advise him."

"What else would you expect from Prussia?"

"The finances are to be controlled by the states who must support and, if necessary, loan money to this government."

Friedrike laughed. "I can just see the squabbling that would ensue. That government will never see a penny."

Johann nodded. "But worst of all it would take away the popular and secret vote and place it only in the hands of the aristocracy."

"That's terrible. And we thought the 'March-governments' settled all that," she exclaimed.

"And that is the trouble. Too many people think that now that we have a constitution and the popular vote it cannot be taken away again. Very few are paying attention to the reaction that is setting in amongst the princes. If we don't watch them carefully we can lose it all over night. Ernst August is going to Potsdam."

"He would."

On 26 May 1849 Hannover and Saxony concluded what was to be known as the Three Kings Alliance with Prussia. Bavaria hesitated and eventually bowed out. Hannover and Saxony joined only reluctantly fearing unrest at home that might require Prussia's help, but they had strong reservations, stating that they would only remain a party to it if *all* German states were to join and also insisting on several changes to the constitution. The conservative delegates to the Frankfurt Diet voiced their approval. Within a few months most, but not all, of the smaller states fell into line.

The alliance was supposed to have lasted for one year but popular elections in February 1850 were so decidedly against it that both Hannover and Saxony withdrew on the grounds that not all the German states had joined. In neighboring Hesse the still cruel and despotic elector dissolved the lower chamber of his parliament when they refused to approve new taxation and tried to impose taxation by decree. State officials and judges would not enforce the unconstitutional decrees and all the officers of the Hessian army resigned their commissions. Hesse, of necessity, withdrew from the union. Later the same year Bavaria and Württemberg concluded and alliance with Austria. Prussia, needless to say, was furious because it had become apparent that her main objective in the alliance was not the union of Germany but the strengthening of Prussia.

Meanwhile in late August of 1849 little Sophie Margarethe put in her appearance a few weeks early. She was tiny but otherwise perfect and seemed to be in good health. The midwife, although optimistic about her chances of survival, pointed out that she would need special care for a few months.

"Why Sophie?" asked Johann as they were preparing for her baptism. "Why not Friedrike?"

"Because I like Sophie. It is my middle name after all," replied Friedrike. "Not only that but it was my dear mother's favorite of all her several names. She always wanted to be called Sophie but no one would. She was always called Kati."

Johann shrugged. "I know we agreed that girls would be your choice for a name and boys mine. At least you've decided on Margarethe for a middle name after my mother. That will make Mama happy. I'm not complaining, mind you. I just wondered."

Friedrike smiled. What a wonderful husband she had. He was so amenable. Who could ask for anything more?

The baby thrived and soon no longer needed special care. By March Sophie was struggling to sit up and Friedrike knew she was pregnant again. This time she vowed there would be no sadness to mar her happiness. Little did she know how wrong she could be.

As spring broke Johann came in one day bearing mail. He was very excited.

"Look, Fritzi. A letter from my old friend Alfred Krupp. I haven't heard from him in years. I wonder what he has to say."

"Well, if you open it and read it, you might know," she replied, not particularly interested.

Johann tore open the missive and quickly scanned it. He then reread it slowly, his face brightening by the minute. Now Friedrike became very interested. She knew that Krupp had once invited Johann to go into business with him in Essen. Johann had elected to stay in Vilsen but she feared the temptation was always there.

"So what does he have to say that is making you so excited?" she asked.

"Listen to this, Fritzi. Queen Victoria has authorized a Great Exhibition to be held in London next year. They are building a huge exhibition hall all of glass and iron to be called the Crystal Palace. It will showcase all the accomplishments and products of English science and industry. But manufacturers and inventors from other countries have also been invited to exhibit—presumably those not in direct competition with England. And Alfred is to be among them. He will show his newest big cannon made from cast steel."

"Cast steel? What is that?"

"Something he has been experimenting with for several years. Said to be ten times stronger than cast iron and no danger of the gun cracking or blowing up."

"So he is still making armaments and munitions. I thought you said he wanted to discontinue that after his father died."

Johann shook his head. "So he said. But that was years ago. He was young and idealistic then. But I suppose he had to go where the money was to be had. With Prussia so militaristic it would be what her kings and generals most desired—needed. Perhaps he was ordered to continue making arms. I wouldn't be surprised. Prussia allows very little freedom of choice. But never mind that. Listen to this, Fritzi. He has invited me to go to London with him to help set up his exhibit."

"London!" she exclaimed. "Why, they are having a terrible cholera epidemic there. Thousands and thousands of people have already died. Oh, no, Johann, you mustn't go there. And besides, what of your own business? You can't afford to leave it for—what—maybe months. And what of me? Expecting another child and you might not even be here for its birth."

"Fritzi, Fritzi, calm yourself. I didn't say I was going to London, just that he invited me. Alfred foresaw that I should probably refuse so he goes on to say, failing that, he would like me to come to Essen for a few days to see his newest creation."

"What is this hold Alfred Krupp has over you?" she cried. "He is like a magician who waves his wand and you jump."

"Fritzi, that is not true and you know it. Alfred was my friend—and mentor—long before I even knew you." Johann knew that in her condition his wife was not seeing things clearly but that last remark angered him.

605

Friedrike knew she had gone too far. She had rarely seen Johann angry and never at her. But she could not help herself. "Even Essen," she went on, "even to Essen you would be gone at least three weeks or more."

"Not necessarily."

"What do you mean? Why, it will take over a week just to get there and another to get back, to say nothing of how long you would be tempted to stay there—just to look at an ugly old cannon."

"Not if I went by train."

"By train? Are you out of your mind?"

Johann tried to reply calmly. "No, Fritzi, I am quite sane. If Hermann or my brother were to drive me to Eystrup in the wagon, I could take the train from there to Hannover from where another one leaves for Düsseldorf and Köln which I'm sure stops at Essen. I can be there in a day or less depending on the schedule and the same coming back. I've never been on a train before. I should think it would be quite exciting. Imagine travelling through the countryside at almost thirty miles an hour."

"And who is paying for this? Your friend Alfred Krupp?" she snapped.

"He might. But in any case it is far less expensive than the fastest stagecoach and gets one there more than three times quicker."

"I still don't think it's safe."

"Oh, come now, Fritzi. You used to be interested in the great engines, as was I."

"Not anymore. Not after I read about all the smoke, ashes and cinders that fly into the cars, ruining your clothes and even setting people on fire."

"They've improved on that a lot since then. They're even putting screens on some of the windows."

She shrugged. "You'd go through all that just to see an ugly old gun?"

"You know I've always been interested in all types of metalwork. And besides I haven't seen my friend Alfred in several years. I believe he's quite wealthy now."

"That's it. You think more of Krupp than you do of your wife and children."

"That's not true. I love you dearly but, Fritzi, you are being unreasonable. I believe you are jealous."

"Mayhap I am." She stormed into the kitchen and would say no more. They ate—or pretended to eat—an unsavory supper in total silence.

After supper Friedrike crawled into bed and wept. Was she being unreasonable? Could she possibly be jealous? Mayhap she was. But why? It was the first serious quarrel they had ever had. How could she make amends? The big bed felt awfully empty without her dear Johann beside her.

Johann sat at the table for a long time, thinking. He could not comprehend Fritzi's reaction to the whole thing. What was a simple, short trip to Essen? It's not as though he were going off to war. She had always been so enthusiastic about any of his projects. It had to be her condition, especially so soon after the first child. And, he reminded himself, she was several years younger than he—still a little immature. After her devastating childhood, losing both her parents at an early age and then her beloved grandmother, she was afraid of being left alone again. That had to be it. He would try to comfort her in the only way he knew how—if she would have him. But he would not back down. He was eager to go to Essen.

He carefully banked the fire in the big iron stove. What a blessing that was compared to the old fireplace. All the new inventions of the modern age fascinated him. What an exciting time to be living in. That was another reason he wanted to go to Essen—to observe how the new, huge foundries functioned. He blew out the candle and another idea occurred to him. Now that brave men were venturing all the way down to the Antarctic, whale oil was readily available and quite inexpensive. Fritzi had always insisted on making her own candles but now he would buy her one of the new oil lamps in Essen—or maybe on the way back in Hannover—as a peace offering. Some of them were quite elaborate with beautiful colored glass shades to shield one's eyes for the light was many times brighter, clearer and steadier than candlelight. She would be so surprised.

With that pleasant thought he tiptoed into the bedroom not sure if she were asleep or still awake. As he quietly undressed he thought he heard her sobbing. He lay down beside her and gently took her in his arms.

She laid her head on his broad shoulder. "Oh, Johann, I'm being terribly selfish, aren't I?"

"A little perhaps but it was too much of a shock all at once. I understand your fears. I promise I shan't stay in Essen more than two or three days—just long enough to see some of these new modern things." It was on the tip of his tongue to say how much he wished he *could* go to that exhibit in London but since there was no real possibility of going that far, why upset her more? "I promise I'll be back home in less than a week."

607

"I know," she sobbed, "but that's what Papa said when he went to Lüneburg and he never came back."

"But I'm not going under some quack's knife. I'm just going to visit an old friend. I'll be perfectly safe. Why don't you and the baby stay with Tiete while I'm gone? I'm sure she'd be happy to have you."

"Nay. I don't want to seem like a ninny."

"A ninny? You? Who was the brave girl who escaped from the highway robbers no but a year ago and who ran to Moor to warn us? My sweet Fritzi, that's who."

In the dark he could not see her face but he sensed that she was trying to smile. "I was brave then, wasn't I?" she murmured. "Then what is wrong with me now?"

"Nothing that a little loving won't cure," he whispered into her hair. He began caressing her body and bit by bit he felt her relax. When he kissed her breast he could feel her excitement rise. Johann had had only limited experience with women before they were wed and had always been told that women were passionless and did not enjoy making love. Either his dear wife was exceptional or those other men were wrong. He knew exactly how to bring her to the heights of ecstacy and he did so now. When he entered her, she rose to meet him and together they soared to delicious realms of rapture.

Later as they lay in each other's arms Friedrike whispered, "Thank you, dearest Johann. You always know what's best for me. Go to Essen and enjoy yourself. I'll try not to be too lonely."

"I have a better idea," he replied. "Why don't you come with me?"

She gasped with surprise. "But what of baby Sophie?"

"I'm sure Mama would be more than happy to take care of her for a few days."

"Nay. You go. Besides I am enceinte. It is not seemly for a woman to appear in public in that condition."

He ran his hand over her still flat belly. "But you're not even showing yet. Wouldn't you like to ride on a train?"

"Someday, mayhap," she replied hesitantly, "but not just yet. And I should only be bored with factories and guns. You'll enjoy your visit with Alfred better without me trailing along. But mayhap one day we could ride the train to Hannover. I should like to see the Duchess again."

Johann kissed her gratefully. He knew he had won that battle.

Friedrike tried to keep busy while Johann was gone. She invented a new design for her weaving—a sort of plaid of blue, gray and red on a white background—and was very pleased when it turned out well. She copied patterns for dresses out of Henriette's Paris Ladies' Book. She took Sophie to visit her Grandma Bruns and also for walks around the village, although the baby was getting a bit too heavy to carry very far. Ocassionally she helped Doris in the spice shop. And in the evening she read her favorite books until she was too sleepy to mind the lonely nights. Thus the time passed swiftly and suddenly it was time for Johann to come home.

Hermann invited her to ride along to the railway station in Eystrup. She was tempted but then thought, no, suppose something happened and he does not come. Then she would be more worried than ever. Best she wait right here at home. They should be here in a few hours. Her eyes kept going to the clock which never seemed to move. For the first time since Johann left the time seemed to drag unbearably.

At last she heard the wagon stop before the house. She ran to the door and there at last was her dearest Johann. She could not embrace him as he was carrying a large wooden box which he promptly set on the table. Only then he swept her into his arms and kissed her soundly.

"Oh, my dearest," she said, "it is so good to have you back safely. And was it a good trip?"

"Very good and very interesing," he replied. "But it is good to be home."

Hermann had followed Johann into the house carrying his brother-in-law's valise, a bottle of something and two small boxes wrapped in oiled paper.

"Now whatever is all this?" asked Friedrike.

"A surprise for my dearest love," relied Johann.

"I can't wait to see it," put in Hermann.

"Do you know what it is?" she asked.

"Ja, he told me but I haven't seen it," replied Hermann. "You'll love it, I'm sure."

Friedrike could hardly contain her curiosity while Johann fetched a hammer and carefully pried the lid off the box. He pulled out reams of old newspapers and gently lifted the lamp from the container and then unwrapped the colorful glass shade.

"Oh, Johann," exclaimed Friedrike. "How beautiful. I've often dreamed about having one of those."

"You have? I thought you insisted on making your own candles," he said in pleased surprise.

"Only because I thought such a lamp was beyond our means."

"They are so commonplace in the big cities that it was nowhere near as expensive as I had thought." He carefully filled the lamp with oil from the bottle. "Now wait till you see what other wonder I have brought. He opened one of the small boxes. In it lay dozens of small sticks each with a colored blob of something on the end. "They are the newest invention called matches. Now watch." He struck one against the iron of the stove and it burst into flame.

Friedrike backed off. "Ooo, it stinks," she said. "It smells like the devil is in here."

"That is the sulphur. It burns off quickly and it is so easy. No more flint and tinder." He lit the lamp and it flared up with a blinding light.

Friedrike covered both her eyes with her hands. "Ach, it is too bright. It hurts my eyes."

"That is what the shade is for." He placed the colored glass shade on the lamp. It directed the light down onto the table and filled the rest of the room with a soft glow. "There is also this little handle," he instructed, "so that you can turn the wick down to whatever amount of light you want but you must always turn it up high when you first light it."

Friedrike uncovered her eyes. A rosy glow flooded the entire room and only on the table was the light bright. "Oh, Johann, it is beautiful. I had no idea. Thank you so much for a lovely gift." And she hugged him with delight. "I hope that oil is not too expensive, for now I shall sit up half the night reading."

"Not when I want to take you to bed," he replied, only half joking and kissed her again.

"But I can't say I like those matches. They scare me a little and they do stink."

He laughed. "You'll get used to them. Now fix me some supper and I'll tell you all about my trip."

"It is the biggest gun I've seen in my life. It weighs two tons, is ten feet long and stands taller than a man. They are having to build a special gun carriage and limber for it. How it will survive the Channel crossing I know not. I fear it will sink the ship."

"And how fares your friend Alfred?"

"Still very much the same and still my friend but I fear he is a man driven, almost obsessed, by making bigger and better armaments. He is concentrating all his experiments and efforts on that now although he still makes a few mundane things like stoves. I hesitated to ask why the change of heart but I am sure much of it is due to Prussian pressure—and also the money. He is very wealthy now, recently married and has a large luxurious home. And the foundry is unbelievably huge."

"And do you still regret not going partners with him?" Friedrike asked.

"Nay, not at all. I never did. But now—and this should make you happy—I am more than ever glad I elected to stay in Vilsen and be a humble pewterer. I have seen all I want of foundries and factories belching forth black smoke that putrifies the very air you breathe. All the houses in Essen are covered with gray grime from the coal dust. Even the most fastidious housewife cannot keep her windows clean. At times the pall hanging over the town makes it seem like twilight long before the sun goes down. Nay, I prefer the pure air and clear water of Vilsen over all the money in Essen."

And Friedrike was overjoyed at hearing that.

A few weeks after Johann's return baby Sophie seemed to sicken. At first Friedrike did not think it was anything serious attributing it to what was often called 'the summer complaint'—diarrhea caused by the new fresh vegetables. She dosed her with some of Dorothea's tried-and-true medicines. But when the child developed a high fever and seemed to be in great pain, in a panic she sent for the doctor.

The doctor shook his head. "It's like nothing I've ever seen here before. If I didn't know better, I'd say it was a form of cholera. But there hasn't been a case anywhere around here for many years."

"London!" gasped Friedrike.

"London?" asked the doctor puzzled. "Have you taken her to London or has anyone in the family been there recently?"

"Nay but my husband just visited Essen and he mentioned that some of Krupp's workmen had come back from there—to help set up the Great Exhibition, you know—and they told how devastating the epidemic there had been. Could it be from that?"

"Nay, nay," replied the doctor. "The men would have to be already sick with it to pass it on to your husband who in turn would have sickened long before the baby. He's not sick, is he?"

"He doesn't seem to be."

"Then it is something you are feeding her. How long have you been giving her solid food?"

"A couple of months."

"Then stop for a while and give her only liquids—plenty of liquids. Are you still nursing her?"

Friedrike nodded, blushing. "But my milk seems to be drying up now that I am carrying again."

"Then wean her off and give her only goat's milk. 'Tis easier for her stomach to digest. She'll be fine in a few days."

But Sophie was not fine in a few days. On 10 May their precious first-born died. Friedrike was devastated. She was as sure it had been cholera as the doctor was sure it was not. And she blamed it all on Johann, who was doubly heartbroken because he could not understand why.

"Stay away from me," she insisted. "I don't want you infecting the new baby. It's enough you killed our Sophie."

"But I didn't," retorted Johann. "I wouldn't have hurt her for the world. There's nothing wrong with me. I am *not* sick."

"But you mingled with those men who had been to London."

"Just barely. And they were not sick. Nor did I touch a one of them nor stand close enough to breathe their breath. Whatever sickened her did not come from there—nor from me."

"But she was perfectly healthy ere you returned from Essen. It had to be from there."

"Fritzi, Fritzi, you are overwrought with grief, as am I. It is a terrible thing losing one's first-born but it happens to many people all the time. You must get ahold of yourself and think of the new baby."

"I am. And that is why I don't want you near me," she replied petulantly.

Bewildered, grief-stricken and devastated, Johann turned away so that she would not see the tears in his eyes. It was not manly to cry but he grieved not only for their daughter but for his lost love—the love of his life. A double burden he did not know how to cope with. What was wrong with her? He would do anything to help her climb out of this abyss into which she had sunk. But he knew not what. She would barely speak to him. They shared silent meals together but she refused him their bed. He threw himself into his work and eventually set up a cot in his workshop and slept there.

The first to notice the change in their relationship was Johann's mother Margarethe.

"Fritzi," she said, "you have got to pull yourself out of this grief. Women lose babies all the time—I have myself. It is not unusual. But they get over it eventually and look forward to the next one. If you keep on like this you may harm the new babe."

Friedrike shook her head. "The grief is too raw. I can't just put it aside. I am afraid."

"Afraid of what? My dear son who loves you more than I've ever seen any man love a woman? You are hurting him deeply."

"I can't help it."

"Yes, you can. You are supposed to be comforting one another. Yet you drive him away."

"He cared more for Alfred Krupp than for me or Sophie."

"That is foolishness and you know it," snapped Margarethe. "Now get ahold of yourself and act like a grown woman instead of a child."

Johann spoke to the pastor who willingly came to counsel Friedrike. "Don't you believe that your little angel is in heaven with Jesus? God will give you strength as you must give strength to your husband."

But his words fell on deaf ears.

Henriette was not much help although she tried to comfort her cousin. But her own experience with men was so limited—she already thought like a spinster—that she inadvertently agreed that the problem must somehow be Johann's fault.

Doris was not so gentle. "You are a fool, Friede," she chided. "You are destroying what everyone thought was the ideal marriage. And everyone considered you to be the brainiest of the family—aside from Georg. Where is your brain now? If you keep on like this you will drive him away—mayhap even into another woman's arms."

"Oh, no!"

"Oh, yes. I learned enough from Oma Dorchen—and so did you—to know that Johann could not possibly have brought any disease from Essen. Get that idea out of your head ere you lose him, too. It would be no more than you deserve. He is too good a man to have to put up with your foolishness. If he didn't love you so much, he'd be long gone already. He is grieving doubly what you are but you are too selfish to see it."

"Oh, Doris, how can you say that?"

"Very easily. And don't 'oh, Doris' me. I'll keep on saying it until you come to your senses. I have to get back to the shop. Call me when your pains start." She flung out of the house before Friedrike could say another word.

Shocked at her cousin's harsh words, Friedrike threw herself on her empty bed and wept.

Several weeks afterward in late October her pains began. The midwife and her assistant, Doris and Margarethe Bruns were in attendance. At first Friedrike bore the pain stoically. It was almost as though she did not care what happened.

The midwife shook her head. "It's not right. She should be yelling by now. It looks to be an easy birth but why is she so quiet? She's not even trying."

Friedrike was only dimly aware of the midwife's concern. The women did not know that she thought she was going to die—even hoping for it, perhaps. But some innate strength kept her from actually praying for it. Life was not worth living without Johann. Now where did that errant thought come from? Hadn't she driven him away? Hadn't she turned herself from him? She did not care what happened to him—or to her. *Let us just get this over with and let me go in peace.* Or so she thought.

Suddenly as the baby's head began to descend a particularly devastating pain tore through her and she began to scream with all her strength. "Johann! Johann! Help me."

"Where is the husband?" asked the midwife. "Why isn't he pacing up and down in the other room like most men?"

"She sent him away," replied Doris. "She doesn't want him near her."

The midwife shook her head. "Well, she does now. Fetch him."

Doris needed no urging. She ran across to Johann's workshop. "Come quickly. The baby's coming and she's calling for you."

Johann could not believe his ears. "She is? She really is?"

"Ja, ja, come on. But wash your hands first."

Johann threw off his work apron and scrubbed his hands. He hurried after Doris. In the bedchamber his wife was still screaming his name. He rushed to her side. He was so overjoyed at being summoned he did not know what to do. He had never witnessed an actual birthing before. The sight before him was quite unnerving.

Thoroughly cowed, he asked timidly, "What can I do?"

The midwife handed him a damp cloth. "Hold her hand and cool her brow with this. She needs you now."

Johann took Friedrike's hand. He was amazed at the force of her grip. Rarely had he felt such strength even in another man. And her hands were so small. But now she calmed down and the heart-rending screams stopped. "I am here, dearest one," he murmured into her ear. "I am here for you." At each contraction she gripped his hand tighter until he thought the bones would break. *My God, what I've put her through,* he thought.

614

I'll never make her go through this again.

At last the baby came rather quickly, popped right out into the mid-wife's waiting hands. She carefully cut and tied the cord and left the after-birth to her assistant. She held the little one up by the ankles and gave a hard slap. The baby let out a loud yowl.

"Well, Mistress and Master Bruns, you have a beautiful and healthy little girl—and a lusty one, too, it seems," she said. She handed the baby to Johann's mother and turned her attention back to Friedrike. No excessive bleeding. Everything seemed to be under control. A very normal and quite easy birth. "Now if you'd kindly leave us for a few minutes," she said to Johann, "we'll change the bedding and get them both cleaned up. Then you can come back and kiss your wife and enjoy your new daughter."

Johann felt drained. He crept into the other room and sat down at the table. He put his head in his hands and silently said a prayer of thanksgiving.

"How will you call her?" asked Doris a little later.

"Marie after the Duchess and Dorothea after Oma," replied Friedrike, "but we'll call her Doris after you. You will be godmother, won't you?"

"Gladly," said Doris.

That night Johann crept timorously into the bed, fearful of being rejected once again. He knew he could not make love to her, however much he wanted to, until the bleeding stopped. But he could kiss her and hold her if she would let him. Without thinking, from old habit, she cuddled into the curve of his shoulder and sighed with pleasure. He held her that way all night although his arm grew numb. Never was he more thankful.

That very same month King Ernst August dismissed his ministers von Bennigsen and Stüve, no reason given. A wave of fear and worry swept over the country. Pockets of unrest quickly arose again. Here and there minor protests and demonstrations occurred. But the king, perhaps fearing open revolt or perhaps just too old to care anymore, did not change or rescind a single one of Stüve's reforms. The new Prime Minister he appointed was one Alexander von Münchhausen, descendant of the great Adolf von Münchhausen who had so ably ruled Hannover back when the first Georges went to England. He was considered a moderate so things gradually settled down again. But the liberal party kept a watchful eye on things in Hannover.

Johann wished he could to to Osnabrück and confer with Stüve but he dared not leave Friedrike again whilst their loving reunion was still so tenuous. Anyway the old king could not possibly live much longer. And so it was. In September of the next year Ernst August began to sicken and on 18 November 1851 he died. He was buried in the royal mausoleum at Herrenhausen.

Everyone had high hopes that under Georg V things would continue to improve. How wrong they were.

19

1852

Friedrike picked up her skirts and ran through the snowy slush of the yard between the house and Johann's workshop. She was so excited she had even forgotten her shawl. But it was not far and the shop would be very warm. She burst through the door. Johann looked up with surprise and not a little annoyance from the delicate mold he was shaping.

"Johann, Johann," she cried. "I know you don't like to be bothered when you're working but the news is so exciting I couldn't wait until suppertime to tell you."

"Then you'd better sit down and tell me." He dusted off a stool and led her to it.

"We've been invited to the coronation."

"To the what?"

"You know—where the king and queen are crowned."

"I know what a coronation is. What I meant, I guess, to the actual ceremony in Hannover?"

"Ja, ja. Here is the engraved invitation with a personal note from Duchess Marie—I guess I should say Queen Marie now—asking us especially to come for her sake."

"Well, isn't that something! No wonder you are so excited. And I suppose you want to go."

"Of course, I want to go. It's almost like a royal command, isn't it? That is, if you'll say we can go."

"When is it?"

"In two weeks."

"Two weeks!" he exclaimed. "I thought they planned those things months in advance."

She laughed. "And I thought it was all over already. Don't they usually crown the new king just as soon as the old one dies?"

"Only if there is a question of the succession or other siblings who might contest it. But since Georg is the only child there can be no question as to his right to succeed. But then they usually wait until the weather is better. Two weeks," he mused. "Doesn't give us much time."

"What do we need to do? Two weeks is plenty of time," she replied. "Oh, but what shall I wear?"

"Your wedding dress, I should think. You haven't worn it since."

"Ja, I suppose that will have to do. Are we expected to take a gift?"

"Nay, nay, never that. We are just peasants to them."

"How can you say that? We are Bürgers of Vilsen. And Marie is my friend."

"Maybe so, but to royalty in Hannover we are just peasants. She probably did not even think of us until the last minute. How long would we be gone?"

"The invitation doesn't say anything about any reception or fêtes or galas. It's just to the church. So I suppose we only need go for the day."

"For the day?"

"Ja, if we take the train you are so enamored of."

Johann laughed despite himself. "So my dear wife is finally agreeing to come into the modern age."

She smiled. "Ja, Marie wrote that they are even running several extra trains just for that day. So you advise your customers and I'll ask Mama Bruns to take care of Doris. Oh, Johann, thank you for agreeing to go. I'm so excited."

Johann did not recall actually agreeing but it was so wonderful to see his dear Fritzi happy again and excited about something—anything—that it did not matter. "Then you'd better write the duchess immediately by the next post accepting the invitation. They have to know that."

"They do?"

"I'm sure every seat in that church is reserved."

"Ach, ja, I see."

On the day in question Hermann drove them to the railway station at Eystrup before dawn. They intended to take the very first train which should already be on its way from Bremen. Johann bought their tickets and they joined the large crowd waiting near the tracks. Friedrike held tightly onto his arm afraid of losing him in the press of the crowd.

"Are all these people going to Hannover?" she asked.

"The majority I should think," replied Johann. "Although the train does make several stops on the way. But I imagine more passengers will be

618

getting on than getting off."

"Where will they all fit? Will there be room for us?"

Johann laughed. "Of course, there will be. This is not a stagecoach, you know. No one will have to ride on top. But seriously, I am told that for these special trains they are adding more cars than usual—as many as the engine can pull."

Friedrike's excitement grew but she was also a little frightened. "I can't believe we shall be in Hannover in two hours."

"Mayhap less," replied Johann. "These special trains may not stop at every little way station."

Just then a mournful whistle wailed from the distance. Friedrike jumped and gripped Johann's arm tighter. "That's it coming, isn't it?"

"Ja, now close your eyes for a moment as the engine passes so you don't get any dust in them."

Friedrike closed them immediately but then curiosity got the better of her and she reopened them to see the behemoth with its funnel-shaped smokestack approaching. It slowed to a crawl as it pulled into the station, still blowing its whistle. The crowd automatically stepped back a little as the monstrous engine crept past them and stopped at the end of the station. As soon as the conductors opened the doors of the carriages the crowd pressed forward again.

"Now let us try to find seats in the middle of the car," advised Johann, tugging her along.

"Why the middle?"

"Beacuse if you sit too close to the big stove you will be sweating ere we reach Hannover and if too far back, we'll freeze."

However, they did not have much choice. The train was already half filled with passengers who had embarked at Bremen. They could not even sit together. Johann found Friedrike a seat next to another woman.

"I'll be right back here a few seats behind you. Don't be nervous. I'll keep an eye on you. Just hold tight to your reticule. Wouldn't want anyone stealing that invitation."

Friedrike gasped and clutched her reticule to her breast as she sat down in the seat. In a few minutes the conductors closed the doors amid much noise and shouting. The whistle tooted and the engine lurched forward. Friedrike almost cried out as she was thrown back against the hard wooden bench but she gritted her teeth and kept silent so as not to appear the fool. She braced herself for the next few jerks and lurches until finally the engine chugged along at a steady pace. Once she relaxed she tried to peer past the woman next to her. The window was filthy with grime but she could see the snow-covered countryside flashng by so fast it made her dizzy. Her companion noticed.

"Is this your first train trip?" she asked.

The woman seemed friendly enough. "Ja," replied Friedrike. "I was a little apprehensive. I didn't know what to expect."

The woman smiled. "I was, too, at first but now I wouldn't travel any other way. It's quite comfortable in winter with the windows shut but in summer, oh my, one must cover one's clothes with a duster and a special shawl over one's bonnet to keep the dust off. Some even wear goggles to protect their eyes."

"How inconvenient."

"Somewhat but well worth it for the time saved."

"I see. Are you going to Hannover?"

"Nay. Only as far as Nienburg. And you?"

"To Hannover. To the coronation."

Her seatmate looked at Friedrike askance. "I think you're wasting a trip," she said slowly. "You'll be lucky if you even catch a glimpse of the royal coach. And standing for hours in this weather just for that? I couldn't be bothered." She felt sorry for this ingénue.

"But we shan't be standing in the street," replied Friedrike. "We have been invited to the actual coronation at the church."

The woman shook her head in disbelief. This gullible peasant woman invited to the church? "You—have been invited—to the church? I'm sure you're mistaken."

"Nay. I have the invitation right here." She was about to pull it out and show the woman but then she remembered Johann's warning and thought better of it. "The duchess—that is, Queen Marie is my friend." Friedrike could see the woman did not believe her so she decided she had better change the subject. "I have not been able to see the Weser yet. I thought the train ran right alongside it."

"Parallel to it but not that close. The ground is too swampy and the Weser floods frequently."

"Ach, ja, I suppose that's true."

"You may catch a quick glimpse of the river when we pass through Drakenburg but that is all. Well, I shall soon be descending at Nienburg. Then your husband can sit next to you."

"Ja, that will be nice."

They rode in silence the rest of the way. Friedrike wondered, do I really look that much of a peasant? But then her innate dignity took over. Mentally she put her nose in the air and thought, Marie will welcome us and let everyone know I am truly her friend.

At Nienburg she had to stand up to let her erstwhile companion out of the seat. She signalled to Johann, who hurried up the aisle to her side.

"Enjoy your coronation," said the woman with a slight touch of sarcasm.

Friedrike merely nodded.

"I see you have made a friend," remarked Johann.

"Friendly but hardly a friend. She doesn't believe we're going to the coronation. She thinks we're foolish."

"Ach, don't let that kind bother you," he said.

"I don't." She slid over to the seat the woman had vacated. "Now I can really see out the window."

"And what do you see?"

She laughed. "Not much really. It all goes by so fast I get dizzy."

Johann patted her hand.

When they reached Hannover Johann tried to hire a hackney cab for the railway station lay quite some distance from the center of town.

"I can't take you to the church," said the driver.

"Whyever not?"

"All the streets are closed to vehicular traffic from the Fürstenhof and the Schloss to the church. Don't want any horseshit to mess up the procession, I guess. Except the horses of the royal coaches. Mayhap they don't shit. Begging your pardon, Mistress," he added as Friedrike blushed at his profanity.

But she smiled. "You're no doubt right. Then take us to the Fürstenhof. I know the way from there."

"But that is still quite a distance," objected Johann.

"I can take you closer than that, if it's the Marktkirche you want," said the driver. "You'll just have to walk the last few blocks."

"That will be fine," they agreed.

When they reached their destination the crowd of onlookers was dense. People glared at them as they pushed their way through. When they finally reached the church they were stopped at the door by a uniformed dignitary who was about to turn them away.

"But I have a personal invitation from Her Grace," said Friedrike, pulling the elaborately engraved card from her reticule.

The man looked at it. "Oh, very well," he said grudgingly. "We didn't expect any of the invited guests to arrive on foot. The usher inside will show you to your seats." He let them pass.

The usher inside consulted a long list. "Bruns. Hmm. Ah, yes, right over here." He led them to the very last pew at the back of the church on the farthest left side. The great church was already packed.

Johann and Friedrike squeezed into their seats.

"Oh, my goodness," sighed Friedrike. "I'll not be able to see a thing with all these people in front of us." Friedrike was not tall and even Johann was only of medium height.

"I'm sure we were the very last names on that list," replied Johann. "We're lucky to even be here. Maybe you could stand up on the seat."

She looked at him aghast. "Do I dare?' she asked.

"Why not? There's no one behind us. But only do it in the most important part else they'll ask us to leave."

She gave him a gamine look. "I'll do just that. What care I if they think we're boorish peasants? We're here, aren't we?"

At last the great organ thundered out a tremendous fanfare. The choir in the loft sang one of Bach's magnificent anthems. Then the stately procession began, led by all the clergy of the city.

"Oh, there's our Georg," whispered Friedrike. "Tiete told me his Orpheus men's chorus was going to perform at one of the fêtes this evening. How I'd love to hear them. We're so proud of him."

People turned around and glared at her. Johann poked her. "Hush now," he chided.

After the clergy came the Cabinet Ministers. Then the most senior of the nobility escorted blind King Georg down the long aisle followed by all the rest of the noblemen. As the king passed, everyone bowed low or curtseyed as best they could in the confining spaces of the pews. A special chamber choir separated them from the next part of the procession. At last came Queen Marie followed by her own extensive retinue of ladies-in-waiting. Everyone bowed again but not quite so deeply as for the king. The bishop and his staff brought up the rear.

Georg was led to a place on the right side of the aisle, Marie to one on the left. On the chancel there were three thrones, the middle one set higher than the other two. The bishop now approached this and he and the other clergy began the lengthy service.

At last came the part everyone was waiting for. Georg was led to the bishop's throne and knelt on the cushion before it. A nobleman carried the royal crown of Hannover on a large velvet cushion up to the chancel.

He handed it to a clergy-acolyte who presented it to the bishop. The bishop took the crown and firmly placed it on Georg's head as he intoned a lengthy prayer. Georg was then led to the righthand throne. When he was seated he was then presented with the royal sceptre, the orb and other symbols of his office. The choir burst into a joyous anthem.

Then it was Marie's turn. A very elderly noblewoman led her to kneel before the bishop. This worthy placed a much smaller diadem on her head and she was led to the lefthand throne. But she was given no other accoutrements. The choir sang another lovely anthem.

As the queen was being led to her coronation Friedrike decided it was time to stand up on the pew. She hiked up her skirts, leaned on Johann's shoulder and climbed on to the bench. The woman next to her gasped with shock but then apparently deciding it was not such a bad idea after all, followed her example. Soon most of the back row was standing up on the pew. The ushers' collective gasp was quite audible but they could hardly create a disturbance now.

The ushers heaved a sigh of relief when the bishop began his homily and everyone sat down. The prelate's sermon was full of praise for the royal couple and he especially enjoined Georg to be a wise and devout Christian ruler, a father to his people and so on and so forth. No one, including the king, paid much attention.

At last the lengthy ceremony was over. The bishop blessed the new king and queen and everyone else. The royal pair was led down the aisle out to the waiting coaches which would take them to the Leine Schloss where they would now live. The nobility and clergy slowly filed out behind them. The congregation was then permitted to leave but only one row at a time starting from the front. Thus Johann and Friedrike were among the last to leave the church. The royal coaches were long since out of sight.

On the train back home Johann asked, "Are you happy we went?"

"Oh, yes." replied Friedrike. "It was magnificent. I'm still full of chills from the exquisite music even if I couldn't see much of the rest of it. I must write Marie thanking her for inviting us. Now I can brag that I am a friend of the Queen not just of the Duchess of Cumberland."

Johann smiled. "What sort of a king do you think Georg will make?"

Friedrike pondered a moment. "I don't really know. I never got to know him as well as Marie. He was always so quiet and withdrawn. He's a much nicer person than his father but one never quite knew what he was thinking."

"He was trained by Ernst August, don't forget."

"There's that, of course. But he's certainly not as cruel a person as his father nor, I should think, quite so reactionary. We'll soon see."

And soon they did see.

When they arrived home it was very late. Hermann met them at Eystrup.

"You know, I've been waiting through three trains," he said. "I didn't know which one you'd be on and I didn't want you to have to wait for me. Did you enjoy it?"

"Ach, very much," replied Friedrike. "The music was outstanding although I couldn't see much."

"No, I meant the train ride."

"Oh, that. Well, I must admit I was a little nervous when it started to get dark. How do they manage to see in the dark?"

"There is a great lantern mounted on the front of the engine with a reflector behind it that shines the light right down the track," explained Johann.

"Ah, so. But the speed, Hermann, is unbelievable. Imagine thirty miles an hour! Only those wooden benches are awfully hard. At least in a coach the seats are cushioned. But except for the stops and starts the ride was much smoother."

When they reached Vilsen Johann said, "Shall we fetch little Doris or would you rather have some supper first? Mama will have fed her by now."

"Oh, let's leave her there for tonight else we'll disturb both their sleeps. Your mama won't mind. Ah," she sighed deeply, "I am still basking in the afterglow of that powerful, majestic music. It makes me feel so passionate." Whereupon she embraced Johann and whirled him around the room in a quasi-dance.

Johann could not believe his ears. He hoped he was hearing her aright. Since the baby's birth Friedrike had no longer turned him away but their lovemaking had been few and far between and it lacked the frenzied passion they once had had. Not knowing what to say, he made an inane remark.

"After that you won't want to hear my poor fiddle anymore."

"I always love to hear your fiddle, especially when you play love songs for me. But come, dearest love, I need you tonight." She led him into the bedchamber.

They quickly disrobed and climbed into bed. He took her in his arms, supper forgotten.

Gently he caressed her and she moaned with pleasure. He nibbled on her breasts and she responded like an eager tiger. She bit his ears and tugged on his penis. As he kissed his way down to her moist womanhood, she took his member in her mouth sucking so hard he nearly went frantic—something she had never done before. At last she spread her legs wide inviting him in. He needed no urging. He plunged into her warm welcoming recesses and she rose to meet him. More, more, deeper, deeper. Did she actually cry that out? Neither knew nor cared. He drove deeper, harder until she screamed with ecstacy and he groaned with pleasure. They climaxed together in a frenzy of passion. Never had it been so good.

Later when she cuddled in his arms, she murmured, "I have not been very good to you lately, my love. The more fool I."

"Never mind that now," he whispered into her hair. "We are back together again. That's all that matters. You won't turn me away again, dearest one, will you?"

"Never, never," she replied. "I want you to love me every night that we can."

"Perhaps we should listen to music more often," he joked, more than half seriously.

"Your fiddle is quite good enough."

King Georg V was not only ultra-conservative but turned out to be even more reactionary and retrogressive than his father Ernst August. He was absolutely convinced of his divine right to absolute rule. Some of his adherents tried to excuse him on the grounds that his blindness left him feeling not in control unless he could be sure of absolute power. But that was no excuse for what came next. He dismissed almost the entire cabinet and appointed Georg von Schele, son of his father's reactionary advisor, as Prime Minister. To give him credit, von Schele tried to steer a moderate course but to no avail. One by one the king rescinded or overturned most of Johann Stüve's hard won reforms and ordered a return to his father's hated constitution of 1840. Moreover he increased the number of jurisdictions in the country from 127 to 175 in order to give the nobility a greater majority in the parliament.

Once again unrest spread like wildfire throughout the country.

Johann, Hermann and Dieter Meyer travelled to Osnabrück to seek

Johann Stüve's advice before open rebellion broke out again.

"There is nothing we can do," replied Stüve to their questions, "but try to keep people calm. The king is as stubborn as his father and is inflated with his 'divine right of kings'. In time, let us pray, he will realize the fallacy of his policies. But it will take time just as it did with Ernst August."

"But it was the revolution of '48 that finally brought Ernst August to his senses."

"Even that did not bring him to his senses," replied Stüve. "But he was intelligent enough to realize that it would destroy the whole country if he did not give in a little."

"So what can we do to bring Georg to his senses?" asked Johann.

"Nothing at the moment except to maintain calm. I predict that this time it will not be a revolution that will solve Hannover's problems but an outside power. The king favors Austria but Austria is weak—rotten from the inside. It will be Prussia, I fear. Bennigsen's son Rudolf and others are forming a new Liberal Party that favors Prussia."

"Prussia!" exclaimed Dieter. "She whom we all hate and fear?"

"Ja, but union with, not conquest by. Like the Prussian Zollver-ein—Customs Union. Hannover has constantly—and foolishly—re-fused to join when it could have brought us so many benefits. Instead she forms her own little Tax Union with Oldenburg, Braunschweig and Schaumburg-Lippe depending on her onetime relationship with Britain to make it work. But England couldn't care less about us. Even Prussia has had to moderate some of her stifling policies in the face of bur-geoning trade and the capitalist investment that makes it possible—all due to the Zollverein.

"But gentlemen, I only explain all this so you can see the picture of what surely is to come. Hannover values—nay, craves—her indepen-dence but under this king she is wandering about like a lost soul. Why, he even has revamped the army after the Austrian model. Whereas everyone knows—as much as we hate to admit it—that Prussia is the model to fol-low—the most powerful army in Europe. But enough of this. I am no longer involved in politics. Ernst August finished my career and Georg has destroyed all I worked for. I'll not try again. It is time for younger men like Rudolf Bennigsen to take over the battle. Go home and explain all this to your folk and tell them to bide their time."

Johann, Hermann and Dieter went back to Vilsen and tried to explain these things to the people. Most accepted it philosophically, more

626

concerned with their personal problems, their businesses,even how the weather would affect the next harvest, although the spectre of Prussia loomed large in everyone's mind. And gradually things calmed down. But Johann worried about Hermann. Hermann was always overenthusiastic about his loves and hatreds — in short, a hothead who could get himself in trouble if not brought to heel occasionally.

For all their frequent and frenzied lovemaking Friedrike had not yet conceived. At first she was grateful but after while she became worried. Could something be amiss with her? Was she being punished for her denial of Johann those many months before and after Doris' birth? She did not think so. But it was puzzling all the same.

That summer in a thick North Sea fog the Gypsies suddenly and sliently arrived long before dawn as was their wont. Every summer it happened. No matter how raucous and rowdy they were during their stay, they always appeared and disappeared as quietly as wraiths on the moor. The town fathers made no attempt to chase them away but kept a watchful eye on their activities. Mothers kept small children close by their sides for they were believed to steal children. And men kept their animals, especially horses, under lock and key.

Yet it was a fun time, a carnival-like break in the routine of the village. People flocked to see their wild dances and hear the soulful music that even as talented musician as Johann Justus could not emulate. Men enjoyed the shooting galleries and lost their money on various games of chance; children begged their elders for a few pennies so they could have a pony ride; and women, for any number of reasons, patronized the fortune-tellers. Many a farmer got a good bargain on a new horse, even though everyone knew the animal had no doubt been stolen a few counties away. The Gypsies stoutly denied this and always managed to have a few foals on display with their dams to prove that they bred rather than stole the animals. Whatever the truth of that, they were renowned as sharp horse traders.

"Ach, come on," Doris urged Friedrike. "I want to go to the fortune-teller just to see if I'll *ever* meet someone who will wed me."

Friedrike laughed. "Ach, Doris, you're not that old yet. Someone will come along when you least expect it."

"Not many men want a businesswoman. It intimidates them."

"But you have a thriving business. That should be some incentive."

"Not the kind of incentive I would want them to have. I want someone who will love me for me, not for the business. I so envy you and

Johann. But never mind that. You need a break. Let your weaving go for a few hours. It will still be there when you come back."

"But what of little Doris?"

"My goddaughter is old enough to enjoy a pony ride," insisted Doris. "I'll even pay the penny or two."

Little Doris was a strong, healthy and very lively child, almost two and into everything. She chattered endlessly and seemed to want to learn as much as she could as fast as she could. Friedrike knew she would love the pony ride.

"Very well," she agreed, "but just for an hour or so. Is Tiete going?"

"Nay. My sister is such a stick-in-the-mud. She's probably afraid the Gypsy will tell her that her Lude will keep on studying until the day he dies and never wed her."

Friedrike laughed. "It's beginning to look like that, doesn't it?"

For a while they strolled around the Gypsy encampment located in a meadow on the edge of the village. Little Doris was enchanted by all the sights, noise and color. She constantly begged her mother or Doris to lift her up so she could better see what was going on.

"Ach, Gott," sighed Friedrike, "she's so excited she'll never sleep."

"She'll sleep," Doris assured her. "Let's put her on the pony ere she gets too tired."

The pony was old and very gentle. Friedrike lifted the baby up on to the saddle while Doris paid the old Gypsy his penny. The little girl's legs stuck out straight on either side.

"Oh, she will fall off," exclaimed Friedrike. "Shall I walk around with you and hold her?"

"Nay, nay. Wait," said the old man. "I have a special saddle for the littlest ones." He lifted Doris down again. The child immediately began to scream.

"I want the pony," she cried.

"Ja, just wait a moment," replied her mother. "The nice man has a special seat that will just fit you."

"That will be an extra penny," said the Gypsy.

Doris grimaced and paid. They could not disappoint the child now or she would scream forever. The man produced a small seat which he placed on top of the regular saddle. It had a back and a strap across her waist to prevent her from falling. Little Doris could even grip it with her knees. The child beamed and clapped her hands.

"Now hold tight and off we go," said the old man as he led the ancient pony slowly around a track that wound in and out of the encampment.

The two women smiled as they watched. "That one knows what she wants already," remarked Doris.

"I know. She is very headstrong," sighed Friedrike. "That is why I wish we would have another one else she'll be spoiled beyond belief."

"Let's see what the fortuneteller has to say," said Doris.

After the pony ride Friedrike had to carry her daughter. The little girl was almost asleep in her arms. They joined the line outside the fortuneteller's tent.

"Goodness," said Friedrike. "I never thought so many women would be interested in their fortunes. I think we should go home. Doris is ready for her nap. It's just a lot of foolishness anyway."

"Ach, just wait a little longer," urged Doris. "See, the line is moving quite rapidly."

A few minutes later Doris emerged from the tent grinning broadly.

"What did she say?" asked her cousin.

"I'll tell you later. It's your turn now. In you go."

Friedrike entered the tent and sat down opposite the Gypsy woman. The place smelt like a well manured barn. She held Doris on her lap, not daring to set her down on the filthy ground.

"And what can I do for you today?" asked the Gypsy.

Friedrike was determined not to give the woman so much as a hint as to where her interests lay. "Tell me what you think is in store for me," she said as she paid her coin.

The Gypsy took her hand, studied the palm for a moment, turned the hand over and back again. "You will have many more children . . ."

"I shall?"

"Ach, ja, but several of them will leave you for a land far away."

Friedrike gasped. "America?"

The Gypsy shrugged. "Who knows? I can't be that specific. But you will live a long and mostly happy life. There will be a time when you fear for your man's life but he will probably outlive you."

Friedrike raised her eyebrows. "Really?"

The woman shrugged again. "Now let me see your daughter's hand."

"I don't have any more money."

"Ach, no charge for the little one. Their future is often not too clear." She took Doris' tiny hand. The child perked right up and Friedrike thought she might scream but instead she watched and listened with intense curiosity.

"Ach, ja," said the Gypsy. "This one will marry wealth and have many sons but beyond that it is very cloudy."

Friedrike thanked her and rejoined Doris outside.

Doris asked, "What did she say? You look happy."

"Ach, unbelievable. But tell me yours first."

"She said that I shall, indeed, meet someone within the next few years, someone totally unknown to me right now. Do I dare believe her?"

Friedrike laughed. "A mystery man is better than no hope at all. You might as well believe her. 'Tis what you paid for."

A few weeks later Henriette came to visit. "I've brought you the latest Ladies' Book from Paris. Just wait until you read this one article. Absolutely astounding the length some women will go for notoriety." She flipped through the pages. "Look at this. Some woman in America, a Mrs. Amelia Bloomer, has said that women's clothing is too confining and restrictive. She advocates that women wear trousers just like men only a little fancier."

Friedrike looked at the illustration and laughed. "Why that's hilarious. It looks like pictures I've seen of the Turkish harem beauties."

Henriette blushed. "We're not supposed to look at pictures like that!"

"Well, I do. But I certainly would not wear them."

"And what's more," continued Henriette, "she and some of her friends actually wore these things to the Great Exhibition in London last year. Imagine being seen in public dressed like that. Quite disgusting."

"So what can you expect from America? A strange country, that." Friedrike laughed again. "But my question would be, how does one go to pee wearing such a strange garment?"

Henriette blushed again but laughed despite her indignation. "Ach, Friede, you are just too risqué."

Friedrike changed the subject. "Well, let me show you something else new and interesting and not at all risqué. Quite a clever idea, in fact. I had a letter from the duchess—Queen Marie—the other day and I did not have to pay for it at all. Not that I usually have to pay for hers. She almost always prepays them. But look at this little pink stamp on the corner of the cover. It has the coat-of-arms of Hannover on it and states that she prepaid one gute groschen to send it. Isn't that something? Johann tells me it is called a postage stamp."

"Hmm," muttered Henriette not really interested at all. "And what did she have to say?"

"Just the usual. She is well, the children are growing and she is so proud of her Georg. She says nothing of politics. I don't think she dares."

"She wouldn't. But I can't say we are so proud of her Georg."

"Oh, Tiete, Tiete, we must be patient. Things will change. Just look at this postage stamp. Isn't that the cleverest thing? Johann says that some man in England thought of the idea a few years ago and that soon every country in the world will be using them. It's so pretty I think I'm going to save it."

"I don't see what good it would be if every country had them. You still couldn't send a letter from one country to another with all the different currencies. Besides I don't think there's one country in the world that gets along with any other."

"Ach, Tiete, don't be such a pessimist. Someone will think of some way to overcome that."

By the middle of the following year Friedrike knew she was finally pregnant again. This time she was overjoyed.

Anna Margarethe Bruns put in her appearance few days before Christmas 1853. And that was truly a blessed, happy Christmas.

1854 "Have you heard the latest?" exclaimed Hermann as he burst into Johann's workshop.

Johann did not like to be bothered by anyone when he was working. Sometimes his brother-in-law's exuberance annoyed him greatly. But Hermann knew how he felt so this must be something important. "What now?" he asked.

"A Prussian delegate to the Frankfurt Assembly—fellow by the name of Otto von Bismarck—has come to Hannover for a private conference with King Georg."

"Indeed? No doubt to pressure Hannover into joining their Zollverein."

"No doubt. But we think there is a lot more to it than that. We mislike the idea of a private conference."

"But that's the way kings are. If anything comes of it, we'll hear soon enough. And if nothing, it will be as though it never happened. And who is this 'we' you speak of?"

"Bennigsen's German National Union party. It's what the Liberal Opposition party is calling itself now."

"Have you actually joined them? Be careful, Hermann. 'Tis not safe to be too outspoken these days except among ourselves."

"Nay, I haven't officially joined them but I'm thinking of it."

Johann shook his head. "I'm in full sympathy with their goals—trying to restore our constitution, again, and so on—but I don't like the idea they have of seeking a Prussian solution to German unity."

"But you certainly don't favor union under Austria, do you? That is the King's stand—even remodeling the army after the Austrian image."

"Nay. I don't favor Austria. I favor Hannover's independence from either of them. If there are other things than the Zollverein discussed at this conference, I am sure this Prussian will try to woo Georg away from his Austrian sympathies. Prussia doesn't like that one bit. What did you say the fellow's name was?"

"Otto von Bismarck. He's said to be a firebrand and a wily diplomat as well."

"Never heard of him."

"I think you will hear more of him in future."

"Then I pity poor Georg. He is so wishy-washy. He'll go with whichever wind blows the strongest and then go back again."

The Prussian Zollverein—Customs Union—was originally organized in 1837. Most of the southern states had joined it as well as most of the smaller states—some willingly, others reluctantly. But now the treaties were due to expire and many of the southern states were leaning toward a similar customs union with Austria. Prussia was working diligently to renew those treaties, keep those current members in the fold and if possible expand the union. Hannover had always held herself aloof from either side, mistrusting them both and had formed her own small Tax Union with a few neighboring states.

The Zollverein paid out its income based on the population of each state. This favored some of the smaller but industrialized states. Hannover, although one of the larger states, was primarily an agricultural country, exporting cattle and the attendant dairy products, grain and above all, linen, but with a relatively sparse population. Moreover, she had been held back from any extensive industrialization by the repressive policies of Ernst August and his son King Georg V. Furthermore, she had always been a thorn in Prussia's side by simple reason of her geographical location. Prussia had always regarded her as the 'bridge' state between Prussia's eastern and western provinces. In addition, Hannover possessed the extensive North Sea coastline—the only country in Germany to do so. And if that were not enough, Prussia eyed jealously and covetously the huge Welf fortune. For almost 800 years the Welf had been, and still were, the wealthiest royal family in all of Europe.

Whether it was Bismarck's forceful diplomacy or Georg's hard bargaining, we shall never be sure, but Prussia offered Hannover such favorable terms and exceptional advantages that she finally relented and joined the Zollverein in 1854. That left only Mecklenburg, Schleswig-Holstein and the three Hanse cities—Bremen, Hamburg and Lübeck—outside the Customs Union.

To give Georg his due, he tried to improve the cultural life of the capital city. His father Ernst August had already made efforts to modernize the ancient Leine Schloss and Georg continued these with extensive renovations and additions to turn the old castle into a modern royal residence. He also built an opera house which was the finest in Germany for many years. He took great interest in trying to make Hannover a maritime nation, improving the harbors at Emden, Hamburg and above all building an entirely new seaport and shipbuilding facility at Bremerhaven, close to the mouth of the Weser, some thirty miles north of Bremen in order to compete with that venerable city. However, the Hanse cities maintained their preeminence in overseas shipping. The Hamburg-America line was founded in 1847 to take advantage of the lucrative emigration trade. Bremen had four smaller lines which later (1857) merged into the Norddeutscher-Lloyd.

An unfortunate result of Bismarck's conference played right into Georg's reactionary hands. The Prussian encouraged him to be much stricter with the Liberal Opposition and take even more of the franchise away from the common people. To this end Georg appointed one Wilhelm von Borries as Prime Minister. This unreasonable, bitterly antagonistic man immediately instituted a police-state, hated by everyone, and especially cruelly persecuted Bennigsen and the Liberal Opposition.

"Now aren't you glad you didn't actively join the Liberal Opposition?" Johann asked Hermann.

"But I finally did," replied Hermann.

"Oh, no!" exclaimed Johann. "I truly fear me that this Borries is about to set up a witch-hunt. You may find yourself in danger."

"I think not—at least, I hope not. Most of his efforts will be concentrated on the more important people in the larger towns. I shall lie very low and keep very quiet. Most of the local police are not enthusiastic about his edicts. A few are even in sympathy with the Liberals and have said they will not enforce his orders at all."

"Maybe so but they will have to or lose their own jobs."

Hermann merely shrugged.

Hermann was partly correct. Not only were the local police reluctant to root out Liberals on trumped up charges—they were, after all, friends and neighbors—but their very paucity made the job impossible. Vilsen had one full-time officer, Bruchhausen one part-time. The chief constable was in Hoya, some distance away, and paid little attention to the two villages as long as things remained peaceful. Therefore Prime Minister Borries was forced to revive and deputize the long defunct local militia. Once again Hinrich Campsheide of Asendorf was called upon to lead them. But this time Hinrich's task was not so easy. Very few recruits were willing to join since most citizens found Borries' policies hateful and in some cases, illegal. Most were on the side of the Liberal Party if not actual members. But as in any similar situation there were always those who were willing to harass their neighbors for the few pennies the government would pay them. The three or four recruits Hinrich was able to gather were the lowest of the low—vagabonds, uneducated ne'er-do-wells, not above committing petty crime and vandalism. Hinrich was ashamed of them but he vowed to train them into some semblance of a police force. Since this would take some time, the Bürgers of Vilsen relaxed and went about their business.

Friedrike heard someone burst into the house. She turned from the bedroom where she had been airing the featherbeds fully expecting to see her brother Hermann. Instead she was surprised to see staid, lady-like Henriette bubbling over with excitement like a teenager. She had never seen her cousin acting like that.

"Tiete!" she exclaimed. "What has happened? It must be something good judging by the look on your face."

"Oh, it is, Friede. Lude and I are to be wed in less than a month."

"Well, that is indeed good news. And about time, I say."

Henriette bristled at that but she was so happy the mood passed in a moment. "After all, he had to finish his studies and then save up some money. Lude is a very cautious person and never does things precipitously—as befits a good doctor."

"Of course. I understand. And I'm so happy for you." Friedrike embraced her cousin. "And when is the wedding to take place?"

"As I say, in less than a month. Pastor will start calling the banns this Sunday. So as soon thereafter as possible. Oh, I'm so excited. And what's more he has purchased the big three-storey house here at the other end of Gartenweg and old Doctor Eichhorn has agreed to sell him most of his practice. He wants to retire gradually."

"Ja. He is getting old. He simply can't handle all the patients anymore. We certainly do need a young, modern doctor here."

"And that means we won't have to leave Vilsen."

Friedrike smiled. "Tiete, that was your intention ever since you met your Lude," she teased, "whether he knew it or not."

Henriette smiled, neither admitting nor denying the allegation. "And I have other news as well."

"Ach, what more could there be?"

"My brother Georg has been called to Harber bei Hohenhameln and will have his own church. A full pastor at last."

"That is good news, indeed. He certainly deserves it. He has worked so hard in Hannover. Any sign of a wedding there?"

"Not as yet. But I feel that now that he is on his own he will be more amenable to marriage. In fact, a pastor needs a wife, doesn't he?"

"It helps."

"And that brings me to another thing I wanted to discuss with you. Now that I'll be moving out, Doris will be all alone in the big Bergmann house. Would you and Johann like to live in part of it?"

"Nay. And I can speak for both of us. Thank you for the offer, Tiete, but we are quite content here."

"But this cottage is so tiny and you may have more children."

"Ah, but we, too, have plans," said Friedrike. "We are going to build a byre onto the house where our garden is now. Johann is already negotiating with old Wassmer to buy that large garden across the way. It is four times the size of our present garden. I've always wanted a cow and a couple of goats, also some chickens and mayhap a ewe. We'll be able to pasture them in the common pasture across Homfelderstrasse and in winter the loft will be cozy enough for the the children. So you see, we've been busy with plans, too."

"So I see. And very ambitious ones, too."

"I think the best thing Doris could do is rent out part of the Bergmann house."

"You're no doubt right. I'll suggest that to her."

"Well, keep me apprised of your plans and if I can help in any way, let me know."

"Oh, I have all the plans already made. Georg will come and give me away and Doris, of course, will be maid of honor. I'm not sure if we should have Johann or Hermann for groomsman."

"Tiete! The choice of groomsman is up to the bridegroom—or it should be," exclaimed Friedrike.

"Oh. I'll have to see what Lude thinks about that. But I'll tell you the very first thing I'm going to do after the wedding is send in our application to the Stockman Foundation in Celle."

Friedrike laughed until tears came to her eyes. "Tiete, Tiete, you innocent. It may be the second or third thing you do but definitely not the first if your Lude has any guts." And she laughed all the harder when that made Henriette blush.

After her cousin left Friedrike got to thinking about the Stockman Foundation. She had never completed the letter she had started almost five years ago. And they could certainly use the extra money now. She vowed to do so immediately before anything else happened.

1855   Friedrich Matthies was working very hard to please his father. Not that he had any love for his father. He hated him. But it was easier to try to please the irascible old bastard than to suffer the constant beatings and canings. Now seventeen, Friedrich had almost completed his apprenticeship at the great windmill, of which Heinrich was so proud. But Friedrich hated the work, too. He had never wanted to be a miller. Like his cousin Hermann Bergmann, he once had dreams of going to university and studying to be a doctor or a lawyer—or anything but a miller. But Heinrich would not hear of it. They were wealthy, could easily have afforded it—not that one would ever know, Heinrich was so penurious—but no. Just because way back in 1785 his great-grandfather Anton Matthies had been awarded hereditary rights to the two mills at Heiligenberg and Bruchmühlen—the windmill was not included in that—Friedrich must slave to keep up the family tradition.

He also deplored the brutal manner in which Heinrich treated his mother. He loved his mother but he had little respect for her. Adi was so meek she had lost any willpower to fight back—if, indeed, she had ever had any. Friedrich admired his elder sister Dorothea who, the moment she turned one-and-twenty, had run away from home.

Heinrich had made no attempt to bring her back. "Let her go," he had said at the time. "Saves providing a dowry."

Word had finally filtered back to them that she had fled to cousins in Westen and was soon to be married. Friedrich would have like to go to the wedding or at least visit her but he dared not broach the subject.

Friedrich was outside the windmill helping a farmer unload sacks of grain when the soldiers rode into the yard. At least he assumed they were soldiers. The captain in charge, who looked vaguely familiar, wore a uniform of sorts but his associates were a ragtag bunch of scalawags, such as one would be afraid to meet in the dark. Friedrich had a sudden recollection of the time he had tattled too much at a birthday party and caused untold trouble to the citizens of Vilsen. In hindsight he regretted his action and yet, strangely enough, it had been one of the few times his father had praised him. This time he would be very careful what he said.

"Heinrich Matthies?" asked the captain.

"My father is within and very busy," replied Friedrich. "May I help you?"

"Is Heinrich Matthies a member of the German Union party?"

"No, he is not," denied Friedrich. "He is a conservative, a strong supporter of the king."

"Does he not favor union with Prussia?"

"Oh, yes. He believes that the strong Prussian discipline is the only thing that can unite Germany."

"Then he must be a Liberal," said one of the scalawags. "They favor Prussia."

"Right," agreed another ruffian. "If he supports the king, he would favor Austria."

Friedrich was bewildered. At his age he paid little attention to politics, merely repeating whatever his father said. What had he said wrong now?

"We would have words with Master Matthies. Fetch him," ordered the captain.

"But—but I told you he is very busy," replied Friedrich.

Just then Heinrich, wondering where the rest of the grain was, walked out of the mill, fire in his eyes. "What are you doing talking to these men when there is work to be done?" he yelled. "Where is Jacob?"

The farmer, not wanting to get involved, had quietly driven off.

"Gone home, I guess," mumbled Friedrich.

"What?" screamed Heinrich. He cuffed Friedrich on the ear. "Get back inside whilst I get rid of these vagabonds." He took his cane and began hitting the horses across their rumps. "Get off my property whoever you are. I'll not have the likes of you corrupting my son."

Hinrich Campsheide stepped up to him. "Master Matthies, I am

637

Kapitän Campsheide, duly authorized police of His Majesty, and I hereby arrest you for disturbing the peace and molesting the King's officers."

"You what?" sputtered Heinrich. "Arrest me for defending my own property when you are obviously trespassing?"

Campsheide ignored that remark. "Furthermore," he went on, "you are known to be in favor of the German Union Party and that could result in a charge of treason."

"Treason?" screamed Heinrich. "Are you out of your mind? I have no use for any Liberal Party. I am more conservative and loyal to the King than you are."

"But your son admitted that you favor Prussia," stated the captain.

"Of course, I favor Prussia. So did our late King Ernst August, God rest his soul. Would you have arrested him?"

Campsheide realized he had gone too far. "No, of course not. However, you will still have to answer to charges of breaking the peace." He nodded to his men. Two of them took Heinrich Matthies by the arms and forced him to walk rapidly between two horses to the magistrate's office.

Dieter Meyer groaned inwardly when they entered his chambers. He recognized Campsheide from the previous fiasco some years ago. He knew about Prime Minister Borries' campaign against the Liberals. And wasn't this Kapitän Campsheide just the one to head it up locally? But Heinrich Matthies? The most outspoken opponent of the Liberals? It made no sense.

Judge Meyer listened courteously to the charges. As much as he disliked Matthies, he could not let an innocent man be accused of their trumped up charges.

"Gentlemen," he said, although he nearly choked over the word, "I fear you have made a grave mistake. Of my own personal knowledge Miller Matthies is one of the most conservative men in the whole county—an *ultra*-conservative, I would say. He has no truck with any liberals and there are any number of upright Bürgers here in Vilsen who can vouch for that. You had no cause to arrest him on those charges."

Once again the captain seethed with frustration. "But he molested my men who were simply doing their duty."

"None of them appear to be injured," said the judge. "In what way did he molest them?"

Heinrich Matthies could no longer keep quiet. "I took my cane to their horses but I did not molest any man. They were trespassing on my property."

638

"See. He admits it," said Campsheide.

Judge Meyer thought a moment. He wanted to be rid of these men ere they turned the case into a full blown persecution of Vilsen. Yet it would not hurt to do something to warn Miller Matthies to curb his temper.

"In that case I shall fine you a half a silbergroschen, Master Matthies. Case closed. Good day, gentlemen."

The fine was only a token—the equivalent of about three pennies—but Heinrich Matthies was fuming. Ten minutes later when he arrived back at the windmill, he had worked himself up into a raging fury. He immediately turned on his son.

"Why did you tell them I favored Prussia, you fool?" he screamed as he started beating the lad.

"But—but Papa—I—I thought it was the right thing to say," stammered Friedrich. "You do, don't you?"

"You leave those things to me and keep your mouth shut," stormed Heinrich as he kept pounding the boy unmercifully.

Friedrich tried to get out of his way but his father was too strong for him, especially enraged as he was. Adi heard the noise and came rushing from the house to the mill. She tried to place herself between her husband and her son but this only infuriated Heinrich all the more. He knocked her out of the way.

"Get back in the house," he roared. "This is no concern of yours."

"But there is no need to hurt the lad so. Whatever did he do?" she cried.

In response Heinrich chased her into the house beating her all the way. Friedrich wanted to help his mother but his head was swimming and his legs would hardly move. He heard her scream once or twice and then silence. Heinrich had knocked her down so that her head hit the hearthstone. Satisfied that she was still breathing and would no longer interfere, he turned from her and returned to the mill. Unbeknownst to either, the edge of her skirt was just touching the hot embers at the front of the fire.

"Now let's get back to work," he growled at his son. "I wonder where that fool Jacob got to with the rest of his grain. Probably scared shitless. Well, he'll come back when he sees the coast is clear. Let's start milling as much as we have here."

Although every bone in his body ached and he could hardly move, Friedrich made the effort, fearing another outburst of temper. After about a half hour he said, "Papa, I smell smoke."

639

Heinrich sniffed the air. "Can't smell a thing with all this flour dust in here. Probably that fool woman burning our dinner."

A few minutes later Friedrich said again, "Papa, it's getting stronger. That's no dinner burning. It's something else."

Greatly annoyed, Heinrich shut down the millstones. In the silence that followed they could hear crackling. They ran out of the mill to the house. Smoke was already seeping out of the windows. When Heinrich opened the door he was met by a wall of fire.

"Oh, my God," he cried. "Run for the pumper. I've got to save the mill."

Friedrich, although his legs felt as though they had been hamstrung, went as fast as he could. The windmill had no near neighbors. Heinrich had wanted it that way but now it was definitely a disadvantage. When Friedrich reached the limits of Vilsen, he accosted the first man he met.

"Fire! Fire!" he yelled. "Tell them to send the pumper, ring the tocsin. I've got to go back and help my father."

The man nodded and ran down the street. He needed no urging. In a village of wooden houses most of which had thatched roofs, fire was dreaded more than anything else. The new fire barn was nearby the church. It had been built to house the extraordinary fire engine that Friedrich's great-aunt Eleonore's husband Theodor Hohnholz had invented. The horses were always ready and eager to run.

Johann Justus heard the tocsin ringing wildly. He quickly damped down his own fires and ran to the fire barn, as did every able-bodied man in Vilsen. The pumper had already left by the time he got there. "Whereaway?" he asked.

"The windmill. Matthies' windmill," he was told. He hurried down the street, carrying his bucket. When he arrived Heinrich Matthies was arguing with the firemen.

"But we've got to save the mill," he screeched.

"We'll try to save your mill if you'll just get out of the way. The brook's too far away for the hoses. We've got to use your well," replied the fire chief. "Now pull that pump out of the well and take the cover off," he ordered, "so we can run the hose down it."

Heinrich stood by looking helpless, temper boiling.

Friedrich asked, "Where's Mama? Could she still be inside the house? And the girls?"

Heinrich seemed to wake up from a daze. "Nay, nay. They'd have run out the back way. The girls were outside anyway—I think."

The firemen wet down the side of the mill and turned their attention to the house. It was already too far gone to save but it was a raging inferno and must be brought under control or the mill would surely catch. Fortunately there was no wind. The men pumped for all they were worth while Johann and others formed a bucket brigade.

Freidrike also reacted quickly to the ringing of the church bells. She knew there would be burns and other injuries for the women to see to.

"Now you be a good girl," she commanded little Doris, "and look after your sister Anni. Oma Bruns will he here in a few minutes." She grabbed her medicine bag and ran to the fire barn. When she learned that the fire was at the Matthies windmill, the first thought that crossed her mind was Oma Dorchen saying years ago, 'It will come back to them'. But little did she realize how horribly true that prophesy would be.

When she and the other women arrived at the scene of the fire, the men had it partially under control. They had saved the mill but the remains of the house were still burning furiously. As Friedrike looked about to see who needed her help Caroline Matthies ran up to her father.

"Papa, Papa, Hanne's hurt, burned. Come quick!"

But Heinrich was busy throwing water on the ruins and paid her no mind.

But her brother Friedrich heard her, as did Freidrike.

"Where is she, Line? What happened?" he asked.

"She tried to go in the house to help Mama but when her dress caught fire, I pulled her back and rolled her in the grass," sobbed Caroline.

"Smart girl," said Friedrich. "I'll come. But where is Mama?"

"Still in the house, I think," cried the girl. "She's not with us. I thought she was with you."

"Oh, my God," exclaimed Friedrich. "Papa, Papa, Mama's still in the house."

Heinrich either did not hear him—or chose not to. He was concentrating so on saving the mill.

Friedrike touched his arm. "He does not hear you. Tell the fire chief. Although I fear me, if Adi is still in there, it is already too late. I'll see to Johanne."

She took Caroline's hand and together they ran around to the meadow behind the house. Little Johanne was lying in the grass, moaning, more in shock than seriously hurt. Her gown was scorched but only

641

the left shoulder was burned away. And, thanks to Caroline's quick-wittedness, the burn on her arm was not too serious. Friedrike peeled away the remnants of the sleeve, slathered salve on the burn and wrapped it in clean linen. She washed the soot from the child's face and inspected it carefully. There were no injuries. Only her hair and eyebrows were singed a little but that would grow back. Only then did Friedrike take Johanne in her arms to comfort her.

"Why did you try to go into the house?" she asked after a while.

"To save Mama," sobbed Johanne.

"Are you sure she was in there?" asked Friedrike. "She may have already run out."

"Nay, nay," objected the child. "I saw her. She was lying by the hearth. She was not even trying to run. But then the fire was so—so big I couldn't get near her. Then Line pulled me back. I wanted to save her, Mistress Bruns, but I could not." The little girl lapsed into soul-wrenching wails while Friedrike held her close.

Friedrike shuddered. What a horrible last memory to have of one's mother. She feared the picture would haunt Johanne the rest of her life. But then another question arose in her mind. Why was Adi lying by the hearth unable to run from the fire? Had Heinrich in his brutal temper finally killed her and deliberately set the fire to cover the murder? No, it had to have been an accident. Even Heinrich Matthies would not go that far. Yet the question bothered Friedrike. Why had Adi been lying by the hearth?

After the child ceased the worst of her weeping, Friedrike said, "Come girls. Line. Hanne. You must tell the firemen what you saw. They don't know that your mama was still in the house." She led them around the still smoldering ruins.

Johanne hid her face in Friedrike's skirt. "I don't want to look," she sobbed. "Oh, Mama, Mama."

Friedrike walked up to the fire chief. "Are you aware," she asked, "that Mistress Matthies was—and no doubt still is—in the house at the time of the fire? Lying comatose by the hearth?"

"She is?" exclaimed the chief. "Ach, Gott, we wondered where she was but Heinrich didn't seem to know. How do *you* know?"

"Johanne here saw her. Tried to get to her but couldn't," replied Friedrike.

When the chief approached Heinrich with this information, he tried to bluff. "She wasn't there when I last saw her. Er—ah—I don't know where she was." And he went back to wetting down the mill.

But Friedrich heard him. He sidled up to Friedrike and whispered, "Mistress Bruns, he is lying. I don't know what happened in there but he was beating me and Mama came to intervene. Then he started beating her and chased her back into the house and suddenly—suddenly it was very quiet—too quiet. Not long after we smelled smoke. I think he killed her."

Freidrike gasped. "Oh, you mustn't say that," she said, although the same thought had occurred to her. "She could have gotten out and be wandering about somewhere in a daze."

"I doubt it," he replied bitterly. "Oh, how I hate him." He started sobbing unmanly sobs. "Oh, Mama, Mama."

With Johanne still clinging to her skirt, Friedrike took him in her arms and let him weep against her shoulder. Oh, God, she thought, what an unholy mess. She reflected back on her own dear mother and her grandmother Eleonore. This family is surely jinxed.

The firemen and others were now digging through the still smoldering ruins. And there they found Adi's corpse, burned beyond recognition, still lying on the hearthstone.

Much later, although everyone knew of Heinrich Matthies' violent temper, they were forced to believe him when he swore up and down that his wife had been alive and well when he last saw her. Who could believe a six-year-old child? It was her vivid imagination. At the most, Adi may have tripped, fallen and hit her head but Heinrich swore he knew nothing of that. But his three remaining children knew better. And Friedrich hated him all the more.

Perforce Heinrich had to go to Ünzen to break the sad news to Adi's family. Before very long a woman there caught his fancy—another Adelheit. Mayhap this one would be livelier. His first Adi had been so dull. Although Heinrich was over fifty, he could not long be without a woman. Within weeks he had her in his bed and a few months later she was pregnant. He could not marry her yet, he made the excuse, as he was still in mourning. Also he had to rebuild a proper dwelling house. The new Adi seemed to accept this without question.

Meanwhile Friedrike took in the two Matthies girls and Doris let Friedrich have a room—rent free—at the Bergmann house. No one wanted Heinrich, so he slept alone at the mill. Although Friedrich went to work everyday, he refused to speak to his father except when absolutely necessary. The only blessing to come out of the tragedy was that there were no more beatings, only verbal abuse which Friedrich could easily ignore.

Meanwhile by late spring of 1856 Friedrike found herself pregnant again. The Gypsy's prediction was certainly coming true but she prayed desperately that the second half of the fortune-telling would not come to pass. It would break her heart if, after having borne and raised them, her children all went away.

Little Doris had first been jealous of having to share her parents' loving care with baby Anni. But soon she realized that Anni was very sweet but also meek, mild and quite malleable—not at all like forthright and gregarious Doris. And Doris was still queen of the roost. Hadn't Papa told her that? But now there was going to be another baby. How would that affect her status? Doris wondered how mamas knew ahead of time that another baby would soon arrive.

Doris loved both her parents but she liked Papa better. Although he worked very hard all day, he always had time to play with his two little girls. He was such fun, especially when he played his fiddle and taught them all kinds of little songs. She already knew more songs than any of her peers and she had not even started school yet. Mama, although kind and loving, was stricter. It was she who doled out punishment when Doris became too rambunctious or mistreated her little sister. Mama was always after her to practice her embroidery when she would much rather be drawing pictures. Everyone said Doris drew very well for her age.

Of her other relatives she liked Tante Doris the best. Tante Doris and Tante Tiete were not really aunts at all, but cousins, Mama explained. But she had been taught to call them Tante and so it was. Onkel Hermann was fun, too. Sometimes he would let her ride in his wagon when he went to deliver a piece of furniture. Or even better he would sometimes let her watch him carve a beautiful piece. Papa made beautiful things, too—out of pewter—but his shop was so hot and smelly, Doris did not like to go there. But the smell of the wood was so—so like out-of-doors, Doris loved it. Sometimes Onkel Hermann would hang some of the wood shavings in her hair and call them curls. Mama did not like that one bit. But Onkel Hermann always seemed to be in a hurry to go somewhere, so she did not see as much of him as she would have liked.

Tante Tiete was no fun at all. Although kind enough, she was always so dignified and ladylike. Doris was told she would do well to emulate Tante Tiete's manners but who wanted to be ladylike if one could not have fun? One time she had heard Tante Tiete tell Mama that this child was too precocious by far. Doris did not know what 'precocious' meant but she did not like the sound of it. And now Tante Tiete was getting very fat and did not look ladylike at all. 'Twas said that a baby would be coming to her and Doctor Lude very soon. Doris wondered why women always got so fat when a baby was expected. Maybe they had to store up a lot of fat so they could feed them later. She wondered if Mama would get fat like that, too.

But of them all Tante Doris was her favorite besides being her god-mother. She was always teasing and joking and making fun of the neighbors. And oh! the delicious smells in that spice shop. Doris would sit very quiet, just breathing in the wonderful scents and odors, while Tante Doris opened fascinating jars and dove into bins as she waited on her customers. And when she was not busy Tante Doris always had a story for her. Not the usual Grimms' tales—Mama read her those aplenty—but funny, and sometimes scary, stories about the neighbors, or long-dead ancestors, or the history of Vilsen or even about the old gods and goddesses—not quite appropriate for a Christian godmother to be telling her goddaughter but interesting nonetheless. Ja, Tante Doris was definitely her favorite. Doris wondered if she would one day have a baby, too. But Tante Doris had always been rather chubby so it would be hard to tell.

In November 1856 Wilhelma Luise was born. She was a rather pretty little thing but to Doris all babies were boring. So she concentrated on her drawing and on teaching Anni little songs. The following year she was going to start school and that was far more exciting than any baby.

1857 Doris was so enthralled with her schoolwork that she scarcely noticed that Onkel Hermann was not around as much anymore. And that when he was, he was deep in serious discussions with Papa, to which little girls, especially precocious ones, were not welcome. She did notice that Tante Doris did not seem to have as much time for her as heretofore but she assumed that that was because Tante Doris wanted her to pay more attention to what she was learning in school than to old wives' tales.

Although Hermann was still living in the Bergmann house, Friedrich Matthies had gone back to live with his father, the new bride and their baby Heinrich at the rebuilt dwelling house at the windmill. Whether there was any reconciliation between the Matthies, father and son, no one could be sure but at least they were tolerating one another. Doris had taken Friedrike's advice and rented the extra bedrooms in the Bergmann house to a few young men. One of these, Christian Möser, a shopkeeper in his own right, seemed to have a growing interest in the pro-prietress of the spice shop.

Doris at first was very leery of his motivation. After all, the spice shop was a very lucrative enterprise and Christian, being a businessman, knew a good thing when he saw it. Also he was more than five years younger than Doris, who at almost thirty, had already resigned herself to being an old maid. But somehow over the next few months Christian must have convinced the astute businesswoman that he loved her as well as her business. And suddenly hardheaded and skeptical Doris was going about with stars in her eyes. To everyone's surprise and delight they were wed the following year.

Meanwhile the political situation grew more tense. Prime Minister Borries' police regime was now stooping to inadmissable and, in many cases, illegal methods to stack the rump parliament in favor of the king. He rearranged the voting districts in order to increase the number of nobility in the upper house. He threatened candidates to the lower house as well as those aspirants to the Civil Lists with 'disciplinary action' if they did not vote as instructed or withdraw their candidacies.

"How much longer are we going to tolerate this?" Herman asked Johann one evening.

"I don't know," replied his brother-in-law. "What can we do? Our hands are tied. This Campsheide and his gang are turning neighbor against neighbor looking for informants. Informants against what, I ask you? People are afraid to think aloud anymore."

"We shook Ernst August up back in '48. Why can't we do that again? We need another Stüve."

"Because in '48 the revolution was all over Eruope and it took Ernst August by surprise. He only gave in to Stüve because he did not want Hannover to become another Berlin or Vienna. But now they are ten steps ahead of us. They have the police regime already in place, Parliament stacked with nobles and they are already persecuting Bennigsen cruelly."

Hermann sighed. "Ja. Did you know they made Judge Meyer resign? The fairest, most righteous justice we've ever had—and a local man besides."

"I heard. He wanted to retire anyway. He refused to go along with their 'disciplinary action'. They'll no doubt appoint one of their toadies in his place. But Vilsen has really been very lucky. I hear it's much worse in the larger towns. But that is why we must lie low and be very circumspect.

Someone, somewhere will do something and then we must be ready to join them."

"Ja, but who? When? Many of us are tired of waiting. I'm more inclined than ever to go to America."

"Hermann! You can't mean that," exclaimed Johann.

"I'm serious. Do you know there is a new shipping line out of Bremen that goes directly to America? One doesn't have to go all the way to Hamburg to embark."

"I didn't know that. I don't pay much attention to what goes on in America."

"Ja. They combined the old Roland Line with two or three others. It's called the Norddeutscher-Lloyd—North German Lloyd. They're making a transatlantic voyage every week and it takes less than two weeks to get there. Can you imagine? These steam vessels are a wonder."

"But Hermann, why would you want to give up a good business and everything you have here for—for an unknown land? Fritzi would be heartbroken."

"Ach, Johann, admit it. Under King Georg we are no better off than the old medieval serfs were. And you know another thing that worries me? Did you know that old King Friedrich Wilhelm of Prussia has finally been declared insane—as if we didn't know that all along—and his brother Prince Wilhelm has been made regent? That worries me. He will certainly renew the push towards Hannover."

"Ja, that worries me, too. Although Wilhelm is not as reactionary as his brother, he is more decisive and assertive. And with our Georg cozying up to Austria, that does not please Prussia at all. Wilhelm is sure to pressure Hannover ere long."

"Ja, ja. So that's another good reason for going to America."

"Nay, nay, Hermann. I'd rather stay right here and fight them both. It's our Heimat after all."

"Fritzi, do you know that Hermann is talking more and more about going to America?" said Johann one spring day.

"Ach, he's always talking about America," replied Friedrike. "It's just spring fever. He needs a wife. He's always so restless and he's not getting any younger."

"I'm afraid he is more serious this time. He's even gathered information about the new transatlantic shipping line out of Bremen. And I know, although he won't admit it, that he is more involved with the Liberal Party

647

than is wise—or even safe."

"I'll talk to him. He promised to be godfather to this new baby. What kind of a godfather would go traipsing off the the New World right after the baby's christened?"

At the first opportunity Friedrike collared her brother. "Hermann, you promised to be godfather to this new baby, especially since I feel sure it will be a boy this time."

"I did and I shall," replied Hermann. "But how can you be sure that it will be a boy?"

"I somehow just know. After four girls, don't you think I deserve it?"

Hermann laughed. "Then you must name him Hermann."

"I intend to. But what kind of a godfather will leave the babe to go off to America? He will need you until he is of age."

"Mayhap I'll take him with me."

"Oh, Hermann, stop teasing. This is a very serious matter."

"I am serious. What better place to bring a young man up? Rich farms, plenty of room—and freedom."

"Freedom? When they're on the verge of having a war over slavery?" Friedrike exclaimed.

"Ach, that's only in the south. That place is so big that out in the west where the good farmland can be had for the taking they won't even know that a war is going on. If, indeed, it comes to war."

"But Hermann, you are a cabinetmaker not a farmer."

"Even farmers need furniture. And 'tis said the forests are endless."

'Oh, Hermann, stop talking America. Promise me you won't leave this child without a godfather."

"Friede, Friede, don't upset yourself. I'm not going tomorrow—if I even go at all. A lot depends on what happens here in Hannover. Anyway I do promise you this much—this son, if it is a son, will always have a god-father for as long as he needs him."

And it was a son. Hermann Friedrich Bruns was born in May 1858.

"Fritzi, Fritzi, what is wrong?" asked Johann. "Why are you weeping? What has happened?"

Friedrike was sitting at the table, silent tears streaming down her face and dripping on a copy of Grimms' Fairy Tales that lay open before her. She shook her head. "He has died," she murmured.

"Who? What?" said Johann, bewildered. He had not heard of any recent deaths in the village. "Where are the children?"

"Out. I sent them out to play. I could not read anymore once I heard."

"But who has died, dearest Fritzi, that you are so overwrought?"

"Wilhelm Grimm."

"And you are weeping so profusely over a man you don't even know?" exclaimed Johann.

"I know him very well." She indicated the book. "I always thought of him as a beloved uncle. My Mama worked for the brothers, you know, for about a year before she and Papa were wed. And I never tired of hearing Oma Dorchen speak so fondly of Wilhelm the time he came to Heiligenberg to collect some of the stories. It was she, you know, who took up a collection for him here in Vilsen when Ernst August dismissed the 'Göttingen Seven'."

"I remember. I even gave a few pennies toward it."

"Although they always signed their work the Brothers Grimm, it was Wilhelm who kept revising and rewriting the stories to make them more suitable for children, more Christian-like. He took out some of the more risqué parts. Although they were fun to read, too." Friedrike blushed at her own temerity.

"I never realized that. I thought once they were written down, that was the end of it."

"Nay. I understand the latest revision was done only two years ago, while Jacob worked on his dictionary. I wish I could have gone to the funeral but it was in Berlin and over before I even heard about it."

Johann smiled. "That would have been a bit far."

She wiped her tears and laughed. "Indeed it would. And do you know what Jacob said in the eulogy? He referred to Wilhelm as 'Märchenbruder'—Fairy tale brother. Wasn't that endearing?"

"Ach, Fritzi. You are such a sentimentalist." He took her in his arms. "With people like you and this book to keep his memory alive, your 'Onkel' Wilhelm Grimm will be immortal long after King Georg and Minister Borries are forgotten. That is the real spirit of our Heimat."

20

1859

Johann Hermann Campsheide did not like his oldest brother Hinrich at all. In fact, there were times when Johann positively hated him. Hinrich was an authoritarian, arrogant prig—perfectly suited to be Borries' toady, harassing innocent people just to make himself look good. And he treated Johann like a serf on their own land.

Hinrich Campsheide had finally married Becke Rabens back in 1849, much to their mother's delight but to the dismay of his siblings. Becke was almost as arrogant as her husband. Although she came from a simple peasant family, she acted as though she were the queen herself. Their sister had married the same year and Johann often suspected it was as much to get away from her brother and his wife as for love of her man. And Hinrich's marriage settlement! It was the strangest Johann had ever heard of. Although he did not know much about such things, having been only eighteen at the time and forced to sign it. Johann had always heard that the usual settlement involving the heir to the property customarily paid a sum of money or goods to the other siblings as their share of the inheritance and that was that.

But no! Hinrich had to be different, as though he would control their lives forever. His sister and two brothers each would be paid a considerable sum—220 Thaler, 11 gute Groschen, 3 pennies—upon the occasion of their marriages. So far so good—but there were strings attached. If any one of them remained unwed or should die before age thirty-five, half of this amount had to be returned to the estate; if any should die after his thirty-fifth year, the entire amount must be given back. In addition, each of the brothers was to be given a coffer whenever he requested it. What, if anything, the coffer would contain was not specified. Knowing Hinrich, Johann did not expect much.

But he did not care. Johann Hermann had plans. Now twenty-eight, he was tired of working for his brother for nothing but his bed and board.

For some time now he had been scouting the countryside for a farmer who would hire him at a living wage and he now had a good prospect. But there was one thing he wanted to do first.

When Becke first appeared on the scene she had been furious that their sister had up and left, leaving Becke with most of the housework. She had immediately wanted to hire a girl to help but Hinrich would not hear of it nor would their mother Adelheit. Adelheit saw to it that Becke did her share, however reluctantly. But Becke was crafty and soon, without realizing it Adelheit was carrying most of the burden. Becke used any number of lame excuses including pregnancy for getting out of work. And she was not very fortunate with her pregnancies either. In all those years she had only two sons living. The others had either been born dead or succumbed shortly after birth. And, of course, she blamed these losses on the heavy housework. Then in 1854 Adelheit died. This had not been in Becke's plans at all. Adelheit was only fifty-five and, in Becke's opinion, had no right to die so young.

This time Becke convinced Hinrich that he must hire help for her. He certainly could afford it. Becke conducted the search herself and soon found a young girl that suited her. Margarethe Möhlmann came from a very poor peasant family in Affendorf, a tiny hamlet consisting of only two farms between Asendorf and Vilsen. Margarethe was seventeen, meek and mild and a hard worker. No one realized that underneath that meekness was a fiery and stubborn personality. Margarethe was so grateful for the work that she took great pains to conceal this side of her character from her employers. Only to Johann Hermann did she occasionally reveal tantalizing bits of her real self. Soon he came to realize that they were kindred souls, put upon by his brother and sister-in-law. Margarethe was now twenty-two, Johann twenty-eight. And Johann had plans.

"Good morning, sweet Gretchen. Isn't it a beautiful spring morning?" he said as he strolled into the kitchen.

"Don't call me that," snapped Margarethe. "You know she doesn't permit it."

"But you like it," he insisted. "Besides she's not here and it *is* a beautiful spring morning." He bent and kissed the tip of her nose. "'Tis the time of year to fall in love."

"Ach, Johann, don't be such a tease." But she blushed as she said it and he knew she liked it. He wished he could kiss more of her.

"But it is spring and at least we can be outside a little more."

"Mayhap you can but she has so many spring-cleaning jobs lined up for me, I don't know where to begin," she said glumly. "Spring, indeed."

"Surely you have a few minutes to sit down and have a cup of coffee with me," he suggested. "I have news."

"Oh? What news?" she asked as she poured the coffee.

"You know I've been looking for work away from here—work that I shall be paid for. There's a farmer over in Barke, name of Heidtmann, who is willing to hire me."

"Ach, then I'm happy for you," she commented but she did not sound too happy. "I shall miss you."

"Well, it will only be part-time at first and I'll still be living home. He needs me to help with the plowing and planting right now and then not again until first haying in June. After that only a day or two a week until harvest time."

"Your brother will not look kindly on that arrangement."

"Too bad for him. If I do well, I think it will be full time next year. Heidtmann is getting old and he has no sons."

"But doesn't he have a place you can stay over there? That would get you out from under your brother entirely."

"There is a tenant cottage but he won't lease it unless the tenant is married."

"Then you had better find yourself a wife right soon."

"I already know whom I want." He reached across the table and took her hand.

"Ach, Johann, don't be foolish. I am not the woman for you. I am no but a poor peasant while you are the son of a great landowner." It broke her heart to say it for she was already half in love with him but she knew what was right and that she would never fit into a highbrow family such as the Campsheide.

"The youngest son only and treated worse than the dirt you walk on. Don't belittle yourself, Gretchen. You are sweet, intelligent, hard-working—everything that a man could want."

"Well, let's see how working for Master Heidtmann turns out." She turned away abruptly. She dared not take him seriously. "I have work to do. And you had better get back out there, too, ere your brother misses you."

The following week Johann Hermann went to work for farmer Heidtmann. It was a world of difference for him. The old man was grateful for the help and treated him kindly, more like a son than his own family had. His brother Hinrich, however, was furious as was Becke. It mattered not that Johann came home three days a week and worked harder than ever for his brother. Hinrich considered him a traitor and was only prevented from throwing him out of the house entirely by their brother Chris, who interceded for Johann and pointed out that he was still doing his share of the chores, even to working on Sundays to make up for his time away.

Becke had long suspected that Johann had designs, as she put it, on her housekeeper Margarethe. So she watched the girl even more closely thus preventing any more liaisons. Things had not gone that far, thanks to Margarethe's hesitancy but Becke did not know that. She suspected every-one and trusted no one. Becke did not realize it but her strictures, instead of discouraging the young people, only made Margarethe long the more for Johann's company—the only bit of cheer in that dour household.

One day in the middle of summer after the first haying was done, Johann dragged himself into the kitchen and sat down for his morning cof-fee. For once Becke was not around.

"You are killing yourself, Johann," said Margarethe, "working two farms. You never have even one day's rest."

"I'm young and I'm strong," he insisted.

But she could see he was not the cheerful, happy-go-lucky man he had once been. She could see it in his eyes and in the way he slumped over the table as he sipped his coffee. "Why don't you just leave here entirely and stay at Heidtmann's?"

"Would you want me to?" he asked. "Then I'll never have a chance to see you."

"For your sake I would," she replied. "Is that the only reason you're doing this?"

"In great part, yes," he admitted.

"Don't. I'm not worth it," she admonished. But then at the woebe-gone look on his face, she softened a little. "Mayhap if you were not here, they would not watch me so closely and we might be able to find a way to meet once in a while."

He brightened at that. "Do you really think so?"

She shrugged. "Anything is possible. Let me think on it."

Johann stood up and took her in his arms. He kissed her soundly, deeply. Margarethe could feel the thrill surge through her. She knew there was no hope for them. Yet her body told her otherwise. She wanted him as much as he wanted her.

"Ach, Gretchen, sweeting, you give me some hope," he whispered into her hair.

"Hrmph."

They broke apart quickly, both blushing. But, thank goodness, it was only Chris. Chris would not betray them.

"Sorry to disturb you," he said with a twinkle in his eyes, "but our esteemed brother requests your presence to help get the last of the hay into the barn ere it rains."

Margarethe did think about their situation. That deep kiss had thrilled her so she wanted more of him. She knew he would never be permitted to marry her but could she not at least have a taste of what love was like—until they found someone 'suitable' for him. And the more she thought about it, the more she realized they never would find someone 'suitable' for him. All Hinrich wanted was the work he could get out of Johann. And so she began to scheme and plan.

The next time they had an opportunity to converse she put forth her idea. "You know I am allowed one day off a week."

"Ja, I know," replied Johann. "So you can go home to visit your parents. And I miss you even more then."

"But I only go home to get a day away from here. They don't really care if I come or not. It is just one more mouth to feed. And, of course, they want a part of my wages."

"So?"

"Barke is only a wee bit further than Affendorf. I could be there in less than an hour. And the mistress need never know."

Johann's face brightened. "You mean you'd give up your day off for me?"

"It would be a lot more pleasant than visiting my parents," she replied.

"Ach, you dear one," he exclaimed. "But—but where would we go? I don't have a room, you know. Heidtmann lets me sleep in the hayloft but not in the tenant house."

"Haylofts can be very cozy. Anyway I'm not planning on sleeping with you," she replied teasingly. At least, not yet, she said to herself.

"Of course not," he replied somewhat abashed. "I wouldn't think of compromising you." But I'd certainly like to, he thought.

On a warm August morning Margarethe trotted along the road that led from Asendorf to Bücken. When she left the Campsheide farm at dawn the morning had been pleasantly cool but now that the sun had risen it was rapidly growing warm and promised to be quite hot ere noon.

654

She wondered if the hayloft would be quite appropriate for their rendezvous. Haylofts would be warm and cozy in winter but terribly stifling in summer. She wore her best shirtwaist, white and crisply starched, with a dark skirt and over it a fashionable but modest short jacket. Already she was beginning to sweat. She would have to take the jacket off if it got any hotter but she hated to spoil the ensemble.

She also wondered if she would be able to find the shortcut Johann had described. His directions had been rather vague. She only knew if she came to Calle she had gone too far, although there was a better road leading from there to Barke. She shifted her basket to the other arm. She was bringing some fresh-baked buns and a little cheese to their meeting—and hoped Becke would not miss them—because she was not sure whether farmer Heidtmann provided Johann with midday meal when he was not actually working.

At last she saw what she thought must be the shortcut. She turned off the Bücken road. It was nothing more than a farm path but it had to lead somewhere. It did not. After less than a half mile it ended in a field of asparagus. Well, she was not going to backtrack now. She knew she was going in the right direction so she hiked up her skirt and trod carefully along the edge of the field so as not to step on the crops. Fortunately there was no fence to have to negotiate. The feathery fronds of the asparagus brushed against her cheek and made her itch and she could feel the sweat trickling down her back and between her breasts. She dared not take her jacket off now or the prickly fronds would make her itch all the more. She crossed another field of ripening oats and then a third which seemed to be pasture or fallow. At last she emerged on the Barke road.

Johann met her in the barnyard. "Ach, it's so good to see you, Gretchen. Did you find the shortcut all right?"

"Some shortcut," she complained. "Look at my face."

"What happened?"

"Traipsing through the asparagus."

"But you should have turned right before you came to that field. There is another path on its far side."

So much for his directions, she thought. "Never mind," she said. "I'm here now."

"Yes, and I'm so happy . . . " He took her hand and led her towards the barn. "I can't wait to kiss you."

"Surely not here in the barnyard."

"Nay, nay. Up in the loft."

655

She shook her head. "You mean we are going to spend the entire day in the hayloft? We'll be suffocating ere noon. Surely on a glorious and hot day such as this there must be somewhere else we can go."

Johann had not thought of that. He was so anxious to get her into his arms. "I don't have a room, you know."

"So you said. But isn't there a shady spot with some trees—away from the house? I brought some things for midday meal." She indicated the basket which he had not even noticed.

"Oh. Here, let me take that." He thought a moment. "There is a little brook between this farm and the next that has some shady spots. We might go there."

"That sounds ideal."

"But you'll have to cross some more fields."

"I've already crossed three. What's a few more?" Lord, she thought, he might be eight-and-twenty years old but he's acting like a teenager. Little did she know he had been planning his seduction and so fearful she would turn him down that he had given no thought to her comfort or to how far she had come just to see him.

He took her hand and led her beyond the barn along the edge of another field. She could see some trees in the distance. The shade looked very inviting. Her blouse was decidedly drenched with sweat by now. She could feel it clinging to her skin.

The brook was tiny but swift-flowing and crystal clear. The banks were lined with soft moss and sweet smelling grass. Margarethe threw herself down in the shade of an old oak tree and leaned her back against its trunk. "Ah, this is much better," she sighed. She kicked her shoes off and Johann stared as she wiggled her toes. "How I'd love to take these stockings off and wade in the brook. I'll bet it's very cold."

"Why don't you?" he suggested.

"Johann!" she exclaimed. "I am no longer a child."

"I'm very much aware of that," he said as he sat down beside her. He took her in his arms and kissed her deeply. His tongue began probing her mouth and after a moment's hesitation she let him enter. The heat she felt was far more than just the heat of the day. She longed to take her jacket off but dared not. She knew he would be able to see right through the sheer lawn of her shirt, plastered as it was to her body. In moments the decision was taken out of her hands as he undid the buttons of the jacket, slipped his hand inside and cupped her breast. The firestorm that surged through her was like nothing she had ever experienced. All thoughts of propriety left her as she leaned closer to his hard, muscular chest. Under the onslaught of his desire she was barely aware that he was unbuttoning her blouse until she felt his fingers teasing her nipples. The shock waves coursed through her body and seemed to center on the lower regions—regions she dared not think about without blushing. Still kissing her, his hand moved lower until he struck an obstacle to his explorations.

He broke away from her. "You are wearing a corset."

How could one discuss such an intimate item of female apparel with a man? "Of course I am wearing a corset," she exclaimed, indignantly flustered.

"But why?"

"Why? But every woman wears a corset. I'd never fit into my clothes without it."

"Nonsense. With your lovely figure you have no need of such—er—props. Ach, Gretchen sweet, I long to feel your naked skin against mine. Will you not take it off?"

She gasped with shock. Embarrassed, she backed away from him. "Nay, Johann. Not yet. Not today. You go too fast for me."

"But dearest Gretchen, I want to make love to you. I'll not hurt you, I promise. You want me as much as I want you. I can sense it."

"Mayhap ja, mayhap nay," she replied slowly. "But not today. I'm not ready to go that far yet. Maybe not ever."

"But why? You know I love you."

"I'm afraid."

"Afraid? Of me?"

"Nay, not of you but afraid I might fall in love with you. And then—then . . . " She hesitated. "Then when you find someone more suitable for a Campsheide, you will break my heart. I can't risk it. I'm not ready to give myself to any man. Not yet, anyway."

"Sweeting, I'll never break your heart. You are the one who is most suitable for me. I told you I love you. I want to marry you just as soon as I have my own farm."

"But that may be—will be—a long time hence." She shed her jacket. What difference did it make now? But she carefully rebuttoned her shirt. "I find I'm awfully warm. I think I shall act like a child and wade in that brook." Carefully she rolled down her stockings and took them off.

Little did she realize how enticing that was to Johann, still so solidly aroused it was almost painful. He knew she was not deliberately teasing him. She was too innocent for that. But he felt like raping her on the spot. But he would never do that. He loved her—and yes, respected her too much for that. Perhaps he was moving too fast. He would simply have to bide his time. She would come around—he was sure of that—if he wooed her more slowly. He watched longingly as she hiked her skirt up to her knees and waded into the brook. Her legs were the most beautiful he had ever seen and his arousal only grew harder. Although to be honest, he had never seen many female legs.

"Ooh, it's icy," she gasped, "but it feels so good. Come on, coward," she teased, "it will cool your ardor down."

Johann was shocked at her brazenness. Mayhap she wasn't so innocent after all. But then he realized she was just being sensible. He had rushed her too quickly. He took off his shoes and stockings, rolled up his pant legs and joined her in the cool brook. He, too, gasped at the first icy shock and his arousal quickly shrivelled. And then he began to feel better. They cavorted around in the water for a while like a couple of children. Then they sat on the mossy bank and partook of their noonday meal.

"Will you stay with me in the hayloft tonight?" he asked timorously. "I promise I won't touch you."

"Nay, not tonight. Mayhap when the weather is cooler. I'd best sleep at home tonight."

"But what will your parents think, you arriving so late?"

"I'll simply tell them that Becke made me work a half day and that I can only spend the evening with them."

Margarethe did not return to Barke for over two weeks. During that time she had a lot of thinking to do. Whenever Johann came home, she avoided him as much as possible, dreading his questions, knowing she did not yet have the answers he wanted. During the day she kept as busy as possible but at night when she lay on her cot in the little cubbyhole off the kitchen her mind kept returning to the thrill of his kisses, to the wonderful erotic feel of his hands on her breasts. And she could not sleep. Her body was aflame with desire, longing for his touch, longing for more.

But she was afraid. Not only afraid that he would use her and then leave her for someone better than she, but what if she got pregnant? Pregnancies before marriage were extremely common in the rural areas and, she supposed, in the towns as well. And nothing immoral or disgraceful was thought of it. But—and that was the big 'but'—they usually occurred after the betrothal when the man—conceited creatures that they were—

wanted to be sure the woman was fertile. Those conceived after a quick roll in the hay with a farm lass or a housemaid were usually ignored—'Ach, he's just sowing his wild oats'—and the woman was left with a bastard to raise by herself, often after having been dismissed in disgrace from her only means of livelihood.

And yet—yet—those deep, aching cravings in her groin cried out for more of him. She wanted to experience that wondrous thing. Having come from a large peasant family where there was little privacy, she knew what went on between a man and a woman. In fact, her mother had told her that she enjoyed the act, although many women did not. Margarethe wanted to know it for herself. After all, she was two-and-twenty—soon would be considered a spinster—old enough and more for bedding and wedding. But would Johann wed her? He said he loved her but was that just talk or did he mean it? She realized now that she was in love with him. Oh, what to do?

Becke noticed the change in her. "What ails you, girl? Now iron those shirts properly. Look at the creases in them. You're drooping around like the last rose of summer."

"I'm fine. Just a little tired is all. I didn't sleep well last night."

"Ach, missing that ne'er-do-well brother of ours. Well, set your sights elsewhere, girl. A Campsheide is not for the likes of you."

And that stiffened Margarethe's spine. Not for the likes of her, indeed. She would show them how much he loved her, how right she was for him. The very next Thursday she went to Barke.

Johann was overjoyed to see her. "Dearest Gretchen, I thought you were angry with me."

"Nay, never that,' she assured him. "I—I just needed some time to think."

"And apparently you've had some good thoughts about us. I've missed you so." He took her in his arms and kissed her soundly.

"Johann! Not here where everyone can see us." But she was pleased just the same.

"It's only old Heidtmann. And he knows about us."

"He does?"

"Ja," he admitted. "He noticed me moping about and asked what was wrong. So I told him."

"And he approves?"

"Wholeheartedly." What Johann did not tell her was that the old farmer had advised him, "Bed her as quickly as you can then she'll want

659

you all the more. Better yet, get her with child. Then she can't say you nay."

It was September. Although the days remained pleasantly warm, the nights were beginning to turn chill. They ate their noon meal by the brook but they did not play in its waters. Johann kissed her hungrily and she responded willingly. But he refrained from caressing her breasts although it was very difficult for him. He wanted her so. He did notice one thing as she pressed against him in a torrid embrace. No corset! It gave him a ray of hope.

As the shorter day drew to a close he hesitantly asked, "Will you stay with me tonight?"

She nodded and fell once again into his embrace. In his gratitude and eagerness he wanted to rush her into the barn right then but he vowed to move slowly so as not to frighten her again. He took her hand and pulled her up.

"Don't you think we should eat some supper first?" she asked.

"But it will be dark by then," he objected.

"That's what usually happens at night," she replied.

Ach, this woman—how she tantalized him. He wanted to be able to see her—all of her—when they finally made love but he knew she was still shy and mayhap a little fearful. He would have to indulge her or she might refuse him again.

They sat down and she handed him some bread and cheese. It was the same fare they had had at noon but it did not matter. He could hardly taste it, his mouth was so dry. And Margarethe could hardly swallow it, she was that nervous. At last they gave up trying to eat and took a long, refreshing drink from the sparkling brook. Neither would admit that there were more important things on their minds than eating.

He led her up into the hayloft over to the cozy corner where he usually slept. Twilight had fallen but twilights were long in these northern climes. There was still sufficient light to see how comfortable he had made his little nook. There was a small coffer for his clothes and a row of books propped on one of the beams of the barn. He even had a feather pillow—probably brought from home—and a blanket against the growing chill of autumn. She wondered if Becke knew. Probably not. She never went near anyone's bedroom but her own. That was Margarethe's job.

"How nice and cozy you have it fixed," she commented.

"Ja. I wanted you to see it," replied Johann. "It's not the tenant house but it will do for now."

She stood there wondering what was going to happen next. He spread the blanket over the hay and sat down.

"Come, sit by me, love," he invited. He enveloped her in ardent kisses. Then he surprised her by kneeling at her feet. "Let me take off your shoes and stockings. May I?" She nodded. Carefully he removed each shoe and set them aside. Then his fingers crept up her leg to her garters. She thrilled to his touch. Gently he rolled down each garter and stocking and began kissing her toes. She had never heard of men doing this. It was a strange sensation, more tickling than exciting. Then when he ran his hands up her legs, she jumped at the sudden shock. That *was* exciting. She fully expected him to spread her legs and place himself between them as she had seen her father do when she and her brothers had spied on their parents. But he did not. He caressed her legs as far as her thighs and then drew himself up next to her and started kissing her again. Oh, I wish he would touch my breast again, she thought. That was really thrilling.

"May I take off your shirt?" he pleaded. She nodded, willingly help-ing him with the buttons. She was that eager for is caress. "And your skirt?" She hesitated a moment at that but then undid the belt and slipped the garment down over her hips. She lay there in nothing but her shift. He sat back and gazed at her longingly. "And now this." He lifted the shift and pulled it over her head. She shivered a moment, not from the cold, but from the heat emanating from his eyes. Sometime during all this—she had not even noticed when—he had shed his own shoes, stockings and shirt. She stared at the hard muscles of his chest. He was broad and strong from all the farm work but not heavy. Her eyes drifted down to the bulge in his pants. She wondered what that looked like. She was eager to see it, feel it but just a little frightened, too. In one quick second he shed both his trousers and drawers and then she saw it. It was large and angry-looking but she could not take her eyes away from it.

He lay down beside her and began caressing her breasts. Ah, that's what she wanted and it was even more exciting with his bare hand against her bare breast than it had been down by the brook. When he teased the nipples she nearly screamed with ecstacy. With one hand still squeezing her breast his other slid down across her belly to the private place she had been so acutely aware of these last weeks. His tongue followed his fingers. He suckled her breast and she nearly died with wanting him. When his tongue found the little rosebud she did not even know she had within that private place, she forgot all hesitancy and fear. Her hips rose to him of their own accord. She had no will of her own. Her body cried out for more, more. She had never expected such ecstacy. But all thought was gone—only exquisite feeling. He did not have to push her thighs apart. They opened wide of their own volition, inviting him into her deepest recesses. He gently eased himself over her and she could feel that rock-hard prick pushing against her. Yes, yes, she wanted him, wanted it.

Suddenly he thrust hard and she cried out from the momentary stab of pain. Then he was inside of her, pushing deeper and deeper. All thought of pain was gone as her hips rose to meet him. She wanted all of that thing as deep as he could thrust it. She could not get enough of it. Oh, my God, how exquisite. Don't let it end. In a moment her body caught the rhythm and she tried to draw him deeper yet into her. He pounded into her, deeper and deeper, harder and harder, faster and faster. When she thought it could not get any better, it did. Suddenly a star burst over her. She was floating off into heaven, fireworks exploding all around her. And again. And again. Then when she thought she could not stand anymore, the most magnificent explosion of all occurred. She thought she cried out in ecstacy. He groaned and collapsed against her.

When their breathing returned somewhat to normal, he murmured, "Oh, my love, you are so beautiful."

All she could do was sigh, "Oh, Johann."

After a bit he suggested, "Let us snuggle down in the hay and put the blanket over us."

"But I'm so warm," she replied. "I don't need the blanket. Besides the hay will tickle."

He laughed. "You'll cool down soon enough. Put your shift under you."

"I could put it on."

"Nay, nay. Don't you want me to love you again?"

"Of course, I do. It was so—so wonderful. But I didn't think . . . "

" . . . that I could?' he finished. "With you in my arms, it will get hard again in no time."

It was fully dark now but she did not need to see. Feeling his strong body curled around hers was enough. It was exciting, yet comforting, too. And sure enough, before very long she could feel his erection poking into her side. This time she knew what to expect and used her hands to caress him. It aroused him all the more and their ardent coupling was even more ecstatic and satisfying than the first time. Exhausted, they fell asleep in each other's arms. And suddenly it was cockcrow.

She jumped up. "I have to leave."

He pulled her down again. "Let me love you once more ere you go. See how I want you." His cock was standing up straight as a soldier.

She leaned over and kissed it. How she loved that thing, wanted it inside her again. Not just now but for the rest of her life. Johann groaned at her caress and wasted little time on preliminaries. He loved her once more, quickly and fiercely.

As autumn and then winter closed in it was increasingly difficult for Margarethe to get to Barke. Yet she was happy with what opportunities they had to be together. Now surely he would marry her as soon as he had enough money saved.

Becke noticed the difference in her housekeeper. It was not hard to guess the reason. "My, you're cheerful these days," she remarked.

"Oh, yes," replied Margarethe. "I am very happy—er—in my work here."

"So you've finally let him crawl up under your petticoat. Foolish girl. Don't think you can lure him that way. My husband would never permit it."

"I have not," denied Margarethe hotly. "I'm just happy that Christmas is coming. That is all."

"Don't lie to me, chit. Let me warn you. The first sign of a child and out you go. Out to the wolves, not to him."

Margarethe tried to ignore her jibes but it was difficult. The woman persisted in making sneering, insulting remarks. How could she demean something that was so beautiful?

When Johann came home for the Christmas holiday she was overjoyed to see him. She was tempted to tell him of her troubles but decided against it. Whether due to his presence or because of the festive season, she did not know, but Becke had finally let up on her for which she was grateful.

Late on New Year's Eve Johann crept into her cubbyhole.

"Johann!" she exclaimed. "You shouldn't be here. Becke will kill us both if she catches you."

"Becke drank so much elderberry wine this eve she is sound asleep in her bed and Hinrich with her. I made sure of that. Don't worry, love. We are safe. I couldn't stay away from you any longer. I've missed you so."

"And I've missed you, dearest Johann. Come and love me. Quickly."

They made beautiful love and afterward as they lay in each other's arms squeezed onto her tiny cot, he said, "I have news. Good news. I couldn't say anything in front of the family because I don't want Hinrich to know just yet."

"Tell me. What is it?" she begged.

"Heidtmann is so pleased with my work that he wants me full-time starting in the spring."

"That's wonderful. I'm so proud of you."

"Wait. There's more. He is going to rent me one field to start my own farm. Aside from the minimal rent I have to pay him, all the profits will be mine."

"Oh, Johann. How exciting. Then can we be wed sometime next—er—this year?"

He drew back from her a little. "I thought you didn't want to marry me. You thought you weren't good enough."

"But I am now," she replied. "You changed my mind for me."

He held her close again. "Well, we'll see about that."

Spring arrived in the land. The warming sun coaxed flowers into bloom and trees into bud. Birds began their fanciful courtships. Calves, foals and lambs were born. And blood ran hot in the young people as well. Margarethe had long wondered why she had not conceived but under the circumstances she was grateful for it. Now that the warmer weather made it easier for her to get to Barke, she and Johann made frantic love as often as they possibly could. Johann had not mentioned marriage again but she trusted him. It was enough just to be together.

There had been quite a scene when Johann had announced to his brother that he was leaving permanently. Hinrich had been furious, called him betrayer, traitor and other less choice epithets. Johann had calmly and politely requested the coffer due him. Hinrich had at first reneged but his marriage settlement was a legal document and he had to abide by its terms. Reluctantly he handed over the coffer. It did not contain much money but it was enough to enable Johann to rent another field close by Heidtmann's.

"Go, get out," screamed Hinrich. "And don't ever show your face here again, you ungrateful pup. And if you think to have my blessing, you shan't have it."

"Ja," added Becke, "and take your doxy with you."

At that Hinrich softened a little. "Nay, don't blame the lass for what he has done. Let her stay—for now." In truth it was not so much concern for Margarethe that prompted this concession as not wanting to hear

Becke complain about having no help.

Johann set a hamper containing his clothes on his shoulder, tucked the coffer under his arm and walked out. As he passed through the kitchen, Margarethe said, "I'll walk to the gate with you."

"Nay, best not. 'Twill only anger them more. Come as often as you can." He kissed her quickly and was gone.

Toward the end of April she missed her monthly course. She should not have been surprised but she was. Now the fat's in the fire, she thought. She did not tell anyone, not even Johann, for another month until she was absolutely sure. Now he'll have to marry me—but will he?

When she finally told him, his reaction was rather cool. "Hmm," he said. "Stay as long as you can. When she tells you to leave—and I know she will—you'll have to come here. But I'm so busy right now, I'm not ready for you yet. Mayhap later when he sees the circumstances, Heidtmann will let us have the tenant house. He's a jolly old soul. He might be understanding."

"But—but," she said, trying to hold back the tears, "I thought you wanted to marry me."

"I do. I do. But, as I said, I'm not quite ready for that just yet."

"When will you be, Johann?" she asked petulantly. "The babe will not wait. Didn't you think of that when you—you seduced me?"

"Seduced? You wanted it as much as I. Didn't *you* think of it?"

"I did but . . . Oh, never mind." She turned away from him in tears.

He pulled her back to him. "Come, sweeting, let me make love to you. That always cheers you up."

For a moment she hated him but she could not resist him. She followed him meekly into the hayloft.

By the end of August what Becke had suspected all along became quite apparent. She had already been seeking a new maid. Now she dismissed Margarethe out of hand. "You'll have to leave by the end of next week," she said. "I can't have you corrupting the children. The new girl will be comimg on the first September."

Corrupting those two spoiled brats, indeed, thought Margarethe. The ten-year-old probably knew more about sex already than his mother did. But she only said, "Very well, Madame."

Late that night she took the last bath she knew she would be able to have for a long while. She packed her few belongings in an old pillowcase and before dawn set out for Barke. She regretted leaving behind her last wages but she refused to put up with Becke's maligning her another minute.

When she arrived at the Heidtmann farm, Johann was out working in the fields somewhere. She put her bag up in the hayloft and climbed down again to face Heidtmann. Although she had waved to him a few times, she had never actually met the man. She would confront him before he had time to do much thinking.

The old man had seen her come and was waiting for her at the barn door. "Well, what have we here?" he asked with a big grin.

"I am Gretchen Möhlmann, Johann's betrothed," she lied.

"I know who you are but I don't think Johann was expecting you just yet. Although it looks like he certainly should have." His eyes swept over her swelling belly.

"I fear I have lost my position and I have nowhere else to go. He told me you are alone, Master Heidtmann. I will clean and cook for you, do the washing and ironing, help with the farm work to earn my keep. I wouldn't want you to take it out of Johann's wages."

"That would be nice. And I wouldn't think of letting you work just for your keep. I can afford to pay you a small wage. Not much, mind you, but something."

"Oh, Master Heidtmann, I truly appreciate that. Johann told me you were a good man. Now just give me a few minutes to change my clothes and tell me where I can start."

"Nay, nay. Rest yourself a while, lass. The dust will keep. Johann will be in for dinner in an hour or two. Then we can talk. And it looks as though we'll have to open the tenant cottage. Can't have you climbing up and down to the loft with a babe in your belly. I'm glad he took my advice and got you with child. I knew that would bring you around."

"What do you mean?" she asked, bewildered.

"He said you didn't want to marry him but now you will, won't you?"

"He said that?" she exclaimed. "I'll admit I didn't think I was good enough for him at first but that was long ago. I changed my mind long, long before the babe happened. Now it's he who doesn't want to wed me."

"He doesn't? Why, that young knave! I'll talk to him. You can be sure of that, Gretchen. You certainly look good enough to me. I like you already, lass. Now go and rest and come by the kitchen at noon. I hope you can stand my cooking. I'm sure you'll do better."

Margarethe was diligently working in the tenant house readying it for their occupancy. She already was in love with the house. It was really too big to be called a cottage, bigger than her own parents' home. She had washed and rehung the curtains on sparkling windows; had scrubbed and polished the floors. The place was ideal, if rather bare. It lacked all but the most basic furnishings. There was a bed and a table with two chairs. That was all. But she loved the kitchen. It had a modern iron stove and a sink with its own pump. No need to go out and chop ice off a well in winter. A big pot-bellied heating stove stood in the front room and there was even a small fireplace in the bedroom. They would be warm and cozy if not yet too comfortable. And the loft was big and high enough to stand upright in the middle. It would be perfect for the child once he outgrew his cradle. A cradle — that was the first piece of furniture they would have to have made.

Suddenly the dogs set up a furious barking. She loved Heidtmann's dogs — a big black nondescript mongrel and an even bigger St. Bernard. They never barked except in cheerful greeting unless a stranger whom they did not like approached. This was someone whom they evidently did not like. She looked out the window and was surprised to see Hinrich Campsheide kicking at the dogs as he approached the main house. She knew that Master Heidtmenn was out in the fields with Johann. She would have to face Hinrich alone ere the dogs attacked him.

She walked out the door, calling to the dogs. "Hush, Fido, hush Barni. It's all right." The dogs came loping over to her and stood about protectively. She patted their heads before she spoke to Hinrich. "May I help you, Herr Campsheide? I am afraid Master Heidtmann is up in the far field."

"So you *are* here. We thought you might be. Good. Saves me a trip to your father's house. Here is the balance of your wages for August."

"Why, thank you, Herr Campsheide. I appreciate your kindness."

"I always pay my obligations. Figured you might need it since you'll have to leave here soon, too. That is, unless old Heidtmann has taken a fancy to a whore."

Margarethe felt like throwing the money back at him but she was too practical to indulge her fury. She gritted her teeth and asked, "Shall I fetch Master Heidtmann for you?"

"Nay. I'll find them. It's my brother I must talk to, not the old man." He tromped away across the fields.

Margarethe turned back to the cottage. She sat at the table and wept. The nerve of him calling her a whore. And what did he mean she would have to leave here, too. She could not bear the thought of that. She felt the baby stir. Oh, I hope he hasn't marked you, little one. The damned bastard. How she hated that man.

She was still sitting there, head on her arms, the money still on the table where she had dropped it, when Johann came in hours later.

"Come on, sweeting, it's time for dinner. What have you fixed for us today?"

She raised her head and gasped. She had forgotten all about dinner. Then Johann realized she had been crying. "Whatever is wrong, sweet Gretchen? Did my brother upset you? Don't let him."

"He called me a whore!"

"Did he? I'll kill him."

"Nay, nay, let it be," she cried. "Take it from where it comes. But worse yet, he said I should have to leave here—and that right soon. Johann, I couldn't bear that. Did you talk to your brother?"

"Ja, I did. And don't worry about any of his threats. Heidtmann has suggested a solution. Come now, we'll talk about it over dinner."

"But I was so upset I forgot all about dinner. Master Heidtmann will surely turn me out."

"Ach, don't be so foolish. We'll make do. Come now," he took her hand, "dry your tears and listen to Heidtmann's idea."

They made do with bread and cheese and a little leftover ham while Johann told her what Hinrich had threatened. "He forbade the pastor in Asendorf to marry us. And since he is the largest contributor to that church, the pastor had to abide by his wishes."

Margarethe was horrified. "Then—then we can never be married at all. But then—then," she murmured sorrowfully, "you never did want to anyway, did you?"

"I do now," Johann replied defiantly. "Master Heidtman had made me ashamed of how I've been neglecting you. And I guess it just took the extra nudge of my brother's prohibition to make me see the light."

"Ach, Johann, love, I appreciate knowing that but now it's too late to be making up your mind. Oh, what can we do? I don't want this babe to be born a bastard."

Heidtmann was grinning from ear to ear. "Easy, lass," he said, "and listen here. After that son-of-a-bitch left—your pardon, Mistress, but that's what he is—I pointed out to Johann that, although his brother may be the richest farmer hereabouts, his *power* only extends to Asendorf. Barke, and Calle too, belong to Bücken parish and the pastor there is a good friend of mine. We share a stein of beer or cider every once in a while. Neither of you have been to church since you've been here. I suggest we all go together this Sunday and I'll speak to him about posting the banns immediately."

"Wonderful!" exclaimed Johann. "We'll do that. I want this babe to be properly christened when the time comes."

"But wait," said Margarethe. "The banns are for three weeks. Aren't they supposed to be so that anyone who wants to object to the marriage can object?"

"That's true," replied the old man, "but I'll tell pastor to slip it in so subtly that only a few of those with the sharpest ears will hear it. Don't worry. No one in these parts likes Hinrich Campsheide and he won't come all the way to Bücken to check on it. He'll be too busy gloating over his little coup in Asendorf to even think about Bücken." Heidtmann grinned broadly. "And then, dear boy, you can collect your inheritance and buy some decent furniture for the cottage or maybe rent another field from me? Won't that kill him?"

"Inheritance?" asked Margarethe. "What is that all about?"

Johann explained, "According to my brother's marriage settlement, each of the rest of us are to receive 220 Thaler, 11 gute groschen and 3 pennies when we marry. Only, knowing my brother, there's a catch to it. If I should die before age five-and-thirty, half of it must be returned to him."

Margarethe laughed for the first time that day. "Then you'd better not die," she quipped. The sum was staggering. She could hardly believe it. "Ach," she joked, "even to the three pennies. Isn't that just like him?"

On 12 October 1860 Johann Hermann Campsheide and Anna Margarethe Möhlmann were joined in holy wedlock at the parsonage in Bücken. It was a very private ceremony, the only witnesses being Chris, Johann's brother, as groomsman and one of Margarethe's sisters. And of course Master Heidtmann. Margarethe's parents did not attend. Not that they were not overjoyed that one of their daughters was finally wed, and to a member of the prestigious Campsheide family at that, but because it was harvest time and they had very little help on the farm. The pastor's wife set out a generous afternoon coffee with delicate little cakes for the company.

On the way home in the little horsecart Heidtmann said, "Well, that's that. Now, son, you had better hie you over to that brother of yours on Sunday and wave that certificate under his nose and demand your inheritance ere the bastard can think of some way to do you out of it."

"Ja," agreed Margarethe. "The first thing I want to do is have a cradle made."

669

"There's a reliable cabinetmaker right here in Calle, I believe."

"There's an even better one in Vilsen, name of Bruns," said Margarethe.

"Ja, I've heard of him. Said to be the best in all of County Hoya," added Heidtmann.

"And his brother is a pewtermaker," put in Johann. "We could do with some more dishes and tableware. I know them both, although not well."

"Good idea. And when is the babe due anyway?" asked Heidtmann.

Johann looked abashed. "I—I never thought to ask," he admitted. "Gretchen, when?"

"Along about Christmastime as best I can figure," she replied.

"Ach, then that will be a double cause for celebration," said the old man.

Two days before Christmas Margarethe's pains started. It was a long and difficult labor although the midwife probed and helped all she could. At last shortly before midnight little Dorothea Campsheide made her appearance. Margarethe was so exhausted all she recalled hearing the midwife say was that it was a girl. She fell into a dead sleep.

The little girl was healthy and perfect in every way but one. On her face, covering most of her left cheek and encircling her eye was a huge purple birthmark. The blemish seemed to skew her eye and it remained to be seen whether it would distort her vision.

The next morning when Margarethe demanded to see and hold her daughter she turned away in horror at the child's face. "He marked her," she screamed hysterically. "He marked her when he frightened me so, telling me I had to leave here. I just know it."

"Nay," said Johann wistfully. "It's because she was conceived in sin. I'm sure of it."

"Now stop it, both of you," the midwife scolded. "It's not anyone's fault. That sort of thing just happens sometimes and no one knows the cause. I've seen it many a time. Now just look at the rest of her—perfect arms and legs, a healthy body and even the rest of her face is quite pretty. See that pert little nose and those rosebud lips. I don't ever want to hear of either of you turning away from this child because of a slight disfigurement. She will need your love more than any other child you may have because life will not be easy for her. And she may just turn out to have the best personality of all your children."

Both Margarethe and Johann hung their heads in shame. The woman was right of course.

"Now put her to your breast and nurse her. She's hungry."

Margarethe took the child again but turned her so that only the good side of her face showed. After the first few hungry suckles with the tiny hands groping her breast, all thoughts of horror left her and Margarethe's heart filled with love. "She is our kleine Dorchen," she murmured.

And Johann watching was amazed at the love he felt for them both.

Meanwhile earlier that same year in Vilsen Johann Justus and Friedrike Bruns had another daughter.

"What would you like to name her?" asked Friedrike.

"You mean you're actually letting me choose this time?" teased Johann Justus.

Friedrike laughed. "Truthfully, after four girls and only one boy I seem to have run out of female names. Just don't say Henriette. Tiete hates her name and I can't say I care much for it. Although she's already used it for a middle name for two of her girls."

Johann Justus thought a moment. "How about Caroline? I've always thought that rather pretty."

"Caroline." She turned the sound of it around her tongue. "It is pretty. But no one in the family is named that."

"Neither is Luise," he reminded her. "You seemed to think that up out of nowhere. Besides Caroline was a very great queen about a hundred years ago, if I recall. Georg II's consort, I believe."

"Ach, then we shall have a queen in our midst. Caroline it will be."

Johann Justus and his Fritzi were still very much in love and adored their growing family. Doris, the eldest, now ten, was precocious, intelligent and very artistic. Pretty now, she would be a beautiful woman when she grew older. Anni, seven, was the quiet one. One never knew what she was thinking. But she had the sweetest personality so far. Luise, four, was totally unpredictable — one minute flying high, the next sad and on the verge of a tantrum. Little Hermann, two, was already enamored of his Onkel Hermann and followed him around like a puppy dog whenever he could. They wondered how Caroline would turn out. Each of them so different. Yet both Friedrike and Johann could see family traits going back many generations. One thing they all shared was their parents' love of music.

21

1862

"So I just received a nice big order for a complete set of tableware," announced Johann Justus.

"That's nice. From whom?" asked Friedrike.

"Remember that young couple name of Campsheide who outfoxed old Hinrich a couple of years ago?"

"Vaguely," she replied. "I shouldn't think you would want anything to do with any Campsheide after the way he treated you and Hermann and even me—almost everyone in Vilsen back before we were wed. I certainly don't."

"This is the youngest brother—as totally different from Hinrich as day and night. This one is a very pleasant fellow, hardworking and ambitious, although a bit of a dreamer. He either ran off with the housekeeper or she seduced him, depending on whose story you believe. But in any event Hinrich tried to prevent the marriage but they fooled him and went to Bücken and were wed there."

"I didn't think you indulged in countryside gossip," said Friedrike.

"I usually don't but I have to be sure they can pay me. This is a large order. They gave me a very small one when they were first wed—just two plates, knives, forks and spoons. This is for a full set complete with bowls, soup tureen, gravy boat, soup ladle and so on. And they can pay. Only thing I think he's being foolish about is that he is renting fields all over the place instead of saving up enough money to buy his own farm—but that's his business."

Friedrike shrugged.

"Well, business is business," said Johann. "And what's more they gave my brother Anton an order for a child's bed. He made their cradle but now they've apparently had another daughter and need the cradle for the new baby." He left to go back to his workshop.

Friedrike was not the least bit interested. She wanted nothing to do with any Campsheide.

672

Meanwhile political unrest was rising to a fever pitch and becoming more widespread. Everyone, even moderate conservatives, hated the oppressive police system of Borries. The entire country was suffering under his corrupt officials and draconian measures. Only in a few places, such as Stüve's Osnabrück, was he prevented from implementing them. Everywhere else the land was seething with dissatisfaction. People were no longer afraid to speak out against him although they did so at risk of life and limb. Here and there demonstrations and protests broke out but they were too small to be effective.

Then a minor and relatively insignificant proposal by King Georg supplied the spark that set off a major conflagration. Some of his bishops convinced him that a major revision and updating of Luther's Catechism was in order. Many people had fallen away from the church, especially in the larger towns, although in the rural areas and villages the church was still the center of their lives. But even those who had not learned it by heart from childhood regarded this tampering with a revered, venerable document as simply too much.

"Johann," enthused Hermann, "we're all going to Hannover in about ten days."

"Who's all going to Hannover?" asked his brother-in-law. "And why?"

"Every Liberal in the country, most moderates, even a lot of conservatives—just about every able-bodied man in the country. We're fed up with Borries and his police regime. It will be a huge rally. We hope to convince King Georg of the error of his ways. It will be '48 all over again."

Johann looked dubious. "'48 all over again? I don't think so. Borries has his police force well in hand. A mob that size will be hard to control. I admit I, too, am fed up with Borries and his cronies and I agree that something must be done. But I fear something like this. It will lead to more violence."

"No violence, I promise you," declared Hermann. "We are all pledged to be peaceful. It will just be to demonstrate our solidarity, to let Georg know how the majority of people feel."

Johann shook his head. "I don't know. I agree with your goals but a mob like that can easily get out of hand when tempers flare. And so can the police."

"Ach, Johann, where is your patriotism? You used to be such an ardent supporter of the constitution and freedom. Come with me. I'll show you how well-behaved this gathering will be."

"I'm still patriotic. Just a little older and more sensible perhaps."

"Ach, come on. Don't be a coward. I'll wager Friede would go, were she a man."

Johann laughed. "She might have once but she has five children now."

"It's for their freedom we are fighting," insisted Hermann. "Paul Meyer is going. He's never forgiven what they did to his father."

"Is he now?" Paul was the son of retired Judge Dieter Meyer—forcibly retired by Borries. He was a very soft-spoken young man, a graduate of Göttingen, now reading law in his father's office. "That's interesting," continued Johann. "I wouldn't have thought he was the type to join a demonstration."

"Everyone is the type when they get angry enough. And he is all for justice," said Hermann.

"He is that," agreed Johann. "Well, let me think on it. And discuss it with Fritzi. When is this going to take place?"

"A week Wednesday."

"Just for the day?"

"Ja. That's all we plan. We all have to work, you know."

Johann talked it over with Friedrike. At first she was vehemently against the whole idea.

"Ach, Johann," she said. "It *will* be '48 all over again. I don't want you to be hurt again."

"They have vowed there will be no violence."

"There wasn't in '48 until those troopers caught us." She lovingly touched the scar on his face.

"But that was only one renegade, whose sergeant quickly stopped him."

"There's always one," she mused. And then she thought for a few minutes. "But Hermann is right. You have always been the leader here in Vilsen for the constitution and for freedom. It would look odd if someone like Paul Meyer joined them and you did not. Borries is destroying this whole contry and the king is too blind—literally—to see it. Ja, I think you should go—if only to keep Hermann out of trouble."

Johann laughed. "That same thought occurred to me." He was glad his understanding Fritzi agreed because the more he thought about it, the more he really wanted to go to Hannover. Something *had* to be done. Their beloved country was a shambles. There was always the chance that Georg might listen.

On the day in question—a perfect June day—people descended on the capital city by the thousands, from every corner of the country, from every walk of life. Although mostly men, there were a significant number of women—not the whores and harridans of the mob of '48—but well-to-do women, some even accompanied by their maids. Some men carried signs and placards, all were shouting slogans—some simply 'Freedom, freedom' or 'Down with the tyrant', others explicitly obscene. Even this early the press of the crowd in the square before the Leine Schloss was so great that Johann, Hermann and Paul could not get near the place. Many were also gathered outside of Borries' house some distance away. The three men and their friends from Vilsen opted to stand along the route that the hated minister must take to reach the Schloss.

At last in midmorning Borries' coach drove out of his courtyard surrounded by a large platoon of heavily armed police. The driver swung his whip to try to disperse the crowd blocking the way but the horses could only move at a snail's pace through the dense mass of humanity. As soon as it passed, the men closed in behind it in order to follow it to the Schloss. Then some started pelting the coach with rocks and all manner of rotten garbage.

"I mislike that," said Johann. "I thought your people pledged no violence."

"Ours in the north did," replied Hermann. " 'Tis probably some uncouth louts from the city itself. I mistrust them."

"As do I," agreed Paul. " 'Twill serve no purpose but to anger him all the more."

Just as the coach was about to pass where they were standing, Hermann suddenly shouted, "Watch out." And pushed Johann back from the edge of the street. A wild-looking, dishevelled man had forced his way through the police cordon and was attempting to climb onto the step of the coach. A shot rang out.

Dozens of voices cried out "Oh, my God!" "He's crazy!" "Run, run."

The coach stopped and the police swung into action, wielding swords and batons indiscriminately on everyone within thirty or forty feet of the coach. Johann and the others tried to run but the press of the crown was so great they could hardly move. Suddenly a police baton connected with Johann's right cheekbone under his eye—the very same spot where he had been cut in '48. But this time the blow was hard enough to knock him out. Hermann had seen it coming and ducked but he was not quick enough to deflect it from Johann. He turned on the officer and kicked him in the groin. The man howled with pain. Hermann bent down to see to Johann who was still unconscious. He tried to heft him to his shoulder just as Paul who had been somewhat ahead of them came running back.

"Here, let me help you," he said. Together they carried Johann, forcing their way through the crowd. "Come this way," instructed Paul. "I know of a safe house not too far from here,"

"You do?" asked Hermann, surprised.

"Ja, Papa made sure I knew about it before we came. He was afraid something like this would happen."

As they were leaving the street, the window of the coach opened, Borries' manservant stuck his head out and announced, "The Minister is unharmed. The shot went wild. But he warns that everyone here today will be prosecuted without mercy." Before he could shut the window, someone threw a ripe horseball. Fortunately the police had no idea how to accomplish that formidable task and no arrests were made except that of the would-be assassin. Johann heard none of it.

As soon as they were free of the worst of the crowds, Hermann and Paul moved swiftly through several back streets carrying Johann to the safe house. The woman there, whose name Hermann never learned, quickly put cold compresses on Johann's face.

"He should see a doctor as soon as possible," she said. "I worry about that eye. And the bone may be fractured as well."

"If you can just bring him around so we can get him on the train," said Hermann, "our cousin in Vilsen is an excellent doctor. We can be there in a few hours."

After a liberal dose of brandy brought Johann to, they managed to get him on the train. He was in great pain and worried about his eye. Herman had left his wagon at a livery in Eystrup and he pushed the horse for all it was worth. When they arrived at the house the children were outside playing.

Hermann shouted to Doris, "Run fast to your Onkel Doctor Lude and tell him to come quick. Your Papa is hurt."

The child was honored to be given the task. She had seen the huge bruise on her father's cheek and his closed eye. She ran down the street as fast as she could, praying all the while, "Dear God, don't let my papa be blind. Don't let him die."

When they brought Johann into the house, Friedrike screamed,

"Oh, no, oh no. It *is* '48 all over again. I had a terrible fear of that." She, too, immediately applied cold compresses.

Lude arrived within minutes. He examined Johann carefully. "There is no damage to the eye," he pronounced. "That will heal in a few days. Put some raw beefsteak on it. It may remain closed for a while but that is merely a defensive mechanism to protect it. The cheekbone is another matter." Johann winced and moaned as Lude gently probed. "There is a very slight fracture there. That will take longer to heal but it will heal if he's careful. Keep the cold on it today. Then tomorrow and for several days put hot packs on it. You'll have to give him some very soft foods for a while so that he doesn't overtax it by too much chewing. He'll mend with a few days rest. And tell him," said Lude only half joking, "to stay out of politics."

"I intend to," replied Friedrike.

But Johann, once he started feeling better, was adamant. "Nay, my dear, don't ask me that. You see, we *did* accomplish something." Because within a week news reached Vilsen that King Georg had dismissed Borries and had appointed two liberal ministers to his cabinet. There was hope again.

But Friedrike wondered for how long.

Johann healed rapidly but, unsuspected by any of them, there was some permanent damage. He developed a tic under his right eye that he could not control. Lude said, "It is nerve damage, and that is something the medical profession knows little about. How the nerves function is still a mystery to us. I wish we did know more. It could alleviate a lot of pain and suffering."

While Johann was convalescing word came to them that Friedrike's cousin, the miller Heinrich Matthies, had died of a sudden heart attack.

"No doubt brought on by another of his fits of temper," she commented. "Just like our grandfather Anton, although he softened up in old age, according to Oma Dorchen, whereas Heinrich never did. He wasn't that old."

"How old was he?" asked Johann.

"Only fifty-eight. I suppose I'll have to go to the funeral but you can use the excuse of your injury, if you don't want to go. I know you didn't like him."

"Not many people did," replied Johann. "But no, I'll accompany you. It wouldn't be right otherwise. What will happen to the children now, I wonder?"

"Young Friedrich is the heir and I'm sure he will take care of his sisters. Caroline is eighteen and Johanne fourteen now. They should manage quite well. But the two little ones by the second wife concern me. They are hardly more than babes and they say this Adi is even less competent than the first one. I never was able to get to know her as well as I knew the first Adi. She is so shy."

"Ach, that's what comes of having had such a domineering man. Now she won't know how to fend for herself. Aren't you glad you have such a kind, generous husband?"

Friedrike laughed. "Ach, Johann, stop teasing. Of course I'm glad." She leaned over and kissed him. "But I truly am concerned about those children. I don't know what the legalities are but Friedrich could easily put them out."

"I doubt that will happen. Friedrich is an entirely different man from his father. He will try to care for them but whether he can afford to is another matter. I have heard that in the last few years Heinrich neglected the two watermills—Heiligenberg and Bruchmühlen—disastrously. He concentrated all his efforts on the windmill."

"Ja, bought with stolen money," she commented bitterly. "Our money. Oma Dorchen always said it would all come back to them and it has. First Adi losing so many babies and then being killed so horribly. Now his own death at too young an age. Serves him right."

"Fritzi!"

"I know I shouldn't say that but it's hard not to. Ask Hermann. He saw the whole thing. He could have gone to Göttingen or somewhere to be the doctor he wanted to be, had they not stolen all our money."

"Hermann denies remembering any of it. He has a good trade now and seems happy enough in it."

She shook her head. "He says not but it affected his whole life. That's one reason he is so restless. My dear brother has never been happy."

"But that's all long past, Fritzi. Let it go. Right now we must think if there's anything we can do to help those Matthies children. They're your cousins, too."

"I know," she admitted remorsefully. "And I shall if I'm wanted. Let's see first what the situation is."

After his father's death Friedrich Matthies was surprised to learn two things. First, that for over a year Heinrich had been trying to sell—unsuccessfully as it turned out—the Klostermühle at Heiligenberg. And secondly, the old man despite his often cruel treatment of both his wives, had appointed a legal guardian for the minor children, one Friedrich Behrens—not only for his two sisters but also for little Heinrich and Wilhelm, his offspring by his second wife. Heinrich had also left instructions that the lawyer was to handle the financial affairs of the three mills. He apparently did not trust his son.

And whose fault is that, thought Friedrich. Friedrich was not unintelligent but his education had been limited to the most basic elementary schooling ending at age fourteen. His father had never shared with him any knowledge of the finances of the mills. He only knew the bullwork. Friedrich had never wanted to be a miller in the first place but he knew nothing else. He hated the work but did not know what to do about it. In his dilemma the young man turned not to Herr Behrens but to Hermann Bergmann.

During his brief stay at the Bergmann house following his mother's tragic death Friedrich had become fast friends with Hermann despite the fifteen-year disparity in their ages. Friedrich looked up to Hermann as to the elder brother he had never had. If there was also some longing for a father-figure, it was easily understood in view of the fact of his hatred for his own cruel parent. Back then Friedrike had approved of the friendship hoping it would help both her brother and her cousin. But now she shook her head. Hermann was the last person anyone in their right mind would ask for financial advice. But she said nothing, hoping that soon young Friedrich would learn to stand on his own two feet.

"I'd like to sell all the mills and go to America with you," declared Friedrich.

"Ach," replied Hermann. "I'm not going to America just yet. Been thinking about it for a long time but somehow, with one thing and another, I've not yet made up my mind. But why don't you sell at least the two watermills? You haven't lived out there for a long time. Would you even know how to operate them?"

"I've never lived or worked in either one. I was born here in the windmill. Papa rented them both out. But as long as I can remember, he would never sell because of that Hereditary Lessee Letter that was awarded to my great-grandfather Anton back in 1783. It was a very precious document that the family was very proud of. Apparently it took Opa a long time and a lot of effort to acquire it. That paper was more sacred to them than—than the Bible."

Hermann laughed. "But you have no heirs to work them for you.

You're not even married yet. Your father was wealthy. Surely between the proceeds of that sale plus your income from the windmill you would have enough to live on comfortably. I say sell them both and be rid of that worry."

"That's what I'd like to do but there are complications. Herr Behrens has just told me that Papa did try to sell one of them—the Klostermühle at Heiligenberg—but he was not able to because according to the terms of thet damn Hereditary Lessee Letter the two mills have to stay together as one unit. Papa actually had a buyer for the Klostermühle but the man either was not interested or couldn't afford both. So the deal fell through. That's why it will be extremely difficult to sell them."

"I see." Hermann thought a moment. "Tell you what I would do. Let some of those payments to the governmant slide. Then they'll soon take notice and mayhap release you from the terms of that letter or even help you find a buyer."

"Do you really think so? I shouldn't want them to take the mills away from me."

"If they threaten that, you can always quickly make the payments."

"Sounds like a good idea. I'll think on it."

Just then Adelheit came into the kitchen to serve them afternoon coffee. Hermann noticed that everyone seemed more relaxed and cheerful since old Heinrich's death. He had never noticed before that she was rather pretty with a full figure and now with a pleasant personality she had kept well hidden before. He found himself growing interested.

Her two little boys, Heinrich and Wilhelm, came bursting into the kitchen behind her. Heinrich jumped on Hermann's lap.

"Tell us about America, Cousin Hermann," the little boy begged. "Is it really so big?"

"Ja, it is bigger than Hannover, bigger than all of Germany. I'd guess as big as all of Europe."

"And you told us about a big river with a funny name. Is it bigger than the Weser?"

"Much, much bigger. Compared to it the Weser is like a little boy's piddle."

"Hermann!" put in Adelheit. "That's not a very nice thing to call our beautiful Weser."

Hermann laughed. "And there are many such rivers and rich farms and thick forests and mountains."

"Tell us about the Indians. Do they eat people?" asked Heinrich.

"I don't think so although they sometimes kill them. But they live in the far, far, west where other people don't live." He hoped he was right in that. No sense frightening them with some of the horror stories he had read.

"Are there lions and tigers there?" piped up little Wilhelm.

"Nay, I don't think so. But there are some funny-looking beasts called buffalo. They look like a big old bull but with a shaggy mane like a lion."

"Ooo, that's scary," said Wilhelm, wide-eyed. "How do you know so much about America?"

"I've read lots of books about it." He forbore telling them that the great land he admired so much was now divided into two countries waging a bloody civil war over slavery.

"I'm going to start school next year," said Heinrich. "When I learn to read, can I—I mean, may I read some of your books?"

"You certainly may."

"And when I grow up, I'm going to America," announced Heinrich.

"Ach, Hermann," sighed Adelheit, "stop putting foolish notions into their heads."

In 1861 Albert, Prince Consort of Queen Victoria of England, had died, plunging the little queen into a lifetime of mourning. The same year mad King Friedrich Wilhelm IV finally died and his brother Prince Wilhelm, who had been Regent for a long time, ascended the throne of Prussia. Almost immediately Otto von Bismarck convinced the king to appoint him Prime Minister.

"And that bodes ill for Hannover," said Johann Justus to Hermann.

"Indeed it does," agreed Hermann. "Prussia has long wanted to take over Hannover—the so-called bridge between her eastern and western provinces—but Bismarck is positively adamant about it."

"But what can he do, short of actual war?"

"I don't know but he'll find some excuse. And look at the foolishness our Georg is getting himself into. That could be just the excuse Bismarck needs."

"I agree. Whyever would Hannover want to annex Schleswig-Holstein anyway?"

"Publicly, he claims he doesn't. Just wants to support his relative the Archduke of Oldenburg for the succession."

"And Prussia doesn't want that. Nor does she support the Augustenburgs, the legitimate heirs. What does she want?"

"What do you think? Another jewel to add to her crown."

The situation in Schleswig-Holstein was extremely complicated and dated back over 400 years to the convoluted fealties and loyalties of the feudal period. At times the two duchies had been ruled by two dukes; at others they were combined into one and ruled by a single duke. Both also owed fealty to the King of Denmark as well as to the old Empire. At this time Schleswig with a population almost entirely German was a province of Denmark; Holstein was a member of the North German Confederation although forced to acknowledge the King of Denmark as overlord. According to the ten-year-old Treaty of London the Danish king had agreed to grant both duchies autonomy with their own dukes and constitutions. This had not been done, arousing great resentment among all the other Germans, especially the Liberals. The Diet at Frankfurt had actually gone so far as to order Hannover and Saxony to send troops into the duchies to solve the problem but they had proven ineffective.

Then Bismarck in a brilliant diplomatic maneuver in order to keep the other signatories of the treaty—England, France and Russia—out of the conflict made an alliance with Prussia's old enemy Austria, ostensibly to solve the problem within Germany, although secretly his ultimate goal was to annex both duchies into Prussia. He offered Austria a joint rule of the two duchies but counted on Austria's weakness and usual disastrous financial situation to make that a short-lived proposition. The Prussian troops quickly dispensed with the troops from Hannover and Saxony and forced them to go home. Bismarck did not want too many fingers in the pie. Austria was willing to help as long as Prussia left the south German states, whom she considered allies, alone.

1863　"Mama! Mama!" screamed Doris as she burst into the house, so startling Friedrike that the newest baby Minna had stopped nursing and started to howl.

It was a hot, muggy July day and the baby had been fretful. Friedrike's patience was wearing thin. "Now look what you've done," she scolded. But then she could see by her daughter's face that something dire, indeed, must have happened. "I'm sorry, Doris. Whatever is amiss?"

"Tante Doris is dead," Doris wailed.

"Dead?! But that's impossible. She was perfectly well and cheerful when I spoke to her yesterday."

"She's dead, Mama," Doris insisted. "I was there and I saw the whole thing happen. Oh, it was awful." And she broke into deep, heart-wrenching sobs.

Friedrike put baby Minna back in her cradle since she had stopped nursing anyway and took her eldest daughter in her arms. "Has your Onkel Lude been sent for?" Doris nodded. "Then tell me what happened." Doris was now a rapidly maturing young lady of thirteen and usually of a sunny disposition. It was rare that she broke down like this.

"I—I was helping her out in the spice shop as I often do in the summer. And—and she was waiting on a customer—Frau Naumann—and all of a sudden . . . " She sobbed uncontrollably for a few moments. "All of a sudden she cried 'Oh, lieber Gott' and clutched her breast like this." Doris demonstrated with her own budding breasts. "And then—and then she fell down on the floor. Frau Naumann screamed—foolish woman—but I ran to help Tante Doris. She didn't seem to be breathing but I tried to revive her. Oh, Mama," she sobbed and Friedrike held her closer. "I held smelling salts under her nose just like you showed me but she wasn't able to breathe it. I even tried slapping her face just a little but her head just flopped. Oh, Mama, it was horrible. Onkel Chris ran for Onkel Doctor Lude and I stayed with her until they came back. Then I ran to tell you." Friedrike held her until her weeping subsided somewhat.

"I must go to help," said Friedrike at last. She instinctively reached for her medicine bag. No, she would not need that, not if Lude is already there, not if Doris is dead. Oh, God, have mercy.

"May I come with you, Mama?" begged Doris. "I want to help, too."

"Nay, Kleine Dorchen, you stay here and watch the baby."

Doris pondered that a moment. Mama had not called her 'little Doris' in years. And now she was the only Doris. "Please, Mama. Anni can watch Minna. I love Tante Doris so much. I want to—to say goodbye."

"Nay," said Friedrike. "A house of death is no place for a young maid. There will be plenty of time for goodbyes at the funeral." She hurried out the door.

But Doris was stubborn—a trait she had inherited from her mother and who knew from how many grandmothers before her. She waited until Friedrike was well down the street. She ordered her sister Anna to watch over baby Minna and crept out the door.

As luck would have it, she met her cousin Henriette hurrying down Gartenweg. She was carrying her newest child, nine-month-old Georg, her first son after four girls. Tante Tiete seemed to regard this boy as the most miraculous thing that ever happened and would never leave him alone. But Doris knew her cousin well.

"Here, let me carry him for you, Tante Tiete, so that you can run faster."

"That's kind of you. But be careful. He's cutting a tooth."

"I'll keep him happy and quiet. A house of death is no place for a baby," Doris paraphrased her mother's words.

"Of course. Thank you, Doris," said Henriette and rushed off down the hill.

Doris, carrying the heavy baby, followed in her wake. She did not enter the spice shop, which was now closed, but went through the house. The big Bergmann house was as familiar to her as her own home. She stood by the back door of the shop watching and praying the baby Georg would not cry. Her mother was just getting Frau Naumann revived from her swoon. The woman was full of questions but Friedrike helped her to her feet and tactfully ushered her out the door.

"Later, Frau Naumann. I can't tell you anything until the doctor finishes his examination." She shut and locked the door behind her and pulled down the shade. "Thank God, we're rid of her," she sighed and turned to where the doctor was on his knees examining Doris. "What was it, Lude? Her heart?" she asked.

He nodded. "As near as I can tell, she had a massive heart attack. It happened so fast, I couldn't have saved her had I been standing next to her. She just allowed herself to get too fat. Her heart simply couldn't take the strain. Let that be a lesson to you women. It's not only men who have heart attacks." He glanced at his wife Henriette, still skinny as a rail, standing there for once speechless and not taking command of things as was her wont.

So that was it, thought Doris, and all this time I thought Tante Doris was going to have a baby but she never did. She looked at her mother. Friedrike's figure was still lovely—perfect in her daughter's eyes—despite having borne seven children. I'll never let myself get fat, Doris told herself. She looked at Chris, Doris' husband. He was standing on the other side of the doctor apparently awaiting instructions. He looked awestruck and unable to think for himself. Doris wondered what would happen now.

She soon found out. Christian Möser inherited the spice shop and the Bergmann house from his late wife Doris. He asked Friedrike not to permit Doris to come and help out in the shop any longer, claiming she was too young. Doris was heartbroken because she was sure she was smarter than Chris and inadvertently made him uncomfortable and nervous. He allowed Hermann to continue living in the house, even offering him a second room when he turned most of the dwelling into apartments.

Not long after acquiring the second room Hermann hired Adelheit Matthies to do for him. What 'to do' meant other than housecleaning everyone guessed but no one commented upon. Everyone liked Hermann despite his political inclinations and as they got to know Adi better most agreed that she was a sweet person well out from under the Matthies dominance. At first she would bring her sons with her but once Heinrich started school she often left Wilhelm behind at the windmill. Soon Chris Möser realized that he could not handle the spice shop alone and hired her for his two busiest days of the week. Although the total wages amounted to a pittance she seemed to be able to support herself—no doubt with Hermann's help—without being dependent on her stepson Friedrich. And Friedrich Matthies was just as glad to have her away from the mill as much as possible. Through no fault of her own she was too much of a reminder of what his father had done to his mother.

And no one commented on any of it. Vilsen was a happy village. Although the Bürgers were devout and pious and much of their lives centered around the ancient church, they were not bigoted. No one raised an eyebrow at the fact that few maidens reached their marriage beds virgin or that many young men left occasional by-blows around the countryside. That was life and life was to be enjoyed as long as a person worked hard to deserve it. Hard work and good pleasure. That was the German Lutheran ethic and it made Vilsen a happy village.

But soon out of the east a cloud of doom and gloom was to dim that happy contentment.

The Schleswig-Holstein question resolved itself almost by default. Bismarck secretly made a treaty with Italy promising to help her acquire Venezia from Austria, who now owned it. At the same time he was encouraging Bavaria to cut her ties to Austria and stand alone as the dominant state in southern Germany. When Austria requested Prussia's help in fighting Italy, Bismarck refused. Diplomatic relations were severed and Austria decided to withdraw her troops from Holstein which were quickly helped on their way by augmented Prussian troops without a shot being fired. Now Bismarck had what he always intended—the complete absorption of the two duchies into Prussia.

The next step in his grand plan was to annex Hannover, Hesse-Kassel, Nassau and Frankfurt—the so-called bridge states between Prussia's eastern and western provinces. All of these states were firmly pro-Austria and wanted no part of Prussia or Bismarck's blandishments. Bismarck knew he first had to eliminate once and for all the Habsburg influence over Germany. He declared war against Austria. It was one of the least known and shortest wars in European history but of utmost importance as it accomplished the final separation of Germany from Austria. Bavaria, to her credit, did not intervene. Hesse-Kassel under its corrupt and frivolous duke quickly succumbed and the two smaller states followed suit. But Hannover would not give in. On 15 June 1866 Bismarck sent Hannover an ultimatum giving her the choice of union with Prussia or being considered an enemy. Blind King Georg opted for 'Christ, Monarch and Welf' and led his army to meet the Prussians at a place called Langensalza in Thuringia. The Hannoverian troops fought bravely and actually defeated a superior Prussian force on 27 June. But after the victory they found themselves completely surrounded by several other large Prussian contingents and were forced to lay down their arms and surrender. Hannover's army was disbanded and the men sent home. King Georg was sent into exile in Vienna.

"That does it," declared Hermann. "Now I know I'm going to America as soon as I possibly can."

"But Hermann," objected Johann Justus, "you are too old to start anew especially in a strange land."

"I am only forty-three. I *want* to start anew. I'm fed up with the uncertain politics here."

"Just wait a bit until things settle down. Prussia is promising us a constitution modelled on hers of 10 June that will have universal—or more or less universal—suffrage."

"Balls! I don't believe a word of it," said Hermann. "Besides even Bennigsen admits that the Liberal Party is finished. How can there be a fair parliament without two parties?"

Johann could not answer that. "There's bound to be opposition. A new party will arise."

"I can't wait that long—if it ever happens. Haven't you heard? Prussia is going to clamp down on emigration. Only a few people will be allowed to leave each year."

"I hadn't heard that. I'm so confused with all their promulgations I didn't pay attention to that one. But I doubt she can enforce it. The big ship owners in Bremen and Hamburg will surely fight it. And if people really want to leave they'll find a way."

"I'm not going to wait for that. Prussia will make serfs of us all again and plunge us back into the dark ages."

"I fear you are right in that. Bismarck is so angry at Hannover's resistance he has threatened to punish the whole country. But how can he punish a *whole* country? We lived through Borries' regime. We'll live through this."

"It will be worse this time. I just know it."

"Do as you wish but I would rather stay here, bide my time and fight for our Heimat," said Johann.

A few weeks later Johann and Friedrike had just climbed into bed anticipating a little lovemaking and a good night's sleep when there was a pounding on the door.

Friedrike was startled out of her wits. "Whoever can that be at this time of night? I don't hear the tocsin ringing."

"You stay here. I'll go and see." Johann lit a candle and stumbled to the door in his nightshirt. He was surprised—although he should not have been—to find Hermann standing there all excited.

"Ach, Johann, I'm glad you're still up. You've got to take me to Bremen tonight."

"Tonight?" asked Johann bewildered.

"Ja. Right now. As soon as you can get dressed and Friede can pack you a little food for the return journey."

When Friedrike heard her brother's voice, she donned a bedwrap and joined the men. "Hermann, you're crazy! Whatever is amiss that you must flee to Bremen in the middle of the night? Have you committed murder?"

"Nay, but I'd like to. They are going house by house and rousing out all the Liberals."

"All the Liberals? And only Liberals?"

"Well, they didn't exactly say Liberals. The way they put it, anyone suspected of fomenting rebellion against Prussia."

"Have they actually arrested anyone?" asked Johann.

"Not yet to my knowledge. But it won't be long. There's a ship leaving Bremen for America day after tomorrow and I mean to be on it. The *Westfalen*, I believe. I already have my ticket but one has to be on the pier the day before to confirm it. Last week I took the precaution of getting a copy of my birth certificate from Pastor and Dieter Meyer issued my passport. A Hannover passport, backdated."

"But that isn't even valid anymore."

"It still is for a while. I understand there is so much confusion on the docks these days with so many wanting to emigrate—why, some got their passports months before Langensalza—that they're accepting anything that looks official, just as long as you have a valid birth certificate."

"Now tell us the *real* reason you want to leave," put in Friedrike. "It's the military draft isn't it?"

"Well, that, too. I don't want any part of that. Prussia is a military state. She knows nothing else. Ninety percent of her people would have no income at all but for the army. That is why her farms are so poor. They are totally brainwashed into thinking that is the only way of life."

"We know all that," she said, "but you are forty-three."

"And they're taking men up to forty-five. What's more, as part of Hannover's 'punishment' they won't pay any of our men until the end of their three-years' service."

"I see." Johann had noticed Hermann's poor old mare already hitched to his wagon standing patiently in the lane. "And what of your horse and wagon? Surely you can't take that with you?"

Hermann laughed. "Nay. Those are yours. I'm giving them to you to do with as you wish. I am only permitted to take what I can carry. I have my tool box and a bag of clothes. That's all. And all the money I own." He patted his waist where apparently a money belt was concealed beneath his trousers.

Once Johann saw that his brother-in-law could not be dissuaded from his folly, he said, "Very well. Let me get dressed. Fritzi, pack me a little food for breakfast. It looks as though I'll have to spend the night—or what will be left of it—in Bremen."

Friedrike was on the verge of tears but she was also so angry at her brother she could barely hide it. "You're a fool, Hermann," she sputtered. "I'll never forgive you for this. And what of your godson? Have you no thought at how heartbroken he will be?"

"You'll forgive me when you see how well I do," replied Hermann blithely. "And as I've said, send him to me when he's grown."

"Ooh!" she spat. "And where in America do you plan on settling?"

"I thought I might try that place called Elgin west of Chicago where your friend lives."

"Ach, I haven't heard from her in years. Who knows if she's even still alive."

"Well, I've heard from others that many Germans from this area have settled there—including some of the Bruns."

"Indeed?"

"It's rich farmland with a pretty little river. An ambitious man could do well there."

Friedrike turned away from him in disgust and started packing Johann's breakfast.

When Johann rejoined them, Friedrike said to him, "Best take your heavy cloak."

"But it's July," he objected.

"Maybe so but I expect you'll be sleeping in the wagon ere dawn. 'Tis said on the days before a ship is to leave all the inns in Bremen are jampacked with people from all over Germany waiting to leave."

"So you do keep track of the latest news," commented Hermann.

"I only know what I read in the newspaper," she replied.

"Ach, Friede, don't be angry with me." He took her in his arms and kissed her. "I'd like your blessing."

Against her will she started to cry. "Harm, Harm," she called him by his childhood name, "I shall miss you so. It's such a terribly long ways away."

"I'll keep in touch, I promise," he said. "You know there's now a cable under the Atlantic Ocean from New York to London. I'll send a telegram as soon as I arrive there."

She laughed despite her tears. "And how will I get it here in Vilsen? There are no telegraph wires out here in the country. You'd better write a letter."

Johann cleared his throat. "We'd better be going if you want to get to Bremen before dawn. We can't push that old mare of yours too hard or she'll never make it back and I don't favor walking from Bremen."

"Ja, of course. Oh, and one thing more ere I leave," said Hermann. "I have paid Adi's rent at your old home for a full year. That should help her until she finds another man."

"That was thoughtful of you." Her voice dripped with sarcasm. But then she shook her head. This was farewell to her dearest brother who, when they were children, had promised to watch over her all their lives. And now she would never see him again. It was not a time for recriminations. "Harm," she said softly, "you have my blessing. Fare thee well and God go with you."

After the men left Friedike was about to go back to bed where she could weep out her disappointment and bewilderment when she heard a scratching sound over her head. "Do I hear little mice up there?" She looked up the ladder to the loft. Three pairs of eyes quickly backed away from the opening. "Caught you," she said quietly.

Doris quickly descended the ladder. Anna and Luise came tumbling after. "Oh, Mama," said Doris, "we didn't mean to eavesdrop but we heard you arguing with Onkel Hermann and—and—he's gone, isn't he?" She rushed into her mother's arms and wept.

"I wanted to go with him. He said I could," cried Anna.

"Ach, you're such a copycat. He never said that," insisted Luise. She could always bait her gentle, elder sister.

"He did, too," replied Anna on the verge of tears.

"Hush now," said Friedrike, "don't wake the little ones, especially Hermann. He will be devastated when he learns. Ja," she sighed, "your Onkel Hermann is going to America. It's what he's always wanted to do. It just needed this little push of Prussia conquering Hannover to set him going."

"And is Papa going, too?" asked Luise, suddenly contrite at having teased her sister.

"Nay, silly," replied Doris, "he's just taking Onkel Hermann to the big ship in Bremen. He'll be back soon." Then, as sudden doubts assailed her, "He *will* come back, won't he, Mama?"

"Don't worry," replied Friedrike, "he will be back some time tomorrow. How late, I don't know. Dearest girls, your Papa and I will always be here for you." She was still holding Doris. Now she hugged each of the others in turn. To Anna she said, "And I don't want to hear any more talk about *you* going to America. Time enough when you're grown and wed." For she knew how strong the lure of that land was to the young men of Hannover. And to Luise, "Now Missy, no more of your teasing. Anni is too serious by far and has no need of that from the likes of a ten-year-old."

"I'm sorry, Mama, Anni," said Luise contritely.

"Thank you," said Anna. "I won't talk about America anymore but you can't stop me from thinking about it," she added in an unusual show of defiance.

"Oh, I'll miss Onkel Hermann so," sobbed Doris.

"There's one thing should make you happy," said Friedrike. "Hermann has given us his horse and wagon. If you're willing to take care of the mare mayhap Papa will teach you to drive." Doris brightened a bit at this. "Now off to bed with you. And don't disturb the little ones. Tomorrow when Papa returns, we'll hear all about his trip to Bremen."

When Friedrike heard the wagon drive into the yard behind the house, she heaved a sigh of relief. She had expected Johann back about noon and here it was suppertime. She wondered what had delayed him so long. No matter as long as he was home safe. She would soon hear.

Johann's first concern was to care for the old mare. He was exhausted but she was more so. Doris met him in the byre. "Mama said if I take care of the horse you will teach me how to drive the wagon."

Johann smiled at his eldest daughter. She was beautiful and so talented, too. Lord, he'd be losing her soon, too. "She did, did she? Then you can start right now. Poor old gal is exhausted. Give her plenty of water and rub her down good before you feed her."

"Do you think your horse will mind sharing the byre?" she asked.

"Mind? He'll be right happy. Although I think she's too old to foal anymore."

Friedrike could tell that someone out there was not happy about the newcomer by the squawking of the chickens. She could hardly contain her own impatience. The minute Johann walked in the house she hugged and kissed him, dirty and sweaty though he was, as if she had not seen him in a year.

"What took you so long? I was afraid you'd gone to America, too."

"Not I," he replied. "You know I intend to stay here and fight, however I may, for a free Hannover." He threw himself down at the table. "But never mind that. I'm hungry. But it was a beautiful ship."

The children were all gathered around wide-eyed with anticipation.

"Tell us about the boat," begged Luise.

"It is big," he began. "As long as from here to Homfelderstrasse."

"It couldn't be that big," exclaimed Anna. "How could it fit in the Weser?"

"The Weser is very big by the time it reaches Bremen. And I assure you it does fit and several others like it with room to spare. It has two smokestacks and four masts and room for hundreds and hundreds of passengers mostly down in the hold. But there are very luxurious cabins for the rich people." He noticed little Hermann looking very downcast among his eager sisters. "Come over here by Papa, lad." He put his arm around the boy.

"I didn't want Onkel Hermann to go without me," whispered Hermann with a sob. "Are you going to go away, too, Papa?"

"Nay, nay, little Harm. I'm not going anywhere," Johann assured him. "But here. Look what I brought for you." He fished in his pocket and drew out a crumpled postcard with a daguerreotype of the ship.

The little boy's eyes opened wide. "Ooo, it *is* big."

"That picture is just for you. Onkel Hermann wants you to keep it until you are old enough to go and visit him."

"Johann!" exclaimed Friedrike. "Don't go putting ideas in his head."

"Ach, he'll forget all about it ten years from now. At the moment it's merely intended to comfort him."

But Hermann did not forget and kept the picture of the ship with all his other little-boy treasures.

"Anyway, what took you so long to get home?" asked Friedrike.

"I thought it best to wait until he was safely on board. The press of the throngs and throngs of people was unbelievable. Hundreds of emigrants plus all their families and well-wishers. It seemed chaotic at first but actually it was quite orderly. It's just that there were so many of them that it took so long. First they checked their tickets against a list; then they checked their papers. Many did not have passports, just birth certificates. Hermann needn't have worried on that score. Then each one was examined by a doctor. Any sign of disease they were not permitted on board the ship. Quite a few were disappointed at that stage. They say conditions in that hold are appalling. You've got to be in good health just to survive. Then came the long wait until about four o'clock they permitted them to board. And that, my dear, is why I'm so late. I waited until I saw him go up the gangplank. And now I'm going to bed and sleep for two days."

Friedrike never got a cablegram from her brother, which she did not really expect, nor did she receive a letter, which she had hoped for, until almost Christmastime. Hermann wrote:

'I am well and boarding on a farm just outside the village of Elgin, Ills. I have obtained work in a sawmill but most of it is out in the woods cutting down the big trees they have here. I am taking part of my wages in fine hardwood which I am saving for when I can start making furniture again. But I may have to take a job as a carpenter ere that as people here are more anxious to have houses built than fine furniture. There are many Germans here, mostly farmers, from our part of Hannover. Not far from

692

here is a new village they have named Hanover. My best wishes to all for a happy Christmas season.

Yr. loving brother,
Hermann Bergmann.'

"A sawmill," exclaimed Friedrike. "How demeaning."

"At least he has work," commented Johann. "You see what he says about people needing houses first before the finer things of life. I expect in a new, raw land like America it will take a while for them to reach our level of refinement."

"I suppose. But from what I've read about New York, it seems quite civilized if a bit rowdy."

"Ach, ja. But this Elgin place is over a thousand miles from New York."

"That far?"

"Ja, and that's only half the country. Beyond that it is still wilderness. They call it the Wild West."

"Ach, poor Hermann in such a place."

1867   Bismarck's punishment of Hannover had little effect on the average citizen except for the drafting of young men into the army. And even that was very limited at first as Prussia was in such dire financial straits she could hardly pay her own troops. In fact, there were even some benefits. The Prussians improved the highway, rail and water systems, drained wastelands and encouraged more scientific agriculture and husbandry, provided welfare and health benefits, insurance and easier credit, and even supported the arts and sciences through museums, libraries and the preservation of historical monuments. However, much of this effort was undermined by the inefficiency of the Prussian civil servants and the great fear instilled by the 'Säbel-regiment' of Governor-General von Falckenstein, he who had been defeated by the Hannoverians at Langensalza and still bore them deep resentment.

Bismarck was careful not to offend the nobility whose support he counted on because they were largely ultra-conservatives. Hannover was given a provincial constitution modelled after the new constitutions of the old Prussian provinces and ostensibly universal suffrage. However, in order to cast their vote, the electorate had to swear an oath to abide by and support the Prussian constitution and this the majority of voters refused to do. What Bismarck simply did not understand was the peculiar loyalties all Hannoverians had to their traditions, their country and especially to their royal family, the Welf. When, fearing Hannover's power, he divided the former kingdom into three Prussian provinces — Niedersachsen, Westfalen and Thuringen — there were uprisings everywhere and, to his surprise, the nobility joined with the small Bürgers and the vast peasantry to form a pro-Welf party. Even Prussian King Wilhelm shuddered at Bismarck's high-handed deposing of the legitimate rulers of all the annexed states as he was a firm believer in the legitimacy of the ruling dynasties. He had been especially in awe of the ancient Welf, the oldest and wealthiest dynasty in all of Europe. Strangely enough, it was the former Liberals, including Bennigsen and Miquel, who gradually accommodated themselves to the Prussian regime.

The most heinous of Bismarck's 'punishments' was the sequestering of all the royal lands and estates, which Queen Marie had been left behind to administer. And in the final blow he seized the entire Welf private fortune in the amount of over sixteen million Thaler. Some of the money he used to shore up his sagging military budget but a great part of it was paid out in secret bribes and illegal transactions, such as a 300,000 mark annual payment to mad King Ludwig II of Bavaria to support his wild building program but in reality to keep Bavaria and the other southern states quiet until Bismarck could consolidate his gains in the north. Because of these clandestine, grossly illegal misuses it came to be known as the 'Reptilienfond'.

Friedrike was flabbergasted to receive a poignant letter from Queen Marie, which said in part, 'You have no idea how distressing the horrendous, illegal deeds of that monster have been. I long for some peace and quiet ere I leave my beloved home. Your description of your lovely village sounds perfect for my needs. Do not answer me as they read all my mail and I do not want them to know where I have gone. I shall be there in a few days. If you cannot accommodate me, please do not fret yourself. I shall understand. Your loving friend, Marie.' There was a great inkblot where she had evidently started to write "R" for Regina after her name and crossed it out.

"The Queen coming here to Vilsen? To us?" asked Johann, astonished.

"Ja, she is," replied Friedrike. "Isn't that exciting? And she doesn't want anyone to know. So don't breathe a word. But, oh, where *can* we accommodate her?"

"We can hardly put her in the loft with the children. Or worse yet, over the byre." Johann thought a moment. "Wait. I think I heard that Chris Möser has one of his apartments in your old home vacant."

"Then I shall go to see him immediately. I'll just tell him it's the lady from Hannover that I used to work for."

"Nay, don't say that. Everyone knows you used to work for the Duchess of Cumberland who is now Queen Marie."

"You're right. Then I'll just say it is an old friend from Hannover who can't climb the ladder to the loft."

"Better."

"Now what can I feed her?"

"The same fare we eat every day," replied Johann. "I think that's what she wants. Mayhap you could add a fancy kuchen or something."

"That's just what I'll do. I wonder how long she intends to stay."

"She said just a few days. She'll soon tire of the simple village life."

Friedrike fully expected a royal coach and four to deliver the Queen to Vilsen. So that when a simple hired hackney stopped before the house, she wondered who it could be. She watched with amazement as the driver helped the Queen alight. He carried her single small valise and a large bundle and deposited them on the stoop. Friedrike flung open the door before he was able to knock and the two women fell into each other's arms. The driver had suspected who his passsenger might be and had been well bribed to keep silent. But now he watched in total puzzlement as this simple peasant woman and his queen embraced like long-lost sisters.

"Return for me in three—no, four days. Saturday morning early," Marie instructed the driver.

"I'll be here, Your—that is, Madame," he assured her.

They entered the house and were greeted by a display and love and loyalty that surprised even Friedrike. Unbeknownst to her mother Doris had trained each of the children in proper court decorum. Each of the girls starting with the eldest curtseyed deeply and bid their former queen welcome. Little three-year-old Minna curtseyed so low she caught her heel in her skirt and would have fallen over had she not been rescued by Anni. This brought smiles to both women. Young Hermann made a very courtly bow, kissed Marie's hand and handing her a bouquet of flowers said, "Welcome to our home, Your Majesty. We hope you will be very happy while you are here."

Marie was so touched by this, it brought tears to her eyes.

695

"What a lovely family you have, Rike," she said as she wiped her face with a delicate lace handkerchief.

"Thank you, Marie. And how fare your two?"

"Well enough considering how distressing this whole thing has been. First the conquest and now the outright theft of all we own. Ernst August is much like his grandfather—good at concealing his true feelings. So much so that even I often do not know what he is thinking. He is playing along with Bismarck in the hope of saving some of what we have lost. I hope it is all pretense but I can't be sure. He has taken that blasted oath to the Prussian constitution and they made him take a further oath to relinquish all claims to the throne of Hannover and to never allow himself to be a rallying point for the pro-Welf party."

"How demeaning," said Friedrike.

"Indeed. Disgraceful. In return he has been allowed to keep his title of Duke of Cumberland. He claims he wants nothing more to do with politics and will retire to the life of a country gentleman with his wife Thyra on his personal estate, greatly reduced in size. As I say, no one knows how he really feels but I am hoping he is just biding his time until Hannover can throw off the Prussian yoke and be independent again. But I'm afraid that is an impossible dream whilst Bismarck is in power."

"I fear you are right. And my little namesake?"

"Not so little anymore. Friederike is taking it all very badly. She has always been a very sensitive child and now she is convinced that no one will ever want to marry her—a disenfranchised princess with no land and no dowry—not even a country anymore. Our cousin Queen Victoria has offered to let her come to England and she may just do that. She does not want to share the disgrace of my exile."

"Your exile?" exclaimed Friedrike. "Then you are forsaking us too?" She knew the moment she uttered it that that was a poor choice of words.

"Forsaking you? Never," denied Marie. "I shall never forsake Hannover. Nay, Rike, I am being forced out. At least my Georg was able to retain a little dignity by being 'allowed' to go into exile. I am being expelled. Mandatory expulsion in one month's time. That is one reason I came here. The servants are even now packing what few possessions I am permitted to take. I couldn't bear to watch." She choked back a sob. "He fears me. That monster Bismarck is actually afraid of my strength. But what can a mere woman do in the face of the vindictive Prussian army? I would not have them destroy our beloved country."

And at that last, the former queen, seated at Friedrike Bruns' kitchen table, broke down and wept.

Friedrike put her arm around Marie and held her head to her breast as she would a small heartbroken child.

After the brief storm was over Marie apologized. "Ach, Rike, I did not come here to burden you with my troubles but it is so good to have a real friend, a friend to whom I can unburden my grief, a friend whom I can trust. You know, kings and queens have very few true friends, only sycophants who seek to bask in the reflected glory of the sun. But when the clouds hide the sun they, too, disappear."

"I shall always be your true friend," Friedrike assured her. "Now let us talk of more pleasant things. What would you like for supper? Since I didn't know exactly when you would be coming, I haven't prepared anything special."

Marie shook her head. "Something very light. I am not very hungry. The journey in the hackney was very wearying."

"Ach, forgive me. Perhaps you would like to lie down and rest a while. Then I shall take you to my late cousin's husband who has prepared a comfortable apartment for you in the house where I grew up. Then tomorrow dinner we shall have our feast."

"A feast," shouted Hermann and Luise together and clapped their hands.

"Now you children remember," warned Friedrike, "you are not to tell anyone who our guest really is — not Tante Tiete or Onkel Lude or Cousin Chris or Pastor or your schoolmaster or any of your friends — not anyone at all. She is just Mama's old friend. It will be our secret, all right?"

Six heads nodded solemnly.

"Thank you," said Marie. "That is a heavy burden to place on children, especially the little ones."

"Ach, every child loves a secret. If they let it out long after you have gone, what difference can it make?"

"It could cause trouble for you and your husband."

"Here in Vilsen? Hardly. I can only think of one or two people who are not pro-Welf. Wait until you meet Johann."

"Ach, ja. I'm looking forward to that," said Marie. "I well remember the night you never came in and an old mare came up missing which miraculously returned the next day. I want to hear the true story of that."

Friedrike laughed. "You shall. Now, children, change out of your 'court' dress. There are chores to do. Hermann, run and tell Papa that our guest has arrived. It's almost time for his afternoon coffee."

Johann washed up as best he could in the horse trough before entering the house. He felt a bit embarrassed at meeting his queen in his work clothes.

But Marie assured him that he should not be. "It is good that you have a solid trade to support this wonderful family," she said. "You can be proud of your work clothes."

The woman was so gracious that she immediately put Johann at ease and he began to relax.

"That I am, Your Majesty—er—or how shall I address you?" he stammered.

"Just plain Marie," she replied as she smiled. And soon they were gossiping around the table like old, beloved friends.

After Johann returned to his workshop, Friedrike asked Marie, "Is there anything special you would like to do while you are here? I'm afraid we don't have much in the way of entertainment to offer you in Vilsen."

Marie shook her head. "Entertainment is the last thing I want. No social occasions, please. But you often spoke of the Vilsen woods, of how beautiful they are. A walk through there might be just the thing to lift this dark mood I've been in."

"Indeed it might. It has always been a special place for generations of this family. My Oma Elli often spoke of a secret place where she would hide from the wrath of her—er—overly strict father. But after Napoleon had the whole woods cut down for his ships it disappeared. It is all second growth that you will see now but it is still beautiful and very restful."

"I think I should enjoy that very much," said Marie. "And what of the ancient mill where you told me you were born? Is that still there?"

"Oh, yes. And still a working mill. It has been there since 1215, part of the old monastery that was there before the Reformation—the only part that still stands. The Matthies family that owned the two mills have recently sold it—just last year, in fact. But fortunately the new owner has hired my uncle Georg Brüning Bergmann to operate the Klostermühle. So we should be most welcome to visit there."

"I should like that. I am most interested in the ancient heritage of Hannover."

"As are most of us here—and proud of it. There are all sorts of stories about the old monks I could tell you and about an old wisewoman who lived in the woods. Heiligenberg is said to have been an ancient Saxon shrine before Karl der Grosse conquered us. Once, before I was born, Wilhelm Grimm came here and asked both of my grandmothers to tell some of the old stories."

"Did he indeed?" said Marie. "Then I should like to see some of this. I well remember how you loved those stories and read them to my children even though the king forbade it because he did not agree with their politics."

After supper Marie finally opened the mysterious package she had brought. "I have a gift for you. I hope you don't mind that they've been used once or twice." She drew forth two exceedingly large linen tablecloths. The first was quite plain. "This is the tablecloth that Herr von Bismarck ate on when he came to Hannover back in '55. I want no part of anything to do with that monster, so I thought you might have some use for it."

"Ach, it is so huge — twice the size that will fit on this table. But I thank you just the same."

"So cut it in half," said Marie. "This other one is the real gift. It is a family heirloom woven over a hundred years ago. So they couldn't take that away from me. I wanted to give it to you on the occasion of your wedding but the king wouldn't hear of it. But now, however belated, it is yours."

Friedrike clapped her hands in delight. "Ach, it is the most beautiful thing I have ever seen. What intricate weaving! I am considered an accomplished weaver but I could never do anything like this." She spread the cloth out for all to see. It was pure white and woven into the design were twelve complete place settings, including plate, goblet, knife, fork and spoon. In the center were platters of food — swans, fish, rolls and other edibles — as well as two bouquets of flowers. "All it lacks is the place cards."

Marie laughed. "I thought you would be pleased. See here in the corner are our ancestor's initials — RW. W for Welf, of course, but even I don't know who R was."

"Thank you, Marie. I shall treasure it always."

After two days of strolling through the woods and around the little village, of early bedtimes and hearty but simple meals, the former queen seemed much refreshed. Although many friends and neighbors suspected who Friedrike's guest was, the conspiracy of silence bespoke their intense loyalty to the royal Welf. As Marie was packing to leave the next morning, she answered the question Friedrike had been hesitant to ask.

"I shall be going to Vienna — at least, at first. Georg is in Paris, as you may know. I may join him there. I'm not sure. Did you know that 800 loyal troops fled Hannover and are there with him? They call themselves the

'Welfenlegion'. But Georg doesn't want any more of war. Nor can we afford to pay them for very long. Anyway what could a mere 800 do against the might of the Prussian army? But he is very touched by their loyalty and support."

"I should think he would be. How valiant of them to sacrifice their lives for you. For surely if they returned to Hannover they would be branded as traitors and probably shot."

"I'm afraid so," sighed Marie. "No doubt the penalty Hannover must pay for always having been a peaceful nation—not like Prussia, always seeking out war."

"Ja," agreed Friedrike. "It makes one wonder what Germany will be like in the future under Prussian control."

Marie shrugged. "I don't even want to think about it. But dearest Rike, I have a favor to ask of you. Feel free to refuse if you do not think it convenient. As you know, once I leave here, I shall never be able to return to my homeland in my lifetime—mayhap not even in death. I need someone to look after my parents' graves. I was the only one left of my family to do it. And now . . ."

"I should be most happy to do so. But where are they?"

"In Altenburg in Saxony."

"Of course. I should have known."

"It's a full day's journey by train from here."

"Oh, my."

"I shall leave you enough money for your train fare and a fee for your time but if you feel it is too much to ask, please say so and I'll try to make other arrangements. You would be away from your family three days twice a year. I'll see that you can stay the two nights at the palace."

Friedrike thought a moment. Although she was very content with her life and happy with Johann and her children, she was aware that she was beginning to undergo the change—she had not become pregnant since Minna's birth over three years ago. She felt she could use a little excitement. It would remind her of her youth spent at the court of Hannover—well, sort of. "Very well, Marie," she said. "I'll do it for you."

"Fine. I appreciate that more than you know." She handed Friedrike two purses. "Here is enough for your train fare and fee for three years and full instructions. And then we'll see what happens. I've taken care of the graves for this spring. You won't have to go until the fall."

"I'll take good care of them and keep them beautiful, I promise you," said Friedrike. "But what is this other purse for?"

700

"Your daughter Doris is a very talented young lady. She wants to study art and I'd like to help her."

"She told you that?" exclaimed Friedrike. "Why, that little minx."

"She deserves it. I've been quite impressed by her. In that purse is enough for her tuition for one year under a good master. Paris would be the place but I don't think that's wise right now. There are many such in Germany. It will be a year before she is eighteen. Time enough to inquire around. But let the decision be hers."

"Marie, you overwhelm me with your generosity. Doris will be thrilled. As will Johann. He is quite artistic in his own way and recognizes her talent but we never thought we could do anything about it."

"Well, now you can. I'm sure Doris inherited the talent from both sides. You yourself are quite talented with your weaving."

Friedrike laughed. "Ach, ja. Tablecloths, bedsheets and curtains."

Just then Marie's hackney drove up. The two women hugged and kissed, both fighting back the tears.

"Thank you, my dearest freind," said Marie, "for helping restore my faith in people. Auf Wiedersehen."

But it was not *Auf Wiedersehen*. It was goodbye. No one in Hannover ever saw their beloved queen again.

Shortly after the queen's visit an epidemic of measles broke out in Vilsen. Friedrike was grateful that it had not happened while Marie was there. Doris and Anni had survived the dread disease some years ago. So she did not worry about them. In fact, Anni was not even there. According to custom, as soon as a child finished school they were sent out to work for other families—the boys to an apprenticeship in a trade, the girls to learn housekeeping, cooking and child-rearing. Anni had just started working for a distant Bruns cousin who had a large farm out in the country and an even larger brood of children. She had been granted one day off to be at home for Marie's arrival.

Friedrike had kept her eldest at home to help care for her own young ones while she worked at her weaving. She was grateful for Doris' help now. Luise was the first to come down with the measles and it seemed to be a particularly virulent case. It quickly spread to the other three but they seemed to have a milder version. Luise succumbed within a week.

Friedrike was so devastated at her loss that she almost cancelled her proposed trip to Altenburg in the fall. But Johann Justus urged her to go.

"It will do you good to get away for a few days," he said. "The others are all well again, God be thanked. Doris can manage for three days."

"I suppose so," she agreed reluctantly.

He took her in his arms. "Don't worry, dearest Fritzi. Tonight we'll make another baby to take Luise's place."

"Ach. Johann, how can you be so crass? No one can take Luise's place."

"Ach, Fritzi, I'm sorry. Of course, no one can. What I meant was the old saying that when one dies another is conceived."

"Don't tease me so. You know I'm into the change. I fear my child-bearing days are over."

"I don't think so. Look, not one gray hair on your beautiful brown head. And here I am a bald old coot with a twitchy cheek and a half-blind eye. Not many teeth left either. Shall I play my fiddle a bit to put you in the mood?"

At last she smiled. "No need tonight. I guess I am in the mood." She took his hand and led him into the bedroom. "Come, love, let us put dear Luise to rest."

Their rapturous lovemaking that night was finer than it had been in a long time.

Friedrike thought the train ride would never end. She was glad she had brought ample crocheting with her, although, to be honest, most of the time her eyes had been glued to the window, watching countryside she had never seen before flash by. She had boarded the train at Eystrup and had to change in Hannover for another to Leipzig. That had been the longest stretch. Then another change to the local to Altenburg. She wished she could have seen a little of Leipzig. It was said to be a beautiful city but there had not been time. Now it was almost the end of the day and she was very tired.

When she descended at Altenburg she did not know what to expect. Marie had promised that she would be met but as she looked around the little station she saw no one. Suddenly a man in livery came rushing up to her.

"Frau Friedrike Bruns?" he asked.

"I am she."

"Come right this way, Madame. I have the coach waiting over here."

He took her little bag and escorted her to the coach. She felt like royalty as he handed her up into the luxurious vehicle. The drive to the palace was very short and the staff welcomed her, not as another servant, but as a friend of their beloved Marie. The palace was old but well kept up. She was saddened to learn that not one of the family was still in residence but the staff took pride in maintaining it as though they were expecting someone, anyone, to return momentarily. She insisted on eating supper with the servants. No way would she sit at that huge dining room table by herself. She soon put them at ease with her earthy questions about the garden and the graves.

"The family cemetery is on the far side of the park," the butler advised her. "There is a mausoleum where the former dukes and duchesses are interred. But as Queen Marie's parents were only a count and countess they are buried outside. The gardener has kept it neat and the weeds off of it but as the Queen always planted the flowers herself, we were not sure what she would have wanted."

"Nor am I," responded Friedrike. "But as she gave me free rein I would say, since it is fall, I should put in some spring bulbs—crocus, daffodils, tulips and the like. But where can I get them?"

"We have a conservatory but I'm afraid . . ." The butler hesitated, obviously out of his depth.

An older man at the end of the table spoke up. "We have them, Madame, although not very many. I am Dieter, the only gardener left here. Since I am responsible for the entire estate," he waved his arms in every direction, "I have not had much time for the cemetery."

Friedrike shuddered as she envisioned the plot overgrown with weeds. She feared she would need more than one day here. "Then if you will take me out there first thing in the morning, I'll see what has to be done," she said.

"Gladly," replied Dieter. "I am grateful for your help. I know the queen would not have sent you had she not been confident of your ability."

That night Friedrike was accorded one of the guest rooms. She felt like a queen herself as she sank into the luxurious featherbeds.

Very early the next morning the cook said, "Dieter is waiting for you. Go and take a look while I fix your breakfast."

Outside she met the gardener. "Good morning, Dieter. I shall need some tools."

"They're already in the gig," he replied.

"The gig? But is it so far that we cannot walk?"

"Quite a ways, Madame."

Friedrike, dressed in her oldest gardening clothes and apron, climbed into the gig, still feeling like a queen at his deference. They rattled off through the extensive park, then through a dense wood, no doubt once a ducal hunting preserve, and finally reached the cemetary. It *was* quite a ways.

The mausoleum, elaborate seventeenth-century baroque, dominated the large area. It looked fairly well kept except that it was blackened with age. Friedrike longed to take a scrubbing brush to the mildew but that was not what she was here for. The ducal tomb was surrounded in all directions by hundreds of lesser graves, some very ancient. The far reaches of the cemetary were badly in need of mowing. She felt sorry for Dieter, having to care for all this plus the park around the palace all by himself. No wonder he concentrated on the area people would see. She doubted anyone came here very often. Dieter led her to Marie's parents' gravesite. It was in better shape than most. She could see the evidence of Marie's loving care. The summer flowers, recently touched by frost, were dry and forlorn-looking but she could see the pattern. She studied it for a moment deciding what she must do.

After a hearty breakfast—so much larger than her usual roll and coffee that she felt she could never eat dinner—she set to work. However, the crisp fall air and the hard work gave her an appetite. She planted various spring bulbs in elaborate designs and felt certain that Marie would have been well pleased. She looked forward to seeing them when she returned in the spring. She finished up in the late afternoon and spent part of the evening regaling the servants with stories of the court in Hannover and how she came to be Marie's friend.

Friedrike had to leave before dawn to catch the train that connected with the mainline at Leipzig. When she finally arrived at Eystrup and fell into Johann's waiting arms, she was so tired that she did not notice how quiet and glum he seemed on the way home.

As she walked in the door saying, "Ach, it's good to be home," a tearful Doris flung her arms about her and sobbed, "Oh, Mama, Mama, it's so awful. Didn't Papa tell you?"

Friedrike looked at Johann. "And what was Papa supposed to tell me?"

"Anni has run away," cried Doris. "She's gone."

Friedrike collapsed into a chair. "Then we'll have to find her. Immediately." She glared at Johann. "Why didn't you tell me?"

He replied sheepishly, "I thought it better to tell you here because it's too late to get her back."

"Too late? What do you mean?" she screamed.

"She's gone to America with my cousin Heinrich's family. We never knew a thing about it until his brother Conrad, to whom he left the farm, returned from Bremen. He brought a note from your daughter."

"Bremen? America? She's your daughter, too. Why didn't you stop her?" Friedrike was almost hysterical.

"We didn't know. And now it's too late. The ship sailed early this morning."

Friedrike thought she would faint. "My God, Johann, she's only thirteen. How could they do this to us? What could Heinrich have been thinking of?"

"She wanted to go," whispered Doris.

Friedrike looked at her daughter. "How do you know?"

"I should have told you before," murmured Doris, "but I thought it was just a childish infatuation. I never expected anything to come of it. Certainly not something like this."

"What are you saying?" asked Friedrike sharply.

"Anni fancied herself in love with Johann Justus, cousin Heinrich's son. She didn't want him to leave without her."

"Ach, at thirteen. What could she know about love?" Then a horrible thought struck Friedrike. "She wasn't pregnant, was she?"

"Nay, I'm sure she wasn't," replied Doris. "She swore to me he never touched her. I think it was quite one-sided. But she is a very determined girl once she makes up her mind to something."

"Ach, Dorchen," sighed Friedrike. "You seem to know your sister better than I. She was always so quiet, I never knew what she was thinking."

"She always wanted to go to America ever since Onkel Hermann left," put in Hermann. "She was always talking about it."

Friedrike glared. "You knew and you didn't tell me?"

"Mama, I didn't think she meant it—not right now," sobbed the little boy startled by his mother's anger. "I—I thought she would wait until she was big, until I was big, too, so I could go with her."

Friedrike gasped and Johann whacked the lad on the rump. "Not one more word about America out of you," he scolded. "Don't upset your mother any more than she already is." Hermann slunk away to join his little sisters in the corner where they had been hovering, the younger ones not quite understanding what this terrible scene was all about, except that they knew they would never see their dear sister Anni again, whom they all loved better than Doris. She had been so kind, reading to them and such-like. Not like Doris who was strict like Mama.

"Hadn't you better read her note?" suggested Johann gently.

Friedrike took the missive from his hand and slowly opened it. She read:

'Liebe Mutti and Papi!

'I am going to America with Cousin Heinrich Bruns and his family. Cousin Heinrich has promised that Johann Justus and I can be wed just as soon as we are old enough and are properly settled. I hope we can find Onkel Hermann in Elgin. Please don't be angry with me as I am very happy and excited to be going to America. I promise to write as soon as we arrive there.

Your loving daughter, Anna Margarethe Bruns.'

"Another Johann Justus," she exclaimed. "I can't keep track of all the Johann Justuses in your family."

Johann smiled for the first time. "Quite a few. Every branch seems to want to bear that honor," he quipped.

Friedrike ignored his attempt at humor. "And how old is this one?"

"Fifteen, I think."

"Two children! God have mercy. And why didn't Heinrich do any-thing to stop it? Why all the secrecy anyway?"

"I think he didn't want the Prussian authorities to know. He detests the Prussians—as do we all—but he made no bones about it. Said he couldn't live under them. He wanted to get out before they tightened the limitations on emigration any further."

She nodded. She put her face in her hands and wept. After a time she said, "I'm going to bed. This has been too much for me. Doris, fix supper for your Papa and the children. I couldn't eat a thing."

After a makeshift supper and the little ones had been sent to bed, Johann and his eldest sat at the kitchen table.

"Poor Mama," sympathized Doris.

"She'll get over it," opined Johann. "It was just too much of a blow so soon after losing Luise. Your mother is stronger than you think. That's why I love her so." He almost sobbed himself and hoped he was right.

Johann wanted desperately to make love to his dear wife but he feared that it would not be appropriate just now. He only hoped she would not turn him away as she had after Sophie's death. After a while he turned out the oil lamp and climbed into bed. He was surprised to see that she was still awake, lying very still, staring at the ceiling. He took her in his arms and held her close to him while she wept out her grief.

Then quite unexpectedly she said, "The Gypsy woman was right."

Johann had no idea what she was talking about. He waited for her to enlighten him.

"You know, Doris and I went to her after little Dorchen was born. She said I would have many children but that I would lose most of them to a far-off land. Anni is the first, not counting my bother. Ach, Johann, how many more?"

He held her closer. "I don't know but try not to worry about it now. They're all very young yet."

"But so is Anni." She lay very still for a long time. Johann thought she had fallen asleep when she said, "And you know something else? Remember the night you said we would replace Luise and I didn't believe you?"

He nodded, suddenly alert. "Don't tell me . . . "

"Ja," she murmured, "I'm pretty sure I'm carrying again."

"Then that's a cause for celebration." He started stroking her body.

"But how can we replace Anni?" she asked in a quivery voice.

"The same way as we have before, I should imagine." He was suddenly kissing her breasts and she could no longer resist him.

Several weeks later Friedrike was in the spice shop—or what was left of it. Chris Möser had remarried a woman named Auguste. Together they had remodelled the store extensively and had radically changed the focus of their main line of business, in part because a real apothecary shop had recently opened up across the street, providing stiff competition. Oma Dorchen's apothecary corner no longer existed and even the spices occupied only a small section of the store. They now sold mostly stationery and what Friedrike deprecatingly called trinkets. She did not like what she saw but business was business. She supposed that everyone had to modernize but she missed the old shop.

She was making her selection of a few condiments that she needed when a woman came in and looked over the display of 'trinkets'. She seemed in a hurry and Chris was busy with another customer. So Friedrike thought to be helpful by saying, "May I help you find what you are looking for?"

"Oh," the woman looked up, "do you still work here? Aren't you Frau—uh—not Bergmann—uh . . . ?"

"Frau Bruns," she corrected. "Nay, I never worked here but my late cousin Doris Bergmann once owned the shop and my daughter Doris Bruns occasionally worked here." Friedrike searched her memory in vain for a name. She knew she had met the woman once but could not place her.

"Ach, ja, of course. I am Margarethe Campsheide. I am looking for a teething ring for my youngest. He is cutting teeth rather painfully and I thought it might help. Do you know if they have any?"

"I don't know. You'll have to ask Herr Möser. But if I may make a suggestion, try rubbing oil of cloves on his gums. It will ease the pain and not cut the gums. I mistrust those rings. The child could choke on it."

"Ach, foolishness," said Margarethe. "That's old-fashioned thinking. I believe in modern methods of childrearing."

Friedrike took an instant dislike to the woman. Modern methods—teething rings—humbug. At last she remembered who the woman was. Her husband was the youngest and least obnoxious of the Campsheide brothers. This Margarethe seemed to fit in well with that family. Then she recalled that he still owed Johann some money on the flatware they had purchased some years ago and, she believed, still owed Johann's brother something on the furniture he had made for them. Mayhap if she were polite she could get a little information as to their ability to pay the debt.

"And how many children do you have now?" she asked, not really caring.

"Four—two girls and two boys. A perfect assortment, don't you think? The latest Friedrich Dietrich was born in August."

"And he's teething already?"

"Well, I think so. He's been awful fretful lately."

It sounded more like colic to Friedrike but she asked, "And how is your husband doing? Do you have your own farm now or are you still renting?"

"We're still renting—four fields now but Johann is doing very well. We'll soon be able to buy out Master Heidtmann. Johann has already spoken to the bank at Hoya about a mortgage. I'm so proud of him."

"Mayhap if you're real sweet to him, old Heidtmann will leave the farm to you." Friedrike could not resist the sarcasm but it went right over Margarthe's head. She laughed but she was not quite sure what the joke was.

On 2 April 1868 Elizabeth Alma Bruns was born. She was such a sweet-tempered baby that she immediately became everyone's favorite.

Hermann, meanwhile, had become fast friends with the two young Matthies boys and, when Adelheit had married a farmer whose holding lay not far from Vilsen, he missed them terribly.

"Mama," he said, "could I spend part of this summer with Heinrich and Wilhelm? They invited me."

"Did they now? But what did their mother say? Does she even know?"

"She said it's fine by her. Please, Mama. I have no other boys to play with. They said I could help with the farm work."

"I'm afraid farm work is a bit heavy for a lad your age."

"But I'm only a year younger than Heinrich and Wilhelm is even a year younger than I. Besides I won't be doing the heavy work—just little things like milking the cows and feeding the chickens and gathering eggs . . ."

"There's plenty of that right here," she interrupted. "I need your help in the garden and later with the flax."

"I know." It was on the tip of his tongue to say that the girls could do all that but he thought better of it. "But I won't be gone all summer—just a week here and there and I'll work twice as hard for you in between. Besides, our garden, big as it is, isn't a *real farm.*"

He was so sincere in his pleading that she felt sorry for him. She knew there were not many boys his age in the neighborhood. Johann had often commented on how difficult it was for a lone boy to grow up among so many females. "Very well," said Friedrike, "I'll speak to your Papa. It will be his decision."

Hermann was overjoyed. "He'll say 'yes'. I know he will."

And Johann did say, "Yes. Let him go. It will be good for him. He needs male companionship. And if the step-father doesn't take to him, they can always send him home."

Doris spent all summer making a new dress, petticoats, shifts and nightclothes. The bustle was coming into style which was a bit tricky to drape properly. But a new invention by an American Ebenezer Butterick, the paper pattern, was a boon to women everywhere.

She also worked diligently on her sketches. Some were of flowers; some were of clothes. All beautiful. The master she had chosen specialized in pen-and-ink drawings and watercolor sketches rather than paintings. Johann could not see the point of this. To him it was not real art.

She tried to explain. "But Papa, a woman—or even a man—could wait for years to sell one painting, and starve in the meantime. This sort of art can be used to illustrate books or even newspapers. Those of the clothes could be sold to couturiers. There are endless possibilities."

He shook his head. "You mean to work? To make a living at that? But women don't do that. Women aren't supposed to work outside of the home."

"Ach, Papa, don't be so old-fashioned. More and more women are working, some even in offices and stores. Tante Doris did."

"But that was practically out of her own home," he argued. But he knew he could not win this discussion with his headstrong daughter, especially when Friedrike agreed with her, in part because the queen had recognized the girl's talent and offered to support it.

But Friedrike did insist that both she and Johann accompany Doris to Bremen. She wanted to be very sure that this master, however brilliant, would be harmless to a young, innocent girl.

"But not in the old wagon," objected Doris. "Why can't we go by train?"

Johann insisted, "By the time we drive to Eystrup we can be half way there. And with the amount of baggage you have, it will be much easier. We'd have to hire a wagon in Bremen anyway to say nothing of the cost of three fares."

And Friedrike added, "The queen didn't give you that money for frivolous things."

Friedrike had not been to Bremen in many years. As they crossed the Weser bridge she was amazed at the number of huge steamships tied up at the wharves, most destined for America and other far parts of the world. She was even more amazed that the old city walls had been torn down and the sites beautifully landscaped. In fact, Am Walle had become one of the most fashionable residential districts in the city. But the artist's studio was in the old city which had not changed in hundreds of years.

Friedrike immediately approved of the old master especially when he praised Doris' talent. Johann was not so sure.

"Those grandfatherly types can be old lechers," he commented when they were out of the man's hearing.

"Ach, don't be foolish," replied Friedrike. "It's the yong male students I should be more concerned about."

She carefully inspected the premises nearby the studio where Doris was to live. It was an apartment shared by three other girls, all of whom seemed quite respectable. She especially approved of their chaperone, a very dignified middle-aged lady who she felt would brook no nonsense. She knew the girls would hate her but that was all to the good.

Friedrike missed Doris terribly. Not that she had not known she would lose her to some suitor eventually. But it had been pleasant to have an almost adult daughter to share her joys and sorrows, just to talk to. Now with only the three little ones home and Hermann gone most of the time the house seemed empty. She toyed with the idea of hiring someone, at least part-time, to take care of the children in order to give herself more freedom. Although she would still be nursing Lise for some time to come, which would limit her to a great extent. Hermann and Line were already in school and Minna would be starting next year. So she had to admit to herself that caring for the children was merely an excuse. What she really wanted was a companion.

One day she took her concerns to Mathilde Meyer who had been so helpful with her sound advice in the past.

The old dame pursed her lips and thought for a moment. "I may just have the solution to your needs," she said. "I have a granddaughter Alma. While she is not yet fourteen, she is highly intelligent, well read and wise beyond her years—but restless for something rewarding to do. She is agitating to go to the gymnasium and on to university. But my son, her father, will not hear of it. It is not seemly for girls, he claims. Although I have heard that a few have succeeded in breaking into that male bastion but it is made diffucult for them. I agree that I should not want her to have to contend with that. She is too much of a lady. But on the other hand I'll not have her farmed out as mere nursemaid to some family. I want her to remain home where I can teach her all she needs to know about manners and housekeeping but I'd like her to have some outlet for her tremendous intellect and energy. Do you know her at all?"

"I know who she is," replied Friedrike, "but I've never actually spoken to her."

"She would make an ideal teacher but I'm afraid our current schoolmaster is a bit stiff in that regard, too. What is it your children miss most about Doris?" she asked.

"Why, reading the stories, I suppose, and devising brain-teasing games, especially for Minna who is not yet in school and feels quite alone. But my Anni was best at that. She had far more patience with them than Doris," said Friedrike.

711

"Alma would have infinite patience. It's really amazing in one so young. I'm sure she would suit admirably. Suppose I send her over to you some afternoon after school and you can decide for yourself."

The day Alma showed up had been a particularly exhausting day for Friedrike. Sweet Lise had not been sweet at all but fretful all day. Minna was being froward, feeling neglected. Line and Hermann had come home from school and, taking one look at the situation, had dumped their school books on the table and had gone outside again even though it was a chilly raw day. When Alma walked in, Friedrike was sweating over the stove, jogging Lise on her hip while trying to fix supper with one hand.

Alma took the baby from her and immediately Lise calmed down. Minna, curiosity about the newcomer overcoming her sulks, came over and sat by them.

"Thank you, Alma," said Friedrike. "As you can see I occasionally need some help."

"Oma said you might. I should be glad to help, Frau Bruns, when I can," Alma replied. Although Friedrike had addressed her in Plattdeutsch—the Low German indigenous to the north—the girl had replied in perfect High German.

Friedrike hoped that did not mean she was going to be a snob. But she did not think so. It was simply the good manners all the highly educated Meyers had been taught. She studied the girl. She was very tall for her age and extremely thin, almost scrawny. She had the long fine fingers of an artist or musician. Her face was long and rather homely but Friedrike looked beyond that and noted the determined chin and bright, intelligent brown eyes. She liked what she saw. Then when the girl reverted to Plattdeutsch to speak to Minna, she was reassured.

"Bring me your favorite book and I'll read you a story while your Mama fixes supper," she said.

The five-year-old ran to the bookshelf and came back with the time-worn copy of Grimm's. Although she could not yet read, Minna knew every picture by heart. She turned the pages carefully until she found the one she was looking for.

"That princess was very brave to kiss an ugly old frog. I'm scared to even touch one."

Alma laughed and started to read. Within a few minutes the two elder children, Hermann and Line, came in, their curiosity about the newcomer more than they could bear.

Thus Alma became a regular visitor to the Bruns household, beloved of the children and welcome companion to Friedrike. She refused to take a penny for her services. Johann bragged to everyone who would listen of the happiness she brought to his family. During the summer after she graduated from school she came even more frequently and spent longer hours with the children.

Everyone was keenly disappointed when at the end of the summer she announced, "Oma has finally talked Papa into letting me attend a finishing school abroad since he won't let me go to the gymnasium or university. I have a choice of England or Switzerland. Which do you think I should choose?"

Friedrike was so shocked at the thought of losing Alma that she barely heard the last question. "Oh, Alma, I shall miss you so. I've come to depend on you. Whatever shall I do without you?"

"It's only for two years and I'll be home for every holiday and for long summer vacations which is when you seem to need me most. Don't worry, Frau Bruns. I'll not desert you. But where do you think I should go?"

Friedrike pondered this. It was not a question she felt competent to answer, never having been outside of Germany in her life. Nor was she exactly sure what a finishing school was. "I should think England," she said at last. "Hannover has always been closer to England than to Swizterland or even to the states of the south. That way you could learn a new language, whereas in Switzerland you would still be speaking German, and not very good German at that." "That was my thought, too. But then I found out that most English girls go to Switzerland. And it would be in the French part, not the German," said Alma.

"Indeed?" Friedrike shook her head. "Then I don't know what to advise you. Most Germans hate the French for the devastation they wrought during the 'French Time'. That was before I was born but both my grandmothers spoke of it often. My Oma Elli was part French and spoke the language fluently. I never had a chance to learn because she died when I was very young—the same year my mother died."

"Then you, too, must have some French blood," said Alma.

"I suppose, but it goes way back—long before the French Time— back to Eleonore d'Olbreuse and the Huguenots who came with her. It's from the Matthies side."

"Oh? I didn't know you were related to the Matthies."

"Distantly," replied Friedrike rather cooly.

Friedrike returned from the post office one day with no letters but

713

with news. As she approached he house she could hear Johann practicing something on his fiddle. It was a lively, lilting melody.

"Look as these new stamps," she said. "Apparently Prussia has bought out the Thurn and Taxis Postal System and now we all have to use these stamps of the North German Confederation."

"And I read in the paper that diamonds have been discovered in South Africa," he replied.

She stopped in midstep. "You're not thinking of going to South Africa, are you?"

"No, of course not, silly. I couldn't care less about either thing. Just listen to the new waltz that has come out of Vienna. Fellow by the name of Johann Strauss wrote it. It's called *The Blue Danube*." He picked up his fiddle again and played a few bars. It was a catchy tune. Friedrike's feet moved to the waltzing rhythm of their own volition.

"Oh, don't stop," she said. "It's lovely."

He took her in his arms. "But I can't play and dance with my dearest love at the same time. I'll sing it to you." They waltzed around the room as he sang in his broken voice, "La-la-la-la-LA—la-la—la-la." And she was back in her youth again.

22

1870

1870 was a year of joy in one family and tragedy in another. It was a year of war against France, Germany's perennial enemy, which aroused fierce patriotism in most quarters and which helped toward the final unification but which instilled deeper hatred and fear of Prussia in many others, especially in Hannover and in some of the southern states, and added to everyone's mistrust of Bismarck.

It was a fine spring day in April and happy-go-lucky, carefree Johann Campsheide was out riding over his fields, deciding what to plant in each. There had been a minor setback to his plans when old Heidtmann had died and had not left the farm to him as he had hoped. The new owner was willing to sell part of it but at a price Johann did not feel the land was worth. So the new owner had promptly raised the rent and there was not a thing Johann could do about that because he needed the income in order to make payments on the large mortgage he had undertaken to purchase some of the other fields he had been renting.

Margarethe had been very upset at that. She may have been poorly educated but she had the peasant's innate shrewdness when it came to money. "That is stupid," she had complained. "The mortgage payments are far higher than the rent you were paying. You should have saved the difference and bought them outright."

"But don't you understand, my dear," he replied, "that when the mortgage is paid, they will be ours, totally ours? And no more payments of any kind to anyone."

"Except the taxes," she said, "which Prussia is raising all the time."

"Ach, that is minor. Gretchen, we have two sons to think of now. Some day this will all be theirs. This and any other fields I may buy before they are grown."

"Any other fields?" she snapped. "Don't even think of it. And they

715

will be well grown long ere that mortgage is paid off."

"Ach, twenty years. What's that?" he had replied.

And Johann was not thinking of any of that on this fine spring day. He was already envisioning the fields thick with healthy crops, his income for next autumn. He was happy also because Margarethe had just presented him with a new daughter, Sophie, just two weeks ago. He was a man without a care in the world.

After he surveyed the fields and decided on the plantings, he felt the need to release some of his pent-up energy. He had not been able to make love to his wife for the past two months and the midwife had warned not for a few more weeks. Well, the hell with the midwife. He was going to demand his conjugal rights tonight. Nay, not demand. He was sure he could coax Margarethe into it. She must be longing for it as much as he by now.

With that happy thought in mind, he set his horse to a gallop along the edge of the field. This particular field was bounded by a dense wood of very old, large trees, many of which actually overhung the field. The horse, glad for the opportunity, flew like the wind. As the horse ran, Johann paid little attention to his suroundings, his mind on planting—planting crops and planting a new babe in Margarethe's belly. The trees flashed by in a blur and his spirit and body were exhilarated by the speed. Johann never saw the thick branch protruding into his path.

The horse saw it, whinnied and tried to swerve. But too late. The branch struck Johann full in the chest, nearly decapitating him. His last thought as he flew through the air was, I won't be able to make love to her tonight. His body hit the ground with a sickening thud that broke his neck.

The horse wandered around, bewildered, for a while and then ambled off to home.

Hours later Margarethe noticed the riderless horse standing in the stableyard. She wondered where Johann was. It was not like him to leave the poor animal still saddled and not in his stall. But she was in the midst of nursing the new baby and still a little weak from the recent childbirth. She waited until the child was sated and Sophie back in her cradle before she went out to check. There was no sign of her husband. Where could he be? It took a while to dawn on her that the horse had come back on its own and Johann must have been thrown. Then she panicked.

She had no idea where to begin her search. Four fields, widely scattered, only one nearby. She searched that one first, calling and calling, but found nothing. She returned to the cottage and called to the big St.

Bernard, the only thing Heidtmann had left them. He was very old but his instincts and his nose were still good.

"Dorchen," she called to her eldest, only nine years old, "watch the little ones. I fear your Papa has been hurt and I must look for him."

"Can I come with you, Mutti?" asked five-year-old Wilhelm. "I'm good at finding rabbits and things. I want to help Papa if he's hurt."

"Nay, nay," she said, afraid of what she might find. "You stay here with Dorchen. If Papa needs help, I'll send Barni back for you. He'll know where to lead you." To the dog she commanded, "Go, fetch, Barni. Find your master." And she set off.

Unbeknownst to her, Marie, a strong-willed seven, and Wilhelm waited until she was out of sight and then quietly followed. Dorchen was too young and mild-mannered to control them and she knew she had to stay with the two youngest, Friedrich and Sophie.

Margarethe searched one field and then another as carefully as she could, calling and whistling to the dog. What was Johann wearing? She could not even remember. She was growing tired, her legs wobbly. She was still bleeding somewhat from the recent birth and she felt herself getting light-headed and weak. Just one more field, she told herself. Where can he be? He must be somewhere. She hoped he had not ridden off in some other direction. Then she would never find him. She had to fight the panic rising in her breast. Keep calm, keep calm. He will need your strength. She plodded on.

Just one more field—and this the farthest, quite some distance from the others. She had always told him she didn't like that arrangement. But never mind that now. Just keep looking and calling. Then as she approached the last field, the dog yipped and ran ahead of her. About half way down the wooded side of the field he stopped and started barking frantically. She picked up her skirts and tried to run. But in her weakened state she tripped over the stubble of last year's crop and fell.

Before she could pick herself up, Marie and Wilhelm were by her side. "Mutti, Mutti," cried Willi, "are you hurt, too?"

"Nay, just the wind knocked out of me and filthy dirty," she gasped. "But what are you two doing here? I thought I told you . . . " The dog's frantic barking finally impinged on her consciousness.

"Shall I go and see if he's found Papa?" asked Marie.

"Ja, go." But then on second thought, she said, "Nay, nay, wait for me. Help me up." She had bruised both knees and her weakened legs would hardly hold her up. Taking each child by the hand she hobbled

717

over to the dog. What she saw almost made her faint.

Johann's shirt was literally torn in half. His chest and throat were covered with congealing blood. But worst of all his head was twisted at the oddest angle. Dropping the children's hands she screamed and ran to him. She never felt her own bruises as she knelt by his side. When she took his hand, already ice cold, she knew it was too late. She threw herself on his bloody chest, kissing him and weeping hysterically as if the sheer strength of her love would revive him. But he was gone. Gone.

On 22 April 1870 Margarethe Campsheide became a widow with five small children at age thirty-four. A widow laden with debt and not even a home to call their own.

Marie, as young as she was, took charge. She knew her Papa was dead and she realized that Mutti had been reduced to a helpless bundle of nerves. She prayed her mother would not die as well from pure grief.

"Willi," she instructed, "run and fetch Herr Stühring and tell him to bring the wagon. Papa's dead and Mutti is sick."

"Is Papa really dead?" asked the little boy, totally bewildered.

"Ja, he is."

"And is Mutti going to die, too?"

"Not if you run fast and get help. I'll stay with her."

"Suppose Herr Stühring is not home?" he asked. "He sometimes isn't."

"Then find out where he is. Run all the way to Calle if you must. And tell Dorchen on the way. She has to know and she will help you. Now go."

Wilhelm ran as fast as his stocky little legs would carry him, the dog at his heels.

"Johann, Johann," moaned Margarethe, rocking back and forth on her knees. "What am I to do now? Oh, dear God, what am I to do now? Johann, Johann come back to me. Oh, dearest love, don't leave me. Johann, dear Johann, don't be dead!" And she kept on in this vein, sobbing hysterically, for the longest time.

Marie desperately wanted to comfort her mother but she did not know what to do. The very sight of her father's twisted body was seared on her brain forever. She did even want to get too close to it. After a long, long while Margarethe finally sat back in the dirt, sobbing great hiccoughing sobs but not as hysterical as she had been. Marie went to her and gently touched her shoulder but she would not look down. Her mother was still holding her father's cold hand. Margarethe started at Marie's caress and slowly looked up.

"Ach, you're still here. Your papa's dead, Marie. Gone," she whispered hoarsely.

"I know, Mutti. Maybe he's with God's angels," said Marie hopefully.

Margarethe shook her head. "What a sweet thought, but I don't know that I believe in angels—or even in God anymore, who took him from me."

"Oh, Mutti, you mustn't say that," gasped Marie, horrified.

"I suppose not but one wonders." She was silent for so long that Marie started to worry again.

"Mutti, I sent Willi to fetch Herr Stühring and his wagon. We can't leave Papa lying in the dirt."

"Did you now? That was a good girl," mumbled Margarethe. "I hope Willi doesn't get lost."

"Barni is with him. They won't get lost."

Margarethe shuddered and started to weep again. Marie took her hand and sat down beside her to wait. And a long wait it was. It seemed to the child that it took hours for help to come. At last they heard the wagon trundling across the unplowed field, the dog in the lead.

Wilhelm jumped down and ran to Marie. His mother seemed to him like an alien being. "Is Papa still dead?" he asked tremulously.

"Ja," sighed Marie. "Nobody comes back from the dead."

"And Mutti?" he asked.

"Mutti is sad. We must help her all we can."

Stühring climbed down from the wagon and looked over the scene. "Hmm. Must have hit that branch there." He pointed to the offending tree but no one looked. "Bad luck, that. Darn near cut him in half. I always told him he was too exuberant with that horse. Too late now."

Marie wished he would shut up and get on with it. But she just kept stroking her mother's shoulder and said nothing.

"Well, let's get him in the wagon. Move out of the way, children, and help your mother up." He made no move to assist Margarethe.

Marie said gently, "Come, Mutti, you've got to get up. Herr Stühring is going to put Papa in the wagon."

Margarethe nodded but made no move. As much as she hated to, Marie reached down to disentangle her hand from Johann's. The touch of that icy cold hand sent an unwelcome shiver through her. Gradually she coaxed her mother to rise and stand aside. Margarethe seemed in a daze.

Stühring picked up the corpse, slung it over his shoulder and, none too gently, threw it in the wagon. Margarethe gasped and made to run to him but Marie held her back. Stühring climbed up onto the wagon seat and said, "Come on, now, let's get him home. I have work to do."

Margarethe sat next to him on the driver's seat but the children had to ride in the back with their father's body. Marie held tightly to Wilhelm's hand. As they started off Barni jumped up to the wagonbed and began licking his master's face. That, more than anything else, clutched at Marie's heart and she let the tears flow freely.

On the way home Stühring said, "You'll have to have a laying-out lady. Do you know one?"

Margarethe shook her head.

"I'll send to Frau Humpelmann. She's fairly good and won't charge you much."

Margarethe nodded.

As they neared the cottage Stühring said, "I'll have to find me a new farmhand now. What a bother. Just at plowing time. You realize, of course, that you'll have to move out of the tenant house."

That woke Margarethe out of her fog. "Oh, no!" she gasped. "Where can we go? Please, Herr Stühring, give us a little time."

He shrugged. "Ja, I'll give you a little time but as soon as I find a new hand, you must leave. Just be aware of that. Don't you have family?"

"Ja, but they could never take us."

"Then I'll send to your husband's brother. He certainly has room for you."

"Oh, no. Not him. Never!" cried Margarethe.

They reached the cottage and Stühring unceremoniously dumped Johann's body on the bed. Margarethe would not go near it. She was so weak from emotional exhaustion she barely had strength to nurse baby Sophie, who by this time was yowling with hunger. Marie helped Dorchen fix a meagre supper but Margarethe refused to eat. That night she curled up with her daughters in the loft. No way would she sleep in the same bed with Johann's cold body.

The minute Hinrich Campsheide heard the news he took charge. He, who had never spoken to Johann but three or four times in all the years they had been married, and never once to Margarethe. He scarcely knew one child from another and he frightened them. He came bustling in with his old friend and part-time lawyer Dietrich Meyer of Barke—no relation to the distinguished Meyers of Vilsen.

He immediately had the old lawyer draw up a document making the two men legal guardians of the five children. "The woman's helpless, can't

720

you see?" Hinrich commented to Dietrich. "We'll have to register this at the county clerk's office in Hoya as soon as possible."

Margarethe, even at her brightest, did not know about such legal formalities but even in her fog of grief she wondered why she could not take care of her own children. But she felt helpless against their assault and merely nodded her reluctant consent.

"We'll find you another house as soon as possible," said Hinrich. "There's no question of you coming to us. I simply don't have the room."

Margarethe knew that for a lie but she was grateful she would not have to live with Becke again.

"I know of a small cottage in Calle that would suit," suggested Meyer. "It's been vacant for a long time."

"I'll look at it," replied Hinrich and they left.

A few days later Hinrich returned bearing a sheaf of papers. "Here is a copy of the writ appointing me legal guardian of your children until the end of this year."

"Just until the end of the year?" asked Margarethe hopefully.

"It has to be renewed every year until each one finishes school or reaches the age of fourteen. Then you can seek apprenticeships for the boys and places for the girls. Or I can do it for you, if you prefer."

Margarethe's face fell. "Let me see it."

"Can you read?"

"Of course, I can read," she snapped. He handed her the paper.

"I also had to obtain copies of the children's birth certificates for my records and a copy of my brother's death certificate which you may have. You will need it to try and collect welfare from the state. That is one good thing that Prussia has come up with."

"I see," she said, feeling more humiliated by the moment. "But why the children's birth certificates? It's all in the church book."

"To prove that they exist and that *I* shall now stand in place of their father. Of course, if you should ever remarry, your new husband could go though the same legal process if he chose. That is why the guardianship must be renewed every year."

"I have no intention of remarrying," she said as she choked back a sob. She was about to add how much she loved Johann but it seemed like profaning his memory in front of this man. "And what are these other papers you have?" she asked.

"This is a list of your husband's debts. I think you will find it in order.

Take a moment to look it over."

Margarethe looked at the final total first and gasped. She quickly sat down at the table and studied the list very carefully. She knew about the mortgage to the bank in Hoya, about the rents owed on the various fields plus a few things she herself had purchased like winter coats for the older children—they were growing so fast—but she had no idea that Johann had borrowed so heavily from other sources as well as owing several merchants for flour and seed. She willed herself to be calm as she checked item by item.

"Here are two debts that are duplicated," she said. "They are listed twice. This is shocking enough but I'll not be cheated."

Hinrich looked over her shoulder as she pointed out the errors. "Of course. You are correct. The clerk must have made a mistake. I'll have Herr Meyer make a note at the end revising the total. Do you disagree with anything else?"

She looked it over again before she replied. She seethed when she saw various clerks' fees for all these damn papers, a charge for Johann's coffin and for the children's birth certificates. What galled her most of all was a debt of two Thaler, five groschen owed to Hinrich himself. Evidently Johann had been paying off that strange marriage settlement ever since he was thirty-five. Couldn't the bastard have forgiven that, she thought.

"I'll have to take your word for it on many of these debts. I had no idea . . . But I could never pay that amount off in my entire lifetime. Even with the adjustments, that's almost three hundred Thaler. What am I to do?"

Hinrich looked about the pretty cottage. "You have far too much furniture to fit in the cottage in Calle. You'll have to sell some of it. Do you have any jewelry?"

She laughed ruefully. "Nothing but my wedding ring and I'll not part with that."

"The cows will have to go."

She was shocked. "But that's my butter and egg money and milk for the children. My only income now."

"Well, perhaps you can keep the chickens." He quickly changed the subject. "Have you looked at the cottage in Calle?"

"Nay. I haven't wanted to."

"You have no choice, Widow Campsheide. It is quite sound except for a few patches of rotten thatch which the owner has promised to replace. It is small but quite ample for your needs now that you no longer have a husband."

She gritted her teeth to keep from lashing out at him. What did he know of her needs?

After he left she was so furious that when she tried to feed Sophie the baby seemed to sense her anger and refused to nurse. Ach, I hope he hasn't soured my milk, she thought. After much coaxing she finally got Sophie to suck a little. At last she gave up and put the child in her cradle. I need some fresh air and exercise to work off my anger. It's not good for the babe, she told herself. I shall go and see this wonderful cottage.

"Willi, stay here and watch the baby until Dorchen comes home from school. I shan't be long."

"Where are you going? Can't I come with you?" Wilhelm was terrified of her leaving him ever since Papa died.

"I'm going to look at our new house. You must stay here and play nice with Fritz. I'll be back in less than an hour. Calle isn't far."

She trudged off down the lane, the dog following. Calle, indeed, was only a little over a half mile away but there were two lanes leading to it. She was not sure which one to take. She decided to take one and circle back on the other. She was bound to find it. Her heart was so heavy she took no pleasure in the sights and smells of spring—the freshly plowed earth and the beautiful apple blossoms on trees that lined so many of the roads in this area. She thought about her children. What would happen to them now with that devil as their guardian? Dorchen, so sweet and helpful, would probably never marry. That horrible birthmark around her eye was sure to turn away any man. And Marie, headstrong and determined, ja, she would do well in life. She did not worry about Marie. Willi was another strong one, constantly inquisitive, always wanting his own way. She hoped he would not turn out to be a bully but she did not think so. He had a lot of good qualities, too. He was caring, for one thing. Little Fritz, not yet three, was her favorite. He was so like Johann it tore at her heart. Quiet, with only an occasional flash of temper, he already loved flowers and animals but he also seemed to be a dreamer—too much like his father. And this concerned her. Well, he was too young yet to tell how he would turn out. And baby Sophie, newborn and not yet showing any personality. She would never have known her father—poor little waif.

She found the cottage. It was located directly on the Bücken-Asendorf road about half way between the two lanes from Barke. Next to it was a large apple orchard. At least that would be some benefit, provided

the owner would let her pick some. She looked with dismay at the building itself. It had a high, steeply pitched roof promising an ample loft but—
and that was a big 'but'—the roof came down almost to the ground. The
few tiny windows across the front were no higher than her chest and there
were no dormers or even skylights in the loft itself. The house would be
very dark and airless. That depressed her already as she thought of the
bright cheery house she would be leaving—and she had not even seen the
inside as yet. A man was working high up on the roof.

She called up to him, "Good afternoon. I am the new tenant. May I
look inside?"

"Go right ahead," replied the thatcher. "Door's open. Never ever
been locked, far's I know."

Oh, my, she thought, wondering what she would find. Just then
Barni raced across the unkempt grass in hot pursuit of a huge rat. Margarethe screamed.

The thatcher looked down and laughed. "I be disturbin' their nests,"
he said. "Quite a few of 'em up here. I'll try to get rid of the most of 'em for
ye. But ye'd best get a cat if'n ye don't have one. That'll scare 'em away."

Margarethe was almost afraid to enter, envisioning the vermin dropping on her head. She gathered her courage and pushed open the door.
The place was surprisingly clean and dry considering the condition of the
thatch. Of course, the dust of ages covered everything and there were little
piles of leaves in the corners, no doubt sheltering mice nests. She was startled when a sparrow flew out of the rafters and darted frantically about
until it found the open door. Oh, my, she thought, this place has been
home to more creatures than humans for a long time.

She looked about her. The cottage consisted of two rooms, one large,
one very small, with a fireplace in between. There was no stove. Well, she
sighed, I've cooked over open hearths before. I'll just have to again. There
was a sink but no pump. She wondered how far away the well was. Back to
chipping ice again in the winter. Cautiously she opened the back door.
The light breeze rustled the leaves about and she fully expected to see
more creatures emerge but none did. To one side of the back door a small
shed was attached to the house, presumably for firewood and hopefully
leading to a root cellar. The back yard was small but good enough for her
chickens and maybe a small garden. But it was so overgrown it would take
a lot of hard work. In the middle she found the well. She let down the
leaky bucket and drew up some water. She tasted it. Thank God, that at
least was pure and sweet. At the far edge of the yard stood a dilapidated

724

privy. She approached it with disgust. Quickly she threw open the door and stepped back. Sure enough, several wasps, angry at being disturbed, roared out. Once they settled down she put her head in. The stench, though bad, was not as overpowering as she had expected. Probably because no one had lived here for so long. It was a two-seater but one of the seats was cracked and the whole board looked splintery. She wondered if Hinrich Campsheide had inspected that. She doubted it. She did not even know who her new landlord was to be but he would have to fix that. The whole thing looked as though it would fall over at any moment.

She returned to the house to inspect the loft. The ladder looked sturdy enough but as she climbed one of the rungs cracked ominously. Another thing to be repaired. She climbed cautiously the rest of the way. The loft was quite large and comfortably high in the middle as she had expected from the pitch of the roof. She could hear the thatcher whistling to himself as he worked over her head. Every once in a while chunks of the old thatch fell down around her as he loosened them. She could smell the mildew. There were two small windows, one at either gable end so the loft was not completely dark. But they did not look as though they could be opened. The floor boards seemed sound enough although they were so widely spaced one could look down through the cracks to the room below. The children would love that and it would allow a little heat from the fire-place to rise up here. She could easily fit two beds and mayhap a chest up here. It would have to do. She had no choice. She climbed down carefully avoiding the cracked rung, shut the door behind her and went home. Home, she thought, not for much longer. This derelict was to be her home for the foreseeable future, perhaps forever.

Doris Bruns was enjoying her new life in Bremen. How different was life in the vibrant city compared to quiet little Vilsen. Not that she did not love her hometown but she was not the least bit homesick. She was too busy. She enjoyed her studies with the old master, although she early came to realize that as talented as she was, her work palled in comparison to the exquisite pieces of some of the other students. But she was determined to work hard and polish her efforts. She enjoyed all the new friends she had made, especially the cosmopolitan Bremers. But most of all she enjoyed the monthly teas — although most of them drank coffee — that the professor held in his home on Sunday afternoons for all his students and many former students.

At one of these gatherings back during the winter she had noticed a very handsome young man staring at her from across the room. He was not staring impolitely but twice when she looked up he was still looking at her, almost flirtatiously. At the third time, she gathered up her courage and smiled shyly. Usually there was nothing shy about Doris Bruns but she was not quite sure how to handle this. After everyone had been served and the guests began to mingle, he came over to her.

"May I join you?" he asked.

"By all means," she replied.

"I am Johann Menten. Hans to my friends. I don't recall seeing you here before. Are you new?"

"Not really. I have been here since the fall. I am Doris Bruns. And I don't recall seeing you either."

"I was away for a time in the fall and only come to these gatherings occasionally. I am a former student of the good professor but I like to attend once in a while to keep up with things. I am working now. However, you can be sure I shall come more often now that I have met you."

Doris looked at him askance. What a smooth-talking knave! But she felt pleased just the same. "And what sort of work do you do, Herr Menten?"

"I'm an electrical engineer."

"A what?" she asked perplexed. "I mean, I know what an engineer is. They build bridges and drive the railroad engines. But what is this 'electrical'?"

He smiled. "It is a brand-new field. Someday electricity will be a major source of light, heat and power. Men are just beginning to learn to generate it and harness its power." At her puzzled look he added, "Think of lightning. That is wild electricity."

"Oh, but that is frightening—and dangerous."

"But once it is controlled, it is not." He pointed to the gaslights on the wall. "Someday electricity will light those lights instead of gas. The horescars in the streets will be powered by electricity." He could see she had no concept of what he was talking about and apologized. "Forgive me for boring a beautiful woman with scientific things. I'm afraid I too often get carried away by my enthusiasm. Women are not expected to understand such things—especially a beautiful woman such as you. Tell me about yourself."

That she could understand. And he had called her beautiful—not once, but twice. "There is not much to tell," she replied. "I grew up in a small village called Vilsen, some miles south of here. My father is a pewterer and my mother, a fine weaver. I am the eldest of six children—six still living, that is. I have always loved to draw beautiful pictures and designs. So here I am."

"It is most unusual for—" he almost said peasants and quickly corrected himself "—for middle class artisans to permit a daughter to study art—or study at all, for that matter. You must have very understanding parents."

"Oh, I do. Both of them are artists within their own trades and Papa is also a musician. He is very—er—lenient. But if it hadn't been for the Queen I should not have been able to come here at all."

He was not sure if he heard aright. "The Queen?"

"I should say *former* Queen Marie. Mama always calls her the Duchess of Cumberland. They have been dearest friends for years."

This really sparked Johann's interest. Perhaps this country girl was worth cultivating after all. And she *was* beautiful. "And what had the Queen to do with it? Do you know her as well?"

"She came to visit us once before she was forced into exile. I met her then and she was impressed with my talent. I feel sad that the Prussians sent her away. She is a wonderful person. It was she who gave Mama the money for my tuition here."

"I am impressed," said Johann, meaning it. "I have never known anyone who hobnobbed with royalty."

She laughed. "Walking through the woods to the ancient watermill where my mother was born is hardly hobnobbing. But the poor woman was so distraught, I think the peaceful country helped to calm her and refresh her soul."

"That is very interesting." The party was beginning to break up around them so he quickly said, "I should like to see you again—before next month, that is. Will you take coffee with me next Sunday afternoon?" She agreed with alacrity. "And now permit me to walk you home."

She was a little more hesitant about that. "It's not far. Only a few blocks away. I can manage, thank you."

"But I insist. Even a few blocks more of your company, I shall cherish."

Oh, you smooth-talking knave, she thought, but she agreed.

Johann took Doris to an exclusive coffee house the next Sunday and to another the Sunday after that. He soon realized that she was not only beautiful but also highly intelligent and well-read. He enjoyed their con-

727

versations on all manner of subjects although he carefully avoided confusing her with talk about his profession. Soon he was escorting her to operas, concerts and intellectual soireés. And Doris revelled in every bit of it. She may have been an innocent country girl in some ways but she was no fool. Although she felt herself falling in love with him, she still did not trust him.

And she would have been right in that. All Johann could think of was how to get her into his bed. He wanted her so badly it was beginning to hurt. He had never had this problem with women before. Usually they fell at his feet. And yet he had never felt this way about a woman before. However, when he invited her to his apartment, she demurred, mumbling something inane about needing a chaperone.

Usually a refusal like that would cause him to drop the lass and seek out another. But he could not. He wanted to be with her no matter what terms she set. He dreamed about her day and night. Could he be falling in love? Perish the thought. And then a fear struck him. Perhaps she did not love him. They had never spoken of any such thing. After several agonizing weeks of debate and frustration, he realized that he truly did love her and that there was only one way to make her his very own.

He proposed.

And to his great joy, she accepted.

When Johann Bruns met his eldest daughter at the train station at Eystrup at Eastertime, he realized that his kleine Dorchen was a woman grown. He watched in awe as a vision in pink descended from the car. Her dress had a modest bustle which only enhanced the slim princess style of the front. The bodice had myriad tucks lined with piping, very narrow lace and tiny seed pearls. A small, perky hat sat atop her pompadour in the latest style. He was afraid to hug her and kiss her as he had intended. She kissed his cheek and then, very lady-like, placed a gloved hand on his arm as he led her to the old wagon.

He dusted off the wagon seat with his handkerchief and then spread it out for her to sit on.

"Can't have you sitting on that old board with that beautiful gown. Did you make it yourself?"

"Nay, Papa. They have ready-made shops in Bremen where the seamstress only has to take a tuck here and there and adjust the hemline."

"Ready-made, eh? My goodness, what next? Your mother will want to hear about that. And did you spend the Duchess' money on that?"

"Only a little bit," she prevaricated. "It wasn't expensive." No way would she admit that it was an engagement gift from Hans.

"And how are your studies going?"

"Very well. I've submitted a few of my illustrations to the *Bremer Zeitung* and am waiting to hear from them."

"You mean they might actually buy them?" he asked astounded.

"I'm hoping so. If I'm to make my living with my art, it would be a good start."

"Your living! Ach, what is this world coming to?" He forbore asking any more questions. He could tell she was bubbling over with some sort of news—he hoped good—which she would undoubtedly share with them once they were home. He wondered what it could be. Mayhap she had already sold one of her pictures. He did not have to ask it she were happy. Her cheerful demeanor told him that.

When they reached home, Friedrike embraced her lovingly and then held her at arm's length. She admired the gown, of course. Immediately alarm bells went off in her mind. That gown was far beyond their means. But then she looked into her daughter's eyes. "You are a woman in love," she exclaimed. "You have a man. Does he love you, too? I can see he has been good to you."

Doris did not blush easily but she should have known her wise mother would guess her secret. "Yes, I do and yes, he does. We are going to be wed in June. I am so happy. I couldn't wait to tell you."

Johann could not believe what he was hearing. How did women know these things? He would never have recognized the signs in a thousand years. And then another thought occurred to him. His eldest about to be wed and Fritzi had recently told him that she was breeding again. Wouldn't that be the height of irony having a son and a grandson at the same time? But he kept these thoughts to himself as he commented, "Rather short notice, isn't it? Is it anyone we know?"

"Nay, Papa," replied Doris. "Hans—his name is Johann, too—is from Bremen. But he wants to meet you both and all the children. With your permission I'll write and ask him to come for a few days during this Easter recess."

"That would be nice. I want to be sure this Hans is worthy of my daughter," mumbled Johann. But he already knew the whole thing was out of his control. He felt defeated.

"Ja, and we must notify Pastor right away," added Friedrike. "It's too bad Anni is away. She should be your maid of honor."

"Nay, Mama," said Doris. "We are going to be wed in Bremen."

"In Bremen?" exclaimed Friedrike. "But how . . . ?"

Doris ignored that and went on, "One of the girls I live with will stand for me. It's all planned. Hans has so many friends, I'm not sure which one he will choose. And don't worry about the expense. Hans is paying for everything."

Friedrike gasped. "But that is unseemly."

"These are modern times, Mama. Hans is wealthy. Let him. But you both must come. I should feel bereft if you didn't. He will pay for your train fare and a hotel room."

Friedrike gasped again. And suddenly there flashed through her mind the Gypsy's prediction. 'This one will marry wealth but beyond that it is cloudy.' The first part of that foretelling was coming true. She prayed fervently that the second half would not.

Hans arrived a few days later. He did not take the train from Bremen but drove his own classy gig. He quickly overwhelmed both parents with his glib talk and smooth personality. He set all Friedrike's fears to rest. He was an expert at handling women. He entertained Johann with details of his profession and explanations of the potential of electricity. And was delighted when Johann understood most of it. He strolled with Doris through the woods and out to the Klostermühle which she had told him so much about.

But even there, he was not interested in the history of the ancient mill but its future potential.

"Someday a watermill like that will be able to generate electricity," he said.

Once again Doris was puzzled. "I know about water power. It's been used for centuries. But I don't see the connection."

"The waterwheel drives a turbine which generates the electricity. In America they are already working to harness the huge cascade called Niagara Falls."

"I have seen pictures of that," she said laughing. "'Tis somewhat larger than this little brook. I have read that many Americans go there for their honeymoon."

At that he remembered his promise not to bore her with technicalities. She wanted romance and she would have it. He took her in his arms and kissed her longingly. In just two months she would be his. He found that he was a romantic as well.

Meanwhile Bismarck was busy trying to consolidate his North German Confederation and to integrate the annexed states into the Prussian module. He knew it would be some time before he could turn his eyes to the southern states because they still looked toward Austria, were largely fervent Catholics and especially as the individualistic independence movements were still very strong in most of them. Their centuries-old fear of France was the only thing that made them, collectively, even consider leaning toward Prussia.

Then an unexpected development in Spain gave Bismarck the opportunity to use his devious, intricate diplomatic maneuvering to achieve his goal — namely to end the French threat once and for all. The Spanish conservatives had forced their dissolute Queen Isabella into exile and looked around to the European royal families for a likely successor. Their choice fell upon the scion of an obscure branch of the Hohenzollern family, a distant cousin of King Wilhelm of Prussia, named Leopold von Hohenzollern-Sigmaringen. This branch of the family was the only one remaining on the ancestral Hohenzollern lands, a small southern state tucked in between Baden and Württemberg. They were still Catholic although Leopold's father had pledged their allegiance to Prussia, the only southern state to do so.

Spain's choice of a cousin of the Prussian king immediately sent waves of indignation through France. France feared, above all, a renewing of the empire of Charles V with Prussia lapping at her southern frontier. Wilhelm had given his reluctant approval to the succession but Bismarck vehemently disapproved, not that he cared much what happened in Spain. He saw it as a chance to aggravate France.

France immediately sent an emissary, Count Benedetti, to Bad Ems on the river Lahn where Wilhelm was taking the waters. The first talks were cordial enough but there was the implied threat of war, which Wilhelm greatly feared, if Leopold did not withdraw his candidacy. Since Wilhelm had not really been in favor of the whole thing anyway, he persuaded Leopold's father, Prince Karl Anton, to announce that his son was no longer interested in the Spanish throne. Since no one really knew Leopold's own stance on the matter, Benedetti suspected trickery. So he added another demand that no further candidacy of a Hohenzollern would ever be considered. Wilhelm balked at this, saying he could give no guarantee for the future and therefore further talks were pointless.

Bismarck was furious at Wilhelm's apparent crumbling before the

French threats. He regarded the French diplomatic triumph as an insult to Prussia. When on 13 July 1870 one of Wilhelm's aides sent the famous 'Ems dispatch' to Bismarck, he outlined the talks with Benedetti in concise detail and left it to the Chancellor's discretion how much to release to the press. Bismarck edited the dispatch he released to the press in such a way that it appeared that Benedetti's last demand was his only demand and that Wilhelm had refused to talk to the ambassador.

The French government took this as a grave insult. They further thought they could count on the south German states to remain neutral and that they would break their defensive alliance with Prussia. What the French did not realize was that the southern states feared a threat from France far more than possible union with Prussia. On 19 July 1870 France declared war on Prussia.

The Franco-Prussian war was to be the bloodiest European war of the nineteenth century. France relied on her more professional army but she still used outmoded cavalry tactics. What she was not even aware of was the rapidity with which Prussia could mobilize her vastly superior numbers and move them into action with far more modern weapons. Although the Prussians won many decisive victories, the conduct of the war was plagued by dissension between Bismarck, the statesman, and von Moltke, the commander-in-chief, as well as interference from King Wilhelm. Thus when the Prussia army reached Paris in January of 1871, Bismarck forbade a direct assault on the city, hoping that a siege would encourage the French to elect a government willing to negotiate peace.

The war was greeted with enthusiastic patriotism in most of Germany, especially by those who did not have to fight in it. The fact that corps and regiments from every state in the North German Confederation including Hannover joined the Prussian war effort was seen as a sign that unification was solidifying. The County of Hoya alone lost thousands of young men, over two hundred from Vilsen. One of the saddest things that stuck in the craw of those at home was that the Prussians took the great bells of their beloved Vilsen church and melted them down for cannon.

Friedrike Bruns thanked God that her Hermann was too young to go; Adelheit Matthies was grateful that her two boys were still minors; Margarethe Campsheide was equally thankful that her two little sons would not know war—at least not yet.

Toward the end of 1870 Bismarck decided the time was ripe to turn his attention to the southern states. They were happy with the German victory over France since they had always been the most vulnerable to

French onslaughts from Charlemagne through Louis XIV to the two Napoleons. They were also aware that with the treaties of the Customs Union, which had been very lucrative for them, soon expiring, Prussia could force their annexation either financially or militarily, if she so chose. Bismarck was very careful to make it appear that they were joining the union voluntarily and not by coercion.

All sorts of plans were put forward including the ancient 'land-grab' techniques, that is, both Bavaria and Württemberg wanted pieces of other states' territories and suggested that Prussia could 'reward' the 'donors' by carving up the newly conquered Alsace. Bismarck rightly wanted no part of such arrangements. He declared Alsace a province of the federal government. Bavaria in particular was a hard nut to crack. Her prime minister and her mad King Ludwig insisted on maintaining her independence. At most Bavaria suggested a South German Confederation to be ruled jointly by Bavaria and Prussia. But times had changed and Bismarck had had his fill of dualism after his experience with Austria some years back. He deemed it wisest to negotiate with each state separately, which he did. On 15 November Baden and Hesse-Darmstadt were the first to sign treaties. By the end of the month Württemberg and Bavaria fell into line, with Bavaria still demanding special privileges and exemptions, few of which she achieved. Bavaria's acquiescence was apparently brought about by a huge secret bribe to King Ludwig paid out of the stolen Welf fund.

Bismarck's next task was to convince King Wilhelm of Prussia to accept the crown and title of emperor over this vast territory. Wilhelm did not want it and considered it meaningless. He was too proud of being King of Prussia. Bismarck knew he would never accept the title from the hands of the various state parliaments as his father had refused back in 1848 to be 'at the mercy of those demagogues'. So Bismarck craftily convinced Ludwig of Bavaria—as part of his handsome bribe—to write a letter to Wilhelm saying how delighted he and all the other princes would be if Wilhelm would accept the imperial dignity. Bismarck himself actually drafted the letter and personally urged each of the other princes to give their consent. Wilhelm still struggled against it until Bismarck explained that, in order to offend no one, he could not call himself 'Emperor of Germany' or 'Emperor of the Germans' but merely 'German Emperor'. Thus on 18 January 1871 in the hall of mirrors at Versailles, surrounded by his cheering army, Wilhelm was proclaimed German Emperor.

Blithely unaware of all this, on 15 November 1870, the same day that Baden entered the union, little Marie Anna Bruns made her way into the world to the delight of her parents Friedrike and Johann, both of whom had thought they were too old for such a blessed event.

23

Right from the start Marie Anna Bruns was everyone's favorite. A tiny baby yet she seemed strong and healthy. Before long her sunny personality manifested itself. Although christened with the dignified name of Marie, after the former queen, she was soon known as Mimi by one and all.

1873 By the time Mimi was three, she was already singing little folk songs that Friedrike taught her and dancing while Johann played his fiddle. This endeared her to her father even more. When she went on walks through the woods with Mama and Lise she found her own special place to pretend to hide. Unlike her great-grandmother before her, she did not choose the flat rock but rather an old stump just the right size for her little bottom. Those walks because of their infrequency became very precious to her. Alma Meyer, too, doted on her. Whenever Alma was home from school on holidays or for the summer she spent an inordinate amount of time with the Bruns children. She delighted in teaching Mimi all sorts of things, even a few words of French. And Mimi was a quick learner.

One day there was a great deal of excitement in Vilsen. For months stonecarvers had been working on a monument to honor the men from Vilsen who had died in the Franco-Prussian war. Some years before the congregation of the church had purchased a large tract of land on the hillside above Gartenweg for a new cemetery. The old burial ground around the church, in use since the dawn of time, had been filled to overflowing. Now a new Prussian law stated that any graves that were not maintained or were older than thirty years would have the tombstones removed. A few bodies were reinterred in the new cemetery but the majority were so ancient that the stones were pulled down and destroyed. This caused a great deal of consternation among the Bürgers as many of them were of great historical value. Many were especially upset when Friedrich Matthies had donated the two boundary stones of his ancestors and paid to have them cemented into the wall of the church tower. The few who remembered old Anton Matthies commented that he must be awhirling in his grave, he who had so rarely attended church. Many of subsequent generations believed they were gravestones and should have been destroyed with the rest until a historian pointed out that they were both dated 1806 and all the parties represented thereon had died long after that.

Now the new monument to Vilsen's fallen heroes was ready to be dedicated and placed in the chruchyard under the great linden tree. And there was to be a parade. A contingent of Prussian soldiers from the Hannover regiment had been sent to fire the salute. Along with them would march several local groups including the Bürgermeister and Town Council, the local militia, the police and fire brigades, the remnants of some of the craft guilds and a large group of youths from the church congregation.

The town fathers had beforehand given out hundreds of tiny flags to the children of both Bruchhausen and Vilsen—the new flag of the German Empire. And therein lay a problem. Bismarck had designed the new banner, black, white and red, by combining the black and white flag of Prussia with the red and white marine emblem of the Hanse because King Wilhelm wanted nothing to do with the old black, red and gold flag of '48. Wilhelm did not even like this new flag until Bismarck pointed out that it was a combination of the Prussian and Brandenburg pennants, discreetly making no mention of the Hanse symbol.

However, there were many in Vilsen, still a dedicated pro-Welf stronghold, who hated the new flag and what it represented. Among them was Johann Justus Bruns.

"I'll not have my children waving that thing," he grumbled to Friedrike, "or marching with Prussians, for that matter."

"Ach, it's just a small thing and the little ones don't understand what it's all about," she replied. "Although I agree with your sentiments, let them have their fun. They've been so looking forward to it."

"That's just the trouble. Few people understand anymore. The Prussians claim this is to be a celebration of the beginning of the French war but in reality it is to commemorate their victory over us at Langensalza. That is a slap in the face to Hannover."

"Ach, Johann, let go. Few people still think that way," said Friedrike.

Minna and Line had been asked to march with the Sunday School children. Now determined Minna joined the argument. "Papa, Pastor asked us to walk with the Sunday School and we promised him we would.

We can't go back on that now."

Even mild Line spoke up. "Ja, that's right. And besides he told us it was to honor the heroes who died and not all those other things you are talking about."

Johann was about to sputter but then he realized that, although it was only seven years since Prussia had conquered Hannover, it was already the distant past to his children.

Lise started to cry. "Please, Papa, let us go."

But it was tiny Mimi who turned his heart. She climbed on his lap and said, "Papi, I've never seen a parade before. All the other children say it's such fun to watch and wave the little flags. We wouldn't want them to think our Papa's mean—when we know he's the best papa in the world." She kissed his cheek and his heart melted.

"Very well, you may go," he acquiesced. But he made up his mind that, when they were old enough to understand, he would carefully explain what Prussia had done to Hannover.

That same year a worldwide financial panic spread across the Atlantic from America. It reached Germany in October 1873. Since most of Germany had joined the industrial revolution very late compared to other countries such as England and huge corporations and conglomerates were only beginning to spread their wings, such a panic would previously have had only a small ripple effect but for two things. A few years before Prussia, in an attempt to play economic catchup, had repealed the law requiring the formation of all joint-stock companies to be approved by the government. As a result a proliferation of new companies, most respectable but poorly financed, many outright fraudulent, occurred and a frenzy of investing took place. The panic swept away fortunes and the savings of many small holders. Although the fall in consumer prices actually benefitted others as the dip in wages was slight.

In 1871 Prussia had introduced the mark in all the annexed states, prohibiting the minting or printing of any more of their thirty-three different currencies. She had given the people and businesses two years to exchange their old money into marks. Now in 1873 it became obligatory to do so and the old money would become obsolete and worthless. The curious name of mark for the Prussian currency dates way back to the dim mists of the early Middle Ages when the Emperor transferred a rambunctious duke in—not of—Saxony to the marches (marks) east of the Elbe to protect what was then Germany from the incursions of the Slavs as well as

737

to make room for Welf Heinrich der Löwe, the legitimate duke of Saxony. As a cash economy gradually developed, most of the western states adopted the Thaler, named for the Jacobsthal where it was first minted, but Brandenburg (later Prussia) called her coins marks. The Thaler had a long and relatively stable history—the Lübeckerthaler of the Hanse, the Reichsthaler of the Empire and, after the French Time, plain thaler of various states. Thus it was trusted and respected by all, and, especially in Hannover where most people tended to hate anything that was Prussian, the mark was totally distrusted.

"Just look at this thing," said Johann Justus, flipping one of the silver coins on the table, "with Wilhelm's portrait on the front and the eagle on the back. Why, that eagle belongs to the old Empire not to Prussia."

"It's now the German Empire," corrected Friedrike.

"It takes more than four of these to make one Thaler. That's inflation," he declared. "I won't use them, I tell you."

"Well, you'd better. If you don't exchange our Thalers, and that right soon," she urged, "our entire life savings will be worthless."

"I know," he sighed in disgust. "Prussia never gives a man any choice, does she?"

1874   It was a lovely May morning and the children wished they were out playing but they sat obediently around the shoemaker's shop while their elder sister Caroline Bruns perched in the shoemaker's great chair to try on her new shoes under the watchful eye of their mother Friedrike. Next Sunday was Pfingsten—Pentecost—and Line was about to be confirmed in the church and graduated from school—a simultaneous rite of passage—and Line was very excited, more about her new shoes and clothes than about the pending ceremonies. More and more in recent years factory-made shoes were undermining the livelihoods of master shoemakers reducing them to the role of mere cobblers—shoe repairmen. Thus Master Schuhmacher was grateful for die-hards like Friedrike Bruns who insisted on only the best for her children. The shoes were expected to last for many years and to be handed down to each of the younger ones in turn.

Minna watched the fitting with envy. They were pretty high-button shoes in soft but sturdy kid. In two or three years they would be hers. Lise worried that they would be old and shabby by the time she ever inherited them. Little Mimi, if she thought about it at all, reasoned that they would be all worn out by the time they would fit her and maybe, just maybe, by the time she was fourteen Mama would buy her a new pair.

In any event, Mimi was more interested in the new arrivals who entered the shop just as Line climbed down from the chair and, walking to and fro, proclaimed that the new shoes fit well and were quite comfortable. Two small children followed a dour-looking, sharp-faced woman who was obviously much younger than Mama but appeared much older.

"Good morning, Frau Bruns. I see your daughter is getting ready for the big day."

"Good morning, Frau Campsheide," replied Friedrike. "Ja, I'm afraid so. With my Doris wed and all the others—er—gone, it's like having a second family with Line the eldest.

"Ach," sighed Margarethe, "at least you still have them with you. They're taking mine away from me—one by one."

Friedrike thought she detected tears in the other woman's eyes. While she had never cared for Margarethe Campsheide and did not know her well, she felt sorry for her, widowed so young. "What do mean?" she asked. "Who's taking them away from you? And why?"

"My brother-in-law, Hinrich Campsheide. Oh, how I hate that man," she exclaimed and quickly put her hand over her mouth. "I should not have said that. But he claims I cannot care for them properly on the little bit of welfare the state gives me. He also implies that because I am a peasant I am not capable of bringing them up to be worthy of the la-de-dah Campsheide name."

"Then why doesn't he help you?"

"Him? He wouldn't give a penny to a dog, much less to me. I had to sell all my lovely furniture, my cows, even the fruit on the trees to pay all my late husband's debts, including a large one to that same greedy brother. He couldn't even forgive that."

"I'm sorry to hear that. But what right has he to take the children away?"

"Within two days after my Johann's death he made himself legal guardian of the children." she sobbed bitterly. "I was so grief stricken at the time I wasn't aware of what it would mean. I thought, as you say, that he would help care for them, see that they had food and clothing and an education. But now," she sobbed again, "now he insists that the moment they turn seven I farm them out to others. My Marie and Wilhelm are already gone and now my little Fritz," she nodded towards the little boy who was visiting with Mimi and Lise, "must go. He will be seven in August."

"That's terrible," commiserated Friedrike. "Do you know where they are?"

"Oh, yes. At least he gave me that much choice—probably because he did not want them in any Campsheide household. Marie is with my Rajes cousins in Haendorf; Willi is with my sister in Bassum. Fritz will go to my other sister in Hoya. Thank God he left me my sweet Dorchen. I pleaded that I needed her help but I think it was really because he felt no one would want her. She is marked, you know. If people would only look beyond that to see what a sweet, loving girl she is and so capable, too. She is being confirmed this Sunday in Bücken church but no new clothes for her, I am afraid." She looked enviously at Line parading up and down in her new shoes.

Fritz, meanwhile, was bragging to Lise and Mimi. "I am going to get new shoes so I can visit my uncle in Hoya," he said.

"Ooo, that's a long ways away," commented Lise.

"Not so far," he said. "It's only a two-hour walk from our house. Probably take you longer because you're still little. I'm going to be seven in August and I'll be starting school."

"I'm not so little," objected Mimi indignantly. "And we're going to watch the Pfingst-ox parade on the day after Sunday," she added, not to be outdone.

"Are you coming to see it?" asked Lise.

"I'd like to," replied Fritz. "I've never seen it. But I'm not sure if Mama will let us."

"She might not but Dorchen will if we're real sweet to her." His little sister Sophie spoke up for the first time. She was only a few months older than Mimi but already she seemed wise beyond her years.

"Do you think she might?' asked Fritz.

"She will if you help her with some of her chores instead of sitting around dreaming all day," replied Sophie.

Mimi and Lise looked at each other. They all had chores, of course, but on Pfingstmonday all chores except the most essential were forgotten. The entire village turned out for the Pfingst-ox parade. Both girls immediately felt sorry for their new friends.

"He doesn't realize," whispered Margarethe to Friedrike, "that he is not going to Hoya for just a visit but for good. He is so sensitive—so like my dear Johann—that I hate to disillusion him."

"It would be better if you did," replied Friedrike. "Give him a chance to get used to the idea while he is still with you. Make it sound exciting, like an adventure."

Margarethe thought about that for a moment. "Perhaps," she said dully.

Friedrike paid for Line's shoes and said, "Come, children, we must go now. Perhaps you'll see your new friends on Monday." She looked pointedly at Margarethe.

"Perhaps," said Margarethe sadly and without much enthusiasm.

As they walked home Friedrike thought to herself, why, that woman does not even know how to smile much less have any fun. How I pity those poor children. Mayhap they are better off away from her. She watched her four, Mimi and Lise skipping along as carefree as could be, Line and Minna trying to act as ladylike as possible. Ach, Johann, we'll need your fiddle tonight, she thought. God be thanked that you have made us such a happy family.

On the Monday people were already lining the streets of Vilsen at first light although the parade was not scheduled to start until almost ten o'clock in order to give the farmers time to bring their beasts in from the countryside. It was no longer as elaborate as Friedrike remembered from her childhood nor as competitive as Oma Dorchen had often described. It was no longer a race at all, simply a decorous parade to display the beautifully intricate floral displays that decorated the homely oxen. In fact, there were far fewer oxen than in years gone by. Most farmers now used horses for their plowing. But the judging was still taken very seriously and a welcome prize awarded to the winner. And it was fun for the children with a picnic and dancing afterward.

"Come on, Line," urged Lise, "you don't have to dress so fancy for a bunch of dumb old oxen. We'll be late."

"I'll dress how I please," retorted her sister. "There's plenty of time yet."

"But I want to go out to the field where the parade starts," said Minna. "That's when the flowers will be the freshest."

"Oh, no," insisted Line. "We are going to stand closest to the judges as possible. That's where all the people will be."

"I'm going to stand next to Papa," put in Mimi, "so he can hold me up so I can see."

Friedrike decided it was time to step into the argument. "We are not going way out to the assembly field nor are we standing near the judges where it will be pure chaos. We'll wait where Papa and I decide is best—

probably at the entrance to the meadow where we can see each ox as it passes." And the girls had to be satisfied with that.

As they were waiting for the first oxen to appear, a little girl dragging her older sister by the hand came up to them. "Hello, Mimi," she said. "Do you remember me? I'm Sophie Campsheide."

"Of course, I remember you, Sophie," replied Mimi. "We met at the shoemaker's. Your brother was going to get a new pair of shoes. Is he here today?"

"He's around somewhere." Sophie pulled her sister forward. "This is my eldest sister Dorchen."

Friedrike was shocked to see the terrible birthmark on what otherwise might have been a comely face and it became even more pronounced as the girl blushed.

"I am Dorothea Campsheide and you must be Frau Bruns," she said shyly, trying to turn her face to the good side. "Mama could not come today and the little ones begged so to see the oxen with the flowers after talking with your children that I felt I just had to bring them."

"It is well worth seeing," replied Friedrike, "as I'm sure you know. The farmers put so much work into the decorations. Many are like works of art, as you no doubt remember."

Dorothea shook her head. "I'm afraid I have never seen it myself," she admitted.

"You haven't?" exclaimed Friedrike.

"Nay. I—er—don't go much of any place."

And no wonder, thought Friedrike. But she tried to put Dorothea at ease. "Then come and meet my other daughters. This is Caroline—you must be of an age. How old are you?"

"Fourteen," replied Dorothea.

"The very same. You could be friends," suggested Friedrike, hoping Line would take the hint and be kind to this unfortunate. "And this is Minna and Lise. Mimi seems to have already made the acquaintance of your little sister."

"Ja, that is Sophie and Fritz . . . Sophie, where has Fritz got to?" she asked sharply.

"He's over there—sulking," replied Sophie.

"Well, go and fetch him. Can't have him sulking on a fine day like this. He is the one, most of all, who wanted to see the flowers."

"I'll go with you," said Mimi to Sophie, taking her new friend by the hand as they skipped off.

742

Line had no intention of becoming friends with Dorothea. In fact, she was repulsed by the girl's ugly disfigurement. "I have friends I promised to meet here," she said abruptly and turned away.

Friedrike was about to call her back and make her apologize for her rudeness but then decided it would only embarrass poor Dorchen further. Minna, however, had no such qualms. She took Dorchen's hand. "I'll be your friend," she said. "My sister is too haughty by far. That's why she has no friends."

Meanwhile Mimi said to Friedrich, "Why don't you come and stand with us, Fritz? We have a good place and Papa is going to lift me up so I can see all the pretty oxen."

"Don't want to," he mumbled. "Don't want to stand with a bunch of girls."

Mimi was too young to know that Friedrich was at the age when boys hated all things female. "But Papa's a man," she insisted. "He's the best man in the world. Come on."

"You're lucky you have a papa," said Friedrich.

"But don't you . . . ?"

Sophie interrupted, "Our Papa died right after I was born."

"Oh," replied Mimi, shocked. "I didn't know. Is that why you're so sad, Fritz? I would be, too, if I didn't have my Papa." But Mimi always tried to look on the bright side. "Come on, why don't you let my papa be your papa just for today?" she suggested.

When Friedrich did not reply, Sophie put in again, "He's sad because he's going to Hoya."

"But why?" asked Mimi. "I should think going to Hoya would be fun. I've never been there."

Friedrich had enough of the inquisition. "Shut up, Sophie," he said rancorously. And to Mimi, "You're too young to understand. It's not for a short visit. It's for ever. Mama is putting us out of the house one by one. My brother Willi is already gone and my sister Marie, too. She doesn't love us and—and—" his voice rose in pitch with every word, "I hate her."

Mimi watched helplessly as the tears streamed down his face. She wanted to hug him, comfort him, but she sensed that that would not be welcome. Very unobtrusively she slipped her hand into his. She felt him about to pull away when someone in the crowd shouted, "Here they come. Here they come." The crowd surged forward and they were trapped. They could not get back to Mimi's parents. Instead Friedrich tightened his grip on her hand and pulled her forward. He placed her right in front of him at the very edge of the street.

When he saw the first gaily decorated ox, his whole demeanor seemed to change. He was enthralled by the spectacle and his love of flowers overcame his dark mood. "Look," he pointed out, "see how the iris are dripping purple on the ox's white coat. And the peonies—they're too delicate for something like this but, oh, they smell so sweet. And daffodils— now where did they get daffodils this late in the spring?"

And Mimi saw an entirely different boy from the sullen creature they had first encountered and she was as enchanted as though he wove a fairy tale out of each beautiful flower.

1876   Two years later a very agitated Adi Matthies came pounding on the door of the Bruns cottage. They still thought of her as Adi Matthies even though she had been married to Farmer Schierenhop for many years and had borne him numerous children. Friedrike stopped her loom and went to the door. It was an extremely hot July day and the sweat was pouring down Adi's face—or was it tears?

"Why, Adi, what a surprise," exclaimed Friedrike, embracing her. Adi's gown was soaking wet. She must have run all the way. "How nice to see you. But whatever is the matter?"

"It's the boys," she gasped.

"An accident? Is someone hurt?"

"Nay, nay. They've run away. My Henni and your Harm. And Schierenhop won't do a thing about it. He says let them go and good riddance. He never liked my two and now—now—oh, I don't know what to do," she wailed.

"Calm yourself, Adi. Come sit down and I'll make some chamomile tea." Friedrike led her to the table and put the kettle on. "I thought you said he was kind to your boys."

"Ach, kinder than old Matthies but I always felt he sort of resented them even though I've given him so many of his own."

Friedrike poured the tea. "Now tell me what happened and why you think they've run away. Couldn't it be just a childish lark? It is a hot day and I'm sure the first haying is done by now."

Adi nodded and tried to control her sobbing. "Willi thinks they've gone to America."

"America!" exclaimed Friedrike. "I know they're always talking about it but they're underage and couldn't possibly have enough money." Then she thought of her Anni who had emigrated at age thirteen. "Or could they?"

"I don't know," sighed Adi. "I know Henni has saved almost every penny Schierenhop paid him and I imagine your Harm has, too." She put her head on the table and wept.

"Come now, Adi. Weeping won't solve anything. Let us put our heads together and think."

"I was hoping your Johann Justus would go after them. They can't have gotten far unless—unless . . . Willi thinks they may have taken the train. We don't live that far from Eystrup."

"Let me call Johann," volunteered Friedrike. "He will know what to do."

Hermann was now living entirely with the Matthies boys and working for their stepfather Farmer Schierenhop. He rarely came home except for Christmas and ocasionally for his own and his parents' birthdays. Since both his and his father's birthdays came in May he usually appeared for the long Pentecost weekend and celebrated both birthdays and the holiday at the same time. But this year he had not come. Johann Justus was deeply disappointed that his only son had not chosen to follow his trade as a pewterer.

"I love farming, Papa," Hermann had said. "I like working with the animals and watching the crops grow."

"But it is hard work and full of so many uncertainties," Johann had said. "I have built up a good business here. We are living very comfortably. You wouldn't be starting from scratch. It could make you very wealthy some day."

"Like your friend Alfred Krupp? Here in Vilsen? Nay, nay, Papa. I prefer working out in the fresh air. No offense, Papa, but I can't even stand the stink of your workshop."

And so Johann had let him go.

Hermann Bruns and Heinrich Matthies descended from the train at Bremen's main station. While Henni stood for a moment to get his bearings, Harm stared in awe at the great building. It was ten times bigger than the largest barn he had ever seen. In fact, Harm had never been to Bremen before. He had been too young when his sister Doris had wed and that was the last time, as far as he knew, that anyone from the family except Papa had been here. And that made him feel a little guilty. He really should visit Doris while he was here but he was too ashamed of the real reason for their trip to face her. On the train Henni had explained what was going to happen.

"We couldn't do it right on your sixteenth birthday," he had said, "as we were in the midst of spring planting. So this will be your birthday present. Papa suggested it and gave me the money for it. He brought me here last year when I turned sixteen and I tell you, Harm, it was the most wonderful thing that ever happened to me."

"He did? It was?" said Harm, full of doubts.

"Ja, he explained that every man should be taught by a professional the first time so that he knows how to fuck a woman properly instead of fumbling around like a fool. It makes the difference between a man and a boy."

Harm had already done his share of fumbling with the neighboring farm girls and most of it had not been very satisfactory. In fact too often he had been so embarrassed he could not even get it up. Maybe he did need this lesson but still something seemed shameful about the whole idea. Mayhap that came from growing up in a house full of females. Women so often had a way of making a man ashamed of—of—just being a man. "I see," he said and straightened his shoulders like the man he was supposed to be.

"Don't be nervous. I was scared to death, too," admitted Henni. "And Papa was laughing and joking all the while, trying to put me at ease but it only made me feel worse."

Henni always called Schierenhop 'Papa' even though he was his stepfather but he barely remembered his own father, miserable old Heinrich Matthies. And Harm knew well how Schierenhop would always be laughing and joking. The farmer was a big, robust, jolly man and Harm liked him immensely but he was glad he was not along today. It would have made him even more nervous.

"Come on," said Henni. "I think I remember the way. We have to go through the Old Town first but not as far as the waterfront. That's where all the seamen's dives are but this is a real high-class bordello. Papa wrote the address down for me in case we have to ask directions but I'm pretty sure I know the way."

They set out into the teeming city. Harm was amazed at the crowds of people and the noise. On every street they had to dodge drays and wagons, beautiful carriages and fancy gigs, ancient hackneys whose horses looked about to fall down from old age. At last they came to the great square in front of the Rathaus. Harm stopped to stare. It was the most beautiful building he had ever seen.

"And that must be the famous Roland," he said, pointing to the huge

746

statue of a medieval knight in front of the Rathaus.

"That it is," replied Henni. "If we have time later, you should really see the inside of the Rathaus. They have huge models of the old Hanse ships hanging from the rafters."

"Why not now?"

"Nay, we've got to find the house first and be sure they know we are here. It may be a little early for the girls yet but we must make an appointment so you can be sure you get Lili. She's the girl Papa picked out for me and, let me tell you, she's great. I've been back to her a few times since and I wish I could afford to come more often."

"You have? I had no idea."

"Well, you were just a kid then. But after you get laid today you'll be a man."

Hermann blushed. He wished Henni would not use such crude language. Friedrike would have killed him had he spoken like that. He wondered what she would think of this expedition.

When they finally found the house Hermann read the discreet sign that said 'Mme. Blaufeld's Young Ladies Emporium'. "What does emporium mean?" he asked.

"It's a place where things are for sale," explained Henni, "in this case the ladies' charms."

Hermann was shocked again but he quickly told himself he must not be. After all, that's exactly what they were here for.

An old porter opened the door. "Too early, lads," he said through a toothless grin. "Girls be sleepin' yet. Come back after four."

"But—but," stammered Henni, not so sure of himself now, "we just want to talk to Madame a minute to make an appointment with Lili. My father wrote ahead."

"That so? A christening, heh?" he joked as he looked knowingly at the younger boy. Harm blushed furiously. "In that case, Madame she be about in a couple of hours. Come back after dinner, around two."

"What time is it now?" asked Henni. Neither boy had a watch.

"'Bout half after eleven," replied the porter. "Go and have some dinner. Ye'll need your strength." He chuckled as he shut the door.

"What do we do now?" asked Hermann.

"Eat some dinner, I suppose," replied Henni.

"I don't think I could eat a thing. I'm too nervous."

"Nothing to be nervous about. You'll love it."

Earlier Hermann had had an erection just thinking about it. Now he was not so sure. "I think I'd like to see the ships that go to America," he said. "Is the waterfront very far?"

"Nay, not far. This way. But there's not always a ship in port. We'll see." Heinrich was willing to go along with Hermann even though he was hungry himself. He wished there had not been this long time gap. They should have taken a later train but it was important they get out of the house before Adi suspected anything. Well, he would try to keep Harm occupied.

They reached the hustle and bustle of the waterfront but only one transatlantic ship was berthed there and she seemed deserted. Hermann was disappointed.

"When Papa brought Onkel Hermann here he said the crowds were so dense you could hardly get through," he said.

"That's only on the day they are leaving," Heinrich informed him. "This one probably came in a day or two ago and they've finished unloading her cargo—most likely wheat from America. Now they have to clean her and make her ready for the passengers. And load her with tons of coal."

"How do you know so much?"

"I've asked. I'd like to go to America, too, some day but not till I'm ready."

"Do you think they might let us go aboard and see it?"

"No way!" replied Heinrich. He was not sure if that were true or not but he was not going to take a chance that his cousin might stow away and sneak off to America.

As they strolled along the waterfront a beastly-looking woman approached them and took both their arms. "You lads looking for a good lay? Real cheap." She stuck her tongue out through the gaps in her teeth.

Heinrich quickly shook her off and said, "Get lost, you filthy bitch."

But Hermann had never had anything like this happen and did not know what to do. The drab put her other arm around his neck and tried to kiss him. "See, your friend ain't so fussy, are you, sonny? I can fuck you real good. Only two pennies." Hermann could smell the alcohol fumes. He tried to shake her off when Heinrich grabbed her by the arm and flung her aside.

"Leave him alone, pig," he yelled, "or I'll call the police."

The whore stumbled, almost fell and finally went away screaming obscenities.

"Henni!" exclaimed Hermann, visibly shaken. "Henni, I don't think I can go through with this if that's what it's like."

"Good Lord, no! It's nothing like that at all," claimed Heinrich. "I'm sorry that had to happen. Madame Blaufeld's girls are ladies—polite and clean. Brush your clothes off in case that pig left you with any fleas. Let's get out of here and have some dinner. I'm starved and it will take your mind off it."

Eating some foot-long wursts and a generous helping of potato pancakes purchased from vendors in the Rathaus Square did make Hermann feel better. Now he was ready for his new experience. Just thinking about it made his groin throb. Promptly at four o'clock, having made the appointment earlier and then having viewed the ship models inside the Rathaus, they presented themselves back at Madame Blaufeld's Emporium. Hermann was amazed at the sumptuous parlor where Madame greeted them. Thickly upholstered couches bespoke luxurious comfort, heavy velvet drapes lined the windows and an exquisite Turkey carpet covered the floor. Madame herself wore a severe but expensive high-necked black gown with leg-o'-mutton sleeves and a prominent bustle. She looked for all the world like the strict headmistress of an elite girls' school.

"Go right on up, Herr Bruns. Lili is waiting for you. Second door on the left."

Hermann took two steps up and once again his courage deserted him. 'Herr Bruns' she had called him. Good heavens! He looked pleadingly back at Heinrich.

Madame was speaking to him. "Henni, we have a new girl you might like to try. Name of Kunigunde. She's quite exquisite."

"No thanks," replied Henni. "Today is my cousin's day. I'll just wait here for him." He could not admit that Papa had only given him enough money for one. He picked up a newspaper and sank into one of the couches. Then he noticed Hermann's hesitation. "Go on up, Harm. She won't bite you."

Hermann blushed and slowly ascended the staircase. Second door on the left. He tapped lightly. No response. She was probably already in the bed waiting for him. Hesitantly he opened the door a crack and peeped in. She was standing in front of the window. The backlight silhouetted her voluptuous figure through the sheer silk of a pale blue peignoir. She was the most beautiful woman he had ever seen—blond, full-breasted, softly rounded hips—although to be honest, he had never seen a naked woman before. The farm girls he had fumbled with had merely hiked up their skirts, closed their eyes tightly and lay still while he fumbled. As she turned to greet him the front of the negligee fell open. He

749

gaped at those lush breasts. His eyes travelled lower to the golden triangle above her thighs. His erection was immediate, almost painful, straining against his trousers.

She extended both hands to him. "You must be Hermann. Come in and make yourself comfortable."

He could hardly move. She took his hands and led him to the bed. "Ja, I am Harm," he stammered. "And you must be Lili." He did not know what to do next.

"Shall I help you take your clothes off?"

"Nay, I think I can manage." But she helped him anyway, quickly, expertly.

"Now lie down on the bed and relax." She shed the peignoir and lay down beside him, gently stroking his penis.

"Oh," he gasped. No one had ever touched him there before. He thought he would die with pleasure.

Although most of the girls did not, Lili loved these 'christenings', as the old porter called them. They were so young and innocent. It was a pleasure to teach them—and no need to examine them for crabs or disease. Often she herself actually became aroused. She continued stroking. But not too far. This one was ready to burst. He had a good-sized organ for a small man and she wanted to enjoy it.

She quickly straddled him and rubbed her breasts against his chest. "Kiss my breasts," she instructed. Hermann was in such a state of ecstacy he barely heard her—and he was not even inside her yet. He took one breast in both hands and kissed it gently. "Suck on the nipple," she said. As he did so, she felt herself becoming aroused. Quickly she guided him into her moist warmth. Automatically he pushed deeper—push—push—push and suddenly it was all over. He felt his semen spurt into her.

"Oh, my God! Oh, my God!" he groaned. And then he realized. "I was too quick, wasn't I?" he said in dismay.

"No matter," she replied kindly. "It will be better next time."

"Next time? But I . . . "

"Just lie back and relax for a few minutes." Lili was no jaded tart. She was basically a kind person who really wanted these young men to enjoy their first time. She thought of all the women who would be pleasured if they learned to do it right. But that was why the other girls did not like these beginners. It was too quick. Lili knew they needed a second time to prove they were men and not out-of-control boys. But most of the girls wanted to charge them double which usually embarrassed them. She also

750

knew that these young ones recovered very quickly.

She cleaned Hermann's penis off with a soft cloth and began fondling him again. To his surprise it soon became rock hard again. This time she kissed it and sucked it and he nearly fainted with shock—and pleasure. He needed no instructions to squeeze her breasts and nibble on the nipples. At last she rolled over on her back and guided him into her. This time he vowed to go slower but it did not matter now that the first pressure was off. He plunged as deeply as he could and it was heavenly to feel her warmth wrapped around him. He drove harder and harder and was thrilled when she bucked and quivered beneath him in her own orgasm. He felt her deep muscles grab ahold of him and pull him deeper into her. At last he could stand it no longer but to his surprise she climaxed again right with him. It was the most exquisite sensation he had ever felt in his life. Now he was truly a man.

Henni had told him merely to lay the ten-penny piece on the dresser and leave. But now he was not sure if it was enough. "Do I—I mean—is that enough?" he stammered.

"Exactly right," she replied, smiling. "We don't count the first time. I can keep this hour free for you every Wednesday if you like."

"Thank you, Lili, but no, I don't think I could come that often. We farmers are busy in the summer." Surely she must know that ten pennies would buy more than three loaves of bread or a gallon of milk or a pound of coffee.

He trod jauntily down the stairs to where Henni was waiting. Henni grinned knowingly.

"Well?" he asked.

"I think we should pay a visit to my sister while we're here. I haven't seen her in ages."

"Won't she wonder what you're doing here in Bremen?" asked Henni.

"She's a grown woman with two babies. She's not shy. I'll think of something."

Henni grinned again. This was a new, confident Harm. Obviously the trip had been a success.

Doris was surprised when the boys showed up on her doorstep but she welcomed them joyously.

"Whatever are you doing here in Bremen?" she asked.

"Well—er—we—er . . ." stammered Hermann.

Henni quickly jumped in. "Papa gave us the day off so we came to see

751

the big ships that sail to America. Harm's never been here."

"Ja, and the inside of the Rathaus and Roland," added Hermann. "It was very interesting."

Doris noticed immediately that there was something different about her little brother. *Perhaps it's that I haven't seen him in so long. Teenage boys grow so rapidly. But, no, it was more than that.* He seemed to have a swagger about him and his eyes shone with a new light that she had only seen in well satisfied men. *Could she be right, she wondered. Doris was a modern women—no Victorian prude she. Well, she would soon find out. But first feed them so they relaxed.*

"We've just finished our afternoon coffee," she said, "but I can make more and there's plenty of cream cake left. Then you must see your two nephews. They've grown a lot since last Christmas."

While the boys stuffed themselves on cream cake, Doris went to fetch her two boys from their naps. Gerhardt, now five, only a few months younger than their own little sister Mimi, greeted them like a little gentleman. Teddi, two years younger, bounded in and jumped on Hermann's lap, immediately putting his fingers into the cream cake.

"Now look what you've done," scolded Doris, not very vigorously. "Lick your fingers off and don't get any on Onkel Harm's good clothes. They're a handful, let me tell you. If I have another boy, I think I'll tear my hair out. Mama doesn't know how lucky she is to have had all girls except you."

Harm thought otherwise. He would have liked to have had a brother. That was one reason he had grown so close to Henni Matthies. Harm wondered if Doris were going to have another baby but it was not something one discussed in mixed company. "Are you—I mean, do you think you might?" he asked.

"Yes, I'm breeding again." Doris laughed at his consternation. "Tell Mama, would you? Because this time I'm going to need some help with the boys. Maybe Line could come."

"Ach, Line is too hoity-toity. Besides, I mean, isn't she too young to—er—know about such things?"

"No, she's not. And neither are you. You're sixteen now, aren't you? And I suspect there was more to this trip to Bremen than looking at ships. It's written all over your face." Hermann blushed. "I hope you chose Madame Blaufeld's. She's the very best—and safest."

Hermann gasped. Henni smirked.

And Doris laughed. "Caught you out, didn't I? Even Hans uses her

752

girls occasionally when I am too grossly pregnant to have him." Hermann was so flustered he did not know where to look. Doris took pity on him. "I'm sorry, Harm. I didn't mean to tease you, little brother. Bremen is such a sophisticated city I sometimes forget it is not Vilsen. Don't worry. Your secret is safe with me."

On the way back to the train station Hermann asked, "How did she know?"

"She told you," replied Heinrich. "It is written all over your face."

"Do you think Mama will guess, too?"

"I doubt it. That is Vilsen. But your papa might unless my papa has already told him."

When the boys reached the Schierenhop farm both Johann and Friedrike were there waiting for them. Hermann almost panicked. Now I'll surely get a whipping, probably from both men.

But Schierenhop, chuckling, boomed, "See, I told you they'd be back tonight."

Friedrike was so relieved, she hugged and kissed her son. "I'm so glad you didn't go to America. I was worried sick."

"We had no intention of going to America," replied Hermann. "Who told you that?"

"Willi did. He had everyone believing it."

Johann Justus took his son aside, out of earshot of his mother. "I'm glad Schierenhop arranged things for you. He knows Bremen much better than I. I've never been to one of those places. Your dear mother is quite enough for me." He put his arm around Hermann's shoulder. "So today my son has become man. Tell me, was she very good?"

Hermann blushed again but then he relaxed when he realized that Papa was not angry but actually happy for him. He nodded and then burst out, "Oh, Papa, it was unbelievable."

It was Willi who got the whipping for telling stories that upset everyone.

1878   Bismarck was a genius when it came to foreign policy, playing potential aggressors France and Russia against one another, letting Austria-Hungary dabble in the Balkans as long as she stayed out of German politics and assuring friend and potential ally England that a strong Germany in the middle of the continent was the best guarantee of peace. But in domestic policies he was completely out of touch with the great social changes that the industrialization of Germany had brought about. In the isolated atmosphere of the Prussian court he knew only aristocrats and on his estates, the poorest of peasants. He had only the vaguest notion of the powerful bourgeoisie that existed in the other states and even less of the proletariat of the industrial centers. His greatest fear was of too strong a parliament with full budget control. He did everything in his power to stymie this.

As far back as 1870 an event occurred which threw Bismarck into a panic. Pope Pius IX and the Vatican council announced the dogma of papal infallibility. Bismarck feared a return to the old medieval status where the church meddled in all phases of life. He immediately reacted by enacting a law separating church and state, which threw him into the arms of his former adversaries, the Liberal Party, which had long advocated such a law. Henceforth, all schools were placed under the jurisdiction of the state. Further, civil marriages were required and the keeping of all vital statistics was transferred from the churches to the government. Although looking at it from opposite points of view—Bismarck from a need for control, the Liberals in favor of freedom of religion or 'freethinking' as some of them called it—both agreed that the 'ideal' German was one whose first loyalty was to the state rather than to any particular church. Whether this was brought about by education or coercion did not matter.

So far, well and good. These reforms were long overdue. But in the eyes of Bismarck and some others they did not go far enough. Strangely enough two laws initiated by heavily Catholic Bavaria forbade the discussion of any matters of state by clergymen and banned the Jesuits from the country—the latter based on the still prevalent fear of the Jesuits dating from the Thirty Years War. Bismarck then turned his ire on the Catholic Church in Prussia although in theory the new laws applied to the Protestant churches as well: all clerical appointees had to have been educated in German schools and universities and had to pass a state board examination in philosophy, history and German literature; papal authority over the church in Prussia was abolished; the disciplinary authority of the church was transferred to the state. Soon bishops and priests were overwhelmed by fines and penalties. By 1876 all the bishops in Prussia were imprisoned or driven into exile. By the following year over a quarter of the Catholic parishes in Prussia were without a priest.

Although most of these and other repressive 'reforms' applied only in Prussia they sent shock waves through the rest of the country. A new political party arose calling itself the Center Party. Although originally formed to defend states rights (i.e., anti-Prussian) and to ease the tax burden, it quickly became the parliamentary advocate for German Catholics. It soon became the second largest party in the Reichstag, due in part to the brilliant leadership of Ludwig Windthorst, the former Minister of Justice of Hannover and an ardent Catholic. Strange as it may seem, whether due to Windthorst's able leadership or to the party's anti-Prussian stance, a large group of Protestant Hannoverians, the pro-Welf party, collaborated with the Centers in parliament and Windthorst became Bismarck's most formidable opponent.

One May evening three pairs of eyes and ears clustered around the top of the ladder to the loft in the Bruns cottage. Minna, Lise and Mimi loved to listen, secretly of course, to Papa and his friends discuss politics. Line was not with them. She was off visiting friends. Now that she was almost eighteen she was allowed to stay up later. But the days were getting longer and the three younger girls did not feel at all sleepy yet. It was much more fun to spy on Papa. Although Mimi did not understand the half of it, she knew none of them dared breathe a word of anything they overheard.

"But Windthorst is a Catholic," said Uwe.

"He is also a Hannoverian and loyal to the Welf," argued Johann Justus.

"Do you really think he can achieve independence for Hannover?" asked Erich

"Probably not. But he can at least keep Prussia out of our hair," said Johann.

"That won't be easy," said Conrad. "Bismarck would love to extend those repressive anti-Catholic laws to the entire country. Windthorst and the Center Party in the Reichstag are our only hope of avoiding them."

"Ja, even our own Evangelican Lutheran Church here in Hannover refuses to obey them," added Erich. "And what's more, she has refused to be united with the Prussian church which is more Calvinistic than Lutheran."

"There is always hope that we might convert Prussia," said Conrad. "Look what happened when they made the new ordinances revising the form of the local governments in Prussia. They copied our Hannoverian formats almost exactly."

"I doubt it will go any further than that," said Johann. "Our towns and villages have always elected their own councils who elect the Bürgermeister. Our schools have been separate from the church since the old Hanse merchants founded them during the Reformation. Our peasants have been free for centuries, whereas Prussia is only beginning—*beginning*, mind you—to free hers."

"Ja," agreed Erich, "and the poor souls don't know what to do. The army has always been their only alternative. So they emigrate by the thousands."

"Indeed," agreed Johann. "Prussia has always been a militaristic state—and always will be."

"What we need is a full scale revolution to free Hannover," said Uwe.

The other men gasped. "Ach, Uwe, never that," exclaimed Johann. "You are too young to remember '48. And even '62 with the Borries regime. I lived through them both and I'm getting too old to go through that again." The tic under his eye twitched uncontrollably at the memory. "And what little we accomplished was only taken away from us again under Prussia."

"And now we have to fight to get those rights back bit by bit," said Conrad, "but the parliamentarian way is the only way."

"Exactly," agreed Erich. "It's too bad he turned Bennigsen down."

"Bennigsen would have been the lone Liberal—and the lone Hannoverian—in the cabinet had he accepted Bismarck's offer of a minister's portfolio," explained Conrad. "He would have been made a scapegoat. Bismarck has a long memory. Bennigsen was right to demand that two other Liberals be appointed to the cabinet with him. 'Tis said that the Chancellor never even answered him."

"I wish Bismarck would drop dead," said Uwe. "He's run this country too long as it is."

"Hush! Don't say things like that," chided Johann. "Although we're among friends here, even the walls have ears."

Ostensibly the men were playing pinochle but their weekly meetings were always political discussions. And always about how to achieve Hannover's independence from Prussia. Their ideas ran the full gamut from young Uwe's revolutionary opinions through Erich's and Johann's moderation to Conrad's sober parliamentarian ideas. Johann, being the eldest, always tried to steer them into conservative thinking but inevitably the discussions ended in frustration at their powerlessness to throw off Prussia's yoke.

The girls were getting sleepy now—and bored. Papa and his friends always talked about the same things, over and over again. Mimi's eyes were getting heavy and Minna urged her to come to bed before she fell asleep where she was and tumbled down the ladder into the midst of the card game. Suddenly there was a knock on the door and the new pastor, Georg Beermann, burst in.

"Why, Pastor Georg, how nice to see you," said Johann. "Care to join us in a hand of pinochle?"

The pastor shook his head. "Nay, not now. Have you heard the news?"

"What news?" they asked.

"An assassination attempt has been made on Kaiser Wilhelm's life."

"Ja, that was in yesterday's newspaper," replied Johann. "That's hardly news."

"And it was unsuccessful. Worse luck," commented Uwe.

"It said they caught the would-be murderer," added Erich.

"Ja, some fanatical Socialist," said Conrad. "Good riddance to them."

"But," said the pastor and paused dramatically, "there was another today—just this afternoon—and His Majesty is gravely wounded!"

"What?!" they gasped collectively.

"How can you know this already if it only happened this afternoon?" asked Johann.

"Have you not seen the miraculous new machine at the post office? It is called a telephone. Some fellow name of Bell in America invented it. Quite amazing," said Beermann.

"I've heard of it but not seen it. My wife usually sends the children for our mail," said Johann.

"The devil's instrument," commented Uwe.

"Nay. A great step into the future," rejoined the pastor.

"You mean you actually spoke to someone in Berlin on this thing?" asked Erich.

"Not exactly," admitted Beermann. "Someone in Berlin called the Obersuperintendent in Hannover who in turn called our superintendent here in Vilsen. I was the one who ran to fetch him to the post office and I stood right next to him as he spoke to the minister in Hannover. It is unbelievable to hear someone's voice from so far away. Superintendent Meyer says he would like to get one installed in his house just as soon as they string some more wires."

"Unbelievable," commented Johann. "I had heard about it but I've not known anyone who actually spoke on it. Most people are afraid of it, I think."

"But enough of the telephone," said Pastor Georg. "The real reason I rushed over here this evening is to warn you . . . "

"Have they caught the new culprit?" asked Erich.

"I believe so. A crazed nobleman this time—also said to be a Socialist."

"So what is there to warn us of?" asked Conrad.

"Because after the first attempt Bismarck rushed a measure through the Reichstag outlawing the Socialist Party."

"So what is that to us? They are troublemakers anyway," said Johann, forgetting for the moment that he, too, had once been branded a troublemaker.

"And after today's attempt," continued Beermann, "the Chancellor dissolved Parliament."

"Oh, no," they gasped.

"But he won't get away with that," declared Conrad. "Windthorst won't allow it."

"Windthorst is powerless without a rostrum to speak from. The reason the minister in Berlin called Hannover first is that it is feared that Bismarck will now turn his ire on the Center Party and especially on the Pro-Welfs. The Superintendent suggested it would be wise if we all lie low—disappear—for several days until we see which way the wind blows."

For a few moments there was a general hubbub, each one expressing his shock at the Chancellor's imperiousness, everything from disgust to outright hatred of Bismarck. Then there was silence, each man thinking of his family and wondering where he should go into hiding.

"I must be on my way now," said the pastor. "There are many others I must warn."

"Indeed," said Johann, "including Superintendent Meyer's own family."

After the men dispersed Johann said to Friedrike, "You heard?"

"Ja," she said dispiritedly, reliving in her mind all the times Johann had had to go into hiding because of his political beliefs. But she had known and accepted that before she even married him. Hadn't they fallen in love when she herself was hiding him? "You'd best go to the Klostermühle. My nephew Jürgen will keep you. They'll never think to look there. It's so isolated."

"I had the same thought."

"Then let me give you some food to take along. They are so poor.

Will you ride or walk?"

"Walk, I think. Easier to hide in the woods and they're sure to spot the horse."

Shortly after Johann left, Line came in breathless. "Mama, did you hear the news? Kaiser Wilhelm has been shot and they despair for his life. He's so old."

"Ja, we heard," replied Friedrike. "And how did you know so quickly?"

"My friend Gerde was at the post office when Superintendent Meyer spoke on that machine they call a telephone. He had to yell so loud everyone heard him. Where is Papa? Had I known his friends had already left I'd have come home earlier."

"Papa may be away for a few days."

"Oh, I see," said Line. When would her dear papa give up his foolish dreams of bringing the Welf back to rule an independent Hannover? But she kept her thoughts to herself.

The three eavesdroppers had come fully awake when they heard Pastor Beermann's tidings. But now they scrambled for their beds. Line could be just as strict as Mama and not always so kind.

The next morning Mimi awoke before the others. Lise lay next to her, still sound asleep as were her sisters in the other bed. She knew it was an opportunity to get washed and dressed for school before the others used up all the warm water. But she lay there instead. Mimi was worried. She had not understood the half of the conversation last night but she did know that some crazy person had tried to kill the Kaiser and now everyone was frightened. Mimi did not like to be frightened. Papa could always calm her fears but now Papa was going away. She did not like it when Papa went away. But Mama had said it might only be for a few days. She would try to be brave until he came back. And she must keep all these secrets. That was a heavy burden for a seven-going-on-eight-year-old.

Mimi struggled through the next few days at school and Papa still had not come home. The schoolmaster noticed her preoccupation. She was one of his brightest pupils.

"Marie, aren't you feeling well?" he asked. She was just at the age to come down with one of the dread childhood sicknesses and he was concerned.

"Ja, ja, I'm fine." She could hardly say she was worried about Papa.

759

"I—I'm just a little tired is all."

"Then you must go to bed earlier. I know it's difficult with the days getting longer but you must."

She ignored that and tried to apply herself to the arithmetic problem in front of her. Arithmetic was her best subject but today the figures seemed to blur on the paper. She could hardly wait until Saturday. If Papa was not home by Saturday, she would—what would she do? She would try and find him and tell him she missed him.

The half day of school on Saturday seemed interminable. As soon as the church bell struck noon she jumped up and ran all the way home. She quickly changed into her old clothes but Friedrike caught her before she could leave. By that time her sisters had arrived.

"Dinner is on the table," announced Friedrike.

"But I'm not hungry, Mama," said Mimi. "I just wanted to take a little walk first. The schoolroom was so stuffy."

"Eat," ordered Friedrike. "Then you can take your walk. Aren't you going to Fräulein Alma's tea today?"

"But that's not till much later." She loved going to Alma Meyer's and was sorry she would miss it but Papa was more important. She picked at her food and finally she was excused.

Mimi trudged up the hill to the woods behind the new cemetery. Before she had fallen asleep the other night she thought she had heard Mama mention the Klostermühle. Papa might or might not be there but it was a good place to start her search. When she reached the woods she slowed her pace. It was so quiet and peaceful here it was hard to believe there were wicked Prussians out there who might hurt Papa. The trees were greening with spring foliage. Birds were twittering and chattering, building nests for their babies. Little creatures rustled through the underbrush. She loved these woods. Mama had told her that she and her grandmothers and great-grandmothers and, Mimi guessed, all the women of their family back to the beginning of time had sought peace here. She followed the path to the well-known short cut.

When she arrived at the Klostermühle her cousin Jürgen was hesitant. "Uh—I don't know where your papa is," he said.

But then she heard Johann's voice from the other room. "It's all right, Jürg. It's just Mimi. Let her in."

She dashed into the parlor and threw herself into Johann's arms. "Oh, Papa, I was so worried about you."

He took her onto his lap and held her close. "There, there, little one.

There's nothing to worry about. Your Papa's safe. But how did you know I was here?"

"I—I just guessed."

His Mimi was a smart one—the smartest of all his very intelligent children except possibly Doris. "Did your Mama send you?"

"Nay, I came by myself."

"Then she will be worried."

"But I was worried about you. I think it's safe for you to come home now. This morning I saw Master Uwe and Master Conrad walking about town as though nothing were amiss."

"Then it's no doubt safe again. Let's go." He set her down.

"Afternoon coffee's almost ready," announced Jürgen's wife. "Why don't you stay for that? Little one must be tired, running all that way."

"Very well, we'll do that," replied Johann, "but then we must go. I haven't seen my wife or even changed my clothes in five days."

Mimi was not tired at all but Jürgen's wife made such good *Butterkuchen*. She hoped she would have some today. She completely forgot about Fräulein Alma's tea.

As they neared Vilsen fatigue finally caught up with her and Johann had to carry her down the last steep hill. When they reached home the household was in an uproar.

"Mimi has disappeared," cried Friedrike. "Oh—you found her."

"Rather she found me," replied Johann. "Don't scold her now. She's exhausted from her adventure. I think it's straight to bed for this little one. We had a big coffee at Jürg's. She won't be wanting supper."

Johann helped his littlest daughter up the ladder to the loft and gently tucked her into bed.

"Papa, sing to me," she begged. "I haven't slept much this week. But now I don't have to worry anymore, do I?"

"Nay, you don't, kleine Mimi. But your Mama is the singer of the family. I do better on my fiddle."

"No, I want you, Papa," she insisted.

"Very well then. Here's a brand new lullaby I've been practicing, written by one Johannes Brahms." And he croaked in his creaky voice,

> "Guten Abend, Gute Nacht,
> "Mit Röselein bedacht . . . "

And Mimi thought it was the most beautiful song she had ever heard.

The next morning at church Mimi apologized to Fräulein Alma. "But it was more important to know that Papa was safe," she said.

"I understand," said Alma. Alma was always so kind and understanding.

In any event Kaiser Wilhelm I recovered slowly from his injuries and lived on for another ten years.

24

1880

Mimi was all excited. Her beloved Fräulein Alma was going to be married. All the Bruns girls loved Alma Meyer and were happy for her. Not so, at first, her own elitist family. Her father was Church Superintendent (similar to a bishop). Her brother was a county judge. With her high intelligence and superior education they had hoped for something better for her than a mere village pastor.

When Georg Beermann first came to the Vilsen church, he immediately noticed Alma Meyer. Not that she was beautiful. In fact she was tall, stick-thin and somewhat homely. But her sparkling personality and brilliant intellect more than made up for her lack of physical attributes. And she seemed to be everywhere helping around the church. She taught Sunday School, sang in the choir, occasionally played the organ. She even voluntaily acted as his secretary as needed. And needed she was. Her fine legible hand far surpassed his hen-scratching. Georg Beermann fell madly in love with Alma Meyer.

Eventually the family relented. They had to. Alma was clear-thinking and headstrong and she knew exactly what she wanted. Georg might be inexperienced, fresh out of seminary in his first parish but she could see his potential. She envisioned a great future for him with her help. Alma, too, had fallen in love.

An elaborate wedding was planned as befitted the leading family of Vilsen. Her sister was to be her maid-of-honor but Alma insisted that all four Bruns girls were to be bridesmaids. And that was why Mimi was so excited. But then she had second thoughts. This would mean that dearest Alma would not have time for her anymore. Even the French lessons would be forgotten.

But Mimi, too, was headstrong and outspoken. She knew it was not the time to ask such a question but she put it to Alma anyway. "I'm going to miss you so, dear Alma. Whatever shall I do when I can't see you anymore?"

"But you will, kleine Mimi," replied Alma. "I'll be right here in Vilsen. You can come and visit me any time."

"But it won't be the same," insisted Mimi.

"Perhaps not quite. But I'll make you a promise. By the time you are fourteen and have finished school, I may have a baby or two. And I'll need you to care for them and help me in the house. A pastor's wife doesn't have much time for housekeeping. The place will be yours as soon as you are graduated and confirmed. That's a promise. And if I should need you before that, I'm sure your mama will let you come on Saturday afternoons and during the summer, just as I did for her when I was in school."

Mimi was overjoyed—especially to have been selected over her elder sisters. "Oh, thank you. Thank you, dearest Alma."

"Just one thing," added Alma. "Once I am wed you can no longer call me Alma. I must be addressed as Frau Pastorin."

Mimi nodded. "Of course." She did not care what she had to call her. All that mattered was that her future was assured.

1881   Friedrich Campsheide lay on his cot in the workshop of his new master and he could not sleep. He was frightened out of his wits. He hated having to sleep here in the back of the shop. Dimly he heard the clock strike twelve. Midnight! Now they will come after me. He pulled the cover over his head and trembled. Nothing happened. Finally from sheer exhaustion he fell into a fitful sleep. But that was worse because then the nightmares started.

Fritz was not entirely unhappy living in Hoya. At first he had been bitterly resentful and hated his mother for sending him away. His uncle was a stern, taciturn man but not unkind. His aunt, Mutti's sister, although a bit of a complainer like Margarethe, was basically much more cheerful. The couple had no childen of their own so she lavished all her frustrated love on young Fritz and tried to be the best mother to him that she was able.

Onkel was just a simple laborer doing all sorts of odd jobs around town but especially gardening for those few wealthy people who wanted beautiful gardens but had neither the time nor the inclination to take care of them. While they were poor, they were not impoverished. Although Tante complained about it constantly, there always seemed to be enough food on the table and warm clothes in winter.

When Fritz was approaching fourteen, having just gone through the graduation/confirmation rite, his uncle said, "Now you must learn a trade.

Is there anything you'd especially like to do?"

Fritz had his answer ready. "I want to be a gardener like you. I love flowers and you've already taught me a lot about vegetables."

"Nay, nay, never that. No money in it. And you'd starve over the winter. It's good enough for a sideline but you must have a real trade. You see, I never had the chance. My father could not afford to apprentice me so I learned whatever handyman work I could teach myself. But ever since you came to us, I've been putting a bit aside so that you can learn a real trade. Do you want to be a farmer since you like growing things?"

"Nay, nay, I'd not be happy plowing fields and such. I only like growing beautiful things like flowers or maybe fruit trees. And I'm not very good with animals except dogs. I love dogs."

"Ach, ja, that mutt next door. Well, what then? Surely you must have been thinking about it."

"Ja, Onkel, I have and I rather like working with wood. Not as a carpenter, mind you, but making small, beautiful things like tables and chairs and such."

"Ah—a cabinetmaker. An excellent trade. And I know just the man to start you off with—my friend, Herr Zimmermann. I'll speak to him tomorrow and see if he will take you."

"Thank you, Onkel. And Onkel, thank you also for putting the money aside. I didn't really think I should be able to learn a good trade. Mutti is so—so . . . ."

Onkel shook his head. "Never mind that now. You're going to be the finest cabinetmaker in all of County Hoya."

And so Fritz was apprenticed to Herr Zimmermann. During the day, when the master was teaching him, he enjoyed the work very much and was learning fast. However, while Herr Zimmermann did occasionally make tables, chairs and such, his main line of work was as a coffinmaker. And therein lay the problem. Very often the bodies of the deceased were left with him for one or two nights in order to insure perfect measurements and Fritz had to sleep in the same room with them. Being a sensitive, imaginative child to begin with and having been brought up with all the superstitions of old Saxony besides, he was terrified—sure that at midnight these ghouls would rise up out of the coffins and perform some horrible rite such as stealing his soul away.

A few weeks later he was seated at a workbench planing a board when he nodded off. The plane clattered to the floor and his head hit the board. He was sound asleep.

"What ails you, lad?" yelled Zimmermann. "If I didn't lock you in here of a night, I'd swear you were out gallivanting with girls." When Fritz shamefacedly explained why he had not been able to sleep, Zimmerman laughed. "Dead can't hurt you, lad. When they're dead, they're dead. It's the living you have to watch out for. Come, I'll show you." He took Fritz roughly by the arm and led him over to two of the current occupants of the coffins. The boy was terrified. The master took his hand and forced him to touch first one then the other. The bodies were ice cold and very stiff. "See, no way could they rise up out of there and hurt you. Now buck up, lad, and get back to work." But Fritz was more terrified than ever.

Just as soon as Zimmermann went into the other room, Fritz dropped his tools and ran home. Tante was in the kitchen.

"Whatever are you doing here in the middle of the day in the middle of the week?" she exclaimed. "Don't tell me Zimmermann turned you out."

"Nay, I just left," he sobbed. "Oh, Tante, please don't make me go back."

"But why? I thought you liked the work."

"I do. But—but—it's the dead bodies." And tearfully he tried to explain his fears.

"Why, you silly, foolish oaf. Dead is dead. They can't hurt you. You'd just better get over that nonsense. Your uncle will be very angry."

Obviously no sympathy there. And Onkel was very angry.

"Do you think I've spent all that money on you which Zimmermann won't return if you've run away?" And he administered a swift and severe beating. "Now you get right back over there and apologize."

"Ach, Onkel, Tante," sobed Fritz, "can't I just stay here tonight? I'll go back tomorrow, I promise."

Tante was beginning to feel sorry for the boy—at least a little. "Ach, let him stay the night. He's been punished enough," she said to her husband. "You go and explain to Zimmermann."

"I'll feel like a fool."

"So? We all have to act like fools once in a while. The lad won't learn well if he's that afraid. So you'll be wasting your money anyway. He'll grow out of it."

After Onkel left Fritz crept through the hole under the fence into the neighbor's backyard. The Birnbaums were a strange family but he rather liked them. It was said that Herr Birnbaum was a Jew but Frau Birnbaum was not. Fritz was not sure about that although Herr Birnbaum certainly looked fierce enough with his thick black beard. And yet their youngest son had just been confirmed with Fritz in the Lutheran Church. It was all quite confusing. But Fritz did not care about any of that right now. He sought solace with the one creature he knew to be his friend—the mutt, Micah.

Micah was a big, shaggy, floppy-eared dog, as black as his master's beard. The moment he heard Fritz coming, he loped over to the lad and put a paw out. Fritz fell to his knees and hugged the dog. Micah was a very intelligent dog with highly developed protective instincts. Probably of Labrador descent, he loved the water and often was soaking wet from his daily swim in the Weser. Today, however, he was dry and silky and seemed to sense the boy's distress as Fritz buried his face in his ruff. The dog curled his big body protectively around the lad and let him sob out his fears.

Sometime later Frau Birnbaum came out to feed the chickens. Usually Micah came to meet her, hoping for a treat for himself. She wondered where the dog was. And then she saw him all curled up over by the fence. She hoped he was not sick for at first she did not see the boy. As she approached Micah lifted his head, shook it and started to lick the lad's face. Fritz was sound asleep.

"Why, Fritz," she exclaimed. "What are you doing here? Whatever is wrong?"

The dog's ministrations woke him and he sat up groggily. "Oh—ah—Frau Birnbaum, I'm sorry. I guess I fell asleep. I'm just so tired. I—uh . . ."

The woman laughed. "I admit Micah makes a nice pillow but whatever is wrong, lad?"

Fritz started to sob again and his whole sad tale spilled out.

Frau Birnbaum put her arm around him. "Come over here in the shade," she said, "and I'll explain something to you." When they were seated on a bench under an old apple tree, she asked, "You like to eat nuts, don't you?"

Fritz nodded, wondering what in the world nuts had to do with his problem.

"When you crack a nut open you pick out all the good parts and eat them, right? And what is left but a hard, empty, useless shell, right?" He nodded. "And you're not afraid of that shell, are you?" He shook his head. "You simply throw it away, right?"

"Ja, but . . ."

"The same thing happens when a person dies. God takes that one's

767

soul and sends it to heaven and nothing is left but a hard, dry shell. Useless—and harmless, right? That is all those dead, empty bodies are—harmless shells, just waiting for Herr Zimmermann to make a coffin so they can be buried. The real person they once were is already with God in heaven and can do no harm to anyone. Do you understand that now, young Fritz?"

Very slowly he nodded his head as her words sunk in. Why could Tante or Onkel not have explained that to him instead of punishing him? He thought Frau Birnbaum was the most wonderful person in the world—aside from Micah, that is.

"One other thing," she added. "Once you are confirmed you're supposed to be a man—and men must be brave. Not that men aren't afraid sometimes. They are. But they face their fears with bravery and courage. That is what makes them a man."

Fritz nodded. "I'll be brave, Frau Birnbaum."

"Good. Now go and apologize to Herr Zimmermann and tell him you'll be back to work tomorrow."

As Fritz was approaching the coffinmaker's shop, Onkel was just leaving. "I'm going to tell Herr Zimmermann I'm sorry. I'll not be afraid of those old nutshells anymore."

Onkel scratched his head in perplexity. Whatever was the lad talking about? He wondered who or what had brought about the change of heart—certainly not the mutt next door. No matter, as long as it had come about.

As the summer grew hotter Fritz could often be found sitting on the riverbank. The cooling breezes were welcome, of course, but it was not the placid Weser itself nor the boat traffic that interested him. Engineers were building a giant railroad trestle across the river. Very soon the railroad would come to Hoya and folk would not have to go all the way to Eystrup to board a train for Bremen or Hannover. Fritz had never been to Bremen nor had he any desire to go there. It was the construction itself that fascinated him. Although he did not care for metalwork, he was amazed at how the huge cranes mounted on barges could so easily lift the huge girders into place. Someday they will build buildings like that, he thought.

And Frau Birnbaum noticed. Although she was unaware of his interest in the bridge construction, thinking he was merely watching the river, she felt sorry for him. He was such a lonely boy. So she decided to plan a surprise for his birthday in August. The Birnbaums had a boat. It was not much of a boat, to be sure — a clumsy old scow — but her elder sons could handle her well and the family often enjoyed picnic outings on the river on her. Frau Birnbaum made sure to seek permission from Fritz's Onkel and Tante before saying anything to the lad.

"I don't know," said Onkel. "He's clumsy and terribly shy. He might get seasick." Onkel had never ever been on the river himself. He mistrusted everything about it. He also did not like the Birnbaums because the old man was supposedly a Jew. But he could not say that.

"Seasick!" exclaimed Frau Birnbaum. "Why the Weser here is as placid as a millpond."

"Ach, let him go," said Tante. "The fresh sir will do him good after breathing sawdust all week. Just 'cause you don't like the water, I'm sure he'll love it. Ja, Frau Birnbaum, you may take him and thank you."

As the day approached Fritz was all excited. He had never been on a boat before. Neither did he know how to swim — in part because of Onkel's fear of the water and in part because there had been no one to teach him. He had often watched with envy as the Birnbaums took their boat out. He was a little nervous but it looked so easy the way they raised the sail and handled the tiller.

"Now you sit right here next to Albert and don't move unless we tell you to," instructed Jacob, the eldest brother.

Fritz did as he was told. He was glad to see that Micah was with them. That gave him a bit of confidence. They raised the sail and soon were out in the middle of the river. What an exhilarating experience to be floating along on top of the water where no man could walk. They sailed upstream for quite a distance and Fritz began to relax.

The Weser is a winding, twisting stream throughout its length but here so close to the sea it broadened out as it meandered placidly through the flat land. As a result there were all sorts of bays, backwaters and eddies in various places where there was hardly any current at all. The Birnbaum brothers anchored the boat in one of these backwaters.

And Jacob announced, "Now we'll all have a nice swim to cool off and then we'll have our lunch." Frau Birnbaum always packed a hamper full of goodies and this time there was even a tiny birthday cake for their friend. But Fritz did not know this as yet.

The boys stripped off their clothing and dove in, followed by Micah. Fritz was left sitting there, slightly embarrassed as he had never seen so many naked men before. Tante had been very strict about things like that.

"Come on, Fritz," they called. "What ails you?"

"I—I don't know how to swim," he replied.

"Ach, nothing to it," said Jacob. "We'll teach you. Just kick your legs and paddle your arms."

Albert sensed his friend's fear and went back to the boat. The vessel listed dangerously as he climbed back on board. Fritz nearly fell overboard. He grabbed the tiller and the boat swung around in a circle.

"Hey, watch what you're doing," shouted Albert. Fortunately the anchor held. "Now get your clothes off. Don't be a sissy. It's fun in the water."

Fritz did not want to be called a sissy. He had promised their mother he would be brave. Besides his Campsheide pride also told him he must be brave. Reluctantly he took off his shoes and stockings, his shirt and pants but he refused to remove his long underwear. He just could not bring himself to do it. No one was supposd to see him *there*.

"Can't I go in like this?" he asked.

"I s'pose," replied Albert, "if you don't mind going home with wet drawers."

Fritz decided wet drawers would be the lesser of two evils. Still he hesitated. He stood on the gunwale holding tightly to a shroud but when he looked down into the water he could not make the plunge.

Albert's patience wore thin. "Jump!" he shouted and pushed.

Fritz felt himself flying through the air. He opened his mouth to scream just as his body struck the water. Instead of a scream he gulped a huge mouthful of water and choked. He tried to pump his arms and legs as he had been told but his panic was so great that he only succeeded in going down deeper instead of up. Albert dove in to help him as the boat drifted out of reach. Fritz's eyes, ears and especially his nose filled with water. The other boys quickly swam over to help but in his terror he fought them off. He went down again. He thought his lungs would burst and his head felt swollen up as though it were not part of him. I'm going to drown. I'm going to die, he thought. And still he fought his would-be rescuers off, flailing so badly they could not grab ahold of him. Gradually his efforts slowed down as he began to lose consciousness.

Suddenly he vaguely felt something tug on the back of his undershirt and pull him up. And then his head was above water. He coughed and sputtered and swallowed more water as he tried to gulp air. But still something kept him from going down again. It was Micah. Blessed Micah. By that time big Jacob was able to reach him. He slipped an arm under Fritz's chest and hauled him up onto his own chest. The dog finally let go but kept a close watch. Jacob swam backwards to the boat where the others were able to help Fritz aboard.

"Lay him down on his belly with his arm under his chin," ordered Jacob. "Got to get that water out of his lungs."

Fritz felt a tremendous pressure on his back. Then it let off and was on again. He could not think clearly. What are they doing to me—trying to kill me? Suddenly what seemed like half the river spewed forth from his mouth and nose. And the pressure kept on. And more water came out until at last he was able to take a breath. Oh, how good that felt. The dog came over and licked his face. It was then that he realized he was still alive and Micah had saved him.

"Oh, Micah, Micah, thank you," he murmured as he gingerly tried to sit up.

Jacob patted him on the back. "How you doing, old boy?" he asked.

"All right, I guess. I almost drowned, didn't I?"

Jacob nodded. "Albert should never have pushed you but we've done it so often with lads who are timid with no ill effects that I'm sure he never gave it a thought. Feel like having lunch?"

Fritz shook his head. He was still somewhat queasy.

"I'm sorry, Fritz," apologized Albert, "but I never thought you would panic like that."

Fritz shrugged. "I'm just glad Micah was there. I've always meant to ask you where he got such a funny name."

"Micah is an Old Testament prophet who wrote that God would always hold your hand and walk with you," explained Jacob. "Since Micah is a rescue dog, Mama thought it would be a good name for him."

"I see," replied Fritz. "I guess it is."

The boys dove into the picnic basket. They were all hungry after their rescue efforts—all except Fritz, although the fresh air was beginning to revive him.

"What about your birthday cake?" asked Albert as he discovered it it the hamper.

"My birthday cake?" asked Fritz.

"Ja, Mama made it especially for you. It was to be a surprise. We can't eat any of it unless you have some. She'll be disappointed if you don't."

Reluctantly Fritz took a few bites. He did not want to disappoint Frau Birnbaum. She was such a nice lady. And the cake was good. He accepted a whole piece and began to feel better. "Thank her for me, would you? But promise you won't tell her what happened."

The Birnbaum boys all agreed. It was to be their secret. But Fritz privately vowed never to go out on a boat again—or even near the water.

A few months later, after the main harvests had been reaped but winter had not yet set in, there was much excitement in Vilsen. For weeks men and boys had been nailing up broadsides on every tree and fence post. They passed out flyers to every house in the village and every farm for miles around. There was to be a great party and rally in the field where the Pfingst-ox judging usually took place in the spring. There was to be a brass band for singing and dancing. There would be free food and free beer for everyone who attended. And most exciting of all, the sponsors were offering free farmland and a partial payment of their passage to all who would emigrate to America. All that had to be promised in return was that they would emigrate within one year of signing the papers and farm the land for a minimum of five years. The sponsor was the Northern Pacific Railroad of Chicago.

Ever since the financial crash of 1873 farm prices had never recovered especially in view of the huge quantities of grain imported from America. Also, as had been true since time immemorial, there were just too many mouths to feed on the small German farms. Aside from financial reasons there was still the widespread hatred of Prussia and fear of her ever insatiable military draft. Many were disgruntled with their lot for whatever reason, others just curious. Hundreds of people turned out for the celebration. Everyone wanted to hear what the Americans had to say. Free farmland, indeed. Unbelievable!

Heinrich Matthies and Hermann Bruns stood in the front row avidly reading the flyers. Now in their mid-twenties, both were very seriously considering going to America. Heinrich's step-brothers, Schierenhop's sons, were now old enough to work the farm and, although he knew his work was appreciated, Heinrich also knew he would never inherit. And Heinrich was still a proud, ambitious Matthies. He refused to accept a future as someone else's farmhand for the rest of his life. Besides there was a girl . . .

Hermann, too, could see no future for himself on Schierenhop's farm—nor anywhere else in Germany for that matter. The country was just too crowded. His only chance of inheriting anything was his father Johann's pewtermaking shop and, as much as he loved his father, he hated the thought of that. Besides he was astute enough to see that, with competition from the great factories of the industrial revolution, these small shops could not possibly compete and would soon be a thing of the past. Hermann loved farming and was good at it. He wanted a farm of his own. He had always heard that America was the land of opportunity and this, today, seemed the best opportunity of all. Free land? There must be a catch. He would have to listen carefully.

The drums beat calling everyone's attention as a tall gentleman with luxurious sideburns mounted the makeshift platform and called for silence. He addressed the crowd in excellent though strangely accented German. After a few introductory remarks he switched to Plattdeutsch. After asking if everyone understood him, he was greeted with a resounding cheer. Here was a man who not only spoke their language but understood their problems—and hopes. He explained that Mr. Henry Villard, the president of Northern Pacific Railroad, was an immigrant from Germany who had done very well for himself and now wanted to help those who also wanted to improve their lot. The free farmland he was giving away was along the railroad's right-of-way in northern Illinois. It was rich soil with plentiful water available. What he did not clarify was that most of it was still woodland or tough, never-before-plowed prairie. The only requirement was that a man or family farm the land for a minimum of five years. He barely touched on the fact that Mr. Villard wanted to establish towns and farms along the railroad in order to increase passenger and freight traffic. He did explain in glowing terms how Mr. Villard had set up aid societies, to which other successful immigrants also contributed, in order to loan the new emigrants money for seed, tools and even houses.

"Five years!" he concluded forcefully. "What's five years to an ambitious farmer? The land will be legally yours to sell if you don't want it after five years. You've nothing to lose. But I guarantee most of you will have a fine, wealthy property to leave to your heirs. Just step right up and sign this paper of intent and the land will be yours the moment you arrive in Illinois."

The offer was certainly enticing. People had dozens of questions which the agent fielded knowledgeably. Hermann wanted to see a map. An aide produced one with a flourish.

"Where is Elgin?' asked Hermann. "And where is this land in relation to it?"

"Aha!" said the agent, delighted. "A man who is already knowledgeable about the country. Elgin is right in the heart of the land we are giving away. Come, I'll show you. Do you already have relatives there?"

"A sister, I believe, and possibly an uncle," replied Hermann. Mama had not heard from Onkel Hermann in years. No one knew if he were dead or alive. But Anni had written sporadically. The family had heard about Elgin ever since Mama's friend Rosa Schneider went there but no one had ever been quite sure where it was. It was exciting to actually see it on a map.

Hermann and Heinrich pored over the map carefully as the agent pointed out, "See, here is Elgin about thirty-five miles directly west of Chicago and this black line is our railroad which runs right through Elgin."

"And where is the land you are giving away?" asked Henni.

"Mostly to the west of Elgin. But not far." His finger followed the black line in a northwesterly direction to a village called Rockford. "Somewhere along in here," he said. The black line continued to the Mississippi River. The young men stared in amazement.

"Is yours the railroad that goes all the way to the Pacific Ocean," asked Henni.

"Not yet. That is the Union Pacific farther south, just joined together a few years ago. Ours will take the northern route just as soon as we complete this bridge across the Mississippi and find a suitable pass through the northern Rocky Mountains. Theirs goes to San Francisco. Ours will terminate in Seattle."

The two friends gaped. They had never heard of these places nor could their minds grasp the vast distances in America.

"We would like to settle as close to Elgin as possible," said Hermann. "We have heard that there are a lot of people from this part of Hannover in that area."

"That is true," replied the agent, "but it's first come first served. So if you're serious, it behooves you to sign up immediately. When you arrive in Chicago our land office will give you your deeds and show you where the land is. Fall is the best time to go. That gives you the whole winter to cut down the trees and build yourself a log cabin. Then you'll be all ready for spring planting."

"What sort of crops do they grow best there?" asked Henni.

"Wheat mostly and corn. But in the area near Elgin it is largely dairy farms, just like here."

The two men looked at each other. "What say you, Harm?" asked Henni.

"It sounds just like we want," replied Hermann. "What we've always dreamed of."

774

"It sounds like heaven to me," said Henni. "Where do we sign?"

"Right here on this paper and I'll add your names to our growing list," replied the agent. "Be sure you put how many in the party so we can advise the steamship line."

Heinrich boldly signed his name with a flourish and stood aside to let Hermann sign. Hermann stared. "Henni, you wrote 'Heinrich Matthies and wife'. You don't have a wife."

"I shall before we leave. Why do you think I've been taking all those trips to Wenden?"

Harm admitted he did not know. "I thought it was to visit your cousins."

"And some time ago my cousins introduced me to a lovely girl named Anna. But I dared not wed her on the pittance Papa pays me. Now I can. She shares our dream of America, so I know she'll be willing."

Harm was amazed. He did not think his best friend had any secrets from him.

"Are you not married yet, Herr Bruns?" asked the agent.

"Nay, not yet," he replied wistfully. "Mayhap I'll find a wife over there."

The man smiled. "I'm sure you will. There are many fine ladies there just looking for a bright, strapping lad like you."

During the two weeks before they were to sail, while Heinrich went to Wenden to wed and collect his bride, Hermann decided to go home—as much to have his clothes washed and mended as in the knowledge that he would probably never see his parents again. Friedrike was heartbroken but not surpised. Harm had dreamed of going to America ever since he was a little boy. She remembered the Gypsy's prediction so long ago. Another one gone. She wondered how many more. At least she still had her four youngest—but for how long? Johann Justus merely shrugged and bowed to the inevitable.

1884 Shortly before Easter of 1884 Henriette, Friedrike's cousin, waddled down Gartenweg to the Bruns cottage. After five children she had become just as fat as her late sister Doris but apparently her doctor husband took better care of her. Tiete had some surprising, exciting and very welcome news and she could hardly wait to tell her cousin. Friedrike was surprised to see her. Tiete rarely exerted herself to even step out of her house.

She carefully seated herself before she gasped out, "You'll never guess what I just received."

"It must be something extraordinary to bring you this far," commented Friedrike. The Schulze house was less than three hundred feet away at the opposite end of Gartenweg.

"I finally received my marriage stipend from the Stockman Foundation in Celle."

"Good heavens," exclaimed Friedrike. "I had forgotten all about that. How long has it been since you applied?"

"Thirty years," replied Tiete.

Friedrike laughed. "Then I doubt I'll ever get mine since I applied long after you did even though I was wed six years before you. I know you kept reminding me but after Sophie's death I did not care about anything back then."

"But you will be getting it in a few years," insisted Henriette. "You are on the list of 'Exspectans' for 1893."

"A few years? That's nine years from now. I may not live that long."

"Of course you will."

"And how do you know all this?"

"Lude has been writing to them constantly for the past two or three years. He insisted we were due some sort of answer from them. And it finally came through. Isn't that wonderful?"

"I'm so happy for you. But how do you know about mine in 1893?"

"Lude was so insistent they finally sent him a list of the 'Exspectans' through the end of the century. Your Doris is listed for 1896."

"Really? She will be surprised to hear that."

"And what's more we also got an answer from the von Sehnden Stipendium in Uelzen. My Georg will get half the student stipend from that in 1886." Georg was Henriette's youngest child and only son. He had recently begun his medical studies at the University of Tübingen.

"How very lucky for you," commented Friedrike. "That will certainly be a great help to him."

"Ja, and I'm going to use mine for the rest of his tuition. It couldn't have come at a better time."

"And may I ask how much they sent you?" asked Friedrike.

"Sixty-eight marks, fifty-two pfennig."

A considerable sum but nowhere near the purchasing power that Hinrik Stockman envisioned for his descendents over 300 years before.

"So that is what old Hinrik's twenty Lübeckerthaler is worth today," commented Friedrike. "Damn the Prussians anyway."

A few months later Friedrike received a joyous letter from her daughter Anna in Elgin. Anni had finally wed her dear cousin Johann Bruns. She also sent regards from her brother Hermann, who was doing very well but was too busy to write.

"And about time," said Friedrike to Johann. "I fully expected several out-of-wedlock babes by this time, them living so close together. I'm glad she had the sense to wait."

"Now, Fritzi," he chided, "Anni always was a good girl even if she did run off as a child. It's Line you have to watch, in my opinion. She's so crazy to have a man and yet no one seems to suit her. And I worry about Minna. She's just the opposite—doesn't seem to have any interest in men at all."

"Ach, she's just taking a little longer to grow up. She certainly isn't shy."

"Nay, she's not. In fact I think she's sometimes just a little too forthright."

"Well, she'll be keeping busy for the next several months—maybe a few years. Doris wrote she is carrying again—her fifth—and she desperately needs help. I am sending Minna to her and Minna is quite willing to go. 'Twill get her nose out of her poetry books."

"Why not send Line?" asked Johann.

"Ach, Line. She doesn't want to be nursemaid to her sister's children. I think she is secretly entertaining thoughts of America, too. Ever since Harm left she has been corresponding with Anni. She doesn't think I know. It wouldn't surprise me if she decided to go all by herself."

Johann shook his head. He could hardly keep track of the doings of his womenfolk. He was just grateful that his dear Fritzi no longer seemed to be so upset by their comings and goings.

In 1885 Mimi, their youngest, finished school and was confirmed. She immediately went to work for Frau Pastorin. Alma Beermann now had two baby boys and Mimi was to be their nursemaid as well as general household helper. But there was more to the relationship than that. Alma was to have a profound influence on her life. Aside from Mimi's high intelligence and bright, cheerful personality, the pastor's wife recognized something unusual about the girl—almost as though there were a touch of nobility in her blood. She did not think that possible attributing it to her mother's long ago contact with the Duchess of Cumberland. And yet—

there *was* something more. None of the other Bruns girls displayed that characteristic except possibly Minna who not only loved poetry but filled notebooks with her own poems. Alma began training Mimi in every aspect of being a lady, in the real old-fashioned sense. The girl loved to read and Alma encouraged that, trying to broaden her education in every way possible.

When Henriette received her marriage stipend from the Stockman Foundation, Alma was very interested in hearing all the details.

"How do you know you are descended from this gentleman?" she asked.

"Mama has a paper from her Oma Dorchen that proves it," replied Mimi.

"I should like to see that. Do you think she would let me see it?" asked Alma.

"I'm sure she would as long as I bring it back. It's very precious."

A few days later Mimi brought Alma the precious document.

Alma unfolded the yellowed paper carefully. "1695," she exclaimed. "That *is* old."

"But it goes back further than that," said Mimi.

"Ja, I see that it does," replied Alma studying the contents. "It is the genealogy of one Cyriacus Albrecht Lindemann. Who was he?"

"He was—let me think," said Mimi frowning. "He was the grandfather of our Oma Dorchen who was my Mama's grandmother. You see it does go a long way back."

"Ja, and this goes even farther. See, here is Hinrik Stockman. And who are these von Sehnden—Anna von Sehnden, Franz von Sehnden, two Lüdeke von Sehnden?"

"I don't know. But there is also a von Sehnden student stipendium. My cousin Georg is going to study medicine under it."

"Then I was right," exclaimed Alma. "You *do* have noble blood in you. Let me explain. Nowadays that 'von' could mean nobility but more and more it simply means the place someone came from. But back then—back then it could *only* be used by true nobility—what is called the *Uradel*—the ancient nobility. I suspected as much. It shows. Oh, Mimi, you must be very proud of your lineage."

"I should?"

"Indeed, you should. And take very good care of that document. It is very valuable."

"I know. I shall."

Mimi was too down to earth to care much about ancient nobility. She was just an ordinary girl in a tiny village called Vilsen. But she enjoyed the adulation from so esteemed a person as Frau Pastorin and vowed to live up to it if she could.

A few months later Johann Justus read an item in the paper that interested him greatly. A fellow by the name of George Eastman in America had invented a special kind of paper that photographs could be printed on. Everyone was familiar with the daguerreotypes — cumbersome things where the image appeared on silvered metal or glass. But this was something you could take home with you, put in a frame and look at for years. He was fascinated by the idea. He went to talk to the local photographer.

Pointing to the article in the newspaper he asked, "Do you have this kind of paper?"

"I have just ordered some from America. It will probably take a month or two to get here. Are you interested in having some photographs taken?"

"Do you know what to do with it?" asked Johann dubiously.

"Certainly, Herr Bruns," replied the man indignantly. "I have been studying all about it ever since Mr. Eastman announced his discovery. It is a revolutionary new concept but quite easy. It will put photographs within easy reach of everyone. No longer any need to spend a vast amount of money to have the family portrait painted."

Johann nodded. "Ja, I am interested. I'd like a picture or two of my daughters," he said and thought, before anyone else leaves. "Perhaps of my wife and myself as well. Let me know when you receive the special paper."

In November of that year Mimi turned fifteen and almost simultaneously the photographer advised Johann that the photographic paper had arrived. Johann arranged to have a picture taken of Mimi and Lise together. Might as well try it out on the younger ones first and see how it comes out. If it turns out well, what a wonderful Christmas present it will make for their dear Mama. He swore the girls to secrecy. And the photograph did turn out well. Friedrike was thrilled.

In 1886 another newspaper article interested Caroline very much.

"Look, Papa," she said, "at this picture of a beautiful statue the people of France have given to the people of America. Look at her crown — just like stars — and the exquisite drape of her gown. And she is holding up a torch to light the way to freedom. She is called Liberty. That should interest you with all your struggles to gain Hannover's freedom from Prussia."

Johann laughed. "For all its beauty I doubt a simple statue would solve our problems here."

Line ignord that remark. "It says here that it is so big they had to ship it across the ocean in pieces and are reassembling in on a tiny island in New York harbor where it is the first thing all the new arrivals would see. It was supposed to be ready in 1876 for the one hundredth anniversary of America's freedom but some sort of political problems in France prevented them from having enough money."

"France is always having political problems," commented Johann.

"But now it is ready. Oh, Papa, how I should love to see it."

Johann laughed again. "You would travel all the way across the Atlantic just to see a statue?"

"No, of course not. But I could visit Anni and maybe Harm, too. I'm not sure how near they are to one another. She has several babies now. I'd like to see my nieces and nephews."

"Well, put that idea out of your head. It is too far to travel for just a visit." But Johann worried. He wondered if Friedrike was aware of Caroline's thinking. She would be greatly heartbroken if another one left.

And then not long after a most unexpected letter arrived from Hermann. Harm usually wrote only once or twice a year and that very briefly. But this time it was an urgent plea for help—for Anni. After the usual statement that he was doing well, he wrote,

'Anni is very weak and tired and, I believe, unwell. I am sure it is from having too many babies, one right after the other. Her husband Cousin Johann is very kind to her and I am sure he loves her but he cannot seem to control his basic instincts. I have spoken to him about this but he as much as told me to mind my own business. But I cannot. Anni would never write to you about this so I am writing to you on her behalf. She needs help badly. Please send one of the girls. I shall even send her passage money by telegraph if you cannot afford it. But send someone soon.

Your loving son, Hermann Bruns.'

Friedrike was shocked—not so much at the dire news but at Harm's blunt language about her son-in-law's 'basic instincts'. "Good heavens," she exclaimed, "we would never have discussed such things much less written them in a letter. But I'm glad he did or we'd never have known. Line, you must go."

Line was so flabbergasted at her mother's turnaround that she was not sure if she heard aright. "I'm going," she agreed. "Anni has invited me for years but I was afraid to ask for fear of upsetting you. And I've saved enough for my passage. Harm doesn't have to send any."

"Keep your money for when you get there," put in Johann. "I can well afford to pay your way. But what I don't understand is what this has to do with having babies. Good Lord, you had nine," he said to Friedrike, "and no ill affects."

"Anni was never strong," said Friedrike quietly, "strong-willed, yes, but not strong physically. And she started too late. Don't forget she was thirty-one when she married. I was glad at the time that she had waited but thirties is not a good time for first babies."

During all the excitement no one had paid any attention to Elizabeth, who was avidly taking it all in. Minna was in Bremen with Doris. Mimi was with Frau Pastorin. Lise would be the only one left at home if Line went to America. Suddenly Lise announced, "I am going, too."

They all stared at her as though she had suddenly arrived from the moon. Sweet, quiet Lise. No one ever knew what she was thinking but there was great depth to her. She was much like Anni in that respect, although much stronger physically.

"Oh, you just want to find yourself a man over there," said Line snidely.

"Maybe I do. But speak for yourself, dear sister," retorted Lise. "You don't seem to have had much luck in finding one here either. But I really want to help Anni. I have enough money saved, too. I'm going."

"But you don't even know Anni," protested Line. "She was gone before you were even born."

"Then don't you think it's time I got to know my sister? I'm going whether you like it or not."

Johann threw his hands up in disgust. "Go, then. Go," he declared. "It will be a relief not to hear you two bickering anymore. But if you're going to travel together, you'd better learn to get along right now or it will be long, uncomfortable voyage for you."

"Now Johann," said Friedrike. "Let us stop all this discussion and start making our plans." Her heart was breaking but she would not spoil the girls' enthusiasm. If they were determined to go, then go they would. After all, they had inherited that determination from her—and from her

own mother and from Oma Dorchen and from long-ago Anna von Sehnden and Lord knows how many other determined female ancestors.

Johann let his womenfolk make all the plans and arrangements for
the girls' departure but there was one thing he wanted to do before they
left. He wrote to Doris asking her and Minna to come home for a few days.
Doris could not come as she was still nursing her youngest son Rudolph
but she could certainly spare Minna for a few days. She promised, however, to meet her sisters at the pier before they sailed. Johann did not mind
that so much as he already had a beautiful pen-and-ink drawing of his
eldest daughter executed by her very talented artist son Gerhardt, who was
only fifteen. Almost as soon as Minna arrived he hustled his four
youngest—Line, Minna, Lise and Mimi—to the photographer's studio for
a picture. And he even paid extra to have five copies made so each would
have one. Then Johann was satisfied. Now he and Fritzi would always
have their girls with them no matter where they went.

1887   Over the centuries the Vilsen Church had been blessed with a
number of outstanding pastors, many of whom had risen to national
prominence. Whether it was the spiritual legacy and proximity of the long
vanished Praemonstratensian monastery or simply the sheer age of the
ancient church itself which had been a religious center as far back as
pagan Saxon times, no one knew or cared, if they even thought about it at
all. Georg Beermann was one of these dedicated men. A saintly but personable man, he was a tireless worker for his parish, striving to rebuild the
congregation from the falling away that had begun with the near atheism
of the French Time, had continued through the materialism of the
romantic poets and philosophers and had grown even worse due to people's hatred of Prussia and her Calvinistic church. Aside from being a fine
preacher and a caring minister, Pastor Beerman had one special endeavor
to which he devoted a great deal of time and effort, helped of course by his
brilliant wife Alma. Everyone in Vilsen loved them both, whether they
were regular churchgoers or not.

Pastor Beermann's favorite project was to raise funds and restore the
great bells which the Prussians had stolen during the Franco-Prussian War
and had melted down for cannon. The church, of course, was not entirely
without a bell. How could folk tell time without it? But the little ding-a-
ling that struck the hours of the church clock was not the deep, sonorous,
reverberating, thrilling sound of many bells that the townspeople had

been used to before the war.

And now the new bells were being installed and the people of Vilsen were once again very excited and happy. For most of the summer scaffolding had surrounded the square stone tower and everyone watched in fascination as a giant crane lifted the heaviest bells and workmen carefully guided them into place. The bells had to be situated precisely or they would not ring properly—might even be off-key. It was an exacting job and as each one was positioned the bellmaster tested it for tonality. And then, to everyone's surprise and delight, the pastor announced that there was enough money left over to erect a steeple on top of the flat, square, eleventh-century stone tower.

As the day of the dedication service approached Alma Beermann called Mimi into the kitchen to help her. She was unpacking a large wooden crate.

"Whatever is that, Frau Pastorin?" asked Mimi.

"A few little souvenirs of this great day," replied Alma as she carefully rummaged through reams of straw and sawdust. Finally she pulled forth the most beautiful porcelain cup and saucer that Mimi had ever seen. Both cup and saucer had a delicately scalloped edge trimmed with gold and on the side of the cup . . .

"Look," exclaimed Mimi, "a picture of the church with the new steeple! It's actually a real photograph, isn't it?"

"Exactly," agreed Alma. "And we—you and I—must try to sell as many of them as possible. But first we must wash every one to get all this sawdust off."

Mimi frowned. "I don't think you should sell them. How many are there?"

"Two dozen—four-and-twenty there should be if none are broken. And why don't you think we should sell them?"

Mimi mused for a moment. "Not enough for everyone who would want one. Besides some folk have given so much money already they should be rewarded with a little gift. Either them or the most loyal, hardworking members of the congregation, which is probably the same thing."

"Pretty much so," agreed Alma.

"Where did they come from? Would they be willing to make more?"

"From Meissen, of course. From the finest porcelain manufactory in Germany. And I'm sure they would be more than willing to make more. In fact they said that the more we buy the better price they can give us."

"Then I should venture to say that if you give some of these away—

783

maybe not all of them, maybe just a dozen or so—you could sell three or four times that many. Because everyone will be envious and want to have one. If you say you only have four-and-twenty, people will say 'I've already given enough. I can see my church everyday. Who needs a cup to look at?'"

Alma thought about that for a moment. "I do believe you are right, Mimi. Someday you'll make a good businesswoman. I'll speak to Pastor about it. I'm sure he will agree that yours is a good idea."

Of course the Johann Justus Bruns family received one of the beautiful souvenir cups. And Mimi and Alma between them sold over a hundred more.

On the day of the dedication service the ancient church was packed. Many people who had not been to church in years came to hear the bells, commenting that now it sounded like a real church again. Pastor Beermann preached eloquently on the verses from Proverbs—'a time to live, a time to die'—how the bells would ring for every important occasion in a person's life—joyously at weddings, solemnly at funerals. He also pointed out how the new steeple was like a finger pointing to heaven and now the church could be seen for miles around. The Bürgermeister said how delighted the town fathers were. He thanked all who contributed and told a little of how the bells had been founded in the great iron city of Essen. The schoolmaster stood up and recited in its entirety Schiller's lengthy poem *Das Lied von der Glocke* (The Song of the Bells) from memory. And then came what everyone had been waiting for. A talented choir of bell-ringers brought from Hannover played all their favorite hymns on the bells. The congregation departed to the solemn tolling of the great bell. Everyone was so thrilled they talked about it for months and Alma was very proud of her husband.

Not long after Johann handed Friedrike a letter he had just received. "A giant has passed away," he said.

"Oh? Who?"

"My friend Alfred Krupp," he replied sadly. Although they had not seen each other in years, Alfred and Johann had remained close friends.

"Do you think he was the one who made our bells?"

"He could have but I don't believe so. Krupp was almost exclusively into making armaments. Alfred never wanted to but he was forced into it—first by Napoleon and then by Prussia. He had little choice in the matter."

"Will you go to the funeral?"

"Nay. His son would not know who I was. At least someone had the kindness to send me this letter. It is like the passing of an era."

And then late in October another black-bordered envelope arrived from Elgin, Illinois. Friedrike was afraid to open it. Which one, she wondered with dread. Johann took the missive from her trembling hand and opened it. Inside was a black printed card, a letter from Anni and a short note from Lise.

"Line," he said.

"Oh, no! Our dear sweet Line," cried Friedrike. "How can that be? She has only been there a year and was in perfect health when she left here."

Johann quickly scanned Anni's letter. "Typhoid fever," he read. "Apparently it was very quick. One of Anni's babies is lost as well but she assures us that no one else caught it and the epidemic has passed. All the others are fine."

"Typhoid fever! What a horrid, filthy place that America must be. Don't they even have clean water to drink?"

"Typhoid can be spread by lots of other things besides water," said Johann. "It's hard to say. I've been told there was a terrible epidemic of it right here after Napoleon's troops passed through after the Russian debacle. And we certainly have pure water here in Vilsen."

"The French spread all kinds of disease," said Friedrike bitterly, "even into the '30s when my parents and Oma Elli died."

"Well, we can just be thankful Anni did not lose all her babies. But look here. Here is a little ray of sunshine amidst the gloom. Read Lise's note."

"You read it to me. I don't think I can."

"She writes that she has met a fine young man name of Friedrich— she calls him Fred—Blanck," quoted Johann, "and that they will be wed next year as soon as the period of mourning for Line is past."

"That's nice. Does she say where he's from?"

"Not specifically. Just that he is German from this part of Hannover. I guess that means more grandbabies that we'll never see," said Johann wistfully.

"Hah!" said Friedrike.

25

1888

Friedrich Campsheide was so talented and skilled that by Christmas Master Zimmermann declared he could teach him no more.

"He is more skilled than I in these fancy carved decorations. A veritable Tilman Riemenschneider," he said to Fritz's uncle, referring to the renowned medieval woodcarver. "He deserves to learn finer things than making coffins. I have given him journeyman status and have arranged for him to go to work with the greatest cabinetmaker in all of county Hoya, one Anton Christof Bruns in Vilsen."

"That's nice," said phlegmatic Onkel. "I'm glad he finally got over his foolish fears of the dead."

"Oh, he has long since forgotten that. He has matured nicely although still a bit shy. You should be very proud of him."

"We are proud of him," answered Tante with a bit more enthusiasm, all the while thinking that was one less burden for them to contend with. "Will he be living in Vilsen?"

"Of course," replied Zimmermann. "'Twould be a bit far for him to walk from here everyday. Anton's sons do most of his work now but the old man still teaches—and very well at that. Fritz should leave here right after Christmas so that he can start work on the New Year."

"That's nice," said Onkel.

"I'll see that all his clothes are clean and mended," said Tante.

Fritz was overjoyed to be going to work for a real and very talented cabinetmaker. Mayhap now he could make those tables and chairs he so longed to do. And the best part was that he would finally be earning a little money for his work.

It was late in the winter before Mimi Bruns became aware of the new young man in town. It had been a severe winter with lots of snow—unusual for this part of Germany—and no one had ventured very far from home. When going to visit her parents Mimi had the choice of two routes. She could go directly up on Gartenweg from the parsonage past Cousin Tiete's house and past Onkel Anton's house and workshop, thence home. But the snow lay deep up there and it was not very easy walking. Or she could cut through the churchyard, the paths of which were always kept clear by the sexton, and then it was only a short distance to her papa's workshop and Johann always kept the yard well shovelled. Thus it was that she had not walked along Gartenweg for over two months.

But this bright day at the beginning of March the snow was melting and tiny crocuses were bravely pushing their purple, white and yellow blooms up through the snow. She passed Cousin Tiete's large house. Her garden was always so beautiful although her girls did most of the work. One of them was sweeping the doorstep. Mimi waved and continued on her way. As she approached Onkel Anton's house she noticed a very handsome young man standing in the doorway of the cabinet shop. Mimi was never shy. In fact, she was quite gregarious and sociable. She was also very curious as to who this person might be. Neither Mama nor Papa had mentioned anything about him.

She waved and said, "Good afternoon," as she strode into the yard. "I am Marie Bruns. Who are you?"

The young man seemed a bit taken aback by her forwardness but she said her name was Bruns. So she must be some sort of relative. "I am called Friedrich Campsheide," he replied.

"Campsheide? Ach, I remember you," she said. "We met at the shoemaker's and then again at the Pfingst-ox parade when I was only three. You've changed a lot since then or I'd have recognized you." She looked at the dark, curly hair, the fine straight nose above a thick black mustache.

"I expect I have. It's been a long time but I remember now. You've grown up, too." He admired her tiny but svelt figure, her pretty, rosy-cheeked face.

"Are you just visiting or are you staying with Onkel Anton?" Mimi was never shy.

So that was the connection. "I am Master Bruns' new journeyman. I have been here since the New Year and already he has taught me a lot. He is a genius with wood."

"Ja, that he is. And so is my papa, his brother, who is the pewterer next house along. I am going to visit my parents right now."

Fritz felt a little twinge of disappointment. "Just visit? You don't live there?"

"Nay." She could see his disappointment. "But I'm not far. I live with Frau Pastorin but I come home every Sunday afternoon and sometimes on Wednesdays—like today."

He felt relieved at this news although why he should he did not know. He had only just met her. But he definitely felt attracted to her. "That's nice." He could not think of anything else to say.

"It must be rather boring living in a house full of men." Anton's wife had died some years ago and he had had all sons as his brother Johann had had almost all daughters. They often joked about it. "Why don't you come to dinner with us some Sunday. Mama is an excellent cook and so am I."

Fritz was a bit nonplussed by this. Shouldn't it be the mother who invited him? But he liked this girl just the same. She was so totally different from his shy, introverted self. "Thank you. I'll think about it."

"Good," she said. "Then I'll be on my way. I hope to see you soon again." And she went merrily on her way home, certain she had made a conquest.

Fritz hoped so too—to see her again, not yet ready to be conquered.

That same March Kaiser Wilhelm I died. He was ninety-one. His son Friedrich was already dying of throat cancer and incapable of governing at all. Thus Bismarck kept a tight hold on the reins of power. In June Friedrich followed his father in death and his son succeeded as Wilhelm II. Wilhelm was not his grandfather nor was he anything like his idol, Friedrich der Grosse. He frittered away his university years in a sycophantic, aristocratic fraternity house. He enjoyed the adulation of the Potsdam guard of which he was an officer for a short time. Crippled from birth with a withered left arm, he was eccentric, erratic and unteachable. He knew almost nothing about how to govern. Almost immediately he and Bismarck were at odds. Wilhelm believed in the divine right of kings and wanted a return to an absolute monarchy. Bismarck, although he was an ardent monarchist himself, was wise enough to know that to do away with parliament would only lead to a violent revolution and the devastation of the country and all he had worked for.

"Those young students who are praising this new Kaiser are fools," commented Johann Justus.

"Ja," agreed Friedrike, "they don't have any idea what we went through to achieve unification."

"Indeed. And now I believe it is more imperative than ever that Hannover declares independence, gets herself out of the German Empire.

Have you read any of his speeches in the paper?"

"Some of them. All he does is praise himself."

"And the military. That is sure to arouse concern abroad."

"But Europe is more or less at peace now. He would have to create his own war to make him look like a hero, which he is not. Do you think he would dare?"

"He's liable to," said Johann in disgust. "It is just the sort of foolishness he is capable of."

"Ach," sighed Friedrike, "as much as we have hated Bismarck, at least he kept the old Kaiser under control."

Johann shook his head. "You know, dear Fritzi, I would never admit this to our children but if we were younger I think I would seriously consider leaving for America."

Friedrike pretended shock but she understood how he felt. "What! And desert Hannover?"

"I doubt Hannover will ever see independence—as much as I have striven for it all my life—and the movement is stronger than ever. But with this young fool on the throne of Prussia . . ."

"Then be thankful you only have two more daughters to worry about."

"Minna I don't worry about at all. She seems quite content to care for Doris' children. And Mimi is too young yet."

"Mimi is eighteen and haven't you noticed? She seems to have taken a fancy to the new young journeyman your brother Anton has hired."

"She has? Nay, I hadn't noticed. You women always see things a man never does."

It was the custom in Vilsen and in most agricultural areas to allow the children three days off from school during haying time. Everyone in the village was expected to do their part except the very youngest and the infirm. Although it was hard work, the whole operation took on a festive air and everyone had fun. The men did the heavy mowing; the women and teenagers tied the shocks, also provided food and ample water for all the workers; and the children gleaned. The best part, in the eyes of the youngsters, was the ride home on top of the hay wagons. And if you were an older lad or lass it was the chance to do some serious courting, snuggling down in the hay where even the couple next to you could not see what went on.

Mimi always liked the fall haying best because in addition to the hayride one was high enough to pluck apples from the trees that had lined the roads into Vilsen for millenia. But this was June—the first haying.

Mimi had not gotten around to asking Friedrike to invite Fritz Campsheide to Sunday dinner as yet but she had talked to him frequently. Every Sunday afternoon and the occasional Wednesday as she went from the parsonage to her home she made a point of stopping at Onkel Anton's for a few minutes to pass the time of day with Fritz. He seemed to enjoy her company during these brief visits. Although still painfully shy, he was nowhere near as reticent as on the first occasion. She felt she was making some progress.

"I never see you in church," she remarked one time. Frau Pastorin had commented upon his absence, urging Mimi to a little proselytizing.

"I don't go to church," he replied. Was it a bit sullenly?

"You don't?" she exclaimed. "But you told me you had been confirmed."

"Ja. I had to go then. But that was the last time."

"But whyever?" she asked. "You could meet a lot of nice people, make some friends."

"Don't care to. My mother doesn't go either. You're my friend, aren't you? That's enough."

"Of course, I am," she replied. She knew he had not lived with his mother for years. She wondered how the woman could have influenced him to such an extent. But she did not dare pursue the matter. Somehow she sensed it was dangerous ground. She would find some other way to get him out of his shell.

Mimi shared what she had learned with Frau Pastorin. It was then that she heard the whole sad story of Fritz's unhappy childhood. She had assumed that he had left his mother to start his apprenticeship—a common enough situation. She was saddened to learn he and two siblings had been sent away at age seven.

"You see, my husband is from Asendorf," said Frau Pastorin, "so I know the whole story. It was not the church's fault. The then pastor wanted to help but that miserable uncle of his would not let him. The poor mother became embittered, with good reason. She has turned into such a shrew that it is probably just as well that Fritz went to live with his uncle in Hoya. At least there was some semblance of normalcy."

"How terribly sad," agreed Mimi. "Is that uncle—the Campsheide one—still alive?"

"Old Hinrich? Ach, ja, he's too mean to die."

Coming from saintly Frau Pastorin that was indeed a shocking statement. Mimi's tender heart went out to her new friend. She vowed to make him happy in any way she could.

And so when it was near time for the first haying Mimi asked, "Fritz, are you coming haying with us? I'll save you a place in our wagon."

He looked at her, puzzled. "I doubt Master Bruns would allow me that much time off."

"What do you mean?" she exclaimed. "Every shop will be closed for at least one of those days. Even the school. Onkel Anton and his sons will be wanting to get hay into their own barn like everyone else. He'll not only allow you, he'll probably insist that you accompany them. And they always help us with ours as we are all women except Papa."

"Oh. I didn't know. I've never lived on a farm except when I was very small and I don't remember anything of that."

"And you don't live on a farm now. But we all have our fields outside the village. How do you think we feed our animals over the winter?" she asked in exasperation. How could he be so dumb?

"I guess I never thought about it. My uncle never had a horse."

"Then you'll come with us? It's not hard work and it's a lot of fun. The men do the heavy mowing. We gather the sheaves and tie them into shocks. Then we all ride home on top of the hay, singing and laughing."

"I suppose." He did not know anything about haying but it would give him a chance to spend a full day or even two with this enchanting girl.

Fritz asked Anton's permission to ride in Johann Justus' wagon instead of his employer's.

"Sure, why not?" said Anton. "It's all in the family."

The June days were warm and sunny and the haying went well. Everyone prayed that the weather would hold so that the hay would dry well. Damp hay could lead to a disastrous fire. The weather did hold and when the hay was dry whole families helped load it onto the wagons. Everyone was tired, sweaty and itching but thankful. Fritz agreed that it had been fun—not the work, particularly. He was more convinced than ever that he was not cut out to be a farmer—but the congeniality. He was not used to people being so nice and friendly.

He climbed up onto the wagon and helped Mimi up after him. She dug a little nest in the hay and snuggled into it, drawing him down next to her. It was true. They could not even see the couple next to them. But they could hear them. The wagon rang with giggles and laughter. Then the singing began. Fritz did not know any of the songs but it seemed as though Mimi, in her high clear voice, was singing directly to him. 'Du, du liegst mir im Herzen . . .' He was slightly embarrassed at the words. Did she mean them or was she just teasing him?

As they passed under the ubiquitous apple trees, Mimi said, "It is even better in the autumn. Then we can reach up and pick all the fruit we want." She got to her knees to demonstrate. Just then the wagon lurched to much screaming and laughter and Mimi fell right into Fritz's arms. He held her for a moment. How nice she felt lying against him. He could not resist. He kissed her full on the mouth.

"Oh, Fritz," she sighed and cuddled closer. She had never been kissed by a man before. The tingle she felt in her heart was beyond her wildest expectations. Ja, his mustache tickled her nose but his lips were so soft and sweet. She wanted to taste them again. "Oh, Fritz," she murmured and let him kiss her once more. This time it was deeper and longer, his tongue teasing her lips. She opened her mouth slightly to let him in and his tongue met hers. She had never known such a thrill. She felt his hand creep around her and clasp her breast. The excitement swept down and centered in her lower belly. Oh, oh, oh! What was happening to her? She melted against him.

Fritz felt himself grow hard. How he wanted her. But before he took her right then and there, common sense took over. He knew how innocent she was. No doubt in her ingenuous teasing, she had no idea that she was driving him to distraction. He did not want to hurt her. Gently he pushed her away from him. Her face fell. It had been so lovely. "Nay," he said. "We must stop this. It isn't right."

"But Fritz," she objected, "it felt so good. How can it be wrong?"

He could see she was on the verge of tears. "Mimi, sweetheart, it is something that can be very wonderful but it is something that should only happen between a man and a woman after they are wed. Right now, it is very wrong."

She seemed somewhat mollified by this but he could see that she did not fully understand. Lord, didn't her mother tell her anything? Probably not. Fritz decided he must keep his distance from her. It was too potentially explosive a situation. Yet he hated to. He had grown very fond of her, maybe even beginning to fall in love. But Fritz was nowhere near ready for marriage and the inevitable babies that would follow. He first wanted to be a master cabinetmaker on his own. Meanwhile he would try to discourage her without hurting her.

Mimi had no such qualms. She was in love. That night she chose to sleep in the hayloft above the byre. When she and her sisters were little they had often slept there when their attic bedchamber was too hot in summer or too cold in winter as the warmth from the animals' bodies rose up to keep the hayloft warmer than their own room. Mimi had not slept there in years. Since her sisters had left and Minna only came home occasionally, she had had the whole big bed to herself. Tonight it was neither too hot or too cold. But Mimi wanted to go to the loft over the byre because the sweet, fragrant hay reminded her of the wonderful thing that had happened on the way home. She hugged an armful of hay to her and dreamt of Fritz.

Or rather she daydreamed although it was nighttime. But she could not sleep. Thoughts of the exciting sensations that had surged through her body kept twirling around in her head. She would have liked to tell Mama and ask her some questions but she was sure Friedrike would only say, ach, you're too young. Time enough for that when you are older. She wished her only brother Harm were still here. He would have told her. She had been too young to realize it at the time but, looking back, she realized that Harm had changed after he and Henni Matthies had made that trip to Bremen. She was almost certain now that it had something to do with those wonderful things that happened today between her and Fritz. Because Mimi felt different tonight. She resolved to ask Frau Pastorin about it.

Alma Beermann was not shocked when Mimi sought her advice but she was wary. She knew that Mimi was a warm, tenderhearted young girl who could easily succumb to the overtures of a young, lusty male. She did not blame Fritz. He seemed a decent enough lad, only following his instincts as any man would. She did not blame Friedrike for not enlightening the girl. In those days mothers did not speak of such things to their daughters except on the eve of their wedding—and often not then. She would try to explain as best she could without going into explicit details.

"You read your Bible every day," said Alma. "Do you remember where Paul said 'it is better to marry than burn'?"

"Ja," replied Mimi hesitantly.

"Well, that burning is what you felt but you are too young to marry and I am quite certain that Fritz is not ready for it either."

Mimi had to agree with that. She knew Papa and Mama would never

793

allow her to marry until she was at least twenty-one even if Fritz were to ask her. And she somehow knew he would not—not yet.

"So," continued Alma, "you must keep that burning under control and the only way to do so is to not let him touch you anywhere on your body—*anywhere*—nor to let him kiss you on the mouth the way he did. Oh, a light kiss on the hand or cheek is permissible once a couple is betrothed, but not until then. And you may place your hand lightly on his arm when you are out walking or dancing in public but never when you are alone with him."

"I see," murmured Mimi dejectedly. There went all her dreams. "But what causes that exciting feeling? I felt like crawling inside of him."

Frau Pastorin blushed at that. But then she smiled. "It is quite the other way around in marriage. Paul also said that in wedlock the two bodies joined together shall become as one flesh. And then, you see, that burning is cooled down, is satisfied."

"I see," said Mimi but she did not really see at all. Like any country girl she had witnessed animals mating and it did not seem very pleasant— both the mare and the stallion screaming as though they were in agony or a dog and a bitch locked together as though they were trapped. But Mimi was not shy. She had to ask. "But how do people do that?"

Alma was not quite sure how to answer that. "Well, you see, men and women are built differently down—er—below the waist. And that is all I can tell you right now. God will reveal all to you when you are wed. Until then keep a tight rein on your emotions—and Fritz's overtures—until you are old enough for marriage."

There it was again—until she was older. How old would she have to be? Until she became an old maid as her sister Minna seemed destined to be. Mimi had no intention of keeping a tight rein on anything—including Fritz—but she realized they would have to be a bit more secretive about their relationship. She also became aware, to her dismay, that Fritz's attitude was a little cooler. He was still polite and friendly whenever she stopped by her uncle's to pass the time of day but obviously he was keeping his distance from her—both physically and emotionally. Mimi did not like that one bit.

Everyone was happy the hay was in when in July it began to rain. And rain and rain. Torrential downpours occurred day after dismal day without letup. The Weser, which always flooded a little bit every year, now rose to alarming heights, inundating not only the watermeadows as was expected but also nearby fields and entering homes some distance from the river-bank. The Eyter brook, usually so clear and sparkling, the source of most of Vilsen's drinking water, ran high, turbulent and muddy. It had not yet overflowed its banks and fortunately was far enough from the town to pose no threat. The brook, which originated at the Sacred Spring at Heiligen-berg, flowed through the large millpond behind the Klostermühle and on past Bruchmühlen, whence it turned north eventually to join the Weser not far above Bremen.

And still the rain came down in torrents without surcease. Clothes and houses were continually damp, shoes covered with mildew. Fires were allowed to go out as there was no dry wood or even dry kindling. People began to think that they would never see the sun again, that there was a curse on the land. Dozens of long-forgotten pagan superstitions were resurrected as though people were turning back to the old gods for help—or for someone to blame.

After about three sodden weeks suddenly a rider dashed into the village shouting at the top of his lungs, "The dam has burst. The dam at Heiligenberg is gone. The millhouse is washed away. Save your beasts in the meadows—and your children."

"Oh, my God," exclaimed Friedrike. "The house where I was born. Does the mill still stand?"

"So far," replied the man, "but it may not be long before it, too, goes. Hurry to the meadows if you have any animals there. The flood is rushing this way."

Everyone ran to help, even those who had no animals pastured out near the brook. Johann rescued his horse and Friedrike her cow. Her goats were running wild. She just hoped they would follow her to the byre thinking it was milking time. Mimi met Fritz on the way to the meadow and for a while they worked hard helping save others' beasts. When all the animals were out of danger, they stood together on higher ground watching the flood surge cover the meadow where they had stood just moments before. Now the debris was rushing past—beams and boards, roof tiles and even bricks.

"How can bricks float?" wondered Mimi.

"The force of the water is so strong it just pushes them along," replied Fritz, his old fear of the water rising like nausea as he stared at the tumultuous flood.

Then they began seeing live things—chickens struggling to swim, unsuccessfully, geese who could but who could not control their direction nor raise their sodden wings. The poor creatures were rolled over and over in the floodtide until many lost their strength and gave up.

"I hope there are no people in there," said Mimi.

"If they are, they are surely drowned," replied Fritz. "No one could swim in that."

"Look, there is a man in a boat. It looks like he's trying to rescue something or someone."

"I don't see anyone in the water but it's hard to see from here."

As they watched a log or a beam hit the small vessel turning it completerly over. Fritz gasped, remembering his own ordeal in a very calm Weser. At first they thought the man was unconscious but then, after flailing about for a moment he started to swim. He was evidently a strong swimmer but he could make little headway against the torrent. People ran to get ropes but then he must have realized that he was over the meadow and the water, though fierce, was not very deep. He struggled to stand up. The water was only up to his thighs but it nearly knocked him over again. At last he reached the high ground and collapsed, gasping, "My baby, my baby is out there." Everyone looked but no one could see any baby.

While others were helping the man, Fritz was staring out over the water. He spotted something large, gray and furry, strugglng desperately.

"It's a dog," he cried. "A dog saved my life once. I can't let that dog die." He stepped into the rising flood.

"But Fritz," screamed Mimi. "You told me you can't swim."

"You saw the height of the water. It's only thigh deep. I must save that dog." Be brave, be brave, he told himself. A Campsheide must be brave. He strode deeper into the flood. As the water reached his knees the force of it nearly knocked him over. He strove to brace himself against it as he waded toward the struggling animal.

When he was still a few yards from the dog he nearly lost his courage. His foot stuck in the muck the meadow had become and he almost fell. The water was up to his crotch. He had no idea where the original bank of the brook might have been and that scared him for then the flood might be over his head. And then he saw it.

In front of the dog, as though the animal were trying to eat it, a white bundle billowed up on the waves. At first he thought the dog had caught one of the floundering chickens. Foolish dog, he thought, more concerned with filling his stomach than saving his life. I ought to let him drown. But as he drew closer he recognized with horror what it was. The long gown that babies of both sexes wore before they were able to walk. He forged ahead and started calling to the dog. The dog heard him and tried to head towards Fritz but it was caught in the vicious current and could not make any progress. He did not know if the baby was dead or alive but that was all the more reason to keep going. The dog was obviously trying to hold the child's head above water but Fritz could see that he was tiring. The water was now up to Fritz's chest.

Thank God, the dog had a collar on, something to grab on to. Fritz made a mighty lunge and pulled the dog and its burden to him and in the process almost fell again. But now he had no thought for himself. He had to save them both. He managed to turn the dog toward the shore—or what was now the shore. He slipped one arm under the dog's heaving chest and with the other hand held the baby's chin above the surface of the water. He still did not know if the child were dead or alive. But then, as the infant sensed the human contact, it started to sputter and choke and then suddenly let out a great yowl. Thank God, thought Fritz, it lives. The big dog, too, seemed to have been encouraged by that and with renewed strength swam strongly now that it had direction. Bit by agonizing bit they made their way towards the high ground.

Men were trying to throw them ropes but Fritz shook his head. Many did not yet realize that the sodden white bundle was a baby. As they reached the somewhat shallower water, Fritz called out, hoping they could hear him over the roar of the torrent and the constant drumming of the rain, "It's not deep. Come and save the baby. I'll take care of the dog."

Most could not understand his words but Mimi, who had been watching the entire rescue carefully—and prayerfully—heard him. When she saw that none of the men were going to act, she hiked up her skirts and plunged into the deluge. They met where the water was just above knee deep—Fritz's knees, not hers. She never gave a thought to the fact that all of Vilsen could see her pantaloons.

"Oh, Fritz, Fritz," she cried, "are you all right?"

"Never mind me. Take the baby. I'll help the dog."

By this time the big dog was beginning to find his footing on the muddy bottom. He would willingly have carried his burden to the edge of the water but he seemed to sense that this female human was the right person to deliver it to. He let go his grip as soon as the baby was safe in Mimi's arms. Slowly they waded the rest of the way, Mimi calling out, "Send for Dr. Lude."

But Dr. Lude, her cousin Henriette's husband, was already there tending to the man who had lost his boat. She handed the baby over to

797

him. "He's still alive—or she." No one could tell with those long gowns. "But he's no doubt swallowed a lot of water."

Lude took the baby, put him over his shoulder and patted his back. The baby choked and spit up some water but otherwise seemed no worse for the ordeal. Then Lude lifted up the gown. "Ach, it's a girl," he said.

When Fritz and the big wolf-shepherd finally reached high ground, Fritz sat down in the wet grass, exhausted and gasping. He was shaking all over from reaction and also because, although it was July, that water had been mighty cold. Mimi was immediately by him and the dog plopped down on his other side.

"Oh, Fritz," she said, "you were so brave. I'm so proud of you."

Fritz merely grunted.

Just then the dog stood up and shook himself violently, splattering water over everyone nearby. Mimi screamed and then burst into laughter. "As if we could get any wetter with all this rain," she said. The dog began licking Fritz's face and the young man hugged him. "See, he's thanking you," commented Mimi.

"Ja," replied Fritz. "I have just paid back a debt."

About that time the man who had fallen from the boat seemed to revive, not that he had been unconscious, merely grief-stricken. "My baby, my baby, my little daughter," he said and ran over to Lude.

"She seems to be fine," said the doctor, "but I should like to take her back to my clinic and check her over completely before you take her home." At the man's woebegone look, he added, "No charge."

The man nodded. "If I even have a home to go back to." It turned out he had a small farm just downstream from Bruchmühlen. When the flood waters started creeping into the house, he and his wife had begun moving what possessions they could up to the loft. Before they could catch it a surge of water had swept baby, cradle and all into the deluge. He had hoped the cradle would stay afloat but the last he saw of it, it had overturned. He had quickly launched his boat, leaving his wife to fend for herself. He had little hope the baby would be alive but he wanted to at least find her tiny body. He had been so benumbed with grief that it took a while for the joy of her rescue to sink in. He stumbled over to Fritz to thank him.

"It was your dog who really saved her," replied Fritz. "I only helped."

"He's not my dog. We don't have a dog," said the man. "I wonder who he belongs to."

No one seemed to know. Since no one laid claim to him Fritz asked

Anton if he might keep him.

"Sure, if you want," replied Anton, "as long as you feed him and clean up after him."

The great shepherd seemed quite content with his new master, following Fritz wherever he went.

Three days after the dam burst the rain finally stopped. People stood about in the sunshine which they had not seen in weeks, simply enjoying its warmth. The flood slowly receded but the meadow was no longer fit for pasture that summer. Many crops were laid waste and farms ruined. It took even longer for clothes, bedding and houses to dry out.

Some weeks later when the roads were once again passable Friedrike persuaded Johann Justus to take her over to the Klostermühle. She usually enjoyed the walk there but she was afraid of what she might encounter. Also she did not trust her emotions and wanted him with her. Her uncle Georg Brüning Bergmann had been miller there for a long time but after he died, Friedrich Matthies had sold the mill to a young couple named Hünnecke, whom she did not know very well.

When they arrived there she stared in horror. Most of the debris that had not been washed away by the flood had been cleared. There was a huge gaping hole where her childhood home had been. Men were busy building a new dam. Then horror turned to joy as she saw that the ancient Klostermühle still stood as strong and sound as ever.

"So, old Anton Matthies' new millhouse that he built for my grandparents could not withstand the elements," she commented wryly, "but the old monks knew how to build — almost eight hundred years old and it's still functional. That is something to be thankful for."

Mimi continued to stop by Onkel Anton's as often as she could even if it was only for a few minutes. She was in love with Fritz and she knew it. But she did not know what to do about it. Fritz, on the other hand, tried to remain cool towards her. But it was difficult. She was the sweetest person he had ever known. Her sunny personality invariably succeeded in lifting him out of his dark moods. Almost too often. Sometimes he wished she would leave him alone. There were times when he liked to wallow in those dark moods. And now she had another excuse to visit the cabinetmaker's shop — the dog. Often she brought bones and other tidbits from home and even from the parsonage.

When it came time for the September haying, Fritz was tempted not to go at all. But then he realized it would look odd if he were the only one to stay away. Someone would surely ask why. During the actual haying he managed to avoid her as much as possible without seeming impolite. But when it came time to go home, she watched to see whose wagon he climbed up on and she was immediately beside him burrowing into the hay to make a cozy nest for them. She leaned against him, wantonly inviting his kiss. He could not resist. If that's what she wants, she shall have it, he thought and took her in his arms and kissed her thoroughly. He could feel her trembling against him.

When they passed under the apple trees he noticed that some were already red. She reached up and plucked one.

"But they can't be ripe yet," he said. "We have not yet had a frost."

"These are early apples and very sweet," she replied. "Here, taste one."

He did and it was, indeed, sweet and juicy. "Ah, the apple of Eve," he commented, "as sweet as your lips." He put the apple aside and reached for her. "Come here, temptress."

He kissed her again and this time she knew what to do. Her tongue explored the recesses of his mouth. He grasped her breast and the expected thrill surged through her. And then—oh, my God—then his hand was under her skirt caressing her thigh. As his hand crept higher, her hips instinctively rose to urge it towards her secret place. Suddenly his fingers were touching something—she knew not what—that made her jump and gasp with pleasure and such intense ecstacy that her whole body quivered and trembled inadvertently.

"Touch me there," he murmured into her hair. Her hand reached down to his crotch and there, straining against his trousers, she felt something rock hard and throbbing as though it had a life of its own. So that's what it is, she remembered thinking seconds before her whole body exploded in such overwhelming pleasure that she was bucking and thrashing in the hay as though she were a woman possessed. She was dimly aware that he, too, was quivering and groaning and with one hard thrust the hard thing seemed to melt and fade away under her hand.

"Oh, Mimi, I must have you—properly—all the way." At her puzzled look, he said, "That prick of mine belongs inside of you—way inside of you as far as it can go—without any clothes in the way. Whether it's right or wrong, I must have you."

So that is what Frau Pastorin was talking about—becoming one flesh. But she was still a little perplexed. "But Fritz," she sighed, "what we just did was so wonderful, how can it be any better?"

"Ach, you might be a temptress but you are still so innocent," he replied. "That was only the beginning, the preliminaries. The real thing is so much more wonderful you won't believe it until I give it to you." I must have her, he thought. He started wondering where and when they could find the right opportunity. She's ready for it now. There would be no objections. Maybe she'll think of something. But by now he was decidedly uncomfortable. His semen had spurted all over his drawers. He could hardly wait to get home and wash himself off.

When they reached Vilsen he gave her a tiny peck on the tip of her nose before climbing down from the wagon. "We'll meet again as soon as I can think of something," he promised. He had grown very fond of her and he enjoyed her company but he certainly did not think he was in love. She was willing. That was all that mattered. And he guessed that she would be very hot in bed, more than enough to satisfy him.

That night Mimi slept once again in the hayloft above the byre clutching the sweet hay to her bosom. But this time the burning had gone away. She was basking in a glorious afterglow. She racked her brain trying to think of how they could meet in private. Mimi had always been an adorable but mischievous little girl, much to Mama's chagrin and Papa's delight. She was a plotter and planner. And she felt that this called for the most important plan in her life. But where? Certainly not at Frau Pastorin's, nor yet at Onkel Anton's. The byre would be the perfect place. No one came here at night. She could sneak Fritz in through the door at the far end that the animals used. But what if the chickens started squawking or the horse neighed at the sound and smell of a stranger. Mama would surely come and investigate. No, that would never do. But she would think of something. She simply had to.

Then all their hopes and dreams were shattered by two unrelated events.

Early in October Anton Bruns pronounced Friedrich Campsheide a Master Cabinetmaker. Legally it was almost meaningless. No longer were any of the old guild tests, examinations or masterpieces required although Fritz was so talented he could have passed all of them easily. Truth was Anton no longer needed his help but he did not want to dismiss the young man out of hand. But a letter from Bremen solved his dilemma. A former journeyman of his who was doing extremely well wrote that he needed help. He preferred to have a partner rather than an employee if the man

801

were talented enough. Anton saw it as the perfect opportunity for young Fritz although he did not know if the lad had enough money to invest in Karl's business. But arrangements could be made—and they were. Fritz had saved almost every penny he had earned. His only expense had been food for the dog and most of that had been donated from the tables of Mimi, neighbors and a generous butcher. Fritz leapt at the chance. Not only was it an opportunity to advance himself and make some real money but it was the chance to get away from Vilsen and the ever increasing temptation of Mimi. Not that he would not miss her. He would—very much. But he also knew that if the inevitable happened, as it was bound to, he would have to marry her. And Fritz had no desire as yet to marry anyone—not for quite some time.

Mimi was heartbroken when Fritz told her the news although she was very proud of him as well. She immediately began wondering what excuse she could make to go to Bremen. The only person she knew in Bremen was her eldest sister Doris and Minna was already well established there taking care of Doris' five boys. She could think of nothing else but she finally did get around to asking Friedrike if she might invite Fritz to Sunday dinner before he left. Other than that she moped, sure that she would never see him again and that all chance for happiness was gone forever.

After dinner when the young couple went out walking, Friedrike exclaimed, "A Campsheide! I'll never let my daughter marry a Campsheide!"

"But Fritzi my dear, you mustn't let your understandable hatred of old Hinrich Campsheide prejudice you against this young fellow. He seems a decent enough lad although a bit shy for my taste. Don't forget, he, too suffered at the hands of that same Hinrich. Imagine forcing the mother to send her children away."

"Ach, and she is a most unpleasant creature, too."

"Then no wonder the poor fellow is so introverted."

"And therefore not suitable for our Marie at all. It's obvious she's madly in love with him. I fear greatly for her if it goes any farther."

"Well, don't worry about it. He's leaving in a few days. She'll get over it. In a few months she'll have forgotten all about him."

"Nay, I don't think so. I've never seen her acting quite like this before. I dread to think what has *already* happened between them."

"Ach, put your fears to rest. I can see that he is nowhere near ready for marriage yet. He'll no doubt put her off and that will be an end to it."

"And that is part of the trouble. She thinks she is ready although she's not either. She is such a determined little person, he won't know what is happening to him. I don't want to see her hurt."

"She won't be. She's too strong for that. In fact, I feel a little sorry for him."

Friedrike had no reply to that. But she would watch carefully. Her thoughts drifted back to the night she and Johann spent in the palace stable loft. Was it really forty years ago? And she still loved him so much. Daughters never realized it but mothers always knew. And Mimi reminded her so much of Oma Dorchen.

Mimi fretted and bemoaned her loss for a while until she realized that everyone, even Frau Pastorin, expected her to get over it and forget him. She never would but she decided it was best to make a pretense of it so they would stop nagging. She busied herself with her fine sewing, beautiful things she created out of her mother's weaving. Of course, she remained at Frau Pastorin's but there was no longer much to keep her busy there. Both Alma's boys were in school now and Mimi had too much time to dream of her Fritz.

Then Minna came home from Bremen for Christmas bearing grave tidings. She could only stay for Christmas Eve and for Christmas dinner the next day and then she must hurry back. Doris was seriously ill—cancer, the doctor said.

"I must go to her at once," said Friedrike.

"Nay, Mama, not yet," said Minna. "It will be at least six months, maybe more. She is still up and about, acting more or less normally, although she tires very quickly. I can tend to her needs very easily right now. When she is forced to take to her bed, then it is time enough for you to come. What would Papa do without you for a half a year or more?"

Friedrike could see the sense in that but she still wanted to see her eldest daughter before it was too late. Her dear Doris, whom she had not even wanted because she had still been mourning her first-born, Sophie, the one she had loved the most, once Doris' brilliant personality and fine artistic talent became apparent. She thought once again of the Gypsy's foretelling—'she will marry wealth but thereafter her future is cloudy'. A frisson of fear swept over her. Suppose it was already too late? She must go, even if only for a few days, to satisfy herself that there was time ere she was desperately needed.

Then Minna continued. "There is one thing that would help. I can care for Doris well enough but not her and the children both, especially the little ones. Hans is so upset by this he is no help at all. He throws himself into his work and is seldom home. Gerhardt also is away much of the time. He is studying to be a marine architect. Teddi and Alfred are fine lads but typically helpless teenagers. It's the two little ones, Henni and Rudi who need someone. Do you think Frau Pastorin would let Mimi come?"

Although a cloud of gloom had fallen over the Christmas festivities, Mimi almost jumped for joy, although she must not let anyone sense that. Here was her opportunity to go to Bremen and actually live there for a time. Although she loved Doris and felt terrible that her sister's impending death was the reason for that opportunity, she did not really know Doris that well. Doris had married and left home the same year that Mimi was born. Her son Gerhardt was only a few months younger than Mimi.

Not daring to let her joy show, she said solemnly, "I am sure Frau Pastorin would not mind. I really don't have that much to do there anymore."

And so it was arranged. They would leave on the first train on Second Christmas Day morning. Friedrike would accompany them to see Mimi settled and above all to visit her dearest Doris. After a few days she would return to Vilsen and await the dreaded summons. She reluctantly agreed that that was best. Johann needed her and she knew she would go crazy watching Doris fade away. She had seen many cancer patients in her time and it was not pleasant.

On Christmas morning while the goose was roasting and Friedrike was making their favorite pudding—Rotegrütze, a delectable concoction of rasperries and currants served with dollops of whipped cream—Mimi ran to the parsonage to tell Frau Pastorin the news.

"Certainly, you must go," replied Alma. "We shall pray for her and for you, too. And Mimi, are you sure you are not going to try and meet your friend Fritz?"

"Nay," she replied. "I have not heard a thing from him since he left." Which was at least partially the truth. She had not had a letter or any news of him at all but that did not mean she was not going to try to find him.

Alma nodded but she was not so sure. She knew Mimi too well. Once the girl set her mind on something there was no stopping her. "Good," she said. "He's best forgotten. Then go with God and send my fondest regards to your sister."

On the way home she stopped at Onkel Anton's.

"Nay," said Anton, "I have not heard a word from him either nor do I know where he is living. But I can give you the address of Karl's atelier. I'm sure Fritz will be surprised and happy to see you. I believe he was at least half in love with you and too shy to admit it even to himself. Enjoy yourself, girl, and give my best wishes to Doris. How sad to be stricken so young."

The minute she walked in the door, Friedrike asked, "Did you ask Anton for that Fritz's address?"

"Nay, Mama, of course not." Another partial lie. "I just wanted to tell him about Doris. Although he did mention that he had not heard a word from Fritz either. So you have nothing to worry about, Mama. I'll be too busy taking care of Rudi and Henni and helping Minna to worry about that knave." There, she hoped that would mollify Mama to some extent.

Mimi was amazed when she first saw Doris' home. She knew Hans Menten was rich but she had not expected such luxury. In the first place it was not a house at all but occupied the entire third floor of a large apartment building in a very well-to-do neighborhood of Bremen. And so many rooms! Doris' and Hans' lavish bedroom was almost as large as the entire Bruns cottage in Vilsen. Mimi and Minna had a room all to themselves. And the beautiful furnishings. And the rich food. Oh my, this would take some getting used to.

Mimi wondered why they did not have a maid and now, a nurse for Doris. But her sister claimed she was still a frugal country girl and wanted no strangers about her, especialy not now. Her sisters were family and would do just fine. Mimi was delighted when Hans offered to pay her some pocket money in return for her help. Pocket money? It was more than Frau Pastorin had been able to pay her in six months.

Mimi soon realized that she would never find Fritz in this upscale section of town. She would have to wait until she got to know the city better. But it was so big she did not know where to begin and she dared not ask anyone. At least not yet. So she took to exploring the city in her free time. Usually she took the two little boys with her on these excursions. Of course, she had to see Roland and the beautiful Rathaus but the children were soon bored.

"Ach, Tante Mimi," said Henni, "we've seen those so many times."

"But I haven't," she replied. "You'll have to be my guide and tell me about them."

"Well, all right. Just this once," he agreed reluctantly.

And chubby little Rudi could hardly keep up the pace.

Henni wanted to go and see the big ships that went to America but Hans forbade her to go anywhere near the waterfront without a suitable male escort.

"Some Sunday afternoon I'll take you all there," he promised.

But when they went it was a disappointment because no ships were in port that Sunday.

What bothered Mimi the most other than the sheer size and confusion of the city was the lack of open space. Not that she expected greenery in the middle of winter and most of the streets were lined with linden and other trees, now bare. But she felt hemmed in. She longed for a meadow or a country lane to run down and play like a child. Not that she would do any such thing now that she was a woman grown. But what of these poor children? Where could they play but in the house or in the street? And Doris forbade the latter.

When Mimi expressed her concerns to Doris, her sister replied, "Ach, forgive me, I should have thought to tell you but I fear my mind is elsewhere these days. Here in Bremen we have a big Bürgerpark—absolutely huge—with meadows, trees and a good-sized lake where they can go swimming in summer and ice-skating in winter. We often take them there of a Sunday afternoon—except that lately I've been just too tired to go. And Hans—well, I guess he wants to spend as much time with me as possible—ever since we found out . . . " She choked back a sob. "I'm surprised Henni hasn't mentioned it."

"He never said a word about it," said Mimi. "He only wanted to see the ships that go to America."

"Ach, foolishness," commented Doris. "But now I realize how selfish I've been. This very Sunday I'll have Hans take all of you there."

"But if you just tell me how to get there, I'm sure I can find it. Then he can stay with you."

"Nay. You have to take the horsecar—two, in fact. You'll surely get lost. Besides it will do him good to get out of the house for a while. He needs some fresh air, too."

Mimi marvelled at how brave her sister was in the face of—what faced her.

When Doris told Hans of their plans, the first thing he asked Mimi was, "Do you ice skate?"

"Fairly well. I only fall down a few times," she joked. "But I never thought to bring our skates with me. Then Minna could have used them, too." The four younger Bruns girls had had one pair of skates among them

806

which they had had to take turns sharing when they had the chance to go to a tiny pond in Bruchhausen, which was not often.

"Ach, no matter," said Hans. "I'll buy you a new pair tomorrow on my way home from work. They're all adjustable now so size doesn't matter and they clamp very well onto your shoes."

On the Sunday, well bundled up against the cold, Hans, Mimi and the four boys set out. Gerhardt was busy with his sketches and Minna chose to stay with Doris. Minna was not the outdoor type, much preferring to read a good book or write her poetry. Mimi had never been on a streetcar before and that in itself was exciting. She marvelled how one sturdy horse could pull a vehicle of that size loaded with people. But the car glided easily along the tracks laid in the streets. When they reached the Old Town they had to change for another car going to the Bürgerpark—all for the same three-penny fare.

"Some day this will all be electrified," said Hans. "New York and London have already electrified most of their main routes and Hamburg is even now converting."

Mimi could not conceive of how electricity could move a vehicle almost as long as a railway car but she forbore asking, fearing that the explanation would be equally incomprehensible.

When they reached the Bürgerpark Henni ran ahead, packed a snowball and threw it at little Rudi, who promptly began to cry even though the ball missed him widely.

"Heinrich," shouted Mimi, "stop that immediately. That was not very nice."

Henni made a face but Teddi grabbed him by the collar and hauled him back to the others. "You little brat," he said. "If you don't behave, I'll give you a whipping when we get home."

Hans looked at the boys in disbelief and said mildly, "Henni, you must obey your Tante Mimi."

Obviously no discipline there, thought Mimi. Henni was always into mischief. She would have to watch him carefully. It's a wonder the others are so well-behaved—or is it just for my benefit?

When they reached the lake, Alfred said, "If you'll excuse us, Tante Mimi, we are going to meet some friends here. We'll see you back here long before it's time to go home."

Mimi nodded. "Don't forget it gets dark very early these days."

"We won't." Alfred was the fun-loving one, Teddi, the elder, was more serious. The two teens took off and soon she saw them whirling around with a large group of young people including several very graceful girls. The lake was crowded with people of all ages. She watched with envy as elderly gentlemen, who probably could not walk very well on dry land, twirled their equally elderly ladies around in lovely dances. She hoped she could do half as well and not make a fool of herself.

She sat the two little ones down on a log and proceeded to fasten their skates to their shoes. Rudi's had double blades so the little fellow could better keep his balance on the ice. Then she put on her own. How wonderful to have a pair of skates all to herself.

Henni started to sulk. "I don't want to skate. I want to build a snowman."

But Mimi was firm. "First we'll all skate. Then, maybe, if there's time you can build a snowman. I have not been skating in years and always had to share with my sisters. You're lucky you have such a generous papa. I want to show him how much I appreciate his gift."

Henni did not know what 'appreciate' meant but he liked Tante Mimi and did not want her to be angry or she might not bring them here again.

She led them onto the ice. "Now you two skate around this little area for a few minutes while I go off by myself so I can get used to these new skates. Then we'll all go around the lake together." She spun off and was soon flying around the lake. The new skates were like a dream. She waved at Teddi and Alfred as she glided by. Then she returned to the little boys. She took each by the hand. "Now we'll go slow so Rudi can keep up."

"I can skate by myself," said Henni. "You don't have to hold my hand."

"Very well but don't go too far from us." she replied.

They made one slow circuit of the lake and by that time Rudi was tired. Actually Mimi was somewhat weary as well. Having to go so slow like that was fatiguing. She would have liked to fly around as she had done at first but her job was to mind the little ones. They sat down on the log again. Some folk had built a bonfire nearby and they basked in its warmth.

Then Henni wanted to skate some more, snowman forgotten. "I'm not tired yet," he said. "Why do I have to sit just because Rudi's tired?"

"All right. Go ahead but stay close by where I can see you." Of course she knew he would not and in minutes he was lost in the crowd. She did not worry overmuch. His brothers were out there somewhere. And sure enough, after a short while Teddi and Alfred appeared dragging a reluctant Henni with them.

"Come on, Tante Mimi, let me take you for a spin," offered Teddi.

"We saw how well you skate. It's not fair that you should have to sit here all afternoon. Al will watch the little ones while we go."

He took both her hands and led her to the ice and off they went. This is more like it, she thought. She was exhilarated. He tried a few fancy dance glides. Mimi, not expecting it, stumbled and almost fell.

"Sorry," said Teddi. "I'll not try anything complicated until you're more sure of yourself. But you do skate very well."

"Thank you. But, you see, I never had the chance to learn to do anything but just plain skate."

As they passed a group of young men at the far side of the lake, Mimi was startled for a moment because she was sure she saw a very familiar figure. She turned to look and almost fell but Teddi held her tightly and they were by before she could be certain.

When they returned to the log and the others, Alfred said, "Now it is my turn."

"Wait a minute until I catch my breath," replied Mimi. "And where is your papa? He disappeared right after we arrived and I haven't seen him since."

"He's bound to be over at the tavern drinking a beer and eyeing the ladies. He does it every time," explained Teddi. "We think he doesn't know how to skate but won't admit it."

"Ja," added Alfred. "Mama used to skate with us all the time until . . ." his voice caught, ". . . until she got sick. So, come on, Tante Mimi, it's my turn to take you out."

Off they went and Mimi had not had such fun in a long time. When they were part way across the lake, she said, "Al, do you see that group of young men over there? I thought I saw someone I knew in Vilsen. Can we go around them real slowly and see if it's who I think it is?"

"Sure. Why not?" Alfred was always ready for some fun. "But I doubt there would be anyone from Vilsen here."

"He moved here last fall—to work here," she explained.

Alfred might have been only fourteen but he recognized the tremulousness that girls displayed when they were interested in a man but were afraid to say so. They glided slowly around the group. He felt Mimi's hand tighten on his.

"That's him," she cried. "That *is* him."

Alfred had no qualms. This could be fun. He steered her right into the middle of the young men. "Show me," he said.

She did not have to. Mimi took the lead and stopped right in front of a handsome young man with a bristly mustache. "Fritz, oh Fritz," she exclaimed. "How nice to see you." And then she blushed at her own forwardness. Alfred knew that this had to be more than just 'a friend'.

Fritz was so surprised to see her his skates almost flew out from under him. "Why, Mimi, whatever are you doing here in Bremen? And who is this handsome lad with you?" And to his further surprise he felt a twinge of jealousy. The lad seemed a bit young for her but then she always was such an innocent.

"This is my nephew Alfred," she replied.

"Your nephew?" he queried.

"Ja, I have come to Bremen to take care of my sister and her children. She is very ill."

"She is very ill and you are out here obviously enjoying yourself?"

"Ja, well, Minna is with her. The children needed some fresh air."

"The children?" Fritz looked at Alfred and Alfred knew immediately what the man was thinking.

"There are two little ones," he explained. "My other brother is watching them for the moment so that Tante Mimi could enjoy a little skating for herself."

Fritz puzzled over this perplexing situation for a moment. 'Tante'? And the lad was almost as old as she was. He knew Mimi had several other siblings but he had thought they were all in America. And now to find her unexpectedly here in Bremen. Whatever the reason, he might as well renew the acquaintance . . .

"In that case," he said to Alfred, "perhaps you would allow me to take her for a little spin around the lake."

"By all means," replied Alfred. "That is, if Tante Mimi is agreeable."

"Ach, ja," she said, "that would be most agreeable."

Fritz took her hands and off they went. He was not as accomplished skater as Teddi and Alfred but, knowing his background, she thought he had probably never owned a pair of skates until he came to Bremen. Nevertheless they managed quite well. Mimi did not care. It was enough that she had found him again.

Alfred watched them for a few minutes and then returned to Teddi and the children.

"Where have you left Tante Mimi?" asked Teddi.

"You'll never guess what. Tante Mimi has a beau," replied Alfred.

"You mean someone she just met? That is certainly not very lady-like."

"Nay, someone she knew from Vilsen. Tante Mimi *is* a lady," insisted Alfred. "She was so excited she could hardly contain herself. Although I don't think he was as happy to see her as she him."

"Life is full of surprises," commented Teddi. "Who would have thought? Our sweet, little Tante Mimi? I hope he's not a knave."

"I don't think so but it was hard to tell. We only spoke a few words. But I do know he has a jealous streak. I could see it when he thought I was her beau. Imagine me—only fourteen." Alfred thought it was a big joke but Teddi was not so sure.

"Look, here they come now," he said.

Mimi had been floating on air as they glided across the ice. It was so thrilling to be holding his hands again. She was so excited she chattered incessantly asking him about his work and a dozen other things. Ja, he liked living in Bremen. Ja, he loved his work. Ja, he was making all sorts of beautiful things. Ja, he was making good money. Gott im Himmel, would the girl never shut up? Yet he longed to hold her in his arms and kiss her but that was impossible in this crowd of people.

When they arrived at the log Mimi introduced him all around. "Alfred you have already met. This is Teddi Menten and Henni and Rudi. They are my sister's sons." At his strange look, she explained, "Doris is the eldest, I am the youngest. There are twenty years between us. Doris was married the same year I was born."

"I see," said Fritz. At last the puzzle unravelled itself. "I must be going. Will I see you again? Do you come here often?"

"This is my first time but now we shall probably come most Sundays as long as the weather holds," she replied.

"Then perhaps I'll see you next Sunday. Auf Wiedersehen," said Fritz and skated off.

Not a very eager swain, thought Teddi but refrained from comment.

Mimi was in a glow as they rode home in the horsecar.

Teddi whispered to Alfred, "I suggest we keep this to ourselves for now. No sense upsetting Mama. Nothing may come of it."

Alfred agreed but it was Henni who next day let the cat out of the bag.

"Mama, Tante Mimi has a beau."

"Does she indeed? And how do you know that when we don't?" asked Doris.

"We met him at the Bürgerpark yesterday."

"Did you now? Well, I suggest you say nothing about it until Tante Mimi sees fit to tell me herself." Henni pouted. His big news had fallen flat. But Doris was curious. Ever since last night she had noticed the change in her sister's demeanor. Like a woman in love. And yet, how could that be if she had only just met the fellow?

Doris was too wise to pose a direct question. She approached the matter obliquely. "You like to read, don't you Mimi?"

"Ach, ja, I love to read," Mimi replied. "I've read most of Goethe and Schiller and lots of poetry—everything I could get my hands on."

"But have you ever read anything light—like romances?"

Mimi shook her head. "Nay. Such things were not available in Vilsen. Frau Pastorin had an extensive library but she said such things were foolishness for an intelligent person."

"Ach," demurred Doris, "sometimes it's fun to read something light and frivolous. Now that you are old enough to realize they are just stories, I have a number of them you might enjoy. Hans doesn't know I have them. He says if a woman is happily married she doesn't need that sort of thing."

"Are you happily married, Doris?"

"Very much so. I adore my Hans and my wonderful boys. But it's still fun to read about others' romances."

"Doris, may I ask you a question? How did you know when you had fallen in love with Hans?"

Doris smiled. "That is a hard question to answer. You're not often aware of it until all of a sudden, there it is. It starts out with good companionship and common interests. Then a great deal of kindness and generosity on his part pushed it along. Then suddenly—I don't quite know how to put this—you want to spend the rest of your life with him and give your whole self to him—something a woman should never do lightly because men are ever ready to take you whether there's any love involved or not."

Mimi pondered all this a moment. "I see," she said slowly. And then she felt she simply had to tell someone and Doris was so much more understanding than Mama would have been. "Doris, I think I am in love," she blurted out.

"Do you now?" Doris was not surprised. "And who is this object of your affections?"

"His name is Friedrich Campsheide. He is very handsome and very nice although a bit shy. But I'm not sure if he loves me or not. How can I know?"

Doris smiled. "Remember the things I just told you. Hmm, Campsheide," she mused thoughtfully. "From Asendorf, no? Mama always hated a family by that name."

"But Fritz was born in Calle and then grew up in Hoya. It was that same wicked uncle that made life so hard for his mother." And then she told Doris as much of Fritz's sad story as she knew.

"I see. Then that would account for his shyness and perhaps some bitterness. You must watch out for that. But is he kind and generous?"

"He's very kind," replied Mimi, "but he has not had a chance to be generous. He was only a journeyman with our Onkel Anton but now he says he is doing very well here in Bremen."

"Then time will tell," commented Doris. "Has he tried to get you into his bed?"

"Oh, no," declared Mimi, shocked until she realized that was exactly what he had been trying to do back in Vilsen. "That is, I don't think so," she ended lamely.

Doris thought she had better straighten this girl out and that right quick before the inevitable happened. "Has he touched you? I mean other than holding hands?"

Mimi blushed. "Well, we've kissed," she admitted, "and—and he touched my breast."

"Anywhere else?" Doris sounded quite stern now. "Did he get up under your skirt?"

Mimi gasped. How did her sister know? "Just once, for only a moment," she replied hesitantly. "But, oh Doris, it was so exciting. It made me feel so good." There, she had confessed all. Now Doris would understand. But she was not prepared for her sister's vehement reaction.

"Don't ever, *ever* let him do that again," she admonished. "He didn't put himself inside of you, did he?"

"Nay, nay, nay. Only that one touch. I'm still virgin."

"Thank God for that," sighed Doris.

"But why, why, Doris? It felt so wonderful."

"As it was meant to," warned Doris. "That is a man's way of making a woman want it so much that she will acquiesce. A woman's body under a man's touch will always betray her. Make sure your mind is always in control of your body and the surest way to see to that is not to let him do any of those things you mentioned. Oh, a gentle embrace or a chaste kiss is all right, but nothing more."

Mimi was almost in tears. In one way she regretted confessing to Doris and in another she was glad. "Am I a very wicked woman, Doris?" she sobbed.

Doris put her arm around her. "No, of course not. Just very innocent. But to answer your question, no, he does not love you—yet. But if you really want him to, he will eventually, provided you keep him at arm's length. Look, if you see him next Sunday, why don't you ask him to dinner the following week—while I am still able to be a hostess. That way Hans and I can get to know your Fritz and see if he is really worthy of my dearest little sister."

At the hint of Doris' impending demise, Mimi wanted to weep all the more. But then she brightened at the thought of inviting Fritz to this beautiful home. "Thank you, Doris. I'll do that."

Fritz, meanwhile, lay on his cot in the loft above the workshop and dreamed about Mimi. He had been so surprised to see her here in Bremen that he had at first given no thought as to whether he was glad or sorry. Back in Vilsen things had heated up to the danger point so that he had been grateful for the chance to come to Bremen and try and forget her. But now that he had seen her again, had actually held her little hands while they were skating, he wanted her again. Oh, how he wanted her. And now that he had his own private room . . . So what if it was in the loft above the workshop. It was clean, warm and cozy. And no dead bodies down below to frighten him—or her. Only the pungent scent of newly sawn wood, wood shavings and sawdust. A fresh, clean smell that reminded him of beautiful forests.

Fritz could have shared an apartment with three other young craftsmen—he could not yet afford to rent a room of his own—but Fritz was a very private person. He would rather be alone. But, good heavens, he thought. If he wanted to bring Mimi here, he would have to make himself a proper bed. They could never make love on this narrow cot. And so his dreams went until he could hardly wait until the next Sunday. He hoped she would show up at the Bürgerpark. He mentally kicked himself for not asking where she lived. It must be some distance away because she had mentioned taking two horsecars.

At last Sunday came. Fritz rushed through his meagre dinner. It was costly to eat out and he was not allowed to have a cookstove in the loft although he did manage to brew coffee on the small iron potbellied stove that heated the place. He was at the Bürgerpark while most people were still eating their dinner. But that was good. With fewer people he would be able to watch for her. In order not to seem too eager for her arrival, he skated around the lake a few times but he was so nervous that he might miss her that he finally sat on the log where he had last seen her and waited. But after a time he started to get cold. No one had built a bonfire as yet. Cold and impatient. Suppose she did not come? In order to quell his nervousness he skated around the lake a few more times and almost missed her arrival. It was Henni who spotted him first.

"Tante Mimi," he shouted, "there's your beau." The lad ran out onto the ice and collided with Fritz knocking him over and falling down on top of him.

Fritz was embarrassed at his clumsiness when he was trying to act the suave gentleman. But he had not expected the boy to come hurtling out of nowhere. He felt less bad when he reached shore and saw that Mimi was blushing.

"Ach, I'm so sorry, Fritz. Are you hurt?" she asked, concerned.

"Nay, not at all," he replied, laughing. "I just didn't expect to be hit with a cannonball."

"Henni, you must apologize to Master Campsheide," ordered Mimi. "And he's *not* my beau. Just a good friend."

As they skated around or rested on the log Fritz noticed something different about Mimi. He could not put his finger on it but it was there. Was it a new-found maturity or had she become less infatuated with him? He hoped it was not the latter but the thought of the former dismayed him a little. It would not be so easy to lure her into his bed. But she was still the same sweet, fun-loving girl he—what?—loved? adored? Nay, not those. Fritz, who had never known love, was not sure what love really was. But he liked her very much and certainly enjoyed her company.

At the end of a very delightful afternoon he was pleasantly surprised when she invited him to dinner the next Sunday. He was about to refuse, not wanting to be put on display before the whole family but then—he had already met four of the five boys and liked the older ones immensely. If the sister was anything like Mimi, it could not be too bad. And for Fritz, who liked to eat, the thought of a real home-cooked meal was irresistible. He accepted eagerly.

Mimi gave him directions and told him to be there at twelve sharp. Hans would not wait his dinner for anybody. Hmm, thought Fritz, *Am Walle*, a very high-class neighborhood. Hmm.

Fritz almost lost his courage when it came time to ring the doorbell. He kept repeating his usual refrain. Be brave. Mimi answered the door herself and bid him a joyous welcome. Doris was a past master at putting people at their ease and he soon relaxed. The dinner was delicious and he gorged himself. It was a long time, if ever, since he had had a meal like that. Hans made polite inquiries about his work and seemed satisfied when Fritz waxed eloquent about that.

"You should get out more with other young men," advised Hans. "It is not good to be alone so much."

"I don't really know many people," replied Fritz, shy once again.

"The only way to meet them is to get out with them," said Hans. "We men play pinochle every Thursday night. We all go bowling quite often. Gerhardt, Teddi and Alfred belong to a Turnverein. You are welcome to join us in all of these things."

The idea appealed to Fritz. They made him feel so welcome. Yet he hesitated.

"Ach, Fritz, you should go," put in Mimi. "You are alone too much and then you brood. It is not good to brood on the past."

That did it. He would not be called a brooder although he knew it was true. How well she knew him. Over time Fritz joined the men in all three activities although he like the Turnverein best. It made him feel more manly. He also enjoyed the skill and mental challenge of the pinochle games. He made more friends than he could have imagined and it all helped take his mind off of Mimi. Not that he neglected her. Every Sunday afternoon was theirs whether they went skating or just walking through the park once the ice and snow had melted. Although he kissed her frequently he made no further attempts to seduce her sensing rightly that she would reject him. In that, the strenuous exercises at the Turn-verein helped burn off a lot of that excess fire.

As winter slipped into spring the signs of Doris' illness became more obvious. Her weight fell off and she turned wan and haggard-looking. Mimi had always considered her the only really beautiful one of all the Bruns sisters but now Doris looked as though she were their great-grand-mother. She became more and more tired and took to her bed often. Although she always tried to join them for meals, it was obviously an effort and she barely picked at her food. As May burst into the full bloom of late spring Doris could no longer rise from her bed. The doctor kept her dosed with morphine so she could endure the pain.

The happy home became a house of gloom. Once jovial Hans him-self began to lose weight from sheer worry. Although he had known for months that his beloved wife would soon leave them, it was agonizing to watch her slowly and painfully fade away. He neglected his work to be with her as much as he could. Minna never left her side except when Mimi insisted she get some sleep. Then Mimi took her turn as nurse. She tried to keep the children from disturbing her too much but there were times when Doris asked for them. But then she would hug them and kiss them, often without saying a word, and then send them away.

The two youngest, Rudi and Henni, did not really understand what was happening to their mother. Teddi and Alfred walked around like lost souls. Mimi tried to keep them busy with their school work but they had not the heart for it. Gerhardt disappeared almost every evening and only returned very late. Neither Mimi nor Hans asked where he went or what he was doing. They understood that he could not bear to watch his beautiful mother die.

Of necessity during this time Mimi and Fritz's social life was greatly curtailed. There were times when Fritz thought, why does the woman take so long to die? And then he was immediately ashamed of even thinking such a thing. What would he ever do if his dear Mimi should die?

At last on 29 July 1889 Doris found peace with God and a surcease from pain. She was thirty-nine.

Then came the long period of mourning. Hans immediately sent Minna home to Vilsen for a while. She had borne the brunt of the nursing and he feared she was on the verge of a nervous breakdown. Mimi, though heartbroken, was more resilient and the children needed her more than ever now. She agreed to stay. Friedrike and Johann had come for the funeral and Friedrike stayed on for a while until taking Minna home with her. All this time Mimi could not see Fritz at all. She dared not even mention him to her mother. And she missed him terribly.

After things settled down a bit, although they were still in mourning, Hans could see how being deprived of any social contact was affecting Mimi's usual sunny disposition. He suggested, "Why don't you ask Fritz over for Sunday afternoon coffee? I know you would enjoy it. Doris would not want you pining after him for her sake."

Mimi smiled. "Ach, Hans, how kind of you. Ja, I would enjoy it very much and I'm sure Fritz will, too, even if we can't go anywhere. You don't mind?"

"Not at all," replied Hans. "Truthfully, I do not believe in these long periods of mourning. I miss my dear Doris very, very much and always will. But I believe the quicker one gets back to work and the boys to school and all of us back to some semblance of normalcy, the quicker we shall get over our grief. Don't you agree?"

Mimi nodded slowly. "I guess you're right. But what will people say?"

"What do I care what people will say? I will have no yearlong gloom in this household. One month is enough. Then off with those black clothes. Put on something bright and gay and enjoy what is left of the summer with your swain."

"My swain?"

"Well, whatever you want to call him. He's obviously taken with you and you with him. But I warn you—no hanky-panky while you're under my roof."

And Mimi had to laugh for the first time since her sister's death.

As Christmas approached Mimi was not sure to what extent Hans wanted to celebrate the holiday. No matter what he said she was determined to make it as happy as possible for the children.

When she broached the matter he replied, "Of course we're going to celebrate just as we always have. Doris would not have wanted it any other way. And don't forget St. Nikolaus Day."

"How could I forget such an important part of Christmas?" she asked.

Hans gave her money to buy little trinkets for their stockings. On the Eve of St. Nikolaus (5 December) it was customary for children throughout northern Germany and Holland to write a letter to Sankt-Niklas (Santa Claus) listing the gifts they hoped to receive from him on Christmas Eve. When Mimi was little it had been the custom to put the letter in one's shoe stuffed with straw (for the saint's white horse) and place it on the windowsill or sometimes on the hearthstone. More recently the practice had changed to hanging one's stocking from the mantelpiece. And of course, a plate of cookies and a glass of milk were left for the good saint.

Since little Rudi was not yet in school Mimi helped him with his letter. He was a bright boy who already knew his alphabet and could write his own name but nothing more. He was quite excited by the whole procedure. Henni was a bit more reluctant.

"I don't think there is any Sankt-Niklas," he declared.

"Henni, you mustn't say that. Of course, there is," replied Mimi.

"Then why did he take my Mama away?"

"But he didn't, Henni. It was God who decided he wanted her among his angels. Sankt-Niklas only wants to bring happiness to children, not sadness."

"Well, I'm not going to write any dumb letter."

"Then you will be the only one in this family who will not receive any presents on Christmas Eve."

That made Henni think but he was still dubious.

Teddi and Alfred overheard the discussion and decided to step in. Teddi said, "That's right. You'll be the only one left out. Al and I are going to hang our stockings."

"But you haven't hung them in years," objected Henni.

"We are this year because Mama would have wanted us to."

That decided Henni. He wrote a lengthy list of desires. He would not be left out.

When Rudi finished dictating his brief letter to Mimi, he whispered, "Tante Mimi, can you write one more thing?" Mimi almost wept at his poignant postscript. "I know Sankt-Niklas can't bring Mama back but could you ask if he would bring just one kiss from her?"

Mimi had to rush out and purchase some new pencils and small school supplies for Teddi's and Alfred's unexpected stockings. Also, to her delight, she found four plump oranges in the fruit market which would nicely fill the toe of each stocking.

As Christmas drew nigh Mimi asked Hans if she might ask Fritz to join them for either Christmas Eve or Christmas dinner. "He will be so alone," she said. "He has no family here or much of anywhere for that matter. It's not good to be alone at Christmas."

"Why of course you may," replied her brother-in-law. "I fully expected him. You didn't have to ask."

When Mimi extended the invitation to Fritz he was delighted. "I'd hoped you would ask me," he replied, "because I have made a small gift for each of the boys. Nothing much but I could hardly come empty-handed."

"Oh, what?" she asked. "Tell me."

"Nay, it's to be a surprise. And I have a request in turn. Could you ask Hans if I may help them trim the Christmas tree? That is, if they're going to have one this year."

"Oh, I'm sure they are. Hans wants everyting to be as normal as possible."

On the afternoon of Christmas Eve Mimi took Rudi and Henni to see the brightly decorated shop windows and the magnificent Christmas display in the Rathaus Square in order to get them out of the house while

Sankt-Niklas was busy.

"Isn't Fritz coming with us?" asked Henni.

"Nay, because this year Sankt-Niklas has chosen him to be one of his helpers."

"Oh." But Henni was still dubious.

Gerhardt's idea of trimming a tree was that everything must be symmetrical. Teddi's was that it should all be neat and precise. Alfred did not care as long as all the favorite ornaments got on the tree somehow. But with Fritz's guidance and help it soon became a work of art. He moved things around to display them best. He placed the candles just so, so that they would show off the ornaments to best advantage.

And then to everyone's surprise Fritz produced a dozen small but exquisite wooden ornaments that he himself had carved and painted. Of tiny animals there was a dog, a horse and a peacock.

"Where did you find a picture to copy those colors so precisely?" asked Gerhardt.

"I went to the zoo and studied the real bird," replied Fritz.

Of fruit, there was an apple, a pear and a peach; a little house, a church and a mill. "That's for Mimi," he said. And then a small Christmas tree, an angel and a wooden cradle with a waxen baby Jesus lying in the straw.

"You are truly an artist," exclaimed Teddi.

Everyone agreed it was the most beautiful tree they had ever had.

"Ach, if Mama were only here to see it," remarked Alfred with tears in his eyes.

When Mimi arrived home with the children, the parlor was shut tightly and in darkness.

"Do you think Sankt-Niklas has been here?" asked Henni forgetting his earlier doubts.

"We'll soon see," replied Mimi. "If you've been good children, I'm sure he has."

"I been good," said Rudi, too excited to eat the light supper.

None of them noticed Fritz slip away for a few minutes to light the candles on the tree. When they could contain their suspense no longer, suddenly a tiny bell tinkled. Hans flung open the door to the parlor. The children rushed in and stopped. Fritz's work of art brought delighted gasps and exclamations. Even Hans admitted he had never seen anything so exquisite.

After they had exchanged gifts—including more of Fritz's carvings: a horse and wagon for Rudi and a fire engine with a real bell for Henni—there was wine and Christmas cookies. Then they all went to church. At midnight the bells of every church in Bremen—and there were many of them—pealed out a joyous welcome to their Savior. Mimi could not believe there were so many bells in the world. The tintinnabulation, though thrilling, was almost deafening.

As New Year's drew nigh the Turnverein announced that there would be a grand party on New Year's Eve celebrating the beginning of the last decade of the nineteenth century. And what a century it had been from the nadir of Napoleon's conquest to the present-day Germany which was now one of the greatest industrial, military and colonial powers of the world. Members were encouraged to bring their wives and sweethearts, their mothers, sisters and daughters, any female they could lay hands on.

Fritz was at first reluctant to go.

"What?' exclaimed Alfred. "Do you mean to leave Tante Mimi alone on New Year's Eve?"

"But I don't know how to dance," admitted Fritz. "I'll only make a fool of myself."

"Then we'll teach you." And immediately the brothers began giving Fritz dancing lessons. "Think of it as skating only without the skates," explained Alfred.

After several hilarious lessons, which Fritz did not think funny at all, Teddi pronounced him good enough to get by. "Just follow the rhythm of the music," he said. "It doesn't really matter what steps you do."

"Ja," agreed Alfred. "The most important thing is not to tread on the hem of her gown."

Mimi, who loved to dance and was a very good dancer, had looked forward to the event with great excitement. She knew full well of Fritz's reluctance to dance but she was happy that she would be able to spend a whole evening with him, even past midnight. So what if he did not know all the steps. She would subtly try to teach him and put him at ease. Fritz might have been an artist with his hands but his feet seemed to belong to another creature—such as an ox. Soon she found they were spending more time sitting on the sidelines holding hands while her feet tapped to the music of their own accord. As often as possible Teddi and Alfred took pity on her and whirled her around the floor. Even Gerhardt and Hans took her out a few times. And that was a real pleasure.

Fritz did not seem to mind at all. Mimi noticed that Fritz drank no beer, only wine and that very sparingly. Mimi's experience with drinking was very limited. It consisted of one small glass of wine with Sunday dinner and the occasional birthday or Christmas toast. Thus after three glasses of wine she felt quite giddy. It was so pleasant to have Fritz's arm around her waist as they danced even if he did make her stumble occasionally. She loved him so, she wanted him to do those wonderful things he had attempted back in Vilsen, all of Doris' admonitions forgotten in a wine-induced haze. She pressed her body closer to him and did not care who noticed. She did not realize that she was driving him to distraction.

At last the clock struck twelve. Midnight! 1890! A new year, a new decade. And Mimi decided it was going to be the best year of her life—with Fritz. Everyone around her was happy and so was she. Dignified toasts were raised among raucous cheers. Every male in the hall kissed whatever female they were with and Fritz kissed Mimi deeply, longingly. As his hand slipped over her breast, she thrilled to his touch and pressed closer to him. And once again all the church bells in Bremen rang out the good news.

After midnight people began to leave although there were many who would party until dawn.

"I think it is time we went home," suggested Fritz. He knew she would be his tonight. He could hardly contain his eagerness.

"Oh, but we're having such fun," objected Mimi. "I don't want to leave yet."

"It's a long walk and there are no streetcars running this late. Come on. The fresh air will do you good."

She hiccoughed and realized she was a little unsteady on her feet. "I guess you're right," she admitted.

The cold air hit her like a blow and she staggered slightly. As she pulled her cloak closer against the cold, Fritz put his arm around her to steady her. She leaned against him. Oh, he felt so warm. After a while Mimi's head began to clear and she noticed something strange.

"Fritz," she exclaimed, "this is not the way home. Where are we going?"

"Yes, it is. We are going to my home. I won't let you sleep alone on New Year's."

Warning bells sounded dimly in her head but she ignored them. "But Fritz. Fritz, it's—hic—not right," she protested feebly. But she was still too exhilarated from the evening, from his closeness—and the wine—to

822

argue. Truth was, she did not want to deny him.

"You want me. I know you do. You've been telling me all evening," he said.

She nodded. "I have?"

He held her closer and they continued on their way through streets crowded with roisterers, lit only by the cold, bright stars overhead. As they progressed through an area of Bremen Mimi had never seen before, she started to get very excited. At last she would see where he lived, at last spend a whole night with him.

When he unlocked the door and bid her enter, she exclaimed, "But this is your shop."

"Right. I live upstairs. It's not much but it is warm and clean—and very private."

She followed him up the stairs—real stairs, not a ladder as she had had to climb in Vilsen. His room was cozy and very neat.

"I'll have it warm for you in just a minute," he said.

While he shook down the fire and added some more wood, Mimi looked about her. My goodness, he even had curtains on the single window. She particularly admired the bed.

"My, what an elegant bed for a lone cabinetmaker."

"I made it especially for you," he replied.

"You made it? For me? But . . ."

"Mimi, sweetheart, I knew that someday—someday you would come here and let me hold you in it."

"You did?" And then she could not resist teasing him. He was so serious. "And I suppose you made that lovely featherbed, too."

He laughed. "Nay, my talents don't extend that far. I had that made—but just for you."

By now the little stove was roaring. Mimi willingly shed her heavy cloak, gloves and bonnet. She sat down on a chair at the small but ornate table.

"Why don't you take off the rest of your clothes? Or shall I? I want to see you in all your beauty."

By now Mimi was almost completely sober. "Oh, Fritz. I—I don't know. I don't think . . ."

He pulled her up from the chair, crushed her to him and kissed her deeply. The thrill was as it had always been—perhaps more so now that she realized what it would soon lead to. But no, she must not let that happen yet. But her fear only added to her excitement—and anticipation.

What would it be like to have him make love to her? But no, no, she dared not even think of that. Not yet, anyway.

His hand clasped her breast and fire surged through her centering in that place below her belly. She melted against him, inviting him to explore her further. He began fumbling with the buttons of her gown. That momentarily brought her back to reality.

"Don't tear them," she cried. "It's my best dress."

"Then you'll have to help me," he murmured.

Though Fritz was no longer a virgin, his experience with women and women's clothing was very limited. The few prostitutes he had used had already been in dishabille. Right now he felt very clumsy yet his ardor was such that he wanted to tear the obstructing gown from her. But he knew that was the worst possible thing he could do. She would never speak to him again. He must use persuasion.

When he saw her hesitation he coaxed, "Just open a few of them so I can hold your breast without all this cloth in the way. You will like that. I know it."

She knew it, too. Ja, she wanted to feel his hand on her bare flesh. Slowly she opened the buttons of the bodice. His hand slipped inside, past the low neckline of her winter woolen shift and—ah! She was totally unprepared for the shock waves that rushed through her entire body when he took hold of the nipple and gently teased it. She grew so weak in the knees that she collapsed back down onto the chair at the same time opening more buttons. She had to have more of that.

Fritz fell to his knees and putting his head against her eased one breast out of the confining clothing and started kissing it. When he nibbled on the taut nipple, Mimi cried out with pleasure. The fire in her groin seemed to explode. Almost unconsciously she slipped the gown off her shoulders and then the shift. He teased one nipple with his fingers while he suckled the other. She lost all will to resist. Why had she not let him do this before? Her excitement was almost overwhelming.

He picked her up and carried her to the bed. She revelled in his strength. Gown and shift fell to the floor. Carefully she stepped out of them and stood before him clad only in her corset, shoes and stockings. Quickly he divested himself of his own clothes except for his long underdrawers. They stood staring at one another for a moment, he drinking in her beauty, her eyes riveted on the large, red thing protruding from his drawers. A twinge of fear crossed her mind again but her curiosity overcame it. Before she had time to think about it, he was on his knees undo-

824

ing her garters. He carefully rolled down her stockings. She sat down on the edge of the bed so he could remove them and her shoes.

"Now what do we do about this?" he asked, indicating the corset. "I must confess I am not too familiar with the intricacies of that—that garment."

Mimi laughed. "The laces are in the back. I'll undo it if you promise to help me put it back on—when—er—later. But if I'm to take my corset off, don't you think you should remove your drawers?"

Suddenly Fritz's innate shyness almost overcame him. Never, even with the whores, had he taken off his drawers. He was so eager for her he would do anything to please her. Ach, Gott, don't let me fail now, not now when it is so close and she is willing. But his rock-hard manhood told him he had nothing to fear. He slipped off his drawers as Mimi wriggled out of the confining corset.

Now he could no longer wait. He pushed her back on the bed, kissing her and sliding his hands up and down her quivering body. When his fingers found that sensitive rosebud between her thighs, she jumped and moaned with pleasure. But this time they were not on a haywagon with a lot of other people. This time there was no holding back, no spilling of his seed in his drawers, no wondering on her part if there was more.

As soon as he felt her grow a little moist, he spread her thighs and aimed his member at that precious cavity. He knew she was virgin, knew he should be gentle the first time but he could not control his ardor. He plunged in. She gave a little yelp of pain, then gasped and he was in— deep, deep, deeply in. In moments, pain forgotten, she rose to meet him, wanting him to fill her, hips writhing in ecstacy. And suddenly, all too quickly, it was over. She felt him explode and then he lay panting on top of her. She wished it could have gone on forever but if that is all there was— then so be it.

After a few moments, he whispered into her hair. "I'm sorry. It was too quick. You are so beautiful I couldn't control myself."

"But it was wonderful," she prevaricated, although she somehow felt there was something missing. She was still excited, still wanted him.

"Next time it will be better, I promise."

"Next time?"

"Ja. Let me just hold you in my arms for a little while. It will come back."

Mimi was not quite sure what he meant but it was wonderful just lying here this close, bare flesh to bare flesh.

In a very short time she understood what he meant. It had indeed come back to life and was poking against her legs. He began kissing her again, slowly and longingly. His hands roamed up and down her body, caressing every part of her. When he once again suckled her breasts she nearly went wild with desire. Her hips writhed about, seeking him.

"Do you want me again?" he whispered. "This time I'll pleasure you."

"But you did," she replied.

"Not enough. You'll see."

He kept caressing and teasing her until she almost went mad.

"Oh, Fritz, please," she begged. "Ja, I do want you."

This time he entered her slowly, tantalizingly, pushed as far as he could and partially withdrew. Back and forth, back and forth until she caught the rhythm. Then he plunged deep, deeper, harder, faster. Her hips rose to invite him deeper still. Suddenly she felt as though the whole heavens were exploding within her, around her. All conscious thought left her, only exquisite sensation. And still he kept riding her, harder and harder until it happened again—and again. She thought she would die from sheer pleasure. And then the greatest climax of all—fireworks, comets, floating off into the ether. She was vaguely aware—and yet not aware, so great was her ecstacy—of his own climax filling her, filling her to the brim. She screamed, he groaned and collapsed on her.

She sensed the final dying twitches of that wonderful instrument as it shrunk inside of her. But it did not matter now. She had had it all—all he had to give her. She had never dreamt such pleasure was possible, even existed. Now she knew, knew what it was to be fully loved, knew that she was no longer a daydreaming virgin but a fully satisfied woman.

They lay panting in each other's arms, he stroking her hair. Her whole elaborate coif had come undone.

"You are so beautiful, my Mimi," he said at last, "but I'm afraid you'll have to redo your hair ere I take you home."

She snuggled closer to him, totally replete, ready to sleep in his arms. "But I don't want to go home. I want to stay here with you." Now surely he will ask me to marry him, she thought.

But he did not.

"As much as I should like to have you," he replied, "I don't think it's wise. Your family will worry. If it weren't for New Year's Eve, we'd never have dared stay this late. But now that you know how much I want you and how much pleasure I can give you, we'll do it again, nev-

826

er fear. Every Sunday afternoon if possible."

Not one word of love, much less of marriage.

Reluctantly she got up and dressed. She rearranged her hair as best she could with a tiny handheld mirror. "Is that the only mirror you have?" she asked.

"It's good enough for shaving. That's all I need it for."

Ach, men, she thought.

They walked the long way home arm in arm. It was bitterly cold but Mimi felt warmer than she had ever been in her life. She thanked God that Minna was already long in bed but Hans was waiting up for them.

"Happy New Year," he said with a broad wink at Fritz, who immediately blushed. "I figured you'd be along sooner or later. Now I can lock up."

Mimi should have felt embarrassed but somehow she did not. It had all been too wonderful. She sensed that Hans knew exactly what had happened and yet would not condemn them. Hans was a man of the world — and *very* understanding.

The next day Minna made some snide remarks about Mimi's sleeping until almost noon. Why pick on me, thought Mimi. Everyone except the two youngest boys had slept very late.

"People will be coming New Year's calling this afternoon," warned Minna, "and dinner will be ready before you've even had breakfast."

"Then I'll skip breakfast and just eat dinner," retorted Mimi. "I won't die from missing one meal." She refused to let her sister spoil that wonderful afterglow.

She wondered if Fritz would call this afternoon but he did not. Probably sleeping all day. Most of the callers were friends of Hans, many seeking to console him on the recent loss of his wife.

"Of course I miss my dearest Doris but she's better off where she is," he would reply. "She would not want us to mourn — especially on the first day of a new year."

And the same many went away perplexed, even shocked, that he should be so jolly, even flippant, so soon after his wife's death. It was not natural. But that was Hans.

The day after New Year's Minna announced that she was going home to Vilsen to visit Friedrike and Johann for a week or two. "It was their first Christmas *and* New Year's alone and I worry about them. I shall stay at least through Epiphany — maybe a little longer. You should be ashamed of yourself, Mimi, for not thinking of them at Christmas. You could have gone. I was here."

"I felt the children needed me more so soon after their mother's death," replied Mimi.

"Ach, you felt your Fritz needed you more," remarked Minna.

"That remark is uncalled for, dear sister," snapped Mimi. "I do believe you're jealous."

"Me, jealous?" retorted Minna. "I don't care a penny for any man. When is *yours* going to marry you? It had better be soon after last night."

Mimi ignored that. But when Fritz arrived the following Sunday, she had to tell him they could not go to his room. She must stay with the children. And so they conversed innocuously in the parlor in the company of little Rudi and Henni. The next Sunday the same thing happened. Fritz was obviously becoming annoyed.

"Why can't one of their older brothers stay with them for one afternoon?" he grumbled.

"Because it is their only aftrnoon off, too, and apparently they have other things to do. Don't forget, Hans is paying me to mind them," she replied.

Fritz shrugged and he left early that day. Mimi was almost in tears. Why did Minna do this to her—just when things were going so well? Then she felt a little guilty. Maybe she had been a mite selfish in not going to see Mama and Papa at Christmas but—but—

Minna finally returned the following week and, to everyone's surprise, was accompanied by Fritz's eldest sister, Dorothea Campsheide—Dorchen of the 'funny' eye. If one could overlook the woman's terrible disfigurement, Dorchen was a very sweet person. How and when she and Minna had renewed their brief childhood acquaintance, Mimi did not ask because Minna was a changed person—happy and cheerful, no more grumbling—almost as though . . .

But how could that be? Mimi's experience with the broader world was extremely limited.

Hans remarked, "So that's how it is, heh? At least they won't seduce my boys." And he guffawed boisterously.

Mimi did not have the vaguest notion what he was talking about but all she cared about was that now she and Fritz could make love again on Sunday afternoons. After the first few rapturous Sundays they did do other things, like skating. But Mimi always sent the younger boys home with their older brothers so that she could accompany Fritz to his room. To their surprise even Minna came to the Bürgerpark a few times as Dorchen enjoyed skating. As spring began to break Fritz took Mimi to the Tiergarten—the zoo—which delighted her no end.

26

1890

In March 1890 news came that shook all of Germany. Many rejoiced, many were saddened, all were shocked, never believing that such a thing could happen. The antogonism between the young, foolish, idiosyncratic Kaiser Wilhelm II and the aging Bismarck reached the boiling point and the great Iron Chancellor was forced to resign.

The bones of contention between the Emperor and the Chancellor were numerous—labor and other social and domestic economic problems amongst them. Many were of Bismarck's own doing, e.g., the restrictions on parliament. Bismarck had always hated having to deal with parliament but in later years he had come to realize it was a buffer between the government and outright revolution by the people. But Wilhelm believed firmly in the antiquated divine right of kings and wanted to do away with parliament entirely. He wanted followers, not leaders. To this end he appointed one Leo von Caprivi chancellor. Caprivi was a former general, a military man used to taking orders, not giving them. Wilhelm did a lot of travelling, often retiring to the seclusion of his estates and did very little actual governing. Yet he refused to share his intentions or even information with his ministers, who were kept in a constant state of confusion and tried to do their best to keep him from embarrassing Germany in the eyes of the world—and of his own people.

The rapid and extensive expansion of the German navy worried his closest ally, England. The new and widespread colonialism concerned both England and France. The huge build-up of the army upset Russia and all the rest of Eruope. And Wilhelm's entire focus, in fact, obsession, was on the military. He cared for nothing else.

And this is what worried people more than anything. Caprivi was willing to cut the required military service from three years to two but Wilhelm wanted to broaden the scope of the draft in order to enlarge the army by thousands and thousands more than heretofore. A benign economic atmosphere, industrialization, greater mobility and improved health care had all contributed to a huge population explosion, particularly of young men of military age. And Wilhelm wanted to seize these all for his expanded army.

But to a great extent his plans backfired. The population figures would have been far higher had it not been for emigration. From the moment Prussia conquered the rest of Germany the number of emigrants, mostly to the United States, reached hundreds of thousands. By the end of the 1880s the figure had more than doubled to almost a million people. As could be expected the majority of these left from Hannover, Schleswig-Holstein and Prussia itself.

And Friedrich Campsheide was worried.

"What do you think of this Caprivi?" asked Hans one Sunday as Fritz came to call for Mimi.

"His new military plan scares me half to death," replied Fritz. "I'm an artist, not cut out to be a soldier at all. I don't know what to do."

"You could marry Mimi," said Hans sardonically. "They're not taking married men yet."

Fritz gasped. "That scares me almost as much, if you want the truth. I'm not ready for that yet. I just don't know what to do."

Hans smirked. "You soon may have no choice in the matter if you keep on doing what I think you have been doing."

Fritz shrugged. "She doesn't seem worried. Women have ways, don't they? The whores never get caught."

"Are you accusing my dear sister-in-law of being a whore?" exclaimed Hans indignantly.

"Nay, nay, never that," replied Fritz. "I hold her in too high regard for that. I just meant she doesn't seem worried."

"Mayhap she's just too innocent," said Hans, turning away as Mimi entered the room.

But Mimi *was* worried.

During the first few delirious weeks of their ardent lovemaking she had not been too concerned, so sure that now he would ask her to wed. When he did not, she counted anxiously the days to her next monthly flux and breathed a sigh of relief when it happened. She tried to think of some way to put him off and still not lose him. But when he held her in his arms and began caressing her, she had no control, all will power left her and she gave in, all objections out of her mind. So far she had been lucky. February, March, bleeding on schedule. Until a new worry crossed her mind. Suppose she was barren! Then he would never marry her.

Easter fell on 6 April that year. They agreed it would not be right to make love on that holiest of days. Although to Fritz it meant very little, not having been inside a church since he was confirmed. Mimi, however, attended services fairly regularly and he knew it meant a lot to her. Besides there was to be a special children's service in the afternoon. The children begged him to accompany the family.

"You've got to come and hear me say my piece," pleaded Rudi.

"I can recite mine better than he can," boasted Henni.

Fritz had to laugh at their constant rivalry. "Very well, I'll come hear you. I can certainly spare a few hours since I intend to spend all day tomorrow with your Tante Mimi."

Easter Monday was a holiday and Fritz had a special surprise planned for Mimi.

"Oh, do tell me what it is," she begged ingenuously.

"Nay, then it won't be a surprise," he teased. "But be ready at eight o'clock in the morning and wear old, comfortable clothes but bring a cloak, too, just in case it turns chill."

The next morning he arrived promptly at eight driving a smart little gig. Mimi was already waiting for him.

She clapped her hands in delight. "Where did you get that?"

"I hired it for the day," he replied. "I thought you would enjoy a day out in the country."

"Oh, indeed I should." And then as he helped her up she noticed a large basket under the seat. "And a picnic, too," she exclaimed. "Oh, Fritz, you are so thoughtful. It will be heaven to get out of the city for a while."

"I thought you liked Bremen."

"I do but I am a country girl at heart. I miss Vilsen."

"Then why do you stay? With your sister Doris gone, Minna could surely cope without you."

"You want the truth?" she asked. "I only stay because of you, dear Fritz." There, was that a broad enough hint, she wondered.

"Lucky girl," he said and patted her hand.

The old livery nag trotted at a leisurely pace, probably all she was capable of. They headed north from Walle. The medieval walls, fortifications and gates of Bremen had been torn down during the Franco-Prussian War. In fact, fashionable Am Walle had been built upon the rubble. But there were still only a few roads leading out of the city. They passed through a sparsely settled suburb, crossed the railroad tracks and then were out in the country, where widely scattered farms, fields and many woods abounded.

Mimi took a deep breath and sat back. "Ah, how good it smells," she sighed. "Where are we going?"

"Not far now," Fritz replied. "One of the farmers who supplies us with wood invited us to come any Sunday or holiday. No workmen will be about. We'll be entirely alone."

"Ach, that sounds lovely. And it's such a glorious day, too. Perfect for a picnic."

Fritz smiled knowingly. He had far more on his mind than a picnic.

As they passed the farmhouse Fritz waved to the forester. "Now he knows we shall be there," he explained. "Double assurance that we'll not be disturbed."

Mimi smiled. He thought of everything but the one thing she wanted him to think of. When they reached the woods he turned the gig onto a narrow path. Giant cut trees lay stacked along the side waiting to be taken to the sawmill. After a bit the forest opened up into a small glen through which ran a sparkling brook. The grass was already velvety and green and just enough sun filtered through the trees to keep the early spring chill off. Fritz stopped the gig and helped Mimi down.

"What a charming place," she exclaimed.

"'Twill be even more charming when I'm holding you in my arms." He fetched a blanket and their two cloaks from the gig and spread the blanket on a grassy spot near the brook.

"What about the horse?" she asked. "Shouldn't you tie her up or something?"

"Nay, she'll be content to graze on this sweet grass. She won't go anywhere."

"And the picnic basket?"

"Best left in the gig until we're ready to eat. Wouldn't want it to get full of ants." He took her in his arms and kissed her hungrily. "Come, let's sit down on the blanket."

"No wonder you told me to wear old clothes."

"Which I'll soon have off of you."

"Fritz! We can't make love here—out in the open."

"What better place—surrounded by nature? Blue sky, a babbling brook, sheltering trees, soft grass. Just as God intended."

"But—but—ooh, Fritz."

833

He was already opening the bodice of her dress, fondling her breast. Her objections faded away, turned to eager desire and she succumbed to the sweet, sensual onslaught. Before she was totally aware of it, he had her clothes off and his own as well.

"I'm glad to see you are not wearing your corset," he remarked.

She saw no need to reply to that as she shivered in the chill. Although the sun was warm, it was, after all, early spring and the air was quite cool. He noticed and quickly covered her with his body. "I'll have you warm in seconds," he said as he continued caressing her.

True enough. In moments she was warm, hot for him, eagerly begging him to take her, all thoughts of chill forgotten. She glanced up at the blue sky, the new pale green buds on the trees and thought she must be in heaven. Seconds later she was, as she climaxed again and again. She felt the hot burst of his seed explode and fill her eager body. They made love twice and then lay back replete and satiated. He pulled their cloaks over them for now even his perspiring body felt the chill.

"Oh, Fritz," sighed Mimi, "I think that was the most beautiful love we've ever made. It must be because it's spring or this lovely place."

"Both, I'd say," he agreed. "Ah, spring, the season of fecundity, or rebirth. Maybe I've planted something in you this time."

Mimi gasped, "Oh, no, not yet! Not until we . . . "

He put a finger over her lips. "No talk of that now. Don't spoil this beautiful day. Time enough when I'm ready."

They retreated in silence each into their own thoughts. She felt like asking, 'But Fritz when will you ever be ready?' But she held her tongue. He would only turn shy and sullen, maybe even angry and she did not want to spoil this idyllic day. He thought of the old country saying, 'Why buy the cow when you're getting all the free milk you want?' But he dared not say it. She would never speak to him again.

As the sun crossed the zenith Mimi suggested, "Don't you think we should get dressed and have our picnic. It is dinnertime and I'm hungry."

"So am I," he said. "You give me a tremendous appetite. But don't get dressed. Just wrap your cloak around you. I want to love you again this afternoon." He went to the gig and fetched the basket of food.

"Did you pack it yourself?" she asked, wondering if it would even be edible.

"Nay, nay. I told you I'm not much of a cook. Fellow in the delicatessen around the corner packed it. He assured me it would be everything you liked. I don't even know what's in it."

834

She laughed. "Then let us find out." She began unpacking the basket. It was truly a feast, more than they could ever eat. A loaf of rich pumpernickel bread, lots of butter and cheese, slices of ham and liverwurst, several boiled eggs, two different salads, lettuce, tomatoes and a cucumber and even a bottle of wine. "Good heavens," she exclaimed. "How many people did you tell him this was for?"

"I didn't," he replied sheepishly.

"Then you'll have your suppers for the rest of the week. Thank goodness he sliced the bread but how are we to eat the salads or slice the tomatoes and cucumber? Didn't you bring any knives or forks? Or glasses for the wine?"

"I didn't think. I've got my penknife to slice the tomato with. We'll just have to eat with our fingers and drink out of the bottle."

Mimi shook her head. "I don't mind eating with my fingers but I'll not drink out of a bottle. You may have the wine. I'll drink from the brook, thank you. And salt? Is there any salt?"

Fritz hung his head. "And I wanted it to be so special for you," he said sadly.

Immediately she felt remorse. "Oh, Fritz, dearest Fritz. I didn't mean to complain. It is a wonderful repast and such a thoughtful surprise. It's just that men don't think of these things. Come, let us enjoy it no matter how primitive. It looks so good and I'm famished."

They ate their fill and repacked the rest. Fritz would have many a supper from the remains. They wandered about the woods for a while and then made love again in the afternoon. They washed up in the icy brook before donning their clothes again to go home. The old mare was asleep in the traces and Fritz had to gently wake her so that she would not bolt. All in all, it was the happiest, most wonderfully idyllic day either of them had ever experienced. They were more in love than ever, although Fritz had a hard time admitting that even to himself—and never to Mimi. Only a remark she made as he dropped her off at the Menten house sent a chill through him.

"Thank you so much for the most beautiful day," Mimi said as she alighted from the gig. "Fritz, dearest Fritz, you need a woman for far more than just making love." She gave him a quick kiss on the cheek and ran into the house.

Two weeks later Mimi watched in vain for the telltale drops of blood in her drawers. She hoped against hope that it had not happened but she

835

could not fool herself. With their ardent and constant lovemaking it was surprising that it had not happened sooner. But Mimi always tried to look on the bright side. Now he would have no excuse not to marry her.

When next they met, she came right out with it as bluntly as possible. "Fritz, I think I am with child—your child."

He looked as shocked as though such a thought never occurred to him. "You think—but you don't know for sure."

"I know," she insisted. "How could it be otherwise? Now you'll have to marry me."

"I—er—it wasn't part of my plans." At the look on her face he quickly amended, "At least not just yet."

"Just what are your plans?" she asked frigidly.

"I—er—that is, I'd like to have my own business and—and a proper apartment first," he stammered.

"You know perfectly well that you are earning enough to support a wife—and now a child. All that other can come later," she snapped.

"But—but—"

"No buts. It's you. You are the most selfish, despicable man I have ever known. What's more you are a coward," she cried as she gathered up her cloak.

Fritz reminded himself of his old mantra, be brave. You are a Campsheide, be brave, but he was so shocked at her vehemence he could not bring himself to say the words he knew she wanted to hear.

"I never want to see you again," she stormed as she ran out of his room, through the shop and all the way home.

"Why, Mimi, you're home early," said Minna. And then seeing her ravaged face, she grew concerned. "Whatever is the matter, little sister? Has he hurt you?"

"Leave me alone," sobbed Mimi. She ran to their room, threw herself on the bed and wept uncontrollably.

Several hours later when Hans came home Minna accosted him. "They've had a terrible row. You must do something about it."

"Who? What?'

"Our Mimi and that Fritz. Oh, why she ever got mixed up with him—with that Campsheide—I'll never know. That's why I want no part of any man. I'll not be hurt like that."

"Calm yourself, Minna. What happened? Did he actually hurt her?"

"Not physically as far as I could see but he has certainly broken her spirit. She's been crying her heart out all afternoon and says she doesn't want any supper. You must talk to him."

"Perhaps 'twould be best if I talk to her first." Hans felt like saying, I'd like to kill that scamp, but he feared Minna would take it literally.

"And what's more—what's more . . ." Minna blushed. "I—er—it's not something to be spoken about in mixed company . . ."

"I'm hardly company," said Hans, exasperated. "Out with it—what's more?"

"I—I think she is—is breeding."

"Hardly unexpected. Let's see if she'll talk to me."

Hans went to the bedroom door, tapped gently and called out, "Mimi, it's Hans. May I come in?"

All was quiet. Maybe, exhausted from weeping, she has fallen asleep. He debated whether to walk in. The door would not be locked—he hoped—for it was Minna's room, too. He called out again.

Finally he thought he heard a faint, "Come, if you want to." He entered.

He was aghast at her red, puffy face. Her hair was a mess. She was still fully clothed, her prettiest afternoon frock all wrinkled. She struggled to sit up on the edge of the bed and faced him defiantly.

"I know what you're going to say, so don't say it," she declared angrily.

"No, you don't," he replied. "You and Fritz did what any normal young couple in love would have done. Only it went on too long without resolution. And now I assume you are with child."

She nodded and began to sob again.

"Do you love him?" asked Hans. "Enough to marry him?"

"I hate him. I hate him. I never want to see him again."

Hans smiled. "Then that tells me you love him very much."

Mimi looked at him amazed. She started to weep again and replied in a tiny voice. "I did love him—very much—but no more because he doesn't love me."

"We'll have to see about that."

"Nay, Hans, don't waste your time. He'll only make more excuses."

Hans shook his head. "We'll see. Now calm yourself down. Wash your face and come and have some supper. You've got a babe to think of now."

Hans let things slide for a while hoping the young lovers would find their own way to a reconciliation. When nothing happened, he approached Fritz one evening at the Turnverein.

837

"Don't see you coming to call on Mimi much anymore," he commented feigning ignorance. "Have you found a new love?"

"Nay, I haven't found a new love or anything else," Fritz retorted. "What is love? I don't believe such a thing exists. I've never seen it." His bitterness was palpable.

Hans gritted his teeth. Mimi had told him something of Fritz's background. Could that mother of his have poisoned his mind so? "I don't think you would recognize love if it hit you in the face," he replied sharply. "Don't you realize Mimi is head-over-heels in love with you? And yet you spurn her. I think it is time you grew up, Friedrich Campsheide." Hans turned and walked away in disgust leaving Fritz to puzzle over his words.

Hans also made sure he personally escorted Mimi to the dances and other social functions of the Turnverein. At first she refused to go but he explained, "Sometimes the only way to wake a man up is to make him jealous. Be sure you ignore him and flirt with all the other young men. You're not showing yet. So no one will suspect that you are carrying his child."

At last she reluctantly agreed. She flirted outrageously and danced with almost every single man in the hall but her eyes kept wandering to Fritz standing forlornly on the sidelines. She noticed that he did not dance with anyone.

It nearly broke Fritz's heart to watch her but he did not have the courage to ask her to dance. He knew she would want answers he was not prepared to give. At times it brought tears to his eyes. At last he stopped coming to any of the social activities at the Turnverein.

When that ploy did not work, Hans said to Mimi, "As soon as you begin to show, I think it best that you go home to Vilsen so that your mother can care for you when the time comes."

"But they don't even know," she objected. "It will be a terrible shock to them."

"Of course they know. Did you think Minna would keep her mouth shut?"

"Then why hasn't Mama written? It's not like her."

"They're no doubt waiting—as we all are—to see if you two can solve the problem between you."

"The problem is Fritz, not me," she replied tartly. "And I'll stay here for a while longer, if you'll have me." Mimi was not about to leave Bremen while there was even the slightest chance Fritz might relent. She knew once she returned to Vilsen she would never see him again. She was certain Fritz was scared to death of Friedrike.

Hans shrugged. "As you wish."

Late in the summer Fritz had some unexpected but very welcome visitors.

"A lady and some others to see you, Fritz," called out Karl from the front of the shop. Fritz half hoped and half feared that it might be Mimi with the whole Menten tribe. At the look of consternation on his face, Karl lowered his voice. "Nay, nay. 'Tis an older woman. Says they were neighbors of yours back in Hoya."

Fritz dropped his tools and ran to the front. He fell into Frau Birnbaum's arms. "Frau Birnbaum!" he exclaimed. "How good to see you. And Albert. And this must be Margarethe. My what a fetching young lady you've become although you probably don't remember me. And this?"

"This is Friede," said Frau Birnbaum introducing a chubby girl of about ten.

"I received your kind birthday wishes," continued Fritz, happy for the first time in months. "You never forget, do you? But you said nothing about coming to Bremen."

"I didn't because I was not exactly sure when we were coming or if we'd have time to see you. You see, we are taking ship tomorrow—emigrating to America."

"Emigrating? To America? Oh, Frau Birnbaum, how could you?"

"Very easily," she replied. "Is there somewhere we can talk—er—more privately?"

"Ach, how remiss of me," replied Fritz. "Come up to my room. It is very small but quite private. Karl, do you mind?"

"Nay, nay," said Karl. "Take the rest of the afternoon off. We have nothing pressing."

When they were seated around the table and on the bed, Fritz asked, "What made you decide to go to America? The Prussian draft? You have three sons."

"That in part," she replied, "but also because of the growing prejudice against Jews. Even though my Jacob is a Christian, everyone says he is a Jew born and that is what they choose to believe. And now, sadly, that is reflecting on my sons. It is hard for them to find work. If they could have gone to university it might have been different. Many young Jews are following intellectual pursuits—doctors, lawyers, teachers, especially journalists—but the craft guilds refuse them admission and others are afraid to hire them."

"How tragic," said Fritz. "I had heard something of that but I never realized . . . " Truth was he had not given it a second thought, never thinking that the growing prejudice would affect someone he loved so dearly.

"So that is why we are going to America—to New York where we understand there are already many successful Jews from Germany. But enough of that," said Frau Birnbaum with a shrug. "Tell us what you have been doing. Some time ago you wrote about this wonderful young lady you are courting—or is that the right word?"

"Ja. Nay. Er—that is—I don't know."

Frau Birnbaum looked at him askance. "What do you mean, you don't know? Are you going to marry her or is it all off?"

"That's just it. I don't know. Oh, Frau Birnbaum, long ago you gave me some good advice which helped me a lot. I need some more of your advice now."

Frau Birnbaum frowned. She could see he was on the verge of tears. This was a desperately perplexed young man. She immediately took charge. "Albert, why don't you take the girls for a little sightseeing? They should see Roland and the Rathaus while we are here. Just be sure you are back to our hotel well before suppertime." When Albert and the girls had left, she said, "Now tell me—all of it."

"I met Mimi—her name is Marie Anna Bruns—when I first went to Vilsen. We got along well right from the start. She is so bright, cheerful and—and kind. I just knew she was the girl for me but she knew I could not make any commitment then. I was only a journeyman. Besides I wasn't ready for that. When I came to Bremen I thought that was the end of it. I missed her but I was kind of glad in a way—that I wouldn't have to make a decision."

Frau Birnbaum nodded sagely but said nothing.

Fritz continued, "Then about a year and a half ago she turned up here in Bremen to care for her dying sister's children. I realized then how much I had missed her and her sunny disposition. She could always get me out of my black moods. We saw each other almost every Sunday and I began to be happy again. Oh, how I wanted her but . . . "

"In lust or in love?" interrupted Frau Birnbaum.

Fritz blushed, surprised at the blunt question. After a moment he admitted, "In lust, of course. But love I don't know about. Her brother-in-law once said I would not recognize love if it hit me in the face. I suspect he's right. All I've known is rejection, discipline and sometimes even cruelty. I've never experienced love."

"Oh, yes, you have," she said. "Remember Micah?"

"How could I forget Micah? He saved my life."

"And in return you risked your life to save another dog."

"But they were just animals."

"It matters not. It's that sort of devotion where you would trust another person with your life—both physically and spiritually. That is a great part of what love is about. You say your Mimi could always get you out of your black moods. That, too, is a part of love—on her part. Any woman can tell you that that is a most difficult challenge. She must love you very much."

"It didn't seem to take any effort on her part. She was just her usual cheerful self."

Frau Birnbaum smiled knowingly. "Indeed. And then?"

Fritz blushed again. "I must admit I finally—er—had my way with her. Not once but as often as we could be together."

"And now she is pregnant."

"How did you know?"

Frau Birnbaum laughed. "The obvious result of concupiscence. And now she expects you to marry her."

"Ja," he admitted, "and that was not part of my plans."

"Just what are your plans?"

"She keeps asking me the same thing. I want to have my own business, a nice house with a garden . . ."

"But no wife," concluded Frau Birnbaum sardonically.

Frtiz hesitated a moment. "Frau Birnbaum, the thought of marriage frightens me to death. Look at my mother. And Tante and Onkel in Hoya were none too happy either. Only you seemed to be happy and now you have troubles."

"But not with our marriage. A strong marriage will help us to weather those troubles. And Fritz, your mother's unhappiness stems not so much from your father's untimely death—in fact, I understand that they were sublimely happy before that—but from your uncle's cruelty in forcing her to send her children away. You should know that. Now, think about that advice I gave you those many years ago."

"You said, be brave. And act like a man."

"Ja, but you're forgetting part of it. I said all men are afraid at times. It is nothing to be ashamed of except when you let that fear overwhelm you.

Then you are a coward. And, Fritz, let me tell you, the thought of asking a woman's hand in marriage frightens many men more than going into battle. It is not uncommon. But once they gather the courage to make that declaration, they find the rewards far outweigh the fears."

Fritz pondered that for a moment. "You really think so?"

"I know so." She paused to let that sink in. "On the other hand, if you really don't feel you want to spend the rest of your life with her, why don't you come to America with us? I think there would still be time to get you a place on the ship."

"Oh, no!" exclaimed Fritz. "I couldn't do that. Not while she's here and there's still a chance . . . "

"A chance for what?" put in Frau Birnbaum. "To get her back in your bed. She's already carrying your child. Why would she want more of that without a wedding ring?"

Fritz hung his head. "When you put it like that, I guess I can see her point," he murmured.

"Of course. And everything you have said tells me that you really love her even though you won't admit it. Now, in the little time I have left, I should like to meet this paragon and see if she is worthy of your love."

"But she is—more worthy than I am of hers."

"Then put on your jacket and take me to her."

"Nay, nay, I couldn't do that."

Frau Birnbaum picked up her purse and shawl. "Then I wish you well in the Prussian army. They will get you soon. Goodbye, Fritz." She turned to leave.

"No, no, wait! I'll take you but—but I'll wait outside while you talk to her."

Frau Birnbaum nodded. "We'll take a hackney. The horescar will take too long."

When they reached the Menten home Fritz waited behind a large linden tree while Frau Birnbaum went to the door. Minna answered.

"Do I have the pleasure of greeting Mimi Bruns?"

"Nay. I am her sister Minna. And who might you be?"

"I am Frau Birnbaum, a former neighbor of Fritz Campsheide from Hoya."

"Did he send you?" asked Minna sharply.

"Nay, he did not. But I am very fond of Fritz and decided I should like to meet this fine young lady of whom he speaks with such great affection."

"Affection? Hah!" said Minna derisively. "Then do come in but I'm not at all sure she will want to talk to you." She led the way up the stairs.

Mimi was seated by the parlor window knitting baby clothes and at the same time telling little Rudi a story. She was tiny and quite pretty—not beautiful but very attractive. She looked almost angelic but for a mischievous smile as she told the story. Frau Birnbaum could immediately sense the strength of character in her and knew right away that this was the girl for Fritz before either one spoke a word.

"Mimi?" she said tentatively. "I am Frau Birnbaum. I and my family have been friends of Fritz since he was a very young lad."

"Ach, ja, he has mentioned you often," said Mimi, "and now you have come to see the fallen woman. I don't know what your purpose is in coming here, Frau Birnbaum, but you can tell him this, that he will never see his son—or daughter—*ever*, unless he mends his ways—a lot. And even then I'm not sure."

"I agree with you a hundred percent, my dear. And I look down on no one. My purpose was merely to meet you and see what sort of person you were. And I like what I see. Do you still love him?"

"I did once—very much. But no more. He has used me cruelly and broken my heart."

"He loves you very much although he is only beginning to realize that."

"He has never said so nor shown it to me," said Mimi defiantly.

"He was afraid of breaking his own heart and yet he has done so through his own foolishness."

"Fritz is afraid of his own shadow and I cannot abide timid people."

"Fritz's heart has been broken so many times since he was a very little child that that is the reason for his fear. He needs you, Mimi. Would you still consider marrying him if he were to mend his ways—a lot?"

Mimi did not answer right away. She could not. She wanted to say yes but she no longer trusted Fritz. Nor did she trust this apparently kind woman who was obviously his ambassadress.

Just then Henni rushed in from school. "Tante Mimi, why is Onkel Fritz standing out there in the street? He pretended not to see me when I said 'hello'."

Minna was furious. She took Henni by the ear and said, "He is not your Onkel Fritz."

"Well, we all thought he was going to marry Tante Mimi," said Henni.

"Henni, shut your mouth and go to your room," said Minna, herding both boys out of the parlor.

By way of apology Mimi murmured, "My late sister's children. That one has been a bit obstreperous since she died." She hesitated a moment. "So, Frau Birnbaum, he did send you because he was afraid to come alone."

"Nay. It was my idea entirely. He was afraid to come at all but I forced him since I did not know where you lived." She smiled. "So, I must be on my way. We are leaving for America tomorrow."

Mimi blinked at that. How kind of the woman to take time to visit Fritz and then her. On the one hand she felt like telling Frau Birnbaum to take him with her. But then she realized with a start that that was why she had put off returning to Vilsen. While she and Fritz were still here in Bremen there was a chance . . . If he were to go off to America — she could not bear to think of it — that chance would be gone forever.

Frau Birnbaum stood up and took Mimi's hand. "It has been a pleasure meeting you, Mimi, my dear. But you haven't answered my last question."

"You may tell him perhaps. But only, perhaps," she replied with a catch to her voice.

Fritz stood on the pier and waved until the ship was far out on the Weser and he could no longer distinguish individuals. Tears were streaming down his cheeks. There went his best friends — the only friends he had ever had. And now he would never see them again.

Last night Frau Birnbaum had invited him to join them for supper at their hotel. When she had emerged from the Menten house he had run up to her, although he tried to feign indifference, eager to hear what she had to say about Mimi.

And Frau Birnbaum had plenty to say. "Fritz, you must not lose that girl. She is sweet, intelligent and above all, strong. Just perfect for you."

"But I have already lost her."

"Nay, nay. She still loves you, although right now you have hurt her so badly she thinks she hates you. You must mend your ways — a lot, is how she put it."

"But how . . . ?"

"First of all, forget the bed-time. There'll be plenty of opportunity for that after you are wed."

"But she . . ."

"I know. She was as eager for it as you. But now she is regretting her folly. Fritz, do you want a good woman by your side or a fly-by-night whore? If the latter, there are plenty around to satisfy your lusts."

"Mimi is no whore," he declared vehemently.

"Of course not. But you have treated her so badly she is ashamed of what she has done instead of rejoicing in a natural result of your love."

"Hans said something like that, too."

"Indeed. You must convince her that you are very proud—and happy—that she is carrying your child."

"But how can I if she won't talk to me?"

"By actions, not words. As I said, forget the bed-time. At first, don't even allude to the child. It will only result in recriminations and blaming one another. Put the whole idea of sex out of your head. Show her that there is more to you than just your prick."

"Frau Birnbaum!"

"Do I shock you? I intended to. Show her that you have a head and a heart and not just that thing dangling between your legs."

"But how . . . ?"

"Treat her like she deserves—like the lady she is. Start courting her like a gentleman as if you had just met. Send her flowers, take her candy, later perhaps little gifts but nothing too intimate. You say she comes from a musical family. Take her to concerts, the theater, when you can afford it. But don't procrastinate. She is already showing and will not be able to go out in public much longer. And tell her how much you love her—often. Not how much you *want* her but how much you love her for herself."

"But—but . . ."

"No buts. Be brave, Fritz. Don't lose her or you will regret it the rest of your life."

And the last thing Frau Birnbaum said as they were boarding the ship for America was, "I shall write you as soon as we are settled and have a house. And I want you to write me back that you have wed your Mimi and that you are very happy. Promise now."

"I—er—ja, I promise," he stammered.

"It would also be nice to know if it is a boy or a girl."

And they were gone.

Fritz wandered home from the waterfront blinded by tears. And he had never really thanked Frau Birnbaum for setting him straight. But he had promised and he was honor-bound to keep that promise. And suddenly he found that he wanted to. Now how to go about it?

Later that week he sent Mimi a large bouquet of flowers. Dahlias, his favorite. They were at the peak of their splendor now. He hoped she liked them as well as he did. He had never asked. He attached a note saying how much he missed the wonderful kuchen she baked for Sunday afternoon coffee and hoped she would take the hint.

She did.

That Sunday he arrived bearing a box of chocolates, which the two young boys would have quickly demolished had Minna not stopped them. Mimi was very cordial if somewat withdrawn. He knew she was waiting to see how he behaved and it made him a bit tense. But the conversation was generally innocuous and he began to relax. She asked if his friends had embarked safely, how his business was doing. Never once was the coming child mentioned.

It was not until the third Sunday that he even dared to place a chaste kiss on her cheek when he greeted her and again when he departed.

Gerhardt remarked, sotto voce, "So at last he is learning to behave like a gentleman instead of like a stallion in rut."

"I noticed and I hope she holds him to it," replied Hans.

Fritz was not supposed to have heard this but he did. He thought about if all the way home. It bothered him but it had been basically the same thing Frau Birnbaum had chided him with. He would show them all, especially Mimi, that he was a gentleman. After all, he was a proud Campsheide. And he finally admitted to himself that he loved her out of mind.

Fritz had no ear for music. Not that he was tone-deaf. He had simply never been exposed to the great variety that Johann Bruns had taught his daughters. He did not think he could stand sitting through a whole concert but he did like the theater. So he decided an opera would be the best combination of both. As luck would have it he chose 'Tannhäuser' without having the slightest idea what the opera was all about. He only knew it was by the great Richard Wagner whom everyone seemed to like. He hoped Mimi would like it, too.

Mimi was thrilled to be going to an opera. She had never been to a whole performance before, although her father had exposed her to many of the great Wagnerian themes. She also knew the story of 'Tannhäuser' and wondered if Fritz did. She doubted it. It was purely serendipitous that this particular opera was being performed at the Bremer Opera House.

She would say nothing and see what his reaction would be.

Yet she was so excited she could not help but hum a few bars of the 'Pilgrims' Chorus' as they rode on the horsecar.

"Have you seen this opera before?" asked Fritz, looking dismayed.

"Nay, nay. I have never been to any opera before but Papa taught us many of the themes. That is why I can't wait to hear the whole thing."

That satisfied him and he patted her hand.

During the performance she stole surreptitious glances at him. He grinned lasciviously during the Venusburg scene but quickly straightened his face when he caught her looking at him. She knew he was recalling their picnic in the woods when the child had been conceived. Later he squirmed in his seat at Tannhäuser's obstinacy as if urging him to make up his mind. She smiled at that. And then—then, when Wulfram sang the exquisite 'O du, mein holder Abendstern', she saw him flick a few tears from his cheeks.

She had won. She knew it. If only they could hold the mood. She silently thanked God and blessed Richard Wagner.

St. Martin's Summer was the brief period at the beginning of November after the first frosts had turned the leaves to fire and gold and everything else to a sere, ugly brown, when it warmed up again for a brief week or two before winter set in in earnest.

All Saints Day was a holiday and Fritz decided it would be fine for another picnic, albeit a very decorous one this time. He felt that Mimi had softened enough towards him to be willing to go, especially if he promised to behave himself. He hired the same ancient livery nag and gig, had the delicatessen pack the same picnic basket but no wine this time, only lemonade. He wanted everything to be perfect as he had something very special in mind.

Mimi balked when she saw the gig. "Where are we going?" she asked.

"I thought to go to that lovely spot in the woods where we went before."

"Nay, nay," she demurred. "I don't want to go there." She shuddered at the thought. She still did not completely trust him. "Let's go to the Bürgerpark. It's ever so much nicer," she suggested and thought, more people around, too.

Fritz was disappointed but he dared not insist or she might refuse to go at all. When they arrived at the park, Mimi led the way directly to the lake. She sat down on the same old log the skaters had used. Today there

847

were a few couples out on the lake in rowboats enjoying the mild weather.

"Wouldn't it be fun to hire one of those little boats?" suggested Mimi.

"Nay!" he exploded. "I told you I'll never go out in a boat of any size again."

"But Fritz, you can't possibly drown here. The lake is so shallow." But then she let it go, seeing his agitation.

He walked around in circles, fidgeting. This was not going well at all. He wanted nothing more than to take her in his arms, kiss her and declare his intentions. The little box in his pocket felt like it was burning a hole in his side.

"Fritz, what is wrong? You seem so nervous." She caught his hand and drew him down next to her. "Come, sit beside me."

"Ach," he sighed. "This is not going at all as I had planned."

She smiled. "Things seldom do, do they?"

He pressed her hand to his chest. "Mimi, I love you so much. I don't want to be without you."

"Ach," she said gently. "I know but it's nice to hear you say it at last. And I love you, too."

He took the little box from his pocket. "I have something for you," he said shyly, handing it to her.

She opened the box and gasped. On the white satin lay a plain gold ring.

"I want to marry you, Mimi," he said. "Will you have me?"

"Of course, I'll have you. You know I love you very much."

"Put it on."

"Nay, it's for you to put it on." She held out her right hand and he slipped the ring on her fourth finger. It was the custom to wear the ring on the right hand for the betrothal. During the wedding it would be transferred to her left.

"I want to take you in my arms and kiss you," he declared, "but there are so many people around."

"Ach, how do they know who we are? We're betrothed now, aren't we? Kiss me, Fritz."

He did so, longingly.

They set the date for her birthday, 15 November.

The Menten boys wanted to have a Polterabend—a raucous, noisy, drunken orgy for the groom and male members of the party—the night before the wedding but Fritz would have none of it. "Humbug," he said.

He did not want to be hung-over on that important day.

Fritz's brother Wilhelm, already serving in the Prussian army, was granted a special two-day leave and came to Bremen the day before. Fritz had invited his mother and sisters as well. Dorchen, Marie and Sophie all came but Margarethe pleaded that her health was too poor to endure the train ride, which was not true at all. Another rejection that Fritz felt keenly.

Mimi had wanted to be married in Vilsen, in the lovely old church of her happy childhood, but Fritz had insisted they be wed in Bremen. She was also disappointed that her dear friend Frau Pastorin Alma Beermann could not attend. Widowed and now living in Hannover, Alma felt that the trip would be too difficult with her two small sons.

As they rode on the train north Friedrike Bruns said to Johann Justus, "Never ever did I think that one of my daughters would marry a Campsheide."

"Now Fritzi, you must let bygones be bygones," replied Johann. "After all, it is over forty years since old Hinrich Campsheide caused so much trouble for us and for Vilsen. Why, he must be in his dotage by now and I understand he recently lost his wife."

"I don't know about that but he's younger than you and you're hardly in your dotage."

Johann laughed at that. "I should hope not. From what Mimi tells us, his uncle treated the lad abominably. It's no wonder his mother is so bitter."

"Ja, her. I feel sorry for the woman but I don't like her. I hope her son has more character than she."

"He seemed nice enough when we met him, if a bit shy. But he's no doubt outgrown that."

"We shall soon see," sighed Friedrike. "I suppose it's better she marries him than have the child out of wedlock. But I tell you one thing. She is coming home with us right after the ceremony. I'll not have that babe born in Bremen where she won't have proper care."

Johann Justus shrugged but made no comment.

The Menten house was already crowded when Johann Justus and Friedrike arrived but Hans made sure that Mimi's (and his late wife's) parents were given his and Doris' bedchamber. He rousted the boys out of their room and set up cots for them in the parlor so that the Campsheide sisters had a place to sleep. Instead of a Polterabend, he gave a great supper

849

for the betrothed and all the guests at a fine restaurant nearby.

The next morning by Prussian law Fritz and Mimi went first to the marriage registry office with two adult male witnesses. (Prussian law did not recognize females.) Fritz chose his brother Wilhelm and a young, recently hired journeyman named Peter because none of the Menten boys were old enough. Hans could have served but he was just so glad that the lovers were finally to wed he did not care who witnessed it. Then in the afternoon the whole company trooped to the Lutheran Church for what Mimi and her mother considered to be the real wedding. This time Hans gave a reception at the house catered by the local bakery which created an elaborate wedding cake and other assorted treats. No way would he let Mama Bruns or Minna near the kitchen on this special day.

Mimi and Fritz sat at the head of the table nibbling on the cake. At least Fritz was picking at it; Mimi was indulging herself heartily. She slipped her hand into his.

"Oh, Fritz, I can't believe we are really married. I'm so happy."

"I can't quite believe it either." He seemed to be in a daze but then he rallied. "I can't wait to show you the lovely apartment I've found for us."

"Have you now? Then I can't wait to see it. But Mama wants me to return to Vilsen with them tomorrow."

Suddenly he asserted himself. "Nay! I'll not have it. You're my wife now. Your parents have nothing to say over you anymore."

"I know. But Fritz, I *want* to have the baby in Vilsen where I'll get proper care. Mama is an expert healing woman, you know, whereas Minna is—well—only a spinster."

"It doesn't have to be Minna. There must be several capable midwives in Bremen."

"I haven't even sought one out since I'd planned all along to go to Vilsen. And very soon I'll not be able to travel at all. I'm already showing too much to go out in public." Mimi was upset. Their first quarrel and that not an hour after they were wed. She changed the subject. "Tell me about the apartment."

"It has three rooms. A real kitchen with a combination gas and wood stove and running water in the sink. Also a bedroom and a parlor. And I made all the furniture myself."

"Except the featherbed."

He laughed at that. "Ja, except the featherbed."

"Oh, Fritz, it sounds luxurious."

"You won't lack for anything. It has gaslights throughout and, what's more, there is an inside privy—it's called a water closet—off the stairwell between the second and third floors."

The first doubt crept into her mind. "And what floor are we on?"

"The fourth."

"Oh, Fritz," she sighed, dismayed, "I soon won't be able to climb all those stairs. I shouldn't even be doing it now. It could harm the babe or even me."

"I'll carry you," he declared, as if that were the end of the matter.

And that evening he did, indeed, carry her up the four flights. Mimi loved the apartment. It was small but bright and airy even though a bit bare without curtains on the windows and a rug on the floor. Only one thing she insisted on.

"We'd better have a chamberpot. You can't be carryng me up and down those stairs in the middle of the night. And what do I do when you're at work and I'm here alone? You know a woman in my condition has to go more often than normal."

"I never thought of that."

Ach, men, she thought. "Even better would be for you to build us a commode. That would solve the problem for both of us."

"Good idea. I'll make one as soon as I get back to the shop next week."

"And I'll start on the curtains. Mama's linen will be perfect for them. It's bound to be drafty this high up once the north wind starts blowing." Friedrike had given them a huge bolt of her finest linen for a wedding present. Johann had contributed a full set of dishes and utensils of his best pewter.

That night they cuddled together under the featherbed. Fritz did not dare make love to her as he wanted to for fear of harming the baby. Also she was getting quite cumbersome and it would have been very awkward. So they fondled each other as much as possible and derived a measure of satisfaction from that. It was enough to hold her in his arms and know that she was really his, forever.

When the newlyweds did not show up for Sunday dinner Friedrike was very upset.

"You certainly didn't expect them to get up before noon today, did you?" said Hans, trying his best to be diplomatic.

When Mimi and Fritz arrived for afternoon coffee Friedrike calmed down somewhat. Fritz had not wanted to come at all but Mimi insisted on saying goodbye to her parents.

"Don't worry," she had assured him. "I don't plan on going back with them today. I want to stay here with you as long as possible." And that had to satisfy him.

But it did not satisfy her mother. "Mimi, do you have your things packed? We'll have to make haste or we'll miss the last train to Hoya."

"I'm not going with you today, Mama," she replied. "Let me have at least a few weeks of wedded bliss with my husband. You are being cruel to try and separate us so soon. I promise I'll come home in plenty of time."

"Bliss? Cruel?" said Friedrike. "He'll injure the baby with his lust."

"No, he won't. I know he won't."

"Now, wife, let be," interjected Johann, trying to mediate. Mimi had rarely heard him address Mama as 'wife'. He must be very annoyed and hopefully, on her side. "When is the child due anyway?" he asked Fritz.

"I—I never thought to ask," replied Fritz.

Friedrike rolled her eyes heavenward and was about to spout off again when Mimi answered.

"Late in January as best as I can reckon. So you see, Mama, there is plenty of time."

Hans decided it was time to step in. "Ach, Mama Bruns, let them have a couple of weeks together. Don't you remember how it was when you and Papa Bruns were first wed? I certainly remember how it was with me and Doris."

He apparently hit the right note for her eyes went dreamy, remembering.

"Ach, forty-two years ago. Do you remember, Johann Justus?" He nodded. "But I wasn't with child."

"That was just pure luck," said Johann. "If that groom hadn't spied on us . . ."

"Now, Johann. Very well," she relented. "A few weeks but no more. It isn't seemly. And I don't want anything to happen to that child."

"I'll personally see them on to that train myself," promised Hans.

"Thank you, Mama," said Mimi and they embraced, both in tears.

Then Johann hugged her as best he could and whispered, "Take care, Doern. I want to see my grandson." And Mimi knew the depth of his emotion. He had not called her Doern—Plattdeutsch for 'little girl'—since she was a small child.

On the train back Johann asked, "Why were you so stubborn, Fritzi? She wanted your blessing, not your criticism."

Friedrike started to weep. "I could only think of the Gypsy's fore-telling those many years ago. She said I would lose them all—some to death, the rest to a far off land. And everything she said has come true. Sophie, Luise, Lena, Doris, all dead and the rest in America. Mimi is my baby. I don't want to lose her, too."

Johann wanted to take her in his arms and comfort her but all he dared do on the crowded train was hold her hand tightly. "I understand how you feel. We have grandchildren in America we've never seen and probably never will. At least we'll see this one, God willing." And his eyes, too, misted over.

In the event it was the week before Christmas before Mimi finally came to Vilsen. And she came alone.

"Where is that husband of yours?" asked Johann as he met the train at Hoya with the wagon. "Your Mama will be furious that he let you travel alone."

"Mama is furious about everything lately," replied Mimi. "The shop is very busy making last minute things for Christmas. Fritz will be here for Christmas and stay the whole week if Mama won't chew his head off."

Johann laughed. "I'll see that she doesn't. She just worries so much about you. We've already moved your bed downstairs by the fireplace so you won't have to climb up to the loft."

"I doubt I could. I feel like one of those hot-air balloons except I'm sure I'd be too heavy to fly."

Fritz came the morning of Christmas Eve. He looked a bit dismayed at the bed in the middle of the parlor but realized the sense of it. They could do nothing but cuddle anyway. The family celebrated very quietly. Mimi was just too tired to help much.

"Oh, I wish he were already born so he could see the pretty tree," she remarked.

"He?" said Fritz. "Are you so sure then that it will be a boy?"

"Mama says so. She claims she can tell by the way I'm carrying it."

And Friedrike was right. Fritz had hardly returned to Bremen when he received a telegram from Johann. 'Son Heinrich born 16 January. All well.' Fritz was overjoyed. He rushed to Vilsen to see his son and thank his dear Mimi.

Mimi was happy. Baby Henni was thriving. Fritz was doing very well in his business. She loved the little apartment although she hoped some day they could have the little cottage with a garden that Fritz dreamed about. And best of all she loved the new gas stove. No need to keep a wood or coal fire burning all summer long. And it was a very hot summer that year. Now she was grateful that they were so high up on the fourth floor. At least they got a little breeze from the river.

She sang little tunes from her childhood as she pulled two golden loaves from the oven. It was really too hot to be baking but Fritz loved her home-baked bread so much. And, she had to admit, she too preferred her own crusty bread and delicate cakes to those of the bakery.

And she also had some exciting news for Fritz. She had suspected it last month but now she was sure. She was with child again. This time she hoped it would be a girl. Fritz would soon be home for dinner. She would tell him then.

But when he came in his face was as grim and dark as a thundercloud. He slammed the newspaper down on the table. He always brought the paper home at noon and expected her to read it so that they could discuss things at supper. Mimi was a fast and avid reader but she much preferred romances and adventure novels from the library. However, she dutifully read the paper every afternoon.

"Whatever is wrong?" she asked. "You look as though the sky has fallen on your head."

"And it well may soon," he replied. "Read this. The foolish Kaiser has changed the draft laws again. There are to be no exemptions at all from sixteen to forty-five except for a farm lad who is the only son of an elderly widowed mother. Single or married with a dozen children, it matters not."

"Ach, Fritz, that is terrible. And here I thought we were so safe."

"No longer. The stupid fool wants to make war so bad but so far he can't find an excuse. He wants to keep England's friendship but the English politicians no longer trust him. He is scared to death of Russia. Of course, there's always France or some foolishness over the colonies."

"Fritz! Don't let anyone hear you talking like that."

"It's no secret. Everyone's talking about it. I might not agree with your parents on a lot of things but your papa is right about one thing. Hannover should be independent. Prussia will end up destroying Germany."

"But we're in Bremen now, not Hannover."

"Ja, Bremen, who still calls herself a Hanse Freistadt. She's no more free from Prussia than any other state of Germany is."

"Well, there's nothing we can do about it except pray that they don't call you."

"There *is* something we can do. We could go to Poland or Holland—or even America. Frau Birnbaum is always writing to urge us to come to America."

"Oh, Fritz, no. I don't want to leave Germany. It's our home. And besides, when my sister Lise wrote to tell us how wonderful it is there, you pooh-poohed the idea."

"Well, I'm thinking about it now."

"Fritz, that is a huge decision to make. We must not act in haste or we'll be sorry."

"We'll be even sorrier if I have to go and be a Prussian tin soldier instead of a respectable cabinetmaker. What's for dinner? I have to get back to work."

All the sunshine went out of Mimi's day. And she had never had the opportunity to tell him her momentous news.

The next day Mimi wrote to Lise. Although they were thousands of miles apart, Lise had always been her closest confidant—more like a best friend than a sister. Although her sister Anna also lived in Elgin, she had left long before Mimi was born and so was almost a total stranger. But Lise she could trust for good advice and so Mimi poured her heart out to her.

Fritz became more and more despondent and increasingly nervous. So much so that he was becoming difficult to live with and Mimi could no longer cajole him out of his black moods. Even the news of the new pregnancy did not cheer him overly much. He just used that as another reason why they must flee Germany before it was too late.

Each week thousands and thousands of would-be emigrants poured into Bremen and while most of them succeeded in leaving for the New World, Prussia tried to put in place every prohibition and obstacle in their way to prevent their leaving. But there was a growing network—almost a conspiracy—of knowledgeable people to help the prospective emigrants overcome these obstacles and see them on their way. Fritz became more and more nervous.

Several weeks later a reply came from Lise who wrote in glowing terms of how wonderful life was in America, particularly in Elgin. She wrote, among other things, that Fritz would have no trouble finding work. There was so much building going on in the area, her Fred (as they had Anglicized his name) never lacked for work. The climate was healthy, albeit a bit colder in winter and hotter in summer than they were used to. And above all the people were so friendly and helpful, especially to new immigrants, because almost all of them were from Hannover.

So much for advice from Lise. Mimi almost did not want to show Fritz the letter but she did and this time Fritz studied it carefully. Mimi hoped another letter from Frau Birnbaum would not come. If they had to go, she much preferred to be with her sister than in a big city like New York. It would be worse than Bremen. Fritz also mused about two of his cousins, sons of his hated uncle Hinrich, who had left home for a place called Nebraska.

"But they are farmers," argued Mimi. "At least Elgin is a small town like Vilsen where there is work for an accomplished craftsman. You are not a farmer."

"Nay, nor do I want to be. And they say the farms there are so isolated you can't even see your nearest neighbor. Let us think about Elgin."

And Mimi was shocked to realize that she had been defending Elgin as a prospective destination when she did not even want to leave Germany.

"Write to your sister again and ask her how we get to this Elgin."

"Fritz, you're not serious!" she exclaimed.

"Never more," he replied.

Half in tears, Mimi said, "It is near a place called Chicago. One takes a train to get there from New York."

Mimi tried to find a sympathetic ear anywhere she could but none existed.

Hans said, "You would be wise to go. I've just crossed the age limit— barely—but I worry about my boys. I'm thinking seriously of sending the older ones to one of your sisters."

Even her parents agreed. Friedrike had long resigned herself to the Gypsy's prediction. She said, "Can you see yourself living alone for three whole years with the possibility of becoming a widow before you are four-and-twenty? And Fritz will lose all the custom he has built up."

"Oh, no, I didn't think of it that way," cried Mimi.

"Then, 'tis best you go whilst you can," added Johann. "Things in Germany under Prussia will only get worse."

Even her beloved Frau Pastorin wrote, 'I am sending my boys to France or Switzerland for their schooling as soon as they are old enough. And I hope they have the sense to stay there. Germany is not what it was.'

Frau Birnbaum wrote to Fritz, 'Tell us what ship you will be arriving on. We'll meet you and help you board the right train to Chicago.'

A month later Fritz came in at noon looking jubilant. Mimi had never seen him looking so happy—certainly not in recent months. He slapped three cards down on the table.

"Here are our tickets to freedom. We are leaving on the first of November."

"What?!"

"I've secured two berths for us on the Norddeutscher-Lloyd steamship *Lahn*. The baby will have to sleep with you. They only charged one-third for him."

"Oh, Fritz, you can't mean it. I didn't think—I mean I hoped you weren't really going ahead with it."

"But we've discussed it a thousand times."

Mimi started to weep. Fritz took her in his arms. He could afford to be generous now. "Now, now, liebchen, it is our only hope. Our chance for a whole new life free from Prussia at last."

She nodded blinking back the tears. She had taken vows to love, honor and obey her husband. Then so be it. She must do so, however much she hated the idea. At last her practical side took over.

"What about all our lovely things? We certainly can't take furniture with us."

"No, we can't," he replied. "We are only allowed to take what we can carry. We'll sell the furniture. That will give us a good stake to get started over there. And Karl is willing to buy back my half of the partnership. That will be a great help. Any of your treasures that you really can't part with, take to your mother. They can always ship them to us later. I shall build us a trunk—as large as I can handle—for our clothes and the pewterware your papa gave us. And, of course, I shall need my toolbox."

"You've got it all figured out, haven't you?" she sighed bitterly. "Well, then I'd best be about sorting things out."

After a few days Mimi resigned herself to the fact that she—they—would be leaving Germany forever. Gradually her innate cheerfulness and practicality reinstated itself. She sorted through things quickly so that she would not weep with nostalgia over certain items. Even the pile of treasures dwindled as she realized that her mother would not possibly have room for all of it.

She also asked everybody and anybody for information about the voyage. Gerhardt Menten gave her the most precise information. He had recently obtained a job as journeyman marine architect with Norddeutscher-Lloyd. He gave her a card with a picture of the ship and all the pertinent date—length, beam, tonnage, two smokestacks, four masts and the number of passengers it could carry.

"Seven hundred in third class!" she exclaimed. "How can they fit all those people in there?"

"In the hold. That's what they call steerage. On the eastbound trip they actually use it for cargo. It may be a mite crowded but that's what you're paying for. It would cost ten times that for second class and almost a hundred times that for first class. But you can be sure it is clean. It is a German ship, after all."

"Oh, my," said Mimi. "And why do they need all those masts if it is a steamship?"

"Just in case the engine breaks down or they run out of coal from being blown off course in a storm," explained Gerhardt. "It's been known to happen although not very often. But don't worry. She carries a full set of sails so you'll get there one way or another."

"That's frightening."

"Not to worry. *Lahn* is a new ship, only two years old. Chances of a breakdown are next to nothing," he tried to reassure her.

"How long is the trip?" she asked.

"Scheduled for eleven to twelve days, two weeks at the very most."

"What about the food?"

"The company says it is ample and nourishing. I can't vouch for that as I've never experienced it but I don't think they would lie."

But other people told her vastly different versions.

"Watered down soup and bread so hard it's almost unchewable," said one.

"Sausages that look and taste like a piece of shit," said another, even more bluntly.

"If possible, take some fruit with you so your teeth won't fall out," advised a third.

"My teeth fall out?" asked Mimi, perplexed.

"Ja, from the scurvy."

And then she was given other advice.

"Have your husband keep all your money in a moneybelt and sew all your jewels into your corset."

"There are many thieves, touts and other unscrupulous characters on board. Don't buy anything from them or believe anything they have to say."

Mimi took this advice seriously. She made a moneybelt for Fritz and, although she had no jewelry, she sewed as many silver marks onto her corset as she could. It made the garment a bit bulky but she did not care. They would have to undress her before they could rob her.

Mimi made her farewells to her parents in Vilsen. Friedrike refused to go to Bremen to see them off, saying she was getting too old for the trip but Mimi knew that it was because the departure of her baby would be too heart wrenching. Which was just as well as it turned out.

About a week before they were to sail Fritz came home with the news that they had to report to the shipping company's departure barracks two days before sailing.

"Two days? Whatever for?" asked Mimi.

"So that the company's doctors can examine everyone for infectious diseases. Apparently the ships' captains are very strict about that. Those that have anything contagious will be sent away and the rest of us will be locked in there so we can't catch anything new."

"Why, that's horrible," she exclaimed. "Oh, Fritz, I don't want to go."

"Come on, girl," he replied. "You've always been the one to give me courage. Where is your courage now?"

That stiffened Mimi's spine. She knew the decision to emigrate was one of the bravest things Fritz had ever done but without her he would wilt. So she encouraged him even though her own spirits were flagging.

They arrived at the embarcation area two days before sailing, as instructed. Mimi was aghast at the huge number of people milling about—people of all sorts and stripes, some so obviously poor and filthy it looked as though they had walked all the way to Bremen. She wondered how they could afford the fare, especially when they were surrounded by six or eight children. Others were dressed more sedately in their Sunday best as were she and Fritz. She quickly spotted several of the touts she had been warned about. Their flashy clothes gave them away. But many of these poor, gullible folk seemed to pay rapt attention to their spiel.

The building itself was like a vast barn with a concrete floor. At either end were a few closed rooms and sanitary facilities marked 'men' and 'women'. Mimi noticed that there were only about a hundred cots provided for all these hundreds of people. And the noise. The babble engulfed them the moment they entered. She had expected that most of the emigrants would be German. And while most of them were, she overheard conversations—and shouting—in every language under the sun—or so it seemed. Among the foreigners, Polish and Russian seemed to predominate as well as that strange corruption of German spoken by the eastern Jews called Yiddish. There were also a large number of Scandinavians and even a few of decidedly Oriental cast, perhaps Taters or Turks. She had no idea.

"Whyever do we have to go through this?" she complained. "Your friends the Birnbaums stayed in their hotel until the last minute."

"Because they went second class," explained Fritz, "and they simply presented a clean bill of health from their own doctor."

"I see." Mimi and Fritz had not had a doctor. They had relied on her mother's home remedies for any minor upset.

"And where are we going to sleep these two nights?" she asked, pointing out the paucity of cots.

"I don't know," replied Fritz. "On the floor, I guess. We'll have to watch what the others do."

"They don't seem to know any more than we do, probably less. I'm so glad we brought our featherbed."

"Just be careful no one steals it."

After some hours the big outer doors were locked and a few officials tried to bring order out of chaos. One shouted above the din in German while others translated his instructions into several other languages. "Line up according to the first letter of your last name." Clerks spread out across the width of the barn holding up cards with the letters A-C, D-F and so on. "Be prepared to show your steamship tickets and your passports or birth certificates." The noise quieted down some as people shuffled into their respective lines.

Six hefty matrons on one side and six of their counterparts on the other gradually took people from the lines and led them to the closed rooms at the ends of the building. When Mimi's turn came she followed the woman into one of the cubicles.

"Strip down to your corset," ordered the woman.

Mimi blushed. "Are you the doctor?" she asked.

"I am a nurse-inspector. If we see anything suspicious we then call the doctor. Now strip."

Mimi did so and shivered in the cold air. The inspector looked in her eyes, her throat and ears. She examined her hands and toes. She put a stethoscope to her chest and listened. "You'll do." She then took a large atomizer and quickly sprayed an acrid, noxious-smelling disinfectant on all her hair—pubic, underarm and head.

"Not my hair," cried Mimi. "I just washed it. I don't have any lice."

"Everybody has lice. If you don't you soon will. You can wash it again when you get to America. You may dress."

860

Mimi did so quickly and fled the room. Henni was crying from the awful smell emanating from his Mama.

"My God, you stink," said Fritz when she returned to him.

"And so will you. Wait till you see what they do to you," she replied.

Every once in a while the big outer door opened when someone was sent away. Sometimes whole families left, unwilling to be parted from a beloved parent or child. Others bid tearful farewell to an expelled loved one. By the end of the day only about a third of the people had been checked by the inspectors. The relief of those who had passed the examination was apparent. Decks of cards and pairs of dice came out. Someone had a concertina and a Lithuanian group started dancing. As darkness fell attendants lit the few gaslights.

"I'm hungry," said Mimi. "Aren't they going to feed us?"

"Apparently not," replied Fritz. "It seems only meals on shipboard are included, not here."

"I'm glad I brought those apples from Vilsen. We'll share one to make them last." Mimi was thankful she was still nursing Henni, although her milk was dwindling due to the new pregnancy. The most difficult part was trying to dry his diapers after she washed them in the wash room. There was no source of heat anywhere in the whole building. It was going to be a cold night. She thanked God again for the featherbed.

Fritz said, "We've got to eat more than a half an apple. We must keep our strength up. Look, here come some vendors. Let's see what they have to offer."

"Probably highway robbery."

The prices were outrageous. So Fritz bought only two cups of coffee and two dry rolls.

The next day was a repetition of the first. Those who had been examined waited around listlessly while the remainder were checked. It proved to be a long, boring day. Here and there fights broke out when someone cheated at cards or dice. There were anguished screams when the touts or swindlers relieved some fools of all their money and quickly disappeared.

Mimi tried to circulate and strike up a conversation with some of the better dressed women but most were so overcome with fear and anxiety that they were afraid to speak freely. No one would feel secure until they were safely on board and the ship left the pier. Fritz found a yesterday's newspaper that someone had discarded and spent the day reading every word. He purchased two sausages for their dinner and although the unappetizing things tasted like sawdust, it staved off the hunger.

Very early the next morning the ship blew its great whistle and every-one nearly jumped out of their skins. Valises, trunks, baskets and bags were quickly repacked and people crowded towards the big double doors that led to the pier. But for the longest time nothing happened.

"Don't let that ship leave without us," yelled someone.

"Cool your balls down, friend," replied the guard. "She ain't goin' nowhere yet. Nor are you."

But half the people did not understand him and the din rose to a fever pitch. Four guards stood across the doors to hold the crowd back but the pushing and shoving kept on.

"Now," said one of the guards at last, "we are going to open these doors a bit to let the stink out but you are still not going anywhere. You have to wait until the other passengers are boarded. Say that in Russki or whatever these fools understand," he instructed another guard. But even that did not quiet the people.

When the doors were opened the crowd surged forward only to find themselves enclosed in a large fenced-in pen close under the shadow of the big ship. On the outside they could see two gangways leading on to the ship—one to the top deck, the other to second deck.

"How come those people are allowed on?" asked someone.

"Those are the first- and second-class passengers," explained one of the kinder guards. "They paid for the privilege of boarding first. Your turn will come. Just be patient."

When the crowd had surged into the holding pen, Mimi almost lost Fritz. Shouldering the big trunk with his toolbox in the other hand he had been pushed forward while she, holding Henni on one hip and clutching the rope that held the featherbed and basket together, struggled to keep up.

"Fritz," she cried out, "wait for me." But he did not hear her. And the crowd closed in around her.

"Stop pushing, lady, you can't go no place," growled a gruff man.

"But I've lost my husband," she replied.

"He ain't goin' no place either."

"May I be of help to you, madame?" asked a pleasant young man at her shoulder.

"I've become separated from my husband," she said, "and he has our tickets and everything."

"Where do you think he is?"

"Up ahead somewhere." She nodded in that direction, having no free

862

hands. "But I can't see over all these heads. He's carrying a big blue trunk. Can you see him?"

The man stood on tip-toe. Fritz was just about to set the trunk down but Mimi's new friend spotted him just in time. "Ja, I see him. He's very close to the gate. Come, I'll help you through the crowd. Stay close behind me and don't panic."

With many apologies, excuse-me's and a little elbowing the young man made his way through the press of people. Although a few grumbled, most cooperated and made way. It was no time or place to be separated. Fritz suddenly realized that Mimi was not with him and was just about to force his way back through the crowd when the young man burst through with Mimi in tow.

"Ach, there you are," said Fritz angry with relief. "I told you to stay close by me."

"I couldn't go that fast," she sobbed, "and then I couldn't see you any-more. This kind young man helped me find you."

Fritz glared at the man who quickly said, "Sir, don't scold your lovely wife. She is so tiny she simply got swallowed up by the crowd. By the way, I am Otto Lindemann."

"Oh, thank you, Otto. I am Marie and this is my husband Friedrich Campsheide."

Fritz stopped glaring and suddenly remembered his manners. "Pleased to meet you, Otto. It seems we shall be shipmates."

Mimi had seated herself on the blue trunk, the basket between her feet and Henni on her lap. "Hmm," she mused, "Lindemann. I have an ancestor by that name. Could we be related?"

"Possibly but I doubt it," replied Otto. "I am from Celle."

"But that's where they came from—originally. But that was hundreds of years ago. So I guess you're right."

"Interesting," said Otto.

Just then the ship's whistle emitted a short blast. Everyone stirred hopefully. A great door opened in the hull of the ship and a gangplank was pushed out onto the pier. On either side stood two officers. At last the gate in the fence slowly opened part way but the guards held the crowd back. "Now slowly and orderly," shouted the head guard. "Only two families at a time. Any pushing and shoving will only delay your boarding."

Half the people did not understand this so they kept pushing and shoving until the guards went among them with truncheons. Then the mob quieted down once they realized they must wait their turn.

Mimi, Fritz and Otto were near the front of the crowd. Fritz picked up the big blue trunk and his toolbox and slowly edged his way forward. "Now, stay with me and don't get lost again," he instructed.

"I'll see that she's right behind you," Otto assured him. He took Mimi's arm. "Here, why don't you let me carry the baby so you can have two free hands for that basket?" he suggested.

"Nay, nay, I'm fine," she replied. Although the young man impressed her as being honest, Mimi was not about to trust anyone not to steal her precious baby in the meleé.

"Then I'm right behind you," he said.

When they passed through the gate, Otto was still with them. One of the officers at the gangplank asked to see their tickets. Fritz put down his burdens and showed them the required documents. Their names were checked off against the manifest.

"Is this young man part of your party?" asked the officer.

Before Fritz could reply, Otto stepped forward and produced his ticket. "Yes, I am," he said. "I am Frau Campsheide's cousin."

The official found his name. "Ach, ja, Lindemann. But you are not listed together with these people."

"We only got together a short time ago," prevaricated Otto. "We purchased our tickets separately."

Mimi was astounded at his fabrication. Fritz was about to sputter when she realized that any discussion could make trouble for all of them. She quickly said, "That is true but we are travelling together. He is my cousin."

And the officer let them go. What did he care as long as they all had tickets?

When they entered they hold of the ship Mimi stared in disbelief at the vastness of the place which yet was so crowded with bunks there was little room to move about. "Hurry, Fritz, and find us a good place—near one of those stoves, if you can," she said.

Another official directed them. "Single men up forward, single ladies aft, families in the middle section."

The middle section was by far the largest. The bunks were in double rows, stacked three high. The space between was barely wide enough to stretch one's legs. The official looked askance when Otto once again followed them. Fritz found what looked to be a good place, nearby but not on top of one of the little stoves. The big trunk would not fit under the bunk so he had to place it between them and the next row.

"No matter," said Mimi. "We can use it as a table and we'll invite our neighbors to share it. That way they can't complain too much. And I shall sleep on the bottom."

"Nay, you are not," insisted Fritz. "How can you guard all our possessions from theft?"

"But then I have to climb that ladder every time," she objected. "And suppose Henni falls out?"

"You'll just have to hold him tightly," said Fritz. "I'll not have every passing seaman or other riff-raff trying to rape my wife while I'm sleeping."

"Oh, Fritz, what a terrible thought." But she could see that he was adamant so she argued no further. She spread her coat and the featherbed on the second bunk while Otto threw his small valise up on the top. They settled down to wait.

Promptly at six o'clock the gangplank was withdrawn and the great door in the hull was slammed shut plunging them into total darkness. Stewards came through lighting tiny lanterns hung from posts. The weak light was only enough to distinguish one person from another but no more. As they passed each group they announced, "Supper will be served at 6:30. We sail on the ebb."

Mimi had no idea what ebb meant but someone explained that it meant about eight o'clock when the tide changed. "Oh, may we go on deck and watch when we sail?" she asked one of the stewards.

"No, ma'am. You canot go on deck until we are at sea and then for only four hours a day. An officer will tell you when you may."

Mimi sank back on the trunk, disappointed. "So," she sighed, "we shall never see Germany again."

Supper was at least edible and filling if not particularly tasty. Everyone was too excited to eat much. Promptly at eight o'clock the whistle emitted four blasts and they could feel the vibration as the great screw began to turn. Tug boats eased the ship away from the pier and the pilot guided her down the long stretch of the Weser to the North Sea. Men cheered, women wept, children raced up and down the aisles in sheer excitement.

Before dawn the next morning the ship paused momentarily to discharge the pilot and then ploughed full speed into the swells of the North Sea. Mimi began to feel squeamish. At first she thought it was the morning sickness returning but she was long past that. Then when the crew came through placing buckets at each row of bunks she realized that many people were getting seasick. The stench of vomit did not make her feel any better. She tried valiantly to fight it.

"Oh, if we could only get some fresh air," she moaned. "It is so stuffy in here."

"They promised to let us go on deck once we were at sea," commented Fritz. "I'll let you go first while I watch our things."

"I'll be glad to watch them for you so you can go together," offered Otto.

"Nay, nay. That's quite all right. Thank you anyway." Fritz still did not trust this newfound 'cousin'.

Finally the forward hatch was opened and the passengers were allowed to go up the iron stairway to the deck. The steerage 'deck' was actually the bow of the ship, a large but confined area. Instead of railings the sides were solid metal walls so that only the tallest men could look over them to the sea. But they could see the sky and breathe the rich tang of salt air and that was enough. Aft and far above them they could see the tourist deck and the first-class promenade, both of which stretched the length of the ship but the steerage passengers were restricted to the bow.

"Slowly now. Watch your step," the seamen kept repeating. "Hold on to your children. Anyone falls overboard we do not stop to pick them up," they threatened.

"Don't let that frighten you," remarked Otto. "They would stop but threats are the only way to get through to some of these people."

Mimi buttoned her coat tightly and pulled her hat down over her ears as she felt the icy blast from the open hatch sweep through the hold. She bundled Henni up and set out with Otto behind her. He helped her up the steep steps. At the top she gulped breath after breath of fresh air.

"Oh, how beautiful," she exclaimed. "I feel better already." She looked in every direction and could seen nothing but the sea. "I wonder where we are."

"Not too far from land," replied Otto, pointing out gulls that were following the ship. "They don't venture too far out. We're probably off the coast of Holland, I should think. Tomorrow we should be in the English Channel and then Southampton."

"Southampton? I thought we were sailing directly to New York," said Mimi.

"Nay. Almost all these Norddeutscher-Lloyd ships stop at Southampton. They will drop off a few passengers and pick up some more."

"Ah, so. I wondered why there were still some empty bunks. See the pretty bird," she said to Henni. The little boy gurgled and waved his arms.

After wandering about a bit she found a sheltered spot out of the wind and watched the clouds scud by. Then her attention was drawn to a pickpocket working the crowd. "Look at that, Otto," she exclaimed. "Shouldn't someone tell the officers?"

He shook his head. "I've been told they will do nothing about petty thievery. They only intervene if someone is seriously hurt. 'Tis best to ignore it and mind your own business."

"Why, that's terrible. Some of these poor people could lose all their savings."

Otto shrugged. "Someone will catch up with him, never fear." And Mimi was thankful for the coins sewn into her corset. She had nothing in her pocket but a handkerchief.

At last it became too cold for her and she went below to give Fritz his turn. "Ach, Fritz, it is just wonderful. Go, it will blow the cobwebs out of your head. But be very careful. There is at least one pickpocket stealing from people and the officers do nothing about it. Go for an hour or so but give me time to go out again for a few more minutes before they lock us in again."

Mimi tried to make friends with some of the other women or at least strike up a conversation with them. She could not understand the Poles or the Russians, nor they her. But even the German families were close-mouthed and seemed afraid to be friendly. No one trusts anyone else, she thought. How sad. When the ship docked at Southampton she noticed several passengers leave and an even greater number surged into steerage. There were English, Scots and many Irish. The bunks next to Mimi and Fritz had been empty but now an English family moved into them. As soon as they were settled the woman tried to converse with Mimi.

"As long as we're to be shipmates, I'd better introduce myself. I'm Marjorie Harley from Kent."

Since the woman obviously was trying to be friendly, Mimi smiled but tried to indicate that she did not understand a word.

The woman tried again. Speaking very slowly she pointed to herself. "My name is Margie Harley."

Mimi was able to figure that out. 'My name' sounded much like 'meine Name'. If there were some words similar maybe it would not be so hard to learn English. She pointed to herself.

"I am Marie Campsheide and I would very much like to learn English. Do you think you could teach me a little before we get to New York?"

Margie lost most of that but she did pick out the words 'English' and 'lernen'. "You want to learn English?" she asked.

Mimi nodded. There was another similar word—'lernen' and 'learn'.

After the ship got underway again and headed out into the Atlantic Mimi spent an hour each morning and another in the afternoon trying to learn English from Margie. Margie was not particularly well educated but she could read and write and they were helped in their efforts by a children's picture book that her young son Russell had brought with him. At first Russell was upset at being deprived of his precious book even temporarily but he soon realized what was happening and joined in the game.

Mimi tried to interest Fritz in the lessons but he refused saying, "I thought your sister said that almost all the people in Elgin were from Hannover. What need have I to learn English?"

"Many but not all," replied Mimi, "and you can be sure they are learning English. After all, it *is* the language of the land."

Fritz shrugged and would hear no more of it. But Otto soon joined in the lessons. Mimi was highly intelligent and quick to learn and the picture book was a good starting place but she soon wondered what use she would have learning about farm animals. She wanted to learn more practical words. Suddenly the similarities between the two languages, the cognates, became clearer to her. Some words were almost identical—'Farm-farm', 'Wasch-wash'—others close enough so she could guess—'Katze-cat', the colors 'rot' and 'blau', even 'und' and 'and'. But she puzzled over some of the English pronunciation. 'Lachen' and 'laugh' looked close enough in print but when she pronounced it 'lauch', everyone burst out—yes—*laff*-ing.

What a strange language English was!

Two and a half days out of Southampton the good weather deserted them and the *Lahn* encountered one of the fierce mid-Atlantic storms so frequent this time of year. November was not the most pleasant month to cross the North Atlantic. The ship pitched and rolled. The passengers were not permitted their time on deck. All the hatches were battened down and even some of the air vents were covered as water trickled down them. They could hear the huge rollers breaking over the bow where they normally took their air. Children cried, women moaned, men cursed. And more than half the passengers became very seasick, Mimi among them.

Fritz quickly relinquished the lower berth so that she could reach the bucket more quickly. And Mimi, for once, had no qualms about handing Henni to Otto. She was too sick to care. Strangely enough Fritz, who once had vowed he would never go on a boat again, did not seem affected by it. Nor was Otto. They and others who were still able valiantly emptied the buckets as quickly as they could but the stench of vomit in the stifling, close air only made everyone sicker. For two days the storm lashed the ship as she ploughed steadily westward.

And then the storm ended as quickly as it had begun. The ship ceased pitching and rolling and all was quiet—almost ominously so. The hatches were thrown open and the air vents cleared but still no one was permitted to go topside. "Too wet and slippery," the sailors warned. "Maybe tomorrow." But several men managed to slip by the crew to see for themselves.

"Fog so thick you can't see ten feet ahead of you," reported one.

"Ja," added another, "if we were under sail we'd surely be becalmed."

"This I must see for myself," said Otto. "Come on, Fritz." Together the men snuck up the stairs. Mimi was content to just lie on the bunk and breathe the fresh air sweeping down the hatch, no matter how damp and cold.

When the men returned a few minutes later Fritz said, "It is as they say—so thick you could cut it with a knife. I hope the captain knows where he's going."

"Ja," said Otto, "and I hope there are no icebergs out there."

"Oh, Otto," cried Mimi, "what a dreadful thing to suggest. You will frighten people all the more."

Otto hung his head sheepishly. "Sorry. I didn't think."

As Mimi started to feel better she said, "Fritz, please take that stinking bucket out of here and bring me a little drink of water. I think I actually feel a little hungry." She had not been able to keep anything down for two days. She dove into her bag and found one of the few apples left from Vilsen. As she munched it, she brightened considerably. "What day is today?"

"I think it is Sunday," replied Otto. "I saw the chaplain preparing for the prayer service. They'll probably have it down here as we are not yet allowed on deck."

"No, I mean what is the date?"

"I'm not sure." Otto started counting on his fingers.

Just then Fritz returned with the water.

"Fritz, what is the date today?" she asked.

"It is Sunday, the fifteenth . . . Mimi! It's your birthday and our anniversary," he exclaimed. He took her in his arms and hugged and kissed her regardless of the apple. "Happy birthday, Liebling."

"And happy anniversary, Fritz." Then she announced loudly to all within hearing. "Today is my birthday and our first anniversary and we're going to have a big celebration."

By this time most of the passengers had lost their mistrust of one another. How could you not be friendly with strangers who emptied your bucket and cooled your forehead when you were so deathly ill? They crowded around, many offering cookies and little cakes, slices of wurst and pieces of fruit from their meagre stores.

"We must sing and dance," suggested one woman.

And the Lithuanian with the concertina was dragged into their midst and gladly played a little jig.

It so happened that one of the kinder stewards overheard Mimi's announcement. He quickly left and about ten minutes later reappeared bearing a bottle of champagne. He put his finger to his lips as he presented it to Mimi. "Congratulations, Madame. It is from the first-class dining salon but they'll never miss it. Let it be our secret. May I open it for you?"

Mimi was overwhelmed. She handed him the bottle and he deftly opened it without spilling a drop. He had also brought two delicate crystal glasses into which he poured the champagne for Mimi and Fritz.

"Thank you, kind sir," murmured Mimi. And then she and Fritz toasted each other. Then they toasted the steward and their 'guests', the captain and the good ship *Lahn* and finally they toasted America. The bottle was passed around so that everyone could take a tiny sip.

The steward whispered, "Don't break those glasses. I have to take them back. They count them."

Mimi laughed. It was the most exciting birthday she could ever remember.

The next day the steerage passengers were permitted to go back on deck. The ship had sailed out of the dense fog and the sun peeped out occasionally from the lifting clouds. People were cheerful again and much more friendly. Women cooed over Henni and introduced their own children. The men discussed chances of employment in the New World. Everyone compared notes on their final destinations. Some had no idea what lay beyond New York. Others, like Otto, had studied maps and tried to explain to them where Boston, Philadelphia and even San Francisco were. Many were going no further than New York where there was already a large German population. But many more, especially those seeking farmland, were going to assorted small towns. And there Otto was stymied unless they knew of a large city nearby.

But underneath the joy that the voyage would soon be over there still lay fears. Everyone reminded everyone else to be sure they had letters from relatives or friends who would sponsor them. Without that they could be considered vagrants and not be permitted to enter the United States.

"Where is our last letter from Lise?" asked Mimi.

Fritz patted his chest. "Right here in my wallet with our birth certificates. Also the letter from Frau Birnbaum. So we're safe either way."

Mimi did not want to think about Frau Birnbaum and New York. She could not wait to see her sisters in Elgin.

And in the back of everyone's mind was the fear of the dreaded eye examination. Anyone who got even a speck of dust in his eye carefully dabbed it out so that there would not be a trace of redness. No one really knew what this dreadful disease was that the American doctors were so concerned about but they all had heard about it. Women chided their children for rubbing their eyes and men cautioned the women not to cry for fear of making their eyes puffy.

The next day the wind blew bitterly cold out of the north but it had blown the remaining clouds away and the sun was sparkling on the water. Mimi was out on deck despite the chill. She wanted to be the first to see America. Besides it still stunk from vomit and unwashed bodies down below.

Suddenly Otto pointed. "Look," he said. Two large seagulls were circling the ship. "That means land must be very close."

"Oh, how exciting!" exclaimed Mimi. "And how big they are—much bigger than our seagulls. I must send Fritz up."

"I'll fetch him and mind your things," replied Otto. "You stay here and watch which direction they fly off to. That is where land will be."

The next day there was even more excitement. Someone had spotted land in the distance. It was nothing but a dim smudge on the horizon but it was definitely land. The ship changed course from westerly to south-southwesterly. And gradually the land loomed larger.

"That must be a part of New England called Cape Cod," pronounced Otto. "It won't be long now."

"Is that anywhere near Boston?" asked Margie Harley. "That is where we are going."

"I think so but I'm not really sure."

That night they could actually see lights twinkling here and there on the shore.

"That must be the Long Island," announced one man. "It's right next to New York."

"But it's over a hundred miles long," countered another. "We've got a ways to go yet."

"Ja, best get some sleep," said his wife, "so your eyes won't be red."

Mimi hurried below to repack their things. She tried to sleep but her excitement was too great. Finally she dozed off from sheer exhaustion.

Before dawn she, and almost everyone else, was awakened by the silence. The constant vibration of the great screw had ceased and it was very quiet.

"Are we there? Are we there?" was everyone's question.

The passengers rushed to the deck. This time no effort was made to restrain them.

Mimi hurriedly dashed some water from the drinking bucket on her face instead of going to the wash room and washing once again in salt water. Won't it be wonderful to have a bath at last, she thought. "Come on, Fritz. Let's go up and see what's happening."

The ship had stopped outside the harbor to pick up the pilot. Now just as dawn was breaking she made her way very slowly as the great bay opened up before them.

Mimi and Fritz with Henni found a place near the port rail of the bow. As it rapidly grew lighter she exclaimed, "Look Fritz, there she is. That is the statue Line was always talking about. Isn't she beautiful? See how she holds her torch high to welcome us."

Just then the sun burst above the horizon behind them.

Fritz put his arm around Mimi. "Look ahead of you, Liebling. See how the buildings have all turned to gold. That is our real welcome—and our future."

Epilogue

1968

The woman, jet-lagged and groggy, left the Bremen airport and drove down the B-6—the highway from Bremen to Hannover that Napoleon had built so long ago. Once she left the suburbs of Bremen the lush green farmland and forests spread out on every side. She felt a sense of déjà vu. It was exactly as Mimi, her grandmother, had described to her so many times. Beautiful, peaceful and welcoming. She experienced a strong feeling of belonging. This was the Heimat—the heart and soul of her ancestors.

At last she saw the sign BRUCHHAUSEN-VILSEN pointing to the left. Her excitement swept away all the cobwebs. She turned off onto the brick-paved road. And sure enough, there were the ancient apple trees still lining every road to Vilsen. Then through a gap in the trees she spied the steeple—'so that everyone would know there is a church here'.

She drove slowly through the crooked, winding streets, her anticipation building in intensity. She parked in front of a variety shop, little knowing then that it was the old Bergmann house where the spice shop had once been. She walked through the gates of the churchyard and stared. There it was exactly as pictured on the church cup that Mimi had given her. She stood quietly, prayerfully, savoring the beauty, the awe.

Just then the greatest bell began to toll and a funeral procession emerged from the ancient church. The deep reverberations touched such a chord of longing in her, thrilled her whole body and soul.

With tears of joy streaming down her face, she murmured, "Nannie, I've come home."

✻   ✻   ✻

Historical Notes

As in the first two volumes of The Saxon Chronicle, all major characters are real people, but so little is known about them, even the more recent ones, that all events, except actual historical facts, are the product of the author's imagination. Even those family legends handed down to me were so vague and nebulous that they required considerable imagination to reconstruct. Some of these: A 'grandfather' built Vilsen's first fire engine—the fire is documented, so it seemed reasonable that Theodor Hohnholz could have been the builder; whether either of the Grimm brothers came to Heiligenberg is problematical, but entirely possible; the robbery at the Klostermühle as well as the friendship between Johann Justus Bruns and Alfred Krupp and the correspondence between the Duchess of Cumberland and Friedrike were favorite and oft repeated family stories.

Even the specific notes in the churchbook records are only tantalizing hints of what really may have happened. Some of those: The horrible death of the young Friedrich Matthies that opens the story; the fact that Catharine was christened Matthies, although the acknowledged father was Theodor Hohnholz; the deaths of Eleonore, baby Hanne and Kati of TB all within a few months of each other—the TB and earlier cholera epidemics are well documented; but why Heinrich Anton went to Lüneburg and of what he died are a mystery; and the book states that Adelheit Matthies burned to death but how is unknown. The windmill stood until the 1950s when it, too, burned down.

Of the Napoleonic period, the pun on General Dupas' name was handed down even to me, although I did not know the connection with the general until doing research for this book. The mandatory church attendance for Napoleon's birthday is well documented as well as the heavy military levies from this small corner of Hannover. From all the conflicting versions of the Russian campaign and the Battle of Waterloo I have tried to simplify and be as accurate as possible. Whether any of the characters went to England to join the King's German Legion is not known, but entirely possible, since troops from Hannover made up the largest segment of the KGL.

The revolution of '48 in Hannover was far less bloody and violent than in other parts of Germany. There were no deaths, as far as can be ascertained. However, it seems to have been more widespread, encompassing many little towns and villages instead of concentrating mainly in the capital. The 'uprising' at Moor is on record as is the quartering of troops in Vilsen and Bruchhausen. Prime Minister Borries' police regime was a dark blot on Hannover's history. And Johann Justus Bruns continued to fight, both openly and clandestinely, for independence for Hannover until his death.

I have in my possession copies of Anton Matthies' Erbzinsbrief, Hinrich Campsheide's strange marriage settlement, his guardianship of his brother's children and the pitiful list of all Johann Campsheide's debts. Calle, a minute settlement, too small even to be called a hamlet (see map), is not to be confused with the city of Celle, over eighty miles to the east.

Bismarck's diplomacy prior to the Franco-Prussian War was so complicated that I have tried to simplify it as much as possible for the general reader. It boiled down to one thing—both sides, especially France, were seeking any excuse for war. The repressive 'May' laws against the Catholic Church which were intended to unite the German people were a dismal failure and only served to create sharper divisions between Protestants and Catholics, between north and south. Likewise, the suppression of the Socialist Party only drove them underground, pushed them towards communism and further enlarged the great divide between laborers and the upper Bourgeoisie. Both of these unfortunate decisions were to lead, indirectly, to the rise of anti-Semitism just at a time when Jews had been granted full rights of citizenship—at least on paper, if not always in practice. Prussia tried desperately to outlaw the railroad recruiters as well as restrict emigration but never could. It was simply the answer to so many prayers.

For details of the Stockman and von Sehnden stipendia, see Volume I—The Capitalists. The Pfingst-ox parade occurred every year much as described. The flood that washed away the mill house at Heiligenberg actually happened but details are imaginary. The friendship between Alfred Krupp and Johann was very real and lifelong. Krupp's great-grandson Alfried was imprisoned by the Allies as a Nazi war criminal but was exonerated in 1951 when it was proven that he, too, was given no choice.

After World War II Germany returned to the black, red and gold flag of 1848. And Old Saxony was finally restored in the name of Niedersachsen in 1946 after 860 years!

Afterword

For those readers who would like a little closure:

Friedrike Bruns finally received her payment from the Stockman Stipendium in 1892—forty-four years after her wedding and less than three years before her death in 1895. Johann Justus Bruns followed her in 1898. Daughter Doris was scheduled to be paid in 1898 but died before she could collect it. Daughter Anna died in Elgin in 1894 and Elizabeth in 1937. Marie (Mimi) was the only one to return to Germany for a visit when their mother was dying. Minna Bruns and Dorothea Campsheide brought Theodor and Alfred Menten to Elgin sometime in 1894 as the two women and Alfred turn up as godparents to Mimi's third child. They apparently stayed through Anni's funeral and presumably Mimi returned with them. I have an endearing photo of her with her father Johann Justus and her own three small children taken in Vilsen shortly after Friedrike's death.

Fritz did not accompany Mimi on this trip, still fearful of the Prussian military conscription as they were not yet U.S. citizens. When Mimi returned she found to her dismay that Fritz, who for some reason did not like Elgin, had moved to New York and was living with the family I have called Birnbaum. (This family existed much as described but I have changed the name for privacy's sake.) Mimi died on Long Island in 1952, Fritz in 1956.

Of the Mentens, Gerhardt is the only one to have remained in Germany. Theodor and Alfred later moved from Elgin to New York and around 1905 Johann (Hans), who was called by the family 'The Sport', presumably because of his numerous affairs after Doris' death, brought Heinrich (Henni) and Rudolf (Rudi) to New York. Hans made several round-trips to New York before the first war to visit his sons and Mimi, as did Minna Bruns.

Of the buildings: The ancient Vilsen church still stands and it is quite easy to read its history in the stones—from the primitive eleventh century original structure through Romanesque, Gothic, the additions after the Reformation and the 'new' steeple commemorated on the lovely church cup, which I still have. The crucifix from 1200 still hangs behind the altar but sadly the medieval frescoes have been covered by many layers of plaster and whitewash. Anton Matthies' two stones, greatly weathered, are still attached to the outside tower wall. Recently its name was changed back to the original—St. Cyriacus.

The Klostermühle at Heiligenberg was still a working mill when I first visited there. After the death of the elder Hünneckes it was neglected but since has been restored as an historical monument by the town of Bruchhausen-Vilsen. The villages of Vilsen and Bruchhausen were united into one political entity in 1952 but Vilsen remains the religious and shopping center while Bruchhausen is the government center. The Bergmann house still stands next to the churchyard, broken up now into several apartments, but the variety shop where the spice shop had been is still owned by descendents of Chris Möser's second wife. Sadly, only a few months before my first trip the Bruns cottage on Gartenweg was torn down to make a garage for the little hotel there. But the owners were kind enough to give me a picture of it.

As for pertinent history: In 1892 Chancellor Caprivi finally convinced Kaiser Wilhelm II to repay the huge amount of interest due on the stolen Welf fund to the province of Hannover in the hopes of soothing the rebellious state. But to no avail. The independence movement continued as strong as ever. In 1920 a group of men even succeeded in seizing and occupying the ancient Leine Schloss for a few days but was quickly put down. The hope for an independent Hannover continued through the Weimar Republic and was only finally squelched by Hitler in 1932.

Friedrike Bruns was the last in my immediate line to have collected from the Stockman Stipendium but the payments continued regularly until 1916. In fact, the list of 'Exspectans' was projected up to 1950 but sadly the terrible inflation of 1922–23 totally wiped out the capital as well as that of the von Sehnden Stipendium and many others.

✻   ✻   ✻

Once again I should like to thank all those who helped with the research to make this trilogy possible—and especially for a few telepathic nudges from Mimi, my dearest grandmother.